PESTILENCE REIGNS

A novel by
Ben Black

Pestilence Reigns

© 2017 Ben Black

First edition.

DEDICATIONS:

To my much loved wife & child, Helen and Ava, and the hours put up with me while I tried to sort this out.

For GrEMbOt, my Co-P who called me out on all the bullshit: Dammit, chief, you got my back, brah.

Darlaz, for pushing for that extra percent every day.

Thanks to friends and family that supported me, and the select test readers who guided me on my journey to make sure what I wrote made sense to others, and not just myself.

In memoriam of the many we lost, and the voids you have left in our lives:
In memoria aeterna manemus

I
SURVIVOR ZERO

"It's a grave situation we find ourselves in. We can't predict for certain the full extent of the spread, but we are confident we can contain it."

"Get out of the way," he screamed, sheer terror threatening to take over his mind. He wouldn't; no, he *couldn't* rest until he'd seen her. His vision swam as he hurtled through the corridor, blind panic making him question if he was even going the right way. He didn't know what was happening or what was going on, he'd taken off halfway through hearing about her illness. All he knew was that it involved his girlfriend; his soul mate, and he needed to see her; he needed to see Jenny.

The run from the office to the toilets had barely been enough to make him out of breath, but Bill could feel his heart hammering in his chest, almost bursting as he skidded to a halt outside the toilets. A small crowd of people Jenny worked with had started to gather around the entrance, murmurs of intrigue turning to whispers of concern, and angst turning to pity as Bill lurched into view, his mind still reeling. Ignoring their looks, he turned sideways and barged into the crowd, shoving people aside before they had a chance to part and let him through. No one protested, no one offered any words of explanation.

He stormed into the room, the normal lemon-fresh scent of the cleaning products used overwhelmed by something else: a foul, vile stench that was unlike anything Bill had ever smelled before. The cloying odour clung to the back of his throat with each breath, his stomach convulsing as he retched, feeling acidic bile tickle his palette. Grimacing, he swallowed it down and looked quickly around the room. There were a handful of people in the toilets, Jenny's closest friends showing more concern than the morbid spectators gathering outside, but also showing something a little more. Fear? Terror? Bill couldn't tell for sure, they all faced one open cubicle and the figure sprawled in the doorway.

She crouched on her hands and knees, head lying limply on the seat, listless eyes staring blankly at the rim of the once white porcelain seat, both her face and the seat speckled with glistening beads of greenish-pink liquid.

Just a few hours ago, Bill had watched her getting ready for work: smiled to himself as he watched her sitting at her dressing table, grooming herself, making sure her hair was just right. While he was at the bottom of the corporate ladder and could get away with throwing jeans and a t-shirt on five minutes before he had to leave for work, she took time to accentuate her lightly tanned skin, full lips and piercing blue eyes with makeup. Not too much, but enough to turn heads when the couple set off for work.

The person that had keeled over the toilet was barely recognisable as a woman at all: a bitter and ragged abomination with rat-tails of sweat-soaked hair plastered to her forehead and perspiration streaming down her face and arms. Wispy black spider legs of mascara crawled down her face, and the whites of her eyes were barely visible through the web of swollen and bloodshot veins. She'd left her suit jacket balled up on the floor by the door to the cubicle, and her shirt was soaked, clinging to her skin. As he neared her, Bill realised that the source of the smell was Jenny, her legs smeared with her own excrement that had pooled around her knees. As he stepped nearer, her body shuddered and heaved, and a belching retch tore from her mouth as her lips parted and she heaved into the toilet bowl, a thick dark substance that seemed to be comprised of blood more than bile, splashing into the half-digested chunks of food already in the toilet.

Bill had seen Jenny drunk, he'd seen her with the flu, and he'd seen her with food poisoning: nothing rivalled the state she was in now, and he couldn't help recoiling himself as he stepped forwards and gently placed his hand on her convulsing shoulders. Both people recoiled at the touch, Jenny in pain and Bill in shock at her temperature: she was burning up, and no amount of sweat seemed to be having any cooling affect on her.

Jenny's eyes flickered to Bill, the barest hint of recognition flashing in them, before she convulsed and vomited again, her lips cracking and tearing at the corner as she did so. Bill was speechless; he wouldn't know what to say, even if he could find his voice. His vision seemed to swim for a moment, and he sank to his knees beside Jenny, the slick of her expelled waste seeping into his trousers, bringing a disturbing warmth to his knees as the sludge oozed across his ankles and sloshed over his shoes. He felt a wave of nausea wash over him as he knelt beside her and sank into the mire, but the moment quickly passed as he steeled himself to touch her back once again, this time prepared for the heat, and kept it there, finally finding a small voice to blurt out the words "I'm here, Jenny, It's okay". As far as reassurances went it wasn't brilliant, but it was the only thing he could think of.

She tried to acknowledge it, tried to force a smile or form a word with her cracked lips, but yet another shudder wracked her body, a wet cough echoing around the curvature of the toilet, amplifying the splatter of escaping fluids and the weak, pitiful moan that followed.

Still leaking and oozing vomit from her mouth, her limbs suddenly gave way, her head bouncing off the pan and her body curling around the seat as her entire body shook, a spasm that brought with it deep guttural roar followed by thick, gurgling noise. Bill panicked, seeing her eyes closed and thinking that she was losing consciousness, and pulled her out the cubicle, a trail of filth and blood streaking behind her as he dragged her into the main area of the toilets. He rearranged her into what he thought the recovery position was. It had been some years since he'd had any basic first aid training, but from what he could remember, as long as he kept her airways clear any and all vomit would slide out her mouth instead of collect in the back of her throat. Her arms continued to flail and her legs kicked wildly, forcing Bill to back off as she spasmed and convulsed on the floor. Finally finding a voice, Bill spun to look at the people gaping at him and snarled.

"Don't just fucking stand there! Get a doctor!"

"We've already called for the ambulance, it's on the way," one of the women murmured. Bill didn't take the time to acknowledge that, or even identify which of Jenny's friends it was. He tried to hold back the tears, but despite his willpower, the barriers holding them back broke. Salty droplets rolled down his cheek, splashing in the acidic mix of bile, blood and faeces that was pooling around the floor. As the filth seeped across the floor, those already in the room retreated closer to the door, their eyes warily flicking from the pool of rapidly increasing bodily fluids to the crowd peering cautiously in through the door. There seemed to be activity outside the room, distant voices that seemed harsh, abrupt even, but Bill didn't take much of anything else in, and he certainly couldn't concentrate on a conversation in another room while his girlfriend lay on the ground looking like she was... What was she, was she dying? He didn't know what was wrong with her, couldn't possibly begin to believe a word he was telling her, even though her knew how important it would be to keep her reassured. He couldn't panic himself, but what could he do? He'd never felt so helpless, so *impotent* before, and unable to say or do anything meaningful to calm either himself or his girlfriend down. "It's going to be okay," he muttered again. "You'll see."

He looked up as the voices outside became louder, more authoritative, and two men charged into the room, both wearing a heavy duty white all-in-one suit and a combination of gas mask and helmet covering their heads. Thick gauntlets and boots protected their hands and feet as the boldly strode into the miasma of vomit and blood surrounding Bill and Jenny, each carrying a portable generator slung over their shoulders on thick nylon straps. They each removed their device, setting them down on the ground and checking dials and controls to make sure they were getting purified air circulated into their sealed suits before kneeling down to look over Jenny. One carried a white metal box with an embossed Caduceus sigil on the lid, while the other held a small portable computer in his hand. The owner of the box opened it and started retrieving instruments from it, while the other started to tap information into the computer with a stylus. Their masks and attire were almost identical; the only way Bill could discern any difference between the two was that one wore a chevron on his left shoulder. What Bill did notice, though, was that both men carried a pistol strapped to their leg, not a common sight in England, not even with police officers on duty, and certainly not on the legs of a medic or doctor.

"Are you this woman's husband?" A harsh, almost metallic and emotionless voice came from the speaker fixed to the side of the mask. Bill looked at him with glazed eyes, trying to look beyond the tinted lenses into the eyes of the man, but couldn't see anything.

"Are you her husband?" he repeated.

Bill stammered a negative response. Marriage was something they'd talked about once or twice before, but nothing they'd acted on. There always seemed like there'd be another day they could discuss it. "Boyfriend," he murmured, watching as the man with the medical chest started inspecting Jenny, taking her temperature and checking for response to different stimuli. Her eyes fluttered violently, though her convulsions had all but ceased. The paramedic gently pinched at her skin, and the surface broke, weeping a thin, pale watery fluid that cascaded down her arm and into the mix of fluids already on the ground. The paramedic looked at his gloved fingers, and then displayed them to Chevron. He pushed himself to his feet, tapped another series of commands into his tablet and motioned vaguely towards Jenny with the blunt end of his stylus.

"How long's she been like this?" Though the voice was muffled and changed by the helmet, the accent was American.

Bill shrugged his shoulders, shaking his head and soundlessly working his mouth. He had no idea what time he'd burst into the toilets, how long had passed since then, or even what time it was now. He glanced pointlessly at his watch, the face smeared in blood and vomit, and he shrugged. He tried once again to look at the man behind the mask, looking up at the towering figure and feeling like a child being chastened by an adult, something he was all too familiar with from his wayward youth. It offered no comfort or reassurance, and the only thing he could see was his own face of utter confusion and shock reflected on the lenses of the mask.

Chevron pulled Bill away from Jenny, allowing the paramedic to work on her from a different angle and turned his emotionless gaze to the few faces still peering through the doorway. "When did this start? How much has she brought up? Has anyone left the floor since this started?"

"About half an hour ago," someone replied. Bill looked over, finally realised it was one of the girls who worked with Jenny. What was her name, Janine? Janice? Janet? He couldn't remember, but did it matter? She looked sickly and pale, too, though not as much as Jenny. Beads of sweat prickled her brow as she stumbled closer into the room and offered more information. "She was complaining about a headache, something like the flu, then she was just sick. We rushed her here, and when we saw the blood… Jesus, is she going to be all right?" She swayed slightly as she spoke, and leant against the wall, rubbing her temples and screwing the palms of her hands into her eye sockets.

Chevron ignored the question. "And she's been vomiting non-stop since then?"

Janine nodded, licking her lips as she did so. Bill nodded his head once to himself; Janine was definitely her name, he remembered that now. She tried to step away from the wall, but her legs buckled beneath her as her feet slipped in the murky fluid seeping across the ground. She braced herself against the wall again, muttering about how it was hot in the room and wiped the back of her hand across her forehead.

"Has anyone else been through here? Left this floor?" Chevron asked, his masked visage moving from her to the kneeling paramedic, who gave a knowing nod in return. "Anyone you can think of?"

"Cleaners?" she muttered, shaking her head. "The corridor's been vacuumed recently…"

"Window cleaner," Bill murmured, watching as Chevron tapped the details into his computer. "Some guy cleaning the windows when I was on my rounds before. He… he wasn't there later."

"Cleaners, are they're hired by the company, or internal?"

No one responded.

"They wouldn't pack up their gear and leave the building, would they?"

Bill shrugged in a non-committal manner, his eyes focussing on Jenny as the paramedic gently withdrew a sterile spatula and scrapped the corner of Jenny's mouth, pulling a wad of mucus and bile away from her lips and slipping it into a Petri dish and setting it down on the chest by his side.

"Did you hear that Merris?" The paramedic didn't respond: Chevron must have been using a radio set into his mask. "Yeah, that's right. Another possible two people. Lock it down; get hold of their schedules. Get three men in the lobby; seal the ducts off," He paused, tilting his head slightly as if listening to a response. The silence seemed to last a lifetime, and for a moment the only noise Bill could hear was the laboured, burbling breath of Jenny.

"I know," Chevron snapped, his sudden outburst startling Bill, an explosive outburst that shattered the quiet and made the paramedic look up from his work, no doubt a questioning glance behind the tinted mirrors. "But no one enters, and no one leaves; no exceptions. We have one definite, and at least another thirty Hot Bodies. Get some testing kits up here."

Apparently signing off the radio link, he looked across at the paramedic again: in one hand he held small square of paper saturated in a solution that he dipped in the sample, then compared it to the chart he held in the other hand. The paper was blue in colour, but it slowly turned black as it soaked up liquids from the bilious sample. He slowly shook his head. "She's too far gone," he confirmed. "Stage four, best we can do is take her in, make her comfortable, then sterilise her."

"She's advanced pretty quickly. At least at this stage there's not long left, right?"

Bill heard the words of the attending men, but didn't understand the true meaning of it all. Nothing that was going on around him really sank in. Another two men pushed their way into the room, both wearing the same thick white suits and carrying a collapsed gurney between them. They set it down on the ground, gently manipulating Jenny on to the mesh fibre that made the surface of the moveable bed: no matter how gentle they were, though, her body didn't agree. Skin flaked away where the men made contact, and where the flesh stretched it cracked and peeled, weeping a pink watery fluid of blood mixed with pus and mucus.

"Might even be stage five," Chevron offered. The paramedic nodded in agreement, and Bill struggled to his feet, his eyes widening in alarm as he saw the strain being put on Jenny's skin, and he tried to voice his concern, tried to order them to stop, to be careful, but his throat locked. He stepped forwards, but Chevron placed a firm hand on his chest without looking, a silent warning to stay back and let his men do their job. After strapping her down, the two men stood and lifted the gurney, the scissor-legs of the device expanding and locking in to position before wheeling her towards the door, watching as the morbid crowd scattered as they approached them.

"I'm coming with you," Bill finally managed to say, taking a stumbling step towards the doorway. His clothes were caked in the filth from the floor, still warm and clinging to his limbs as he moved, and the tiles beneath his feet were slick with spilled liquid. He stumbled over to the set of basins and clung to them while he tried to regain his composure, his filthy hands smearing the ceramic with bloody handprints and smudged fingerprints. He fumbled for the tap, rinsed his hands and splashed his face, then numbly stared at the bloody stranger staring back at him in the mirror.

"We wouldn't leave you like that," Chevron motioned towards the gore covered clothing and bloody effigy in the mirror before taking hold of his lower arm and guided him out the room, effortlessly moving across the slippery surface like a man who'd done this a thousand times. "You're a biohazard yourself."

As he was ushered out the room, Bill turned to Janine and reached out to touch her arm. His fingers made contact with her skin, and she recoiled, not in revulsion from his bloodstained hands, but from the pain the contact made on her suddenly delicate flesh.

Janine looked at the decrepit form that had once been Jenny McClaren, her friend and workmate, now glassy-eyed and listless; clothing and hair matted and thick with vile-smelling bile and mucus, watery blood trickling from her gaping mouth. She could tell just by looking at Jenny, that there was no pulling around from this: every shudder brought a fresh moan of agony from her, each retching heave bringing more vital fluids. Even with these thoughts of Jenny's condition, and possible expiration, Bill managed a choking plea. "Phone Brian for us, let him know we might be late for drinks tonight." The gravity of the situation hadn't even come close to registering in Bill's mind: everything was happening too fast, but his thoughts were jumbled by the shock of the events unfolding, or just a naturally optimistic disposition that let him see the silver lining of every cloud. In his eyes, in his inability to grasp the serious nature of the situation, the couple were going to be late for a social event. Bill's eyes seemed to glaze over for the briefest of seconds as a thought formed in the back of his head, then nodded. "No, just tell him we'll see him tomorrow."

Janine's response was a slight nod as she slowly raised a shaking arm up and placed a pale hand in front of her mouth, stifling a choking cough that escalated into a rattling fit. Pulling her hand away from her mouth, she frowned at the bloody spatters in the palm of her hand and then looked expectantly up to the paramedic. Without missing a beat, he dropped his chest and opened it back up, retrieving another Petri dish as Janine broke into a fit of coughs and the crowd at the door shuffled back even further. Chevron slapped the paramedic on his shoulder as he motioned past, dragging Bill with him as he exited the toilet and into the crowded hallway.

The corridor seemed more alive than it ever had before: doors to offices were open, and people were milling around them, half drunk cups of tepid coffee in their hands as they gawked at the men in white, the wheeled frame that was being pushed down the corridor, and the gore-covered Bill as he stumbled along behind him.

"Get back in your offices," Chevron shouted, his voice crackling over the speaker as he looked around and motioned to the largest crowds murmuring to one another. They didn't move, looking over Jenny's prone form, them turned back to look at Bill's dishevelled appearance. They spoke in hushed tones, but loud enough for Bill to hear them as they walked past.

"Looks like she's been beaten up," the first of the wild accusations came, something so far from the truth it was almost laughable.

"That's her boyfriend," another whispered, pointing to Bill with an outstretched finger of a hand wrapped around the handle of a mug. "I heard he was high on drugs, took a knife to her." The office rumour mill seemed to be quick off the mark, no matter how far off target. "Jesus, will you look at all that blood."

"Look at his eyes… he looks like he's still off his face, doesn't know what the fuck he's doin'."
"Crazy bastard… Are they the police?"
"No, I've seen them on the news. Soldiers. Marines. They're all over now…"
"No wonder they called the Marines in, the fucker's covered in blood… Jesus, what did he do?"
"What are *they* doing here? Why not the cops?"

"Get back inside," Chevron stopped mid-stride, turning to face the trio of men and motioning towards the office behind him. His voice no longer seemed flat and emotionless, but threatening, a voice that wasn't used to having people disobeying him. He squared up to the men, feet set shoulder width apart, hand resting a few inches from his holstered pistol: the office workers didn't push their luck any further, slinking back into the office and turning to their colleagues, helping to spread rumours amongst the uneducated. No doubt the story would spiral out of control, but Bill didn't care, he was more concerned with Jenny's wellbeing.

"Is this what's happening in London? What's been in the news?"

Bill looked up at the woman who approached the men – the Marines – as they marched towards the lift and the two men holding the doors open; guarding them, maybe? He didn't recognise her as someone that worked in Jenny's office, but she seemed concerned. Bill didn't know what she was talking about in London, though: he didn't pay much attention to local news or current affairs.

"Stay in your offices until further notice," Chevron said, offering no further explanation and pushing past her, continuing to tap details into his computer and making sure Bill followed the gurney: he needn't worry, Bill had no intention in leaving her side.

The lift was cramped already with the wheeled stretcher and the two men charged with transporting Jenny: it was even more of a tight squeeze as Bill was ushered into the cage by

Chevron, who held his thumb down on the button to hold the doors as the paramedic returned up the corridor, his cleansuit dripping with fresh bloody bile from his shoulder and chest where someone had recently vomited on him: Janine was no where to be seen. His shoulders were slumped forwards and his steps staggered, and he motioned towards the toilets behind him while absentmindedly wiping some of the vomit.

"Another one, stage three," even through the distortion of the speaker, he sounded tired. "In this corridor alone, I've seen another three people who look like they're on the verge of stage two, and maybe a handful at stage one."

"Okay, keep everyone here, lock it down. I've got a squad working its way up from the ground floor. Call it in, Code Black; initiate Damocles protocols and key in the locus for home base to catalogue."

"Hey, what the hell's going on?" a demanding voice shouted from the other end of the corridor, loud and authoritative that seemed to silence the murmuring crowds that were starting to spill out into the corridor. A man in his late fifties wearing a grey suit and a tie as red as his enraged face glared angrily at the blood-soaked carpet and men in the elevator. A few groups of people seemed to melt back into their offices, making themselves scarce, while those workers that were more brazen lingered in the corridor, eager to see how the confrontation would play out. "Some of us are trying to work here!"

"I'll handle this," the paramedic said in a lowered tone through the speaker in his helmet, slapping Chevron on his shoulder before turning and walking back up the corridor, dropping his medical chest to the ground and resting his hand on the butt of his holstered pistol as he walked. "I need everyone to remain in their offices."

"I demand to know what's going on," the man didn't raise his voice any more, but he didn't lower it, either, his shrill tone cutting through the low buzz of conversation that had struck up as the paramedic stepped forwards.

The two men guarding the lift stepped forwards and flanked the paramedic on either side.

"It's not your concern," the paramedic's calm voice seemed louder now. Was he raising his voice, or had he just turned his volume up? "Remain in your office until further medical assistance arrives. You will all be briefed when they arrive."

"You'll tell us now," the vocal man demanded, striding purposefully down he corridor, making sure he kept to one side of the blood trail.

"You will all be briefed," the paramedic repeated, "When they arrive."

"It's like that stuff in London," muttered someone close to the paramedic. He turned to look at them, neither confirming nor denying the statement. "Jesus, it is… I… I've got to call my dad."

As one, a number of people still in the corridor reached into their pockets or bags, pulling out a wide variety of mobile phones and expertly flicking through menus or tapping numbers in, raising them to their ears and waiting expectantly for an answer.

"I've got no signal," the first of many people shouted up, complaining that they, too, were unable access a network connection. Another screamed in dismay when they discovered the landlines had been cut off, too. The man with the red tie reached into his jacket, pulled out his palm computer and tapped at the screen, then threw it down to the floor, snarling as he did so.

"What have you done?" he demanded. "Did you do this? How?"

The rest of the corridor erupted with similar accusations, and they people started to step forwards, angrily waving useless mobile devices, each protesting their own case that they should be entitled to phone their husband, their wife, their brother, their mother to tell them what was going on, to ask if they'd heard anything. It was typical mob mentality, the rest following the lead of the alpha pack leader when they knew they outnumbered the paramedics and his friends.

Calmly, the paramedic drew his pistol, raised it and fired above the heads of the crowd, the deafening gunshot instantly silencing the crowd. Some dropped to the floor, others dropped their mobiles and displayed open palms, as if the devices were weapons and they'd been told to disarm; some stifled screams by covering their mouths with balled fists, and others simply stared open-mouthed at the paramedic's smoking weapon, and the two troopers beside him that slowly raised their submachine guns, panning them slowly back and forth across the crowd.

"You will *all* be briefed," the paramedic slowly reiterated his previous statement as he turned his head from side to side, "When further medical assistance arrives."

The doors slid shut and the lift jolted before slowly dropping down the shaft, the dumb-struck silence of the corridor mirrored in the cage as it lowered from the floor and down towards the ground level.

"Fuck," Bill muttered, to himself more than anything else. What was going on?

He looked down on Jenny as he waited for the gentle, warm voice of the lift to announce their arrival, and noticed that her eyes were sealed with a build-up of puss and blood that seemed to be scabbing over. Her breathing was short and laboured, her body shaking as if she were cold, though she remained hot to touch, and her skin still continued to rip and joints where her unconscious form was jostled by the journey. He still couldn't understand what was wrong with her, how she'd changed so much in the few hours he'd spent away from her, from a healthy, lively young woman to someone who looked like she was moments away from death's door.

They'd been looking forwards to going out tonight, their mid-week meeting with their friends for a meal and some drinks. Bill hoped that Janine would pass the message on to Brian and explain what had happened: he really didn't feel like explaining everything to him, he'd rather someone else did that for him. In the maelstrom of her violent illness, it was all he could do to cling to something relating to the normalcy of their life: this whole scenario hardly seemed real, and he could barely process events unfurling around him: the discharge of the gun had left him feeling numb and confused, even more so than when he had upon first finding Jenny in the toilets.

The lift announced they'd reached the lobby, and the doors cycled open, splitting down the middle and parting to reveal the lobby.

It wasn't the lobby that he and Jenny had arrived for work in. The black marble floor, large reception desk and low glass coffee table were still there, as were the collections of up to date newspapers and magazines for visitors to read through while waiting for their appointment, and the pair of receptionists that manned the desk. Both were friends of Jenny, though whether they wore the same concerned expression others on the upper floor had, Bill couldn't tell. The route from the lift to the main doors had been cocooned in a tube of rigid polythene, a sterile corridor with hollow inflated walls that connected the lift directly to the main doors and sealing the rest of the building off from the casualty and her escort. At the end of the corridor, Bill could see where the security turnstiles had been uprooted and cast aside to make way for the opaque tube, the gaping holes in the floor where the barriers had been torn up hastily repaired with quick-setting foam sealant to keep the floor as close to level as possible. A pair of men, wearing the same white cleansuits as every other intruder in the building Bill had seen, were finishing off the refurbishments at the turnstiles, a collection of crowbars and hammers being hastily pushed into a tool chests so the way was clear for the procession of Bill, the gurney and the three men to pass. Chevron pointed to them, indicated to the lift behind them with a nod of his head, and they reacted to the unspoken command by grabbing a pair of bulky assault rifles from a supply rack near the corridor wall and charging into the lift.

The distance from the lift to the exit wasn't that far, but Bill felt like it was an eternity as he plodded along behind Jenny, unconsciously reaching out to brush aside a strand of hair that was stuck to her forehead, and recoiling when the very contact of his fingers with her skin made the her flesh peel and crack, bringing a fresh stream of pink watery pus sluice down her temple and spatter on the floor.

"Stop touching her," snapped Chevron, opening a pouch on his belt spraying a white circle of paint around the seepage, leaving it as an indicator for an orderly to come and clean it up. Bill murmured an apology and continued to follow them, watching with half an eye as outside the sealed corridor, he could see the shapes of other people in white suits marching back and forth, the opaque nature of the walls making the appear like phantoms moving on another plane of existence, watching from the other side as they approached the front door.

They cycled open automatically as they approached them, splitting down the middle and revealing what had once been the main car park outside. Bill had come in to work this morning with Jenny and they'd parked there, the same spot they'd parked in for years: Bill certainly didn't remember the oversized polythene tunnel that had been bolted to the concrete frame around the door and embedded in the floor, nor did he remember the thick mounds of sealant surrounding the door to make sure the building and tunnel remained perfectly airtight. The corridor extended for twenty feet ahead of them, the vestigial remnants of the car park outside as ethereal as the shadowy figures inside the building: Bill couldn't help but look to his left, as if he expected to be able to make out their car still parked up in their space: instead, there was nothing but a blur of shapeless colours and more white figures striding purposefully back and forth.

The procession came to a halt at the end of the short corridor, an obstruction made from a solid inch-thick rigid plastic that slowly ground open as a soldier outside operated a set of controls on the hastily erected structure. Chevron ushered Bill into the room first, then guided the gurney in after him before turning to the two soldiers accompanying him.

"Go back upstairs, help out with the lockdown. I've got this."

The pair nodded and spun on their heels, jogging back the way they came and vanishing back into the building, leaving Chevron alone with Bill and his girlfriend in the enclosed chamber. The door cycled shut, and machinery outside the room started rumble to life. Bill looked feverishly around, and although his escort showed no sign of being startled or wary of the noises, he felt on edge, looking from left to right as a row of lights flickered to life just below the ceiling, then panned downwards, a purple beam of ultraviolet light that swept across his skin, a tingling sensation washing across him as the sterilising light scoured his skin. He looked at his hands as the light left them, noticing a fine white powder that coated his skin. He looked down on Jenny and could see similar residue on her, though these were stained with spilled blood.

"Just burning off any surface infection we may be carrying on our skin or clothes," Chevron explained, his gaze remaining fixed on the opposite wall, and the sealed door that could only be their destination. "Might be too late for you and her, but there's more than just the two of you involved here. Stay still."

A spurt of white, ice-cold gas sprayed up from the grated floor, a sudden gust of air tainted with a chemical, antiseptic taste that clung to Bill's mouth as he spluttered at the sudden jet of air. The miasma lingered in the chamber for a few seconds, then with a deep droning sound, the tainted air was flushed from the room and replaced with fresh. Bill gasped at the air for a few seconds, coughing up the taste of the thick disinfectant as the second set of doors rolled open, revealing a short length of polythene tunnelling linked to the opened back of a large transit van.

The interior of the vehicle was a flat metallic black in colour with a handful of bulbs fixed to the side panels, with space for a gurney on the left side of the vehicle, and four fold-down seats running along the right hand wall; another paramedic already occupied one of them. He nodded at Chevron, then stood up and moved towards the opening, the low roof meaning he could only do so in a crouching shuffle. The two men lifted Jenny up into the van and locked the gurney down in to place, then ushered Bill into the vehicle, pushing him down into one of the seats. While the medic went about his business of attending to the catatonic woman, Chevron pulled out his data pad and started to tap the screen, banging on the wall of the van with his other hand to signify that they were ready.

The rear doors swung shut and there was a pop-ripping sound as the entrance tunnel was torn away, and the lights flickered slightly as the engine of the vehicle growled to life, a deep and powerful sound that shook the confined space of the van as it shuddered and pulled away. The jarring movement shook Jenny on her gurney, resulting in her skin tearing more, the lesions weeping more pale pink fluids. Chevron motioned towards the wall behind Bill, and he numbly acknowledged him as he fumbled with numb fingers for the seatbelt. He finally clicked it into place, and Chevron looked down as his computer, his fingers dancing over the touch -sensitive screen. Without looking up from his work, he spoke to Bill.

"We're supposed to interview everyone we pull in that we can. Build a case history; map out locations, project disease vectors, work out the R0 number, things like that. So, I'm going to ask you a few questions about you and the patient…"

"Jenny," Bill interrupted him. "Her name's Jenny."

"Of course," Chevron said, still not looking up, then went on, resorting to inputting details into the computer with a stylus again. "Fucking machine, it's never been the same since they forced through the firmware update last week."

"Maybe it's been affected by the iron curtain dropping on the office?" offered the medic attending to Jenny, looking up from his task at hand long enough to offer a shrug. "With the network there smothered, it could be picking up interference from the proximity of the dampening cloud. My readouts have been crashing too often in the last couple of days."

"Maybe," Chevron returned the shrug, lowering the computer back into a pouch hanging from his webbing. "Some genius makes us update to an untested firmware just as the shit really hits the fan, only Military Intelligence could come up with that."

"Maybe it was *because* the shit was hitting the fan."

"These things are meant for light field-work, op reports and observations, shit like that, not cataloguing hundreds of infected and working out the next potential hotspot," Chevron growled, grabbing a clipboard hanging from the back of the door. "Sometimes you just can't beat version one. Okay, names?"

"Bill," he answered, his eyes fixed on Jenny. "Bill Reddings. She's Jennifer McClaren. Do you need me to spell that?"

"I'll manage. My name is Sergeant Hankins, that there is Medic Technician Allman."

Bill watched mesmerised as Allman continued to go about his business, hooking up intravenous feeds and applying dressings to her opening wounds. He registered the introduction with the briefest of nods and murmuring of an incoherent acknowledgement.

"Can you remember when the patient may have started displaying signs or symptoms of this disease?"

"No. Nothing. I mean, I don't know. What… what are they?"

Hankins shook his head with an audible sigh that carried over the speaker, then handed Bill a laminated sheet of card. Bill took the sheet, but didn't look at it, instead keeping his eyes fixed on Jenny. Hankins continued to talk. "You haven't seen any of these pinned up in work, or in newspapers? Not heard about it on the news?"

Bill slowly shook his head, his eyes briefly flicking down to the card as he skimmed through the first few lines of text. Inflamed nasal membranes and bloodshot eyes, aches and pains, blood that took longer to clot; diarrhoea and fever, nausea and vomiting: ruptured lesions, bruised flesh, and organ failure. With a shaking finger, he pointed to the first handful of symptoms. "She had a cold a week ago, with dry eyes and a streaming nose. None of the others that I can remember."

"You're sure?" Hankins made a note of it on his chart, and the medic stopped attending the sick woman while he stopped and looked over the sergeant's shoulder. He pointed to the clipboard with a bloodstained glove and murmured something Bill couldn't hear. Hankins continued; "Once the first signs start, they normally go through them all. It burns through their metabolism."

"So maybe she doesn't have this… this *thing* after all?" Bill looked up; hope creeping into his voice and handing the card back over. The van jostled as it rolled over a bump in the road, bringing a fresh tear to Jenny's skin and another gout of watered blood spraying across the opposing wall. The medic hastily returned to her, and Hankins shook his head again, making another note on his clipboard.

"Mister Reddings, I assure you that Jenny has contracted this disease, and we will do everything we can for her. I still need some answers to some questions."

Bill shrugged his shoulders, watching Jenny as her body shuddered with pain, a deep sigh turning into a burbling groan as a spray of blood gushed from her mouth and splashed the medic and the wall.

"Have either of you come in to contact with anyone who may have had these symptoms?"

Bill didn't respond; his gaze remaining fixed on Jenny. Hankins grabbed him by the shoulders with a vice-like grip and physically turned him to face him, then adjusted his seat, trying to block Bill's view and keep his attention focused. He repeated the question, and Bill responded with a nod.

"Richard," Bill muttered. "Jenny's Dad. He's been ill, like the flu. It's been hanging on him a couple of days. We're supposed to drop some medicine off for him after work..."

"Richard McClaren, I see. What can you tell me about him? About his... flu?"

"He travels a lot for his job. Something to do with sales and conferences; he was in London a few days ago. He blames the plane for his being ill, travelling in a tin can and breathing everyone else's air: his words. Flying disease machines, he calls them."

"When was this?"

Bill shrugged his shoulders, looking down at his feet as he shuffled them back and forth. Hankins nodded, wistfully grabbing his computer once more tapping a series of commands into his computer. He couldn't access any passenger manifests from his portable terminal, he'd have to wait until he arrived at their destination. "Where does he live?"

"Saint Aves Gardens. Number seven. It's in Edgly. Can you see that someone get him some medicine? Jesus, and Jenny... Tell them about Jenny... Their number's in my phone... Ah shit, my phone's in my locker..."

"We'll sort everything out, don't worry," Hankins tapped at his keyboard and fed in the address details, knowing that as soon as the details were confirmed in the system, a squad similar to his own would swoop on their home and control the situation there by whatever means needed. His masked face looked back up from the computer. "You mentioned London. Do you keep up with the news? Do you know what's going on in the capital?"

Bill shrugged, his face a blank slate. "I don't watch the news that much. I prefer the music channels in the morning. Jenny, she used to get too worked up at the news, she followed bits and pieces here and there." A smile played across his lips as a memory flickered in the back of his mind; he even laughed softly to himself. "I remember she got really pissed when Kilmer took over from Anderson in the United Government. Shouted at me like it was my fault an American president was still in power over more than half the world. Then she started to scream on that it was Anderson and his private militia of bullies that made the world a lot more dangerous. Bred terror, didn't control it." He held his hands up in mock surrender. "That was Jenny, that was what she was like: easily wound up, full of opinions, and not afraid to speak out. That's why I tried to avoid the news." His smile cracked, and he quickly returned to his dour mood, eyes fixed on Jenny's prone form.

"Well, if it wasn't for bullies like me... forget it. You people..." Hankins shook his head, angrily stabbing more details into the keyboard. "London, a couple of weeks ago, people started exhibiting these symptoms. It's a virus, burns through the body's immune system, then the body: sometimes the mind. A fever, the brittle skin and weeping sores like she has there. So far, the mortality rate has been one hundred percent."

"Fuck," Bill whispered, as the situation finally seemed to hit home.

"There's no easy way to say this. I'm afraid to say that there's no chance of survival, and it's almost certain that you're infected. And you'll go the same way."

"Need to work on your bedside manner, Hankins," the medic said as he sat back from Jenny, casting a glance over his shoulder at Bill, "Poor fucker's shook up real bad."

"It's not my job to act the concerned doctor, and it's not my job to sugar coat the truth. It's my job to bully the world and breed terror. That's what your girlfriend thought, right?"

Bill shrank back from the conversation and felt his shoulders droop, sitting in silence as he dropped his eyes and stared listlessly at the watery blood that pooled on the floor around his blood-soaked trainers. The rest of the journey passed him by in a blurry haze of meaningless conversation, the constant drone of the engine and the rocking motion of the vehicle as it mounted speed bumps and dipped into potholes.

II

Queen Victoria General Hospital had been open for business for over a hundred and fifty years, steadily growing in size over the decades as the size of the city around it expanded. Though there were other hospitals in and around the city, Victoria General had always been considered the main hospital that housed most local specialist departments. Originally a squat, two-floor construction with a large portion devoted to mental health wards, the building had undergone a series of renovations, the most recent being a ten year project that had culminated in a fourteen storey building made of steel, concrete and glass that towered over the surrounding buildings, providing a grand view of the surrounding city for any of the occupants of the building. The architects had wanted to build higher and spread further, but local residents had protested the planning permission. With the construction complete, the finishing touches now involved landscaping the grounds to make the mounds of barren earth more presentable, and to clear away the piles of rubble and inert machines that had been left behind by the construction crew.

The ambulances would normally drop off their casualties at the front of the building by the accident and emergency entrance, but the van continued around the side of the building, and Bill lurched in his seat as the vehicle pitched forwards and trundled down a ramp. It lurched to a halt, the engine idling as Bill could hear muffled conversations outside, and then the rattle of chains as a shutter was hauled open. The vehicle moved again, and Bill could hear the shutter closing behind him. The van continued on its downward journey, listing from side to side as it doubled back on itself, then stopped once more, this time the engine cutting out with a gurgle. The lights flickered once more, and there was a flurry of activity outside, followed by more voices and thumps on the side of the vehicle. The rear doors swung open, flooding the van with blinding light more intense than the internal lighting had been. Bill held his hands up to his eyes and almost fell out the vehicle, stumbling as his feet came in to contact with the pitted tarmac outside.

Bill had been to the hospital a few times in his life: visiting a sick friend, the odd broken or dislocated finger, and once with Jenny for a failed pregnancy, barely two months in. There'd been a lot of blood then, during the miscarriage. They hadn't even realised she'd been pregnant until she'd lost the baby. At least then, Bill knew what the cause of the bleeding was. Now, though, it was a mystery.

He'd never seen the subterranean storage unit that served as both the ambulance storage and delivery bays, but even if he had, he wouldn't have recognised them. The drab grey walls had been painted a clinical white, and recently, too: the smell of fresh paint still lingered in the air, mixed with disinfectant and a heady mix of exhaust fumes from the vehicle. Rows of halogen lamps had been set up every fifteen yards, each on a frame seven feet high and angled outwards towards the centre of the cavernous room. Pipes ran the length of the ceiling in all directions, some hastily boxed in with sheets of plasterboard, others wrapped in grimy lagging that hung from the conduits in lazy loops. Bill gathered his senses and looked around him, looking over his shoulder at the entrance ramp he had presumed the van had entered, and the shutter being rolled back down and locked into place. Bill assumed that it was identical to the shutter at the top of the ramp, a silver barricade with a second, smaller door the right size for a person built in to it. As the final bolt was locked in to place for the shutter, the access door opened and a pair of men dressed in identical white HAZMAT suits stepped through, each cradling a submachine gun in their arms; not the standard medical equipment Bill would have expected to see.

All around him, men in similar clothing were milling around the loading bay, some armed with weapons, others carrying computer tablets similar to that one Hankins carried. There were a handful of doors running along one wall, each sealed with sheets of thick polythene and barricaded with large packing crates or stacks of equipment; the only exit leading out of the bay other than the large shutter over the roadway was a pair of double doors to the far north, guarded on each side by a pair of stoic armed guards and painted freshly with a black triple-bladed biohazard symbol on a red background.

Technicians and medics burst through these doors, three of them almost collapsing over one another as they fumbled with an out-of-control gurney. They quickly attended to transferring Jenny from the back of the van, while another medic rushed to Bill's side, grabbing his wrist and checking his pulse, then looking at the monitor attached to his forearm. Bill glanced at it through the corner of his eye, noticing that although he couldn't understand most of the display, there seemed to be a lot of flashing green and amber numbers. One of the medics pulled a strip of plastic from their terminal and slapped it around Bill's wrist, the white material covered in a series of numbers and holding a black microchip that each technician and medic took turns to scan the device.

"Bill Reddings," announced Hankins as he calmly stepped out of the van and made space for more people to rush in and attend to Jenny. People feverishly typed into their keypads while he attacked his own terminal, sending what data he had on to the other people, and then handing over the paperwork with the rest of the information. "Most of the information's in these files already. If there's anything corrupt or missing, well, blame the genius behind the updates.

"The patient is Jenny McClaren. I'm assuming it's short for Jennifer. It looks like patient zero in this case is her father, Richard, recently returned from London on a business flight. Details are in the files, I need someone to access the flight manifests for that flight and track down all the people on there. I've got a containment squad going out to do a snatch and grab on their house. We can't afford anyone to slip through the net on this. Call in other centres if we need.

"They work at the Colecs building down town. There's a lockdown in place there, I'm expecting people coming in from there within the hour. Sort this guy out; I'm going to have to arrange an overflow. Fuck me, we're not set up to cope with this."

Hankins spun on his heel, the last comment aimed and only himself, and left Bill in the company of the medics: some peeled away to wait for the next load of potential patients, while others guided Bill and Jenny across the annex towards the double door they entered through. Bill stayed close to the gurney, gripping the side of the trolley and blinking rapidly, trying to fight back the tears as he vowed to be strong for his girlfriend. Behind him, a two man crew rushed to the van they'd just travelled in and sprayed the interior with a high powered steam cleaner, swilling the interior out and watching as the watery blood washed out the back and gurgled down the drainage trough that ran along the centre of the annex. The sights and sounds of the room vanished behind him as the doors swung shut, and Bill found himself in a long corridor lined with doors on either side, each secured with a sheet of steel secured to the door and bolted in place with heavy deadlocks. Numbers and letters were painted on the doors, many of them fresh and still glistening wet, as though they'd just been applied. Beside each door, an electronic readout lay embedded on the wall, some blank and inactive, others populated by a collection of words and numbers that Bill couldn't make out through a combination of moving fast and eyes blurred with tears. His hand was peeled off from the gurney as Jenny was wheeled into one room, and Bill led into another. He murmured a wordless protest and tried to follow her, but a pair of guiding hands clamped around his shoulders and kept him on track into the examination room. Before he could turn around or protest any further, he heard the sounds of locks snapping into place.

"Strip," one of the men demanded, producing a plastic sack from a pouch hanging from his webbing and opening it. Bill looked at him; slack jawed as he tried to work out the basic instruction he'd been given. He prompted him again with the simple one-word command, and Bill slowly cooperated, fumbling at his belt and shirt with numb fingers and handing each piece of blood-soaked clothing across to the waiting man. When the sack was full, and Bill was left naked and shivering in the sterile room, he was pulled roughly over to wall and told to stand with his feet outstretched and palms pressed against the wall. Without warning, a lukewarm liquid splashed against his back, a constant stream of something that had an overpowering smell of disinfectant. It had a thicker consistency than water, almost slimy, and Bill spluttered as the stream swung around and sprayed his face before working over the rest of his body.

As suddenly as it had began, the spray stopped, and Bill stood naked and shivering, teeth chattering as he leaned against the wall, feeling violated and as if *he'd* done something wrong. He wasn't sure if he'd have the strength to keep upright if he were pulled away from the wall, not even sure he could move even if he knew where to go. He could hear hushed whispering between two people, and the soft tapping of keys, and he waited for the next instruction, feeling the thick liquid slipping own his face and dripping off his nose and chin, splashing in the pools forming around his feet. He felt a thick, soft robe being draped around his shoulders, then was pulled away, guided towards a low examination table and pushed gently down to a seated position. He pulled the robe in tight around him, embracing its warmth, and watched as the two medics looked over him and compared notes on each other's terminal. While they did this, Bill looked around the room, taking in what he could while he wiped his eyes with the back of his sleeve.

The examination table he sat on was central to the room, with a low table to one side that held a silver tray and an assortment of medical instruments, all sealed in plastic pouches. In one corner there sat a chemical toilet and a sink, and in another, a low table and stool. A grid of thick black metal pipes mapped the ceiling, with a nozzle pointing towards the floor every fifty centimetres, and a trough running around the perimeter of the room, linked to a drainage system. Bill had no idea what the nozzles were for, but suspected that they'd be used for cleaning, similar to the steam cleaning that had been employed in the back of the van. Despite the overpowering stench of disinfectant that clung to his skin, he could still detect something else in the air, an underlying and unpleasant scent he couldn't place.

"The infected person is your girlfriend," said the taller of the men, setting down his datapad on the table and picking up a sealed set of instruments. "Hauffman's Degenerative Syndrome is extremely contagious, especially in the early stages: when was the last time the pair of you had intercourse?"

"This morning," Bill murmured, a hot flush of embarrassment washing over his face.

"And how many times during the last week?"

Bill scratched at his head then shrugged his shoulders, working through things in his mind. He didn't keep a mental record on every time he and Jenny had been together. "Four," he guessed. "Maybe five times. I don't really keep count."

"And have there been any other partners during that period?"

"What? No!"

"Just asking the standard questions. No need to take offence. Any children? Pets? Anyone else you shared the house with?"

"None," Bill shook his head, "No. Just us."

"We're going to need to run some tests," the talkative medic announced, peeling open the plastic pouch he held and producing a needle from it, flicking it with his forefinger and motioning for Bill to lower his robe and expose his arm. "You not allergic to standard needles, are you? Or anything else?"

Bill shook his head, and the medic quickly jabbed the needle into his arm and flushed the contents of the syringe into Bill's system. The liquid was cool, jolting his nerves as the foreign material rushed through his system, and he instantly felt his arm begin to tingle.

"Well, it wouldn't matter anyway, you'd get the shot regardless: just nice to ask. I need you to lie down, and we're going to start running some tests."

"Tests?" Bill murmured, his words already starting to slur and his jaw becoming sluggish, unresponsive even. He lay back on the bed… or was he helped back? His mind was starting to fog over, his senses tingling as if they were slowly being shut down, and he couldn't keep track of what was happening. He struggled to keep his eyes open, trying to watch what the medics were doing as they broke open each sealed packet and laid their contents out on the tray. One of them looked down on him and motioned with a slight nod.

"He's fighting it."

Bill's eyes closed, his mouth working soundlessly as his eyes flickered behind his eyelids. He felt drunk, dangerously close to unconsciousness, but he managed to fight and maintain some level of consciousness. He could feel electrodes press against his chest and being taped in place, needles being pressed into his body, and cold metal instruments pressing against his flesh.

"Give him another shot, he can't fight it forever."

Another rush of cold liquid found its way into his system, and Bill gave an involuntary shiver, and the swimming quickly turned into a sinking sensation, as he seemed to slip further away.

"How far along do you think he's gone?" the words were distant and ringing with an echo to them, sounding like they were talking into a tube, and became fainter and fainter with each passing second. "Ten bucks say he's not here a day before he hits stage five."

"You kidding me? The poor bastard was covered in that shit, look at his clothes. Twelve hours, tops. Easy money, my friend, easy money. And you know where that money's going, right?"

"I can't keep track. Is it Crystal? Or Jill? Which is the stripper of the month now?"

"Fuck you, I'm putting that girl through college; I think of it as a public service."

"And that's what you tell your wife?"

"I tell her I need to buy my own food because the shit they serve in the mess tastes like dog shit. And lets face it, that's not too far from the truth, is it? Pass me the…"

Bill lurched upright with a startled yelp, clutching at his chest where he thought the monitoring equipment had been attached, then rubbed at his arm where he thought the sedative had been injected: he felt nothing but bare skin. He looked around, bleary eyed, and reached out to one side, fumbling for the bedside lamp and flicking it on.

He recognised his bedroom instantly, the walls a warm pastel orange in colour, the wooden furniture a natural oak with flooring to match. Orange curtains drawn shut over a roller blind, a large television hanging from the wall with a blank screen, and stack of paperbacks balanced precariously on his nightstand. He sat motionless for a moment, looking at his shaking hands, then pressed them against his face, visions of his nightmare still swimming in his head. He fished around on the floor, grabbed a half-empty bottle of water and took a swig, swilling it around in his mouth before swallowing it.

"Jesus," he growled to himself, looking to one side and at Jenny who lay beside him, fast asleep and as perfect, in Bill's eyes, as she had been last night when the two of them had returned from drinks with Brian.

The ordeal of the testing procedure and the events leading up to them still haunted Bill, even days after. He was sure that eventually they'd be put behind him, but the vivid memories were currently burned into his mind, and he couldn't shake them while he slept. Jenny, it seemed, was able to still get a sound nights sleep, but she was still recuperating: the doctors had said she'd take days before she was back to normal, but the sedatives would help her sleep and recover. Maybe Bill would help himself to a couple of those pills, if it would mean he would get decent nights sleep.

He rolled on to his side, grabbing one of the paperback books and thumbing through the aged yellow pages, finding the ripped piece of paper that acted as a book mark, and started reading, hoping it would help him drop off. It was a trashy science fiction book he'd had since he was a child, the storyline predictable the first time he'd read it, even more so the seventh time he'd read it. A few minutes passed, and he found he wasn't really reading any of it, skimming through the pages, missing paragraphs out or even reading the same line three or four times before realising. Letters swam on the pages, swirling around one another, and he rubbed his tired eyes. Sighing, he closed the book and tossed it back on the pile, smiling as he felt Jenny roll over, snuggle into the back of him and drape her arm limply over his waist. She kissed his back, murmuring softly into his spine as she pressed herself closer and asking what was the matter.

"Can't sleep," murmured Bill. "Bad dreams."

Another wordless murmur came from Jenny, and she scratched weakly at Bill's stomach, her long nails tickling him in a not-unpleasant sensation. Her hand slid down, and he twitched involuntarily, grinning at the intimate contact and the sensation of Jenny pressing herself even closer. She kissed his neck, nibbled playfully at it, clambered over him and pinned him down on his back, brushing back the blankets as she lay on top of him. She was warm to the touch, almost burning up. Her hands were slick on his shoulders, soaked with sweat as she moved in rhythm with Bill, rolling her head and continuing to murmur to herself as she leaned forwards and planted a kiss on Bill's forehead, leaving behind a thick smear of what Bill thought to be lipstick, her lips smudged red as she grinned, the skin around her mouth cracking and trickling blood. Panicking, Bill wiped his face and looked at the blood that stained the back of his hand, then back to Jenny.

The flesh around her neck and shoulders was tearing again, cracking and peeling, sloughing away in strips to reveal muscle and bone. He felt a warm wetness wash over his thigh and groin, and he looked down in terror as he could see blood oozing across the bedding, soaking in to the mattress and pooling around him like a leaking waterbed. Despite her deterioration, Jenny continued to writhe, screaming as her body twitched and convulsed, her stomach clenched and she spewed blood and bile across Bill, the harsh acrid stench of vomit and blood catching in the back of his throat and making him gag.

"Mister Reddings."

Bill's eyes flickered open, his muscles contracting as he tried to lurch upwards from his prone position on the bed, but he couldn't more, a tight band of nylon cutting across his shoulders, another across his stomach and a third pinning down his ankles. "Mister Reddings," the voice repeated again, a blurry white figure circling him as he felt the restraints loosen and fall away from him. Bill's brain slowly kicked into gear, the sedative he'd been given still clouding the edges of his mind as a pair of hands slowly raised him to a sitting position. Another needle pressed against his arm, a new cocktail of drugs introduced into his system, and he could feel the cloud begin to dissipate and the events before rushed back to him in crystal clarity: Jenny's illness, the underground facility he was in, the hose down with the disinfectant... he pressed his hands to his chest, realising that he was no longer naked, but instead he wore thin paper clothing: a shirt and a pair of trousers with an elasticated waist, and a pair of thin soled slippers.

"Mister Reddings," the medic stood before him: he couldn't tell if it was one of the two that had stripped and performed tests on him, or a new one: the uniform clean suits and external speakers of the masks made it hard to differentiate one person from another, and all the medical personnel wore the Caduceus sigil on their shoulder: the only person he'd been able to identify amongst the crowd so far had been Hankins, and there was no sign of him in the room: just a single medic and pair of armed guards standing motionless behind him.

"You can come and see Miss McClaren now. You need to hurry up if you want to say your goodbyes. I'm afraid she doesn't have much time."

He slipped off the bed, his legs shaking and weak as the remnants of the drugs in him continued to seep out his system. He pressed the balls of his hands into his eyes, screwing them tight and rubbing away the crust of sleep that had built up there, then scratched furiously at his chin: there seemed to be more than a days worth of stubble on his chin, but that wasn't possible, was it?

"How long have I been here?" he asked, his mouth dry and his throat feeling like it had been stripped.

"Nearly forty hours," the medic barely looked at his watch. "Miss McCalaren's lasted a lot longer than we'd anticipated, but it seems like she's nearing the end of her time here."

"Where's she going?" Bill asked numbly, stumbling towards the open door and passing the two guards, both of them seemingly involved in a conversation they'd decided to keep private: their head nodded or shook, and the larger of them shook his shoulders slightly in silent mirth.

"I can get a wheel chair if it would make it easier for you," the medic offered, but Bill shook his head, half-tripping out into the corridor. He felt strong enough to walk if he took his time; if he moved too quickly his head would swim drunkenly, and he'd have to stop and lean against the wall to recover.

"I've got other patients to attend," the medic said as he stepped into the corridor behind Bill, tapping one of the armed guards on the shoulder "Can you take him and bring him back?"

The tallest nodded, snapping his submachine gun up and fall in step behind Bill, nudging him in the small of the back with the muzzle of his weapon, even though he showed no sign of hesitation in going onwards. His companion followed his lead, his speaker snapping and crackling as he nudged the controls for it, activating the external output.

"I have to say goodbye," Bill muttered, his mouth still dry. "Are they taking her somewhere? Special care? A specialist doctor?"

The larger of the armed guards chuckled dryly to himself, motioning onwards with his weapon and pointing him towards another pair of guards that stood by a door at the far end of the corridor. "She's in there still, but if she's a real good girl, she'll be going upstairs soon," he answered, his voice a slow, American drawl that Bill had only heard in films before now, typical of the southern states.

"Is that where the specialist is? I want to go with her…"

"Boy, you'll be joining her upstairs real soon, don't worry about that now. See, that's where the ashes are dumped, all the dead get burned, and the remains disposed of with the rest of the medical waste. She's as good as dead, and Christ, you're probably next."

He chuckled, a deep and throaty laugh, and his companion turned his masked face to stare at him. Though Bill couldn't see his face, he could tell by the body language that he was visibly upset. "Jesus fucking Christ, Jason, keep that shit on a secure line; mouthing off in front of this guy or anyone else… show a little fucking professionalism, or at least some common fucking courtesy, you heartless son of a bitch. That's his girlfriend in there, how'd you like it if your girl…"

"Big fucking deal, Mike, she should already be dead, you heard what those squints have been saying in the barracks. This is that one they were talking about, the one crawling with the disease. Like a dirty whore, like she's fucked every infected person in London before they died. Maybe even after. They're surprised that she's still alive. Three minutes time that bitch croaks, we torch the room, flush it out and deliver the remains for disposal while another poor bastard is dragged in here and forced to wait out the end of their days in there. In the mean time, this bastard here's sitting in his room, waiting to start bleeding out his ass, then he gets char-grilled and the circle starts again. You know this ain't what we signed up for, Mike, you telling me looking after the sick and dying is what you signed up for? Lock 'em up and let 'em rot, that's what I say. I ain't no babysitter."

Anger and rage built up inside Bill, something he hadn't felt so strongly in years, and curled his fingers into a tight fist, his hands shaking and knuckles whitening as he felt his muscles tense. He raised his fist and lunged forwards with a deafening scream, his fist connecting with the abdomen of the larger man. He was wearing armour beneath the sterile suit, which absorbed the brunt of the blow, but the sudden action was enough to make the large American stumble back and falter. He tripped over, and Bill went down with him, raining a flurry of useless and ineffective blows against his armoured torso then scrabbling for the mask, his finger seeking out the catches of the protective casing.

The two guards by the door sprang to life, diving on to Bill and pulling him up, while the soldier referred to as Mike grabbed Jason and pulled him up to his feet, keeping his body between him and Bill as the opinionated American fumbled for his weapon.

"Stand aside, Mike, I'm gonna plug this fucker now, save us all some time."

"Back off, you insensitive shit," screamed Mike, knocking him back with both hands and keeping him well away from the still-snarling form of Bill. "If he didn't do something, I was sure as hell going to. There's a line, Jason, and you crossed it."

Without warning, Bill broke free from his captors and lunged again, this time swinging a right hook around, connecting with the large man in the side and finding an opening in the armour pads. He stumbled again, but this time kept himself up by toppling against the wall.

"That all you got?" he snarled, lowering his weapon and stepping forwards. "Your girlfriend hit me harder than that when I was fucking her last night!"

"What the fuck is going on here?"

The familiar voice of Hankins boomed down the corridor, and everyone froze, spinning to face the man at the far end of the corridor. He strode purposefully towards the rabble, his hand instinctively lowering to his sidearm, as he looked first from Bill, to Jason, then back to Bill. "We are here to do a job, you ignorant bunch of assholes, and our job is look after the people here, make sure infection is contained. It is *not* to taunt, degrade or belittle the prisoners, and I hope, Miller, that this is not your bullshit again. Fuck up one more time, and you'll be scrubbing the rooms of the infected out using your toothbrush. Your name's already been mentioned in more than one report going to TacCom. They can see to it that you're stripped of rank, and I can see to it that you're stripped of your protective clothing, do I make myself clear?"

"Crystal, sir," Jason Miller reluctantly saluted, and as he did so, Bill leant over and spat a wad of phlegm on to his visor. He showed remarkable restraint, not flinching or even attempting to wipe it off. He turned to face the corridor he'd just walked down, holding his weapon tight against his chest.

Hankins leaned closer to Miller, the communication travelling through a closed circuit between the two. Hankins' head wobbled as he talked, and Miller nodded solemnly before reaching up with a gloved hand and wiping his lens. Finally finished with the soldier under his command, Hankins turned to face Bill. He reached out, grabbed the flimsy coverall that Bill wore, then pulled him in closer to him, close enough that Bill could hear the slight crackle of the external speakers and the gentle rasping breath of the man behind the mask.

"My men here have a job to do, Mister Reddings, and to be honest, breeching protocol and taking you half way across the complex to go and see your girlfriend is not standard procedure. This is a courtesy I've extended to you, you ungrateful bastard, and behaving like this is like throwing it all back in my face. If you pull any more shit like this, I won't have to pull any of my men back off you because I'll personally blow your diseased brains out all over the fucking wall, do you understand?"

Bill nodded numbly, feeling intimidated by the closeness of the soldier and the butt of the weapon strapped to his belt that pressed against his stomach. He motioned to the door at the far end of the pushed Bill in that direction, and then nodded to the gathered soldiers to fall in line behind him and follow in a loose formation. The rest of the short walk was conducted in silence; the only noise he could hear was the soft squeak of army boots on the tiled floor and the rustling of Bill's paper garments. All the doors they passed were locked, the electronic readouts embedded on the wall beside each door flashing red with the word "purge" on display. As he moved, Bill could hear a clicking accompanying each step, and he looked down to one side, he could see Jason Miller nervously playing with the safety catch of his weapon.

He's afraid of me, Bill thought to himself, *afraid of me, and Jenny, too. He's afraid of everyone here; he doesn't want to catch what we have.*

It was the first clear thought Bill could remember having since finding Jenny, the first moment of clarity amongst a sea of jumbled thoughts, and of course it made perfect sense. If the situation was reversed, he'd be scared, too, scared of what he might bring home to his family.

Only Jenny is *my family*, he thought as he stopped in front of the door. Hankins reached out with his gloved hand, punched the code into the touch screen and watched as the word "unlocked" flashed up, accompanied by the sound of the deadbolts as they slipped out of place.

Bill reached out, placed his hand on the door, but paused as Hankins grabbed his arm, the physical contact almost making him jump. He turned to look at him, and maybe it was just a trick of the light, but Bill was sure that, after all the attempts he'd made, he could finally see a glimpse of the man behind Hankins' mask: he thought he could see fear.

"Mister Reddings, I must warn you Miss McClaren is seriously ill. We've been monitoring her, and as I told you, her condition hasn't been getting any better. The damage the viral infection has done is irreparable. Her kidneys and liver are failing, and we're unable to keep her hydrated. She's not the first to suffer from this plague; there's been hundreds of infections, mainly in London, but now they're spreading quicker and further than anticipated, despite our efforts to contain it."

"I've already told you, we don't watch the news," Bill muttered, casting his gaze at the door again.

"Yes, that's right," Hankins consulted the datapad still fixed to his arm and tapped it with the tip of his forefinger. "Of course. There's been so many through here... All infections have one hundred percent mortality, the final moments of life can be... there's no way to sugar coat this, but you need to be aware: horrific and painful for all parties concerned. There'll be convulsions, and she will suffer; she'll actually be in agony. Any painkillers we administer don't do anything at this stage, the body losses liquids, including drugs, quicker than they can be administered. The only way we can make it quicker..."

Bill's eyes dropped to the pistol hanging around his waist and nodded, his vision blurring as the true gravity of the situation sunk in to his confused mind. "Remember, this is a major breach in protocol; ordinarily, you'd never be able to see anyone once they're in the final stages, but in this case..."

"I'm dead already," Bill felt a half-hearted laugh burst from him. If Hankins was surprised at the speed in which Bill had grasped the fact his partner was dying, and that he would be following shortly after, he gave no indication of it as he cycled the door open and guided Bill into the room.

"Fucking miserable bastard," Jason Miller muttered to no one in particular, still flicking the safety catch of his weapon as he watched Bill and Hankins slip into the quarantine chamber and the door slid shut. "What's the plan, keep the fucker in there are let him burn with his bitch? Kill two birds with one stone."

"Until he shows signs of being infected, we can't just kill him," scorned Mike, his vacant helmeted gaze staring at him. Jason could imagine him rolling his eyes, like he did when they played poker and he told a bad joke or story. "And you better keep your shit in line, Hankins'll run your ass ragged if he catches you mouthing off again. I don't think he can strip you naked, but he can make sure you wind up looking after the corpses, or wiping down the holding rooms."

"What the fuck ever," snorted Jason, making a show of inspecting his wrist. Though he couldn't see his watch, he knew that it was coming up to his shift change. "I've got better shit to shovel than watching some weirdo fuck a corpse that's still warm and bleeding. I've got a game of poker to thrash some rookies at to pay for my next night of leave."

"Still trying to hook up with that nurse?"

Jason smiled, nodding his head. Both movements were hidden by the helmet and mask, and as he saw another pair of soldiers appear at the far end of the corridor to relieve them, he lowered his weapon and raised his hand, offering Mike a high-five. Reluctantly his friend returned the gesture, and the two walked away from their guard duty, lazily saluting their replacements with just the tip of their fingers brushing the brow of their mask before returning to the decontamination chambers.

"That nurse *will* be mine, trust me. And I hear she likes to have her temperature taken with a rectal thermometer, too, if you know what I mean."

"You're as subtle as a sledgehammer," Mike shook his head grimly. "I know what you mean."

Bill stood by the closed door, sensing Hankins shifting his weight from side to side behind him, and stared at the figure lying on the bed before him as he took a tentative step forwards. He looked back over his shoulder towards Hankins, as if seeking approval to approach his girlfriend, but the mirrored faceplate was as emotionless and blank as always, with not even the barest hint of body language to indicate it was okay. He took a chance, taking a short step forwards and focussing on Jenny.

She wore a white gown made of the same paper material as the clothing he wore, and had a thin white sheet draped over her legs and distended abdomen. Her limbs were painfully thin, with pale, opaque skin pulled tight and splitting across joints and oozing blood diluted by pus and mucus. Bill tried to ignore these, tried to pay no attention to the pink stains on the sheet that were slowly seeping across the clothes and sheet. He kept his eyes focussed on her face, a sallow and gaunt countenance that looked less like Jenny the closer he got, until she slowly twisted her neck and flickered open her eyes, each movement of her head, each fluttering of her eyelids flaking away more skin and weeping more watery blood.

Bill stopped at the head of the bed Jenny lay on, casting a glance down to the surgical tray beside her and the empty vinyl pouches that lay scattered on the surface: some were labelled as plasma, some as platelets, and some saline. Electrodes snaked out from beneath her clothing and into the portable ECG unit that hung from the side of the bed, the sound turned off but the illuminated screen flashing with a slow, weak pulse that barely registered on the machine. The only noise Bill could hear in the room, other than the continuous thumping of his heart in his chest and the rush of blood in his ears, was the rasping and laboured breath of Jenny.

Her eyes eventually fixed on Bill, and he could just make out the washed out and cloudy pupils pulling in to focus, barely distinguishable from the lifeless, pale grey irises; a stark difference to the effervescent, bright blue shine Bill was used to seeing staring back at him. It took her a while to recognise him, and even longer to draw her pale, parched lips into a slight smile, or at least that was how Bill decided to interpret the motion. They scraped back across dry gums, cracking in the corners and washing teeth already gummy with dried blood with another coating of watery fluid. Her mouth returned to its relaxed, normal state and she gave a rattling sigh, her lungs filling with mucus and blood. Bill instinctively reached out for her hand and took it in his own, instantly regretting it as her skin flaked and cracked at his touch, her raw weeping flesh coating his hand with more blood. Jenny didn't seem to notice her skin tearing and flaking away, and despite the warning that Hankins had given him, he could only hope that she had still been given some painkillers to take the edge off her suffering.

Bill stared at the helpless form his girlfriend, racking his brains as he tried to think of something to say. But what *could* he say? Jenny clearly had enough of her wits about her to recognise him, so it was more than likely that she would know what was happening to her as she lay dying. He opened his mouth, a torrent of words and emotions that he wanted to say but couldn't. How could he summarise the years they'd shared together, the love and affection, the tender moments they'd shared? Any sentence he tried to string together seemed to become awkward and clunky, choking him as the stumbled and stammered through a long string of wordless noises. His eyes began to blur again, tears streaming down his face as he tried to blink them away, then wiped the back of his sleeve across his face. He could feel his lip trembling, and he tried to fight it back, opening his mouth as he tried again to speak, but this time his words came out in intangible moans and howls of anguish and pain. He shuffled forwards, his tears trickling over his tear and dripping off his face, splashing on to Jenny's parched skin. Where each droplet fell, her skin flaked and cracked, peeling apart and exposing raw flesh, looking as Bill imagined a gunshot wound would: puckered skin surrounding bloody, ragged flesh seeping with fresh blood.

With slow, agonising movements, Jenny's arm twitched, and she slowly lifted them, reaching out with her hand and curling her fingers around his. Her skin ripped and tore apart, skin flaking away and dropping from her like desiccated rose petals. Bill managed half a smile, saw the corners of Jenny's lips pull in the slightest inflection of a smile, and finally found his voice.

"I love you," he muttered, wiping at his nose with the back of his free hand and smearing blood across his lips. It wasn't much, but it was all that Bill could think of saying. He just hoped it would be enough. There'd never been any doubt that the two didn't love one another, and the words were bounced back and forth between each other every day, but Bill had never meant the words more than he did at that point, when he felt it mattered the most.

"Love…" Jenny choked on her words, her voice breaking as her throat strained to work. She paused momentarily, trying to swallow and moisten her tongue, grimacing as she did so. "Love… you…" With a gurgling cry, her voice cut out as her vocal cords snapped, turning her words to thick, choking wordless shrieks, as piercing as the screams of a banshee.

Her hands pulled away from Bill's, startling him as they spasmed and twitched, flailing wildly and tapping out a silent death tattoo in the air. Each movement snapped skin and tore ligaments: her fingers sagged and drooped as tendons ripped and ruptured, spraying what little diseased blood she had left in her across both Bill and the floor around him. Bill dropped to his knees, sobbing uncontrollably as he watched his girlfriend writhing on the table, watched her wasted flesh peel back and split, exposing wet, raw muscle tissue oozing with watery pus. Even if he shut his eyes, he could still hear her thrashing, hear her blood spatter and drip on the floor, hear her skin rip and peel away as it brushed against her clothing.

Footsteps approached Bill, and he looked up briefly, seeing Hankins stride purposefully across the room and unsnapping the fasteners of his holster, pulling the pistol free and drawing back the slide, the clicking of the weapon drowned out by the tortured screams of Jenny as another spasm tore through her body, and she sat bolt upright, her midriff shredding with the exertion and becoming slick with gore as her internal organs started to seep through her ruined body. Bill turned away, closed his eyes again, weeping into his hands and trying to block out what was happening.

Blam!

The sounds of Jenny's death throes ceased after the crash of the gunshot, and for a moment Bill thought he had lost his hearing altogether. Then, the sound of a brass bullet casing dropping to the ground, the tinkle of metal on ceramic tiles, followed by the sounds of a different kind of empty shell slumping to the table, this one fleshy and lifeless.

Bill felt a heavy hand clamp down on each shoulder, hauling him to his feet, turning him away to avoid having to look at the dead body on the table. Though he couldn't see Jenny any more, he could see the fresh blood and brain matter spattered on Hankins' clothing.

"What now?" Bill asked numbly, looking down to his hands, turning them over and looking at the blood that he, too, had been splashed with. "Do I… Do I have to sign something?"

"The room gets purged and cleansed, the remains sealed up and disposed of. Then…"

"Can I watch? Bill asked, stopping at the door to the room before Hankins could open it for him. "I want to watch."

"Outside," Hankins opened the door and pushed him through, slamming the door shut behind him and locking the bolts in place, sealing the room shut. He stepped over to the control panel beside the door and thumbed a short sequence into the pad, pointing to a metal hatch in the door and motioning for Bill to flip it open, revealing a porthole no larger than his fist. He pressed his face up to the glass, focussing on the fresh bloody copse that dominated the viewport. "Are you sure? It's nothing spectacular."

Bill nodded a definite, feeling that he needed closure, or at least a certainty that Jenny's suffering had well and truly ended. He watched as Hankins finished inputting the code, then turned his attention back to the room, watching as the black pipes that spanned the ceiling started to rattle and shake, the nozzles dropping an inch from their housing and spraying a thick, gelatinous liquid into the room, coating the floor and walls, while a second set of nozzles hosed the bed and its occupant with a concentrated stream of the same viscous liquid. Each nozzle ignited with a spark, and Bill recoiled from the window in surprise as the fluid coating everything in the room burst in to flames, instantly turning the room in to a raging inferno. Bill's vision blurred with tears, and the shape of Jenny became obscured by the conflagration, flames wrapping around her and consuming what was left of her corpse. His body shaking uncontrollably as he wept, Bill collapsed against the door, his head pressing against the glass and his palms pressed flat against the door. He could feel the barest glimmer of heat from the other side, and his hand slid down the door, reaching for the door handle as the thought flashed through his mind that he should be in there with Jenny. Hankins snatched his wrist, pinning it to the door, then tried to pull him away, but Bill shook his head. "I have to see," he insisted. "I need to see."

"Don't do anything stupid, then," Hankins hissed.

Bill continued to look through the glass, watching the incandescent white and yellow flames danced around the room, scouring the room for what seemed like hours to Bill, until they sputtered and died. Thick smoke curled towards the ceiling and the extractor fans that activated upon the flames extinguishing, clearing Bill's view into the room.

The previously sterile walls were ashen and charred, coated in a layer of soot and grime, while the scorched bed held the blackened remains of a skeletal form surrounded by mounds of ash and debris. The nozzles retreated back into their enclosure, then a second set lowered in to place, a set that gleamed silver that Bill hadn't seen before. They opened up with powerful jets of steam, the high-pressure gas wiping the soot from the walls and floor as their slowly panned from side to side, before jointly turning their attention to the remains on the table. Ash spurted into the air and the scorched, brittle bones were knocked from the table on to the floor, cracking and shattering as they impacted against the tiled floor. In agonising slow motion, Bill watched as the skull bounced once, then fragmented into a handful of misshapen pieces, leaving nothing recognisable left of the woman he loved.

"Jenny!"

He fell to the ground and let out a keening wail, burying his face in the floor as more tears streamed from his eyes, and he felt more hands grab him, pulling him up on to his feet. He didn't put up any restraint, but he made no attempt to help himself, allowing himself to be lead back to his room, his feet slapping the floor as he marched in a catatonic state. The door to his room – his cell – was pulled open and he was pushed in.

"We'll get some clean scrubs for you," Hankins said as he pulled the door shut. "Wait here."

Bill sunk to the floor, still sobbing and nodding to himself.

Wait.

Wait for fresh clothes.

Wait until a bullet would scramble his brains and his body incinerated in the basement of a hospital.

Waiting was all he could do.

III

The monitor room stank of stale sweat and cheap coffee, with a lingering haze of tobacco that hung thick and heavy in the humid air. The air conditioning hadn't worked since the outpost had been set up beneath the hospital; the reason Hankins had been given for the unit not working had been to ensure contamination didn't leech in from the outside world. The truth, in Hankins' mind, was that the United Government Marine Corps had more to deal with than a malfunctioning fan. Still, despite the cloying and uncomfortable surroundings, it was one of the few places on base that Hankins, or any other soldier, could be without their HAZMAT suit. He didn't mind watching the security feeds or filling in his daily reports if he could do it in the comfort of his skivvies: the suits they had to wear were didn't allow the body to breath for a reason, but that didn't mean that Hankins was comfortable to sit and fester in his own sweat for hours on end. At least in the monitor room he could enjoy a good cigarette, a foul cup of coffee, and the air on his skin, no matter how humid.

He stared at the bank of twelve monitors that covered one wall of the room, three screens tall and four across, the datapad that controlled the feeds propped up on his knee as he tapped the cycle button at a leisurely pace. The top row of monitors was blank, linked directly to the holding rooms: Hankins didn't need to see those rooms, he knew exactly want was happening in those chambers of disease. Each room packed with twenty corpses apiece, ready for cremation and disposal. In the last couple of days, the rate of infection and contamination had rapidly increased, not just around his base of operations, but the rest of the country. So much so, that Hankins had been given a field promotion to Lieutenant seven days ago while this particular disposal facility was under his command. Men were spread thin across the country; with multiple facilities having men stripped out and transferred to new facilities every day.

He took a long drag from his cigar, tapping the ash from the smouldering stump into the crystal ashtray he'd placed by his side and studying the active screens. One monitor showed three of his men unceremoniously piling corpses into one of the holding cells: with many of the infected people now dying before they could even record any details, the single person disposal method was no longer a viable solution, and mass sterilisation and cleansing had become part of the norm as far as operating procedures were concerned. Sometimes, there still looked to some vestigial trace of life in the fresh cadavers as they were loaded into the incinerators, but Hankins knew that had to be an illusion, or just the final death spasms of the unfortunates. He'd stopped overseeing the cremations now, completely removing himself from interaction with any infected. There was too many to keep track of now, anyway, and he didn't want to waste his time trying to catalogue the dead before they were fed into the flames. His gaze flickered to the next pair of monitors, both showing different views of he entrance to the compound. A pair of guards, one on either side, waving and directing the now-continuous flow of body-bearing vans. Any doctors, technicians and medics still on site were now nothing more than porters and corpse handlers: cure and cause was no longer an issue for TacCom, just control. They were fighting a losing battle to keep the spread of the disease confined, and for just a few moments, Hankins found himself wishing he were still in Brazil. He may have been under enemy fire there, but at least his enemy was a tangible threat he could actually see and shoot at, and he didn't have to wear a HAZMAT suit in the jungles and favelas.

The bottom-most row of monitors displayed the main annex of the facility, and the large pile of corpses that lay in the centre of the compound, a mound that was constantly added to with each van arrival.

"Fucking ridiculous," he growled, stubbing the cigar out in the ashtray and moving it to the surface of the black lacquered desk before him. He kicked his feet up on to the surface and screwed the balls of his palms in his gritty eyes. "Just stop sending the bastards here, send the fuckers to another hospital, for Christ's sake. We ain't got no fucking space for any more dead."

"We're in the same position as every other disposal facility in the country. Actually, there's some places that are worse than here. The numbers of the dead and infected are mounting up, and none of the other facilities have the capability to deal with the volume. Have you read the daily reports?"

Hankins turned slightly so he could make out the shape of Mulligan, his second in command, standing ever-patiently behind him. He could make out the shape of the data tablet he held in his peripheral vision, and held his hand out, accepting the device but placing it on the desk without giving it a second look.

"I know you've already read it, Mulligan, so why not just give me the general rundown and save us all some time?" Hankins sipped at his cup of instant coffee and grimaced. The cups were polystyrene and were always too hot to handle until the coffee itself was lukewarm. Hot coffee, like many other things, was a luxury. He scrolled idly through his own datapad, bringing up a shot of outside the base's armoury and the guard standing vigilant over the weapons store.

"Most reports are the same, content wise. Increase in activity, rise in infection, nothing we don't already know ourselves, to be honest. General Maxis…"

"Am I supposed to know him?" Hankins raised a hand to stop Mulligan mid-speech. Mulligan sighed, snatching up the datapad from the desk and tapped a short series of commands into it, replacing the monitor screen displaying the armoury with a picture of an older man, grey haired and with a face lined with deep wrinkles and creases. He was clean-shaven, but looked as stern as any General that Hankins had seen in his time in the Marines. "He's the doctor in charge of all the information we're compiling, the driving force behind mapping out the spread and predicting the trends for future infection. He's the one that distributes the reports every morning."

"Not interested," Hankins sighed. "I don't give a fuck who pulls this shit together. Over the past three days, how many corpses have we burned? Seven hundred? A thousand? Two thousand? Nobody knows, because we're not keeping accurate records: we're too frigging busy to do anything like that, I doubt anyone's keeping accurate records. Probably just blowing smoke up the old man's ass to keep him sweet. As long as the Brass has someone dancing to their tune, they don't care."

"Other facilities aren't taking the same blasé attitude you are," Mulligan tapped a command into the datapad he held, brought another report up on screen and motioned towards it. Hankins scanned over the first few lines of the report before turning away, his attention quickly waning: he had other things on his mind. "General Maxis has confirmed the bodies are still considered hot after death. We were already working on that assumption. But, there's been a few cases of corpses vanishing from the larger stations in central London."

"Vanishing? Missing corpses?" Hankins scratched absentmindedly at his head, then grimaced as he swallowed the last of his fetid coffee. "Who the fuck in their right mind is going to lift a diseased corpse?"

"Intel suggests that it may be terrorists. Maybe even the Cartel," Mulligan scrolled the report on-screen down a few paragraphs. "The most basic form of biological warfare. Throw one out of a helicopter over a densely populated area, or wire one to explode and dump it in a subway during rush hour…"

"Wait, do they think this whole plague is something that's been engineered by the Cartel?"

"That was a theory that was debunked four days ago. It's all in previous operation reports."

"Yeah, those bastards spend days on end cooking up recreational drugs in tin pans in jungle huts, I guess something this viral and deadly is too complicated for a meth lab jockey."

"So they're treating these facilities as high security risks now. We're stepping up to Priority Omega for security, which means unlocking the armoury and breaking out the heavier weapons: automatic shotguns and assault rifles. It's also going to mean our guys pulling double shifts for duty, which I know they're going to grumble about. We need to keep a lookout for suspicious characters, make sure no one just wanders down here and helps himself or herself to a cadaver. I know, what are the chances?"

"Anything else on cures or vaccines?"

"Nothing. Whatever it is, it's got everyone stumped. There's still no one that's survived ten days after exposure to the disease."

Hankins nodded to himself, taking control of the monitors once more and bringing up a new view. All twelve monitors flickered to life to show the images from the one holding cell that still held a sole survivor. A man wearing grubby paper clothing, his hair unkempt, his face covered in dark stubble and his eyes surrounded by heavy shadows stalked moodily from one side of the cell to the other. Every now and then, he'd bang on the walls or the door or brush some dirt from the bench before sitting on it, only to leap back up to his feet and prowl the confines of his room again.

Bill Reddings had certainly looked better.

"Nine days he's been in there," Hankins said, rubbing his jaw thoughtfully. "I've not mentioned him in any of our reports, but I think it's going to be something Maxis here wants to know about as soon as possible. In another twenty-four hours, he should be dead. But he doesn't look like he's dying, does he?"

"He looks pretty healthy, to be honest," Mulligan agreed with a cursory nod.

"And that's what I don't understand. This guy here is what I've been spending most of my time puzzling over. This is what I'm thinking about; fuck reports from Essex about bodies that they've miscounted and people working out that corpses are still carrying diseases, we knew that shit from day one. We've got a fucker right here who, for all intents and purposes, is immune to this fucking thing."

"Mind if I ask why you've not mentioned him in any reports?"

"If I say we've got a guy who's immune, and then he haemorrhages out in transit, I waste everyone's time, and we all look like assholes. This promotion gets stripped off me, then the next thing we know some shit-for-brains fresh out of the academy has us polishing our boots while we're off duty. At least tomorrow we'll have proof of someone who's *immune* to this."

"We still don't know that he's immune yet," Mulligan shook his head.

"I'm pretty fucking confident he is," Hankins said, grabbing his own datapad and compiling all the notes and observations into one file and encrypting it before sending it on to General Maxis. He smiled and Mulligan. "I'm that confident. Look at that guy; he fucked his girlfriend the morning she died. He should be just as dead as her days ago."

Hankins stared at the screen with the prowling figure of Bill Reddings for a moment longer, then sat back with hand hands behind his head.

"Imagine if this guy's the key. Imagine if this is the cure; this is where the answer lies. And we found him." His chest swelled with pride as he spoke. Maybe the temporary field promotion would become a more permanent thing if this were the case.

His thoughts were broken by a shrill alarm that pierced the still of the room and one of the monitors sparked to life with a flashing message advising of an 'incoming communication'. Hankins smoothed down his closely-cropped hair and thumbed the accept button, looking directly at the lens of the camera that was positioned in the centre of the array of monitors, watching as the screens flickered and cut to the face of General Maxis. Wearing a combat helmet and with a respirator hanging loosely around his neck, the man before him was a far cry from the file photo of him. Dishevelled, bleary eyed and with a dark spray of stubble over his jaw line, he looked less like a paper-pushing general and more like a front-line private who'd spent the last week just spitting distance from enemy lines. Hankins gave a short, smart salute from where he sat, but Maxis returned it with the briefest nod of his head.

"Am I speaking with Lieutenant Hankins?

"Yes sir," he had the sudden urge to fidget, to adjust his collar or check his hair: talking to higher ranking officers always made him uncomfortable, and he never knew what to do with himself. He gripped the console in front of him, allowing himself to drum his fingers. At least then, with the camera focused on his head and shoulders, the nervous motion that would be reflected in his arms would look like he was typing.

It was all about the image he was putting across.

"These files you've sent. Tell me. Is this for real?"

"Of course," Hankins nodded. He was cut off before he could end it with the formal addressing of the General: he clearly wasn't in the mood for trivialities or protocol.

"Tell me why you didn't feel it was important to tell me about this until now? You've been holding this man for nine days now, and there are no visible signs of infection still? Why is this coming to light now? This could be the break we've been looking for."

"Or it could have been nothing, sir. With all due respect, how fucked off would you be if I made you travel halfway across the country just to watch *another* man die? I had to be sure. We still aren't one hundred percent sure..."

"Certain enough to throw this information into my data feed now, though. Twenty-four hours until we know for sure: you're undoubtedly read the reports, the missing bodies."

"Of course," Hankins nodded, noticing Mulligan roll his eyes at the response.

"If this person does hold the key to a cure, or even a vaccine, then the bio-terrorist threat is almost instantly negated, and the country can get back to normal. It's... it's just what we need. There are a lot of things I need to tie up here, gather a surgical team and a virologist: with all air traffic grounded, even for a General, it's going to take me a while to get up north to your station; ten hours at least. Make sure there's a room prepped for the vivisection..."

"Vivisection?" Hankins flicked his eyes from the screen to Mulligan, then back to the video screen.

"It's the only way; we'll have to check each system, compare them to those of an infected person. We'll need to catalogue organs, freeze blood samples; the whole process will need to be documented on video. What about his family?"

"It's all in the files," Hankins said, fighting to maintain his composure and make sure that his voice didn't break. He had no idea that unveiling a cure to the disease would actually entail cutting up the man while he was still alive. He watched as General Maxis frowned and looked down at the files before him, but he decided to fill in the blanks. "No siblings, no parents, his girlfriend is already dead, her parents are, too. He won't be missed by anyone."

"That makes this easier for us at least," Maxis nodded grimly, then sighed. "Make sure you get everything prepared. You have ten hours. Until then, keep him comfortable"

The screen flickered and died, and Hankins let out a breath he didn't know he'd been holding, rubbing furiously at the back of his head with sweating palms and trembling fingers, then looked at Mulligan. His face was a pale as Hankins imagined his own was.

"Jesus fucking Christ," Mulligan finally broke the silence between the two men. "They're going to cut him up alive?"

"Yeah," Hankins muttered, shrugging his shoulders, then slouched back in his seat, returning the view of one of the monitors to the feed from within Bill Reddings' holding chamber. "Poor bastard."

"It doesn't feel right," Mulligan agreed, watching as Hankins went about the business of stabbing his data pad with his forefinger, accessing the hospital database and securing an operating theatre. They couldn't risk transporting the patient up into the hospital itself, but a couple of technicians could disassemble the room and set it up in a more secure environment. "I mean, are we just going to go with this?"

"What *can* we do? We can't let him go; an order's an order. Jesus, I know this is fucked up, but what choice do we have?" Hankins rubbed his eyes, then reached into a drawer beneath the desk and pulled out a battered silver hipflask. He popped the top, took a swig of the potent mix, then offered it to Mulligan, who accepted and knocked back a mouthful himself before handing it back.

"Okay," Hankins finally muttered, playing idly with the cap to his flask. "Get out there, oversee this prep for the surgery, and get someone to clean him up, too. I'll… I've got some reports to write."

Mulligan nodded and left, leaving Hankins to wrestle with his conscious. While he was right and he couldn't stop Maxis from the planned dissection of Bill Reddings, whether he was alive or dead, that didn't mean it didn't weigh heavy on his conscious. If it hadn't been for him submitting the report…

No, he thought to himself. *Just doing my job.* If the death of one man could save millions, then wouldn't the sacrifice be worth it? He turned his head to look at the notice board he'd erected by the monitor, the few collected trinkets and photographs he'd managed to pack before being withdrawn from Brazil. He raised his flask, tilted it towards the one picture he had of his old squad taken moments before a Cartel had launched a mortar attack on them.

"Fucking Brazil," he muttered, knocking back the remaining contents of the flask and his eyes scanning the collection of trinkets and trophies. His gaze fell on the central piece of his montage, a tattered and dog-eared postcard of the colossal statue of Christ the Redeemer looking down on Rio de Janeiro from his perch atop Corcovado Mountain. He grinned grimly, opening his drawer and pulling out the half-empty bottle of vintage whiskey, the one he used to top up his flask. "I guess I know what God would do," he said, pulling the cork stopper from the bottle with his teeth and spitting it on the floor. He toasted his previous squad once more, then turned to the monitors and toasted his prisoner and potential harbinger of the cure. "I know what *I've* got to do…"

Hankins woke up, the acrid tang of the whiskey still thick in his gummy mouth. He'd barely had two sips from the bottle before falling asleep in his chair; he wasn't surprised he'd fell asleep, though; it had been almost forty-eight hours since he'd last had any rest. He rubbed his eyes, grinding the balls of his palms in his eye sockets, and then checked his watch. He'd been asleep for five hours; Maxis would be on well on his way now, he hoped that Mulligan had taken care of the preparations while he'd been resting.

He looked over the bank of monitors once more, focusing on Bill Reddings in his cell first. He'd taken to doing exercises in his room, something he'd done sporadically throughout his incarceration: probably more out of breaking the boredom and monotony than anything else.

Beside that screen, more visions were displayed of the mounds of corpses outside the incineration rooms. They didn't seem to have changed much in the last five hours, which meant that either the facility had shut down while he'd been asleep, or the number of infected and dead had continued to steadily climb. There didn't seem to be anyone tending to the corpses, nor was there anyone operating in the loading bay. In fact, the loading bay seemed to be vacant, the main door closed and locked down. He cycled through some more images, finally coming across the camera facing the entrance into the armoury. Mulligan was there, the doors cranked open all the way, and he was in the process of handing out assault rifles and shotguns amongst the soldiers gathering around him.

"What the fuck?" he demanded, fumbling for his headset and spinning on his chair, storming towards the airlock seal between the communication and surveillance gear and the outside world and pulling his suit on. "Mulligan, what the fuck's going on out there?"

"Jesus, I've been trying to get in touch with you for ten minutes, you've sealed yourself in there and not been responding to anyone," Mulligan's words were rushed and urgent. "I made a call in your absence, we're breaking out heavier weapons."

"What the fuck for?"

"We've lost contact with other incineration stations: there's reports of riots happening out in the town, there's a large crowd gathering and making their way towards the hospital: that's why we've sealed off the loading bay."

Hankins scowled as he hammered some commands into his datapad, bringing up a view of the exterior of the loading bay's sealed shutters. Sure enough, a crowd of about twenty or thirty men and women had gathered outside the entrance. Some stumbled around listlessly, the camera catching their vacant expressions as they pawed at the shutter, while others rapidly paced back and forth, savagely snarling at each other, occasionally swiping at one another with hands shaped like claws. They jostled, pushed and pulled their way to the front of the crowd, battering the shutter with their hands, then wandered away for a moment before starting the whole process again. They acted as if they were on different drugs, Hankins able to identify more than a one different user from his time served in the favelas of Brazil: he'd seen it all there, and seemed like he was seeing it all over again.

"Fuck me," he'd seen enough, sealing up his suit and pulling his helmet on, hooking it up to a fresh air filter. The confines of the mask meant that his whiskey-tainted breath soon overcame him: though he hadn't had that much to drink, the fumes and the aftertaste was still overpowering, and he could feel the alcohol sweating out his body beneath the airtight suit. "Has there been anything said from upstairs? The hospital?"

"They've locked it down, closed off Accident and Emergency. They've asked for a couple of men to keep an eye on things, and to keep the patients already sealed in under control."

"Makes sense," Hankins admitted as he stepped out the control room, into the corridors and rushing to the armoury. Less than fifty metres away, and around a pair of blind right-hand turns, he almost crashed headfirst into a trio of soldiers as they rushed for the elevator and the hospital upstairs. They were all gripping Hammersmith TAC1 assault rifles, the urban choice for the Marines and the weapon they were most familiar with since they'd all used them everyday in Brazil. Some of the weapons still bore traces of jungle camouflage, a reminder that it hadn't just been a large number of personnel that had been pulled out with little notice. All the weapons were loaded with a single thirty round magazine and fitted with a laser target, but none of the men seemed to be carrying any extra ammo. There was no indication that there was any need for more ammo, but if what Mulligan had said was correct, and there were riots moving towards the hospital – and the crowd forming around the sealed entryway into was a clear indication that something was happening – then they needed to be prepared.

"I'll send someone up with a box of ammunition," Hankins promised, lightly slapping one of them on the shoulder as they passed by, "Just in case."

By the time he arrived at the armoury, Mulligan was the only man left there, an assault rifle slung over one shoulder and another held in outstretched arms, waiting for Hankins to arrive and relieve him of the weapon.

"The closest station to us is about ten miles north: we can't raise that on secure coms, not even using conventional phones. Our datapads are getting nothing from any servers, either internal or external: communications within the building are patchy at best, breaking up, and we're not sure how long we'll have those."

"Damocles protocols," Hankins murmured, tapping his datapad: just like he'd been told, there was no connection to anyone outside the immediate communication network. It was as if the protocol they employed on infected buildings in an attempt to neutralise panic amongst the potential infected and their families, or to stop tip-offs reach the fear-mongering press, had been employed on themselves. "Have we tried to work around this?"

"Only for the last hour," Mulligan muttered, tossing him his datapad. Hankins scrolled through the pages of override commands and code that had been input, all to no avail. "We can't break through to the external servers to upload the commands to lift the block. Maybe if we had a hardline out here…"

Hankins dropped the datapad and grabbed the assault rifle he was offered; slapping a magazine into the weapon and hauling back on the cocking lever to make sure the weapon was primed. "There's a crowd gathering outside the main loading bay, I need some men on there: make sure they're kitted out with shotguns, though, it's close quarters down there."

"You don't really think we're going to need to open fire on them?"

Hankins grunted, shrugging his shoulders. "You haven't seen them, they look pretty stoned out their skulls. Warning shots above their heads should be enough to scare them off. If not… well, no one said our job was going to be easy. And make sure we have a couple of guys working on the bodies; they're starting to stink this place up, and fuck knows what they're still festering with. Now, walk with me Mulligan: what do we think they may be advancing on the hospital for? Any reasons we can think of?"

The pair marched away from the armoury, Hankins leading the way as he navigated the labyrinthine corridors of the underground facility and wandering aimlessly towards the main hub of the sprawl, the loading bay. Mulligan shrugged his shoulders,

"Panic? Stress? Maybe they want to see their dead families one last time. Maybe someone spread some bullshit propaganda about there being a cure or a vaccine."

Hankins stopped outside the sealed door leading to Bill Redding's cell and paused, looking at the heavy door, the flaking biohazard symbol that had been painted on it already fading. The paint used on the markings all over the facility was only ever meant to be temporary, and re-applying the markers and warnings was low on list of Hankin's priorities. He went to rub at his face, forgetting about the helmet he wore and tapping his gauntlet against the glass faceplate. "You think it's possible word about him got out? Someone that's immune?"

"Not likely: three people know he's still alive; you, me and General Maxis. No one else."

"Maxis," Hankins sighed, looking at the datapad still strapped to his arm, at the time ticking by on the main interface. "He's less than five hours out, and with coms down, we can't warn him about the riots.

"If there's anything serious happening out there, the convoy he's travelling in will pick it up, reroute to a new destination until trouble blows over."

"I just hope it does," Hankins nodded, continuing on to the unloading bay, pushing his way in through the double doors and looking at the mounds of bodies still piled up in the area: overflowing from the wooden pallets they were stacked up on. A handful of corpses had started to turn, the shrunken limbs sticking out the pile of varying ages and colours: the disease didn't discriminate against age, sex or race. "There must be a way to get a message out of this, or to get something from the outside. Get someone up on the roof with a portable radio, see if we can piggyback the signal from the local police force."

"Miller's the radio expert," Mulligan responded somewhat apprehensively. "He'd be the best man for the job."

"Well, where is he? Get him up there."

"He's… he's out," Mulligan shuffled his feet nervously. "He had a pass for the night."

"I didn't authorise any passes to be handed out, especially with the quarantine we're supposed to be enforcing," Hankins growled. "We're spread out thin on the ground as it is, people being reposted left, right and centre. Its just madness to let anyone else wander off base; especially with the increased cases of infection."

"I've been dealing with them," Mulligan announced, his shoulders drooping slightly. "Jesus, John, you keep these guys cooped up in here for a weeks without any form of R&R, they're going to go crazy. Remember when Miller almost took down Reddings when he first brought him is? You keep people cooped up all the time, there's going to be all kinds of crazy flying around. Even in Brazil, we got time off, right?"

"Using my first name won't appeal to my better nature for this one," Hankins warned him, pointing a finger and poking him in the chest. "And in Brazil, leave meant we'd go to the local village, hit the bar and then hit on the local girls. The only thing we had a chance of picking up was crabs or gonorrhoea, not something that bleeds you from the inside out."

"You were going to the wrong bars," Mulligan laughed softly to himself. "Look, I'm sorry, I may have over-stepped my margins…"

"Forget it, it doesn't matter; for now, at least. When's his pass run out?"

"He's due back on duty at oh-six hundred hours."

"There's still a few hours to kill then," Hankins sighed, tilted his head and leaning against the wall. Beyond the piles of discarded bodies, the locked shutters were rattling and squealing, protesting as the crowd on the other side pressed in close to them and tried to push through. "Hopefully those shutters hold out for long enough. Christ, Mulligan, what the fuck is going on out there? Can't even send out a runner to have a look, it's not safe. If we can't get a radio tech on the roof, at least get me a sniper and a spotter; someone who can tell us what's going on up there. We'll need to see if we can get the internal intercoms working reliably, at least we'll be able to communicate with other floors."

Mulligan didn't have a chance to answer: a sudden noise rattled down the elevator shaft and echoed around the walls of the facility. It was a muffled sound that Hankins instantly recognised, and he could tell by the way that Mulligan reacted that he, too, recognised the sound for what it was: a gunshot. He held his breath, hoping that it had just been an accidental discharge: though his men were professional, even the most disciplined could drop the ball, especially if they were stressed or tired from pulling double shifts of duty. He waited for a moment, hearing muffled screams; the obvious reaction most civilians would make, and then another shot: then another, and a fourth, followed up by the rapid-fire banter of an assault rifle.

"That doesn't sound like a warning shot," Mulligan turned back the way they'd came, but Hankins stopped him, placing his hand against his chest to stop him from moving.

"Keep an eye here, make sure those bodies get burned and that we keep at least two men on guard duty: I'll go check upstairs, and keep an eye out for Miller. If you see him first, get him up on the roof with a radio mast."

Hankins didn't wait for the response, setting off back down the corridor, towards the command centre, then past it to one of the lifts that would take him up to the hospital proper. He hammered the call button and waited, the sounds of the gunfire almost continues and almost drowned out by the echoes of his breathing trapped in the confines of his helmet. As an afterthought, he hammered the datapad on his wrist, seeing if he could activate the emergency alarm for the base. The system didn't respond, and he knew he'd have to activate it manually from the command centre; he turned to go back towards it, but the lift arrived, and he quickly made the decision to stop into the cage, thumbing the button for the ground floor: Mulligan could activate the alarm.

The ascension was quick, and it reached the pinnacle of its journey within seconds, the doors grinding open on to a hastily erected airlock that doused Hankins with an antiviral spray. The intensity of the gunfire increased, the sounds of screaming intensified, and Hankins forced his way through the airlock, his need to see what was going on in the foyer overriding any safety protocols that had been drummed in to him. A long corridor lay before him, dark and vacant, terminating at the foyer. Normally filled at any time of the day with visitors, patients and medical staff, the atmosphere of the corridor seemed oppressive. Doors to wards and off-shooting corridors had been sealed tight, and behind dark glass, the barest flicker of movements could be seen: people sealed away, safe from the conflict. A small child pressed himself up against the glass of one of the doors as Hankins strode purposefully by, a young boy who gave a small, curt salute to the passing officer. Hankins smiled behind his mask, remembering the awe he felt the first time he saw soldiers in a parade when he was just a young boy. A pale hand appeared around the boys shoulder, ushering him away from the window. A ghostly visage of a young woman appeared higher up in the window, her face showing more fear and anxiety than the young boy, before she quickly retreated into the murky darkness of the room beyond. They were relying on him and his men for protection: while Hankins had been left in charge of the disposal facility, he'd never dreamed he'd be dealing in a combat situation. Feeling his heart beating faster and his breathing become deeper, he tucked the stock of his rifle in tight in the crook of his shoulder and stepped in line behind the soldiers already in position.

He felt his throat lock as his eyes fell on the scene of carnage before him; the thundering blasts of the shotguns, the rapid stutter of the assault rifles, the screams of moans of the crowd outside as they slowly advanced on the shattered glass windows that made up the front of the building. Glass had shattered and spread over the people who had already fallen under the gunfire, sparkling like stars scattered over the corpses and twinkling with the magnesium-white muzzle flashes. Despite the downed bodies, the crowd seemed undeterred by the carnage, and continued to press onwards towards the hospital. Hankins stumbled and lowered his weapon, the sight before him overwhelming him as another two solders appeared behind him, one lugging a crate of ammo, the other a clutch of grenades in a green canvas sack.

Lost in the heat of the moment, Hankins dropped his rifle from numb fingers and tried once more to blindly operate the pad on his forearm, his eyes fixed on the scene before him: if ever he needed to reach the outside world and call in reinforcements, now was the time.

"Holy fuck…"

II
HAUFFMAN'S DAWN

"That being said, the rate of infection is quite unfathomable, and the mortality rate unprecedented."

I

"Get up, you miserable shit!"

Jason Miller was torn out of his blissful dream and blearily rubbed his eyes with the back of his hands, finding himself unable to control his grin as he looked around the dimly lit bedroom. One of the two bedside lamps was on, casting a warm orange glow over the immediate area and illuminating one side of the pale skin, raven haired beauty straddling him. She leaned closer to him, her face inches from him as she sat over him, and his grin broke out into a wider smiled as he slowly reached out and stroked her face, caressing her check with the back of his fingers. "You want some more already?"

"Get up," she scorned, slapping his hand away and rising from the bed. "We have to go."

Miller rolled his head to one side, saw that it was early, and he lashed out, grabbing Elaine's waist and pulling her back down to sit beside him. "We've got plenty of time, we don't have to go anywhere yet."

"I've been called in to the hospital, I have to go. You're going to have to come, too."

"That's exactly what I was planning" Miller grinned, his hands slowly moving up her body and pulling her closer.

"Listen," Elaine pushed herself away and pulled part of the sheet up to cover herself. "Listen to what's happening out there. Can you hear it?"

Reluctantly, Miller stopped his advances and sat still, breathing through an open mouth as he tried to listen what was going on outside. He could hear shouting and screaming, loud bangs and crashes, sirens and the sounds of vehicles racing back and forth. He shrugged his shoulders, shaking his head. "Saturday night, this shit's normal, right? Party night, the weekend's here, everyone's happy and cuts loose. Isn't this place the self-proclaimed party capital of the north?"

"No, it's not normal," Elaine hissed, locking Miller's gaze with her own piercing soft blue eyes. "It's far from fucking normal. Off-key singing, yes, *maybe* the odd drunken cock-swinging competition: *that's* what happens on a weekend. It's fucking chaos out there. Up here, we're ten floors up, it shouldn't be this loud. It's all over the news."

For the first time, Miller noticed that it wasn't just the bedside lamp illuminating the room; there was also the soft glow from the large monitor that was fixed to the wall above the double set of drawers that dominated one wall of the large room. All the furniture was made from wood and metal, mahogany and rustic ironwork that was a stark contrast to the lush red walls and complimentary drapes that covered the window and part of the canopy bed's suspended frame. Miller remembered that when he'd first entered the room, it had reminded him of a brothel. Not one of the cheap ones he'd been forced to frequent in Brazil, but more like one of the classy establishments that had been stationed just outside Fort Jackson where his basic training had been carried out in. Bootcamp had been a bitch, but the ladies in that place had been anything but. Unless you *paid* them to be a bitch

Of course, Miller hadn't vocalised the comparison when he'd entered the room, and even now he had to bite his tongue as he watched Elaine storm out the bedroom and into the bathroom. His eyes were fixed on the rhythmic sway of her hips as she moved, unable to look away until she vanished into the room, then he finally diverted his attention to the muted television.

He'd seen it all before up close and personal in his active service, but watching it happen on the screen made it feel unreal, almost as if he were watching a film: streets thick with cloying clouds of smoke, buildings gutted by fires, windows shattered and what goods that were left spread across the pavements. In another piece of footage, people beat one another relentlessly, the faces of those that were visible showing nothing but a barbaric ferocity that Miller recognised as people fighting for their lives. More footage of angry crowds clashing with men in uniform as the two opposing sides rushed in to one another with a the same ferocity: there was no sound coming out the speakers, but Miller had policed those kinds of civil disputes before, he knew the sound of batons on flesh, bones being smashed by riot shields and the steady thump of safety bullets being launched into the crowd. The footage changed once more, this time showing fires ravaging the front of a block of flats. Some people were trapped on higher floors, waving for help to the people below, while others decided to take their chances by leaping over the edges and crashing hard to the ground where people rushed to their aid. Again, the scene changed, this time to show an unruly crowd running headlong into a cordon of armoured police officers dressed in riot gear. Some of the charging people peeled off to break into nearby stores, deciding to loot instead of fight.

"Fucking Brazil," he shook his head, sitting back and watching the footage. "I'd recognise shit like that anywhere. Another Cartel-staged protest?"

"It's not Brazil, you fuckwit," Elaine shouted from the bathroom above the sound of the shower. "That's the local news, didn't you listen to me? That's outside, it's happening now!"

"Yet you're having a shower before you leave?"

"I'm not going in to work smelling like…. Well, like you, to be honest."

"I smell fucking great," Miller muttered before sitting bolt upright as something new in the footage drew his attention, something that was familiar. It looked like one of the areas in the city centre that he'd seen groups of kids hanging around at, a large expanse of grassland with a stone war memorial in the centre and surrounded by a handful of independent shops and stalls. He couldn't remember the name of the green, but sure enough he was seeing footage of it now. The flat grassy ground had been churned up into a muddy quagmire by the hundreds of people congregating on it, the stores had been ransacked and torn apart, and the war memorial defaced by graffiti and burning garbage strewn around the base of it.

"That's here," he muttered, clambering off the bed and grabbing his jeans from the discarded pile of clothing on the floor and fumbling his way into them. "That's just down the road!"

"It's all just down the road," Elaine said as she stormed out the bathroom and back into the bedroom, throwing open her wardrobe and slipping into the plain blue trousers and top that consisted of her nurses uniform. "Down the road, or around the corner." She fastened the buttons of her shirt as she stood watching the footage on the screen and scooped up her security pass from the top of the drawers. "Jesus, I can't believe this is happening…"

"What's happened? I thought midnight was the witching hour; everything was fine before, now all of a sudden it hits four in the morning and everyone goes fucking mental?" Miller asked as he popped his head through the neck of his T-shirt and rolled the crumpled material down, tucking it into the waistband of his jeans. Elaine shrugged her shoulders and waved her hand, the gesture bringing the volume up on the television before leaving the room, leaving Miller to finish off getting ready.

"…Across city, with reports coming in from both sides of the river mirroring the looting and fighting in the streets. Although similar reports are coming in from towns and cities up and down the United Kingdom, it's uncertain if all these riots are linked. With the state of emergency currently announced by parliament, the police are not yet supplying us with any statements at this time, but we have confirmed reports of armed police officers on the streets of London, Manchester and Edinburgh at this time, with other cities deploying police officers wearing riot gear, utilising whatever resources they have available. With looting and rioting spreading through the streets, the unrest is impeding the United Government Marine Corps as they attempt to keep to keep on top of infection and body disposal."

The image flickered and changed to show a different street, this one devoid of any looting or rioting, but not of corpses. Bodies littered the ground, left twisted and mangled on the pavement or hanging out of smashed vehicles. The picture quality wasn't great, and was quite shaky, a clear indication that it was zoomed in from quite a distance, ensuring that the camera operator was far away from the seven men in HAZMAT suits that stalked the streets, spraying the ground with fire from the portable incinerator units they carried on their backs.

"With the riots hampering their attempts to keep on top of infection containment and quarantine, the Marines in larger cities have resorted to foot-based patrols to dispose of any infected that may be left in the wake of some of the riots, in some cases sweeping behind the main movement of the lawlessness and dealing with anyone infected with Hauffman's Degenerative Syndrome in this way. This has provoked outrage amongst some members of the public, and it's believed that this treatment could actually be contributing to the increased amount of rioting that has spread across the country. As with the police force, the UGMC have yet to release any official statements regarding their actions."

The image of the incineration squad cut out as a gloved hand covered the lens of the camera, then it cut back to the studio, showing a man dressed in a dark blue suit and white shirt sitting behind a large desk. The previous footage of the riots carried on in the background in a loop, but the presenter carried on with his announcement, his eyes scanning back and forth as he worked through the off-screen teleprompter. "We're hearing now from the press office of the United Governments' president, Arnold Kilmer, that there will be a statement and briefing issued within the hour. As normal, we'll have our political correspondent Kimberly…" Miller gave a dismissive wave of his hand, lowering the volume once more. Pulling his boots on, he stepped out the bedroom and into the main living area of the apartment. He didn't remember much of the room from the night before; it had been a whirlwind journey from the front door straight to Elaine's bedroom. The room was large, larger than his whole apartment back home, and was open plan, the kitchen and dining area situated in one corner and the main living area sprawling across the rest of the room. A leather settee occupied the centre of the room, large enough to sit five people, and faced a screen that dominated most of one wall. Miller gave a low whistle, aware that the price of a screen that large would take years for him to save up and buy. And even then, he wouldn't have anywhere to put it.

"It's not mine, this is my fathers' apartment," Elaine was standing by a large wooden door, tapping digits into an electronic lock that sat beside the frame. "I live here when he's away on trips, business or otherwise. At the moment, he's out at his country retreat; I've spoken to him already to let him know I'm okay."

The lock beeped and disengaged as Elaine input the last digit, and she pushed it open, but didn't enter the darkened room. "There's a gun cabinet in the back of his office, I've got the code, and we have to get to the hospital."

"Gun cabinet? What the hell does your father do?"

"He's a surgeon at the hospital, but he likes to go hunting in the country. That's what he's there for now. I need to get to the hospital, and you do, too."

"A gun?" Miller stepped forwards and entered the room, the lights flickering on as he entered. He felt himself jump, startled as a hundred pairs of black beady eyes glared at him from the stuffed creatures and heads mounted on wooden plaques around the wall. There was an assortment of different animals either on desks, cupboards, or shelves that ran the length of the walls. He could recognise most of the different species on display, if not the specific types. Mice and other rodents; partridges with their colourful plumage on display; a fox with a limp creature hanging from mouth and a badger mounted on a faux stone plinth were just a handful of the ones he could take in before turning around to look at Elaine.

"You couldn't warn me I was walking into this?"

"It freaks me out, has done since I was a kid. Taxidermy, it's just one of those things that he does. I just don't like going in there," Elaine shrugged as she slipped a pair of trainers on and motioned towards the cabinet that sat in the corner of the office. Approaching it, Miller knelt down by the combination lock and looked at the series of dials. "Do you know the combination for this?"

"It's my birthday," she said. "Two seven zero one."

"I'll remember to send you a card," Miller muttered as he cycled the dials to the combination and smiled as the lock clicked open. The door swung open and he stepped back, looking into the gaping cabinet. He reached in and pulled out the only weapon that was in there. He sighed, shrugging his shoulders.

"Well, it's better than nothing," he said as he looked the weapon over: long and unwieldy, the rifle has a scope attached to it, though the lens was cracked and the dull wooden stock looked burnished and worn. "Looks like it'll at least still fire, if I need to," he grabbed the cardboard box filled with rounds and loaded five of them into the empty magazine, slammed it home and worked the bolt, then made sure the safety was on and pushed the rest of the bullets into his pockets. "Hopefully I won't have to use it. I assume this means that I'm your armed escort back to the hospital?"

"I don't want you to shoot anyone, that's just going to mean more casualties to deal with in the hospital. More work for me."

"More paperwork for me, too," agreed Miller as he slammed the cabinet shut and exited the office. "Look, I still don't know what the fuck is happening here, but that shit on the television, that's like what happened in Brazil, only worse. It's fucking chaos. And if that's happening outside, here, now, I don't think we should be leaving here. I'll just radio in to base let them know what's going on, and we'll sit tight here. How's that sound? We can lock this relic back up, go back to bed, and… well, fuck each other's brains out until we're given the all clear. C'mon, that's the best offer you've had in some time, right?"

Elaine didn't answer, simply shook her head as she approached the front door and grabbed her keys from a dish on a small table by the door. "I'm going to work, where I'm needed. I can either go on my own, or you can come along too."

"I'm coming," he sighed, slinging the rifle over his shoulder, "Just let me make sure I've got everything, okay?"

He slipped back into the bedroom, his eyes roving over the bed and floor, and grabbed his datapad that he'd left on the nightstand, then paused. As an afterthought, he scooped up a pair of black lacy panties from the floor, sniffed them, and then stuffed them into one of his vacant pockets. He went to turn the television off, but paused, noting that the condition of the host on the muted screen had degraded somewhat since Miller had last seen him. His face was covered in a fine sheen of sweat, the top button of his shirt was undone and pulled open, and he'd discarded his jacket, showing that the fabric of his shirt was drenched, clinging to his body as he moved. Miller knew instantly that the host of the show was infected; he was displaying signs of the fever that accompanied the last few days of the disease. Miller was so focused on the screen that he hadn't realised Elaine had come to see what had distracted him.

"This is a local news station, you said?"

"That's right. Station's about two miles from here: maybe three. Is that guy all right?"

"He's infected, " Miller pulled out his datapad and tapped the screen, trying to link up with the network and report in to his headquarters. "If he's infected, everyone there could be. Even if no one can get out to them now, they can at least try to lock it down remotely. They could at least knock the station out with…"

Miller stopped talking as the picture on the screen blanked out, leaving a plain blue screen with the words 'no signal' flashing in the top right hand corner. "Guess it's already on lockdown. See what else is being said on other channels. It was talking about other towns and cities being overrun with riots, too."

Elaine nodded and started to cycle through the channels, but stopped quickly when it became apparent that there wasn't any signal being received from anywhere.

"No channels work." Elaine shrugged her shoulders. "Must be the weather? It's an old system, dad never paid to get it upgraded. He never really watched television so he didn't see the point. Why?"

"Curiosity. If you insist on making me follow *your* ass out there, I'd at least like to know what I'm getting *my* ass in to. Fuckin' civvy shit, I'll see what I can find on the military network…"

Miller sat down on the bed, stabbing the touchscreen of his portable device, clicking his tongue as he worked. He shook his head and lowered the tablet when he couldn't connect to any networks, military or otherwise.

"Piece of goddamn worthless shit," he mumbled, rubbing his temples. "No network available."

Elaine moved towards the nightstand and grabbed the phone, lifting the receiver to her ear and paused. Frowning, she pressed a couple of buttons, then listened again. Miller snatched it from her and listened to the silence: no dial tone, no soft electronic purr indicating he should hang up and try again, nothing. He slowly replaced the phone in its cradle and sighed.

"Maybe the phone's not working because the exchange is overloaded," suggested Elaine.

"Maybe," Miller tapped idly at his datapad. "This thing should be able to find something. But it can't."

He stood up, looking around the room once more, then nodded towards the door to the apartment. "If you really want to do this, then lets move. Stay close to me, and do as I say. If it's as bad out there as the news said, it shouldn't be too hard to avoid the main trouble spots, but that doesn't mean we can be careless. I'm used to shit like what's going on out there, but I've normally got another eight or nine experienced soldiers covering my ass. Let's go."

II

Miller stepped out the foyer of the apartment block and paused, his eyes adjusting to the dim light as he crouched down and surveyed the streets and urged Elaine to do the same. It was still an hour before sunrise, and the skies overhead were thick with clouds, spraying a light misty rain across the city. It wasn't enough to extinguish the fires that littered the street, the guttering flames casting long flickering shadows from their nesting areas amongst overturned refuse bins, burnt out cars and shattered buildings. Doors to homes and shops alike had been ripped from their hinges and left lying trampled and battered on the ground, though one or two had been left hanging from the frame by a pair of resilient hinges. Other than a handful of stray dogs that rifled through the overturned bins, the street was deserted, a stark contrast to the noise and discourse that seemed to have dominated the streets just five minutes ago.

"Where's everyone gone?"

"Looks like the party moved on," Miller slowly paced down the set of stairs from the foyer on to the debris-littered street, cradling the rifle in the crook of his left arm while idly fingering the safety catch. He motioned for Elaine to follow him, looking one way up the street, then the other, noting that the destruction and carnage was mirrored regardless of which direction he looked. "Which way?"

"Hospital's that way," Elaine nodded her head in one direction, indicating a path that would take them past the large pack of foraging dogs. "There's a few shortcuts I know, they'll cut about ten or fifteen minutes off our journey."

"We stick to main roads and wide streets," Miller confirmed as he started to walk down the street, stomping his feet as he went. Startled, the pack of wild dogs looked up and arched their backs, snarling and growling as if daring Miller to challenge them for ownership of the rubbish they were rooting through. He knelt down and grabbed a handful of loose stones from the path and hurled them in the direction of the dogs; he wasn't intending to hit them, merely scare them off, but one stone bounced and skipped across the concrete surface and struck the front paw of one of the creatures. It growled, yelped, and started to back away, reluctant to turn its back on Miller until it felt it had sufficient space between them. With the fur along the ridge of its spine standing up, the creature finally bolted away, its pack close on its heels. Miller relaxed a little, pleased that they'd gone. He'd seen feral animals being submissive to potential threats to their territory, but he'd also seen people ripped apart by packs of wild animals in the outskirts of the favelas of Brazil.

"But with the shortcuts, we can be there in no time."

"If we run in to trouble, we won't have room to manoeuvre or avoid it. A wide street like this, we've got a lot of potential, we can move around, put obstacles between any trouble and us. In back alleys and side streets, we'd be confined; restricted. Fucked, really."

"What about a car?" Elaine looked up and down the street. All the vehicles in the immediate area were unusable, but there was every chance that around the corner there was something that could still be used. Miller dismissively shook his head without any further explanation.

"Why not?" Elaine pressed the matter, urging him to explain himself.

"Cars break. Cars stall. Cars can easily be surrounded by an angry mob and the people inside can be trapped and ultimately have their heads caved in with the curved end of a tire iron. It's not pretty, but I've seen it before."

Elaine paused mid-step, frowning at the back of Miller's closely buzzed scalp as he continued to stalk down the street, still sweeping the rifle around as he went. "Your time in Brazil really fucked you up, didn't it?"

"War does that to you, you just have to find a way to cope," Miller countered with a shrug as he stopped at the junction at the end of the street and shrank back, lowering to his knees and urging Elaine to follow him and do the same. He spoke again, this time in a low voice as he nodded up the street towards a small group of people that were milling around the shattered entrance of a shop. "If it doesn't fuck you up in the head, then there's probably something wrong with you and you shouldn't be in the armed forces." He looked up the other direction of the street, seeing that it was devoid of life. He nodded towards the group. "We have to go past them, don't we?"

"Yeah," Elaine nodded. "That's the way we have to go. The other way heads into the city centre."

"Probably want to avoid that at all costs, too," Miller agreed, aware that was where most of the rioting would have happened. Shifting his weight slightly, he watched the small group of people as they pawed weakly at the ground, picking idly at some of he debris that littered the street. With the sun on the verge of rising, the streets were still shrouded in darkness, and he couldn't see exactly how many people were there, nor what they looked like; it was just their basic shapes merging in with one another that he could pick out. From what he could see, though, there was plenty of space in the street to circumnavigate the crowd.

"Keep close," he warned, gripping the weapon in one hand and reaching out to take Elaine's hand in the other. Stepping tentatively out into the street, he pressed himself against the walls of the buildings on the side opposite to the group of people. Rough brickwork pressed against his back, and he tried to move slower in a bid to attempt to minimise the noise he made. Even though his eyes had adjusted to the darkness, his vision wasn't perfect and he had to pick his way carefully through slivers of glass and broken wooden frames that were scattered across the ground, each footstep placed with precision while he kept his gaze on the group of people. They seemed to be fighting with one another now, jostling one another as they fought over possession over whatever goods they had gathered from the ground. Their words were inarticulate grunts that Miller couldn't understand, but that being said, he had happened across a handful of people here that he had trouble understanding the thick, local accent, though their broad slang had sounded very different to the guttural mutterings of the crowd.

The two continued to move through the shadows of the street, an unspoken understanding between them as they edged closer to the group, to the point that Miller could smell them. Heavy smoke and soot permeated the air around them, telling him they'd been close to a big fire, but that could mean anywhere in the entire city at this point in time. There was also a faint, unpleasant aroma of faecal matter, as if one or more of the people had been rolling around in waste, and something else that Miller struggled to place, but he could see in the dim light of the rising sun that

Elaine registered disgust and recognition on her face, too.

Focusing on the task ahead, Miller held his breath as he inched past the group who were too intent on whatever they were handling to take any notice of anything else, until someone distracted them.

Out of breath, a pair of men stumbled into the street, laughing and celebrating, their arms heavily laden with boxes of electronics and hessian bags filled with bottles of expensive wines and spirits that clanked together as they moved. Miller froze and Elaine instinctively copied him, watching as the group of people looked up from their own loot and towards the other men. As one, the crowd dropped whatever mysterious objects they held and lurched forwards towards the overloaded men. Panicking, the first man flung his armload of goods at the approaching people and turned and bolted, the bottles he carried smashing as they struck the ground and knocking over two of the attackers. They dropped to the floor, crunching the glass of the broken bottles as they writhed and rolled amongst the discarded boxes, pawing through the contents and hurling the most battered of boxes while babbling uncontrollably to one another. The rest of the crowd fell on the second man, who remained rooted to the spot, terrified as the group bore down on him. He hit the ground at the same time as his boxed goods, screaming and groaning as the group laid into him with well-aimed kicks and punches, falling on him and smothering him as he squirmed and tried to wriggle away. Miller froze, temporarily stunned by the sudden acts of aggression by the previously docile looters, and gripped his weapon, working out if it was worth taking the shots: the rifle was bolt action and slow to fire, he'd have to manually work free each shell and even in the relatively large street, he'd not be able to fire rapidly enough if he needed to. He still wasn't even sure how many people were in the group.

"Do something," Elaine hissed, moving forwards and wrapping her fingers around his arm, her fingernails digging in to his arm and drawing blood as she watched the beating, unable to pull herself away despite the brutality of the violence.

"Move," he whispered, pushing her in the direction they had been travelling in. "I'll be right behind you." Elaine seemed reluctant to move, until Miller pushed her roughly in the back and shouted. "Move!"

She bolted up the street, past the beating and vaulting over the spilled boxes and bottles, and Miller followed, wading in to the fight blindly, taking down the first two people who were still pawing through the discarded boxes with a sharp crack to the back of their skulls with the butt of his rifle: not enough to kill, but enough to incapacitate them and keep them facedown on the ground while he swung the heavy wooden rifle around like a club, connecting it with the bodies of the people still pummelling the downed looter. They snarled and growled as they tried to turn on Miller, but the Marine was trained to deal with all manner of combat scenarios, and the solid wooden construction of the rifle was enough to give him the advantage, scything through the violent attackers indiscriminately in the darkness, feeling the thumping impact of each blow against the attackers as the shock rattled up his arms. Taking advantage of the confusion, he grabbed the comatose victim by the scruff of his jacket beneath his neck, twisted it once, then pulled him free of the melange of bodies lying prone or incapacitated on the ground. Already the first two that he'd laid out with blows to the skull were coming to, gathering their senses and clambering over one another to get back to their feet.

Miller looked down at the man he'd blindly pulled from the fray, and quickly assessed his condition as he continued to move, lifting the rifle and pointing it towards the other people. He could see that both arms had been broken, the left one bent awkwardly beneath him indicating he'd fallen on it, the forearm of the right pierced where both ulna and radial bones had burst through the skin, oozing blood that seeped from the wound and spread out behind him. His chest was deformed, parts of the ribcage having been pushed in, while other sections of the body distended outwards, as if the organs inside were struggling to burst out. His mouth was bloody, a rictus grin of yellowed teeth spattered with bloody saliva, and his eyes were blank, staring off into the distance. Part of his scalp had been torn away, the dull bone beneath cracked and fragmented, a well placed kick having destroyed the brain case and allowing a small scrap of bloody-pink material to seep out. Disgusted, Miller released the hold he had on the man's jacket, his head fell to the floor with a dull thud, the dead man feeling no pain as Miller stood and followed Elaine, seeing the woman had stopped a few metres down the road.

"C'mon," Miller shouted, grabbing her roughly by the arm as he thundered past. He could hear the group he'd attacked were already pulling themselves together; could hear them taking up pursuit, and glanced behind him, seeing the shadowy figures following them with great loping steps.

"Don't look back," he urged Elaine, the buildings on either side of him blurring as he focussed on the end of the street and curved around vehicles, some having crashed into buildings and other vehicles, others having been seemingly left abandoned in the middle of the road. Some had their windows smashed or had been left with their doors wide open, while others were stained with blood and pitted with dents. He could see that the street ahead ended in another junction, and he called out to Elaine as they neared it. "Which way?"

"Le… Left," her response came, ragged and uneven, clearly out of breath and out of shape; the run had barely covered fifty metres, and Miller had assumed that she would be more fit than she was. He mentally shrugged, aware that an athletic body didn't automatically mean an athletic person. A plan already forming in his mind, he tore around the corner and hurled himself at the first vehicle he came across, rolling over the bonnet and bringing his rifle up to meet his shoulder as he rested his elbow on the bonnet of the car, steadying his aim. The first of the pursuing people bounded into view, and Miller just had enough time to take in the bloody, beaten face of the man before squeezing off a round, hitting him in the shoulder. The sound of the gunshot bounced off the walls around him, and Miler grimaced, wishing that he'd thought the foresight to bring a pair of ear defenders; but then, how was he supposed to know he'd need any? His target stumbled to the ground, rolled and bounced up to his feet, blood seeping from the fresh wound. Miller quickly worked the brass loose, retargeted and placed the round in his leg, another deafening blast knocking him back down to the ground. This time he stayed on the ground, his leg rendered useless by the ragged exit wound of the bullet. He still crawled along the ground, but quickly became ensnared in the feet of the others that were behind him.

"Fuck this," Miller grunted as he stood up and worked the bolt again, turning to follow Elaine, who was still running. He didn't have enough time to take any more shots, and even if he did, he wouldn't have enough time to reload: he counted another six people in pursuit, and the rifle held five rounds even when it was fully loaded. With two shots already gone, Miller knew his limitations, knew when to fight and when to run. He quickly caught up with Elaine, aware that more of the looters were stepping out of the shattered shop fronts as they passed, some dropping their illicit goods as the two stormed past, others peering cautiously around for the origins of the gunshots. A couple blindly joined in the pursuit, muttering inarticulately as they tried to catch the pair.

"How far to the hospital?" Miller asked, shrugging the sling for the rifle over his shoulder as he ran and blindly thumbing the safety catch on.

"Not far," Elaine managed to say in one breath. Miller could see that she was terrified, tears streaming down her face, and she stumbled as she ran, he flat feet slapping the concrete with each step. Her running form was terrible, and Miller hoped that she was right about the distance to the hospital. And then she was gone; one minute she was running beside him and the next, she'd vanished. Miller stumbled to a halt, spinning around to see a woman on top of Elaine, clawing at her arms with dirty fingers and battering at her face with clenched fists. Miller stormed back towards her, leading with a sweeping roundhouse that caught the woman on the side of the head, hurling her from her perch atop Elaine sending her sprawling across the ground. Without missing a beat, Miller scooped Elaine up in his arms, threw her over his shoulder and ran with her. Although she was by no means light, he'd certainly ran with heavier packs of equipment and ammo in his time, and he felt he was able to move quicker like this. He didn't need to ask for directions, now, either; as he ran around the corner of a large department store that had been gutted by a fire, and could see the tower of the hospital complex, an illuminated finger pointing towards the sky that gave Miller a sense of direction, a beacon that indicated to Miller where he needed to go. He charged towards it, aware that the streets of the city snarled around the base of the hospital like a nest of snakes at some points, but as long as he could see the building, he should be able to find his way to it.

"You okay?" Miller asked, and although Elaine didn't say anything, he could feel her nodding her head. He could also feel warm liquid seeping through his clothing. "How bad are you hurt?"

"Bad," she finally muttered, and Miller readjusted her weight on his shoulder before deciding that they needed to tend to her wounds.

A darkened doorway came in to view to the his right, a heavy door left invitingly open and promising that inside there was a stairway leading up to a tattoo parlour. Miller decided to take his chances and swerved into the open passage, throwing Elaine on to the floor immediately in front of him and slammed the heavy door shut, fumbling with a handful of deadbolts and chains set in and around the doorframe. He exhaled heavily, leaning against the door as the pursuing looters hammered against the barrier. "It's a solid door, and they'll soon get tired and move on. Are you okay?"

Elaine didn't say anything, and the passageway was too dark to see anything. Miller pulled out his datapad, using the glow of his screen to cast some light, and he could see her nodding her head while cradling her arm. The scratches weren't too deep, but Miller knew from his time in Brazil that any wound left untreated could go bad, especially bites and scratches caused by humans: they were normally rife with germs and bacteria. "C'mon," he said, clipping the datapad to his belt and angling it to act as a light as he started to climb the stairs, bringing the rifle up to target the top of the steps. Holding his breath as he moved, he reached the landing and felt himself relax.

Parlour was being generous to the tattoo shop: it was a single room, occupied by a bench able to seat three people, a small desk littered with needles and inkpots, and an adjustable chair in the centre of the room, with a number of lights and magnifying glasses nestled above it like a dormant insect poised over the seat. A green metal cashbox lay on the ground, broken open with only a handful of coins scattered around it. A small cupboard sat beside the desk and beneath the only window in the room, the doors broken open and the contents spilling out on to the floor: more pots of ink, needles sealed in their wrappers, and a handful of bandages, sterile dressings and bottles of distilled water. He scooped some of the supplies up and motioned for Elaine to take the seat positioned beneath the array of suspended tools. He reached up and turned the lights of the unit on, angling one of the posable heads so it cast the most light on her scratched forearm. He unclipped the datapad and handed it to her while squirting some of the distilled water over her arm.

"I'm going to clean it up while we're somewhere reasonably secure. See if you can hack into a network with that, find an update for what's going on."

"Do you know what you're doing?" Elaine asked through gritted teeth

"Please," Miller shook his head. "Basic combat training covers dealing with gunshots, amputations: a couple of scratches ain't nothing to worry about, I'll get it clean. How's it going?"

"Still no network to connect to. Look, I don't know how to work this thing…"

"They give those things to every ground-pounder that goes into combat, they can't be too hard to work out."

"Wait, I think I've got something… what the fuck is this?"

Elaine kicked and pushed Miller back while she stared at the illuminated screen of the device, at the naked bodies that were writhing before her. Her eyes widened, and she hurled the datapad at him, missing and smashing the device against the wall behind him. "You filmed us having sex?" she shouted. "You dirty bastard!"

"You enjoyed the sex," Miller ignored her protesting as he continued to work on her arm, wrapping a sterile dressing around it and securing it tightly with some medical tape. "I did, too. I like to think of it as a reminder. A souvenir."

"Like my underwear you stuffed in your pocket before leaving the flat? I saw you do that, I'm not blind, you know. And I'm not fucking stupid."

"Well, you should think yourself lucky. I was stationed with a guy in Brazil who fished used tampons out of the bins of the women he slept with. Said the smell of a woman on her period really got his juices flowing. *He* was a dirty bastard, let me tell you."

"And how many other unsuspecting women do you have saved on that thing already?" Elaine looked at the dressing once Miller had finished, tucking in a ragged corner and glaring at the Marine as he retrieved his datapad and tapped at the screen, trying to reactivate it. The screen flickered as it came back on, and it still worked, but remained unable to connect to a network. Miller quickly erased all but the offending video in question, and shook his head.

"It's just you; you're special. Trust me."

"I'd rather not fucking see you right now, yet alone trust you. Sooner we get back to the hospital, the better." She looked out the window, nodding towards it. "It's just out there, look. So close."

"Isn't it just," grunted Miller, leaning his head against the window and staring at the hospital looming in the murky distance, then lowering his gaze to the network of alleyways behind the tattoo parlour. Despite what he'd thought, the ferocity of the crowd of looters hadn't died down yet. If anything, it seemed to be increasing. "We're going to have to go out there; into the alleys. I really didn't want to have to, but…"

"Well, I can get us there," muttered Elaine, nursing her wounded arm. "Don't worry about that. And then you can fuck off. I expect you'll delete that video, too, you pervert."

"Expect all you want," he muttered, working over the controls of the device again before shaking his head and sighing: he was still unable to find a signal, which didn't seem right. Acting on an impulse, he rifled through the contents of the desk and pulled out the telephone, lifting it to his ear and thumbing on the power as he did so. He shook his head, dropped it back to the desk. "No signal either. This… this isn't right. First the TV goes out, I can't get a signal on any network, not even the military's. Now, even the fixed line's dead. This isn't right. This is… mother fuckers," he snarled as realisation dawned on him, and he swept his hand across the desk, sweeping it clear so he could work on his pad, setting it up on the table and sliding out an additional keyboard from the underside. He worked at it furiously, shaking his head and muttering incoherently as he did so, before finally pushing it across the desk with a sneer. "Those sons of bitches, they've dropped the curtain on us. All these signals being knocked out, it's Damocles."

"And what's that?" Elaine pushed herself up from the seat and stumbled over to the desk, wrapping a bandage around her arm and strapping it to her chest to immobilise the limb and keep it elevated. She placed her free hand gently on Miller's shoulders, before remembering that she was in a bad mood with him and removed it, hooking her thumb over the waistband of her trousers instead.

"We used it all the time in Brazil when we were taking on Bebops. Ah, the Cartels, rather. There's a network of satellites up there, they can neutralise all forms of electronic communications. Disables wireless networks, cuts off fibre-optics, phone lines. The only thing it doesn't disable is line of sight shit like semaphore or Morse code with lights. Which is next to useless, and barely anyone knows now, anyway. We'd use it when we attacked to knock out a target base or whatever to make sure they couldn't get word out for reinforcements."

"And they're using it here? Why?"

"We started using it on buildings here to isolate cases where infection occurred. Out there, it was for our protection: here, it was for media control. Keeping news of the infection and its severity out the public eye to keep everyone calm. We could target one building; we could target a compound. Seems like… like we're targeting the whole city, though…"

"Why would you do that?"

"Fuck knows," he muttered, slamming the extended keypad shut and pocketing the device once more. "And it wasn't me that did this, trust me."

Pushing the desk to one side, he unlatched the lock of the window and jiggled the frame, working loose the dried paint that had sealed the wooden sash shut and heaving the window open. The clean, almost antiseptic smell of the parlour was quickly washed away as the morning air rushed in to the confined space, the smell of the dampness brought by the rain thick with the cloying stench of burning debris. Thick palls of dark grey smoke were starting to rise all across the city: from his vantage point, he could count six, all of them snaking lazily towards the sky. Though the rain clouds were starting to dissipate, these smokestacks continued to obscure the morning sun, casting a muted pale palette over the buildings. The alleyway was still as dark as it had been before, but now he could see a metal ladder and railing bolted to the wall, descending into the murk below.

"We're going," he finally announced, swinging his leg out the window and testing the sturdiness of the ladder before slinging the rifle over his shoulder and starting to descend into the darkened streets below. "You want me to carry you down?"

"I'd rather jump," she muttered, adjusting her bandage. "I'm sure I'll manage."

"Fuck it, then," Miller shrugged as he slowly clambered down the ladder a rung at a time, taking his time as he descended and allowing his vision to become accustomed to the murk as he went. He dropped the last couple of feet, his boots splashing down in the puddles littering the ground. Bringing his rifle up and tucking the stock under his shoulder, he stood motionless in the dark backstreet as he waited for Elaine to clumsily make her way down the ladder. He glanced up at her to check on her progress and smirked as she slowly made her way down the ladder.

"Shame you're not wearing a skirt, this would make a fine video," he grinned as he spoke before returning his attention to the alley.

Elaine gave a wordless grunt by way of response as she dropped to the ground, her step faltering as she nursed her injured arm, but shrugged off the guiding hand of Miller as he tried to help steady her. Blood was still oozing through the dressing on her arm, and she seemed to be visibly shaking from the exertion of the climb.

"You sure you okay?"

"Fine," she said with a shake of her head, motioning towards the end of the alleyway in the distance. It was the only main source of light in the enclosed space, leading out on to a main street that, hopefully, wouldn't be as filled with as many rioters as the previous. The waning light picked out the barest hint of the grimace that was etched on her face: pain, determination and maybe a touch of hatred directed towards Miller. "Let's go," she muttered as she started to venture slowly down the back alley and towards the main street it opened up on.

Miller had seen hell on the streets of Rio de Janeiro almost a year ago, when a Cartel had managed to rally up enough local support to incite a violent demonstration directed towards the Marines' main base of operations near one of the main ports there. That had seen civilians both young and old take to the streets, men and women rioting alongside children. Ninety percent of those people had been armed with guns, making it an incredibly dangerous period of time. As those riots had proven, there was little skill in killing simply by pulling a trigger. Most bodies recovered in the aftermath of that riot had been shot, some multiple times, to the point where gunshot wounds no longer fazed him: he'd seen enough in his time. It was the bodies of people who had been beaten to death that moved him more. A primal, violent way to go: there was nothing quick about it, nothing painless. The streets closer to the hospital were thick with these bodies that turned Miller's stomach, lying on either side of the road, or in some cases in the middle of it. Broken necks were the main cause of death in most of the bodies, their necks snapped and hanging at an unnatural angle: one particularly gruesome body of a young girl about no older than fourteen had parts of her spine poking out from a bloody wound that ran down her back. Others were covered in bruises and footprints, as if they'd been victims of a stampede. It seemed that the closer they got to the hospital, the greater the number of bodies lying around.

The only saving grace for the travelling pair was that there was no sunlight or heat to spoil the bodies: the streets were dark and miserable, glistening wet from the downpour of rain that drummed against the pavement. It had looked like there was going to be a break in the rain at one point, but instead it had started to come down heavier, much to Miller's chagrin; it pelted his cropped head and plastered Elaine's hair to her forehead. Miller looked over his shoulder every so often, aware that they were just around the corner from the brutal mob that had already beaten one man to death in front of his eyes. He couldn't imagine that it had been just that one group of people that had killed all the others that they had passed by, but he didn't want them or any others to sneak up on them while they gently picked their way through the streets of the dead.

"Fucking animals," Miller spat the words with grave contempt.

"Why the fuck would people do this?" Elaine asked, finding herself stepping closer to Miller and taking his hand in hers. She was more than willing to put her grudge to one side when faced with such macabre sights.

"Mob mentality," he spoke again, his voice low as he looked over his shoulder again and caught the briefest flicker of movement within the doorway of a shop they'd just passed. Tightening his grip on the weapon, he picked up the pace, almost tripping over a pair of corpses interlocked together in a perverted version of a hug, gnarled fingers coiled around each others throats, bloodied faces snarled and vacant eyes staring blankly at one another. A smashed laptop lay on the ground beside them, clearly the reason for their fight to the death. "Once you get pulled into a pack... it only takes one or two people to make a shit decision before they all do it. Course, if you can take those leaders out, sometimes it'll pacify the mob."

"You've dealt with things like this?"

"Similar," Miller nodded as the road leading up to the hospital came into view. Already he was starting to feel a little relieved, but he couldn't afford to relax when her could sense people moving around in the shops around him; no doubt the vestigial remnants of the looters that had already moved on, or perhaps people that had sought refuge after the initial violence had broken out. Either way, Miller didn't want to be there when a crowd of scared and angry people emerged from their hiding places and found a pair of armed strangers standing in a street of dead bodies. As with all mobs that he'd dealt with, all it would take would be one person to jump to the wrong conclusion to create another riot. Lost in his thoughts and paying more attention to the buildings around and behind him, he was brought to a jarring halt as he stumbled into Elaine, who now stood on the threshold of the main entrance to the hospital itself.

The main entrance to the building had consisted of a set of double doors beside an ambulance bay, with the front of the building consisting of a collection of large glass windows that gave natural light to the waiting room, reception and administrative areas of the hospital. These glass windows were now covered with heavy metal shutters pulled down and locked into place with thick, heavy padlocks. Parts of the shutters were dented, other parts painted with crimson and scarlet gore, with bullet casings scattered on the ground amongst the dead bodies riddled with gunshot wounds. These were the dead bodies that Miller was more accustomed and familiar with, though none of them were armed. He knelt beside a corpse of a young black man riddled with bullet holes, ignoring the vacant eyes gazing at him from beneath a gory loophole through his head and grabbed a handful of the metal casings, rolling them thoughtfully around in his hands.

"These are our rounds. These people... they were killed by Marines. A hundred yards away, people were slaughtered by one another with bare hands. Here..."

"Here they were cut down by machineguns," finished Elaine.

"Not a good day for civilians," Miller mused as he quickly counted the dead bodies he could see along the front of the building. He stopped counting at fifty, lowering his rifle and approaching the one ambulance that was still parked up in the bay. The interior of the rear was painted in gore, holes ripped through the skin of the vehicle and the grizzly remains of three women slumped over one another furthest from the door. Inside the cabin of the vehicle, the driver lay slumped over the steering wheel; his head missing and his gaping neck wound trickling blood across the dashboard.

"Not too good for your friends, either," Elaine pointed towards the only opening in the shutters, a doorway large enough to admit two people into the main foyer. By the door there lay two bodies, both men wearing the white HAZMAT suits that Miller was familiar with. Bullets had smashed both their masks in, a bloody soup of gristle and gore seeping out their ruined faceplates. Their suits were ripped open around the collar, arms and stomach, exposing flesh that was pitted and gouged by fingernails. For whatever reasons these soldiers had opened fire on the civilians gathering around the hospital, the civilians had at least fought back. Miller wasn't sure how to feel about that as he stood over the corpses of his fallen comrades, and then dropped to his knees, searching their corpses for anything he could use. Any ammunition or weapons they had carried had already been stripped off them, which made Miller feel uneasy. If it had been the other Marines that had removed the weapons, they would have taken care of the bodies, too. He quickly looked over his shoulders, suddenly aware that he could be in the crosshairs of anyone that may be sitting across the street who now had access to military weapons, before grabbing Elaine and diving into the darkened interior of the hospital.

III

Elaine lay peacefully on the floor beside Miller in the observation room on the seventh floor of the tower block, a view that overlooked the city towards the green-blue river that snaked lazily through the city. It was the room that the pair had set up as their makeshift apartment after Miller had cleared the lower levels of the hospital as best has he could: he was only one Marine, the rest of his squad were nowhere to be seen, as was their equipment and weaponry. He hadn't attempted to access the armoury; even if he had the codes, he'd wanted to avoid the lower levels as much as possible, although he knew he had to go down there now.

He carefully rose to his feet, stretching his legs and shuffling over to the window, pressing his hands flat against the glass as he stared off towards the buildings that lined the shores of the river, and the smouldering ruins that stood where the marina had once been. He knew that if he were to walk around to the other side of the building, he would be able to see the destroyed remains of the airport there, too. The first night the couple had spent in the observation room, the two of them had held each other close as they watched the military bombers swoop overhead and obliterate the marina just hours after the communication blackout had lifted with a looped message telling people to make their way towards marinas, sea and airports to arrange for screening for disease and aid to be administered.

As soon as the bombing run had stopped, so too had the emergency broadcasting signal.

Elaine had wept that night, but Miller hadn't felt moved by the display of wanton violence and destruction. In fact, Miller hadn't felt anything other than mild irritation as he managed to attach his datapad to the military network at that point, only to find that access to all files and folders he'd previously been able to access were no longer available: apparently he was trying to log on with the credentials of someone that had been reported KIA. All that he could glean from his brief connection was that the entire island was being quarantined, though he couldn't find out how before the network went down again.

The observation room had been the place they'd watched the military wipe out potentially hundreds and thousands of people; the place they'd had sex once more.

The room that Elaine had died in.

Though he wasn't sure how Elaine had contracted Hauffman's Degenerative Syndrome, he was sure that it had something to do with the scratches she'd picked up in their journey to the hospital: the wounds shown signs of infection, and the disease had burned quickly through her system in a matter of days: four days, to be precise. Miller had seen people take longer to succumb, but he'd also seen people die a lot quicker. In the end, he hadn't been able to let Elaine suffer. He'd seen the infection enough over the past three weeks to know the signs, and know that there was no coming back. He'd killed her while she lay in a fitful coma with sweat pouring from her body and watery blood oozing from her eyes and mouth. Miller had taken care of her by putting a bullet in her head while she'd slept, a round from the rifle that had entered through her open mouth and cracked her head open at the back. When he'd moved the body and wrapped her in a sheet, the bullet had burst clean through the floor beneath her. He'd carefully mopped the spilled blood up and slung the sheet on a metal gurney, then had sat by Elaine while he'd watched the sun set and rise once more.

He was alone now; Elaine had been his only company while the city outside had turned into chaos on the streets, violence that dwarfed the previous riots by comparison. Those that hadn't been in the right place at the right time and died in the military surgical strikes now wandered aimlessly in the streets, attacking one another. Even worse was the fact they were infected too; no doubt spreading it to anyone they in turn came in contact with. HDS had mutated from an infection into a deadly plague, and although Miller couldn't say for sure, he was confident that the same story was being carried out in every other major town and city across the United Kingdom.

Now he was alone, and he had to dispose of Elaine's body.

Which meant he had to go into the lower levels of the hospital, to where he had previously been stationed with his friends. Somewhere he'd previously been unwilling to go to.

He grabbed Elaine, hauled her up on to the metal gurney he'd gathered in preparation and paused, looking at her face for a few moments. She was at peace, he supposed, which was at least something. She'd been spared a painful and traumatic death, and she didn't have to see what had become of her home city. He pulled the sheet over her face, then rested the rifle on her covered chest and pushed the gurney out towards the elevator in the hallway.

The halls up here weren't as messy as the lower floors. When the rioters had swept through the lower floors of the hospital, they hadn't managed to make it beyond the third floor. The corridors on those levels were bloody and grim, a testament to the wanton violence that had spread through the hospital in his absence, and he didn't like to spend too much time there, especially now he was on his own. With no one to offer him any kind of backup, he didn't want to have an infected sneaking up on him. Not that the infected were capable of moving without making too much noise.

The doors of the lift rolled open and Miller pushed the gurney in, fumbling with a ring of keys he'd pulled from the body of one of the soldiers he'd found dead outside the empty maternity ward. In his mind, Miller liked to think that his friends had managed to evacuate as many of the patients as possible before the rioters had broken through their defences and slaughtered those that were left in the hospital. Where they were evacuated to, he didn't know, and although he'd accepted everyone he knew in the hospital was dead, he didn't feel the need to pull facemasks of dead bodies to put a name to the corpse. Inserting one of the keys into the control panel of the lift, he clicked it a quarter turn to the right, and then started the journey into the lower levels. The doors slowly ground open once it came to a halt, and Miller instinctively reached for the rifle again.

The floors were covered in blood, tacky and dried in some places while slick and wet in others. With footprints leading back and forth, mixed with scuffmarks that suggested something heavy had been dragged across the floor. The lights that ran along the corridor flickered randomly, reflecting on the scattered brass casings that littered the floor further up the corridor. He slowly pushed the trolley out into the corridor and made his way through the dark tunnels, nervously looking from side to side as the echoes of trickling water and clanking pipes surrounded him. He had to get Elaine's body to one of the incineration rooms to dispose of her body; he'd managed to burn most of the bodies in and around the hospital using rags and surgical spirit more for sanitary reasons than anything else, but he hadn't been keeping on top of that recently. And now, a dignified send off for Elaine was the least he could do for her. Something clean and total, rather than the haphazard bonfire he'd managed to ignite in an enclosed garden on the other side of the hospital.

The corridors here were more familiar than the rest of the building, but it felt strange for Miller to be wandering around the facility without a respirator on. He didn't let his mind wander too much as he navigated his old base, keeping a vigil for any signs of anyone else, living or dead. He hadn't cleared the lower levels out, so there was every chance that there could be someone else down here, either friend or foe, that he may need to help or dispose of.

He rounded the corner and saw the door to the armoury cracked open, and his heart leapt as he forgot about the body and the rifle lying on the gurney, rushing into the opened room with a grin on his face.

The grin died as he found the previously secured room empty. The door showed signs of stress and tampering around the locks and hinges, and a pair of power drills lay on the ground, surrounded by buckled drill bits, chisels and hammers. The racks had been stripped of all weapons, ammunition and grenades that had been kept on site: Only the empty green duffel bags that lay on the ground gave any hint as to what had been in there previously. Whoever had cleaned out the armoury had taken their time to break in and take what they wanted, and they wanted everything. It had to have been a large group of people, a couple to work over the door and pack everything up, a couple to stand guard, and a few more to carry it all out. Miller cursed himself for not plucking up the courage to come down here sooner, but what would have happened if he'd stumbled upon the robbery armed with only a bolt-action rifle?

Muttering wordlessly to himself he returned to the gurney, navigating through the corridors and moving towards the incineration chambers, the clanking of the pipes slowly giving way to something else: a slow, purposeful sound of an object striking a door. He felt himself tense up as he neared a turn in the corridor with a set of double doors hidden behind large sheets of hanging plastic: he knew that through the set of doors, he would be able to access the parking lot and the vehicles left there. Even if the looters who'd stolen the weapons had left them behind, where would he be able to go? Another Marine outpost? There was a station similar to this one every ten of fifteen miles, trying to keep on top of the bodies that were racking up through the spread of the plague, but Miller was certain they'd all be in similar situations: the riots and looting, the bombing runs of densely populated buildings across the country, it wasn't just confined to this city here and now. Gripping his rifle, he stepped closer to the doors, cracked the seal and pushed one of the doors open slightly, pressing his face against the thick plastic and peering into the chamber on the other side.

His initial suspicions were right: all the vans had been taken from the loading bay, and the halogen lamps that had previously been set up there had all either been knocked down or smashed. The room was in near darkness, the only light coming into the bay from the ramp on the other side leading out. In the dim gloom, he could see a couple of figures milling around the entryway. The new sound wasn't coming from there, and Miller hissed in annoyance. The sound was coming from further in the compound, and even if Miller wanted to, he couldn't get out through there. He gently closed the door and slipped the deadbolts in place, securing the door before turning his attention back to the corridor.

The sound was coming from one of the holding cells further down the corridor. Leaving the gurney by the locked doors into the loading bay, Miller tucked the stock of his rifle under his shoulder and stalked down the corridor, zeroing in on one of the holding cells where the banging was coming from. He approached the barrier, reached out with shaking fingers and touched the door controls for the lock, thumbing in what he remembered as an override code, then levelled the weapon roughly at head height and disengaged the powered locks.

The door burst open and a figure stormed out into the corridor, reeking of stale sweat and urine and clutching a piece of metal pipe that had been ripped from the smashed toilet and wash basin that lay in pieces in the far corner of the room. Miller's finger twitched over the trigger, but he didn't fire: something was different about the man.

The figure faltered and dropped the pipe the moment he saw the weapon pointing at his face and lifted his hands above his head, looking around blearily eyed as he peered over Miller's shoulder. He licked his parched lips, taking in the dilapidated state of the blood-soaked corridor and flickering lights.

"What's going on?" he finally demanded, his gaze returning to the wavering muzzle of the rifle. "Where is everyone?"

"Stay back," Miller warned, lifting his free hand and holding it out to ward off the newcomer to his world. "Who the fuck're you?" it was the first time that Miller had spoken since he'd dealt with Elaine, and the words felt awkward and cumbersome as he spoke.

"I'm Bill Reddings,"

The armed man gawked at Bill as he stood in the doorway, his hands frozen in position above his head as the barrel of the weapon remained fixed on his face. Bill could see the confusion on his face as he shook his head slowly. "No way, he'd be dead now. It was two weeks ago he was brought in. He should be nothing but ashes now."

"I'm telling you, that's me!" Bill was adamant, but he could see that the man wasn't convinced.

"Well, if that is the case, you can just fuck off back in there, sit down, and wait for your end to come. If you are him, you'll be infected, and it's only a matter of time until you end up going the same way as everyone else, trust me. In fact, putting a bullet in your brain right now would probably be the best thing for you. Stops you bleeding out your ass and coughing up your lungs. I ain't no fucking babysitter."

Bill froze, frowning.

"Say that again."

"Say what? That I'll shoot you, it's for the best, or I'm not your fucking babysitter."

"Yeah… Yeah, that's what I thought you said. Miller, right?"

"How the fuck do you know that?

"I didn't recognise you without your gear on. You finally get stripped of your uniform and put on corpse detail?"

"It fucking is you, isn't it? You're the asshole that tried to knock me out," Miller said, finally acknowledging the facts laid out before him. He didn't move his rifle, though, keeping it trained on Bill as he squared off against him. "So how the fuck are you not dead?"

Bill wasn't sure what he could say, so he just shrugged his shoulders. He motioned to the rifle, but Miller didn't move it. "Get back, away from the entrance. In fact, no, fuck that: grab that gurney over there; wheel it in to your room. C'mon, move."

Reluctantly, Bill stepped out the confines of his room, a sudden sensation of vulnerability as he left the safe cocoon of his holding cell and shuffled down the corridor towards the gurney covered by a white sheet that was behind Miller. He placed his hands on the frame, pushed it, and was surprised by the weight on it. As he moved, a pale hand flopped out from beneath the sheet, and Bill recoiled in horror, uttering a wordless and inarticulate scream as the dangling limb pointed towards the floor with loose fingers.

"C'mon," Miller insisted, motioning with the rifle. "Get her in there. She needs to…. I need to… I have to get the room primed for firing. Move."

Bill continued his task of moving the trolley, returning to his enforced safe haven and leaving the trolley next to his bed before turning to face the doorway to see Miller working at the control box by the open doorway. He gulped, thinking for a moment that the Marine was going to lock him in with the corpse and dispose of both him and the body at the same time. He stepped back from the control box and looked at the trolley before finally addressing Bill. "Well, you want to get out of there now, or are you going to stay and get fucking burned, too?"

Bill shuffled out the room quickly and watched as Miller hauled the door shut, latched the deadbolts into place, and cycled the controls to start the immolation procedure. The black nozzles that ran the length of the room – the same nozzles that Bill had watched for days, waiting for a fiery end that never came – burst to life, spewing their thick gelatinous contents over the room and its contents: the ceramic floor tiles he'd lay on each night, gripping himself and crying until he was asleep: the bed he'd raised up and used for exercises, one of the few things that kept his mind off everything that happened. With the thick gel coating everything, including the sheet that now clung wetly to the body beneath it and defined the clear figure of a woman lying on her back, the nozzles sparked as they had when it had been Jenny on the other side of the door. The flammable coverage instantly became ablaze, burning the contents of the room: licking tongues of crimson, orange and yellow that lashed at the sheet covering the body and the pale corpse within. Bill stepped away from door, feeling the heat press against it, but Miller shuffled closer towards it, pressing his hand against the small glass porthole and staring at the figure as the intense fire consumed the gurney and the body lying on it. Material dropped away in flaming strips, skin beneath it blackening and charring. Miller was lost in the moment, but Bill was lost in his own memories of what had happened to Jenny. It seemed like a lifetime ago, and he felt his eyes stream tears as Jenny's final moments came rushing back: the spasms, the splitting skin, the harsh snap of a pistol that had ended it and the fire that had cleansed the room. It may have rinsed away the physical evidence of Jenny having ever existed, but the memories were still with Bill, burned indelibly into his mind's eye.

Bill snapped out of his train of thought as the dying whispers of the steam jets died away, and Bill expected Miller to turn back to him, but he stayed against the door, his head pressed against the viewing window for a further five minutes before he finally pulled himself away from the door. His face was red, a perfect circle of inflamed skin where he'd been pushed up against the viewing window, and he simply stood and stared at Bill, as if daring him to speak. Neither man said anything for a further minute, staring at one another and waiting for the other to make the first move.

"You were close to her?" Bill finally asked. This time Miller shrugged, slinging his rifle over his shoulder and sliding his back down the wall until he was sitting on the ground amongst dried blood and bullet casings. Bill lowered himself to the ground, squatting on his heels while flicking a couple of used cartridges out the way.

"I don't know," Miller shrugged again, sighing as he pulled out a battered cigarette carton from his pocket and offered it to Bill. He refused, and Miller sighed again. "Not one of those fucking health freaks, are you? I'm in no mood for lectures on how it's bad for you."

"I just don't smoke," Bill shook his head.

"Yeah? You should. It's fucking awesome." His voice was monotone as he spoke, then he stopped and looked at the cigarette he held in his hands for a few seconds, seemingly going somewhere else in his mind. "We smoked these after we'd had sex. Fucking awesome." He placed it between his lips and fished a lighter from his other pocket, lighting the cigarette and taking a deep pull on it. He grinned, holding it in before forcing it out through clenched teeth.

"She was you girlfriend," Bill nodded his head knowingly.

"I don't know what she was," Miller confessed. "We'd only been out for one night. That's when everything happened. We've been together since. Riots. Shootings. Fires. Raids…"

"Hell of a first date," Bill mused, trying to piece together what Miller was talking about.

"Hey, fuck you," shouted Miller, pointing a shaking finger at Bill. "You think it's fun watching someone you're close to being burned? Shooting them in the head to stop their suffering?"

"You want compassion?" Bill laughed incredulously. "Lock 'em up and let 'em rot, those were your exact words. Your exact fucking words. Where was *my* compassion when that was Jenny in there?"

Miller lowered his hand, flicking one of the bullet cases, watching as it skittered across the floor. He didn't say anything else for a couple of minutes, and Bill finally had enough, pushing himself up from the ground and walking down the corridor.

"Where the fuck are you going?"

"I'm getting out of here," Bill shouted. "I've sulked and mourned on my own for something like two weeks, I'm not about to sit and watch someone else do it, especially if you're going to be an arsehole about it all. You didn't tell me what's going on, so I'm going to go and find out myself."

He stopped by the locked set of doors and looked at them, tried rattling the handles, then reached for the deadbolts.

"Jesus Christ," Miller stumbled to his feet and lurched forwards, arms outstretched and barrelling into Bill, knocking him backwards and slamming him into the wall beside the door. "Don't open that fucking thing!"

"It leads to the car park, right? The way out? If you're not going to answer me and tell me what's going on, then maybe someone else will."

Miller lashed out, grabbed Bill by the wrist and wrestled his arm back from the door, wildly gesturing at the door. "If you go out there, you're dead, you hear me?"

"Get the fuck out of here," Bill laughed, snatching his arm back and placing his hands on the door again. "I've been here long enough. Let me go."

Before Miller could do anything to stop him, Bill unlocked the door and swung it open, stepping out into the loading dock. It was darker than it he remembered it, making him halt in his tracks, but even if it hadn't been dark, the overpowering smell would have made him stop and think twice about continuing: it was a thick, acrid smell, something that reminded him of the ashen remains of a barbeque. The halogen lamps had been dropped to the floor and the vans were absent: there were large shapeless mounds scattered around the ground, but in the dim light of the underground loading dock, he couldn't make anything out. In fact, the only thing he could see were a handful of figures gathering around the entrance ramp.

"Get back inside," Miller hissed as he stormed into the loading dock after Bill, gripping his rifle and shepherding him back into the corridor. "Do as I fucking say, you ignorant shit, or you're going to die!"

Although he was keeping his voice as hushed as he could, it was enough to draw the attention of the people at the foot of the ramp. They slowly turned towards the two men and started to make their way towards them, each trudging step a soft, scuffing tap in the relative quiet of the chamber. Miller shouldered the rifle and fired three times, quickly working the bolt on the side of the rifle between shots.

The first gunshot almost deafened Bill as he stood mesmerised by the Marine opening fire, muting the next two into a dull roar, but it was what the muzzle flash illuminated that disturbed Bill the most: each successive burst of light from the discharging weapon picked out details of the mounds that scattered the floor. A hundred twisted corpses, their flesh blackened and charred, each face peering at Bill with a permanent leering snarl where the heat of the fires that had consumed them had shrank back their skin. Bill couldn't take in any more details, his thoughts swimming as he was barely aware of being bundled through the doors or hearing them being locked behind him.

"Maybe next time you'll listen to me," Miller grunted as he lay against the door. The reek of cordite from his rifle was overpowering, at least helping to remove the thick stench of burnt human flesh from Bill's sinuses. "That could've been a lot worse. If there was more of them... Jesus, we could have been swamped."

"Maybe next time I ask you a question you should fucking answer," snapped Bill. "What the fuck is going on here? Where the fuck is everyone, and why are you just…. Just firing your fucking gun at people? And what happened to those people in there?"

"Monitor room's just around the corner," Miller motioned with a nod of his head and wiping his sweat-beaded brow with a shaking hand. "Maybe we can get all your answers there. But first, help me barricade this door. I don't know if I got them, scared them off, or what: I was too busy looking after your dumb ass. Now c'mon, grab some shit and stack it against these doors. We're not coming back here if we can avoid it."

The command room was cramped and warm, with a smell of stale tobacco lingering in the thick air as Bill and Miller pushed through the opened airlock and made their way into the oppressive chamber. There was barely space for the two men; between the banks of monitors that dominated most of the room, the black desk and the notice board covered with postcards and trinkets from Brazil. Miller squeezed into the chair in front of the desk and pulled the keyboard across the desk, tapping one of the keys and grinning as one of the monitors blinked to life, displaying a page of pale green text on a black background.

"Yeah, still no connection to the network," he muttered to himself as he hammered some commands into the keyboard, and then sat back with a grin on his face. "I can still access the server on site, though. Sword of Damocles can't cut a hardwire, eh?"

Bill looked quizzically at him, but he just shrugged and carried on typing, his lips moving silently as he read the words appearing on the screen. "Doesn't matter. Looks like you were lucky. You were due to be cut up five days ago. They wanted to see what made you tick."

"That's impossible," Bill shook his head. Miller shrugged, pointing at the screen.

"Says it right there. Vivisection of subject Reddings; Bill on the orders of some high-up Brass, some fucking general from down south who was on his way up here to watch, take notes. Here's some internal notes to get surgery prepped and to get you cleaned up."

Bill leant against the wall, feeling his shoulders sag as the truth of what Miller was saying dawned on him. "Someone did come to the cell they were holding me in; brought clean clothes and watched me shave. Made sure I didn't… you know?" he made a gesture of drawing a blade across his throat. "Why'd they want to cut me open?"

"Isn't it fucking obvious? If I can see it, then why can't you? You're fucking immune. This plague that's killed everyone out there, there's something inside you that makes you immune to it all."

"Well that's… wait, what did you say? Everyone's dead?"

"You wanted to know where everyone was," Miller activated the rest of the monitors and thumbed the control panel for the security cameras. Most of the monitors displayed nothing but static, but a couple did show corridors in the hospital above: hallways smeared with blood, littered with bodies piled up on top of one another, some looking as if they were clinging to each other. Some bodies were partially burned, while others seemed dried and desiccated.

"I was trying to keep on top of them," Miller admitted. "There's a courtyard in the centre of one of the wings, some fucking garden area designed to be therapeutic. I was burning them when I could, but once Elaine started showing signs of infection I… I stopped. Guessed I wanted to spend time with her before she…"

Bill was silent, his eyes fixed on the screens as he took in their details, shaking his head. The burned bodies out in the loading dock, and then all these other bodies left in the corridors, were just too much for him to take in. He closed his eyes, burrowing his face in his palms as he tried to block them out. There was no unseeing what he'd already seen, though, and the rictus grins of the charred mounds staring back at him. "Shit," he muttered to himself. "Everyone's died of the disease? *Everyone*? This is fucking unbelievable."

"It gets better than that," Miller sneered, coughing into his curled palm and absentmindedly wiping it on his trouser leg. "Much better. Those fuckers I shot in the loading dock, they were infected. And if they got hold of you, then I'm sure you'd be infected, too."

"But I'm immune," Bill argued, not entirely sure about what he was saying. "How would I be infected?"

"Shits changed," Miller continued tapping the keyboard, then snorted and pushed it away, shaking his head. "That's what diseases do, right? They change. What's the word, mutate? Well, this fucking thing's all different now. A whole new ball game. It doesn't just bleed you out, it…"

Miller stopped as a barrage of coughs rattled form his lungs and he lifted his hands to his mouth, catching a thick wad of reddish-green phlegm that dripped from his hand and on to the black polished desk. He looked in shock at the bloody mucus dripping through his shaking fingers and remained silent for a few seconds before finally uttering the word: "Fuck."

III
REBIRTH

"We're overwhelmed by the sheer volume of the dead and have no way of keeping track of them."

Miller slept on the floor of the seventh floor observatory of the hospital, a thin sheet plastered to his sweating body as he shivered, despite the heat of the sunlight streaming through the large windows, while Bill stood motionless by the largest pane of double-glazed glass, looking over the city outside. In the five hours since he'd been released from this cell and his reacquaintance with the Marine, Bill had seen more dead bodies than he'd ever expected to in his lifetime, both in person and through the live security feeds Miller had managed to access in the monitor room; he'd listened to Miller's lucid ramblings over the last couple of hours, he'd seen the man degrade from healthy to someone who appeared to be close to their deathbed. He reminded him of Jenny in her final moments, but at least at the moment he was just sleeping. There had been no bloody vomit. Yet.

On a table by him, Bill looked at his meagre possessions that had been retrieved from his locker at work and brought here for disposal. His clothes had been cremated not long after arriving, along with his wallet, but a small strong box labelled with a biohazard symbol had been kept aside with the things that couldn't be safely destroyed on-site. A wristwatch, a mobile phone, a handful of coins and a pair of keys, along with a metal chain with a pair of military dog tags attached to the end. He opened the box and pulled out the tags, working them over in his hands. Of everything left in the box, he was pleased that the dog tags were still there: they were the only link he had with the family he'd lost as an infant. He'd never known them, but his father clearly had high hopes for his son: the military-style dog tags were the only things that had survived the car crash they were killed in, but Bill didn't know the true significance behind them until much later, when he discovered his grandfather had been a highly decorated soldier in his youth: though Bill's dad hadn't made it into the service, it was clear that he'd hoped Bill himself would carry on the tradition that had skipped him. The dog tags had actually been his grandfathers, and he'd been named after him.

He probably would have been a real disappointment to him now, if he were still around.

But then, if he were still around now, Bill's life would have been completely different. No foster parents, no leapfrogging from one care home to another.

He probably wouldn't have met Jenny in the first place.

And he probably wouldn't be standing in a hospital, wearing a dark grey t-shirt, a pair of blue jeans and heavy boots pillaged from a dead man's locker, looking after a dying soldier and trying to work out which parts of his story were true, which were hallucinations, and what exactly he'd be doing once his companion died. Were the stories he'd been told simply the products of the fever running through his delirious mind? His tale had been rambling and disjointed at the best of times.

"The plague's changed," Miller's words echoed in his head as he mindlessly slipped his keys and loose change into the pocket of his blue jeans. "It still does a number on you, bleeds you dry. But don't end there. Can you believe that? Even the dead can become infected."

Bill couldn't believe it, and had been more than willing to express this fact, but Miller had been adamant, right up until he fell asleep.

"Makes no sense," Bill muttered to himself as he stared down into the street. It was coming up close to noon, at least according to his wristwatch it was, and there would have normally been a lot more traffic outside. There may have been some remnants of truth to it all: How else could Bill explain the aftermath of the carnage he'd seen out in the hospital on the way up to the seventh floor? Blood had been liberally splashed all over, some wings of the building were simply locked up and Miller offered no excuses as to why the doors were locked. Instinctively, Bill powered on his phone and tried dialling a couple of numbers, but wasn't surprised when the screen boasted there was no signal. He dropped the phone back on the desk and started moving towards the door, deciding he was going to explore the hospital on his own.

"I wouldn't go too far," Miller coughed as he slowly pulled himself up and looked at the green glow of the datapad he clutched in his hands. He muttered something incoherent about thirty minutes, then sat up and looked towards the desk and the discarded mobile phone.

"Still no signal, right? Yeah, I gave up trying a few days ago."

He tapped at the pad he held, reviewing the files he'd downloaded direct from the server again before casting the device aside. He grabbed one of the cans he'd rescued from a vending machine a while back and downed the contents in one gulp, complaining he was thirsty and wiping his lips with the back of his sleeve. Bill dropped to the floor as he watched him drink and sighed.

"You say I shouldn't go out there. What the fuck can I do? I can't stay in here for the rest of my life."

"No," Miller laughed softly. "No, because I'm going to be dead soon, then you're going to have to make a decision then. Sit in here with my rotting corpse, or go out there prepared for what's waiting for you."

"Which, you've said, is more rot?"

"Rots," Miller nodded. "I'm in charge here, that's what I'm calling 'em. It's like when someone discovers a star or a creature or something, they get to name it. First there were the riots, and then they started to rot. Like when something's been dead for long enough for an eye to fall out. You get it?"

"No," Bill shook his head. "No, none of that makes sense. I've been thinking about what you said before you blacked out. None of it makes sense. I just don't know what to think."

"You don't *need* to think," Miller insisted, pulling himself to his feet and grabbing his rifle from where it leant against the wall. "You just need to react and listen to what I've told you."

"What you've told me? In the past five hours you've told me that everyone in the city, probably the country is dead: that the Marines, the people you work for, attempted to gather as many people as they could into major target areas just so they could bomb the shit out of them, knocking out transportation and stopping the spread of infection, and then you tell me that the dead don't even stay dead any more?"

"That's right, it was Hauffman's," muttered Jason. It was the clearest that Miller had spoken since the pair had broken in to the monitor room, but even as he spoke, the edge of his mouth started to seep watery blood. "The syndrome, that's how it mutated. Everyone thought it just killed anyone infected, and the bodies were always disposed of. With the riots, some of the bodies were left unattended. They'd never been left long enough to see what happened *after* death, no autopsies were ever conducted, it was obvious what killed them, and the shit that killed them is still active even *after* death. Once we lost control, let if get out of hand and we couldn't keep up with the volume of corpses to be disposed of... the syndrome takes you beyond death. Bites. Blood. Death..."

Miller turned his head to look out the window and seemed to phase out again, lost in his thoughts. He stifled a yawn with the back of his hand and went to lie down again.

"So fucking tired," he confessed, closing his eyes. "Do me a favour: I'm going to catch a little shut-eye, then I'm going to show you what you need to do with that," he motioned towards the rifle that leant up against the wall with a wave of his hand. "While I'm out, have a look through the lockers where you got those clothes, find me some painkillers or a pack of smokes or something. Something to take the edge off the pain. I need... just a little bit of rest. Got some stuff I need to teach you, Redman. Fucking... fucking Willy Redman. Heh."

He was out almost instantly, and Bill reluctantly moved towards the door leading to the nearby locker room.

Bill didn't want to move too far from the observation room: If Miller woke up and started talking again, he wanted to be there to see if he could piece together more of the bizarre things that he was coming out with. The syndrome taking you beyond death didn't mean anything to him at the moment. Miller had insisted that the dead were coming back to life: that the syndrome had mutated into something no one could have predicted, and that potentially the entire country had been affected by this mass-scale infection, to the point where potential carriers of the disease had been indiscriminately gathered up and exterminated. Nothing of it seemed real in Bill's eyes, but he knew that this hospital was always busy, and the city outside was normally busy, yet since being released from his cell, he hadn't seen anyone, other than the people Miller had fired on in the loading dock.

He sighed inwardly as he entered the locker room and started to pry them open with the small crowbar Miller had provided him with when he'd originally been looking for clothes. One by one, the metal cupboards popped open and yielded the contents until Bill had gathered three cartons of cigarettes, four plastic bottles of aspirin and paracetamol, and even a small plastic bag with a couple of buds of marijuana in. He'd never done any drugs himself, but he knew what they looked like, and what they smelled like, and figured that Miller would have been grateful of anything that would help dull the pain. He gathered everything up into a plastic carrier bag returned to the observation room.

As he entered the room, he could see Miller lying on the floor, his body wracked with spasms and twitches as he lay on the floor in a seizure. Bill dropped his bag and rushed forwards, dropping to his knees beside the fitting Marine and watching helplessly, uncertain of what to do. More memories of Jenny flashed through Bill's mind; the final death spasms that twisted her body until she'd graciously had her suffering ended with a bullet to the brain. He looked over to the rifle, licking his lips as he sized up the weapon and glanced at the twitching Marine. His eyes were open now, gazing blankly at the ceiling, and Bill thought for one moment that he'd died mid-seizure.

"Fuck," Miller croaked, slowly rubbing his temples. "Fuck me, that was…. Fuck."

"I thought you'd died," Bill muttered.

"Me too," Miller nodded, slowly pulling himself upright into a sitting position and cradling his head in his hands. "Did you find anything?"

Bill nodded, kicking the bag across the floor so Miller could inspect the contents. He tipped them on the floor and broke open the plastic bottles, stuffing a handful of tablets into his mouth and crunching them before swallowing them with a grimace. He washed his mouth out with a sip from his opened can before swallowing, then he went about dismantling the cigarettes and mixing the tobacco with the marijuana before rebuilding it into a large joint.

"Want one?"

"I'll pass," Bill shook his head, watching as Miller lit the cigarette and took a deep drag of it before grinning. "Your loss. That's some good shit."

He held the cigarette out, but Bill still refused it. He shrugged, took another mouthful of pills, then another drag. He suppressed a coughing fit with the back of his hands, wiping the bloodied phlegm on the back of his trousers, before leaning over and grabbing the rifle. He released the magazine, worked the bolt to eject the round in place, and then tossed everything on to the floor before motioning towards it with a nod of his head.

"Wipe it down, there's some rags and spirits over in the corner there. Wipe it down, and I'll show you how to use it. Without firing, of course. Don't have the rounds to waste on target practice; I guess accuracy will come later in the field. Baptism of fire, right?"

Bill reluctantly did as he was told, retrieving the spirits and wiping the weapon down before taking it up in his hands and adjusting the weight and balance of it in his hands. Miller grabbed the bottle of surgical spirits and took a sniff of it, then a small swig.

"That'll help wash the pills down," he said through gritted teeth. "One way or another, I don't have long left. Let me go through what you need to know to use that."

Bill lifted the rifle and tucked the stock in under his shoulder, sighting through the scope and squinting as he tried to see through the crack that split the lens. He teased the trigger with his finger, surprised at the stiffness of it, before lowering it and looking at the rifle as a whole. It looked a lot more like something from an old war film, and not what he'd imagine that the Marines would be armed with.

"It's… basic," Bill wasn't sure on what he could say without offending Miller. He shrugged, clearly agreeing with him.

"Yeah, it is. It's old, too. It's a hunting rifle; it's nothing that anyone here would be equipped with."

"Well, where *is* the stuff you were equipped with here? When I was brought in there were pistols, machineguns…"

"Submachine guns," Miller corrected him and shook his head. "By the time I got here, everyone I was stationed with were either missing, or their corpses had been looted. Like the armoury in the basement, that's empty, too. Looks like some fucker and his crew opened it up and emptied it out, which means somewhere, out there, there's a group of psychos with military hardware. So you need to be careful out there."

"Zombies and psychopaths," Bill grumbled. "It's going to be fun, right?" Miller ignored him, rubbing his eyes instead while he tried to remain focussed on the task at hand. While he spoke again, Bill noticed that Miller's eyes were pink and watering, with thin blood trickling from his tear ducts and rolling down his gaunt face.

"It's bolt-action, with a clip that can hold seven rounds. Thirty-naught six calibre; not the easiest rounds to find, especially in this shitty country: but then, what is here? There's a few better weapons out there. Most of them are probably in the hands of others by now. Scope's just a quad magnification, and there is a crack in it, but it still works. Still puts a lump of lead in the brain if your aim is on."

Miller stopped talking, a rattling cough shaking his frame that brought about a tremor through his body. Skin around his neckline and hands cracked and wept as he convulsed, and watery blood seeped and oozed from his fresh lesions. He finally stopped, regaining his composure and indicating towards the rifle with a shaking finger while he spoke.

"Bullets go in the magazine. That little box, yeah. They click in place, pointing forwards. Slap it in to the body, pull back the receiver bolt…"

Bill slowly did as he was told as he was walked through the procedure, smiling a little as the bolt snapped back in place.

"Fucking awesome," Miller managed with a choking cough. "You'll be a fucking badass out there, Michael. Just you wait and fucking see."

"Bill," he corrected him. "It's Bill, Bill Reddings, remember? You've called me William Redman, now Michael…"

"No," Miller shook his head, "No, I don't remember. This thing… this plague… it fucking hurts. Hurts so much. In here," he tapped himself in the centre of his forehead rapidly, his fingertip flaking off skin with each successive knock. "I can't remember your name. It's all I can do to remember what I'm telling you now. A lot of it's… it's blurry. Did I tell you about what's happening out there? The fucking… the plague, its mutation."

"You've told me," Bill nodded, lowering the rifle slowly.

"That's a good rifle you've got there, though," Miller nodded. "Nothing like the military, but it's pretty decent enough. Where'd you get it?"

Bill sighed inwardly as he slung the rifle over his shoulder. "Do you have any rounds for this?"

"I don't think so," Miller grunted as he absentmindedly patted himself down, then stopped, pulling out a handful of brass-cased bullets from one of his pockets. "Look, I guess I do, yeah. Here," he pushed them back into his pocket and grinned, showing teeth flecked with pink spittle. "Pretty… pretty fucking lucky, huh?"

"Yeah" Bill nodded as he took count of the rounds before they vanished back into Miller's pocket. Five bullets, with the seven that were already in the magazine… Twelve bullets in total.

"If you get the shot right, you can take the top of a Rot's head clean off with that thing," Miller laughed to himself as he had a moment of clarity. Then his features softened as he coughed again, wrapping his arms around his gut as he felt his body clench.

"Fuck me, it hurts Dean. It hurts really bad. I think…"

Miller was cut off as vomit burbled up his throat, a thick crimson soup of blood, bile and frothy pink foam, speckled with white flakes of tablets and reeking of pure alcohol. Miller grimaced, fumbled for the bottle of spirits and took a second drink, making a visible effort to swallow.

"Fuck me… It fuckin' hurts bro… Don't… Don't make me beg… C'mon…"

Bill fingered the trigger guard of the rifle, standing over Miller as he convulsed on the floor, a second wave of nausea washing over him that brought another torrent of blood-tainted vomit. He tumbled on to his hands and knees, his back arching as he heaved and retched. Bill had seen this before, and it was bringing a wealth of unwelcome memories back to him: Jenny, curled up on the floor of the bathroom, oozing blood from her very pores, vomiting uncontrollably. There was nothing Bill had been able to do then, nothing he could do to end her suffering. He could act now, though. Watching as Miller heaved another bloody load on to the ground, Bill lifted the rifle – his rifle – and levelled it with Miller's head, then lowered it again. He wasn't sure he could do what needed to be done. Miller fell on to his stomach, splashing into the bile, and rolled on to his side, his eyes meeting Bill's as he looked up at him, feebly grasped the muzzle of the rifle and lifted it up to his face, pressing it against his forehead and mouthing his pleas.

Bill turned his head, and coiled his finger around the trigger.

"Thank you," whispered Miller, a bloody tear trickling down his cheek.

Bill jumped in surprise at the deafening blast as the rifle discharged and bucked wildly in his hand. Miller's body slumped to the floor, and an acrid odour lingered in the room, like sulphur; a thick haze of blue tawny smoke hung transfixed in the air where Miller had once lay. Fresh blood and thick pieces of ruddy grey matter splashed across the floor. Bill didn't look at the body, though; he didn't want to see what he had done. Was it wrong? Miller had quickly degraded in front of his eyes, from someone able to hold a conversation with to someone who was quickly losing his mind. He supposed that Miller had known what he was asking for, on one level or another. He'd dealt with enough victims, seen them degrade himself. With the agony that Miller had been in at the end, the bullet had been the only option available to him: and with the size of the rifle, there was no way he would have been able to turn the weapon on himself, certainly not in his delirious state.

That's what Bill would have to keep telling himself.

Remembering his lessons well, Bill worked the bolt action, ejecting the spent casing. It crashed to the floor, the gentle sound of brass tinkling against floor tiles seeming magnified in the dying echoes of the gunshot.

Six in the mag, thought Bill, blinking his eyes and trying to focus on something other than the body lying on the floor. *Plus another five spare makes eleven…*

Bill realised that he hadn't been given the other bullets, which meant that they had to be on Miller somewhere. He swallowed hard, realising that the convulsing death throes and the memories they stirred had left him stunned and he'd forgot where Miller had put the rounds: he was going to have to search the corpse to find whichever pocket the bullets were in. It was a ghoulish notion, though something he was going to have to do if he was going to get through this. He lowered the still-smoking rifle and sank to his knees; his eyes fixed on the open window looking out over the city. He couldn't take his eyes off the view outside, which could only have been a good thing. Better to look at anything other than the clammy body his hands were probing. Sealed pockets held nothing of interest: a handful of coins, some chewing gum, and an unused condom. His blind fumbling revealed the handful of rifle rounds, as well as a lighter. With one final flourish, his fingers worked up the body, tentatively prodding areas of pooling blood, until he felt the soft metallic edges of the Marine-issued dog tags. He ripped them from around Miller's neck, then backed away, the whole scene finally becoming too much for him. He turned to one side, dropped his treasures, and tried to vomit, though nothing came up. The dry retching made his stomach ache, and he dropped to the floor, feeling a cold sweat prickle the back of his neck and his brow as he tried to regain his composure. Breathing deeply, he felt a couple of shudders run through his body, and he managed to open is eyes, looking at the pale-faced reflection that stared back at him from the scarlet pool of bodily fluids that coated the ground.

"What the fuck are you looking at?" he snarled, slapping the liquids. Ripples spread across the surface of the pools of blood, but as soon as they stopped, his blank, expressionless face was still there, staring back at him. "Fuck off," he muttered, hauling himself to his feet. Carrying his meagre possessions with him as he went, Bill exited the observation room and slammed the door behind him. As he pushed the rounds and the lighter into his jeans pockets, he looked at the dog tags before removing one of them and attaching it to his own, then hooked the chain of the remaining one over the door handle and turned away.

II

Standing in the elevator as it slowly descended to the ground floor, Bill was silent as he waited for his journey to end, pulling out the magazine of the weapon and replacing the spent round. His mind was swimming with a thousand different thoughts, all of them revolving around what he could do now, or where he could go. If what Miller had said was true, and he was stepping out into something short of a warzone, then his options would be very limited and restricted. If Miller had been wrong, or embellishing what had really happened, then Bill would be stepping out the hospital a murderer.

With a muted electrical bleep, the lift doors rolled open and Bill stepped out into the foyer, faltering as he took his first steps as the smell assailed him. He was by no means fresh himself: he'd spent a fortnight locked up in a cell with a blocked toilet and wearing the same clothes for days on end. Even though he had managed to change now, his skin still felt grubby. The smells he'd been locked up with had been strong, but nothing had been as overpowering as the potent stench of rot and decay that lingered in the foyer, so thick that he could almost taste it.

The tiled floor was coated with dried blood and littered with pieces of bodies: dismembered limbs and chunks of unrecognisable meat were rife with maggots and buzzing flies, while the white walls were sprayed with the same bodily fluids that coated the floor. While Miller may have been disposing of the corpses, he clearly hadn't decided to break out a mop and clean up the detritus left behind from his whirling dervish of death and destruction. Bill took a tentative step into the foyer, clutching the weapon close to his chest and moved cautiously towards the reception.

The reception area had once been a combination of pale pastel shades, but now the soft whites and light blues had been covered over with a new hue. What should have been an idealistic waiting room to Bill was actually a hideous painting by Bosch, a canvas awash with blood and entrails. Thinly padded seats previously bolted to the floor had been uprooted and piled up against the doors and windows. The knee-high coffee tables had been torn apart and used to board up what the chairs couldn't cover, and the old magazines and thin romance paperbacks that had previously been gathered on the tables now lay in bloody pools on the ground. A large oak-finished reception desk looked out across the whole room, facing the barricaded doors, the paperwork and computer that had previously rested on it cast on to the floor. Despite the boarded windows, there was still enough light filtering in through the boards to pick out the grim details of the room; the deep scarlet and dark crimson that splashed the walls was just the beginning. Ruddy grey matter had been spread across the ground, and innards of various colours lay coiled around chair legs and tabletops, looping lazily from one to another. White fragments of bone and cartilage littered the floor, picked clean of flesh and gristle. Despite the amount of offal spread around the room, there wasn't a single body that Bill could see, a further testament to Miller's body disposal. He stood, transfixed with the sight, unable to move for a few minutes while he drank in the details of the room until he felt his head start to swim with the overpowering stench and daunting vision. Even as he closed his eyes, the blood and viscera still burned his retinas, his eyes permanently defiled by the remnants of the violence he had witnessed. Steeling himself with deep, shaking breaths he reluctantly stepped into the room, gripping the walls as his feet slipped on the slick surface. The heat of the world outside mixed with the meaty remains invaded his sinus cavity, a dizzying mix of sweet and sour, and the stifled buzz of a hundred flies nestling amongst the feted remains tickled in his ears. He slowly made his way across the room to the reception desk, where he looked in disgust at the three curled fingers lying atop a bloodied register of patients.

"Where to go," he whispered hoarsely. He turned, looking at the choices he had. He didn't want to head back towards the lift, back to the basement, but he certainly didn't want to stay in the reception area, with the filth and the dirt. The reception area had two other corridors leading off in different directions, both of which were as uninviting as the next. Miller had bragged the hospital was clean, though, that he'd dealt with the immediate threat. It didn't mean that Bill would let his guard down, though.

"Police," he suddenly screamed, the loudness of his voice startling him. He scrambled for the bloody phone, grabbed the receiver then hammered the tacky pushbuttons. He held the handset to his ears, but there was no dial tone. Cursing to himself as he forgot about the blocked signal Miller had mentioned, he slammed the receiver back on to the cradle. Sighing, he leant against the desk and casually looked to his left, then his right, judging which corridor would be best to take.

"Fuck it," he spat, jiggling the rifle so it sat more comfortably on his shoulder.

Without a second thought, Bill made his way into the corridor to the left, hoping that it would offer him some form of guidance to his misdirected life. He read once in a book that when faced with a decision, most people chose to go right, while the mentally imbalanced and deranged took the left. Something to do with frontal lobes and the way they operated, he never really understood it.

Or was it the other way around? Bill mused, casting a quick glance over his shoulder, before shrugging and pushing on.

The corridor was well lit, and thankfully didn't stink of the blood and carnage the reception area did. It wasn't very long, ending at a large pair of double doors with a fire exit sign above it. They had been barricaded with tables and filing cabinets, while chains and padlocks had bound their handles. The walls, a subtle shade of pink and white, bore no marks of bloodshed or fighting, and the two doors in the corridor, one leading to an office, the other to a ward, were each unlocked.

Looking at the barricade, Bill decided that it would take hours to try and remove the stacks of furniture himself, and even longer to hunt out the keys for the padlocks. He could always go back to search Miller again to see if he had any keys on him, but he didn't relish the idea of that. Sighing heavily, he turned to face the ward, gently pushing open the door and poking his head around the corner. It was empty, naturally, the beds ruffled as if recently slept in. Covers had been hastily thrown back, intravenous drip stands knocked over, and life support systems left abandoned. Bill strolled into the room, looking around slowly. Miller had mentioned he'd been hopeful that patients had been evacuated before the hospital had been invaded, for lack of a better word. Maybe they had, though the ward showed some sign of disruption it certainly didn't show any signs of the gratuitous violence that the reception had.

Bill left the empty ward and slid into the office, not surprised that it was as empty as the ward and didn't show any signs of conflict or struggle. The desk was neat and organised, pens and pencils sitting erect in a china mug with the words "Number One Dad" written on it in a colourful writing. A leather-bound diary lay open on the desk, displaying the date for five days ago, with a list of patient names and a staffing rota. It must have acted as a register, as a number of staff had ticked their names off of the list. It looked like most of the people checked in had been starting at the midnight rota: just another fact that seemed to lend credence to Miller's story. Beside the diary was a pile of charts, and a few unopened envelopes addressed to Doctor Levins. The name meant nothing to Bill, and he just shrugged it off, leaving the room and heading back to the corridor. Without going through the process of unblocking the crude barricade, he decided it would be better checking out the rest of the hospital.

"There has to be more than just the one exit," he muttered, tapping the muzzle of the rifle against the wall, scrapping off some of the wallpaper.

Back through the waiting room, Bill entered the as-of-yet-unexplored second corridor. To his left there lay a closed doorway to a female toilet, and to his right the male. Pushing open the male toilet, the nauseating odour of backed up toilets and spilled blood struck his nostrils, and he released the door quickly, unwilling to go in and look. He didn't even consider looking in the female toilets. The next door he came across was the locker room, and he quickly made his way into it, propping he door open behind him as he went.

Larger than the doctors office, the room was lined on both sides by metal lockers, most of which were left wide open, displaying personal effects that had been left hastily in a rush.

Or in a blind panic, thought Bill as he worked his way through the lockers on this floor. Although there was a wide collection of clothes and personnel artefacts, there was nothing that would be helpful to Bill. There was one other door in the room, and looked to be leading into the staff shower room. Bill grabbed the handle and opened it, grinning as it pushed inwards into an immaculately tiled white room. He tried the tap, and his smile spread as a hot stream of water trickled out the showerhead. It wasn't much, but it would be enough to clean him up a little, at least to wash away the sweat and blood he'd collected in the last five days.

He quickly stripped, throwing the clothes on the floor outside the shower and propped that door open too, making sure he had a clear view to the corridor outside it he needed to, and propped the rifle up in the corner of the shower room, making sure it was within grabbing distance, just in case he needed it.

Standing under the water, he gritted his teeth as the streaming hot water scorched his scalp and shoulders, trickling down his face and body as he scrubbed himself, first with the soap from the dispenser on the wall, then with a sponge, then eventually he was down to his fingers, rubbing and scratching with his nails, until he felt himself drop to the floor, riving at his skin and sobbing uncontrollably. He felt lost, alone, and confused; he'd lost his girlfriend, the only person he really had in his life, and now he had the fact he'd killed someone lodged in his mind: the fact that he had ended someone's life, regardless of how doomed he had been, weighed heavy with him. There were some things that the shower couldn't wash away.

III

After showering and recovering his clothes, Bill had returned to the main corridor and backtracked to the doctors office, resting in the wide chair before the desk and sat with his head in his hands, slowly shaking it from side to side while he went through everything Miller had told him, about the plague and the riots. The fact that the whole of Britain seemed to be dead, or dying, and no one was prepared to lend a helping hand to anyone still alive; in fact, it seemed they were more than willing to wipe people out rather than help them out. Of course, none of it seemed real.

"Is this some fucking joke?" he muttered, looking at the rifle propped against the wall. He didn't keep it next to him; he didn't want to touch the weapon any more than he had to, his thoughts clouded with what it – what *he* had done to Miller. "Some sick fucking joke?"

He drummed his fingers impatiently on the tabletop, as if waiting for someone to respond. No one did. He couldn't just sit in the hospital, though. Despite what Miller had said, there may be someone out there that may be able to help him. He banged his fist on the table and stood, knocking aside his chair. He strode to the doorway, then paused, looking down on the inert weapon. The muzzle still carried with it the smell of discharged cordite, and Bill weighed up his options. He didn't like the weapon, or what it was capable of, but he'd have to take it. He snatched the rifle and gripped its stock, finger resting outside the trigger guard.

He made his way through the corridors of the hospital, each as bloody as the last, following signs to the adjoining multi-storey car park. Miller should have barricaded that entrance just as he had the hospital itself, but he thought the top level of the multi-storey might be more open and accessible than the main entrance. Even if he couldn't get out, then he might at least be able to get a better idea of what he should be expect outside.

Once he found the stairwell, he wearily climbed three sets of stairs, still following the signs for the exit. Bill was sick of the sight of blood. Pooling on the floor tiles, streaking across the walls, splashed against doors. So much blood, yet no bodies that Bill could see. Or rather, no *whole* bodies that he could see. While the odd limb was lying around here and there, there didn't seem to be a full corpse. Miller had certainly been thorough with his cleanup, and he hoped he wasn't going to wind up seeing one of his makeshift funeral pyres.

Much to his surprise, the exit to the multi-storey wasn't actually barricaded. Bill couldn't understand why and tightened his grip on the rifle, cautiously approaching the door and grabbing the handle. He twisted the handle.

It wasn't even locked!

The door swung open, and Bill stepped out the hospital, seeing natural daylight and feeling the heat of the sun beat down on him for the first time in a fortnight. He squinted, shielding his eyes with his spare hand and looked from side to side. From what he could see, the city was normal. All the buildings, at roof level at least, seemed normal. He inhaled deeply, the nauseating stench of decay and rotting flesh overpowering him and making him dizzy, and he stumbled forwards a few feet, quickly mimicking what he had seen Miller do and use the rifle as a support. He sunk to his knees for a couple of minutes, allowing his head to clear and his senses to accommodate to the new and overpowering surroundings. With a silent nod to himself, he slowly stood and made his way to the edge of the car park, looking out across the surrounding land.

Trees and grasslands surrounded the hospital, its grounds designed to look like a peaceful park and hiding other wards behind trees and foliage. The area of the city that the hospital was located in wasn't completely alien to Bill, but it wasn't one of his most often visited areas. Everything seemed to be in order, though. Parked cars lining the street, shops and restaurants shuttered and locked up. It was eerily quiet. The very fact that the shops were seal didn't sit very well with Bill: even if it was Sunday, shops would still be open. He studied the vista from his vantage point, slowly turning his head from right to left. At first, nothing moved on the streets. No students going in to university; no people travelling to work, no doctors or nurses walking around on hospital grounds. It didn't surprise Bill, but despite the fact he'd been warned about it, it still unnerved him.

Then, something moved in Grey Street, a main road that ran parallel to the hospital. One of the side streets leading off from it erupted into a frenzy of activity as someone lurched out of it, walking quickly in sharp and jerky movements. Their legs didn't seem to be working correctly, unable to bend at the knees. Bill tried to concentrate on them, trying to make out the details, but the distance was too great. Hesitantly, Bill knelt down, rested the muzzle of the rifle on wall, and lowered his eyes to the shattered scope.

Finding himself looking at one of the shop fronts, he repositioned himself and swung the weapon around, bringing it about on to the person. He kept his fingers well away from the trigger, not wanting to shoot someone who was okay. After a few seconds, he finally managed to get the person in the scope.

Miller had mentioned the Rots, but Bill wasn't sure what to expect.

He certainly hadn't expecting the visage he saw.

"The motherfucker was right!" Bill whispered incredulously to himself, feeling sick to the pit of his stomach. "The crazy motherfucker…"

Nothing was normal about the creature he looked at. The reason its legs didn't bend properly was because they were purple and swollen, filled with blood that had settled there after its heart had stopped pumping. Its stomach had been torn open, exposing pale innards and inert organs that seeped digestive liquids. Moving the scope further up the body, bypassing the exposed rib cage and mangled arms, Bill set his sights on the head of the Rot.

Its skin was pulled tightly over the skull, sparsely decorated by the mapping of thin veins empty of all fluid, and gave the face a skeletal quality that Bill found disturbing. Its eye sockets were darkened and sunken, and each jerky movement spilled a handful of maggots from the vacant orifices. Its mouth worked constantly as if chewing something, exposing yellowed teeth smeared bloody pink. The clothing it wore was stained reddish brown where its liquids had dried, and these patches seemed to congregate mainly around it's cracked and exposed joints.

Where they'd moved after the Syndrome killed them thought Bill, *or during their convulsions.*

Bill lowered the rifle and turned away from the stumbling figure. In his peripheral vision he saw another two figures stumble on to Grey Street. He didn't check their dilapidated state with the scope; he had no interest in what *they* looked like. He rubbed his eyes and sat with his back to the wall, deciding what to do.

The first thing he had to do was make sure that the multi-storey was secure. Miller had left the doors unlocked, and that must have been for a reason. Bill thought that the soldier must have had enough training to make sure everything was safe and locked up tight, and he'd certainly went to great lengths to make sure that no one could break in or out. He wanted to make sure that was the case, and that the Rots hadn't kept away from the entrance just by chance. Gathering his senses and trying to put the nightmare image of the creature he had just seen behind him, Bill grabbed the rifle and ran towards the ramp leading down to the next level. It was a clear run to next one, and Bill realised that there were no cars on the top level, nor this one. He trotted to the ramp, stumbled down, and chanced a glance over the side of the building. He was only one level above the ground, but he could see that Miller hadn't forgotten his training after all.

The only entrance to the car park had a large coach parked up in front of it, surrounded by numerous different cars. The vehicles had effectively barricaded the entrance ramp, and they seemed too well placed to be anything but an intentional blockade. Bill grinned, then took his time getting down to the next level, knowing that he was safe at the moment. The closer he got the street level, though, the stronger the smell of decay became. He made it down to the bottom level and paused, his eyes stinging with tears induced by the scent. He had come this far, but now what could he do? Peering over the wall and the surrounding barricade he could see that in the time it had taken for him to come down from the top, seven more of the Rots had appeared. That meant that there were ten already, waiting for him. Even if he could take aim, and score perfect hits every time, then that would leave him with a single bullet.

Enough for me, he thought grimly, though he knew he couldn't physically turn the weapon on himself because of the size of it.

He moved back into the shadows of the ground floor, keeping out of sight from the Rots, and listened to their gurgling moans and wails. He'd come this far, but now what? Surrounded by Rots, and beyond them would be whatever was left of the riots. He couldn't leave the country because of the quarantine enforced by the outside Marines. There was nowhere for him to go and nothing for him to do.

IV
CHILDREN OF THE SCOURGE

"The disease has spread exponentially already, raging out of control…"

Sitting cross-legged in the shade of the parking lot, the rifle lying across his lap, Bill cradled his head in his hands and mulled over his predicament. Though no more Rots had approached the building in the past fifteen minutes, there were still ten of the creatures lingering outside the barricade of cars. Their gangrenous and bloody hands battered constantly against the bonnets and windows of the hastily parked cars, in a bid to try and batter them down so they could feast on the fresh meat. One had tried to climb over the pile, but its mutilated leg hadn't been able to support it properly, and it had fallen to the ground. No other Rot had attempted to climb over. Bill had experimented a few times with them, moving from side to side, and they had shuffled with him in response, their limbs cracking and weeping blood as they moved.

They've got me pinned in here. Maybe they're waiting for me to make my move, thought Bill, his gaze still lowered and transfixed on his rifle. *But what is my move?*

With the ammo he had, Bill would be able to clear a path through these Rots, but beyond that he'd be practically defenceless. And where would he go from there? Where could he go? Everyone he knew would be dead.

He needed to make a list of things he was going to need. He didn't know how long this thing was going to last, or if it was even going to blow over at all. He might be stuck in this situation for the rest of his life; especially if what Miller had said was right. The Government or its Marine forces certainly wouldn't attempt a rescue, especially if they were enforcing a strict no-go quarantine on the island and levelling any buildings that may hold a way off the island. He would need things like food, water, and any kind of weapon he could get his hands on. The only thing was, the rest of the country had a five-day head start on him. The time he was holed up in the quarantine cells, the riots had commenced, possibly even beyond the dead rising. With everyone wanting to survive through this just as much as the next one, it was only inevitable that there would be fights for supplies essential to survival. The chances of finding anything at all that he could use were slim to none, though on the up side, he wasn't expecting much resistance from anyone else still living.

"Still got you dead fucks to contend with, though," he growled, lifting his gaze to the closest Rot. It didn't respond directly to the insult, just glared at him with a milky-white eye and a stream of drool trickled from the corner of his mouth. There was always a chance he could outrun them, but this was his first encounter with them. He had no idea how quickly they could move, if properly motivated. He had seen films where zombies stumbled and shambled, but at the same time he had seen films where zombies ran and leapt over obstacles.

Zombies, Bill shook his head. He'd accepted that fact as soon as he'd seen the first of the Rots in the street: it was hard not to. He wished he'd listened to everything Miller had said now: even through the craziness, it seemed that he was still speaking the truth and there may have been something important he'd just put down to the plague burning through his brain that he'd just disregarded. It was hard *not* to accept the truth when a clutch of walking corpses were just a few feet from him now. *And my survival hinges on titbits of information I've gleaned from cheap horror films and ten minutes weapons training with a crazy Marine,* he thought glumly.

And eleven bullets.

He knew that he couldn't just sit where he was and wait. If the hunger didn't kill him, then the Rots would probably find a way through the barricade, eventually. He would need to get to the closest store and see what had been left for him, if anything. The best place to look would be Grey's Square, the town's central shopping mall. It was only about half a mile from the hospital, but it was half a mile he would have to cover on foot and the countless side streets and back alleys would no doubt harbour more of the Rots.

And once he got to Grey's Square, what then? What if the whole shopping mall was infested with the Rots? The confines of the shopping precinct would be nothing short of a tomb if they could move fast, or work in a team, and Bill was unsure about both these factors. And the answers weren't going to present themselves if he just sat around.

He had always been poor at making decisions, but at this point he had no choice. There was no one around to make the decision for him; it was normally Jenny who decided for him. She never would make any more decisions for him, though.

What would she say? Thought Bill. Faced with a situation such as this, he was sure she would make the right decision for both of them. But now he was on his own, and he couldn't begin to think what Jenny would do.

Don't think, just act.

He rose to his feet, eyes locked on the group of Rots on the other side of the barricade. They all seemed close enough to one another, bunched up tightly, and barely acknowledged the fact he had risen. He slowly walked to his left, and the group of the dead followed his movements, stumbling over each other in a bid to keep sight of their potential meal. Keeping his gaze locked on them, he boosted himself up on to the concrete wall surrounding the lower car park, lifting his weight up on to the wall and balancing precariously on the barrier. Slinging the rifle over his shoulder, he slowly stood up and gingerly climbed on to the large coach acting as the main part of the barricade. He looked out towards the edge of the hospital grounds, where it merged on to Grey Street. It was an open stretch to there, and beyond that would be no different. There were plenty of cars lining the street that he may be able to break into, possibly even hot-wire if he could remember how he and his friends had done it as kids. But the time it would take him to even *try* something like that might be all it took for a Rot to catch up to him. He could almost make out the shopping mall from his position, between the spire of a church and the side of a department store. Shifting his gaze, he peered over the edge of the coach to the Rots below. Their blank, disfigured faces stared back, tilted up and watching his every move, their bloody hands still pounding and tearing at the cars.

Now he had his plan, he had to work out the best method to execute it. They followed his movements, as if they were keyed in to his mind, mirroring his every move. He cast his mind back to the quick briefing that Miller had given him, about how they ate any flesh: dead *or* alive. He didn't have many choices; he'd have to make a run for it. But he'd need a distraction, and those were in short supply. Shouldering his rifle, he sighted down the scope, the magnification of the lens picking out all the disfigurements of the targeted creature.

"Head shot," he muttered, raising the rifle slightly and fixing the disjointed crosshair on the centre of the bloodshot eye of the Rot. He could shoot the Rot where it stood, but then he'd have to get down to street level, and *then* make a run for it. Lowering the rifle, he scanned the surrounding cars, looking to see if there was a quicker way down other than dropping straight to the floor. A beat-up van stood beside an old family estate car; certainly enough to act as a makeshift staircase for someone who wanted to get down from the top of a coach in a hurry. Shouldering the rifle a second time, he chose his target as the largest Rot in the group, lined up square on the eyes, and then tensed his muscles, ready to move. In his mind, he could see the coach, the van and the car he would have to use to get down to the street, the direction he would have to run in to hit the street, then the location of the shopping mall.

At one with himself and his path, he squeezed the trigger.

The blast of the rifle echoed in the silence of the city, then the keening wail of several Rots followed suit. The rifle kicked him in the shoulder, and the image of the Rot's head in the scope erupted into an explosion of scarlet liquid and white shards of bone. Lowering his rifle, he sprang into action, leaping from the coach to the van roof, then the estate car, and on to the floor. He set off at speed, casting a wary glance over his shoulder at the diversion he had attempted to create.

The headless Rot he had shot lay on its back, the dead weight pinning three other rots beneath it. Two others had sunk to their knees and quickly started chewing on the gristle of the fresh kill, ripping into the body and tearing apart what sinewy muscle was left on its frame. The remaining four Rots had elected to give chase to Bill, however, and though two of them seemed to be stumbling awkwardly, the other two moved with the speed of a normal man. Their upper limbs waved wildly as they ran, joints cracking and splashing tainted fluids as they moved almost spasmodically, their mouths frothed as they increased their speed, ever closer to their next meal. They obviously preferred fresh meat to dead meat, and were willing to go that extra yard to fulfil their desires.

Bill ran with all the energy he could muster. The rifle was cumbersome to his movements, and already his chest burned with each breath, reminding him of a childhood plagued by asthma. He gulped air like a goldfish in its tank; each breath he took bringing with it the hideous acrid tang that lingered in the city's air. His heart hammered in his ears, pounding almost as loud as his feet slapping against the concrete: but nothing could drown out the hideous moans and groans of the pursuing Rots. By the time he had reached Grey Street, the two stumbling Rots had given up their pursuit and elected to return to their fallen comrade, but the running creatures seemed to be edging even closer.

Still half a mile to go, thought Bill, suddenly regretting leaving the sanctuary of the hospital. As he ran, he passed by all the cars that he previously thought had been parked. From his vantage point, he hadn't been able to see the driver doors ripped open, the shredded seats, the spilled blood, decapitated bodies left to spawn thousands of maggots, nor had he been able to smell the fierce stench of the festering dead. The odour was dizzying and nauseating, attacking his senses and making him stumble mid-stride. He stooped low, placing his hand against the concrete to steady him and pushed off straight away. He recovered and endeavoured on, fighting the urge he had to turn around and look. Though he hadn't stopped, surely it had slowed him down. Had the running Rots gained any ground on him?

In a flash of inspiration, he flicked his eyes to one side, catching his speeding reflection one of the shop fronts, and a little way behind him, the two chasing creatures. He almost gave a sigh of relief, when the shop window he was looking at shattered into a thousands shards of glistening silver, and a bloodied and half-eaten body tumbled through it. Bill dived to the side, tumbling to the ground and slamming into an opened car. The smell of decay washed over him, and he felt a cold and slippery hand topple on to his shoulder, frantically snatching at his hair. Screaming, he knocked aside the hand of the agitated corpse strapped to the driver's seat, then looked towards the approaching Rots. There were only a few feet away now. Panic getting the better of him, Bill grabbed the rifle and fired blindly into the oncoming Rots, frantically working the bolt action between each shot. The first two rounds went wild, missing the zombies by a wide margin. The third punched a hole in the first of the creatures' stomach, then the fourth ripped into the midriff of the same creature. Its spine shattered by the two rounds, the creature toppled to the ground, paralysed from the waist down, though it continued to claw its way towards Bill, dragging its shattered carcass behind it. The remaining Rot took the final bullet in the thigh, ripping through the leg, shattering the bone and almost severing the limb. It too toppled to the ground, and instantly tried to regain its footing, drooling and moaning as it did so. Bill clambered to his feet, his eyes fixed on the damaged creatures. He pulled the magazine free from the weapon, and then started feeding the bullets into the empty receptacle, each round clicking as it snapped into place. A grin spread across his face as he eyed the flailing corpses, a feeling of superiority suddenly washing over him. This was what he had to contend with?

"Bunch of fucking stiffs," he muttered, slamming the magazine home and working the bolt. Maybe the rest of his journey to the mall wouldn't be as deadly as he had originally thought.

I'm down to my last five rounds, though, he thought, cradling the rifle. Despite the fact he had loathed the weapon a few hours ago, he now had a new respect for it. It had put an end his pursuers, though not permanently. The crawling corpse was only a foot away now; its dirty and rotten nails inching ever closer to his foot. Without a thought, Bill slammed the butt of the rifle down on to the head of the creature, then again and again, the dry skin peeling away from the bone as it cracked and shattered, exposing the pale grey matter beneath the shell. The skull cracked, and the shrivelled brain crumpled beneath the onslaught of the wooden stock. Retreating from the pool of blood and fragments of bone, he turned his attention to the floundering Rot still trying to regain its footing on its remaining limb. He prodded it with the stock of the weapon, knocking it on to its back, then stepped closer, about to perform the same act of violence.

In a matter of minutes he had gone from nervous, apprehensive human wreckage to a seasoned killer of Rots with two notches on his belt. Three, if he included the untimely death of the infected Miller. The seasoned killer, however, had grown overly confident, and had forgotten about the chewed body that had burst through the plate-glass window.

The weight of the mauled Rot took Bill by surprise as it picked itself up from the shattered remains of the window and threw itself on to him. The rifle clattered to the ground, landing amongst the remains of the shattered head, and Bill stumbled forwards on to the bonnet of the car, the weight of the chewed creature pinning him down. The bloody stumps of its fingers probed Bills neck and back, joints cracking and seeping blood as they did so. Recovering from the shock of the assault, Bill shrugged off his attacker, throwing back the ravaged body and diving for the rifle. He rolled to his feet, and with a scream of triumph, he brought the stock of the weapon up into the bloodied chin of the attacking Rot, snapping its head back. It reeled from the blow, stumbling back and slipping on the spilled brains of the first creature and crashing to the floor, rolling in the fragments of glass and smearing its blood on the pavement. Knowing when he was beaten, Bill turned and ran, leaving the rots with their dead counterpart. Casting a glance over his shoulder as he moved, he watched as a handful of Rots gave up their pursuit then turned on their fallen kindred.

The partially eaten Rot, obviously already a victim of the same cannibalistic rite, had found itself face down in the opened cranium of the dead Rot on the ground and had proceeded to gorge itself on the not-so fresh meat. The remaining Rot floundering around with one leg practically blown off had dived into the open car and attacked the creature still strapped in the seat. Blood covered the interior of the windscreen, pooling around the opened vehicle as chunks of discarded meat slipped out the grasp of the frenzied Rot as it worked at the struggling corpse.

Taking as much advantage of this distraction as he could, Bill turned and ran for the mall.

The shutter covering the main entrance was still down, locked in place in both corners and at the middle by large silver padlocks. They all looked scuffed and dented, as though someone – or something – had tried to break them to get inside. Whatever it was had given up and decided instead to go for the direct approach, tearing a hole through the metal. The edges were stained a dark red in colour with flayed strips of skin and muscle hanging from the ragged tips. Bloodied footprints led into the darkened interior. Some stains were clearly defined, others nothing more than a dragging smear of a useless limb. Over the top of the blood and dirt were clear-cut impressions of boots. All these tracks led *into* the building. None came out.

Leaning forwards slightly, Bill peered into the gloom. He could see the glint of the discharged brass bullet casings on the tiled floor, surrounded by splashes of blood and fragments of bone. He counted fifteen shells, and that was just in the small space he could see.

"Fifteen shots," muttered Bill, standing up straight and pressing his back against the shutter, his eyes scanning from left to right, keeping an eye out for any movement. The street was littered with overturned refuse bins and discarded boxes, and a few crashed cars. Even if any Rots were in the vicinity, Bill would hear them approaching him as they clattered through the obstacle course. That didn't mean he wanted to give them any chance, though. He knew now that they moved at different speeds, and they probably varied in strength, too. "They went in there and fired off fifteen shots, and *still* didn't come out. At least, not the way they went in. Fuck that."

Bill kept his voice low. The fact he was talking to himself wasn't anything new. He often muttered to himself as he went around work. It wasn't a sign he was mad, or at least not in his eyes. In his eyes, it just showed that he had an active mind. Though now, his mutterings to himself may attract unwanted attention from many an undead admirer. He had no idea about how well they could hear, but he didn't want to take any chances. The gunshots he'd fired previously hadn't attracted any Rots yet, but then, maybe just the slow ones had good hearing. There could be a deluge of shambling monstrosities converging on him as he stood and thought things through.

On that happy thought, Bill pushed himself off the shutter, the metal grating clanking and clattering in its tracks. The sound of the clanging metal rattled out across the empty city, fading into the distance. As if in reply, a long and keening wail sounded in the distance, a Rot in answer to Bill's accidental call. He couldn't tell how far away it was, but he didn't want to wait and see. The fact he had received an answer to a noise he had made merely made him want to get out of there was soon as possible. The last thing he wanted was for the hearing population of the city to key in on him and track him down. The run from the hospital to the mall had tired him enough; he doubted he could manage another marathon sprint like that. True, it hadn't been a marathon, just an eight hundred-metre sprint, but Bill wasn't an athletic character, it had taken it out of him. He needed somewhere to he could rest until he both recovered from his run, and worked out what he was going to do.

Summoning a mental map of the town in his mind, Bill ran down a list of places that he could go, slowly walking away from the entrance to the mall and spinning in circles. His ideal place had been Grey's Square: it was large, would have had plenty of supplies inside, and he thought that it would have been secure. If he had been wrong about that, who was to say he was wrong about the supplies? It could have been raided days ago, and most likely had. There were plenty of food shops around town, but they would have all been raided, too.

"Fuck," he muttered, banging his fist on the bonnet of one of the closest cars. Again, a droning response, the muted wails of a clutch of rots, this time much closer than the previous. Bill knew of a few shops that doubtless would have been amongst the first of the shops hit by raiders and looters, beyond the obligatory jewellery stores. The town had a few sporting goods stores, a lot of equipment used for fishing and hunting: rods, lines, and knives. A few even had hunting rifles. The chances of any of these stores still having anything remotely useful to Bill were extremely slim, but other than the large mall, he knew of four different kinds of shops in the town. Sporting goods was one of them; another was a computer store. The remaining two sold women's clothing, and women's shoes respectively. Of the four types of shops he knew, he figured only one would help him.

The closest to Grey's Square was a large shop called Haversons & son. Although it only spanned one floor, unlike almost every other shop of its kind in the town, it had a wide collection of utensils and equipment, wider than any other shop of its ilk. A brisk ten-minute walk from the shopping complex he was outside of would have normally been quickest way, cutting through the various back alleys and side streets. As it was, he didn't know where Rots would congregate more: dark streets or open spaces. Again, his only knowledge and experience of this matter came from horror movies. They mostly gathered in darkened areas, such as alleys. That way, the whole budget of the movie wasn't spent on makeup. But Bill knew it wasn't a movie: that the disease that inflicted the Rots had an unlimited budget to spend on sickening and horrific effects, and the Rots probably went wherever they wanted, which was probably anywhere a normal human went. As if to confirm this, he watched as a trio of stumbling corpses shambled out a clothing store, one practically toppling through the shattered window as its damaged leg almost buckled with each step. Bill froze as the creatures entered the street, feeling his muscles clench. He instinctively went for the rifle, but refrained from grabbing it and bringing it up to bear on the triplets. His ammo was sparse, and he didn't need to kill these yet. They hadn't even noticed his presence.

They continued out into the street, then as one paused mid-stride. Without sniffing the air, without making any noticeable signs they had heard or even seen Bill, they turned and glared at him in perfect synchronicity. They opened their rotting mouths and muttered a guttural moan, then began to stumble towards him, almost tripping over each other as the thought of the meal whet their appetite. Drool began to pour from their slack jaws, a myriad of pale and bloody liquids, thick, tacky and speckled with flecks of white and yellow: fragments of bone and teeth. As they made their way they bounced harmlessly off the abandoned cars left in the streets, leaving bloody smears on the metal and fibreglass bodies. They were clustered reasonably close to one another, and Bill quickly assessed his options: through or around. Lurching to one side, he leapt up on to the bonnet of the closest car and danced on to the roof. The Rots automatically swivelled and spun to face him, but he was too quick for their corrupt and damaged limbs. He was down off the car and running away from them before they could fully turn and alter their course. Casting a quick glance over his shoulder, he noted that the undead creatures were stumbling after him, not breaking into a run like his previous pursuers. He slowed down a little, not wanting to completely tire himself out should he need the sudden burst of energy.

He moved quickly, listening intently to the low moans and shuffling of feet within darkened doorways as he passed. No more creatures lurched out on to the street in front or behind him, and no other entourage of the dead dared rear their disfigured head before he reached his destination.

"Haversons," he muttered, looking at the smashed windows and the door ripped from its housing. The display windows now held nothing but torn boxes and shredded clothing. He had expected it to be raided, but he had hoped something had survived. He made his way up to the doorway and slowly made his way into the shop, his feet crunching on the shattered glass and splintered wood. "Even a penknife will help me out," he muttered. But what were the chances of there being anything left of use?

The shop had been turned upside down. Display cabinets had been torn from the walls; the contents spilled on to the floor and kicked around, the best prizes plucked from the store. The glass cabinets lining the left side of the shop had also been broken in to, smashed and raped of anything worthwhile. Behind the counter, there were boxes of bullets and shotgun shells, already the victims of the pillagers. No box bragged to be the same calibre as his rifle, though, so it was no loss. He knelt beside the first cabinet, rummaging through the pile of leftovers. A compass and a magnifying glass were first to catch his eye. He quickly stuffed them into his pockets, and instantly knew he needed to find a bag before he got any further. He rose to feet and turned; looking for something he could use, and saw a shadow-cloaked figure in the peripheral of his vision.

Charging headlong, he lunged at the person, lowering his shoulder and ramming it into the gut of the figure. The abdomen crumpled and cracked, shattering beneath his weight and splitting the mannequin in two. The legs parted and fell to the floor, and the torso landed on Bill's back, pinning him down. He pushed the plastic effigy off, then stood and looked at the jigsaw of remains. It had been a simple mistake, of course. A humanoid figure standing motionless in the shadows, any features obscured by the veil of darkness it wore. He sparked the lighter to life and looked closer at the dummy. Blank eyes glared listlessly at the ceiling, painted on the thin shell of a head. It still wore a cap on its head, a camouflage pattern of dried leaves and twigs printed on the fabric. On its partially destroyed torso it wore a green jacket, and on its back, a rucksack in the same green colour. He may have looked like an idiot, charging the mannequin, but it had proven to be prosperous for him. He stuffed the compass and magnifying glass into a side pocket on the bag before returning to the cabinets. His search brought up a few various trinkets that he thought might come in handy, including a block of flint and a small basic medical kit. The other cabinets contained nothing of interest; just gloves and various camouflage netting and jackets. Camouflage wasn't a priority, not with the apparent intelligence of the Rots he was facing, plus the faux greenery wouldn't fit in too well with his urban surroundings. He continued his search behind the counter and cabinets, finding a pair of small metal cylinders, each six inches long and lying in the deepest recess of a draw. He pushed aside the toppled cash register, noting that it had been emptied by one of the opportunistic looters that had passed through, and found a leather sheath, hiding within it a ten-inch blade. Though a knife meant he would have to get close, he'd rather use the stainless steel hunting knife to pierce a skull than have to instigate a fistfight with one of the rotting bastards. Fixing the sheath to his belt, he looked over one of the six-inch solid cylinders in his hands. What *were* they?

A small button secluded on the base of each device intrigued Bill to the point of pressing one, purely to see what it would do. As he applied pressure, it suddenly occurred to him – were they grenades? Too late, he realised, as the button released the spring within the device. It exploded outwards and quadrupled in length as it instantly transformed into a baton. Impressed, he waved the weapon around, before resetting the device and placing the weapons into another pocket. It was certainly an improvement on what he had previously been armed with. A few more shots and he'd have nothing but a large unwieldy club. Grabbing some of the least tattered clothing available and a few roles of duct tape before stuffing them in his bag, he looked around the shop one last time. There didn't seem to be anything else in the way of equipment for him. He took a second look behind the counter, and something caught his eye. Something lying beneath the empty cardboard boxes and discarded packaging. A glint of metal from beneath scuffed paint, an attempt to blend in the handle of a trapdoor on the floor. Kicking aside the scattered debris, he tried the handle, but it was locked down tight.

He pulled the knife and pressed the blade into the thin gap between the trapdoor and the floor itself, working at the joint and making it bigger. Slivers of wood and paint scraped up and peeled away, which Bill constantly swept away as he worked. The hole increased in size to a point where Bill could see the dim glow of a flashlight beneath the floor. There was someone down there, hiding. Maybe someone who'd be able to help Bill, or someone he could help himself.

"Hello," he called as he continued to work the gap, the blade now carving slices and chunks from the hatch. "Hey down there!" Given the conditions, he couldn't think of anything else to say while he feverishly worked at the floor. Finally, he could fit his hand into the hatch. Straining with all his might, he worked at the latch, listening to the creaking wood as the locking mechanism strained against the frame it was set in. With a final scream as pain tore through his already-damaged hands, Bill stumbled backwards and into a display cabinet, the wooden hatch coming away in his hands. Clambering from the remains of the cabinet, Bill rushed over to the hole, flung his bag down, and then clambered down the ladder after it. He glanced around the chamber, looking for any signs of the people who had locked themselves there.

"Fuck," he shouted.

The room was no more than six feet across and eight foot deep, barely enough space for a grown man to lie flat on the concrete floor, which was littered with newspaper and tattered carpet tiles. Empty shelves lined three of the four walls, and some were still labelled with what they once held. Bill noted that the thirty-naught six calibre shelve was particularly bare. At six foot tall, Bill had to stoop slightly to avoid the iron girders that criss-crossed the ceiling as he made his way towards the sole resident of the room. A figure propped up in the far corner of the room, surrounded by books, piles of material, unopened packets of batteries, and a series of flashlights, each one turned on. A black plastic radio lay beside the figure, smashed open and exposing the simple circuitry of the useless device. One limp hand that rested in the person's lap held an opened book, while the other lay by his side, a handgun lying inches from it's opened palm. The back of the person's head had been obliterated by the well placed round that had been fired point-blank through his own mouth, and a large red smear covered the wall behind him. The corpse didn't smell as bad as the rest of the city did, although the smear of excrement beneath it didn't sweeten the odour of the room. Crouching by the body, Bill looked at the face of the man. He looked maybe ten or fifteen years older than Bill. He had probably been the owner of the shop.

He reached out and took the book from the corpse, discovering it to be the record book for gun sales. Putting it to one side for now, Bill grabbed one of the blankets from beside the body and tossed it over the remains, so he wouldn't have to look at the shattered head of the corpse. Shuffling a few steps back, he grabbed one of the flashlights and played the beam over the opened pages of the book, reading the lines of text. The sale figures themselves proved interesting in their own right: they indicated that up until five days ago, no one bought a gun that often. Then the day after there were over seventy units shifted. And then, there were no sale figures after that day. It must have been when the riots started proper. Turning the page, Bill found something he hadn't expected, tucked amongst stock figures and sale totals.

It was a suicide note, belonging to the dead man sitting opposite him.

Carol,

I know you know about this storeroom, and I expect you to find me. I hope you can realise that I'm sorry, and that I thought of you and our kids right up to the end.

There was nothing you could do for me. I realised that I was infected this morning, and the news said there was no cure. Rather than spread it to you, I thought…

Take the kids to your mothers. The riots seem to be centralised in the cities, so you should be okay out there. I tried to phone; to talk to you, to hear your voice one last time, but the phones weren't working. Take my weapons with you. I hope you won't need them, but…

Please forgive me.

Love, always,

Ted.

Bill dropped the book, the hard cover slapping the concrete floor. The letter provided no new information for Bill. It mentioned the riots, which Miller had told him about. It only served to remind him two things: like his own close-knit family of Jenny and himself, many families had been torn apart, and somewhere out there, at one point, there had been a couple of hundred of armed people in the city. Maybe it had been enough to wipe out a large portion of the Rots that lived in the area. Or, maybe like in the films, the firepower had gone to their heads; they had become overconfident, and had fallen at the hands of the undead.

Stupid frigging movies, he thought, flicking off the flashlight he held and stuffing it into his bag, scooping up a selection of batteries and doing the same. Slowly leaning forwards, he grabbed the pistol and ran his fingers over it, finding the catch to release the magazine. He slipped it free, then pulled out the bullets left in the magazine. Almost full, it still held twelve rounds. It still wasn't an amazing amount of ammunition, but he had almost trebled his current stock. The note had mentioned weapons, the plural. But short of the pistol, what else was there that he could use? There was no more ammo on the shelves, nor any other knives or batons he could use. What else could he possibly…

He stopped moving as he surveyed the room, his eyes falling on something hidden beneath one of the piles of fabric. What looked to be the butt of a second rifle: a hard walnut construction the same size as that of his current rifle. He reached forwards and grabbed it, pulling the weighty object from its cover. It wasn't the rifle he was expecting, but a large crossbow. Bill looked over the weapon, careful not to point it directly at himself, nor get any part of his body in the way of the bolt already in position on the cocked weapon. The weapon looked like a custom design, it didn't look like any other crossbow he had seen before: although he had passed by the shop many times, and seen the variety of weapons on display, he had never seen anything as heavy-looking and destructive as the crossbow he held. He lifted the weapon, shouldered it then sighted through the mounted scope on the top of the weapon. It didn't magnify as much as the cracked scope on his rifle, Bill figured it may be two-times magnification. His finger touched the trigger, coiling around the metal protected by a large doubled trigger guard, similar to the old Winchester rifles in the Old West. The trigger was tight, had no give as he squeezed and squeezed, testing for the breaking point.

The weapon jerked, the trigger clicked and the stock kicked into his shoulder as Bill finally found the release point for the trigger. The bolt launched from the weapon and struck the concrete wall, embedding the barbed tip deep within the brickwork. Still startled from the silent discharge of the weapon and the accuracy of it – the bolt had struck exactly where he had been aiming – Bill strolled forwards and lowered the weapon, tugging at the bolt that had pierced the concrete wall. It was wedged deep, and refused to move.

"There'd better be more of you bastards," he said, poking the bolt as he turned back to the piles of fabric. He disturbed each pile of materials, hoping to find something of use. He uncovered two quivers of crossbow bolts, a pair of hiking boots that just fit him, and a leather belt adorned with hooks, pouches and pockets. He strapped on the belt, attached what he could to it, including the bolts and the pistol, then plucked one bolt and dropped it into position on the crossbow. He tried pulling back on the wire to cock the weapon once again, but it bit into his fingers before he could pull it back. Running his hands over the weapon, Bill grabbed the Western-style trigger guard and yanked on it, cocking it automatically as he cranked the handle.

"Very smooth," he muttered, gathering up all the objects he had found, before picking up a brown leather jacket from the piles of clothing and slipping it on. Despite his late entry into the game, Bill was both surprised and pleased that he had managed to find weapons that would help to protect him, and the leather jacket, while not a perfect fit, would certainly offer a little more protection from the advances of a Rot. If not, it would still mean he'd never have to feel their cold and clammy hands over his arms. Should they ever get close enough again. *Which I doubt* thought Bill, cradling the crossbow in the crook of one arm as he started back up the ladder. He re-emerged in the main area of the shop, and found himself still alone, much to his relief.

Outside the shop the sky was darkening. The coming of the night, accompanied by a foreboding rainstorm, didn't sit well with Bill, especially as he knew he had to go out into the city to hunt for more supplies. He didn't want to have to trawl through streets and shops in the dark. The Rots would be harder to see, and he would have to use a torch, making him more visible to anything with eyes. Food and water had now moved to the top of his priority list. He wanted medical supplies too, though at the moment he didn't need them. The rifle loaded and strapped to his back, pistol cocked and hanging from his utility belt, and his crossbow primed and ready, Bill left the ruined shop and stepped back into the streets.

II

The closest place to get food was a good five minutes walk away, but on the way there, Bill passed a large chemist. Going by the name of Grahams, it was an independent store, though one of the largest chemists in the city. The shattered windows obliterated by the various bricks and stones lying within the threshold, told the tale of heavy looting. Bill expected to find nothing of use within the store, but curiosity got the better of him. Pushing on the broken doors, he entered the store and went for the flashlight hanging from his belt. He paused. Would it be wise to broadcast his location by shining his light around the area? If he wanted to find anything of use, especially in the mess that had been left behind, he was going to have to. The beam cut through the darkness of the shop, illuminating the debris and glittering on the fragments of glass lying on the ground. He played the beam from left to right, the bright stream of light picking out details of smashed bottles, hastily discarded cardboard boxes and overturned display cabinets. Blood had sprayed across walls and shelving units, though no bodies of the dead lay on the floor. Amongst the glass splinters, other objects added to the sparkling effect. Trying to keep an eye on everything around him, Bill sunk to his knees and grabbed one of the mystery objects, holding it between his index finger and thumb.

A brass bullet casing, the edge crimped and blackened, smelling of burnt powder. It wasn't warm, meaning it hadn't been fired recently. He turned around, shining the beam across the floor and illuminating several other shells, most the same size as the rounds in the pistol he carried. He rolled it around, looked at the small writing on the base around the primer. A nine-millimetre round. That was the magic number he was looking for, though he doubted he would find any lying around in the chemist.

He tossed the spent round back on to the ground and returned to his search. He found a small bottle of aspirin that had been kicked under the counter, and slipped that into one of the empty pouches of his utility belt. A small roll of bandages was his next find, stuffed in the furthest reaches of a store cupboard between two boxes of sanitary towels. Bill grabbed one of the boxes too; tapping the lid with his middle finger in deep thought, before casting the box back into the cupboard. He didn't have a great deal of knowledge about those kinds of things, but figured they'd be no good at stanching a serious wound. What he'd found would have to suffice. There didn't seem to be anything else worth taking, unless he wanted to survive off cod-liver oil and…

Bill froze at the door, flashlight poised as he considered turning it off and leaving the shop. Something else he'd need to have to survive; something he'd need if he couldn't get hold of any food straight away. Vitamins and minerals: enough to keep his body going. He'd still need to eat food to get his energy, but if the only food he could get hold of was junk food, then he would start to suffer from serious vitamin deficiency. Scurvy and rickets would be just two of the various diseases he'd have to contend with. Having to worry about the interjection of Rots in his business was enough to keep him preoccupied, he didn't want to keep track of how many teeth he'd lost, or how his steps were degrading into painful shuffles, too. Given enough deficiencies, he would probably be able to pass himself off as a Rot, albeit a non-cannibal version.

He found a large stockpile of vitamins near the checkout, and scooped as many bottles of multi-vitamins as he could carry. The cardboard display box boasted a picture of a family of five, showing two parents, a young boy, a young girl and a baby in the arms of the mother. They all smiled at the camera, and big friendly writing proclaimed that these were the perfect choice for all ages of the growing family. Part of the sign had been splashed with blood, and what looked to be a bullet had torn through the chest of the young boy. Bill paused as he grabbed the final bottle of tablets, wondering what fate had befallen that happy family. Had the magic vitamins protected them from the terrors of the syndrome, or were they wondering around the streets of Britain now, each hungering for an alternative source of nutrition? The picture did nothing more than remind Bill that the horror of the plague had swept across the country and tore families apart, wrecked lives, and killed thousands. He was reminded of his own loss, and how his own world had been torn apart. At least he could take some consolation in the fact that Jenny had been disposed off the right way, and she wouldn't be stumbling around the city now.

Putting his loss to the back of his mind, he turned from the family picture as something shifted in the debris near the back of the shop. Whoever or whatever it was, was revelling in the gloom. Every muscle in his body tensing, Bill slowly turned around, lifting both torch and crossbow as one, pointing in the direction of the noise.

The torch revealed the static form of a woman dressed in the white coat of a pharmacist, standing behind the counter, near where Bill had discovered the bandages. Her coat was far from pristine, spattered with blood and grime, tattered and frayed along the hems of the material. The blouse beneath had been torn to the point of being just a collar and a few buttons down her front, holding together a collection of scraps and threads. Parts of her breasts were clearly visible, though the gnawed and half-consumed bosom of the woman offered no titillation to Bill whatsoever. Beneath the shredded meat lay the exposed ribcage, stained in blood and speckled with what seemed to be tooth marks. The skin of her cheeks looked to have been eaten away, exposing grimy yellow teeth even though her mouth was firmly shut. Her vacant, milky eyes glared lifelessly at Bill, though she made no movement towards him. Bill resisted unleashing the bolt, not wanting to waste any ammo unless he specifically had to. The female Rot kept it's gaze fixed on Bill as it blindly pushed it's twisted fist into it's opened thorax and tugged out a piece of flesh, shovelling the piece of its own body into the drooling orifice.

Bill slid along the counter towards the windows, eyes locked with the woman's, and came to a halt against the slight step up to the window display. He climbed up on it, crossbow held ready and backed out into the street. Glass crunched beneath his boots as he went, and he hoped he wouldn't attract too much attention with the noise he was making, no matter how slight. The street was still empty, the lowering sun crowning one of the larger buildings and casting long, lazy shadows. His torch still on, Bill slowly backtracked from the chemist, pleased at the fact he had evaded combat with one of the creatures. He'd saved ammo in doing so, and prevented creating any kind of commotion that would result in attracting any more of the Rots to his location.

A shrill scream tore through the silence of the city, the origin of it from the woman within the chemists. The creature exploded out from the shop, her movements kicking up glass and fragments of wood as she moved, limbs splitting and spewing watery blood with each twist of its body. The whirling dervish stopped in the middle of the street and twisted her head around, looking from left to right, cracking and tearing the skin around her neck as she did so. Her white eyes fixing on Bill once more, she made a move for him, arms outstretched and hissing in the back of her throat, the sounds becoming gurgled as blood welled up in the back of her gullet.

Bill shouldered his crossbow once again, sighting through to scope at the partially eaten face of the Rot, lining up the crosshair on the forehead of the fast approaching creature. His finger tensed, squeezing the trigger and releasing the bolt as the weapon kicked back. He was prepared for it this time, and quickly lowered the weapon, cranked the handle and replaced the bolt with a fresh one before drawing a bead on the still standing Rot.

Bill almost fired again, but paused as he looked at the neat hole that had appeared in the centre of the head of the female creature. It had stopped moving, and now stood motionless, eyes glaring blankly at Bill. It swayed slightly for a few seconds, then slumped to the floor, joints cracking and rupturing as the dead weight toppled in on itself. Thin watery blood trickled from the fresh wound, splashing on the concrete surface. The eyes still glared at Bill, white and unblinking. He kept the weapon levelled on the body, waiting for it to make another move, like they always did in the films, but it didn't do anything.

Flicking the flashlight off, Bill quickly ran from the scene, leaving the body behind him. If any other Rots turned up to investigate the hideous scream, he'd rather not be there, and he certainly didn't want to bring any more attention to himself by shining the torch around. It would be dark soon, and he'd need to find somewhere to spend the night. He doubted he would sleep, but he'd feel secure if he were surrounded by four walls and a roof, at least that would offer him some form of protection from the cold, and any wandering Rots. There weren't a lot of houses in the city centre, far from it in fact. A few shops had single bedroom flats above them; it was just picking a shop that hadn't been torn apart or looted. The more secure the building, the safer he'd be.

He moved quickly through the streets, looking from left to right as he went. Soft wails and moans echoed in the vacant streets, and figures shifted in the gloom of the decimated buildings. His senses as alert as they ever had been, Bill felt his stomach lurch with each alien sound: felt his guts heave with each new smell of putrid rot, and nervously looked for somewhere he could find some cover. The rioters and looters had attacked all the shops: even normal bookshops and furniture stores had been given the once over, the contents shredded or scattered across the grounds of the building. Nowhere seemed to offer him enough protection as he moved, and he found himself to be running out of options. The sun had all but vanished now, but the night was cloudy, hiding the silver moon from the city. None of the streetlights along the road he walked on were lit, and Bill's vision was failing fast. The flashlight in his hand ached to be turned on, but he refrained from doing so, not wanting to act as a beacon to every unliving thing in the city. He would have to make a decision, and make it now, while he could still make out the edges of doorways and windows.

He stopped outside a small newsagent. Like every other building around it, it had been trashed, but its layout made it an ideal place to hold up. It was a small and claustrophobia-inducing shop, barely seven feet wide, and not much deeper. A wooden counter, a shattered refrigeration cabinet and a few smashed shelving units that once held magazines made up its meagre contents, but the thing that attracted Bill to it, was that it had no windows, just the solid wooden door that hung from one hinge on its frame. He stepped into the dingy room, flicked on the flashlight and gave the room a quick once-over. Nothing moved in the room, it was empty and devoid of any sign of Rots. He placed his gear on the countertop, then grabbed the door and heaved it back into its place in the frame, slamming home the variety of locks and bolts that adorned the inside of it. With one hinge it may not hold out against a barrage of attacks from outside, but if he dragged the fridge over to the doorway, it would act as an effective barricade. His work complete for now, he played his torch beam over the room, getting a better look at it. Naturally, everything of any value had been taken: cigarettes, lighters, matches, magazines, and drinks. There was an unopened bottle of whiskey behind the counter, beneath the empty cash register, but it didn't interest Bill. The last thing he wanted to do was dull his senses with alcohol. He left it where it was, and picked up one of the tattered sheets of trampled newspapers and looked over the headlines. It looked to be an early edition from days ago, and although it was a local paper it seemed to be willing to divulge news from distant cities.

"Riots hit country's capital," he muttered to himself, brushing the dusty footprints from the paper. He scanned down the page, but it didn't mention anywhere about the dead rising. It hinted at people infected with Hauffman's running riot, but nothing about people trying to eat each other. It talked about groups of rebels rising against authority figures, though, about how they were stopping the right people getting through to the infected to treat them. Nothing of any help to him, though. No paragraph about where any survivors should gather, no emergency telephone numbers to ring.

"Telephone" he said, throwing aside the paper and looking around the small shop. There had to be a phone somewhere behind the counter, for the shopkeeper's use. Maybe he was able to use something outside the hospital, as if the jamming were only concentrated on that building. If he'd thought to bring his phone, he would have been able to keep trying, at least until the battery ran out. He'd had photographs on there, too, of Jenny. He faltered a moment, thinking if he should return to the hospital tomorrow to retrieve it.

Beaming with pride, his mood altered as he found a telephone beneath a pile of rubbish in the corner of the room, and heaved it on to the counter. The line was dead, though, no matter how many times he hammered the cradle or yelled for the operator. His hopes that the phenomena was centralised around the hospital were dashed, and he cast it aside, then took up the torch and finished his search around the room. There was a single door leading out of the shop up into whatever living quarters sat above the room. Something he probably should have checked before locking himself in, really. Grabbing the pistol and keeping hold of the torch, he opened the door, peeling back the heavy barricade and exposing more darkness behind it. A narrow staircase ascended ten steps, up to a mid-level floor, which doubled back on itself to a new staircase. Bill carefully stalked up the sets of stairs; flashlight and weapon poised in front of him, and found himself faced by another door, this one slightly ajar. He pushed it open and slipped into the blackened room.

Apart from the sofa lying beneath the window looking out into the street and a vacant recharging station for a pair of laptops that were missing, the room was empty. It must have been used for simple storage, or maybe as a break room for person running the shop. Maybe they retired up here for their lunch. At least it was something to sit on. He made his way back down the stairs, double-checked the strength of his barrier, then gathered his equipment and dragged it upstairs. He lowered himself to the sofa, and relaxed as the cushions welcomed his frame. He flicked his torch off, and found himself in near darkness. Glints of moonlight came in through the window, giving a silvery pallor to the walls of the room. Bill laid his head back, closing his eyes, going through the events of the day. He was tired, but he felt that he wouldn't be able to sleep, not knowing what demons were prowling the streets below him. Did the Rots rest at night? Did the dead need sleep?

These were the last thoughts that went through Bill's mind as he dropped into a restless sleep.

His dreams plagued by visions of dead lovers and undead friends, Bill awoke with a start, the sudden jolt of his body dislodging him from the seat on to the floor. Groggily, he climbed to his feet and looked around. His jacket lay on the floor; he'd obviously taken it off during the night. Sunlight glared through the window as he swept up the garment and slipped it on. He strolled over to the window and looked out into the street.

It was much the same as the previous night, only this time he could see more details. Cars abandoned, windows shattered, shops looted. A few shambling creatures stumbling around the streets, occasionally lunging at one another and tearing chunks from each other's rotting corpses. A heavy layer of smoke hung in the air, thick dark clouds billowing up from behind the buildings to the right of the shop, on the opposite side of the street. Was the fire an accident, or was it a survivor, sending a signal? Hurriedly gathering his equipment, he shrugged the bag on to his back, checked the webbing to make sure everything was there, then grabbed his crossbow and stormed down the stairs, into the pitch-black of the windowless shop, where he quickly began to work moving the cabinet. Trying to make as little noise as possible, he managed to get the fridge upright and away from the door, before silently unlocking the bolts. He paused, the crossbow heavy in his hands. The minute he got the door open, any Rots in the area would be on him straight away. Maybe the crossbow wouldn't be the right choice, especially if they were close together. Slinging the weapon, Bill drew the pistol from its holster and pulled back on the slide, gripping it in sweating palms as he unlatched the door's bolts. Slowly pulling the door open, he allowed sunlight to flood into the shop.

He had forgotten about the overpowering stench of rot that permeated over the city, and his night in the sealed house had cleansed his senses of it. He almost retched at the smell, but held it back. There was something different about the smell, something sickly and sweet, something familiar from normal life. As he slowly made his way into the street, casting wary glances from left to right, his memory worked overtime, trying to place the scent.

Saturday nights with their friends, Brian and Louise, in the middle of summer. The music turned down low so as not to disturb the neighbours. Patio furniture had been arranged on the lawn, and the table bedecked with an assortment of fresh salads and dressings. Louise and Jenny sat at the table, an opened bottle of red wine shared equally between them in two large glasses, while Bill and Brian stood over a flaming barbecue, cans of beer in hand. Fresh steaks on the grill hissed and spat as the flames licked at the bubbling meat, slowly cooking the slabs of flesh.

Cooking meat.

Burning meat.

To the right of Bill, human shapes stumbled out the smoking shop, undead human torches vacating the burning premises. Their blazing visages turned to face Bill; smoke rising from their rapidly charring corpses, then they began to move towards the only living human on the street. The flames that licked their lips and slipped into their throats seared their inner flesh, stealing their pitiful moans. Shuffling footsteps dislodged loose chunks of burning flesh from the walking torches, the flaming flesh splattering the ground with boiling blood. The fear gripping Bill subsided, and he stepped away from the zombie flambé, keeping his distance as the intense heat neared him. He could feel the prickle of the flames against his skin, the sweat roll as it began to bead on his forehead. As they moved, they attracted the attention of more Rots, drawing the creatures from shops and alleyways. One lumbering beast lunged at Bill, its skeletal fingers tearing the hem of his jeans, and lay on the ground, moaning pitifully, grieving at the loss of its meal, then as it became trampled underfoot by the advancing horde. The minute the foot of the flaming rots touched the prone creature it took to the flames, creating another of the burning dead.

They're gonna burn the whole place down, thought Bill as one of the faster flesh-eaters appeared behind the bulk of the crowd and charged through the rabble, its wildly flailing arms knocking one of the pillars of fire and instantly setting its own tattered rags and peeling flesh on fire. Bill lifted his weapon and fired at the creature as it neared him, the weapon bucking in his tight grip. The first round caught the running creature in the shoulder and spun the animal, the second and third cracked the head and splattered its putrid, smoking brains on the crowd behind it. The momentum of the running animal kept the creature going for a couple of yards before it tumbled to the ground. The lead two creatures instantly dropped to their knees, clawing at the flaming corpse and igniting their own bodies. *They don't even know they're on fire,* he mused, *and they're totally unfazed by it.*

Turning from the scene, Bill ran from the advancing creatures as the flames began to spread. If the Rots were this stupid, and if they had infested the whole city then there was no telling what damage they could cause to the city, or themselves. If they didn't sink their rotting teeth into them, they might just burn him alive, or even bring the buildings down around him. He had to get out of the town centre, and fast, but what would be the best way? Roads would surely be densely populated with the undead, and he really wanted to avoid as much open space as he could. He also wanted to avoid as many confined spaces as he could. That didn't leave him with many choices. The city had literally hundreds of roads leading away from it, what were the chances of him choosing the right path? What else did the place have that could be of use to him? There had been an airport in the area, about fifteen miles from the centre, but Miller had assured him it had been bombed into non-existence like the port had. It was also fifteen miles away, and that was a distance along the motorway he didn't want to cover. It wouldn't have been so bad if he could drive, but he wouldn't even know where to begin: Jenny had been the driver of the couple, and he certainly didn't feel like learning in the middle of a zombie apocalypse.

He stopped his running and tried to get a bearing on his position, taking note of the shops around him. A couple of designer clothing stores, two large bookstores, and one of the larger chains of chemists in the town. All had been torn apart by looters and gutted by fires, the embers of which still glowed amongst piles of debris. Each store stood on the corner, forming the points of a star around a large towering pillar of stone, topped by a carved figure. Bill craned his head back and looked up to the stone figure and the maintenance balcony surrounding it, a series of long white banners that had been draped from the railings. Squinting, he read the words to himself.

For fucks sake, save us!

Bill shook his head glumly. It must have been put up at the beginning of the infection; it was obvious that no help was coming now. He wondered where the flag-makers were now. They'd either had their brains splattered on a wall behind themselves, or were trying to feed on someone else's brain.

Still, he knew were he was. Davison's Monument was the centre of the town, more or less. Its base was a large flat concrete podium, about forty feet square, and often used as a makeshift pulpit by the religious bodies and other street performers to preach and entertain the public on their daily shopping routines. All that remained of the former entertainers were a few discarded and shattered instruments, a bloodied sandwich board, and the headless, armless body lying facedown amongst the instruments. Blood had dried around the body, a large rusty pool, and its clothing was tattered and torn, revealing patches where flesh had been stripped clean from the body. At least it was headless, which meant it wasn't going to get back up and attack him. Stepping over the shattered case of a broken guitar, Bill looked at the bloodstained sandwich board and looked at the large handwriting, white chalk on the blackboard.

"God Will Save," he muttered. It certainly didn't look like *He* had any plans to save anyone in the imminent future. It looked more like *He* had turned *His* back on the whole island, as had the rest of the world.

Twenty feet from the podium, there was a stone staircase leading down beneath the streets to the underground railway system that linked various parts of the city together, a scaled down version of the massive New York transit system. It was an old system, though one of the more reliable forms of public transports. Bill looked thoughtfully towards the darkened opening, weighing up his options. Could he follow the tracks by foot? While most the rail tracks were underground they did lead outside sometimes, though even then the tracks were hemmed in on both sides by the either steep embankments or large walls. It would be like travelling in corridors, which was certainly favourable to wandering around in the open grounds of the city and the surrounding areas, but most of them were wider than the roads, at least giving him a chance to avoid any Rots he encountered if he did. The only thing that gnawed at his mind about such a venture was the fact the tunnels could well be teeming with Rots, who would give their decaying right arm to gnaw at *his* mind. The soft wailing moan of a Rot as it stumbled out one of the bookshops, tattered scraps of paper stuck to its bloody carcass, served as a subtle reminder to Bill that there were going to be Rots wherever he went, all of them hungry. Stepping closer to the opening into the underground railway station, he peered at the stairs, where the light of day bled off into the murk of the underworld, and holstered his pistol before shrugging off the bag and pulling out the flashlight and the roll of duct tape. Keeping one eye on the paper-clad Rot, he hurriedly tore strips of tape off the roll and strapped the flashlight to the underside of the crossbow. He turned the beam on, cast one last look around the city, and then waved casually to the stumbling Rot as if he were parting company with an old friend.

Taking slow and uncertain steps, Bill made his way down into the subterranean structure, turning his back on the outside world.

Two things struck Bill when he entered the underground station.

The first was the lack of the foul smell of decay that seemed to permeate the rest of the city. The second was the cooler atmosphere, which he welcomed after the heat of the morning sun. The lack of the sun probably accounted for the lack of the decay, though Bill hoped it was purely because there weren't as many Rots down here with him

It was pitch black inside, and his torch was the only source of light. Like the rest of the city, the station was suffering the same lack of electricity. Trying to remain as alert as possible, Bill attempted to remain silent, experimenting with the way he moved to try and minimalise the noise he made with each step. He'd have to be vigilant in the darkness, especially as a Rot made no telltale noise such as breathing. Bill suddenly felt the cold hand of fear grip his lower intestinal tract, and suddenly got the feeling that coming down into the darkness wasn't a good idea at all. The torch cast just enough light to make out the shapes of a few things in the manmade catacombs, such as turnstiles and ticket machines, but there were plenty of places that one or more Rots could hide in. If they even had enough intelligence to hide, which Bill doubted. If they were dumb enough to walk through fire, then they certainly wouldn't have the gumption to hide, at least not knowingly. If anything did surprise him, it would be just pure chance. But he didn't want it to come to that, anyway. He moved quickly in the darkness, banging his knee against one of the turnstiles as he began to climb over it. It was slick and wet; cool liquid coating the metallic barrier. He lifted his hands to his nose, smelled them, and wiped them on his jeans. He didn't know what it was, but it certainly wasn't water.

On the other side of the turnstiles, there was a large open chamber, like a foyer. The floor was awash with dark crimson and deep scarlet, tacky and glistening in the faint light. Footprints spattered the blood, dwindling around in circles before leading off to other areas of the station. Some led to a large dark blue door, claiming it to be staff only. Probably just their rest room where they had their tea breaks. Bill didn't want or need to go in there, so he gave it a wide berth, shining his light to his right and reading the map of the railway lines fastened on the wall. Where did he want to go? Most stations were deep in the heart of residential areas, or surrounded by shopping districts. All had as much chance of being Rot-infested as the next, which was something he was trying his best to avoid. He stepped closer and traced all the routes from the Davison's Monument Station, sequentially eliminating each and every station as he went, until his finger came to a halt on a small station labelled "Golden Nexus". He furrowed his brow, tapping the map thoughtfully. Golden Nexus Trading and Industrial Estate was a good twenty or twenty-five mile hike out of town, and was nowhere near any housing estates. While there may well be *some* Rots out that far, their number should be a lot less than in the city centre. Maybe a couple of hundred, if that. A couple of hundred Bill could possibly evade in an industrial area such as Golden Nexus, at least until he found a secure place to hold out for a while, gather his thoughts and plan out the rest of his survival. There were plenty of decent, large-scale stores there, most of them electrical goods or linen stores, even a cinema; there would have to be somewhere out there that would offer him some protection, even if only for a couple of days. If it were twenty-five miles away, once he got down to the tracks themselves it should be no longer than a seven-hour walk, providing he had no nasty surprises to encounter. He felt safer walking the twenty-five miles far beneath the city than covering the same distance in streets and on roads in plain few of all and sundry.

Turning around, he shone the beam of the torch from left to right, looking for the stairs that would lead him down to the tracks for the coastal line. As he searched, his beam played over a hunched mass on the ground, a vaguely humanoid shape. At first Bill thought it was a Rot, the smell lingering around it certainly backed up his assumption. Prodding the mound with the tip of his boot, his foot sunk deep into it tearing the delicate surface and spilling the watery contents over his leg; a foul stench of rot and decay assailed his nostrils as the garbage inside the refuse bag toppled out. Hopping backwards and shaking his leg, he brushed off his jeans and returned to the search for the stairs.

He found them towards the back of the area, beside the sealed elevator doors. There were three sets of stairs: two escalators, one on either side of a central set of steps. The escalators to the right promised access to the Central line. This would take Bill back the way he'd come through the city so far, past the hospital, and towards the football ground. He'd never been a fan of the sport, and standing in the centre of a large field with Rots coming at him from all directions certainly wasn't his idea of fun.

The left escalator had an arrow pointing downwards, boasting access to the Coastal line. He made his way over to the stairs, crossbow raised and poised. It occurred to him that the blood on the barrier might have been from Rots escaping *from* the station into the town itself. This didn't mean he was going to let his guard down: one moment with his mind off guard, and he could end up with a bite: the same infectious thing Miller had warned Bill of during one of his moments of lucidity.

The platform, much like the rest of the station, was completely devoid of life. A few spatters of blood on the on the tiled wall, a single bullet casing lying amongst the tattered scraps of paper and loose garbage, and a bloodied jacket was all that indicated that someone had passed through here. Unlike the rest of the station, though, dull red bulbs were positioned on the walls, casting a soft red glow on the tracks illuminated the tunnels leading off from platform. Obviously running on a back-up generator, the emergency lighting along the tunnels provided a little more light than his own torch, and he welcomed the muted tones of scarlet. Shuffling over to the edge of the platform, Bill took a good look at the tracks before dropping down over the edge.

The tracks themselves were thick with dirt, slick underfoot with the combination of grease and moisture. It was noticeably cooler in the tunnels than the rest of the terminal, mainly from the cold breeze that gusted down the shaft from outside, bringing with it a slight trace of decay. Stepping into the centre of the track, finding himself surrounded by paper and empty cans of lager and carbonated drinks, he decided on his direction of travel and moved off, feeling the cool of the decay-riddled air press against his face.

Navigating the tracks was no simple feat, especially in the gloom of the underground tunnels. He decided to keep in the middle of the tracks, judging it to be the safest place to move. The distance between the shadows of the sides of the tunnel and the centre was further than one man could leap, so any lunging corpses couldn't surprise him. This didn't make his movements any easier, though, as the middle of the tracks were riddled with miscellaneous equipment used for the running of the trains: abandoned tools, lumps of discarded metal, even the odd pool of human waste expelled from the toilets aboard the train. The further he advanced into the complex, the greater the heat and humidity.

Pipes running the length of the tunnels, filled with steam and hot water, made it almost too hot to bear. Even with the wind in his face as it was channelled down the dark corridor towards him, beads of sweat still formed on Bill's brow, trickling down his face. He wiped his brow with the back of his arm, then stopped and removed the backpack before unfastening his jacket and slinging it off, tying it on to the straps of his sack.

"It'd help if I wasn't carting around so much shit," he muttered, hefting the pack back on to his shoulders. The breeze against his bare arms was more refreshing, more invigorating, and gave him a second wind. Pushing on with his journey, he tried to pick up the pace. He had a lot of ground to cover, the vast majority of which would be in near darkness beneath the surface of the diseased city. He'd never suffered from claustrophobia before, and he wasn't beginning to suffer from it now. However, although he felt no fear, he was certainly beginning to feel uncomfortable.

He froze, a noise up ahead making him stop mid-stride. Crossbow gripped in sweating palms, he paused. The noise again, a gentle hissing sound. Was it simply steam escaping from the pipes, a leaking joint somewhere, or something else? Images of a Rot, crouching in the shadows somewhere and watching Bill with hungry eyes, flashed through his mind. He panned his weapon from left to right, playing the beam over pipes and conduits. Nothing seemed out of the ordinary, and there certainly didn't seem to be anything hiding in the shadows. The red glow of the lighting didn't illuminate anything abnormal, either. He paused for a few minutes, waiting for the noise to sound again. Nothing came. Maybe it had just been his imagination, or maybe it had just been an echo of his own movements. Either way, there was nothing there now. He took another step, and his footfall was followed by the clank of metal scrapping across gravel.

That definitely wasn't me, he thought, glancing down to his feet. The only metal near him was the track, and he certainly hadn't kicked that. He shouldered the crossbow, and then performed a full circle on the spot, the beam of the torch picking out few details. Whatever, or whoever it was, it was clearly out of range of the small torch, and it stayed out the pools of crimson murk shed by the emergency bulbs along the alls. Bill stood his ground as another noise sounded, this time a clank of metal on metal. The acoustics of the tunnel betrayed his senses, confusing him and making it impossible to tell where the origin of the sound was. In front? Behind?

Two sounds this time, both almost simultaneous. The sound of liquid splashing in a puddle, accompanied by the sound of something stumbling on the gravel. Realisation dawned on Bill as it suddenly struck him: they were on both sides of him, front *and* behind. The first of the creatures stumbled into his light, lurching out of the dark side of the tunnel with its bloody hands outstretched, gnarled fingers twisted and contorted. Blood oozed from the multiple bullet holes that peppered its body, fluid sloshing out the wounds with each jarring step. Sighting the weapon, Bill loosed a bolt, and watched in disbelief as the Rot actually attempted to dodge the projectile, turning to one side. The bolt still hit its target, though instead of piercing the brain it merely tore through the cheek and ocular cavity of the Rot. It wasn't fazed by the injury, and continued to advance. Cocking the weapon and slipping a fresh bolt into the groove of the weapon, he fired blindly from the hip with the animal inches from grabbing him. Again, it tried to dodge the projectile, but the small arrow struck the shoulder of the rot, the force of the blow dragging the Rot backwards and pinning it to one of the pipes behind it. The tip of the bolt pierced the pipe, and with a tremendous squeal, a jet of scalding steam burst from the tear, smothering the struggling Rot with the intense heat. The vapours scalded and blistered the flesh of the animal, boiling the meat from the bones of the undead creature. Despite the torment the creature was undergoing, it still struggled, still tried to reach out for its meal. Backing away from the pinned zombie, Bill reset and reloaded his crossbow, spinning on his heels to see if he could see the second creature. The approaching noise seemed to be coming quicker now, but still he couldn't see anything. Flashing the light from left to right, there was still no sign of movement, and nothing else could be seen on the tracks.

The dripping sound of liquid splashing against the ground drew his attention, sounding as if the source of the dripping liquid were moving, blood dripping from a wound. But there was no one in the tunnel that he could see. Bill stepped backwards, away from the still struggling Rot, and stumbled, almost falling back over a rail. As he did so, the torch lifted towards the curved ceiling of the tunnel, and he caught a flash of movement amongst the pipes.

"What the fuck," he moaned, lifting the light on to the ceiling proper and playing it over the pipes and thick cables that lined the surface. Of all the things he had seen in the past forty-eight hours, the improbable tales of the dead walking, the sights of the carnage that had been left in the streets, the last thing he had expected to see was this.

Wrapping its fingers around wires and coiling cables around its limbs, the Rot on the ceiling moved impossibly, joints cracking and weeping pus-diluted blood on to the ground far below. Its muscles tensed beneath its skin and it supported its weight, the thin and brittle layers peeling away and revealing the taut muscles beneath. Its movements were slow but steady, and every so often it would pause and twist its neck, transfixing its pale white eyes on Bill and dripping translucent pink drool from its partially eaten lips. Bill loosed the loaded bolt, missing the scaling Rot by a wide margin, and fumbled to reload.

He cocked the weapon, but his trembling fingers dropped the bolt. It clattered to the ground and the Rot followed, releasing its grip and untangling its limbs from the cables and toppling to the floor, landing heavily on the tracks with a sickening crack. Lowering the crossbow, and focusing the beam of light on the ground, Bill drew his pistol and aimed for the floundering Rot as it tried to right itself. Limbs now shattered beyond usefulness, it tried to heave the weight of the decaying creature up, but the bones simply shattered and splintered, tearing through the splitting flesh and shredding muscle, thinned blood oozing on to the ground. It tried to pull itself along the ground towards Bill, rolling over and showing the freshly exposed spine, partially severed from the impact of the skeletal frame on the railway lines. He could easily blast a hole in the floundering Rot, but doing so would waste a bullet, and also attract unwanted attention of anything else living in the tunnels. Stepping back from the crawling abomination, Bill holstered his pistol, drew the machete, and gripped the handle tight, towering over the creature. Without a second thought, he plunged the blade into the skull of the creature. It sliced its flesh and glanced off the hardened bone, but didn't stop him. Bill tried again, hacking at it instead of stabbing this time. Again, the flesh of the head was sliced open, and more bone became exposed, but the blow still didn't penetrate the skull. He tried again, and it was clear that each blow certainly caused some damage to the Rot, though not enough to completely incapacitate it. He quickly decided on changing his tactics, now moving the knife strikes from the skull to the neck, working his way through the gristle surrounding the spine of the creature. The sound of steel hacking wetly through meat changed to the sound of a metal blade striking gravel, and Bill finally sliced through the neck of the creature. The skull rolled from the body, dark crimson oozing from the headless torso, and he stepped back, wiping the blood from the blade on his jacket sleeve.

Bill staggered back from the grisly scene, gripping the knife with one hand and looking blankly at the carnage he'd created, his body numb with the shock of what he'd unknowingly been able to do, and his mind reeling from the barbaric act he'd just committed.

With one Rot decapitated on the ground, and the other still pinned to the wall with most of the flesh steam-cleaned from its bones, Bill turned and began to make his way again, this time picking up the pace. There was no telling what else would be lying in wait in the tunnels, but he wanted to avoid as much confrontation as he could. Retrieving the fumbled bolt and replacing it in the groove of the crossbow, he continued on his journey, sweeping the weapon and the light from the left to right, this time also checking the walls and ceiling.

III

After an hour of negotiating the underground tunnels, the seemingly eternal near-darkness that Bill had voluntarily embraced gave way to a pin-prick of light, gradually growing in size as he neared it.

The walls of the tunnel opened out into two steep embankments made of shale and pebbles, one on either side of him. A length of seven-foot tall chain link fence ran along the top of each embankment, shreds of bloodied flesh clinging to the metal barrier. From the tracks, Bill could just make out the roofs of the houses running parallel to the line, though he felt no need to climb the embankment and check on the condition of the houses. He had no urge to look in on the back gardens of houses in fear of what he may find.

Bill lifted his hand to his brow, shielding his eyes from the intense sun after his stint in the darkened tunnels, trying to allow his eyes to readjust to the light levels. On a whim he patted down the jacket and found a pair of sunglasses in the inside pocket, pulling them out and looking at them. They were a little too round for his liking, and they probably didn't complement the shape of his face, but he wasn't trying to win any fashion awards. He slipped them on, and lowered his hands, removing the torch and flicking it off before returning it to the rucksack.

His hands were still shaking from the encounter in the tunnel. The Rots were very different to what he would expect. He hadn't expected them to be able to run, and he certainly hadn't expected to find one *climbing* along the roof of a tunnel. Each undead creature seemed to be as different as the next, just like when they had been people. Some were fast, some were slow, and their strengths varied. He'd seen them run, now he'd seen them climb: the way the creature had used it hands, coiling the cables around its limbs to keep it up off the ground, indicated, to him, some form of intelligence, perhaps the vestigial memories of its former life. There seemed to be no limit to the surprises they were capable of. For all he knew, one of them could leap over the fence and chase him down as easily as a dog would a rabbit, which was why he didn't lower his guard.

He followed the tracks as they snaked lazily from left to right, slowly winding through the various housing estates. Once every few hundred metres, a thin footbridge spanned the gap between one embankment and the other, and Bill paid particular attention to these as he passed under. If they couldn't leap over the fence, they could certainly topple over the railings on the bridges. Picking up the pace, Bill tried his best to cover as much ground as he could. He didn't feel safe in the tunnels, and he felt just as insecure in the open. The sooner he got to the Nexus, the better. At least once he got there, he hopefully wouldn't have to face anything like…

"…This," he muttered, grinding to a halt and staring at the derailed train carriage that he was faced with. A train wreck was the last thing he wanted to have to deal with.

Large and yellow, the carriage lay on its side, resting on an angle so that it blocked off the entire track. The only way Bill could possibly get by would be by entering the carriage through its opened back door, and working through to the other side. It was too high to climb up outside, but inside he'd be able to use whatever remained of the seats to climb out through the windows. Externally, the damage didn't seem too bad to the train car. Moving closer to the metal tube, he peered inside.

Sunlight poured in from the shattered windows above him, illuminating the torn seat and the few dead bodies lying on the ground, limbs buckled and twisted beneath one another. There were four bodies, two males, one female and a small child of about seven or eight years old. None moved, and none showed any sign of agitation or excitement as most Rots did when Bill was around. There was a smell of decay, though, but no sign of disruption amongst the dead, or even bite marks on them. Tentatively stepping into the train, crossbow trained on the closest of the bodies, Bill looked up to the safety glass coverings above him. Most of it had fractured when it had rolled over, but not broken completely. Only one window had completely caved in, and that was at the far end of the carriage. Beneath it, there was a second door leading out the carriage, though it had been buckled and twisted beyond use. Picking his way over the dead bodies, swatting away the small crowd of flies that had taken to buzzing over the largest of them, he looked up towards the opening. It wasn't going to be the easiest of climbs, not with all the equipment he was carrying, but it was certainly possible. Holstering all his weapons, he grabbed the seats and hauled himself up one, then the next, then coiled his hands around the edge of the frame. The remains of the thick glass cut into his palm, but he held on, hauling himself up and through the hole: it seemed that the exercise regime he'd come up with in the holding cell was paying off. With a grunt, he knelt on the top of the carriage and tried to catch his breath. The smell of decay seemed stronger atop the blockage of the track, but he couldn't figure out why that would be. And then, looking slowly to his left, the reason became clear.

Twelve Rots milled around on the track, blocking off his direction of travel. They didn't look up at him; they were too busy tearing apart the weakest of the pack. A small creature, probably only five-foot tall, lying on its back and squirming as the other eleven tore flesh from its body, peeling back skin and muscle, gorging themselves on the festering innards as they tore them from the body. One of the bulkier Rots shuffled away from the feeding frenzy and grabbed one of the larger stones that made up the embankment, dragged it back to the feast and hefted it above its head, before bringing it down on to the skull of the prone creature. Again and again, the stone came down, until the bone cracked open and spilled fresh blood, exposing the quivering grey matter within. The large creature tossed the stone aside, and almost fell face-first into the opened skull, forcing the creature's brain into its mouth faster than it could swallow. As with the other creatures, it kept choking as it tried to gobble more flesh than the rest.

Bill lifted his hand to his mouth, feeling vomit press against the back of his throat. He'd seen them eat before, but never so many, with such ferocity. Nor had he ever seen a half-rotten man destroy another man's skull and stick its head in the grisly remains. The remaining eleven creatures finished off their meal, and then stumbled away from the stripped carcass. Bill dropped silently to his stomach, drawing the rifle from the rucksack and laying it down in front of him. They hadn't seen him yet, and he planned on keeping it that way, but if it came to it, the rifle would be the easiest way to take them out from atop the train. At least until he ran out of ammo, that is.

A flash of movement to the left of his peripheral vision made Bill spin his head. A medium sized dog bolted through a small hole in the chain link fence, its jaws drooling a thick pink liquid and the joints of its body tearing and spilling blood as it ran. Bill couldn't decide whether it was undead or not, but from the cracking joints and pink watery blood, he could tell it was definitely infected. It reached the body of the dead Rot, and picked at the bones, finding chunks of meat that had been left. The Rot closest to the body moaned and wheeled around on the spot, lunging at the canine. The pair quickly erupted into a fight, snapping at one another, sinking teeth into flesh and tearing chunks away from bodies. While the two fought, the other Rots ignored them, slowly making their way up the track, in the direction that Bill intended to go.

Bill must have only travelled about four or five miles, so far, and now he was going to have to follow a troupe of Rots for another twenty miles. He didn't like the idea of that, nor did he like the idea of trying to run through the crowd.

Below him, the baying howl of the dog below signalled a victor of the fight, and it trotted away from the fight, the throat of the Rot hanging from its foaming jaws. The Rot hadn't been completely killed, but the dog had gnawed the best part of the creature's face and neck off, and it could barely move. Bill sat upright on the carriage, making sure he wasn't placing any of his weight on the glass. With the possibility of the entourage of the dead up ahead, there was no way he could simply break through. A glance through the scope on the rifle revealed that they hadn't really covered that much ground in the time they'd finished their meal. Was it possible that with a full stomach, they were slower? Maybe with a full stomach, they wouldn't even be interested in eating him? It was a possibility, but not a theory he wanted to put to the test himself.

So what can I do?

Sitting on top of a derailed train carriage wasn't an activity he wanted to indulge in for too long. His search for food and water had been swiftly forgotten in his rush to leave the city, and although he had a large supply of multivitamins, he couldn't survive too long without any. Hunger was starting to set in, and he could feel his stomach growl and groan. For a brief moment, he found himself envying the Rots. At least they could eat whatever they wanted, and had a plentiful supply of meat if they turned on the smallest of the pack all the time.

Bill sighed. It suddenly struck him that he was never going to have a good burger again, or a decent hotdog. Meat in general seemed to be off the menu, especially if any other animals could carry the plague. That also meant the hunting down and eating any vermin running through the streets was also out the question. Not that he relished the thought of burning a rat or a cat over a fire. Food was just as big a problem as water, now. Any water source was sure to be infected, that was something he was going to need to be careful about. A sealed bottle would be the only way forward now; any other liquid could be tainted.

A deep rumbling sounded in the distance, a rolling of bass, and Bill looked around, expecting to see thick smoke rise from somewhere along the horizon. It was what he'd expect an explosion to sound like. There was no sign of any smoke, though, and none of the Rots seemed agitated by the sound. Another rumble, louder this time, and enough to rouse one of the remaining Rots. It twisted its head up to the sky, cocking its head at a distant memory, and lifted a deformed hand. Bill followed its gaze, and caught a tiny drip of water on his forehead. In the tradition of British summertime, it was beginning to rain. Another drop of rain dripped on to his chin, and then a third on his cheek. Grabbing his rifle, Bill dived back through the window, landing roughly back in the cabin with a grunt. He scrambled back into the car, beneath the intact windows, and listened to the rain as it began to spatter the metal and glass of the carriage. He didn't want to walk out in the rain, it may contain the taint of the syndrome, but at the same time, the smell of the dead in the carriage was too strong. He unpacked a white T-shirt from his bag, tore off three strips, and wrapped one around his face and the other two around his hands, before dragging the corpses out the door he came in, pushing them through the door rather than dragging them out and getting wet himself. Closing the door and locking it shut as best he could, Bill stalked around in the darkness, listening to the rain as it pelted against the skin of the train car. It was really coming down, and there was no telling how long it was going to be.

Dropping his rucksack, he grabbed one of the less secure seats and worked at it, prying it from the wall and slamming it down amongst the dried blood on the glass floor. Taking a seat, he slumped over and supported his chin in his hands, elbows pressed against his knees. He tilted his head so he could see the grey clouds through the shattered window, and sighed. They weren't as dark as they could be, but it certainly didn't look like it was just a passing shower.

"Just take your time, man," he said aloud, then lowered his gaze back to his feet. "I've got all the time in the world."

Three hours later, the constant thrumming of the rain slowly dwindled to a slight rapping, and then nothing at all. Startled at the sudden silence, Bill leapt to his feet; his boots splashing in the two inches of water that had accumulated on the base of the car. He climbed up through the broken window as he had done before, and clambered up on to the roof. Looking down the tracks, he noted that the Rot that had been cannibalised still lay on the tracks, while the creature that had lost the fight to the dog had crawled its way up the track. It now probed the body with bloodied fingers, trying to find any morsel that had been left behind, and forcing them down its mouth. It didn't get beyond the bloody hole in its throat, though the animal seemed oblivious to that fact. Whatever it tried to eat dropped back on to the floor, though it often found its way back up to its mouth in another frenzied shovel of food.

Bill guessed that the feeding Rot down there wasn't up to moving much, and the gaggle of the undead couldn't be seen around anywhere. He guessed he had a clear run for the next three hours or so, which would get him roughly another twelve miles closer to the Golden Nexus. With all his equipment back in its place, he climbed down the underside of the carriage, finding handholds amongst the network of suspension springs and axles, finally setting foot on the loose gravel to the side of the track. The loose stones crunched beneath his feet, and the feeding Rot rolled its head to one side, catching a glimpse of Bill from the corner of its eye. With a fresh stream of drool trickling from its mouth, it started to pull its weight towards him, mumbling softly. Bill lifted his crossbow, sighted the head of the creature, and paused. Did he really need to put an end to the Rot? It wasn't in the greatest condition now anyway, and the next group of undead that stumbled upon it would probably pick it apart. Doing so would be merely a mercy killing, though it would be the humane thing to do. Without a second thought, he loosed the bolt, the projectile piercing the skull and lodging in the spine. The Rot slumped to the floor, dead again. Bill cocked and reloaded his weapon, then started on his march along the lines.

The tracks trailed trough the housing estate for another couple of miles before vanishing back into the darkness of another underground tunnel. Bill froze, fumbling back in his bag for his torch. He didn't want to go back underground, especially knowing that he was only a couple of hours behind the group of Rots: the tracks between the derailed car and the tunnel mouth were fenced off, and showed no sign of any Rots trying to climb over or break through. Nor had there been any more bodies along the way, showing that the group hadn't turned on one another again.

Finding his torch, he flicked it on and pointed it into the darkness. The beam didn't seem as bright as it should have been, so he unscrewed the base, tossed aside the batteries, and then replaced them with fresh ones before fixing it to the crossbow again. Better he change the batteries *before* entering the darkness instead of fumbling in the darkness. As ready for the gloom as he'd ever be, he pulled off his sunglasses and plunged into the tunnel.

The emergency lighting seemed stronger here than the previous tunnel, though he still needed the torch to make out details. The tunnel was clear of anything undead, the walls lined with sagging power cables and thin pipes. Making his way through the tunnel, he could see a faint flickering glow up ahead, just around the curve of the passageway. He increased his speed, making sure to check the walls and the ceiling with each step, before reaching the source of the flickering light.

The station had been wrecked, benches torn from walls and thrown to one side, posters ripped and shredded, litter strewn across the platform. This station had electricity; at least enough to power the three fluorescent tubes hanging from the ceiling, flickering wildly and swaying from side to side. They gave enough light to illuminate the ten rots lying dead on the platform, each having been either decapitated or shot in the head. Bill froze, flicked off his torch and danced to the back of the tracks, slipping into the shadows where he couldn't be seen. He crouched down, pressing his body close to the wall, and waited, not wanting to make any move in case he was discovered by whatever or whoever had killed the rots. Minutes passed, and still no sign of anything in the station to indicate whether the slayer of the Rots was still in the area or not. He was about to make his move, when he heard footsteps on the platform. He held his breath and moved from left to right, trying to see the owner of the footsteps.

"Did you see that fucking head roll?" said one voice, loud and deep, gloating at his kills.

"Very nice," came the reply. Not as loud or as deep as the first, though unmistakably that of a man. "But it's easier to mop up a splattered brain then it is to clean up your decapitations."

"Not with your weapon it's not. That fucking shotgun makes just as much mess as my axe. It's a fucking woman's job, anyway, cleaning up this mess. Why isn't Anna doing this bullshit job?"

"Because Derrick's in charge, and at the minute, he's fucking Anna. *And* Donna. So, it's up to us to clean up this shit."

"Well leave it, wait until he's finished. Then get one of those bitches down here to mop this shit up!"

"Fuck you, Norman, I'm not sitting down here on guard duty with these dead mooks rotting under my nose. Fuck knows how long Derrick's going to be with them, anyway."

The first speaker, Norman, finally came into Bill's field of vision. He wore tight leather trousers and a black sleeveless T-shirt, and had an assortment of chains and straps wrapped around his body and arms. He carried a large, heavy axe in one hand, and had his other hand wresting on a dagger tucked into his belt. His head was shaved bald, and his face adorned with a collection of rings and studs. He stood over one of the severed heads, lifted his axe above his head, and brought it down on to the skull, lifting it up and swinging it over his shoulder. "Where are we throwing these bastards now?"

"Derrick says to start throwing them outside the southern tunnel entrance, and to burn them. Says they're attracting too many rats."

"Derrick can drag these fuckers there himself, I ain't dragging them way out there. There could be anything waiting out there in the tunnels."

"It's all right, we'll load them up on the cart, just pile them up first. We'll go through their pockets before we load them up."

Bill watched as the second speaker strolled into view. Wearing jeans and leather cowboy boots, he didn't have any top on, proudly displaying the various tattoos of naked women and demonic skulls that he had. In one hand he held a large gardening fork, and in the other he held a large grey shotgun. A bandoleer of shotgun shells hung over one shoulder, several missing from the strap, and his long black hair was pulled through the back of his baseball cap. Bill remained silent, unsure as to whether he should announce his presence to the two men or not. He wasn't sure what to make of them. After all he'd heard and read about the riots, he was pretty sure that these guys were the offspring of the looting and pillaging. Would there be space for him with them? He watched as the man in the cap speared one of the Rots lying on the platform through the stomach, then heaved it up and tilted it back, looking at the body and face.

"Hey, the face of this one's not too fucked up. What do you think?"

Norman dropped his axe and looked at the Rot pierced on the fork, then pulled out a pair of thick gloves from beneath one of his straps. He gripped the chin of the Rot, tilted the head from left to right, and then nodded approvingly. He plucked at the hair, gave it a good tug.

"Pretty enough. I'm guessing twenty-eight, twenty-nine. Blonde. Let's see what she's built like."

Norman reached forwards and tore open the ragged clothing that hung to the frame. He took a step back, his shoulders sagging. "Shit, no good. Some fucking mook must've chewed on her. Throw her on the pile, Vern."

Vern sighed, and threw the body on to the largest pile of the dead. Bill stared at the pair, unable to grasp what they were doing. Were they sifting through the dead, looking for the best looking corpse? Bill gripped his crossbow, his throat dry, his mind confused.

"What about this one?" yelled Norman, pulling a corpse from the corner of the platform. "Body's intact, but the head's fucked, thanks to your shotgun. What about this body," he muttered, dropping the body and retrieving his axe, then pointing it at the pile of corpses, "with *her* head?"

"Works for me," said Vern, donning his own pair of gloves and stripping the new corpse of all clothing. "Very nice, it's just her arm that's been chewed, the rest's almost untouched."

With a grunt of exertion, Norman removed the head from his first find and carried it over to the naked corpse, sitting it atop the shoulders. The pair stood around the corpse, smiling and looking at their creation. With their backs turned to him, Bill watched in morbid curiosity, as the pair seemed to unfasten their trousers, grab their crotch…

"What the hell?" muttered Bill. He decided it would be best if he didn't introduce himself to these particular people. He didn't go in for threesomes or gangbangs, nor did mix-and-match corpses turn him on like they did the pair of sick bastards on guard here. "This is fucked up," he whispered to himself.

"Did you hear something?" asked Norman, pausing and turning his head slightly to one side. Vern paused, then put himself away and grabbed his shotgun. "Grab the lamps. I think we might have missed one."

"I hope it's a nice-looking redhead. We haven't had one of them through here yet," laughed Norman as he walked towards a storage cupboard towards the back of the platform. He returned with a large halogen lamp, the power cable trailing from the rear of the device and leading back into the cupboard. He flicked it on and the station was instantly bathed in a bright white light.

"Fuck me," screamed Vern, shielding his face with his arms, "Don't point the fucking thing at me, point it out there," he scorned, waving one arm out towards Bill. Lowering his crossbow, Bill grabbed his pistol, tried to take aim at Vern: He was the one with the ranged weapon, and could easily take out Bill from where he was. He held off on loosing the round, though, he didn't know why. Maybe it was because it wasn't a Rot he was shooting; it wasn't something that was once human but now dead. Maybe it was because what he was now targeting actually *was* human, albeit the lowest form of sadistic human scum.

The halogen lamp spun around to bathe Bill in both light and heat, and the two men on the platform looked startled momentarily. Vern reached for his shotgun, bringing it up to bear on Bill, and the survival instinct kicked in. Bill squeezed off a round, the roar of the weapon almost deafening in the confines of the tunnel. It caught his target in the gut, making him double over in pain and drop his shotgun. Recovering from the recoil of the weapon, Bill aimed again, and unleashed a second round, this time the pistol not bucking as wildly in his hands. Again, Vern screamed, this time dropping to the ground and clutching his shoulder as a spurt of fresh blood splashed across the wall and floor.

"Get the fucker," he screamed, holding his wounds, coughing blood on to the already bloody platform. "Get him!"

Norman nodded, hefted his axe and lunged forwards, leaping on to the tracks and rushing for Bill. He tried to track and follow the axe-wielding maniac, loosing three successive shots from the pistol, and then dropping it as the axe came swinging towards his head. The blade narrowly missed his head, and from his crouched position, he drew his machete and lashed out, the blade biting into his kneecap and remaining lodged in the bone there. Norman dropped his weapon, lowering both hands to his injury and screaming in agony as Bill rolled away, bringing the pistol up to bear on Norman's face. Adrenaline still pumping through his system, he unloaded a round into his face, splattering blood and brain against the tracks, then pulled the machete free from the wound. A grim expression of determination on his face, he turned back to Vern, who was lying on his back, gulping air and fumbling for his shotgun. Bill climbed up on to the platform and kicked away the weapon from his grasp, before circling the floundering man. Blood gushed from the hole in his stomach, and it was obvious that even now as his blood mixed with the infected fluids on the ground, Vern had been exposed to the Syndrome. His features were pale and gaunt from the sudden blood loss, and he knew that one way or another he was dead. Looking down on him, Bill felt no pity for the sick pervert, no remorse for killing Norman or causing the probable infection of Vern.

"Kill me," pleaded Vern, looking distantly up towards Bill, trying to plug the hole in his stomach with one of his fingers. He was close to tears as he spoke. "Kill me, please."

"Let's see," said Bill, kneeling on the floor and looking him in the eyes. "Should I go through your pockets now, or wait until you're dead? Then maybe I'll strip you down, leave you tied up for those two women with Desmond up there."

"Derrick," corrected Vern, blurting out the name as blood oozed from his lips. It was a dangerous move to correct him, he was undoubtedly trying to provoke Bill into finishing the job.

"I don't give a shit. What kind of sick perverts are you?" scorned Bill, strolling away from the wounded man and stooping to pick up the shotgun. It was large and heavy, its body made from metal and the slide made from a hard, varnished wood. Bill looked at it, hefted it to his shoulder and sighted down the barrel. He was impressed, liked it a lot. It was a little bulky and heavy, though he was sure he could get used to the weapon. He could hear Vern blabbering away, no doubt trying to defend his case, but he didn't take in any of the words. He wasn't interested in anything the dying man had to say. He returned to Vern, plucked the bandoleer of shells from his body and slung it over his own. He looked down on him, then grabbed by the scruff of his neck and hauled his torso off the ground.

"What cart were you going to use to move the dead bodies?"

"There's a… A small cart just… Just next to the security hut over there. It's motorised, makes the job… Makes it easier."

Bill nodded, then stood up and looked over to the small hut on the far end of the platform. It originally had the words 'Security' written above the open doorway, though this was now partially covered by graffiti proclaiming it to be 'Norm & Vern's Shack', and the wall next to it proudly boasted that 'any mook trespassers would be fucking killed'. Beside the hut there was a small cart sitting upon the tracks. It had a large engine and a leather seat, along with a basic control system consisting of two levers.

"Maintenance cart," Bill mused as he strolled closer, stroking the engine. It was warm, suggesting that it hadn't been too long since it was used. There was an ignition for the engine, though the key was missing. "Where's the key?" called Bill, half looking over his shoulder. No reply came back to him. He asked again, this time turning to face the prone body on the floor. The eyes were glassy and distant, staring blankly into the halogen lamp and the blood had stopped pumping from the hole in his stomach. Bill returned to him, looking down on the dead body. He'd taken the location of the key to the grave, which was annoying. If it worked, it would certainly help Bill on his way, almost like his own personal train engine. He couldn't hot-wire the engine; he wouldn't even know where to begin, it looked nothing like the steering column of a car. On a whim, Bill jogged over to the security shack and peered in. He wasn't sure what to expect to find, but it certainly wasn't a collection of Polaroid photographs pinned to the wall, a montage of various Rot bodies propped up on the station outside, all female, all stripped naked. He tore the pictures down and flung them outside, not wanting to have to look at the obnoxious pair's idea of pornography. The rest of the shack contained of a pair of foldout beds, a desk and a small folding chair. The floor was littered with empty cans of alcohol and half-eaten bags of crisps, and the desk held a portable television connected to an old digital camera. A collection of tapes lay beside the camera, but Bill didn't feel compelled to check any of the labels on the cassettes, yet alone the contents. A small hook screwed into the wooden frame surrounding the door held a single key attached to a thin metal chain. It looked the right size, and Bill plucked it from the hook, twirling the chain around his finger.

Sick fucks, he thought as he walked over the discarded photographs, making his way back to the maintenance cart. The key fit perfectly, and he turned the engine over. It started first time, and Bill climbed into the seat, looking at the two levers. They were clearly labelled so even the dimmest of workers could use the small, one-man transport. The left controlled acceleration and braking, while the right lever indicated whether the cart would go forwards or backwards. Knocking the gear into drive, Bill settled down in the seat and slowly eased the accelerator forwards. The cart shuddered, then slowly pulled away from the station, easing towards the darkness of the tunnel ahead.

The driving of the cart took no intelligence at all. Bill kept his eyes open, scanning from left to right with his new shotgun, but encountered no more Rots. He even found the controls for some lights aboard the cart, so at least he wasn't travelling in darkness. As he trundled along, he found himself reflecting on his behaviour in the station. He'd been sickened by the behaviour and attitude of the two men. Their nonchalant approach to looting and stripping the corpses had been ghoulish, and their use of the dead in one of the vilest manners imaginable had been more than sickening. It had only been five or six days since the whole Syndrome had escalated into the killer of civilisation within Britain, and already the people who had survived were becoming unhinged and unbalanced. How much longer would it be before he would follow?

He already didn't like what he'd become. First he'd killed Miller in cold blood, despite the fact he'd been infected with the syndrome, and he'd taken down a few Rots in his short journey, too. He could live with killing the Rots, purely because they were dead already: any trace of who or what they once were had died the moment their brain ceased functioning. That was how he justified putting the Rots out their misery, though he didn't know if he could apply the same logic if he were to come across any Rot that used to be someone he knew. It was the fact he'd been able to open fire on Vern in the first place, the fact he'd been able to hack Norman's legs then shoot him point blank in the face, that was what had shaken him. Once the rush of adrenaline had worn off, the killing of Norman and Vern had hit him hard. He'd reacted in self-defence, that was how he'd justified it to himself, but it still didn't sit right with him. He'd killed one man outright, and the other he'd left to die from a wound he'd inflected. He hadn't even found it in his heart to finish the man with a bullet to his brain and in a day or so he'd probably be back on his feet, roaming the city and looking for a fresh source of meat. Yet Bill didn't regret that. Maybe it was because of their attitude towards the Rots themselves. He'd killed some, true, but he didn't strip them, didn't rob them of any personal belongings they still held, didn't feel the need to commit any acts of self-abuse over the corpses. The daunting thing was that if he'd encountered one group of men that would willingly attack him, then he was sure to meet another. It if it came down to it, he'd probably do the same thing again. But would he still feel like shit after killing *them,* even if they'd pulled a gun on him?

With the cart trundling along the tracks at a speed of a little under ten miles an hour, the journey to the Golden Nexus station took less than two hours after acquiring the cart. He pulled into the station and slowed the cart to a grinding halt, stepping off and on to the clean tiles of the station floor. In comparison to the other stations he's passed through, this one was in pristine condition. No piles of litter, blood splatters or bodies, not even a severed limb in site. Gripping his new shotgun in his hands, Bill stalked up the stairs of the station, clambering over the ticket turnstiles at the top and exiting the transit system all together.

The station emerged in a small car park, only large enough to hold seven cars. The lot was empty, however, and it looked as if it had been for some time. It was situated beside a dual carriageway, though this too was empty, devoid of any sign of life or unlife. Despite the absence of any Rot, he could still hear their distant moans and groans, floating to him on the gentle breeze. Strolling out into the middle of the road, shotgun swinging lazily from side to side, Bill tried his best to get his bearings. He pointed up one way of the road, then the other way, muttering to himself all the time, before dashing all the way over to the other side of the road, leaning his head over the concrete siding. Below him was a massive parking lot, its capacity seemingly limitless. A few cars had been left in the lot, and lonesome Rots stumbled into them as they aimlessly wandered through the opening. Lining the lot, there were a number of large shops, most of them the size of a warehouse, their shutters torn open and their windows shattered. The three electrical goods stores, the trashed remnants of their wares shattered and left on the pavement, promised nothing of use for Bill. A few other stores held nothing Bill imagined he could use in order to survive, either: bed linen, curtains, and various potting plants. There were four car showrooms, each holding a stock of luxurious sports cars and bikes that cost more than Bill could ever hope to earn in his lifetime. Again, his lack of driving expertise meant the showrooms held nothing but large and overly expensive paperweights and he certainly didn't feel like drawing attention to himself by driving around in the car park and weaving between the cars in a bid to teach himself how to drive.

Behind the main bulk of the shops there was a larger warehouse, larger than any other in the trading estate, and covered in faux wood panelling with an external metal structure painted a garish orange. It stood out more than any other store in the estate, and it instantly struck a cord with Bill. A do-it-yourself emporium, it was huge, and would certainly have been raided by any looters in the riot, but the store had one advantage over any other of the pillaged shops: it would have the tools and material needed to rebuild and reinforce the shop front from any Rot assault. From where he stood, he couldn't picture the route to get down to it: with Jenny being the driver, she took note of the road signs and which way to go. Bill would normally sit in the passenger seat and read a good paperback or the instruction books for whatever gadget or game he'd bought, and not pay a blind bit of notice where he was going. He couldn't see any turnoffs from his immediate location, but there was a grassy verge that he could drop down to if he was prepared to take the plunge. It was a ten-foot drop from the concrete barrier he leant on, and looking down, Bill felt he couldn't simply jump down to the verge without damaging himself.

"Stupid bastard," he grunted, mounting the wall and flinging his legs over the edge. The drop was ten foot, but he was six feet himself. If he dangled off the edge, the drop would only be four feet. His mind made up; he dropped the shotgun down, making sure it landed on the grass, then followed suit. His arms shook and trembled as he lowered himself, steadied himself, and then dropped to the ground, bending his knees and rolling as he landed. He scrambled for the shotgun, brought it up to bear on the closest Rot, and waited. Nothing had noticed him, but that didn't mean he was going to go unnoticed for too long, especially seeing as he didn't know how they sensed others anyway: many had one or no eyes at all, others had their noses or ears torn off. He went to move, and felt a twinge in his left leg. He gripped his leg, gritting his teeth and holding back the scream of pain that was building in his lungs. He raised himself up, using the shotgun to lever himself upright, then looked quickly from left to right. The quickest way to the DIY store was straight ahead, through a large crowd of Rots who had decided to hammer and pound against a large white van.

Why are they doing that? He wondered, lifting his shotgun and getting ready to move. Should he have to open fire in such an open area, he'd rather have something powerful to open up with. While he wasn't sure whether the rifle would be more powerful then the shotgun or not, he had five times as much ammo for the shotgun as the rifle, plus he knew enough about guns to know that shotguns had a wider cone of fire than a rifle. The only thing was, once he started firing he couldn't stop until he reached somewhere safe, and even then he'd have a job to make sure his target store would be secure. Glancing from left to right, he tried to work out the best way around the group. To his left lay an open expanse of parking lot, populated by a few stumbling Rots who tried to take swipes at one another, trying to snatch handfuls of flesh and dangling organs from one another. To the right of him the car park ended about ten-foot away, where the shattered shop fronts began. Their interiors were dark and mysterious, and could hold any number of Rots. If he were going to skirt around the group, he'd rather go to the left. What was that old saying, better the devil you know than the devil you don't? At least he could count all the Rots in the car park. In total, there were about twenty Rots in the lot. There could be more than double that hiding in the shops. Maybe they'd tried to hide from the downpour; a distant memory imprinted in their dead minds, and hadn't come back out.

Making his move, Bill slowly started to make his way across the asphalt surface, eyes darting from left to right. The Rots by the van continued their pounding on the vehicle, shaking it. The sides of the van were heavily dented, spattered with blood and dirt kicked up by the tyres, and the windows on the inside looked to be cracked, coated with dripping gore *inside* the machine.

Whoever had been trapped inside had ended their own misery before the Rots could get their hands on them. Bill couldn't blame them. Pinned into a vehicle like that, he'd probably have done the same. He edged past the gathering of creatures, weapon aimed high at those with their back to him. One of the creatures on the other side of the van stopped the hammering, fists raised in the air mid-pound, and looked directly at Bill. He'd been discovered, though it had happened much later than he thought it would. Sweating fingers coiling around the weapon, he backed away from the Rot, his gaze locked with its blank glare. It didn't make a sound, just shuffled sideways, away from the van and around to the front of the vehicle. Lowering its arms to its side, its fists still clenched, the Rot stood motionless, ignored by all its brethren but the focal point of the one living person in the area. In a fluid motion it knocked its head back, arched its back and screamed, a piercing sound that tore through Bill and made his ears ring. All the other Rots in the yard stopped, turned to face it then, one by one, they spun to face Bill. No one paused once eye contact was made.

Bill spun and launched into a run, his heavy equipment banging against his body as he went. Behind him he could hear the moans and groans of twenty undead disease carriers, some dropping behind as their decrepit bodies couldn't take it, some gaining ground with their unprecedented speed. He could see the entrance to the parking lot reserved exclusively for the customers of the DIY store, and between it and him, a few parked vehicles, cars left deserted and overturned motorbikes lying on their sides. Leaping over one of the bikes, he landed heavily on his left leg, but carried on, running up the front of one car and straight back down the other side. Some Rots tried to follow straight over the parked vehicles, and created a mass of shattered limbs and broken bodies as they piled into the unforgiving steel chassis. Others bounced and rolled around the cars before continuing their chase. Chancing a glance over his shoulder, Bill saw that almost half of the Rots were unable to keep up with his pace, while half as much again had fallen over either bikes or ploughed into the car. There were six creatures behind him, gaining ground fast. Leaping on to another car, Bill tried the same again, running up the bonnet and leaping down from the rear.

This time only one Rot attempted to follow Bill, and it managed to emulate his movement, launching from the back of the car and hurling itself at Bill, bloodstained fingers scraping his rucksack and snagging in the straps. It yanked Bill back, and it was all he could do to stop himself from falling on to the struggling zombie. Kicking away from the fallen creature, Bill spun around and moved backwards, the butt of the shotgun resting against his hip. He fired point blank at the creature on the ground, its head cracking open in a spatter of blackened brain and thin watery blood. The sound of the weapon was immense, far louder than the sounds of the pistol in the tunnel had been, and the butt of the weapon kicked hard into his hip, bruising the skin and almost cracking his hip with the recoil. Regaining his composure, Bill lifted the shotgun high, braced the weapon against the bone of his shoulder, and squeezed the trigger, aiming at the closest of the running demons. The trigger refused to budge, so he tried again, this time with greater force. Still the trigger wouldn't move, and Bill shook the weapon, hoping to shake loose whatever had jammed. He tried firing again, but with the same anti-climactic result. Backing up to try and keep the distance with the salivating animals, he stooped low, knocking the weapon against the ground in a desperate bid to remove the jam. He tried again, and swore as it still refused to fire. *Think, damn it,* he told himself. He'd relied on movie knowledge so far, what could he remember about guns? His memory suddenly kicked in with an image of a bulky man dressed in leather, gripping a shotgun and yanking on the slide on the muzzle. It had looked like a different weapon, but surely all shotguns worked the same. He grabbed the wooden slide, dragged it back with a 'ratchet' sound, and ejected the shattered plastic shell from the side of the weapon. Bracing the weapon again, he fired.

The grinning skull-like head of the closest Rot vanished in an explosion of gore, the headless body tumbling to the floor, joints cracking and severing as they twisted and bent the wrong way beneath the dead weight. With two of the undead down, Bill turned again and made a dash over the final distance to the welcoming doors to the DIY store. He could still hear the thuds of the four remaining Rots that gave him pursuit, though a cursory glance over his shoulder told him that the vast majority had now turned on one another. The parking lot behind him was nothing but an orgy of cannibalism and violence now; Rots turning on one another, tearing each other limb from limb, feasting on putrid flesh. The only creatures that seemed to be paying any interest in Bill were the four running zombies directly behind him.

With his legs aching and lungs burning, he finally made it to the open doors of the Barkley's DIY warehouse. A large cartoon image of a brown dog with black floppy ears had been painted on the wall beside the door, an eight-foot tall canine standing on it's hind legs, its body hidden by a large pair of blue dungarees. It had a collection of tools hanging from a tool belt and a red baseball cap with a white 'B' on it. Ordinarily, Bill would laugh at the sight of Barkley, remembering the long running adverts that were shown on the television. He was just as pleased to see the comical dog, though this time it wasn't the thought of the cartoons that made him smile inwardly, rather the fact it may grant him sanctuary from the quartet of flesh-eating Rots behind him.

With the doors open, he dived into the foyer of the shop, turning in mid-dive, sliding along the tiled surface on his back with the shotgun pointed at the opening he'd just burst through. The first of the Rots stumbled into view, and Bill opened up with the shotgun, obliterating the left half of its head and upper torso. As the blood and bone shrapnel showered down on the pavement, two more Rots stumbled into view. Working the slide on the weapon, Bill unloaded a second shell, this time catching the heads of both creatures with one shot. They fell on to the first creature downed at the entrance, their bodies twitching and oozing blood and partially demolished brains, while the forth creature shambled into the doorway. Bill worked the slide once more, freeing the spent casing, then squeezed the trigger. It didn't respond, so Bill worked the slide again: still no response. The creature had now stepped over the bodies, and was trying to keep upright as it slipped and skidded on the spilled gore. Bill lowered the weapon, then grabbed his handgun and squeezed the trigger, again and again, until it clicked empty. The Rot stared down at Bill, one of its eyes punched through by a round, its teeth smashed in by another. It wavered from side to side for a moment, then slumped to the side, crashing into a cardboard display stand and scattering the leaflets it held all over.

Slipping the pistol back into the holster, Bill fed shotgun shells into the magazine tube of the shotgun, then pumped one into the breech. Clambering to his feet, he moved forwards and kicked the bodies out the foyer of the shop, rolling them out the doorway before dragging the large doors shut. They'd been automatic at one time, though they didn't work any longer, either because their electronics had been damaged, or more likely, they were receiving no power. They also had a keyhole, suggesting that they may also be locked, though Bill couldn't see any keys anywhere near the door.

"Probably kept in the manager's office," he muttered. The door would just have to hold until he could find the keys. They'd been heavy to drag, and although there was a chance the Rots would be able to open them again, the majority of the creatures didn't seem to demonstrate enough intelligence to try opening doors themselves anyway.

Moving away from the foyer, weapon in hand, Bill looked up and down the aisle of the shop. Everything was clearly marked and labelled. Kitchens, bathrooms, tiles, lumber and building materials: providing looters hadn't hit the place too hard, there would be plenty of materials and equipment to secure the building. He needed food and water, too, but that would come later. There was no point in getting a stockpile of supplies, only to have to abandon them at the first sign of danger. Plus there could still be some Rots lurking around in the store itself. He needed to flush out anything that was in the building, secure it, *then* consider stocking up on supplies.

He didn't know where to begin looking. It would be a hard job searching the whole store on his own; he could easily miss something. One of them could double back on him, surprise him from behind. Not a particularly happy thought.

Grabbing one of the maps from the upturned leaflet holder, Bill glared at the layout of the shop, planning his route, all the time listening for any telltale sign of life in the building. There were twenty-four aisles in total, running from left to right; each intersected at three points by an aisle that ran the entire length of the warehouse. There was any number of opportunities for a Rot to circle around him, and just as many places to hide. There was only the one door into the building, or at least only one door for use by the public. There would be a number of doors out back, used by the staff for receiving goods and deliveries, though these wouldn't be on the map he held. There was an outdoor garden section to his left, and a yard used to display bricks, fences and sheds to his right, though these were all surrounded by walls about fifteen feet high and topped with coiled lengths of razor wire. He knew from his journey through the tunnels that they could climb, or at least some of them could, but he also knew that anything trying to get through the wire would slice itself up. Even if that didn't stop them, there'd be a lot of rattling noises, which would act as an early warning for him.

He sat down on one of the swivel chairs positioned behind one of the fifteen checkouts and sighed. He dumped the shotgun on the conveyor belt, then idly prodded at the keypad. Maybe it wasn't such a good idea to hold out in the warehouse after all. He rested his hand on the weapon, drumming his fingernails on the metal body. Already he could hear the scratching and tapping on the doors he had shut.

The inside of the shop could wait. The sooner he got the door sealed up, the better,

IV

It was hard for Bill to juggle the materials he needed with the equipment he was carrying, so he ended up leaving the rucksack and all but the shotgun by the smashed vending machine near the door. It had been ransacked of all food, though there had been a can of Klassic Kola left jammed amongst the innards of the machine. It had taken five minutes work with his knife to work the can free, but the sugar-laden beverage had been worth it, and helped wash down the cocktails of vitamins and minerals. Feeling revitalised, Bill had fashioned a strap for the shotgun from a length of power cable from one of the cash registers, then carried it and the bandoleer of shells as he gathered materials.

He'd tried do-it-yourself around the house before, but it had always taken too long, and Jenny had often ended up complaining about the speed at which he moved, or how he never would quite finish a project. Despite his lackadaisical attitude, he'd always managed to get the job done. True, it had been little jobs like painting the walls, filling gaps with plaster and cement, and the occasional flat-pack furniture: he'd never had to seal up a large shop door made from ninety percent glass.

After two hours of shifting and juggling, Bill looked at the collection of materials he had gathered. A few large sheets of plasterboard, a bundle of wood, an acetylene-welding torch, and a loading palette stacked with bricks and rocks from the gardening department, along with a pile of tools. He'd taken nearly twenty minutes choosing the finest power tools, but had realised after getting them to his work area that he couldn't use any. These tools now lay piled up in the corner of the foyer, beside the vending machine and his equipment.

Bill surprised himself with the speed at which he worked. Not wanting to go looking for the keys in the offices just yet, he had decided to simply weld the door shut. He didn't have any proper welding equipment, just the little gas torch he'd found in the plumbing department, and a few strips of metal used to seal copper pipes. He melted these pieces of metal to the doors where they met, then heated up the locks themselves to the point where they started to drip and run in their housings. He did the same to the runners, wiring and motors of the doors, turning them to slag, before going about the chore of wedging as much wood as he could between the door and their frames. Once the metal and wood had been wedged into place, Bill finally shifted the plasterboards into place, pleased that he no longer had to look at the rotting faces pressed up against the glass as the Rots watched him work. One power tool he had found and could still use was an industrial, gas powered nail gun, loaded with six-inch nails. It was fully loaded, which was just as well, as he couldn't work out how to reload it. He used this to secure it to the frames around the door, and then piled as many bricks and stones up as he could at the base of the barrier. With a flash of inspiration, he gathered a few bags of cement and a couple of buckets of water from a still-working tap in the garden department, then mixed up a quick batch of cement and dumped it over the base of the barrier. Bill stood back, examining his handiwork, then retrieved his equipment. It wasn't the greatest of constructions, but it would certainly keep out unwanted guests.

Bill returned to the garden department and sat on a wooden bench there, inhaling the scents of the many blossoming flowers. It was a pleasant sensation, though the cloying scent of decomposition outside the confines of the walls could still be detected, and would be even more so when the flowers started to die. He stretched out, suspiciously eyeing the tap he'd gotten the water from to mix the concrete. There had been a notice attached to the underside of the tap, boasting that it should not be used as drinking water, and it was for irrigation only. He nodded to himself, remembering the chemical tang to it as he'd mixed the concrete, and decided that it wouldn't be a good idea to drink from it. The only thing he would be able to drink would be anything in sealed containers: bottled water, cans of juice, anything that couldn't be tampered with or infected by outside sources.

He closed his eyes, listening to the wailing outside the compound that carried over the walls. He was pretty confident that there were no Rots trapped inside the building, or at least if there were they were deaf. The noise he had made erecting the barrier at the door would surely have attracted the attention of anyone of anything living in the store, though he still intended to check the shop floor, just to make sure. He'd also need to check on the offices of the store, wherever they were, and make sure the loading dock was secure. Sighing, he rose to his feet and headed back into the building.

He walked around the outer aisles of the building, catching a glimpse of the full range of merchandise available, shelving and storage units towering high above him and stocked with a multitude of different brand names. In one corner of the building he stumbled upon a small dining area, obviously installed for the hardcore DIY enthusiasts who would spend hours buying what they needed. This, too, had seen some looting and pillaging. Tables had been turned over, chairs broken and scattered, and the glass display cabinet smashed open. A blackboard above the counter boasted fresh bread baked daily, and a variety of sandwiches made to order; though the only evidence of this was a few brown lettuce leaves lying on a white plastic tray. Bill looked at the mouldy salad remains and felt his stomach growl. He needed something to eat, but the remains of a sandwich didn't tempt him.

There was a door next to the dining area, thick and heavy, with three signs fixed to the door: one was the shadow of a man, the other a woman, and the third the word 'Staff'. Bill pushed the door open, casting a wary glance over his shoulder, then entered the small corridor on the other side.

It wasn't very wide, obviously not designed for a man laden down with weapons and supplies in mind. Walking at a slight angle, Bill checked the male toilets first, making sure he checked each individual cubicle as he went. Both were empty, though one of them hadn't been flushed the last time it had been used. The water was a brownish-yellow in colour, and the smell that accompanied it was foul, almost as bad as the reeking body of a stumbling fresh Rot. As a subconscious act, Bill lifted his foot and brought it down on the flush of the toilet, draining away the foul mix of liquids. The call of nature suddenly beckoned, a combination of the Kola and the sounds of the running water, so Bill took a moment to relieve himself. It was a quick procedure, but a procedure he tried to rush through. He didn't like the thought of having his back to the door while he went about his business, and certainly didn't want to spend the last seconds of his life with his eyes fixed on a urinal as something crept up on him from behind and pounced on him.

Relieved, he left the men's and entered the women's toilets, the cubicles here noticeably cleaner here than they were in the men's toilets: there was a mirror in here too, positioned on the wall above the sink. Bill looked at the figure that stared back at him, and barely recognised himself: hair unkempt, dark facial growth, eyes puffy and bloodshot, face streaked with grime and sweat. He barely resembled the person who had left his home to go to work just over two weeks ago. Rubbing the hair on his chin, he decided it would have to go. Something he would deal with at the next available opportunity.

With the toilets checked, Bill moved on to the third door, looking at the red letters on the door boasting that entry was restricted to members of staff only. Bill looked at the door, then at the silver metal keypad set at eye level on the door. The set of twelve small metal keys were engraved with nine digits and three symbols, and Bill wouldn't have a clue where to begin with the code. He didn't even know how many digits the code would be. Still, he didn't have to worry about it. Pulling out his machete, Bill used the tip of the blade to loosen the screws, and then pried the keypad off, exposing the workings of the lock. Snapping the wires, he tossed aside the keypad and worked at the lock itself. He stopped in the middle of trying to jiggle the bolt, then grabbed the handle and pushed the door. It opened inwards, revealing the corridor behind it

A pale blue carpet covered the floor of the passage, and the walls painted a similar colour to match. The corridor extended for about ten metres, ending in a large wooden door with a plaque on it, engraved with the word 'Branch Manager: P Marlins'. On the left side of the corridor there were another two doors, one for the locker room, another for the break room. Bill made his way down the corridor, entering the locker room first.

Metal lockers lined all four walls, some open, some closed. Bill inspected those that were open, and found identical uniforms for use by the staff. Blue dungarees, a white T-shirt and a red baseball cap. He grinned inwardly at the thought of having to dress like a cartoon dog for work, but stopped as he caught sight of one of the pictures pinned to the door of one of the open lockers. It depicted a young blonde woman, maybe a couple of years younger than Bill, sitting in a hospital bed. She was grinning at the camera, and cradling a newborn baby. Again, the harsh reality of the situation struck Bill, and for a moment he paused, thinking about Jenny, and his friends, who were probably also dead. If not dead, then undead. He reached into the locker and retrieved the baseball hat, toying with it. He slipped it on to his head, then left the locker room.

The break room was next, and like the locker room it looked completely normal. A few low-level coffee tables, a collection of plastic and metal stools positioned around them, with a pile of magazines and books on the centre of each table. A row of benches ran along one wall, the worktop holding a kettle, a microwave and a toaster. Everything looked new and clean, and they probably were. With the exception of the electrical appliances, everything else would be furniture taken from the shop's stocks. If Bill wanted to, he would probably be able to go outside and find everything on the shop floor. He didn't want to, though.

Another vending machine had been situated in the break room, this one still holding a vast amount of chocolate, jelly sweets and crisps. Nothing especially nutritious, but they would do for a while. He patted the glass front of the machine, then left to check out the final door. He tried the handle, but found it to be locked. He leant up against the door, trying to see if it had any give. He'd have to break down the door if he wanted to look in the manager's office, but he'd seen it done in films before, he knew how to do it. Taking a few steps back, he lunged at the door, throwing all his weight against the door.

He slid to the floor, leaning against the door and the wall, gripping his shoulder and nursing it. It had been a harsh lesson, but he'd learned that movies were a load of bullshit. This never happened in the films; they always just burst straight through the doors. Clambering to his feet, clinging to the walls, Bill kicked the door. It didn't sound too thick, just locked up tight. Raising the shotgun, he smashed it against the brass handle, then again, and again, until it came away. With the handle gone, Bill tried kicking the door, only harder this time. There was a soft thump on the other side as the handle inside fell to the floor, and the door seemed to have a little more give. Bill tried again, this time directing the force of the blow directly where the handle had been. The door rattled, then with a final kick the door smashed open, clattering against the wall inside the office as it struck it. Bill strode into the room, shotgun raised. It was small, decorated with much the same colours as the corridor. A large wooden desk sat in the centre of the room, covered with a clutter of paperwork and folders. Behind the desk, there was a large leather seat, and on it sat the manager.

Bill lifted the shotgun, but the person on the seat didn't move. He stepped closer, but still the person didn't move. Bill looked at the person; her eyes shut and head lolling to one side. He cleared his throat, thinking that the woman may be asleep, but still there was no activity. Bill walked around the desk, deliberately thumping his feet on the desk, though still training the weapon on the manager. Once he could see her from the side, he understood why she hadn't moved when he'd entered.

The carpet around the base of the seat was a deep red, saturated with blood. The woman had sliced her own wrists, not just horizontally, but vertically too. The craft knife she had used to cut herself lay amongst the pool, with dried blood tarnishing the blade. Dried blood also stained her wrists and fingers, indicating the paths the fluid had taken. Another suicide, the second find in as many days for Bill. She had no bites on her, which at least meant that she wasn't going to get back up. Despite that, Bill didn't like the idea of sharing the break room with a corpse. He would have to remove her, and the fact the chair had wheels on it made it easier to do so. It also meant he didn't have to touch the cold flesh of the dead woman, too. He wheeled her out into the main area of the shop for now, promising a cremation for the woman as soon as he had cleared out the store. If there were any more Rots in the building, he may as well dispose of all the bodies at the same time. Leaving the staff room for now, wedging the door shut tight behind him, he continued to check the rest of the building out, moving on to the yard packed with building and fencing material. It would be an ideal place to build a funeral pyre for the woman he'd just found, and any other creature he found lurking in the confines of the building. Though every minute he spent unmolested by the living dead made him think that his initial thoughts about the empty building were right.

The yard was larger than the gardening department, with a large metal shutter-door in the far-left corner of the building. This door was set further back than the back wall of the shop, suggesting that this was the door that led to the loading dock of the shop. It seemed to be intact, and still shut tight. Bill tried the handle, and found it opened with ease. Raising his shotgun and retrieving his flashlight, he rolled the door open slightly and stepped inside.

The loading bay wasn't in the complete darkness Bill had expected it would be, as a series of skylights allowed a fair amount of sunlight into the room. It extended a considerable distance, and ended where he thought the gardening department ended, meaning the bay practically ran the entire length of the massive shop. It could easily hold two or three delivery trucks, the large articulated wagons, though at the moment only one truck was in the bay. The doors to the truck were wide open, though there was no sign of the driver. Bill neared the trailer cab and peered warily into the interior. It showed no sign of struggle, or bloodshed, and the driver was nowhere to be seen. There was no sign of any bodies, moving or otherwise, anywhere in the bay: Bill accounted this to the fact the heavy-duty metal door was still securely in place and locked tight. At least he knew that nothing would be getting in here, either. Still, morbid curiosity got the best of him, and he strolled over and checked the door. It wouldn't budge, and an electrical motor opened it, so without power it wasn't going to open. He turned from the door, and his eyes fell on a row of bicycles, all chained up and padlocked to a line of steel railings cemented into the ground. It wasn't the bicycles that caught his eyes, but the shining red motorcycle parked up beside them. It was in perfect condition, and looked almost new. Bill climbed up on to the bike, his weight sinking into the padded leather cushion beneath him. He'd always wanted to have a motorbike; he'd even had a few hours practice on a friends bike once, but once he found himself to be in the position to buy one there'd always been something in his way preventing him from doing so. When he was younger, it had been the lack of money, and then later on in life, Jenny had deemed it 'not worth it'. After all, you couldn't carry the monthly food shop home on the back of a sporty bike. The bike was locked and clamped, so like the other bikes it wasn't going anywhere at the moment.

Dismounting the bike, Bill looked around the loading dock once more, smiling to himself. He was happy enough to believe, for now at least, that the DIY store was secure, and no Rots would be able to break in. He still had a few things to sort out before he could settle down and relax. The corpse of the employee still needed to be disposed of, and he'd have to set up a proper area to make sure the fire didn't spread. A further search of the area would be in order as well, just to double check for any other zombies. But after that, he would be able to settle down for a nice, nutritious meal of crisps and sweets. He smiled to himself.

He'd found a new home, somewhere secure he could spend a few days, until either his supply of junk food ran out, or until…

His smile cracked.

There was no alternative.

He was on his own.

V
RANKS OF THE UNDEAD

"I recommend that the UGMC maintain whatever cordon they have around the island and sustain Damocles Protocols."

I

Albert George Colebrook stood with his back pressed against the wall of a small hut made from metal and wood. The windows had been put out, leaving jagged fragments of glass embedded in the frame, like the teeth of an ageing person. The cloying heat was thick, and he could feel the warm sweat trickling down his brow and along the ridge of his spine. The salty liquid stung his eyes, and he quickly rubbed at them with the back of his sleeves. The sweltering sun of the Brazilian summer was making his brow ache from frowning, even though he wore dark sunglasses, and his mouth as dry as the soles of his boots. He longed for a nice, cool drink of water, or even better, an ice-filtered cold beer. There was a small café just across the road, the door wide open, offering promises of alcohol and air-conditioning.

Not even twenty feet away, total refreshment.

Apart from the fact that if he walked out across the street, he'd be cut down by heavy gunfire.

Sergeant Colebrook had been on a recon mission deep in the jungle with his squad of eleven other men for over three days, and the finding of a small shantytown in the middle of nowhere had been a pleasant surprise. The locals had seemed nice enough, smiling at the collection of soldiers, nodding, talking to them in a mixture of the local dialect mixed with a few English words. The local branch of one of the drug Cartels must have had a lookout, though. Ten minutes after entering the town and sitting down to a cold drink, all hell had broken loose, and Private Dean Miller had been the first of his squad to die. Taking a burst of gunfire in his back and slumping over on the table, his body had been left in the heat, blood seeping out the wounds on to the chair and floor around him. The rest of the squad had scattered after the initial attack, and were now pinned down in various positions around the main street, while ten men had taken up a central position in the town square, producing sandbags and heavy machineguns from the backs of trucks and cars. Within minutes, Al and his squad weren't outnumbered, but they had the tactical disadvantage while the ten Cartel members peppered the town with suppressive fire. They hadn't been discriminative with the shootings, either, and several villagers lay dead or dying on the ground.

"Goddamn Bebops," he screamed as a salvo of bullets drummed against the side of the building. None had penetrated the shell yet, but it would only be a matter of time before the building was Swiss cheese and Al along with it. There was nowhere for him to make a break for; moving anywhere else would leave him an open target. "Does anyone have a clear shot? Anyone got a good line of site on those bastards?"

The radio attached to Al's flack jacket spewed a stream of replies. All but Ping came back with a negative answer.

"I can just make out the back of one of their heads. I'm not getting much fire over here, so I don't know if they saw me in the scatter."

"Where are you?" screamed Al, patting down his jacket and pulling clear all the spare magazines he'd had. Conflict in the jungle had been minimal, so most of the squad still had the five magazines they set off from base camp with. That, plus the four magazines he had for his sidearm and the three grenades, meant that they'd be able to put up a good fight, just as long as they could get in the position where they could retaliate.

"I'm south-east of the Cartel, maybe a hundred yards. There's a lot of debris between me and them, I'm gonna try climbing up on to one of those huts and see if I can get a better look at them. Is there any chance of any covering fire?"

"You heard the man," said Al, "Can any of you worms give our man some cover?"

"I got you," sounded a response. Al recognised it over the rattle of gunfire as Jon Mantel, or J-Man as the squad had dubbed him. He was pleased J-Man was going to be the one offering cover, as he was one of the squad members who didn't carry the normal assault rifle, but a belt-fed light machinegun. He didn't need to see the target, either; he could just pop the weapon out from over his cover and fire blindly.

"Ready, J-Man? Ping? Do it!"

The chatter of the Cartel's machineguns was drowned out as J-Man opened up with his own weapon, spraying high-calibre gunfire towards the encampment. Al knew enough of the local language to understand expletives, and that's all he could here from his hiding place.

J-Man's retort ceased, and the Cartel opened up again, now concentrating their firepower on J-Man's position. Al took a chance, leant out from his hiding place and fired a burst from his assault rifle. Al hadn't taken into account how high they'd built the sandbags while he'd been hiding and his rounds simply chewed into one of them, spilling sand and nothing more. He still counted ten men standing, too, so none of the shots J-Man had fired had taken down anyone. It had still given Ping enough time to get out from hiding and climb on to the roof of a hut. Al could see his Kevlar helmet just above one of the rooflines before he had to retreat again. Another salvo of bullets, and this time a few finally punched through the walls. Al could see the phosphorus blaze of the tracer rounds as they just missed his legs and smacked into the ground.

"What do you see, Ping? Tell me something good."

"Ten men, armed with AK-47's and USAS-12's, but they seem to be favouring the mounted point-fifty calibre at the moment. They're got five of those beasts, and they've got a whole stack of ammo crates with them. They're not planning on moving any time soon."

"You got any forty mils?" he asked. Most of the squad had assault rifles with under-slung grenade launchers, but not everyone carried shells for it. He didn't wait for an answer, though; he knew Ping always carried at least four in his webbing, and a spare in his rucksack. "Fire one off, aim for the centre of the group. Everyone else, get ready to break out and advance. Weapons ready, Ping, don't take your time."

After a few seconds pause, Ping's grenade launcher opened up, and the high-explosive shell collided with one of the cars forming the barricade. As the explosion rocked the ground and tore through the Cartel's encampment, Al swaggered out from his hiding place and screamed a wordless war cry, lifting his assault rifle and keeping the trigger depressed, spraying bullets from left to right. As he walked forwards, the rest of his squad emerged from their hiding places, bringing their weapons about to bear on the machinegun nest. Bullets ripped into the billowing smoke clouds as the squad of marines advanced on the Cartel's position, accompanied by a few screams. There was no way of knowing whether everyone inside was dead or not, other than waiting for the smoke to clear. An eruption of gunfire sounded off from inside the cloud, and the whole squad dropped to their bellies, a few rolling of to one side and taking cover, bringing their weapons about to bear on the smoke screen. It was probably the crates of ammo cooking off in the heat, but there was always a chance that someone had survived the initial explosion, then the assault Al had mounted.

A few minutes passed, and the sounds of gunfire died down. For the first time in what seemed like hours, silence had fallen in the small town. The only sound that could be heard was the crackling of fires within the smoke. Al cautiously stood, then held up his hand as he ejected his second empty magazine. He replaced it with a fresh one, cocked the weapon, then pulled out a battered packet of cigarettes and placed one to his dark lips. The final wisps of smoke cleared, revealing the small fires and dead bodies of the Cartel members, and Al nodded, content. There seemed to be about ten dead bodies, though it looked like a few had been melded together in the explosion. He moved close to the scene of destruction, then leant forward and lit his cigarette on a small fire busy consuming one of the sandbags.

The remains of the equipment were exactly what Ping had said. Assault rifles, automatic shotguns, and the mounted machineguns. There were also the smashed and shattered remains of a radio in the middle of the destruction, spattered in blood and partially obscured by a dismembered arm. Somehow it was still functioning, or at least partially functioning, as it sputtered streams of static dispersed with random words unintelligible to Al. "Leo," he growled, motioned to Private Li

Yung, the squads' communication and linguistic specialist. The young Asian was fluent in six different languages, had a very good grasp of another four, and had more than a basic understanding of the local dialect.

"They got a message off to their friends," he said, straining to hear the words through the haze of static. "They must've asked for backup!"

"Fuck," said Al, kicking at one of the bodies. "How long before they get here, any ideas?"

"They say they're five minutes away."

"Okay, men," screamed Al, climbing on to the blackened bonnet of a pickup truck and disturbing the collection of discarded bullet casings that had landed there. "Leo say's these dead Bebops've got a group of friends coming to help out. They're going to pretty friggin' pissed off when they find all these guys dead. We've got eleven men, any injuries? Good. We need to fortify our position, get these stinking carcasses out of here, someone get Miller covered up. Leo, on the radio now, call base camp. We need backup, fast, more men, maybe some light air support."

He drew his sidearm, a heavy Desert Eagle magnum, and cocked it, surveying the shattered remains of the town. "These bastards want some action? We'll show them some action."

Now this is the life of a marine…

II

…Not babysitting some fucking quarantined island, Al thought to himself as his memories of the buzz of combat faded away.

The cold winds of the North Sea and the fine drizzly mist that clung to the air had been a complete system shock to Al and his squad, especially after the four years they'd spent in and around Brazil and it's multitude of rainforests. It wasn't just the environment that Al missed, though; it was everything about the place. The locals, their fine blends of alcohol, superbly rolled cigars, and unique culture. But most importantly, he missed the combat. All the cigars, alcohol and loose women in Brazil couldn't make up for the adrenal buzz of intensive combat.

He'd joined the marines to fight. He'd joined to make a difference. He hadn't joined to freeze his ass off as he stood on a miniature oil platform in the middle of nowhere, watching over some backwater island while it's inhabitants either died of a hideous disease, or rebelled against the government. And while he stood babysitting the island, there was roughly a quarter of the United Government's Marine Corps stationed on the island itself, enforcing marshal law and, generally, doing everything Al had been trained to do.

"Bastards," he muttered, spitting a wad of phlegm over the edge of the railing he gripped with his giant hands. He watched as the green mucus spattered on the faux concrete floor, and sighed heavily. He still couldn't believe they pulled him out Brazil, a combat-heavy environment with the UGMC beating down on the many various drug Cartels that had sprung up in Southern America since twenty thirty-seven. With the eventual demise of the drugs barons in sight, a lot of squads were pulled out from Brazil and placed in Britain just as the plague, whatever the scientists were calling it, reared it's ugly head. Then, about a week later, more squads had been pulled from the tropics to be placed on the various different guard towers that had been erected a few miles off the coastline at regular intervals. They acted as sentinels, destroying any unauthorised air or sea craft leaving the island.

At first, Al had thought it to be overkill, and unnecessary. Though, after considering the fact there was no way of guaranteeing whether an escaping craft contained infected people or those people that were rebelling against the government, Al couldn't help but agree with the actions. Better that the spread of this plague is stopped, or the escape of any potential rebel 'terrorists' is thwarted. It was a well known fact that the Marines didn't give in to terrorist demands, and the fact these rebels were holding up major places like power stations and transport depots meant they were nothing more than that: Terrorists.

"And those bastards on the mainland are getting all the fun."

Al pushed back from the railing, spun on his heels, then moved towards the hatchway leading back into the outpost.

The outpost was the same as every other marine outpost that had been hastily set up with the massive spread of the plague across Britain. Anchored in the seabed the same way as oil platforms were, the base of the outpost was nothing more than a large collection of concrete dumped and sculpted into a shape reminiscent of a natural rock formation. On this base, the buildings had been constructed.

The main building was a two floor construction, the first being a storage and supply warehouse, the upper the barracks, mess hall and armoury, encircled on the outside by a balcony. The top of the building was crowned by a railing, coming up to Al's waist, and that was where the outposts primary offensive weapon was: A quad-barrelled rocket launcher, bolted down securely to the roof and controlled by the single-man seat attached to the rear. That was one of the reasons Al spent so much time up on the roof: the proximity of the implement of mass destruction. Up to three days ago, the weapon had been fired at least ten or eleven times a day, but since then, there had been nothing.

The other building on the miniature island was a tower, four stories tall and topped by a cylindrical chamber, its roof crested and bristling with radio masts, satellite dishes, and radar equipment. Inside, it was alive with satellite feeds, constant radio conversations between various towers and patrolling gunboats, and the occasional spate of shoreline activity. It was never a great deal, normally just an unruly mob slowly sweeping up and down the water's edge.

Al slammed the hatchway behind him, then thumped his way down the stairs and into the barracks. It was nothing special, just a collection of six beds, six footlockers, and six wall-mounted lockers, each one emblazoned with either a name or a custom motif. As he strolled into the room, the sole occupant looked up from the paperback book he was reading and nodded towards him.

"Up on the roof again?"

Al nodded his shaven head, a wordless response, then lowered himself on to his bed and leafed through the magazine on his pillow. It was the latest edition of his favourite read, a healthy dose of naked women holding big guns, and not a lot of words. With pictures like those, he didn't need anything else to complicate the matter.

"You morose mother fucker," grinned the soldier, closing his book and tossing it casually on the floor. "Still lusting after a hearty dose of combat, eh?"

"You were in Brazil, J-Man, you got the same buzz I did. We're killing machines, meant for combat!"

"I was there, yeah, and I saw a lot of good men get whacked by those Bebops. The frigging Cartels weren't as much of a pushover as the Brass figured, and they made a rash decision by throwing the brunt of their forces into one conflict. One bloody, violent and pointless conflict that lasted for six years. That was five and a half years longer then Intelligence predict it would be."

"Fuckin' politics, man, the lot of it," muttered Al, scratching his thick black goatee beard. "I asked the wrong man."

"Don't get me wrong," carried on J-Man, rising from his bed and hauling open his footlocker. He pulled out a packet of cigarettes, took one, then offered one to Al. He smiled and took two, placing in his mouth and the other behind his ear. J-Man twisted his face, about to protest.

"You know you owe me one, so don't get all fuckin' bitchy on me for stealing your smokes," scorned Al, pointing a thick finger in the face of his friend. "It wouldn't have been so bad if they'd stuck the whole damn squad in here together, but *they* decided, in their infinite wisdom, to split the squad of twelve between two different towers. We're here, on the rest of our guys or in some tower on the other fuckin' side of the island."

He stood and went to his own footlocker, retrieving a silver metal thermos and two tin cups. He poured two equal measures of his moonshine into the cups, then handed one over to J-Man. "I mean, at least we're back together with Johnny C, but the whole friggin' squad should be together. What about Billy-Mac, Davis, Milo, and the rest of the squad? We can speak to them on a good day, when the sun's not to bright, which it never fuckin' is, or when there's not too much humidity or moisture in the air, which there always fuckin' is."

"You've had enough?"

"Have you ever read The Shining? It's about cabin fever, stir-crazy ape-shit stuff. I'm going that way, J-Man. No combat and no loose women make Colebrook go crazy, you know what I'm saying?"

"I didn't know you could read. I thought you just looked at pictures of assault rifles and asses."

"I'm a man of many different hidden talents, what can I say?"

The two men sat back in silence, contemplating the conversation. J-Man knew that what Al was saying was true. He himself couldn't believe that The Wolvers, the squads' nickname for themselves, had been split between two different towers and over two hundred miles difference. Like Al had said, though, it was refreshing to be with their lieutenant, Jonathan Clarity. Johnny C hadn't been sent on tour in Brazil: he, like most commissioned officers, had spent their time planning troop movements and crop burning.

"Fuckin' bastards," muttered Al, still brooding over the troops stationed on the mainland. He finished off his moonshine, rinsed out the cup in the small sink, then casually tossed the mug into the footlocker before knocking the lid shut. "Where's everyone else?"

"Leo and Ping are playing one of those stupid video games in the mess hall, and Johnny C and Rookie are up in the tower, keeping an eye on the controls. Last I heard, they were getting in some kind of signal, a top priority one from one of the frigates down south."

"Signal?" asked Al, suddenly interested. "What kind of signal?"

"I'm not the radio man, don't ask me."

Al sighed, then stood up and lurched forwards. He paused, his head swimming with the shot of potent alcohol, mixed with possibility of combat. A priority signal could mean one of many things, but he was hoping it meant some form of action.

"Fine. I'll go see the kids, see if they have any ideas about what's going on. Leo's communications, why's he not up there with them?"

"Leo's too green, he doesn't have enough rank to hear the stuff coming through. And besides, he reckons he's on his way to beating Ping's top score on that damn games machine of his."

"Fucking kids toys," he growled, walking towards the door of the barracks. "You coming?"

"No, thanks, I'll stay here. I've got some reading to get through. Lisa's sent me another parcel of magazines and books, plus a few new photos of her and little Sally. It's her birthday next month, I've put in for some leave."

Al smiled and nodded then left the barracks, making his way through the cramped corridor towards the mess hall. The passageway was cramped, lined with pipes and wires, and was certainly no place for a muscle-bound man just less than seven feet tall. There were parts of the corridor he had to shuffle sideways to make progress. The rushed manner at which all the observation towers had been built had meant that a lot of the finishing touches hadn't been applied, and as such, there was a lot of equipment and conduits exposed that shouldn't be. All the materials needed for adding the finishing touches were in the storeroom on the ground level, but Johnny C had insisted that the squad didn't touch them. His men were for killing and fighting, not for carpentry and metalwork. There were technicians and builders to do that.

Al swaggered into the mess hall and leaned against the doorframe, watching the two youngest squad members as they sat and played on the games console. He shook his head in silent mirth, unable to see the attraction of video games.

The machine had been hooked up to one of the large monitors the pair had found in the storage room, and had been the source of many hours of entertainment for the two people. It had also been the source of hours of arguments on behalf of Leo and Ping.

To the left of the set-up sat Peter Ian Nigel Grem, or Ping as he had been dubbed by his fellow squad members. Almost as tall as Al, but nowhere near as muscular, he'd allowed his hair to grow slightly into a short, spiked mess. The hair was longer than the regulation crew-cut of the corps, but the time served in the heart of the jungle, and then the immediate evacuation to the watchtower, had meant that the men had gone for some time without any access to hair clippers or scissors. The only thing they had with them was their combat knife, and a few razorblades, and no one felt the need to hack their hair off with their knives. Ping had only been in the squad for two years, but both of those years had been in a combat scenario in Brazil.

To the right sat Leo. At only five foot four, he was the shortest and youngest member of the squad, but was by far the most intelligent. He could speak six different languages perfectly, which was five and a half more than most other marines, not to mention the four he was still learning. He had a slight limp, a wound that he'd picked up in Brazil when a training mission using live ammunition had gone wrong and he'd taken a shot to his calf, and he'd made himself a crutch out of a few of the metal poles from the storage room. It was enough to cause pain in cold weather, which was the only type of weather they experienced on the tower, but it wasn't bad enough to be taken off active duty. His face, normally happy and full of joy, was screwed up in a hateful and pained expression. For a moment, Al presumed that the wound was playing up, until Leo flung the blue plastic controller he held down on to the floor at his feet.

"Stupid frigging controls," he complained, kicking the control pad with the toes of his good foot. He paused for a moment, then snatched it up again. "One more go, winner takes all."

"Hmm, I don't know," muttered Ping, feverishly tapping buttons to set up a new game. "You already owe me three months pay as it is. But, if you really want to kiss all that green goodbye, then I'll happily take your money. Just make sure your mamma can afford to fork it out all at once, huh?"

Leo didn't reply. He already held the controller in his hands, fingers twitching over the buttons.

"Hey, kids, have you heard the news?"

Al strolled forward and climbed into the seat between them. He looked at the computer graphics on the screen for a few minutes, waiting for a reply. "Did you hear the news? There's some kind of radio signal coming through?" There was still no reply from the pair locked in competition. He wasn't going to get anything out them with their attention focused on the game. He leaned forwards and switched the machine off, smiling as the screen blacked out. The two younger soldiers dropped the control pads and stared at him. Leo cracked a smile, then stood and walked away from the room.

"Oh well, the game's abandoned. We'll call it a draw, and everyone's equal. Good game. We'll have to play again some time!"

He had left the room before Ping could break his dumbstruck silence. He glared at Al, furrowing his brow and flaring his nostril.

"Do you have any idea what you've done?"

Al nodded, smirking. In Ping's eyes, Al had lost him hundreds of dollars. But in Al's eyes, he'd saved Leo a lot of money and a lot of grief.

"There was four hundred dollars at stake on that game! And you just lost me it!"

"I'm not going to give you any money, kid, so don't start getting any crazy ideas about playing me for the money. If you want to play games, I've got a couple of games you could play. Like dodge the point fifty calibre," growled Al, drawing his Desert Eagle and resting it in his lap. He caressed the metal for a moment, then slipped it back into the leather holster. "There's a radio signal coming in…"

"Yeah, I know that," scowled Ping, coiling up the cable of the controllers and laying them on top the machine. He flicked off the monitor and glared at Al. "High priority, top level, too much for little

Leo to hear. That's why he was here playing games. You probably could have gone up there with Johnny C if you weren't being moody on the roof."

"The signal," continued Al, "Is sure to mean some kind of action for us. Even if it's just going out in a patrol boat for an hour or three, it'll get us off this fucking manmade island."

Ping made a guttural, wordless response, then stood and started to make his way towards the door. "Jesus, are you that desperate to get out of this place? It's a cushy little set-up we've got. And besides, I get seasick easily. I'll stay here, cook our dinner," he joked.

"I've tasted the shit you cook, kid, I'm not going to let you poison the rest of the squad. C'mon!"

"Where are we going? We're not going to wait for Johnny, are we? Ah, come on!"

Al didn't answer, just made his way towards the open doorway leading to the staircase. It was the only way into the barracks from the tower, and as soon as the Lieutenant came down, he'd be ready. He didn't have to wait long. The six-foot, blond haired squad Lieutenant appeared at the doorway just as Al started to lean against the wall, his sunglasses perched, as always, atop his head. An unlit cigarette dangled from his lips, and he was nodding his head in agreement as the soldier behind him talked in a low voice.

David Rook was also a Sergeant, like Al, but not as experienced. He'd only been in the Marines for six years, while Al had been in for the best part of fifteen years and a Sergeant for seven. He was the complete opposite to Al; only five and a half-foot tall, nowhere near as muscular, and his skin a pale and milky pallor, unlike Al's dark skin. Where Al provided the brawn and heavy weaponry knowledge, Rookie provided the brains and tactical planning to the squad. Al had earned his rank through combat experience and battlefield promotions, while Rookie had sat through the multitude of courses, lectures and exams that they now needed for promotion.

"Hey Johnny, what's the word?"

"Al, Ping, come to the barracks. Are the other two there?"

"Last I seen, J-Man was reading his book in there. I don't know where Leo went."

"We'll see when we get there. I'll tell everyone together!"

"Action?" asked Al, a smile creeping across his lips. "We going into action?"

"Barracks, Al, c'mon!"

Al followed the Lieutenant to the barracks and flung himself on to the bed. Leo had came here to lick his wounds after his humiliating defeat, and was reading through a games magazine, trying to glean hints and tips to aide him in his next game against the resident games player. As Johnny C strolled into the room, both J-Man and Leo put down their books and magazines and looked towards the Lieutenant. He held the attention of everyone for a few minutes, then sat down on his own bed. He took out a match and lit his cigarette, took a few drags, then tapped out the ash on to the steel floor.

"I guess it's safe to say that everyone knows we've received a high priority signal from one of the command stations. Me and Rookie took the call, and we've got the rundown for you." He took a second drag, longer this time, and dropped his cigarette, crushing it out beneath his boot. "You all know about the quarantine that's been enforced on the island, nothing enters, nothing leaves. Well, we're going to do both."

A murmur went up between the three Privates. After a few seconds it was Ping that fully verbalised their concerns. "Won't that mean we'll be exposed to this plague, too? I mean, how contagious is it? Won't we…"

Johnny held up his hand, silencing him. "You know we've got sealed suits, filter masks, plus we're not actually touching down on the ground, it's just a pickup. There's a General Maxis on the mainland, he was trying to get to a pre-arranged evacuation site so he could be airlifted out, but he ran into trouble on the way there. He's currently stranded in one of the pre-fab outposts in Cumbria."

"Whoa there," said Al, raising a huge meaty paw and pointing a finger toward Johnny C. "Marine

Command is breaking quarantine rules, their *own* rules, to get one of the Brass out? Jesus, are we a two-tier structure? There's us grunts, then they're the fucking officers, and they all got their own rules to abide by. Sorry, Johnny, I know you're one of them. But why the fuck should we risk our asses to go and haul out some fucking General?"

Johnny pulled out a packet of cigarettes, removed one himself, and then passed them around the squad before continuing. "General Maxis is one of the few high-ranking Marines who were around when this plague started. Apparently, he's been spending the past three weeks compiling as much information about the plague as he can, and he's got a lot of information for the science boys to digest."

"Fucking bullshit!" muttered Al, clenching his fists. "Typical fucking bullshit lies. They just want their man out, so *our* men can continue to do the hard fucking work. And what 'problem' did this guy run into?"

"Intel was a little vague on that. From what they could decipher from his frantic reports, his convoy was attacked by a rowdy group of civilians, and they were forced to make a detour. There's a chance that it could be an armed militia group, like the various rebels that have been trying to seize control of the ports and power plants. If that's the case, then there could be some kind of armed resistance, though we don't know what kind of weapons they've got. Like I say, he's waiting for us at an outpost in Cumbria. We're going to get picked up by a Cavalier Gunship in twenty minutes, we're going to provide support, pick him up, and then bring him back. We meet on the roof in fifteen. Get suited up; grab your weapons, load them up, we'll go through final details."

"Gunship," muttered J-Man, opening up his footlocker and removing a box of his homemade shotgun slugs from it and strolling out the room. "Jesus, I hope it's not Dick. If it is, I'm staying."

Ping and Leo followed, leaving Al and Rookie with Johnny. "I thought you'd be happier than this, Al. Combat, it's what you've been wanting!"

"It's not combat, though, is it?" he muttered, unholstering his magnum and slipping the clip out, counting the rounds before slamming it back home. He grabbed another three clips and a handful of loose rounds, then pushed them into a black leather pouch and clipped it to his belt. "It's sitting in the back of a fucking helicopter for a couple of hours, while some high-ranking piece of shit who's gotten himself in trouble gets picked up by us, then looks down his nose at us working guys while we drop him off somewhere. It's barely a promotion: instead of babysitting an island, we're babysitting this fucking Maxis character and his precious documents."

"You don't like authority, do you Al?" muttered Rookie, strapping up his boots tight. He grinned, then shook his head. "I agree, it stinks…"

"It's not the authority I got a problem with," sneered Al, storming over to the door. "It's the fucking bullshit they feed us!"

"Al, leave the magnum," cautioned Johnny C. "It's not standard issue, you shouldn't even have it with you on the station. It stays behind."

Al glared at his Lieutenant, knitting his brow into a frown. "The Colebrook Cannon is my good luck charm, Johnny, you know I don't leave it anywhere. Where I go, it goes."

"Lock it up in the weapons locker. Don't make me tell you again."

Al snarled a wordless response, then turned on his heel, and marched off towards the armoury, leaving Rookie and the Lieutenant on their own.

"What do you think?"

"Well, if you're asking me, it's all wrong. We can evac a General, but the rest of our boys are left there? Last I heard, it wasn't looking good for us. The rebels take a port, we bomb it, and they take another one. Off the record, Rookie, we're getting wiped out over on the mainland. When I'm up in the tower, I get snippets of different signals. Some are coded, some are scrambled, but some aren't. They're normally the ones that are sent out in haste. The men and women sound terrified in those ones. Crazy things like riots, armed rebels, someone even mentioned 'unstoppable' once.

Whatever's going on over there, we're not being told the whole story."

Rookie finished tightening his boots, then nodded in agreement. He'd heard similar radio transmissions while he had been on duty in the tower. "We can whack the well funded, well organised drug pushers in Mexico and South America, but when it comes to restoring and maintaining order in a civilised and urban area... It's hard to swallow, isn't it? I think your right." He grinned, then continued. "Maybe we could give Al a heavy machinegun, a few thousand rounds of ammo, and drop him off on the way there. Maybe that'll even the odds!"

"Yeah, or we could carpet bomb the whole place with nuclear warheads, it'd have the same effect. Come on, we have to get ready."

The bitter winds that had previously nipped at Al's skin couldn't penetrate the thick neoprene suit that he now wore, or the armour that covered his chest, shins and forearms. The suits had been specially designed for use in hazardous and infectious areas, specifically with mobility and protection in mind. It was one of the better things that the techs in the research department had developed in the past ten years, or at least it was in Al's eyes. It wasn't just sealed against the microbes of a virus; it was also sealed from the elements. Maybe on his next leave he'd invest in a neoprene shirt or vest. It would certainly help keep him warm when he stood out on the roof.

Leave, he thought, smiling grimly. *There's an alien concept to the UGMC.*

No one could see his smile, because his head was encased in a Kevlar helmet and a heavy filtration mask. The mask covered his whole face, and he could only see the world through the two round goggle lenses in the mask. There was a radio headset that linked the whole squad together; the bulk of the electrical workings for it stored in the padded rucksack they each carried. Each man apart from J-Man carried an M-16 assault rifle strapped over their shoulder: he had been designated the squads' gunner, and as such, carried one of the Marines' heavier weapons, an M249 SAW. All were armed with a Glock-17 handgun as a sidearm.

"Everyone ready?" came Johnny C's voice over the com system. Everyone gave a verbal affirmative, making sure his equipment worked. "The copter should be here any minute now. You've all got your weapons, just in case. The best-case scenario is that we touch down, grab the General, and get out of there. We shouldn't need them. Okay, copter positions. Rookie, you sit up front with Davis. Al, you take back left gun, Ping, you got back right. Leo, you and J-Man take the front weapons. I'll watch our tail.

"Davis?" said J-Man. "Richard Davis? Dick's our pilot? Fuck this shit, Johnny. I'm staying right here. You know I can't stand that self-righteous son of a bitch. You get Command on the line and tell then to send in a different pilot."

"Too late," muttered Al, pointing towards the distance, and the fast-approaching shape of the helicopter. As it neared the outpost, the features of the bulky transport ship became clearer.

In Brazil once, Ping had referred to the Cavalier as "a flying turd". His choice of wording hadn't been at all inaccurate. The shape of the machine itself was bulky and irregular at the front, the cockpit and body bristling with netting filled with equipment, mounted weaponry and cooling vents, while it tapered off into the tail of the machine. Its rotor blades were a blur of motion as the vehicle neared the outpost, and the pilot expertly manoeuvred the machine around, avoiding the tower and hovering above the roof. The swirling wind tried to shake and buffet the machine, but its weight combined with the skill of the pilot was enough to keep it almost perfectly still. The drab olive skin of the hull parted as the hatchway slid open and three rope ladders tumbled out the opening. Al, Rookie and Johnny C each grabbed one of the ladders, secured them to the moorings on the roof, then nodded to the rest of their squad. Ping and Leo scrambled up the ladders, racing one another to the top, while J-Man reluctantly grabbed the ladder and looked towards the helicopter above him. He turned to look at Johnny. "If he pisses me off, can I kill him?"

"After the mission," said Johnny, nodding and smiling behind his mask. J-Man's shoulders slumped forwards, and he slowly began his ascent, muttering to himself as he went. The in-mask microphones picked him up clearly. "Maybe this Maxis character can fly a helicopter. Maybe we can swap him for Dick, leave him on the island. Maybe I could just fake airsickness and sit this one out..."

"You're next, Al. First, though, gimme the gun!"

"What gun?" asked Al, indignantly.

"Christ, Al, I'm not blind, and I'm not an idiot. Your Desert Eagle is in your shoulder holster, there!" Johnny pointed to Al's body and the shoulder holster, which he was trying to keep hidden beneath the strap of his rifle. "That stays here."

Al slipped the gun out the holster and reluctantly handed it over to Johnny, muttering numerous curses under his breath as he did so. Relieved of his illegal weapon, Al began to climb the ladder into the helicopter, pausing only briefly to cast a look over his shoulder to the outpost below him. He was pleased to be getting out of the prison-like tower, but only wished it were under better circumstances.

"Seems a little light, Al," Johnny C called out, dropping the weapon to the floor with a clatter and kicking it off to one side of the helipad. "You still carrying the ammo clips?"

"Still carrying the gun, *sir*," he called out once he was halfway up the ladder, well out of reach. "Replica was a decay. Dumb bastard."

Grinning to himself and clambering into the body of the helicopter, Al swaggered over to his designated gun emplacement and strapped himself into the harness, giving the thumbs-up signal to Ping first, then Johnny C when he pulled himself up into the helicopter, before giving a dismissive 2-fingered salute to the back of the pilot's head. Rookie stumbled by him, slapped his hand down, then clambered into the seat beside the pilot and nodded a greeting.

"Are we ready to go?" asked the pilot, his nasally voice coming loud and, unfortunately, crystal-clear over the built-in radio sets. If Al wasn't strapped into the harness, he would have seriously considered taking off his pack and tampering with the communications equipment to block out Lieutenant Davis' signal. Although Dick Davis was a good helicopter pilot, his arrogance and cockiness was legendary amongst Al and the men in his squad. He'd served as their lift into and out of hot zones in Brazil, and had become one of the most disliked Lieutenants in the corps. "Sergeant Rook, do you have the co-ordinates?"

"Come on, Dick, just get moving," shouted J-Man, swivelling around in his harness. Al didn't doubt for one moment that if there were room in the helicopter amongst the wiring, tubing and equipment that was carried as standard, J-Man would have tried to bring up his weapon and shoot Dick. He'd threatened to do so on many different occasions and not all of them when he was drunk.

Oblivious to any of the hard feelings, or maybe he just didn't care, the pilot flicked a handful of switches by his side, releasing the ladders from their moorings below before lurching forwards, and then a rolling to the right. The helicopter peeled away from its hovering vigil over the watchtower and headed inland towards their target.

III

The deep blue colours of the cold sea rushed away from Al and turned into the drab grey-brown mix that denoted they were passing over a town or city. Al watched the landmarks and sights pass him by with interest, making out details that suggested to him that martial law wasn't being enforced at all. Shattered and destroyed buildings, abandoned vehicles, and even at the speed he was travelling, the unmistakable shapes of people stumbling through the streets. There were fires raging in every other street they flew over, and even the filter mask and the rushing air around him couldn't block out the stench of the towns below.

"Fuck, Johnny," he muttered, tugging on Johnny's sleeve. "Is this command's idea of martial law?

It's like a fucking war zone down there!" There was no verbal response from Johnny, he didn't even turn to look at Al, he just nodded his head.

"Where's our boys?" asked Leo, sweeping the barrel of his weapon from left to right absentmindedly. "Where's the squads out on the streets, where's the law, where's the order? And how come there's people out on the streets?"

"Looks like you were right, Johnny," muttered Rookie, putting aside his maps and notes to gaze down upon the world below him. "Despite what Intel tells us, we don't have control. It looks like the rebels have control over this place!"

"That's right," confirmed the pilot, his masked visage fixed on the controls. "It's like this all over, Sergeant Rook. The rebels are running riot in the cities, their interference is preventing treatment getting through to the sick and dying. The dead bodies are left to rot, attracting rats and vermin. It's a total mess down there. Meanwhile, our guys are held up in whatever outpost, base or fort they've been assigned to."

"Why aren't they out there taking back the cities?" asked Ping, scratching at his suit. Al felt the same way: though the bodysuit was warm and sealed, it didn't allow the body to breathe. He was too warm, and the trickles of sweat that rolled down his back were irritating the hell out of him.

"Look at that down there," said Dick, banking the aircraft to one side. To the left of them, far below, they could see a massive crowd of people surrounding a large building: possibly a warehouse of some description. At a quick estimate, Al would have guessed there to be two or three hundred people down there. "It's like that all over, civil unrest, massive crowds surrounding buildings. I don't know, it's like some sick bastard's stockpiled all the food in the area, and is selling it on for extortionate prices. There's always an opportunist, looking for a quick buck. When all this shit's cleaned up, he or she'll be rich. Would you go into an area like that and try to restore law and order?"

"Fuck, yeah," said Al, without a pause. "No worries."

"You're an idiot, Colebrook," said the pilot, correcting the course of the helicopter and continuing on the journey to the pickup zone.

"Yeah, and you're a dick, Dick," muttered Al, sinking back into his harness.

The rest of the journey was carried out without a word exchanged between the squad. The visions of the towns and cities in ruin, streets on fire, cars left in ruin. The scenes he'd seen were reminiscent of the urban warfare he'd experienced in the streets of Brazil, and doubtless the rest of the squad were thinking the same thing. Preoccupied with his thoughts, he lost track of time until the speakers of the radio squealed to life, bursts of static and staccatos of gunfire filled the interior of the helicopter.

"What the fuck's that?" shouted Johnny C, raising from his seat and swinging his way to the front of the helicopter. The transmission died to a hiss, then burst into static again. Gunfire still punctuated the transmission, but it seemed further away, and not as frequent.

"This is General Maxis of the UGMC, currently located at outpost KDL-76, where the fuck is my evac 'copter? Are you out there! Where the fuck are you? God-damn it, is anyone out there?"

Johnny patched his radio into the helicopters' transponder, signalling to Rookie to look at his maps. "This is Lieutenant Clarity, my squad has been assigned to your pick-up. We're currently…"

"Five minutes, tops," muttered Rookie, getting a confirming nod from Dick.

"We're currently five minutes away, Sir, just hold tight!"

"For fuck sake, hurry, man. They're getting closer every minute. I don't know how…"

The radio squawked, then died. Johnny reached forwards and twisted a few dials on the radio, trying to regain the signal. Dick batted his hands away from the dials, shaking his head. "*They* lost radio, not us. There's nothing we can do to get in touch with them again."

"Well, can we hurry up?"

"We can try," said Dick, adjusting the controls of the machine. "We can certainly try."

"Okay, men, listen up," said Johnny, returning to his position at the rear of the helicopter. "Something's going down at the outpost we're going to. We don't know what, exactly, they've lost their radio. If it's a civilian threat, then there's no way we can open fire. Warning shots, maybe, but not direct fire. So everyone ease off on the guns until we can assess the situation."

"What if they're armed," asked Al, throwing back his hands from the gun in disgust. "What if they open fire on *us*?"

"That's something we'll have to deal with if and when it happens. If it comes to it, we've got a few smoke grenades we can drop, hopefully add a little confusion. If they are armed, then it'll only be things like shotguns, handguns, and maybe a few hunting rifles. Nothing that'll puncture the armour of this beast."

"We're approaching the outpost, Lieutenant," shouted Dick, casting a glance over his shoulder. "I think you should see this!"

Johnny rose from his seat and swaggered towards the front, gripping one of the handrails that hung from the ceiling. He stared at the scene that filled the windscreen, his mask hiding the dumbstruck look on his face.

"Jesus Christ!"

Al twisted his head around to catch a glimpse of the windscreen, and froze. He understood the reaction Johnny had.

In the centre of the screen there was the outpost they were heading to: a square based pyramid with the top cut off, leaving a flat top. The top was crowned by a metal fence, and had a small, one-man observation tower position in the centre of the tower. There was enough room to allow the twelve men stationed there to occupy the roof at the same time, which was just what they were doing now. Twelve soldiers lined the perimeter of the roof, each wearing the same sealed suits as Al, and armed with various different weapons. They were firing these weapons wildly into the crowd of unarmed civilians that had gathered around the base.

"What the fuck are they doing down there?" demanded Rookie.

"Jesus, they're shooting them! What's going on?"

"Maybe they're using rubber bullets?" suggested Ping, unhooking himself from his mounted weapon and leaning closer for a better look. The interior of the helicopter became awash with a muted orange light as an explosion flowered to life amongst the middle of the civilians, setting people on fire and flinging them upwards and outwards. Those that were on fire didn't seem to panic, just continue moving towards the building.

"I didn't get any memo from the Brass indicating we'd started using safety *concussion* grenades," Johnny sneered. "What the fuck are they doing?"

"How many is there down there?" asked Leo, gripping the controls for his weapon tighter. "There must be hundreds of them!"

"Stand down from your weapons, men. Just because they're firing on them, it doesn't mean we need to."

"I'm bringing us in for pickup," said Dick, wiping his hands over a control panel and turning on all the internal and external lights on the helicopter. "Open the hatch and get ready to throw that ladder out. I think I can see Maxis on the roof. He's the only one not firing a gun!"

"No fucking surprise there, then," grunted Al, standing up and helping Ping with the ladders. "Why would a general possibly consider doing any work when there's another twelve guys to do it all for you?"

"Is he going to make us just pull the ladder up with him on it?"

"Don't even joke about it, kid. If he does, I'm gonna drop the bastard in the crowd."

The hatch trundled open, and both Al and Ping recoiled from the overpowering stench that flooded the cabin: a foul and potent stench of rot and decay, thick and cloying even through the masks. The two marines stumbled back, and kicked out the folded up ladder with both feet. Al watched as it tumbled over the edge, then turned to look at Johnny.

"The ladder's out, Johnny, but shit, it stinks out there."

"We can all smell it, Al," said Rookie, turning back to face him. "Now, get ready to help him up if he needs any assistance."

Al gave a half-hearted salute, but the mask hid his expression as he twisted his face in disgust.

Fucking babysitting, he thought in silence as he stuck his head out over the edge of the helicopter and watched the marines on the outpost fire wildly into the crowd. *I wanna be down there!*

Mike Taylor was the only soldier in the one-man observation tower, and currently manning the mounted Vulcan cannon, sweeping it from left to right and chewing into the advancing creatures. He didn't know where they'd come from, only Maxis seemed to have any idea about that, but he'd barely spoken to him since he crawled into the base two days ago. Maxis had been wounded when he'd arrived, but hadn't told anyone how it had happened, nor had he mentioned what had happened to the rest of his convoy. As soon as he'd arrived, he'd been whisked into the small medical room, and hadn't spoken to anyone but the commanding lieutenant. He certainly hadn't had the time of day for any of the Privates in the outpost.

About thirty-six hours after he'd arrived, the medic had confirmed that he could be moved, and a priority signal was sent out to one of the command bases off shore. Then, the creatures had arrived. Danny, another Private, had told Mike that he'd overheard Maxis talking, and that they were actually zombies. Mike hadn't believed a word of it, until they'd opened fire, and seen the damage just one of them could take before dying. Now they were surrounded by whatever they were, and they were outnumbered at least ten to one.

At least the rest of the squad's doing something about it, Mike thought to himself as he lowered his masked glare at the general, standing in the middle of the platform. The leg of his suit was bloodied and torn, although the wound itself had been dressed and bandaged. He wasn't wearing a helmet or mask, now, and insisted that the plague was no longer airborne. Maxis looked tired and weary, his hair grey, his eyes bloodshot. He'd refused any form of weapon, and simply stood staring at the skyline, waiting for his pickup. Once the gunship appeared on the horizon, Maxis seemed to relax a little, and why shouldn't he? He had a ticket out of here, a one-way ride off the island, and Mike was going to be left here, surrounded by the creatures that were trying to crawl their way up the slanted sides of the building.

The helicopter was closer, now, close enough for Mike to make out the masked faces of the pilots, and a third masked face peering out the side hatch, one arm trying to keep the ladder straight and steady as the machine approached the outpost. Maxis raised his arms as the ladder came closer, his fingers coiled around the first rung…

…Just as the first of the creatures leapt over the railing and dived on one of the soldiers, Mike couldn't see who it was. As soon as the mask came off, the creature was on to his face, teeth sinking into flesh and scraping against the bone of the skull. Another soldier turned and fired on the feasting creature, peppering its body with gunfire, only to be assaulted from behind by another creature and pulled back over the barrier. By now, Maxis had hauled himself a quarter of the way up the ladder, and already the helicopter was beginning to pull away from the building. The outpost was lost to the creatures now, as another five clambered over the railings and took down more soldiers, their bodies dropping to the floor amongst spilled blood and discarded bullet casings, and Mike didn't like the idea of being left behind. He left the controls to the weapon, pulled himself from the frame out of the lookout, then leapt out and up, hands reaching for the lowest rung.

If only he could reach it, then he'd be pulled to safety, away from the fallen base. His hands brushed the metal rung, his fingers coiled around it, but his sweating palms slipped straight off the slick material. He found himself plummeting towards the mob at ground level, and found himself wondering whether the impact on the ground would kill him first, or whether it would be the creatures.

He landed heavily on the head of a creature with a sickening thud, and the animal crumpled beneath him. He felt bones pierce his flesh, though whether those bones were his or the creatures he'd landed upon, he didn't know. He was aware of fingers probing and ripping at his flesh, and could feel teeth sinking into his body.

The sight of the helicopter flying away into the distance was the last thing he saw, before one of the feral animals sunk its rotten fingers into his eye sockets and plucked out his eyeballs.

"Fuck!"

Al and Ping were in the process of pulling the ladder up, assisting the general in his climb, when the civilians overran the outpost. Al watched as the people climbed up the side and ripped into the soldiers, then stared in disbelief as the person in the lookout took a leap of faith, trying to reach the rungs of the ladder, but missing and plummeting to his death amongst the riotous crowd. He couldn't take away his gaze as the crowd ripped the mystery jumper to pieces.

"What the fuck is going on here? What the fuck are they?" demanded J-Man, swinging his weapon from side to side, flitting from target to target on the ground. He was anxious to open up with the weapon, avenge the death of the twelve fellow soldiers in the outpost who had suffered a bloody death.

"Here's the little fuck that may be able to tell us," growled Al as he and Ping grabbed the collar of the general and hauled him up into the cabin. They carelessly dumped him on the ground, cycled the hatch shut, then returned to their gun stations. "Permission to hose those fucks, Johnny."

"I'm already on it, Al," Johnny said, settling down to the controls of his weapons array and cranked the fire selector around to 'automatic'. While the rest of the squad manned heavy machineguns, Johnny was in charge of the rear-mounted grenade launchers. As he squeezed the firing controls, a salvo of explosive shells plunged into the mass of flesh-eaters and erupted into a flaming explosion, tossing aside the creatures and obliterating those caught at ground zero. He left his controls as the helicopter flew out of range, then looked down on the general. He was a wreck, he looked like he'd gone through hell, his leg had been injured, and he wasn't wearing any breathing mask like the rest of the squad, or those that had been stationed at the outpost.

"Thank God," muttered the general, rolling on to his knees and leaning against the side of the cabin. "Thank you, all of you, you've rescued me. You'll all receive medals for this. God, thank you!"

"You want to tell us what the fuck those things were?" asked Johnny. "And where's you mask? We don't have a spare…"

"The syndrome's not airborne, it hasn't been for weeks, now. Maybe it never was, I don't know for sure. And those… those *things*… are what the carriers turn into."

Al looked at the general, at the state of his face and the wild look in his eyes, and decided it would be best to keep his own mask on for now. He didn't want to take advice about the contagion of the syndrome from someone who looked as unhinged as Maxis did. No one else made a move to remove his mask, either.

"You look like shit," offered Leo. The dishevelled appearance of the man didn't inspire any respect in the men. His features were gaunt and sallow, and his reddened eyes were heavily lined with puffy bags of tender flesh.

"He looks like a crack-addled paedophile," offered Ping. He said this quiet enough so only the microphone picked it up, and transmitted it to the rest of the squad. Al managed to suppress a laugh, but he couldn't stop a slight grin spread his face.

"Get me out of here," ordered the general, closing his eyes. A grimace of pain spread across his face, and he moaned softly as the wound on his leg seeped a pale pink fluid, pooling on the floor amongst a coil of thick insulated wiring. With a gentle sigh, he drifted off into a restful sleep.

"Remember when you said we weren't being told the whole story?" asked Rookie, facing Johnny.

"That little shit probably knows the whole damn tale. Why don't we pressure him for the real deal?"

"Because if he tells us, what good is it going to do?"

"Johnny's right. We're still going back to that stinking prison. We're still going to be babysitting this frigging island. We're still going to be doing the exact same thing we do every day. Why do we need to be bogged down with more information than we need?"

"All right, everyone get back to your stations. We're due to rendezvous with the gunboat *Narcissus* in half an hour."

Twenty minutes passed by, the helicopter zigging and zagging through the air as it returned towards the sea. The deaths of the soldiers at the outpost hung heavily in the minds of the Marines as they travelled, each unable to comprehend what they'd seen. The general had remained silent since falling asleep, he hadn't stirred once, even when the 'copter had passed through some rough turbulence.

"We're coming up on a built up area," said Dick, breaking the silence of the journey. "We're not far off from the rendezvous. We're going to be early."

"Okay, Dick," murmured Johnny absentmindedly. "Circle for a little bit. Keep us steady, don't want to wake sleeping beauty."

"Looks like there's a storm coming in. Winds picking up and the clouds are darkening. We're going to get rain, it's probably going to get a little rough…"

"Well for fucks sake, Dick, do something! Take us lower! Jesus, do I have to tell you to do everything? Use your friggin' initiative!"

Dick didn't respond, simply lowered the helicopter, so it was only a few hundred feet above the ground. He held it at that level, lazily circling the city below.

"You could have given us a better view, Dick," grumbled Al, looking at the city with heavy eyes. He would be quite happy to doze for ten minutes, but knew that his snoring would tip off the entire squad. He turned to look at their sleeping cargo, and saw him twitching slightly, weeping pink liquid from the corner of his mouth. Relinquishing his grip on the machinegun, he stepped back and kneeled down beside Maxis, slowly reaching out and prodding him. Maxis shuddered, and spasmed slightly. His skin cracked around his neck, spilling thin, watery blood.

"Infection," stammered Al, standing up and backing away from the general. He'd paid enough attention to the briefings about the spread of HDS to identify the signs of the plague. "Maxis is infected. Shit, what do we do?"

"There's nothing we can do," said Ping, edging closer and trying to look into the eyes of the general. He uttered a single, drawn-out moan, then keeled forwards and slumped to one side. Laboured and heavy breathing stopped all together. "Jesus, he's dead. Not airborne anymore my ass!"

"That's it?" asked J-Man, scratching his body subconsciously. "That's the drawn out death that we've read about in the files?" He sounded a little disappointed about it.

Ping gently rolled the body of the general on to its back, and unsheathed his combat knife and prodded the wounded leg on the bandage. If oozed yellowish-red pus, and he gently pried the cotton dressing up and over. "Looks like his wound was bad. Heavy bleeding, maybe that increased the plagues progression."

"Does it work like that?" Leo asked.

"How the fuck should I know?" snapped Ping, "I'm not a medic. Jesus, don't we have a medic?" He turned from the body to look at Leo, and everything happened at once.

"Activity on the ground," snapped Dick. "On the rooftops, ten o'clock."

Al leaned over to one side to look out the window, and could see a small group of about seven people. They all seemed to be armed with various shotguns and handguns, though one of them seemed to be lugging a large wooden crate between them. "What the hell've they got down there?"

he muttered as he leaned closer to the window. The end of his question was drowned out by an ear-shattering scream that tore through the internal speakers and made his ears ring. He spun around and saw the dripping and bloody body of Maxis draped over Ping, writhing frantically and splashing contaminated blood all over the interior of the machine.

"What the fuck?" screamed Al, almost losing it at the young soldier. Surely he wasn't as insensitive as to mess around with a fresh, infected corpse like that.

"That bastard isn't dead," screamed J-Man, leaping on Maxis and trying to knock him off Ping's back. He was still screaming in pain, and the general seemed to have his mouth pressed against his shoulder. "He just leapt on him!"

Chaos erupted in the helicopter as each marine blindly fumbled for his weapon. There wasn't enough room in the cabin for everyone to bring their rifle up at once, so each had to rely on their sidearm. Of all the members in the squad, Al had the quickest draw, and before anyone could lift their Glock, he had already opened one of the pouches on his webbing and pulled out his immense handgun, the black metal of the magnum he'd smuggled aboard he helicopter glinting in the poor light. He brought the butt of the weapon down hard on back of the skull of the general, then grabbed his shoulder and heaved back with all his might. The general peeled away from Ping, taking with him a large chunk of flesh from his shoulder, then spun to face Al. With lightning quick reactions, he lifted his magnum and fired twice, point blank into the torso of Maxis. The thunderous fire of the weapon was magnified by the confines of the helicopter, and the bullets tore though both the body and hull of the helicopter with ease. Maxis stumbled back with the power of the impact, then lurched towards Al, a malevolent smile on his bloodied face. Al fired again, this time lifting his aim and planting a round square in the centre of the general's forehead. The top of his head cracked open, ruddy brains and blood spattered against the cabin and the general keeled over backwards, dead.

"I thought he was fucking dead," muttered Al, grabbing Ping and dragging him to the back of the helicopter. He leant him against the wall, and looked at the wound inflicted by the general. "You all right kid? We're going to get you some help, okay?"

"Activity, rooftops, ten o'clock," screamed Dick, his voice unusually high and panicky as his fingers danced over the communications console. "Will someone check what the fuck they're doing?"

"J-Man, Leo, get to your weapons," ordered Johnny. "Al, you look after Ping, okay? And keep away from that corpse. I don't know what the…"

Johnny was cut off as the helicopter wildly bucked and shuddered, and was flung towards the front of the vehicle as an explosion outside lit up the dark sky.

"Rebels, sir," reported Leo, bringing his mounted weapon about aim at the rooftops. "They've got RPGs, and they're not shy to use them"

"Well were the…"

Johnny C's final words ended there as a pair of rockets tore into the front of the helicopter and ripped apart the armour and windshield, bathing the interior with heat and light. The cabin was filled with acrid smoke and the sounds of a hundred emergency sirens going off at once. The engine of the machine choked and died, and with a sickening lurch, the vehicle plummeted towards the ground, smashing against the concrete surfaces of the streets.

VI
LEFT TO ROT

"Tests have proven the body remains rife with disease and remains highly contagious even post mortem."

I

Fuel, crash, fire, rain, sparks, gun, Maxis, Johnny, squad, helicopter, explosions!

A collection of confused thoughts ran through his mind as everything slowly came back into focus for Al. A pair of rockets that had exploded on impact had grounded the helicopter, making it crash on the ground, in the middle of the streets. Johnny, Rookie and Dick had taken the brunt of the explosion, and had been flash-fried almost instantly. From his position on the floor, Al could make out three smoking and blackened corpses near the front of the cabin. Behind them, he could see the twisted and broken shapes of J-Man and Leo. J-Man had broken his neck in the fall, his head now hanging limply to one side, while the head and upper torso of Leo had been crushed between the frames of the machine as it had crumpled on impact. The body of Maxis had fallen out mid-crash, and Al couldn't see it anywhere. Beside him lay Ping, his shoulder seeping blood, though he was still breathing shallowly.

The air inside the helicopter reeked of smoke and the pungent odour of leaking fuel, while the shattered control panels at the front of the machine sparked and hissed violently. It was raining now, so at least the water would dilute the fuel a little bit, but Al had to get out the 'copter and far away from it as soon as he could. His mask had been torn off in the crash, and now hung uselessly from one side of his helmet, so he tore both helmet and mask off and threw them aside. If Maxis had been right about the syndrome no longer being airborne, then he'd be all right. But if he wasn't... Well, he was dead anyway.

"Hey, kid, you all right?" Al asked, raising himself up from the floor and tapping Ping on the shoulder. He moaned, then slowly nodded his head. He reached for the clasps on his mask, then pulled away the rubber front, leaving the helmet on and discarding the front. He coughed, then dragged himself to his knees, looking at the remains of his squad. "Christ, Al, what happened? Johnny... Leo... J-Man..."

"We got shot down," muttered Al, forcing open the hatch to the cabin and looking out into the street. Rain splashed to the ground, and the smell of fuel intensified. Despite the downpour, it wasn't doing much to dissipate the fuel. "We've got to get out of here. The fuel tanks have been ruptured, we're pissing fuel, and those sparks won't do much good if they hit it. Grab your gun and get out!"

"What about you?" muttered Ping, hauling himself to his feet and fitting the butt of his rifle beneath his shoulder. He hobbled out the hatch, then rolled away from the crashed machine. "What are you doing?" he yelled, raising his own voice so he could hear him above the torrential downpour thrumming against his helmet.

Al didn't pause to give answer to Ping, he was trying to work as quick as he could. He didn't relish the idea of stripping his dead friends of ammo and weapons, but he had to face facts: both Ping and himself were in more need of it now than they were. J-Man was the first to be plundered, Al knew him too well. Not only was the soldier armed with the heaviest weapon, the M249, he also carried custom shotgun shells. Al had never seen him fire them, nor had he been privileged enough to watch him make them, but he figured if he'd protected them so much, then they had to be worth something. Stripping him of all the ammo he carried, Al cut the dead marine's rucksack free, emptied it out, and piled the ammunition into it. The only other marine he could salvage anything from was Leo: any magazines the rest of the squad had been carrying had been set off in the heat of the explosion. Grimly, Al snapped the dog tags from around each of the corpses' neck, then turned back towards the hatchway. The rain was coming down hard now, maybe it would give him a little extra time to get some more equipment out the downed machine before it went up.

He tumbled out the opening, dragging the sack of ammunition and juggling his assault rifle and the machinegun, trying to keep them both tucked under his arm as he ran towards Ping. The young marine hadn't even tried to help the Sergeant, simply backed up against one of the buildings surrounding the crash-site and taken point, sweeping his weapon from left to right.

"Nothing to report," he yelled, wiping his eyes clear of the rain that pelted against his face. It was cold, but not as cold as the spray they were used to out at sea. "Whoever brought us down is taking their time to come and have a look!"

"They'll come," muttered Al, dumping the weapons and ammunition beside Ping. "If we brought a helicopter down, we'd want to have a look at it. Get that machinegun ready, kid, make sure it works for me. I'm going back for some more."

He ran back, delving into the helicopter. Thick wisps of smoke were now beginning to snake lazily from the control panels towards the door, tugged out by the wind outside. The sparks were coming more frequent, and Al guessed that he might have a few minutes before it went up. Certainly not enough time to detach one of the two remaining mounted weapons that looked like they still worked, but possibly enough time to drag out one of the boxes they'd been sitting on.

Large and heavy, the box was a pale brown in colour, with each face of it stamped with the UGMC logo, denoting ownership of the box and the equipment inside. Heaving it through the hatchway and back into the street outside, Al dragged the box behind him as he went, muttering and cursing under his breath as the cumbersome container rattled and clunked with each jarring movement. He'd covered half the distance between the helicopter and Ping, when he felt himself be picked up and tossed aside by an immense shockwave, followed shortly after by a deafening explosion. The vehicle erupted into a fiery ball of explosive heat as fuel and spark finally found one another and celebrated their unity in a frenzied blast. Pieces of the machine sailed up into the air and tumbled to the ground, flaming debris punched through walls and windows of surrounding buildings, and Al tumbled along the ground until the side of a building stopped him. He curled into a ball, trying to protect himself from any additional damage that flying shrapnel could inflict, and waited for the sounds of tumbling metal to stop. Gingerly lifting his head up, he looked around the damage zone.

The helicopter had crashed in the middle of a street, and the front of the smoking machine lay embedded in the front of a now-ruined shop, though the explosion that had annihilated so much of its contents had damaged it more. To the left and right of the shell were more shops, just a few stories tall, their windows shattered by looters and, most recently, flaming shrapnel. Behind the ruined machine there was a deep trench in the asphalt road, two feet deep and twice as wide. Hunks of useless metal and scattered equipment lay behind the helicopter, the remains of what had been jolted loose by the violent crash. Already the fire was hissing and spitting beneath the downpour. Al stood up, looking around the crash site, and slowly took out a silver cigarette case, placing one of them in his lips and absentmindedly patting his pockets down for a light. Returning the case to one of the pouches on his webbing, Al was resigned to the fact he didn't have a lighter, though he kept the cigarette clenched between his lips anyway.

He turned towards his only remaining comrade, and strolled over to Ping. He still lay on the floor where Al had left him, surrounded by pieces of broken machinery and the few supplies he'd managed to get out before the explosion. He seemed to be enjoying the rain splashing against his face, and had a slight smile on his face. The rain trickled down his helmet and dripped into the wound on his shoulder, the chunk of flesh Maxis had tore out of him before Al had shot him, and flowed over on to his uniform, staining the dark fatigues with a slight red tinge.

"You all right, kid?" he asked, grabbing the rucksack and slinging it over his shoulders. Ping simply nodded his head, neglecting his task of sentry duty.

"We've got to move. If that thing crashing didn't attract the attention of every man woman and child in this city, then the explosion will. Grab your shit and we'll get out of here."

Nodding, Ping clambered to his feet, slinging his own rifle and arming himself with Al's, leaving the sergeant to use the machinegun. "What about that?" asked Ping, pointing to the heavy box Al had tried to drag from the helicopter. The green casing was heavily blackened and bashed in, a corner buckled and hinges bent. It smoked an unhealthy, choking cloud.

"Whatever was in, I don't think it's going to be worth having!"

"Bullshit," muttered Ping, lurching over to the saved cargo. He tapped it hard with the butt of his rifle, then again, until the lid popped open. He peeled it open, and stepped back as a revolting smell assailed their sense: The scent of burning rubber and melted plastic. "Rations," he muttered, pulling out his knife and poking around in the contents of the box. "I'm not touching this shit, we're leaving it."

Grinning, Al swung up his weapon and panning it from left to right. There was only one main road out the crash site, but there were numerous back alleys leading away from the street, and into secluded sanctuary.

"Which way, then?" asked Ping, lazily aiming is rifle in no particular direction. "Where are we?"

"We need to find some kind of radio. The one on the helicopter's trashed, and our own communication gear hasn't got the ranging to get off shore. C'mon, this way," growled Al, swinging to the right and entering the first alleyway he came to. As he left the smoking debris, the smell of smoke and fuel faded out and a stronger smell took over, a stomach-churning bittersweet scent of what Al could only describe as a rotten body. He'd found his fair share of bodies in his time in Brazil, and the heat in South America hadn't done anything to sweeten their scent. The odour that lingered in the alleyway wasn't at all dissimilar to that, though much more potent.

As the pair moved they took care where they placed their feet. If there *was* a corpse lying in the alleyway, the last thing they wanted to do was to plunge their boots into the opened chest cavity of a dead body.

"What the hell is that stench?" asked Ping. The further into the alley and away from the smoke they went, the stronger the smell became, up to the point where it became overpowering.

"Smells like the whole town's been left to rot," muttered Al, leaning against a wall and keeping his gun trained on the pathway ahead of him. He urged Ping to do the same thing behind them. "It makes sense, though, I guess. These armed rebels, guerrillas or whatever the hell you want to call them; they're pulling the shots here. If they're running this place, and they're not letting the proper help get through, then the sick are going to die and the bodies are gonna be just left. And dead things rot."

"Why'd they shoot us down?"

Al shrugged. "I haven't got all the answers, kid. I wish I did. C'mon, let's move. The sooner we get to a radio, the sooner we can get out of here."

The pair carried on deeper into the alleyway, eventually coming out the other side on an open area of land. Like most open expanses of land in a town or city, it had become a car park, though now looked more like a graveyard for machines.

Vehicles left abandoned, their doors wide open, windows shattered and bodies battered and dented. Some had been parked up carefully, others had simply ploughed into the sides of others, their bodies and bonnets fused together by fire and twisted metal. An eerie silence hung in the still of the air, the only sound the pair could hear the drumming of rain atop the roofs of the vehicles. Al paused and held up his hand then hefted his weapon. He felt like he was being watched, though he couldn't say for sure. The carcasses of the vehicles held so many possible hiding places for any number of people. Ping didn't question his actions, he knew enough to know when and when not to make any noises, and especially knew when not to question orders. Slowly, Al stalked out into the area and stepped into the small trenches between the cars.

Mud splashed up beneath his boots, though he tried to roll his feet to minimise both splash and noise. He made it past four of the cars, the paused and held up his hand, signalling to Ping to advance on his position. He splashed his way through the mud, sloshing to a halt beside the sergeant and looking at whatever Al had his gaze focused on.

"Someone there?" he whispered through tight lips and clenched teeth. Al didn't respond, simply lifted the muzzle of his weapon slightly. Ping did the same, grimacing as pain from his wound flashed through his arm.

The area they were aiming at was a dark opening on the side of a building, easily wide and tall enough to drive a truck trough. Smashed wooden crates lay around the entrance, and a few scraps of whatever used to be in them littered the ground. The interior was too dark to make anything out other than the sparking junction box to one side of the doorway.

"What's wrong?"

"I thought I heard something in there. At first I thought it might have been that fuse box, but I'm not too sure now. Gimme your goggles," growled Al, keeping his gaze locked on the doorway but holding out one of his hands, not making a move for the pair dangling from his own belt. Without shifting his own gaze from the doorway, Ping pulled a small pair of goggles from his utility belt and passed them over to Al, flicking them on as he did so. He took them with a nod, and pressed the whining device to his eyes, not bothering to strap them on.

The black darkness of the doorway was transformed into a lurid mix of blues and purples, the darkest of colours representing the coldest of regions. The junction box pulsated with a steady red-orange, while the deepest recess of the garage seemed to dance with a mix of almost black-blue shapes. He spun on the spot, casting the heat-detecting visor over the assortment of cars and vehicles parked around him. Thin streaks of cold grey lashed down before him, and each car seemed as cold and dead as the rest. He thought he might have found a car with the bonnet still glowing, indicating that there might have been someone here, but nothing gave him any indication of that. He turned back to Ping, and handed the goggles back to the multicoloured creature that stretched out its hand towards him.

"Nothing in there," he muttered, watching as Ping took a quick look through the goggles before returning them to his belt. "Looks really cold, though. Probably used to be a meat locker or something. Come on, it may be cold, but at least it'll offer us some shelter from the rain."

Trudging through the puddles around him, Al lead his companion through the vehicle graveyard, still swinging his weapon warily from left to right. Just because there wasn't any sign of anyone when he had scanned the goggles, did mean they hadn't crept up on them since then.

As they neared the open doorway, the sounds of swinging chains clanking against one another told Al that his initial thoughts were right, and it was indeed a large freezer for a butcher. A sign beside the doorway, partially obscured by dirt and blood, read "Hursts Master Butcher: Deliveries Only". Al stopped and slipped a small magnesium flare from a pouch on his belt, then sparked it up and threw it into the darkness.

With the eruption of light there came the flurry of movement, and the darkness of the building roared to life as a hunched-up figure darted towards them, lips smothered in blood, eyes yellowed and bloodshot, fingers dirty and stained a dark brown. He made a coarse, gurgling sound in the back of his throat, lurching towards Al and Ping with open arms. Both soldiers raised their weapons, but none opened fire straight away, their trained eyes scanning the man for any weapon. He wasn't carrying any gun or melee weapon, though one hand seemed to be gripping a handful of dripping meat. His teeth gnashed together as he swayed forward and a feral look in his eyes reminded Al of General Maxis in his final moments of life. Ping reacted quicker than Al, having already been on the receiving end of someone in this condition, and fired a three-shot burst into the stomach of the man. He stumbled back, his fresh wounds oozing a watery pink substance, but didn't fall to the ground, didn't react the way the Marines had expected a man taking three point-blank shots in the gut. Again, he lurched forwards, arms flailing and fingers curling into a claw-like shape, dropping the bloody mess it held in anticipation of a fresher chunk of meat. Still wired for action, Ping flicked the selector switch on his rifle to automatic fire and unleashed a stream of bullets into the man, jerking him backwards and tearing his body open. The man fell back to the floor, but he was still alive, despite the fact his ribcage had been shattered and his internal organs torn apart. He groaned incoherently, arms twitching and mouth still gnawing at thin air.

"What the fuck is going on here?" screamed Al, lowering the muzzle of his heavy weapon towards the paralysed man. He wasn't going anywhere, and certainly posed no threat to the pair of soldiers as long as they kept their distance. With a grimace, Ping drew his Glock and fired a single round into the face of the man. As soon as the bullet pierced his skull, the man ceased all movements. The pair towered over the corpse, inspecting their kill. All the joints on show seemed to be flaking, the flesh torn and seeping a watery pink fluid. The ragged clothing he wore was steeped in dirt and blood, and he smelled like he'd been swimming in raw sewage. He also had a slight odour of rotten flesh. Ping sunk to his knees and gingerly pressed his hand against the forehead of the man. "Christ, Al, he's stone cold!"

"Course he's cold, he's been sitting in a freezer chomping on whatever shit *that* is for God knows how long," argued Al, waving the muzzle of his weapon towards the pile of discarded meat. Ping shook his head.

"Look," he said, making a show of taking in a deep breath, then blowing out. "This freezer isn't working, not properly at least. He wouldn't be iced to this temperature this quick…"

"Bullshit," murmured Al, turning back to look towards the collection of cars outside the delivery room. "Britain is a fucking cold place, kid, I used to live here for a while. People are this cold all the time."

Ping shook his head, then rose to his feet, holstering his handgun and ejecting the empty magazine from his assault rifle before replacing it with a fresh one. He let the empty clatter to the floor, then kicked it aside.

"You know, you're supposed to keep those," muttered Al, kneeling down and trying to light his damp cigarette with the sparking junction box. He gave that up quickly, and tried to do the same with the flare. He succeeded, and grinned as he took in his first drag. "It saves the military hundreds of thousands a year."

"If they want to take it up with me they drag their asses over here and pick me up to court-martial me," Ping growled, wincing as he lifted his arm too much and sprayed blood from his wound on to the wall beside him. "Shit, that hurts, Jesus," he muttered, clamping a hand over his injury.

"We're going to have to find somewhere to settle in for the night, kid. You need to rest that for a bit, then when the sun comes up, we'll find some high ground, get a good picture of the town, and try to work out where a radio is most likely to be. Worst comes to the worst, we'll make our own."

"Can you do that?"

"Me?" sneered Al, moving deeper into the freezer room, searching for a door other than the large one they'd entered through. "Shit, no. You're the brains of the group, aren't you?"

"If that's the case, we're fucked," smirked Ping, joining Al in his search.

II

Moloch and his band of followers were on a winning role. They'd cleared most of the zombies out the town… correction, *his* town, and although there were a few rival gangs still fighting over the territory, he had the upper hand, and was about to add another ace to it.

The local police station had been an invaluable source of supplies, and as such had been a first class base of operations. While other gangs had set up their bases in houses or old pubs and bars, grounds that they were familiar with, Moloch had vouched for the police station. It had been hard to take at first; there'd been a few soldiers guarding it at the time with a bunch of civilians holed up inside, it'd been a tough fight, but they'd finally took it and converted it to fit their needs. Soldiers and civilians, those that couldn't provide 'entertainment' for his men, had been quickly disposed of, and their weapons distributed amongst his followers. Among the soldiers' own specialised armoury, there had been a heavy box containing a number of disposable, one-shot rocket launchers. They had tipped the balance of power between his gang and the other major player in town, a joker by the name of Eddy, and now, another of his wonderful toys had brought down an honest-to-God Marine helicopter. The same helicopter that lay in Horsley Street. And if the reports he'd had over the radio system were correct, then it, like the young seventeen-year old he had tied to the bed in his office, was just waiting to be gutted and used. He just had to make sure his men got there before anyone else. He impatiently strolled from one side of his room to another, a yellow plastic radio in his hand, as he waited for an update on the situation. He paused, looked out the window of his office. He could see the rooftops around Horsley Street from here, and could see the thick black plume of smoke trailing into the sky, indicating the resting-place of the downed bird. He cast a glance over his shoulder, back to the young girl, and smiled. The police station was perfect for so many reasons. It had prison cells to store his mounting collection of Gold and other valuables, and came with a bountiful supply of handcuffs. Handcuffs that came in very handy to fasten the limbs to bedposts. Four limbs, four bedposts, the maths worked out just right. Moloch stroked his jaw as he looked the young girl up and down. She was sleeping: the five hours of screaming and trying to loosen her bonds had tired her out quite a bit, and she wasn't as young as he preferred: her sister had been quite accommodating, and he hoped she would be just the same. Maybe it would help pass the time if her woke her up, amused himself for a while...

A flash of light illuminated the window behind him, and he spun on his heels just in time to see the death of an explosion as thick black smoke covered the rooftops of the buildings in Horsley Street. As he snatched up his radio and screamed into it, the thunderous blast of the explosion rattled his windows.

"Jimmy, there's been another explosion, Horsley Street, what the fuck's going on? Are you there yet?"

"Not yet, sir," sounded the reply. It was ragged and broken up, as if the speaker was running. "We're three streets away now, we can see the explosion."

"Shit," muttered Moloch, kicking the one of the bedposts. The girl, startled by the knock, awoke; her eyes darting nervously from left to right. Her sobbing, muffled by the gag tied around her head, started up once again. Moloch cursed inwardly. Now was not the time to annoy him with more constant crying.

"We can see the helicopter now... Jesus, it's trashed."

"Nothing salvageable? Nothing at all?" asked Moloch, grabbing a length of material with one hand and eyeing it up. Maybe it would help silence the girl a little more.

"Nothing... Jesus, wait a minute... There's a survivor. Wait, two of them, two Marines."

"Marines?" scowled Moloch. "That's great. It was bad enough evicting the soldiers that had taken up residence here. A pair of Marines parading around the town is the last thing we need. Can you take them out?"

"No way, not from back here. They're moving on, through the alleys, looks like they're heading to the back of Hursts."

"Get closer, sift through the wreckage. There must be something there we can use. And kill whichever dumb bastard fired that rocket, they fucked up. I will not tolerate fuck ups."

Dropping the radio to his desk with a clatter, Moloch's spirits sunk. His haul had been lost, his town compromised by a pair of Marines, and now his mood dampened by the bad news. If Jimmy didn't come back with anything worthwhile, somebody was going to pay. Wrapping the length of material around his fist and advanced on the captive girl. Sure, he could just beat her without the padding, and it would make him feel much better to vent his frustration, but he didn't want to bruise the kid.

At least, not yet.

Jimmy released the radio he held, then slipped it back into the pouch on his belt. He drew the knife that dangled next to it then turned and pushed it into the throat of the man beside him, all the way up to the hilt. He hadn't known his name; he didn't feel it necessary to learn all the names of the people in Moloch's gang. They were all just soldiers, after all. Moloch was the general, he was his second in command. Anyone else was below him. He smiled as the man crumpled to the floor, silently trying to pull the blade from his throat, his life force slowly seeping on to the ground.

"That's a message from Moloch to all you guys," he said in a hushed voice. "Anyone else fucks up like that, the same thing'll happen to them."

Jimmy grabbed the hilt of the knife, working it from side to side, until he finally hacked through the neck and pulled the head clear. He rolled the head far to the left, making sure the corpse was damaged in such a way no other zombie could reanimate it should they happen across it, then turned back to the helicopter. The marines had gone now, leaving them with the charred remains of the helicopter. He stood and motioned for the remaining five people to follow him. They strolled through the darkened street, heading towards the ruined vehicle with a confident swagger in their step. This was their town; they ruled the roost. They didn't need to fear anything

As they neared the helicopter, the smell of roasted flesh was easily recognisable, along with that of burning fuel. Jimmy's eyes lit up as he found a battered and blackened crate that had been thrown clear of the explosion, and for a moment, he though he had discovered something they could use. His spirits sank as all he could see inside was a collection army rations.

"They stink like shit," muttered one of the men behind him, trying to keep his voice low and directed at his counterparts.

"Too bad, you've just volunteered to carry them. We can use if to feed the bitches. You and you, see how close you can get to the helicopter. You two, keep an eye out for anyone else approaching."

Jimmy retired to a smashed shop front and brushed aside the glass on the sill, lowering himself down and pulling out his hipflask. Unscrewing the cap, he took a quick nip of the potent alcohol inside, savouring the warm, tingling sensation as the liquid washed down his throat, into the pit of his empty stomach. He didn't take too much, though, he needed to stay alert. He gave the men plenty of time to work through their tasks, and was about to call them in, when the still of the night was shattered by gunfire. A short burst of three, then the continuous chatter of fully automatic followed by a single gunshot after a brief pause. Jimmy's men were quick to react, bringing up their weapons and dropping their current tasks at hand. Jimmy dropped his hipflask, then stood and raised his own weapon. It was obviously the Marines, but who or what had they run into? A rival gang? A few of the zombies that had been missed in their culling? Either way, it was his job to check it out. If he didn't, Moloch would cut his balls off and make them into a necklace for his latest entertainment to wear.

Without saying a word, he strolled into the alleyway the Marines had vanished down, knowing that the rest of the men would follow. The dark passageway opened up into an area filled with derelict cars, most of which Jimmy had supervised the moving of. It had been Moloch's idea to have as many cars as possible in one place, so that when the group began building and maintaining vehicles, they'd have a massive supply of parts nearby. He stood in the entrance to the opening, scanning from left to right, looking for any sign of the soldiers. He froze as his gaze fell on the opened delivery door for Hursts, one of the local butchers, and the two figures within. One seemed to be clutching his shoulder, possibly wounded during the crash. The other man, towering like a giant over the first, seemed fine.

Jimmy paused for a moment, mulling the situation over in his head. He could call for backup, but the better option surely would be to tackle the situation himself. That way would gain favour with Moloch, and what better to present his leader with the corpses of the two marines? They'd have equipment with them, too. His tactic decided, he raised his weapon, drew a bead on the taller of the two, and fired.

He watched, grinning, as the large marine clutched his chest and toppled to the ground.

A loud crack shattered the silence, and Al stumbled backwards, away from Ping, gripping his chest. He felt like he'd just been punched, and the armour he wore smoked, hot to the touch. As he stumbled, a crumpled piece of lead toppled to the ground, splashing into the blood of the man the Marines had already slain. The round hadn't pierced his armour, but it was sure to bruise: whatever weapon had been fired at him wasn't too powerful, but it had enough of a kick behind it to wind him through the plating.

"Take cover," he wheezed, rolling to the ground and taking up position behind the car closest to him. Ping was already on the move, sliding across the ground to hide behind a second car. Al tried to recall the layout of the junkyard, and where their attackers would most likely be. The crash would have attracted unwanted attention, so anyone exploring it would have came the same way the pair of soldiers had, providing there weren't any other back alleys Al hadn't seen at the crash site. He slowly edged his head above the bonnet of the car, and tried to focus on the alleyway. It was too dark to make out any distinct shapes, but with the aid of the thermo-optic goggles, he could see a few orange shapes lingering around behind a car. A single bullet casing lay on the roof of a car, glowing yellow in the infrared scope. At least his guess had been right, and he knew where he had to aim.

"Got any forty mils?" asked Al, keeping his scope trained on the car the gunmen were hiding behind. There hadn't been any more gunfire, nor any movement that would normally indicate a band of approaching attackers. The sooner they could retaliate, the better, before they had a chance to call any backup. "Same as Brazil, remember that shantytown? Time to smoke some Bebops."

Ping grinned, slipping a grenade into the launcher of his rifle and priming the device.

"Same place we came in through, don't aim high, go for the car they're hiding behind. Quick, before they move."

Ping poked his head above the bonnet of the car, eyeing the battered blue estate car that the men were hiding behind. He couldn't see them, but then, he hadn't put on his infrared goggles like Al had. Closing his left eye, aiming with his right, he squeezed the forwards-mounted trigger for the grenade launcher, bracing for the impact.

The weapon kicked in hard, jarring his injured shoulder and bringing a fresh, intense wave of pain to him. He managed to stay up long enough to see the grenade strike his target, and feel the heat of the explosion wash across his face before he fell back to the ground, dropping his smoking rifle. A wide grin was spread across his face as the dying echoes of the explosion slipped away, and waited Al's confirmation of the kill. Another explosion rocked the ground, and then another. He thought he heard Al swear, then heard his goggles drop to the ground and felt a meaty hand roughly grab the scruff of his neck and drag him across the ground, deeper into the freezer. The world rushed by him, explosions continuously blossoming to life, and amidst the chaos, the banter of Al's machinegun. Chunks of plaster and loose rubble rained down on Ping, and the next thing he knew, he had been dragged through a ragged hole in a piece of plasterboard, and was in a new, pitch-black environment. He lay his head back, dizzied for a moment, before rolling on to his front and clambering to his feet, looking at the breathless form of Al, leaning against a wall. A layer of sweat had appeared on his forehead, and he wiped the back of his arm across his brow, panting from the exertion. Outside, explosions still sounded, but they weren't as loud or intense as before.

"What the... what the hell was that? Al, what weapon did they have?"

"Christ, kid, that was your grenade," muttered Al, wiping his eyes with his thumb and forefinger. The heat from the explosion had played havoc with his heat vision, and his eyes were still suffering from the effect of the intense display of colours. "Christ, if the Marines had forked out the extra couple of hundred on *real* night vision, I'd be fuckin' blind by now. God bless the cheap shits in charge of equipment," he muttered to himself, sinking to his knees and pulled his armour off, inspecting the dent in the breastplate, before returning his gaze to Ping. "Your grenade hit the car and blew it up. The explosion took another two cars, they both took two more, it was like a chain reaction."

"A reaction that you didn't take into account," countered Ping, listening as the final explosion died, and silence reclaimed its hold on the night. He unfastened his helmet and placed it on the ground, then watched as Al performed a slow sweep of the room, left to right with the muzzle of his gun. He shrugged nonchalantly.

"How was I supposed to know they all still had gas in them?" he said, poking at the dent in the armour. It was still usable: at least the penny-pinchers hadn't skimped out on quality protection. He stripped off the top section of his suit, and prodded gently at the tender area of flesh that had taken the beating from the deflected round. "Shit, that's gonna hurt tomorrow."

"Are they okay?" muttered Ping, motioning towards the tattoos on Al's chest: One was the head of a wolf, with the letters UGMC beneath it, and the other a naked young blond woman, seductively reclining and maintaining her modesty using only her hands. They were both decorations he'd gotten when he first joined the Marines: one to prove his commitment to the marines, the other a memento of the woman he'd left behind. It had cost two months pay, but it had been worth it. Al nodded, brushing at the hairline of the female tattoo.

"Mariah's fine," he muttered. "It hit too high, and too far to the left. She's safe."

Ping smiled, and hobbled to his feet. He'd lost his rifle, but Al had a spare waiting for him. He grabbed it, ran a few checks over it, then slammed a fresh magazine into the carbine.

"Can we hold up here during the night?" he asked, helping Al as he started to heave furniture over to the hole he'd made in the wall, blocking it back up. "I mean, is it safe?"

"Not here, no. Fuck only knows how many guys are out there, whether they're the armed shits that shot at us, or the crazies who keep trying to eat us. Kid, what the hell is going on here?" Ping didn't answer, merely shrugged his shoulders. "Okay, then, plan of action," said Al, taking charge of the situation and replacing his top and armour. "We rest as long as we can, but not here. We have to move. If those jokers back there had any friends, they're sure to come and inspect the explosion. If there's anything left to identify, then they're going to come looking for us. We head west, looking for cover or high ground: if possible, both. C'mon, find the door to this place, or maybe somewhere we can get a good view of the street."

Al found the first window, a small decorative porthole no larger than a foot across. Its view was restricted, and no good for their needs: they could neither see much of the street, nor clamber through it. Ping found the next, its location given away by the gentle breeze flapping the drawn curtains as the wind whispered through the hole in the glass pane. Cautiously pulling the curtains aside, Al peered out the window first, while Ping tried to break open the sealed lock. "Better to open it than break it," Al had warned, and with good cause. The sound of the breaking glass would carry for miles in the quiet city. With a click, the latch unfastened, and the window moved outward slightly.

"The street seems clear," muttered Al, slowly pushing the window open and lifting one leg out into the street. He winced as his foot knocked something, the dull metallic clang of a boot scuffing an empty dustbin. He eased himself out, then helped Ping clamber out, gently moving the bin to one side and shutting the window behind them. Each Marine ran in a low crouch from one side of the street to the next, flitting from shadow to shadow, taking advantage of the cover provided by both shop doorways and darkened side streets. The smell of rot and decay didn't seem so bad as it had before, the cool of the night mercifully offering a break from the odour.

"Shit, it's freezing now," muttered Ping after five minutes of navigating empty streets. As he spoke, his breath frosted in the cooling climate, looking as if he were smoking. "It's not too bad," exclaimed Al, looking at the pale colour of his friend in the moonlight. "You've lost some blood, you're going to feel the cold more than anyone." Al pulled out another cigarette to replace the one he'd lost in the escape from the explosion, and found himself patting his body and pockets down again for a lighter he didn't have. He was about to replace it, when he rolled around the corner, weapon raised, and froze mid step. He grabbed Ping by the arm, making sure it was his good one he grabbed, and sunk to the floor, hiding behind one of the piles of rubble that littered the street. He held his finger to his lips, and listened to the sounds coming from the other side of the barrier.

Wet sounds of splattering liquid and smacking of lips, of raw and bloody meat being chewed in opened mouths could be heard. Al had seen the people making the sounds before hiding, but peered around the barrier, just to make sure what he'd seen was right.

Three people, their sexes indeterminable in the darkness, seemed to be squatting around a prone body, scratching and tearing at the figure on the floor and stuffing their faces with chunks of meat.

Al reached around behind his back, and grabbed his own pair of goggles that were still wrapped up and secured to his webbing. They may have lost Ping's, but at least they still had one working pair between them. It was probably just as well they had lost Ping's, anyway, the explosions had probably permanently damaged the electronics. He slipped the equipment on, then tried to focus on the crouching figures, if only to get a definite count on them.

The goggles showed nothing in the streets, just dark blues and purples.

He waved one of his hands in front of his face, watching the coloured limb sway past, then turned to look at Ping. He was no longer the bright colours he had been before, they were more muted as the cold claimed his body, but he still had some trace of green and orange among him. Al adjusted the goggles as best he could, then looked again at the crouching people. Still, he could see nothing. He handed the goggles back to Ping, and motioned for him to just reattach them to his webbing.

"They've got no body heat," he muttered, bemused by that fact. "What's going on?"

Curiosity and intrigue getting the better of him, Al blindly ignited another flare, lit his cigarette with the sparking end, then tossed the flare over the barrier, towards the feasting group. He heard it hiss and bounce as it rolled to a stop, but the chewing sounds didn't stop. Al slowly lowered his weapon and peered over the barrier, making out what he could in the white glow of the sputtering flare.

Three people, as he'd already seen, crouching beside a prone figure. They were ripping and tearing at the corpse, pulling chunks of dead meat from it and shovelling it into their mouths, occasionally squabbling between one another if both laid their hands on the same piece of meat. In the dim light, Al could make out the features of only one of the people, covered in dried blood and dirt, partially covered by ragged clothing. Its fingers were caked with grime and covered in pieces of entrails, and its mouth quivered and drooled heavily with each expectant mouthful.

"What the hell?" muttered Ping, leaning slightly on Al's back and peering over his shoulder. "What are they eating?"

Their food source, despite having been ripped open and most of the insides eaten, didn't appear to be dead yet. Its legs were twitching, and one of its arms prodded and poked around inside it's own opened torso, grabbing scraps of it's own organs and forcing them into its mouth.

"This never happened in Brazil," said Al, watching with morbid curiosity as the trio continued their meal, unaware they were being watched. He took a long drag from his cigarette, trying to blow the smoke down so it remained behind the barrier. As he did, the illuminated figure stopped eating. It slowly turned its head, glaring over its shoulder and fixing one yellowed eye on the mound of rubble the soldiers hid behind. It made a visible effort of smelling the air; the ragged flesh around its noseless face quivering and twitching. It stumbled forwards, all the time hissing to its counterparts as it did so. The other crouching figures stood and made their way after the leader, each with a wound to their bodies that give them a limp or made them hobble. Miraculously, the person on the floor they had been feasting on rolled on to its front and started to drag itself after the advancing horde, trying to keep up.

- 129 -

Al and Ping stood up and backed away from the rubble, the Private gently shouldering his rifle and the sergeant hefting the machinegun.

"I didn't want to open fire unless we had no choice," growled Al, suspiciously eyeing the oncoming creatures. As they moved, their limbs wept watery fluids and their skin stretched and tore apart. "Jesus, they're carrying the plague, too. They're all carriers!"

Ping sighted the closest of the carriers, but didn't fire first, waiting for the official word from his sergeant. They may have been carriers, but in the eyes of the marines, they were still civilians until they attacked.

Al also stood motionless, weighing up the situation. Cannibals, badly damaged at that, slowly advancing on his position, with a crazy, *hungry* look in their bloodshot eyes. "Back up, kid, *slowly,* you hear me?" Ping nodded his head quickly, and started to slowly move back up the street, towards the junction they entered through. Once there, they'd be able to make their way into another street.

A bloodcurdling moan split the air behind them, and Al glanced cautiously over his shoulder to see another five people standing behind them, watching them back up towards them.

"A pincer move," he muttered to himself. Just because they looked crazy, it didn't mean they were, and this tactic proved it. "Get ready to cut loose, kid, they've got us trapped," he said, taking a final drag from his cigarette and flicking the smoking filter to one side. The lead creature in front of them followed the arc with its head, its gaze lingering on the discarded stick before returning to the pair of Marines. It licked its lips, then took another step forwards, curling its fingers into a claw.

Al fired off a single round from his weapon high into the air, acting as a warning shot and showing the creatures that they meant business. Only one reacted to it, slowly looking up towards the sky, trying to see what he'd shot at, before returning its bloodied face towards the pair. Lowering his weapon, Al unleashed a salvo of bullets into the leader of the cannibals, catching it high in the chest and knocking it on to the ground. He sprayed suppressive fire from left to right, cutting through the torsos of the other two in front of him, before spinning to deal with the creatures behind them.

Ping had already dealt with two of them, and was lining up a shot on a third, firing single shots and blasting the animals in the head, when Al joined in and hosed his weapon back and forth. The gunfire and acrid smoke dying away, Al surveyed the carnage he and Ping had created, then lowered his weapon and scratched his head, puzzled.

All around them, the twisting and squirming bodies of the carriers writhed and twisted, their torsos riddled with bullets and shredded by hot lead. Despite their fatal wounds, they were still alive. The only creatures that were truly dead were the few Ping had shot cleanly through the head. Ping noticed this, too, and stepped forward and chose the most intact of the creatures, unloading three rounds from his Glock into the body of the downed carrier. Still it squirmed, moaning and gurgling, despite the three lead projectiles freshly embedded in its heart. Nodding, Ping raised the handgun and let loose a fourth round, this time into the ragged and bloody eye socket. The creature instantly stopped moving and grey matter spattered from the opening, crashing to the floor with a wet slap.

"Shoot them in the head," he said, absentmindedly. "You have to shoot them in the head!"

"Don't talk shit," screamed Al, stalking out amidst the killing field and kicking one of the corpses. "Head shots? Do you think this is one of those dumb comic books Leo reads? The only way they can be killed is by shooting them in the head? Are you even listening to the words coming out your mouth?"

"Look at the facts," said Ping, sitting on the mound of rubble and waving to the bodies. "The massive crowd of people attacking the outpost? Eating other people, impervious to anything apart from trauma to the head. They don't show up on the thermo-optic goggle. They've got the plague, who's to say…"

"You're talking about fucking science fiction, kid. You're trying to say they're frigging zombies! Do you know how crazy that sounds? Hey, it's night time, maybe they're vampires instead?"

"No, it was daytime when we saw them at the outpost," countered Ping. Either he didn't pick up on the sarcasm in Al's voice, or he chose to ignore it. "Is it so hard to believe? In modern times, where we tamper with DNA, mess with genes…"

"Oh, for fucks sake, kid, you know me well enough to know that I don't get involved in conversations like this, and I certainly don't believe in zombies. Whatever the fuck these freaks are, they're not zombies."

"Just remember this, Sergeant, you're the one who gave them the title of 'zombie', not me."

"You know I've read Leo's comics," replied Al, keeping one eye on the young Private and another on the surrounding streets. Gunfire had attracted unwanted attention once already, he didn't want to get shot again: The next bullet might be aimed a little better than the last. "I know that's what you were hinting towards. Fucking zombies, don't make me laugh. The real cause is that they're probably carriers of the plague, and they're loaded with painkillers. Now come on, we're going to find somewhere to settle in for the night."

The first suitable building they came across was a simple two-story building with a thick wooden door barricaded shut from inside, the only decent-looking building in a long row of terraced houses. A few metal spikes poked out the door at irregular intervals, giving Al the impression that the other side had been blocked up with various pieces of wood and nails in a hurried attempt to bar the outside world from entry.

Just like those zombie films, he found himself thinking absentmindedly as he pushed on the windows of the ground floor. They, too, had been boarded up shut from the inside. He could see the boards from the outside, could see the hurried way in which they'd been stacked and nailed. One of the windows on the upper floors was easily accessible, even for Ping in his weakened condition, and took no effort for the pair of trained soldiers to climb up, using bins and ledges to offer extra leverage to their ascent.

Al tumbled in first, dropping his weapon and leaning back out to help Ping make his way up the final few feet. With a muffled groan and his muscles straining, Al heaved his partner into the room, then rolled up to his feet and reclaimed his weapon.

The room was just like a normal bedroom, or rather, a normal bedroom that had fell victim to a burglary. A large double bed claimed the centre of the room, while to one side there lay a wardrobe, its doors open wide and displaying their scattered and shredded contents. A dressing table stood at the foot of the bed, the large mirror cracked and bloody at the centre. Jewellery boxes lay open on the countertop, all empty, and the draws had been pulled out and emptied on to the floor. Other than the blood on the mirror, there were no physical signs that anyone had been in the room for a while.

"Do we check out the rest of house?" asked Ping, leaning heavily against the wall and gripping his aching shoulder.

"Stay here," ordered Al, moving towards the closed bedroom door and placing his hand on the doorknob. "I'll check it out, make sure the place is secure. You keep an eye on the street, but stay back in the shadows, make sure no one sees you."

Turning the handle, Al opened the door and strolled out into the landing of the house, grimacing as his first footstep made the floorboards creak and groan. He started to roll his feet as he moved, slipping into the lessons he'd first learned in survival school all those years ago when he'd first joined the Marines, shifting his weight slowly and quietly as he went.

There were another three doors on the landing, two of them open and the third shut. The two open doors were bedrooms belonging to children, one to a girl, the other to a boy. Toys covered the floor, some broken and crushed underfoot, any draws or cupboards left open and searched. Al checked the beds in both rooms with a grim expression on his face, hoping he wouldn't find anything like the corpse of a child. A few flecks of blood marked the sheets in the girls' room, with a larger pool of blood on the floor beside a small human form. Al's heart lurched into his stomach as he stopped and lowered himself to the ground, reaching out a hand and tentatively grabbing the body. He sighed with relief as his fingers wrapped around the cold leg of the large plastic doll, and he lifted it with ease. The toy had one eye missing, and its hair was plastered to its head, matted by the blood it had been lying in. Al dropped the plastic infant to the ground, wincing as it called out "Mama", bouncing once on the wooden floorboards. The boys' room, other than the emptied draws and broken toys, was clean.

Returning to the landing, Al advanced on the closed door and tried the handle. With a click, the lock released, and the hinges squealed in protest as the door opened up into a bathroom.

The bath, formerly a clean white in colour, was filled half way with a thick, dark red liquid, and the enamel above that stained heavily by the numerous splashes of blood. These splatters also carried on up the wall, across the tiles and over the interior of the cracked windows. The basin had been pulled off the wall fittings, and the toilet smashed to pieces, no doubt by the bloody and grimy sledgehammer that had been left on the floor beside it. The smell of the room was pungent, enough to make Al turn his face to one side and cover his mouth, though not enough to make him gag. He stepped further into the room, feet crunching on chips of tile and toilet, and looked into the murky water. Something bobbed beneath the surface, a dull white bone stripped of flesh and muscle, glinting in a sliver of moonlight that filtered through the windows.

"Jesus, it looks like something out of one of my games," muttered Ping, silently appearing behind Al.

"Who's watching the window, kid?" asked Al, resisting the urge to pull the plug out the bath and see just what exactly was lying in the viscose fluid. "Because unless your zombies have made our dead comrades rise up and take their turn at guard duty, someone's left a gap wide open in our defences."

Ping trudged away, back into the larger of the bedrooms, while Al turned from the bathroom, closed the door behind him, and headed downstairs, keeping one free hand firmly on the wooden banister and swinging the muzzle of his weapon as he went.

The lower floor comprised of three rooms, a living room, dining room and kitchen, and other than boarded windows, doors and the rooms' looted appearance, there wasn't anything that really stood out as out of the normal. The living room had been ransacked, naturally, a vacant space in the corner where the television had once sat. Draws pulled open and emptied into the middle of the floor, piled up the kicked aside in a hurry. A black and white photo lay on the ground, crumpled up by careless hands as it had been pulled free from a picture frame, no doubt a valuable one. Al sunk to his knees and looked at the photograph. A man, a woman, two kids and a dog, the four people smiling, the dog sitting obediently by the man's side: the stereotypical image of an English family. He absentmindedly pushed the photo into his pocket, then left the living room, and pushed on into the dining room. A large wooden table, four places set out, with cutlery, plates and empty glasses. The cupboard here had also fallen foul at the hands of the pillagers, the doors pulled off and anything of value pulled free from it.

The kitchen had been hit the hardest. Open cupboards left with crumbs and damaged containers, draws smashed on the floor, spoons and forks left, but all knives taken. Washing powder had been spilled in one corner of the room, a small pile of fake snow, perfect and untouched in the chaos that had erupted around it, and a few pieces of ragged clothing hung loosely from the open washing machine door.

Al returned upstairs, entering the master bedroom and lowering his weary body on to the double bed, watching Ping as he looked out the window. The young Private sat with his back to the room, his head swaying slightly from left to right, then rolling forwards so his chin rested on his chest. He jumped, startled, and lifted his head, then slowly repeated the process. Al smiled, stood, and then rested his hand on Ping's good shoulder.

"Get some sleep, kid," he said, slowly guiding him away from the window and on to the bed. "I'll take guard duty. You need the rest more than I do."

Ping didn't argue with his superior, he simply sunk to the bed and fell asleep the moment his head touched the pillow. Grinning, Al grabbed one of the sheets on the bed and draped it over his friend, almost as a coroner would a corpse. Taking up a seat by the window with his weapon lying across his lap, and drew his magnum, polishing the heavy barrel with a leather chamois he pulled from his pocket. Movement out in the street caught his attention, and he slowly eased himself up of the seat, peering over the window ledge as two people stumbled by, tripping over their own feet and flailing their arms wildly. Any other time, Al would have thought they were simply drunken people stumbling home from the local bars, or a late party. But now, after seeing the things he'd seen in the past hour or three, he knew better. Or at least, he thought he knew better.

Before crashing in the middle of hell, Al had always been under the impression that cutting a person in half with a machinegun would certainly kill them. He thought that a soldier emptying a full magazine of five point five-six rounds into another mans body would have killed him outright. He hadn't dreamt that the *only* way to put someone down would be to blow his or her head off. He watched, bemused as the couple stumbled off down the street, watched as the smaller one tripped and crashed to the floor, and the larger one sank to it's knees and started to tear shreds of flesh from the protesting creature.

Was it even remotely possible that Ping was right? His wild theory about zombies seemed too farfetched, and Al had seen his fair share of strange and unbelievable things in the combat he'd lived through. He'd seen some people get up after taking a few bullets, but not a full clip. He wasn't even sure he believed his own theory about plague carriers high and overdosing on painkillers.

"Christ, I don't know what to believe," he muttered, watching as the larger of the people in the street gurgled a scream of rage, and pulled away holding an arm. It stumbled away, cradling the severed arm and gnawing at the flesh on show. He'd lost all track of time working over the conundrum of the creatures in the street, it seemed like he'd been thinking it over for hours. His back could certainly attest to that, aching from the way he'd been sitting, and it would certainly take longer than just a few minutes for someone to pull another persons arm off. "What the hell are you guys?"

"Maybe I can help you out on that, sir!"

III

Al leapt from his chair, his heavy weapon clattering to the floor and adopting a classic firing stance, feet shoulder-width apart with his left hand cupping his right, and pointing the magnum at the darkened figure standing in the doorway.

"Who's there? Show yourself!" He stepped forwards, raising a leg and nudging Ping with his boot while keeping his gaze – and weapon – trained on the doorway. "Get on the clock, kid, we got company!"

Ping moaned slightly, then rolled to one side, off the bed. He sleepily grabbed his rifle, then knelt on the floor and propped himself up on the bed, rifle trained on the doorway. He was still half-asleep, but that didn't mean he wasn't on the ball. Al had seen other soldiers behaving like this, people running on automatic, and they could be just as deadly and effective as someone wired on pure adrenaline.

"Identify yourself, before we open fire!"

The figure shifted, then strolled into the room, casually dragging a wooden seat over to him and sinking into it. He crossed his legs, resting his hands calmly on his lap, and smiled.

He wore a fedora hat that sat perched atop his head, and a pristine grey business suit and white shirt. He smiled casually, a sly-looking grin, and his upper lip was hidden behind a greying moustache. His eyes were obscured by the shadows of his hat, and he held a pipe clenched between his teeth. A monocle hung from his breast pocket, which he carefully cleaned with a red silk handkerchief, watching the Marines as they watched him. His grin widened, and he nodded courteously, knocking the brim of his hat with his forefinger. The light from the window caught his eyes briefly for a moment, and Al thought he saw a glimmer of malevolence in them.

"Finally, it's jolly good to meet someone else who hasn't turned, or who isn't trying to kill me! My name is Stilgoe Furlonger, and I'm very pleased to meet you," he said, allowing a charismatic smile to spread across his face and extending one hand. Neither Marine went to accept the offering, so he made a dismissive gesture with his hand and returned it to his lap. His accent was English, and sounded like he was laying it on with a trowel, coming across like a stereotypical English monarch. Al had to concentrate to understand some of the words he said.

"Okay, Furlonger…"

"Mister Furlonger, if you please," he said, raising a finger and waggling it from side to side.

"Okay, Furlonger," repeated Al, ignoring the request. "You want to tell us what the fuck is going on here?"

"Well, I'm afraid it's all my fault."

"Your fault?" stormed Al, taking a menacing step forward. Stilgoe Furlonger didn't react, didn't even flinch. "All this shit is *your* fault?"

"Well, in a way, yes. But not directly," he said as he stood up and made his way to the door. Al let him move, knowing that he'd have no problem plugging him from where he sat. He turned his back on the soldiers, then turned back, now holding a china cup filled with a dark liquid. "Firstly, I have to ask you, do either of you chaps recognise me?"

"Are we supposed to?" asked Al, sitting back down, but keeping his weapon trained on the man. Stilgoe took a sip of his drink, then smiled and licked his lips.

"Fucking tea guy," murmured Ping, still half-asleep, but slowly coming around. "Tea man, Johnny's tea man." Stilgoe smiled, nodding towards the kneeling soldier.

"Johnny's tea man," muttered Al, rubbing his jaw absentmindedly with one hand. It finally dawned on him, and he nodded slowly. "Right, that's right, kid. Johnny C used to have a special tea sent to him, he said it was the only tea he'd drink. He kept saying the rest tasted worse than cat piss. Furlonger's finest blend of Chinese tea. Furlonger, is that you?"

Stilgoe nodded. "Years ago, my grandfather perfected the finest blend of Chinese tea. For three generations, the Furlonger family name has been linked with tea, making the finest drinks from only the finest tealeaves. Each generation has added an extra ingredient, and modified the recipe slightly, to make for a better tasting product. The secret recipe has been handed down, and I carry it with me now as I speak, in my case." As he spoke, he motioned towards the brown attaché case standing in the doorway. "And that's what all this is about!"

"Your tea is responsible for those flesh-eating freaks and the bastards with the guns out there?" Al demanded, confusion once again clouding his mind. "How?"

"Not my tea *directly,* you must understand chaps," said Stilgoe, finishing his cup and placing it on the floor. He pulled out a lighter from his pocket, and lit his pipe, thoughtfully puffing away at it. Al motioned towards him, and Stilgoe tossed over his lighter. Finally able to light his cigarettes, Al joined the strange gentleman in smoking and waited for the rest of the story.

"Blow that shit away from me," growled Ping, looking up towards Al. He'd woken up now, and seemed to be back in the land of the living. Or rather the land of the unliving, depending on how you looked at their situation.

"Where was I?" he muttered, gazing off into the distance and talking to himself. "Ah, yes, that's right. The tea industry can be ruthless and dangerous at times, my friends. Ruthless. The main competitor and rival of Furlonger's Finest was a young German entrepreneur who goes by the name of Baron Von Hurricane. He offered to buy out Furlonger's Finest, and when I refused, he must have put a contract out on me, and that's where the men out there with the guns come in. Hit men. You see, he tried to emulate our secret recipe, but it went hideously wrong. Anyone that drinks his tea contracts the plague and turns into one of those creatures, so he needs our recipe to counteract the negative effects of his own brew, and pass it off as his own."

"Thanks, man, thanks, you've cleared up a lot for us," Al smirked, looking towards Ping and rolling his eyes. "Thanks for that."

"Mind if I make another cup of tea?"

"Go for it," said Ping, raising the muzzle of the rifle and following the man as he left the room and headed into the bathroom. Once he was out of earshot, Al lifted his magnum and sat back.

"The guy's a total fucking mad bastard!"

"Crazier than a rat in a shithouse," countered Ping. "What could make Stilgoe Furlonger think his tea is responsible for creating thousands of zombies?"

"If he's who he says he is," Al grunted, slipping his handgun back into its holster and retrieving the M249. "If he *is* crazy, he could be anyone. Poor bastard…"

"Would you boys like a fresh cup of tea? I've got a batch on the brew, my finest brand. It will help you heal young man, and will even grant you some partial invisibility from the Baron and his men. That's how I've survived so long, you know. My tea, it has magical powers," he announced, returning back into the bathroom, muttering to himself as he went.

"So how do you know we're not this Hurricane's men?" called Ping, grinning and humouring the man while listening to the water splashing and dripping into cups. Stilgoe staggered back into view, a fresh cup of tea in his hand and a grin across his face. "Simple, you're black, and the pair of you are wearing green. The Baron can't abide black people, and he's allergic to the colour green, in burns him. That's why the wrapping of all my tea is green, it keeps his hands off it."

"Perfect sense," agreed Al, speaking in a tone of voice he normally reserved for speaking to children.

"What do we do with him?" muttered Ping, watching as the man stumbled around the room, muttering to himself and pointing towards people only he could see and hear. "He's a liability if we take him, but we can't leave him…"

"I say fuck him," muttered Al, scratching his beard. "Him and his damn magic tea have survived this long. He may be crazy, but he's got enough smarts to stay alive. He had something the poor family that lived here didn't."

"Family?" shouted Stilgoe, putting his cup and saucer down on the dresser and removing his hat, dusting off the rim with the collar of his jacket. He replaced his hat, then slipped his hand into his jacket pocket, rummaging for something. "Oh, yes, the four unfortunates that once lived here. Dashed shame about those fellows."

"Did you know them?" asked Ping, clambering to his feet and glancing out the window. There wasn't much activity out on the street, just a single creature lying on the ground, its arm missing and surrounded by blood.

"Knew them?" asked Stilgoe, advancing on Ping from behind and sinking his finger into the open wound on the Private's shoulder. The Marine screamed in agony, trying to wriggle free from the grip, but only succeeded in causing more damage. "Knew them? I had to kill the poor souls. Baron's men, you know. But their eyes were of the highest quality!"

As he spoke, Stilgoe moved from left to right, keeping his impaled hostage between Al and himself. The giant soldier had his machinegun up, but couldn't get a clear shot at the insane man.

"Let him go, you crazy bastard," screamed Al, trying to out-manoeuvre the pair and get a clear shot. "Let him go or I'll kill you were you fucking stand, you miserable shit!"

"I can't let him go," retorted Stilgoe, increasing the pressure on the wound. Ping had stopped screaming, now, and had lapsed into unconsciousness through the pain. "I need his eyes for my blend. I use only the finest, he should be honoured." He pulled his hand out of his pocket, showing a glinting silver scalpel in his hand, and brought it down in a sharp stabbing motion, piercing Ping's eye and spewing blood and vitreous fluid. The sudden attack jolted Ping awake once more, bringing another ear-shattering scream out the lungs of the young Marine. With a jerk, Stilgoe removed the scalpel and released his captive, admiring the shapeless eye skewered on the blade. The moment Ping was released he fell to the floor, giving Al an opportunity to open up.

The heavy weapon thundered to life, pounding round after round into Stilgoe and knocking him back. With a bloody scream, the man was pushed out the window by the force of the bullets, toppling to the street below with a sickening crack. Al rushed to the window, peering out on the street below at the twisted remains of a twisted man. Blood pooled around his bent form, and it looked like he'd landed on his head first, his neck twisted and broken. Not taking any chances, Al levelled off his machinegun and loosed a single shot, cracking open the skull of Stilgoe and ensuring he didn't rise again. He spun and knelt beside Ping, helping his friend regain his feet. Blood trickled down the gaping eye socket and he shook viciously, the shock of the event hitting his system.

"Jesus, Jesus, sweet fucking Jesus," he moaned, cradling his head in both hands and gritting his teeth. "He took my frigging eye."

Al nodded, not knowing what to say, and looked around the room. The cup of tea still sat on the dresser, and Al looked at it, picking it up and swilling it around. The liquid was an earthy red in colour, and smelled vaguely familiar: blood. As the liquid moved, something pale surfaced in the murk, and Al poured the contents out on to the dresser. He recoiled in disgust as a pair of eyeballs flopped out, splashing into the spilled blood. Al made his way towards the door and grabbed the case Stilgoe had carried, opening it up and searching for something to use as a bandage. He pulled out a heavy white wad of material, and it unfurled into a straight jacket, buckles tinkling and clattering as they clashed together. He tossed the opened case on to the bed, then returned to Ping and cut up the straight jacket, folding and dressing both wounds, attending to the eye wound first, then the shoulder.

"You good to go?" asked Al, holding one finger up for Ping to focus on. He waited for a while, then nodded. "Between your screams and my gunfire, we're probably going to attract the attention of every rebel and creature in this town. How d'you feel?"

"A little weak, shaky, light-headed. God, it hurts, *shit* it hurts."

"Who would've thought having your eye poked out by a madman would've hurt as much?" said Al, helping his comrade to his feet before rooting through the rest of the case. A green packet of tea, bearing the same name as the man lying dead outside the window and depicting an illustration of a man in a suit, smiling and offering a cup of tea. Al launched it out the window, then grabbed a clear plastic bag filled with a disturbing miasma of blood and eyeballs and threw that out behind it. Wrapping an arm around his friend's waist, they made their way down the stairs and towards the front door. It was still locked up, and Al couldn't help but wonder where the madman had been hiding when he'd done a sweep of the house. Maybe there'd been a cupboard he'd overlooked, or maybe the house had some kind of loft or attic that he'd missed. Whatever the answer was, he knew that he had messed up, and because of it, his friend was in an even worse condition than he had been before.

"Sit there, I'll get the door open," said Al, lowering Ping to one of the broken armchairs while he started to pull away the planks from the door.

"I could... I could use a grenade," laughed Ping, the grin on his face turning into a grimace of pain. "Blast our way out."

"It'd take half the house down around us," grunted Al, tossing aside each piece of wood he managed to pull, apart from one particular plank that was about four-foot long. He tossed it to Ping. "It should work as a crutch."

Five minutes passed, and the front door was finally unblocked, allowing the pair to emerge into the morning sun. The rising sun had brought a pleasing warmth, and also the fetid stench of rotting flesh baking in the heat of day. The smell was stronger than it had been the night of the crash, almost to the point of making the duo retch as they stumbled through the streets.

"So, what's the plan?" asked Ping through ragged breaths. His homemade bandages were already soaked with oozing pink liquid and grimy sweat, and the trek through the street was quickly taking its toll on him.

"Same as before. We need high ground, medical supplies, and a radio. And food. Lots of food. Once we find high ground, somewhere we can dig in and protect ourselves, somewhere that isn't already inhabited by a fucking crackpot, I can leave you there and get what we need. We need to keep you as stationary as possible to give your body some time to rest."

Supporting the young Private, Al carried on deeper into town looking for a good place to hold out.

"It's not exactly the Hilton in New York," said Al, striding along a concrete balcony and half-carrying his companion. On one side of him there were rows of windows and doors, some kicked or smashed in, while others had escaped the wrath of any passing vandals, and on the other a ten-foot drop to a vacant parking lot. "But it's not covered in blood, doesn't smell like shit, it's completely empty, and looks pretty much untouched. Plus, there's only one way in and out, so with a little ingenuity, we can set up traps all the way along here and really dig in."

They reached the front door of a small first floor flat and pushed it open, peering inside. It was a stark contrast to the house they had left a few hours ago: where it had been bloody and ruined, this place was almost untouched. The bed was ruffled and unmade, and some newspapers left lying carelessly on the floor, but other than that, it was fine. The only thing that really spoiled the one bedroom flat was the potent smell of urine and dampness that lingered in the carpet. Ping wrinkled his nose at the smell, but nodded.

"We've certainly slept in worse places," he confirmed. "Like the barracks."

"At least the barracks is around the corner from an armoury," muttered Al, lowering his friend to the bed then softly closing the door. He locked up the door, then dropped his machinegun to the floor. Thanks to the local undead denizens of the town, his weapons were a few hundred rounds down, and Ping was on his last magazine. They hadn't used their handguns much, but weapons like those were of little use when surrounded by ten or twenty of the creatures.

"How many rounds you got left?" asked Ping, motioning towards the silent M249. Al kicked the box of bullets attached to it, then looked at the other two boxes in his bag.

"Five hundred rounds, give or take. Enough to see us through, providing we can keep out of trouble until we can get to a weapon cache. Or a working radio that can reach one of the towers."

"Yeah," smiled Ping, easing himself back on the bed. "Didn't you once say trouble comes looking for you?"

Al nodded, remembering the night in the rainforest that he'd first bestowed that jewel of truth on to his squad. It had been in a makeshift camp in the heart of the jungle, and only seconds after a Bebop scouting party had encountered them and tried to smoke them out with napalm. "Get some more rest, kid. I'll look for some fresh material to clean your wounds. Maybe even try the taps and test our luck for running water."

"If we're relying on our luck," said Ping, lying back and closing his eye. "It'll be piss coming out the taps."

Al grinned, then stood and started to root through the contents of the house, making a pile of anything they could use and discarding the rest. The first thing he laid his hands on in the kitchen was a shining green foil packet, with a distinguished looking gentleman on the front, smiling and proffering a cup of freshly brewed tea. Al opened the front door, spat on the packet, then hurled it outside, sending it on the same journey the last packet of Furlonger's Finest had gone on. He returned to his search, wiping his eyes and rubbing away the dust and debris that had found its way into his face during the search.

Hours passed, and Al had kept himself busy by sorting through the piles of junk into separate mounds he'd labelled 'useful', 'maybe' and 'crap'. He'd also changed Ping's dressings while he slept, and he hadn't stirred. The wounds didn't seem so bad now even the missing eye was just seeping a fine, translucent pink liquid. He'd exhausted all his menial tasks, and finally set about the actual task of constructing a radio. There was a number different household appliances that he needed to make a radio, most of which were still in the flat. Anything else he needed, he'd managed to plunder from the adjoining flats. He now sat cross-legged on the floor, surrounded by wires and circuit boards, holding a dismantled telephone in one hand and his knife in his other. Beside his right leg was a large box with a mass of wires and transistors, a tangled mess of electronic components. With a triumphant grin, he tossed aside his knife and looked at his creation. It was a hideous device, with controls torn from a television, a heavily bastardised radio and a mishmash of electrical gubbins. He'd wired it up to a car battery he'd found in one of the flats, a hovel that previously belonged to a mechanic or an electrician, and lashed the aerial into the small satellite dish attached to the side of the house. He wasn't sure if the dish would be any good for his needs, but the only way that he was going to find out was to fire up his creation.

"What's the worst that can happen?" he muttered, hand hovering above the large and cumbersome power switch he'd torn from a kitchen blender. He mulled it over, then nodded to himself. "At best, it'll work and I'll arrange an evac. At worst, it's going to blow up and fry all the circuits, and I've just wasted…"

He looked at his watch and whistled

"Fourteen frigging hours! Jesus, time flies when you don't know what the hell you're doing!"

He flicked the switch, then grabbed hold of the device and started twisting the dials. Static and squeals faded in and out as he adjusted the machine, picking up a wide variety of sounds and signals. People speaking French, the voice of a lone man talking to himself with a heavy and pulsing engine in the background: Al paused on that channel for a moment, listening to the voice and thinking it may have been a Marine. The lack of radio etiquette and incoherent rambling made him think otherwise, and he quickly switched to another frequency.

"What the fuck?" screamed Ping, jarring awake and sitting upright, eye glazed and expressionless. He gripped his rifle tightly, staring blankly into the darkness across the room from him.

"Zombies," he growled, lifting his rifle and squeezing the trigger. The weapon had been left empty, and remained silent, unfired. The world around him slowly came into focus, then faded back out as unconsciousness reclaimed him.

The static of the radio cleared, and for a moment there was silence, then the banter of two men, Marines on sentry duty in guard towers somewhere along the nearby coast. Excitedly, Al grabbed the sender and spoke clearly into the microphone, hoping everything was wired up right, otherwise it was going to be a boring, one-sided conversation.

"This is Sergeant Colebrook of the Wolvers, my serial number is… uh… seven five nine seven six two five, urgent evac required, repeat, urgent evac required, over."

There was a pause, some muffled conversation as if someone were speaking with their hands over the microphone, and then a pause. "Sergeant Colebrook, this is Watchtower eighty-six-delta, we roger your request. What is your current location, over?"

"Location is unknown, repeat, unknown. Our bird was shot down. We're in hostile territory somewhere along the coast, the north of England. I have an injured man in need of immediate medical attention. Over."

"Standby."

The line went silent for a moment, and Al thought the radio had died, his poor workmanship giving up the ghost and ruining his chances of further contact. There was a slight clicking, and then a new voice came on the radio. This new voice seemed to exude power and confidence, obviously an officer of some ranking. He also wasn't a great fan of radio etiquette.

"Who am I speaking to here?"

"Sergeant Albert Colebrook, United Government Marine Corps, serial number…"

"This is Major Carter," announced the voice, cutting off Al and confirming his initial suspicions. "Where is your commanding lieutenant? Uh, what was his name…" There was a rustle of papers as Carter thumbed notes, looking for the information. Al's training had taught him better than to offer the information voluntarily. "Jonathan Clarity. Lieutenant Clarity, yes, where is he?"

"Dead, sir. Everyone died in the helicopter crash, apart from me and Ping. Ah, that is, Private Grem, sir."

"Dead, I see," muttered Carter. "What about Maxis? We lost contact with KDL-76 shortly after they reported seeing the helicopter approach."

Al froze. He'd forgotten all about Maxis, their reason for getting into a helicopter and attempting to breach quarantine. He could tell the truth and admit that he'd been killed, or try and bluff his way out of it. Thinking it would be easier to lie, Al swallowed hard and took a chance.

"He's with us, sir, but he's the one who's seriously injured. He's out cold."

"I thought you said only you and Grem had survived?"

"I did," said Al, not missing a beat. "From our squad, I meant. We managed to drag the General from the helicopter before it exploded."

"Then he's alive, and his research intact?"

"Yeah," said Al, shrugging his shoulders. If that's all they were wanting Maxis for, then saying he still had it would only add another card to his hand. "Yeah, he's alive. And he's got some kind of briefcase attached to his wrist." It sounded like something that would be done with sensitive documents: It always happened in films like that.

"Good. If you open the case, there should be a brown manila envelope that's sealed with a wax seal. Open it, and confirm the priority command override code. Read it out to me."

"Uh, I don't have the key," stammered Al, trying to stall for time.

"Break the lock, Sergeant," said Carter, his voice sounding bored, and maybe a little condescending. Al looked around, still trying to play for time, and brought his fist smashing down on to a pile of spare circuit boards. Hopefully, it sounded like a briefcase being smashed open. He sifted amongst the wreckage, then cleared his throat.

"I've got it, sir," he said.

"Well, read it soldier. I assume you can read."

"Max evac forty-three," muttered Al, already knowing that he'd had his bluff called.

"Nice try, soldier," laughed Carter. Al could imagine his face, cheeks swollen, flushed red from laughter and cognac, hair greyed from all the worrying about where his next crate of expensive brandy was coming from. "Did you really think you could pull the wool over my eyes? A sergeant, outsmart a major, really. No, that pilot managed to send out a message moments before the rebel fire hit the helicopter. Said a Marine by the name of Colebrook blew the general's head off with an illegal magnum smuggled aboard the helicopter. Are you that same Marine?"

"He attacked one of my squad," scowled Al. "He bit a fucking chunk out of the kid, what was I supposed to do?"

"Restrain him, not kill him. You dumb bastard. Maxis had all the information we needed on the plague, its spread and the state of Britain. He had figures, detailed reports on the symptoms…"

"Here's some statistics for you, you piece of shit. It's not airborne anymore, the whole country's gone to fuck, there's some crazies running around with guns and RPGs, and those carrying the plague have turned into zombies. I know what you're thinking, and I don't believe in fucking zombies either, but I believe in what I see, and I've seen people that are carrying the plague eating each other."

"You're obviously suffering from delusions, more than likely brought on through contraction and exposure to the plague. For that reason, Sergeant Colebrook, I'm afraid you're going to have to remain under quarantine until we can be sure. You and 'Ping' will have to sweat it out until we can confirm you are not infected. Why don't you call back in ten days, then we may be able to arrange some details for your court martial?" Carter said, laughing as he finished his sentence.

"Yeah, why don't you go fuck yourself, you pompous cocksucker," spat Al, making sure Carter was still on the line before drawing his magnum and firing a round into the radio. The blast was deafening, and Al hoped that it gave the officer on the other end a splitting headache. Despite the loudness of the gunshot, Ping didn't stir from his slumber.

Left high and dry thought Al as he kicked aside the remains of his radio. *You give them nearly twenty years of your life, and how do they repay you?*

"They kick you in the balls when you're down," he said aloud, answering his silent question. "You expect this kind of shit from a woman, but not the Corps."

He sunk to the floor, pulling the magazine from the magnum and replacing the round he'd fired.

Whatever happened to semper fidelis?

Ever faithful… what a load of bullshit.

VII
CITY OF GHOSTS

"The implementation of martial law has been vital in maintaining some form of order within the larger cities and maintaining our operations. Civilian losses remain within acceptable tolerances during these operations."

I

The four days Bill had spent in Barkley's Warehouse since arriving had not been wasted or squandered. At least, not in his eyes.

The first day had been spent burning the bodies in the compound, then double-checking the barricades keeping the undead horde out. This had only taken a few hours, and after rationing out the food left in the vending machine, he'd slept for almost the rest of the day. He'd awoken confused and bewildered an hour before midnight, convinced he could hear someone in the store crying out for help. He'd searched the building over twice, before finally giving up and realising it was all simply in his mind. He'd wandered back to the staff room, the place he'd decided to live in, and tried to settle back to sleep, but to no avail. He'd decided to clean out the lockers for anything that would prove useful, grabbing a claw hammer from the shop floor to aid him in his search.

Most of the lockers didn't hold anything of particular interest, a lot of photographs of family and loved ones: Bill was trying to keep himself distanced from anything like this, any pictures that reminded him of the fact hundreds of thousands of families had been torn apart. He had enough to think about with his own family of two being torn asunder; he didn't feel like taking on the emotional baggage of a hundred other families along with that. The only thing he found of interest was a large ring binder filled with pages and pages of computer printout, some of it vaguely recognisable to Bill as chemical equations and formula. He pulled up a chair and browsed the contents of the file, taking in as much as he could. A lot of it seemed to be a foreign language to him, but the short period of time he'd spent in his chemistry class in college gave him some understanding of the text.

"Explosives," he muttered. "Sweet Christ, some crazy fuck was trying to make explosives."

He rushed back to the locker he'd gotten the binder from, and found a second book, a small, leather bound book filled with delicate and ornate handwriting. It was a journal, and made for just as interesting a read as the anarchist's handbook he'd discovered. Locker, book and binder had belonged to a particularly disgruntled employee who was extremely unhappy with every aspect of his life, and had decided to take it upon himself to exact his revenge on the world. He'd researched various weapons, their maintenance and construction, the creation of explosives, techniques of unarmed combat, traps and tactics that only a soldier or a guerrilla would need to know. The journal proclaimed that the young employee had elected to hide the binder and its forbidden knowledge in his locker at work because his mother wouldn't find it there. Bill grinned as he read this, pleased to see that even a lunatic held a healthy fear for his own mother. The journal detailed potential targets for his frustration and anger, including a pompous store manager, the bitch on the checkout who had belittled him when he'd made advances towards her, and the entire north east of England, who he planned on ruining with his ill conceived acts of petty terrorism. Luckily they'd never come to fruition.

And so, the second day had seen Bill experimenting with the book of destructive lore, gathering what materials were at hand in the warehouse and dedicating one corner of the massive building to explosives production. Gunpowder was the easiest to make, and the mixture that Bill spent the best part of the morning. He'd filled and sealed several wooden barrels with this mixture, and pushed them outside for use later. He'd then moved on to other substances listed in the book, including the fast burning thermite, slow-burning napalm and a fertiliser bomb. Although there were also procedures for plastic explosives and dynamite, he didn't have the ingredients, nor the desire to tamper with anything as unstable as the book claimed it would be.

Further reading in the binder provided Bill with some insight into how to enhance some of the weapons he already had. He took five of his crossbow bolts, cut off the ends with a junior hacksaw, then filled them with gunpowder before breaking open some of his shotgun shells and gluing the primer to the tips. The book claimed they would explode on contact, though it didn't state how large the blast radius would be. He stored these carefully, then went on to spend the rest of the day creating a full size model of a human.

The morning of the third day, he read through some more pages of the binder, then stripped down to only his jeans and launched into a full assault on the dummy, employing every technique described in the book, practising first accuracy, then strength of the blow. He had to stop after seven hours, his knuckles bleeding and his shins and elbows heavily bruised. He stepped back from the dented and battered dummy, breathing heavily and helping himself to his whole days ration of food and drink. He'd done himself some damage, and the dummy certainly didn't offer any resistance, but he felt confident that he could hold his own in a fight. He could've always corralled a Rot in to the building to take on, but he didn't really want to go hand-to-hand with a shambling zombie that could well pass the infection on to him. But it was good to know he could easily lash out at someone and gouge their eyes with his fingers if he needed to.

The rest of that day was spent reading up on weapons, allowing him to brush up on what he didn't know about his implements of destruction, and identify those that he owned: The handgun was a Beretta, a reliable handgun used by a lot of armed forces and law enforcement agencies. The shotgun was called a Benelli Tactical, again used primarily by law enforcement agencies, but he couldn't find anything to identify the hunting rifle or the crossbow. He stripped down the handgun and shotgun and reassembled them, then did it again and again, familiarising himself with their construction, his aching fingers trembling and throbbing with pain. While working with the weapons, he went on to construct his own from various lengths and diameters of plastic drainpipes, electrical wiring and gas canisters, following the detailed instructions in the file. He didn't test it, though, simply stowed it away with his rucksack.

On the fourth day, Bill practised a few more combat moves in the morning, rested for an hour or two, then spent the afternoon going through a few targeting exercises with the dummy and the crossbow, using his unmodified bolts and retrieving them when necessary. He was about to settle down to a late meal of stale crisps and a few squares of chocolate when the low, constant moaning of the Rots outside was interrupted by a new sound, a thunderous drone of an engine overhead. His heart racing, Bill ran from the break room out into the gardening section, grabbing a ladder and slamming it against the wall, clambering up on to the roof and tilting his gaze skyward.

An unsightly machine, irregularly shaped and covered by nets and bristling with weapons, flew overhead and tilting slightly to one side as it buzzed low. Bill waved his arms frantically, jumping up and down, shouting and screaming at the top of his voice, trying to attract the attention of the pilot of the machine. He had no flares, and certainly didn't want to fire one of his weapons into the air: he didn't have the bullets to spare and he'd left them in the break room. And even if he had brought them out with him, he figured opening fire on an attack helicopter would probably be a bad idea. It would get him noticed, but probably shot at, too.

The helicopter faded out of sight, and Bill stood motionless, watching as his ticket off the island faded into the sunset. He could only hope that they'd fly back overhead, and if they did, he'd have to be ready for them. He'd mixed up some home-made napalm with some petrol he'd siphoned off from various heavy-duty power tools and a few petrol canisters stored in the loading area, maybe he could use some of that to set up a beacon on the roof.

He made his way back to the ladder, but paused as he reached it. The sounds of the Rots waiting patiently in the car park below seemed louder now he was on the roof, and the smell of the decaying bodies, something that hadn't been all that prominent in the warehouse itself, was overpowering outside. He shuffled closer to the edge of the roof, peering into the crowd, and froze.

"Christ almighty," he muttered, confronted by hundreds of Rots below him, waiting to get into the warehouse and tear him apart. In the four days he'd trained and prepared in the store, he'd not once considered the possibility of more creatures stumbling towards the warehouse. As he watched, small clusters of the Rots turned on one another, four or five taking one of their own kind down to the ground and regaining their feet, now covered in the blood of their fallen comrade.

Closer to the walls of the building, the animated corpses scrambled over one another, bloody hands scraping against the brickwork and trying to find a way to climb the wall. Shaking his head, Bill rushed back to the ladder and almost tumbled down it, desperate to get back into the building itself.

"Why are they all here," he growled, gathering some of the explosive devices he'd constructed and dragging them out to the opened garden area. He'd made some basic devices, simple Molotov cocktails and glass jars filled with gunpowder. Although there wasn't enough to take out all the creatures, he hoped that there'd be enough to water down their numbers. Making three trips up the ladder, he managed to gather all his explosives on the roof, and igniting a blowtorch, set off the fuses and hurled the glass projectiles into the crowd. Explosions blossomed in mid-air, raining down red-hot glass shrapnel, while other bottles smashed on contact and doused the creatures in thick, flaming liquid. Flickering fire illuminated the undead crowd, showing the number of creatures that Bill had managed to take down with his initial assault and allowing him to take a body count. He counted about ten taken down by glass shrapnel, their faces and torsos shredded by the fragments, and maybe another thirty lying static amongst the fires, bodies burned to a crisp. There were still hundreds left, though, too many for him to kill with the amount of explosives he had left. He made his way back to the ladder, reaching to grab the blowtorch and bring it back down with him. As he did so, his fingers brushed the wrong part and he quickly withdrew his hand, blowing on his burned fingertips and shaking his hand. The burner fell from the rooftop, clattered off three rungs of the ladder, then rolled to a stop…

…Inches from the storage containers of Bill's homemade gunpowder.

"Fuck no!" shouted Bill, half-falling down the ladder into the courtyard. Already the heat of the flame was burning through the container: he wouldn't have time to get to the stockpile and prevent it from blowing up, he'd just have to make a run for it.

He was halfway across the warehouse when he was knocked from his feet by an explosion and a wave of heat, sliding across the polished surface and crashing into a display stand of paint tins. He flipped over on to his front and looked towards the explosion, what had once been his store of powder, and instead of seeing a mound of barrels and a sturdy wall, saw only small fires and a gaping hole in his defensive perimeter. The Rots closest to the wall had obviously been smashed to pieces by the blast, but those that had just been knocked over were already clambering back to their feet, while those further back were beginning their advance. Some moved with slow, ponderous steps, while others moved quickly and with jerking, rigid limbs flailing from side to side. As they advanced on the hole, they didn't move to avoid the flames, simply stumbled through them, bringing the fire further into the shop itself.

Bill scrambled to his feet, looking for the first weapon that came to hand to fend off the advancing creatures until he could get to his own arsenal, back in the break room. One of the faster Rots was already on him, leg on fire and gnarled fingers dripping putrid flesh. Bill swung out with his right hand, landing a solid blow to the head of the zombie with a tin of paint, then dropped it and scrambled to the next aisle, the power tools aisle. He grabbed the first thing he came to, one of the few petrol-driven chainsaws he hadn't gotten around to draining, and revved it to life, spinning around and slowly backing away from the door, moving towards the break room. There was a large contingent of the undead advancing on him, but all around he could hear the dead as they swayed and lurched through the store, crashing into shelves and smashing displays.

The pack ahead of him broke up, and the lead Rot rushed forwards, moaning and groaning, drooling in anticipation of a kill. Bill brought the chainsaw he held upwards in a wide arc, the whirring blade slicing through skin and cartilage. It glanced off the ribcage, the bones deflecting the blow, and Bill brought up the unwieldy weapon for a second attack, this time slicing clean through the neck. The body toppled to the floor, preceded by its head, leaving room for another attack. A pair of the creatures rushed him, the first of them instantly dropping to the ground as Bill's chainsaw sliced open its skin and ground through two inches of skull and brain, before sputtering to a halt. Bill relinquished his grip on the weapon, knowing that by the time he pulled it free it would be too late, and grabbed a second tool, this time a battery-powered circular saw. Hoping it would be strong enough he raised the weapon just in time to fend off a blow from the second of the pair. Rotten fingers vanished in a spray of crimson gore as the circular blade chewed through them, but that didn't stop the creature. Bill raised the saw higher as the Rot advanced, the blade biting through the jawbone of the undead and dragging up into the frontal lobe, cracking open the skull and ripping its brain apart. Bill dropped the saw, then kicked away from the Rot and ran, navigating the aisles and making his way back to the break room.

Bursting into the room, he forced the binder into his bag, pushed as much of the junk food that he could grab into it, then swung it up on to his shoulder and grabbed his weapons. With his rifle slung over one shoulder and handgun sitting snugly in its holster, he ran from the room with his shotgun in one hand and his crossbow in another, still loaded with normal bolts from target practice that morning.

Of course, Bill had a plan for escaping the building. The loading dock still held the motorbike he'd found when he first arrived, which he'd freed from its shackles with a pair of bolt cutters, and had made sure was fuelled and ready to go, in case a situation such as this happened to rear its ugly head. He'd never gotten around to opening the door, though, because he'd never wanted to leave an opening exposed. Now, though, he had to open it and fast. But without any power, doing so was going to be a tough job. He'd never thought through that part.

The aisles of the warehouse were now filled with zombies, almost wall-to-wall, and Bill had to loose a shell from his shotgun the moment he returned to the shop floor. The blast tore through the midriff of the closest creature, knocking it back into another three, which in turn knocked down another two. Taking advantage of the domino affect he'd created, Bill swung himself up on to the closest shelving unit and clambered on to the top. There were about twenty aisles between his position and the way out to the loading dock, which meant going through the building material yard. At least the Rots hadn't breached at the same end of the shop as his escape route.

Running crouched along the top of the shelving, his arms outstretched to keep him balanced, Bill reached the end of the row and paused. There was a ten feet gap between each shelving unit on all sides, separating rows and aisles. He knew there was no way he could jump that: even if he could, there was no guarantee he could land on the three-foot wide raised shelving without sliding off the edge.

Fortune had smiled on Bill, though: The wheelbarrow he had mixed up his own napalm in lay at the foot of the shelving unit, a thick opaque liquid spattered with a few flecks of polystyrene that hadn't fully dissolved in the petrol. The fumes from the mixture were pungent this high above it, but the presence of the flammable liquid was enough to inspire him. Fumbling with his crossbow, he gingerly unloaded the bolt and replaced it with one of the customised bolts, hoping it would work the way the binder had boasted. He dropped down to floor level, the closest of Rots less than three feet away, and kicked over the barrow, spilling the fluid. He backed away, moving towards the lumberyard and carefully taking aim. With his target clear in his mind, he closed his eyes, squeezed the trigger, and prayed the book had been correct.

The bolt didn't create a huge explosion, though it certainly would have enough to cause massive damage to a Rot, had it struck one.

The bolt struck the floor, at the centre of the pool of rapidly spreading liquid, and the shotgun primer attached to the end sparked to life, igniting the gunpowder within. Shrapnel and burning powder showered the liquid, and it instantly burst to life, flames spreading across the floor and igniting Rots the moment they blindly stumbled into the flames. The fire consumed them, but didn't stop there: plastic packaging melted, dripping into the mass of flaming liquid, wood smoked and burned, while the spreading fire licked ever-closer towards the large selection of aerosol paints on display in the paint section.

Bill didn't see any of this, though, the minute the napalm had ignited he had turned his back and ran towards the lumberyard. The first inclination he had of the true extent of the damage he had created was when the containers of pressurised paint cooked off in the heat. A deep, thunderous blast exploded within the shop, shattering windows and spreading flame and debris, blowing a cloud of dust and fragments out the opening and into the lumberyard. He stumbled mid-stride, though he didn't stop and scrambled frantically into the loading dock. There was no way of knowing for sure how many Rots he'd stopped, or how difficult it had made it for the lumbering creatures to follow, but he certainly didn't want to hang around and find out.

The loading dock was eerily quiet. After days of hearing the monotonous droning of the creatures outside, or their bloody and festering hands pounding the doors, it didn't seem right. Still, no sounds of the Rots pummelling the metal shutter meant his escape route was at least clear. The bike was ready, sitting facing the door, though the door itself still remained locked. Mounting the bike, he loaded a second of his customised bolts into his crossbow and aimed at the power box to the door. It struck the box with an explosive blow, destroying the motor within, destroying the counterweight mechanism and loosening the shutters. It slowly ground up halfway, exposing the small delivery road leading away from the shop. It was clear, devoid of any shambling corpses, and Bill revved the bike to life, slowly nudging the vehicle forwards and rolling both the machine and himself out the dock. Kicking the resting stand up, he revved the engine and slowly rode the machine away from Barkley's Warehouse and the fiery wrath that consumed it.

II

It was the first time Bill had tried to ride a bike in years, so he decided he'd keep to a safe speed. Once he'd left the DIY store far behind him, he'd pulled up by the roadside a few miles away and gathered his senses. The events in the warehouse had left him shaken slightly. The plan for his escape had worked out, though a lot of it had relied on luck. It was pure luck the shutter had opened first time, that the counterweights and chains still worked, and it had been just as lucky that there had been no Rots on the other side of it. The fact his wheelbarrow of napalm had been exactly where it needed to be at the right time had been even luckier. He'd had no contingency plan had anything gone wrong, and he knew that if anything *had* gone wrong, he wouldn't be sitting on a bike two miles away from a Rot hotspot, contemplating what he should and shouldn't do in the future.

"Gotta plan everything out in the future," he muttered, glancing from one side to another. The motorway was miles from any town or city, but he wasn't going to rule out the possibility of a surprise attack from any lurking Rot, or even one of the deranged men he'd encountered in the underground station. "Need to have backup plans for my backup plans. I can't afford to fuck up, not once," he murmured.

He pushed on, the engine of the bike stalling as he kept his balance and tried to ride the vehicle. It was an unusual experience, trying to remember the basics he'd learned and subsequently forgotten in the years since he'd last had a lesson. He kept to a moderate speed, getting to grips with the clutch and the gearshift of the machine, riding back and forth on the empty road. The sun had now almost sunk beneath the horizon, and Bill found the controls for the headlamp, flicking it on. He didn't want to teach himself anything else in the waning light, he needed to find somewhere he could rest, or at least wait until daylight returned.

The best place he could find was an old articulated truck that had been left abandoned, a further five miles down the road. The rear of the vehicle had been torn apart, the edges of the metal sheets coated in tacky and dried blood, the wooden crates it had carried left lying on the ground around it, torn open and revealing their scattered contents. Parking his bike next to the to front cab, Bill killed the engine and heaved open the door. The interior stank of stale sweat and dried faeces, but other than that it seemed clean. The discarded cargo of the lorry had been nothing more than linen: bed sheets and towels lay on the ground, some spattered with blood, most trampled into the ground, but a little searching allowed Bill to find a few blankets and sheets that he could use. He slipped into the cab, slammed the door and locked it behind him, then wrapped himself up in the blankets. He didn't intend to sleep, just keep warm and safe while the cool of the night passed.

Morning broke, and so too did the window of the passenger door as the bloodied hand of a Rot smashed against it, showering nuggets of the shattered safety glass against Bill's head. Startled awake, he instinctively grabbed the pistol from his holster and tapped a round into the opened window, the round hitting the Rot outside square in the face. Bill wiped the sleep from the corner of his eyes and looked in awe at the smoking weapon in his hand, unable to recall any other time he'd had reactions like that. Unravelling his legs from the blankets around him, he cautiously opened the door he was leaning against, pistol sweeping from left to right in search of any other undead creature. Nothing else seemed to be there, and he holstered the pistol, then grabbed the rest of his weapons and mounted the bike. He cruised away from the trailer cab without a second thought, and found another stretch of open road before him. Clenching his teeth, he motioned the bike onwards, accelerating all the time, seeing how fast he could go before he either lost his balance or his courage to do so. He was approaching seventy miles an hour when the stretch of road suddenly curved off to the left.

A cold sweat of panic washed over him as he weighed up the options. He could either try to stop in time, or attempt his first high-speed turn. With a determined grin, he slowly turned the handlebars, gentle movements to go into the turn, then started to lean slightly into the corner, fighting the urge to close his eyes as the barrier of the road rushed to greet him. It rushed away from him just as quick as it had to greet him, and Bill quickly stopped the bike, stepping away from it with shaking legs and sinking to the floor.

He still didn't know how to ride a bike properly; he'd almost lost control of all his bodily functions doing that turn. He needed to do something about that, but without the proper training facilities available to him, all he could do was try to remember the basics and fill in the blanks himself.

Yeah, sure, he snorted in his mind. And w*hy not? You taught yourself to fight from a book. Why the hell not?*

He spent the next few days going back and forth on the highways, riding his bike and siphoning off fuel from abandoned vehicles as and when he needed to, while spending the nights locked up in cars. After hours of practice and perfecting his manoeuvres, Bill felt he was confident enough to cruise the roadways at a steady speed of fifty miles an hour, kicking it up a notch if and when he needed to. Instead of driving up and down the same stretches of road, he moved on, navigating the roads and finding himself on a long stretch of tarmac leading towards a town Bill was familiar with.

"Edgly," he muttered, scratching the thick and itchy whiskers that covered his chin. It was a town he'd spent most of his childhood in, somewhere he'd gone to school in. Could it be that he'd been subliminally drawn to his old hunting grounds, the streets he'd roamed as a youngster, without him knowing? Would going into such a familiar place be a good idea? Seeing all his old hangouts torn apart by Rots or shredded by gunfights didn't really appeal to him… but Jenny's parents lived there. He felt like he should check on them, at least, make sure they were okay. And by okay, he meant dead, not undead. He also wanted to pick up a photograph of Jenny, just so he'd have something to carry around with him, something to remember her by. He'd rather go to her parents to get one instead of their flat. Her parents' house wasn't filled with the same memories their flat had been: memories of love and intimacy, of plans made to last the rest of their lives.

Edgly had been no more interesting a place to grow up in than any others Bill could remember, though it was the place he first met Jenny. He slowed the bike to a crawl as he entered the suburban areas of the town, finding himself surrounded on both sides by barren expanses of land, patchy fields of crab grass and weeds. Ahead, there lay the beginnings of a housing estate: rows of terraced houses standing vacant and dormant, their windows smashed and doors torn off. Bill stopped his bike at a fork in the road, looking at his choice of routes. One road skirted around the town, avoiding the bulk of the built up area, while the other plunged straight into the heart of the development itself. Though he would have loved to give the whole place a wide berth, he wanted that photo. And more to the point, he *needed* some food. His supply of the sugar-laden junk he had liberated from the vending machine back at Barkley's hadn't lasted too long out on the road. He was down to his last bar of chocolate, and was hoping against hope that there'd be some kind of food left in the town centre. Gunning his engine on, he took the left fork, sighing inwardly as he did so.

The McClaren household was in just as much disarray as any other house Bill had passed since he'd entered the town. Their abode was situated in Claybrook Street, in the New Farm housing estate; one of the southern-most regions of the town, and one of the more desirable areas to live in. Each house differed slightly in appearance, some had a porch, some had an extension built on the back, others a conservatory. Each family had tried to make their home their own, had spent thousands on decorating, building or landscaping. All the hard work and effort had been wasted now, as windows had been shattered, doors and their frames removed, brick walls knocked down by crumpled vehicles still lying embedded in the masonry. Blood spattered the streets in varying quantities: large pools formed in some places, trickling along the guttering and down the drains, while smaller splashes simply dried in the heat of the summer sun. Bill dismounted his ride and stood at the foot of the driveway leading up to the house, drawing his shotgun and slowly easing himself up the pathway. The building was one of three in the street that still had its doors intact, and Bill hesitated when he placed his hand on the handle. He felt the urge to add a little normalcy, to knock before he entered. He did so, but didn't wait for an answer, nudging the door open with the barrel of his weapon.

He entered the hallway of the house, and casually removed his jacket and hung it on the banister at the bottom of the stairs before proceeding with his inspection.

The lounge and dining room had been knocked through into one, and seemed more-or-less normal. Jenny's mother had kept the house to a very high standard, and couldn't abide clutter of any description. Consequently, the only personal artefacts in the house were photographs, framed perfectly and hung on the wall. The largest of the hanging pictures was of Jenny, dressed in her graduation robe and holding her diploma. Surrounding it were various other photos of Jenny and her parents, at various ages and on different holidays. All these were too large for Bill to carry around with him, but he knew the photograph albums were kept in one of the dressers. He moved over to the largest of the oak constructs (a unit Jenny's father had pieced together himself, DIY was something he liked doing in his spare time), and opened the door, pulling out a leather-bound book and started to flick through it. He skipped through as much of it as he could, his eyes misting with the memories the pictures stirred within him.

He found his prize, a small glossy photograph with the grinning face of his dead lover, and paused for a moment, his finger lovingly tracing the lines of her face, her smile. Pulling the neck of his t-shirt up over his face and wiping his eyes, he slipped the picture into his bag, keeping it pressed between the pages of the binder, and returned to searching the rest of the house.

Leaving the living area, he moved into the kitchen. This was one of the room's Mrs McClaren had loved the most, and it was also the room that had been hit the hardest. Cupboards had been torn off the walls, doors ripped off, and draws smashed on the ceramic-tiled floor. Every cupboard had been emptied of both foodstuff and cutlery; not a trace of any had been left. Bill moved on to the utility room, but found the same sorry tale there. Everything of use had been taken, suggesting to Bill that scavengers had hit this house and probably every other house in the street, knowing exactly what they wanted and where it was. They hadn't wasted time on the senseless trashing of the buildings. Bill took a stroll up the stairs, and found to his surprise that the bedrooms had also been ransacked, and all valuables had been taken. Someone had not only been planning ahead for their imminent survival, but also for their life after the trouble died down. Somewhere out there was one fat, rich character that was just sitting tight, waiting for the Rots to keel over and die and for this whole mess to clear up.

Bill snorted at the idea. He knew that there was no chance of something like this just *blowing* over. He also knew in the back of his mind that he was going to die on this plague-infested island.

So why delay the inevitable? He pondered silently, sinking down on the double bed in the master bedroom and looking at the shotgun he carried. It was smaller then his rifle and he'd be able to pull the trigger himself. And if he couldn't, he always had the handgun. *Why not just turn the weapon on yourself now? End all your suffering…*

"Because Jenny wouldn't do that, and she wouldn't want me to," he muttered to himself, looking towards the bedside cabinet on his right and seeing a simple plastic frame, where both he and Jenny smiled back. He remembered the day it was taken, a picnic one unusually sunny day in early June…

He shook his head. Memories were all fine and dandy, but not a luxury he could afford right now. He had to keep himself in line and focused, and doing so meant not getting lost in his thoughts.

He left the house, bypassing the bloodied bathroom: an obvious sign that Jenny's family had died of the plague. He remembered Jenny's father, the symptoms he'd been suffering, and that he was probably the person responsible for the bloody mess. He was sure that Jenny's mother would have been escorted to a facility like the one he and Jenny had been taken to. Hopefully, they both would have been disposed of before the rise of the undead.

Bill snapped out of it and grabbed his jacket, pulling it on and returning to his bike. He had what he came for, but he still needed food. He started the bike and kicked away from the curb, leaving the street and the McClaren household behind him.

He drove slowly through the silent city, lazily meandering from side to side, along main roads and down cramped and dirty alleyways. No matter which direction he looked in, all the paths and buildings had the same motif of spattered blood and ruined structures. The buildings eventually gave way to more and more open fields, and for a moment Bill thought he had lost his bearings and managed to work his way back out the town. He knew he was still in Edgly once he realised he had just wandered into Edgly Common, a large expanse of fields where the younger children had once played. The tyres of the bike chewed the soft ground, making both acceleration and control nearly impossible for Bill. He quickly headed for the footpath and stuck to the firmer ground there, and as he moved on the openness of the field was slowly choked as thick clumps of wooded areas took over. Soon, the footpath was surrounded on all sides by the trees. They offered some protection from the heat of the sun, which he was glad for, and he rummaged through the contents of his pack to find a plastic bottle filled with a once-fizzy liquid. He sipped at the flat coke, fighting the urge to gulp down the bottle in one, then replaced the bottle. He grinned as he did so, looking at the trees closest to him and remembering days in his youth where he and a group of friends would dive into the thickest of trees and bramble patches to set up makeshift forts and camps. Later in life, the same group of friends had skulked into the same trees and shrubs to drink bottles of cider or an old thermos flask filled with whatever dregs of alcohol wouldn't be missed after a family party. Now, he didn't dare venture into the scrub in fear of what he would find.

The pathway emerged from the cover of the trees into a small car park, large enough for seven or eight family saloon cars. No vehicles occupied the lot, but a collection of shattered safety glass and spatters of blood suggested that there had once, until someone had decided to move them. Running the engine of his bike down to a halt, Bill dismounted the machine and grabbed all his weapons, before stepping towards the first of the two large buildings beside the car park.

The first of the buildings was a small café, a business going by the peculiar name of Spoonface's Café. There was a small wooden veranda surrounding the building, playing host to a variety of different sized tables. Those that still stood upright were covered over by red gingham tablecloths, the tattered and crumpled sheets held down by heavy vases filled with dead flowers. They fluttered in the gentle breeze, like patterned ghosts of the people who once visited here. Stepping on to the veranda and following the platform around, Bill found himself looking at the collection of steel and rubber climbing frames and swings about a hundred metres away. Another of the favoured meeting places for the children of Edgly, he felt no urge to walk over and examine them. He didn't want to find a group of partially devoured children or anything that may hint at the possibility of children Rots.

He entered the café itself, pushing aside the upturned stools and table that had been used in a feeble attempt to block the door. Thanks to the abundance of windows it wasn't that much darker inside than out, which allowed Bill to see the spatters of blood pooling around the main counter, the glimmering splinters of glass lying by the window frames, and the stack of menus that had been scattered across the floor. He stooped down and picked up one of them, looking at the comprehensive list of food that had once been available. If he remembered the café as well as he did, he knew that their chicken breast in peppercorn sauce was the best he'd ever tasted. He also knew that he'd never taste it again. He flipped the menu over in his hand, and smiled at the cartoon mascot. It was a cross between a human and a goat, a bastard offspring that was too surreal to exist in the real world. Though, having said that, Bill wouldn't be at all surprised if old Spoonface himself came wandering down the street. The figure was badly drawn, a human figure hunched over and pointing in different directions with each hand. Its face was shaped like a spoon, with one eye larger than the other and a shock of blond hair. A small horn stuck out from each side of his head, and it smiled up at Bill with an inane grin on its face. There had once been a large plastic version of the mascot outside the café, but neither the elements nor the drunken clientele from the adjacent building had been kind to it. First it had just been damaged paintwork, then graffiti. The statue had been placed into storage by the management after an incident involving a large concrete penis and a tin of white emulsion. Bill smiled. He'd had the privilege to be there that faithful night, and at the time it seemed to be one of the funniest things in the world. He and his friends had been only seventeen and drunk on cider at the time. Looking back, it wasn't as funny…

Bill gave the kitchen a quick once-over, not expecting to find anything and not at all surprised when he didn't. He left he restaurant and moved over to the next building, looking up at the sign and rubbing his chin. The Hawk Inn was a small pub, and had once been the favoured watering hole of Bill and his friends. Stalking into the building, a wave of memories washed over Bill, nights out with his friends, their numerous attempts to hook up with a woman, and the same number of refusals. The bar now still looked familiar, but only the way he remembered it after a particularly violent brawl one night. A brawl that had left; several tables broken, the entire collection of spirits smashed and lying on the floor, stools lying broken over bodies, windows put out and pool cues snapped in half. The only thing that was different this time around was that the large stuffed hawk that had once sat above the bar with it's wings spread wide didn't end up on the roof of Spoonface's: it lay broken and torn on the floor before him. Bill sank to the floor and stroked the stuffed carcass. He didn't search the pub, he simply turned on his heel and left the building.

"This was a mistake," he muttered as he returned to the bike. "I didn't need to come here, not to this town."

He kicked the bike to life and trundled off, leaving the parking lot by the small road that lead away from the park, making his way deeper into the town. He knew he was kidding himself, and that he did need to go into the town and search for food. He just didn't want to.

The bitter tang of the salty sea air seemed to take away the pungent aroma of decay and rot, for which Bill was grateful. He'd had the intention of heading directly into the town centre, but instead had taken a detour and visited the beach first. Parking his bike out by an old and decrepit ice-cream truck (empty, of course) on a flat pad of tarmac overlooking a large play area, Bill had scrambled over the dunes, across the flat stretch of cream-coloured sand, and made his way out on to a small wooden pier. The end of the wooden platform had been smashed and burned by something, the frayed planks at the edge turned charcoal-black. Could this be the result of something that Miller had mentioned back in the hospital, the ports being bombed? Edgly itself had been a large port town at one point, specialising mainly in importing fossil fuels for the nearby power station. Once that had closed down, the port unofficially shut down along with it, and the once-bustling port now played host to the occasional passing submarine or frigate: mainly Russian or English vessels, it was very rare anything else dropped anchor in the port.

A port such as Edgly also held host to a few fishing boats used by local fishermen: it would surely be a prime target for a tactical strike. Maybe if Bill hadn't been trapped in a hospital for the first fourteen days of the plague, he would have been able to get a boat, and maybe escape from the island.

Or maybe if I hadn't been locked up for a fortnight, I would be dead by now. Eaten by those things or… or worse.

Bill stood motionless on the pier with his eyes fixed on the distant horizon. Waves crashed into the sandy shore, washing up planks of bleached wood and black seaweed. Some of the pieces of wood looked not at all dissimilar to pieces of smashed and ruined boats: curved pieces of a hull, the darkened and twisted shape of a steering wheel, a partially blackened lifejacket. Bill sighed, stepping down from the shattered platform and stooping to pick up a few flat stones, skimming them across the rolling ocean. He was just trying to kill time, now, trying to avoid re-entering the town.

He stood motionless on the sand for a little longer, the sea turning a dark green as the clouds darkened overhead. There was another storm coming, though Bill had long since outgrown his fear of the rain carrying any form of the disease. He'd been rudely awoken one night when the battered roof of one of the abandoned cars caved in and spilled almost three litres of stagnant rainwater over him. The initial shock had subsided to fear, and then the fear into annoyance. He was cold, wet, and he didn't get back to sleep for the rest of that night. With his blankets soaked and clothing wet, he'd picked up a really bad cold, though he seemed to be getting over it now.

A distant rumble sounded, and a single jagged fork of lightning flashed in the distance. The wind picked up, and the ocean began to froth, the foam splitting as tiny droplets of rain splattered against the surface. Although he didn't fear the rain, he didn't want to get another drenching, and he certainly had no desire to catch another cold.

"I may be stupid," he muttered, swinging himself away from the beach and clambering back over the dunes, towards his bike. "But I've got *some* common sense."

The town centre was only a short ride away, and once there, there would be a wide selection of shops and buildings he could search through for food. It would also offer some protection from the rain. Mounting his vehicle, he kicked the engine into life and cast one last look around the parking area of the beach. He tried his best to not think about the summer days he'd spent here with his friends. He also tried to avoid the thought of Rots as they shambled over the dunes, covered in the blood of sunbathers and merrymakers, dripping in gore and…

Stop it, chided Bill, closing his eyes and trying to block out the visions. Closing his eyes only made it worse. Trying to push aside all his visions of death and any doubts about his upcoming jaunt into the town, Bill took the bike slowly away from the destroyed pier and followed the coastal route, into the town centre.

Brinkly Way was surprisingly void of the cars and bodies Bill had expected, especially after the carnage he'd already experienced on his journeys. True, houses were just as badly damaged and boarded up: some broken into, others left alone by the hordes of living dead. Splashes of blood stained the paving stones; some punctuated by scattered bullet casings of different sizes, others by chunks of partially decaying organs. The mile-long road curved around, just on the outskirts of the harbour, and terminated at Edgly Market, an opened expanse of concrete and cobbled streets where market stalls were set up every Friday and Saturday. At the moment it was completely empty: no stalls, no bodies, no abandoned cars. Bill rolled the bike to a stop and dismounted, grabbing all his weapons and making sure he had everything with him before deciding on his course of action.

Numerous shops surrounded the marketplace, most of them larger department stores, though there were a few smaller independent traders that could afford the higher property rental for a central location. Bill grabbed his flashlight and dived into the first shop, playing the beam over the ruined shelving units. As he moved on through the store, he realised that it wasn't just food that had already been stripped from the store. Almost everything that would have any use had been removed. Bill passed shelving units that had once housed lightbulbs, garden spades, clothing: even the books had been ransacked, children's books had been left behind, while anything that had a practical application had been taken. After ten minutes, Bill left the store gripping a single tin of dog food, stroking it thoughtfully. He'd found it beneath an upturned pile of dolls and their plastic accessories, and it promised a healthy coat and stronger teeth, though whether that were true or not would be a different matter. Placing the tin in his rucksack, he played the light over the names of the rest of the stores in the waning light, then flashed the beam over the shop fronts. They each told the same tale of a ransacked store. Muttering under his breath, Bill returned to the bike and perched on the seat, deciding what to do next. He didn't even need to check the rest of the shops surrounding the marketplace, he could tell just by looking through the windows that they were all just the same. He'd be lucky if he'd find another tin of dog food in the entire town, and even then, he wasn't looking forward to opening or eating it.

There was one more building adjoining the market, a large shopping complex filled with a number of different shops. Bill couldn't see anything from outside, but the doors seemed to be in one piece: the glass panels hadn't been smashed, nor had the doors themselves been broken down. The shops inside would probably be just as demolished and empty, but there was always a chance that *something* had slipped through the hands of the looters.

Bill left his bike again and trudged over to the shopping centre, trying the doors and cocking his head when he discovered they were locked. It didn't faze him, however, and one panel was quickly removed with the butt of his shotgun. Dusting fragments of glass from the weapon and debris crunching underfoot, he strode into the building, flashlight in one hand and shotgun in the other.

The interior of the shopping complex was cleaner than Bill had anticipated. If he hadn't known better, it looked like someone had attempted to clean up the building. Thick pools of blood had been partially wiped up, more than likely by the grime-encrusted mops that were sitting amongst other cleaning products and piled in the doorway of a cleaned-out butcher shop. As Bill ventured further into the compound, the cleanliness gave way to mounds of unused building materials and equipment, and as he looked from shop to shop, he realised why all of them were so empty. The shopping mall was under refurbishment at the time of the plague, all the shops had been emptied and builders brought in to extend the centre by adding a second floor. He vaguely remembered Jenny's father talking about it once over Sunday dinner, but he figured that Edgly would never be a big enough a town to warrant a luxury such as a larger shopping centre. As it transpired, he'd been wrong.

Picking his way through the building material, Bill carried on into the depths of the building, hoping that one of the builders had left one of their lunchboxes lying around. A stale sandwich would be better than a tin of dog food. A few metal and plastic boxes were scattered amongst metal containers of paint and plastic bottles filled with cleaning solvents. There were a few crumbs, but nothing he could eat.

The renovation of the shopping centre had also included adding on a small, three-screened cinema: something the town had been in dire need off since Bill could remember. It was almost twenty miles to the closest cinema, and had often proven to be too much of a journey for a young teenager to take a would-be date for a night out. Consequently, Bill had missed out on a lot of films and a lot of possible dates. Gripping his weapons, he stalked towards the large doors leading into the cinema. They were elaborately decorated wood panels, with frosted glass and ornate gold-plated handles. The walls were decorated with posters for upcoming movies and future attractions. A few appealed to Bill, though he knew deep down he'd never get to watch another movie again. Still, the cinema may well play host to a number of snacks that be may benefit from. His mouth watered at the thought of fresh popcorn lathered in warm caramel sauce, and jumbo hotdogs covered in onions and mustard. He knew he was torturing himself, knew that he'd probably never eat a decent meat product again… or even a hotdog.

Setting his thoughts aside, he tried the doors. They were locked, but a little persuasion from one of the workman's discarded tools broke the lock and the door swung open, the scent of stale and trapped air washing over his face. There was an underlying taint to the air, a gentle bittersweet tang of rotting flesh, and Bill readied his weapon, knowing that he was sure that one of the undead creatures that had seemingly been entombed in the building.

He stepped into the foyer of the building, the wet carpet squelching beneath his feet and displacing spatters of spilled blood: the matting was sodden with dark blood and piles of cast-off skin flakes lay on the ground, confirming that at least one of the creatures was in here. The foyer was elegantly decorated, carrying on the theme of plated gold from outside. A sweeping staircase rose to the left and right of the entrance, following the curve of the wall and joining at their apex to form a balcony. The banister was made of the same metal as the door handles, gold in colour, and merged into the back of a small statue of a woman either side of the staircase, each figure holding up a glass sphere which emitted a dim glow. Evidently, parts of the town seemed to still have some power: maybe a backup generator?

To the left of Bill lay the ticket office, a small alcove whose walls were covered in old posters and price guides, while in the centre of the room there was a small stall, made of wood and glass, the refreshment stand for the cinema. Bill rushed over and searched the stall, but didn't find anything other than a bloody smear on the glass display panel. Shaking his head, Bill made his way to the foot of the stairs to his right, then slowly climbed the stairs, his weapon raised and preceding him. The interior of the picture house was as quiet as the rest of the town was, and not a creature was stirring.

"Not even a mouse," he muttered, sliding along the balcony and resting against the railing, looking into the pair of doors that lead away from the balcony, through the bar area and into stalls. He stepped forwards, pressed against the doors, tried to force the barriers open. The hinge creaked, a shrill and piercing scream announcing his arrival to anyone that lay in wait in the bar area.

He pushed on into room, sweeping his weapon from left to right, scanning each of the alcoves that lined one wall. Each alcove had a wooden table, surrounded by a bench coated in padded faux-leather. Thick wood-chip coated all the walls, painted a creamy, dirty white. The walls themselves were irregularly shaped, curving at the corners and sweeping around into two separate bathrooms. These offshoots were dark and foreboding, their fluorescent tubing flickering wildly. Bill identified these as the most dangerous areas in the room, and stalked towards the bar, keeping his eye trained on the curve leading towards the male toilets and the muzzle of his shotgun pointed towards the opening for the female toilets. As he neared the bar, a heavy oak construct littered with cardboard tablemats and dirty bar towels, a pungent odour assailed his nostrils, sickly sweet with a metallic tang. He knew the source of the smell as soon as he reached the bar, and couldn't believe he'd overlooked the most obvious place for someone to hide.

He stepped back, bringing his weapon about to bear on the space above the bar, and the collection of glass shelving behind it. Before he could do anything else, a dark and rotting mass sprang up on to the counter, an agile Rot crouching atop the bar and knocking the shotgun from Bill's grasp. It glared at him with beady eyes and curled back what remained of its lips, hissing and spattering the countertop with bloody drool. It lunged forwards from its crouch, curling its talons around Bill's shoulders and toppling him, pinning him to the ground. He struggled with the squirming dead body, fending off the salivating jaws and yellowing teeth, managing to get one hand loose and slide it down his body to the holster hanging at his hip. He drew and fired a shot as he did so, plugging the cadaver in the hip and spinning it to the side, grimacing as blood, cold as the grave, washed over his hands and stomach. Kicking back from the squirming body, Bill rolled to his feet, stayed in a crouching position, and raised his pistol, cupping his left hand around his right, steadying his aim and plugging a second round into the base of the corpse's skull. The Rot ceased its movements, blood slowly oozing from the wounds and soaking into the carpet.

Replacing his pistol in the holster and retrieving his shotgun, Bill prodded the body with the muzzle of his weapon, rolling over the corpse and keeping the shotgun pointed squarely at the head of the creature, at the hideous visage that had been smashed by the round from the pistol. Teeth and shards of bone flecked the bloody pulp of the face, swimming amidst a pool of gore and spattered brain matter. Rushing over to the bar, Bill grabbed the only bottle he could find, a cheap brandy in a clear bottle stashed at the back of a cupboard and hidden beneath a pile of rags, and doused his hands in the fluid, trying to clean off the blood of the corpse. He splashed the remains of the bottle over his clothing, trying to remove all trace of the Rot, before turning back to the room. His hands reeked of the alcohol, but he preferred that in comparison to the stench of death and decay that lingered on the corpse.

A quick and cautious search of the remaining bathrooms confirmed that the bar was empty, the only other place to look at was the door leading into the stalls themselves. Bill carefully made his way over to the doors and pushed the heavy barrier inwards. Fetid air oozed out from behind the doors, a damp and mouldy breath from the tomb inside, and Bill worked his way in, up the short flight of stairs and finding himself surrounded by a graveyard of empty chairs.

He stood in the centre of the seating area, with twenty seats on either side of him, ten rows before him and another ten behind him. Each row in front of him was a step down, while those to his rear were raised a step. He made his way up into the seats behind him, gripping the wooden barrier separating the chairs from the stairwell leading back down into the bar, and gently lowered himself into the uncomfortable plastic and sponge frame. The wooden floorboards beneath the seat were surprisingly sticky, coated in spilled beverage and discarded wads of chewing gum. Though Bill longed to savour the cool and minty taste of a fresh piece of chewing gum, he didn't feel like peeling one of the discarded pieces from the floor and testing to see if they still had their taste. He was pleased, though, when he found an unopened bag of chocolate-covered peanuts lying tucked beneath the seat beside him. The packaging was a bilious yellow in colour, and Bill could make out words on the packet, a claim that the milk chocolate would only melt in your mouth, not in your hand.

Be that as it may, thought Bill, tearing one of the corners open and popping one of the small round treats into his hand. *The colour of the crisp shell still runs in your hand. Blues, greens, reds, all the colours of the rainbow in palm of my hand...*

He flicked the sweet into the air, watch as it arched high, then caught it in his open mouth, crunching though the shell and chocolate, halving the peanut inside and smiling as he swallowed. He slipped his rucksack from his shoulders, opened it up and slipped the sweets into the bag, beside the tin of dog food. He grabbed a multivitamin tablet and swallowed it whole, then kicked his feet up on to the wooden banister before him, resting his chin on his chest.

Memories of past visits to the cinema rushed into Bill's mind, trips he and Jenny used to make to go and see the latest blockbuster films. Either comedy or horror, the couple had a passion for those genres of film. It was a different passion, however, then made sure the couple never saw the end of a film. Bill smiled and closed his eyes, folding his arms over his chest and remembering the kisses and embraces from each visit.

Her arms wrapped tight around me, lips brushing my own. Fingers caressing, brushing my brow…

III

Trails of blood and flakes of skin left on me, joints cracking and weeping as she takes my hand in hers. Her lips cracking, fresh wounds gushing blood, and a harsh and alien voice trying to talk to me.

Bill flicked his eyes wide open. He hadn't intended to sleep, surely he hadn't been out long. Ten, maybe fifteen seconds, it couldn't be any longer. Could it?

He glanced at his watch, but the face of it was cracked and it seemed to be missing the hour hand. Whether it worked or not was an entirely different matter altogether. He had to accept that it could have been seconds or minutes: possibly hours. He was trying to pull himself together and gather all his wits, when the door leading into the bar just beneath where he stood squeaked open. Bill froze, holding his breath as he slipped the last strap of his bag over his shoulder and grabbed his shotgun. He hadn't even bothered to search the seating area he'd carelessly fallen asleep in, had there been someone else already there? Or had someone else entered the room? Sinking to the floor amongst the chewed gum and spilled drinks, he pressed his body flat against the floor and wooden barrier, listening at the footfalls on the stairs leading from the bar. There seemed to be two pairs, meaning two people. Bill could also hear their breathing, indicating that there weren't Rots, and the smell that accompanied them was not the decay and putrid smell that lingered around the corpses. Tobacco and alcohol mingled with the heady and intoxicating stench of sweat. Real people, standing just below where he hid, and he was about to announce his presence, when flashbacks of the sick acts of necrophilia in the transit tunnels sprang to mind. Instead, he waited and listened.

"You think that cock-sucking Nigger's in here?" sneered one man, a nasally and high voice. For a moment, Bill was reminded of an old teacher in his high school. He didn't think it was him, though, even though he had lived in this town. There was no way the teacher who had taken religious studies could have turned into such a racist.

"There's that bike out front, it's not one of ours. It must be his." A gruff voice, the voice of a man who smoked a lot of cigarettes and drank a lot of whiskey.

"Oh, I hope it is. That bastard's killed a lot of our men, when I catch him I'm gonna shoot that little shit right here!"

"You ain't shooting no-one, Higgins. Remember what Moloch said, he wants him alive so *he* can pull the trigger. We catch him alive and in once piece."

"Fuck Moloch," muttered Higgins. "If he wants this little shit so much, why doesn't he get up off his arse and do something, instead of sending out patrol after patrol? This fucker keeps wiping us out."

"Moloch's busy, he's got other things to attend to."

"Bullshit," replied Higgins. Bill summoned up the courage to peer over the top of the wooden barrier, and tried to get a look at the men. One was a little over five foot and was wearing tatters of denim and leather, kept together with lengths of chains and rope and a head shaved bald. The second man stepped into view, almost six and a half foot tall, showing his shoulder-length black hair and long leather coat, dragging along the ground behind him. The short man turned to face his companion and prodded him with a finger. "Moloch's got nothing better to do with his time. He's killed all our bitches in the prison cells and we've got nothing for our own entertainment. He's got a hard-on for this Negro bastard because he killed his friend, and he wants revenge."

"Fuck you, Higgins. If he hears you talk like that, you'll be next. Now, are you going to search high, or low?"

"I'll take low," muttered the bald man, stumbling down into the lower stalls. The tall man made his way into the higher seats: directly towards Bill's location.

Grasping his shotgun in sweating palms, Bill shifted his position and listened for the heavy footfalls approaching him. The movement stopped, and the hem of the long black leather coat swayed into view, quivering slightly as the tall man looked from side to side. "I don't think he's still in here, and he could've smoked that lurcher out there in the bar days ago if he came through here, searching for food. C'mon, let's get out of here. Hey, what the…"

Bill looked up, saw the white painted face of the tall man glaring down on him, and watched as he reached for the machinegun dangling from his belt. He lifted the machinegun and squeezed off a short burst of three rounds, each bullet hammering into the ground in front of Bill. He raised his shotgun and fired in retaliation, unloading a round into the face of the man as he scrambled away from him. He screamed as his face instantly became a battered and bloody pulp, and crashed on to the chairs, bones and joints cracking as he smashed into the rigid structure. Bill snatched at the machinegun, tore it from the strap and fumbled for the catch of the belt of the fresh corpse, relieving him of the ammunition strapped around his waist.

As he sorted out his new find, Higgins opened fire with his own weapon, spraying the higher seats with automatic gunfire. Lead pellets tore through the wooden barrier, and Bill scrambled feverishly forward, wooden splinters raining down on his back as he crawled onwards.

"Come on out, you little black bastard, I know you're there!"

Bill cautiously peered over the top of a chair, trying to get a fix on the man attacking him. Down from his position, and to the left, the man in denim and leather stood on one of the seats, nursing his smoking assault rifle and panning his head from left to right. He pulled the empty magazine from the weapon and slammed a fresh one into place, cocking the weapon and opening up again. The muzzle flash illuminated his snarling face as he sprayed the same area again, destroying more of the barrier that had previously protected Bill: he obviously hadn't worked out that he'd moved. The firing stopped again, and Bill took his chance, standing up and loosing another round from his shotgun. He worked the slide, and fired again, both shots knocking the man back and making him drop the weapon. Taking a step forwards, over the back of a chair and down into the next row, Bill fired again, this time his target toppling backwards over the chair and swearing as he bashed his limbs against the floor or other seats. As soon as he saw the man vanish, Bill launched into a run, tumbling down the rows of chairs and swinging into the stairwell leading back into the bar, blindly thumbing shells back into his weapon. He slammed into the door, yanked it open, and burst into the bar, eyes frantically searching from left to right.

The corpse of the Rot had been dragged to one side, the meat hook embedded in the spine the obvious method of shifting the body. One man crouched beside the bar, rummaging through the piles of debris with the barrel of his shotgun, his back turned to Bill. The hair of the punk had been died blue and cut short, but he also wore a long leather coat. He span around as the door slammed shut, standing up and narrowing his eyes, licking his lips as the pair eyed each other up, weapons dangling by their side. Feeling like he had been transported back to the Wild West, Bill wasn't quite sure what was going to happen next. He'd never had any experience in drawing, especially not the bulky shotgun that he knew was ready to go: but at the same time, he knew that Blue Hair had just as bulky a weapon, a double-barrelled shotgun.

"You're not him," he muttered, his voice harsh and dry. He brought his weapon up, but his preliminary words had snapped Bill out of his trance. Already, he had lifted his shotgun and drew a bead on his would-be assailant, coiling his finger around the trigger and hammering a shell into the chest of the man. He stumbled back, screaming and clutching at his bloodied chest as he crumpled to the floor, his weapon clattering to the ground. He keeled over on to his wound, a hideous burbling sound wheezing from the gushing holes in his torso. He tried to scream, tried to open his mouth to bellow a warning or utter his dying words, but the only thing he could manage was vomit a little blood.

The shotgun blast itself was enough to attract unwanted attention, however. A pair of men dressed in tattered clothing entered the bar, one from each of the entrances into the adjoining toilets; each armed with a different weapon. At the same time, the bald man in denim from the stalls burst into the bar, assault rifle dangling from his hand and blood trickling down the side of his face, his forehead spattered with a collection of dimples and cuts from the shotgun blasts.

"Kill the fucker," he slurred, pointing a finger towards him and lazily circling it in the air. "Kill him, shoot him!"

Bill slunk low to the ground, lowering his shotgun and instinctively lifting his other hand, squeezing the trigger of the machinegun he held. The weapon shuddered to life, pulling wildly to the left and upwards, dragging a stream of bullets across the wall, punching holes in the wall and showering debris down on the ground. All three of the punks dived to the ground, rolling away and trying to hide from the wild gunshots as the weapon emptied its clip. Bill lowered his weapons, affixing them to his webbing and taking full advantage of the distraction his wild shots had created. He smacked the doors behind him, retreating to the sanctity of the foyer of the cinema…

…And found himself in a nest of vipers.

The foyer was alive with numerous men dressed in various scraps of leather, denim and lengths of chains, their hairs died different colours. Bill didn't have time to take in any of their details; he barely had time to count the three men climbing the stairs to his left, or the two men to his right. With only his pistol ready to fire, there was no way he'd be able to take on all of the men at the same time, he'd have to run: but to where? There had to be a fire-exit somewhere, but that would probably be in the stalls. His closest escape route was the main door ahead of him, but he was going to have to go through one group of armed men: the three men carried knives of various sizes, while the pair to his right carried fire axes. He didn't feel like going up against either of the groups and his mind quickly weighed up his options. A piece of advice Brian had told him one day at work flashed momentarily into his mind.

Always go for the hidden third option: there's always one!

Bill rocked back on his feet, then charged ahead, vaulting over the barrier at the top of the balcony and sailing through the air, his bulky and equipment-laden form crashing into the confectionery stall in the centre of the room. The frame folded in half around Bill, shattering the glass and showering him with debris. His ankle had twisted and buckled beneath him on landing, and his muscles ached with each movement, feeling like he'd torn it with the impact, or maybe that a sliver of wood had pierced his leg. He didn't have time to check on himself, though, not with the punks advancing on him with murder on their mind. He plucked himself from the damage stall and hobbled for the door, rolling through the opening and slamming the door shut behind him. He slapped blindly at his webbing, detaching one of the telescopic batons he'd picked up in the hunting store and flicked his wrist, extending the weapon and forcing it between the door handles, jamming the barrier shut behind him. He knew it wouldn't hold for long, the glass had already been smashed by one of the men brandishing the axes, but it still bought him a few precious seconds. Those precious seconds would hopefully give him enough time to charge up the staircase under construction and look for somewhere to hide, or maybe attend to his possible wound.

The sound of the smashing glass and a few wild gunshots had attracted the attention of the other men in the building, and Bill could see a collection of ten people hanging around the main entrance. There was no way he could break through there, he'd need to avoid them, or at least check and reload his weapons. Stumbling up the stairs and rolling into an open doorway of the floor under construction, Bill loaded as many of his weapons up as he could, pulling the curved magazine from the machinegun and slamming a second one home, then forcing more shells into the shotgun. Below him he could hear sporadic bursts of gunfire, screams of anger and rage, and questions about his location.

"It's not the Nigger," screamed the unmistakable voice of Higgins. Though Bill couldn't see from his hiding place, it sounded like all the men were gathering in the centre of the shopping mall, just below his position. "Moloch doesn't know about him, he doesn't want him alive, this is one fucker we get to kill ourselves! He's already killed two of us, and he's well armed. Looks like he's injured, though."

Bill glanced down at his left calve, and saw the dark red stain on his jeans, along with the piece of wood sticking out his leg. He clenched his teeth and grabbed the wooden sliver, pulling it out and letting it drop to the ground. He needed to find something to tie off his leg, a tourniquet that would staunch the bleeding, but he could only do that once he'd found a safe hiding place.

"Split up, you lot upstairs, the rest search down here."

Bill gripped his weapons and stumbled away from the staircase, lifting his new weapon and training it on the top step as he went. He was delighted to note that pressing lightly on the trigger of the machinegun activated a small laser target, the red dot wavering wildly. He watched the target dance, trying to keep it just below the lip of the step to keep it out of sight of the men climbing to the second floor. He licked his lips, suddenly aware he was in desperate need for a drink, and cast a glance over his shoulder and around him. The upper floor held a large number of packing crates and discarded building materials, enough to offer some form of cover from his pursuers, though obviously nothing that would offer any real protection from a bullet. Looking back on his actions, Bill decided that clambering upstairs hadn't really been a good idea after all. He'd manage to reload his weapons, but he didn't think he'd have enough ammunition to take out all the armed men.

A plume of red hair rose over the lip of the staircase, and Bill snapped out his thoughts, raising the wavering dot, placing it in the centre of the hairy mass, and hammered a single round into the head of the approaching man. He screamed and fell back, the crunching sounds of his body smashing against the concrete steps and the dying retort of the single gunshot echoing into a deathly silence. Bill knew there were still people on the ground floor, and they knew he was up there.

"What are you doing," muttered Bill, listening intently to the sounds beneath him. Shuffling feet, the occasional murmur or cough, a clank of metal against metal. "Come on, you miserable racist shits, show yourselves!"

Without warning, a salvo of three silver canisters arched over the edge of the new floor, bouncing on to the tiled surface and rolling to a stop. They were nowhere near his hiding place, but devices looked a lot like grenades to Bill. Would their explosions reach Bill, or would he be a safe distance from the flying red-hot shrapnel? He watched, frozen in terror as the top of each grenade cracked open and belched thick grey smoke, masking the only way up in a thick haze of smoke.

"Tricky bastards," Bill growled. He didn't want to fire randomly into the mass, he wanted to try and keep as much of his ammunition as he could. Dark shadows began to move and dance within the swirling smoke, but Bill had no way of deciding what may be a man and what could be a shadow. He'd effectively backed himself into a corner, with no way to escape other than straight through the armed gang below him. True, there were a few windows he could bail out of, but would he be able to survive the drop to the ground floor? And if he did survive, would he escape injury and be able to run to his bike without his assailants catching him?

He feverishly looked around again, searching his immediate surroundings for something he could use, maybe something to cushion his fall. Amongst some of the packaging crates, there were some rolls of fibreglass that would be used for insulation. Enough of the material would certainly offer enough protection for a single-story drop. The insulation was next to a boarded-up window, and Bill hastily made his way across to it, running in a low crouch and firing off a few bursts of gunfire into the smoke cloud, just to keep any approaching people at bay.

Metres away from the crates and insulation, he dived to the floor, sliding along the slick tiled surface and crashing into one of the wooden boxes. He leapt to his feet, grabbing his shotgun and smashing the butt of the weapon against the wooden boards over the window. They cracked along the centre, then fell away, revealing a view looking out on to the market square, and his silent motorbike. The machine was surrounded by a collection of four dark and monstrous vehicles, cars with bodywork enhanced by welded steel pipes, barbed wire, spikes and large weapons. One man strolled back and forth, a large rifle cradled in his arms and his head twisting from the vehicles towards the shopping mall. He seemed torn between staying at his post and rushing to help his comrades, but he hadn't seen Bill opening the window. He was certain he'd see rolls of bright orange insulation tumbling to the ground, and he'd definitely see a six feet tall man dropping out the window.

Behind Bill, gunfire began to erupt from the dissipating smokescreen, wild shots that were nowhere near their mark. It wouldn't be long until someone hit lucky, though, or until the smoke cleared enough so that a clear shot could be made. Bill sprayed the remaining clip from the machinegun into the cloud, ejected the empty magazine and slammed a fresh one home. He pulled back on the T-bar, then lowered the weapon and placed it on the floor before drawing the rifle from his backpack, quickly setting up and resting the weapon on the window ledge, lining up the patrolling guard in the kaleidoscope-like lens of the rifle. He squeezed the trigger once, and caught the man in the shoulder. Stunned, the target dropped his weapon and stumbled around, rushing to take cover behind the closest car. Bill feverishly worked the bolt, ejecting the spent brass and took a second shot, this time hitting his mark and caving the face of the man in. He lowered the rifle, tied it back in place and grabbed the machinegun, spraying the thinning cloud with rounds as he blindly forced insulation rolls through the window. As he forced the forth and final roll out the window, men emerged from the cloud, sweeping their weapons back and forth, their rounds chewing through crates and punching holes into the unpainted plaster walls. Bill didn't waste time trying to return fire, he simply dived through the window, aiming for the pile of fibreglass. As he sailed through the opening, he felt a sudden stinging sensation in his left thigh, felt blood seeping over his leg and cool air whistling against raw flesh. He'd been hit, but it didn't feel bad enough to cripple him, at least not now while adrenaline was surging through his system.

He slammed into the insulation and rolled to the side, moaning in agony as his fresh wound pressed against the concrete. Already itching from the contact with the agitating material, he bolted for his bike, hearing men scream and gunfire erupt behind him. Bullets smashed into the ground around and behind him, the pavement vomiting chips of concrete into his wake as he dived over the bonnet of the first car and tumbled on to his bike. He kicked his bike into life, and looked hastily around. There didn't seem to be anyone else outside the mall, but he had to get out of there as soon as he could, and possibly delay the men so he could get a good lead.

He grabbed the drainpipe cannon he'd made while in Barkley's and dropped a small glass bottle into the opened muzzle, lighting the rag and bracing the weapon against his hip. He squeezed the handle together, waiting for the chamber to fill with gas. Just as he thought he'd wasted his time, the weapon kicked to life, simultaneously knocking Bill from his perch on his bike and spitting the Molotov cocktail out the barrel, smashing in front of the shopping mall and blocking the doorway with thick sheets of flames. Clambering back on to his bike, Bill gunned the engine and sped off from the market square, swerving wildly from left to right to make a harder target in case any of the gang members tried to take a shot at him.

The flames from the Molotov hadn't lasted as long as he'd hoped. Already he could hear powerful engines growling to life, accompanied by sporadic bursts of gunfire. He chanced a brief glimpse at the cracked mirror on the bike, saw the black machines of death grind their way around the corner behind him, and tried to make the bike go faster. The winding roads twisted and turned through shopping areas and housing districts, main roads slipping into side streets and alleyways before re-emerging on main roads. No matter where he went, or how he tried to shake his pursuers, the four vehicles stayed right behind him. Every so often one of the men riding on the vehicles would try to take a shot, but Bill's erratic driving and 'tactful' evasive actions prevented him from being in anyone's sights for too long.

He managed to gain a little ground just as he reached the field near Spoonface's Café, and slid sideways into a mound of shrubbery and greenery. He managed to completely cover himself and the bike as he rolled to a stop, finding himself in an encampment similar to those he'd spent his childhood days in. He'd made it just in time as the four pursuing cars trundled to a stop in the middle of the field surrounding the café. The loud engines gurgled and died, letting silence fall on the area once more. The men dismounted from their machines, forming a cordon around the vehicles and the only way Bill could get out.

"He's out there, somewhere," one of the men said. Even with the distance there was between them, Bill could still hear their conversation. "He's still out there, he must be hiding in the bushes."

"You think he's with the Nigger?"

"I can smell the filth on him, I don't doubt it for a minute. But Moloch doesn't know he's here, so he's ours. Spike, you and Dave smoke the fucker out there."

Two of the men split off from the defensive line and moved to the bushes, the weapons they held bursting to life and spewing orange-white flames over the greenery. The bushes ignited the minute the flames touched them, the conflagration slowly spreading towards Bill and his secluded spot. With nowhere to go, he'd have no other choice *but* to get back on his bike and try to break through them. He levelled the machinegun in one hand, drawing a bead on one of the men with the flame-throwers, and drew his handgun with his left, holding it out and trying to target the other man with the incinerator. He'd seen it done in films, he'd even tried it out in the arcades once or twice: how hard could it possibly be?

He jerked both trigger fingers, bursts of gunfire pounding into the man on the right. He spun around, dead fingers convulsing on the controls of his weapon and dousing one of the vehicles with flames. The shots from Bill's second weapon were way off target, but they were enough to make the man drop to the floor.

The fire consuming the vehicle was enough to send a wave of panic around the men, and they ran from the fireball, some diving into the remaining cars and backing up while the driver from the flaming car toppled out, skin bubbling and blistering beneath the heat of the inferno. Screaming as he rolled from side to side, Bill kicked his engine into gear and revved up, shooting out the burning shrubbery as more and more of the greenery was consumed by the fire. Screams of panic and confusion turned to rage and frustration as Bill cruised by them, the heat of the flames washing over his body. Sporadic bursts of gunfire erupted behind him, and bullets struck the ground around his bike. Again, Bill began to swerve and sway, hoping to make a harder target.

He found himself back in the streets of Edgly, heading back towards the town centre. It struck him that this could go on all night and well into the next, and he needed to do something to remedy the situation. An explosion blossomed behind him, and a quick glance in one of his wing mirrors showed the smoking remains of the car that had been caught in the unfriendly fire.

"One down," muttered Bill through gritted teeth, trying to work out the best way to get rid of the pursuing gang. If he couldn't lose them, he'd have to try and take them out, or at least disable their vehicles.

His machine careened down one of the main streets, wheels smoking and engine choking, sounding like it was beginning to give up the ghost; it was either out of petrol, or the engine was starting to seize up. Regardless of the situation, he was going to have to stop. And without any garages open for business, it was going to be a while until he could get his machine serviced. He tried to keep the vehicle moving, but with a grinding crunch, the engine completely died, and the bike rolled to a stop. Cursing, Bill kicked himself off the bike and scuttled across the ground, ducking into a shop storefront as the pursuing vehicles droned by. He heard the men aboard swearing and pointing out his location as they sped past, then the screech of the brakes as they stopped and tried to turn around.

Bill grabbed his crossbow, slapped one of his modified bolts into the groove, and dropped it to the floor before bringing up his machinegun, instantly firing off a burst at the men as they clambered out their vehicles. They ducked behind the machines, blindly firing over the barriers, and forcing Bill to retreat behind the masonry of the store. Stone and plaster rained down over him, but at least he'd got them to hide behind the vehicles, which were his main target. Grabbing the crossbow again he made sure the weapon was ready to fire, then waited for a lull in the barrage of gunfire. A second of silence gave Bill the time he needed, and he stood, shouldering his weapon and unleashing the bolt into the closest car. It struck the rear wing of the vehicle, and bounced harmlessly off with a dull thud. Bill dropped to the floor, cocking the weapon and pulling out the two remaining explosive bolts. One had been twisted at one point, the casing cracked and leaking the gunpowder. That left him with just the one powerful metal arrow, and if *this* one didn't work, he'd have to rethink his whole strategy. A second wave of gunfire pummelled his hiding place, this time the chatter of automatic fire and the booming of shotguns dispersed with laughter and obscenities. Again, a lull in firing, and Bill lifted his head and the crossbow, striking the same target. This time, the bolt exploded on contact, illuminating the darkened street with a pale orange light. The primary explosion itself wasn't enough to kill anyone, but once the intense burst of heat and its shrapnel pierced the petrol tank of the vehicle, it did the rest.

Bill was tossed to the floor as the first car exploded, causing a chain reaction and taking out the remaining two cars, sending bodies crashing from the scene and smashing them into the surrounding buildings, fire consuming their clothing and igniting any ammunition they carried. Bill lay dormant on the floor, his hands frantically working with the mechanism on the weapon and reloading it. His ears were ringing, and a permanent imprint of the explosion seemed burned into his retinas. Everything he looked at seemed to be covered with a greenish-red blur, though it seemed to be dissipating with each blink. Still dazed from the explosion, he lay amongst the debris in the store, eyes gazing at the doorway and his weapon lazily pointing from side to side. As his ears regained some normalcy, the ringing of bells turned into the crackling of fire, sounding like dried leaves beneath a heavy boot, and the smell of grilled meat lingered heavily in the air.

Stumbling to his feet, Bill hobbled out to the street, the adrenaline of the chase finally dying and the pain of his bullet graze reminding him he'd been shot, albeit a minor wound. Blood trickled from his wound, and he slowly made his way to his bike, the machine lying on its side. One half of the vehicle was blackened and dented, though it still looked like it would work, if only he could get it started. Bill righted the machine, deciding he would have to hunt down a book about bike maintenance in the morning then leaned against the battered bike while he looked around the charred blast crater. Here and there, burned corpses lay crumpled against walls or bent around lampposts, while severed limbs littered the ground. Some looked like they had been cut off, while others looked like their bodies had simply disintegrated.

"Jesus Christ," he muttered, watching as a limbless torso flopped around on the ground, skin blistered and dark brown in colour. Bill reached for the butt of his pistol, contemplated putting a bullet through his head and ending it's suffering.

He refrained from drawing his gun, simply turning away and limping along with his bike. It was going to be dark soon. He needed to find somewhere warm and secure for the night.

IV

Darkness had claimed the town by eleven, and the absence of any power or working streetlights meant that the only source of light was the moon, and the yellowing light from Bill's torch. He'd tried to get the headlight for the bike working, but it hadn't lasted longer than five seconds before flickering and dying. He wasn't afraid of anything being attracted to his light, he and his now-dead friends had been racing around the town a few hours ago. If there was anyone or anything left here, they would have been attracted to the noise, and certainly the explosion.

Winding streets and alleyways led Bill to a housing estate, a one he was vaguely familiar with. Or, he thought he'd been familiar with it. The roads leading into the central area of the estate were as Bill remembered them, still strangely devoid of parked vehicles or decaying bodies. The roadways curled around to a large car park situated behind a squat building; the doors and windows of the ground floor were boarded up, while those that could be seen over the metal barrier of the upper-floor balcony seemed to be covered with wire mesh.

The car park itself had been transformed into a battleground. Mounds of cement, bricks and the twisted skeletal remains of shopping trolleys seemed to be laid out in random patterns, the surfaces facing Bill pockmarked with craters and scorched by burns. Bullet casings littered the ground in massive quantities, like there had been a snowstorm of brass, while blood spattered the ground here and there. As Bill made his way through the mounds, he noticed that the other sides of them weren't as badly damaged, and there didn't seem to be as much brass. It looked like the parking lot was the site of at least one major battle.

Laying his bike down to rest against the wall, Bill drew his shotgun and slowly made his way up the concrete stairs, up on to the balcony. The building had always been a block of flats, and the balcony had always been a perfect place for Bill and his friends to play. Now, though, as Bill stood atop the staircase and looked along the balcony, it seemed too clean, especially in comparison to the haphazard design of the parking lot. He cautiously began to shuffle along the balcony, crouching low behind the concrete barrier lining the balcony and keeping out of sight. He tried each door as he passed it, but all seemed locked. He finally reached the last of the line of doors, and grinned inwardly as it clicked open, the well oiled hinges silent. He'd expected them to squeal and moan, like they always did in the films: it was a classic scenario that he was surprised to see didn't play out. Sliding into the building, he closed the door and locked it behind him, fumbling with the catch in the darkness. He pulled out his flashlight and flicked it on, partially covering the hood of the device to smother some of the light, and shone the beam around the room.

It didn't look like it had been lived in for a while. The linen had been stripped from the bed, the table overturned, and a large collection of electronic goods had been smashed and dumped in the centre of the room. The stale smell of tobacco lingered in the air, easily a few days old, and an ashtray amongst the electrical debris held the butts of three large cigars. Whoever had been living here had stopped doing so a long time ago. Clambering over the table and chairs, Bill moved into the kitchen area, and slung his pack on to the bench. Various dishes and plates had been left in the sink, encrusted with pieces of food and stained with dried sauces. Bill didn't feel like eating from a soiled plate, and rummaged through the cupboards. He came up triumphant with a metal dish, engraved with the word 'Bonzo'. Quite appropriate, considering what he was about to eat.

He pulled out the tin of dog food he had found, then retrieved a clean fork and rolled it between in his thumb and forefinger, eyeing the tin. It had a ring pull on top, making it easier to open. It wasn't going to make it any easier to swallow, though. Chunky pieces of tripe with jelly wasn't his favourite meal, but when faced with either Woofy Chunks or starvation, his options were limited. He peeled back the lid, grimacing at the odour of tinned meat as it slowly drifted into his nostrils. It certainly didn't smell appealing, nor did looking at the quivering meat on the end of his fork whet his appetite any.

It tasted surprisingly bland, but it wasn't the taste that repulsed him, it was the texture of the meat in his mouth. Slimy and cold, almost as if it didn't need to be chewed. It slipped down too easily to warrant as food in Bill's eyes. He swallowed another two fork loads before casting the tin aside on the bench. He'd give it a few hours, maybe sleep on it and see if he could keep it down. If he could, then he'd try to eat some more for his breakfast. He opened the fridge, noted that it was well stocked with cans of beer and other alcoholic drinks, then made a space for the opened tin. He was half asleep, and rationalised that whoever had previously lived here had only recently fled. Either that, or the looters hadn't made it into the building yet.

Returning to the main room of the flat, Bill half-heartedly checked the latch on the door once more, lay down on the bed, using his pack as a pillow, and lay out his weapons within easy reach. He'd acquired a machinegun now; maybe that would give him a better chance in the crazy world he now lived in.

With a body aching and a bullet wound beginning to throb a dull pain, he closed his eyes and Bill quickly slipped into a dreamless sleep.

VIII
MARINE CORPSE

"Soldiers stationed on the island are faced with horrors worse than anything any Cartel in Brazil could throw at them. This is a true test of their mettle."

I

Sleep gently subsided into the waking world, and Bill found himself staring at the ceiling of the flat. In particular, a naked woman, reclining and smiling seductively while sitting behind a bulky black weapon: maybe a different type of shotgun to the one Bill had. For a moment, Bill felt a familiar stirring within him, but the thought of Jenny lying on a table, vomiting blood and tearing her flesh apart with each movement, quickly put an end to that. The poster must have been there when he went to sleep; he'd just been so tired he hadn't noticed. It had also been pitch black.

"Caitlin Dillons," he muttered, deciphering the black handwriting on the poster. "Fire off a round and think of me... Christ, who thinks up that cheesy shit?"

"I did, when she signed it for me."

Startled, Bill sat bolt upright and blindly patted the bed beside him, fumbling for his weapons. His crossbow, rifle, shotgun, pistol and machinegun, all gone. He backed up against the wall, ignoring the twinges of pain from his tightly bound limb and trying to see where the speaker was. It sounded like he was in the kitchen area; there was also the sound of tinkling china and cutlery in the flat, and no one sat in with Bill.

His heart racing, Bill quickly assessed the situation. His limb was bound now, he'd noticed that as soon as he'd moved. It was painful, but not debilitating. It had been dressed and cleaned, and it felt like it had been stitched. His weapons were on the table at the other side of the room, all of them unloaded and some of them stripped down to their constituent parts.

"You know," carried on the unseen speaker, his accent laced with an American twang. "I don't know what repulses me the most: the fact you actually ate that shit, or the fact you put it in the fridge with my beer. I've made you some proper food. Get it eaten, it might be a while until you get fed like this again."

The speaker strolled into the room, a seven-foot, muscular black man carrying the same metal dish Bill had found the night before, with a cloud of steam rising from it. He set it down on the bed in front of Bill, and motioned to the dish. He sniffed it tentatively, his mouth watering with the smell of the succulent meat and gravy, though he didn't move to eat it.

"I know what you're thinking. It's meat, so it's infected. I found it in one of the flats downstairs: it was in the freezer. It's about six months old, so it's older than the plague. It's fine. I've been eating it for days. That's the last of it."

Bill looked at the face of the man, and tried to judge him by his appearance. His face looked strong, his chin hidden by a thick growth of styled beard and his head shaved bald. Dark eyes glared at Bill, flitting from his face to the dish of stew. He sunk into a chair beside the door. "Shit, if you're not going to eat the damn food, I'll eat it. I'm no master chef, but it's better than the tasteless Marine rations they make us carry."

"What isn't?" grinned Bill, remembering the stale bricks of dehydrated food he'd been given in quarantine. At least he'd learned that this man was a soldier. The black man smiled, showing a mouth filled with perfect white teeth. "Marine, huh? What division you in? You certainly ain't no Wolver, maybe you were one of them Eagles..."

"Division? No, I'm not a Marine."

"Army?" he asked, curling his lip into almost a sneer.

"No, just a normal guy. I worked in an office."

"But you're not an Army soldier?"

Bill shook his head slowly, all the time keeping his eyes fixed on the muscular man. He wouldn't stand a chance against him in a fight, especially with his injured leg. Was he going to attack him because he wasn't part of the armed forces?

"Why the tags, then?" he asked, motioning towards Bill's T-shirt, and the metal dog tags that currently hung out its collar.

"They're just a keepsake. They were my grandfathers. I think."

"Was he in the Corps?"

Bill nodded. "Sure," he added. *Why not?*

"So you're not part of the Army? Well that's a fucking relief," grinned the Marine, standing up and thumping over to the table with the weapons on. He looked over the collection of weapons and smiled, nodding. "I should've known, though. The Army doesn't have as good a choice in weapons as you."

"it wasn't through my own personal choice," muttered Bill, slowly placing a piece of the meat into his mouth. After a diet of snack food and the experiment last night with dog food, it was like a piece of heaven on his tongue. He smiled and nodded, appreciating the cuisine.

'Still, MP5, M92F, Benelli, very reliable and durable. Not quite as good as my own collection, though. I'm not sure about the crossbow and the rifle, either."

"A Marine gave me the rifle," said Bill, a little hurt at this new man insulting his armament. "You know, one of *your* men."

"Must've been fucking desperate to use a relic like that. Anyway," he said, changing the subject and sitting back down on the chair. "You're the little hellion that tore through the town and killed a few of Moloch's guys?"

"And you must be the cock-sucking Nigger they mistook me for," said Bill, grinning a little as he absentmindedly blurted out the first thing that came into his head. The Marine lunged across the room with lightning speed and grabbed Bill, knocking aside the bowl of meat and pinning him to the wall by pressing his thick muscular forearm against Bill's windpipe.

"Listen to me and listen good," whispered the Marine, leaning in close to Bill, his hoarse voice tickling his ear. He was close enough that Bill could smell the onions and gravy on his breath. "If you use either of those words to describe me again, I'm going to gouge you a new asshole with my bayonet, stuff you with dynamite and kick you off a building, do you understand?"

He released his hold over Bill, but slammed him against the wall to reiterate the threat. Bill made a mental note not to annoy or insult the man any further.

"You mind your mouth around me, motherfucker, or you'll find yourself on the wrong end of a sniper rifle. Now I'm a reasonable guy. I know you've probably been through hell over the last couple of days, and you're obviously not thinking straight. We're going to start again. *You* must be the little hellion that tore through the town yesterday."

"Um, yeah, that's right. My name's Bill. Bill Reddings."

"Al," said the Marine, nodding his head slightly. Bill extended his hand in a sign of friendship, but it wasn't received very well. He withdrew it before the soldier decided to cut it off. The silence between the two was uncomfortable, and Bill felt like he should say something, but he wasn't sure what.

"Why are they after you? One of those guys kept talking about somebody called Malcolm wanting to kill you."

"Moloch, yeah," agreed Al, his face grim and emotionless. "He's the guy in charge, and he's pissed off at me. I keep killing his guys, I've raided a few of his ammunition depots, stolen some of his weapons. These guys are a bunch of fuckin' amateurs. They're holed up in the police station, they had a few prisoners but they've all been killed since. They kept bringing out bodies and burning them." Al finished his speech by flipping a cigarette into his mouth and igniting the tip, inhaling a deep breath and letting smoke seep out though his dark lips.

"They had prisoners? Other survivors? And you just let them kill them?"

"Don't judge me, mother fucker," scorned Al, standing over Bill and pulling the cigarette from his mouth, gripping it between two meaty fingers and waving it in his face. "I'm not stupid, one man can't take on a whole station filled with psychopaths. If I went in there, I would have wound up dead, and that wouldn't benefit me any. It was all very fucking sad, I agree, but ultimately nothing I could do. If I still had my squad, we could have stormed it no problem. I don't, so I couldn't do anything. And besides, from what I heard, Moloch has an appetite for raping and beating prisoners to death anyway."

A deluge of questions poured into Bill's mind, he instantly wanted to ask about Al's squad, and how he knew so much about the workings of the gang. Instead, he asked something that had sprung into his mind when he first heard Higgins talking in the cinema.

"What kind of a name is Moloch, anyway? It sounds biblical, is he a religious guy?"

"Moloch is the name of an effigy the Canaanites used to offer sacrifices of children to," said Al, stepping backwards and returning to his seat, not turning his back on Bill for a second. "The reason he's called it is probably twofold. From all accounts, he likes his women young. The other reason is it's probably more intimidating than being called Peter or David."

"How do you know all this?" asked Bill, scratching his head. Al seemed to have a lot of information at his disposal, and was very generous handing it out, which instantly rang an alarm bell in his head. Was this man who he said he was, or simply one of Moloch's men lulling him into a false sense of security? Bill tried to keep the scowl off his face as he watched Al talk.

"Like I said, I've raided a few of their depots. I've killed a few of their men. I've also wounded some and got the information I needed from them." Al sat back and finished off his cigarette in silence, dropping the smoking filter on the floor and crunching it beneath his heel. "One of the most painful and prolonged ways to kill a man is to shoot them in the stomach. Something to do with stomach acids eating away your internal organs, I don't know, I'm no biologist. If you offer instant death, though, sometimes they'll spill their guts."

Al grinned at his comment, the unintentional joke obviously tickling him.

"Course, sometimes they'll tell you to go fuck yourself, or insult you and your parents. Those I leave to die. There's no chance of them being food for those fucking pus-bags, the group of rebels have done a good job of keeping the place relatively clean."

"They didn't check out the cinema very well," muttered Bill, remembering the feral creature that had tried to attack him.

"So, between the two of us, I figure we've probably killed maybe half of their manpower," said Al, scratching his chin and kicking his feet up on the bed. He looked towards the metal bowl filled with meat, then casually picked it up and began to finish it off. Bill grabbed his rucksack and fished out one of the bottles of vitamins, helping himself to a couple of the tablets. He offered them to Al, who refused them. Instead, he pulled out a battered silver hip flask and took a sip from it. He offered it to Bill, who in turn, refused.

"With their numbers decreased as much, things are going to start changing a lot around here. They can't spread themselves around as much as they do, so they're probably going to concentrate on protecting their base." Al swallowed another gulp of alcohol, then replaced the cap and pocketed the flask. "That means they're going to pool all their resources, pull back any little outposts and guards they have, and protect their headquarters."

"Wait a minute," said Bill, raising his hand. "How do you know their numbers? How do you know how many of them I... I killed?" It sunk in at that moment that Bill had killed people: not just creatures that had formally *been* people, but actual *living* people. He'd thought about it beforehand, but he'd never verbally acknowledged it. He looked at his hands, imagining their blood on them...

"I tracked your movements through the town. I'd just taken out another depot, grabbed some ammo and some rations, and that's when I heard you ripping up their town. I climbed one of the steeples, watched your path of destruction. You must've taken out about four or five of their vehicles. Normally two or three people per vehicle, that's fifteen rebels, give or take. Add that to my score, and our magic number is in the high forties. My reconnaissance work suggests there's about one hundred of those bastards, so we're looking at about an estimate of about fifty left." He seemed smug at this, though Bill couldn't tell if he was pleased at his mathematics or the number of people that had already been killed. He didn't come over as a cold-blooded killer, but at the same time he didn't seem like the worlds greatest pacifist, either.

Bill gave a low whistle. If the Marine's figures were correct, it was surprising. He hadn't figured there'd be as many people who had survived, and certainly not all gun-totting psychos living in the same place. "So what now?"

"I know when I'm beaten. I've tried to get by on the odd supply run, but nothing more. I've been trying to arrange pickup by the UGMC for a few days now, but I can't seem to reach anyone. I've got a mess of wires and metal up on the roof here, I'm going to try and make a radio mast and boost my signal a little further, possibly to the rest of Europe, beyond the range of the coastal guard towers. They're not so much blocking our signals now, more filtering them. keeping us in check."

"Damocles is down?"

Al eyed him suspiciously, slowly nodding his head. "You know your shit. If I can't get anything here then we move on and try elsewhere."

"No one will come to pick you up?" asked Bill, though he wasn't entirely surprised, not from the information that Jason Miller had told him.

"Bastards keep making reference to potential infection, spreading the disease… Jesus, I've been here for days now, I don't know how long, but surely the fact I'm not showing any signs of the plague must mean *something*. I mean, it was the fucking Brass that sent me over here in the first place, they were the shits that made me breach quarantine rules. They can bend the rules to get me *on* the island, but they can't do the same to get me *off*."

Al clenched his fist, dropping the dish to the floor and kicking it away from him.

"If I can reach the mainland on the radio, maybe I can get out someone to send out help…" his voice tailed off, obviously addressing himself. He rose from the chair and grabbed a red metal toolbox, making his way for the door. "I'm going up top to do some work on my radio. You know how to put your weapons back together, right?"

He didn't wait for an answer, he just opened the door and left, slamming it behind him. Bill slowly clambered to his feet and strolled over to the collection of gun parts on the table. They all had a strong smell of oil on them, it was clear that Al had cleaned them during the night. It took Bill a while to reassemble the different weapons, making sure that each piece went with the right one. The rifle was no problem, he'd had that drummed into him by Miller. The Beretta and shotgun posed a slightly tougher challenge, though one that he completed after about twenty minutes. This didn't include the time it took for him to find one of the springs after it catapulted across the room. He decided to leave the machinegun for Al to reconstruct: he was so unfamiliar with the weapon he wouldn't even know where to begin.

Replacing weapons in their holsters and finding a load of ammunition the Marine had left for him, Bill stepped out the flat and back on to the balcony outside.

The summer heat wasn't as bad as it had been the day before, and as such the smell wasn't as bad either. As Bill scanned from left to right, surveying the desolation around the flats, he could hear the hammering and thumping from the roof, accompanied by cursing and grunts of annoyance. The sounds stopped for a few seconds, and then a voice from above. "You keep an eye on things down there, y'hear?"

Bill muttered a response before clearing his throat. "I've left the machinegun on the table, I can't figure it out."

"I'll do it later. Here, take this."

The butt of a large grey weapon appeared over the lip of the roof, and Bill hooked the dangling strap with his right hand, accepting the weight as Al released his grip on it. "Same as the rest of them; point and squeeze. And watch out for the kick."

The hammering and swearing continued once more, and Bill took it as red that the conversation, short as it was, had ended. Bill sighed and casually strolled along the balcony, trying to adjust to the oversized assault rifle he had been handed. Maybe for a seven-foot muscular giant it was in scale, but in Bill's hands it felt overly large.

He's a strange one, he thought to himself as he raised his gaze towards the edge of the roof. He wasn't exactly sure what to make of Al. He'd been quick to divulge some information, much of what had been going on in the town. He'd quickly glossed over any information relating to his squad, only making a passing comment about his former team. He wondered what had happened to them, though the fact the man was on his own seemed to tell the story itself. One way or another, his squad had been killed. And it was a safe bet that Al had been witness to all of it. Not surprising that he didn't want to talk about it, really. That being said, though, he hadn't given anything else away about his personality.

"You're not exactly an open book either, Bill," he muttered, recalling his role in the conversation. He hadn't been very responsive to Al, but the whole situation had been a little bewildering. Bill couldn't remember the last time he'd been woken up with breakfast in bed. Though on second thoughts…

One year ago, it was my birthday. Jenny woke up before me, went into the kitchen and prepared breakfast. Bacon, sausage, scrambled egg, accompanied by toast and a cup of coffee to follow. Then she'd slipped off her dressing gown, showing off her naked, perfect figure. Skin pale and almost translucent, tearing along shoulders and elbows where she moved her arms, embracing me, lips pressing against my neck, teeth sinking in, tearing…

"Fuck," shouted Bill, snapping out his trance and stumbling back from the edge of the balcony. It was bad enough his life had turned into a nightmare, now even his memories and dreams were tainted by the touch of the Syndrome.

"What's going on down there?" demanded Al, sticking his head over the side of the roof, a cigarette hanging from his lips and a pair of black sunglasses covering his eyes. "Do you see someone coming?"

Bill stared in bewilderment for a few moments at Al, then shook his head. "Nothing. I… I was just thinking. About all this shit that's happening. About how it's changed everything."

"Yeah," muttered Al, turning away and returning to his work. "Ain't it a bitch?"

Bill turned and looked along the balcony, at the doors leading to the rest of the flats. He supposed Al had checked them out, so he didn't feel the need to start poking around inside. He made his way along the balcony towards the stairway, stopping and pressing himself against the wall before easing his head around the corner. Everything seemed safe enough; nothing seemed to be moving in the outlying area. He lifted the rifle Al had passed down to him and rested the butt against his shoulder, sighting through the scope mounted atop the rifle. It wasn't as powerful as the scope attached to his own rifle, but the fact the lens didn't have a crack running its length made it easier on the eyes. He lowered the rifle and strolled back and forth along the balcony, scanning for any sign of life.

Nothing moved.

After twenty minutes of patrolling the balcony, Bill stopped and slumped to the ground, resting his back against one of the doors leading into another flat. He sat and listened to the sound of Al above him, working on his project and swearing at the pieces of machinery that didn't work the way he expected them to. A gentle rattling, and a low, muffled moan also accompanied the hammering and grunts, though Bill accounted for this as simply noise from the radio. As he concentrated more on the moaning, though, he realised the noise was coming from *behind* him: from the room behind him.

He turned around and inspected the door handle, finding the key snapped off in the lock and sealed in with a lump of solder. Pulling his knife from its scabbard and wiping the blade on the leg of his jeans, he jammed the tip of it into the thin gap between the door and its frame, silently picking away at the wood and exposing the locking mechanism beneath it.

With enough of the metal housing exposed, Bill could start to excavate the bolt from the frame. Slivers of wood peeled away from the frame, each stab of the knife embedding more and more splinters into Bill's fingers. Swearing, pausing every few seconds to pull chunks of the frame from his hand, he finally managed to break the lock open. Gripping the door, he gently pushed inwards, again finding the hinges well oiled and responsive. As it opened, a fresh stench of decay washed across Bill, a feted odour of rot that could only be produced by a shambling corpse.

"I think I've been to this party already," he muttered to himself, lifting the rifle and swinging it uneasily from left to right. As soon as he opened the door all the way, the noise intensified. Gentle moans and soft rattling of metal became agitated moans and clattering of chains. Bill grabbed his flashlight and flicked it on, slowly panning from left to right, picking out the details of the room.

In appearance it was the same as the flat he had occupied at the end of the row, where he had slept and fed. The upturned furniture and scattered personal artefacts told the same story that the rest of the town had already told Bill; a story of carnage and struggle.

He stepped deeper into the room, his heart hammering faster and faster, his breath coming in ragged and heavy bursts. He lifted the collar of his T-shirt over his nose and mouth, the material doing little to help mask the smell. His eyes watering, Bill reached the back of the flat and found the source of the smell.

A Rot, as he'd expected, dressed in tattered green rags. Flesh had started to drop from the thin body, hair and scalp sloughing to one side and exposing the gleam of a bloodied skull, and it stared at Bill with one bloodshot eye and one vacant eye socket, each opening trickling a watery bloody fluid. Its left shoulder was ragged and bloody, home to a throbbing mass of squirming maggots. Chunks of its own flesh lay scattered at its feet, some partially chewed and gnawed on, surrounded in a pool of thin pink blood. A thick silver chain had been wrapped around its neck and arms, fastening it to the bulky kitchen appliances that had been bolted to the walls and floor.

The creature moaned and shuffled, trying to get up and make its way towards Bill. The chains rattled and clanked, the padlocks clattering against one another as the Rot tried to get up, putrid flesh cracking and tearing with each jarring movement.

"Poor bastard," murmured Bill, raising his crossbow and levelling the decaying face of the Rot. At this range he didn't really need to sight his target to ensure a hit, but he checked anyway, just to make sure. At such a close range, the scope intensified the putrid and mottled appearance of the animals flesh, the glistening rivulets of watered blood and seeping pus. He lifted his aim slightly so it targeted one of the vacant black eyeholes.

Bill squeezed the trigger, the loaded bolt crashing through the skull of the Rot and pinning it to the cupboard behind it. The creature spasmed and thrashed for a few moments, before finally shuddering to a halt. Bill turned his back on the carcass and walked away, returning to the outside and closing the door on the feted stink behind him.

He stood on the balcony once more, staring out into the town around him. The green tatters the Rot had been wearing were reminiscent of the uniform Al had been wearing, or at least those that Bill could identify beneath the layers of faeces, blood and chunks of flesh that had fallen on the clothing. Had the creature been one of Al's squad members, the same squad that Al had refrained from talking about? Why the hell had he just locked him up in the room and left him to suffer?

Bill hadn't been sure what to think of Al at first, but in light of this new information the thought that Al was slightly unhinged sprang to mind. He decided he was going to have to confront the Marine about this; and confronting the seven-foot giant wasn't something he was looking forward to doing.

II

"Jesus friggin' wept," muttered Al, tossing aside the welding torch and hammering the twisted metal shopping trolley with the sole of his boots. He'd gathered as much metal and wiring as he could on the roof, but welding wasn't his strong point. The aerial, though a stroke of genius, was proving to be more trouble than he had anticipated.

After repairing the radio unit after venting his anger and frustration, he had first tried boosting the signal and adding extra power to the unit. He had managed to reach one of the towers a couple of hundred miles north, near the coast of Scotland somewhere, but had ended up speaking to the same pompous and arrogant Major.

"Not ten days yet," he'd scoffed, then simply killed the connection. So Al had decided to try and reach out further.

Days later, the flat roof was now littered with coils of wire, metal shopping baskets, bike frames, and any other metal objects he could throw or carry up, along with a number of car batteries and generators. He'd managed to extend the signal a little further, and had managed to speak to someone in Ireland, first. They had merely confirmed that the situation over there was exactly the same as it was in Britain: zombies running amok, gangs of rebels armed with various weapons, soldiers abandoned. He'd tried to keep in touch with that Irish man. He spoke lovingly of the family he was trying to protect, his wife and his daughter. Until a few days ago, when the undead overran the building they were holding out in. Al had killed the transmission that time, the signal dying in the middle of a young girl screaming in terror or pain.

Now he had managed to increase the range, but all he could get was a French operator, babbling in a language Al couldn't understand. No matter how he reconfigured the mounds of metal and wire, he couldn't boost it any further.

He kicked at the metal trolley again, then sat back and lit a new cigarette, tossing the empty crumpled packet on to a pile of blackened circuit boards. He rubbed his temples, frowning at the machine that he was now considering the bane of his existence. He tore his sunglasses off, folded them up and slipped them into one of the pouches on his webbing as he saw a brown-haired head rise over the roofline. He lifted his weapon and pointed the magnum until he could confirm the identity of the head as Bill. Holstering the weapon, he grunted a greeting. Bill threw down his assault rifle and stormed over to Al, grabbing his shoulder and spinning him so they were face to face.

The movement wasn't particularly powerful, but it caught Al off guard. He stood up and glared down at Bill, wondering what was wrong. There was a bitter underlying scent clinging to his clothing, a cloying scent of death and decay. Though a similar scent permeated across the whole town, it seemed stronger on him. Bewildered by it all, he watched bemused as Bill poked Al's muscular stomach with his finger

"What happened to your squad?" he demanded. Despite the difference in height, Bill was in no way intimidated by him. He smiled a little, impressed at the balls this young man had. With his size and strength, Al knew he would easily be able to defeat him without breaking a sweat. Yet he still confronted him.

"Don't smile at me, you stupid bastard. What happened to your squad?"

"My squad, *my* business. Now fuck off," he growled, pushing Bill backwards. He stumbled back a single step, but regained his balance and advanced once more.

"I've just dealt with some of your 'business' in one of the locked flats beneath us. What happened to them? Are they all Rots? Does each flat hold a different squaddie?"

Al froze, his gaze locked with the cold and accusing eyes of Bill.

"You killed Peter?" It was the first time he could recall actually calling Ping by his first name. "You killed Ping?"

"He was already dead, Al. I just finished the job. Something you couldn't do."

"You killed him?" he repeated, his fists clenching. "You killed my only remaining squad member?"

"Rot, Al, he was a fucking Rot! A zombie, whatever you want to call them."

Al slammed Bill with both palms, knocking him to the ground and pushing him inches from the edge of the roof. "I help you out, I feed you," he yelled, grabbing one of the metal poles from the poorly welded structure and swinging it back and forth like a baseball bat. "I clean up your wound, and you repay me by killing my one remaining squad member?"

Bill leapt to his feet and altered his stance, adopting a fighting stance. Al grunted, then spat out his cigarette and tightened his grip on the pipe.

"Batter up, you ungrateful…"

"Mother fucker," the marine spat, the morning sun glinting off the shining metal he held.

Bill swallowed hard. This whole plague and the subsequent post-apocalyptic nightmare he was living in had consistently provided a number of tough lessons that could only be learned the hard way. He'd already learned about planning things out to perfection, and he'd learned not to just dive blindly into any given situation.

He'd also learned not to confront a giant Marine about issues that didn't really concern him.

Already Al was advancing on Bill, pipe swinging wildly from side to side. Bill reached behind him, unclipped the one remaining metal rod from his belt, and flicked out the metal telescopic defence stick he'd picked up all those days ago. It wasn't as thick as the pipe, nor was it as long, but it would certainly be good enough to block a couple of blows. And then, after that, he'd probably have his arms and legs shattered by a pissed-off soldier.

The first blow came directly towards his head, and Bill barely managed to knock aside with his baton. He was already running through the combat moves he had read in the binder, backing up a step and assessing Al's stance. He was well defended; all the potential weak spots that Bill could take advantage of in the melee were protected or hidden from his view. His training had obviously prepared him for a situation like this, and it only reinforced Bill's notion that his hot-headed approach had sealed his fate.

"Piece of shit," muttered the marine, taking a wild swing at Bill's legs and smashing some of the slate tiles on the roof. The surface they stood upon creaked and groaned as Al took another swing, again missing his target and taking another chunk out the roof. "Kill my fucking squad, will you?"

Bill avoided another attack, then stepped to one side and smacked his weapon against the back of Al's knee, his leg buckling slightly. He was already breathing heavily, and wasn't sure if he'd be able to last much longer. Fighting a dummy made of wood and stuffing was certainly different to a living, breathing opponent. Al drew back with his weapon, winding up for what could be the final assault, then paused for a moment, cocking his head to one side and listening, pressing one finger to his ear. Seeing his one chance, Bill took advantage and lashed out with his weapon, the temple of the Marine his target. Without blinking, without even looking, Al blocked the attack with his forearm, grabbed Bill's wrist and twisted his arm, the sudden move making him drop his baton and drop to his knees. Al lashed out once more, his boot making contact with the back of Bill's skull and dropping him to his back. Al rested one of his boots on Bill's throat, pinning him down and choking him at the same time.

"Attacking me when I'm distracted," he muttered, pressing down with his boot and throwing his pipe aside. "Dirty fucking trick from a dirty little bastard."

Bill could only reply with a series of splutters and coughs, he could feel himself slowly loosing conscious as his airway was crushed. Al scratched his beard thoughtfully, looking out across the town around him. "Do you hear that?" he continued, oblivious to the fact he was slowly killing Bill. He lifted his boot and stormed over to the discarded weapons, retrieving the rifle he had previously handed out and making sure there was still a round in the chamber, ready to fire.

"There's a vehicle approaching. Jesus, they're going to attack in the daylight?" he said, slinging the rifle over his shoulder and beginning to descent from the roof. Bill rolled on to his front, coughing violently as he tried to regain his breath and slowly clamber to his feet. He stood up, the sudden movement and rush of air to his head inducing a sickening feeling of nausea. He lurched over to the large aerial and gripped it, watching as Al vanished over the edge of the roof. He paused for a moment, but couldn't hear anything.

Bill felt totally bewildered by the sudden change in Al's behaviour. Grabbing his own discarded weapons and replacing the defence baton back in his bag, he followed Al back down to the balcony below.

He touched down on the concrete platform in time to see Al as he vanished into one of the flats. It wasn't the one Bill had slept in, but it wasn't the one the Rot had been held captive in. He followed, intrigued by the confusing movements, and found himself in a room with a single vacant table in the centre of the room, all the walls lined with metal crates and racks of weapons, some partially covered with green tarpaulin.

"What the hell are you doing?" asked Bill, watching as Al replaced his rifle in a rack containing three other weapons of the same design, then grab a large and dangerous-looking machinegun, cradling it with two hands. He slammed it on to the empty bench, then tore the ammunition feed open and threaded a belt of rounds into the chamber before slamming it shut and working the action, feeding a few rounds through without firing them off. Al looked up at him then cracked open one of the cases beside the table, pulling out a thick cigar and lighting it up.

"This little spat between you and me, this can wait. Those fuckers're approaching this place, and I'd rather take care of them before I have to deal with you. They're a hell of a lot more dangerous than you are. Now, grab a gun and pick a side, you got two choices: You're with me, or against me. If you're against me, then as far as I see it you're one of Moloch's men, in which case I should blow your head off right now."

Bill swallowed hard as the barrel of the machinegun slowly rotated around to point directly at his stomach.

One of the most painful and prolonged ways to kill a man is to shoot them in the stomach, he recalled, the conversation that had taken place between the two men flashing back into his mind. He gingerly lifted his hands in mock surrender, looking around the armoury. "I'm on your side," he said, confirming his allegiance.

"Grab something decent," said Al, jerking his head towards the main bulk of the weapons he held. Bill nodded and moved forwards, grabbing the first weapon he saw. Al shook his head, tutting at the choice.

"That's a shotgun, Bill. Crap range, no good for long range. You don't want these bastards to be close enough to use a shotgun. Grab an assault rifle. M16 should do you good. I doubt you'll be ready to handle the grenade launcher attachment."

Bill nodded and grabbed the weapon Al pointed to, passing it over to the Marine. He quickly loaded it up, passed three spare magazines with a radio headset, then stormed out the flat. "Fan out. You get down there and take cover behind one of those concrete barriers. I'm going back up to the roof and take them out from there. I should be able to pick most of them off, but anything that gets through is for you to take out."

"How many can we expect?" shouted Bill as his companion disappeared on to the roof again.

"I don't know," shouted Al, his voice fading as he ran along the edge of the roof to his sniping position. "All of them?"

"Great," muttered Bill, slipping the radio headset on and returning into the armoury to take another look around. He grabbed a small metal crate beside the door, the dull green case stencilled with the yellow marking "M16/ M203". Bill didn't know what the latter was, but the former had been what Al had called the weapon he now held. He certainly didn't feel like three magazines would be enough, should a few slip by the soldier's watchful gaze. It wasn't Al he didn't trust, but himself.

Taking his weapon and crate of ammo, Bill ran down the stairs and took a position behind one of the concrete mounds, crouching down and opening the case. In it were eight additional magazines, and two large cylindrical devices, with rounded metallic grey caps. They looked about the right size for the large device attached to the underside of the rifle, and Bill took a chance and slid one of the projectiles into the breech.

"Grenade launcher," he muttered, removing the remaining magazines from the box and laying them out on the ground around him. He sat back and waited. Minutes had passed, and he still couldn't hear anything in the silence that hung over the town. Five more minutes passed, and Bill could feel his legs numbing with cramp.

"Where the hell are they?" he said to himself.

"Two miles away, approaching from the East. One vehicle, probably a humvee running silent, and a number of foot soldiers," whispered a voice in Bill's ear. He spun around, muzzle raised, expecting to see Al right behind him. No one was there, and Bill suddenly remembered the radio he had been given. Bill returned to his vigil, frowning.

"How do you know all this?"

"My radio's keyed in to several motion detectors I've placed around the city. Standard Marine procedure when securing a safety zone: Keep it safe, keep it monitored."

"That's how you knew," smiled Bill. "I thought you had some kind of sixth-sense."

"I get it," agreed Al. "Well, as a Marine you have to be alert at all times. But you thought that because I'm black, I had some kind of weird Voodoo mojo going on?"

"That's not what I meant," said Bill, trying to defend his actions.

"Don't shit yourself, Bill, I'm messing with you. Now get ready. Five hundred metres, they've entered the estate. They're going to be here any minute."

Bill shook his head, unable to understand the erratic moods and behaviour of Al. One minute he was up, the next he was down. "Here they come."

The road leading into the car park was suddenly alive as figures rushed for cover behind walls and fences, none making any verbal communication, but Bill could make out a few hand signals flashing between one man and another.

"Three men on the left, two on the right," reported Al, his voice hushed and quiet. "It looks like an additional small group of about six are trying to skim around the outskirts of the battleground, to your right. You're going to have to take them out if I can't reach them."

Bill glanced to his right, but couldn't see anyone moving behind the surrounding houses.

"And there she is. Christ, she's a beauty. No wonder they're attacking in the daylight!"

Bill moved his gaze forwards once more, and saw five men walking in front of a large green vehicle, the machine heavily armoured and sporting even heavier weaponry. The one weapon mounted on the bonnet was a large multiple-barrelled machinegun, and Bill was instantly reminded of the guns mounted on helicopters. That couldn't be a good sign, and neither could the two smaller machineguns mounted on the rear of the vehicle. "Marine Corps classic," relayed Al, giving Bill all the information he needed, and some that he didn't. "The Landmaster series seven, with reinforced tyres and three powerful engines running it. It's got a large cargo capacity, good armour and an excellent selection of weapons. Try your best not to hit it."

"Affirmative," said Bill, shouldering the rifle. "Just tell me when it's time to open fire."

Al's answer came in the form of a short burst of gunfire, bullets tracing along the ground and tearing through one of the men surrounding the vehicle. Although the bullets were close to the vehicle, none hit.

The men approaching the flats screamed and fell behind whatever cover they had, opening fire with their own weapons, shots firing wildly in all directions. A few stray shots hit the barricade Bill hid behind, forcing him to duck behind it and stay low. Without looking he lifted his weapon above the barrier and squeezed the trigger, blindly spraying bullets from left to right. He heard a few screams, but he couldn't be sure if they were from his wild shots or Al's concentrated and well-aimed bursts. Bill ejected the empty magazine and fumbled for a fresh one, slamming it home and blindly spraying the gunfire once more. No screams came this time, but a lot of expletives followed.

Again, the magazine was empty, and Bill ejected it, tossing the empty clip aside.

"That's some random shooting you're doing there," commented Al. "You're doing a good job, they're laying low and presenting a perfect target for me. I can count about seven bodies. Jesus, behind you, there's a group behind you."

Bill looked up from his reloading, and saw a group of four men charging towards him, running in a low crouch and brandishing their shotguns. Bill lifted the rifle, but hadn't yet replaced the magazine. Panicking, he coiled his finger around the secondary trigger on the mounted launcher, and squeezed.

The rifle kicked into his stomach, winding him and buckling over with the sudden pain. The grenade streaked through the air, struck the front-most gang member, and exploded on contact. Although they were far enough from Bill for him to avoid any major injuries from the blast, the wave of heat didn't escape him. As it washed over him, the vision of four men vaporising in a cloud of smoke and flames permanently etched itself into Bill's memory. The sounds of the battle were drowned out by blast of the explosion, and then as his hearing returned, gunfire was still obscured by the maniacal laughter of Al in his ear.

"Out-fucking-standing," he screamed. "Un-fucking-believable! Where'd you get the grenade from?"

Bill didn't reply, he couldn't find the words in him. The shockwave of the explosion had left him temporarily stunned, and it was all he could do to try and shake his head clear. With shaking hands, he replaced the empty magazine and slowly turned around, the muted rattle of gunfire around him still obscured by the swirling blood in his ears. Men charged into the parking lot, but all were cut down by Al's well-aimed bursts. Bill tried to contribute with his own barrage of automatic fire, but his swimming vision made it hard for him to concentrate on any one target.

The large vehicle, which had remained silent for so much of the battle, suddenly opened up with a barrage of gunfire from its various weapons. The men on the mounted machineguns swung their weapons around and tore into the concrete barriers littered around the lot, the large calibre rounds chewing through the material and turning them to rubble.

"Get the fuck out of there, Bill," screamed the Marine over the radio. "Those heavy guns are obliterating the barriers."

Bill had already decided to move, and was stumbling across the parking lot to the flats even as Al spoke. Bullets whizzed past him, some destroying the ground around him, others narrowly missing him. His own momentum, mixed with his dazed senses, created erratic movements that made for a hard target. He crashed into the door of one of the lower flats, the wooden barrier giving way beneath his weight. Sliding across the ground, Bill flipped on to his back and pointed his assault rifle at the door, cursing at the fact he'd left the rest of his ammunition outside. He dropped the rifle and pulled his shotgun clear from his webbing, levelling the muzzle at the doorway and waiting for the gang to advance on his positions. Outside, the sounds of battle died. Gunfire slowly rattled to a halt, screams of the wounded gurgled and died, and the droning thunder of the humvee's engine cut out.

Silence.

Bill clambered to his feet and stumbled to the doorway, shotgun in one hand and assault rifle in the other. He slowly poked his head around the corner: thick clouds of smoke slowly settled over the killing grounds, a heady and acrid scent lacing the air.

"Don't you just love the smell of cordite in the morning?" shouted Al, grinning from ear to ear as he jumped down from the humvee. He was covered in dark red blood, and carried a shining curved knife, its blade coated in the same thick liquid. Al wiped off the blade on one of the lapels of the dead bodies, then slipped it back into his holster. "I had to finish the rest of them off by hand, I didn't want to damage the machine. We did it. I count about twenty, give or take a couple. Still, the hummer is ours for the taking. Now, lets get that son of a bitch loaded up and move out."

Bill lowered his weapons and shook his head, watching as Al heaved the bodies out the vehicle and dragged them into a pile, away from the vehicle. "So what's the plan?" asked Bill, still feeling the effects of the grenade and leaning against a bullet-riddled wall.

"Pack my shit up, head south. Maybe I can reach further afield than some bastard speaking a foreign language. Try and convince them that we're okay, that the plague isn't airborne. Maybe try and arrange an evac…"

"Do you really think that someone will come and rescue us?" asked Bill. He couldn't hide the disbelief in his voice. "After everything you've said?"

"I'd rather be rescued and court-martialled for killing an officer than spend the rest of my days on this friggin' island," muttered Al. "The plan remains the same, we head south. You going to give me a hand with my stuff?"

"Two minutes," begged Bill, holding up his hand. "I'm still recovering from that blast."

"Brilliant," said Al, clambering up on to the bonnet of the machine and pointing to the smoking black mark out in the car park. "That was a brilliant move. Totally unexpected, I didn't think you'd be able to handle a grenade launcher like that."

"I wish I hadn't," smirked Bill, rubbing his temples. "Feels like I'm hung over."

"That was awesome. I haven't seen something like that since… shit, probably Brazil. Ping was big on grenades, always using them whenever he could. That kid wasn't afraid of getting his hands dirty, either. You remind me of him."

Al slid off the bonnet and strolled into the field of bodies, pulling the magnum from his holster and slowly turning from side to side, aiming at the dead bodies. Bill shrugged, and drew his own Beretta and slowly followed him.

"You've been here since the start of the plague, right?" asked Al. Bill nodded slightly. "So you've lost everyone you knew. Did you ever watch someone close to you turn?"

Bill shook his head. "I watched my girlfriend die naturally of the plague, that was enough. Then I was put into quarantine for a fortnight. By the time I got out, the country was like this."

"Jenny, right? You kept muttering her name in your sleep. If you'd sat and watched her die, then rise from the dead, would you have been able to kill her?"

Bill looked at his feet and shook his head. He knew what Al was getting at. He knew that was the reason the Rot had been chained up. One of his squad had been bitten, then turned, and he couldn't bring himself to shoot him. Bill closed his eyes, finally understanding the Marine's motives, and why he had been so angry when he'd put an end to the Rot's existence. He felt a large hand grip his shoulder, and he tensed, instantly thinking it was going to be the conclusion to the rooftop battle. He held his pistol, and he knew Al carried his own weapon. Was it going to be a shootout to decide the winner?

"Thanks," Al said, quietly. "You helped me out here, and you took care of my friend. You did good, Bill. You did real good. Kid."

Bill smiled warmly. He didn't reply, just nodded his head.

The silence between the two men was suddenly broken by the ear-shattering explosion of the magnum Al held. For a split second, Bill thought he had been shot, and he spun on his heels, bringing up his pistol to fire before the pain of the wound disabled him.

He saw Al, his weapon smoking and pointing down towards the headless corpse oozing blood at his feet. Al grinned, then looked towards Bill. "Bastard was just wounded, trying to crawl to his gun. Come on, we'd better start loading up. I want to get out of here before nightfall."

III

"Almost loaded up," said Al as he pushed the final crate into the rear of the humvee and forced the door shut. "We just need to strap that bike of yours on, and we're ready to go."

"Do we really need all this shit," asked Bill as he reloaded one of the rear-mounted machineguns, following Al's instructions to the letter. He cocked it, then spun it slowly on the mount, making sure it was ready to fire.

"It's better that we take everything and not need it, then need something and not have it," Al grinned as he tightened the ropes that secured the barrels of fuel to the roof. "Anyway, if we take the bike, we can either use it for spare parts, or maybe get it fixed up. It's all useful crap. Now, are you going to get in *The Colebrook*, or not?"

Bill paused and looked curiously at his companion. "The Colebrook?" he asked. Al nodded, and drew his magnum from the holster, slamming it carelessly on to the bonnet of the vehicle.

"See this," he said, pointing to the weapon. "This is the Colebrook Cannon. It's my gun, so I named it. It's my good luck charm, and it's saved my ass on numerous occasions. That," he continued, pointing to the vehicle, "That is my new vehicle, so I name it. *The Colebrook*, named after me."

Replacing the weapon on his belt and with the final preparations complete, Al admired his handiwork and nodded approvingly. By working together and sacrificing most of the space normally reserved for additional personnel, Al and Bill had managed to pack away nearly all of the contents of the stolen armoury. The Marine had also convinced Bill to swap some of his weapons for the more durable armed forces versions. The rifle had been the first to go, Al cursing the poor construction and damaged scope and dubbing it as the worst weapon he'd ever had the misfortune to handle. He'd taken great pleasure in dismantling it using a hatchet and part of a brick wall. "What we can't take, we destroy so any survivors can't use it against us," he'd explained.

He'd also persuaded Bill to swap his Benelli for a large robust shotgun, heavy and made from sturdy plastic and metal. "SPAS-12," he'd said, explaining the functions of the weapon. "Semi-automatic, you only need to work the slide if it's jammed. It's solid, it's heavy, and it can split a zombie's head open with a single shot if you've got a good eye. Good as a battering device, too."

As the sun started to sink in the western sky, the pair climbed aboard the fully laden vehicle and sat in the front seats, the engine grumbling to life as Al gunned the accelerator. He gripped the steering wheel, then paused and looked at Bill.

"Where to?"

"I thought the plan was to go south!"

"I'm new to these parts," said Al, "What *is* south?"

"A lot of fields. Couple of small villages. Further beyond, there's some larger places like Leeds, Manchester, then London. "

"Fields, eh?" muttered Al, taking a sip from his hipflask and offering it to Bill once more. "Fields must mean farms. Perfect for moonshine, which is a good thing, because I'm almost out of whiskey. Lets go, kid."

"What about all the beer you got?"

"You fucking deaf, or just stupid? I said I'm almost out of whiskey. Beer is for a pleasant buzz, whiskey is for total annihilation."

"It's going to be dark soon," noted Bill, ignoring Al's comments and looking towards the sky. "Won't we be safer if we wait until the morning? The Rots don't seem to have any problem hunting in the dark, they have an advantage over us."

"Here," the Marine said, throwing a pair of cumbersome goggles into Bill's lap. He took another sip from the flask, the tutted and cast the empty container over his shoulder. "Night vision goggles. Expensive little things, I pried them off a couple of dead rebels. They're more useful than the thermo-optic goggles they equip us with, the dead don't give off heat. I discovered that the hard way, friggin' dead bastards."

Bill smirked and pulled the goggles on, but before he could power them up Al yanked them off. "Don't waste the batteries," he warned. "The little bastards suck power like a two-dollar whore, and a recharge is hard to find, at least in this place. Hopefully we'll find some areas in Britain that have power left, or maybe a portable generator. Now, let's drive before Moloch and his remaining boys decide to pay us one last visit."

With a wide grin on his face, Al knocked the vehicle into gear and rolled out of the conclave.

The black of night enveloped the fields around the village of Little Slumberton, light provided by the pinpricks of the stars in the clouded sky. An eerie orange glow deep in the heart of the distant settlement told the tale of a fire raging out of control, slowly eating away at the buildings.

Bill stood beside Al, looking at the unfolded map on the bonnet and casting nervous glances over each shoulder every five seconds. Al had parked the machine in the middle of a field of corn, the crop almost five feet tall.

"So this is the village," whispered Al, his dark finger pointing to a collection of buildings surrounded by fields. "The closest farm is over here," he continued, tracing a road from the village to an even smaller collection of about three buildings, with the label of 'Green's Farm'. "That's where we head, as soon as the sun rises."

"What?" asked Bill, absentmindedly. He turned, looked at the map, then nodded and muttered an affirmative.

"For fucks sake," Al growled, climbing back into the humvee and gently closing the door. 'We're parked up in a field for a reason. It's all dried up, so anyone or anything approaching us is going to make a lot of noise. Now, get up on the back, take watch, and wake me up in four hours."

Bill clambered up on to the back of the vehicle and grabbed the controls of one of the machineguns, sitting on the roof of the vehicle and staring vacantly out into the surrounding darkness. He grabbed the goggles dangling from his webbing and slipped them on, flicking the power switch and smiling grimly as pitch black slowly melted into muted tones of green and grey. Corn wavered and swayed in the breeze, the gentle bobbing of the crops the only movement that could be seen for miles in all directions. Bill sighed, listening to the sounds of the bulky Marine snoring in the vehicle, and tapped the goggles. They also displayed the time in the lower left corner of his vision, and although he didn't really think it was half past seven in the morning, he figured it was going to give him a good measure of time to go by.

"Roll on half eleven," he murmured, resting his chin in his hands and sighing heavily. "Jesus, these things really strain your eyes…"

The heavy pounding of the rear-mounted machineguns startled Bill to life. He grabbed his combat shotgun and fell out the interior of the humvee. He leapt to his feet and brought his weapon up to shoulder height.

"Where are they, Al?" slurred Bill, sleep lingering in his mind and clouding his thoughts with a thick blanket of fog.

"Nowhere," grinned the Marine, looking down from his mount atop the vehicle. "I was bored, thought I'd do something to keep me busy. But, since you're up…"

"I've only had two hours sleep, you bastard!" shouted Bill, throwing his weapon back into the vehicle and glaring at the digital chronometer on the dashboard.

"Two hours?" laughed Al, locking off the machinegun so it remained fixed during transit. "Don't you remember me waking you up last night? You fell asleep on the watch, wasting battery power for those goggles. I tried to chew you out about it, but you told me to fuck off and crawled into *The Colebrook*. I figured I would wait until the morning to give you some shit about it."

"Well, do it on the move. C'mon, we're already behind your schedule. We'll have to make tracks if we want to get to this farm of yours. I doubt there'll be any moonshine, you're not in America now."

"We'll see," smiled Al, clambering into the driving seat and turning the engine over. "We'll see."

With a sickening lurch, the vehicle trundled through the field, flattening the crop before it and crushing it beneath its large tyres. The field gave way to a single lane country road, barely wide enough for the vehicle to travel down without its wheels slipping into a ditch or catching on a rock.

Al didn't pay as much attention to the road as he should have, concentrating more on the map on his lap. Despite this fact, he wasn't as surprised as Bill was when the vehicle ploughed through a group of six Rots. The vehicle bucked and swayed as it made quick work of the walking corpses and carried on as if nothing had happened.

The road ended at a large wooden gate at the foot of a large grassy hill. Gunning the engine on, the humvee burst through the barrier and slowly crawled up the steep incline, tyres digging into the damp earth and slipping every so often, even with four-wheel drive. Finally, the vehicle crowned the hill, and Al stopped the vehicle and climbed out. He pulled out a sheet of metal from behind his seat, followed by an aerosol of red paint, and slammed his homemade stencil against his open door.

"How many of those rotten bastards did I hit?" he asked, watching as Bill climbed out his own door. He shrugged. "Six, I think."

Al nodded, then sprayed six of the stencils on his door and slammed it shut. Grabbing his weapons and standing beside Bill, he looked down into the grassy valley and nodded, scratching his beard. "Green's Farm. Think anyone'll be home?" Bill shrugged his shoulders, and watched as Al lifted a pair of binoculars to his eyes. He swept his vision from left to right, then passed them down to Bill so he could have a look.

From this distance there didn't seem to be anything untoward with the farm.

It was comprised of three buildings; one a barn constructed of plates of corrugated metal, one a small wooden shack, and the third a large, single-level house made from bricks and wood. None showed any sign of fighting or struggle, and the land around the building seemed to be free of blood. A winding road leading up to the house from their current position seemed to be lined by piles of blackened ash, and one small area of ground behind the house seemed to be littered with small wooden sticks erected in the uneven ground.

"Shall we take a look?" asked Al, resuming his position behind the steering wheel. Bill nodded and went to climb back in, but the Marine pointed to the machineguns on the back. "Why don't you stay up top and keep an eye out for anything that doesn't look right. And try and stay awake this time, you lazy bastard."

Bill climbed up on to the back, sighing as he went, and grabbed one of the weapons, strapping himself into the safety harness just as Al powered down the hill. Bill closed his eyes as the wind whipped in his face, and felt his stomach sway and clench with each seemingly out-of-control movement from the cackling driver.

At least someone had some fun, he thought as the vehicle bounced off the hill and powered along the bumpy surface towards the building, screeching to a halt in front of the metal barn. Bill jumped down from the rear platform and grabbed his shotgun, sweeping the muzzle from left to right and waiting for Al to emerge from the cabin of the humvee.

"You can almost hear the banjos as I speak," he grinned, slamming the door shut and nursing a double-barrelled shotgun. He cracked it open and pushed two blue-cased shells into the breech, then snapped it shut.

"Banjos?" asked Bill.

"Yeah, you know, banjos," said Al, holding his shotgun and imitating the movements of plucking strings. "Inbred country yokels, moonshine distilleries, livestock abuse…"

"You Yanks are very strange," Bill grinned, shaking his head in mirth. "I think you'll find the farmers here are just like normal people."

Al snorted, then glanced from one building to another. "Where do you want to start?"

"I'll check out the house, if that's okay with you?"

"Go for it," muttered Al, motioning to the building of Bill's choice. "I'll start with the barn. Meet back out here in ten minutes. If anything happens, or if you need a hand, you've got your headset, keep it live."

Bill nodded, and made his way towards the front door of the building, pressing on it lightly. The hinges of the wooden barrier squeaked slightly, then gently swung inwards into the uninviting gloom within.

"I want to look in the barn instead," he whispered, fumbling for the flashlight dangling from his belt and flicking the power switch. The white light cut through the darkness of the interior, picking out a few details and casting menacing shadows on the walls and floor. With a final glance over his shoulder, and a mock salute to his companion, he took a deep breath and stepped into the building.

IX
BODY HARVEST

"The media's portrayal of the way we handle each new outbreak only helps sensationalise the whole situation."

I

Upon crossing the threshold of the farmhouse, Bill found himself in a long hallway lined with three doors: one halfway along the corridor on the right side, the second directly opposite it, and the third at the far end. A pale green floral wallpaper had been used to cover the walls, and surprisingly enough it hadn't been splashed with blood or punctured by bullet holes. He tried the door on the right first, pulling it open and shining the beam around the contents of the small cupboard he had found. Large green Wellington boots lay on their side on the ground, while a thick green wax jacket hung from the rail. A long wooden shepherd's crook had been propped against the wall, with a cloth cap hanging on the hook of the stick. Closing the door on the farmer's clothing, Bill spun around and tried the second door opposite the cupboard.

This opened up on a kitchen, dark and gloomy, the windows covered by thick heavy sheets to blot out the sun. Stepping into the room, Bill slowly swept the flashlight and the muzzle of his weapon around from left to right, drinking in the details of the room. Glass-fronted cupboards above the large ceramic sink were filled with dishes and plates, while the drawers beneath them were filled with silver eating utensils. A dining table stood against one wall, with three chairs surrounding the heavy wooden structure. Bill stood in the centre of the room and lowered his shotgun, letting it hang from his webbing and putting one hand out to lean casually against the bench. He swore and spat in agony as his palm came into contact with the scalding hot burner of the gas cooker, and he backed away, thrusting his hand into the sink and the three inches of lukewarm water left in the bottom. Cupping his hand and pulling out some of the water, he threw the liquid on the stove, watching as it hissed and spat upon contact with the hot surface.

"Christ, Al," whispered Bill, clicking his radio twice to get the attention of the Marine. "There's someone living here. Stove's hot, it must have been used recently."

"I know," replied Al, his voice as low as Bill's. "There's a petrol generator out here, it's not running at the minute, but it's warm, too. Whoever lives here must've seen us coming and went into hiding, turning everything off before they went."

"You think they're just hiding, or do you think they've ran off?"

"We're going to have to assume they're still here," Al said. "Carry on sweeping through the house, I'll come and join you when this barn Is secure."

The radio went dead, and Bill nodded silently to himself, confirming his actions. Carefully lifting his shotgun with his red and tender hand, he returned to the entry passage and made his way to the final door, pushing it open and finding himself in a large living room. A settee and three armchairs were arranged in a semicircle around an oval oak coffee table, each seat pointing roughly towards the metallic television set pressed against the wall. With the rustic appearance of the building and the furnishings within, the modern television set seemed almost alien, as if it didn't belong. Bill stepped forwards and looked at the china plate on the table, at the mouth-watering meal that had been freshly prepared by whoever lived here. He had the urge to help himself, even if it were just for a taste, but visions of a mousetrap sprang into his head: a form of instant death which lures its prey to their doom with promise of a free meal.

The living room also had a large wooden staircase leading up to a landing. Puzzled by this architectural anomaly, remembering that the building was only a single-floor structure from the outside, Bill cautiously made his way over to them and looked back at the room he had ran across. The room had no other doors to it, and the windows had been boarded up from the inside. Lightly placing his foot on the first step, he slowly made his way up the stairs, intrigued as to what he'd find.

It was a second floor he found himself looking at, but not a conventional one that most other houses had. The loft space of the house had been constructed and renovated in such a way that it housed two bedrooms and a bathroom, the latter of which Bill could see from the landing, the door left wide open. He cautiously made his way towards the first bedroom, gently nudging the door open and peering in. A skylight flooded the room with natural light, a pleasing alternative to the dimming torch that he held. Flicking the device off, he stepped into the room and looked around.

Pale purple wallpaper, mostly covered with posters and pictures of various animals and musicians, lined the walls, while a single bed lay to the right of him, a large collection of soft toys covering the pillow. A dresser directly beneath the skylight held an unusual amount of glass bottles and makeup, some of which he was familiar with through Jenny, others were completely alien to him.

Leaving the bedroom, he headed towards the second bedroom, tried the handle, and pushed it open, finding himself…

…In an empty room. The walls had been stripped and the furniture and carpet removed. Puzzled, Bill scratched his head and returned to the landing, idly making his way towards the bathroom. It looked as if whoever was living here had flown the coop before he and Al had arrived, unless they were hiding in the bathroom. Which wasn't a very clever place to hide, it being a dead end. Still, he had to check, if only to keep Al off his back.

Strolling along the corridor towards the bathroom, his mind not quite focused on the task ahead, his feet stumbled through a thin wire stretched across the ground at ankle level. Bill felt the resistance of the metal string before it snapped, and looked down in time to see a small device fastened to the wall, a red light blinking rapidly.

Although Bill wasn't up to scratch with proximity mines and tripwires, he had seen enough movies to know that obscure devices attached to the wall with flashing red lights never meant anything good. He spun on his heels and launched into a sprint seconds before the corridor behind him erupted into a blossom of fire and thick smoke.

Al finished his study of the generator and turned around to survey the rest of the equipment piled into the barn. Most of it seemed to be an eclectic mix of farming equipment: scythes, sickles, and spades mixed with more industrial machinery such as combine harvesters and tractors. The heavy vehicles didn't seem in too bad a condition, either, especially in comparison to other vehicles he had passed on his journey.

Around the lower floor of the barn were huge mounds of hay, some covered with white canvas sheets, others simply tied down with lengths of rope. He was about to ascend the wooden ladder to the second level when the ground shook around him with a deafening explosion.

"What the fuck is that?" he shouted, all thoughts of further exploration were put aside in his mind as he leapt from the ladder and scuttled out the building, clinging to his shotgun and bursting through the front door of the house, finding himself in an entry hallway. He slapped the first door open, found a storage cupboard, then opened the second behind him with a powerful back kick, knocking the door from one of its hinges. He looked briefly around the kitchen, then pulled back out the room and charged into the final door, his shoulder making contact with the door tearing it clean off the frame. Rolling to a stop and bringing his weapon up, levelling the shotgun against his shoulder and bracing for fire, he looked to his left and saw Bill lying motionless on the ground, parts of his clothing charred and smoking.

"Christ, kid, are you okay?"

Bill moaned incoherently, but managed to lift his hand and make a weak gesture of thumbs-up, then pointed towards the top of the stairs and the shattered banister he had been flung through.

Nodding in understanding, Al gripped his shotgun and carefully made his way up the stairs, poking his head above the final step and scanning the environment.

Plumes of light grey smoke rolled across the ceiling, and the familiar smell of plastic explosives tickled his nostrils, giving him a rough idea of what had happened. Bill had set an ambush off, that much he was sure of, but he couldn't see where, and he didn't want to just dive into the smoke and hope for the best.

He unclipped one of the goggles dangling from his belt and slipped them on, powering up the device and watching as the world exploded into a myriad of thermal colouring. Shifting clouds of blue and purple gave way before him as he ventured into the smoke, and he could make out an orange and red doorway before him, the heated remains of a line of C4 that had been moulded around the corridor. Beyond it, there seemed to be another room, devoid of any heat signatures as if it had been padded out with insulation material to absorb the heat and the shockwave of the explosive. Ripping the goggles from his face, he lifted his weapon, charged through the clouds, and into the bathroom, rolling in low and spinning left first, then right, the muzzle of his shotgun finding empty air on both accounts. Al stayed low, listening carefully to the near-silence that hung in the air and holding his breath. He could hear his own heart drumming in his chest, but above that, he could hear the weak moans of his friend lying on the ground outside, and a slight rasping sound, similar to breathing.

"Shit!"

Before he could look up and see the figure sitting in the rafters above him, it leapt on him. Although it wasn't particularly heavy – Al would be able to bench-press at least twice as much without breaking a sweat – the surprise of the sudden weight was enough to make him topple to the ground, the grip on his weapon releasing and sending it crashing into the bath beside him. He was already going for the knife holstered in the sheath on his belt, ready for a melee encounter, but was surprised when the person leapt up and ran from him, making tracks for the landing and stairs.

Retrieving his shotgun and clambering to his knees, Al lurched forwards and trained the weapon on the woman's back. It was definitely female, as the first thing that registered in Al's mind was *nice ass*, followed by *Shame I have to kill you*.

His finger ready to coil around the trigger, he almost fired until he watched her vault over what remained of the banister, landing on the ground with a gentle thump. Al, not wanting his target to escape, followed in close pursuit, approaching the balcony and intending to jump the same way his prey had.

By the time he had reached the landing that looked down on to the living room, it suddenly occurred to him that it was higher up that he had thought, and that maybe jumping wasn't such a good idea. But even if he tried to stop, the momentum would keep him going over the edge. Trusting his body to the pull of gravity, he launched himself from the hole that Bill's body had made, and hoped for the best.

He sailed through the air with the grace of a cement block, and landed with just as much elegance, touching down on one of the armchairs. The wooden frame buckled and cracked beneath his weight, then tipped forwards, carrying Al forwards into a roll. He tucked his shoulders in tight, rolling with the appalling landing and ignoring the pain that shot through his right calf, then raised his shotgun and unleashed both barrels into the back of the fleeing woman.

"Got you, bitch," he said, wheezing heavily and pulling out a home-rolled cigarette. He lit it, smiling as his tired body accepted the nicotine rush, then cracked open the weapon, replacing the spent shells with two fresh ones. "I got you, you crazy fuckin' bitch!"

He looked to his side and saw Bill slowly crawl on to his stomach. His movements were slow and looked painful: it was obvious to Al that he'd been close enough to the explosion when it went off to be knocked senseless, and probably winded him. Which also meant that if he was that close to the explosion, then he'd been thrown quite a distance.

"Are you okay, kid?" he asked, repeating his previous question. Bill slowly nodded his head, then stumbled to his feet, clinging to the wall for support. With a grin, Al slung the muzzle of his weapon over one shoulder, gripping the stock, and wrapped his arm around Bill, pulling him from the wall and heading towards the front door.

"Let's get you some fresh air," he said, skirting the body lying on the floor. He stopped, staring at her. Had the corpse moved when he'd neared it?

"Some kind of super-zombie," he muttered, lowering his weapon and firing a single shell into the small of her back. She moaned in pain and tried to move, fingers slowly working and trying to pull herself away. Bemused, Al cracked open the weapon once more and glared at the remaining shell that hadn't been fired.

"Fuckin' J-Man," cursed Al, dropping the shell and grabbing his magnum from his holster, levelling his aim with the base of the undead woman's skull. He'd held on to the shells he'd retrieved from J-Man at the crash site, but had never had the need to use a shotgun before now. He'd always thought that J-Man had been creating the ultimate shotgun shell, but it turned out that some of them, or at least the blue cased ones, were the homemade alternative to a safety bullet used for crowd control exercises. He was about to fire his handgun, when Bill jerked to life and lashed out with his hand, knocking the pistol high and to the side. The round smashed harmlessly into the wooden floorboards, inches from the woman's head.

"Jesus, Al," choked Bill, pushing away from the Marine and sinking to the floor beside the woman. "She's alive! Hold your fire, she's alive!"

"Alive or dead," shouted Al, grabbing Bill and pulling him to his feet with one hand, "The bitch tried to blow you up, got the drop on me, and now you made me waste a round! It's not easy to come across shit for this weapon, you know, especially not in this ass-backward country."

Al levelled off the magnum once more and smiled.

The crazy son of a bitch is going to kill her in cold blood! Bill managed to piece some of the random and incoherent thoughts that swirled around in his confused brain, the fact that he'd just been almost blown up not fully registering in the swirling vortex of thoughts in his mind. The image of Al towering over the body of the woman and levelling his pistol with her head slowly came into focus, and drawing all the strength he could muster from his battered body, Bill stumbled forwards, tackling Al by wrapping his arms around his waist and pushing him to the ground. Bill's senses were still foggy at best and his muscles ached with every movement, and he shook his head, trying to dislodge the concussive blast that hung over him.

"We can't kill her, not like this."

"Why not?" hissed Al, pushing Bill off him and standing up, retrieving his shotgun and replacing the blue shell with a pair of standard red ones.

"Because… because," stammered Bill, trying to wade through the jumble of thoughts that were swimming through his mind.

"That's not a good enough reason," snapped Al, "An eye for an eye, a tooth for a tooth. She tried to kill us, why don't we kill her?"

"You mean execute her," spat Bill, finding a bloodied tooth and pulling it from his mouth. He tried to focus on Al, then tried to put a stern expression on his face. Whether he succeeded in any of these tasks he didn't know, but he liked to think that he had. "Don't the Marines have a code, guidelines to follow regarding prisoners? I'm sure they don't advocate cold-blooded killing."

"What do you know about the Marines," snapped Al. He was hostile and riled up, but he holstered his weapon as he spoke. Pulling out some nylon cable ties and strapping the woman's arms up behind her back, he picked her up and propped her against the wall. "Fine, how's this? You got a prisoner. I hope you're pleased with her. Now, you deal with this little whore as you see fit. I'm going to secure the rest of the farm, see if there's any more rebels around here. We've wasted enough time here, we're going to have to secure the area and settle in for the night."

Al grabbed his weapons and stormed out the hallway, slamming the door behind him. Bill could hear him muttering and cursing to himself as he stalked away from the farmhouse. Taking a few minutes to gather his senses, Bill leaned against the wall opposite the woman, resting his hand on the butt of his pistol and breathing heavily. His vision slowly started to refocus, and as it did so he could make out more of the woman's features.

She was smaller than Bill by about half a foot, and wore a thick denim jacket and heavy blue combat trousers, the pockets bulging with clanking metal objects. A thick scarf had been wrapped around her head; no doubt to protect her from the heat of the explosion, while a pair of dark glasses hid her eyes. The two stared at one another for a few minutes, until Bill had regained enough of his senses and strength to clamber unaided to his feet. He looked down on her, then reached out and helped her to her feet, leading her back into the living room. She didn't put up much of a fight, but all the time she seemed to be working against the bonds on her wrists. Bill motioned towards the sofa, inviting the woman to sit, but instead she stood in defiance. Bill shrugged, then skirted his way around the ruined armchair, settling into one of the intact seats and sighing. The woman stood silently, the emotionless gaze of the glasses somewhat disturbing, reminding Bill of something from his past.

Soldiers at the incinerator plant. The people who killed Jenny…

"Do you mind if I take your glasses off?" he asked as he stood and reached out towards the woman. She flinched and shuffled back to avoid the contact, tripping and slamming herself down into the seat behind her. She was obviously terrified of Bill, unsure of his motives or intentions. Bill tried his best to reassure her that he didn't want to hurt her. The only time he could remember trying to do anything like that had been with dogs. Drawing a blank on any other movement he could do to display his true intentions, he showed his opened hands and edged closer, slowly reaching out and teasing the glasses away.

"It's okay," he said, his voice soft and low. "I'm not going to hurt you."

With the glasses removed, the woman started to shake her head violently from side to side, the scarf starting to come away. Bill took it as red that she wanted to remove that, too, so he also grabbed that and started to unwind it. The protection removed, Bill returned to his seat and studied the woman from the comfort of the armchair.

Piercing green eyes studied him back, eyelids half closed and brow furrowed. Her skin was a milky-white in colour, and she licked her pale lips. Her auburn hair had been tied back in a ponytail, with a few loose hairs above her forehead forming an untidy fringe. Bill smiled a little at the young lady, but she didn't return the favour. Although she was scowling, Bill could tell she was good looking, he couldn't deny that, but even the slightest thought relating to how attractive she was instantly summoned an image of Jenny, suffering on her death bed, the sounds of her gurgling blood-filled lungs.

"There," he said, dropping the scarf to the to ground and shaking the image of his dead lover from his mind. "Is that better?"

The woman didn't respond, simply stared coldly at him. She snapped her head to the left as Al stumbled into the room, an assault rifle in one hand and a wooden crate in the other. "I've secured *The Colebrook* in the barn, out near the petrol generator. Now, I'm going to clean this here rifle, and drink some alcohol. Where's the bedrooms?"

"Upstairs," Bill said, waving towards the staircase and the broken banister. "There's two of them, but only one has furniture. The other's been stripped bare."

Al nodded, then trudged up the stairs, his dark eyes fixed on the woman on the sofa. She, in turn, returned the cold gaze. "Just a fucking child, anyway," he muttered, then announced as he reached the landing "I'll take the bedroom, hold up there for the night. It should have a good view of the road leading up to here. You, keep an eye on her. If I wake up in the middle of the night and find that little whore trying to gut me with a knife, I'll kill her, then I'll kill you, if you're not already dead."

He turned and vanished from Bill's vision, his disappearance shortly followed by the slam of a door. The woman's eyes remained fixed on the landing for a few seconds, then she turned to look at Bill. He shrugged by way of an apology, then rummaged through his rucksack, pulling out one of the capsules containing his vitamin tablets and swallowed one. He offered one to the woman, but she simply closed her eyes and lowered her face. He replaced the tablets, then fished out an aluminium drinks can, breaking the ring pull open and setting the opened drink on the table. He motioned to it, offering a drink, but his prisoner simply shook her head.

"If he messes with any of my things I'll skin the bastard alive," she muttered under her breath. Bill looked at her, startled, but her emotionless expression had not altered. Had he imagined it?

"Do you want anything to drink? Anything at all?"

The woman simply snorted a negative response, keeping her head lowered

"Something to eat, maybe?"

"I made something just before you got here," she whispered in a low voice. Bill grimaced at the memory of the cooker hob, unfurling his fist and looked at the red and angry flesh on his palm. "Yeah, I know," he muttered in response. "Well, is there anything I can get for you?"

"You can get me out of these handcuffs," she said, raising her voice and keeping her tone harsh, but failing to hide the hope in her words. She lifted her cold gaze and fixed her stare on Bill. He shrugged again.

"I would do, but I fear for my personal safety. Not from you, but from him. He's a little unbalanced," Bill grinned, jerking a thumb towards the ceiling. The cold and hard stare of the woman finally cracked slightly, the edges of her lips lifting into a slight smile. "It's okay, his bark's worse than his bite."

She stifled a chuckle, struggling to maintain her composure. "So what *is* his problem?" she asked. She finally spoke in her normal voice, a soft and gentle tone that Bill found easy to listen to.

"He's a Marine," Bill answered. The woman nodded knowingly, and Bill felt like he didn't need to explain any further.

"What about you?" she asked. "Are you one of his squad?"

Bill laughed softly, shook his head. "I'm no Marine. I like to think I'm different to those gung-ho types," he confessed. The women smiled and nodded a little. "I think you are."

"He's too fucking soft," shouted Al, his voice carrying down from the upper floor. "Now shut up, I need to concentrate on this!" Bill twisted his face slightly, turning around to glare at the top of the staircase, then returned his attention to the woman.

"He's been through a lot of shit," said Bill, leaning closer and speaking in a more subdued tone. "He lost his squad. He hasn't told me all the details, but I know at least one of them turned into a Rot."

"A what?"

"A fucking zombie, you dumb bitch," shouted Al. Bill coughed, then cleared his throat and spoke in a lower tone. "I had to kill it; he couldn't finish the job. Which I guess is understandable, it's hard to kill someone you're close to."

"Like your parents," muttered the woman. Bill shrugged his shoulders.

"I don't know, I never knew my parents, I lost them at an early age…" Bill said, his voice trailing off as he realised she was referring to her own parents. He swallowed hard, realising he'd lodged his metaphorical foot in his mouth, and found himself lost for words.

"Is this your farm?" he finally asked, breaking the silence. The woman nodded.

"My parents were given this farm by my grandparents almost thirty years ago. It's been in our family for generations. When the plague first came, my Dad had said we'd be okay out here. He said we were far enough from the village or any major town to ensure that we wouldn't catch it. He told all the people who came in to work for us to take a break. All the sheep had been sheared, and we weren't due to start harvesting for a couple of months, so there wasn't really a lot of work to do. Dad had always said it was just going to last a few weeks. He kept me back from college, but he'd promised it was only going to be until the contagion cleared up."

The woman stopped for a moment, clearing her throat as her voice cracked. She tried to reach out and grab the can on the table, forgetting that her restraints prevented any movement. She sighed, and Bill grabbed the knife hanging from his belt, making a move to sever the cuffs. The woman recoiled, a look of terror in her eyes as she saw the light glint on the silver blade. Bill smiled slightly and lowered the weapon, grabbing the nylon tags and pressing the blade to them.

"Don't tell him I did this," he whispered as the plastic snapped. He returned to his seat, looking at the bewildered look on her face. Had it been possible that she assumed he had something else on his mind? Shaking slightly, but keeping her eyes fixed on Bill, she reached forwards and broke open the drink, taking a sip and clearing her throat. She spoke again, her voice still shaky.

"When the riots started, my Dad started to try and prepare us. We brought together all the livestock so they surrounded the house, gathered his shotguns and the shells he had for them, then sat in here, trying to get the television or radio working so he could check for any news relating to the outbreak. Or the riots.

"It was surreal," she remembered, thinking back to the days locked up in the farmhouse, a glazed look in her eyes. "Dad would sit here, one shotgun being cleaned and checked while the other was loaded and sitting by the door. My Mam just went about things as if they were normal, as if riots threatening the local community were just an everyday event. She still made our meals, did the washing. The only thing that was different was she'd hang the washing out around the back with a shotgun resting on the clothes. And me, I'd sit beside my Dad, reading my notes for my course. I was studying to be a veterinary surgeon, you see."

Bill nodded, listening to the story. It was far more detailed than any information that had been offered by Al. He'd been happier to gloss over his whole ordeal.

"What information that *did* come through on the radio before everything went off was mainly about the riots, and how the Marines couldn't cope. By the time we started to hear about the walking dead, about how they seemed to home in on living people, no one knew what to believe We were told we should gather at ports or power stations, apparently the Marines were to arrange the pickups for survivors before we were completely overrun. Mam and Dad said we'd just sit it out."

"Fucking bastards," muttered Bill. He looked at the woman, then shook his head, raising his hands in mock surrender. "Sorry, not your parents. I was told by someone I knew that the Marines had been planning to target power stations, air and seaports with bombing runs in order to reduce any survivors chances of… well, surviving. Sorry, go on."

The woman smiled courteously, then continued.

"Anyway, my Dad decided we'd have to get rid of our animals. They said that the living attracted the dead, so he thought that the more living things there were, the more chance the dead would find us. That's why the cities were so dangerous, or at least that's what the radio said. Like a beacon, Dad had said. So we took all our animals and killed them, burned all their bodies."

She paused, wiping her eyes with her sleeve.

"It was hard to kill them. I've always loved animals; that's what made me want to be a vet. It was the same day that one of them stumbled into the farm; I guess the smell of the cooking meat attracted it. We didn't see it until it was right at our door. It didn't even try to open the door, just stood outside, waiting, motionless. As soon as my Mam opened the door, the creature was on her. Took a chunk of skin, right out of here," she said, circling the lower part of her thin and pale neck with her index finger. She drained the rest of her can and dropped it to the floor. Her eyes were glazing over again, but this time they started to weep tears.

"Like everyone who ever knew someone infected, we thought she'd pull through if we washed out the wound, looked after her. We kept her in bed, looked after her. The quality of the meals degraded, I'm not a brilliant cook. But that didn't matter, when she stopped eating she just kind of faded away, she just wasn't herself. Then one day, I heard her moving around, after days being laid up in bed, and thought she might actually be pulling herself around. She wasn't, though, she… she bit my Dad. I knew straightaway that what had happened to my Mam was going to happen to him. I locked them up in separate bedrooms, and ran to get my Dad's shotgun.

"I couldn't do it, though, not straight away. How could you shoot someone who raised you? Who you love? It seemed like only yesterday my Dad carried me on his shoulders across the south field, or I helped my Mam in making jam with the bruised berries from our crop. It was easier to do once they'd changed, with their dead eyes… No, actually. It wasn't easier, not at all. But I had to do it."

She broke down in tears, burying her head in her hands, sobbing. Bill nodded to himself, but wasn't sure about what else he could say or do, if anything. She'd had to kill both her parents, and from the sounds of it, in their bedroom. That was probably why the second bedroom had been emptied and gutted, stripped of anything that would remind her of the event. After a few minutes the woman stopped crying, wiped her eyes and her nose on the sleeve of her heavy jacket, then sat back, looking at Bill with reddened eyes.

"So this was your parent's farm. The were the Greens, I assume."

"I'm Angela. Angela Green," she said, adjusting her ponytail and nodding slightly. She made a visible effort of trying to put aside the memory of slaying her parents, but Bill knew it would take a lot to do that. "My friends called me Angel."

"My friends called me Bill," he offered with a slight grin. "The asshole upstairs is called Al."

Angel nodded slowly, but she still kept her untrusting gaze fixed on Bill. He shrugged slightly, then curled up on the armchair, trying to get comfortable on the seat.

"It's been an eventful day," he said. "I'm aching all over from that explosion. How about we get some rest, we can talk in the morning."

"That explosion," she said, waving upstairs, "That wasn't meant for you."

"You were expecting someone else to stumble blindly through your house and hunt you down?" Bill asked, smiling as a new thought occurred to him. "You didn't set up a similar trap in your bedroom, did you? Maybe a bomb under your bed?"

Angel shook her head.

"Shit, it may have knocked some sense into that stubborn old bastard. Shame. So, if it wasn't us you were expecting, who exactly *were* you expecting?'

"There's a gang, they've been trying to get to me for days now, maybe a couple of weeks, I don't know. When I heard your jeep coming, I thought you were one of them. My trap was already set, I just had to hide there and hope for the best. I hoped that you'd just think I'd left."

Angel curled up on the settee, unfastening her heavy jacket as she spoke. Bill kept a wary eye on her, making sure she wasn't reaching for any secluded weapon, but she simply tossed the jacket aside, revealing the tight-fitting vest she wore. "I know they'll be coming soon, they turn up every few days, but I normally manage to ward them off."

How can this girl keep a gang at bay? Bill wondered, especially in light of the class of people he could recall from Moloch's minions. Al had seemed to manage on his own for a while, but he had something like twenty years of marine training. This girl barely looked old enough to order a drink in a bar.

The two people sat in silence for the next five minutes, lost in their own thoughts. Angel was the first to show any signs of lethargy, her eyes sagging and struggling to remain open. Finally losing the struggle, her eyes remained closed with her mouth open slightly, a soft rasping breath coming with each rise and fall of her chest. Bill sighed heavily, watching his prisoner while he evaluated what to do next. He wouldn't be able to reapply the handcuffs without waking her up, but he didn't feel he needed to. The little body language he knew about indicated that although she was fearful at first, she was now more relaxed, especially if she was willing to go to sleep. There was a chance she could be faking the sleeping, and planned to murder both Al and himself in the night, but he didn't think that she would. Unpacking the blankets from his rucksack and rolling them out, he gently placed one over the sleeping girl, then the other over himself, propping his feet on the table and casually flicking through the binder filled with explosive recipes and fighting techniques. He found a blank page in the book, then unearthed a pen from the depths of his rucksack and started to add his own notes to the tome of knowledge.

II

Dawn broke, the dreary darkness of the small room being chased away as the sun crested the peak of the hills surrounding the farm. Bill's eyes fluttered open as daylight warmed his skin, and he slowly opened them, rubbing grit from them and closing the open binder in front of him. Minute particles of dust flitted to and fro in the shafts of light that found their way into the room, trapped in eddies in the circulating air currents.

Replacing the heavy binder and pen back in his bag, he carefully stood, not wanting to make any noise and rouse the sleeping girl on the couch, and started to skulk around the room, pulling back one of the curtains and glaring out on to the surrounding countryside.

It seemed quiet enough; nothing seemed to be moving in the immediate vicinity. With the exception of the sole Rot that had passed the infection to Mrs Green, Angel's father seemed to have had the right idea about the location of the farm and its distance from civilisation. It was just a shame that the sanctity of the hills hadn't also provided cover from the gang Angel had spoke of the previous night. Bill turned his head to one side, looking at the form of the sleeping woman and the blanket she had cast off during the night. She looked peaceful and rested, and Bill imagined that she hadn't slept much in the past few weeks. Holding a large area such as the farm from both Rots and gangs was obviously a tiring job, and up until now, she may not have felt safe enough to have a full nights sleep.

Bill smiled, his eyes resting on Angel for longer than he intended. She stirred, turning over in her sleep, and he quickly looked away, suddenly feeling embarrassed that he'd almost been caught staring at her. She remained asleep though, and Bill sat back down at the table, his eyes coming to rest on Angel once more. She looked just as attractive in the morning as she had the night before, if not more so, but again Bill found his mind plagued with images of Jenny in her final moments of life, before the pistol sounded, and before the flames washed her away.

He stood, folding up his blanket and replacing it in his bag before slowly ascending the stairs, carefully lowering his foot with each step and trying not to make too much noise. He reached the landing, inspected the frayed and shattered banister he had been catapulted through the day before, then slowly made his way back towards the bathroom, and the piles of debris and dirt that littered the broken part of the corridor.

The bathroom itself hadn't been damaged too badly: Bill had read enough in his book to know that a shaped charge had been used to aim the force of the explosion away from the bathroom, but how Angel had also known that was a mystery. Picking his way through the small piles of shattered tiles and charred fragments of wood, he stood in front of the basin and looked at the reflection that glared back at him. An alien face with a thick and scraggly unkempt beard, a tangle of dark hair on top of his head. He scratched his chin, unaware of how irritating the growth was until he actually saw it. He rummaged in the cabinet behind the mirror, unearthing a disposable razor sealed in its plastic wrapping. He didn't want to chance using anything from the tap to aid his impending shave, but half a can of shaving foam beside the razor would provide enough lubrication for a quick cleanup.

The first stroke was rough against his skin, nicking him and splashing a few drops of his blood in the basin. It took him almost twenty minutes to finish his shave, he'd certainly had quicker, but the end result was just as clean, if not as bloody.

Tossing the razor aside, Bill inspected his work before leaving the bathroom. Rubbing his naked jaw, he paused outside the door to Angel's bedroom, listing to Al as he huffed and puffed his way through his morning exercise regime. Leaving the burley man to his training, Bill descended the staircase somewhat more elegantly than he had previously, and walked out through the living room and into the kitchen, setting himself down in one of the chairs at the dining table and sighing to himself.

Surely there had to be some way that he and Al could help Angel out, or maybe convince her to come away with them. Of course, it wasn't just Angel he had to talk around, it would be Al, too, as they would need to dump or leave some of his various weapons.

"It'll never happen," he muttered to himself, able to picture Al's face if he suggested that they leave some of their armament behind. He stood and wandered over to one of the cupboards beneath the sink, pulling the door open and looking at the contents of the cupboard. He smirked slightly, then stood and dusted off his jeans. He was sure there was something he'd be able to rustle up from his book of magic tricks, but he'd have to double check before he started to pull out ingredients and try making something he wasn't familiar with. He returned to the living room and grabbed his binder, flicking casually through the pages, and nodding silently to himself as he found what he was looking for.

With a grin, he returned to the kitchen and started to rifle through the contents of the cupboard.

Al stopped his final set of push-ups and sat on the wooden floor, pulling the sheet off the bed and wiping the sweat from his body before tossing it back on to the bed and pulling on his armoured vest. He stood in front of the mirror and looked at the tattoo on his stomach for a moment before fastening up his clothing and grabbing the rifle he'd cleaned during the night.

He'd thought Bill had more sense and balls than he'd displayed last night. Maybe he *had* gone a little overboard when he was going to kill the woman, but in his eyes, she had tried to kill him, or at least Bill. He was more pissed off at the fact she had got the drop on him, maybe that was why he wanted to kill her.

He grabbed the collection of documents he'd found in the bottom of one of the draws, tucked them beneath his belt and strolled out the room, his rifle slung over his shoulder. He clambered down the stairs, looking at the form of the sleeping woman on the settee, and couldn't help but notice her restraints had been removed. He shook his head grimly, resting one hand on the butt of his holstered magnum and skirting around the room, eyes trained on the sleeping woman.

He exited the living room and headed towards the kitchen, suddenly aware of an overpowering smell, a bittersweet and acrid tang that he found strangely familiar. Unable to place the smell, he strolled into the kitchen and found himself engulfed by clouds of steam carrying the same cloying scent. He could see the source of the odour, two large metal pots on the stove filled with a bubbling clear liquid, each with an opaque film forming on the top. He saw Bill sitting at the table with his back turned to him and surrounded by small black tubes and glass jars.

"Jesus, kid," spat Al, struggling through the clouds of steam and helping himself to one of the seats. "What in Christ's name are you doing?"

"I'm cooking," the young man grinned, putting down the battery operated drill and plastic end cap he'd been working on. "Just a meal for some friends. I've got plastique boiling away in those pans over there, those bottles over there are a few Molotov cocktails, and at the minute I'm preparing a desert of pipe bombs."

Al smiled, impressed at the ingenuity of his friend, picking up one of the finished pipe bombs and testing its construction. It seemed rigid enough, it looked like the kid had done a solid job on it. He stood and turned off the hob, opening a window to let the acrid vapour escape the confines of the room.

"I'm impressed, kid. Where'd you learn all this shit?"

Bill closed the thick white binder and slid it along the table towards him. Al grabbed it and started to casually flick through it. A lot of it was stuff he already knew: some from when he was twelve or thirteen. The rest looked like the type of information survivalists back in America had posted on the Internet years ago so other paranoid fucks could benefit from it. A few pages even described tactics and explosive devices used by terrorists and militias.

"I bet those Bebop bastards all had a copy of this," he muttered, then passed it back to Bill. "Where'd you get it? Did that crazy little bitch have it?"

"I found it in the store I was holed up in before I met you," he confessed. "Christ knows what they wanted it for, but it was stashed in some dumb bastard's locker."

"This here is a lot of dangerous information," Al said, tapping the cover of the book. "If anything like this has fallen into the hands of our friends out there, guys like Moloch and his bunch of shits, it's going to make our lives a lot harder."

"I know," agreed Bill, sitting back in his seat and rubbing his eyes.

Al was silent for a moment, then glanced towards the kitchen door.

"So, I see you released Sleeping Beauty in there."

"I was wondering how long that would take," sighed Bill, scratching his chin. His cleanly shaven chin. Al didn't mention it. "She's had a rough time, you know."

"Yeah, her and every other poor bastard that isn't pushing up the daisies or eating the next guy that tries to pass them by. When are we going?"

"She's in trouble, Al. Shouldn't we help her?"

"Sure," snarled Al, standing up and stalking around the kitchen, peering out the window and making sure the area was still secure. "Why don't we help out every little whore that tries to kill us? That girl isn't *in* trouble, she *is* trouble, plain and simple."

He pulled out the papers tucked beneath his belt and tossed them on to the white binder. A passport lay on top of the pile. "Girl's called Angela Green. Seventeen years old."

"Seventeen?" asked Bill, surprise in his tone.

"Last month, actually, but that's beside the point. This isn't the Colebrook Dedication hour; this is me, delivering the facts. You, I stuck with for two reasons. You reminded me of the kid, and you seemed to be able to take care of yourself. I mean, you walked into an ambush upstairs, but you're just a newbie, I can let that slide. That little bitch out there…"

"That 'little bitch' is being hounded by a gang. You know, a group of rebels like those in Edgly?"

"That little bitch is a fucking cocktease, and has probably brought it on herself."

"And what do you base that on?" laughed Bill, shaking his head in disbelief. "You're just pissed at her because she got the drop on you."

Bill's comments stung, maybe because they were close to the truth, but Al was too worked up to care. "Maybe you just want to help her to score a few brownie points. Bill, the big hero, waltzes into her life and saves the day. The bad guys are dead, there's celebrations all around, she's very grateful and fucks you senseless. Hence the impromptu shave."

Bill's face took on a sudden look of resentment and shock, though Al figured he was trying his best to hide the fact that he'd hit a nerve. He had a slight tremor in his hands as he reached forwards and opened the binder, knocking the passport on to the floor and pulling out a photograph. He pushed it in front of Al, tapping one of the corners with a pale and shaking index finger. He looked at the image of an attractive woman, maybe the same age as Bill, with long dark hair.

"You see her," Bill said, his voice quiet but faltering in tone. "Up until about a month ago, I was going to spend the rest of my life with her. And now, she's dead. Do you really think I'm interested in sparking up a relationship with a fucking *kid*?"

Al backed away from Bill, shaking his head. "I don't know who you're trying to convince, kid, me or you."

He turned away, and felt something barrel into his back, a writhing and squirming mass of limbs that was pummelling him and pinning him down to the floor. Confused, he managed to roll on to his back and tried to reach for one of his holdout pistols secluded in his combat webbing. He paused mid struggle, and was more than surprised to see Bill sitting on top of him, a look of fierce determination set on his face. He held a knife in his hand, and it was dangerously close to Al's throat. He nodded and grunted a wordless sound, then tossed the blade to one side and stepped away, returning to his work at the table. Al clambered to his feet and almost retaliated, but held back. Maybe he had been too harsh, and jumping him would certainly be a bad idea if he were in the middle of making explosives. He'd let it slide for now, and take it up with him later. He spun on his heels, and saw the girl standing at the doorway, her face passive.

"I'm going outside," he muttered, keeping his eyes trained on the woman and talking back over his shoulder to Bill. "There's a bad stink in here. And it's not the shit you've been cooking."

He stormed past the girl, pushing her aside and leaving the farmhouse, heading back towards the barn and the generator he had found yesterday with the intention of firing it up and recharging the batteries of the various pairs of goggles he carried.

The generator had cooled down now; it had been inactive since their arrival, and Al discovered it had been drained when he tried to turn it on. He rapped on the fuel gauge of the machine, looking around from where he stood for an extra can of petrol to refuel the generator. There had to be some in the barn, somewhere close to the machine itself.

"Maybe stashed behind the hay," he muttered to himself, starting to make his way around the building, his mind swimming with thoughts about Bill and this new whore that they'd met up. "Maybe teaming up with the kid was a bad idea. I might just piss off now on my own, leave the pair to get on with screwing each others brains out while I…"

His words trailed off as his search for fuel climaxed in the discovery of three plastic containers, partially obscured by a loose mound of hay. He pulled aside a clump of the dried grass, and stopped in his tracks, looking at the wooden crate the petrol containers had been placed on. Shaking his head, he spun on his heels and ran back towards the house, his mind swimming with his find.

Bill watched as Al barged past Angel, pushing her roughly and disappearing from sight, the front door slamming behind him as he left the farmhouse. He looked down, returning to his work and trying his best to ignore the questioning looks of the girl. He didn't want to acknowledge her presence, unsure of exactly what Angel had seen or heard. He heard soft and gentle footsteps on the wooden floor approach him, then the slight creaking groan of one of the vacant seats as it became occupied.

"Do you always have this many problems with your friends?" she asked, her voice soft and low. She looked cautiously over her shoulder as she spoke, watching for the large Marine's return. "I mean, not that it's my business or anything…"

"He's a strange one," agreed Bill, concentrating on his work. "He's just not a morning person I guess. He's in a bad mood, too. I don't know how much he drank last night, he may be hung over as well."

Angel nodded solemnly, playing with one of the empty plastic tubes on the table.

"How much of our conversation did you hear?" Bill finally asked.

"I heard none of it," she replied. Bill knew she was lying, but he smiled and thanked her anyway. There had been a lot of raised voices, she must have heard them talking: the fact of the matter was they had probably woken her up in the first place. "I just saw him get up off the floor and storm out."

She reached out and replaced the plastic tube on the table, then turned around the photo on the table and looked at it.

"She's pretty. So that's Jenny?" she asked. Bill nodded, then looked up from his work, a puzzled expression on his face. How had she known that? She looked up at him, noted the puzzled on his face, and smiled. "Sorry, I just assumed... You talk in your sleep, did you know that?"

"I've been told that, yes," said Bill, reclaiming the photo and staring at it longingly before replacing it between pages in the binder. "Al told me. Jenny used to say the same thing. Jesus, I miss her."

Angel reached out, placed a small cold hand over his and nodded. "We've all lost people that are close to us," she whispered. "We just have to remember them, that's all we can do."

Bill nodded, then looked up, startled at the sound of the front door slamming open and smashing into the wall, followed by heavy pounding footsteps. He reached for his handgun, knowing it was Al before he even entered the kitchen.

"Looks like it's time for round two," he muttered.

Al approached the table, and with lightning speed lashed out and grabbed Angel, lifting her from her seat, throwing her against the bench and wrenching her arms behind her back. He fumbled at his belt and pulled a pair of metal handcuffs from their pouch, clapping them on to her wrists and binding her. He pulled her from the bench and pushed her on to the ground, lifting his foot and resting the boot against the small of her back, the same place she had been shot the previous day. She moaned with pain, oblivious to the fact that he had now drawn his Desert Eagle and had it levelled at her head.

"Much as I hate to break up this very cosy little scene," he growled, spitting his words and pressing down harder with his foot, "I'd like to take this opportunity to point out to this thieving little whore I've just found her dirty little secret out in the barn. And it's no wonder there's a bunch of guys out baying for this bitch's blood."

"Christ, Al, be careful," scorned Bill, grabbing him by the shoulder and trying to pull him off. He didn't move. "Jesus, what are you talking about?"

"You're girlfriend here… What did I tell you? She said there was a gang of rebels after her, she didn't mention why, did she? She's using you, Bill. There's more than just hay and animal feed out in the barn."

At the mention of the barn, Angel's face blanched, and a fine bead of sweat trickled down her brow and dripped on to the floor. She twisted her head around tried to look at Al first, then at Bill. She could barely manage either move. Al grinned at the look on her face, waving the muzzle of the Desert Eagle towards her panicked features. "That's not exactly the expression of a child who's as innocent and helpless as she tries to make out, is it?"

"Calm down, Al, you're not making any sense!"

"Then come on, out to the barn. See what I'm talking about," offered the Marine as he motioned towards the door. He removed his foot from Angel's back, rolled her over and pressed his weapon against her lips. The panic on her face turned to fear, and she pressed her eyes closed, tears seeping from them as she shook nervously. "And you, bitch, stay here or I'll blast your fucking head off, you follow?" She nodded with a whimper, and Al stepped away, firing a round into the floorboard inches from her head and making her jump in terror, rolling under the table and curling up beneath it. "Now stay," he commanded again before turning to face Bill.

"You coming?"

"I've got no choice, have I?" he asked. Al shook his head.

The pair marched from the house towards the barn, both moving in silence while Al stormed ahead. He burst into the barn, navigating through the stacked bales of hay and stood motionless in front of a large wooden crate. Bill stood beside him and looked at the wooden box in silence for a few moments before breaking the silence.

"It's a crate. Am I supposed to be impressed or intimidated by it?"

"Look inside it," he said, motioning to the loose lid. Bill reached out for it, then noticed the wires and metal contacts surrounding the crate itself. "She's wired it to explode, hasn't she? You open it."

"I've already disarmed it," muttered Al, reaching forwards and yanking the wooden lid off, throwing it across the room. Bill leaned forwards, peered cautiously into the box, and saw a large collection of dark metal objects. He looked at his friend, and shrugged.

"What am I looking at here?"

"Ignorant shit," growled Al, diving into the box and pulling out some of the larger components, slapping them together and locking them into place. He grinned at the massive weapon he had constructed and gently placed it on the ground. "This is an M82, one of the most powerful sniping rifles in the world. It makes that pissy rifle you had look like a pellet gun. This is a military model. That stamp on the side of the crate is the Marine emblem. There's shit in there to make machine pistols, automatic shotguns and heavy machineguns with enough ammo to blow up a small frigate. There's even a couple of one-shot disposable RPGs in there. Now can you explain how the fuck that thieving whore has come to possess this little haul?"

Bill shrugged. "She didn't tell me anything about this. Just mentioned that some gang was out to get her."

"I know," Al said, nodding. "I've heard all the conversations you've had with her. You keep leaving your radio on," he said, slapping Bill's headset with the palm of his hand. "Next time you want a private conversation, turn this frigging thing off. Or at least switch to another channel."

"You could've just taken your own headset off," said Bill, removing his headset and letting it hang around his neck. Al shrugged. "Why should I? It's my damn equipment, I'll do what I want with it. And now, this shit is mine, too."

"Hey," Bill said, reaching into the crate and pulling out a machine pistol. "You think the gang that's been bothering her's been the Marines, trying to get their stuff back?"

"Doubt it," snorted Al. "Us Marines take no shit from no one. They would have splattered that whore all over before she could even think about fighting back. It has to be someone like Moloch and his band of idiots: disorganised, no solid command structure."

"He's right," confirmed Angel. The pair spun around to see her standing behind them, the handcuffs dangling from one wrist. Al drew his sidearm, bringing the muzzle of it up to point at the face of the girl. This time she didn't flinch. "I don't know who this Moloch is you're talking about, but they're certainly not organised like the army would be."

"Marines," corrected Al, scowling at her. "This crate of shit you've stolen is from the Marines."

"I didn't steal it," she protested. "There was some kind of cargo plane that flew overhead a few days ago. It dropped this and three more crates like it."

"Supply drop," muttered Al, nodding his head. He turned to Bill, but kept the pistol trained on Angel. "Standard procedure for the corps, dropping supplies behind enemy lines. There must have been some troops stationed near here: drops have never been especially accurate. I remember once in Brazil my squad had to walk for miles to find an ammunition drop, we were completely dry. We had to make it through seventeen Bebops armed with only our knives and whatever we could find in the jungle…"

"Focus, Al," Bill said, clicking his fingers. He turned to Angel and smiled. "So four crates were dropped around here?"

"That's right. I found this out in south field, and another landed in the north field. The other two landed just outside the village, but those two were captured by the people who live there."

"Wait a second," muttered Al, holding a finger up and frowning. "You have two of these crates?"

She nodded. "Yeah, the other one's up in the hay loft."

"Wait here," he said, turning to Bill. "Draw your piece, point it at her head. If she moves, blow it off." With a flourish, he holstered his magnum and broke into a sprint, looking for a ladder up into the second floor. As soon as he was out of earshot, Bill apologised for the Marine's behaviour.

"So, they want these two boxes of weapons to complete their set, as it were?" asked Bill. Angel nodded gently, smiling slightly. "And they've tried to get these before?" Again, she nodded. "How'd you fend them off?"

"I'm good with a rifle," she replied. "And I used some of the crates contents a couple of times. Nothing really big or anything that didn't come with instructions, of course. I've lived out here all my life, looking after fields of wheat and tending to livestock, I never got much of a chance to play with explosives."

"I was a city kid," said Bill, smiling and leaning against the bale of hay beside him. "We never had the opportunity to play with this kind of shit, either. Al, on the other hand, is American. He was probably born with that handgun of his in his hands."

"Jesus frigging wept," Al's voice boomed down from the loft above them. "How many grenades have you used, bitch?"

Angel grinned and shrugged, looking at Bill. "I've seen films, I know how to use grenades."

Bill smiled, laughed slightly, but his grin died as he heard something in the distance: a steady, low droning sound. Angel opened her mouth to talk, but Bill placed his finger to her lips, silencing her as he slipped his radio headset back on. "Al," he whispered in a low voice. "Do you hear that noise?"

"Roger that," came his response. Only Bill could hear him now: it seemed that he too had started to whisper into his headpiece. "I can't see anything from up here. I'm going to climb on to the roof, see if I can get a better look."

"Be careful," Bill said, then removed his finger from Angel's mouth. "It sounds like something's coming. Can you hear that noise?" She nodded, her eyes wide with terror. "Do you know what that could be?" This time she shook her head.

"Do you know?" she asked hopefully. Bill shook his head, moving back towards the entrance into the barn.

"It could be one of two things: a gang of the rebels, as Al calls them, or an army of Rots. Either way, it's not good, and it's going to cost us a lot of ammo. Grab whatever weapon you favour and get ready for some shit to hit the fan."

The pair stormed out the building, Angel running into the farmhouse while Bill turned and looked up towards the roof of the barn, seeing Al balanced precariously on the tin plating, his binoculars pressed to his face. "Do you see anything yet?" he asked him, cupping his hands around his mouth and shouting up towards him.

"The radio, you dumb bastard, you don't need to shout. And you're not going to fucking believe what I can see."

III

"Moloch?" asked Bill as he rushed around the kitchen, gathering some of the explosive devices he had made that morning and placing them in a large plastic box. "Are you sure?"

"I'm sure, I recognise those bastard vehicles his guys parade around in."

"How the hell did *he* find us?"

"Well how the hell should I know?" Al responded over the headset. He had directed Bill and advised him to set up a defensive line of traps around the house while he prepared all the weapons that he felt would be useful for the impending attack. Bill couldn't help but feel he'd been given the worst job. "How could he track us?"

"Well, it's not as if we've travelled hundreds of miles," Bill replied, passing the crate on to Angel and motioning for her to carry it outside.

"Who is this Moloch?" she asked, dragging the container and trying to readjust the strap of her military rifle. It wasn't as monstrous as the rifle Al had made, and it didn't seem as bulky, either. It was probably just as well; from the looks of her, it didn't look like Angel could even pick up the weapon, yet alone fire it.

"You tell that bitch to shut up and stop pissing around, get those things outside now!"

Bill nodded towards the door, indicating for her to leave with her load and started to load up a second box, this one for himself. "Maybe they followed our tracks?"

"Through the grass and mud? It's a possibility, but they still had to find it first. We stuck to roads for the best part of the journey… Shit!"

"What?" shouted Bill, almost dropping the Molotov cocktail he held.

"The damn hummer. They followed *The Colebrook*. Jesus, how could I forget? The armed forces, ever since thirty-six, have fitted every machine they've ever made with a tracking device. I mean everything: bikes, planes, helicopters, tanks, *everything*. They must have tracked us by that. If they were holed up somewhere previously held by the army, who's to say they don't have the equipment to track us? Damn, shit, fuck, why didn't I think of that?"

"Because you're human, Al, and we all make mistakes."

"Bullshit," he spat. "I'm more than human, I'm a Marine. We don't make mistakes."

Bill shook his head and finished off packing his box, carrying his load out and meeting up with Angel, who knelt on the ground about a hundred yards away from the house. Bill looked over his shoulder to see Al storming back and forth on the roof of the barn, an assortment of various mounted weapons bolted haphazardly to the metal roof, like quills on a porcupine's back. "How far away are they?" he asked, having learned his lesson about shouting down the radio. Atop the roof, the Marine lifted his binoculars to his eyes once more and sighed. When he spoke he didn't sound afraid, but he didn't have the casual and laid-back tones he normally had.

"They're on the other side of the northern rise. They've stopped for the moment, looks like they're readying their weapons."

"Do they have much?" asked Bill. He still didn't know that much about weapons, but he trusted Al and his judgement.

"They've got enough," muttered Al, lowering his binoculars and finalising his preparations for his weapons. "When they're ready to charge, they'll be on us in about two minutes. Now get that shit ready down there, like I told you."

"Are you sure you know how to use those weapons?"

"I'm a Marine," scoffed Al, pausing mid work to casually flick one finger towards Bill.

"That's not the question I asked you. Can you work them?"

"Of course. Don't patronise me."

Bill nodded, then rushed over to watch Angel as she placed one of her charges in a small hole on the dusty road, covering it over with loose dirt and small shrubbery.

"How are you doing?" he asked, setting his own box down and beginning to plant similar charges. She nodded grimly, but didn't say a word, too busy with her work to speak. Al had obviously finished his own preparations, and resumed his vigil on the imminent threat.

"Still checking their weapons, getting ready to storm this shitty place. You nearly finished with those explosives?" he asked, then continued without missing a beat. "You know, I've got the controls to those C4 charges up here. I could quite easily blow that little whore up, if I wanted."

"Why don't you shut up," scowled Bill, covering his final charge and motioning for Angel to return back to the farmhouse. "Why don't you see if you can take those bastards out with that sniper rifle you found?"

"Tried it, can't get a clear shot," said Al. "And besides, that'll give away the fact we know they're coming. I don't want to give our biggest weapon away. Surprise, it's a key element in most conflicts."

"Surprise?" mocked Bill, slamming the farm door behind him slamming all the locks into place. "The barn roof is riddled with various heavy weapons, most of them pointing in their general direction. That's not going to tip them off?"

"Yeah, well the thing about that is… Wait a minute. They're starting to make their move," said Al, all trace of humour seeping out his voice as the sound of a weapon cocking came over the headset. "Get that bitch ready, remind her not to fire until the fireworks begin. Concentrate your fire forwards, I'll keep an eye out for any of the bastards trying to flank us."

Bill nodded to Angel, and the two of them ran through the house, upstairs to the bathroom and the shattered windows. Angel slid her rifle through one of the opened panes, crouching on the ground and resting the barrel on the wooden frame, while Bill placed his bag on the ground and opened it up. He removed the store of magazines for his MP5 and waited, holding the submachine gun close to his chest and staring out into the surrounding land. He tried to look to his side to see if he could check on Al, but the barn was just out of sight.

The drone of the engines slowly increased in intensity as the vehicles parked over the ridge slowly crawled forwards, and the first of the vehicles came into view. It had at one point been an old black sports car, but the body panels had been pulled from the frame, leaving a skeletal car and exposing the mechanics of the vehicle to the elements. Chains and barbed wire had been wrapped around the exposed frame, and various weapons had been mounted on the vehicle. Two men occupied it; the driver perched behind the steering wheel, while the second man stood in the back, his hands wrapped around the firing controls of the mounted machinegun he seemed to favour. As more vehicles came into view, Bill could see that had all been modified in the same way.

"I think the shit in the back of the lead car is Moloch," muttered Al. "We'll see what he does."

The entourage of vehicles stopped just outside the ring of explosions, and the man in the back of the front-most car raised his arms with fists clenched, signalling to his followers to kill their engines. They died with a rattling gurgle, and the apparent leader clambered out his car, strolling forwards and grinning. He wore dark blue body armour and jeans, his eyes hidden by a pair of dark goggles and his head by a black helmet, an orange letter 'M' stencilled on the front.

"I know you're here, Nigger," he called. Another few steps forward, and now he was only a few feet from the explosive charges. "You have something of mine. Me and my friends want it back."

"Hold your fire," whispered Al as the leader edged forwards. "This asshole is mine."

"If you hand the vehicle over, we'll let you go in one piece," the man shouted, then turned and muttered something to the men in the vehicles behind him. They all laughed at him, one or two of them cheering and applauding at his comments. Al laughed softly over the radio, muttering incoherently to himself. The man outside took another step forwards, reaching for the weapon dangling from his belt.

He vanished behind a cloud of dirt and a lick of flames as one of the explosives hidden in the ground burst to life. Another explosion followed, then another, and the men in the vehicle began to scream and panic. Some opened up with their weapons, firing randomly through the rising smoke and debris from the explosions: others began to turn their engines over, trying to reverse out of the ambush.

"Open fire!"

Al's loud voice carried over the sounds of gunfire and the dying retorts of the blasts, and was quickly followed by the sounds of his own collection of weapons barking to life. Both Bill and Angel held back on their weapons, unable to see through the clouds that lingered around the battlefield.

"I can't see anything," said Angel, slowly panning her rifle from side to side.

"I know," said Bill, standing over Angel and peering into the battleground. He lifted his machinegun, cocked it, and unleashed three random bursts into the fray. "Maybe Al can see stuff from his vantage point, but we're blind down here."

"Twelve o'clock," Al shouted between bursts of gunfire. "One, two, and ten. Christ kid, just fire into the cloud. You've got enough ammo, take the chance."

"What about Angel? She hasn't got as many bullets as me."

"I could do with a coffee," laughed Al. "Tell her to stick the kettle on. Milk and two sugars. Maybe a biscuit?"

"What's he saying?" asked Angel, still waiting for the first sign of a clear target. Bill fired off the rest of his magazine into the target area, roughly in the directions Al had told him. He ejected the magazine, letting it drop to the floor and snatching up a fresh one in a single fluid motion.

"He wants you to make him a cup of coffee," he confessed.

"Sexist pig," she muttered, hoisting her weapon and tightening her grip.

The smoke finally shifted and parted as a single figure stormed out the clouds, a rusty hatchet in one hand and an assault rifle in the other. He fired off random shots, though none were aimed towards the roof of the barn and the true source of the resistance. Bill swivelled around, readied his aim and prepared to fire, but Angel beat him to it, squeezing a round off from her rifle and striking the man square in the face. He crumpled to the floor, his head destroyed from the powerful bullet.

"Nice shot," Al said, sounding casually impressed in the heat of the battle.

"That was Angel," confessed Bill.

"Terrible, completely amateur," Al sighed, sounding exasperated. "Where's my damn coffee?"

Bill grinned and tore the headset off in a bid to ignore the string of abuse that Al started to hurl, concentrating more on the battle as the smoke finally dissipated enough to make out details of the killing field. Vehicles had been riddled with bullet holes, and already a large number of casualties lay on the ground, many having their limbs severed by the rapid fire of the large calibre weapons. Bill could see some of the men crouching behind the husks of the machines, each looking feverishly around to identify the source of attack. With the smoke clearing, it would only be a matter of time until they could see the bulky man on the rooftop and his collection of weapons. Bill took careful aim and squeezed off a three shot burst, striking one man in the arm and chest. He tumbled to the ground, screaming in agony, but his death throes were silenced as Angel released a second round from her weapon, obliterating his throat. Bill looked down to see her face: she wore a grim expression, her jaw clenched and eyes staring blankly ahead. She shouldered the rifle again, and took out a third man, this time blasting his arm off at the elbow. He sunk to the ground, screaming and holding the bloody stump with his one remaining hand. A volley off gunfire from atop the barn ended his suffering, shredding his body and spreading his internal organs across the ground around him.

Emptying magazine upon magazine of ammunition and spraying the ground and the remains of the vehicles with gunfire, Bill ducked away from the window as the dwindling numbers of the gang managed to pinpoint the location of their attackers. Panicked screams went up amongst the lines, instructions to concentrate their fire on the farmhouse and the barn.

Angel dropped to the floor as a barrage of bullets tore through the bathroom window, smashing into the tiles behind them and showering them with heavy ceramic debris.

Cursing, Bill pulled his jury-rigged drainpipe cannon out and slipped one of the Molotov cocktails into the gaping barrel, lying on the floor, bracing the weapon against his hip and aiming for the opened window, gently squeezing the trigger. There was a slight pause, then the weapon kicked into him, sliding him a few feet backwards across the ground. He heard the bottle shatter, but didn't hear the agonising screams he would have expected from a firebomb smothering a small gathering of people.

"You didn't light it," hissed Angel, rummaging through her pockets and throwing him a cigarette lighter. He caught it, grabbed a second glass bottle and lit the rag, bracing and aiming again, the recoil hammering his hip once again.

This time, the smash of the bottle was followed by the agonising screams he had anticipated, and he couldn't help but grin slightly. Now, the gang members were too busy trying to extinguish the either the fires or themselves to return fire. Bill stood and opened up with his machinegun, spraying the charred, smoking ground and anyone lying on it. Angel reclaimed her own position, taking careful aim and punching round after round into the bodies and vehicles in the annex of the farm.

Bill paused in his firing, comparing Angel's face with what he imagined Al's would be at that moment in time. The Marine loved his job, loved his weapons, and he also seemed to have a penchant for killing people. At that point in time, Bill couldn't think of anyone in the world who would be having as much fun as Al.

He grabbed his headset and slipped it back on, listening to the whoops of joy and excitement as he continued to fire.

"How many of them are left, Al," Bill shouted to be heard over his cursing and weapons fire.

"Not many," confirmed Al. "About thirty came, give or take a few. Most of them are dead, now. A lot of the others seem to be mortally wounded. They're all rolling around, drying out in pain and begging to be killed. Shit, it's just like back in Brazil. Of course, if Ping was still here, this would have ended about five minutes ago. The kid loved his grenade launcher. Of course, *grenades...*"

"Okay, Al, that's great. How long until we're clear?"

No response came from Al, and for a moment Bill thought he had been shot down while he'd been remising about days gone by. An eerie absence of gunfire descended over the battlefield, leaving only the tortured screams of the severely wounded to carry across the opening. Bill slung his shotgun over his shoulder, reloaded his MP5 and grabbed his final magazines, tucking them into his back pockets and running on to the landing and almost falling down the stairs. He kicked the door open, hearing Angel following close behind him, and swung his weapon from left to right. Angel barrelled to a stop beside him, rolling to the ground and providing low cover from anyone that may still be standing.

They were just in time to see three metal spheres arcing down from the barn roof, one landing in the middle of a small fire and the other two bouncing into an opened car chassis. Bill dropped to the ground, pulling Angel down with him and partially shielding her from the battlefield as the devices exploded. The two in the car did the most damage, rupturing the fuel tank and igniting the mixture of flammable liquid and gasses within, the explosion showering debris all over the farm. Smoking chunks of twisted metal and flaming rubber slammed into the ground around them and bounced off the farmhouse. A few charred lumps of debris sailed through the windows of the house; Bill could hear them smashing whatever furniture they landed on within the building. Angel heard, too, and winced as a particularly loud crash echoed through the house.

Once the rain of shrapnel had ceased, Bill climbed to his feet and grabbed Angel's wrist, helping her up.

"You okay?" he asked, smiling. She nodded and brushed the stray hairs out her face, slinging the rifle over her shoulder and looking at the crackling and smoking remains of the battleground.

"There's a lot of dead people out there," she muttered. "Are you okay?"

"I'm a little numb, to be honest," said Bill. "I've never done anything like that."

"It's not over yet," shouted Al, strolling over from the barn with an assault rifle slung casually over his shoulder and his hand resting on the butt of his holstered magnum. He brought his assault rifle around and waved it loosely in the direction of the remains of the gang "Some of those shits aren't dead yet, just wounded. We have to wade through them and finish off whoever isn't already dead. It'll be easier to do that then have one of those half-burned, half dead bastards crawl up to you in the middle of the night trying to cut your throat with a rusty knife. Come on, clean up duty. After we kill 'em, we get to burn the bodies."

Bill sighed and lifted his shotgun, moving towards the smouldering blast crater and cradling his weapon. Angel followed closely behind, warily eyeing the charred and smoking twitching corpses. Bill drew his handgun and offered it to her, aware that she couldn't hope to perform any of the mercy killings with the massive and unwieldy weapon. She refused it, drawing her own from a holster the back of her belt and cocking it. It didn't look like his own, so he didn't know what type it was. Al cautiously eyed her as they walked, nodding as he noticed her choice of weapon. If Al seemed impressed by it, then it must have been a good choice.

Either that, he thought to himself, *or it was the only one she could assemble from the box of pieces.*

The snap of Al's assault rifle echoed first in the still of the air, the sound of a single round smashing into one of the heads of the dying men silencing one of the few cries of agony still carrying over the battleground. Bill found his first suffering victim; a burned man almost cut in two by the shrapnel of the explosion. He grimly lowered his shotgun and pressed the muzzle against his temple, slowly squeezing the trigger.

The blast tore the head apart, splattering ruddy fluids and fragments of skulls across the scorched ground. Bill turned away feeling slightly sickened by the execution, and carried on his search for tormented survivors.

He didn't find any more, though Al found another three in the space of two minutes as he quickly ran around the killing ground, finally calling for an all clear once he had reached the other side of the scorched earth. Bill nodded slowly, then looked towards Angel. She stood over a single twitching body, her weapon dangling from a limp hand as she stared down on the writhing body. Her face was pale and she was shaking slightly. Bill cautiously made his way over, his own weapon raised and pointing low at the prone rebel.

Skin heavily burned, blisters popped and oozing pus, the man had to be in terrible pain. His head was surrounded by pieces of cracked plastic, the remains of the helmet he had worn, and dark plastic of his goggles fused to his face. What remained of his trousers still burned with a small flame, slowly consuming the skin on his exposed shins, while his shredded body armour displayed the numerous lesions that flying shrapnel had inflicted on him. Bill didn't fire, didn't ask Angel what was wrong. He lifted his head and called out to his partner.

"Al!"

The Marine ran through the field of the dead, holding salvaged rifles close to his chest as he went and grinding to a halt beside Angel.

"What's the matter, bitch," he taunted, looking at the pale girl standing beside him. "You can plink a man from a hundred yards, blast his face off at thirty paces, but you don't have the balls to put a bullet in his brain close up?"

She didn't say anything to defend herself, simply pointed with her free hand. Al sighed and glared down on the dying man, frowned, then knelt down and picked up a fragment of the shattered helmet. Black in colour, it had an orange marking on it, something that at one point could have been the letter M.

"You said you wanted to kill this guy," said Bill, slowly pulling Angel back and stepping in front of her. "Well, here he is. If you hadn't caught him in that explosion, he may have survived this attack."

"Moloch," growled Al, snarling as he spoke. He pulled the knife from his webbing and sat on the ground beside the corpse before looking up.

"Give me some time alone with this piece of shit," he said. It wasn't a request, but an order. Bill nodded silently, then pulled Angel aside and headed towards the barn. "We'll go and get some tools to start clearing these bodies up."

The aftermath of the battle still played through Al's mind as he sat beside the squirming body. Adrenaline was finally dying off, returning his heartbeat to normal and allowing him to concentrate once more. The finding of the girl's weapon cache had been a massive boost to his morale, and the opportunity to test them out an even bigger boost.

And now, with Moloch dying beside him, Al felt complete.

"You know, you little shit, this is all your fault," he growled, digging the knife into the blackened ground and idly picking at his nails. "If it hadn't been for you and your idiotic worthless followers, all my squad wouldn't be dead. We wouldn't have crashed the helicopter, we could have been kickin' up our feet on that damn tower."

He laughed softly to himself.

"That tower. You might have done me a favour in that respect, I suppose. Doesn't mean I'm going to thank you for it, though, you worthless bastard. Under your orders, your men shot down our bird, and killed all my friends in the process. Well, now all *your* men are dead. Stinks of shit, doesn't it?"

The floundering man managed a choking, gasping gurgle, coughing up thick, dark red blood. Al looked at him.

"And now I'm stuck on this friggin' island with those two as company," he muttered, jerking a thumb towards the barn. "I mean, the kid's not too bad: he seems have a decent idea of what's goin' on, and he's a quick learner. I don't like his new girlfriend, though. Still, you dying on the floor beside me has really made my day, you racist fuck."

He replaced his knife in its pouch and drew his magnum, casually removing the clip and checking the barrel before slapping it back together and cocking it. He pressed the muzzle against the head of dying man and grinned. "This one is from me and all my 'Nigger' brothers back home. And my squad. And every one of your prisoners you beat and raped to death. Burn in hell, mother fucker."

Al pulled his weapon away, then took aim once more and squeezed the trigger. The slide of the magnum snapped back and spat a smoking brass shell from the top of the weapon. Moloch screamed in agony as the heavy round smashed into his gut, tearing through the lining of his stomach and splashing bile and blood over the edges of the fresh wound. Al chuckled to himself, then clambered to his feet. He looked down on the quivering and moaning man, then spat on him.

"We're going to burn the bodies, now. If you're not dead in four minutes, you're getting burned alive anyway."

He spat once more, then spun on his heel and slowly walked away.

"C'mon, kid," he shouted at the top of his voice, calling towards the barn and waving his arms. "Lets get these bastards on the barbecue. We ain't got all day."

IV

The sun lowered over the western ridge surrounding the farm, washing the building with a pale orange glow and casting long shadows across the ground. Thick curling wisps of smoke gently rose from behind the ridge, the smouldering remains of the burning bodies still glowing red and lacing the air with a taint of burning meat.

Bill and Al sat on two bales of hay in front of the farmhouse, watching the lazy sun as it slowly sank out of sight. Bill held an opened can of lager in one hand, taking the occasional sip and looking over the collection of home made cards that the Marine had produced from his pocket. Al held half a bottle of whiskey in one hand, with an empty at his feet, and glared at his own hand of poker. A thick and smouldering cigar hung loosely from his mouth, obscuring his face with a cloudy haze of tobacco smoke.

"What've you got?" he growled, flicking ash by tapping his cigar with his tongue. Bill scowled at the collection of cards in his hand, not really impressed by the various pornographic pictures that had been torn out of magazines and pasted on to credit card-sized pieces of card.

"Not much. Two pairs: threes and nines."

"Four aces," grinned Al, throwing his hand down on to the ground in front of him. "That's another game to me."

"Yeah, I must owe you, what, six hundred?"

"And the rest. I'll take your firstborn child as a down payment."

"You can wait that long?" asked Bill, finishing off his can of lager and opening another one. Al took another pull of his whiskey, then collected in the stack of cards.

"Another hand?" he asked, already shuffling the cards. Bill waved his hand in a dismissive gesture and Al shrugged, replacing the cards in his pocket. The two men were silent for a few minutes; each lost in their own thoughts.

"You know," muttered Al, removing his cigar and stubbing it out beneath his boot. "You know, I've been a Marine for almost twenty years. Twenty years, that's almost as long as you've been alive. And I'm still a Sergeant. All this time, and I haven't been promoted beyond that. And do you know why?"

Bill shrugged his shoulders and shook his head. Al took another pull from his bottle and wiped his mouth on the back of his hand.

"I'll tell you why. Above me is an officer. And I can't stand the pompous, arrogant bastards that they pick to be officers. They think they're so friggin' important and that they shouldn't have to get their hands dirty, you know what I mean? And the fact of the matter is that without people like me and you, kid, without us grunts, they'd be doing the dirty work themselves. The ignorant bastards that they are, they probably wouldn't even give you the time of day."

"You have a problem with authority figures?" Bill asked. Al shook his head and held up his hand.

"Hey, don't get me wrong. Johnny C was a great guy, he was a Lieutenant, but he was a brilliant guy. We got on like a house on fire. He was the exception to the rule. Officers are assholes.

"However, desperate times call for desperate measures. And if the dead getting up and eating other people while a bunch of fuckin' rebels armed with my weapons isn't a desperate time, then I don't know what is. In light of this, and the fact I'm the senior ranking person here, I'm going to give myself a battlefield promotion. As of now, I am Commander Albert George Colebrook. And you, kid, can be Sergeant Bill. How's that grab you?"

"Okay, I guess," Bill said. His surprise promotion didn't make him feel any different. "What about Angel?"

"Long-range scout," slurred Al, finishing off his bottle of whiskey and dropping it to the floor. "When we leave tomorrow morning, she can stay here."

Bill was quiet. Al smiled and nodded, realising he'd hit a nerve.

"I'm going to get some sleep. We have an early start tomorrow, and I want to make sure we get as much of that stuff in the barn packed up as we possibly can."

"We're going to take *everything* from her?"

"Why not?" grunted Al, climbing up from the bale of hay and turning to face the farmhouse. "None of it's hers, it belongs to the Marines. I'm a Marine, so it's mine."

"What about defending herself from the gang?"

"They come here, the bitch lets them in, shows them she hasn't got anything, they leave her alone. Christ, I'll give her our forwarding address if she wants."

Bill nodded, then watched as he walked towards the house and his chosen bedroom.

"Hey," he called after his new commanding officer. Al paused mid-stride and looked back over his shoulder, cocking an eyebrow. "You've lost people, haven't you? Close friends, people you're close to. You've lost them in combat, right?"

Al nodded slowly, grimly.

"How do you deal with that? How do you deal with losing people you're close to?"

Al rummaged in one of his pockets, and pulled out a silver metal ring with several metal dog tags attached to it. He looked over it, then casually tossed it to Bill.

"People deal with it different ways. Some are desperate for revenge. Me? I never forget them. I'll get it back off you in the morning. Night, kid."

Remember them, he thought. *Just like Angel said. Don't forget.*

Bill sat and looked through the collection of tags he had been handed, reading through the names, ranks and serial numbers on each tiny piece of metal. Mantel, Clarity, Yung, Grem, Rook, Davis, Miller... names of his lost squad members? The last name he read stirred a memory, and Bill patted down his pockets, pulling out the single battered tag. He traced the letters of Jason Miller's name, and compared it to that of Dean Miller's.

"Wonder it they were brothers," he muttered, clipping the tag on to the ring, effectively laying him to rest with his fellow Marines. He slipped the ring into his bag, then look up at the sky. The sun had finally set, leaving behind the black cloth of night spattered with pinpricks of light. Lost in his thoughts, Bill didn't hear the sounds of boots crunching on the ground, or the crinkle of hay giving way beneath the weight of someone sitting down.

"You okay?"

Startled by the question, Bill had to look around to identify the speaker, as if the soft and feminine voice wasn't enough of a give-away. He smiled at Angel, nodding softly.

"Just thinking to myself. You know, lost family, lost friends."

"You said you'd lost your parents when you were young. How did you cope?"

"It was easy for me. They were killed in a car accident when I was three months old. I never knew them to miss."

"What about Jenny? Did you have to kill her?"

Bill swallowed hard, then shook his head. "She was amongst the first to go. The plague took her, near the beginning of the spread. She was killed and cremated by the Marines. All I had to do was watch it all happen, then dwell on it for days in quarantine."

Bill crushed his can and dropped it to the floor, letting it land on the two empty whiskey bottles with a clatter. He sighed heavily, then returned his gaze to the darkened heavens.

"Since this all began, I've always thought about Jenny, and about her being dead. I never thought about my friends. Christ, everyone I know is dead. Or undead. Jesus, everyone… they're all dead."

"There's a chance that some have survived, though, isn't there? I mean, we survived, right?"

Bill grinned. He knew she was just trying to make him feel better. "We survived for a reason, though. You were way out of here, in the middle of the country, away from the mass crowds. Al was offshore in a guard tower somewhere, watching over the island. And I was trapped in quarantine for a fortnight. If I hadn't been in there, I would probably be dead by now."

"You were lucky then," said Angel. Bill laughed softly to himself.

"Look around me, Angel, do I look like a lucky guy? My life's turned to shit, everyone I know is dead, I've just spent the last four hours dragging dead bodies over to the other side of that hill to set fire to them… Is that lucky?"

"You're still alive," she said. "And not everyone you know is dead. You know Al. You know me. Come on, inside. The sun's gone down, and it'll be getting cold soon. C'mon, I'll make you something to eat."

Bill rose from the bale of hay and stumbled after Angel into the farmhouse, closing the door behind him and shutting the cold of the night out behind him.

Another day dawned on the farm, and Bill found himself awake first once more. He and Angel had sat on the sofa late into the night, the two of them talking about their lives before the plague. Bill had tried to make his own existence sound exciting, but he could only dress up the fact he was an internal postman so much before he sounded like an incredibly boring person.

Well, Junior Head of Post Distribution, he mentally corrected himself.

He'd talked about Jenny for a while, then his friends, then about Jenny again. He'd held back his tears as best he could, but he knew some had managed to find their way out his glazed eyes and down his face.

Angel, in turn, had spoke of her life on the farm, her college course in veterinary medicine and surgery, and her family. She also had shed a few tears during the course of her story, and Bill had wrapped an arm around her, trying to comfort her.

That was how he had woken up: a blanket draped over their legs and his arm over her shoulder. She lay her head on his chest, her eyes closed and her hand gripping a handful of T-shirt. For a moment Bill smiled, remembering lazy Sunday mornings with Jenny. Then the memory died, and a sudden flash of guilt washed over his mind. He slowly and expertly moved out from beneath the sleeping girl, making sure there were enough cushions to keep her comfortable and asleep, before moving out to the exterior of the farm.

Rain lashed the ground, a thick grey haze of fat raindrops splattering the dirt around the house and turning it into a thick quagmire of mud. Sheets of water poured from over the edge of the roof, forming a transparent wall around the house. Bill removed his jacket and strolled out into downpour, allowing the water to wash over his face and hands. The smell of gunpowder had clung to him long after the battle, and the arduous task or removing the dead had worked up quite a sweat. Sweat and cordite mixed with the cloying scent of the burning dead wasn't an especially pleasant smell to carry around on your clothing, and Bill was pleased to have the chance to rinse off the stench. A couple of water barrels beside the front door were slowly filling up, so there would be plenty of water for Al and Angel should they decide to have a wash themselves.

Lightning flashed in the distance, and after a brief pause, a rumble of thunder rolled across the valley. Returning to the front door and grabbing his jacket, Bill returned into the house and shook himself off. A cool chill hung in the air, and he could feel his flesh prickle and pucker in the slight draft that circulated the room. He returned to the living room, saw that Angel was still fast asleep, and sat down in one of the armchairs. He noticed a single red dot of light dancing over the blanket still wrapped around Angel's legs, slowly working its way up over her stomach, up her arm and resting on her forehead.

"Put the gun away, Al, and get down here."

The Marine at the top of the stairs grunted and slung his rifle over his shoulder, slowly making his way down the stairs and grinning. He only wore his trousers, proudly displaying his muscles and tattoos.

"Very tasteful," muttered Bill, pointing to the reclining woman on Al's stomach. He grinned, tracing the hairline of the woman, and nodded.

"Still raining?" asked Al, nodding towards Bill and his soaking clothes. Bill nodded grimly and wrung out the lower part of his dark T-shirt, splattering water on to the floor.

"It was raining last night when I got up to go for a piss," Al commented. "When I got up and went outside, I couldn't help but notice you and her were pretty frigging cosy. All wrapped up and hugging each other."

He strolled out towards the front door and opened it up, crouching down and digging the blade of his knife into the floorboards, wedging the door open. A brief flicker of lightning crashed into the ground in the distance, shortly followed by another thunderous crash. The windows rattled slightly, shaking the spatter of water already on the pane and creating obscure patterns.

"Damn, it's really coming down out there," he said before Bill could protest about his remark. "It's going to be a real pisser trying to travel in this. At least until we get over the ridges and fields, back on to the proper roads. We're going to get soaked loading those crates up into the hummer, too. Shame we didn't do it last night, we could have just made off now and left her to get on with it herself."

"Jesus, we can't do that," Bill hissed, glaring over his shoulder and keeping his voice low, making sure Angel was still asleep. He gently pulled the door to the living room shut behind him, then turned back to face Al. "You're still hell-bent on leaving her behind, aren't you?"

"Typical frigging English gentlemen," Al scoffed, pulling a small cigarette from behind his ear and searching his trouser pockets for a light. "Always with the chivalry and what you think's right. We can't bring her, there's barely enough room in there as it is for all the weapons. And you mustn't have seen my bumper sticker. It says 'No bitches or whores allowed'. We take the loot and leave her."

"Well, why don't we leave some of the weapons to make room for her?"

"What?" choked Al, a look of astonishment on his face as he turned to look at Bill. "Leave weapons? Christ, kid, are you mad?"

"C'mon, Al, how many machineguns and grenade launchers do you really need?"

"All of them," he growled. "Every last one. Why don't you let her drive your bike?"

"It doesn't work," Bill said. "You know that as well as I do."

"Yeah, but she doesn't," he smiled sadistically. "Let her find out the hard way."

Bill sighed, looking back at the closed door, then at Al again.

"What if we get a bigger vehicle? Something that would carry all the weapons and the three of us comfortably?"

"Last I head Uncle Bob's Used Car Emporium closed for business about a month ago. Think about it, kid, where are we going to get a working vehicle bigger than the humvee? Anything that was half-decent would have been taken and used by the rebels for their own diabolical needs. That, and we don't have the time, tools or expertise to stand around in the middle of no-mans land surrounded by zombies and rebels and shit knows what while we tinker with whatever machinery lies underneath the hood."

Bill sighed heavily. "Well why don't we tow something with it?"

"Because I don't want her coming with us," yelled Al. "Jesus kid, what's it going to take to get that into your thick skull?"

Angel opened her eyes to the sounds of raised voices in the kitchen and sighed. The duo only seemed to argue and bicker with one another, much like an old married couple. She grinned as the thought of an old married couple conjured images of her parents, sitting by the fire after a hard day of work. Her father, sitting on one of the armchairs and reading through the daily newspaper, smoking his pipe with Buster, the old sheepdog, curled up at his feet.

Buster had been getting too old to round up the few sheep they had, but Lexis, the young bitch they'd got to act as a replacement, was too young to be trained at the moment. She liked to run around in the kitchen, always looking out for any scraps of food Angel's mother dropped on the floor.

Her mother and father always seemed to get on, but every so often they'd have the occasional argument: tracking in mud from the fields, or leaving pieces of his shotgun lying on the table when he was cleaning.

The same shotgun she'd used on both parents when they'd become infected.

She closed her eyes, trying to shut out the vision of their heads cracking beneath a point-blank shell from the shotgun, but those images were permanently burned into her mind, a grotesque scene that she knew she would be taking to her deathbed.

Wiping the tears from her cheeks, she stood up and cast aside the blanket that covered her, grabbing her handgun off the table and replacing it her back-drawn holster, moving towards the door and lightly placing her hand on the doorknob. She opened it slightly and listened to the most recent argument.

"You've seen her fight, Al, seen her with a weapon." Bill's voice came first. Angel smiled. The soldier may not like her, but at least she had a friend in the young man. "She's a good shot with a rifle, even at a distance," he finished. Angel blushed slightly at the comment, then opened the door a little more to hear Al's response. His voice was low and stern.

"She balked when it was time to shoot someone at point-blank range, though. It's hesitation like that that could get us all killed. I don't care what her bullshit story is with her parents: I have to see it to believe it."

Angel felt a surge of anger rush through her. He probably didn't have any idea what she'd gone through. She clenched her fists tight, her nails nipping the flesh of her palms as she listened to him continue.

"That being said, she does have a lot of food and water stored. More than she would ever need. If we had a larger vehicle, we *could* take a lot more stuff with us."

"Bastards," she muttered. They were going to just take everything they could and leave her with nothing. No food, no weapons, nothing. She'd expected this much from Al, but she didn't know how Bill would deal with it. She opened the door fully and crept into the hallway, edging towards the doorway into the kitchen: she knew the house well enough to avoid the creaking floorboards.

"And what are we going to leave her with? A kitchen knife and a box of crackers?"

Angel grinned at Bill's defence. At least he was still on her side. And after the story he'd told her the previous night, about Jenny and how much he missed her, she knew there was no ulterior motive behind his actions.

"Don't be stupid," muttered Al. There was a pause as the sounds of cupboards opening and closing filled the air. "I'll be taking the knives, too. You never know when I might need one." Angel shuffled closer, trying to hear what was going on without being seen.

"So we're going to leave her unarmed and without any food?"

"She lives on a friggin' farm, Bill," Al shouted, angrily slapping his hand on the bench. "What we take she can grow again."

"What we take will leave her dead in a couple of days, if that. I'm a Sergeant, now, remember that?"

Angel frowned. What did Bill mean? Was he a soldier, too? Something he'd left out his tales, maybe? She heard Al groan then a tapping sound of a heavy boot against the wooden floorboards. "Stupid damn alcohol, always making me say stuff I shouldn't. Okay, so I made you an honorary Sergeant. Temporarily, I may add. I can revoke that status at any given moment. What of it?"

"If I'm a Sergeant I need a squad. Just like you had one. And I want Angel in my squad." She smiled, happy that she was wanted by at least half of the team.

"That's not how the Marine Corps work, Bill. It's not like picking teams for soccer."

"It's called football over here," Bill ventured quietly to himself. Al scowled at him, though the Marine's look didn't deter him from continuing the argument.

"Teams or not, she's coming with us. If she wants to, that is. And if you're going to take all her weapons and food, then she isn't going to have a choice in the matter."

"What did I say about my bumper sticker? No bitches or whores," said Al. "And besides, the little cocktease has probably got a nuclear warhead in a cellar somewhere. Let her deal with her shit herself."

"No nuclear devices," said Angel, entering the kitchen. She'd heard enough of the argument to know what was going on. Al wanted to take everything and leave her behind, but Bill didn't.

"What?" said Al, spinning on her heel and glaring at Angel. "Where the hell did you crawl out of?"

"I was only in the next room. These walls aren't soundproof. And there's no nuclear weapons hidden in the cellar, just five barrels of wine."

Al raised his finger, pointing his finger aggressively in Angel's face, and was about to launch into a tirade of insults when his features broke.

"Wine?" he asked softly. "You have wine in a cellar?"

"I'll show you," she offered, sinking to her knees and rolling back a corner of the rug. Al whipped his heavy pistol out from the holster and levelled it with Angel's left eye. He casually flicked the safety off and motioned towards the floor with it.

"Take it really slow," he cautioned. "I wouldn't want to have to put a bullet in your brain." He smiled, then turned to face Bill, raising an eyebrow.

Angel rolled back the rug and grabbed the handle for the hatchway into the cellar. She twisted it, then heaved it open, exposing the dark depths of the chamber below the kitchen. Al sunk to his knees, peering into the gloom of the pit.

"Is it safe? No traps, no explosions, no nasty sharp rusty things waiting to stick in my feet?"

Angel shook her head. "There is one explosive charge, but that's at the other entrance to the cellar."

"Other entrance?" asked Bill, squatting down beside the hole. "Where's the other entrance?"

"The wooden shack between here and the barn. This place is almost a hundred and fifty years old; it's been in the family since it was made. During one of the wars it was modified with the addition of a bomb shelter. After the war was over, the bomb shelter became a cellar, used to cure meat and store anything else that couldn't be left out in the barn. My Dad made his own wine, and stored it down there."

"The wooden shack?" muttered Bill, turning to look at Al. He shrugged.

"I didn't check it out," he confessed, lowering his legs into the hole and slipping into the darkness. "Is there a light down there?"

"Switch is here," Angel said, pointing to a small plastic button set into the wooden frame around the hole. She flicked it on, then quickly turned it off again and smiled as Al stumbled down the steep stairs in near darkness, landing with a thump at the bottom. Bill caught sight of the smile and grinned back.

"I think you've found his Achilles heel," he whispered, winking. Angel smiled and felt her cheeks flush. She peered back into the cellar and could see Al sitting on the ground, eyes fixed in the direction of the wall that had the five casks of wine lined up. "What have you got down there?"

The Marine was speechless, his find obviously too much to take in all at once. After a couple of minutes he clambered back into the kitchen and flicked the light off, then replaced the hatch and rolled the rug back into position. He sat down at the table with an idiotic grin on his face, scratching his beard, his eyes glazed and distant. He finally looked over to Angel.

"Elderberry wine, marrow rum; do you how to make that shit, bitch?"

"Yeah," Angel nodded. "I used to help my Dad out all the time."

Al nodded, then grinned and turned to look at Bill.

"We're going to need a bigger vehicle."

X
RIGGED TO KILL

"I don't know how many are dead now. Millions, certainly…"

I

The torrential downpour of the rain had died down to a fine drizzle by dinnertime, giving both Bill and Al an easier task of loading equipment into the humvee. The outlying fields would still be unstable and muddy, but shouldn't prove too much of a problem for the heavy army vehicle.

"Are you sure you'll be okay on your own?" asked Bill, looking down on Angel as she finished off cleaning her weapons and pushing them aside. She smiled, then nodded her head.

"I'll be fine. One of us needs to stay here and keep an eye on the weapons."

"And the alcohol," shouted Al as he marched through the hallway outside the kitchen.

"And the alcohol," agreed Angel, sighing. "Talk about a one-track mind."

"He's a man of few thoughts, and a lot of words," agreed Bill, smiling. "I could stay with you, if you want. Or maybe you could go with him on this search."

"It makes sense that the two of you go. And if I go with Al, I don't know who would be pissed off the most, me or him. No, you go I'll be fine. Just as long as you're not going to be too long; the rest of that gang's still out there, they're still going to want their stuff back."

"We'll try to get back here in about a day or two. We won't be away too long, I swear."

Angel smiled, nodded her head. Bill removed his radio headset and handed it to her. She looked at it, puzzled, then looked at Bill.

"I don't know what range it's got," he confessed. "Al normally has it on channel two. Keep it on channel six for now. If he finds out I've given you this he'll probably tear some of my favourite things off my body and feed them to the zombies out there. Put it on soon as we leave."

Angel grinned, then folded up the headset and placed it in one of the pockets on her trousers. "If I get into any trouble, I'll hide in the cellar. That's where Al's stored the weapons that he's leaving."

Bill nodded, then started to make his way towards the door leading out the kitchen. Angel lashed out, grabbing him by the arm and pulling him back.

"You *are* coming back, aren't you?"

Bill smiled, then patted her hand with his own before removing it. "We've both got reasons to come back for you. Al wants his liquor and weapons. I want someone to have a decent conversation with. Don't worry, Angel, we'll be back. Promise."

Leaving the kitchen, Bill exited the farm and saw Al sitting in the driving seat of the humvee, waving frantically to him and motioning towards his head. Bill shrugged and tapped his ear with his finger. Al shrugged and hammered the dashboard, finding the air horn of the machine. Turning once more to Angel, Bill smiled then ran towards the vehicle, clambering aboard and strapping himself into one of the vacant seats in the front.

"I've been telling you to hurry your miserable ass up for ages. Did you turn your headset off?"

"I've lost it," muttered Bill, fidgeting with his fingers and looked down towards his feet. He'd never been brilliant at lying, and he hoped Al wouldn't be able to call his bluff. "It must've fallen off when we were shifting the dead yesterday, and I didn't realise it."

"Damn it, Bill, that's an expensive piece of military hardware, paid for by taxpayers. Do you have any idea how much they cost to replace?"

Bill shrugged his shoulders.

"They're dirt cheap," laughed Al, opening a compartment beneath the dashboard and pulling out another headset. "But that doesn't mean you can just go around losin' them all the time. You have to take care. Now, have you said goodbye to your girlfriend?"

"She's not my girlfriend," scorned Bill, pointing a finger menacingly at Al. He laughed and knocked his hand aside, turning the engine over and grinding the gear stick into drive. "How many times do I need to tell you?"

Al laughed aloud then pressed down on the accelerator, tyres churning the muddy ground beneath the heavy vehicle before lurching away.

"Let's see if we can do this a little easier than we did comin' in," muttered Al, slowly tracking the soft and slippery road leading away from the farm. The vehicle gently meandered from side to side as it followed the dirt track road, the rear wheels spinning and occasionally drifting out wide to one side.

"Easy," muttered Al to himself, licking his lips and gripping the steering wheel. "Easy… Gotcha, you little bastard!"

With a triumphant roar of the engine the vehicle crested a small rise and slid to a stop on a glistening black concrete road. Bill followed Al's gaze as he looked from left to right, slowly checking the surrounding area for any sign of danger. He pointed a finger towards the road ahead of them, and at a small crowd of moving dark shapes.

"We go that way. If the compass on this piece of fine military hardware is correct, which it should be, then behind us is Edgly. We've already been there, I don't think there's anything around there that can help us out. And I sure didn't pass anything on the way in here."

"So those things up ahead of us are Rots, right? And we're going to go through them?"

"It's the only way, really. I'd be inclined to check out Little Slumberton, but that bitch of yours says that village is where the rebels are hidin' out. Do you feel confident enough to conduct a full-scale assault on a nest of vipers?"

"Shit, no," said Bill. "But I bet you do."

"There's a fine line between confidence and arrogance," Al announced, running his hands over the controls on the dashboard and flicking a seemingly random collection of buttons. The heavy weapon mounted on the front of the vehicle shuddered slightly, emitting a few creaks and groans. "I'm confident enough to say the Vulcan cannon on the front there will rip those dead shits apart. I'm also confident enough to say I'll be able to smash them to a pulp beneath the tyres of this vehicle. I'm not arrogant enough to think I can conduct an unplanned assault on a whim with just you as my backup."

Al gunned the engine and slowly rolled the machine forwards, edging closer to the shambling corpses in the distance. He motioned wordlessly to a small control panel in front of Bill, and the small nub of a joystick. Bill looked at it and gently nudged the controls. The weapon responded by moving in the direction the controls were pushed. He smiled, then tried some different movements, panning the barrels of the weapon slowly from left to right, nudging them up and down.

"It's more like a miniature anti-aircraft gun," Al announced, keeping his speed below ten miles an hour as he coasted along the road, trying to line up the gaggle of ghouls with the front of the vehicle. "It's a smaller calibre, but it would still shred a chopper in a couple of minutes. You don't need to raise it much; it should already be levelled with their heads. And you might want to put those goggles and ear protectors on, though. The son of a bitch can be loud when it kicks in, probably pop your eardrums at this range."

Bill watched as Al flicked his own pair of tinted goggles on and pulled on an old pair of ear protectors. Bill copied him, knowing that if the battle-hardened Marine was quick in protecting himself from the impending weapons fire, then he'd be an idiot not to copy.

"Ready?" asked Bill, resting his thumb on the firing control and slowly rotating the weapon to the left. He looked over and saw Al nod solemnly, biting his lip and gripping the wheel with his giant hands.

Bill looked forwards and scanned the group of undead, drinking in the details of the group.

Each of the rotting creatures before him served to remind him that they had been living breathing people up until a month ago. Amongst the gathering he could see a man dressed in a bloodied white doctors coat, face gaunt and features sunken: beside him was a pale-faced man, a red grin smeared across his face. Bill thought for a moment that it was the bloody remnants of its last meal, but the garish and ragged clothing he wore suggested he had been a clown in his former life. Bill shuddered. He'd never been overly fond of clowns, and the hideous and garish atrocity that lingered in the crowd didn't help renew his love of them.

One of the closer of the Rots, a young man of about eighteen, turned to look at the approaching vehicle and stopped, milky white eyes fixed on the gleaming windows and the warm meat behind them. The one arm he had was clutched around his midriff, oozing a thick dark red liquid. As he saw the vehicle he reached out with his limb, opening his toothless and bloody maw and uttering a low, keening wail. He took an unsteady, lurching step towards the humvee, the movement dislodging blood and offal from the tear in his stomach: a snake of scarlet organs and intestines slopped out the hole, spilling stagnant blood and caustic juices from the ruined vital parts. Fluids dripped and spattered on the pavement, slicking the already wet surface and affecting the balance of the creature.

"What're you waitin' for, kid?" asked Al, grabbing a small revolver from the floor and cracking open the chamber, counting the rounds before slamming it shut, spinning it with a flourish and aiming it at the young man through the glass. "Hose the bastards."

Bill nodded and pressed down on the firing button of the weapon. The barrels of the weapon began to spin, and for a moment he thought that Al hadn't loaded the device, but he should have known better then to doubt the Marine.

The weapon screamed to life, a deafening and thunderous retort that hurt Bill's ears, even through the protectors. The muzzle flash from the weapon seared his eyes, and he lifted one arm to shield his eyes. Even through the windshield he could feel the heat against his face and hands: the few drops of rain that still fell from the sky hissed upon contact with the whirling metal, instantly evaporating.

Bill slowly nudged the control from left to right, showering the crowd with the lethal rounds before the ammunition reserve dried up, leaving the barrels spinning but ejecting no projectiles. He looked at Al and shrugged. Al nodded grimly.

"Fun," Al smiled. "Looks like that's the main cannon out of ammo. It's amazin' how quick it can chew out a full load of five hundred rounds. Okay, that's dry for now. Get out back and man one of those mounted machineguns."

Bill glared out the window and saw that some of the Rots still stood: though their torsos had been chewed and destroyed by the rounds, they had managed to stay upright, and had started to make their way towards the static vehicle. He flung the door open and toppled out on to the ground, slamming it shut and frantically clambering on to the back of the vehicle. He chanced a glance over his shoulder and saw the faster of the group of Rots begin to break away, their joints stiff and oozing fluids with each jerking movement.

He grabbed the controls to one of the machineguns and hammered on the roof of the humvee, indicating he was ready to go. The machine shuddered forwards, gaining speed as it barrelled for the oncoming group. It smashed into the front-most creatures, and Bill could hear Al laughing maniacally as their bodies were torn and shredded beneath the heavily armoured machine. Severed limbs rained down on the ground and bounced off the bonnet, fingers twitching and grabbing at the vehicle. Bill slowly panned the weapon from left to right, tapping off bursts from the weapon at any of the decaying creatures that shambled too close to the sides of the humvee.

"You're doing good, kid," said Al, his voice calm and quiet, as if ploughing through a crowd of walking dead were an everyday event for him.

"Don't hold back on the speed on my account," said Bill, his voice the exact opposite to Al's. "How long do I have to stand up here?"

"Until we get where we're going," barked the Marine, guiding the large vehicle beyond the few undead left standing.

"We don't have a destination, though, do we? We're just randomly driving until we find something we can drag."

"Well then, keep your eyes open. Think of it as an incentive."

Bill grumbled to himself, then flicked the radio headset to channel six, listening to the gentle howl of white noise: the telltale sign that he'd wandered out the signal range. He flicked it back to two, listening to the low whistle of the driver as he guided the vehicle along the road. It was a tuneless melody, though Bill found it strangely familiar. Maybe identifying it would help kill some time while he was on lookout.

After a few minutes the whistling stopped, and Bill found himself engulfed in semi-silence once more, the wind whipping around him as the machine moved onwards.

"When do I get my turn driving?" he eventually asked. "I know you like firing your weapons, are we going to take turns?"

"Can you drive?" asked Al.

"Not really," answered Bill. "But how hard can it be? I mean, it's not as if there's any traffic on the road, is there? I can't cause an accident."

"I'm not trustin' *The Colebrook* to you if you can't drive. It's bad enough I had to ram those dead shits and stain the bodywork in the first place, but for to put it in the hands of an amateur… what, do you think I'm fucking stupid?"

"Do you want me to answer that?" muttered Bill beneath his breath.

"Microphone, kid," Al scorned. "I can hear everythin' you say. Now keep your eyes open for anything we can use."

Bill slowly turned from left to right, snagging his crossbow and lifting it to his shoulder, using the scope as a makeshift telescope as he scanned the surrounding countryside. Hills scattered with craggy rock formations and covered in thick foliage surrounded him, with giant steel skeletons standing guard over the dead countryside every so often, inert pylons that had been raped of the electrical charge they carried. "So I'm looking for anything like a trailer or a caravan, something we can hook up to the back of this machine."

"Even if it's just a cart big enough to carry five casks of home made wine, I'll be happy."

"What about Angel?"

"Fuck her," said Al, then he laughed to himself. "Of course, you probably already have."

"Microphone," mimicked Bill. "I can hear you."

"You were meant to. That's why I said it aloud."

Bill continued his vigil, trying to pinpoint something that they'd be able to use in their voyage. "Anything like a cart… trailer… hey, what about an articulated lorry?"

"Where the hell are we going to find one of them out here?" mocked Al. Bill could imagine the degrading and belittling smile on his face as he spoke. He smirked himself as he answered. "Looks like there might be a one over to our left. I think we should swing by and take a look. Providing this machine of yours can pull something that heavy."

"*The Colebrook* can pull anything, you annoying little shit. Now, what time?"

Bill shrugged to himself and looked at the watch on his wrist. The glass face had been cracked, and one of the hands seemed to have come loose and got lost in a scuffle at one point. "I don't know, maybe one or two o'clock. Why?"

The vehicle slowly swayed off to the right, away from the vehicle Bill had spotted in the distance to the other side of him. He banged on the roof of the vehicle and yelled for Al to stop and turn around. The gurgle of the engine died, and the machine rolled to a stop.

"What's wrong, damn it?" spat Al, leaning out the drivers window and craning his neck around to look at his partner. "You said two o'clock."

"It was just a guess, my watch is broken. What does that matter, anyway?"

"Idiot," shouted Al, opening the door and clambering out the machine. He looked at Bill, but pointed his hand straight ahead in the direction the vehicle was facing. "Twelve o'clock is that way, dead ahead. Left is nine, right is three, and backwards is six. Work out the rest of the angles yourself. Now, where is it?"

Bill turned to his left, then lifted the scope of his crossbow and scanned the distant horizon.

"Uh… I'd have to guess at about maybe seven, now."

"Fuckin' amateur," muttered Al, climbing back into the vehicle and turning the engine over. "I'll have to teach him how to wipe his ass next."

Grinding dirt and grass beneath thick heavy tires, Al spun the vehicle around in one fluid motion and headed towards their intended prize.

II

It was another lazy afternoon for Gareth Lloyd Arthur Asfeld, just like every other afternoon of the past month had been.

He sat in the cabin of his articulated lorry with a thick smoking cigar hanging from one hand, wisps of acrid smoke curling up the length of his arm and tickling his nostrils. The smoke mixed with the heady scent of his own musk, trapped in the confines of the cabin with no means for it to escape. Though it was a pungent odour, it wasn't as bad as the overpowering scent of rotting flesh that lingered over the countryside outside. He tried not to leave the confines of his cramped living conditions unless he needed to: it was normally just the need to relieve himself that forced him to exit the cab and expose himself to the sights and smells of the decaying countryside.

The lorry had been a state-of-the-art vehicle when he first purchased it, with an on-board computer loaded with the latest in satellite navigation software and a digital copy of most road maps for the European continent. Garth had never really trusted the satellite information, and preferred his own collection of paperback A-Z books to the digital copies. The first thing he had done after getting the lorry off the forecourt had been to erase the hard drive and fill it with his music. Every song he had, on every format, the procedure took him over three days to complete, including the day he spent hunting through his belongings in the storage locker he'd rented in Spain to find the older vinyl records he'd been given by his parents.

"After all," he'd said to himself while in the process of waiting for the information to transfer. "I didn't buy it for the gadgets. I bought it because I like the colour."

That hadn't been the real reason he'd bought the vehicle, though. The real reason was more tragic then that.

Up until three years ago, Gareth Lloyd Arthur Asfeld, Garth to his friends, had been married to his wife Laura, and was the proud father of Anna, a thirteen year old who was top in nearly all her classes, bar physical education. Garth himself was no fan of physical exertion, as his ample frame testified to, so the fact something like that seemed to be dragging Anna's grades down didn't annoy him that much: he knew she excelled in what really counted.

Garth also excelled in what he did as the managing director of his own shipping and transportation firm. GA Shipping was a highly successful firm, delivering millions of pounds worth of goods and equipment globally each year. With his earnings, Garth could afford to take his family and buy a new house in Spain, providing a life of luxury for the two women he loved.

Three years ago, business seemed to slow down as rival firms took his business away. It was about this time Laura also started to cheat on him, indulging in an affair with an advertising executive. The marriage soon fell apart, and the resulting lawsuit saw Laura gain custody of Anna, the house, and half of the business. Through a series of further unfortunate events, Garth was forced to sell his business to a rival firm in order to cover maintenance payments and lawyer bills. With nothing remaining of his company, and what was left of his money rapidly dwindling, Garth had no option but to look towards a source of income to keep his money-hungry ex-wife happy.

Having worked in shipping his whole adult life, he figured it would only make sense to stay in the business. Pooling as much money as he could, he bought his lorry, fully loaded with the gadgets and gizmos, and became a driver for the haulage firm EuroTruck Ltd, formally known and GA

Shipping.

"That bitch Laura," he swore, idly tapping his feet in time to the drumbeat of the current song. "If it hadn't been for her, I wouldn't be working as a driver, or stuck on this frigging island. Soon as I get out of here, I'm going to retire. The bitch has got more of a chance pissing into the wind then getting another penny out of me."

He shook his head, knowing that wasn't true. As long as he thought his money was helping Anna, he couldn't stop sending money. Though at the moment, he had no choice. His own desire to take the highest paying jobs meant he had volunteered for a delivery from Italy to Scotland, a long and arduous journey that many drivers shirked away from. It had left him exhausted, and now stranded in a hostile environment where it looked like he had no hope of escaping from. If the living dead didn't get him, then the people running around with weapons would.

Garth grinned and patted the sawn-off shotgun lying on the seat next to him, a weapon he'd liberated from the body of a partially eaten young woman. It wasn't the most pleasant way to acquire a weapon, but it had saved him numerous times.

His relaxed attitude quickly changed, as the soothing sounds of his music became drowned out by the heavy and thunderous sounds of an approaching vehicle. Grabbing the shotgun and sinking low into the foot well, he tried to peer into the cracked and shattered mirrors on either side of him. He fumbled with the shotgun and cracked it open, making sure both barrels were loaded and primed before snapping it shut. Clenching the smouldering cigar between his teeth, he lowered the volume of his music and listened to the sounds outside.

The pulsing engine drew closer to the truck, then ground to a halt. The sound of a single car door opening, then slamming shut, was followed by a low murmuring voice. Then there came slow, deliberate footsteps in the gravel surrounding the parked vehicle. From where he was crouched, he could see the reflection of a shaven head, the skin dark and glistening with moisture from the fine spray of rain in the air. Another hushed whisper came from the large figure, and then a gentle continuous hissing. The butt of a large rifle battered against the passenger door window, then again. The third blow smashed the window, and a small grey canister bounced into the cabin, the tapered end spewing a thick yellow smoke.

The minute Garth smelled the gas his eyes began to stream, the hideous acrid odour burning at his sinuses. He flung the driver-side door open and fell the three feet to the ground, coughing violently and dropping his weapon, rubbing at his watering eyes with the palms of his hands.

"Flushed him out," called a deep American voice from the other side of the vehicle. "Head's up, he's on your side."

"Got him," came a second voice, this one English and not as loud, but closer. "He's on his knees, looks like he's crying."

"Tear gas will do that to you," laughed the American, his voice carrying over the crunching of gravel beneath his feet. "Knock that shotgun away from him, make sure he can't grab it. And keep him covered with your own weapon."

Garth rolled on to his back and tried to look around, but could only make out two blurry figures. One was taller and darker than the other and he seemed to be the source of the American voice. He felt a heavy boot press down on his chest and saw the opened muzzle of a weapon pointing directly at his face: his eyes were still too bleary to make out any further details.

"Who are you?" grunted the American, pressing down harder with each word spoke.

"Garth," choked the lorry driver. "My name is Garth Asfeld."

The pressure from the boot didn't increase any further, but it didn't decrease.

"What's in the truck?"

"Not much," stammered Garth, blinking rapidly as the chemical burns to his nose slowly started to ease. He hadn't inhaled enough of the gas to cause any lasting damage, but there was enough in his system to keep his eyes blurring over. "A few crates left over from my last run. Some soap, deodorant, toothpaste, tampons… nothing you fellas would be interested in."

"We'll be the judge of that. Check it out, kid, see what he's got in there."

"The keys are in the cabin," called out Garth, squirming beneath the boot of the American.

"He's a little keen on us looking, Al, are you sure this isn't a trap?"

"I hadn't though of that," confessed the American. He removed his foot and grabbed Garth by the collar of his EuroTruck uniform shirt, pulling him to his feet.

"You're going to open the truck for us, pal."

"Get me the keys," demanded Garth, allowing the man pulling him to guide him, albeit roughly, towards the rear of the large vehicle.

"What's so special about these keys?" demanded Al, pushing him against the back of the truck and pinning him by pressing the muzzle of his weapon against his windpipe. "Do you have a key ring with a concealed blade? Maybe a small throwaway holdout pistol?"

"It's got the key to the padlock on, you dumb bastard, so I can open the truck up," spat Garth, pushing Al away from him. The dark skinned man staggered back a step, then lifted his weapon and jammed the muzzle in Garth's stomach. He continued his speech, oblivious to the threat of the weapon. "It's bad enough that my fine vehicle is riddled with bullet holes, burn marks and dented from the impact of the walking dead, the last thing I want to do is bust open the back with a frigging *crowbar* just to please the Spanish frigging inquisition. Who the hell are you guys?"

"Got them," shouted the English man, running around to the back of the vehicle and shaking the keys. He tossed them to Al, who made a show of examining the plastic key ring, obviously searching for any concealed blades.

"Wine them, dine them, then sixty-nine them?" he asked, before handing the keys over. "Very nice, very classy. Now open the truck up, I want to see what's inside."

Garth took the keys and sighed, then turned and unlocked the padlock, letting the heavy device drop to the ground. He unhooked the latch, then grabbed the handle to one door and hauled it open, displaying the cavernous and empty cargo hold.

"Check it out, kid," commanded Al, waving into the darkness. Garth watched as the young man hoisted his body into the gaping maw of the trailer and vanished into the darkness. A faint glimmer of light sparked into existence near the back of the cargo hold, accompanied by sounds of wood scraping against metal.

"Checks out," came his muffled response. He returned from the darkness with a toothbrush hanging from his mouth and a fleck of toothpaste on his lips, nodding to Al. "Toothpaste, shaving cream, the lot."

"Well we don't need to carry the soap around," confirmed Al, turning around and looking at the large green military vehicle parked up behind the lorry. "We can dump that here, one of us drive the thing back to the ranch, the other takes *The Colebrook*. Can you guess what you're driving, kid?"

"I'm guessing it's not your humvee," laughed the young man. Garth felt a sudden flash of anger, and he stepped forwards, his fists clenching.

"Hey, you can't just come here and think you can drive off in *my* lorry, you miserable pieces of shit. One reason is because it's broken, but the other reason is its mine. You can't just claim my lorry as yours, what gives you the right?"

"I've got a couple of guns," Al grinned, then waved towards the man accompanying him. "He's got a couple of guns, too. That makes us in charge, and means we can take pretty much anythin' we want. Now, what's wrong with it? Why doesn't it move?"

"Something to do with the engine," muttered Garth, shrugging his shoulders. "She's always been a temperamental bitch, and required regular tune-ups and overhauls. With every single motorway service station and garage closed indefinitely, it was only a matter of time before she froze for good. Now she's stranded, and so am I, until I can get either a new engine or some replacement parts."

Al stroked his chin thoughtfully, then nodded. "How heavy does she weigh?"

By now, the gas was starting to wear off, and Garth was beginning to make out details of the duo. The dark skinned bald man wore military clothing, and the weapons he carried seemed to come from the same source. About seven foot in height, he towered over Garth's short stature, and his muscular build an opposite to his slightly overweight frame. His companion, a shorter man with a pale complexion and brown messy hair, wore a battered leather jacket and dirty jeans, with a green rucksack strapped to his back. The weapons he carried didn't seem as advanced as Al's, but they would certainly be just as dangerous.

"An empty load, she'd probably be about ten tonnes, give or take. Why?"

"I think we might be able to help each other out," Al said, motioning towards the bulky green vehicle. "That vehicle there is one of the military's finest. It can pull massive weights, I'm talking heavy artillery cannon and fully loaded tanks. I'm guessin' it may even be able to drag your dead machine, given enough time. We've got a base set up back that way, a little farmhouse. What say we drag the machine back there, then see what we can do about fixing it?"

Garth thought his options over. If he agreed, he'd be teaming up with a pair of complete strangers, but the fact one was a soldier was certainly an appealing notion: if anyone knew what they were doing and how to survive, he would. Plus, if he declined the offer, the pair could easily wipe him out and take his vehicle anyway.

"Do we need to repair it?" asked the younger man. "If you can pull the rig with the hummer, why bother?"

"It will be a crawl, Bill, I'm talking a maximum speed of maybe five miles an hour. It'll burn through any and all petrol we have just to get us back. We have no choice."

"And you need me to drive it," confirmed Garth

Al looked at him in surprise, lifting an eyebrow as if questioning him. "Do we? It can't be that hard."

"Like I said, she's temperamental at the best of times. Plus there's over eighteen gears on that thing to work through. You need to know when to use what gear."

"Eighteen?" muttered Al, leaning out to one side and glaring at the front cabin of the lorry. "That many, eh? Well, I guess we do need you, after all. Give Bill a hand in fixing it up to the back of *The Colebrook*. I'll keep watch."

Garth nodded slowly and wandered around to the front of the lorry, leaning in and grabbing his red cap from the foot well of the passenger side, whistling to himself as he went along.

"Keep an eye on him," muttered Al, a wary eye trained on the movements of the lorry driver.

"He hardly seems like a threat," countered Bill, slinging his shotgun over his shoulder and grabbing a small toolbox from the back seat of the humvee. "He was pretty quick to break down and confess to everything the minute he was down on the ground. To be honest, he seems a bit of a coward."

"Maybe he is. So don't be surprised if he tries to do what a coward does and shoot you in the back when you're not looking. Now, I'll back up *The Colebrook* so you can get these two vehicles fixed together, I'll man the machineguns and keep an eye out for any of the dead shits you might have missed. C'mon, I want to be on the move in a couple of hours, maximum. And as soon as you get within communication range of the whore, tell her to look around for some kind of acetylene cutting torch and a toolbox. I think I saw something like that in the cellar."

Bill stopped what he was doing and looked at Al, trying his best to look puzzled, as if he didn't know what he was talking about.

"Lost your headset?" questioned Al, shaking his head. "Did you think I'm friggin' stupid, or that I came down in the last shower? You have it on one minute, talk to that bitch for ten minutes, then come out and you've lost it? Did you think I would buy that for one minute?"

"You wouldn't have given her a headset if I'd asked," said Bill, waving his hand in a dismissive gesture. Al nodded in confirmation.

"You're right. Because I wouldn't trust anything with that bitch if my life depended on it."

"Who?" asked Garth, pulling on his hat and interrupting the middle of the debate.

"Bitch," repeated Al. "A girl who lives in the farmhouse. An irritating little whore, about seventeen years old. Nice ass, but that's about all she's got going for her. Not really worth bothering with, and I wouldn't, if she didn't have a shit load of weapons and alcohol I want. No, I correct myself, weapons and alcohol I *need.*"

Al spat on the ground by his boot, then retreated to the humvee and clambered in, turning over the engine and beginning the process of manoeuvring the vehicle into position behind the trailer. Bill handed a selection of tools to Garth, then waited for the trucker to make the first move: after all, Bill didn't have a clue what he was doing.

"What's his story?" asked Garth, leaning into the back of the trailer and pulling out a large metal frame, speaking in a low tone so Al couldn't hear him. "He sounds awfully aggressive towards this girl. Is he gay? A woman hater?" Bill smirked and shook his head, lending a hand with the cumbersome frame.

"His main problem is he's too damn proud. The way I see it, Angel got the jump on him, she could have killed him outright if she wanted, and he knows that. He's pissed with her about that. Judging from his tattoo and the magazines and posters he insists on carrying around, I'd guess he's not gay, either. He's a Marine, he's proud of that, and I don't think he likes the fact his training failed him against a seventeen-year old civilian."

Garth nodded, slowly lowering the frame on to two bolts on the rear of the lorry and tightening one bolt. He motioned to Bill to do the same. Finishing off his own bolt he pulled his cap off, wiping his brow with a grimy handkerchief. Bill looked up at him, at his shaven head and bloodshot eyes, then the bulge of his stomach. He looked overweight, but not obese or unhealthy. The shirt he wore was a deep red in colour, with his name embroidered on the left breast pocket with blue thread. EuroTruck's corporate symbol covered the rear of the shirt, the name in thick black writing with a yellow and orange flame burning in the background. The red hat he wore bore the same logo, and both shirt and hat were just as grimy as the handkerchief. He pulled a silver tube from one of his pockets, unscrewed it and placed a dark brown cigar between his teeth.

"Another smoker, great," mumbled Bill. "You know, those things stink like shit."

"They may stink like shit, but at the moment, I have to confess you do as well. And your friend, too. Besides, I'd rather have a fine cigar beneath my nose instead of having to smell this country air tainted with decay and rot. If you can, I suggest you try and convince him to keep the toiletries. Especially if there's going to be four people sharing the cabin. It'll get a little ripe in there, if you know what I mean. Summer, the heat, the air conditioning doesn't work all the time... Just see what you can do."

Bill smiled and nodded. "I'll see what I can do."

"Bill, right?" asked Garth, holding out his hand in a formal greeting. Bill extended his own hand and took the lorry driver's hand in his own. He shook it, and Garth nodded, evaluating the shake as if he had once been in a job where doing so had been a regular turn of events.

"Let's get this son of a bitch moving," shouted Al, the humvee rolling to a stop behind the trailer. Dismounting from the vehicle, he made his way around to the back where Bill and Garth stood, and looked at the work they had done so far.

"Jesus, what have you been doing all this time? It looks like you've just been talking between the two of you like a pair of housewives. Christ, if you want something done you have to do it yourself."

Al snatched the tools from Garth and Bill and started to tighten the bolts already secured, then hitched the tow bar to the rear of the humvee himself, grunting and muttering under his breath every few minutes. He stepped away from the rigid fixings, looking at the mass of wiring and hoses hanging from the underside of the metal frame.

"What's all this wiring for? Hey, buddy, what the hell's all this for?"

"Hydraulics, braking systems, it'll give you more control over the rig you're towing. Do you want me to hook it up?"

"No, I'll do it," snarled Al, dropping to his back and wriggling under the rear of the vehicle, grabbing a handful of wires and looking for something that they would attach to on the underside of the humvee. Bill signalled to Garth by jerking his head to one side, and stepped away from the busy Marine.

"He's pissed off that he's having to do the work, isn't he?" asked Garth. Bill shook his head.

"He's a perfectionist. Even if we'd done it perfectly, he would have checked it over, then decided it wasn't good enough and done it himself. And besides, the humvee is 'his'. He'd probably bite your hand off if you tried to mess with the connections. So, how does this work, will you have to sit in the rig and steer?" Garth shook his head.

"Those tubes and wires he's connecting up work the brakes on the lorry, so when we stop, it doesn't just ram into the back of us. I can lock off the steering in the lorry so it's effectively just one massive trailer to be pulled. That'll make it a heavy and bulky load, pretty cumbersome, which is another reason Al's going to have to take it slow and steady. Problems with lorries breaking down aren't unheard of, especially on long hauls."

"So I guess we'll be riding in the humvee itself, so if there's anything you want to carry with you, grab it from the lorry and stow it in the back seat."

"There doesn't look to be much room in there," commented Garth as he peered in the back seat of the vehicle. "But then, there's not much I want to have by me. Just cigars, a photograph and a bottle of whiskey. Medicinal, of course. I'll lock off the steering while I'm up there."

Garth ran to the front of the vehicle and rummaged around in the cabin, leaving Bill to his own devices. He discreetly flicked the radio headset to channel six, but again received nothing but static and white noise. He turned the device off just as Garth returned clutching a small wooden box, a curled and crumpled piece of paper, and a clear glass bottle half filled with a golden, amber liquid. He placed the bottle and box on one of the seats, lodging it between a metal box filled with ammunition and a wooden crate marked with the words 'explosive'. He smoothed out the photograph and pressed it against the bonnet of the vehicle. "That's Anna, my daughter. One of the smartest kids in her class."

Bill nodded his head grimly. "Is she dead now?"

"No, she's fine, she lives in Spain with my ex-wife, she's well out of harms way. But I get the feeling I'm never going to see her again."

Bill looked at the smiling raven-haired young girl in the photo, then opened up his rucksack and pulled out his own picture of Jenny.

"This was my girlfriend," he muttered, staring longingly at the photograph. "She was… She was lucky, I guess. She went before the dead started walking."

Al, having finished tying the ropes between the two vehicles, pushed his way between the two men holding photos. He grabbed a tattered magazine from inside the vehicle and flicked through it, stopping on an image of a young red-haired girl, naked except for the military helmet she wore. He pointed at the panel of writing beside the pictures of the woman.

"Alicia Waterford," he announced. "Twenty one years old. She lives in Missouri with her dog Boxy, and her favourite drink is Tequila. I know enough about her to feel like she's *my* family. She might be dead, she might not be. I'm never gonna see her. It's a sad, but true story, and you don't hear me complaining about it all the damn time. Now stow that sentimental bullshit and climb in, I don't want to be reminded of any of the shit from 'the good old days'. Now hurry up, it's a long way and it's going to be a slow journey."

When Al had said it was going to be a long, slow journey, he hadn't been lying.

The humvee had struggled with pulling the trailer from the very beginning, and the off-road sections of the journey proved to be an even tougher challenge for the machine. Bill had watched Al as he concentrated on the journey, and found it bewildering to see the attentive gaze on his face. His fingers were locked tightly around the wheel, and he seemed to wrestle and fight for control of the vehicle. He didn't even try to engage in any conversation with the other two people in the vehicle.

Garth didn't say much, either. He kept looking over his shoulder, making sure his lorry was still okay, then checking on Al's driving. Every so often he would remove his hat and pat down his sweat-covered brow with his handkerchief, then return to his vigil over driver and vehicle.

Bill had nothing to do. He'd flicked through most the magazines Al had elected to carry, and didn't feel like he could look at any more naked women holding weapons or draping themselves seductively over a tank. He'd tried the radio headset several times to see if he could contact Angel, but nothing could get though, so he presumed he was still out of range of the devices.

"How much longer is it going to be until we get back?" he finally asked, drumming his fingers anxiously on the dashboard. He was starting to feel edgy and guilty about leaving Angel on her own.

"It's gonna take some time," muttered Al, licking his lips. He quickly glanced over to see Bill's fingers tapping the dashboard. "It'll take even longer if I have to stop to break all your fingers. Besides, it'll be dark soon. I don't want to attempt pulling this thing in poor lighting, we're going to have to stop for the night."

"Do we have to?" asked Bill, glancing and the glowing clock set into the dashboard. "We should try and get back as soon as we can. The sooner we get back, the sooner we can start working on it."

"Al's right," said Garth, watching the lumbering vehicle behind them and biting his lower lip as it leaned to one side. "If the rig tips over, we aren't going to be able to set it upright."

"I know you're eager to get back to the whore," continued Al, slowly drawing the vehicle to a halt. The brakes of the lorry squealed and hissed as the command to stop was carried along the wires and tubes that Al had connected. Garth quickly clambered out as soon as the vehicles had come to a halt, rushing to check for damage on his truck. "And who knows, the little bitch might be eager to see you, too. But darkness is drawing in now, and I don't want to have to drive with the headlamps on. We're a big enough target as it is, I'd rather not be lit up like a Christmas tree, and if someone did try to attack us we'd be a sitting duck. Dragging that dead weight behind us means we're about as manoeuvrable as a drunken cow with three legs."

Al made sure the brakes were applied, then clambered out and looked up and down the road. The sun was beginning to set now, a heavy orange ball of fire in the distance, and casting long shadows across the countryside, and the Marine nodded to himself.

"Garth, run over to the cabin of the lorry, make sure the parking brake's on tight, the last thing I want is to wake up in the middle of the night and find it half way down the road. Bill, we're going to spend the night in the rear of the lorry, it'll give us some warmth, so see about maybe getting some light in there. I'll get some weapons set up, form a perimeter around the vehicle. Now come on, move."

Bill muttered under his breath as he opened one of the back doors of the humvee and trawled through the small box marked 'Not Weapons' in Al's handwriting. It had two small first aid kits inside it, both with the seals unbroken, and a small portable lamp with three spare bulbs. He looked it over, tried the power switch, and screamed in surprise as the bulb burst to life, searing his eyes with bright white light.

"Christ, kid," shouted Al. Bill looked up, bleary eyed, and saw the Marine about fifty yards away from the vehicles, a long barrelled rifle in his hands and braced against his shoulder. "Why don't we just erect a giant neon arrow pointing to us? There's a reason I wanted the lights *inside* the lorry, you dumb bastard."

Bill sighed and dragged the lamp and bulbs into the rear of the lorry.

Garth was already inside, either kneeling down or sitting down on one of the two wooden crates and smoking his cigar: all Bill could see was the warm glow of the tip of the cigar, and smell the pungent smoke as it filled the trailer.

"Shield your eyes," commanded Bill, setting the lamp down and flicking it on once more. It wasn't as bright the second time around, and after a few minutes he finally became accustomed to the harsh glow. He rubbed at his eyes, then sat back on the cold metal floor and looked around.

The trailer was empty apart from the two crates, one of which Garth sat upon with a contented smile. The bottle of whiskey he clutched had the top off, and there seemed to be a considerable amount missing, more then there had been before. The walls of the trailer were metal, painted a matt white and dotted with rivets surrounded by brown rusted metal. One of the walls had been redecorated with numerous posters and pictures, some of naked women, some of trucks and cars, and others a mix of both. Bill stared at them, trying to quickly count an estimate how many there were.

"I'm a simple man," confessed Garth, a wide grin on his face as his eyes roved over the array of pictures, lingering on some photographs longer than others, "I like drink, I like a good cigar. Women and a good truck, too. As long as I have them, I'm happy."

Bill nodded. He wasn't uncomfortable with the large collection of naked women polishing the bonnets of trucks with their breasts, but he had the idea Angel might not be too impressed.

"Room for one more?" asked Al, clambering into the trailer and stomping over to the wall covered with posters. He unrolled his own poster, then placed it on the wall, sticking down the corners and standing back to admire the poster of Caitlin Dillons, the same that had greeted Bill the morning he had woken up in Edgly. Garth looked over the poster then nodded, impressed.

"Okay," announced Al, his eyes still fixed on the poster. "We take turns on watch. Bill, you're first, take a rifle up on the roof. Garth and me'll keep ourselves occupied. You play cards?" asked the Marine, pulling his deck of cards out his pocket and laying them on the crate in front of Garth. He smiled and casually shrugged his shoulders.

"I've been known to win a few hands of poker," confessed the lorry driver.

"Well all right, then," said Al, grinning and shuffling his handmade cards. "Ante up."

Bill turned and left the trailer, closing the doors behind him and finding himself in the darkening countryside.

He grabbed an assault rifle, the same kind he'd used when defending Al's flat from Moloch's men, and clambered up on to the roof of the trailer, crouching down low then sinking to his stomach, lying flat on the roof and lifting the rifle. He looked at the heavy scope attached to the body of the rifle, then flipped the covering off and flicked a switch on the side. It hummed to life, bathing his face in a putrid green light, and he closed one eye as he squinted into the illuminated scope.

"M16," he muttered, recalling the name Al had given the weapon. "With night vision scope. Better to see the dead with," he repeated the words of the burly Marine, trying his best to recall everything he'd been told so far: these were things he was going to have to remember for the future. He panned the illuminated scope from left to right, scrabbling around to cover a full circle, slowly scanning the countryside for any sign of movement.

"How's it looking up there?" asked Al, his voice crackling slightly in the earpiece.

"Really quiet," muttered Bill, rolling on to his back and zipping up his jacket before resuming his position. "Completely dead."

"Better dead than undead," muttered Al, then "This guy is better at this then you are. I almost lost a hand there. I'm keeping an eye on him."

"What's he like?"

"He likes fine cigars, loose women and alcohol, he's like the brother I never had."

Bill heard Garth laughing in the background, and allowed himself to smile slightly. Maybe with a new best friend, Al wouldn't be so harsh or aggressive towards Angel in the future.

"What time are we setting off in the morning?" asked Bill, trying to zoom in on a distant rock formation, sure he'd seen something moving behind it.

"We'll see what time we wake up," said Al. "Until then, I'll see you in, say, five hours. And don't go to sleep, you miserable bastard, or I'll make you walk back to the bitch's farm."

Bill nodded, but didn't verbally respond to the soldier inside the truck, he was concentrating on the rock formation ahead of him. A blur of motion almost made him squeeze off a round, but he refrained from doing so, checking the target before he fired. A small and mangy dog pounced on to the rock, its tail sagging and fixing Bill with an emotionless stare. The eyes of the hound were an eerie green in the night vision scope, vacant and soulless, but it wasn't this that gave away the dog's undead condition: all eyes appeared the same way in night vision, Bill had seen enough films and documentaries to know that. The main indication was the absence of the canine's lower jaw, and the ragged entrails that hung from the torn abdomen. It looked at Bill and moaned pitifully, a watery gurgling sound oozing from the broken mouth.

"Poor little bastard," muttered Bill, bracing the rifle against his shoulder and squeezing off a single round, shattering the skull of the creature as the lead projectile destroyed the top of the head. The creature didn't have time to yelp before the spindly limbs gave way beneath it, slumping over and sliding down the rock, lying in a crumpled heap on the ground.

"What's happening," quizzed Al, his thumping footsteps as he made his way to the door audible even outside the trailer.

"Nothing," confirmed Bill, looking around for any sign of another creature. He knew that dogs were normally pack animals, and the Rots seemed to follow the same animal instincts, but this particular mongrel seemed to be a loner. Maybe it has last the rest of its pack, or maybe they had abandoned it.

"Nothing," he repeated again. "Just an undead dog. I've taken care of it. I didn't mean to disturb your poker game."

"See that it doesn't happen again."

The sun rose, bathing Al in a pleasing warm glow. He opened his eyes and stared into the sky above him, at the large white clouds drifting by overhead. He stretched slightly, then rolled over to one side, and almost fell off the roof of the trailer. Swearing and muttering under his breath, he clambered to his feet and looked over the edge of the roof.

"Fell asleep," he muttered, slapping his head with the palm of his hand and rubbing it, rolling the other way and pushing himself to his feet. He stretched his back, raising his arms above his head, then collected his scattered weapons, opened can of beer and half-smoked cigar, and made his way back down to ground level. He dumped his gear in the back of *The Colebrook*, then wrenched open the door of the rear of the trailer and clambered in.

"Wake up, you bunch of pussies, it's game time. Grab your shit and we'll get on the road. C'mon, Bill, I know you want to rush back and see your bitch."

The trailer was empty. Al rushed through to the back of the container, raising an eyebrow and smirking at his poster as the flash of flesh caught his eye.

"Where the fuck are you," he muttered, returning to the humvee outside. He could see moving shadows in the front of the vehicle and rushed forward.

"You're more eager to get away than I thought," grinned Al, marching up to the door and wrenching it open. "C'mon, move over. I'm driving."

"It was a different story in Brazil," uttered a familiar voice. Al crouched and peered into the interior of the vehicle, unable to comprehend the fact J-Man was sitting in the driver's seat. He slowly turned to face Al, a grin on his lopsided face. His head hung slightly to one side, an exposed ring of cartilage poking out through the flesh of his neck. He grinned, then motioned towards the seat beside him, his head swinging lazily on the broken neck.

Al didn't recognise the soldier sitting beside J-Man. The torso and face of the person were hideously mangled; a bloody mess of raw meat oozing scarlet fluid and quivering as the human carcass raised it's one good arm and gave a mock salute.

"Say hello to Leo, Al," croaked Ping, leaning into the cabin, grinning at the bloodied mess. He tore a strip of flesh from the pulp and shovelled it into his decaying mouth, yellowing teeth shredding and tearing at the meat while his vacant eye socket examined Al. "What's wrong, are you too good for your old friends now? Wait until I tell Johnny C."

Al spun on his heel, and saw a towering figure manning one of the mounted machineguns on the back. Skin blackened and charred, the only way Al could identify this person was by the mark of a Lieutenant on his left sleeve. The figure grinned, showing white teeth behind burned lips, and saluted. Al shook his head and stepped away from the vehicle, unable to take in the obscure chain of events that were unfolding.

"We're in a new army, now," gurgled the burned corpse, making its way down from the rear of the vehicle and taking a shambling step towards Al. "We're getting bigger every minute. Take a look around you, Al, see what the new order has to offer you…"

Al spun around and found himself confronted by a crowd of the undead, hundreds of faceless creatures surrounding him, reaching out with bloody and dirty hands, eager to tear him apart. He peered over his shoulder, looking towards his dead comrades for help, but both the remains of his squad and the vehicle had vanished, replaced by more of the crowding undead. Their cold and probing hands found his own skin, and he tried to fight back but there were too many of them. Flesh tore as the creatures groped at him, and screamed in agony as hundreds of teeth sunk into his muscles.

"Fucking dead bastards!"

Al jerked awake, the dreamscape around him shattering as he regained his senses. He sat bolt upright, gazing into space as the remnants of the nightmare slipped away from his mind, and he lifted a shaking hand to his face, rubbing the sleep from his eyes and exhaling deeply.

"Jesus Christ," he muttered to himself.

"Bad dream?" asked Bill, sitting on one of the wooden crates and looking distastefully through the playing cards. Al laughed by way of response, and slowly clambered to his feet, kicking the empty bottle of whiskey at his feet.

"I guess Garth gave me a bad cigarette," he confessed, looking at the pile of crumpled cigarette butts lying in a small metal ashtray. He tentatively sniffed the remains and the piles of ash, then wrinkled his face and nodded.

"Frigging bastard," he muttered, fishing out one in particular and nipping the end, breaking open the paper and sniffing the tobacco inside. He offered it to Bill, who refused it with a wave of his hand. "The shit laces his cigarettes with marijuana. Between the two of us we must've smoked twenty of them… Jesus, no wonder my dream was fucked up. Where is he now?"

"He's outside, on guard."

"Why didn't you wake me? I'd rather I was on watch instead of an overweight pot head."

"I've been trying to wake you for five hours," confessed Bill. "You've been dead to the world."

"I guess it's all catching up on me," Al confessed, shrugging his shoulders and gathering his weapons from the ground around him. "C'mon, it's time to move out. I'm awake, the sun will be up by now, and I know you're eager to get back to your whore."

Bill didn't respond to the jibe and Al smiled to himself. Giving the kid a hard time was something all Marines did to the rookies, and Al didn't see why he should be any different. It normally took weeks to find a suitable weakness to exploit, but Bill's protectiveness towards Angel provided an ideal target.

Al threw the doors to the trailer open and stepped out, the freshness of the morning tainted with the foul stench of nearby death.

"You killed a dog last night?" he asked, climbing down on to the ground and double-checking the tow bar between *The Colebrook* and the lorry, ensuring the wires and tubes were still tightly in place. "Did you think about moving it away from the lorry?"

Bill shook his head. "I didn't want to touch the thing. It's rife with the plague, I didn't want to catch it."

"So you thought you'd leave it to rot and attract the unwanted attention of flies and other undead flesh eaters?" replied Al, grabbing a light machinegun from the back of the vehicle and making his way around to the carcass of the animal. He smiled slightly, impressed at the single bullet that had put down the living dead, then kicked it with his boot. "Well it stinks of shit, and it's probably going to attract the attention of every shambler in the immediate vicinity. Where's Garth?"

"Up here," came the familiar voice of the lorry driver. Al looked to the roof of the trailer, and saw Garth perched atop it, a pair of binoculars pressed to his eyes as he slowly scanned the horizon. "There's a copse of trees maybe a couple of miles away to the right, that might offer some cover to the walking pus bags, but that's the only place that might keep them out of our line of sight."

"It might only be a couple of miles," said Al, opening the door to army vehicle and throwing his weapon inside. "But I've seen some of those bastards reach quite a speed, despite their fragile and dead appearance, and I know that the kid has seen some pretty frigging unbelievable things, too. Now get down here, buddy, we need to keep moving. We might make it back to the farm today if we push on."

Al watched as Garth clumsily made his way down from the roof, dropping half his equipment as he went, then bundled it in the back of *The Colebrook* before hauling himself in to the front seat. Al jumped in beside him, then turned to face the portly man.

"Next time you give me anything to smoke, I want you to tell me what it is."

Garth grinned, tapping the silver cigarette case that poked out his trouser pocket. "It's good stuff, right?"

"Bad shit, is what I'd call it. One is fair enough, but ten of them fucked with my head. Next time, warn me and I'll go easy. Dope and drink doesn't agree with me, buddy, so make sure it never happens again."

Garth nodded understandingly, and pushed the case deeper into his pocket, his cheeks a bright pink as if he'd just been told off.

"You're on the guns again, kid," shouted Al as he turned the engine over and looked in one of the rear view mirrors, watching as Bill sighed heavily and climbed on to the opened back of the vehicle. Giving him time to find a comfortable position, Al released the brakes and slowly eased the vehicle forwards, towards their distant goal.

III

"Back on the guns," muttered Bill as the vehicle lurched away from the night's resting spot. Still, at least Al was restricted in his driving because of the heavy load he was towing. He couldn't reach the speed he had last time, meaning there was less wind to ruffle his hair or catch his breath. The drive up to the trailer the previous day once Bill had spotted it had been a sickening journey, and he'd almost fell out at one point. At least now he didn't need to hang on for his life.

"Stay on the clock," muttered Al, the omnipresent voice filling his ears. "Dead bastards could be anywhere, and at this speed we'll be easy pickings."

"Jesus, look at those!" Garth screamed, his voice carrying up to Bill on his sentry position, the arm of the man sticking out one of the windows at the front of the vehicle.

"Got them," said Al. "Bill, four o'clock. You see them?"

"I can't see shit from here," shouted Bill, rotating the mounted weapon he straddled, the position indicated by Al obscured by the large trailer. "How many are there?"

"I don't know," responded Al. "Take the wheel, buddy, I'm going out."

The vehicle and its payload swayed slightly as control was handed over to Garth, and Al clambered out the open window, throwing his weapon on to the roof before he hoisted himself up after it. "Keep it at this speed," he confirmed, and then slowly rose to his feet. "There's a big crowd of the dead, maybe twenty strong, and they seem to be slowly gaining on us. Looks like our buddy was right about the trees offering cover to them. You sure you can't see them?"

"I'm sure," confirmed Bill, disengaging from the mounted weapon he manned and slowly climbing on to the roof beside the Marine. From his new vantage, he could see the horde of dead, and lifted his shotgun as he tried to target the front-most zombie. Al lowered the muzzle of the weapon with his hand, shaking his head.

"Range is too far, kid, haven't you learned anything yet? Get down on your knees and use your MP5. I'll rip into the bastards with this," he said, stroking the large machinegun as he swung the barrel around so it trained on the advancing dead.

Bill obeyed the order and dropped to his knees, lifting the submachine gun and trying to target the head of the lead zombie. At the distance they were, the head was an impossible target for a man of his inexperience to hit, but their bodies and legs weren't. If he couldn't kill them outright, he could at least incapacitate them.

"Fire at will," screamed Al, releasing a burst of gunfire into the oncoming crowd. Bill watched as one of the heads of the creatures erupted into a fountain of crimson gore and the body toppled to the ground. Some of the approaching Rots stumbled on the downed corpse, losing their pace, while one decided to sink down and begin eating the remains of their fallen comrade. Bill followed with his own burst of gunfire, catching two of the pursuing animals in their chests. They stumbled with the impact of each bullet, but neither fell to the ground.

"Heads or nothing," screamed Al over another burst of gunfire, cutting down another pair of Rots. "That doesn't have enough penetration to do anything at this range. Don't waste your ammo."

Bill let the machinegun hang from its strap, then scuttled back to the mounted machinegun, seeing if they were within view of the weapon yet. Al swore, then lowered his own weapon. "They're moving back."

A loud thumping sound came over the headset. "Hello?" crackled a new voice within Bill's head. "Does this thing work?"

"What's happening, buddy?" asked Al, responding to Garth's radio transmission.

"It looks like they're sweeping around the back, I can't see any of them in the mirrors."

"Does it look like they're slowing down? Maybe they've tired themselves out."

"Don't count on it," Bill murmured, gripping his submachine gun and looking from the left to right. "They might be coming at us from the other side."

"They don't have the intelligence to do that," growled Al, raising himself to his full height and trying to lean out to either side in an attempt to see if he could catch a glimpse of them. "They're not on either side," he confirmed. "They must've dropped back behind us."

Bill relaxed slightly, loosening his grip on his weapon, but listening for anything that would indicate further attacks. The steady drone of the humvee's engines, the grinding sound of gravel and dirt beneath the vehicles' heavy tyres, and a gentle thumping sound: like a weight being applied to sheets of thin metal.

"You hear that too, kid?" whispered Al, stepping alongside Bill and lifting his machinegun. "What the hell is that?"

"Footsteps on the roof," hissed Bill, lifting the muzzle of his shotgun towards the top of the trailer. "Jesus, how could they be up on the roof?"

"Bastards," Al said, shouldering his weapon and aiming high. "They dropped behind us so they could climb over the rig!"

"They're not that clever, are they?" screamed Garth, his tone near hysterical. "Shit, I never seen any of them act like that."

"These assholes are moving quickly," said Al, his finger resting lightly on the trigger. "If they move like that, they can probably climb shit, too."

"I've seen one of those bastards hanging upside-down on the ceiling of a tunnel," agreed Bill. "Where are they?"

The padding and thumping had stopped now, and still there was no sign of the creatures. Bill edged forwards, contemplating crossing the tow bar and climbing up the outside of the trailer. Al grabbed him by his arm and pulled him back, shaking his head.

"Why don't we stop so we can wipe them out?"

"There might only be the one or two up there," said Al, eyes fixed on the roof. "If we stop, we could get overrun by the stragglers."

"Jesus, I can see them," bellowed Garth, deafening both Al and Bill with his amplified scream. "Two on the left side."

Bill peered around the edge of the trailer and saw two Rots dangling from the roof, shimmying along the trailer and leaving a bloody smear along the side where they went. He took aim with his shotgun, loosed a shell and caught one of the Rots on its arm. The slug tore the limb in two, knocking the creature clean from its perch. He fired again, this time only managing to cause a shower of sparks as he struck the side of the trailer.

Al's weapon burst to life, too, though none of his bullets struck the second hanging Rot. Bill spun around, saw him firing wildly at the roof of the trailer, then followed his gaze. Four rots stood on top of the trailer, soaking up bullets in their bodies and limbs. As one took a shot to the head and toppled to the ground far below, another clambered into view. Bill scrambled back towards the centre of the humvee's roof, then lifted his weapon and fired blindly into the crowd, ignoring the dangling Rot for now and concentrating on the most dangerous threat.

He fired the final shot from his weapon, then dropped it to the floor, favouring his MP5 instead of taking time to reload. He took aim and squeezed off a single burst, knocking one of the Rots off the trailer. It slumped forwards, bouncing awkwardly off the humvee and trailer, then vanished beneath the tyres, the dying moans of the creature drowned out by the sound of its spine snapping and ribcage cracking.

Al finished spraying the creatures with his rapid-fire weapon, then dropped it and grabbed the mounted machinegun, raising the aim and opening fire, shredding the dead with the heavy gunfire. Limbs and battered torsos fell from the top of the trailer, a rain of grasping fingers and twitching feet, snapping teeth and pale watery blood, crushed beneath the wheels of the trailer as it continued it's slow pace.

From the roof of the trailer a blood-curdling scream pierced the air, and a pale blur streaked over the edge of the trailer, landing on the roof behind Bill with a thud. Before he could turn to react, the still-screaming Rot lashed out, knocking the weapons from his grip and wrapping its arms around him, pulling him down. The sensation of the dead flesh enveloping him made Bill retch, and the thunderous sounds of the gunfire fading as Bill was suddenly aware of only the sounds of his blood rushing through his ears. The creature continued to wrestle with Bill, trying to work out how to keep hold of its prey and bite it at the same time, while Bill desperately tried to escape the clutches of the attacker.

With a scream equal to that of the frantic Rot, Bill rolled over and pushed it away with his arms, tumbling over and over until there was a brief sensation of weightlessness in the pit of his stomach…

Then both Bill and the zombie landed on the road with a crunch, and in a moment of weakness, the dead creature released its grip. Bill pushed himself away from the struggling creature, then rolled to his feet and cast a glance over his shoulder, watching the trailer and humvee roll slowly away.

"Jesus, we've lost Bill," screamed Garth, his voice once more deafening over the radio headsets.

"Fuck, kid, are you okay?" asked Al, his voice barely audible over the gunfire that was picked up over his microphone.

"Fine, I'm fine," growled Bill, drawing his pistol and levelling it off at the Rot. The creature leapt to its feet, then dived on to Bill again, throwing him back on to the ground and pinning his arms down, a hideous grin on it's bloated and festering face. The rabid animal chattered its teeth as it tried to lower its rotten mouth to Bill's neck. Struggling frantically, Bill managed to push his leg up into the soft and oozing abdomen of the creature, then heave with all his might, pushing the Rot away from him. It broke its grip on his arms, and he managed to bring his pistol up, drawing a bead on the pale and leathery forehead, directly between its sunken eye sockets. He hammered a round into the bloody and rotten face of the screaming creature, silencing it but not ending its spasmodic death throes as it toppled on to its back.

He regained his footing and started to make his way back towards the slow-moving vehicle, leaving the twitching corpse behind him and breaking into a run. After a couple of steps, he felt a painful twinge in his left thigh, felt blood slowly seeping down his leg, and he knew that his old wound had been torn open in the tumble from the vehicle. His jog quickly broke down into a hobble, but despite his impairment he was still slowly gaining on the escaping vehicle, keeping his eyes on the roof of the trailer. Every three or four steps he had to stumble around a crushed limb or a bullet-riddled torso, grisly remains from the battle conducted by Al.

"How's it going?" he asked, pain tearing through his system as he tried to catch up to the vehicles. "Are we winning?"

The continuous sounds of gunfire over the radio ceased, but the silence was short-lived as Al gave a celebratory whoop of excitement.

"Score another twenty points for *Team Colebrook*," he laughed. "What about you, kid, are you okay?"

"I'm injured," muttered Bill, "You want to slow the thing down?"

Garth didn't verbally respond, but the convoy slowed to an eventual stop, allowing Bill to hobble up to the humvee and lean against it. He looked into the front of the vehicle and nodded to Garth, who responded with a courteous nod of his head. His face was paler than before, and he seemed to have a slight shake. Bill nodded back, then turned around and looked at Al, who stood on the mounted podium on the rear of the vehicle. He leaned casually against the weapon, a cigar clenched between his teeth and a grin on his face. He waved towards the trailer and Bill followed his gesture.

The rear of the vehicle, which had previously been smooth and in fairly good condition, was now battered and bloody, punctured in numerous places by the heavy calibre rounds Al had been firing from his weapons. Bill nodded, his adrenaline-fuelled mind suddenly forming the question: *is Garth so pale and shaking so much because of the combat, or because of the damage to his trailer?*

"You want to get back on the guns for the rest of the journey?" asked Al, patting the weapon one hand.

"Fuck off," muttered Bill, hobbling around the humvee and clambering into the passenger side. "My leg aches, and my face feels like it's been pushed against a belt sander. I'm sitting down for the rest of the journey, *you* can man the damn guns."

Al shrugged, then banged on the roof of the humvee, indicating he was ready to go.

"Well let's get this shit moving again!"

Bill tried to get as comfortable as he could in the vehicle, pressing hard against his leg and leaning back, carefully resting his raw face against the shoulder of his jacket. He casually flicked over the channel on his headset with one hand as the vehicle slowly built up to its maximum speed of five miles an hour.

"Jesus, Jesus, where are you?"

"Angel?" whispered Bill, pressing his finger into his ear and trying to increase the hushed tones of the panicked young girl. Garth looked over at him, a questioning look on his face.

"You can speak to her?"

"The bitch is on channel six," shouted Al from his mounted weapon outside.

"Angel, what's happening?"

"Thank God you're here," she hissed. "Jesus, Bill, where have you been? Christ…"

"Easy," cooed Bill. "Take it easy, Angel, what's happened? What's wrong?"

"They're here," she said, her voice low and almost inaudible. Bill found himself straining to hear her words. "They're here, and they're in my house. Jesus, they're tearing the place apart looking for the weapons. How far away are you? How long will you be?"

"Not long," promised Bill. "Where are you now?"

"I'm in the cellar. It's only a matter of time before they find…"

The comlink cut off. Bill frantically hammered his radio, then placed his head out the window, looking out at Al.

"What happened?"

"I dunno," he said, scratching his head. "Maybe the power died on her headset. Maybe someone sliced through her head with a knife, and caught the unit. Shit, we can only hope."

"Did you hear what she was saying?"

"I don't listen to anything whores have to say."

"They're already there, the gang, they're at the house and they're looking for the weapons."

"Well, we should probably pick up the pace. How far to go?"

"I don't know," admitted Bill, withdrawing back into the humvee. "What're you thinking?"

"Ditch the trailer, leave it here for now. Cover the last leg of our journey at a decent speed, storm the house and wipe the fuckers out. What do you think, Garth?"

Garth looked at Bill, shrugging his shoulders. "Hey, he's the soldier, he knows what he's doing."

"He claims he does. Okay, Al, let's do this your way."

"Quick and painless," muttered Al, leaping down from the rear of the humvee and unfastening the towing frame. "We'll make this operation quick and painless."

XI
KILLING FIELDS

"Smaller towns and villages have been almost wiped off the map; those that are too far from our facilities that we've been unable to reach have been entirely lost."

I

"Slow and painful," snarled a gruff voice from above her. "When I catch up with that bitch, I'm going to fuck her, then gut her. And it's going to be really slow, and *really* painful."

Angel sat in the darkness of the cellar, surrounded by the damp and earthy smell she had loved as a child. When she was younger, she used to spend hours at a time in the cellar, sometimes playing with her toys, sometimes just sitting and thinking. The happy memories of her childhood, hearing the heavy footsteps of her parents in the kitchen above her, the merry banter between both adults as they talked to one another, oblivious to the fact their daughter lay hidden beneath them.

What had once been her childhood sanctum was now her adolescent sanctuary, a secret hiding place that had kept her alive and out of reach, up until now. The trapdoor was hidden out of view by the rug above her, and the second entrance to the small subterranean catacomb was well hidden by a mass of wood and stone rubble, but that didn't mean the gang above wouldn't find her or the weapons. She'd tried her best to barricade both entrances, and now hid behind a pile of thick and musty cloth sacks filled with seeds. She gripped her pistol with sweating hands and tried her headset once more. There was still no response; not even a whisper of static. It must have been either a loose connection inside the delicate device, or a flat battery. Either way, she didn't have the necessary resources, technical skills or adequate lighting to try and fix it.

The gang above her had moved in towards the end of the previous night, only a few hours after Bill and Al had left her alone to her own devices. It had seemed to be the whole gang when she looked out the windows, and she'd quickly weighed up the options. She could have tried to defend her homestead with what weapons Al had left behind, ran from the scene, or hid and hoped they would lose interest. She'd chosen to hide, and was now regretting not just grabbing her stuff and running for the hills.

The men and women that had passed through the kitchen had been an unruly and rowdy collection of people, each making just as threatening and disturbing empty threats, while she had been forced to listen to them all. She knew there was no way she would be able to take on all the gang on her own, and that she'd have to contact Bill as soon as she could.

It had just been blind luck that Bill had tuned in or come into range when he had. Angel hadn't even had time to tell Bill how many there was before her radio died. For the brief seconds she was able to speak to someone, she had felt hope, but now with her radio dead, she was alone once more, and forced to sit and wait out the eventual appearance of Bill and Al.

She had no fears of the pair running into trouble outside. Despite his arrogance and derogatory attitude towards her, Angel could tell that Al knew exactly what he was doing, and that he was obviously a skilled soldier. Bill seemed competent enough to follow orders as they were given out by the giant, so she thought the pair would easily be able to get through to the rear entrance of the cellar. She didn't think they'd be foolish enough to try an all-out assault on the building, but deep in the back of her mind, she wouldn't be surprised if they did.

Time passed for Angel, what could have been either hours or minutes, she couldn't tell in the darkness. The voices and footsteps above her continuously came and went, more and more insults and threats indirectly targeted at her, mixed with small talk and meaningless conversation.

Her senses already heightened by the long time spent in the darkness, she heard something behind her, down the stone passage leading to the rear hatch of the cellar, the sound of boots scraping on the metal rungs of the ladder, then followed by hushed voices and soft footsteps. Gripping her pistol tighter and pressing herself against the wall, Angel waited for the two figures to step into the antechamber. It may have been Bill and Al returning from their journey, but she couldn't be too careful: after all, it was conceivable that a pair of the gang members had managed to find the door hatch.

Moving as silent as she could, she crept up behind the pair, drew a second smaller pistol from her utility belt, then pressed the muzzles of both weapons to the base of the skulls of each man. Both men froze, the smaller man lowering his head slightly, chuckling softly while the taller man drooped his shoulders and shook his head, swearing underneath his breath. Angel felt a smile creeping across her lips, and removed the pistol from the head of the shorter of the two, keeping one weapon trained on the tallest man.

"I'm always getting the drop on you, soldier boy. You want to start watching your back more."

Al whipped around and lashed out, trying to grab the pistol from Angel, but she nimbly stepped back out of reach, grinning to herself. Bill quickly stepped between the two, holding his hands up and trying to keep the peace between the two.

"Will the pair of you stop pissing around?" he hissed. "They're going to find us before Garth attacks."

"Who the hell's Garth?" muttered Angel, turning from Bill to Al.

"It's a long story," whispered Bill. "We've got another man on our side, now. He's in the humvee, waiting on the other side of the southern ridge. As soon as we give him the signal, he's going to come over the rise and cause a distraction with all the weapons we've left. Vulcan cannon, grenade launchers, mounted machineguns. He's got enough equipment with him out there to flatten almost the entire farm."

"Do you trust him?" asked Angel, finding it hard to comprehend the fact the two had managed to find another survivor in such a short period of time. He must have been sleeping on her back door, and she hadn't even known.

"Not particularly," grunted Al, turning away from Angel and walking towards the staircase leading up into the kitchen. "*The Colebrook* and his lorry's rigged up with explosives. If he doesn't carry out his side of the deal I blow his miserable cowardly ass to kingdom come. Now, what's the deal with the rebels upstairs? How many is there?"

"I don't know," said Angel. "I haven't been able to count them. A lot of them look or sound the same."

"Sure they're *not* the same, you dumb bitch?" whispered Al, pressing his eyes against the trapdoor and trying to look through the cracks and the rug above it. Angel casually lifted her weapon, aimed at the back of the Marine, and imagined how easy it would be to stop his complaining and constant ridiculing.

"Okay, I think there's about three people in there, two at the table and one by the stove. It's hard to make anything else out through the weave of the rug. We'll have to do this quick and quiet to keep our element of surprise. Here's my plan," said Al, making his way back down the stairs and sitting on the lowest step.

"Garth's out there, over the ridge, waiting for the signal to attack. He launches a full- scale assault on the place, flushes out the Bebops from upstairs. They rush him, leave their backs wide open to attack, and we give them a suppository they'll never forget. But first, we need to have control of a room in the house. The kitchen's the best place."

He opened a black bag he carried, handed a pistol fitted with a silencer to Bill, then looked at Angel. He removed the last two pistols and threw the empty bag to the ground, cocking both suppressed weapons and gripping one with each meaty hand. Angel extended one hand, waiting for him to hand over one of the weapons. He didn't, electing to keep both weapons to himself.

"You stay here until we've cleared out the kitchen, bitch. I can handle two pieces at once. You with me, Bill?"

"Give her a gun, Al, we can't afford to take any chances with you playing the big action hero."

Al reluctantly handed over one of the weapons. Although it was dark, Angel could imagine the sour look on his face.

"Okay then," said Al, slowly making his way back up the stairs and working the latches as silently as he could. "You two lovebirds take the shits at the table and I'll whack the guy at the stove. On my mark: three two one… Mark!"

Al rose to his full height, pushing open the trapdoor with his broad shoulders and turning to his left, lifting his weapon and releasing a single round into the head of the large bald man standing by the cooker. At the exact same moment the round smashed into the man's skull and splattered his brains across the kitchen wall, both Angel and Bill lifted themselves up and fired their own weapons. Bill fired three rounds, two catching the woman sitting down in her chest, the third round crashing through her skull. Angel fired five rounds, only two of them finding their mark and shattering the final man's collarbone and upper arm. Al sighed, then casually turned and fired a single shot, catching the man's jaw and splattering the window with fragments of teeth and blood.

Al clambered out of the hole first, dragging the bodies one by one into the cellar, while Bill and Angel kept watch, Bill at the door and Angel crouching by the window. In the light of day, Angel could see the weary expressions wore by both men, and the bloodied leg and face of Bill.

"Jesus," she whispered as Al vanished into the cellar with the final body. "You're hurt, what happened to you?"

"A slight accident," said Bill, keeping his eyes trained on the passageway beyond the door.

"He was lying on the roof of *The Colebrook* while we were moving," said Al, re-emerging from the cellar and closing the hatch, readjusting the rug to cover it. He looked at Angel, then grinned. "You know, thinking about you. He was jerking himself off, he must've jerked too hard, and fell off. Dumb bastard."

Angel felt her cheeks flush and quickly returned to the window, looking out into the courtyard that only a couple of days ago had been the site of a bloody and violent battle.

Looks like there's going to be another one, she thought, watching men and women rush back and forth between vehicles and the barn.

"I count maybe ten or fifteen out there."

"There's another seven or eight in the barn," muttered Al, peering out from behind one of the curtains. "More than likely a couple of snipers. There's probably still a few in the house, too. Hopefully we can flush everyone out at once when Garth hits the green switch marked 'go'. You there, buddy? Kitchen's secure over here, what's it like at your end?"

Both Bill and Al cocked their heads slightly, listening to the voice coming through on their headsets. "Yeah, that's the plan," confirmed Al. Angel plucked her useless radio from her ear and dropped it to the table. Al looked up, scowling at her, then eyed the device.

"That's mine, and I want it back. You're gonna pay for breaking it, too."

"I didn't break it."

"We'll discuss it later, bitch. Get ready. You may want something more powerful than that pistol, too. Bill, give her your MP5, you use your shotgun instead. Get ready, buddy. Roger, I hear you; we're still good to go. In three, on my mark. Three…"

Garth sat in the driving seat of the humvee, leafing through one of Al's magazines, looking up every so often to make sure no one had managed to approach him and break through the web of infrared motion detectors and claymore mines Al had set up around the vehicle.

"Last line of defence," he'd said as he finished laying the last of the mines. "If they make it past here, there's a modified flare gun loaded with a single hollow point slug fastened just beneath the dashboard. Use it on yourself, it'll be for the best."

Those had been Al's last words before leaving with Bill, heading towards the farmhouse situated just over the ridge. Over half an hour had passed since he'd last seen the men disappear, and now he was starting to get edgy. He knew they hadn't just left him; Al loved his magazines, his weapons and his vehicle too much to just walk away and leave it with a stranger.

"You there, buddy? Kitchen's secure over here, what's it like at your end?"

Garth jumped, startled as the voice of Al sounded as if he were just behind him. He looked over his shoulder, through natural instinct, but wasn't surprised when there was nobody there. He cleared his throat, nodding to himself.

"Yeah, I'm here. Ready to roll. Are you sure this is going to work? Just press the button we're ready for action, rolling in with guns blazing?

"Yeah, that's the plan," confirmed Al. Garth sighed and turned the engine over, grinning to himself as the vehicle roared to life. Garth looked at the small keypad just beside the gearshift, at the green button Al had labelled by tearing a word out of one of the erotic stories in his magazine.

"Get ready, buddy. Roger, I hear you; we're still good to go. In three, on my mark. Three…"

"Whoa, wait a minute," yelled Garth, gripping the steering wheel of the vehicle with both hands and locking his lips. "What about the motion sensors, the mines, won't I get blown to shit?"

"The vehicle's fitted with an IFF decoder, it emits a frequency that overrides the… shit, you don't need to know the technology behind it all, just drive."

"You'd better not be trying to get rid of me," muttered Garth, crunching the gears and slowly edging forwards.

"If I wanted to do that, I'd detonate the twenty five pounds of explosive charges that I planted on the humvee and the trailer. Now move, before we're discovered."

The line went dead, and Garth slowly edged forwards, cautiously eyeing the mounds of dislodged earth that marked the location of each mine. Gritting his teeth, Garth closed his eyes as he rolled over the mines, expecting the worst. Ten seconds passed, and he was pleased to find that he hadn't been blown up yet. Applying a little more pressure to the accelerator, the vehicle slowly began to pick up speed as he approached the rise, an uneven ploughed field between him and the hill that Al had told him to ride over. He fumbled with the controls of the vehicle, making sure it was in four-wheel drive, then gunned the engines on, hitting the furrows of the field and bouncing from side to side with each bump. He had to wrestle with the controls just to keep the machine travelling in a straight line, and constantly looked around from side to side, making sure there were no guards on duty.

He made it to the small hillock and pressed down hard on the pedal, pressing it flat against the floor as the machine strained to ascend the incline.

"C'mon, you piece of shit," muttered Garth, striking the gearbox with one hand. "Move it."

Staring straight ahead, the front windscreen became awash with blue sky, spattered with thin wisps of candyfloss. For a brief moment, Garth could forget about everything around him as the sky filled his vision: memories of sunny days at the beach and lying on his back in the park rushed back to him, happier times with Anna when she was younger…

The Colebrook clambered over the top of the rise, and the sky was quickly replaced with a large farmhouse, a metal barn and a dilapidated wooden hut between the two. People swarmed around outside the buildings, each stopping in unison to look towards the sound of the powerful engines and the new interloper on their territory. Garth swallowed hard as some started to make their way towards him, while others ran to the collection of parked vehicles and began to strap themselves in.

"See the tube lying beside you?" said Al, his voice louder now than it had been. Garth nodded, oblivious to the fact the Marine couldn't see him. "It's a guided rocket launcher, primed and ready to fire. Grab it, get out The Colebrook and take out those vehicles before they get them working, they're your most dangerous threats."

Muttering and swearing beneath his breath, Garth grabbed the weapon Al had left in the front seat and climbed out the vehicle, shouldering the weapon and focusing his attention down the aiming reticule.

"What if I miss?"

"The rocket goes wherever the launcher's aimed at. Keep the weapon pointed at the vehicles until you see the explosion, don't lower it before it gets there otherwise it's a wasted shot."

Garth steadied the launcher, concentrated, then slowly squeezed the firing pin.

There wasn't a massive amount of recoil from the launch, a series of vents and an open back to the weapon meant it lost a lot of recoil, meaning Garth could keep the weapon aimed at the vehicles. The first of them was about to pull away, when the explosive projectile reached its target and swallowed the metal shells and their operators in a fiery blossom. Garth dropped the weapon, grinning at the sounds of Al whooping and hollering, then giving the signal to Bill and the girl to mop up the remaining foot soldiers.

"Come on down," shouted Al, his deep voice almost drowned out by the chatter of his assault rifle.

Garth reluctantly climbed back into the machine and drove forwards, hitting the button marked 'go' as he went. He felt the seat begin to vibrate as he reached the bottom of the hill, then watched as the Vulcan cannon seated on the bonnet spun to life, slowly tracking from side to side. Although the barrels were moving, they didn't seem to be firing any shots, simply panning from left to right, then back again. For a sickening moment, Garth imagined the weapon hadn't been reloaded and suddenly found himself sweating profusely at the thought of being caught by the gang. One of the approaching men, brandishing a large machinegun similar to the one Al had favoured during the zombies' attack, stopped about ten yards away from the vehicle, raising his weapon and pointing the muzzle of the weapon roughly in the direction of Garth. Before he had the chance to react, the cannon swivelled and opened up with a deafening burst of gunfire, the blinding flash of the muzzle temporarily obscuring Garth's vision. Rubbing at his seared eyelids, he looked up to see the shredded remains of the man, his torso nothing but a scrambled mix of torn flesh and bone.

"Bring it in," hissed Al, his voice still obscured by gunfire.

His confidence suddenly boosted by the automatic targeting of the heavy weapon, Garth rolled further into the farmland, grinning as the men and women didn't know who to attack, the heavily armed tank approaching them, or the three people wiping them out from behind.

Well, not a tank thought Garth to himself. *But as good as one*

His seemingly indestructible vehicle fuelled his courage, and he rushed to meet the battle head on. His good spirits died as the ammunition from the weapon ceased, but the spinning barrels continued to track targets, unable to pick any off.

With his main offensive weapon out of commission, Garth found himself in a very uncomfortable position, surrounded on all sides by panicked screams and sporadic bursts of gunfire.

"They're holding out in hiding places," reported Al. "Get over here, buddy, we need a new plan."

Garth surveyed the battlefield, and made out a seven foot giant by the front of the house, the person partially obscured by the thick sheets of black smoke that drifted across the opening from the shattered vehicles. He pushed on, through a group of three men huddled together on the ground and sweeping their weapons from side to side. Two of them looked up and barely registered the sight of the massive vehicle before each of their heads were knocked off by the front bumper, while the third rolled to one side. He leapt into action and lunged at the vehicle as it passed him, catching the wing mirror on the passengers' side and gaining a foothold on the wheel arch, struggling to angle his weapon through the open window.

Struck with terror, Garth grabbed his double-barrelled shotgun and squeezed the dual triggers, releasing both barrels into the snarling face of the man. His head crumpled in a spray of blood, and he fell with a spasm, his arm snagging on the mirror and cracking with a sickening sound. Garth drew the vehicle to a stop by the front door of the house, the sound of the feet of the fresh corpse dragging along the ground audible even over the sounds of battle. It reminded Garth of a hunter dragging the carcass of his kill behind him, of a killer taking a trophy.

"Nice kill," muttered Al, nodding towards the corpse as he lowered his frame behind the humvee, using it as a barricade. "Did you have to bring it with you?"

Garth didn't say a word as he stumbled out the vehicle. He caught a glimpse of himself in the mirror as he moved, noted he looked pale, and felt about as nauseous as the expression on his face.

"You okay?" asked Bill, joining Al in a crouch behind the vehicle as bullets bounced off its armoured hide. Unable to say anything coherent at that time, he simply nodded, feeling his cold sweat trickle down the back of his neck. He would have preferred to meet the attractive young girl beside Bill under different circumstances; somewhere he could have introduced himself, made a few charming jokes, then proceeded to get her drunk, or if not, tipsy. As it was he didn't even try to speak, unsure whether the first thing to leave his mouth would be words or the bile churning around in his stomach.

The hectic crossfire of the battlefield didn't agree with him, of that much he was sure.

"There's about eight or ten of the bastards left, I think. A few of them are using the destroyed vehicles as cover, but we should be able to penetrate those with the mounted machinegun on the back. The rest seem to be hanging around the entrance of the barn, but again, the flimsy metal of the building doesn't offer much protection from a large calibre round. I think there's still a pair of snipers on the roof of the barn, though, they keep dipping out of view."

Garth nodded feverishly, hoping Al was going to ask him to do something like keep the engine ticking over. The Marine was either psychic, or could tell from his shaking form that Garth was not ready for combat on such a large scale.

"You, take the wheel of *The Colebrook*, keep her moving. It'll be a harder target if we keep moving. I'll take the weapon on the back, try my best to wipe those fuckers out. Bill, take the bitch here and sweep through the house, double-check for any stragglers we may have missed, then see about working back through the cellar, out through the ruined outhouse. And for Christ's sake, kid, watch your back. From them…"

Al waved the muzzle of his weapon towards Angel. "And from her."

Nodding, Garth slowly clambered back into the vehicle, feeling safer as soon as he found himself surrounded by a cocoon of reinforced-steel armour.

"I'm not cut out for this," he managed to mutter under his breath.

II

Bill quickly ran through the house, first checking the storage cupboard in the entrance hall, then charged up the stairs, making sure the stripped bedroom and bathroom were empty.

"All clear," Angel confirmed, skidding out of her own room, her breathing shallow and her skin flushed red. At least this time, it was the exertion that was making her flushed, and not Al making her blush with inappropriate comments.

I can think about that later, Bill thought to himself, making his way back down the stairs and ripping up the rug. He flung the trapdoor open, then slowly descended into the murk of the cellar, this time flicking on the light as he went. Their cover had been well and truly blown now, there would be no harm in turning on the light.

"What's the plan once we get outside?" asked Bill, picking his way through the mound of corpses at the foot of the stairs, then turning around and helping Angel down from the higher steps. She looked at him, then shrugged her shoulders. Bill smiled, then motioned towards his headset with one finger. She nodded, understand that he wasn't addressing her.

"Break out the outhouse, you should be able to get a better view of the roof and the bastards sniping at us. If you can, kill the fuckers. If you can't, then move so you can. There's no way I can get them from down here, but we can provide a decoy target. They'll be too busy… Jesus, buddy, watch where the fuck you're going!"

The signal died, and Bill ripped the headset off, looking at the power indicator.

"It's dead, too," he muttered. The army needed to invest in some decent batteries in the near future. Bill would be sure to remember to write a strongly worded letter as soon as he got off the damn island he'd been trapped on.

The pair rushed through the narrow stone corridor leading to the second hatchway out of the cellar. Above him, he could hear muffled shouts and bursts of gunfire, accompanied by the constant drone of the humvee's engine.

The passage ended in a concrete tube, with a series of metal rungs about a foot apart leading up towards a heavy metal hatchway, locked in place from the inside. Bill twisted the round handle, unfastening the deadbolts, then pushed the hatch open, shielding his eyes as the light filtered in through the shattered wood making the walls of the outhouse. He turned, leant back into the hole and grabbed Angel's wrists, hauling her up out of the cellar. She was surprisingly light, and he didn't struggle too much with her, despite the added weight of ammo and weapons.

Crouching low in the ruined building, paying careful attention to the numerous bullet holes that peppered the thin and rotten walls, Bill shuffled to the open doorway, keeping as much of his body obscured by the building as he could, and peered out into the battleground.

The humvee seemed to be out of control, spinning around in tight and frantic circles, looking as if it were ready to tip at some points. The only thing that made Bill think that everything was okay was the fact he could see Garth gripping the wheel through the cracked and shattered windows: they were bullet proof, but only to a certain extent; enough bullets smashing into them would eventually do some damage. The vehicle still had the dangling corpse attached to the passenger side, but it had also picked up a bloody torso that had been impaled on part of the broken grille. It now also had part of a burnt-out car that seemed to be welded fast to the rear of the vehicle, a flaming tail swinging wildly with each frantic turn.

"Jesus, he's a maniac."

"Not as much as Al," Bill observed, pointing to the shape of the bulky Marine on the rear-mounted machinegun, a single safety strap the only thing that kept him from falling out with each bucking movement. He had a wide grin on his face, and randomly fired bursts of gunfire towards the direction of the barn roof. The darkness of his face was split by the glint of his white teeth, a wide grin testament to the thrills and excitement he was currently experiencing.

Lifting his gaze, Bill could barely make out the shapes of two heads atop the building, ducking in and out of view, firing bursts of gunfire towards the circling vehicle. He lifted his submachine gun, trying to draw a bead on of them, but he couldn't. Angel tried the same with her rifle, but had the same result.

"How do we get on the roof?" asked Bill, motioning towards the barn. "We can't get them from down here, we need to go up there."

"There'll be some ladders inside, unless you want to climb the outer wall."

"There could still be a couple of stragglers in there, we'll go up the wall. I'll try anything once."

"You won't be able to do it," said Angel, placing her rifle on the ground. "With your leg like that, you won't be able to get half way up. I've climbed it before, I used to when I was little. Let me do it."

Bill was about to protest, but felt the pain in his leg, and the look of determination in the young girl's face told him that he wouldn't be able to sway her decision.

"Here," he said, offering her his own handgun. "It's more compact. I don't know if it's as powerful as yours, but it'll be easier to carry than the shotgun."

"I'll be okay," said Angel, quickly dropping to her knees and unfastening the strap from the rifle and fixing it to the shotgun. Strapping it to her body, she broke into a sprint, leaving the seclusion of the outhouse and running to the barn. She reached the metal building and leapt at the wall, finding purchase on the smooth walls and slowly inching up the surface. Bill watched anxiously, his mouth dry as he watched Angel work her way upwards.

"Be careful," he whispered to himself. Within a minute, she had reached the top of the giant structure, and hauled herself over the lip of the roof, vanishing from sight. Bill waited, the sounds of gunfire exchanging between Al and the snipers continuing all the time.

Another burst of gunfire, this time different in tone to the rest, and a hushed and eerie silence fell over the battleground.

"Did we win?" called Garth, his distant voice shaking as he drew the humvee to a halt. Al unfastened himself from the mounted weapon and leapt down on to the ground, his Desert Eagle drawn and aimed casually towards the roof of the barn. Bill smiled and stepped out from behind the outhouse, carrying Angel's discarded weapon as he went. Al nodded towards him, then looked at the weapon he carried.

"Does that mean she's dead?" asked Al, unable to hold back a smirk as Bill approached him. He shook his head, turning his back on Al as he reached him and lifted his eyes skywards.

"That would make your day, wouldn't it?" shouted Angel from atop the barn. She tossed down a coil of rope, then slowly began to descend the building. Garth joined Al and Bill, then looked up towards Angel, following both men's gaze.

"You were right about one thing," agreed Garth, his eyes fixed on Angel. "She's got a nice arse."

"Ass," corrected Al. "Nice *ass.*"

"It's the same thing," muttered Garth as he watched Angel approach them. Al smiled at Garth and playfully punched him in the shoulder, then looked towards Angel, his face stern and emotionless.

"So, you did that, I guess."

"I did," she admitted, handing the shotgun back to Bill and exchanging it for her rifle. She swapped the straps back over, then looked at Garth.

"Fucking typical of a reckless young bitch."

"You must be Garth," she said, ignoring Al's slanderous remarks and nodding curtly. He nodded, then wiped a hand against his trouser legs and extended a hand. She held up her hands, both bloodied and raw. "You'll forgive me if I don't shake."

She slowly made her way back towards the farmhouse, leaving the three men behind.

"Not much of a conversationalist, is she?" asked Al, watching as she turned and vanished into the farmhouse.

"But a firm arse, none the less," confirmed Garth.

"Ass," muttered Al.

"Jesus, this could go on some time," said Bill, slowly making his way towards the farmhouse.

"It's all clear here, anyway, thanks for asking," called Al. "Me and buddy'll go fetch the truck. You get your shit ready, and see about digging out that welding torch."

Bill responded simply by waving over his shoulder, listening to Al as he started to remove the dead bodies from his vehicle.

He found Angel in the kitchen, running her injured hands beneath the tap, the water pooling in the sink an unhealthy pink, similar in colour to the blood of a plague carrier. She was trembling slightly, then looked up out the shattered window at the sound of the humvee growling to life. Still trembling, she returned to tending her wounds.

"You okay?" asked Bill. She jumped, obviously unaware she was being watched, then nodded, sniffing quietly to herself. Bill stepped forwards, grabbed a couple of pieces of cloth and stood by Angel, watching as she finished cleaning her hands. She kept her head tilted low, hiding as much of her face as she could while she worked.

"I guess I'm not as light as I was when I was nine," she announced, laughing slightly as she spoke. There was a tremor in her voice, and she slowly turned to face Bill. She smiled weakly, and her eyes were red and puffy, glazed with tears. "I cut my hands on the climb. Burned them on the way down. My hands sting, feels like I've rubbed them in hot glass."

"You've been crying," said Bill, lifting one of the pieces of cloth he held.

"Because it fucking hurts," snapped Angel, snatching the cloth and gently wrapping them around her hands. "That's why I came in here. If that arrogant bastard saw me like this, I'd never hear the end of it. You know what he's like."

Bill nodded in agreement as Angel laughed softly, the motion dislodging a fresh trickle of tears.

"Maybe it's more than just that," she continued. "Maybe it's everything getting on top of me. My parents, the farm, that bunch of arseholes…"

Feeling awkward, Bill wasn't sure what to say or do in this situation. If Jenny were like this, he'd reach out and hold her, try to comfort her. Was this something he should try now?

He stepped forwards awkwardly, opened his arms and gently wrapped them around her shoulders. She pressed in closer to him for a moment, rubbing her head on his chest and sniffing. He held her for a moment, then she nodded and stepped backwards, rubbing her face and drying her eyes. It hadn't been a moment too soon, either: Bill had felt a familiar stirring while he held her, a feeling that although was welcomed, wasn't very appropriate.

"Thanks. So, where've they gone to?" she asked, casually changing the subject of the conversation and nodding towards the window.

"They've gone to get the lorry. Garth is the driver of an articulated lorry, complete with trailer. The only thing is, it doesn't work. Al seems to think that if we drag it back here we can fix it up. He said there's a welding torch in the cellar, is that right?"

"Yeah," agreed Angel, nodding. "Dad used it to fix up the barn, and the tractor, patching over the rust. I don't know how long it will last, though."

"Well, the only way to find out is to get it ready for those two. Will you show me where it is, give me a hand?"

"I'll show you," sighed Angel, wiping her tears away with the back of her hands. "But I don't think I'll be able to help you carry it."

"That's ok," said Bill, making his way back into the cellar and grinning. "As long as it's out ready for the boys when they return, it'll keep them of our back."

The sun had settled for the night behind the surrounding hills, giving way to a clear night sky speckled by a field of bright stars. Both Bill and Angel sat on a wooden box by the front of the house, each with a thick blanket draped over their legs. The cool of the night had crept in a few hours ago, and the chill was enough to make Bill's hands and feet numb with cold. Looking at the pale colour of Angel's lips, he'd figured she felt the cold the same way, and it had been his idea to unpack his blankets.

"Busy couple of days," muttered Bill, surveying the remains of the carnage from the battle. There had been too many dead bodies and too much structural damage to the buildings to even think about beginning a clean up.

"I've had busier," Angel said, smiling thinly. It was all a show, Bill knew that much, but he couldn't blame her. In the past four days her home had been downgraded from a farm to a shell of rubble. The two battles had taken their toll on the buildings, and Bill thought there'd be no chance of finding an intact window anywhere on the farm. The walls of all the structures were riddled with bullet holes and burned from explosive damage: some blasts had taken large holes clean out the masonry, effectively making the house a large slab of Swiss cheese.

"I'm sorry about your home," said Bill, taking another look around the farm from his seat. "It's going to take a hell of a lot to get this place fixed up."

"It's not home," said Angel, her voice dull and quiet. "Not now. Everything that made it home's gone."

Bill didn't respond. She didn't have her parents any longer, but up until four days ago, she still had her home filled with her memories: now she didn't even have that. He was still trying to think of something to say when the distant growl of the humvee filled the night.

"It should be Al," said Bill, grabbing one of the weapons beside the couple as he spoke and slowly rising to his feet. He shouldered the rifle, aiming towards the rise the vehicle should be coming over.

Sure enough, the powerful headlamps of the humvee peered over the ridge, slowly crawling over the hill and pulling the leviathan vehicle behind it. The vehicles drew to a halt, the hissing and screeching of the truck's breaks confirming that the convoy had stopped. The doors to the humvee opened, and both Al and Garth spilled out, laughing raucously and each carrying a thick smoking cigar.

"So I said 'Jesus, girl, just because it's twice as big, doesn't mean you have to charge twice as much'," Al shouted. Garth doubled over, dropping his cigar and gripping his side as he laughed uncontrollably, rolling around on the floor. Al continued to laugh as he met Bill's glare. Still smiling, he managed to control his laughter and waved at the lorry. "We've got it," he managed to say, maintaining a straight face for a couple of seconds before bursting into laughter again.

"Christ, what is it now, drunk or stoned?"

"Stoned," admitted Al. "I'd never drink and drive."

"Apart from that time in Brazil, eh?" Garth shouted, retrieving his cigar and stubbing it out before tucking it behind his ear, jamming one end between his head and his hat. Al grinned and pointed to Garth, nodding.

"That's right, buddy," he agreed. "That's so right. And that's why I don't do it."

"I suppose we're sorting this out tomorrow morning, then," asked Bill, watching as Garth grabbed a wrench from one of the toolboxes in the back of the hummer, then fall to the ground and look at the device he held, laughing softly at it.

"Why not, we've got all the time in the world," said Al, grabbing a magazine from the front of the vehicle and marching towards the house. "I'm going to bed. I've got some reading to take care of, and you two lovebirds can get back to snuggling under the moonlight."

He stumbled towards the house, looking down on Angel as he passed her.

"Evening, bitch," he muttered, before vanishing into the house. "Jesus," he continued as he thumped through the entrance hall and into the living room. "This place is a fucking pigsty! Have you two just been screwing each other all afternoon?"

Bill ignored him, looking over the humvee and its heavy load.

"You managed it okay, I presume."

"Piece of cake," Garth announced. He licked his lips, then looked towards the house. "I'm really hungry, actually. I'm going to look for some snacks in the kitchen. Want anything?"

"I'm good, thanks," said Bill, waving him away. He returned to his seat by Angel and recovered his blanket, listening as Garth rummaged through the cupboards in the kitchen.

"I'm sorry for this," Bill said.

Angel shook her head. "You don't have to apologise. I know Al's not my number one fan, and it's clear he's a bad influence on Garth. I'm going to find somewhere to sleep."

"I'm really tired, too," agreed Bill. The adrenaline from the battle had worn off some time ago, and he'd been fighting the lethargic feeling that had been washing over him for a couple of hours. "I think I'll join you. Sleeping, I mean. That is…"

"I know what you mean," said Angel, standing up and wrapping the blanket around her shoulders. "I'll see you in the morning."

She entered the house, leaving Bill alone outside. He wrapped his blanket around him and sat down on the ground, listening to the eerie silence of the night. No insects, no wild dogs howling, nothing.

Feeling his eyes grow heavy, and not wanting to fall asleep out in the open, Bill wearily trudged back into the house, closing what was left of the front door and jarring the rifle against it, wedging it shut.

Al will bite your head off if he sees that, the voice inside Bill's head volunteered.

"So fuck," he muttered his response aloud. "Let him."

He looked in the kitchen first, checking to see if anyone had decided to settle down there for the night. The cupboards had all been opened, their contents disturbed and cast aside, spilling out on to the floor. The entrance to the cellar still lay open, but Bill didn't think that anyone would have ventured down into their to spend the night, especially with the three corpses lying at the bottom of the stairs. He closed the trapdoor, replaced the rug over the covering, and left the room, moving on towards the living room.

He made his way into the living room, where he found Garth curled up in a ball amongst the ruined armchair, gripping a packet of opened biscuits in one hand. His snoring was deep and rattling, and Bill was surprised it hadn't woken Angel, who lay stretched out on the settee, the blanket tucked around her body.

Bill lowered himself into the intact armchair and closed his eyes, slowly drifting off to sleep despite the snoring of his new companion, his dreams plagued with the sights of battle, the sounds of the dying, and the smell of the rotting undead.

III

By the time Bill woke up, the rest of the farmstead was a hive of activity.

Both Al and Garth we busy fixing the lorry; he could see the pair working over the vehicles from the window. Both men seemed to be working efficiently as a team, and neither of them seemed to be suffering from the effects of the previous night of dope smoking.

"How's it going?" he shouted, cupping his hands round his mouth to carry his voice. Al lowered the welding torch he held and lifted the heavy black mask that shielded his face.

"Morning, Sleeping Beauty. No problems here," he yelled in response. "Buddy and me got this covered. Been up since dawn. Looks like we're almost there with the repairs, too."

"Might even get around to fixing your bike," announced Garth, his face streaked with oil and sweat. "If you're a good boy, that is."

Leaving the pair to their work unsupervised, Bill walked away from the window and headed into the kitchen, finding Angel packing what food that was left into boxes and bags.

"Is there much left to do?"

She shook her head, stepping back from the box and closing the lid. "That's the last of them. You've slept through the best part of the morning."

Bill shrugged his shoulders by way of an apology, looking around the packed food. He counted three large boxes and two bags: enough to last the four of them a couple of weeks, if they rationed if out properly.

The silence of the farm was broken as a deep and thunderous engine roared to life, accompanied by the deafening blast of an air horn.

"Sound's like they fixed it," Bill said, stating the obvious as Al stormed into the kitchen with a wide grin on his face.

"Was there ever any doubt?" he asked, running his hands beneath the tap and rinsing off the dirt from his fingers. "You see, me and Garth are a killer team, we work together brilliantly. You should think about joining our team, kid, it's a winning combination, you can stop fraternising with the whore."

"We're all in one team now, Al," Bill reminded him. "Regardless of whether you like it or not."

"Are the rest of the *team* ready to load all this stuff into the trailer? We've already put the heavy stuff in the back, so it's just the food now. Can I leave it in your hands to supervise? Or do I have to do this as well?"

"I'll do it," muttered Bill, stacking one box on top of another and slowly lifting it, juggling the load and tilting his back so the weight rested on his hips. He slowly edged out the room, down the entrance hall and out into the courtyard, dragging his feet so he didn't end up tripping over the tools and loose debris left lying around the ground. He reached the lorry, hefted the boxes on to the raised edge of the opened trailer and pushed them deeper into the container.

"What do you think?" Garth asked, sitting in the rear of the trailer on a familiar-looking seat. Bill climbed up into the new and improved trailer and looked around.

The interior was now illuminated by three evenly spaced light bulbs running the length of the trailer. The wooden crates of toiletries that had been previously used as seats had now been removed and replaced by the back seat of the humvee. In order to create the space required for the five barrels of alcohol from the cellar, Al had decided to hang as many of the weapons up as he could. There were still two crates filled with weapons and ammunition pressed against one wall, but the two long walls of the trailer had been covered with hooks and ledges, each of which held a weapon of some description. Some Bill recognised, but others were completely alien to him. Bill also noted that a hole had been cut in the roof of the trailer, and a hatchway had been fastened on. The hatch looked exactly the same as the one that had been in the outhouse, leading into the cellar.

"We pulled that from that wooden shack," said Garth, confirming Bill's suspicion and pointing up towards the hatch. "Next time we get boarded by a troop of those acrobatic zombies, we can just pop up there and blast them with a shotgun. Or the mounted machinegun Al's transplanted up there."

"We'll need a ladder," said Bill, waving in the direction of the hatch. "That must be ten foot off the ground, even Al would struggle reaching that."

"He mentioned something about a rope ladder in the back of *The Colebrook.* I don't fancy my chances of climbing a rope ladder when I'm moving, but then, I'm just the driver."

"We take our turns driving," grunted Al as he pushed the last of the boxes into the rear of the trailer. "Hey kid, you take it easy over there, I know you've been busy all morning, you deserve a break. Me and the bitch have handled moving the food out, here she comes now."

Angel appeared beside Al, slowly hoisting her bags on to the trailer and wiping her forehead with the back of her arms. "Heavy," she said by way of an explanation to a question nobody asked.

"So, what now?" asked Bill as he dragged the bags further back into the trailer and stashed them between the barrels and the crate. "I mean, we've put this thing back together."

"And your bike," added Garth. "We've strapped it to the side of the trailer."

"And my bike, thanks. So, what are we going to do with '*The Colebrook*'? I mean, are you going to leave it behind?"

"Fuck, no," said Al. "Just because we've stripped things out the engine, doesn't mean we're going to leave it behind. It's still got a couple of weapons in working order. I can't remove the Vulcan cannon, and there isn't a chance in hell I'm going to leave that behind. We're going to tow it behind, facing backwards. Like a mobile gun platform."

"Sounds plausible," agreed Bill. "So, two in the back, two in the front, I presume that's how it's going to work."

"That's the deal," agreed Al, motioning for Garth to follow him. "And seeing as the pair of you can't drive, you and her don't need to be up there at any time. I'm sure you'll be able to keep yourselves entertained. And you might want to get strapped in. Is there anything else you want to get before we go?"

Angel shook her head, but stepped towards the open doors anyway, looking at the ruined house while Al and Garth slowly made their way towards the cabin. She leaned against the wall of the trailer and sighed, looking at the demolished buildings.

"You okay?" asked Bill, gently placing his hand on her shoulder. She nodded slowly.

"I knew I'd be leaving home one day, I just never figured it would be like this. I'd always thought that when I left, I'd be able to come back if I wanted to."

"Not much to come back to, is there?" said Bill, gently squeezing Angel's shoulder. She shook her head grimly. Grabbing the handles of the door and heaving them closed, Bill and Angel made their way towards the seats at the back of the trailer, hammering on the walls as they went to indicate they were ready.

The vehicle shuddered to life, the trailer shaking with the power of the engine and rattling the weapons hanging from their mounts.

"We fitted an intercom, too," came Al's voice, fuzzy and distorted through the small grille attached to the wall behind the seat. "It'll come in handy if I get bored with the miles and miles of endless roads ahead of me."

"Does it have volume or a power switch?" asked Bill, turning around to look at the clunky and cumbersome device.

"Yeah," confirmed Al. "We fitted both of those. Garth didn't want to, but I persuaded him. I didn't want to have to listen to the pair of you fu…"

Bill flicked the power switch, closing his eyes as the Marine was cut off.

"Now all we need to do is get one of those installed on the real life version," muttered Angel, waving back to the controls for the intercom. Bill laughed, and couldn't help but agree.

"They could've given us a window to look out of, that would have helped pass the time. Too damn cold to it travel in the hummer, though."

"We can always play cards," suggested Angel. "I mean, I watched you and Al playing poker the other day. I may not be as good as him, but I'm sure *I* wouldn't lose my first born child."

"That's funny," he said. "But I don't think you'd appreciate Al's deck of cards."

"I brought my own," she said, pulling a pack of cards from one of the pouches hanging from her belt and placing it on the seat. "Now, what's your game? Happy with poker?"

"Why not," said Bill, sitting back. "It's always good to get some practice in."

"You're not driving too fast, buddy. What's wrong, you think you still getting paid by the hour?"

"The fix isn't one hundred percent," Garth said, slowly rolling the steering wheel from left to right "She's temperamental, like I said. I figure if I take it over forty, she'll blow a gasket, or the engine will start pissing smoke, and we'll be stranded out here, in the middle of nowhere, until two jokers with assault rifles show up and drag this thing thirty or forty miles back down the road."

"You're still bitter about that?" asked Al. "Jesus, we didn't even rough you up too much. I shot the bitch in the back about three times."

"Yeah, well I can't speak for her, but I don't want to go through that experience again. I'd rather take it easy and not chance wrecking the engine again."

Al shook his head slowly, watching as the road slowly rolled by.

"Jesus, forty miles an hour. I may as well walk there."

"Where are we going, exactly?" asked Garth, drawing the vehicle to a halt at a slip road that fed on to a dual carriageway. "I mean, I know I'm the driver, but I get the feeling that you're the guy pulling the strings and making the decisions here."

Al nodded, smiling as he did so. Garth was right, though he was sure Bill would be loathe to admit to it. The kid seemed to have a free will, an attribute that wouldn't fit in with the Marines, or at least the grunts like himself. It seemed to be a trait the arrogant bastard officers seemed to look for, though.

Maybe I should promote him to a Lieutenant, he though to himself before dismissing it. He didn't want the give the kid a sudden promotion like that, thinking it would give him a big head.

"We plan on going south," confirmed Al, rummaging in his pocket and bringing a compass out of pocket, placing it on the dashboard.

"South, that narrows it down slightly to about two thirds of the British Isles. Anywhere in particular?"

Al rubbed his chin, scratching absentmindedly at his beard, before shrugging his shoulders. "What do you suggest?"

"Well, what's your aim?"

"I'm carrying a radio in *The Colebrook*," he said, still going with his initial plan of contacting someone outside the plague quarantine zone. "I'm trying to boost the signal to reach someone who might be able to help us get out of here. I need somewhere further south so I'm closer to my target audience. I'm also looking for something to boost my signal with. Any ideas?"

"Yorkshire has a lot of hills, maybe a higher point of transmission?"

Al shook his head, knowing that the radio needed more than just height to get over the North Sea and past the non-English speaking population.

"Manchester, then. Last I heard they had a reasonably large television studio out there, maybe something there could be rigged up to an antennae."

"Television," muttered Al, scratching his beard thoughtfully. "Always wanted to make a television show. Maybe we can do something like that. You any good with electronics?" he continued, not relishing the idea of returning to his soldering iron and metres of wiring.

"I get buy," confessed Garth. "I've been known to fix a few electrical goods around the house."

"Then you're the electronics man of the team. Have you ever thought about joining the Marines?"

"With this pot?" Garth said, smiling as he rubbed his overweight stomach. "I don't think I'd be able to pass any of the fitness tests."

"Well, there is that," said Al with a grin. "But Jesus, you're a veteran of this shit. You've survived this long, you've still got use of all your limbs and you're not one of those fucking zombies. Baptism of fire, and all that shit. You handled the hummer pretty good back at the farm. You see I'm a Commander now, and I made Bill a Sergeant. Now he's got this crazy frigging idea that he's a real Marine, and he's demanding to have his own squad to control. Naturally, his first selection was that crazy whore in the back, which I think was a decision made purely with his dick. Shit, they're probably in the back screwing each other right now."

"Jealous?" asked Garth with a grin. Al shook his head.

"Just pissed off, I don't like her. Anyway, if he wants a squad, he can have one. But I get some say in it."

"Well, you're his commanding superior," confirmed Garth. Al cocked an eyebrow and pointed to Garth with one finger, a lopsided grin on his face.

"Damn right. Now, as a squad we need to have different people with different key skills. Bill's role is to keep the team together. I guess that whore's role is to keep the mood of my men up and maybe turn a few tricks for some money. Between that, I'm sure she can cook and clean up after us.

"In my old squad, before they were all… Well, we had different specialists. J-Man was the driver of the group, he could handle anything the Corps threw at him: hummers, those crazy-bastard bikes R&D came up with, cars, tanks, the man was a natural with vehicles. Couldn't make fucking bullets to save his life, though," he added, recalling the safety bullets he'd used on Angel upon meeting her. "Anyway, you remind me of him: a shorter, fatter version of him. So, how'd you fancy being a Corporal?"

"Was he a Corporal?"

"No, just a private. But there was another guy that got put in another team, Milo; he was the electronics genius of the squad, he could make a clock out of a lemon and some chewing gum wrappers. He was a Private, too. So you're taking the place of two Privates, that makes you a Corporal."

"Is that the way the army works?" asked Garth, slowly moving the trailer on to the dual carriageway and following the floating needle in the compass. "Corporals are worth two men, Sergeants worth more?"

"Well, I'm a Commander," repeated Al. "And I'm a one-man squad of destruction. So it must. Now get moving. It's a long way to Manchester. Especially if we're stuck at going forty miles an hour."

"Do you want to tell our passengers where we're going?" Garth asked, pointing a thumb back towards the trailer behind them before gripping the wheel once more, carefully weaving between the random scatter of abandoned vehicles lying about the roadway. Al watched as his chauffeur piloted the vehicle with grim determination, clenching his teeth as he barely missed the parked vehicles.

"I'll tell Bill later, he can pass it on to the whore if he wants. Remind me to tell him before we pull up. The last thing I want is for the couple to stumble out the trailer half naked and find themselves surrounded by those dead fucks."

"You think we're still going to be bothered by the Rots?"

Al grinned. It seemed Garth had quickly picked up on Bill's names for the zombies, which he supposed made sense. If they were all going to be working together, they would need to have a generic terminology for each thing they were going to encounter.

"The population of Britain was something like seventy five million people, give or take a few hundred thousand. Of those people, how many do you think died of the plague, or ended up as zombie-fodder?"

Garth shrugged his shoulders.

"Well, I don't know either," confirmed Al. "But I'll bet my magnum that it's over ninety percent. And of that ninety percent, how many lived in towns or cities? No matter where we go, we're still going to be knee-deep in this shit."

"So you're saying we're completely fucked?"

"Unless we can get off this island. Hence our trip to Manchester. Now, you're sure we can't get this piece of shit to move any faster?"

"I'll try," grinned Garth, "But I make no promises."

XII
DEAD AIR

"The ability to dampen and control what can be seen and broadcast from hot zones will be a boon to our operation."

I

Two long and monotonous days of travel crawled by for the band of four people aboard the vehicle. Towards the evening of the second day, the smoking ruins of Manchester slowly scrolled into view.

From where he sat in the cabin of *Colebrook's Runner,* Al's name for the vehicle, Bill lifted a pair of binoculars to his eyes and glared at the dark shapes of the ruined buildings that made up the outskirts of the city. Amidst the gloomy buildings, he could see figures lurching amongst the rubble; almost dancing around the hundreds of small fires that burned in the ruins. Thick clouds of smoke rolled across the city, heavily laden with the ashes of ruined buildings and the remains of any creature or Rot that had come to rest in the flames.

"Is that the place?" asked Angel as Bill passed her the binoculars. She sat between Garth and Bill in the front of the cabin: it wasn't too cramped, as the vehicle was wide enough to comfortably accommodate three people, and it was a lot better than sitting in the trailer with Al as company. "It doesn't look too promising. Are those creatures running around in the ruins?"

"Certainly looks like them. The place is crawling with the bastards," said Bill, nodding slowly. "Do you think we can talk Al out of finding this damn television studio?"

"You know him better than me," said Garth, shrugging his shoulders. "Can you talk him out of *anything*?"

Bill shook his head slowly. "He's a stubborn bastard, there's nothing I could say to change his mind."

The vehicle slowly ground to a halt, the brakes of the vehicle hissing and screeching until it came to a complete stop. Garth sat back from the steering wheel, stretching his arms and back as he tried to work the cramp out of his muscles. He stifled a yawn with the back of his hand, then pulled his hat off and rubbed his gleaming pate with his wrist before slipping the cap back on. He grabbed a cigarette from the crumpled box lying on the dashboard, placed it between his lips and flicked out the lighter from the dashboard. He lifted it to his mouth as if to light the cigarette, then caught sight of Angel and her disapproving glare. He sighed, then replaced both cigarette and lighter.

"Well, do we go any further, or wait out the rest of the night here?"

"You're asking me?" asked Bill. Garth nodded.

"With the Commander asleep back there, you're the next man in charge. So, do we wait, or dive in?"

"We wait," confirmed Bill. "Let sleeping beauty get his rest. I don't want to go in there now, not so close to nightfall. First thing in the morning, we move in closer and have a look around. I'll take first watch up top, swap over in about four hours."

"Forget it," said Garth. "I'll take watch first. It'll give me a chance to have a decent cigarette without having to worry about poisoning your lungs."

"You've been driving for over twelve hours, you of all people should be getting the most rest."

"I've been doing this kind of shit for years," muttered Garth, opening the door and stumbling out the cab, grabbing his packet of cigarettes and rummaging amongst the junk food wrappers and crumpled maps for a box of matches. "It's not the first time I've pulled an all-nighter, and it certainly won't be the last."

He opened the box of matches and lit one, taking a drag from the stick and smiling. He smile turned to a frown as the skies above opened up with a deafening clap of thunder and a sudden downpour of cooling rainwater.

"Won't be able to smoke your cigarettes now," said Angel, smiling slightly as she moved over into the driver's seat and slammed the door shut. "Too bad,"

"Like I said, I've been doing this for years," he said, flicking the peak of his cap. "Keeps the sun out my eyes and the rain off my smokes. Catch you in four."

Bill watched Garth disappear in the mirror, then tried to adjust the settings on the seat, pushing back with his weight and managing to recline it slightly. He gave up on it, and watched as Angel swiftly adjusted her seat, reclining fully and stretching out. She looked at Bill and grinned.

"Must just be well worn."

"Been doing it for years," Bill said, repeating Garth's words before he'd went on lookout detail. He laughed softly to himself, then closed his eyes, welcoming the feeling of lethargy as it washed over him.

"Bill?" asked Angel, her voice quiet.

"Hmmm?"

"How long do you think this will last? The dead walking, I mean."

Bill shrugged his shoulders, then realised that if Angel had her eyes shut, as he did, then she wouldn't have been able to see his response. "I don't know. It could be weeks. It could be months. They could all keel over tomorrow morning."

"Which wouldn't be too bad if we're going in there tomorrow morning. Here."

Bill opened his eyes and rolled his head to one side. Out the corner of his eyes he could see Angel's outstretched hand and the plastic bottle she gripped. He took it from her, sipped at the sweet blackcurrant juice, and handed it back with a murmur of thanks.

"Do you really think Al's plan will work?"

"He seems convinced it will. He's been trying to arrange a pick up since he crashed in Edgly, him and his damn radio project. It's the one of the reasons I tagged along with him; he seemed to have a goal, a reason to get up every morning."

"If this plan *does* work, and we get picked up by the army, what do you think will happen to us?"

"Quarantine, probably for a couple of months: doctors will probe, take tests, look to see if we're infected, they'll try to work out why we're not. We'll probably have to sign some kind of government secrets act. Might even be given new identities."

"We won't be superstars, then?" asked Angel. "No way we can sell the rights to our stories, no movie deals?"

"The rest of the world has been told there's a plague, and that's pretty much it. Could you imagine the panic if word got out about the dead rising? I'm not that familiar with any religious texts, but I'm pretty sure that's part of Armageddon. There'd be panic on a global scale."

"There were probably a lot of people here that thought the same; the priests and their devout followers."

"A sign of the end times," Al's voice crackled over the intercom.

"How long have you been listening?" sighed Bill, looking over to the small metal grille on the dashboard.

"Long enough. You made a decision and gave an order. Not necessarily the decision I would have made myself, but you were in charge."

"You would have took us into the city in the dark, knowing that there were Rots lumbering about in there?"

"No, I would have sent *you* into the city, I would have remained here, provided you with covering fire."

Bill nodded slowly, imagining the mischievous grin on Al's face. He knew he was joking, and that even *he* wouldn't have taken them into the city this close to nightfall.

"We'll move in at first light. I'll take the second watch cycle. Doubtless you and the bitch will be to busy from…"

Bill flicked the intercom off and lay back, sighing heavily.

"He's an arsehole," Angel announced. Bill smiled and nodded slightly.

"Be that as it may, at the minute he's our only chance of getting off this island. Come on; get some sleep while we've got the chance. It'll be a long day tomorrow.

The first light of day broke through the windows of cabin, waking Bill the moment the light hit his eyelids. Deciding he preferred sleeping in the windowless trailer, he sluggishly raised his body from the seat and fumbled for the handle to the door. He moaned as his stiff joints creaked and snapped, his numb legs almost giving way as his feet touched down on the asphalt outside.

He still wasn't used to the unnerving silence of the morning. The absence of the dawn chorus of singing birds that normally heralded the beginning of a new day seemed to only add the surreal situation Bill found himself in. He didn't know if they'd fled from the carnage, were off scavenging some easy carrion, or if they were just dead themselves.

"Morning, kid," Al's voice shattered the silence as he strolled around from the rear of the trailer, his arms laden with a load of white material. "Take five minutes to pull yourself together. Garth's fixed up some coffee for us all. Once we've got that, I'll go through my idea. I've been working out the details to my scheme while I was on guard duty last night. I think I've got a flawless plan."

"What's that you've got there?" asked Bill, motioning towards the pile of white material in Al's arms. He grinned.

"I'll tell you in five, I told you."

Bill shrugged his shoulders and made his way around to the rear of the trailer, where he found Angel and Garth sitting on the edge of the opened trailer, each holding a ceramic cup filled with dark steaming liquid. Both mugs they held seemed to have pictures of women in bikinis on, and Bill assumed they were both the property of the tanker driver.

Angel smiled and reached behind her, grabbing a third cup of coffee and passing it on to Bill. He tentatively sniffed the dark liquid and twisted his face slightly at the bitter smell.

"I suppose it's too much to ask for milk or sugar?"

"Got some powdered stuff," Garth offered.

"I'm not touching that fake shit, I'd rather have the real deal."

"Milk comes from cows, and most of those are infected or dead. And we don't have any sugar," responded Angel with a sympathetic expression on her face before taking a sip of her steaming drink. The shudder of repulsion suggested that she didn't just drink her coffee black.

"I do have a couple of pieces of chocolate," said Garth, extending his hand and displaying a small sweet that nestled in his palm, round and wrapped up in a shinning purple wrapper. "Just drop a piece in. Tastes a little strange, but it takes the edge off."

"I'll pass on that, thanks," said Bill, waving his hand in a dismissive gesture. Garth shrugged and unwrapped the piece of chocolate before dropping it into his own drink and taking a big gulp. Bill smirked at the grimace that crept across Garth's face, then clambered up on to the humvee attached to the rear of the vehicle and rested his feet on the tow bar.

"So, what do you think the big guy has planned?"

"Shit knows," said Garth, taking another drink of his coffee before pouring the contents out on to the ground. Three soft, half-melted lumps of chocolate slipped out the mug and slapped to the ground. "Ever since I mentioned that television studio he looks like he's been plotting and scheming for something."

"Jesus," muttered Angel. "He could be planning to do *anything*."

"The man's obsessed with guns, tits and alcohol," agreed Garth, leaning forward and lowering his voice. He removed a cigarette from his crumpled packet and lifted it to his mouth, catching Angel's look. He lit it, then pointed his finger at her and scowled. "Don't give me any shit, you hear me? We're outside so I can smoke however much I want. You got a problem with it now, fuck off over there."

"He must have something in mind, but I dread to think what," Angel continued, trying her best to ignore Garth and the rings of smoke he deliberately blew towards her.

"I always wanted to make a snuff movie," announced the Marine as he returned to the small gathering, throwing the mound of material he carried into the rear seat of the humvee. "But I never really had the weaponry, the filming equipment or someone I really wanted to kill to hand. Now look at me! I'm going to visit a studio, I've got plenty of weapons, and I know of someone I'd happily kill. It's turning out to be a fantastic day."

"What's this plan you've been working on? Something reckless and stupid?"

"You remember I told you how I wound up on this damn island? Rescuing that damn bastard Maxis from his tower, all that shit?"

Both Bill and Garth nodded their head, while Angel shook her head and shrugged her shoulders.

"Good, that saves me telling that part of the story," he said, lifting himself on to the humvee and clambering up on to the one remaining mounted machinegun. He stood erect and rested his forearms on the weapon, mimicking a pose Bill had seen the lecturers assume so many times in college before he was thrown out. He quickly leaned forward and whispered to Angel: "I'll tell you the details later." She nodded quickly in understanding.

"I tried to keep it from that bastard I spoke to that Maxis was dead, but he already knew. Dick had managed to send a transmission before the helicopter was shot down. But what if Dick had been lying? What if the transmission had been rushed and incorrect?"

"But you blasted the Rot's head off with a magnum," countered Garth, waving wildly with the hand that held his cigarette. Angel batted the hand away, scowling at him. "You killed him outright."

"Maybe so," said Al, pointing to Garth. "But wouldn't they have to think different when Maxis appears on their screen and tells them to pull their fingers out their asses and organise a pickup?"

"What?" asked Bill, jumping down from the humvee and scratching his head while craning his neck to look up at the soldier. "What are you talking about?"

"General Maxis. He's going to have a videoconference with Carter, tell him to stop being an asshole and arrange a pickup. After all, that God damn gunship he sent never turned up."

"I think I understand," said Garth, smiling and nodding his head. He jumped down from his perch at the rear of the trailer and circled the humvee. "They send a helicopter out to rescue him, but the troops there are really pissed off at having to break quarantine, or what have you. They make up some half-ass bullshit story about killing Maxis and ditch the helicopter, then go AWOL. They'd had enough of the fighting they'd seen in Brazil."

"Something like that, yeah," said Al, pointing a dark finger at the short man. "We make it sound like I spun some yarn just to get out of the assignment. I doubt it's the first time a Marine has bullshitted just to get out a mission."

"And one of us looks like Maxis, right?" asked Bill, half-skipping over to where Garth had once sat. "This man looked like me? Or Garth?"

"Honestly, I can't even remember what the old bastard looked like. I remember seeing him from behind as he was chewing on my friend, and I remember seeing him covered in blood," admitted Al as he clambered down from the weapon and grabbed the mound of white material. "But that doesn't matter, because everyone knows the plague is airborne, and everyone has to wear these."

He unfurled it to display the material as both the shape and size of a regular human male, with a head constructed from metal, rubber and glass. Bill flinched at the sight of it, the expressionless gaze of the empty suit reminding him of the soldiers that had toiled around him and Jenny, the men who had patrolled the confines of the hospital where he had been quarantined.

"Suits," he muttered, more to himself than anyone else.

"Environment suits," Al announced, tossing it into Bill's lap, grabbing another two more and passing one to Garth, then reluctantly handing one over to Angel. Bill stared glumly at the featureless helmet resting on his lap, and remembered for one brief moment that the last time he had seen someone wearing a suit, his lover had been alive.

"I found these in one of the crates the bitch had stashed in her farm. You put these on and you look like every other dumb fuck soldier that was left to rot on this island. Only thing is, you're the

General, Bill. He's your Corporal. And she's… well, you can imagine what a General would have a little whore like her traipsing around with him for."

Angel didn't verbally respond, but the look she gave him was icy cold. Al chose to ignore it.

"You really think we can pull this off?" asked Garth.

"Hey, I'm genuinely excited about this plan," said Al, bubbling over with enthusiasm. It was certainly the most excited Bill had seen him since they first claimed the humvee as their own. "What's not going to work? We drive on into the city, guns blazing, knock down a few Rots, make our own little show, and arrange for a pickup. By the time they realise, it's too late, and we're on the way out of here."

"He really thinks it's going to work," Garth muttered, shaking his head and looking at the suit he held. "When do we go?"

"No time like the present," suggested Al, waving towards the front of the trailer and the open cab doors. "Put them on now, don't be afraid to get them dirty. It needs to look like you've been doing nothing but breathing, pissing and shitting in these suits for weeks. If they're too clean, they're gonna smell a rat. Roll around and smear some dirt on you. You," he said, pointing to Angel. "You're a dirty bitch, anyway, just act normal."

"You like me really," grinned Angel, opening her suit and stepping into it. Bill watched her out the corner of her eyes as he clambered into his own suit, and caught himself wondering what it would be like to watch it in reverse, to see her stepping *out* of her clothing. He checked himself as he removed his jacket and tossed it into the back of the trailer before fastening up the suit. He stretched out his arms and spun around, showing the result to Al. The Marine didn't seem impressed.

"Very pretty, kid. Now come on, get aboard and we'll get on our way."

He made his way to the wooden barrels loaded in the humvee and helped himself to a mug of wine, smacking his lips as the dark liquid worked its way down his throat. Bill waddled over, struggling slightly with the cumbersome suit, and stood beside him as he watched Angel clamber into the rear of the trailer.

"Like you really?" he muttered, refilling his mug and swilling the liquid around in the bottom of the cup. "Your ass, maybe. The rest of you, I could do without."

"Little early for that, isn't it?"

"Never too early," Al replied, downing the second cup.

"What's your roll in this, anyway?" asked Bill. "I notice you're not wearing one of these clown suits."

"Someone needs to work the camera and the rest of the stuff."

"Do you know how to work that stuff?"

"Do *you*?" Al asked with a smirk, walking away towards the cabin. "Now climb aboard, before we leave you behind."

II

The oversized vehicle had some trouble negotiating many of the narrow roads and crowded streets, even with the expert driving skills of Garth behind the wheel. Where he had first tried to avoid the numerous cars that littered the roadways, or the many dead that wandered aimlessly along the streets, he had eventually gave up, and the front of *Colebrook's Runner* was now battered and dented, splattered with blood, while the front grille now carried a collection of severed fingers, arms and flayed strips of skin, each of which flapped and swayed in the breeze.

"How long until we get to this damn studio?" growled Al. Garth sighed and continued to drive through the streets in silence, keeping his mind focused on the task ahead. It had been some time since he'd been to Manchester, and he'd lost his road atlas for England a long time ago. He was sure it was deeper into the city itself, closer to the city centre, it was just getting there. If only he hadn't dumped all the navigation equipment in favour of his songs, at least then he'd be able to get a fix on his position. All he needed was some kind of landmark he could recognise

There, he thought to himself, catching a glimpse of a large shopping mall in the distance. He forgot its name, but he knew that he had to take the next right.

As the wheel slid through his hands, Al slapped the dashboard with his open hands and stomped his feet.

"Jesus, that's the fourth consecutive right turn you've taken. You're going around in fucking circles, *buddy.*"

"Will you give me a break?" snapped Garth, temporarily turning his attention from the road as another shambling flesh eater vanished beneath the thick tyres. So many had gone under now that the slight bump was barely recognisable. "How long until we're there? Where is it? Do you know where you're going? It's like going on holiday with an impatient kid. We'll make a deal. I'll keep my mouth shut when you're firing guns, you keep you mouth shut when I'm driving."

Al didn't reply, but looked glumly at the back of his hands, tapping his fingertips on the dashboard.

The rest of the journey was conducted in total silence, and Garth knew that the Marine was sulking. His daughter had done the exact same thing when she had been younger.

He breathed a sigh or relief as the television studio rolled into view; the gates locked shut and security barrier down. Grinning to himself, he revved the engine and looked over to Al.

"Hold on, y'moody bastard, I'm going through."

Al perked up and grabbed the submachine gun that lay on the ground beside his feet, cocking the weapon and tucking the stock in against his shoulder.

"Outstanding," he said, winding down his window and allowing a cold blast of feted air to seep into the cab. It mingled with the stale stench of sweat already trapped in the cab, creating an unpleasant cocktail of nauseating odours. "Soon as we're through I'm going out there, clear and sweep the parking lot, get the gates secured. You park up as close as you can to the building."

He reached over and thumbed the intercom to life.

"I realise you're probably busy right now, kid, but we got a job to do, so pull up your pants and listen. I need you to get on the machinegun on the roof as soon as the vehicle stops and give me some covering fire. If the bitch wants to be helpful, she can climb on the back of *The Colebrook* and operate its gun. We're coming up to the studio, and I want the parking lot secured before we enter the building. And hold on, there's going to be a bit of a bump.

"Hit it, buddy!"

Garth nodded slowly and gunned the engine, building up to his top speed of forty miles an hour, seconds before the front of the cabin collided with the security gate, buckling the protective bars and rending the steel of the gate with a spine-jerking shudder. This was for more noticeable than any jolt they had received from running over a Rot, and Garth's vision suddenly became obscured by a thick cloud of steam that spewed out the front grille. He swore beneath his breath and wound his own window down, sticking his head out and trying to make out the details of the car park.

A few cars still littered the lot, many of them high-performance sports cars belonging to the executives of the studio. A few less impressive cars had also been abandoned: these were obviously the chariots of the men and women who worked in the studio. Garth didn't discriminate between the rich or the poor; he smashed into the sides of every vehicle that got in his way as he tried to regain control of the cumbersome trailer.

"Jesus Christ," Bill's voice crackled over the intercom, "what the hell are you doing up there?"

"Broke through the security gates," hissed Garth through gritted teeth as he practically stood on the brakes. They weren't responding as they should have, which suggested to Garth that not only had the radiator blown, the brakes had decided that moment to give up the ghost at the same time.

.

Is that how it works? The two things aren't connected, he thought to himself, sideswiping one of the sporty cars and activating the car alarm. The screeching wails of the alarm made him wince, and it was an unpleasant reminder of the society that had crumbled around him. Maybe he'd miss some aspects of the Old World more than others; waking up at three in the morning to the high-pitched drone of a car alarm was certainly something he wouldn't miss.

"The damn thing's pissing steam, I can't get it under control, that final blow must have caused some major damage. Temperamental bitch that she is… just hold on!"

Bill muttered something in response, but the muffled response fell on deaf ears as Garth tuned out the world around him. He finally managed to bring the vehicle to a stop by using two television vans as buffers, and sat back, grinning triumphantly. He turned to face Al, his smile still fixed in place, but instead of the Marine he saw only a vacant seat and an open window.

"Al?"

The screeching of the car alarm drew to a halt, but instead of silence following, there came a rapid burst of gunfire, followed by another, and a third.

"Bill, hurry up and give Al some cover out there," Garth spat, fumbling for the tool box beneath his seat and grabbing the largest wrench he could find and grasping blindly at the bonnet release. He wanted to get the problem sorted out as soon as possible, before it got worse. If they needed to make a quick exit it would be no good if the vehicle didn't work.

He tried to look in the cracked mirror, then through his window, to see if he could see the Marine and judge how he was doing, and realised where he had managed to stop the vehicle.

Between Al and the vehicle, there stood the television studio. He'd managed to park on the *other* side of the building, meaning Bill and Angel couldn't possibly provide cover from the mounted weapons. He revved the engine, knocked the gear into reverse and tried to move. With a spluttering wheeze, the engine died. Garth swallowed hard and removed his hat to wipe his brow, which had suddenly broken out into a feverish sweat.

He'd fucked up.

The minute the lorry hit the gates to the studio parking lot, Al pushed open the door and slipped out the moving vehicle, tucking his shoulder in and rolling across the gravel.

The minute he stopped rolling, he leapt to his feet, bringing the stock of the submachine gun tight against his shoulder as he panned the weapon from left to right. Already, the Rots that had been trapped in the parking lot started to stumble towards him, arms outstretched, throats burbling with hungry moans. Al quickly evaluated the situation and guessed there had to be about fifteen Rots in the lot, but with the gates destroyed and wide open, any number of Rots could stumble in off the street. He had to seal off the entrance before he could begin the secure the lot.

What can I use? He thought absentmindedly as he squeezed a burst of three rounds into the head of the closest Rot, a man dressed in a long white doctor coat that flapped in the wind and exposed the bloodied and flayed limbs of the creature. It collapsed in a twisted heap, fragments of bone piercing the peeling skin of the creature as it keeled over.

He targeted the next Rot, waiting until it was a little closer to ensure a clean kill and minimal ammo expenditure. This one was a nurse, her head hanging at a crooked angle, spine protruding from the twisted neck and blood dripping from the ragged skin hanging loosely from her frame, the pale pink liquid drawing spiralling patterns with the infected fluid on the concrete floor.

Must be a hospital around here, he thought absentmindedly as he tapped off another three rounds, shattering the ribs and skull of the nurse.

The gunfire was sure to attract Rots in the area from outside the studio parking lot, and Al had to work fast to seal up the opened gates. He scuttled towards the closest car, a sleek black sports car with tinted windows, and ducked down behind it, listening to the stumbling footsteps and moans of hunger that were slowly approaching him. At least once *Colebrook's Runner* had stopped the kid and his whore would be able to provide him with some covering fire. Maybe he'd be able to move a few of the less sexy vehicles littered around him into the gateway: the large people carrier opposite his current position, near the door leading into the studio, seemed to be a particularly good choice for that, however its shredded tires quickly ruled that out as a viable option.

"It would have been easier to have just opened the gates," he muttered to himself, rising from behind the car and removing his cigarette case, casually resting it on the roof of the low sports car and removing one. He lit his cigarette and smiled, casually cutting down another two Rots just as a car alarm started to sound. Startled by the sudden noise, he jumped and sent a burst of gunfire into open air. He cursed himself for wasting bullets, then looked towards the source of the car alarm, just in time to see the trailer vanish behind the other side of the building.

"Where the fuck is he going?" he muttered, firing blindly at the gathering of three Rots slowly lurching towards him while he backed away from the car. He snatched his cigarette case and slid it back into his pocket, watching as a new clutch of Rots stumbled through the gates and instantly homed in on the lone Marine. He fumbled for his headset and flicked it on.

"Christ, Bill, what gives? Where's that mad bastard going?"

"Jesus Christ," Bill's voice carried smoothly over the headset, his voice laced heavily with panic. "What the hell are you doing up there?"

Al pressed one hand against his head, trying to make out the garbled reply over the intercom. Frustration set in as he realised he couldn't understand a word that was being said.

"What's he saying? Don't keep me in suspense, kid."

"The trailer's shot," answered Bill. "He said that it's pissing steam, or some kind of technical talk like that."

"I need you to bail. I'm going to have to get some big and heavy vehicles blocking the gates, the dead fucks are already coming in here, and I need some cover. Don't take your time, kid, I need you here yesterday."

Sounds from the rear of the trailer played over the headset as Al continued to gun down the approaching creatures: expletives, metal tearing against metal and heavy crates toppling on to one another.

Emptying the rounds from his current magazine, he quickly dropped the empty one to the floor and slapped a new one in, hastily counting the number of creatures now in the courtyard. The continual influx of creatures from the outside meant that there was now thirty of the undead and this number continued to increase every minute. Lowering the submachine gun, Al snatched one of the grenades hanging from his belt, primed it and casually tossed the device into the largest throng of Rots, covering his head with his hands and turning away slightly. The blast tore through the bodies and sent chunks of smouldering flesh flying through the air, showering Al with gore and smoking concrete.

"Grenade?" enquired the voice in his ear as he lifted his weapon and sprayed gunfire from left to right.

"Fuckin' a," grinned Al. "You hurrying up back there, or are you still busy screwing that whore?"

"We're coming," Bill confirmed. Al's grin broadened; that was *too* easy to even pass comment on.

"Get up there," he heard Bill say, his breathing laboured. "I'll go down around the front, see what I can do from there. Just be careful."

"I've handled this before, I'm not a total amateur," Angel responded. Al sighed and sought refuge behind a large and clunky-looking family saloon car. He traced the contours of the bonnet thoughtfully, deciding if it would be a good choice for the gate. He decided to worry about that when Bill got to him.

Which was going to be a tough job, counting the number of Rots between Al and the corner the trailer vanished behind.

"I count about fifty, now," he hissed. "Where the fuck are they coming from?"

"They're coming in from all the back streets, stumbling out the shops. The city's crawling with them…"

"I don't think I asked you," muttered Al.

"Well you asked someone. And Bill can't see much more than you down there."

"Down there?" asked Al, taking the head of an almost-skeletal Rot with a single, precise shot from his submachine gun. "Christ, bitch, where the hell are you?"

"Roof. Bill sent me up the fire escape around back…"

"Clever bastard, I'm impressed. And here's me thinking he was just trying to take you from behind… he's starting to think and act like a Sergeant. I'll make a Marine of him yet."

"What makes you think I'd sign up?" Bill cut in. "After this shit is over, I don't ever want to see or handle another gun, and I certainly don't want to see another corpse, walking or otherwise."

"Yeah, yeah. Cut the crap, kid, it's game time. Where are you?"

"Far corner of the car park, some of them have seen me, they're breaking off and are heading towards me. Jesus, how many are there?"

"I get sixty," said Angel. There was a loud report of a rifle, and one of the Rots in the middle of the gathering crumpled into a pile of bloodied inanimate meat. "Fifty-nine."

"Do we have a plan, then?" asked Bill. The blast of his weapon joined the cacophony of moans and gunfire, creating a deafening symphony of explosions and pain.

"I'm running low on ammo," warned Al. "I didn't think it would be as intense a battle as this."

"Clear me a path, I can get through to you. I've got one of your weapons for you."

"If I could clear a path," sighed Al, "I'd have enough ammo, and wouldn't *need* to clear a path for you to bring me more ammo."

"That made no sense," confirmed Bill. "Angel, can you help us out?"

"Take cover," she warned. Al tried to see where she was on the roof. He saw a cluster of four small spheres arc over the edge of the building, and instantly knew that Angel had helped herself to some of his grenades.

"Fire in the hole," screamed Al, hoping his warning made more sense to Bill than the simple 'take cover' command Angel had given. The small devices clattered to the floor in the midst of the crowd of corpses, and for the few seconds that followed that, Al thought Angel had neglected to activate the grenades. Al couldn't blame her for that; she was inexperienced, and his own grenade throwing action was so smooth and seamless that the casual observer could easily just assume that throwing them was all there was to it.

The grenades in the crowd bloomed into a chain of explosions, maiming those that were at ground zero and catapulting those that weren't far from the blast, crashing bodies into buildings and smashing them through the windows of the parked cars. One car took the brunt of one of the explosions, the fire shredding the front of the vehicle and raining burning fragments of metal and plastic into the gathering of corpses.

Al stood and panned his weapon from left to right, taking note of the number of Rots that had been obliterated and those that simply seemed stunned by the blast. Many corpses seemed to be trying to pick themselves up out the flaming rubble that surrounded them. The grenades had done their job, however, and Al made out a figure dressed in a brilliant white suit bolt across the lot, diving over flames and randomly discharging his weapon at any squirming corpse that tried to grab him. With a triumphant scream, he leapt the last six feet of his run, landing on the bonnet of the saloon and sliding across it, crashing into Al and knocking him off his feet.

"Get off me," he grunted, almost throwing Bill off the top of him. "What you got for me?"

Bill didn't respond, just handed over the heavy weapon that was slung over his shoulder. Al took it from him with a grin, tossed his submachine gun to the ground, and cocked the heavy mechanism of the M249. He hadn't really touched it since winning *The Colebrook* from Moloch's men, and it had been neglected even more since the discovery of Angel and her cache. But it was a welcome weapon at this time and place.

"Thanks, kid, it's just what I need. Now, what say we mop up the rest of these bastards and get the yard sealed?"

Bill nodded his head, gripping his shotgun and licking his lips as he peered over the roof of the car. Those that hadn't been killed in the explosions were already on their feet. Some were homing in on Al and Bill, while others wandered away to the walls of the building, pitifully scratching at them with their fingers, trying to climb up and get to the third person up on the roof. These were the first to be dispatched by a combination of Bill's shotgun and Angel's rifle. Al shrugged as he cut into the swathes of the undead; he would've happily left those until last, they didn't pose any immediate threat to him.

A grin slowly crept across his face as the kick of the heavy weapon hammered into his upper arm and shoulder as it rapidly ate through the belt of ammunition coiled inside the magazine. He slowly strolled into the midst of the Rots, his weapon making him feel almost invulnerable as he kept the undead creatures at bay.

"The car park's nearly clear," Angel announced between rifle shots. Each shot marked the demise of another Rot, but they were few and far between now. The grenades had been extremely effective, as had Angel's marksmanship. Although he hated to admit it there seemed to be more to the bitch than just a pretty ass: she was good with a rifle, though she still hadn't made him the coffee he'd asked for back on the farm when they were facing Moloch's men. Nice ass, but with a crap memory. "You could probably start blocking the gates now."

"There's nothing here that's suitable," said Al, lifting his finger from the trigger and casually leaning against the wall, the smoking muzzle of his weapon pointing skywards. He looked slowly from left to right, searching for any vehicle that may work, or any sign that one of the Rots may be playing possum. "The cars are too small, and there's no decent vans big enough to block the gateway."

"What about just blocking the doors to the studio? If we lock ourselves up in the studio, it'll be easier to secure," Bill asked, pointing to the heavy doors at the front of the building.

"It's possible," muttered Al, scratching his beard. "We can't just lock ourselves in and hope for the best, though. We need to have another escape route. Ask your bitch if there's a hatchway up there, or doors to a stairwell or something."

"It looks like there is, I think," Angel confirmed, her voice accompanied by the rattling sound of her trying to open the hatch. "It must be locked."

Al sighed and looked impatiently at Bill, motioning for him to speak to Angel. Now it was Bill's turn to sigh.

"She says yes, but it's locked. Christ, Al, why do I have to repeat everything she says?"

"Chain of command," he grinned. "Okay, there should be a few of the larger cars we can use to block up the doors, maybe set a few traps with some grenades, like an early warning system or something. We'll go in through the top, blow the hatch, I don't think there'll be to many of those Rot bastards out there who can climb up the fire escape, but just to make sure we'll destroy the fire exit behind us, set up a zip line directly to *Colebrook's' Runner*. Tell the whore on the roof to cover us while we work, we'll be up there in about ten minutes."

"Tell him to piss off," said Angel. Al grinned to himself as he began to work on the barricades to the studio.

III

Major Samuel Carter sat behind the cheap wooden desk that had been installed in his office aboard the gunboat *Narcissus,* and sighed heavily. He'd much rather be sitting in his own office, behind his own desk and smoking one of the fine Cuban cigars that were lying in one of his locked draws. He didn't enjoy being on the boat as it circled the British Isles, hated it when the vehicle passed by close to the shoreline, and despised it when the vehicle had to sail through the body of water between England and Ireland.

This was the current location of the boat, and Carter sat on the edge of his seat, nervously glancing at his watch. It normally took a few hours to pass through, and until they were clear, he wouldn't be able to relax. He rubbed his hairless head and squirmed uncomfortably, looking at the digital clock, willing all the digits on display to advance by three hours.

"Major Carter, Sir?"

Carter looked up at the young soldier standing at the open doorway, a dark skinned man with short black hair and wearing plain green trousers and a shirt. He saluted smartly, the tips of his finger brushing his thick eyebrows. Carter lazily returned the gesture, trying to regain his composure and hide his discomfort about his current situation. He knew the man to be the communications officer, he'd sent numerous reports through him on several occasions. What was his name, Levins? Lowens?

"Lewins," he remembered, sitting up and straightening his jacket, trying to look calmer and less agitated than he felt. "What is it? It had better be important."

"We're getting a signal sent directly to us from the mainland. It's got audio and visual, looks like it might be a television signal."

"Television signal?" Carter asked, raising an eyebrow. Could it be that one of the more resourceful of the groups of rebels on the island had managed to bring together enough brain cells to figure out how to send a television station? No doubt, in a bid to send a distress call to anyone outside the island who may be able to organise a rescue operation.

Fat chance in that happening, he mused to himself, suppressing a grin. *We own the island; we say who goes and who doesn't.* But still, if their signal *did* manage to leave the island and hit the coastal areas or Europe... He couldn't let that happen.

"I've already jammed the signal, just to make sure," confirmed Lewins, almost as if he had read the mind of Carter, "But I didn't need to. It's coming in on a military signal, bouncing off one of our satellites; high priority. They're asking for you by name."

"What?"

"The man doing the talking claims to be General Maxis. Sir, what should I do with the transmission?"

"Patch it through to my office," he muttered, slowly scratching his head. The report he'd received from the gunship sent to pick him up said the Marine who kept trying to reach other towers and arrange evac had killed Maxis. That same sergeant had tried to get in touch with a few other towers, but the signal had always been re-routed to his office, where he would take great pleasure in deriding the arrogant and cocky soldier. When he was cooped up in a gunboat such as the *Narcissus*, he had to take whatever entertainment came his way.

He turned to the flat screen monitor that hung on his wall beside his desk, leaning forwards in anticipation of the signal that would be fed through. The green glow of the monitor, which currently displayed the schematics of the boat, blanked out, then became replaced with the television signal.

A man sitting at a desk, wearing a grimy and blood-spattered HAZMAT suit, his head covered by a helmet with a gold-tinted faceplate, reflecting a distorted view of the television studio around him: a single camera, light blinking red, and walls lined with cables and junction boxes. The headgear certainly matched up with what a General would have been issued with in the field. Behind him stood a pair of soldiers, each in the same dirty attire, only their faces were obscured by the more traditional gas mask. One male, the other female, they both cradled an MP5, the light assault that most of the troops on England had been provided with before they had been stationed. The trio had positioned themselves in front of the UGMC's flag, a red banner with a map of the world embroidered in gold.

"This is Major Carter," he finally announced into the small microphone sitting on his desk. His palms suddenly felt very clammy. "Who am I addressing?"

"Carter?" asked the central figure. The only way Carter knew this was the man speaking was his body language. While he spoke and moved, the two soldiers behind him remained rigid, their heads slowly scanning from left to right, as if searching for a threat. "It's about frigging time. I don't know how long this signal is going to hold, or how much power we have in the generator here, the last thing I want is to be stuck on hold while one of your grunts decides what to do with my transmission."

As if on signal, the screen flickered and faded, vanishing behind a covering of static before reappearing.

"You know who I am," the central figure continued, pointing a finger towards the camera. "I'm the son of a bitch you left stranded here. Where the fuck is that air support you promised would be coming to collect me? I've been waiting for weeks; we had to abandon KDL-76 not long after I managed to get in touch with you the first time…"

"We sent a Cavalier Gunship to collect you weeks ago, we were informed by the pilot that your were killed by one of the Marines aboard, and then the helicopter was shot down."

"Do I look or sound dead?" shouted the speaker, pounding a fist on the desk. "Christ only knows how I'm not already, do you have any idea what the fuck is going on here?"

"The creatures," muttered Carter, nodding his head. He wasn't sure whether this man was telling the truth, and that he *was* General Maxis, or whether it was someone trying to pull the wool over his eyes. "We've received various reports confirming your initial observations, and these were later confirmed by…"

"You're wasting my time," growled the speaker. "Are you going to arrange an evac? Preferably with a team and a helicopter you can trust to carry out their job this time."

"You still haven't answered my question," said Carter, leaning closer to the microphone. "Who am I speaking to?"

"General Maxis," confirmed the man, sighing heavily. "Now, can we talk about a gunship?"

One of the soldiers that had remained stationary for so long, the woman, leaned forwards looked at Maxis, obviously communicating on a secured channel.

"The area is hot, the Rots are heading our way, and we can't hold the position any longer. We have to go. Do we have a confirmed evac?"

Carter sat back and rubbed his temples deep in thought. It was certainly his call; he had to make the decision. There was no way that he could be sure whether it was Maxis or not. He supposed it was conceivable the crew aboard the Cavalier that had originally been dispatched had just concocted a story and landed somewhere, maybe for some shore leave. Once they'd realised the error of their ways, and the truth behind what was actually happening on the island, Colebrook had constantly tried to arrange a pickup…

Fuck it, thought Carter, nodding his head and grabbing the stack of reports that sat on his desk. *If it's not Maxis, we can always shoot them, burn the bodies, or leave them to die at the hands of the creatures.*

"Where are you?"

"Manchester," answered Maxis, slowly nodding his head. "Does this mean…"

"Three days," he agreed, finding a report and circling a name with his pen, passing the sheet over to the awaiting Lewins, who still stood by the desk. "There'll be a squad in the outskirts of Manchester in three days, a small clearing called Greyson's Park. Make sure you're there."

The picture on the monitor flickered and died, the image being replaced by static and a flashing message informing that the signal had been lost. Carter turned to look at Lewins, motioning to the piece of paper he held.

"That's one of the first special ops teams we're sending in. Make sure they're at Greyson's Park in three days. If it's Maxis, they throw him in quarantine. If it's not, they shoot to kill. Make sure this order is understood."

Lewins saluted sharply, then spun on his heel and left the office. Carter sighed and opened one of the draws of the desk, willing a cigar to appear. He had no such luck, and closed his eyes, finding himself wishing once more to be in his office and smoking one of his fine cigars.

IV

"And the signal is dead," bellowed Al from the control room of the studio, stumbling out the control room and chewing heartily on a bacon sandwich he had found in a drawer in one of the offices. Bill shook his head silently, unable to comprehend the fact he was still eating it, despite the fact the bread was hard and crispy, and the meat turning a subtle shade of green.

"Are you sure?" asked Garth, placing his gun on the desk and reaching for his helmet, then hesitating.

"Camera's turned off," confirmed Al, swaggering over to one of the junction boxes and heaving the cables out their sockets. "I killed the signal so they won't be getting anything but dead air. Now we just need to survive another three days, and find this 'Greyson's Park' that Carter was talking about. You did good, kid, real good. I think we fooled them."

"And what's going to happen when they come to pick us up and realise that I'm not Maxis?"

"I've got another three days to think of that," Al grinned as he pushed Angel roughly to one side and pulled down the flag he had erected as a backdrop. It hadn't been necessary, but it would have looked really good on camera.

Bill slipped the cumbersome facemask off his head, dropped it to the table with a clatter, and wiped his face down, breathing a sigh of relief. It certainly felt good to be able to breathe fresh air again. He couldn't imagine what it would be like to keep something like that on for days at a time. If his had been uncomfortable, he could only imagine how uncomfortable Garth and Angel found their own. As if to confirm this, Angel tore hers off and flung it on to the ground, cracking one of the lenses as she did so.

"Should've kept it on," muttered Al, barging into her with his shoulder as he walked past. "Improved your looks no end."

"You're very funny," smiled Angel, placing her gun on the desk and hoisting herself up on to it. "So we need to find a map from somewhere. Any ideas?"

Al was about to suggest one of the garages they had passed on their way to the station, when Bill held up his hand, an order for silence. Years of training made him instantly remain quiet, while Garth had to ask what it was he'd heard.

A few moments of silence passed, and for a moment Bill thought he had just imagined it. He shrugged it off, then reached for the fasteners of the white coveralls, when the sound came again: a spluttering, wheezing noise.

"Christ, it's a car," hissed Al, drawing his magnum from its holster and running out the studio. Bill turned to see Angel struggling out her suit while simultaneously trying to grab the gun she'd been posing with on camera.

"Better hope these work," hissed Garth as he grabbed his own weapon and followed Al.

"I don't understand," said Angel as she stumbled out her suit, almost losing balance. Bill rushed forwards and caught her, kept hold of her arm while she struggled with the clinging and thick material. "Are the Rots trying to start one of the cars be used to barricade the studio with?"

"I don't know. Remember the stories I've told you? I wouldn't think anything was beyond their capabilities. Come on, we'll go find Al and Garth, see where it is they've rushed off to.

"Security office," Al's voice carried over the headset. "Main corridor, first right. I'm trying to get a fix on the security cameras out in the parking lot. I think you need to see this."

Bill and Angel found the office quickly. It was a small room, about eight-foot square, with one wall covered entirely by security monitors; it reminded Bill of the command centre in the hospital, and for a moment he was back there in his mind. Of all the monitors, only three were active, showing different scenes in the car park. A group of about ten people, seen from three different angles. They were standing around the one large van Al had managed to park up next to the main door, and looked as if they were trying to move it aside to get to the front door.

"Rots?" asked Bill hopefully, though he already knew the answer even before Al shook his head.

"Looks like a small group of rebels," said Al. "They must have been drawn here by the gunfire and explosions."

"That was hours ago," said Angel, glancing at her watch to prove her point. "What took them so long?"

"I don't see any vehicles with them," said Garth. "Maybe they walked over?"

"Just casually walking through a Rot-infested city?" questioned Al, flicking his eyes towards Garth momentarily, then quickly shifting them back towards the monitors. "Even *I* wouldn't make someone do that. No, they'd have to park up somewhere. Walking would just be suicide."

"They're breaking through," Bill felt compelled to commentate on the events on the monitor, even though everyone could see for themselves as one of them clambered into the van and slowly reversed it away from the door. A few of the people seemed to be celebrating this, with congratulatory pats on the back, or slaps of one another's hands.

"Grab your shit," growled Al, pushing himself away from the desk and knocking over the chair he sat on with a clatter. Bill jumped at the sudden noise, though something told him that there was going to be a lot more loud sounds to follow. "They're going to be coming in through the main entrance. I can't raise any of the other security cameras in the yard or the building, so there's no way of telling where else they could be coming from."

Al made his way for the doorway to the security office, when the lights suddenly flickered and died. He swore as he blindly stumbled into the wall, then fumbled in his pockets. With a click, his lighter blossomed to life, barely illuminating the doorway he stood in.

"They cut the power," muttered Garth, panic lacing his voice. "Jesus Christ, they cut the power!"

"Bullshit," hissed Al, his face eerily lit by the flickering flame he held. It disappeared with a second click, and Bill could hear a rustling sound. "The generator's just died. It's not them; it's just bad timing. Here, take these."

Bill felt a bulky metallic object pushed into his hands, and could recognise them just by the shape. He'd worn a pair before, or rather a pair similar to it. Instead of washing the world with an opaque green-grey tint, this created a swirling mix of colours, ranging from blue to white.

"Heat vision," muttered the blur of colour that Garth had become. Bill looked towards him, and saw the portly shape looking at his own hands, as if it were the first time he'd ever seen them. Bill did the same, out of curiosity, though didn't stare at them for as long as the truck driver did.

"You're giving me one?" asked Angel. Bill turned to see a large and muscular mound of colour handing a dark purple object over to a small and thin band of colours. "What's the special occasion?"

"I don't want you shooting my damn head off in the pitch black."

"You think that'll stop me?" asked Angel. Though he couldn't make any of her facial details, Bill guessed she was smiling. Al grunted, then turned back towards the doorway and lifted one of the weapons sitting idle by the doorway.

"Why not night vision?" asked Bill, feeling slightly nauseous as he jogged a couple of steps. The swirl of colours was too much for him, and he felt like he'd been injected with a very powerful hallucinogenic drug.

"Gunfire creates light, so do explosions. They make heat too, but not enough to blind you in total darkness," He seemed to pause, as if thinking about something that happened in the past. "Well, not smaller ones, anyway. They might have flash grenades, too."

"You think of everything," said Garth, obviously impressed.

"That's why I'm the Marine in total control of this rag-tag squad. Now come on, we might be able to make it to the hatch without running into them."

Bill followed closely behind Al, trying his best to ghost his movements and mimic his stature. Despite his size, he could move almost silently when he wanted to, and that was certainly a trait Bill wanted at that moment in time. Al froze as he reached one of the numerous junctions, and raised his left hand, clenching it into a fist. Bill stopped moving, assuming this to be one of the Marine's special hand signals designed for silent operations, and made sure Angel and Garth didn't just stumble into them.

"What's wrong?" whispered Angel.

"Someone's here," muttered Al, the microphone of the headset barely picking up his voice. "Around the corner. Wait here, don't go anywhere."

Without further warning, Al leapt silently out from behind the corner, turning in mid-flight, then coming to a rest at the other side of the cross junction, his back planted firmly against the wall.

"Are we dancing, now?" asked Angel, sarcastically.

"Two of them, fifty yards down the corridor, standing either side of the stairwell. We're not going up that way. We need to find another way around."

"Silenced pistols?" suggested Bill. "We've done it before."

"Fifty yards," repeated Al. "Can you shoot a man's head at fifty yards?"

"I've never tried," Bill confessed.

"I have," said Al. "And I couldn't: at least, not at first. If I couldn't, what chance do you think you have?"

"Let me have a go," Angel said, slowly creeping towards the junction. Al lifted his hand and held it out, a sign to stop where she was.

"If you even try to do it, *I'll* shoot you before you manage to squeeze a shot off. I'm not going to have you jeopardise this whole operation just because you want to prove yourself to your 'boyfriend' there. We get out of this one conflict free: when the odds are more favourable, we fight on *my* terms. Got it?"

Angel didn't verbalise her response, but she slunk to the back, behind Garth, and nodded slowly.

Bill stepped across the junction to the other side, quickly snatching a glance at the two men who Al had reported seeing. Large in size, though not as large as Al, they seemed to be standing back to back, looking to either side: their heads were moving, as if having a conversation, though at this distance Bill didn't have a chance in hell of hearing what they were talking about. He also decided that he *wouldn't* be able to shoot a man in the head at fifty yards. Maybe even ten yards would be pushing his still-developing talents. Lost in his thoughts, his mind wasn't on the current situation at hand and he waded through a small pile of papers, the rustling almost deafening in the silence of the dead building.

"Who's that?" shouted one of the men, lifting a dark purple tube and pointing it in the direction of Bill. He couldn't make out any fine details of the device, but he figured it was a torch, as it was aiming directly at him and he wasn't dead yet. The second man didn't respond, simply lifted his own purple device, this one most definitely a weapon, and trained it on Bill. The reality of the situation kicked Bill into action, and he leapt to the side, rolling forwards and out of the line of sight of the men. Gunfire sprayed the floor where he had previously stood, showering chips of concrete and tufts of carpet into the air.

"Stupid dumb fuck," shouted Al, roughly pushing Bill aside and cocking his assault rifle with a loud crack. He peered around the corner, ducked his head back so it wouldn't be taken off with a burst of gunfire, then fired blindly down the corridor with his own weapon. Bill watched on, mesmerised as the white-hot casings tumbled to the ground, the carpet around them slowly changing in colour, from a dark purple to a warm red.

Garth and Angel returned fire before Bill managed to pull himself around, their dark weapons spitting bursts of fire and excreting casings. Slowly pulling himself together, he grabbed his own weapon and sluggishly made his way towards the battle and its accompanying din of gunfire.

"If you'd let me shoot one of them, we'd be better off now," Angel said, her voice carrying over the communication headsets. Al simply responded with a grunt, continuing to fire down the corridor.

As Bill made his way to the fray, gripping his submachine gun and raising his aim, he saw the flickering shape of another five people appear at the far end, their heat signatures making them appear as nothing more than multicoloured spectres.

"More of them," shouted Garth, fumbling with a magazine from the safety of the side corridor. "We're outnumbered."

"We've got something they don't," said Al, and Bill could imagine the grin on his face as a plan slowly formed in his head.

"You?" suggested Bill as he loosed a burst of gunfire towards the group of people.

"Fuckin' A," agreed Al, removing the second assault rifle that was strapped to his back and fumbling with its magazine. He pulled a small cylindrical object from his belt, placed that on the floor beside him, then looked towards Garth, motioning with the second assault rifle as if he were going to throw it.

"You'd better catch it," he warned, then tossed it through the air.

With a grunt, Garth caught it and stammered backwards with the weight, Angel helping to keep him upright.

"I'm going to cause a distraction," confirmed Al, retrieving the cylinder and removing a small metal pin, dropping it to the ground. "Soon as I throw this, you and me advance. Got it?"

"Fuck that," hissed Garth, turning around and thrusting the rifle into Angel's hands. "I'm not walking up a shooting alley just because some crazy-bastard psycho Marine says I have to. She can go, I'm not doing it."

"Coward," Al grunted, hauling back with his right arm and flinging the cylinder out into the corridor. "I don't have time to argue. Bitch, cover me."

Seconds after throwing the device, there was a loud bang, and the men at the other side of the corridor seemed to cease their firing. Instead, they now screamed and moaned in agony, with mutterings of blindness rising from their ranks. Al casually strolled around the corner, rifle tucked in high and tight against his shoulder, and let off multiple bursts, while Angel followed behind him, crouching low and keeping to one side. Both Bill and Garth stepped out from behind their corners and watched as the two slowly made their way up the corridor, working efficiently and as a team. Garth covered his microphone with his hand and leaned in closer to Bill, eyes fixed on their comrades.

"Even through these weird goggles, she's still got a nice arse."

"You're spending too much time around Al," Bill laughed as he slowly began to work his way up the corridor, weapon primed and ready.

"Not enough, the spineless bastard," quipped Al. "You two cover our tail, make sure no clever little bastard tries to sweep around behind us. I count seven bodies up here, I figure there's another three in here somewhere."

"Copy," Bill replied, spinning around and slowly walking backwards, both he and Garth sweeping their weapons from side to side.

"Still heading for the hatch up top?"

"I don't know," muttered Al, his voice broken by several gunshots as he squeezed of single rounds. Bill glanced over his shoulder to see Al firing a final shot into one of the cooling bodies lying on the floor.

"We're not far from the main doors, now; we could just make our way out there and run around to the trailer. We might stand a better chance out in the open," suggested Angel.

"Dumb bitch," muttered Al. "If you'd served for even five minutes in Brazil, you'd know that the open ground can be your worst enemy. I heard tales out there of half a squad cut to ribbons by heavy weapons fire when they crossed a clearing in the jungle. We're best sticking to the shadows in here."

"Sticking to the shadows," muttered Bill, nodding his head. "Keeping it low-key, you mean, so we don't attract attention to ourselves?"

"Exactly," agreed the Marine, kneeling down by the fallen people and stripping their weapons of ammunition, then pulling apart the weapons and tossing the pieces in different directions. "And I know this is all going to bring down a lot of heat on our position. So quit talking, and move, upstairs. Come on."

Bill hurried along the corridor, guiding Angel and Garth up the stairs, while watching Al as he continued to manipulate the bodies lying on the floor. "Are you coming?"

"Two seconds," he said, raising a finger as he positioned the last of the bodies in his morbid arrangement. "Okay, let's go. Before their friends turn up."

"What did you do?"

"Lets just say when they ID their friends, they'll get a blast."

"Grenades under the body," said Bill, nodding his head. "I saw that in a film once. Does it really work?"

"I'll tell you in about two minutes."

Bill and Al ran through the corridors of the upper level, stumbling over objects left lying on the floor that didn't generate enough heat to register on the goggles. Bill gingerly lifted his goggles, and saw that although it was gloomy on the second floor, it wasn't the total blackness of the lower levels. He tore them off, pleased to get rid of the nauseating vision, and took the lead over Al, guiding him across the debris strewn across the ground.

"Ah, shit," Garth's voice hissed over the headset. Bill turned to corner and saw him standing at the far end of the corridor, head tilted towards the ceiling, with Angel balancing on the small pile of crates they had used for a platform to originally get in through the hatch.

"What's up?" asked Al, ripping his goggles off and lurching into a sprint.

"It's not opening, looks like something's been put on it outside to keep it shut," Angel said, jumping down from the crate. Al scowled and pushed her aside, then climbed the crate and hammered on the hatch.

"Fuckers," he spat, pounding it once more with his fist before turning around and sitting on the crate, his legs dangling over the edge. "It's not opening. Looks like they've put something on the hatch to keep it locked down."

"Kind of exactly what I said," Angel said, but Al chose to ignore her intentionally. "So they want to herd us out the main door after all. It's a fucking set up."

"Like lambs to the slaughter," agreed Angel. Al leapt down from the crates and punched the wall in anger, cracking the plasterboard surface and leaving an impression of his fist in the wall. "What do we do now?"

"Load up and tear them apart," said Al, gripping his weapon in both hands. "There can't be that many. How are we for ammo?"

"Plenty of shotgun shells," Bill confirmed, stroking his bandoleer, then patting his jacket down. "Another two magazines for the MP5. Garth?"

"I don't know," he muttered. "Two, maybe three?"

"Well, I grabbed what rounds those assholes down there hadn't fired, most of them seem to be five point fifty-six, a perfect fit for the rifles, we should be able load a few magazines from that. We're going to break through the front door. Kid, you and buddy try to take aimed shots at whoever's out there with an MP5, keep low. The bitch'll lay down covering fire with me using the assault rifles. Sound like a plan?"

"It's a plan, yeah. A suicidal one, though."

"I wish I could think of something better," muttered Garth, slowly making his way back towards the stairwell.

"Don't knock the bodies as you pass them by. They're rigged to blow," warned Al, before leaning over towards Angel and thoughtfully scratching his chin. "Feel free to kick the bodies as you pass by."

The four cautiously returned to the ground floor, Al carefully picking his way over the bodies and making his way down the jet-black corridors until they arrived at the main foyer. Light streamed into the entrance from the opened doors, picking out the blood-spattered details of the wall, the scattered papers on the reception desk, and the upturned chairs carelessly thrown across the floor. The odour of the dead Rots drifted in from outside, an overpowering stench of decay and the lingering scent of smoke and spent gunpowder.

"Okay, take it easy, keep your head, pick your targets," Al said as he danced lightly over the floor and tried to peer out the door. He couldn't see anything, and waved over to Bill to join him.

"On three, we break out there. Bitch, you cover the left, I'll take the right, just like we discussed. Three two one, go!"

Bill and Garth leapt out the door first, rolling to a stop three feet outside the doorway, while Angel and Al stormed out, standing upright behind them, with the stocks of their weapons tucked in beneath their shoulders. No one fired as they'd planned.

The parking lot was still littered with the corpses of the dead, but these were now joined by fifty erect figures, men dressed in red trousers and shirts, covered in stains and rips. Some had redecorated their clothes with patches of leather and denim, while others had chosen to remove parts of their clothing all together. They all carried the same assault rifles as Al and Angel held, and they all seemed to be pointing them in their direction. One of the men stepped forwards and looked the four up and down then made a downward jerk with his assault rifles.

"Drop your weapons, mother fuckers."

Bill looked at Garth first, then twisted around to see Angel and Al, as if asking what to do.

"Shit."

XIII
JAILHOUSE ROTS

"Though the island may now be nothing more than a prison, it's imperative that this disease remains confined."

I

"Drop your weapons," repeated the man, his voice gruff and deep "Then get on your knees." His dark, beady eyes were fixed on the quartet, quickly and carefully assessing each one. Bill removed his own gaze from Al, and reluctantly dropped his weapon to the ground. Garth followed suit, followed by Angel. Only the Marine stood defiant, gripping his weapon and keeping it trained on the speaker of the group.

"Drop it," urged Bill, sinking to his knees and looking back over his shoulder. "Christ, there's fifty of them, do you really think you can take them *all* on?"

"I've faced worse odds," he responded, almost casually.

"You heard him," shouted another of the men, storming forwards and smashing the butt of his weapon against the side of Al's head. With a grunt of pain, he stumbled and fell to the floor, releasing his weapon and gripping his head in agony.

One of the men covering them rushed forwards and retrieved the discarded weapons, then systematically checked one after the other, removing any additional weapons and ammunition they were carrying on their person before shackling their hands and feet with heavy manacles linked with thick chains.

"How'd you get here?" asked the apparent leader, slowly walking towards the kneeling quartet. Al looked up from his kneeling position; his brow knitted into a frown and he spat some blood on to the pavement.

"We caught the fifty-eight bus. It was a bitch to track down, and we didn't have the right change, but I managed to convince the driver to let us on for free. We got off at…"

Al was silenced as the leader lashed out with his foot, catching him in the face with the side of a heavy steel-shod boot. He crumbled to the floor once more, though this time he couldn't protect himself with his hands.

"We walked," confirmed Bill, watching as Al struggled to regain his composure. The leader kicked Bill now, this time in the gut. Bill gasped for air, gulping with each breath and watching as the aggressor advanced on him.

"There's a trailer around back," shouted Angel. "We came in that."

The man spun on his feet and looked down at her, nodding his head slightly.

"Quick learner, aren't you? How many more of you are there?"

"One more," hissed Al, finally managing to get himself into an upright position and glaring at the speaker. "There's one more of us, we left him inside, buried amongst the bodies of your friends. He was injured in the fire fight, we told him to stay there and keep out of sight until we'd secured a route to evacuate him."

"Check it out," snapped the man, glancing quickly to three men standing idle by the open doorway. They nodded and jogged into the building, each fumbling with flashlights as the disappeared into the murk. Al barely managed to keep his face straight, looking towards Bill and winking slightly.

Barely two minutes had passed when the ground shook with a muffled explosion, and smoke billowed out the open doors, engulfing the four friends and their captors in a plume of debris and soot. While Bill remained motionless in the thick cloud, he could hear the sound of rattling chains, flesh making contact with flesh, and bodies dropping to the floor. He knew what was happening even before the smoke settled, and the bodies of four men lay at the feet of the bloodied and battered Marine, who had been restrained by a further four men, one clutching each manacled limb. The leader had managed to stay away from the blind fight, and slowly advanced towards Al, making sure he kept his distance.

"A strong willed soldier," he confirmed, appraising him. "Think you're pretty fucking smart for pulling that, eh? Intelligent, a good fighter, somewhat lacking in discipline, though. An ideal addition to the army: were it not for that fact, I would shoot you where you stand, you miserable bastard. Put them in the van and take them home. It doesn't look like any of the Chosen are left standing here."

With that, they were marched towards the main gate of the car park, out through them and into the streets beyond and into the rear of a large blue security van.

It was large enough to carry several people: the rear of the vehicle was fitted out with eight cages, each no larger than an adult man. Of these cages, the twisting and squirming Rots that were being held captive already occupied three of them. Bill looked them up and down as he was herded into one of the metallic tubes, feeling as if the walls were pressing in against him as the door to the cage was slammed shut and padlocked shut. Angel was pushed into the one next to him, and Garth managed to squeeze into the one opposite him. The armed escorts tried to place Al in one of the cages, but it became apparent that his bulky frame and height meant he wouldn't fit in the vessel. They had obviously dealt with oversized customers before, as they quickly and efficiently lifted his hands and lashed the manacles to one of the white metal bars running the width of the van's ceiling, before exiting the vehicle and slamming the door shut.

The soft glow of a yellow bulb provided the only light in the windowless environment, which was enough for Bill to make out the shadows of his three friends, and of his three undead enemies. They gurgled and moaned softly, bony and rotten fingers tapping lazily against the bars.

"They're going to release those Rots and let them eat us," hissed Garth. "Jesus, what do we do?"

"If they were going to let them eat us, the sick bastards would have done it in the open so they could watch. I know their kind," Al said, his shadowy form slowly pacing back and forth along the cabin, his wrists still attached to the ceiling. "We're being hauled off somewhere, shit knows where. This is a vehicle used for transporting prisoners. I've driven one, I've escorted one, carried out raid and rescue missions on them. And now, I've ridden in one."

"Really?" asked Garth. "Raid and rescue?"

"Back in Brazil," said Al as the vehicle shuddered and roared to life. He tried his best to keep upright, wrapping his hands around the ceiling bar and stumbling forwards as the machine jerked away from its parking place. "The shit really hit the fan that day. Bullets flying in all directions, grenades, rockets, man that was a good day. I figured between me and my boys we probably got about twenty of the bastards."

"You keep count of your kills?" asked Angel, sounding repulsed at the notion.

"Christ, yeah. Am I the only one here who does? Kid? Buddy?"

Bill muttered a wordless response, while Garth coughed and shuffled his feet.

"None of you? Shit, c'mon, it's not like I'm killing people in cold blood here, they normally open fire first."

"What about the Rots?" asked Angel. "You keep track of those kills? Does it count when you kill something that's already dead?"

"Now there's a thought," mused Al. Bill knew he was aching to rub his beard as he thought it over. After a couple of seconds, he nodded. "I'd have to say yeah, it still counts. It's a threat; I eliminate it, one point for Colebrook. Simple maths, that's all it is."

"So, what do you think your lifetime kill count is?"

"I dunno," muttered Al. "Since the whole Brazil thing it's probably went up hell of a lot. I'm guessing over, shit, three hundred? Yeah, that probably sounds about right. Three hundred confirmed, I'd say."

"A mass murderer," muttered Angel. "Strung up in the back of a prison van. I think we've finally found your position in life."

The dim yellow gloom of the mobile room was briefly pierced by a bright luminous green, lighting Al up as he tried to manoeuvre himself to look at the small illuminated wristwatch strapped to his wrist.

"Got somewhere you need to be?"

"Just wanted to get a bearing. Time means nothing now, but there's always going to be a north. It's all GPS tech, I just wanted to know where we're headed."

"So where are we going?"

"East. I don't know, they could be taking us anywhere."

He released the button, and the green glow faded. As it did so, the three confined Rots quivered and rattled, moaning softly to themselves.

"The thing I don't understand, is why they're carrying those dead shits around," said Bill, motioning towards them by nodding his head in their direction, though he doubted anyone knew that he was making the relative movements.

"Right," agreed Garth. "What could they possibly want with Tom, Dick and Harry?"

"Entertainment?" suggested Al. "Some kind of weird and twisted form of arena combat? Rot against Rot? Man against Rot?"

"Something tells me we're going to find out. And not like it."

The conversation died at that point, with the rest of the twenty-minute journey conducted in silence. As the vehicle ground to a halt, the dim yellow light flickered off, instigating another bout of mutterings from the Rots, which exploded into howls of rage and frustration as men rattled and banged on the outside of the van.

The doors rolled open, flooding the interior of the cargo container with muted sunlight and filling Bill's ears with sounds of what could only be described as a wild and raucous party. He lifted his hand, shielding his face from the glare of the intense light, and made out the shape of several men clambering aboard the van. They carried thick wooden batons and broken pieces of scaffolding, playing them maniacally across the bars of the cage while laughing at the top of their voice.

"What do we got here?" slurred one of the men, listing from side to side as he stammered up towards the cage Angel stood in. "Shit, girl, ain't you got it all in the right places?"

He pressed his hand against the cage, wiggling his fingers at her in a mock-wave. Angel lashed out without warning, catching the tip of his fingers and bending them back over themselves, snapping the joints with a sickening crack. The man stumbled away, gripping his hand and sobbing to himself as he rolled away.

"Keep away from her," warned one of the men: the same one who had briefly questioned them outside the television studio. "You know they gotta be unspoiled before they're presented to Steele. Once he's finished with her, *then* she's fair game. Get these four out first, bag them up and take them to the main hall. Get a few handlers up here, we still have some Chosen to take to the Baptist."

The doors to the Bill's cage were opened first, and he was guided out by two of the unruly mob, their hands roughly dragging him from his hovel and checking the manacles before forcing a sack made of an irritating material over his head. The light was taken from him again, and he was pushed from the back of the van, landing awkwardly on the soft mud around the vehicle. He groggily tried to rub at his face, to try and remove the bag from his head, but one of the men laughed and pushed down on him with his foot, keeping him squirming on the ground. He listened as his friends were obviously given the same treatment, sounds of bodies hitting the floor and gasps of surprise and pain. Only Al seemed to refrain from any cries of pain, making Bill think he was used to this treatment, or that he had suffered like this at least once before.

Of course, there was the possibility he *had* conducted similar behaviour on captives of his own in the Marines. What did he refer to in his story? Bebops, wasn't it?

"Get on your feet, you miserable pieces of shit," screamed a new voice. "Get up before we throw you to the dead bastards in the pit. C'mon, get it together. Johnson, chain them all to the big man, that might keep him calm. And keep your eye on him, he's a quick one. Carver, give me a look at your fingers."

Bill listened in frustration as uneven footsteps slowly made their way across the ground, accompanied by whimpers of pain and clanking of chains.

"You're lucky, Carver. Any worse and you'd have to pay a visit to the Baptist."

"Fucking bitch," stammered the man whose fingers had been snapped by Angel. "I should slice her up…"

"If you even *touch* her, you know Steele will chain you alive to the wall in the dead pit. Wait until he's finished."

"I like the sounds of that guy with the busted fingers," whispered Al. "We might be able to find a common ground with him."

"Shut up and get moving," one of the men ordered, nudging Bill in the small of the back with a baton.

Blinded by the sack Bill stumbled onwards, his senses confused as they were guided left first, then right, then left again. The soft mud of the ground changed to concrete, then wood, then concrete again before becoming metal. It seemed as if they were nearing the source of the party, as the constant rhythmic pounding of the drums and shouts of pleasure and delight intensified.

With his vision taken from him, Bill could only imagine what kind of building he was being taken to. His mind conjured an image of hell, of demons perched high above the gathering of people far below, fire all around them, groups of men and women who were interlocked in positions of passionate love, yet at the same twisting in their death throes.

Their movements ceased, and Bill could hear a low conversation, taking place between one of the escorts and someone new to the party; a voice he hadn't heard yet. He couldn't make out words, just a murmuring that suggested a conference, and then there was a deafening creak as if a pair of giant gates had been opened.

Pushing onwards, the giant gates rolled shut behind them, blocking some of the din from outside. It now seemed they were inside, their footsteps had a slight echo to them, though a lively tune still seemed to carry towards them on the hot air within whatever tunnels they journeyed through.

"We're inside," hissed Al. "Try to remember which way they travel so we can backtrack."

But Bill didn't find it that easy to keep track of his directions. The twists and turns they took were too numerous to remember, and when the journey began to take the entourage of prisoners up and down staircases, Bill gave up all together. He heard Al, still trying to keep track of the journey, but the numerous expletives he muttered meant he was having just as much luck as Bill.

The march had them heading towards the source of the lively music, and at one point Bill completely forgot where he was and what he was doing, humming along softly to the tune. He stopped himself, and conducted the rest of the journey in silence, the source of the music seemingly his goal.

The acoustics of the area changed once more, giving the impression of space, and Al muttered something to himself about being in a large hall, more than likely the main hall one of the captors had mentioned when they had pulled up. The music here was louder, as was the sound of cheering and hollers of joy.

The bag was pulled roughly from Bill's head, and he squinted, expecting to be blinded by the light of the hall he stood in. Instead, he saw a massive room, gloomily lit by flickering torches affixed to the walls, casting eerie shadows and large pools of darkness across the walls and floor.

The room itself was about thirty feet wide and almost a hundred feet long, with a catwalk running the full perimeter of the room fifteen feet from the floor; beyond that, the ceiling towering far off into the darkness above it. Two thirds of the floor was littered with tables, each holding between four and eight men, all clutching metal mugs and craning their heads around to look towards the final third of the floor, which had been cleared of all tables. In this space, six young women clothed only in golden bikini briefs, frantically danced in time to the thundering rhythm of the music, which came from speakers hanging from the underside of the catwalk. Beyond the dance floor and the entertainment, a single man sitting on a large chair made of a dark black material watched on, his head hidden by a brown shroud. Behind the throne, a large statue of an oversized man pinned to a cross loomed menacingly over the chair, all of which were hemmed in by a large circular stone surround.

"I think I could fit in here," said Al, mesmerised as he watched the dancing women spinning, gyrating and leaping from side to side. "Guns, grog and girls. Did I die and end up in heaven?"

"Shut up, dog," hissed one of the guards beside him, nudging him in the ribs with the muzzle of his shotgun. "Entertainment's nearly over, for now at least. C'mon, get up front."

"Gladly," whispered Al, rubbing his hands and storming forwards, almost dragging his friends as he moved through the clearly defined path that wound through the crowd of tables. Men cursed and craned their heads to see around Al as he bounded down the path, though many a gaze was drawn away from the dancers as Angel stumbled by. Bill grimaced at the remarks and single-entendres that were passed between men on the tables. He shuffled closer, subconsciously trying to keep himself between Angel and the leering men.

"You okay?" he asked quietly. She didn't say anything, but nodded slowly.

They reached the line where the tables stopped and the dancing started, then were forced down on to their knees by the armed guards. Both Al and Garth watched the dancing girls, oblivious to their surroundings, while Angel looked glumly towards the floor. Bill's eyes remained fixed on the man on the throne.

Although he was now close enough to make out more details, his face still remained hidden by the brown leather hood that hung over his head. He wore a pair of orange-red trousers, the same colour as the clothing their captors had worn, and like his dancers, he had decided to go topless. His body was well built, with muscles clearly defined; it looked to Bill as if he could possibly match Al in a fight. The right half of his chest was covered by an intricate tribal tattoo; a web of lines of various thickness, while his stomach bore a black cross with the word 'Christ' running through the horizontal bar, and the word 'Frank' down the vertical, the two words intersecting on the R. A cape of dark material hung over his broad shoulders, seeming to be attached to his flesh by two round clasps. He sat with his hands out on the armrests, and Bill frowned as he tried to make out more details. Had his hands been pierced by spikes attached to the throne?

The music died, and the dancers quickly left the dance floor as the men around burst into applause and cheers. All but two of the women vanished into the darkness of the stone opening surrounding the throne. These remaining women, one with black hair cut into a bob, the other with short red hair loosely styled, quickly sunk to the floor by the throne, one on each side. As they lowered their heads, a routine they appeared to have followed for some time now, two armed guards emerged from the shadows either side of the seated man and fastened a length of chain around their necks.

A hushed silence fell across the hall, broken only by the occasional cough or clearing of a throat. The man on the throne lifted his head and slowly turned it from side to side, appraising each of the four prisoners before him. He slowly rose from his throne, carefully moving his hands free from the armrests, and slowly strolled across the dance floor, his naked feet thudding against the polished surface with each powerful step.

"Prisoners?" he asked in a voice deep and rumbling; raised just enough so that the entire room could hear him. The guards motioned to the four captives, nudging them with their weapons to get to their feet. They reluctantly cooperated.

"Yes, Lord. We found them far from here, in a television studio."

"And they have killed the Chosen?"

"Over fifty that we could identify."

A muttering of disbelief went up amongst the men at the tables. The hooded man raised his arms, a command for silence that was swiftly met by his courtiers. He took a step closer and stopped in front of Al first, looking the giant up and down. The top of the hooded man's head was level with

Al's eyes, and he had to look up slightly to search his face.

"A soldier," said the man. "A killer. Perfect for the Chosen."

"And who the fuck are you?" asked Al, leaning closer to the man so his face almost vanished into the folds of the hood. Without warning the cloaked man launched a single punch into Al's stomach, making him buckle over and gulp for air.

"Insolent maggot. I am Alpha and Omega," he announced, raising his hands towards the prisoners and displaying the open wounds in his hands. Holes the size of a man's finger had been bored through his skin, weeping dark blood and exposing the dull glint of yellowing bone beneath. "The beginning and the ending, saith the Lord, which is, and which was, and which is to come, the Almighty."

"Jesus Christ, what are you talking about?" wheezed Al, clambering back to his feet and attempting to square off against the hooded man. His bonds restricted his movements, and knowing that he couldn't possibly defend himself against the leader, he stepped back slightly.

"That's *exactly* what I'm talking about," he said with a slight nod of his head, taking a step to the side and appraised Garth next.

"Fat," he hissed. "No doubt a coward. I can see the fear on your trembling face. The Baptism can remove that, though. The tears of God will wash the fear from you. Your bulk will make for a strong and resilient member of the Chosen."

He came to Bill next, and as he looked at him, a flare of firelight briefly illuminated the twisted smile and glare of cold eyes filled with hatred. He reached out, wrapping his fingers around his throat and turning his head from side to side.

"Worthless. Nothing. Food for the Chosen, that's all this one is good for."

He stepped over to look at Angel, and a deep laugh rolled out of the shadows of the hood. He flexed his fingers and gently reached out, taking a handful of her hair and rolling it between his fingers, leaning forward and breathing deeply.

"My, what do we have here? A sweet child, reeking of innocence. A lady travelling in the company of knaves. Tell me, child, why do you travel with such a band of brigands?"

"They protect me from shits like you," she hissed, snapping her head back away from his caress. He snatched at her hair again, pulling her closer and leaning in to her, his deep voice rumbling softly close to her ears. Bill couldn't hear what he was saying, despite his proximity, but it was enough to make Angel squirm and writhe beneath his grip. She finally managed to pull back from him, and gain enough time to spit directly into the shadows of the hood. He recoiled, releasing her from his grip and pausing just long enough to wipe his face with the back of his hand.

"Sick bastard," she hissed, still struggling, though this time against her chains. "Leave us alone."

Now both Bill and Al lurched forwards; Bill to protect one of his friends, while Al went for him with the intention of settling the score for the punch he'd received. Just as they almost laid their hands upon him, the guards leapt on Al, obviously intending to try and incapacitate the largest threat first. Bill managed to make contact with the hooded man, but he quickly and efficiently blocked his attack and kicked his legs out from beneath him. Bill fell, back on to the floor, beside the fallen Marine and looked up at the malevolent man.

"Forgive them," he shouted, turning away and looking up towards the oversized statue of the crucifixion and lifting his arms above his head. "Forgive them, father, for they know not what they have done!"

"Guy's crazy," whispered Al, slowly regaining his composure and clambering to his feet. "Sounds like he's quoting from the bible or something."

"Crazy?" asked the man, spinning around on his heels and gripping Al's face, a clawed hand on either side of his head. As he continued to speak, his voice continuously rose in volume, until he was shouting at the top of his voice at the end of his speech. "Over two thousand years ago, they said I was crazy; they hung me from the cross to die. But it was promised I would return to the living in the End Times, to lead an army against evil. For I am he that liveth, and was dead; and behold, I am alive for evermore. Amen, and I have the keys of Hell and death. Amen."

"Amen," the hall echoed in unison.

"Jesus," muttered Garth, looking around at the men sitting around them. "He thinks he's the Son of God, and these dumb shits believe him! Christ, this is too fucked up."

"Enough," hollered the man. "Enough of these blasphemous insults. Mine ears bleed with each profane sentence your cursed mouths utter."

"C'mon," shouted Al, turning around to face the men seated at their tables. "This guy's clearly a fucking nutcase! Who's really in charge?"

Bill shook his head. He wasn't sure if Al had suddenly tried to start an uprising, or if he'd just lost his senses at that moment in time. One of the men gathered at the closest table stood, raised the metal mug he held above his head, then brought it crashing down on Al's, once again knocking him to the floor.

"Stay on your knees, bitch," spat the man, a burly creature made mostly of muscle and tattoos. "The Messiah has guided us where others failed. We were left to rot in this stinking shit-hole of a prison; while the guards abandoned their posts, we were left locked in our cells, with no food or drink. He helped us, guided us. Saved us. Men that society had given up on."

"He is the son of the whore of Babylon," insisted the man dubbed The Messiah.

"Nobody talks about Mom like that," Al said, trying to make another attack, though his time he was stopped by the sight of an opened muzzle wavering in his face. The Messiah laughed maniacally, then continued to talk.

"Surely only the power of the Baptist can cleanse him. Take the men to the holding chamber. The girl… she will stay as part of my Seraphim."

"Wait a minute," shouted Bill as Angel was detached from the links of chain and carried away towards the dark throne. Though she tried to struggle, the two men escorting her simply lifted her from the floor and carried her with the minimal of fuss. The remaining armed guards started to shepherd Bill, Garth and Al away from the hall, each having their heads covered once more by their bags.

"What's going on?" demanded Al as they were herded away. "Where are we going?"

The Messiah simply laughed as they were removed from the hall, before the music started to play from the speakers once more.

With that, the three blindfolded and bound men lead were away from the hall and back into the myriad of corridors and passages, taken up and down stairways, past sliding metal gates and heavy slamming doors. The guards didn't say anything as they moved, simply spurred on the trio by nudging them with their weapons.

The journey ended after five minutes of walking, and Bill felt the manacles around his arms and legs finally released. Before he could do anything to act upon it, he was pushed roughly through a doorway and on to a hard stone floor. He fought to remove the sack from his head, just in time to see Al and Garth also pushed through the doorway. The door, a thick and heavy iron construction with a small grilled window four inches square, slammed into position and the locks slid home consecutively; Bill counted five locks in total.

Al slipped the sack off his own head, lunging at the door and pounding it with his massive fists.

"Let me out, you mother fucking pieces of reeking shit. Open up, you sons of a bitches."

Garth struggled out of his bag, repositioning his cap and sinking to the floor beside Bill, watching the Marine continue to hammer the door.

"Should we stop him before he breaks his fists?"

"Let him tire himself out first," said Bill, clambering to his feet and looking at the room they'd been thrown into. It was a gloomy chamber, illuminated by two dim light bulbs hanging from the ceiling by their flex. The walls were made from large blocks of stone, possibly sandstone, and the tiles of the floor were cracked ceramic, an orange in colour. The room itself was ten feet square, and had a large table pushed against the wall opposite the door, its surface littered with books and papers. Two bunk beds were affixed to the walls, one on either side of the door.

Each bunk held a darkened figure, one of which seemed to be stirring.

"Al," hissed Bill. "We're not alone. Save your strength."

"What we got, kid?" he asked, wheeling around on his heels and stepping into the centre of the room, his fists swollen and bloodied, though he held them up ready to fight.

"We got two men," muttered one of the men on the bunk. "Two men who are trying to sleep."

The man who spoke slowly pulled himself up from his bunk and swung his legs over the side of the bed, looking at the three new interlopers to his domain. As the denizen of the cell looked the three men up and down, Bill did the same, appraising the cell's dweller.

He wore black trousers and a black T-shirt, with a white piece of cloth sewn on to the neckline, much like a priest's dog collar. His hair was short and blonde, spiked and kept off his forehead by a thick band of red leather, tied in a heavy knot at the rear of his head. His face was pale and round, with wide blue eyes and a gentle expression. He smiled at the three men, then stood up, stretching out one arm and stifling a yawn with the back of his other hand. He was a little shorter than Bill, though his spiked hair seemed to make him taller than he actually was.

"I see the heathen has sent down more prisoners," he said in a nonchalant manner, extending his hand in a sign of friendship. "Father Clive Ridgedale." Neither Al nor Bill went to accept the hand, but Garth dived forwards and shook it.

"Always good to meet someone in the same boat as us," he grinned enthusiastically. Al was very hesitant, not trusting the new person.

"Look like a preacher man to me," he said, waving to the white square of cloth. "You the Baptist? That crazy psycho said he was sending us to see him. I couldn't get to him, but I don't see any armed goons protecting you…"

"The 'Baptist' is almost as sadistic as the 'Messiah'. Almost," said the priest, his hand remaining outstretched. Al continued to ignore the gesture. "The Messiah claims to be the Second Coming of our lord Jesus Christ, and he seems to genuinely believe that himself. Just like other mass murderers and serial killers before him, he truly believes that his killings are justified."

"Mass-murderer?" questioned Al, sitting down on the bed that the man had vacated. "Sweet fucking Jesus, man, where the fuck are we, who is that crazy bastard with the towel on his head, and what in God's name is going on?"

"Blasphemy," Clive muttered to himself, shaking his head.

"I've heard it all before," Al insisted, patting his body down for his cigarettes. He groaned as he remembered he'd been stripped of all his belongings outside the studio, "Small minded man who can't express himself without resulting to expletives. Jesus, who do I have to kill for a cigarette?"

"More profanities," Clive said, slowly walking across the room and sitting down by the second sleeping man.

"You talk just like that shit up there," hissed Al, jerking his head in the vague direction of the door. "You sure you're not part of his demonic fucking cult?"

"I assure you," the priest confirmed, his voice soothing and comforting. "I've already told you my name. I was father of a local church before the dead rose. Though I study the same religious texts as Frank Steele, I have very different views on the way they are perceived."

"And Frank Steele is this Messiah guy, right?" asked Al, sitting on the floor and leaning against the door. Bill relaxed slightly, seeing that as the big Marine was calming down and warming to Father Ridgedale, he seemed to be winding down. The lack of cigarettes meant he had nothing to do to keep his mind occupied or his nervous fingers busy, though he had quickly started to chew at them, absentmindedly biting at his nails.

"Frank Steele," cut in a new voice, as the man by Clive slowly pulled himself up from his prone position on the bed and swung his legs out on to the floor. "Frank Steele is a convicted mass murderer, a serial rapist, and a self-confessed paedophile who should be burning alive in the depths of hell."

"Another of the God Squad?" asked Al, tipping his head towards the man as he pulled himself together.

He wore dark blue jeans and a white polo shirt; both garments of clothing dirty and covered in splashes of grime and blood. His long hair was dark and matted with grease and dirt, tied back in a tight ponytail, keeping any strands of hair from his square-jawed face. His bloodshot eyes were sunken in his eye sockets; the skin beneath them coloured a dark purple. He slowly rubbed his stern face, yawning as he did so, then slowly rose from his bunk. He was the same height as Bill, though his muscles were more developed.

"Not the God Squad, just someone who's extremely pissed off at the son of a bitch out there. hell's too good for him, anyway."

He looked at the three new occupants of the prison cell before lowering his gaze to the floor, at his tattered trainers and the stone tiles beyond them

"How long have you been in here?" asked Bill. He wasn't expecting a large number of days; the men didn't look too malnourished or mistreated and he couldn't imagine that the gang would happily feed and clothe their prisoners.

"More or less since the beginning," muttered the as-of-yet-unnamed man.

"How'd you get here?" asked Garth, sidling on to the ground by Al and emptying his pockets out on to the floor, searching through the bundles of fluff and thread for pieces of loose tobacco.

"Not much of a story," promised the man. "But it's not like we've got anything better to do around here."

II

Monday mornings had never been quiet in his garage; Sylvester McThurton always had at least two cars in for repairs at any time. This Monday was unusual in that the seven cars sitting outside the repair shop had all been fixed for a number of days. Their owners had just neglected to turn up and collect them.

Of course, he'd tried to get in touch with the owners, using all the contact numbers he had before resorting to contacting insurance companies and arranging tow trucks to take the vehicles away. In his eyes, it didn't look good to have a large parking space in front of the vehicle repair shop filled with other cars. He knew they were repaired, but the casual observer didn't. To Joe Public, the garage was booked solid, they had too much work, so they'd take their car to one of the over-staffed, high-priced chain of garages that populated southern Manchester.

"Try phoning the police," suggested Terri, her head buried in the thick book the garage used to keep track of income and outgoing expenses as she tried to balance the figures. Sylvester shook his head, wiping his hands down on a white rag and slipping it into the back pocket of the blue coverall he wore.

"I tried that on Friday. They told me to piss off, they had more important things to deal with."

"Like trying to control an epidemic," Terri muttered. "Imagine the health of half the population of England taking precedence over your business. What *is* the world coming to?"

"Life has to go on for everyone else. Fish gotta swim, birds gotta fly."

"Doesn't it worry you that there's hundreds of people dying from this weird disease?"

"It worries me more that business is suffering because nobody's coming to collect the damn cars when I've fixed them. We must be a few hundred down this week because of this."

"Isn't that a little cold? It hasn't occurred to you that the owners of these cars have suffered a loss through this plague? Maybe a relative down in London, or up north near Scotland, and the last thing they want to think about is paying for a repair job when they have to arrange funerals and memorial services. Did you ever think about that?"

"I know there was a reason I married you," Sylvester said, strolling into the office and unfastening his coveralls a couple of buttons. "I mean, I *know* there was a reason for doing it. Was it because of your level-headed approach to life?"

"I could balance your books," she said, closing the ledger and grinning as she wrapped her arms around Sylvester. "You only married me for my brain."

"At least you know I'm not shallow or only into your looks."

"Intelligent, but plain," she teased with mock hurt in her voice.

"You know I wuv oo," Sylvester grinned, playing his finger up and down across her mouth, flicking her lip as he did so.

"Get out of here," she laughed at the sound of an electronic buzzer: the alarm of someone opening the main door to the shop. "There's a customer coming."

"Good," Sylvester grinned as he left the office, keeping his eyes trained his wife while stepping backwards through the machine-filled workshop. "Maybe I can charge them extra for a live sex show, recoup some of the business we've lost from those damn cars outside. Hey, maybe a topless car wash would help, too."

He spun around, and his grin melted into a mixture of surprise and shame as he saw the shape of a young man dressed in black, with spiked blonde hair and a stiff dog collar wrapped around his neck. Sylvester smiled gently as he approached him, but the priest didn't return the gesture.

"Clive," Sylvester said, grabbing his hand and shaking it. "It's good to see you. Can I help you?"

"I'm glad you're both here. We need to talk. Can you lock up the shutters?"

"Sure," muttered Sylvester, running over to the open shutters and pulling them closed, then fastening them in place with a pair of large padlocks. "Not as if it's going to scare away all the customers. Terri's in the office, c'mon. Do you want a drink of coffee? Tea?"

"I'm fine, thanks. Morning Terri."

"Morning," Terri said, pushing her books and calculators to one side and looking up from the table, seeing the worried priest. "Clive, what's wrong?"

Clive sat at the table and waited for Sylvester to enter the office, then removed a hip flask from his pocket and took a small sip.

"I've just come from the hospital," he finally announced, his hands shaking slightly as he fumbled with the cap of the flask. "I've been there since last night, giving the last rites to five of my parishioners. They all died early this morning."

"Jesus," Terri said, reaching out and taking Clive's hands, then apologising for her outburst. "What happened?"

"They had contracted the plague. Agony barely describes their final tortured moments of life."

Terri nodded in understanding, while subconsciously removing her hands from his and wiping them her trouser legs. Sylvester helped himself to a cup of coffee and sat down on the bench, pushing aside a pile of spare parts and greasy fast food wrappers to clear room for himself.

"Is it as bad as the news says it is?" he asked, feeling a sense of morbid curiosity playing with his mind. Clive slowly nodded; his gaze fixed on the back of his own hands, a glazed look in his eyes.

"Like leprosy," he muttered. "A modern day Black Death. Spilled blood, weeping sores, flaking skin… perpetual agony, right until the end."

Sylvester looked into his cup of coffee then pushed it to one side, no longer thirsting for the dark liquid.

"I overheard one of the soldiers at the hospital talking, though. He says there's no signs of the plague dying off; the spread of it to here in Manchester only adds fuel to that fire. He said it's worse in London than the news says, with almost seventy percent of its population dead or dying. He says only those isolated from the city itself seem to evade contagion. That's why I'm here, to warn you two. It won't be long until seventy percent of Manchester goes the same way."

He turned to Sylvester, idly scratching his head

"Sly, you saved my life once before. Now it's my turn. Take Terri far away from here, out into the country. It should be pretty clean out there. Stay out there until the plague has gone, or at least it's under control."

"Don't be so dramatic," laughed Sylvester, leaping down from the bench and clapping Clive on the back. "I hardly saved your live, just doing my job…"

"And so am I," Clive countered, his voice raising slightly. "Please, take her and go."

"It all seems a little too much," Sylvester growled to himself.

"My uncle has a cottage out in the countryside," confessed Terri, grabbing him by the hand and pulling at it playfully. "And it's not as if we're incredibly busy. He won't mind if we stop by there for a few days. What harm can it do?"

"What about you?"

"Just as you have your family to look after," Clive said, waving towards Terri, "I have mine. I'll try to get my message across to my flock in my sermons."

"If it's all as bad as you say it's going to be, do you think anyone will even *bother* to come to church?"

"Jesus saves," the priest replied, pulling himself up from the table. "In times of dire need, who do you turn to?"

"I have close friends, you may have heard of them. Like Jack Daniels," muttered Sylvester. "Jim Beam, you can normally find them in any good bar…"

"And others choose God. They'll come to me, where I can help them. Please, go. You have my telephone number in case you need me, and I have yours. I'll keep you up to date. I'll also take care of your business, if anyone turns up."

"You're not going to take no for an answer, are you?"

"Not really," Clive admitted. "Go on."

After collecting some of their belongings from their home, Sylvester and Terri got in their car and took the two hour drive out to the little cottage in the middle of the countryside: a picturesque house surrounded by hills, fields and small copses of sycamore trees.

The silver sports car ground to a halt as the dirt road they had been following turned into a gravel path, and Sylvester climbed out the car, grabbing the suitcase from behind the seat and lugging it behind him as he made his way down the path.

"So which uncle is this," he asked Terri, calling back over his shoulder. "The alcoholic or the bigamist?"

"Neither. The gay fashion designer uncle."

"Ah, Uncle Marc. How could I possibly forget him, after he turned our wedding into a fashion disaster."

"It wasn't that bad," Terri smiled, a small rucksack over her shoulder as she jogged across the stones to catch up.

"The man wore a gold tuxedo and top hat with diamond-studded gloves. More people were looking at him than us," Sylvester said, knocking politely on the front door.

"Marc's harmless. He's just an extrovert."

"He's not in," he said, pressing his head against glass of the door and peering into the gloom of the building. "Nobody's home. What now?"

"Can't you break the lock? Work it open?"

"Do I look like a professional crook?" he said, crouching low beside the door and reaching into his jacket pocket, withdrawing a flat bladed screwdriver. He pushed it into the lock, jiggled it about, and twisted it. With a click, the lock gave way, and the door swung wide open, allowing the couple to stroll into the house.

Despite the flamboyant nature of the occupant and the clothing he wore, the house had been decorated with a minimalist approach. Walls painted cream and floor laid with a matching carpet; a few pieces of modern art hung from the wall, and the occasional sculpture stood erect in the centre of the room.

"Where is he, then?"

"Fashion shoot?" suggested Terri, working through the house towards the kitchen. "Maybe he was called in for a big meeting. So, how long are we going to stay here?"

"Clive said he'll phone when he's heard something, or when we've been given the all clear. Until then, I guess. Probably just a few days, then the whole thing will have blown over."

Clive stood by the altar in the church, watching over the candles burning around him.

It had been four days since he'd sent his two friends out to the country, and in those days, those mourning the loss of family members or those who knew people falling ill came and lit a candle. They put the slow burning flames where the large wooden statue of Jesus Christ could watch over them. Clive sighed heavily to himself as he looked at the number of candles that had blown out overnight. It wasn't a good sign, for him or his flock. And the fact that fewer and fewer people had come to his sermons over the last four days wasn't a good sign, either. If it wasn't the plague keeping them away, then it could be the riots.

"More casualties," he whispered to himself. He hadn't heard anything from Sylvester since he'd left for the countryside, and no matter how many times he tried to ring them, he could never get through; he was always informed there was no signal. He hoped that everything was all right with them, and that hadn't sent them to just another hotbed of contagion.

Clive had first met Sylvester in Strangeways Prison four years ago, before the mechanic owned his own repair shop and not long after Clive had been given his first flock to tend to. He had been visiting the minister in the prison chapel, hoping to gain an insight to the people of the area, and as he was leaving, one of the prisoners had attacked him. He'd been armed, of course: like every other prisoner he had made a shiv, a home made blade fashioned from whatever junk and materials were lying around and wouldn't be missed. The attack had been ill thought, a spur-of-the-moment action that, once executed, couldn't go any further. While other guards had tried to talk down the excited and agitated prisoner with soft words and soothing promises, one prison guard had stalked up behind the prisoner and swiftly disarmed him by breaking an arm with his baton.

That guard had been Sylvester McThurton; referred to as Sly by the other guards. Five weeks after that event, Sylvester left the services of Strangeways Prison: the two incidents weren't linked, he had intended to leave to start his own business anyway.

After leaving his job in the prison, getting the business off to a start had been a risky affair, and there had been several times that the whole deal looked as if it was going to fall through. During those rocky days, Sylvester had lived with Clive, the pair living as an odd couple: the humble priest and his friend, the drunken mechanic.

Once the garage had finally opened, and business had started to trickle in, Sylvester finally saved enough to leave Clive's house and move in with one of his employees, Terri Moore. The relationship between man had women blossomed and moved quickly: unlike other men and women who saw less and less of their friends as two lives became one, Clive played a large part in both their lives, even acting as the minister at their wedding a year later. He was considered as one of the family, and always welcomed at their house. A friendship that had blossomed from an act of violence that had spanned almost half a decade, and showed no immediate sign of degrading as others had in the past.

Clive lifted the telephone handset to his ears once more, punched in Sylvester's number, and sighed as he got the same message relating to the lack of signal. He slipped the phone into his pocket and sighed, looking up towards the wooden model of Christ. He closed his eyes and found himself in silent prayer, asking that the Lord watch over his friends, but a banging and rattling at the large oak doors of the church disrupted the prayer. He'd locked up the doors the previous night, and had completely forgotten about them. How many parishioners had been turned back from the doors of the House of God while he had neglected to unbar the doors? How many had been trapped out in the riots while he neglected to keep his doors open? Maybe that was why the church had been strangely devoid of anyone this morning.

Shuffling down the central aisle, he reached the door and grasped the heavy iron bar, sliding it to one side and slowly opening the door.

He instantly recognised the person on the other side of the door as one of his older flock, Mrs Beaton. Though last Clive had heard, she had been on deaths door, stricken by the plague. She lumbered forwards, as if to enter the church, and he recoiled, part in disgust at the foul smell that lingered around her, part to avoid the raking movement of her blood encrusted fingers as they cut through the air, inches from his face. He back-peddled away from the door, watching as the woman stumbled through the opening, a vacant and lost expression on her face as she looked from side to side. Another person stumbled into the church; Clive identified him as the youngster who had been paralysed in a car crash earlier that year. He couldn't remember his name, though he remembered sitting by his bedside for a couple of days at his parents' request while he slept in a coma. The doctors had declared he would never walk again, yet there he stood, flesh flaying from his shaking legs with each jerking step he took.

The two people veered towards Clive, who had already made his way back towards the altar, and fumbling for the bible lying open on the table of worship. He had been reading it that morning, recounting the tale of Jesus as he healed the lepers, showing his flock that faith in the almighty would save their loved ones. It appeared it had worked in one way, though the way in which these two people were moving, particularly in the condition they were in, suggest that the Devil had been at work instead of God.

"Get back," he commanded, lifting the book and displaying the embossed golden cross on the cover. "Get back!"

The two people chose to ignore him, continuing their approach. While the old woman swayed to one side, skirting the rows of pews, the youth nimbly pulled himself up on to the wooden seats, balancing with cat-like precision on the backrests and dancing lightly over them, edging ever closer. The simplistic look on his face told a story of dementia, though the grin suggested he seemed to be enjoying his newfound agility, despite the massive trauma to his spine he had already suffered and the bloodied injuries his legs displayed.

Hurling the book across the void between himself the advancing people, he caught the youth in the stomach, knocking him backwards and sending him tumbling into the pews behind him. The silence of the church echoed with the sickening crack of bones, though amazingly enough he did not cry out in pain. Clive didn't have time to worry about it, at least not now: Mrs Beaton was almost upon him, bloodied talons flexing and toothless mouth wetly opening and closing. She gave a low mewling moan, then lunged forwards, arms outstretched.

Clive grabbed the first thing he could, trying to add some obstacles between himself and the mad woman, finding himself gripping one of the four foot ornamental candle holders that surrounded the altar. She knocked aside the candles with her hand, her tattered grey hair catching one of the flickering flames and starting to smoulder, then impaled herself on the candelabra, arms flailing blindly for the priest. He lifted the candlestick, trying to get some leverage between himself and the crazed woman, watching as the smouldering ends of her hair burst to life, rushing up the dry and wispy hair, the orange and white flames licking at the sagging flesh of her skull. She didn't seem to notice the flames that had engulfed her head, still frantically scrabbling for Clive.

"Devils," he muttered, pushing back on the human torch and guiding her away from the altar. He had to get her out the church before any of the ancient woodwork took to the flickering flames, and he also needed to get the front door shut, in case any others like her decided to pay homage to God.

With strength he didn't know he had, he guided the woman, still unaware she was afire, from the church. Heaving her from through the wooden door, candelabra and all, he threw the human pyre from the church, slamming the door shut and slipping the heavy metal deadbolt back into place.

Safe for the moment, he grabbed the telephone from his pocket and thumbed at the buttons, trying to get in touch with the police. All he got was the busy signal: he hung up and tried again, but got the same response. Keeping calm, he tried to call Sylvester, pressing his back against the stone wall and keeping his eyes on the centre of the pews where the youth had toppled. The phone still refused to connect, and he hurled it down in a fit of rage, the plastic device splintering on contact with the stone floor.

He circled the room with his back pressed against the wall at all times, and tried to look into the rows of pews, hoping to see the youth still lying prone on the floor.

Blood, strips of skin and material told Clive where the boy had fallen, but much to his surprise the youth wasn't there. He could hear a scraping and tapping sound, but the acoustics of church meant he couldn't place the exact position of the noises. He rushed for the altar, skirting around the outskirts of the pews and stooping low to grab the bible on his way. He barrelled into the heavy table, backed up against it, and looked feverishly from side to side. He couldn't think what they were, the creatures that had entered the house of God, but he felt that there had to be something in the book to help him. He leafed through the pages with trembling hands, all the time accompanied by the click-slide of the youth still trapped in the church.

Maybe exorcism, he thought to himself. *Surely the devil has possessed the poor boy.*

It didn't seem like something that was real, especially in this day and age, but what else could possibly account for the previously crippled youth now lurking somewhere in the shadows of the church? Gripping the bible, he started to mutter what little he could remember of the relevant verse. It hadn't been required reading for his priesthood, but he *had* looked into it; like every other person in his class, curiosity got the better of him.

The clattering seemed to become closer, and the Latin words stuck in Clive's throat as the twisted remains of the boy crawled into view. His legs had been broken once more, this time twisted and shattered: shards of bones glistening a dark pink in the light as they pierced the flaking flesh with each jagged movement. His arms had the suffered the same kind of injury, with his fingers either bent back or snapped off completely. He screamed, a ghastly gurgling sound, then somehow managed to flip himself up, standing erect on his shattered legs for a second, before lunging down on to Clive, flailing its useless hands, knocking aside the book held out for protection.

As he struggled with the slobbering abomination, he heard a heavy thumping on the locked door. He couldn't remember if he shouted or not, he was too busy trying to keep the broken boy from latching on to his throat with yellowed teeth.

The thumping ceased, though Clive barely had a chance to contemplate whether it had been friend or foe hammering on the doors. If the youth and his incredible resilience were anything to go by, it had probably been Mrs Beaton, flaming head *et al.*

The trill of glass shattering was the next sound he heard followed by the heavy footfalls of a well-built man powering across the stone floor. The weight of the boy was suddenly heaved off Clive, and he watched as the interloper to the church flung the body across the room, levelled a double barrelled shotgun with the creature as it scrabbled over the damaged pews, and unloaded both barrels into the bloody and broken mass. It wordlessly slumped to the ground, pale blood oozing from the corpse, though it still quivered and shuddered, bones cracking against the wood of the chairs it lay upon. Clive clambered to his feet, leaning heavily on the altar and watching as the man strode over to the shuddering mass, cracking open the weapon and letting the two smoking shells drop to the floor. He reloaded, aimed at the creature once more, and fired point blank into the skull, splashing brain matter and blood across the floor in a spatter of gore.

"We're not in the clear yet," grunted the man, reloading once more and slinging the shotgun over his shoulder. "Place is surrounded by them, and not just the church. The whole damn countryside is crawling with them."

"Sylvester," Clive said, his face a mix of bewilderment and joy. "What's going on?"

"We don't have time for that. Terri's waiting for us outside; she's keeping the engine ticking over. C'mon, out the window."

"But the boy... Mrs Beaton..."

"If that's the old woman who was on fire outside, I drove over her, then backed up to make sure I'd done the job. Out the window, move, they'll be here soon."

"I don't understand," protested Clive, retrieving his bible and being guided to the broken window by his friend. "What's happening?"

Clive half-jumped, half-fell from the opened window and thumped to the thick grass below. Sylvester followed behind him, and urged him onwards towards the BMW waiting at the front of the church. As the pair ran to the front of the building, Clive stumbled to a halt and looked around the streets surrounding him. Buildings were empty, windows smashed, the path dotted with the occasional corpse. He had spent the past four days and nights in the church, and knew he had lost touch with the outside world, but for this much to change... it seemed unreal.

It seemed like hell...

"C'mon," shouted Terri, hammering the car horn. Sylvester rushed to the vehicle and held back her arm, urging her to stop.

"You'll have them running to us like flies to a piece of shit. Clive, get in, we don't have time..."

Clive acknowledged him by slowly moving towards the car, gripping his bible and spinning around as he walked, taking in the details of the street: derelict buildings, abandoned vehicles. In the distance, he could see figures slowly stumbling up the street, though they appeared only as shadows.

"Can you use this?"

Sylvester grabbed Clive by the arm and drew a black handgun from the waistband of his trousers. Clive looked blankly at it, but took it anyway, looking at it in confusion as Sylvester bundled him into the passenger seat of the vehicle. Taking one last look around the place, Sylvester clambered into the back of the car, perching on the folded canopy of the two-seater convertible, and gently squeezed Terri on the shoulder, an indication to move on. She revved the engine and took off at an alarming speed, making Clive grip at the dashboard with whitened knuckles.

"What's going on?" he yelled, the wind snatching at his face and catching his breath as Terri wrestled with the wheel of the vehicle. "You can't drive," he announced, finally realising who was driving the vehicle. "You don't have a licence!"

"She's learned quickly, a crash course," Sylvester said, leaning closer and gripping his shotgun. "You been holed up in that church for a while, have you?"

"Since you left. I've spent day and night there... What's happened? What was wrong with those people?"

"They were dead," Terri answered, bluntly.

"Dead? I don't understand."

"Nobody does," said Sylvester, bringing his weapon up to aim at a group of people as the car rushed by. "But it seems that people dying from the plague are coming back to life. And they're trying to eat people."

"Demons," Clive muttered, lost in his thoughts. Was this all a dream? Some feverish nightmare brought on by his contraction of the plague? Had he unwittingly caught the disease, and now lay in a state of delirium within the church?

"You thought we'd be safe out in the country," shouted Sylvester, trying to contend with the howling wind around them. "We were, up to a point. If the dead bodies are left untended, they rise. With nobody to collect or dispose of them out in the countryside, they were left to fester. Then they rose from the dead. Five hours ago, we were attacked by a farmer out at Uncle Marc's house."

"Where *is* Marc?"

"We've not seen him. As soon as we got there a farmer attacked us. We tried to phone out, but the landlines must've been down and my phone couldn't pick up on a signal, so we had to drive to the closest farm. Which happened to be the farmer's point of origin, and it was a bloody scene of violence. His animals and family had been torn apart. We found his shotguns and pistol, but still couldn't find any phone. We just got in the car and came here, we knew you'd be in your church."

"I'm sorry," Clive muttered. "I sent you out there, I thought it would have been safe."

"Bullshit," Terri said, scorning him. "You probably *did* save us. Since entering the city, we haven't seen another survivor. Not one. If we stayed in our house, we'd probably be in the same position as the rest of the city."

The three sat in silence as Terri negotiated the streets of the city, weaving between the parked vehicles and keeping a wide berth of the blurred figures shuffling along the roadside.

"Where are we going then?" Clive finally asked. Terri slammed her foot down on the brakes, the vehicle screeching and sliding to a halt. She looked over her shoulder to Sylvester, who simply shrugged.

"Hell if I know," he admitted. "I just told Terri to drive."

"Well we can't just ride around until we run out of petrol," Terri said, warily eyeing the surroundings of the car. Sylvester nodded in agreement, then leant forwards to look at the amount of fuel still displayed on the dashboard's readouts.

"Quarter of a tank," he confirmed. "Maybe less. Still, it should be enough."

"Enough for what?"

"Strangeways Prison," he announced, pulling back his long hair into a tighter ponytail and tucking it beneath the collar of his grubby polo shirt. "I know the guards there, they'll help us out. I still keep in touch with them; we played regular games of football. We'll be safer in there than out here."

"The prison?" asked Terri. "Locked up with the convicts?"

"It's built to keep them in, why wouldn't it keep those creatures out?"

"Monsters on the outside, monsters on the inside. Either way, we're screwed. Better the devil you know," agreed Clive. He looked at Terri, who had a look of disbelief on her face. "I know it's not ideal, far from it, and I can think of places I'd rather be than that place, but it could offer us sanctuary, at least until we work out what we're up against.

"Zombies," Sylvester murmured, levelling of his shotgun and unloading one of the barrels into the face of a slowly approaching creature. Though Clive was too late in looking to make out any of its facial features he could plainly see the ragged bite marks that covered the upper limbs of the fallen creature.

"Zombies?" Terri asked, knocking the car into gear once more and pulling away. "You really think so?"

"Soulless creatures," agreed Clive. "Hollow Men."

A short and clipped conversation carried on between Terri and Sylvester, though Clive didn't take in much of the details, his mind swimming with a thousand thoughts about what had happened.

"Sounds like you took it all relatively well," Al said, leaning back from the edge of his seat. During the telling of the tale, the Marine had stood and walked around the room, coming to rest on the second bunk. He'd picked up a handful of papers from the table, had rolled them into a cigarette, and was now looking for something to light it with. He was aware it had no tobacco in, but he wasn't doing it for the nicotine, just the very action of lighting up and smoking. "I mean the dead walking and all."

"I believe in what I see," Clive said, his face impassive.

"And you believe in God?" Bill asked curiously.

"I believe in what I see," Clive repeated. "I see God all around us."

"So where's this Terri?" asked Garth, focusing on only the parts of the story that interested him.

"By the time we got here, the prison was under the control of the prisoners," Sylvester said, pulling a box of matches from his pocket and tossing them to Al.

"As soon as the plague showed signs of being totally out of control, the guards left their posts and went home to spend their last days with their families. Can't say I blame them, to be honest. If I still worked here, I probably would have done the same thing.

"So the guards abandoned their posts. Left the inmates locked up in their cells. No food, no fresh water, they were as good as dead. The prisoners obviously didn't like this, of course, and tried to escape their cells. With all the authorities gone, they didn't have to be subtle about it. Breaking bars, tunnelling, chipping away at blocks of stone, they tried them all. The more they tried, the more energy they used. With no food, they quickly tired themselves out.

"In the end, one man escaped, and he released those who promised to follow him."

"Let me guess," Al grinned, snapping his fingers. "That fuckhole upstairs?"

"The very same," Sylvester nodded. "They brought Frank Steele in when I worked here. He'd openly admitted to countless charges of rape of both men and women of all ages, from six months to sixty, laughed in court as they listed the murders he was linked to. He even insinuated there were other murders that the authorities didn't even know about. He claimed to be delivering a message from God, that his 'seed' was that of the lord, and only those who received it may enter the kingdom of Heaven when the end times came. Those he killed, he said were done in the name of God."

"He was mad before capture," Clive cut in, standing up and walking over to the table littered with papers. "After spending a month in captivity, his claims became even more obscure. He announced he was the Second Coming of Jesus Christ. You can probably imagine how the church took that. His madness continued, right up to and beyond this infestation of the walking dead. During his unsupervised incarceration, he was the only prisoner who kept himself nourished by eating his own faeces."

"Fuck," muttered Al. "He ate his own shit, and that gave him enough strength to break out? Does it work like that?"

"Frank Steele was incredibly strong anyway, you've seen how much muscle he has. He's actually lost some bulk since I last saw him. Of course, he plays on his escape as divine intervention."

"And Terri?" repeated Garth, still waiting for his answer.

"Terri was kept back by Frank, claiming that she was a gift from God for doing his bidding. That's what he claims all his Seraphim are."

"That's what the bitch will be doing," Al grinned. "She'll be all right, she'll fit right in with the rest of those cock teases."

Without warning, Sylvester lunged on the Marine and grabbed him by the collar, pinning him against the wall. "One of those 'cock teases' is my wife, you tactless bastard. Think before you speak."

"I don't need to think," snarled Al, refusing to back down. A slight smile crept across his lips, but he tried to fight it. "Only officers have to think, and I'm not one. At least not a real one, anyway. "

Sylvester released his grip on Al and returned to his seat, muttering to himself.

"You have a friend that's been added to the Seraphim?" Clive asked, placing a comforting hand on his friend's shoulder. Bill nodded slowly. "Angel."

"Seventeen years old," Al said. "Nice ass but that's about all she's got going for her. A nice little piece of fuck-meat, really. Fuck her once or twice, but not so many times that I'd have to meet the parents."

"Her parents are dead, Al, did you forget that she had to kill them?"

"Did I mention that she had a fiery temper on her?" Al grinned.

"What the hell is a Seraphim, anyway?" asked Garth.

Shaking his head, Clive opened the black book he had retrieved from the table. "The highest order of angels. They're mentioned a few times in different religious texts. Of course, not one of them describes them as topless dancers. Those that can entertain, he keeps for his own pleasure. Pray for your friend's sake that he doesn't find out her real name, or he'll take great pleasure in *taking pleasure* from her. He treats all the women like objects, and uses them as he sees fit. If they don't respond to his desires, or fail to obey his orders, they get sent down here to await their Baptism, just like us."

"I'm guessing that's not a good thing," Bill said. He'd never been a follower of any religion, and the man that had cast them into the holding cell certainly wasn't doing anything to make him think otherwise.

"You don't even know the half of it," Sylvester said, rubbing his chin.

III

The small room that Angel sat in had once been a pair of prison cells designed to hold two men. Now, its wall had been knocked through and it housed seven young women, including herself. Two of them slept on the bunks, deep in a peaceful sleep, while the rest went about their normal business of washing, preparing their meals and preening themselves. Angel sat on a wooden chair in the corner, a blanket draped over her shoulders, shivering and clutching a steaming mug of coffee, unable to understand what was happening.

After her friends had been marched away from the large assembly hall, she had been dragged up in front of the throne and forced to her knees, where she had been restrained by two guards and stripped naked at the lecherous hands of The Messiah. He hadn't physically assaulted her, but the humiliation had been enough to leave her shaken and distressed. The two women who had been chained up were released, and instructed to take her away and prepare her for the next performance. One of them had prepared a warm drink; another presented her with a pair of the same gold bikini briefs the each wore, and a third had covered her in the blanket. None of them had spoken more than a few words to her since she had arrived in the cell.

"Do you smoke, sweetie?"

Angel looked up from the dark cup of liquid to see one of the women had taken time to come over and talk to her. She was the red-haired woman who had been chained to the chair and one of the two who had guided her the short distance to the cell. She carried a small white and red box, with one cigarette hanging out the edge, waiting to be plucked from the container. Angel shook her head. The woman nodded and sat on the edge of the lower bunk, leaning forwards.

"I didn't, not until I was caught by these guys. It helps me relax, you know, just normal smokes laced with dope. You'll find something to relax you, something to dull your mind. You'll have to."

"What do you mean?"

"The Messiah. He likes to fuck, and he likes to do it hard. It won't be so bad for you, not at first. You're the new girl, so you'll just be with him first, but he'll soon pass you around his followers when he grows tired of you. That's why we all have our little vices. Dulls the pain. Helps us blank out the reality of the situation."

"And if I don't do what he says?"

"You'll be Baptised, just like your friends. And trust me, that's not something you want to happen," answered the woman. Her eyes were already dilating from her fix of potent drugs: Angel could smell the pungent tang of the narcotic from where she sat.

"Jesus, Bill! I forgot about them. What is the Baptism?"

"Something you don't want to experience yourself. He's already sent one of us to see the Baptist because she wouldn't do as he demanded. He made us watch it happen… It's just another reason to keep taking the drugs. Poor girl, she was one of the first."

The woman took a final drag from her cigarette, then tilted her head back and lay down, curling her body around the legs of the girl already lying in the bed. Angel watched as the rest of the girls wound down from their schedule, each slipping into a comatose state as their drug of choice kicked in.

Angel sighed and rose from her seat, stepping into the briefs she had been given, but keeping the blanket wrapped tight around her shoulders. She had to find some way out the prison cell and meet up with her friends, and together try and escape from the place. She didn't know what the Baptism entailed, and the drug-taking woman hadn't been very specific as to what it meant. She remembered that he had mentioned that Bill would be fed to the Chosen, and that the other gang members had referred to the Rots as Chosen… that meant they were going to feed Bill to the Rots. But why would they voluntarily feed the undead creatures?

She wandered over to the large vanity table and looked at the collection of makeup and hair-sculpting products, littered with crumpled cigarette packets, empty alcohol bottles, plastic bags filled with residual amounts of white powder and dirty syringes. She looked distastefully at the collection of used drugs, and slowly sank to the chair, looking at her reflection in the cracked mirror.

Angel awoke from the small space on the floor she had managed to curl up in with a dull aching in the small of her back. It had been a cramped and uncomfortable night, and although she had resisted falling asleep for as long as possible, she had eventually succumbed to the lethargy and slipped into a light, fitful sleep. The night had been constantly broken by footsteps patrolling back and forth in the hallway outside the cell, the small metal grille in the door opening every now and then as the guards outside decided to stop and leer at the captive women.

The morning saw one of the jailers throw open the door and stand menacingly at the opening: a large man, red trousers tattered and covered in grime, wearing a white muscle shirt and a leather bondage-style face mask. He stormed in, a shotgun resting in his hands as he surveyed the sleeping women, lingering looks resting on each woman before moving on to the next. Angel quickly closed her eyes and kept her head down, facing away from the door and trying to remain anonymous.

She knew she'd failed as heavy footsteps thundered their way towards her, and a large hand wrapped itself around her hair, heaving her to her feet and pulling her towards the door. She screamed, more in surprise than pain, and vainly struggled with the grip, stumbling out the room and being led down the corridor. It wasn't the way she had been brought to the cell, so she knew she wasn't heading towards the main hall.

"Where are you taking me?"

The man responded with a grunt, dragging her towards a large oak door painted with a golden cross. Angel felt a cold chill run down her spine, knowing that only one man in this prison could reside behind that door. They reached to door, and the man tore it open, flung her in, and slammed it behind her.

Shaking her head and tentatively touching her scalp where her hair had been pulled, Angel groggily clambered to her feet and looked around the room.

It was about twice the size of the cell that held the women, and had undergone extensive redecoration. While other cells had been left with bare concrete walls painted white, the walls of this room had been covered by heavy velvet drapes, running from floor to ceiling. A thick red carpet had been laid on the ground, which had softened her impact on the floor somewhat. On one side of the room sat a large desk, littered with large flickering candles, papers and an opened leather-bound book. She crawled over to the desk, pulled herself up and looked at the book in the waning light.

She recognised it as the bible, left open on one of the later chapters right at the end of the book. The loose papers were covered in an illegible scrawl in various different coloured pens, and Angel couldn't even begin to make out the writing. She turned around and looked at the other piece of furniture in the room: a large king-sized bed, covered with fur throws and large cushions. Angel carefully walked over to it and sat on it, taking one of the throws from the bed and wrapping it around herself. It wasn't as cold in the room as it had been in the cell, more than likely due to the soft furnishings that had been scattered around the room.

The door opened and The Messiah strolled in, his cloak billowing behind him as he marched across the room, turning his head towards where Angel sat. He reached up and pulled the hood from his head, revealing his malevolent face. A hook-like nose, sunken dark eyes and a bald, flat head looked down on her, lips twisted into an expression that was half sneer, half smile.

"On the bed already," he murmured in a low voice as he removed the clasps of the cloak from his chest, pulling the pins from his flesh and wiping away the trickle of blood that followed. "Your feigned modesty intrigues me."

Angel leapt to her feet, clenching the throw tightly around her and backing away from him, coming to a stop as she hit the curtains surrounding the wall. The Messiah grinned, looking her up and down, nodding in appreciation.

"Surely my work is in the name of God," he announced, dropping his cloak to the floor and stepping forwards. "Lest he would not send such divine gifts unto his servant as a reward."

"You're fucking crazy," she whispered, spinning around and leaping over the bed, trying to keep a barrier between herself and the crazed man.

"You doubt me," he grinned, standing in the same place, refusing to chase after her. "Many before you have doubted me, just as Thomas did. Bow down upon your knees and put you fingers in my wounds, for I am Jesus reborn."

As he spoke, he stretched out his hands, displaying the bloodied scabs in the centre of his palm. Angel didn't lean forward to get a closer look; she knew the wounds were self-inflicted anyway, having seen the arms of his throne, and the metal spikes he rested his hands upon. "You really think you're the Son of God?" she asked, slowly trying to edge along the wall towards the closed door while keeping him occupied.

"He talks to me," admitted The Messiah, grinning and unbuckling his trousers, letting them drop to the floor and revelling in his nakedness, displaying another tattoo, this one of flames extending from his groin, licking at the base of the cross on his stomach. "Behold, the devil shall cast some of you into prison, that ye may be trialed. And trialed we were. Those that passed, surely are the men of God, and shall be marked with the holy seal."

"You can talk all you want, you're still crazy. It's not enough that we've got to contend with the Rots at every turn…"

"Rots?" he asked, shaking his head and climbing on to the bed, lying on his back and grinning. "The dead? Surely you mean the Chosen? Merely children of God, sent to aid the judgement. They of the people and kindreds of tongues and nations shall see their dead bodies for three days and a half, and shall not suffer their dead bodies to be put in graves. And the nations were angry," he said, looking towards the ceiling and closing his eyes, arms outstretched in the form of a crucified body. "The nations were angry, and thy wrath is come, and the time of the dead, that they be judged.

"And he gathered them together in a place called in the Hebrew tongue Armageddon," he continued. He waved his arms around as if to illustrate the building they were in. "But it was commanded them that they would not hurt the grass of the earth, neither a tree; but only those men which have not the seal of God on their forehead."

"What?" asked Angel, halting her gradual edging towards the door to stop and look at the man on the bed. The words he spoke made only partial sense, and reminded her of the old Shakespeare plays she had been forced to read in school. It was also similar to what little of the bible she could remember. She cast a quick glance to the open book on the desk, and understood that he was trying to relate everything that was happening to stories in the bible. Her mind worked through what he'd been saying, trying to piece it together into something she could understand.

Rots in the van, the gang called them the Chosen... Gathered them in a place... Hurt those without the seal...

"Christ, you think you can control them?"

Without another word Angel turned and ran for the door, hoping to make her escape with The Messiah relaxed on the bed. No sooner had her hands made contact with the door handle than the large man was behind her, clammy palms wrapped around her waist and pulling her away from the door, ripping away the material draped around her and throwing it to one side. Without any discernible effort he lifted her from the ground and heaved her across the room, throwing her on to the bed. He approached, leering at her and starting to play with himself as he moved.

"Them, my Disciples, my Seraphim, I can control them all. Just as I will you."

He pounced on to the bed, holding down her legs with his own and grabbing both her arms, wrapping a large hand around both wrists and completely pinning her to the bed. He slowly started to work his way up her body, straddling her and keeping her pinned using his superior weight and strength. She almost retched at the sensation of his cold and sweat-covered skin as he slid up her body, twinned with the alcohol and musk-like stench of his body as he neared her face. He sat on her chest now, and try as she might, no amount of squirming and fighting could either dislodge him or enable her to kick him with her flailing legs. She could barely breathe properly; she was panicking to the point of hyperventilating, the heavy weight on her ribs was doing nothing to help her breathing.

"New additions to the Seraphim," he said, "You always fight so much. I like that. Reminds me of the days before the Judgement."

Angel didn't say anything to respond; she knew that it was impossible to fight the weight of the man.

"And I say unto thee take it and eat it up; it shall make thy belly bitter, but it shall be in thy mouth sweet as honey."

Angel closed her eyes and pushed her head as far back into the pillows as she could, squeezing tears from them as she braced herself for whatever came next. She felt cold, hard flesh press against her mouth, pushing though her lips and meeting her teeth. He kept pushing, uttering a deep and throaty laugh as he felt he was on the verge of completing his degrading task.

His laughter turned to a shrill scream of agony as Angel quickly opened her mouth, then bit down hard, teeth grinding through flesh and filling her mouth with blood. The Messiah leapt up from his bed, cupping his groin and cursing, giving Angel the chance to roll off the bed and spit the mouthful of blood on to the bed.

"Fucking bitch!" screamed The Messiah, hobbling over to Angel and smashing her face with the back of his hand, sending her crashing across the room and landing sprawled near the door. He stormed over to her, picked her up by her neck and tossed her across the room, sending her crashing into the table and scattering the papers, knocking candles over and spilling hot wax on her.

The door burst open, and Angel looked up, hoping to see her friends standing at the opening, ready to save her. Instead, it was the jailer who had dragged her to the room.

"Lord?" he said, rushing forwards towards the Messiah. He looked up, a feverish glare in his eyes, and he pointed a shaking finger towards Angel.

"And I gave her space to repent of her fornication; and she repented not. Take her to the holding cell, she can be Baptised with the rest of the heathens. Take her from my sight. I'll watch the

Baptism myself later. Now go."

"And he actually thinks he can control the Rots?"

"He's a fucking nutcase, all right," agreed Garth.

Bill offered nothing to the conversation. He found it difficult to understand that any man, no matter how crazy, could delude himself into thinking that he could control the Rots for his own gain. He also found it hard to concentrate on the scale of the madman's delusions while all that he could think of was Angel, being recruited into his band of sex slaves.

"And that's what he's going to do to us?"

Sylvester nodded in agreement. "We've been locked up for so long, we were probably the first of his captives. He just hasn't got around to sending us to the Baptist yet. I'd say he's forgotten about us, but they keep sending us food. True, it's only the slops that they've mopped up from the kitchen floor, but it's food none the less."

Silence settled over the cell as the conversation fizzled out. The quiet lasted for five minutes, until a pair of heavy footsteps sounded outside the door, coming to a halt with the sounds of a minor scuffle. The bolt was worked open, and Al sprang to his feet, standing by the door and raising his hands above his head, ready to bring them crashing down on the guards when they entered the room. The door opened, and a figure was quickly pushed into the room, a tumbling flash of skin and gold, accompanied by cursing and moans of pain. Al was too distracted by the whirling dervish to strike out at the guards, and by the time he realised what had happened the door had slammed shut once more, locked secure. Sighing, he returned his attention to the new captive in the cell, and was just as surprised to see Angel lying splayed on the floor, naked except for a pair of golden briefs. She quickly gathered her senses, covering herself up and scrambling back into the corner of the room. Bill leapt to his feet, unfastening his jacket and shrugging it off, ducking down on to the floor and dropping it over her shoulders. She looked up at him from behind a swollen and black eye and barely managed a smile.

"What happened to you?"

She didn't say anything, just slipped into the jacket and fastened it up, wiping the tears from her face with the back of her sleeve.

"A Seraphim's first night," Sylvester said grimly. "It's the novelty of a new woman in the ranks."

"Did he… did he force…"

Angel shook her head, wiping her eyes again. "He tried, but I bit him."

As if to punctuate this statement, she spat on to the floor beside her, the saliva tainted red from the blood still in her mouth. After a few minutes, Angel managed to calm down and went through her story, from the humiliation in the main hall to the attempted rape in The Messiah's quarters.

"We've got to get out of here," said Bill, standing up and pacing the length of the cell.

"It's a helluva story," muttered Al, leaning over so only Garth could hear him. "I liked the part about the room filled with almost naked women. I think we should break out and go there."

"We have to break out," repeated Bill, "Before we get sent to this Baptist. There's no way they're going to turn me into a Rot just to add some muscle to his deranged army."

"He's not even turning you," Garth reminded him with a mischievous grin. "You're just going to be food for us."

"We've looked all around the room," said Sylvester. "The only way in or out is through that door. It's a prison. Each cell is locked up pretty tight, how are you going to get out?"

"Air vents," said Al, turning his gaze up towards the ceiling. A metal grille in the ceiling, about fifty centimetres square, spewed cool air into the cell. Bill hadn't noticed it before, but as he stood beneath it and looked directly up into the opening, he caught the faint scent of rotten flesh. "Have you ever tried the air vent?"

Sylvester circled around beneath the grille, looking up at the metal covering. "Only the lowest cells in the prison have the vents in the ceiling. These cells were rarely used when I worked here; they were just used for storage more than anything else. Those bastards probably don't even know about the airshafts. Not that it matters."

"We couldn't fit in there," Clive said, confirming his friend's comments. "We're both too big, we tried that. By the time one of us managed to get up there, and size ourselves up we realised neither of us could fit."

"Me and buddy won't be able to fit either, then. Bet the bitch can fit up there."

Bill looked at Angel, knowing that she would easily be able to fit, but he didn't think she'd be able to manage after going through what she had. That only left one option.

"I'll go."

"It'll be a tight fit," Al said, "You sure you can do it?"

"Just get me up there, I'll manage. Just tell me what the plan is after I get up there."

"Get out of here. They've probably brought *Colebrook's Runner* to this place, or at least they will have if they're got any common sense. Find it, grab some weapons and come back, we'll blast our way out back to the rig and drive to our rendezvous. Don't take all day, now, we've only got two days left until our pickup. If the *Runner* isn't there, you'll have to grab some weapons from somewhere and we'll have to steal one of their vans, then find what they've done with our gear."

"A pretty big task, then," muttered Bill as he helped drag the table under the vent. Al leapt up on to the wooden desk and worked at the vent, managing to pry it from its fixings and letting the metal grille drop to the floor.

"Here, take this."

Bill watched as the Marine unfastened his trousers and let them drop to his ankles. Beneath the combat trousers he wore tight fitting black underwear, which had a holster built into the briefs. He unclipped the fastener and drew a small pistol, half the size than any handgun Bill had used or seen. Al dusted it down and handed it over.

"It's a holdout pistol. Four shots in there, one in the chamber and three in the magazine. It's not amazingly powerful, but it'll be enough to break through someone's skull."

"How do you still have that?"

"Heterosexual men rarely thoroughly check a man's groin for weapons. I just exploited a weakness, and now it's going to work in our favour. Now get up there, you're wasting time."

Bill nodded, slipping the pistol between the waistband of his jeans. He clambered up on to the table, waited for Al to replace his trousers, then braced his foot between the interlaced fingers of the Marine and vaulted up into the opening of the airshaft.

He found it was a very tight fit; he wriggled and wormed his way up the vertical shaft, bracing his weight on either side with his boots and trying to find a purchase on the slick metal. He decided it might not have been such a good idea to just dive into the shafts without thinking. The vertical shaft soon opened up in a wider horizontal shaft, and Bill clambered over the edge, heaving himself up over the ledge, puffing and panting as he lifted his legs up and over the lip.

"He's up," Al's voice echoed, bouncing up the metal walls. "C'mon, kid, you can do it."

"Good luck," another voice called. Angel. Bill smiled to himself and started to push himself along the floor of the shaft.

It was warmer in the shafts the deeper Bill went, surprising considering the initial cold gusts of air. He was glad that he only wore a T-shirt, and not the thick padded jacket he had left with Angel. The further he went along the shaft, the thicker the smell of rotting flesh. He figured he was going the right way: the smell of rotting meat was obviously coming from the outside, which was where he needed to be.

He also found that, the further along the shaft he went, the more it opened up. Each junction he crawled across gave him another ten centimetres to move in. After about twenty minutes of scratching and scrabbling, Bill found that he could actually move on all fours; instead of snaking across the floor and tearing his fingernails on the joints of the shaft, he could crawl on his hands and knees. Once he could do this, he found his speed increased dramatically. He got so carried away with his momentum he almost pushed his hand into the opened chest cavity of the body lying prone in the shaft.

He paused, his face inches from the upturned face of the bloodied body. The gloom of the shaft didn't offer much light to make out any details, but that didn't bother Bill. With the increase in space, he was able to reach around to his back pocket and pull out the lighter he had picked up all those weeks ago after breaking out of quarantine. He flicked it to life, holding the flickering flame close to the body out of morbid curiosity.

The features were unidentifiable, the flesh of the upper body and face having been shredded by hundreds of tiny sharp teeth. Small footprints led away from the bloody pool around the body, rodent tracks leading away from the corpse and in the direction he intended to travel. Its legs had been smashed and splintered, bone protruding from the grey flesh and covered in rivulets of dried blood.

Bill placed the lighter on the duct floor and sighed heavily. He was pissed off that he hadn't thought about anything else tracking through the vents like a pack of rodents, but now he wasn't sure if he'd been following the rotten stench of the outside, or just the ripe odour of the rotten body.

There wasn't any identifying marks or any other way to identify the body, he could barely tell if it was male or female. He didn't relish the idea of following the pack of rats that had chewed on the body, but short of breaking his neck and his back to turn around, he had no choice but to keep on going.

He pushed back the body, sliding it into one of the offshoots from the main shaft, then crawled past the bloodied corpse, continuing on his journey into the depths of the darkened shaft, snuffing out the lighter and slipping it back into his pocket.

"This was a bad idea," muttered Bill, the thick blood on the floor already congealing. He couldn't tell how long ago the person had been killed, but it was long enough to render the blood clay cold and thicken it. "Next time Al gets an idea like this, *he* can crawl through a pipe and follow bloody rats."

He continued to follow the duct, staying in the largest of the pipes. Even beyond the body, the scent of rotting flesh still seemed to be getting stronger, so he knew that he was still heading in the right direction, or at least towards the *next* dead body in the shaft. The smell had also become accompanied by something else, a low bass-like rhythmic sound of a drum twined with a high-pitched screeching. Bill winced as he heard the piercing sounds, trying to determine what it could be. It was a sound that made him think of rats. Was he heading towards the pack of vermin that had partially devoured the body? He paused mid crawl, trying to peer into the gloom ahead of him, and blindly fumbled for the handgun, drawing it and aiming it into the darkness. He knew he didn't have a chance in hitting something the size of a rat in the gloom of the tunnels, but holding the weapon made him feel a little better and steadied his nerves. He tried to work out whether the squeal was coming closer or moving away. It seemed to be staying in one place; it's origin the same of the beating drums.

Bill continued on his journey, nearing the alien sounds and imagining giant rats pounding huge tribal drums, waiting for their next kill to stumble upon their lair. He shook his head, trying to dislodge the thoughts from his mind on concentrating on escaping from the shafts.

"Dentists," he muttered to himself after another minute of shuffling and crawling. He'd finally placed what the screeching was, and it wasn't giant man-eating rodents. It was the sound of a dentist's drill, boring into someone's tooth. He shivered at the thought, not sure if he was happier heading towards a giant rat or a dentist; he wasn't too keen on either of the two.

The shafts took a sharp right, and then slowly started to descend in a gentle slope. It meant he was getting closer to the ground, which also meant that he should be getting closer to the way out, hopefully: if he was lucky, it would be a grille. If he was unlucky, it would be something like an industrial air conditioner unit. The intensity of the smell increased, as did the whine of the bone drill and thumping of drums.

The end of the shaft slowly came into view, a small pinprick of dim light that gradually got larger and larger with each shuffle, bringing with it a warm breeze laced heavily with the smell of death. Bill almost gagged at the stench, but tried his best to keep his stomach under control, knowing that any retching he did now would be dry, and bring nothing but bile up. He soldiered on, his head down and eyes fixed on the ground, and finally reached the grille, pushing on it with all his strength. He found he was unable to shift it, the bolts holding tight. Even with the extra space the past hundred feet of conduit had granted, he couldn't turn around to kick at the grating. He placed his head on the grille, slowly pushing it as he walked his legs closer and closer, hoping to force his way through. He could feel the mesh buckle and bend; felt wire dig into his scalp and snapping metal lash and cut him. The frame of the grille bent, and with a loud snap, the top half of the mesh covering came away from the wall, leaving the hinged and buckled lattice like a broken drawbridge.

Panting and gently touching the fresh wounds on his head, Bill tumbled out the shaft and found himself in a dark and damp pit, the walls and floor made from cold and roughly cut blocks of stone. He pressed himself against the wall by the opening of the shaft, breathing heavily despite the thick taste of rot in the air. It felt good to be out the shafts, and he cautiously stretched his limbs, the sound of his joints cracking lost in the cacophony of drills and drums. Bill slowly raised his gaze upwards, towards the ceiling and the source of the noise. Suddenly, the thought of returning to the shafts didn't seem like a bad idea.

XIV
THE DEAD PIT

"Our facilities are completely overrun with bodies waiting to be disposed, but even working around the clock we can't keep up with demand."

I

From where he crouched, Bill could see that the ceiling high above him was constructed from metal poles and wooden planks creating a catwalk around the perimeter of the room. A network of pipes and a metal grid filled the gap between the catwalks, acting as a platform. From what he could see through the gaps in the scaffold, he could make out movement and flickers of light and shadow. Curiosity got the better of him, and he made his way towards the structure supporting the platform, slowly and silently clambering on to the metal poles and gradually making his way towards the upper floor. He twisted his face in discomfort as the bullet wound he had received in Edgly decided to flare up once more, but pushed the pain aside as he reached the very top of the climb. Wrapping his arms around two lengths of pipes, he peered through the grid that formed most of the barrier above him.

The chamber above him looked similar to something from a bad horror film, like Doctor Frankenstein's laboratory. By twisting himself around in his perch, he could see that three of the four walls were lined with benches. Each held a dizzying array of rusted and bloodstained tools, bottles of murky fluid and vials of glowing, neon chemicals. The fourth wall had a door leading out the room, and either side of the door there stood a Rot, limbs chained to the walls and floor, a gag held fast in each of their mouths by oversized screws that were painfully inserted into their jawbones. The centre of the room held a large metal table, silver in colour and surrounded by numerous trays, each littered with bloody instruments of surgery. A naked female Rot lay pinned to this table, arms and legs restricted by leather straps, with a thick metal chain keeping the head of the squirming creature face down. A large black and battered stereo lay by the head of the Rot, the vibrating machine source of the constant drumbeats.

Around the table strolled a man, almost naked except for the lengths of leather and chains that were tightly wrapped around his torso, and the black leather briefs he wore. Attached to this bizarre costume was a flap of leather hanging down the back of his legs, like half a skirt. Tools hung from his belt, bloodied instruments of the twisted and bizarre surgery he was busy conducting. Bill watched in morbid fascination as the man circled the creature restrained on the table, prodding the mottled grey flesh of the Rot with the scalpel he held. Bill couldn't tell if the man was enjoying his job or not: the customised rubber gas mask he wore had a death-like skeletal grin painted on the surface; the lower jaw of the skull seemed to be a real and bloody jawbone, dripping with gore.

The man stood at the end of the table, by the head of the Rot, and pulled at the white latex gloves he wore before slicing into the flesh at the base of the zombie's skull, making a small incision to expose the bone. The surgeon retrieved a curved and twisted piece of metal, placed it against the exposed bone, and grabbed a power drill, affixing the plate to the Rot's head with three short screws. He continued to add metal plates to the head of the creature until its skull was encased in a protective metal shell. These actions were accompanied by the shrill sound that Bill had thought to be a dentist's drill as the metal bored into the bone.

The doctor laughed silently to himself, the shaking of his broad shoulders the only indication that he was deriving pleasure from the obscene operation, then flicked the stereo off. As silence fell across the operating theatre, the man placed the tools he held on one of the benches and returned to the figure, running his gloved hands over the body, gently massaging the upper thighs and lower calves of the creature. For a moment, Bill thought he had stumbled across another necrophile like those inhabiting the tunnels of the underground railway he had walked through. The man proved him wrong as he unfastened one of the leg restraints and wrenched back the leg, the knee of the woman popping with a sickening crack. He worked through the rest of the joints of that leg, fastened it back down, and performed the same actions on the next leg.

"Work that rigor out, Chosen one," the man said in a gentle voice muted by the mask, his tone soft and soothing as he massaged the muscles of the creature. "The Army of Christ welcomes you with open arms. May your sins in life be forgiven, and your soul received in the Kingdom of God: your mortal vessel shall continue to serve."

Bill remained frozen on his perch, feeling his fingers numb as he feverishly held on to the pipes, trying to keep low and out of sight, but also trying to keep an eye on what was going on above him.

The Baptist stepped back from the prone figure on the table and stalked over to the door, caressing the heads of each the bound zombies before opening the door and leaving the room. As he left, he flicked the lights off, leaving Bill alone in near darkness with the three Rots above him.

The door clicked shut, and Bill released his breath, not even realising he'd been holding it. The darkness was suffocating, and the fact he *knew* there were three creatures sharing the dark with him didn't help alleviate the feelings of dread that hung over him. He needed to get out there as soon as possible.

Bracing his back against the jumble of pipes, Bill slowly pushed one of the wooden planks, finding a loose panel that he could work at in a bid to try and get up through the floor. He managed to find a collection of loose nails, and gently tapped them with the butt of the holdout weapon, wincing with each clink the weapon made against the metal pins, aware that even the slightest noise may bring the Baptist back to his demonic workshop.

Smiling inwardly as one of the planks gave way and lifted from its housing, he slowly eased himself up, replacing the plank and pushing the nails back into their place so his actions wouldn't attract too much unwanted attention.

Bill found himself standing at the head of the table, looking down on the metal shell that encased the skull, and tentatively reached down and rapped softly on the construction. The female creature murmured softly in response, but didn't fight against her restraints. Turning on the spot, Bill looked over the collection of tools and trinkets that lay on the wooden bench, picking those that caught his eye. A golden crucifix attached to a long chain, etched with the words 'For Cassandra', a heavy and expensive wristwatch, and a collection of rings, belonging to both men and women: one item, a locket, seemed to call to him, and he picked it up.

Turning the locket over in his hands, he traced the contours of the necklace and triggered the release mechanism. The spring-loaded hinge yawned open, a smooth action revealing the picture of a young couple inside. One was a woman, young with dark, shoulder length hair and a soft smile, the other a grinning man with long hair tied back in a ponytail.

"Love you forever," he read the inscription aloud to himself, voice barely a whisper. "Always yours, Sly."

The only explanation he could think of was that the locket had belonged to Terri. His gaze lingered on the photo for a while, and for a moment he was reminded of his life with Jenny, the countless photographs they had posed for, the numerous photograph albums they had at home. All the good times and memories, captured forever, never to be relived.

"Trinkets from the Chosen before they were baptised," announced a muffled voice. Bill wheeled around, dropping the locket back on to the bench and seeing the Baptist standing at the doorway, arms outstretched and a hand resting on each Rot standing by the door. "The Chosen have no need for them. They know nothing of remorse or loss. They only know to serve. As you will, soon enough."

Bill didn't say anything; he stood motionless, eyeing up the man, and gripped his pistol tight in one shaking hand. He didn't raise it to fire or even take aim, not wanting to create any unnecessary noises in case he roused the attention of any guards that may be in the area.

"A lost child," the Baptist said, moving forwards as he spoke. He reached out and caressed the legs of the restrained creature, invoking the same muted groans Bill had earlier. "Her time had come, the soul of the poor wench didn't have the strength to live on through this ordeal. The will is weak, but the flesh is strong; it will continue to serve. To be Baptised is to sacrifice your own spirit in order that your body may continue under God's will."

Bill didn't say anything, simply took a step back and shook his head. The Baptist picked up one of the sterilised cutting tools that lay arranged neatly on a metal tray, then slowly and methodically began to make his way around the table, like a snake spiralling in on its prey. Previously mesmerised by the voice and movement of the man, Bill quickly recognised the threat and started to move, trying to keep the table between himself and the demented surgeon at all times.

"There's no need to fear God," the Baptist said, his voice a soft and gentle coo, the knife in his hand twirling gently from side to side, rolling between fingers and thumb. "He welcomes us all, when our time comes. Take pride in knowing that even in death you continue to serve in the name of Christ."

"Fuck you," Bill finally managed to say, his voice trembling slightly. Finally lifting the weapon in his hands, Bill lifted the pistol and pointed it at the masked visage of the man. The hell with any guards nearby, this man was enough to make his skin crawl. The Baptist didn't flinch, didn't try to avoid the weapon, but he stopped moving and stood his ground. His hands lowered to the tabletop, the scalpel clattering against the metal surface as he released it.

"Does your God condone such blasphemous remarks?" he finally asked. Bill looked at the painted skull on the mask, at the glistening jawbone affixed to it, but couldn't read anything into the words or posture of the man. Any emotion like fear or anger was lost behind the rubber and metal construction on his face.

"Does yours welcome murderers into his kingdom?" Bill finally countered, finger twitching near the trigger of the weapon. "People who freely kill others to fuel the dementia of one man crazy enough to eat his own shit?"

"Lies!" shouted the Baptist, lifting his hand in a flourish and slicing the skin of Bill's wrist. Startled, he dropped the pistol, though the Baptist made no further advance, or any motion to retrieve the dropped weapon. Bill suddenly felt very vulnerable. "He is a great man, and has guided us through this. He has shown us the way the world has turned, shown us that it is God's way, that everything that has happened so far has been predicted in the Book of Revelation. He prepares us for the battle with Satan."

"Bullshit," hissed Bill, "He's a fucking nutcase who you're all terrified of. A killer, a rapist, and a child molester who you'd rather follow than turn your back on."

"Who better to carry the message of God than a reformed doer of evil?"

Bill didn't respond; there was nothing he could say or do. If the Baptist believed he had a real purpose, and that by infecting people with the plague he was creating soldiers for the army of God, there was nothing he could say or do to counter that. In Bill's eyes he may have been crazy, but in his own eyes, the Baptist was only two steps away from God. Bill wasn't educated in theology in the way Clive may have been, and he certainly wasn't self-taught in the same way the Messiah claimed to be, but he couldn't imagine any god of any religion would encourage the killing and infection of so many people. Nor would they applaud screwing pieces of metal into the skulls of their victims.

Without warning, the Baptist lunged forwards again, twirling his scalpel and catching Bill as he dodged to one side, this time opening a wound on his temple. Bill stumbled back, wiping his brow with the back of his hands and realising if he'd been any slower he would have lost an eye. He continued with his silence, realising that any words he contributed to the discussion would only help to incense the deranged surgeon.

Again the Baptist advanced, and Bill lunged for the metal tray on the bench, sending instruments clattering across the floor and bouncing through the gaps in the floor. The scalpel bounced harmlessly off the tray, but the blow forced Bill to take a second step back, ever closer to the two Rots chained by the door. He didn't want to get too close to the creatures, especially if he was involved in a fight with the Baptist.

He quickly looked across the floor, trying to locate the pistol he had been forced to drop.

There, behind the Baptist; beneath one of the benches.

There was no way Bill could slip around the man and retrieve the weapon, and fire it, without being cut open with the scalpel. His wrist and brow were awash with a constant stinging sensation, thick and wet with blood, while his thigh pulsed with a dull, numbing sensation. Pistol or no, he wouldn't last long if he received another cut, especially if they were closer to any vital arteries than his previous wounds had been. At least with the man wielding a smaller scalpel it was tougher to score a direct hit.

As if he had read his mind, the Baptist let go of the scalpel and retrieved a pair of large and bloodied bone saws, dripping with fresh gore from a recent 'autopsy'. Bill tensed, realising that taking a cut from a clean scalpel was one thing, but any wound from one of the dirty instruments would end his life, either through trauma or infection of the plague.

Bill had to make a move, he needed the pistol to end the fight as soon as he could. He made his move as the Baptist raised his pair of cutting tools high above his head, lunging forwards and barging into the muscular man. His shoulder made contact with his assailant square in his stomach, knocking him backwards and sending the instruments he held flying from his grip. Bill tumbled to the floor, slid along the grating, and slammed into the bench, his outstretched arm slipping beneath it and his fingers coiling around the butt of the pistol.

As quick as his aching body could manage, Bill spun around so he was lying on his back, lifted his arm and fired off a single round into the back of the recovering Baptist. The pistol bucked slightly in his hand, and a blossom of raw flesh and blood exploded outwards, splashing Bill and the corpse on the table with spatters of gore. He sunk to the floor, trying to nurse the wound on his back as he moaned and hissed in agony.

Bill clambered to his feet, looked at the smoking weapon he held, then at the writhing man on the floor, at the blood trickling through the grating to the ground far below.

"Jesus f-f-fucking Christ," hissed the man, clawing at his wound with one hand and fumbling for the catches of his mask with the other. With a scream, the mask toppled from his face, and his breathing, previously subdued and muted by the heavy mask, came in heavy rasps and groans. "Fucking s-sh-shot me bastard."

Bill felt himself grinning, felt his grip tightening on the pistol as he stalked closer to the squirming man as he flipped on to his back and stared listlessly towards the ceiling. The pupil of one eye was dilated and distant, the other a tiny pinprick of black amidst an iris of pale blue. His face, twisted in pain, looked to be not much older than Bill himself. As he neared him, the Baptist snarled and spat at him.

"Get the fuck away from me," he snapped.

Bill laughed, felt his shoulders shake slightly as he did so. The foreboding aura that had previously radiated from the man seemed to die as the youth lay bleeding to death on the ground. Without the grinning countenance of the grotesque mask, he didn't seem very dangerous at all.

"Where's your Messiah now?" mocked Bill, tucking the still-smoking weapon beneath the waistband of his jeans. The barrel was still warm against his skin, and he made sure the metal wasn't too close to any of his more sensitive areas. "Shouldn't he be all-mighty and omnipotent, and know exactly what's going on? He's a fraud, just like you. Without this mask," Bill said, retrieving the discarded headgear and shaking it at the downed man. "Without this, you're nothing."

The Baptist didn't respond, just shook his head and moaned to himself, looking at his bloodied fingers as he withdrew his hands from the wound. He paled in colour and seemed to shake more as he realised just how bad the wound had been. Bill was no biologist, but he figured the bullet has struck somewhere important, like maybe near the kidneys or his stomach. The bullet hadn't come out the other side, so the projectile was still lodged solid in him. Whether from lead poisoning, shock or blood loss, the young man was going to die, of that much Bill was sure, and from the look on his face he wasn't going to put up much of a fight now.

Rubbing his raw skin from where he slid across the grating, Bill carefully edged over to the door, keeping himself as far from the chained Rots as he could while trying the door handle. It wasn't locked, and the creatures didn't seem too agitated by his proximity, unlike any of those he had encountered in the wild. He glanced over his shoulder, at the shivering and pale man dressed in his bizarre sadomasochistic surgery gear, then back at the restrained corpses. Could he have actually tamed the Rots; could they have become accustomed to the presence of a live human? It seemed like a bizarre thought to have, but then, two months ago the notion of a walking corpse was just as bizarre.

He turned back to the man, about to ask him about the Rots, in time to see him plunge one of the retrieved bone saws into his own stomach, a deranged grin spreading over his face as he voluntarily infected himself with the bloodied tool. He quickly faded as blood gushed from his new wound, washing over his hands and the dirty knife. Bill shrugged, feeling that nothing had been lost in the death of the morbid surgeon as he grabbed the golden locket, opened the door and dived between the pair of chained Rots standing guard, slamming the door shut behind him.

The corridor outside the surgery was brightly lit, and extended far to both the left and right of him, each vanishing out of sight as they turned a corner. The walls had originally been painted a drab grey colour, though it had since been painted over with various forms of graffiti and splashes of dirt and blood. Doors were dotted along the corridor walls; some closed, others hanging from their hinges, their dark openings uninviting. Litter and debris had been scattered across the floor, and a trail of muddy boot prints had been tracked back and forth along the dirty ground.

Faced with a multitude of choices, Bill didn't know where to start. He knew he had to get out of the prison complex and see if they'd brought their vehicle with them. If they hadn't, then he had to find some weapons from somewhere else to get his friends out. Knowing his mission didn't help him decide which way to go, though. His original plan in the air vents had been to follow the scent of rotting meat, but it turned out that plan hadn't worked as well as he had hoped. At least he was out the shafts, though. All he had to do was decide on a way to take. The majority of the boot prints seemed to be going one way, so he decided to follow those, pistol drawn once more and raised in one hand, pointing upwards as he crept through the passages.

The thought of returning to the surgery room to grab another weapon, something heavy or sharp, did occur to him, but he didn't want to go back in that room unless he had to. The presence of the three Rots was enough to deter him, but at least they were locked up. Bill had never encountered anyone that had died before the syndrome claimed them, and knew that even after death the virus or whatever it was remained active, reviving the body. He didn't know how long a dead body would take to reanimate, and he didn't want to take any chances by going back in there. He could easily put a bullet in the brain of the Baptist, but what if he encountered three armed guards after that?

"Three guards," he muttered to himself. "Like I'm that frigging lucky."

He followed the footprints around the corridor, and found they took him to a heavy metal door bearing the slogan 'Recreational Facility', locked by three deadbolts on the inside. He opened them up, starting on the top one and working his way down, then swung the door open on to the cool night air. The stench that assailed his nostrils forced him backwards, away from the door, and for a moment he considered returning to the Baptist's chamber to retrieve his mask, before reconsidering. He was working to a tight deadline, and he couldn't afford to keep doubling back on himself. For his sake, and his friends.

Steeling himself, he took a deep breath, and stepped through to door into the foul-smelling night.

II

The door opened on to a metal catwalk that looked like it ran the length of the building's exterior, overlooking the prison's recreational grounds. The catwalk, though slightly rusty in a few areas, seemed structurally sound, and halfway along its length there looked to be a metal staircase descending to the ground below. Despite the fact it was now dark, the walkway was well lit by a series of halogen lights fixed to the wall. Conscious that he may be an open target, Bill tried to sink back into the shadows as much as he could.

Leaning over the encompassing barrier, Bill looked at the ground, and tried to judge how far it was to the ground, in case he needed to suddenly vault over the edge if someone opened fire on him.

He decided that wouldn't be a very good idea.

Whenever he had seen prisons in films, their recreational yards had been expanses of concrete flooring littered with weightlifting equipment, or maybe a couple of fields to play some ballgames on. Although this prison may have had something like that once, it didn't any longer.

Four large walls, completely enclosing the area, surrounded the yard, though the yard itself looked like it had been drastically altered through the use of the three heavy-duty excavators that were to Bill's left, which had no doubt been brought in through the large and heavily secured gates that were on one wall. The ground had been churned up, dried mud and chunks of concrete sculpted into the lip of a large circular pit with a raised hillock in the centre of it. The pit was illuminated by several halogen floodlights towering high above the ground, picking out the shapes of figures stumbling around in the hollow, knocking into one another and having the occasional scuffle. Bill thought back to when they had first been brought to the prison, and one of the gang members had mentioned the dead pit – was this that place? And if so, did it mean that the people down there weren't really people, but Rots?

"It's his army," hissed Bill, watching entranced as one pair of creatures spun on each other. He couldn't make much detail out from his vantage point, but most of them seemed to have misshapen heads, as if they wore some kind of uniform for Christ's Army.

Lifting his gaze from the Rots in the pit to the hillock in the centre, he could see a tall building with a large flat roof, upon which the two men stood. One was stationed behind a large mounted machinegun, the other behind a spotlight that was played over the crowd in the dugout. It looked like a security or watchtower; something to mind over the creatures and make sure none of them escaped.

"Security," Bill wondered aloud, knowing that there would be more weapons for him to use, and if there were only those two men stationed, then it should be easy enough for him and his three bullets to cope with. He had to get there first, though, and from where he crouched it didn't look like there was any way to get to the building other than the small metal ladder fastened to one side of the hill. This ladder didn't even extend to the ground, and looked like the bottom rung was a good eight or nine foot off the ground, obviously kept short in case any of the creatures remembered how to climb. To get there he would have to take a trek through the pit filled with the undead.

"Fuck that," said Bill, slowly making his way along the catwalk and past the stairway leading down. He didn't care if they had all the guns in the world in that security tower, he'd need more than three bullets just to get through the Rots; what would he do once he was facing the men on the tower? He followed the bulwark, hoping to find a door leading back into the prison building, but instead he found the end of the platform, a ragged tear in the metal grating which lead uninvitingly down to a pool of dark water in the dead pit. It looked like the only choice he had was for to return back the way he'd come, back into the building and try one of the other doors he had ignored: he'd been too busy following the footprints to bother looking anywhere else. He could have just walked past a fire exit sign.

That'd be right, he thought, carefully sneaking along the raised pathway. *Too busy concentrating on where I'm* going *instead of taking any notice of where I* am.

As if to prove himself right, his foot came down dangerously close to the hole in the catwalk that lead down to the staircase, and he could feel himself teetering on the edge. He tried to regain his balance, tried to step over the hole with his other foot so he stood astride the gap, but it proved to be too wide for him. Spinning in the air, he felt himself falling, and tried to let his limbs slacken: he knew there was no way he could save himself from the fall, and could only hope for a soft and forgiving landing.

He landed with a muffled thump on his back, knocking the wind from him, and feeling the uneven mounds of rubble and dirt beneath him. As he lay on his back, he saw the bright white searchlight sweep over the catwalk above him, and thought for a brief moment that he as lucky to have taken a fall as he had avoided detection. However, he soon remembered where he was, and that it was like being trapped between a rock and a hard place.

He slowly rolled on to his front, knowing that he had to get up and move as soon as he could. He was grateful that he hadn't killed himself in the fall, and vowed silently to himself, not for the first time, to pay a lot more attention to his surroundings in the future.

Crawling up the wall beside him, he pulled himself to his feet and dusted himself down before stooping to retrieve his dropped pistol. His movements induced a heavy wave of nausea, and he tentatively pressed his hand against the base of his skull, hissing softly in pain and drawing his fingers away to see they were covered in blood. He could only assume that it wasn't a major wound, and that he would be able to go on until he could get someone to look at it.

Taking a few steps on aching limbs, Bill tried to get his bearings, working out roughly the direction of the security tower and setting off towards it. Though the pit had looked just like a large hole from above, it turned out to be more than that, with various troughs and peaks making some areas a maze and other areas like a valley. He stumbled blindly through the pit's haphazard layout, grateful for the small miracle of no Rots being drawn to his presence, though the sounds of his heavy footsteps dislodging the loose rocky material beneath him would surely attract their attention sooner or later.

"Better later," he muttered under his breath, climbing a rocky verge and catching a glimpse of the top of the security tower. He was going in the right direction, which he supposed was one good thing. He could also see several Rots lumbering towards him from the right, making him decide to skirt around them and spiral to the left. Noticing that several of the shambling figures seemed to perk up and increase their stumble towards him, he broke into a jog, vaulting over mounds of rubble and leaping across the smaller ditches.

The still of the night air became alive with the moans and groans of the undead, as if they were communicating with one another, informing the crowd that there was live meat in their enclosure.

Looks like the Messiah was right about my fate, he thought to himself as he narrowly avoided one Rot scrambling out from one of the darkened recess of the pit wall. *I might yet end up as meat for the Chosen.*

But then again, he may not. He'd noticed that a lot of the creatures had misshapen heads, though none of these seemed to indicate trauma: in fact, they looked as if they were wearing armour or helmets on their head. Much like the metal plates the Baptist had been fixing to the woman in his surgery.

Bill stopped running as he found himself in front of a steep wall of debris, catching his breath and looking over his shoulder to see how many creatures were following him. He counted six, and all but two of them had a helmet or metal plating covering their head.

He's protecting them, he thought as he started to climb the mound of rubble and dirt in front of him. *The only way to kill them is to destroy their brain, and he's making it harder to do that.* The Messiah was protecting his soldiers, and with their mouths hidden or wired, they couldn't bite any of their handlers.

"Crazy bastard," he muttered as he grabbed a handful of tarmac and hauled himself up, pushing with his feet as he half-climbed, half-crawled up the incline. He reached to top and rolled himself up, noticing that he was now balanced precariously atop a precipice overlooking the other side. He looked down behind him and saw that although the creatures had followed him to the rise, they hadn't attempted to climb up behind him. Instead, they stared up blankly at him, glazed eyes and expressionless faces, some hidden behind steel, others naked and rotten. He decided to get out of sight quickly, before one of them decided they should follow, and rolled off the edge of the mound, lowering his legs down behind him and gently dropping to the ground.

He landed with a splash as his boots sunk into the muddied surface beneath him, and quickly sunk to his knees, hoping to possibly soften the sound of his landing. He was in the dark, which he supposed was a good thing at the moment, as there seemed to be about ten Rots between him and the hillock in the centre, which was about forty metres away. None of the creatures had seen or heard him as he landed, and he remained deathly still where he crouched, not wanting to attract any unwanted attention until the very last minute, when he finally decided to make his move.

He could see the ladder from where he hid, the lowest rung glistening in the light of the powerful lights overhead. He'd have to take a running jump to get to the ladder and give himself enough of a boost to scramble up the sheer face until he could get a foot on the rungs. Which meant he'd have to run through the throng of Rots as fast as he could, and with the ground all around him being muddy and waterlogged in some places, he didn't fancy his chances of weaving between them all before reaching his final goal. Although they were pretty spaced out in the opened area, he had to remember that some of them could run at quite a speed, and jump quite high and long.

They can climb, too, he thought, looking back up towards the lip of the cliff he'd just dropped from, but was pleased to see that nothing had decided to follow him. Yet.

He slowly rose to his feet and adjusted his positioning for the best start he could get, his boots schlepping wetly as he moved his feet from side to side. He took a deep breath, prepared himself, then took off, trying to power through the mire towards the shining ladder at the end of his run. He managed to take three awkward steps before crashing down into the mud face-first, trying his best to keep his mouth shut and prevent himself from swallowing any of the foul earth. Flopping around on the floor like a fish out of water, he finally managed to drag himself back on to his feet and carried on his journey to the ladder.

Strangely enough, the sound of him toppling into the mud hadn't attracted any attention from the creatures, but as soon as he got back up and carried on with his jog, all the Rots in the annex slowly turned to face him. Each uttering a soft and gentle moan before shuffling towards him, the undead began their advance, teetering from side to side as they slogged through the quagmire. One of the creatures further away from Bill keeled over in the mud, limbs becoming ensnared in the thick soup, and one of the creatures ceased its advance and dropped to its knees, tearing at the struggling zombie. As it hunkered down, Bill noted that it was close to the ladder, and a bizarre idea blossomed to life in his mind. Sure it was crazy, but so was wading through a field of mud, surrounded by flesh-eating undead cannibals.

Not cannibals, he corrected himself as he feinted to one side, narrowly avoiding a gnarled hand as it swiped at him. He stumbled, felt his hand sink into the dark mud, and pushed himself off once more, bringing up a handful of slop and flinging it in the face of another creature. It reeled backwards, acting as if it had been shot, and clawed at its face. Bill rushed on, ducking and weaving between the creatures, powering through the mud and rushing towards the crouching Rot.

Holding back a scream he longed to release, he leapt forwards and planted one of his feet on the ragged and bloody back of the creature, attempting to use it as a springboard. The creature stumbled forwards, its feast disturbed as its spine cracked and splintered, and Bill leapt from the creature with all his might, sailing through the air and reaching out for the lower rung of the ladder.

The kneeling carcass of the Rot proved to be just the extra spring he needed, and his hands wrapped around the lowest of the rungs. His body bashed against the wall, and he hissed in pain as he was winded. Undeterred by the sudden jarring pain of his injured leg as it smashed off the roughly cut wall, Bill frantically scrambled upwards, legs kicking as he slowly pulled himself upwards. He could feel the burning pain across his shoulders and upper arms as he tried to pull his weight up the ladder, and found himself wishing not for the first time that he had spent more time in the gym instead of sitting at home and watching the television. He had started to carry a little extra weight over the past couple of years, and the wet mud surrounding his limbs didn't help. Sweat beaded on his forehead, and he could feel his arms shaking and quivering, almost to the point where he felt he was going to drop back into the pit, and the hungry carnivores below. His flailing legs kicked and scrambled at the uneven surface, until he finally managed to haul up his body and gain footing on the lowest metal rung.

With a lopsided grin, Bill climbed the rest of the ladder with ease, hauling himself over the lip of the cliff face and rolling on to his back on the raised walkway, lifting his legs uneasily and spreading his arms out wide, breathing heavily as he recuperated from his slog through the mud. He lay in that position for a few minutes, a pose reminiscent of the giant marble statue behind the throne of the Messiah, until he finally managed to drag himself back to his feet. Stumbling the five metres from the edge of the mound to the wall of the security tower, Bill carefully leant against the construction, the corrugated iron wall sagging slightly as his weight pressed against it. As the metal gave, it released a soft and hollow clunking sound, and Bill gritted his teeth, trying to be as quiet as he could while he breathed in and held his breath, praying that the sound of the metal giving didn't carry up to the sentries on the roof.

"What's that?"

Bill silently mouthed an expletive, pulling the holdout pistol from his jeans and silently pulling back the slide, checking there was still a bullet in the chamber, ready to be fired. If only Al had the foresight to secrete a silencer on his person, Bill wouldn't have been so hesitant about firing the weapon. The dead of night had carried the sound of the bending metal well enough, especially over the gentle moaning of the denizens of the pit. A single gunshot would carry well into the prison, probably right to the lair of the Messiah himself. It would lead to his escape being known, certainly, and that could lead to the premature execution of his friends.

Of course, the Baptist was now dead, so they'd have to throw them all in the pit. At least they'd have a fighting chance…

"What's what?"

Bill snapped out of his thoughts, listening to the voices of the two men above him. The bright white beam of the searchlight atop the tower swept across the stumbling creatures below, illuminating their deformed and twisted forms as they slowly dispersed from the opened ground near the ladder.

"Fuckin' shufflers."

"They're spooked tonight. Must be something down there. Cat, maybe? Stray dog?"

"The metal-heads can chase them all they want, they're not going to get anything through their helmets. Maybe one of the normal ones'll get it. We might see some bloodshed yet."

"Christ, I hope so. Do you remember when that badger managed to find its way in to the pen? Rabid little fucker took three of them down before it was ripped apart."

"Hmm," muttered the other man. "Good times. Good times."

The conversation died at that. Bill slowly let out his breath, then looked around. There was a doorway leading into the tower, an opening surrounded by metal poles gleaming in the moonlight, and Bill had to evaluate which way would be best to go. There was a long metal walkway leading from the hillock, over the pit and to the far side of the prison. He hadn't been able to see it from the catwalk he had fallen from, but it was the only way he could go. It was pretty long; maybe thirty or forty metres, and he didn't feel like just trying to run across. He'd be an easy target for the men on top of the tower, and he'd be cut down before he could get halfway there.

Resigned to the fact he was going to have to take out the tower, Bill lifted his weapon and slowly slid into the building, weapon raised and ready.

The interior of the tower hadn't been what Bill had anticipated. He had thought there might have been a small room, with a short ladder or staircase leading up to the roof. What he had found was simply a tall shell of a structure with a wide wooden ladder rising towards the open hatch in the ceiling. There was a small wooden crate at the base of the ladder, which held a half-eaten sandwich and an open packet of biscuits. Bill hungrily helped himself to the biscuits while his gaze remained fixed on the hatch, his pistol raised and aimed in the direction of the opening.

"Hey, shouldn't we have a replacement by now?"

Bill's ears pricked up as the two men struck up their conversation once more.

"Are you serious? He's had the dancers out all day and night, from what I've heard. No one's going to come away from that party. We're stuck looking after these dead shits for the rest of the night; Frank knows how to throw a party."

The conversation degraded into a conversation detailing previous encounters with the dancers, who Bill presumed were the Seraphim that Angel had come so close to joining. He looked around the small shaft, grabbing a dusty rag and shaking it before tying it around his mouth, Bill started to casually whistle and slid the pistol into his back pocket before climbing the ladder.

Christ, I hope this works, he thought as he started to climb, then casually called up: "Hey guys, I've come to replace you. Anything happened?"

"About fucking time," announced one of the men as Bill crawled through the hatch and stood up. The roof was cramped, with just enough room to comfortably allow two men to stand on guard. One wore the tattered remains of the prison coveralls, the other a pair of black jeans. Neither looked directly at Bill when he climbed on to the roof. "Christ, where you been?"

"Party overran," said Bill, avoiding any eye contact with the two guards and casting his gaze over the dead pit and the creatures within. "Anything happen tonight?"

"Something down there, wild animal or something."

"Another badger?" asked Bill casually. The guard wearing the coveralls laughed by way of confirmation, then finally turned to look at Bill.

"Hey, wait a minute…"

Shit, thought Bill, assuming he'd been recognised as one of the prisoners.

"Shouldn't there be two of you? Where's our second replacement?"

"On his way," said Bill, his mind working overtime as he tried to come up with a reason why he was on his own. He said the first thing that came to his mind, trying to remember the details of the dancers from the Messiah's entourage. "He's still fucking the red head. Get going, I'll take watch until he gets here."

"That'll be Mikey," laughed the man wearing jeans and slapping his companion on the chest with the back of his hand. "Always had a soft spot for the red heads. We'll get going, don't want to miss any more then we have to."

"Hey, what's with the rag?"

"Sun'll be up in a few hours," said Bill, waiving down towards the pit. "And those rotting bastards stink like shit. Anything to keep the stench out."

"I hear that," laughed the one in the coveralls, clapping Bill on the back with a heavy hand. "If they're the soldiers of God, you think they'd smell better. Take it easy, brother, I'll see you around, and we'll tell Mikey to hurry up if we see him."

Bill nodded a vague confirmation as the two men made their way down the ladder, their banter between one another fading away as they slowly made their way down the walkway and away from the tower.

Bill tore the rag from around his face and dropped it to the floor. He couldn't believe that his ploy had worked with the two guards, but he had to move quickly in case they really did bump in to Mikey and send him over to check out the guard tower.

The tower itself hadn't provided Bill with any weapons like he had hoped. He supposed that finding a submachine gun or a shotgun was too much to ask for, but he thought he would have at least found a pistol, or some more ammo. The only weapon he could find was the machinegun that had been mounted to the railing of the guard tower. It seemed to be the same weapon that Al had favoured, but the welding of the stand held fast, and there was no way he could remove it.

Sighing heavily to himself, he climbed back down the tower, grabbing the remaining biscuits as he went, and slowly made his way over the walkway towards the door leading back into the prison. He didn't know how far he was from the car park, which was hopefully where the rig was stored, but he knew that he didn't have much time.

III

"He's been gone for too long," muttered Al, pacing back and forth in the cell, casting the occasional glance at the heavy locked door of the cell, then back to the opening on the ceiling. There had been a sound before that had travelled through the shafts, a distant banging that could have been a gunshot, but could just as easily have been a heavy door slamming shut. Al was desperate to find out what it was that had made the noise, and whether Bill was all right,

"What's it been now, a couple of hours?"

"I don't know," muttered Garth, looking grimly at the silver device wrapped around his wrist. "My watch is broken. It's been five to twelve for the past month now."

"At least it's right twice a day," muttered Sylvester dryly as he stared glumly at his feet. It was a half-hearted attempt to make light of the current situation, and it tugged at the corners of Al's mouth, but he didn't have to fight hard to keep a straight and emotionless face.

"Give him more time," insisted Clive. "We don't know how long the shaft goes on for, or where it brings him out. He could be on the other side of the prison by now, looking for a way to get back."

"Or we could always face facts and acknowledge he may be dead," whispered Garth.

"The kid'll be all right, he can look after himself," Al said, trying to convince himself just as much as anyone else in the room. "Just have to give him more time."

"How much time can we afford to give him?" argued Garth, nervously tapping his feet on the stone floor. Al glared at him, then his feet, then back at his face. Garth swallowed hard and stopped tapping his feet, though his left leg continued to jiggle slightly.

"We've been held here for days," said Clive. "It could be another couple of days until they remember about us."

"Or it could be in the next ten minutes," Al sighed, then wearily lowered himself on to one of the benches, fumbling blindly for one of the pieces of paper he had been mindlessly rolling since Bill had left. He looked down at Angel, who still sat on the floor, wrapped in Bill's jacket and hugging her knees.

"You all right?" he finally asked. He surprised himself at how sincere he sounded when he spoke to her. She slowly raised her head and looked at him, eyes half-closed. No one had spoken to her since Bill left, and she hadn't volunteered anything towards the short conversations herself. "You've been unusually quiet."

"Fine," her muttered response quiet and weak. "Why?"

"Just asking, that's all."

Al didn't say anything else. Since Bill had left, he'd been warming more and more towards Angel: maybe it had been because she hadn't said anything, or maybe it was because she was practically naked. Catching a glimpse of her body had been a nice distraction for a while; it gave him something to think about, other than the fact he was going to be turned into a Rot in about two or three hours. Since seeing her almost naked, he'd certainly started to think about her differently. Just as long as she kept her mouth shut she was tolerable, he guessed. But still, it wasn't something he was going to broadcast. "You think you're up to climbing in there and following him?"

She glared at him, but didn't respond.

"Well?"

She still did say anything, just lowered her head again, resting her forehead on her knees, sighing heavily.

"C'mon kid," he muttered, rising to his feet once more and pacing the length of the cell. He stared at the door, then lifted his head lazily up towards the grating on the ceiling. "C'mon, where the hell are you?"

"Where the hell am I?" muttered Bill, standing in the shadows of a damp corridor. His aimless wanderings had taken him away from the dead pit and into the lower depths of the prison once more. He had been lucky enough to stumble across a map of the current building, which had been fastened to the wall with thick heavy bolts. It had been helpful enough to point out where he was, and that the exit was currently on the other side of the building. If he thought for one moment that the arrow pointing to his location would follow him as he moved, he wouldn't have thought twice about prying it from the wall and carrying it around with him. As it was, he would have to try and remember the layout as best as he could.

As he moved through the building, there had been several times where he had almost been seen by the patrolling guards; he had managed to slip into the shadows of the corridors or one of the opened cells that lined some of the corridors before anyone could see him. Stealth wasn't his forte, and he knew it would only be a matter of time until his luck ran out and he was caught. He would have to find a way out of the prison as soon as possible

From what he could remember from the map, the exit that promised to lead to the outside world was on the other side of the complex, and that required taking a stroll through an empty and dark prison block.

He stood on the threshold of the opened room and looked in; almost half the size of the main hall the Messiah resided in, the cellblock was lined on its two longest sides by rows of iron bars. Some doors to the cells lay open, leading into vacant cells, while others remained closed off, sealing emaciated corpses in their tombs. A steady buzzing sound filled the room, and Bill could see the shapes of large flies as they lazily floated from one side of the room to the other, passing through the muted shafts of moonlight that entered the room through the skylight overhead.

Bill cautiously entered the room and kept his back against the wall, slowly making his way around the perimeter of the chamber. The smell of the dead bodies was overpowering, and the persistent droning of the flies seemed to vibrate within his very skull; a sickening sensation he couldn't shake, that seemed to worsen the further into the room he went. The sounds and the smells became too much, and his slow and careful steps quickly turned into hurried steps. There was a distance of fifty metres between him and the doors at the other side, and his hurried steps took him stumbling past a corpse that was lying half out its cell. In the darkness, Bill couldn't see the twisted and fragile limbs snaking out the bars and across the floor, and his legs became tangled in them as he passed by, grimacing as the arms and legs of the corpse cracked and groaned around him as he stumbled to the floor. Cold and wrinkled flesh skimmed his hands and face, and Bill felt a sudden fit of panic as a swarm of maggots dislodged themselves from their rotting feast and cascaded across his skin. Though the corpse in the cell hadn't been reanimated, he imagined briefly that it was a Rot attempting to snare him, and for a moment his mind got carried away, imagining that he could feel its dry, gnarled fingers coil around him in a last-ditch attempt to pull him in to its cell.

Panic leant his body a burst of pure adrenaline, and he bolted to his feet, running the last stretch of the room to the doors at the far end and rolling through the open doorway, brushing off the squirming maggots as he moved.

He sunk back into the shadows of the darkened corridor he now stood in, and paused for a moment, taking time to catch his breath, to regain his composure, and keep his runaway imagination in check. It also gave him enough time to make sure the sounds of his panicked run hadn't brought any unwanted attention. For five minutes the cellblock remained silent, and Bill gave a sigh of relief.

The darkness of the passageway surrounding him was broken by a flickering strobe light at the other side of the corridor, and next to that light, about a foot below the ceiling, there hung a dim green sign. It depicted a white silhouette of a man running towards the outline of a door, and Bill silently made a fist and pumped his arm up and down, realising that he had finally found a way out. If the map he had seen had been correct, it would lead to the car park, and hopefully *Colebrook's Runner* and the cache of weapons it carried.

He scuttled along the floor to the sign, found the door beneath it, then fumbled with the handle until it came away with a satisfying click. The door swung open, and Bill spilled out into the cool night air once more, this time the stench of death not as noticeable as it had been around the Dead Pit.

He was on a flat stretch of ground, the far expanses of the opening surrounded by either walls or towering barbed wire fences. A raised watchtower rose to the right of him, and as with the guardhouse at the pit, it had a white searchlight sweeping from side to side. The beam danced over the rows of inert vehicles, picking out details of cars, vans and bikes. One of the vans Bill recognised as the vehicle that had been used to bring him to the prison. Others were no doubt used for similar purposes, as most of the vehicles seemed to be bristling with mounted machineguns or crude weapons ideal for ramming other vehicles or ploughing through crowds of Rots. As the beam conducted its long, slow sweep, it picked out the telltale shape of a trailer, bulky and attached to an olive-green jeep, the combined vehicles armed with a pair of heavy machineguns.

"There she blows," whispered Bill, silently counting the length of time it took for the beam to conduct its sweep. There wasn't enough time to allow him to run to the trailer, but there was certainly enough to allow him to dive behind one of the other vehicles. He could work his way through the labyrinth of vehicles after that.

The light swept by once more, and Bill rushed for the closest car, quickly recovering after a stumbling start and rolling the last few feet, tucking his shoulders in tight as he did so. The concrete wasn't as forgiving as the wet mud of the pit, and he managed to tumble to a stop behind a battered old pickup truck just as the light flashed by. His leg ached around his wound, which had constantly taken a battering since he first received it, and he knew that he wouldn't be able to run very far or very fast. He mentally mapped out his route, waited for the next sweep, then moved, making it to a second hiding place, this time behind a low sports car. Could this car belong to Sylvester? Remembering the story, Bill peered inside, hoping that maybe one of the shotguns had been left in the vehicle, but it had been stripped bare of anything useful: even the seats were missing. He shook his head, and returned to the task at hand.

After another two timed run-and-roll movements, he was behind the trailer, and looking at the driver-side door of the vehicle. Smiling to himself, he limped around towards the back of the trailer, but then froze as he heard low voices.

He had been so busy concentrating on the task of getting to the trailer, he hadn't thought about whether there would be any additional guards in or around the vehicles. He dropped to the ground, his leg protesting in agony, and slowly rolled under the vehicle, listening to the voices of the men inside.

"Fire off a round and think of me," one voice chuckled, "Jesus, that's a good one. Who comes up with that shit?"

"Stop pissing around," a second voice scorned. "The more time you spend looking at those pictures of naked women, the more time we spend missing them dancing in there. Now grab the other end of that crate, help me move it."

A pair of heavy boots appeared on the ground by the door, crunching on the tarmac as they spun around and slowly backed away from the opened vehicle. The shuffles increased in speed and the owner of the feet cursed as the crate he carried slipped through his fingers and crunched to the floor. The wooden box cracked open along the side, a thick panel giving way as a clutch of bullets and pistols spilled out and clattered across the dark ground. Bill smiled as fortune cast a favourable hand, and a silenced pistol skidded under the vehicle, inches away from his hand. He reached out and grabbed it, hoping that it was already loaded. Drawing back the slide, he tilted the weapon to catch a glint of light from the patrolling beam, and smiled with satisfaction as the dull gleam of a brass case flashed at him.

"You stupid bastard," shouted one of the men. "Too busy eyeballing those fucking posters. Get down here, you dumb shit, pick up those weapons and put them back in the box. Jesus, why did I have to get stuck doing this with you?"

Another pair of heavy boots appeared by the crate, and a hand dipped into view, grabbing handfuls of bullets and tossing them back into the opened crate.

"Keep cleaning up, I'll go get the trolley. I don't trust you to help carry that. You'll probably get distracted, drop it on my foot and break it. Keep cleaning it up."

One of the men walked away from the vehicle, brisk steps, leaving the clumsy one to carry on retrieving the spilled contents. Bill saw his opportunity, and carefully rolled back out from beneath the vehicle, coming up on the side of the vehicle and rolling himself around the vehicle.

"Arsehole," muttered the man left to retrieve the contents of the crate. "Just because he wouldn't know what to do with a pair of tits if they had the instructions written on them. Fucking puff."

"No way to talk about one of your friends," Bill said in a hushed tone, stepping out from behind the vehicle and levelling the silenced pistol with the man's head. "Make one sound and I'll blow your head off. Now get back into the vehicle, c'mon, move."

The man looked up, and for a moment he paused. Bill thought that he might consider rushing him, and readied his trigger finger, not sure his aim would be on target in the darkness, despite the point-blank range. The man sighed, shrugged his shoulders and lifted his hands, clambering back into the vehicle and resigned to the fact he had been caught out. Bill followed, and slammed the man down on to one of the chairs, grabbing a nylon cable tie from Al's supply and wrapped it around his prisoner's wrists. He found an oily rag that Al normally used to clean his guns, and pushed it into his prisoner's mouth, securing it with a strip of duct tape.

Bill left his charge to sweat on the seat and grabbed a flashlight, forming a hood over the torch with one hand and rooting through the items that had been left in the vehicle. Grabbing a canvas bag, he filled it with what supplies he could find; bullets, handguns, medical supplies and a spare change of clothing for Angel. He pulled out a second canvas bag and trawled through the case outside, filling it with heavier weapons such as submachine guns and shotguns, before pulling out the large automatic weapon that Al seemed to favour. Slapping a drum of ammo in place and threading the chain of bullets through the awaiting receiver, he primed the weapon by heaving on the cocking mechanism before setting it down on the floor beside his feet.

"Jesus, Ellis, where the fuck are you?"

Bill flicked off the torch and spun around and glared at the opened doors to the rear of the trailer to see the second man approaching, carrying a folded metal gurney. He dropped it to the floor and approached the doors, unable to make out any of the details within the darkened vehicle. "Man, if I come in there and find you tugging at yourself, I'm going to rip your balls off and throw 'em in the dead pit."

Bill brought up his silenced pistol and levelled it off at the approaching man. He, in turn, reached for the combat shotgun that was slung around him. Was it possible that he had seen Bill's movement? He took a step closer, reaching for a plastic tube attached to his padded jacket and flicking a switch, a beam of light cutting into the darkness of the trailer and illuminating the startled shape of Bill and the prisoner on the chair. He froze, like a startled rabbit staring into a pair of oncoming headlights, and felt his heart hammer against his ribs as the man lifted his shotgun.

Survival instincts kicked in, and Bill snapped out of his stunned state, raising his aim and firing into the figure.

The weapon kicked in his hand, a muffled whisper followed, and a round from the weapon lodged itself in his target, making him stumble backwards and drop his shotgun. It wasn't a mortal wound, but with the light glaring in his face Bill had known he wouldn't score a lucky hit. He stepped forwards, following the recoiling man as he stared blankly at his wound, and fired again and again at him. The man spasmed and jerked as lead projectiles hammered his body, twisting and writhing as bones smashed and ruby red liquid splashed across the tarmac. A pair of bullets obliterated the man's head, and the partially decapitated corpse keeled over to one side, twitching sporadically before ceasing moving all together.

Bill spun back to face his captive, letting the spent magazine tumble from his smoking pistol, and then replacing it with a fresh one from one of the bags he had packed. Retrieving his flashlight, he switched it on and saw the fear-stricken face of the man, eyes flicking from the weapon to the opened doors, and where his friend had once stood.

"Keep your mouth shut and that won't happen to you," hissed Bill. What he had just said and done didn't feel right: it didn't feel like anything he would *ever* say or do. He'd never considered himself as a bully or a killer, but he'd adapted to this crazy world remarkably quick, and it seemed like he was becoming someone he never considered he would be. He never though he'd turn a gun on another human being, yet alone… how many had it been, thirty? Forty? And then there were all the undead on top of that. It was something he would have to reflect on later, when he had the time. When the lives of his friends weren't in danger.

"You know where they took us? A prison or a cell somewhere on the other side of the dead pit?"

The man nodded, his dark eyes wide with terror.

"Take me there. Try to mess this up and you can join your friend. Now get up and no sudden movements. Go on."

XV
BACK INTO HELL

"Sometimes we're too late and we need to burn the whole place down. Everyone is potentially infected: none can be allowed to leave."

I

"He can't be much longer," Angel finally announced, pulling her jacket - Bill's jacket - tightly around her body. The cold of the concrete she sat on was numbing her legs, and no one else had offered her any further protection from the chill of the cell. Only Clive had offered her a seat on the bench, which she would have accepted, despite the fact it had been next to Al. The moment Clive had risen from the seat, however, Al had stretched out and lay down on the bed, his hands clasped behind his head and a grin on his face.

Bastard, she thought to herself as she looked at the reclining Marine. He was fast asleep now, or at least pretending to be.

"Must be dead," muttered Sylvester. Angel scowled at him, but his gaze was fixed on the ceiling. He hadn't said much since she'd been thrown into the cell, he'd only asked about the dancers she'd been locked up with, one with dark hair who went by the name of Terri. As soon as she told him she'd only spoken to a woman with red hair, he didn't approach her for any other conversation.

"I've told you, the kid can look after himself. He's a good fighter, and he's got balls. Ask the bitch, she'll tell you."

Angel looked towards Al. She knew he hadn't really been asleep, just taking in the meagre conversation and waiting for the right time to throw his comments in.

"You all seem to have a lot of faith in this one man," said Sylvester, clambering to his feet and sighing heavily. "You may know him really well, but I've only known him for a few hours before he vanished off into the air vents. Jesus, how do we even know he's going to come back here for us? Who's to say he isn't just going to drive out of here on whatever you rode in here on?"

"He will come back," sighed Al, opening his eyes and standing up. He waived to Angel, motioning for her to take possession of his vacant seat. She smiled by way of acceptance, then quickly climbed up on to the bed before the Marine decided to change his mind. "Firstly, he's my Sergeant, an honorary Marine, and we don't leave anyone behind. He'll come back for his commanding officer. He'll come back for buddy there," he said, pointing to the snoring tanker driver who had propped himself up in the corner. "He'll come for him because the two of them are friends. And he'll come back for the bitch, too, because who's he gonna fuck if he hasn't got her? He'll come back, and he isn't dead. Just gotta have faith, isn't that right, Father?"

Clive put down the black book he read and nodded gently. "He will come back for his friends," he said, then turned towards Sylvester. "I know my friends came back for me."

"And what about when he does get back?" asked Sylvester. "What do we do then?"

"Break out. Get our gear together and break out of here."

"And Terri?"

"If she's with the dancers, then we'll get her out, too, with all the other dancers. Shit, I'm not leaving a roomful of pussy behind for the antichrist out there."

"Such a nice man," muttered Angel, his choice of words not especially flattering towards the females she had briefly met.

"Wassat?" shouted Garth, his head lolling over to one side and cracking into the wall. He snorted and sat upright, eyes wide and focused. He glared at Angel, his eyes wandering from her face, down to her exposed thighs, then back towards her face. "Still not back yet?"

"Not yet," she whispered, suddenly conscious of how much of her goose-bumped flesh on show, and trying to cover as much as she could without making it obvious. None of the other men in the cell had really shown any interest in her other than Garth, and his not-so-subtle glances were starting to annoy her just a little.

A sound broke the silence of the cell; two thumps on the other side of the door. Everyone froze, suddenly aware of the flurry of activity outside the cell, and threw confused looks at one another. Al stormed over to the cell door and pressed his head against the barrier that stood between them and freedom, trying to make out any further sounds from the other side.

"New plan, he announced, holding up his hand and trying to get the attention of everyone in the room. "I think someone's coming, sounds like just a couple of people. They come in here, then we jump the bastards and take their guns. Get up, buddy. Preacher-man, you and Spanners get over here, too. Hey bitch, you ever punched a guy?"

Sylvester rolled his eyes and slowly climbed to his feet, motioning to Clive to do the same. Angel pulled herself up and hung back behind Clive, not for protection from the approaching men, but so Garth couldn't get an eyeful of her behind. Clive looked over his shoulder and nodded slightly to her, obviously thinking that she was seeking physical protection. He winked, then looked back to the door, and waited.

Seconds passed.

Locks slid noisily to one side, and the door swung open, followed by a blur of motion as two dead men and a third man still alive was thrown into the cell: face battered and bloodied, mouth filled with a rag and taped closed, his wrists shackled together with a nylon tie. He rolled around on the ground, moaning and groaning quietly, and looked painfully over his shoulder, at the figure standing in the doorway and pointing a silenced pistol towards the ground, smoke curling up from the muzzle of the recently discharged weapon.

"Told you he'd be back," grinned Al, stepping towards Bill with his arms outstretched. He reached out and took the heavy machinegun from him, cradling it in a loving embrace as a parent would a child, before stepping aside and allowing his friend access to the room.

Bill sighed heavily, then dropped the two bags on to the floor, opening them up and handing the weapons out to everyone. He produced a mound of clothing and offered it to Angel, smiling awkwardly as she accepted it.

"I got you some clothing," he said, blushing slightly as his eyes danced briefly down to her thighs. "I thought you might need them."

She smiled back. At least his glances weren't as obvious or lingering as Garth. Strangely enough, she didn't mind Bill looking as much as she did anyone else. She turned around, removing the jacket and tossing it over her shoulder while she clambered into the clothing Bill had brought her. It was a tight, one-piece body suit, a deep purple in colour. While it covered her skin, it didn't leave anything to the imagination regarding the actual shape of her body. Bill seemed to blush even more as he realised what he'd brought, and offered a shrug by way of explanation.

"I just grabbed the first thing I could find. I didn't have much time. I guess this is why I never bought any clothing for Jenny."

"It'll do," she said, grabbing one of the submachine guns Bill had brought. "At least, until we get out."

"Okay," announced Al, who had taken up position at the open door, his oversized weapon swinging lightly from left to right. The two guards who had kept watch over the door had both been shot in the face, and Al and quickly relieved them of their weapons, strapping the assault rifles over his back. "We find our stuff, get the girls, and blow this shit hole. We've got an appointment with the Marines to keep."

"Find our stuff?" asked Angel, not quite sure what Al meant. "We've got all the weapons we need to get out of here, why do we need to find any of our other stuff?"

"They've got my handgun, for a start," said Al, looking down on the squirming man that had been left on the floor to his own designs while the rest of the group helped themselves to the weapons cache. "You know where they've taken our gear, asshole?"

The man on the floor stared at Al, but didn't respond.

"I want to know, I want my handgun back."

"Jesus, Al, we've got enough weapons to get us out of here, what's so special about that gun of yours?" asked Bill as he dished out a handful of magazines.

"The *Colebrook Cannon* is my lucky charm. I don't go anywhere without it."

"This is the gun you had on you when your helicopter was shot down?" asked Bill, pausing in his duties and lowering himself on to one of the beds as he replaced his jacket. Angel couldn't help but notice that the wound he carried had opened up again, staining his already dirty jeans with fresh blood. "The same lucky charm you had with you when we were captured by these guys? It doesn't sound like a good luck token to me."

"My gun isn't the only thing they've stashed," said Al, leaning closer to Bill and lowering his voice. Angel strained her ears to hear what was being said. "I didn't want to mention this in front of your new girlfriend, but they also took your rucksack, which has a picture of your old girlfriend in it. The only photo you have, if I remember rightly. Are you still happy to blow this joint without grabbing your gear?"

Bill didn't say anything to further the argument. With a grin, Al leant forwards and tore the gag from the captive, levelling the barrel of his large machinegun with his head. "Where's our stuff?"

"Guard station," the man blurted out, eyes fixed on the wavering barrel of the weapon. "Everything was taken to the guard station. I can take you there," he added, hopefully. Sylvester shook his head, replacing the gag and moving Al's weapon to one side. "I used to work here, I know where the guard station is. We can leave him here, we don't need him to help us."

"So I can kill him?" asked Al, grinning sadistically and grabbing one of the pistols. "Seems a shame to waste one of the big rounds on him, especially when there's all these spare weapons. Just a quick nine millimetre between the eyes should do it."

"You can't kill him in cold blood," hissed Angel, stepping in front of the Marine and raising her arms to protest. Clive agreed, and stepped forwards so he stood beside the protesting woman.

"I wouldn't think twice about blowing a hole through Bill's whore," said Al, reluctantly stepping back, "But I wouldn't shoot a man of the cloth. I've got enough enemies around here to worry about a vengeful God wanting a piece of my ass. So what do we do with him?"

"We leave him locked up in the cell," said Bill, standing up and dragging one of the dead guards from outside into the increasingly cramped room. Garth nodded to himself and stepped up to the opened doorway, reluctantly grabbing a second corpse from outside and tentatively dragging it in.

"Jesus, he's still warm and soft," moaned Garth. "Feels disgusting."

"Stop whining," hissed Al, replacing the gag in the mouth of the squirming and protesting prisoner. Angel wasn't sure if he was talking to Garth or the man on the floor.

"What if he manages to wriggle out his ties?" Angel asked, watching as the burly Marine tightened the nylon tag around his wrists. Al looked up briefly, snorted, and returned to his work. "You hear something, Bill?"

"Christ's sake," Bill muttered, slowly looking from Al to Angel, then back again. "I thought you would have got over this shit by now."

"Apparently we haven't," smiled Al, grinning more to himself then anyone else.

"She's right," said Sylvester, oblivious to the game Al played when it came to Angel talking to him. "I've seen men dislocate their shoulders to escape straightjackets, break their thumbs to slip a pair of handcuffs. All he needs to do is get his hands free and he can rip that gag from his mouth and scream blue bloody murder until someone comes and lets him out. Then we're screwed, our cover's blown, and we've got the whole prison looking for us. They catch us, and it's a one-way trip to the Baptist and his twisted workshop."

"The Baptist's dead," Bill muttered casually, loading his submachine gun and clearing the breech. "Shot him in the guts, left him to die, but he infected himself. He's probably going to be up and active in a couple of hours again. Other than that, the Messiah needs to find himself a new right-hand man."

"Way to go," Al said, smiling and clapping Bill on the back before returning his attention to their prisoner. "No, we'll have to make sure that son of a bitch can't get free, and if he does, that he can't remove his gag."

Without a second thought, Al grabbed the mans hand, and with a nauseating crack, wrenched one of his fingers backwards so it was at ninety degrees with the back of his hand. His eyes bulging wide open, he managed a muffled scream of agony from behind the tape over his mouth before blacking out. Feeling sickened, Angel turned away from the Marine so she couldn't watch the torture any more, but counted another nine stomach-churning cracks before the Marine announced he was finished. From the corner of her eyes, Angel could see a pair of pale hands, fingers twisted and broken, bent at painful and unnatural angles.

"Was that really necessary?" asked Garth, a disgusted expression on his pale face.

"Couldn't kill him, could I?" said Al, "The preacher and the prostitute wouldn't let me. I had to incapacitate him some other way. By breaking his fingers, he can't get the tape off *if* he escapes the ties, and he certainly wouldn't be able to fire a gun or help aid in any search for us. Plus, he passed out after the first finger, so he won't really feel the rest until he wakes up."

"Sadistic bastard," muttered Sylvester, hefting the shotgun he held and storming out the cell. "C'mon then, the station's this way. And don't forget to lock the door after you. Last thing we want is for that cripple to come crawling after us."

II

Sylvester moved quickly through the corridors of the prison, occasionally taking the wrong turn and forcing him and the group to backtrack. Al muttered and cursed each time Sylvester took them back the way they came, often insinuating that they be better off getting there themselves without a guide. Clive had taken him to one side, advising that it had been some time since he had been in the prison, that the released prisoners had carried out some considerable renovation work since then, and he shouldn't be so hard on him. While Sylvester appreciated his friend looking out for him, he knew he could fight his own battles, and unlike some of the other people in the group, the large Marine didn't intimidate him.

He remembered the stories Al had told them while in the cell, tales of guerrilla warfare in Brazil and the many prisoners the Marines took. He couldn't help but wonder if the people Al had labelled 'Bebops' received the same hospitality as the man Bill had brought, and for a brief moment he thought that Al was more monstrous then the gang. Then he remembered Terri, her being forced to dance and perform for the self-proclaimed Son of God, and decided while he was certainly barbaric and maybe a touch sadistic towards people he didn't care about, there were people worse than Al.

The corridors of the prison leading towards the guard station were strangely devoid of life. If the man had been telling the truth about the location of their equipment, he couldn't work out why it wouldn't be well guarded, especially in a building predominantly inhabited by thieves. A few people did stumble into their path, some heavily intoxicated and reeking of alcohol, and each didn't prove to be in much of a state to put up a fight. Al, Bill and Angel were pretty quick to put a few bullets in them using the silenced pistols Al had insisted upon. Both Garth and Clive seemed reluctant to turn their weapons on the gang members, the latter because of his firm religious beliefs, the former because of his apparent cowardice. They didn't shy from the duty of hiding the bodies in shadows or smaller storage cupboards, however, and this gave Clive the chance to bless the body and perform the sign of the cross in a hastened version of the last rites.

"We're here," Sylvester finally announced in a whispered voice, coming to a stop at a T-junction in the corridor. "It's to the right of this junction, a heavy metal door. I've stopped here because it's bound to be guarded."

"Okay," whispered Al, sinking to his knees and motioning for the rest of the group to come and join him. It appeared to Sylvester that Al tried to maintain control over his group, but the balance of power often swayed over towards Bill: Garth seemed reluctant to give any orders, and Angel was all but ignored by Al. "What's the plan?"

Sylvester laughed softly to himself and looked towards Bill, guessing that this was one such switch of leadership. Bill simply shrugged his shoulders, and looked around the group, offering the decision to anyone else who felt brave enough to make the decision.

"Full frontal assault," suggested Angel. "We open up with our big guns."

"That's a brave move, you crazy bitch," Al said, smirking. "See, this is why you're never asked your opinion. They're always wrong."

"Jesus, they're going to know we're free sooner or later. Won't if be easier to just blast the living shit out of them instead of skulking around in the shadows?"

"She's right," Sylvester said. "We've come this far without the alarm being raised, but once we get all your stuff, what are we going to do? If it's easier to just open up with the heavy weapons…"

"Three goals. Kill that fuckhead Messiah," said Al, raising three fingers as he began to count off his aims. "Get the dancers out their holding cell, and kill as many of these bastards as we can so we get a clear run to our rendezvous."

"All those goals mean exposing ourselves to the gang," said Bill, looking from Al to Angel as he talked, "But it doesn't mean that we have to do so before we need to."

"Fuck, no, I say go with the bitch's idea," said Al. Both Bill and Angel looked at him in surprise, and Sylvester couldn't help but join in with the confused looks. From what he had seen, this occurrence was a rarity in itself. Al responded by shrugging his shoulders by way of an apology. "At least this way I get to open up with the old SAW," he said, stroking the lengthy barrel of his heavy machinegun. "Kill any guards there, break into the room, grab our stuff. Then the fun begins."

"And how do we go about the rest of your master plan?" asked Sylvester. He tried to keep the sarcasm out of his voice, but got the feeling that he failed as Al scowled at him.

"Just storm the prison with guns blazing."

"That's an original plan," said Clive. He didn't try at all to hide his sarcastic tone, but Al chose to ignore that. Without another word, Al plastered a wide grin on his face and stood to his full height, manually cycling a round into the chamber of his weapon and strolled around the corner of the junction, finger coiling lightly around the trigger.

The Messiah lay back on a plush red couch, his fingers coiling and twisting around the dark hair of the Seraphim who currently had her face buried in his groin. The sensation that she created wasn't at all unpleasant, and especially soothing on the wound inflicted by the auburn harlot who had come so close to castrating him. The girl currently servicing him had been warned to be gentle, or else she too would meet the same fate.

The Baptism, he mused silently to himself. He had grown tired of watching the surgical procedures after the first seven or eight conversions at the skilled hands of the Baptist, and hadn't viewed any since then. The conversion of the woman and her friends, however, would be one he would take great pleasure in watching. He would convert all but one, who would be forced to watch his friends turn. They, in turn, would feast on him before their protective shrouds were attached.

A smile crept across his lips as he thought of the woman's flesh puckering, flaking apart, and weeping a pale pink liquid, all happening as he watched the agonising transformation. The smile broadened as he felt his excitement build, felt his muscles tense and twitch, then shudder as he felt his climax release. He tilted his head back and moaned slightly in pleasure, his hands gripping the head of the woman and keeping her down. She started to struggle, tried to lift her head, but *he* was in charge, not the girl, and he would say when she could move.

With a grunt, he finally let go, and she shifted her weight so she was on her knees, wiping her mouth with the back of her hand, and looking expectantly at the Messiah. He smiled, reached forwards and traced the shape of the cross on the girl's forehead. His fingers made contact with beads of sweat, and he drew his hand back to his mouth, tasting the sweetness of her perspiration.

Sweet as honey, he thought. All his Seraphim tasted as sweet, weather it was their sweat or their body. Far sweeter than any woman he'd had before the coming of Armageddon, which only proved to him that they were gifts from his father, the Lord. He still missed the women from before the awakening of the Chosen, their appetite for life and the fight they put up. He knew that the Seraphim had access to all manners of drugs and stimulants, many chose to use them to dull any pain he may chose to inflict on them. The Messiah felt the drugs only enhanced experiences such as this, and the sensations augmented by drugs only brought him even closer to God. This particular one had filled her system with opiates, expecting a hard time, and had been lucky so far. She was expecting it. It would be a shame to not deliver.

With a sudden flurry of movement, the Messiah leapt to his feet and lifted the woman to her feet, knocking her across the room and pressing her face against the wall. He kicked her legs open, pressed himself against her, tried to force himself on her…

Then cast her roughly aside. She was too compliant, the drugs was beginning to take all of the Seraphim's will to fight. Maybe he would consider restricting their access to drugs.

A loud banging on the door drew his attention from the girl. He looked up, grabbed his cloak and wrapped it around himself, then stood beside the fallen woman.

"Come," he bellowed in an authoritative tone. The door creaked open, and one of his guards skulked into his room, his head bowed low and eyes locked on the floor. Ordinarily, his guards were not ashamed to try and catch a glimpse of whichever Seraphim he was currently 'entertaining'. This behaviour was not at all characteristic of the guards, which suggested something had happened.

"Why do you disturb me?"

The guard shuffled his feet uncomfortably, then gingerly lifted his head.

"I have some disturbing news, sire. We were taking one of the Chosen to be Baptised but when we got there, we found the Baptist was… well, he was… he's been shot."

"Dead?" asked the Messiah, feeling his heart quicken.

"Undead, sir," the guard muttered, returning his gaze to the ground. "It looks like he tried to Baptise himself."

"Where is he now?"

"We managed to get him into the dead pit," the guard admitted. The Messiah nodded solemnly to himself. It was a fitting end for his first officer, to be placed in the ranks of the Chosen, of so many soldiers he had anointed. But who would possibly dare to slay his right hand man? In a building full of murderers and rapists, everyone was a suspect, but who would have the balls to go up against the orders of the man who commanded them all? Anyone who he felt may be a threat to his leadership, he had Baptised first.

"Has the killer been caught? Any witnesses?"

"No witnesses," the guard said, shaking his head slowly. "But there's more.

"We had two men unloading the captured vehicle. One of them has been found dead in the vehicle. The other found gagged and tied up in one of the holding cells with another two dead bodies. That was in the holding cell the prisoners were held in,"

"They're escaped?" The Messiah asked. He knew the answer already, and he could feel his blood begin to boil. He didn't know how they had managed to do it, and didn't care. All he cared about was that he got hold of the escapees and threw them kicking and screaming into the dead pit. Especially if they had the heretic with them: he had forgotten all about him and his 'friend', though he remembered the woman that had came in with them.

The radio hanging from the belt of the guard blared to life, a staccato of noise and static, a cacophony of blasphemes and gunfire as some of the guards stationed in the prison were assaulted. The deliverer of the bad news lifted the unit to his ear, twisted his face as he tried to make out the words that came through, then dropped it to the floor.

"The prisoners, lord, they're at our armoury."

"They come for my weapons, they seek to steal what is mine. Thou shalt not steal, even the heretic should know that. Don't just stand there; get them. Take as many men as you need."

The guard nodded and spun on his heels, ran from the room and hurriedly spoke into his radio as he went. The Messiah turned his attention to the woman on the floor, who had been taking in the whole conversation, and noted that her eyes were no longer as dilated as they had been. Perhaps the drugs were beginning to wear off, which meant that she might put up more of a fight. Grinning to himself, he clenched his fists and made his way over to her cowering form, his excitement rising at the prospect of a conquest just like the good old days.

"Hurry up," shouted Al as he knelt by the doorway to the guard station, crouching by the body of the single guard that had been on duty and sweeping the barrel of his machinegun from side to side. "Grab what shit you need and get moving. The talk box on that dead Bebop's spouting all kinds of shit about backup and they know we're loose. They also know the Baptist's dead. They're gonna come down on us like so much shit…"

"Stay calm," Bill shouted, finding his rucksack and checking to make sure all his possessions were still in it. Binder, change of clothing, photograph, vitamins, everything seemed to be there. He grabbed a handful of the pills and tossed them into his mouth as he watched the rest of his friends appraise the cache of weapons. He was quite surprised that Al had only chosen his own handgun and none of the other weapons on display. Having said that, the Marine already had an extra two assault rifles and a silenced pistol, as well as the heavy machinegun. Bill supposed even the gun-happy Marine had a limit to what he would use. Or what he could carry.

"I'm ready," announced Angel, slinging her rifle over her shoulder and hefting a pair of submachine guns, their stocks extended and braced against her forearms. Al glanced over his shoulder and saw what she carried, and laughed, shaking his head.

"Crazy bitch. Two guns at once? This isn't some fucking Hong Kong gun-fu movie, bitch; it's real life, you really think you can fire two at once?"

Angel didn't respond; she simply made sure she had enough ammunition stored in the pouches on her belt before joining him in his watch. Garth followed suit as he took up position with his own assault rifle, then leant over and grabbed the sputtering radio from one of the dead guards. He held it up to his ear, listening to the constant chatter that came through.

"Are you guys nearly ready?" he asked, "The locals are getting restless."

Both Clive and Sylvester nodded their heads, each totting weapons of their own choice. Sylvester carried a bulky shotgun similar to the one Bill had, with another strapped over his back and a bandoleer of shells strung over his shoulder. Clive had a single handgun tucked into the waistband of his trousers.

"You might want to grab something a little more powerful then that, Preacher-man," Al said, waving towards the handgun.

"Killing people may come easy to you, but for someone like me, it's not an option. The bible states thou shalt not kill," he said. Al shook his head in disbelief.

"It also says you should do unto others as they would do to you, doesn't it?" he asked. "Jesus, man, that book's full of contradictions, you can use it to back any argument. Like that religious shithead out there. You've gotta be able to adapt in this game, preacher, and that means you gotta be able to do things you wouldn't normally, am I right kid?"

Bill looked up from the loading of his weapons and nodded. Clive remained unconvinced, and didn't make a move to collect any other weapons. Al stood from his vigil, grabbed one of the larger and bulkier of the handguns and thrust it into the stomach of Clive, not hard enough to wind him, but hard enough to make him clutch at his stomach and grip the weapon.

"Automatic handgun," Al said, returning to the doorway. "That bulky thing on the top's the magazine. Hundred rounds, rapid fire. If you don't take anything else, take *that*. Now come on."

Clive followed to the door, shaking his head slowly as he left the room. Sylvester followed, and Bill grabbed his arm, pulling him back. He produced the locket he had previously found and handed it over.

"Sly, right?"

He nodded, and accepted the locket. He turned it over, flicked it open, and grinned at the photograph. "Was this in here, with everyone's stuff?"

Bill didn't answer.

"Bill?"

"No," he finally answered. Better to tell the truth then to string him along. "It was on a bench in the Baptist's operating room." He didn't say anything else; he didn't feel like he had to. Sylvester wrapped the golden chain around the locket, slipped it into one of the pockets of his jeans, and wiped his eyes. Tears trickled down his cheeks faster then he could mop them up, and he sat down on a large green metallic crate, sobbing gently to himself. Bill stepped back from him, stood by the door with his submachine gun drawn and aimed towards the junction. It was the only way into the guard station, which worked as both a blessing and a curse to them while they stood and waited. Though no one could sneak around behind them, it meant they would have no alternative escape route, should they become grossly outnumbered. Al had taken great pleasure in pointing this out as soon as he had taken the watch, and had urged everyone to hurry up several times. Again, he lumbered into the room and opened his mouth to urge everyone to hasten their preparation.

"We're waiting for you, Spanners, c'mon, hustle."

"Give us a minute," Bill said, standing up and placing a hand on Al's chest, pushing him back. "He's just found out Terri's dead."

"Who?"

"His wife," hissed Bill, "Christ, don't you listen to people's stories?"

"Only those that interest me," he admitted, shrugging his shoulders. "She's dead, we're not. He can mourn later, tell him to grab his shit and we'll get going."

"You really are an insensitive prick, aren't you?"

"Grade A asshole," he said with a grimace. "We've all got mourning to do, but we'll do that on the helicopter that gets us out of here. If he doesn't pull himself together, we'll leave him here."

He stormed back into the corridor outside, and Bill followed, leaving Sylvester on his own.

"Preacher-man," Al growled, tapping Clive on the shoulder, "Your friend needs you. You've got two minutes to pull him around, or else the pair of you get left."

Clive nodded and jogged into the station, leaving the four friends alone in the corridor, each fumbling with their weapons. They stopped as soon as they heard the thunderous sounds of footsteps nearing the junction, accompanied by shouts and expletives.

"Here they come," shouted Al, taking refuge behind one of the large metal crates he had removed from the weapons store to use as barricades. Bill hunkered down beside him, and urged Angel and Garth to do the same behind the second box, bringing his weapon about to bear on the opening.

The first of the approaching men rounded the junction with his weapon aimed high, and was instantly cut down as Al opened up with his weapon, smashing the body with high calibre rounds. More men followed, and each met with the same fate from the high-powered weapon.

"Ha, just like a fucking shooting gallery! That's right, keep 'em coming," shouted Al, rattling through more rounds. The corridor wasn't very wide, and it wasn't long until mounds of corpses, surrounded by a blanket of bodies had blocked the way. This made the approach for the attackers difficult, and their onslaught quickly changed from a full assault to one or two men trying to pick their way through the piles of the dead.

"There can't be many more," insisted Bill, inserting a fresh magazine into his weapon. Al nodded in agreement, and pulled a small brown cylinder from the combat webbing he wore. "Flash-bang," he muttered. "Close your eyes and cover your ears. This'll stun the bastards, making an easy mop-up for us."

Without another word, he twisted the tube and flung it into the opening of the junction, smiling as it bounced off one of the corpses and tumbled to the ground on the other side. With his eyes shut tight, Bill heard the muffled thump of the device as it went off, and uncovered his senses to hear the confused screams of their would-be assailants.

"Easy pickings now," Al said as he stood and swaggered towards the junction, drawing his pistol with the intention of putting down the incapacitated assailants. Taking aim for his first shot, he was knocked to one side as Sylvester barged forwards and stepped in front of Al, playing his weapon from side to side, pouring white-hot flames into the corridor, bathing the confined space in fire. The sprinklers running the length of the ceiling burst to life and doused the corridor with a thick mix of water and foam, hissing as the liquid came into contact with the crackling flames and quickly extinguished the fire. By then, the fire had done the damage, and not one of the attacking men had been left alive. Bill made his way towards the junction, and gently pried the portable incinerator from Sylvester's hands. Al followed behind him, and looked down the corridor at the mounds of smoking and partially charred corpses. A few writhed and moaned, and Al quickly dispatched these with a spray of machinegun fire before lowering his weapons and taking the flame-thrower from Bill.

"Where'd you get this from?" he asked, carefully turning the device over in his hands. "High quality, looks like Marine-tech. Didn't think we were allowed to use these outside the rainforests, it must be here from the black market... But who the fuck would want to buy an incinerator unit?"

"Marines used them to burn the dead in the streets during the riots," Garth muttered. "I saw it once..."

Bill ignored Al, and instead placed a hand on Sylvester's shoulder. He shrugged it off, but didn't make a move to step away; he kept his gaze fixed on the smouldering corpses of the gang.

"You all right?" asked Angel, coming up on the other side of Sylvester and laying a gentle hand on his other shoulder. He didn't make as much of an effort to shrug off her hand. He didn't acknowledge either Bill or Angel, simply strolled off into the corridor.

"Hey, Preacher-man," hissed Al as Clive walked past. "Keep an eye on your friend. I think he's flipped out. Try and keep a leash on him, at least until we get out."

"He's just learned his wife was turned into one of the Messiah's hollow men," said Clive. "He's got every reason to be acting the way he is."

"He's going to just walk into that hall and try to put a cap in the religious nut's ass. He's going to walk out there like he's some kind of unstoppable killer robot, and not stop until either he's dead or the crazy in charge of this nuthouse is. He strolled out there and deep-fried them with a flame-thrower, oblivious to the fact they were stunned: if they hadn't been, he'd be dead right about now, and you'd be wiping his brains offa the wall."

Clive didn't respond, but jogged off down the corridor after his friend. Bill and Angel retired to the proximity of Al, who motioned Garth to join with them.

"He's a loose cannon," hissed Al in a low tone. "More so than me. A Goddamn liability. If the Preacher-man can't keep him in line, then I'll have to do something myself."

"Like break all his fingers?" asked Angel, ejecting the spent magazine from one of her submachine guns and replacing it.

"Fuck you, bitch," Al snapped, flicking his middle finger at her before carrying on. "The four of us work good as a team. Despite the fact the three of you aren't as experienced in combat as I am, buddy here's a coward and you're a prick-tease, you can all look after yourself. If he doesn't pull his shit together, we'll have to leave him behind."

"That's a bit callous," said Bill. "Christ, we've all lost someone close to us, but that happened weeks ago for us, we've got through it. If you met me when Jenny died, you would have said the same thing about me."

"Whatever," said Al, turning from the conversation and returning into the guard station to retrieve the crate Sylvester had previously sat upon. "We've got some explosives in this here box," he said, "Military grade shit, with detonators and everything else we need. Should be enough to shake up this prison and maybe rock the foundation."

"You've got a plan?" asked Garth, gently handling the incinerator and attaching a leather strap to it before slinging it over his shoulder. "I bet it's suicidal."

"Only if I get killed doing it," he laughed, tearing open the crate and unpacking the rectangular blocks of white explosives before attaching timed detonators to them and handing them out. "Twist the dial to set the detonator, just like an egg timer. Stick them somewhere vital, but make sure they're out of sight. We're looking for key positions, or in areas of heavy traffic. Main corridors, passageways or densely populated areas: the meeting hall that they watch the dancers in could be a prime target, if we can set any there. You want to take that room, bitch?"

"What about the place they keep the dead?" asked Sylvester, reappearing at the junction with his friend by his side. "You said the recreation yard, right? What about blasting a hole through to there and letting the dead run through the building? Use his twisted delusions against him."

"Damn fine idea," admitted Al, tossing him a few explosive charges towards him. "You get there and set the explosives, take the preacher as backup, make sure the dead get in. They'll hunt out the living from there; it's what they do. We need to find the dancers. If the bitch can tell you the rough location, you think you can give us directions, and meet us in the hall when I give the signal? You'll know the signal when I give it. I'm not very subtle."

Sylvester nodded, and after listening to Angel's brief location of the cell he drew a map on the back of a piece of crumpled paper retrieved from Bill's binder and pushed it into Al's hand. He exchanged it for a pair of radio headsets, and motioned for them to put them on.

"Radio silence," he cautioned, "Just to make sure we're not detected until we *want* to be detected. Stick to the shadows, watch your back. And preacher, keep an eye on Spanners, if he wigs out, then you can break the radio silence to tell us. Other than that, stay sharp and keep 'em peeled. Now go."

Clive and Sylvester took some extra explosive charges, then after that vanished through the corridor of smoking dead.

"Think we're going to see them again?" asked Garth. Al shrugged his shoulders.

"Maybe, maybe not. C'mon, there's some damsels in distress, and we've got a shitload of explosives we need to use. Don't drag your heels."

"Yessir," muttered Angel, falling in line behind Al and mock-saluting him. Bill grinned inwardly, and headed off back into the bowels of the prison behind the Marine and his hand drawn map.

III

"Told you we'd get here," whispered Al, crouching in the shadows of a long corridor leading to a cell guarded by one man armed with an assault rifle. "Apparently the Messiah doesn't value his prized dancers as high as I thought. Just the one guard."

"I can take him out," whispered Angel as she reached for her sniper rifle and brought it about to bear on the guard. She adjusted the screen on the lens and lifted it to her face, a pale green light washing across her eyes as she sighted her target.

"This thing kitted out with a suppresser?" asked Al, tapping the muzzle of the weapon with one of his fingernails.

"Of course," Angel replied, her hushed voice laced with a hint of false hurt. She squeezed a single round off, and Bill watched from his hiding place, impressed as the man crumpled wordlessly to the ground.

"Rest of the corridor empty?" Al asked, motioning to Angel to scan the area with the enhanced scope on her rifle. She did so, and nodded, adding a verbal confirmation in case Al couldn't see her movements in the darkness that shrouded them. Bill tried his best to make out any details himself in the dark corridor, but couldn't come up with anything other than the few meagre details picked out by the swinging bulbs that lined the ceiling. With a little concentration and the minimal use of his imagination, Bill could almost imagine that he was in a corridor deep in a rocking boat in the middle of the ocean. If only he were: he could deal with the seasickness he was prone to far better than bouts of intense life-or-death combat.

"Snap out of it, kid," whispered Al, clicking his fingers next to Bill's ears and bringing him out of his trance. "We're going in. Weapons up, eyes open."

Bill nodded and slowly advanced on the doorway and the fallen guard, weapon flitting between the door and the corridor beyond.

"I can't wait to see these women," whispered Al. Bill could see the gleam in his eyes, and the glimmer of dull light reflecting on the moistness of his lips as he almost drooled in anticipation. "Red heads, brunettes, blondes, I'm not fussy, I'll fuck 'em all," he muttered, hand coiling around the doorknob and working the device, pushing it open into the room and slowly stepped inside.

The first thing to strike Bill was the harsh and acrid stench of smoke as it rolled out the confined room. Part of the odour Bill identified as marijuana, knowing the smell from Al and Garth as they both smoked the occasional joint together at night. He couldn't identify the rest of the smells, but the myriad of different bouquets swirled around his head and rested heavily in his mouth, bringing a bitter taste and an unpleasant swirling sensation in his head. The air was heavy with drugs, and he felt the longer he stood around in the room, the more intoxicated he would become.

The inhabitants of the room sat or lay on the few pieces of sparse furniture that decorated the room. Each still wore their skimpy golden briefs, though some had managed to get hold of a negligee or a silk dressing gown. Al's eyes almost doubled in size as he took in the details of the room, and Garth whimpered softly to himself.

"Say, darlin', I thought you'd be dead by now, for sure."

Bill looked around and saw one of the women approach them, sporting coppery-red hair and a smoking cigarette in one hand. As she approached, the lace gown she wore slid open, and Bill wasn't quite sure where to look. No matter where his eyes flickered to, he always seemed to end up looking at something he didn't feel he should. The woman pushed past him and addressed Angel directly, reaching out and taking one of Angel's hands in her own.

"Laurie said you'd been taken to be baptised, hon. What happened?"

"They took me," Angel agreed. "Put me in with my friends first, though."

"I broke them out," Al said, stepping between the two women and holding out his hand. "Sergeant Colebrook, at your service. Friends call me Al, you can call me anytime."

The woman looked at his hand, but didn't accept it.

"It's all right, he's with me," Angel said. "We've come to get you out. We're breaking out, and you're coming with us. All of you."

A murmur went up along the crowd of women, and they started to move, some with more stability than others: clearly some of the women had filled their system with so much drugs they couldn't move properly. They went through draws and cupboards, gathering what few belongings that they had and tried to dress more appropriately: this was nigh on impossible, as most of their personal belongings, including clothing, had been stripped from them before being locked up.

"That's right," said Al, slowly guiding the women out the door and into the corridor. "Stay quiet, stick behind Bill and Garth. Bill's the guy who looks like shit at the minute, Garth's the little fat bald guy with the cap. Do as we say, we'll get out no problem, okay?"

As they passed Al by, some of the women smiled and nodded their thanks. One stopped beside him and leant on the wall next to him, arms folded across her chest to both increase the size of her breasts and hide the needle marks in her arm. She smiled softly at him, leaned her head to one side, then shifted her weight so she was resting on him, and not the wall. She beckoned to him, stood on her tiptoes so her lips were just centimetres in his ear, then whispered something Bill couldn't hear. He could only guess what it was that she had said, but the smile that spread across his face and the vigorous way in which he nodded his head only suggested that she had offered Al easy access to one of his favourite things. She didn't look like she had any guns or alcohol, so it must have been some kind of sexual favour.

With the six dancers outside their cell, Al slowly guided the party onwards towards where he thought the entrance to the hall would be. The woman with dark hair who was practically clinging to his arm promptly corrected any wrong direction he happened to take, and kept whispering promises to Al, who grinned and chuckled every so often.

"Stoned floozy," muttered Angel, who walked close to Bill, her rifle raised. Bill looked at her in surprise, raising an eyebrow.

"Jealous?"

"Just pissed off," she replied. "He made such a big deal about Sly losing it for a second, but flash a little flesh at him, and he's worse than him. At least Sly pulled himself together after a couple of minutes."

"Yeah," said Bill, nodding his head and finding himself secretly relieved at the fact she wasn't jealous. "Crazy bastard."

The journey through the corridors leading to the cell was carried in silence, apart from the occasional chuckle from Al and the high-pitched titter from the woman who clung to him.

They reached the final stretch of corridor that would lead them ultimately to the main hall, and Al held his hand up to call for a halt.

"Okay girls, you all hang back here, wait for us to give you the signal. Spanners, Preacher-man, you two there?" Al said, breaking the radio silence and clicking his radio to life. There was a pause for a moment, and then finally a response.

"We read you, Al," Clive's muffled response came over the airwaves, accompanied by a low buzz.

"Are all your explosives set?"

"Affirmative. They're all set to go off in about six minutes from now. We managed to put some in some interesting places. And you?"

"All but two are positioned," Al said, gripping one of the charges in his hand and patting the second that hung from his belt. "We should be ready for our grand entrance in a couple of minutes. Sit tight until then."

Al turned his headset away from his mouth and nodded towards the woman with dark hair, indicating he was talking to her. "How much further to the main hall?"

"The end of this corridor," she slurred, drugs still flowing in her system. "We'll be coming out behind his throne."

"Perfect," grinned Al, tossing the explosive charge over his shoulder. Bill stumbled forwards and caught it, glaring at the back of the Marine's head for acting so careless. "Hey kid, make sure that gets stuck on the back of Mister Jesus' throne. I want to make sure he gets a personal demonstration of what twenty pounds of plastic explosives is capable of."

Bill nodded, and started to knead the edges of the block of explosive as Al had shown him previously, preparing to adhere it to the wall behind the Messiah.

The darkened corridor twisted once more, and then the end of the tunnel could be seen. There wasn't the sound of music as Bill had expected, but he supposed it made sense, as the entertainment had been locked up. Without the dancers, what possible pleasure could the gang hope to achieve from just listening to music?

"It's quiet," hissed Al as they began their approach to the entrance. Firelight seemed to flicker in the room beyond, casting frightening and curious shadows across the threshold of the stone flooring. "Could be asleep?"

"They normally sleep in the hall," whispered the woman leading Al, "They get so drunk they can't move, so they sleep where they sit."

"Could work to our advantage," grinned Al. "Storm in, slaughter them all while they're sleeping, they don't put up a fight. Makes our lives easier."

"You'd willingly kill people as they sleep?"

"Not just anyone," hissed Al, trying to defend his actions. "That bitch is still alive, and I've seen her sleep plenty of times. Now, get that explosive in position. Then we'll give these bastards a wake-up call they'll remember for the rest of their life. All two minutes of it."

Bill did as he was told, lightly stepping forwards towards the opening and pressing the explosive charge against the wall beside the doorway. As he worked, he could hear the gentle murmur of conversation coming from the room beside him. Crouching low, he waved his friends on towards him. Al slipped the woman off his arm and quickly jogged forwards, his heavy boots making a gentle taping noise on the concrete ground. Angel followed him, then Garth, leaving the dancers to stay back together in a group. Al shuffled forwards and peered his head around the opening, quickly scanned from left to right, then took cover once more.

"Looks like they're getting ready for war. Armour's being handed out, guns loaded and primed. Looks like you're public enemy number one kid. I'd hate to be in your shoes right now."

"What do we do?" asked Garth, his voice shaking slightly. Bill knew he wasn't the most enthusiastic when it came to confrontation. If they had all been asleep, Garth would probably prefer to tiptoe through the sleeping masses. Combat definitely wasn't his forte.

"They're *getting* ready," said Al, bringing up his machinegun. "I didn't say they *were* ready. We can still get the drop on those sons of bitches, kill a few with an initial sweep, then put a shotgun against their leader's head and walk out. If they value the life of their head honcho, they'll let us leave unmolested."

"And if they don't?"

"If they don't, the explosions going off will hopefully create enough of a diversion for us to make our getaway. The trailer's still out there, isn't it?"

"Car park, I think," said Bill. "Outside, Sylvester should be able to get us out there."

"Great, " muttered Al. "Okay, same rule as with the Rots, aim for their heads. They're getting armoured up, so we're looking at people wearing Kevlar platting on their bodies. I figure there's about four minutes until the first explosions go off. C'mon, people, let's do this."

Without another word, Al stood and strolled through the doorway into the next room, his weapon barking to life as he swept it from left to right. Bill followed next, aiming his own weapon high and cutting back and forth across the crowd of men. They dived to the floor and rolled under tables, screaming and cursing as they were forced to take cover before retaliating with their own barrage of returning fire.

The pair rushed over to the nearest of the metal tables, and Al kicked it over, lowering himself behind the barrier and spraying the room with gunfire. Bill lay beside him, leaning out to one side and occasionally firing poorly aimed bursts of bullets towards the men. Al laughed as he fired his weapon, pausing momentarily to reload, then continued his relentless suppressive fire. From his vantage point, Bill could see there were already a few small mounds of dead bodies, many of which were being used as additional cover.

Al's continuous drone of gunfire became accompanied by deep shotgun blasts from the other side of the room, and Sylvester calmly strolled into the fray, firing shell after shell into the unprotected flank of the gang. Confusion went up along the enemy ranks, many not knowing what had hit them before their skulls were cracked open by a point-blank shotgun shell.

"Flanked the bastards," muttered Al, watching as Sylvester danced from overturned table to upturned bench, his gun continuously speaking. "Out-fucking-standing. Look at that bastard move."

"Where's Clive?" asked Bill, trying to get a clear shot at the rival gang members. With Sylvester on the other side of the room, he didn't want to risk taking any more shots in case he hit the wrong person. "Shouldn't he be helping us?"

"Probably sitting in the corner saying a little prayer," Al snarled bitterly. "At least his friend's worth a shit when push comes to shove."

Clive appeared on the other side of the room, running along the wall and sliding down on to the floor and vanishing behind a table. Bill couldn't help but notice he still carried the weapon Al had forced upon him, but he refused to lift and fire it.

"Where's Frank, anyway?" hissed Al, nodding his head towards the vacant throne of the main hall. The towering marble figure of the crucifixion still loomed over the black throne, dead eyes glaring down on the empty seat. "Shouldn't he be there, lording over his gang of rebels?"

"Might be dead already," suggested Bill. "Maybe he was in the middle of the crowd, picking his weapon out when you burst in."

"Because we're that fucking lucky, aren't we kid? And where are those two?"

Al glanced towards the opening behind the throne, waiting for Garth and Angel to emerge to join the fight, but there was still no sign of them.

"Are they guarding the girls?" asked Bill, seeing the direction of his partner's gaze and the confused look on his face. "I thought they'd be out by now."

"Son of a bitch," hissed Al, lowering his weapon to the ground and peering hard into the gloom of the corridor beyond. "We've been out-flanked."

Bill stared into the corridor from his cover, trying to see what Al was talking about, and saw the flap of a flowing white gown in the dark. He couldn't remember any of the dancers picking up a white robe, but at the same time he couldn't remember anyone *not* picking one up. Everything was moving pretty quickly, and Bill knew that they were all working against the clock with less than four minutes until the bombs started to cook off.

Bill wasn't at all pleased when he heard the booming voice of the Messiah calling to cease the fire, and watched as Angel and Garth marched out of the opening, followed by the dancers, and four armed men. The quartet wore long white cloaks and heavy looking Kevlar armour covering their thighs and chests. Their heads were covered with white helmets decorated with golden crosses painted on the sides, and the assault rifles they carried had also been painted white.

"I suggest you all hold your fire," growled the Messiah, his voice coming over the speakers dotted around the hall. "My paladins are the finest warriors the prison has to offer, and they're very proficient with their weapons. They could easily cut you all down before you even lift your weapons."

"I'd like to try that theory out," muttered Al, grudgingly lowering his machinegun. Bill lowered his own weapon, and saw in his peripheral vision that Sylvester and Clive did the same. They were all herded into the centre of the room at gunpoint, while the men in white took up a sentry position by the throne, and a hushed silence fell across the room as they awaited the arrival of the Messiah.

"Where is he?" whispered Al, looking briefly at his watch in annoyance. "I want to see his face when…"

"Shut up," growled one of the remaining gang members behind him, ramming the butt of his rifle into the base of his spine. Al half-snarled a response, pulled himself to his feet and looked towards Angel and Garth as they stood, hands placed on top of their heads.

"I'm glad you two were watching our six, it could've got ugly if someone managed to creep up behind us, stupid bastards."

"I told you to shut up," hissed the gang member again, this time pulling a knife from his belt and pulling it in towards Al's throat.

"Leave him," hollered the Messiah, appearing at the entrance behind the throne and sliding on to his cold seat, laying his hands down on to the arms of the chair and making sure the metal spikes pressed through the fresh wounds on his palms. He too wore white robes, with his hood pulled up over his head. He cleared his throat, closed his eyes, and seemed to mutter a prayer to himself before turning his attention to the recaptured prisoners.

"My Baptist is dead, my Seraphim tainted. Members of my army have been slaughtered at your hands. The Devil has sent his acolytes unto me to undo my work. Wolves in the clothing of sheep, I know the blasphemy of them which say they are Jews, and are not, but are of the synagogue of Satan."

"You quote the book," screamed Clive, taking a step towards the Messiah before being dragged roughly back by one of the gang members. "You quote it, but you don't know what it means."

"Heretic!" shouted the Messiah, pointing a curled and bloody finger at him. "Get thee behind me, Satan. Behold," he continued, peeling back the hood from his head and revealing a blond wig crowned with a wreath of barbed wire. Blood stained some of the pale tresses a deep red in colour, and he stood, arms outstretched in the dramatic recreation of the crucifixion that he often adopted. "His head and his hairs were like white wool, as white as snow, and his eyes were as a flame of fire; and his feet like unto a fine brass, as if they burned in a furnace, and his voice as the sound of many waters."

"Crazy fuck," muttered Al, glancing at his watch absentmindedly. Smiling to himself, then his friends, he nodded as the first of the explosions were set off, a distant blast muffled by the thick concrete walls of the prison. A series of further explosions sounded, seeming to get closer with each blast and the room they stood in started to shake. The Messiah looked startled, head spinning from side to side as he tried to pinpoint the location of the noises, then looked directly at the group of prisoners he had gathered before him.

"This is the Devil's work. The heretic, the harlot, the coward, the black man, all of them. What form of trickery is this?"

"C4, you crazy bastard," hissed Al, uneasily shifting from foot to the other. "Explosives. A bunch just sitting in your cache, not being used. Probably didn't even know what it was for."

"We put some above this hall, too, on the roof," Sylvester whispered to Bill. "We're going to have to get the hell out of here soon, before the roof starts coming down."

As if on queue, the first of the explosions above the main hall sounded, and a shower of heavy stone and debris spilled down into the room from above, followed by a thick black plume of smoke and soot as it drifted lazily down into the hall. Flaming wood toppled in through the hall, clattering to the ground and sending showers of sparks and spatters of flames across the ground. The gang surrounding them scattered, screaming as they tried to find some form of cover from the explosives.

The deep and resonating detonations above continued, cracking the ceiling wide open and showering heavy chunks of masonry into the hall, smashing tables and crushing anyone unlucky enough to be caught in one of the downpours. Even the Messiah's elite guard moved and sought cover, leaving their master exposed and alone. Bill, Angel and Al quickly recovered their discarded weapons, while Garth and Sylvester gathered the panicking dancers together and tried to guide them away from the rapidly deteriorating room.

"What's happening?"

"You like quoting from Revelation?" asked Clive, standing defiant amidst the crumbling ruins and falling chunks of smouldering rubble. Bill paused from his task of retrieving the weapons to watch Clive, and for a moment he had a vision of a defiant preacher amidst the apocalypse, with smoke and fire raining down around him. His eyes darkened, obscured by the shadows cast from the flickering flames that were rapidly consuming the room. "The first angel sounded, and there followed hail and fire mingled with blood, and they were cast upon the earth."

The whole scenario couldn't have been choreographed better if it had been planned out for a movie stunt. As soon as Clive had finished speaking, the explosive charge on the wall behind the throne burst to life, breaking down the wall and sending chunks of masonry crashing into the back of the Messiah. He stumbled forwards, tumbling to his knees as the obsidian throne and the decorative figure behind it toppled over, pinning him to the ground beneath marble and black stone. He squirmed for a few moments, twitched, then remained still. Blood slowly oozed out from around the Messiah, his white wig matted with a thick red liquid.

"Is he dead?" asked Sylvester, making his way across the broken room and clambering over a large concrete block that had landed beside Bill. He looked down on the bloodied man lying on the ground, and slowly raised his pistol, taking careful aim at head of the fallen leader. "Have to make sure."

Bill caught a blur of motion to the far left, heard the banter of gunfire, and dived forwards, knocking Sylvester down and rolling over the mound of concrete as bullets tore through the air.

"They're pissed," Al's voice crackled over the radio headset Bill wore.

"Their leader's dead, their home's falling to pieces, and now they want a piece of us. They're really pissed off. A couple of the dancers and me are secured at the doorway, but we need Spanners to guide us out."

"You hear that?" Bill shouted over the sounds of explosions and exchange of gunfire. Sylvester tapped his own radio and nodded an affirmative. "Go get them out of here. They need your help."

"I want to finish him," Sylvester said, his voice cold. "I need to make sure."

"He's buried under rubble, his head's split open," Bill said, making sure his submachine gun was ready to fire. "Even if he's just knocked out, he's not going to get back up before the Rots work their way through here. Now go and help Al."

Reluctantly, Sylvester nodded and slowly started to pick his way through the tumbling rubble, returning fire to the few gang members that had elected to stick around and avenge the demise of their leader. Bill opened up with his own weapon, playing it across the far side of the room and feverishly looking from side to side, trying to get a fix on the rest of his group. Al and two of the dancers were by the opened main doors, hunkered down low behind a mound of smouldering rubble, Al trying to gun down the men on the other side of the room. He seemed to be making a better job of hitting people than Sylvester was, who had since started to crawl across the floor, slithering between rubble and keeping as low a profile as possible.

Behind Bill, Garth and Angel were providing covering fire with their own guns. Bill was quite impressed to see that Angel was trying her best to fire with both guns at the same time, and he took great delight in pointing it out to Al. He briefly glanced over at her position, and snorted.

"Bitch is just showing off. She's not hitting anyone. Anyway, Pam here says she can't see any of her other friends, other than Laurie here. Can you see any?"

"I can't see anyone else on our side, it's getting crowded in here. It looks like the yellow-bellied bastards that initially ran off are coming back with their friends."

"Just have a look for her friends, okay?"

Mumbling to himself, Bill slowly performed a sweep of the immediate area, then started to crawl across the uneven surface to see if he could find any more survivors. By now the room was thick with dust and smoke, the taste of burning wood and gunpowder mixed with an acrid tang.

"I'm already on that," Clive announced, his voice crackling over the headset. "I've only found three so far. Both crushed beneath some rubble, I'm sorry. I'm in the middle of their blessings now."

"Jesus, Preacher-man," argued Al. "There's a time and a place. Bill, find that other dancer, quick. We've got Spanners now, we're ready to move out."

Grumbling to himself once more, Bill moved further towards the back of the room and the smoking mass of rubble that had once been the throne and it's dais.

"C'mon," Bill muttered, sifting through the smaller piles of rubble and moving the larger pieces that he could manage. "Give me a sign, damn it."

Rubble to one side of him shifted, pushed to one side, and the woman with red hair attempted to pull herself out, her body streaked in blood and grime.

"Found her!" hissed Bill, reaching her and grabbing her arms, heaving her out of the mound. He smiled quickly at her, then motioned for her to get down on the floor to avoid taking a hit from a stray bullet. "Okay, Al, pull everyone out, we're on our way."

Just have to get back there, Bill thought to himself as he judged the distance between his location and the doors Al guarded over. It was a long way, and seemed even further since he knew he and the woman would have to crawl and slither their way through mounds of rubble while avoiding more debris and heavy gunfire.

Another round of explosives tore through the ceiling above the main hall, sending another shower of debris down into the room. Supports creaked and groaned with the immense strain and pressure they were under, until they finally gave way, tearing free from their housings and crashing down to the floor. Metal catwalks were wrenched from the wall, twisted and warped by the constant battering of the toppling rubble. As the room disintegrated around him, Bill frantically tried to plot his escape route through the decaying chamber.

"Jesus, it's no good," Al's voice said, panic clearly lacing his voice. Bill hadn't heard him sound as on edge as he did now. The fact the normally unshakeable Marine sounded scared didn't sit well with Bill. "There's too much rubble kid, you're never going to make it out this way."

"You can get out the way we came," Sylvester offered over the radio.

"Shit," muttered Bill, keeping his body pressed low against the ground as a salvo of bullets tore over his head. He glanced at the woman beside him, and blindly drew the handgun from his back pocket. "Can you fire this?"

She accepted the weapon cautiously, looked at it dubiously, but didn't return any fire.

"Here come the Rots, " Al said, his signal starting to fade and wash over with static. "Looks like Spanners and the preacher did their job. We have to move."

"I'll keep you right with the directions," Sylvester added. "Just remember to stick to the…"

The radio headset Bill wore Beeped once, then crackled and died. Cursing, he pulled the device from his head and threw it to the ground, not wanting to be over-burdened by any failing equipment, then peered over the mounds of rubble he had been using as a shield. The attacking men had turned their attention from him to the throng of rotting creatures that were starting to scamper and crawl across the mounds of fallen masonry. Some of the creatures stumbled blindly over mounds of rubble, their heads encased in artificial shells, while others leapt and vaulted over the debris in their wake, their bodies riddled with bullets as the gang turned their weapons on the more immediate threat.

Seeing his chance, Bill leapt to his feet and grabbed the woman's arm, running and leaping towards the opening behind the destroyed throne.

"Come on," he said, casting a glance over his shoulder to the battles between the Rots and the gang. It seemed to be a one-sided battle now: the gang had resorted to hand-to-hand combat with the carriers now, and they looked to have sustained large casualties. Creatures sat atop fallen men, their fingers peeling back flesh and wrenching apart limbs, snapping them at the joints. Those that hadn't been fitted with the protective helmet gorged themselves on the meat from their fresh kill, moaning and groaning in delight as they forced bloody chunks of meat down their throat. A few looked up from their meals, thick and bloody strings of drool dangling from their slack jaws,

"Come *on*," Bill urged, pulling harder at the woman's arm. It slipped from his grip, and she stumbled and fell to her knees, cursing softly to herself. "Get up!"

"My feet hurt," she complained, waving to the bare soles of her feet and the bloodied cuts and grazes that criss-crossed them. "It hurts too much."

"It'll hurt more if those bastards chew your feet off," muttered Bill, heaving her back up to her feet and motioning to the advancing undead behind them. "Now move!"

The confines of the dark tunnel swallowed them up as they left the hall through the ruined corridor. Bill swung his weapon vaguely from side to side as he ran. He was pretty sure that there wouldn't be much in the way of opposition when leaving the hall: most of the gang had been assembled in the hall when the explosions had detonated, and Rots seemed to have an uncanny sense that allowed them to home in on living creatures. If most of the living had been in one room, it would only make sense that most of the Rots would swarm there.

Most, Bill reminded himself. *Not all*.

"Do you know where we're going?" asked the woman, her steps faltering as she tried to keep up with Bill. The corridor was dark, so Bill wasn't sure if she could see the shrug of his shoulders.

"I got a rough idea," he lied as he tried to recall the maze-like outlay of the prison. Bill struggled to remember any details though, and tried to think if there was any way he could overcome the labyrinth he was faced with.

"Pick one wall," offered the woman, taking a break from the running to lean against one of the walls.

"We don't have time to fuck around," Bill said, pulling at her arm to urge her on. "We have to go, we need to meet up with my friends!"

"Pick a wall," she said again. "Didn't you ever do any puzzles when you were young? When you do a maze, you pick one wall, and follow it around. You'll eventually find the exit. A lot of back-tracking, but it works."

"Pretty smart," Bill admitted, sweeping his weapon around from side to side, trying to keep both angles covered. He lowered his weapon for a moment, gestured towards the pistol, and took it back off her. It was painfully obvious she wasn't going to fire it.

"I used to visit all the different halls and manors with my parents when I was younger," she said, patting down her body as if looking for a cigarette. She looked towards Bill, but he didn't have any to offer. "They had all the gardens, with the bushes sculpted to look like horses and peacocks, and those big mazes made out of giant hedges. I'd spend hours at a time wandering around those mazes. That's how I know it works."

"We'll give it a shot," Bill said. "What's the worst that can happen?"

XVI
END OF THE LINE

"There comes a time when you have to sever all ties with the rest: maintaining the façade of someone who cares benefits no one here…"

I

"Bill? Bill, can you hear me?"

"It's no good," Al said, spraying the men on the other side of the room with machinegun fire, cutting down gang members and Rots alike: He didn't want to take any chances, and he knew that one could be just as dangerous as the other. "I think his radio's died. Battery's out of juice, more than likely. The explosions and amount of crap in the air won't help with the signal, either. Spanners, you and the bitch secure the next junction, make sure it's safe, we're getting out of here."

"What about Bill?" screamed Angel, hiding behind the doorframe and spraying random shots across the room. She still held on to both submachine guns, and Al couldn't believe she actually thought she would be able to use them like that. She hadn't even tried to fire with her left hand yet, but he wanted to be there when she did, just so he could laugh at her.

"The kid can take care of himself, you know that. Don't worry, your bedtime buddy'll meet us up at the trailer. At the minute, my number one priority is to get me and these lovely ladies out of here."

Al waved Angel off, and continued to lay down heavy fire on the gang and the Rots. He knew he *could* wait and let both opposing sides rip into each other: after all, one of his commanding officers had once told him the enemy of his enemy is his friend. That being said, Al couldn't see himself sitting down for a beer with either of his opponents once the killing had ended. He had enough drums of ammunition to wipe out both Rots and rebels, and had it been only himself, he would have happily stayed until he was down to his last round.

"Position clear," Sylvester's voice crackled through the radio. Al frowned and tapped the headset, trying to clear the signal up. The smoke, dust and debris lingering in the air was interfering with the signal more than it should, but at the same time the walls of the prison were pretty thick. Even if Bill's radio hadn't died, he probably would have lost the signal before he got too far away.

"Okay, move. Preacher-man, get these girls out of here."

Clive nodded, took the hands of each of the liberated dancers, and took them from the hall. Garth went to follow, a look of relief on his face, but Al grabbed his arm and held him back.

"Not yet, buddy. We've got a job to do."

"Jesus, they're coming for us now," he said, pointing across the hall to the shambling undead that were starting to lumber over the rubble towards them. They had quickly dispatched the gang, and those that didn't have their heads encased in helmets or steel plating were busy feeding on the fallen gang.

"God-damn tin-pot fucks," muttered Al, peppering the approaching creatures with bullets. Some rounds glanced off the head protectors, but some managed to penetrate them and put them down. "Bunch of animals. Still got that flamethrower?"

Garth blindly fumbled for the weapon he had slung over his shoulder and passed it to Al. He wasn't especially familiar with the weapon; he'd never used one before, but it couldn't be very hard to use. Point and squeeze, the same principal as any other weapon he'd ever used in the Marines. Even the heavier anti-tank artillery worked off the same principle. He gently squeezed the trigger, and a jet of flame spewed from the nozzle, the thick gel-like fluid spraying over the already-burning rubble and adding to the smaller fires in the room.

"You missed them all," hissed Garth, shouldering his rifle and slowly backing away towards the door. Al shook his head and passed back the weapon.

"All animals fear fire. It's a primal instinct, it'll keep them back for a while. I don't know how long the fuel burns for, but it should give us enough time to get out of here."

"Guess again," said Garth, pointing to the curtain of flames as the undead shambled through the fire. Any tattered clothing they wore burned and smoked, their flesh blackened and blistered, oozing watery pus and blood from open sores. They seemed completely unfazed by the fire, ignoring the blaze as they mindlessly stumbled through, moaning and groaning in anticipation of another kill.

"Time to bail out, buddy," Al called, waving towards the doorway. Garth ran to the opening, barely taking the time to look over his shoulder to see if he was following. Al shook his head, slowly picking his way through the rubble and making his own way out the main hall. As he went, he continued to lay down a suppressive field of fire, obliterating the heads of those Rots who hadn't been armoured, and destroying the legs of those that had, trying to incapacitate as many of the creatures as he could.

"How's it looking there, Spanners?" he asked as he ducked down by the opening of the door, unwrapping the second of the explosive charges that he had held back and moulding the charge into place before setting the timer for a quick countdown.

"Corridors are clear of people," Sylvester replied. "Starting to fill up with smoke, though. It's getting hard to see or breathe."

"But you can get us out, can't you?"

"We'll be outside in three minutes, tops. We're not far from an exit."

Finally, thought Al to himself as he ran around the corner of the corridor, away from the timed charge as it exploded and sealed off the main hall. *A little good luck.*

He caught up to Garth at the end of the corridor, a tunnel lined with open cell doors and slowly filling up with thick rolling clouds of dark smoke, showers of dust and plaster raining down from the cracking ceiling above. He was taking his time walking behind the rest of the group, and for a moment Al thought he had actually taken up the position of Tail End Charlie to the group, making sure no one managed to creep up them by surprise.

"Watching our ass?" he asked, prodding Garth in the small of the back as he approached.

"Just theirs," Garth said, nodding towards the two women that clung to Clive as they followed their guide. "That's one of the finest sights I've seen in a long time."

"Pair of perverts," hissed Angel, scowling over her shoulder at the Marine and his cohort. Al grinned back, leaning closer to Garth as he spoke. "Ignore her, she's just jealous that we're not talking about her ass for a change. Bitch's got competition now."

"Almost there," Sylvester said, abruptly stopping and holding up his hand. Everyone stumbled to a halt, and Sylvester turned around, motioning for the group to huddle together. "Just beyond this corridor there's another hall, a foyer smaller than the main hall we've just left, which has an exit leading out. From there we should be able to find our vehicles, then we can get out of here."

"Like the plan," said Al, nodding and scratching his beard. "We'll have to be careful, though, soon as we get outside we may encounter more trouble. Rots, or maybe there's some guards out on patrol. Last thing we need is to get to the trailer and get shot by one of the guards on duty."

"Who's to say they're still there?" asked Angel, her question aimed directly at Al. Without Bill present, Al would have to field to question himself. He missed him already, without him it would prove harder to wind her up. Harder, but not impossible. "I mean, once all these explosions went off, wouldn't they all leave their posts, to see what was going on?"

"Maybe, maybe not. If it was me on guard duty somewhere where explosions were going off all over the place, I'd stick where I was told until the location of the attackers was confirmed. But then, I'm a professional and I know what I'm doing. The shits running this place now are nothing but thieves and killers: the scum of society. They wouldn't know a procedure if it bit them on their ass."

"Finished?" asked Sylvester, marching down the corridor and making his way towards the exit. Al grunted, then followed, trying to pick up the pace and keep up front with the guide. He didn't mind so much when Bill took charge of a situation, he could deal with that, but he couldn't help but feel that this new guy was trying to muscle in on his authority, maybe even belittle him in front of the new women.

"Much further?" Al muttered, sweeping his weapon back and forth, "We've got a schedule to follow here. We need to get to Greyson's Park, and we've probably got another two days or so to get there."

"I know that place," said Sylvester, nodding his head, stopping at a pair of heavy doors and placing his hand on one of the thick metal handles. "It had a lot of good bars in the area. I used to go all the time with Terri."

"You know that place too," muttered Al. "That's very frigging convenient. How far is it?"

"From here, it's probably about three or fours hours drive. At least, that's what it was like in rush hour traffic. If the roads have been cleared, it shouldn't take as long. If there's a lot of stationary vehicles out there blocking the roads, it could take longer."

"With our vehicle, we can plough through pretty much anything," Al bragged, grinning and winking to the dancer with dark hair who had called herself Pam. She had shown a lot of attention towards him, even in the heat of battle, and Al could see himself getting on quite well with the dancing girl. "It's big and has a lot of power behind it, really good for ramming."

"Providing the trailer is working," Garth said, reminding Al that the vehicle had given up the ghost shortly after arriving at the television studio.

"Hey," said Sylvester, jabbing himself in the chest with an extended thumb. "You seem to forget I'm a mechanic. Whatever you have, I can fix it, make sure it works."

"I can fix it myself," countered Garth, "I've done it before, I can do it again!"

"And that was such a brilliant fix, wasn't it, buddy? Let the grease monkey have a go at it when we get there, we'll hold off any would-be attackers while he tinkers with the engine. What's the worst he can do? Now let's get out of here."

Sylvester nodded and pushed open the door to the foyer, and froze as he saw the crowd of undead that lingered in the hall. Al barged past Sylvester into the room, his weapon raised high, quickly evaluating the layout of the room and the cover. He stood in the open, but none of the undead creatures seemed to take any notice of him: they all seemed to be crouching down, leaning over fallen gang members and tearing them apart with their blood-soaked hands. Many of the victims had already died, but a few of them still screamed in agony as their flesh was ripped and torn.

"Feeding time in the zoo," muttered Al, slowly panning his weapon from side to side. "If our luck holds out, we may just be able to sneak through the bastards. Look," he said, lifting a hand and lazily tracing an imaginary path through the clumps of feasting creatures. "Apart from that bloody corpse propping open the front door there, it's pretty clear. They seem more interested in the feast than us. Haven't even batted an eyelid."

"Those that have eyelids," hissed Angel, lifting her machineguns and quickly switching between targets.

"Okay," whispered Al, turning around to face the remainder of his group. Clive seemed to take the whole scene in with relatively calm, sweeping his weapon from target to target, while Sylvester nervously tapped the tip of his boot against the concrete floor. Both Angel and Garth tried their best to reassure to two dancers, who huddled together and looked anxiously from side to side, their eyes wide with panic. Al grinned inwardly as he saw their bodies shiver and shake, a combination of fear and the cold that gave their exposed breasts a gentle and pleasing jiggle.

Keep your mind fixed on the current situation he scorned himself, shaking the thoughts from his head.

"Move quickly and silently, single file. Bitch, you go first, you're the bait. If they don't attack you, we know it's safe. Next up is you, buddy. Once there's two guns covering the exit, we follow. Hey, Preacher-man, you cool if the shit hits the fan and we have to shoot these Rots?"

"The hollow men have no souls," Clive said, nodding his head. "I have no problem in shooting them."

"Well praise God," Al muttered sarcastically, stepping back from the huddle and motioning for Angel to make her way across the room. He didn't watch her as she moved through the heaving crowd: although he didn't get on well with her, he knew she could take care of herself. He was busy trying to keep the dancers calm and collected. Even Clive and Sylvester had some combat experience, but the two girls probably had minimum contact with the undead; they had probably been rounded up as soon as the prisoners broke out.

"Here goes," announced Garth, slowly stepping out into the mass of feasting creatures and picking his way through the sprawled cadavers. His bulk made his movements slow and cumbersome: where Angel could jump or pounce, he needed to waddle or shuffle. His heavy feet landed mere inches from the squirming and feasting dead, and halfway across the room he paused to remove his hat and wipe his brow, absentmindedly flicking beads of perspiration off him and on to the crowd around him. The creatures around him stirred and mumbled an incomprehensible growl, but didn't turn from the twitching corpse they were stripping. His cowardly nature getting the best of him, he bolted for the open door Angel stood by, lunging through the opening and bringing his weapon up to sweep across the room.

"Yellow-bellied shit," muttered Al, motioning to the two dancers that they were next and that he would accompany them. He went first, making sure each dancer put their feet where he placed his while keeping an eye on the creatures all around him.

"Smells horrible," commented Pam, still clinging to Al as they moved. She was right, of course. A cloying mix of sweet rot with a heavy underlying metallic tang: blood and decay.

"Stick close," whispered Al, feeling he needed to say something, anything. "Try not to look at them, either. Neither of you are used to this yet."

Too late, the second dancer turned to one side to look at one of the packs of feasting animals, and saw the final death throes of one man as a drooling Rot took his head in its hands. With an unnatural strength Al had seen in only a few of the creatures, it managed to tear the skull open, spilling the blood and brains of the body and shovelling scraps of the jelly-like matter into its mouth. It also managed to get a few fragments of bone past its snapping teeth, cutting the insides of its mouth adding to the bloody mess.

The dancer screamed and vomited, unable to keep her gorge down, and stumbled blindly back, retching and muttering to herself. Before Al or anyone else could react to it, she had made her way into the middle of one pack of feeding Rots, who quickly lunged on her, pulling her down to the ground. Her terrified screams turned to a gurgling choke as rotting fingers probed her mouth, first one, then three, then six. Her lips split and tore, teeth and blood bubbled out of her mouth as pieces of flesh were torn from her cheeks.

"Laurie!" screamed Pam, moving to grab the flailing arms of her friend. Al grabbed her around her waist, and with one fluid movement lifted her up on to his shoulder and started to move towards the door, carrying her as a fireman would carry an injured person from a burning building. As he went, he brought up his weapon and panned it around. A few of the creatures had finally finished their meal and now rose to their feet, turning to face the living people now occupying their dining hall.

"Get the fuck out of here," bellowed Al over the screams of the woman slung over his shoulder. "Don't be scared to shoot the bastards in the head on your way out. I want a path secured to Colebrook's Runner, and I want the engine running when I get there. Spanners, break off with buddy there, make sure its good to go. Bitch, you and Preacher-man are with me."

"We have to save her," Pam protested, repeatedly thumping Al's back with clenched fists. "We need to get her out of there, she's still alive!"

"She's gone," said Al, opening up with a burst from his heavy weapon and hosing it across the gathering of undead. Each bullet gave birth to a spray of gore as they struck the creatures, and they stumbled forwards, but they didn't fall down. Al wasn't able to take the time to carefully aim for the kill shot, just to lay down a suppressive field of fire to allow the rest of his group time to escape from the room. He made sure a couple of rounds found the twitching body of the dancer, just to make sure that she wouldn't rise up again like the rest of the inmates scattered around the feeding ground. The way Pam hung over his shoulders, she wouldn't have been able to see, and he slowly backed out the room, sweeping his barking weapon from side to side. He was pleased to see Clive had kicked into action, and contributed to the suppressive fire, slowly making his way towards the exit.

"Exorcising the demons, huh?" asked Al, grinning at the holy man as he cut down a trio of the undead. Clive didn't respond, his attention focussed on the job at hand. "Well you're no fun," Al muttered.

Slowly backing out the foyer and into the cool night air, Al kicked aside the corpse propping the door open and nodded towards Angel, indicating that she should close the doors behind them. She did so as Al lowered Pam to the floor, then secured the door in place.

Outside it was dark, and a gentle drizzle washed across the ground. The fine mist lingering in the air magnified the cool of the night, and after the heat of the battle the cooling sweat that covered Al's skin only intensified the chill he felt.

"We're going to catch our death of cold," muttered Angel, lowering her weapons and rubbing her arms, trying to keep the circulation flowing. Al nodded in agreement, and looked around the immediate area. It must have been the visitors' car park they had come out in, though all vehicles had been removed from the vicinity and replaced with two machinegun nests, the weapon emplacements protected by a barricade of sandbags and wooden support beams. The operators were nowhere to be seen; presumably they had rushed into the foyer once the Rots had found their way there. It certainly didn't look to Al as if the creatures had entered through the front, otherwise there would have been a few bullet-shredded carcasses lying on the floor.

"Which way's the trailer?" Al said, looking from left to right. The surrounding fence had three gates; one to the left and right, with the third being the main gate directly opposite the doors leading into the building. The main gate was locked up securely, but those on either side of the compound were wide open, meaning that Garth and Sylvester could have gone either way. The Rots within the foyer were already hammering on the door, and he knew the barricade wouldn't hold forever, especially under the relentless force of the undead. He didn't want to go the wrong way and have to double back just to find a group of flesh eaters waiting for him with open arms and even wider mouths.

"You there buddy?"

The radio headset crackled slightly, then the tanker driver replied. His voice was ragged, and he seemed out of breath.

"We're there," he managed to confirm, gulping the air as he talked. "We found the trailer, there's a lot of blood just lying around back here. Looks like Bill's left his calling card, but I can't see a body. Sly says the vehicle looks pretty sound, he gave it the once over. Says it's a wonderful piece of machinery…"

"Where is it?" Al said, cutting of Garth before he lost track of the current situation. "The Rots are contained, but I don't know how long for."

"We broke left after leaving the foyer, and then… I can't remember; most of it's all a blur."

"Fuck," said Al, spitting the word and kicking the ground with his boot. "Okay, what about sounding the horn? Give that a blast, see if we can get a fix on you from that."

The silent night was split by the powerful scream of an air horn, not too far away. It sounded like it came from the right, but the acoustics of the crumbling prison could easily make it sound like it was coming from anywhere. Al knew that the pair had made for the left gate, though, so he had something he could work with.

"This way," he said, storming off towards the open gate to the left. "Stick close and move fast. You okay?"

His question was directed to Pam, who appeared to be in shock. Her eyes were wide open, fixed on the closed doors as they rattled and shook.

"I'm okay," she managed to say, distantly. "Shouldn't we open the doors and let Laurie out? It sounds like she wants to come out."

"Laurie's gone," Al sighed, placing a large hand on her shoulder and gently turning her away from the door."

"But she'll come back, won't she?" asked Pam. "The Baptised always came back."

"I made sure she wouldn't," Al confirmed in a gentle voice, guiding her towards the open gate. Pam nodded softly to herself, lips moving but no words coming out as she worked through what she'd been told. Al removed his hand from her shoulder and passed her on to Clive, who took control of her stumbling walk.

"Just you and me now, bitch. Ready to cover our ass and keep the dead shits away from us?"

"Always am," Angel said with a smile.

"What's so funny?" asked Al, irritated by the unpredictable good mood of the young girl, "Do I amuse you?"

"No more than usual," Angel grinned, slowly backing up beside him and sweeping one of her weapons from side to side as they moved. "It's just unusual to see you treating a woman with some degree of respect or genuine concern. Makes you appear almost human."

"Fuck you," he said, feeling his cheeks burn. "She's had it tough, I'm just making sure she gets out alive."

"I can see you," Garth's voice interjected, breaking up the conversation between the pair. Al was glad of the interruption, and shot Angel an apologetic look. "We'll discuss this later," he said, even though he had no intention of doing so. "Buddy says he can see us!"

Casting a glance over his shoulder, Al could see the trailer parked in the distance, amongst a myriad of parked cars. The lights along the front flickered on, casting long shadows across the darkened parking lot, and the engine shuddered to life with a choking growl. "It looks like our mechanic friend can work his magic on the temperamental beast that is *Colebrook's Runner* after all. Secure a path, I'll cover our asses and make sure nobody follows us."

"Except Bill," Angel said, "We're going to hold on for him, right?"

"We'll hold on as long as we can," Al said, nodding slowly, "But I can't make any promises. The minute a shit-load of Bebops come down on us, or a pack of Rots, we're out of here. We can't risk the lives of six people for one or two, even if it *is* the kid and another dancer."

"So we're just going to leave him?" Angel asked incredulously, refusing to make her way across to the waiting vehicle. "After everything we've been through?"

"Tell you what, *I'll* secure a path, you watch our tail."

Al started to make his way to the trailer, weapon raised and pointed towards the roofline of the prison and any snipers that may attempt to take a few pot-shots at the escaping group.

"I can't believe you'd do that to your friend," Angel said, following close behind Al, ignoring the possible threat of enemy fire. Al shook his head slightly, unable to comprehend why Bill was so hell-bent on keeping a woman who couldn't follow orders as part of his team. Clearly if he *were* a Marine, he would be able to make better judgement calls for his treasured squad.

Fucking civvie.

"All's fair in love and war," Al said with a shrug, wandering over to the trailer and motioning to the ropes and chains that fastened the motorbike to the side of the larger vehicle. "We'll leave the kid's bike so he can make his own way to the rendezvous. We'll get there first, secure the area, and keep it clean until he gets there."

"And where is that?"

"Millfield Place," Al replied, a smug grin on his face.

"I thought you said it was Greyson's Park," Sylvester called as he shuffled out from beneath the trailer cab, wiping down his oily hands on a rag and tucking it into his back pocket.

"I did," said Al, stowing his weapon in the opened trailer and climbing up on to the roof of the cargo module, inspecting the mounted machinegun and making sure it was loaded and ready.

"Well, which one is it?" asked Sylvester, stepping back away from the vehicle and craning his head up so he could see the Marine standing on top of the vehicle.

"One of those two, yeah."

"You said Greyson in the holding cell," Sylvester said, raising his hands in frustration. "And now it's Millfield?"

"Well it must be fucking Greyson, shit, I don't know."

"If you don't know," shouted Angel, helping Pam into the rear of the trailer and guiding her to one of the seats welded down to the floor plate, "What chance does Bill have?"

"The kid's magic, he's a frigging genius, he'll be able to remember the name of the place. Yeah, definitely Greyson, without a doubt."

"Leave a note on the bike," suggested Angel. "Just to make sure."

"You dumb bitch," scorned Al, making his way back down to ground and starting to help Sylvester lower the bike down from the side of the trailer, unfastening the chains and lowering it to the ground. "If any of the Bebops in there burst out of the prison lusting after our blood, instead of this monster truck standing here they find a motorbike with a note attached. That note reads 'gone to Greyson's Park, wait for you there, love Angel'. It won't be long until we're knee-deep in the shit again. We may as well just weld a neon sign to our ass."

"I just want to make sure Bill gets rescued with us."

"I'll make sure the kid does, trust me. Now, leave a few rounds next to the bike in case he needs to reload on the fly," Al said, kicking down the resting stand and dusting off the leather seat of the vehicle. He wished that there was a way of leaving a message for Bill, but there was no way to guarantee that it wouldn't be picked up by a bloodthirsty prisoner, or worst case scenario, an intelligent Rot that can still read.

Stranger things have happened.

"Where's Preacher-man?"

"In the back," confirmed Sylvester, giving the bike a once over and confirming that it was roadworthy. "He's trying to calm down Pam, keep her from freaking out. She's not made of strong stuff, not like Angel. She seems pretty fragile, and she looks like she's not taking it well."

"As long as he's not trying to move in on her," Al said defensively, fixing a quiver of crossbow bolts to the rear of the bike and strapping the crossbow to the handle of the bike. Bill seemed to favour the weapon, though he couldn't figure out the appeal of it himself. Acknowledging Bill's love for the more robust and modern weapons, he also dumped a metal box of shotgun shells beside the rear wheel, hoping that he'd see them before riding off.

"Don't worry, the claim you seem to suddenly have on her should hold fast. Clive took a vow of celibacy as part of his faith," Sylvester said, dropping what tools Garth carried around into a cloth sack and slinging it over his shoulder. "He takes his faith seriously, so she's in no danger of being wooed by a randy priest."

"Celibacy? I always knew the church was filled with crazies and whack jobs. Crazy son of a bitch: no sex? Ever?"

"He's devoted to his religion," said Sylvester with a shrug, heading towards the opened trailer cab, and the waiving form of Garth.

"Can we go now?"

"We wait for Bill," Al shouted, climbing back up on to the roof of the trailer and bringing his weapon about to bear on the pathway leading back towards the prison. "Give the kid as much time as possible."

"Wait?" screeched Garth incredulously. "Are you fucking crazy?"

"You knew that before you climbed on this ride," hissed Al, wrenching on the lever on the weapon and cocking it. "Now sit tight, and keep your hands inside the vehicle until I give you the say so."

"Jesus," muttered Garth. "This never happened when *I* was in charge."

II

The corridors of the prison were worse than any maze Tara had been to when she was younger. At least when she did get lost in the tangle of hedges at the stately homes she'd visited, she could always climb up on to her sister's back and peer over the top. Maybe if she'd told that to Bill before he'd taken her sage advice, he would have thought differently.

She still carried the handgun: he'd given her it back at the first sign of trouble, but despite the numerous zombies and prisoners they'd stumbled across, she was yet to fire it. She didn't even know if she'd be able to raise the weapon against another human and fire it, as Bill had on several occasions. Killing seemed to come easily to him, but she didn't think it was anything she'd be able to do, despite the current situation.

In fact, the only person Tara thought she *would* be able to kill was now lying in a crumpled heap in a burning room, possibly being picked apart by a horde of the dead creatures.

Couldn't happen to a nicer man, she thought to herself, remembering all the times The Messiah had abused her, before throwing her to the mercy of his men. Though his men had also taken advantage of her, all of those had also perished in the great hall, either in the resulting fire fight or under the bloodied talons of the decaying creatures: sweet karma.

"This is taking a lot longer than I thought it would," Bill said. He often said something to try and break the silence between the two, mostly with dry wit to try and ease the tension. "How big can a prison be?"

Tara didn't answer. She didn't feel like talking much, not after losing most of her friends in the hall. At least two had escaped with the rest of Bill's group, but she didn't know who had survived.

"Quiet girl," Bill observed, pausing to look around the room they currently stood in; a large chamber, with holding cells running along both sides. Decaying corpses with fat flies buzzing and humming around the rancid dead bodies, occupied some cells, while others were vacant; their doors wide open. Tara tried not to look at any of the bodies, instead focussing on the darkened skylight above her.

"I don't have much to say," she confessed, her voice quiet and soft in the harshness of the opened space. The cool of the prison at night hadn't affected her much until now, and it was only once she'd stopped moving that the chill reminded her she was almost naked. It was also unusual that Bill hadn't noticed this as much as any other man would. Despite the gravity of their situation, Tara thought he would have cast more than the occasional glance at her body.

"Cold?" he asked, watching her as she rubbed at the goose bumps appearing on her flesh. She nodded with a weak smile, and watched as Bill removed his jacket and handed it to her. "Here, take this." She took the brown garment, sniffed it, looked it up and down.

"It smells a bit," she said, absentmindedly. "What's this, blood?"

"Jesus," Bill scowled tearing off his T-shirt and flinging it at her, then taking the jacket back and slipping back into it. Tara smiled sheepishly and looked at the black shirt. It reeked of stale sweat, but that was better than the cloying scent of decay and death that lingered in the blood-spatters and ground-in dirt of the jacket. She tried to give Bill an apologetic grin, but he had chosen to ignore her and return to his investigation of the prison, stalking deeper into the building.

"Stick close, this place looks familiar," he called back over his shoulder. She rushed to catch up, wishing not for the first time since breaking out of the holding room that she'd taken a handful of cigarettes to remain calm and collected.

After handing over his T-shirt, Bill didn't say much else to her, barley grunting to indicate a change in direction. He still seemed to be sticking to the same plan, though he did deviate from the occasional offshoot from the main corridors, seeming sure with himself that he knew it wouldn't lead to an exit.

She hoped she hadn't offended Bill, especially as he was going to be her guide until they escaped the prison. It wasn't a personal comment or insult directed at him, but a habit from her previous life she couldn't shake.

Before the dead had started to walk, Tara Kingsley had been a high-flying lawyer for one of the larger law firms in the city. Her job had been very well paid, and because of her income, she was used to only the expensive things in life: perfume, food, and clothes. Although her captivity had been against her will, she had been kept in some degree of luxury. The jacket she'd been offered by her saviour, no matter how good his intent, still reeked like a month-old dead animal. She would have rather remained naked than wear the foul-smelling garment.

"I didn't mean anything by it," she eventually said, the solitude between the two finally getting to her. "The jacket, I mean."

Bill raised an eyebrow, but didn't look her way, too busy stalking the corridor with his submachine gun drawn and tucked in tight against his shoulder. He moved like he knew exactly what he was doing.

"You a soldier?"

"Not even close," he said, shaking his head, but keeping his eyes focused on the corridor ahead. "I used to deliver internal post in a government office."

"That makes me feel a whole lot better, like I'm in safe hands."

"Really?" snorted Bill. "And what did you do?"

"I'm a lawyer," she said, matter-of-factly.

"*Used* to be a lawyer," he said, correcting her. "So you're used to dealing with scum like The Messiah and his men?"

"Hardly," she said, laughing softly. "I dealt with divorces, mainly, the worst I used to deal with was adulterers; no murderers, rapists or thieves. What about your friends, what do they do?"

"A Marine," Bill said, striding down the corridor and relaxing a little. It has been almost twenty minutes since they'd last encountered anyone, and it looked like he was accepting the fact that another attack may not come. "Al's a Marine. There's Garth; he drives an articulated truck. Sylvester, he fixes up cars and shit like that. Clive's a priest. And Angel... she's just a kid."

"At least someone there knows what they're doing then."

"Trying to say I don't?" asked Bill. Tara almost snapped back, but saw from the lopsided grin on his face that he was playing with her. "Still, I suppose the plan was Al's idea."

"What plan?"

"We're trying to arrange a pick-up, a chopper should be collecting us in a couple of days. We just need to get to the rendezvous point in time. Al had this whole plan set up to dupe the Marines into getting us off the island."

"Where is that? The rendezvous, I mean."

Bill stopped mid-stride, his brow wrinkling as his mind worked overtime. "I can't remember offhand. Grimm's Peak? Gavin's Park?" He tapped his teeth with one of his fingers while he tried to think of the name, then shrugged. "Doesn't matter, Al remembers it. Once we meet up outside, we'll roll out in the trailer. It might be a little cramped, but it won't be for very long."

Tara didn't say anything else, but felt a faint flutter of hope tickle her stomach. If what Bill was saying was true, and Tara couldn't see any reason why he'd lie, then she might actually escape from the infested island. Leave the diseased land behind her; maybe start her life over again. She'd always liked France, had done ever since she'd first visited it when she was twelve. She could probably make it out there. All it would take would be a little money to get herself back on her feet, and she knew she had quite a hefty sum in an offshore account: a trick that she'd picked up from her clients more scrupulous partners.

Yeah, that seemed like a good plan, all she had to do was stick with Bill and his friends.

Garth looked up from the map he and Sylvester were studying, placing the cap on the fluorescent highlighter he held and tapping it on the dashboard. It looked like dawn was starting to break, turning the sky from dark purple to a deep shade of pink. Garth figured it to be coming up to four in the morning, though he had no way of checking. The clock in the cabin had stopped working a long time ago, the digital readout frozen on 88:88.

"Jesus, Al, how much longer are we going to wait?"

"It's only been half an hour," the Marine responded, his deep voice calm and cool. He'd been standing on watch from the weapon mounted on the roof of the trailer all night, and barely said a word. Deep down, he knew that Al wanted to go back into the prison and look for Bill, and he was quite surprised that he hadn't done so yet. The occasional explosion still rocked the building, either delayed charges or further structural damage caused by the first salvo of explosions.

Over the radio link, Garth could hear the Marine sigh. "Rots seem to be coming towards us now. I've been watching them for ten minutes; they've been milling around to the north of us. Looks like quite a large crowd, about twenty or thirty."

"You've been just *watching* them for ten minutes?" cried Garth, feeling sick at the thought of the proximity of the Rots. "And you haven't killed any yet?"

"Gunfire'd attract more than it's worth. I don't think we can hang on much longer. Get this piece of shit moving, buddy."

"Really?" asked Garth, trying to hide the excitement from his voice. The sooner he could get away from there, the better. After all, Bill was a level-headed guy; he knew what he was doing, where he had to go. Slipping the vehicle into gear, Garth slowly guided the vehicle around the mass of parked vehicles and out the prison yard, grinning to himself as a couple of the stumbling dead managed to lurch in front of the moving vehicle. Garth chuckled under his breath as the skeletal bodies crunched beneath the tyres, and his grin turned into a full beaming smile as the vehicle hit the wide tarmac of the road.

"Okay, Sly," he said, flicking his eyes between the road and map in front of him. "I'm relying on you. Keep me right, okay?"

Sylvester nodded an affirmative, smoothing out the map and tracing the highlighted route with a grease-coated finger.

Over the intercom, Garth could hear a gentle, tearful sob. Shrugging to himself, he pushed the vehicle onwards, blindly fumbling for the controls to his music player to drown out the sound of the sorrowful woman behind him.

Bill and Tara finally emerged from the prison, squinting as the light of the morning sun blinding them as it crested the eastern horizon. The air was tainted with the heady aroma of decay and death, and Bill found the prison grounds, hemmed in by a chain link fence topped with coils of razor wire, crowded with an unnerving number of Rots. Though the number of the creatures didn't take him aback, Tara seemed horrified, gripping his arm and squeezing it tight.

"How many of them are there?"

"Maybe more than I can shoot," Bill confessed, quickly working through the sums. He had a couple of rounds for his shotgun and three full clips for his submachine gun. He also carried two spare magazines for his handgun, which he was probably going to retrieve from the young dancer before long: she hadn't made any effort to even lift the weapon. Although he had enough ammo to cut through the swarm of undead if he was lucky, he still didn't feel confident enough to take them all on, as he knew there would be more than just this crowd of the dead he would have to face.

The moment one Rot turned towards him and glared at him with its one good eye, they all seemed to notice him, turning as one and sending a low moan of hunger and anticipation along the ranks of the dead. Some began to stumble and sway forwards, while others broke into an awkward loping gait, limbs stiff and flailing wildly from side to side as they moved. Those creatures that had lost use of their lower extremities clawed their way across the ground, their bloodied and raw fingers seeking purchase in the flat tarmac and curling around loose stones.

Tara began to squirm uneasily beside Bill, and gently stepped back from the advancing Rots, back into the prison they'd just left. He held her arm, holding back her retreat, and nodded towards the chain link fence on the other side of the opening. It had a gate in it, locked up and bound with a chain and heavy padlock, and a metal sign fastened to the hinge, lopsided and covered in spatters of blood and dirt.

"Car park, main foyer and exit," he muttered, reading the writing while simultaneously keeping an eye on the advancing Rots. He lifted his finger towards the gate, crouching down slightly next to Tara so she could see exactly where he was pointing. "We're heading through that gate. C'mon, hurry."

"We're going *through* them?" she asked in disbelief, dragging her heels as Bill half pulled her. He didn't respond, just raised his weapon and sent a three-round burst into the closest of the creatures. Bullets smashed into its shoulder, neck and head, toppling it with a bloody gurgle as it died again. Undeterred by the death of their brethren, more of the creatures began their advance, moans and groans accompanying their shambling movements.

Bill lowered his submachine gun and raised his shotgun, the tight grouping of the encroaching Rots providing ideal targets for the spread of the shot. With a deafening roar from the stout weapon, he fired off three shells into the group, downing another five more of the creatures with a splash of tainted blood. He looked at Tara, who stuck close by him, but still didn't raise her weapon to defend herself.

"Are you going to use that?" he growled, lowering the shotgun's muzzle and blasting at the midriffs of the creatures. Instead of going for the kills, he had decided to incapacitate the creatures instead. With the creatures advancing at a relatively quick pace, it was easier to put them down by causing massive trauma to the bodies, rather than aiming for their relatively small Achilles heel.

"I've never fired a gun before," Tara shouted over the sound of the booming shotgun and the moans of the dead toppling to the ground.

"Are you ever going to give it a try?" Bill shouted in annoyance, letting his spent shotgun dangle from its strap and retrieve the submachine gun. Flicking the selector switch to automatic, he hosed the weapon from side to side, tearing bodies apart and knocking them back. Casting a glance over his shoulder, Bill could see Tara behind him, gripping the pistol in one hand and trying to protect her ears from the sounds of the battle with the other. Behind her, a partially decayed Rot lumbered towards her, yellowed teeth glittering with blood and drool, ragged fingers eagerly coiling and flexing as it advanced on its prey.

"Jesus, look out!"

Tara spun and saw the advancing creature, and ducked to the floor, dropping her weapon and screaming in terror. Inwardly sighing, Bill spun and brought his automatic weapon about to bear on the creature, squeezing the trigger: the weapon clicked, empty. With a fluid movement, Bill ejected the empty magazine and brought another into play, slamming it home and heaving back on the mechanism, before pulling the trigger. Bullets tore through the creature as the muzzle of the weapon climbed, punching a hole through the forehead of the creature and knocking it down to the pavement.

"Get up," he said angrily, grabbing Tara by the arm and roughly pulling her to her feet. She had retrieved the pistol, her hands gripping it tight and her knuckles whitening. She stared at him, her eyes wide with terror and confusion, and tears trickled down her face. He knew he was being harsh with her, but he couldn't help it: the number of surrounding Rots seemed to be increasing, as if the creatures were crawling out of the ground around him. He couldn't keep one eye on himself, another on the creatures, and a third on the helpless woman he was trying to get out of there: he'd given her the pistol so she could be a help, not a hindrance.

Bill looked back to the area around him, at the path towards the gate that was littered with squirming corpses, their midriffs shredded by the rapid-fire weapon. They heaved themselves towards him, clawing at the asphalt and dragging their ruined carcasses behind them. There were still a few creatures left standing, and more of them had been attracted by the bursts of gunfire, their weight pressing against the wire fence on either side of him. They tried to climb the fence, shredding their hands on the razor wire as they gripped the coils and tried to heave themselves up and over the barrier. The fence held them back for now, but it was only a matter of time until the barrier gave way: luckily, they hadn't yet made their way to the gate, which remained clear.

For now.

"Move," ordered Bill, making his way towards the gate and stepping carefully over the few corpses he had permanently put down. The crawling Rots tried to veer off towards him, though a few decided to turn on one another, tearing chunks out of each other and gorging themselves. Lowering his submachine gun, Bill snatched the pistol back from Tara and put it to good use, executing the downed corpses that still squirmed and reached for him as he moved. With each discharge of the weapon, Tara visibly jumped, trying to step on clean spots on the ground, twisting her face as her bare feet splashed in the pools of tainted blood. Bill strode through spilled liquid without hesitation, knowing that it was only ingestion of the blood or a bite that could possibly infect him at this stage.

He paused halfway through his journey to slam a fresh magazine into the handgun, and checked to make sure Tara was still behind him. She was about five feet behind him, tentatively picking her way through the corpses, cautiously eyeing each of the Rots that had been put to death. Sighing, he returned to her, turned around and bent his knees.

"Climb on," he sighed.

"What?" she asked, confused at his offer.

"You ever had a piggyback?" he asked, adjusting the webbing he wore to make sure her ride would be as comfortable as possible. "Climb on, if you're that worried about your toenails."

"The ground's covered in their blood," she complained, awkwardly climbing up on to Bill's back and wrapping her arms around his neck, coiling her fingers around one another. "Isn't that how it's spread?"

"Only if you drink it," grunted Bill, tucking his hand under one of Tara's thighs to keep her up off the ground, while exterminating the few Rots that remained in his way. "Or if one of the little bastards nick your ankle."

Finally reaching the gate, Bill lowered Tara to the ground on a relatively clear patch of land and grasped the chain, testing the padlock. He didn't think he'd be able to pick the lock, not without any picks at hand, nor did he have any other tools to pry the lock apart. He picked up his shotgun, rummaged through his pockets and found he had a single shell left. He fed the shell into the shotgun, cranked the slug into the breech, then levelled off the weapon and fired, point blank, into the lock.

The padlock split apart under the power of the solid slug, the broken pieces dropping to the ground with a hollow clank. Bill pulled the chain free, tore open the gate and pushed Tara through, veering off to the left as the arrow on the old sign indicated. As Bill pushed the gate shut, the fences the Rots pushed against began to creak and give, their supports finally giving to the immense weight and pressure of the pack of the undead.

"We have to get out of here," Bill said, breaking into a run and hoping that Tara could manage the same without complaining, whining or waiting to be carried. She seemed to be able to hold her own, at least when it came to running away. Maybe she'd be a good companion for Garth...

Bill and Tara followed the winding roadway, littered with the smashed corpses of Rots: creatures that looked as though they had fallen beneath the tyres of a heavy vehicle. Bill tried to ignore the festering road kill, his heart skipping a beat as the thought of who or what could have caused this carnage. He knew Garth was partial to rolling over the slower of the mobile cadavers, and had seen the damage that *Colebrook's Runner* was capable of dealing out. His breathing became ragged and laboured as he neared the parking lot where the vehicle had been left, then staggered to a halt. Not looking where she was going, Tara barrelled into the back of Bill, sending him stumbling forwards as he stared in disbelief at the vacant space the trailer had once stood in.

"No," he muttered, breaking out into another jog as he moved towards the maze of cars. "No, no, no."

"What's wrong?" asked Tara, keeping pace and looking from one side of the lot to the other. A few Rots lingered in the distance, but none seemed to have noticed them yet, and even if they did, they'd have to lumber around the maze of cars.

Unless there's more of those bastards that can leap over the cars, Bill thought to himself as he remembered his first days of his freedom after his incarceration and his chase across a parking lot in the Golden Nexus.

"It's gone. God damn bastards have left us."

"What?" she asked, seeming more panic-stricken then Bill felt. "I mean, are you sure? Would they do that?"

"Jesus, yes I'm sure. It was parked there, they've left my bike and they've abandoned me!"

"And you can't remember the meeting place?"

"I didn't *need* to," Bill growled, "That was Al's job. Shit."

"At least they've left the motorcycle," she said. "You know how to drive?"

"Of course," he said, storming over to the bike and looking over it. Someone had left his crossbow and his quiver of bolts, along with a metal strongbox filled with shotgun shells. It was good to see that someone had thought ahead enough to provide him with some form of supplies, no matter how meagre, but there wasn't enough to keep him going for too long. Enough ammo to stop a few Rots, certainly, but no food or water.

"Climb on," Bill ordered, loading up his weapons and securing everything where he could before hoisting a leg over the machine and lowering his weight on to the seat. It felt good to be back on his bike: it had been too long since he'd last taken a ride on the vehicle.

Since Edgly, he thought to himself, remembering his hometown and the carnage he had witnessed there. How long ago had that been? Days? Weeks? Maybe even months; it certainly felt like it was.

Tara perched herself on the rear of the bike, wrapping her arms around his chest and grabbing his jacket with both hands. She pressed her face against his back and nodded gently, as if confirming she was ready to go.

"Where are we going?" she murmured.

"If Garth's been his usual and careful self when driving, I can follow the trail of the dead lying on or around the roads. If he's not, or if someone else has been driving… I'll think of something."

With a squeal of tyres and the smell of burning rubber, the bike lurched away from the prison, carrying its passengers away from the decaying building and its undead inhabitants.

III

The cold chill of night crept in around Bill as he huddled closer to the fire he had built on the top floor of the derelict department store, rubbing his hands together and holding out his palms towards the fire.

As dusk settled over the ghost town of Manchester, Bill had finally given up on his futile search for the day. He'd had to refuel the bike a couple of times, which was easily accomplished once he had found a length of hose to siphon off petrol from the many abandoned cars lying around the streets.

Although the search had at first seemed like a daunting task with the size of the city being the main problem, Bill quickly found that the choices he had were more limited than he had thought. After all, the wide behemoth couldn't fit down narrow back alleys or car-filled streets as easily as his bike could, so he knew to stick to the wider tracks if he wanted to find his friends.

After reluctantly giving up on the search for the day, Bill had guided Tara into one of the larger deserted shops, making sure the building was devoid of any Rots or any other potential threats. He had then cleared out a small area of the upper floor, beneath a hole in the ceiling, and set up a small fire to keep the pair warm through the night. While he warmed himself by the fire, Tara had went on a journey to find something to provide a little extra protection against the elements, and had returned wearing a pair of tight-fitting trousers, and a sleeveless top. It wasn't exactly practical clothing for biking and hunting undead creatures; in fact, it looked more like the type of clothes worn by someone when they were going out for a night on the town.

"Got a hot date?" asked Bill with a smirk as she strolled into sight, tossing his T-shirt back at him. She didn't reply, simply sat down opposite the fire and stared into the dancing orange flames. Bill grabbed a piece of wood from the pile of bricks he was perched on and prodded the pile of burning debris, making sure all the kindling took to the flames. "Couldn't find a pair of jeans and a jumper?"

"It just so happens these are the latest fashion from Los Marcos' range of designer clothing. I wouldn't wear anything else. This would cost a fortune to buy."

"Designer clothes," Bill snorted, tapping the glowing embers and creating showers of sparks. He withdrew the stick and crushed it underfoot, extinguishing the flame before tossing the smoking piece of wood aside. "There's something I won't miss. Extortionate prices and poor quality."

"Philistine," muttered Tara, adjusting her clothing and wrapping a thick blanket around her shoulders. They hadn't been able to find anything edible, but Bill had managed to unearth three bottles of water while he had secured the department store. Tara took a sip from one of these bottles as she stared into the flames, swilling the water around in her mouth before swallowing. Bill took a moment to give his companion a good looking over, something he hadn't been able to do until now, now that he was out of the heat of battle.

Her red hair was styled in a loose manner, her fringe swept back and over to one side of her face. The colouring of her hair looked too red to be natural, and the shine suggested it had been died and enhanced by various chemicals. Her eyes were round and dark, the most prominent feature on her oval face. There seemed to be some chemistry between the two of them, though not good chemistry, not the way he and Angel had it. If anything, it was more reminiscent of the way Angel and Al acted. Bill could see why this might be: he and Tara came from different sides of the track, she was obviously more accustomed to the finer things life could offer. Maybe a little stuck up for his liking.

"So apart from wearing expensive clothing and playing the role of legal eagle, what else did you used to do?"

"What else do you do when you're young? We had a good time. Went out clubbing, went for meals. Drinking. Dancing. Me and my friends used to go to all the best places in town."

"All the exclusive clubs, right?" Bill cut in, taking a small sip from his own bottle of water and grinning. Tara looked at him with an expressionless gaze, shook her head and carried on with her story, ignoring his comments.

"It was probably all the time I spent in the clubs that saved me, I guess. *He* liked his women to be able to dance.

"Once the dead started to walk, I locked myself up in my flat. I had plenty of food in my kitchen; I thought I'd be able to last until help came. As the days went by, though, it looked as if there wasn't any help coming at all. The radio played nothing but the test signal, occasionally broken by the national anthem, and the television was dead. I couldn't even get on to the internet, no matter how hard I tried. Not long after that, the riots seemed to stop, and I decided I couldn't take being locked up any more. I left to look for anyone else who'd survived. I wasn't out for ten minutes when the

Messiah's men captured me. I mean, at first I was quite excited, seeing other survivors. When I noticed they were all men, and not the most pleasant looking of men at that: I mean, they just looked mean, I realised there was something wrong, and that I was in trouble."

Tara shuddered slightly at the memory of her capture, and decided not to talk of any of her ordeals in the prison. Bill didn't need any of these, though. He knew from the stories Sylvester and Angel had told him exactly what would go on behind closed doors in the prison. He could also guess that the prisoners were involved in the same rape and torture that the Messiah was. Instead he just nodded slowly in understanding, and decided to bring up another topic.

"You were around when the dead started to walk, weren't you?"

Tara nodded slowly, taking another sip from her bottle.

"What was it like?"

Tara didn't answer, staring into the dying embers of the flames with glazed eyes.

"Tara?" Bill said, leaning in closer, trying to dip his face into her line of sight. She turned away from him, avoiding eye contact.

"Why do you want to know?"

"Morbid curiosity, I guess," he said with a gentle shrug of his shoulders. "I lived in a city, just like Manchester. All my friends lived in the same city, but while the whole zombie thing was going on, I was locked up in a holding cell. I just wanted to know what it was like. I suppose I just wanted to know that it was... was quick for my close friends."

"It was hideous, okay?" she finally answered, snapping at him. She replaced the top on her bottle and stuffed it into a mound of blankets beside her. "I had to watch my friends and family die of some fucking plague that ate away the flesh around their joints, some disease that made their skin tear and spill blood. Then their dead bodies *stood up* and walked around. Hundreds of corpses stumbling through the streets, attacking hundreds more. The riots. Thousands more dying; the raping, looting, people unable to grasp the true horror of what was going on until it was too late... I stayed away from it all as much as I could, my flat was on the eighth floor of a luxury block of apartments. After what I've experienced, though, sometimes I wish I had died in the initial outbreak."

"Sorry," murmured Bill, looking sheepishly at the back of his hands. "I didn't mean to..."

"Doesn't matter," Tara said, dismissively waving her hand. "Just memories. They'll heal, with time. It's just... I mean, this is the first chance I've had the chance to just *think* about stuff like this. Without having to think about the Messiah, or when he wanted to see me next."

With that, Tara lay down on the ground and pulled her blankets tight around her, closing her eyes. Bill nodded silently to himself, knowing that tomorrow they'd have a busy day as they searched the city for any sign of Garth and his giant vehicle or the trail of destruction it may leave. Standing up, he gathered his submachine gun and strolled over to the top of the staircase, overlooking the ruined department store beneath him and holding his weapon one-handed, resting the extended stock against the ball of his shoulder, muzzle raised towards the ceiling. If only Bill could remember the name of the pickup, it wouldn't be so bad - he could head straight for there and meet up with his friends. Maybe tomorrow, he could stop by one of the many tourist and information offices dotted around the city and browse a few maps: maybe seeing the name in print would jog his memory.

A rustle and a clatter outside the building alerted Bill to the presence of something outside, and he snapped his weapon down ready, panning it from left to right. Outside, he could see the shadow of a Rot as it pressed itself against one of the shattered windows of the shop. Flaking flesh and tattered clothing caught on the splinters of glass as it stumbled by, a brief sliver of moonlight picking out the deformed details of the hulking creature. It paused by the open doorway, tentatively sniffing at the air in a quizzical motion. Bill readied himself, finger poised over the trigger, and waited. If he could avoid it, he wouldn't shoot, as the sound of the weapon discharging in the still of the night may well attract every Rot within the city limits. True, it may also alert Al to his location, but the last thing Bill wanted to do was to fight his way through a city of undead in the middle of the night.

As if hearing his mental plea, the Rot shuffled on, blissfully unaware of the meal it may have just missed. Bill relaxed slightly, lowered his weapon, then sunk to his knees, taking up a vantage point on the landing. Although he was both physically and mentally drained, he decided it would be best to stay awake and on guard. Tara was obviously inexperienced, and Bill didn't think she'd be able to hold her own if she were left to keep a watchful eye over the two of them.

"A long day's night," he whispered to himself, casting a glance over his shoulder as Tara muttered a series of grunts and incoherent words before snoring gently. "Why couldn't I be stranded with Al, or Angel. Hell, even Garth would have been a help in this situation."

He lowered his head, shaking it in silent mirth. "God damn rookie."

Al lay back on the wrecked bar that dominated most of the ransacked Midas Bar that overlooked Greyson's Park, holding half a bottle of whiskey in one hand and a smoking cigar in the other. Sylvester had got them to Greyson's Park pretty quickly, within three hours of leaving the prison in fact, leaving Al with plenty of time to hunt through the multitude of bars surrounding the area to stockpile all the consumables he could find. They hadn't seen a lot of Rots during the day, though that may well have been because all the creatures in the city had been herded together in the prison by the Messiah and his men. With the prison being so far from the city centre, Al figured it would be a long time before even the fastest of the creatures found their way back into the city limits.

With Bill missing and the morale of his men down, Al had decided to offer everyone the night off, as a form of relaxation: though there was no guarantee that there weren't any creatures around their current position, it was a chance Al was willing to take. Garth had gladly taken the offer, and now lay curled around the padded seats of one of the booths around the edge of the room, three empty glasses lying beside his sprawled form as he snored loudly. Pam lay on the floor beside him, sleeping light, waking every five or ten minutes and looking around her surroundings in bewilderment, before smiling and returning back to sleep. Al couldn't begin to understand what she had gone through while she'd been held captive by the Messiah, but he'd managed to have a quiet word with her before she'd went to sleep, advising that if she wanted to talk, he'd be there to listen. She'd smiled and nodded, but hadn't taken him up on his offer.

Give her time, he thought. *She's been through a lot.*

After finding a generator in the basement of the bar behind a stack of kegs and getting it running, Sylvester had promptly taken apart the pool table, prying open the mechanism that kept back the balls from would-be players until they inserted the correct change required for a game. Both he and Clive had spent the rest of the evening playing pool, their conversations carried out in hushed voices.

Al had spent his time in the bar making short work of the spirits that he had managed to pilfer from Midas and the other bars surrounding Greyson's Park, perching on the bar where he had a good view of the only entrances to the bar, and the large window that overlooked the grassy field outside.

He could imagine Greyson's Park had once been a picturesque area families gathered in, or young couples walked around while their dog chased a ball. In winter, he could imagine children gathering with their friends, meeting up for snowball fights. Although he was only four or five when he moved from England to America, Al still had some memories of the few winters he had spent in his English home.

He smiled as he took another swig from the bottle he held, then screwed the cap back on and placed the bottle on the counter. The only person he hadn't seen since the band had taken over the bar was Angel, and try as he might, he couldn't get her to respond to any taunts or name-calling over the radio headset.

"I'm going to check on the bitch," he announced, swinging himself down from the counter and grabbing a couple of packets of bar snacks from the small cache of stale and expired food Garth had uncovered from the beer cellar. "Spanners, you and Preacher-man are in charge. Keep an eye on the window and doors, you see any movement, give me a shout."

Neither man verbally responded, but each gave a slight nod, before returning to the game they were currently engrossed in: they took their turn to glance out the window and the darkening scene outside between lining up shots

Happy that they were doing their job, Al left and headed for the small staircase behind the bar, following the winding steps to the thick metal door set at the top. He heaved the iron barrier open with a piercing screech and stepped out on to the roof.

The scent of rot and decay seemed to be magnified on the roof, as if the pools of water littering the tiled roof were teeming with the viral taint of the plague, even though Al knew that wasn't the case. He made his way over the gentle sloping of the roof, clinging to any handholds he could find between the cracking and bleached tiles, until he reached the flat roof where Angel sat, her back to the Marine as she watched the streets below. She sat with her rifle resting on her knee, and an opened box of rifle rounds beside her. As he approached, Al could see that she was working on five empty magazines, reloading them methodically and putting each to one side as she filled it.

"Expecting a war?" he asked casually, dropping slowly to his knees and watching as she worked. He had to admit to himself that he was impressed with the way the young girl worked, in particular the way she handled herself in combat. Any doubts he had initially regarding her ability to handle herself had been put to rest during the prison escape. The fact she had willingly stepped into the fray with a pair of submachine guns had impressed him, though he wasn't going to let *her* know that. She was still just the bitch with a nice ass.

"You still here?" she asked without looking up from the reloading. "I haven't heard from you for about half an hour. I thought you'd just abandoned me. You know, like you did with Bill."

"Still pissed about that, eh?" sighed Al, shaking his head and grabbing one of the bullets from the box, turning it end over end.

"You left him," Angel said bitterly, sniffing as she talked.

"I left a perfectly capable soldier on his own to extract a civilian from a combat zone," Al said. Ordinarily he wouldn't defend any of his actions to his troops, but then again, his troops wouldn't normally be as emotional as Angel was at that moment. She didn't say anything, so Al carried on. "Bill's a good kid, a strong fighter, and he's got a sensible head on his shoulders. If I didn't think he could look after himself, I would've held on a little longer. But at the same time, I had a trailer full of people to evac from the hot spot."

"We're not soldiers, Al," Angel said, her voice quivering as she spoke. "We're all civilians, in case you forgot. Bill is no more a soldier then me or Garth."

"He's more of a soldier than a lot of men I've commanded. Like I said, he's good at what he does, even though he's got no formal training. Everything he knows may be from a book, or second hand information, but he puts it to good use."

"That doesn't fill me with confidence," hissed Angel through gritted teeth.

"Is there *anything* I can say to fill you with confidence?"

"Not really," she said, finishing her final magazine and turning her back on Al.

"Bill's a fine soldier, whether he had a real rank or something I just gave him one drunken night. He's out there on his bike somewhere, probably hiding out until morning to get his ass over here, because he knows that if he drives through a city in the night, he's going to draw all the dead fucks out after him, and possibly compromise our safety. I've seen this guy operate more than you have, he's good. Like I say, he's got a sensible head on his shoulders, you could do a lot worse than him."

Angel sighed in exasperation, then shook her head slowly. "He's just a civilian, Al, just a normal guy."

"Bullshit," Al swore. "Everyone here now is a survivor, and they've lasted a lot longer than the rest of the country. I look on you all as my men, as my own squad of soldiers. And much as I hate to admit it that includes you: you're good at what you do. Sniper. A little stealthy. You got a fire in you that others don't, it keeps you alive."

Angel didn't say anything, but looked over her shoulder, her eyes swollen and red, as if she'd been crying.

"He'll turn up in the morning, trust me on that."

"Providing he remembers where we're supposed to meet up. The all-mighty Marine couldn't remember where *he* was supposed to go."

Al sighed, shaking his head and muttering to himself, "Can't believe I'm thinking this," then said aloud "Tomorrow, at first light, me and Spanners'll go look for him. How's that sound?"

"I want to go," she said, wiping the back of her sleeve across her eyes.

"And who's going to look after the pacifist, the coward and the dancer? No way, someone has to stay to look after the *real* civilians. Now, I don't want to hear any arguments from you."

Angel said nothing else, simply worked the bolt on her rifle, cycling the first round into the chamber, then shouldered the weapon, peering through the scope and slowly panning from left to right.

"Perimeter secure?" asked Al, feeling that Angel had decided to stop the conversation there. She muttered a response, but Al couldn't tell whether it was a positive or a negative one. He shrugged and carefully returned to the door, stumbling through the frame and down the stairs before returning into the bar itself.

"Nothing to report, sir," muttered Clive, a mock salute accompanying a lop-sided grin before he lined himself up for his next shot on the pool table. Sylvester didn't say anything, his eyes focused intently on the layout of the table before him.

"She still pissed at you?" Garth muttered, clambering to his feet and nimbly stepping around the sleeping form of Pam. Al nodded, scratching the back of his head and looking around the ruined bar.

"Yeah, she's still pissed, but, with an ass like hers, I can't stay mad at her for long. Spanners, you and me are going out first thing in the morning, do a quick recon, see if we can find the kid. I'll leave her in charge, she can keep watch."

Sylvester nodded absentmindedly as he chalked his queue.

"I can keep watch myself, you know," Garth whined, rubbing his bleary eyes and stumbling over to the bar. Grabbing a ceramic mug and flicking the dented chrome kettle on, he ripped open a sachet of coffee and emptied it into the cup. "I'm not a complete invalid."

"Yeah, right," snorted Al, "At the first sign of anyone coming, you'd run with your yellow tail between your legs."

"Survival instinct," Garth said with a grin, pouring the now-boiled water from the kettle into his cup and swilling the mix around. "Kept me alive so far."

"Ain't much use in running away from our military escort, is there?" asked Al, taking over the seat by the sleeping dancer. "Which reminds me, we need to go over the plan for the morning. We've still got the heavy-duty HAZMAT suits from the crate in the trailer. We should probably slip into those now, or as soon as possible, in case the Marines come early. Spanners, you take on the role of the General, unless Bill turns up before they get here. There should be enough suits for the five of us here."

"Five?" said Garth, pointing a finger at each person in the room, counting them off, before flicking one digit towards the roof. "I get six, including Angel."

"The bitch is our insurance, she'll stick around up there until we're absolutely sure it's not a double cross. She's a sniper by nature, eyes like a hawk. It's one of her most redeeming features, other than her ass. If we can't find Bill, we hold on as long as possible. The golden rule is we don't go until the kid turns up."

"When he turns up, he'll be out of uniform, won't he?"

"That's when we'll have to bluff them. Inoculated scout, a mole from one of the gangs of rebels. Jesus, I'll think of something if and when it happens. You can probably see how important it is to find the kid *before* the Marines turn up, though."

"With lame stories like that, yeah, I can," Sylvester said, a grim expression on his face. "An early rise, then?"

"Yeah, so we should probably get some sleep, take a leaf out of Pam's book here and get rested."

"All of us? What about posting a guard?" asked Garth. "Aren't we going to take turns in watching for any movement outside?"

"No need," said Al, climbing on to the seat beside Pam and curling his legs up. "Angel's on watch for her boyfriend, she'll be up all night, she'll keep an eye out for any Rots or gang-bangers, isn't that right, bitch?" his last statement was directed into his headset, but he didn't get any response. "You see? Now get some sleep."

IV

Angel had been up on the roof for hours, so long she'd lost track of all time. The sun was just starting to peer over the vacant buildings to the east, long shadows cast across the cityscape she overlooked, and a gentle misted rain washed across the town, soaking her as she lay on the edge of the tiled roof, her rifle tucked in against her shoulder. Despite the coldness of the night, and the harshness of the morning elements as they soaked her, she refused to move, her eyes transfixed on the column of dirt that had been moving around in the distance.

"Get up," she hissed into her microphone. "Get up, you miserable shit, why aren't you awake?"

After several minutes of cajoling, her radio headset crackled, and Al responded with an audible grunt.

"Looks like they're on their way, Al. A big cloud of dust, heading this way in a zigzag pattern."

"Must still be securing this area of the city," muttered Al, his voice accompanied by the sounds of other people rousing from their slumbers. "How far do you think they are?"

"A few miles, at the moment. Too many buildings in the way to make out any of their details, like how many people or what kind of vehicles they have."

"We'll get ready, sort out the suits. Keep me updated," Al said, then the line went dead. Angel kept the rifle trained on the cloud of dirt as it patrolled from left to right, trying to get a good view of the source of the disruption.

"Damn buildings," she muttered to herself.

"What've you got up there?" Al called as he left the sanctity of the bar and worked his way across to the trailer parked outside, heaving open the doors to the rear of the vehicles and handing out the suits to Garth, who rushed them inside. "Just the rifle?"

"Handgun, too," Angel said, patting her thigh where the weapon sat. "Not much else."

"I'll send someone up with a load of weapons for you; grenades, shit like that. I've got a bad feeling about this, I don't think it's going to go down well. How far?"

"Still as couple of miles, they're taking their time. Must've run into a little trouble."

Al didn't reply, but carried on with the unloading of the vehicle. The light drizzle quickly turned into a torrential downpour, and Al vanished back into the bar, cursing under his breath as he moved. Angel didn't' move, remaining stoic despite the rain as it pelted the tiles around her. She heard footsteps behind her, and quick as a flash, she drew her handgun and pointed it behind her, looking over her shoulder at her target. Pam shrieked, leaping back and dropping the small box she held. Grenades tumbled from the crate and rolled around the roof, some coming to a stop beside Angel. She quickly stood and gathered the explosives, replacing them in the box and apologising for the frightening experience. Pam nodded, her face as white as the all-in-one suit she wore, and quickly retreated back into the bar.

"How's it looking," Al asked as Angel returned to her vantage point overlooking Greyson's Park.

"A little closer, but I still can't make anything out. It's definitely them, it's too large to be Bill's bike."

"Sorry we couldn't get out and find your boyfriend," Al said over the sound of weapons loading and equipment being locked into position.

"And I'm sorry I scared the shit out of your girlfriend," Angel replied with a smile as she imagined the look Al would have on his face. "Bill will turn up, I'm sure of it. Just make sure you stall them long enough."

"We won't leave without him, bitch, I promise."

Angel didn't answer, tensing herself as a motorbike rolled into the clearing of Greyson's Park, grinding to a halt on the muddy grass of the clearing. The vehicle itself was painted in the regular urban camouflage distortion pattern, and held two men dressed in environment suits similar to those that Al was handing out below: one was clearly the driver, facing forwards and toying with the machinegun fixed to the handlebars. The second man appeared to be the main gunner, sitting in a metal cage attached to the rear of the bike and facing to the rear, with a pair of heavy machineguns affixed to the cage.

"What the hell is that?" she whispered, more to herself than anyone else.

"It's a gyro-bike," muttered Al, his voice given an echoing quality by the helmet he wore. "The bastard offspring of a bike and a gun platform. Some bright spark decided it would be a fantastic idea to give an extremely mobile vehicle a couple of heavy weapons and a second person, at the expense of their mobility. The cage at the back has dual mounted weapons, and is set up on a gyroscopic rig; it was supposed to increase aiming while on the move. One of my guys, J-Man, was involved in the initial testing of the vehicles, said they handled like a dead cow, and they looked like a bike with a giant wart on its ass. Looks like they went into production despite his comments and criticism."

"Are they dangerous?" asked Garth, his voice cutting in. "They look pretty heavy duty."

"The most dangerous thing the UGMC has is a Marine and his rifle," Al swiftly responded, and Angel could picture the pompous smile that would undoubtedly be on his face. "From what J-Man said, these gotta spin a one-eighty before they can get a shot off. By then, we'll have popped their heads clean off, neutralised the threat. Now, shut up and switch to secured channel nine, that's what they should be operating on. Maintain radio silence until my mark."

Angel quickly switched her radio to the designated channel, and instantly picked up the relentless chatter between the bike and their support troops, still kicking up a cloud of dirt and still hidden by the range of buildings before her. Angel couldn't follow the banter going back and forth, and tried her best to tune it out, lining up the crosshair of her scope on the armoured head of the driver, then quickly flitting back and forth between the soldier on the rear gunner seat, getting a feel for the potential targets.

As the dust storm closed in, the buzz of military code words and numbers subsided and a rough voice cut in. "Home Base, this is Scout One, location reached and possible civilian presence confirmed. One large vehicle, cargo-class, parked up alongside one of the bars. Marine weaponry and equipment present, suggesting commandeering of civilian resources. No signs of life at present, we may still have time to set up, over. "

"Roger that, Scout One. Dismount and secure entrance to clearing, ETA is three minutes. Do not engage until Home Base arrives, over."

"I copy that, Home Base."

The meaningless banter ceased, and the two soldiers removed themselves from the bike, each pulling the heavy machineguns from the mounted cage and lightly running off to either side of the road they'd driven in on. They didn't talk, simply communicated with simple hand gestures and nods of their helmeted heads. Angel knew from what few civilised conversations she'd had with Al what some gestures meant, and understood they were securing the park before their command base rolled into view.

After perching on the roof for a further three minutes, tentatively swinging from one target to another, the vehicle responsible for the swirling dust cloud trundled into view, and Angel felt her breath catch in her throat.

The vehicle was in three segments, one cab and two trailers, each joined by a series of hydraulic pistons and black accordion-like joints. The cab itself was one and a half times bigger than Garth's own, taking up more than a single lane of the road. The giant caterpillar tracks of the cab seemed to press into the tarmac of the road, the immense weight of the vehicle damaging the man made surface. The top of the cab was bristling with weapons and an assortment of spikes and razor wire, no doubt to hold back any of the Rots that may manage to get that close. One man sat in the opened turret on top of the vehicle, scanning from left to right with a pair of binoculars and periodically checking the conditions of each weapon, while the thick and heavy doors on the side of the engine swung open with a piercing screech, and more soldiers clambered out. Angel could already count seven soldiers, and licked her lips in anticipation. If anything *did* go wrong, they were already outnumbered.

The second part of the vehicle was large enough to host two storeys, and the fact that a metal catwalk ringed the construction only gave evidence to that argument. Three soldiers patrolled the walkway, with another two manning the weapons that covered the top. With a loud crunch that seemed to echo throughout the park, a large plate metal door trundled open on the side of vehicle and another five soldiers leapt out, forming a line beside the vehicle with their machineguns at the ready.

The rear-most section of the vehicle wasn't as tall as the middle, but it was just as long. Other than the obvious tracks along the side where doors would roll open and shut, it was very non-descript in comparison to its sibling sections. While the other two segments of the vehicle were alive with activity, this final trailer was ominously silent.

"It's a set up," whispered Angel, lowering her scoped weapon as another five soldiers clambered out from the middle trailer. She grabbed two of the grenades she'd been given, holding them close against her chest and watching as the squadron of soldiers peeled off in separate directions, some checking on the deserted buildings around them, while others set up a defensive perimeter around the oversized machine.

"Hold your fire," announced an all-too familiar voice, and Angel peered over the edge of the building to see the forms of three men and a woman, dressed in the sealed HAZMAT suit and helmet, swagger out the bar, cradling their weapons but not pointing it in any particular direction. "We weren't expecting you for another few hours yet, we didn't get around to properly securing the area."

"Hold it right there," countered one of the soldiers from across the open land as all their weapons were snapped up and brought about to bear on Al. Angel swallowed hard and found herself chewing her lip, impressed with Al's matter-of-fact and casual attitude, despite the overwhelming odds he faced if his bluff failed. "Who goes there?"

"Corporal John Carlson," Al shouted back, lowering the muzzle of his weapon so it pointed to the ground. It wasn't threatening, but Angel knew he could snap it up into action at a moments notice. She'd never seen another Marine in action for comparison, however, but she had a feeling that this was going to see pretty soon. "Sweet Jesus, is that one of the Bailey mobile command centres? Man, I've never seen one up close before. They took me out of Brazil before my squad was due to get theirs shipped. They're supposed to be a lot more comfortable than the old Samson models, or at least a lot roomier. Look at the size of that thing... I hear they were so big, they had to outfit Landmasters with cutting equipment to clear a route for them sometimes. Off-road capabilities or not, the engineers had their heads up their ass when they made these… Must've been the same fuckwits who came up with those bikes, right?"

"Where's the General?" asked the same soldier, ignoring Al's banter. She assumed it was the same, Angel couldn't see who was speaking as everyone's face was obscured by masks and helmets.

"The Old Man's asleep in the bar, he's not young any more, and he can't take all the excitement of combat like what we can."

"How many men do you have in there?"

"We got enough," Al answered, trying not to give too much away. "Standard cover for a General; his three personal guards, a back up squad, minus a few casualties of course. We've got a scout out in the field, too, we're waiting for him to come back. Once he gets back, we should be good to go. What kind of window do we have to work with?"

"There's a Cavalier Gunship ready to make the pick up once we send confirmation to one of the relay stations offshore. You mind if we step in and see Maxis?"

"Like I said, the Old Man's sleeping. Last thing I want to do is disturb him, he can be a crabby bastard if he doesn't get his sleep."

Angel watched one of the soldiers step aside and confer with another of the squad, placing their helmets together to converse without polluting the airwaves.

"They're not buying it," muttered Angel, curling her fingers around the pins of the grenades. "They're not buying it, Al, do something."

"I'll take a walk back in, see if he's up to visitors."

"Then I'll come with you," said the main talker from the opposing squad as four men stepped forwards. "Time is a crucial factor in this extraction, we need to get moving before this rain breaks out into a full storm."

"The Cavaliers are like flying bricks, a little rain won't do them any arm," countered Al, taking a small step back towards the opening of the bar and motioning for the rest of his crew to do likewise. "But I know the General can suffer from air sickness a little. I'll go get him," he announced, then he turned to address his three companions, communicating in a low voice and with a variety of hand signals before he returned inside.

After close to a minute, the door to the stairs burst open and Al lumbered out on to the rooftop, his helmet removed as he crouched low to avoid detection. "You still here?"

Angel didn't answer, she kept her eyes fixed on the scene below as it played out. Soldiers marched across the wet mud, their boots splashing in puddles as they moved with a purpose. "What're they doing?"

"Gimme a look," muttered Al as he crawled towards the lip of the roof. "Looks like they're spreading out into an offensive pattern, ready for a pre-emptive strike. See the way they're forming a crescent around us? They don't believe a word I'm saying, just buying time until they're ready to make their move. I'll try to buy us a little time ourselves, see what Sylvester can pull off. Okay, plan of action: the biggest threat is that giant machine they've got, there's enough weapons on that beast to wipe out half of Manchester. I want the men on the guns neutralised, but I don't want the machine damaged if we can help it. When we win, that vehicle's ours. Can you get them from up here?"

"No problems," she said, nodding. "I guess we're not leaving, then."

"Not until your boyfriend turns up. But from the looks of things, he's going to miss the party."

"I'm sure he'll survive."

"Okay, bitch, remember the plan. Take out the men operating the weapons on the vehicle first, three clean shots, then see what damage you can cause to their men with those grenades."

"There must be about fifteen, sixteen of those soldiers down there, we're outnumbered, do we stand a chance?"

"There's more than that," Al said, shuffling back from the ledge. "As they pulled up, another five troops dropped out the rear trailer and started to work their way around to flank us. They should be close to the back door now. Soon as they open it, the whole back alley'll tumble down around them. A little trick I learnt from the Bebops back in Brazil. And they're not soldiers, they're Marines."

"What's that mean?"

"It means we're outnumbered more than you think. Just do what you can."

With that, Al retreated to the door and vanished back into the building, shortly reappearing down on the ground with another person beside him, wearing the suit and helmet they used in the television transmission as Maxis.

"What in God's name is going on here, Marine?" Sylvester bellowed over the radio headset. "When I tell my men that I'm not to be disturbed, I expect not to be disturbed. What is going on here?"

"General Maxis?" questioned the main voice of the soldiers as he half-saluted. Several of his men reluctantly imitated him.

"Didn't Carlson tell you I was asleep?"

"Did he inform you of the window before the storm?"

"He told me we're getting picked up in a Cavalier, can't the pilot handle a little cross-wind?"

"I guess he can," blurted the Marine, shrugging his shoulders in response.

"Well get on the God-damn horn and ask! Jesus, I've got two men out there scouting the city, and we're not leaving without them. I don't leave my men behind."

"Yessir," stammered the soldier, and he spun on his heel and rushed to the open door to the trailer, hooking his communication gear into the console inside.

It looks like we may pull this off after all, Angel thought to herself as the troops who had been encircling the bar seemed to be backing off, moving back towards the vehicle. She silently shook her head in disbelief, watching through her scope as the soldier finished his conversation and disconnected from the long distance radio.

"Pilot says he should be able to handle the winds, it doesn't look like it's going to be that bad. Oh, and Major Carter just wants to make sure you still have the briefcase containing your research material and evac codes."

"Briefcase?" asked Sly, going to scratch his head but coming into contact with only his helmet. "Yeah, it's locked up safe in the bar!"

"Fucking idiot," screamed Al, bringing up his machinegun and loosing an unaimed salvo roughly in the direction of the bulk of soldiers before diving for cover behind *Colebrook's Runner*. "Take the shots, bitch, do it!"

Angel nodded to herself as she swung the muzzle of her rifle around to bear on her target and unleashed a burst of gunfire, four shots she tapped off one after another. The first missed its mark, but the next three scored a direct hit, smashing the heads of each heavy weapons operator atop the vehicle. She dropped her rifle, then grabbed the crate of grenades, priming and hurling them as fast as she could. By the time she had managed to do that, the Marines had scattered, meaning the explosives inflicted only minor injuries.

"Alpha omega nine," screamed one of the soldiers, and the radio channel suddenly erupted into a blaring scream of feedback, forcing Angel to switch the channel to another.

"Jamming their channel, the bastards," shouted Al as he unfastened his helmet and tore the cumbersome filter mask from his head while pulling at his suit, trying to get some movement back from the restrictive clothing. "Where'd the bastards scatter to?"

"I didn't see," confessed Angel, lifting her rifle up and panning from left to right. "Sorry!"

"We'll have to wait and see where they open fire from," hissed Al, "Which won't be too long."

His prediction was correct, as the opposing soldiers opened up with their own weapons, a cacophony of sound and a barrage of gunfire that tore through the thick hide of *Colebrook's*

Runner, shattering the glass of the bar. Screams of terror from Pam and rage from Al filled Angel's headset, and she tore it from her head, casting it aside and opening fire on the few soldiers she could see, trying to take down the soldiers that ran to operate the mounted weapons.

This could have gone better, Angel thought to herself as she fumbled for a fresh magazine, ducking back from the edge of the roof as a few of the Marines finally found her perch and raised their aim, the air around her suddenly filled with live ammunition.

"I didn't want to have to do this," Al shouted, his voice fading in and out over the gunfire. "The fighting's going to attract any Rots left in the city."

Angel snatched up the headset and fumbled with it, replacing it so she could join in the conversation below her, trying her best to ignore the incoherent ramblings of Pam. A deep resonating blast sounded behind Angel, and the roof she stood upon shook slightly as a thick serpent of smoke coiled up around her, blocking the light from the sun above her. Choking and spluttering, Angel stumbled to the door leading down into the bar, half-falling down the stairs as she went.

"Christ, they're at the back," the rogue Marine yelled excitedly, "Someone cover the rear, make sure the explosion wiped them all out!"

"I'm on it," she shouted, drawing her pistol and slinging her rifle over her shoulder. She marched through into the bar, looking towards the smoking hole in the roof and the small fires that burned merrily on the carpets and bar. Beyond the hole, she could see the shadows of the alleyway, and dark shapes lurching about in the thick miasma of smoke.

"What's it like back there, bitch?"

"Multiple survivors," she muttered, thumbing the safety off her pistol and dragging the slide back, making sure it was cocked and ready to fire. "Can't see how many, but they're out there."

"Use any grenades you have, make sure you finish them off."

Angel blindly patted herself down as she kept her eyes trained on the opening and the shadows that seemed to be coming towards her. "Damnit," she muttered, looking back towards the direction of the staircase, "they're upstairs."

She was about to turn and retreat to retrieve what grenades she could, when the first shape emerged from the smoke cloud, and Angel snapped up her piece.

A ragged figure, flesh blackened and sloughing from its skeletal frame, lumbered into the room, twisted and broken limbs outstretched as it slowly made its way towards Angel. Without a second thought, she squeezed off three rounds, clipping the shoulders of the creature before finally smashing through the skull and scoring a clean kill. It slumped to the floor with a gurgle, only to be replaced by another two creatures, each as horrific as the first. Angel fired wildly, emptying the clip in less than five seconds and slamming a fresh one home, backing away as more and more corpses shuffled into the bar.

As she backed up, she knocked a table, disturbing the smoking cigar and bottle of brandy that had been abandoned; no doubt the remains of Al's nightcap. She grabbed the darkened glass container and hurled it towards the closest Rot as her weapon ran dry again, hoping against hope that it would faze the creature it struck. Though it didn't stop it, the bottle smashed on impact, covering the front most creatures in the flammable liquid as they stumbled mindlessly on towards her. The liquid took to the fire, igniting those unlucky enough to be splashed and flames spread around the bar area, cooking the small cache of alcohol Al had found before igniting the rest of the room. Both the intense heat and the threat of the creatures pushed Angel back, and she quickly made her way out the front of the building. She sighed with relief as she exited the cloying heat of the burning bar, the rain cooling her skin: her relief was short lived as the air around her became alive with gunfire, and she dived to the ground, rolling across the cement flooring until she bumped into Al. He looked over his shoulder at her as he sprayed his bulky weapon from side to side, and took the time to nod towards the bar, the dark depths of which now had a warm and inviting orange glow.

"What's going on in there?"

"We're in trouble," she said, helping herself to Al's oversized handgun and spinning back to face the bar. With the weapon held in both hands she squeezed off a round, obliterating the top of one of the Rot's head with the bullet and almost knocking herself down to the ground with the recoil.

"It has a way of finding me," Al confessed, and not for the first time. "What's happening?"

"Wasn't the Marines breaking into the back, it was a bunch of Rots."

Already the flaming creatures had stumbled through the bar and tumbled out into the streets, their charred and smouldering flesh hissing and spitting as the rain pelted their blackened hides. A quick look around the courtyard revealed that these creatures weren't the only ones, and they seemed to be overrunning the park: pale, half-rotten creatures were pulling themselves from their hiding places around the opening, some veering off towards Angel and her group of friends, other making a beeline for the retaliating armed forces.

"We're surrounded," screamed Garth, nearly hysterical as he rapidly switched between different targets, either hidden soldiers or lumbering corpses. "We're fucked!"

"Show them no fear, people," Al screamed, tearing his headset free and casting it to the ground before raising himself to his feet and bracing the butt of his weapon against his hip, firing frantically in a full circle. "It's a beautiful day to die!"

XVII
DEATH IN THE FAMILY

"We see families torn apart every day: loathe as I am to admit it, our men seem immune to their suffering now: young, old, man, woman, it's just more kindling for the fire…"

I

Bill lurched awake with a start, blindly fumbling for one of his weapons that lay beside him. Grabbing the shotgun, he leapt to his feet, listening intently to the spatter of rain and the rumble far off in the distance.

"Thunder," Tara said without looking up, stoking the fire with a metal rod and retrieving a tin kettle from the flames and wrapping a thick padded cloth around the handle. "Tea? Coffee?"

"Are you sure that's thunder?" he asked dubiously. "How long's it been going on?"

"Of course I'm sure, it's pissing it down out there. It started a few minutes ago. Now, do you want a drink? I managed to find a large can of sealed coffee granules down in the store."

"Please," he said, staring dumbly towards the direction he thought the thunder was coming from. "Milk and one sugar."

"Milk?" Tara laughed. "You've got high hopes, haven't you?"

"Black then," he muttered, crunching around the debris that littered the floor and trying to look out one of the shattered windows of the store. "What about the sugar?"

"I don't think so."

"Garth used to use chocolate to sweeten it," Bill offered.

"Milk, sugar, chocolate, Jesus you're optimistic. You're going to find nothing like that around here. I went through hell to find this alone."

"Just give me the coffee," he said, admitting defeat. "That doesn't sound like thunder, Tara, are you sure?"

"Jesus, yeah, it's thunder," she scorned, stepping forwards and offering a chipped ceramic mug. Bill accepted it graciously and sipped the steaming and bitter liquid, still focused on the distant cityscape visible from the store. Flashes illuminated the furthest reaches of the city, followed by the distant roll of a drum.

"Doesn't look like lightning," Bill commented. "Looks more like..."

He froze, his mug inches from his mouth, trembling and spilling coffee from the tilted lip.

"What? It looks like what?"

With a crash, the mug slipped from his grip, splashing boiling coffee over his legs as he rushed around the small camp and gathered his belongs, bundling what he could into bags while motioning to Tara to do the same.

"Thunder and lightning," scoffed Bill, throwing his handgun to Tara and slinging his weapons over his shoulders. "It's fucking gunfire and explosions. Jesus Christ, it's Al, it's my friends."

"And we're going *towards* the fighting?"

"It's the only way we're going to find them," Bill shouted as he tumbled down the stairs, throwing his equipment on to the back of his bike and motioning to the silent machine. Sighing heavily, Tara reluctantly clambered on to the vehicle and watched as Bill did the same, lifting his arms as an offer for her to cling to him.

"Hold tight," he said, kicking the engine to life. "We might not have long to get a fix on the gunfight."

Bill couldn't remember much of the journey through the streets of Manchester; he was so focused on tracking the origin of the battle, he barely took any notice of the roads and shopping districts as he hurtled through them at breakneck speeds.

After ten minutes of driving the overwhelming sounds of gunfire ceased, and Bill drew the bike to a sudden halt, suddenly realising that his fevered driving had left him lost in the middle of an alien city.

"It's stopped," he finally muttered, wiping the rain from his eyes and looking blearily around the street. "Where the hell are we?"

"I don't know this area very well, just a few of the local hotspots," Tara confessed, shrugging her shoulders and lowering a foot to the ground as Bill dipped the vehicle to one side.

"Well, where *do* you know?"

"Bars, clubs, a few restaurants, but that's it."

"Al likes a drink, a bar's as good a place as any to start looking," Bill sighed, still listening intently for any audio clue that may give the position of his friends away once more. Even the retort of a single gunshot may give enough of a clue for Bill to get a fix on his companions. "How many bars are there?"

"Too many. They're bunched up in groups around here, set up around different landmarks and monuments."

"Like what?"

"Parks, shopping centres, places people naturally gathered in."

"Parks?" Something struck a chord with Bill, a memory sparked to life, and he twisted to look over his shoulder. "What are they called?"

"Jesus, I can't remember them all. You want to stop, get a road map, that's fine with me."

"Just tell me what you can remember, anything that might help."

"Okay, let me think," Tara pursed her lips as she thought it over. "There's a few down the road there: Stanley Park's one of them, that's the biggest one. I used to hang around there when I was younger, kids go there to drink. Further south from here, there's the Acres, that's where they play football. Sunday league, mostly. Then you've got Morton and Greyson's park, they're mostly just open grassy areas, nothing special really."

"That's it!" Bill shouted, a sudden rush of adrenaline flowing through his system. "Tara, I could kiss you. Greyson, that's the place, that's where we're meeting up. Can you get us there?"

"It's about half an hour away, maybe a little less. It's in the direction you were going, just keep on heading the way we're facing."

"You're sure?"

"Yes, I'm sure, what's the point in asking me questions, then questioning my answers? It's that way."

With a burst of elation, Bill revved the gurgling engine of the bike back into life and kicked off, following Tara's directions as best he could: she was often too late in telling him when to turn, meaning there were a lot times he had to find somewhere to turn the bike around, as the streets were tightly packed with debris and abandoned vehicles. The time it took for Bill to do so seemed like an age to him, sometimes having to drive for several metres to circumnavigate the crashed and blackened vehicles that littered the streets and almost doubling the time the journey took.

The streets of the city were eerily quiet, a fact that played heavily with Bill's mind as he piloted the bike between blackened buildings and through the ground floor of derelict buildings. Even if the Messiah had his men working around the clock, Manchester was a massive city and they couldn't possibly round up all the undead and keep them confined to their holding pen. When he'd passed through the dead pit, although there had been quite a few undead, there certainly hadn't been a city's worth. Even during his time at the Golden Nexus and Barkley's, he had encountered massive numbers of the cannibalistic horde. Where could the creatures possibly be hiding?

Finally, the bike rolled into Greyson's Park, and Bill quickly killed the engine, climbing from the vehicle and staring in astonishment at the scene of carnage before him.

Two shattered and blood-spattered vehicles lay before him, one the familiar shape of *Colebrook's Runner,* the other a vehicle of unknown origin, though from the general appearance of it, it seemed to be of Marine design. Pale blue-grey smoke rolled across the muddy ground, the thick smell of burning rubber and flesh tainted with the underlying tang of spent cordite charges heavy in the air. Black specks circled the air above, carrion-feeding crows waiting for their turn to feast on the dead bodies that scattered the clearing once the current wave of scavengers had took their fill.

Bill instantly lifted his shotgun, trying to count the number of the dead that swarmed over the clearing. Obviously attracted by the thunderous fire fight, the pale corpses picked and fought over lumps of flesh and severed limbs as they gorged upon the recently slaughtered men and women in the opening. Mesmerised by the scene, Bill watched as a zombie dressed in the tattered remains of a grey business suit fought savagely with an undead police officer over a disembodied head, each taking their turns to smash the skull against the ground in a bid to crack it open. Finally, the policeman succeeded and lifted the opened head to its lips, slurping at the grey yolk within until the other zombie attacked once more, snarling in fury and knocking the head far from the scuffle, their prize forgotten as the businessman overpowered the officer and delved its fingers into the bloodied mouth of its victim, tearing out tongue and teeth and shovelling it into its own mouth. The policeman tried to fight back, raking at sagging flesh with tattered fingernails, but to no avail as the creature in the suit pulled away the lower jaw of the zombie, settling down away from the fight and tearing at the meat surrounding the jawbone.

Bill tore his gaze from one scene of carnage to another, a legless soldier crawling away from the smoking ruins of a motorbike, bloodied stumps gushing blood as he tried to escape the Rot that stalked him, a smoking limb gripped in its white-knuckled hand. With a guttural roar, the hunter lifted the limb high above its head and brought it crashing down upon its prey, the impact of the weapon jolting the soldier and sending a wave of pain through his body. The corpse attacked again and again with the bludgeon, a relentless assault until the soldier finally stopped moving and became another meal for the undead, his environment suit offering no protection against the killer.

All around him the dead feasted on the bodies, and Bill took care to make sure none of the animals noticed him, grabbing Tara and hunkering down behind the motorcycle. The engine block was scalding hot, hissing slightly as the gentle patter of rain splattered against it, but it could barely be heard over the chomping and ripping of flesh, the crepitus sound of teeth grinding against bone, and the moans of the injured and dying as they accepted their fate.

"Jesus," Tara murmured, raising her hand to her mouth fighting back the urge to vomit. "God, it's disgusting."

"The same scene played out in every town and city in Britain," Bill said, peering over the top of the bike, feeling his reactions were somewhat cold in comparison to Tara. "Where the hell is everyone? Must be holed up inside a bar."

"Could they have left?"

"Not without transport. They're supposed to meet up here with the Marines for evac. Rots must've rushed them, taken them by surprise. I'm going to see how close I can get, they should have a sentry somewhere with a clear view of the courtyard. If I give your this, will you use it?"

Bill gently cocked his pistol and handed it over with an extra magazine. Tara took it, but looked warily at it.

"I've never fired one before," she said. "What if I hit you?"

"Well, don't point it at me," Bill said with a smile as he crawled out from behind the bike, picking his way through the spent brass and muddy puddles while trying not to make any excessive noise. The Sounds of the slobbering creatures forcing meat down their neck would mask some of his noises, but not all of it.

A good sentry position, Bill mused as he wallowed through a pool of warm bloody water. *Something like a roof or a tall building. Al can really pick them.*

He froze mid-crawl, eyes coming to rest on a discarded Marine helmet. The thick yellow sponge padding inside was stained a deep crimson in colour, and a piece of paper could be seen inside, wet from the rain and the spilled blood, flapping in the slight breeze. Idle curiosity took hold of Bill, and he reached out, slipping the paper from the hat and slowly opening it up, fold by fold.

The face staring back at him was strangely familiar, a woman he'd seen before, though not in person. Racking his brains, he finally recognised her as the woman from the posters that Al carried around with him. A chill crawled across his skin as he unfolded more of the photograph, and he realised it wasn't just a normal nude photograph that any Marine would treasure. The woman, her name eluded Bill, grinned seductively at the camera, holding the familiar muzzle of large black handgun in one hand: the butt of the weapon was held by the Marine beside her, a grinning dark skinned man with a goatee beard.

"Al," he whispered, holding the photograph in trembling hands. Al's photograph, taken from the blood-spattered and dented helmet lying in the midst of a herd of Rots. What had happened here suddenly became crystal clear. The Rots hadn't just swarmed the park, they'd *wiped out* both the Marines and all his friends, and were now probably feasting on them around him. And if they didn't finish off the bodies in the course of the meal, they'd rise from the dead themselves. Bill looked up from the photograph, wiping bleary eyes with the back of his sleeve, and looked again at the two dormant vehicles. The skins of each had been perforated by trails of gunfire and blackened by explosions, blood spattered the vehicles, and the driver-side door of *Colebrook's Runner* hung off one hinge, exposing a large figure in a white suit hanging from the cab, still partially strapped in to the seat. One of the undead creatures gnawed on the driver's leg, noisily ripping through the material of the suit to get at the soft meat.

"Fuck," he whispered, realising his friends and his rescue party had been overwhelmed by the horde of the dead. A surge of anger rushing through his system, Bill glared at the field of cadavers and living corpses. Much as he longed to wipe out all the creatures, there was no way he could possibly hope to kill even half of them before they swarmed over him. And he couldn't forget Tara, who had no combat experience and would be no help at all.

He quickly retreated to the sanctity of his bike, where Tara was waiting anxiously, chewing her lower lip and toying with the weapon in her hands. "What's wrong, is this the wrong place?"

"They're dead," Bill muttered, replacing his weapons in their holsters. "They've been wiped out. All of them."

"All of them?" Tara said, almost shouting as her voice broke and trembled, blind panic threatening to take over. Bill had to keep her calm and quiet as much as possible, knowing that too much noise would quickly attract unwanted attention. "What're we going to do?" she demanded.

Bill shook his head slowly, leaning against the bike and wiping his eyes.

"What... what do we do now?" demanded Tara, her eyes wide and glassy, close to tears and starting to shake uncontrollably. While Bill was close to tears because of the death of his friends, he suspected Tara was upset because her ride off the island had just left without her. He couldn't blame her, of course, she barely knew the people who had been his family for the last... how long had it been? Weeks? Months? Still, the last thing he needed was a hysterical woman.

"Get on," Bill said, clambering on to the bike and motioning to the seat. "I don't know where we're going, or what we're going to do, but we can't sit around here and talk about it." He was hoping that the firm and authoritative tone he used to talk in was what it would take to stop her from breaking down entirely. It appeared to do the trick.

Tara clambered aboard as Bill revved the engine to life, attracting the attention of the closest Rots to him as the machine thundered and sputtered to life. They rose, their interest in their current meals lost as they lumbered towards the fresher source of meat. Keening wails and hungry moans filled the air, and as each Rot uttered a growl, more and more creatures clambered to their feet, or whatever bloodied stumps passed as their legs.

Without another word or a parting glance, Bill spun the bike around and returned the way he came, leaving his fallen friends behind him.

II

Bill found himself sitting around a campfire once more, prodding at the crackling embers of the flames with his one remaining extendable baton, stirring up white-hot ashes and releasing showers of glowing sparks. Since leaving Greyson's Park, he hadn't said more than two full sentences. Tara watched him from the small grassy mound she sat on, not sure if there was anything she could say or do to even try and make him feel better. There was always the fact that they were both still alive, but Bill had spoken fondly of Al, Angel and Garth, and figured that this fact wouldn't help gloss over the loss of his friends. She, too, had lost a friend; Pam, one of the women dancers she had been locked up with possibly just as long as Bill had known Al.

Upon reflection, Tara didn't know where she was better off. In the Messiah's palace, she was constantly beaten, raped and humiliated on an a regular basis, and she wouldn't wish that upon her worst enemies, but at least the drugs she had access to numbed her to most of the torment and helped her go to that special place in her mind. She's read about it in magazines, all the rape victims that said they locked themselves away in their own special place in their mind, building a wall to keep them separate from the abuse. She'd never really understood what that meant until it happened to her. But she knew that if she did as she was told there she would be fed and kept alive, and not served to a horde of living dead. Though she didn't doubt Bill and his ability to keep them both alive, she knew he would have to be in the right frame of mind. Since finding the resting place of his friends that morning, he had been a different man, his mind preoccupied, lost in his thoughts. Maybe he was retiring to his own special place?

Twenty miles past the city limits, after countless hours of driving, he had finally stopped the machine and threw his belongings down, ordering Tara to build a fire while he sat on guard. She'd done as instructed, and returned to tell him that, only to find him looking morosely at his handgun; as if contemplating suicide.

Though she hated guns, and didn't know how to use one, she had offered to take it off him and act as a guard while he got some rest. He'd reluctantly agreed to it, and handed over the weapon, though he'd just sat and stared into the fire since then.

Gotta adapt though, she thought to herself, lifting the weapon and sighting down the barrel, aiming at an imaginary zombie and touching the trigger lightly, trying to get a feel for the awkward device. She knew she'd have to learn how to use it in order to survive: after all, the only other choice was to *not* survive. But how long *would* she have to survive? Could she look forward to another month until she finally saw a helicopter coming to collect her, or was she to be left on the plague-infected island for the rest of her life?

"I'll never get the hang of this," she muttered, lowering her weapon and sighing heavily.

"You will," Bill said, crouching down on the ground beside her and motioning for her to raise the handgun again. "You have to, because if you don't, you won't live."

"I was just thinking the same thing," Tara said with a smile, turning to look at him. His eyes, still glazed from the tears he'd shed, reflected the flickering light of the fire, while some of the dirt on his face had been washed away by the tracks of his tears. "Are you okay?"

"I will be," he answered with a solemn nod. "In time. Now, show me how you handle it."

Tara lifted the weapon again, this time cupping it with both hands, and aimed it into the distance.

"Try for that tree," Bill said, motioning towards a large oak tree just on the periphery of the fire's glow. Tara nodded and brought her weapon about on the tree.

"Confident?" Bill asked. Again, she nodded.

"Then fire."

She jerked the trigger, jumping with the deafening gunshot that echoed off into the night and the sudden kick of the metal device, almost dropping the weapon. The bullet hurtled off into the night, missing the thick trunk of the tree and vanishing into the darkness.

"Try again," Bill said, coming around behind her and wrapping his arms around Tara, cupping each hand in his own and adjusting her stance. "This time, don't aim, but point it. And squeeze the trigger gently: when you jerk the trigger, you jerk the weapon. Try again."

"Won't this attract any creatures in the area?"

"It's too open around here," Bill whispered, leaning in close as he spoke. "Nothing will be able to home-in or pinpoint this weapon. They'd probably be drawn more to the fire than anything else, but I'm not going to die of hypothermia. Which is why I want you to be able to handle yourself. Now try again."

Tara nodded once more, this time following the advice she'd been given and releasing another round, this time grazing the bark on one side of the tree.

"Try it like this," Bill said, raising her aim and pulling the weapon over to the left. "Keep firing, use the whole magazine. Use each shot to readjust for the next shot. See if you can hit the knot in the trunk."

Tara did as she was told, squeezing off round after round until the weapon clicked unresponsively, then lowered the weapon and looked at the result of her weapons training. Of the fifteen bullets she had fired, only ten of them had hit the tree, and of those only three had come close to the knot as Bill had instructed. Bill slowly guided her through reloading the weapon, then told her to aim at the tree once more, only this time to fire off the whole magazine as quick as she possibly could. She did as she was told, but stopped halfway through, dropping the weapon and sunk to her knees, flexing her firing hand and rubbing at her eyes with her other.

"You okay?" asked Bill, pulling out his bottle of water and splashing some on to her hands, encouraging her to clean her eyes with the water. "It's okay, it's just residual gunpowder. It happens when you fire like that. We'll look for a pair of sunglasses for you tomorrow, that'll help protect your eyes."

"My hand couldn't take it," she complained, massaging her wrist and cracking her knuckles. "I don't have to fire like that all the time, do I?"

"Only when we're in deep shit," Bill said, shaking off his hands and wiping them on his jeans. "You've done well, but we'll try again tomorrow. I might even let you have a go of the shotgun."

"I can't wait," Tara said, her tone sarcastic.

Bill shrugged nonchalantly, replenishing the bullets in the pistol's magazine and handing it back. As he did, Tara reached out and held his wrist, keeping his hand close.

"Look, I'm sorry," she said. "This is all so new to me, I've got a lot to take in, a lot of changes to make. I know I can be a little snappy sometimes, maybe a little..."

"Snooty?" offered Bill. Tara laughed. "I guess snooty, yeah. But it's just who I am."

"I'll get used to it," Bill said, smiling slightly and placing his hand on top of hers. "If I can get used to an arrogant, annoying and sexist Marine, I'm sure I can get used to a short tempered and stuck-up lawyer."

"Hey, I didn't say stuck-up," Tara said, pretending to be hurt by his comment. She looked at him for a moment then turned away, pulling her hand free. "You get some sleep, you look wasted. I'll keep watch for a couple of hours. It looks like there's some rain on its way, so get wrapped up."

"You'll be okay?" Bill asked, raising an eyebrow. Tara nodded, patting the warm pistol that lay on her lap. "I can use this now, I'll be able to watch over us. Go on, get some sleep."

The blanket wrapped around Bill wasn't the thickest of material, and the ground certainly not the most comfortable mattress in the world, but he was too tired to care. His sleep was strangely pleasant, considering the day's events, and remained undisturbed until the early hours of the morning, when an assortment of wet chomping sounds roused him. He rolled over on to his front, supporting his weight on his elbows and angling himself to see Tara lying on the ground five feet away from the dying fire, her hand convulsing and clutching for the discarded pistol that lay beside her.

A creature squatted atop her, bare feet pinning down her shoulders and bloody talons digging at her face, tearing her flesh to shreds and squeaking against the pale bone of her skull. Bill leapt to his feet, fumbling first for his shotgun, then his machinegun, only to find all his weapons were missing. He dropped down to the floor, fumbling blindly for Tara's pistol while keeping his gaze fixed on the feeding creature. His fingers groped the ground, but he couldn't find the weapon. He looked down, saw the pistol, and grabbed it, bringing it back up and aiming at the Rot.

It wasn't there, only the remains of Tara lay at his feet, her bloody face slashed to ribbons, eyes plucked from her skull. Bill looked around, and could hear the footsteps of the creature as it ran from the scene. He lifted the weapon and fired blindly into the darkness, five unaimed shots that vanished into the gloom as quick as the Rot had.

He rushed forwards and knelt by Tara, feeling a wave of nausea wash over him as the woman rolled painfully over. Her breathing was laboured and rasping, a thick gurgling in the back of her throat the only sound she could make as she tried to talk. He knew there was only one thing he could do to help her, and levelled off his weapon on her torn face, trying to find it within him to put an end to her suffering.

A gunshot sounded in the distance, and Bill dropped to the ground, thinking he was under attack, though no other shots came. He looked up from his hiding place, and saw the rifle round hadn't been fired at him, but at Tara, and it had obliterated the front of her skull and ended her torment.

"You did the same thing for me with Ping," hollered a familiar voice, far off to Bill's left. "It's about time I paid you back, kid."

"Al?" Bill muttered, then raised his voice. "Al, is that you?"

"The one and only," he called. "Me and the whole gang's here. We heard a shit-load of gunfire a few hours ago, took us a while but we finally found you. Shame it wasn't sooner, we could have saved her, too."

"Where are you?" Bill shouted, circling around in the dark and trying to pinpoint his friend. "You got a torch? Give me a sign!"

"Jesus, kid, didn't you learn anything from me? Instead of a torch, we gotta use night vision. Spook eyes don't give our position away like a big beam of light. Just walk forwards, I'll intercept you. And don't worry, that Rot's long gone."

Bill shrugged and started to march forward, leaving the dim circle of firelight and stumbling over his own feet as he trusted himself to his friend in the darkness. Not far from the campsite, he felt a pair of ice cold hands clamp down around his neck and give him a friendly pat on the shoulders.

"I gotcha kid, don't worry."

"Shit, Al, I thought you were dead."

"Let me tell you kid, it was close. Garth took a bullet in his flabby ass, and Preacher-man almost went to see his God because the dumb shit still refuses to open fire on another living being. The bitch kept her head, though. She's got guts, I can't fault her for that."

"So what happened?"

"I won't lie to you kid, I don't have a fuckin' clue. One minute we're talking all nice, trying to stall a pick-up until you turn up, then the next thing I know there's bullets and explosions. You ever had that whole red-mist in combat? When everything goes red, you go berserk and you can't remember anything?"

"I try not to get like that," Bill said, finally seeing the lights of the trailer cab in the distance.

"It's not often a professional does. Now come on, get in the back, Garth wants to talk to you."

"Garth's in the back? Why's he not driving?"

"I told you," Al said as he guided Bill around to the rear of the trailer. "Poor bastard got tagged in the ass, he can't sit down. Me and Spanners take turns in driving. He's back there with Pam and the bitch.

The doors on the trailer squeaked open, and Bill climbed into the opening, saying his thanks and goodbyes to Al as he returned to the front of the trailer and climbed into the cabin, the engine growling to life and the lights flickering to life in the cargo hold.

Both Angel and Pam were huddled together, a blanket wrapped around them, and Garth lay on the floor beside them, looking up as Bill took a seat beside the two sleeping women.

"Hey Bill, I'd get up to shake your hand, but I'm sure Al told you I got shot. Still, better my arse is ruined instead of Angel's, am I right?"

Bill was flustered, didn't answer, and looked uncomfortably at the sleeping form of Angel.

"Hey, don't worry, she can't hear you. Isn't that right, Clive?"

Bill turned around as Clive clambered into the trailer, his bare feet slapping against the metal floor and fingernails scraping the surface as he clawed his way in. He rose to his feet, looked towards Bill and nodded casually.

"I got these for you," he said with a smirk, holding out a bloody hand. Bill tentatively reached out and shivered as Clive poured the contents of his clenched fist over his outstretched palms: thick liquid trickled over his hand, dripping through his fingers, and two perfect spheres dropped into the murky liquid he held. He looked at his hands.

A pair of eyes looked back.

Tara's eyes.

"The whore was tasty," sneered Clive. Bill noticed for the first time that his mouth was smeared with blood, as were his razor sharp talons. "But not as tasty as those two bitches."

Garth grabbed the blanket and tugged it downwards, revealing the tattered remains of Pam and Angel. They had both been stripped of flesh and muscle in several places, their bloodied bones protruding through torn skin, while both their abdomens had been sliced open and hollowed out.

"The bitch had a nice ass," Al growled as he appeared at the end of the trailer, displaying his battle wounds: one missing eyes, exposed rib cage, intestines hanging out slashes in his stomach. "But it was her guts I was more interested in. But don't worry, we saved the best part for you."

Garth dragged the carcass of Angel down to the ground beside him, the sudden jolt of the body dislodging the head that had been precariously balanced atop the corpse. It rolled across the floor, coming to a rest at Bill's feet. Shaking, he bent down to pick up the head, his fingers coming into contact with the cold flesh of the dead woman.

Without warning, the head opened her mouth and clamped down on his fingers, snapping off the last knuckle of each finger with a sickening crunch. He fell to his knees, gripping his hand and fighting back the tears as his undead friends closed in around him, drooling in anticipation of another fresh meal.

"Fucking dead bastards!"

Bill lurched bolt upright, casting aside the blanket and grabbing his shotgun, rolling to his feet and aiming out into the distance with his weapon.

"Where the fuck are you! Damn bastards, where are you pieces of shit? C'mon!"

"Bill!" shouted Tara, grabbing his arms and turning him around. The sun and risen, and even though it was early in the morning, the ground had started to dry a little, and the rain had died off completely. Bill stared at Tara for a few minutes, his weapon still raised and quivering from side to side, his fingers wrapped tightly around the device.

"You're not dead?" he finally asked, eyes starting to focus and his brain starting to come to life. "You weren't attacked last night?"

Tara shook her head, and Bill dropped to the ground, holding his head in his hands and muttering, "It was a dream. Stupid nightmare, it wasn't real."

He stood up and began packing up his belongings, motioning for Tara to do this same.

"We're going now? Don't you want a drink, or maybe something to eat?"

"We have to get going," he said, looking out in the distance towards the outskirts of Manchester. "We have to move before they come here. They'll be on their way."

"Who's coming?"

"Rots," Bill said, climbing on to the bike and anxiously looking over his shoulder. "Are you coming or not?"

"Jesus," muttered Tara, clambering on behind Bill and gripping his jacket as he revved the engine to life and rolled away from the encampment. "You're not a morning person are you?"

For the next three hours Bill drove non-stop, every now and then looking over his shoulder for any sign of a pursuing trailer cab filled with undead friends, but none came.

His nightmare had mentally scarred him, and had made him realise that the longer he hung around near the city his friends died in, the more chance he had of meeting their undead form. He didn't think he'd be able to put a bullet into the head of any of his friends, and that uncertainty could jeopardise either Tara's life or his own. True, the chances of that happening were pretty remote, as there was no guarantee that his friends had turned. The chance *was* there, however, and that was enough to motivate Bill to get up and move.

Could he explain this to Tara if she asked? Maybe he could, and maybe she'd understand. *Maybe.*

"We need to stop," Tara finally said, the first words she'd said since leaving the campground.

"Stop?" asked Bill, looking at the dials on his bike. Most of them were cracked or broken; the only one that was working seemed to be the one for the petrol gauge, which seemed to be dangerously low. He needed to find some petrol, and although they'd passed several stumbling creatures and quite a few dead bodies, the frequency of motor vehicles had somewhat dropped. Having said that, he might be able to squeeze a few more miles out of the tank before having to refuel.

"Can't it wait?"

"Not unless you want me to pee all over you and the bike."

"I'll pull over then," Bill grudgingly said. "There's some bushes over there..."

"I may be desperate, but I'm not going behind the bushes. Find a house or something."

"Christ, you're fussy," Bill said. "There's no houses around here, it's just fields and hills. I won't watch."

"Fussy or stuck up? Anyway, what's wrong with that?"

Tara extended her arm, pointing across the fields to their left and the small cottage in the distance, partially hidden by a copse of thick green trees and shrubbery. Bill shrugged, slowly turning the vehicle towards the mystery building and trundling across the vast greenery that lay between.

Although he hadn't noticed it before, the urban roads and streets had turned into picturesque country lanes and winding dirt tracks. If it weren't for the lumbering undead creatures that they passed every so often, Bill could have mistakenly thought the plague hadn't spread this far into the countryside. He knew otherwise, recalling Sylvester's tale of his relative's country retreat.

The journey across the fields came to an abrupt halt as Bill, lost in his thoughts, guided the bike into a ditch, the vehicle vanishing into a forest of grass and half-submerging in a foot of stagnant ditchwater.

"God damn fucking bike!" Bill screamed, smashing the handlebars with the palms of his hand in frustration. He revved the engine, trying to manoeuvre the back wheel of the bike and gain some purchase on the sides of the ditch. The machine gurgled and groaned as it tried to comply, then sputtered and died. "Shit," Bill muttered, pulling himself from the bike and turning around to help Tara out the water, then retrieving his equipment. "It's going to be a bitch to haul that out."

"Can't we move it?" Tara asked, brushing down her clothing and grimacing as each step made a wet squelching sound. Her movements were sharp and restricted, indicating that she was more desperate than Bill had anticipated.

"Not without some rope. It's still a fair distance to the house," he said, raising his hand and shielding his eyes from the midday sun, "Maybe another five or six minutes. If you're that desperate, I don't think you're going to make it. Just go in the bushes or something."

"I can make it," Tara insisted, looking towards the house.

"Once we get there I'm still going to have to secure the house, make sure it's safe."

"Jesus," Tara muttered, storming over to a small patch of shrubs and vanishing behind them. "Stay over there. Jesus, what am I, an animal or something?"

Bill ignored her complaining, and took this opportunity to wander over to the other side of the field and relieve himself, leading by example. Once he'd finished, he returned to the ditch, where Tara had reappeared, waiting for him.

"I haven't done that since I was five," she glowered, looking over her shoulder towards the bushes with a disgusted expression on her face. Bill smirked slightly, but quickly hid it when she returned her gaze to him.

"C'mon," he ordered, beginning the slog across the waterlogged field and waving to Tara, hefting his shotgun and machinegun, one in each hand. As they neared the house, Bill began to crouch low, moving cautiously from bush to tree and urging Tara to do the same.

"This is disgusting," she moaned, looking at her mud-covered hands and turning them over, tutting and examining her nails. "See, look, I've broke a nail. Jesus, this is horrible. This isn't my idea of a good time."

"It's not mine, either," Bill said, scowling at her and holding out the shotgun. "Hold this."

He lifted his crossbow and placed its butt against his shoulder, peering down the scope and taking in as many details of the house as he could. The garden seemed well-tended, neat rows of plants and flowers surrounding the winding path leading to the heavy wooden front door. It was a one-story building, the windows boarded up from the inside, and the blackened remains of an off-road vehicle lay at the foot of the path. Through the cracks in the boards on the windows, he could see only blackness and shadow.

"Looks like there's nobody home."

"So why am I on my hands and knees in the mud, and not sitting on a settee in there?"

"Because it *looks* like it's empty, I didn't say it *was*."

Bill sat down on the ground, his back to the building, and exchanged his crossbow for the shotgun.

"Stay here, I'm going to check out the inside, make sure it's safe. If it is, we go in there and spend the night, maybe even find some food. In the morning, we'll drag the bike out the ditch, maybe even find some petrol in that jeep."

"That burnt-out vehicle there?"

"It's a plan."

"It's a pretty crap plan," countered Tara.

"But it's still a plan. Now stay here, keep an eye out for any Rots. You got your gun, right?"

Tara nodded weakly, and Bill turned, crouching low and slowly making his way towards the house, continuing the pattern of moving from side to side, keeping himself hidden from the house until he reached the foot of the path leading to the door. Now, between the door and himself, there was no cover. If anyone *was* hiding inside and they happened to be looking out the window, he'd be in plain view. Not that he was overly confident in his stealth-like abilities; a six foot man in a brown leather jacket and blue jeans, carrying two weapons in broad daylight, was difficult to hide no matter how skilled a soldier. If the front of the house was under guard, and someone was watching after the commotion of the bike rolling into the ditch, then he would present himself as an open target.

Taking a chance and swallowing hard, he bolted for the door, tumbling to a stop as he made contact with the heavy front door. The wooden barrier gave the moment he touched it, swinging inwards on perfectly oiled hinges. Bill snapped his shotgun up, letting his submachine gun dangle from its strap and slowly panned the business end of the device from side to side. Although he hadn't been sure what exactly to expect from the house, Bill didn't think he'd find one of the most inviting rooms he had seen in months.

A thick, plush carpet, deep navy blue in colour, covered the floor of the living room the door opened into, matching with the blue theme that seemed to run through the whole room. A dark blue leather settee occupied the middle of the room, with two matching armchairs, each pointing towards an antique dark mahogany television cabinet. The only other piece of furniture that occupied the room was a large sideboard, also mahogany, with a range of framed photographs on top. Bill stepped forwards into the darkened room, sweeping his weapon around, and stepped closer to the cupboard, looking over the variety of pictures on offer. A man with shoulder length curly blond hair stared at Bill from one, wearing a black suit and standing beside a blonde woman, who wore a white dress with a veil flowing behind her in the wind. Next to that, there was a picture of three children in their school uniforms, one dark haired boy and two blonde girls, the girls obviously twins. These children were the main subjects of the remaining photographs.

Bill felt a pang of sorrow for the family, knowing that they, like everyone else, had their lives torn apart by the plague. He wondered how many of the five people that had lived here were now buried in the ground, and how many had been destined to wander the streets and fields as an undead flesh eater. The photographs also reminded him of his own past life, before the scourge had wiped out the population of Britain. And of his own photograph of Jenny. Did he even have that now? Was it in his bag, or back in the abandoned trailer? Maybe it had even been left in the prison. If that were the case, he would never see it again.

He pushed the door shut behind him, and stood in the darkness for a moment, allowing his eyes to readjust to the gloom of the interior. The sunlight that crept into the room through the cracks in the boards wasn't much, but allowed Bill to navigate around the room with the minimum of fuss, coming to a stop at the only door in the room and resting his hand on the glistening doorknob. It wasn't cool as he'd expected it to be, as most metal objects left untouched would have been, but slightly warm. As if someone had held it recently.

The door clicked, then swung effortlessly open into a second room as large as the first, this one holding an oblong dining table and six chairs, and decorated in a similar fashion. While the windows at the front had been boarded up, those in the rear had been left without barricades, allowing the light to flood the dining area with a soft yellow glow. A vase of flowers sat upon the table, giving the room a delicate splash of colour. Bill pulled out a seat from beneath the table and sat down, scratching his head in bewilderment. Had he stepped through a time warp the moment he'd passed through the front door? This building looked practically untouched by the plague, other than the barricades covering the windows. Bill couldn't help but wonder if he'd found a sanctuary: a place where the diseased hands of a carrier, or the deranged minds of gangs or prisoners didn't go, didn't even know about.

Could it be a new home to settle down in?

He grabbed his weapon and stood up again, looking from side to side as he tried to choose which doorway to take next. Other than the entrance he'd used, there were another two doors, both identical to the one he'd previously opened. He tried the door to the right, his closest, and pulled it open, stepping back and trying to peer into the darkness. A shadowy figure loomed within, not as tall as Bill, but nevertheless it seemed undaunted as it lurched forwards, a hard and heavy weight suddenly pressing on Bill and toppling him to the ground, pinning him down as he struggled to free himself. He finally managed to bring his shotgun around and unloaded a shell point-blank, sighing heavily as the dead weight fell limp and the top half slid noiselessly to one side.

Bill clambered to his feet, hauling his weight up on the table and glaring down at the decimated figure at his feet. Without missing a beat he whirled on his feet, sensing another presence in the room and working the slide of his weapon as he moved.

"You killed an ironing board," Tara said, clapping softly as she entered the room and prodded the wooden remains with the point of her toes. "I'm very impressed."

"What are you doing in here? Didn't I tell you to stay outside until I said it was safe?"

"I'd rather poke around a dark abandoned house with you instead of hanging around outside on my own. Haven't you seen the movies where the attractive woman left to fend for herself winds up as the slasher's next victim?"

"Is that the same movie where the couple in the old house get sliced up with a chainsaw? Listen, this shit isn't like the movies, it's real life. I learned that pretty fast once I'd escaped from quarantine."

"I'm not going back out there while you decide if this place is clear or not. And besides, it's raining out there, I'm not spending another night out in the pissing rain. C'mon, one door left to check in this room."

"I'll go first," Bill said, taking the lead and reaching out to open the door.

"Careful," Tara whispered, and Bill froze. Had she heard something on the other side he'd missed? "There might be a coat stand on the other side. I hear they can be tricky."

"You're a real funny woman, you know that?" Bill scorned, opening the door and stepping into a small antechamber, about half the size of the living room and holding a table and a wardrobe. Bill cautiously opened the doors to the cupboard, stepping back from the opening and finding it empty. Other than the two pieces of furniture, there were three doors, two of them leading off to bedrooms, one blue, and the other pink. The pink room seemed to have a few toys spread across the floor, as if the children had been in mid-play before being whisked off, while the blue room remained immaculate. Bill moved on from the bedrooms, taking the final door and finding himself in a kitchen, well kept and clean just as the rest of the house. Three dishes lay in the sink, encrusted with dried food and left to soak in a shallow pool of water, and a single empty coffee mug stood by the shining silver kettle. It had a spoonful of coffee granules heaped in the bottom, though the kettle itself was stone cold.

"Back door?" questioned Tara as she stepped across the room and opened the last door of the house. Bill nodded and strolled outside into the fine drizzle that now fell from the sky, looking at what seemed to be a large vegetable garden. Stepping out on to the well-worn path leading up the middle of the garden, Bill carefully picked at a few random vegetables, coming up with a carrot and some potatoes. A small greenhouse at the rear of the plot looked to hold more crops, and as Bill neared them, he could see tomato plants and marrows. Adjacent to the glass building, there was also a small wooden building, an outside toilet serving as the only amenities to the property.

"Well, we eat tonight," Tara said with a grin. "Real vegetables, none of the tinned crap."

"Isn't this *too* convenient?" Bill asked, gesturing towards the vegetables, then the house. "Nice house, fresh food, almost as if we stumbled in on someone else's own slice of paradise."

"What's the problem? A family lived here, they obviously bolted from here once the disease spread into the countryside, left things as they were."

Bill listened to Tara as she spoke, but tried to tune her out as he knelt down by a patch of earth beside the greenhouse, where two stone tablets had been laid on the ground, one with the word Tommy painted on, the other with Susan.

"Parents or children?" he asked as he traced the outline of the two words, then stopped halfway around the second letter of Susan. "Parents? Hey, Tara, you counted two bedrooms, right? Both looked like they were kids rooms?"

"Yeah, what about them?"

"Where did the parents sleep... we've missed something, a room... but where?"

"What? Jesus, are you just looking for faults?"

"There's another room," Bill said, pointing to the house they'd just exited from. A flicker of movement on the roof, and Bill saw the tiles, or what he *thought* to be tiles, slide over to one side. "Did you see that?"

He didn't need to ask again as the flicker of a patterned curtain slid aside and the bore of a rifle slipped out a crack in the skylight, followed by the short and muffled discharge of the weapon. A plume of dirt leapt up from the ground, as high as Bill's shoulders, and he ran for the house, submachine gun raised towards the roof and firing in short bursts, hoping to persuade the unseen sniper to stop firing on them. Tara was close behind him, muttering and praying as she went, trying to keep up with Bill as he slammed into the back door and rolled into the kitchen. With both his weapons drawn ready to open fire at a moments notice, Bill stormed out the kitchen into the anteroom, looking from one bedroom to another, then into the dining room. What was he missing? Above him he could hear muffled footsteps, and then random bursts of gunfire, each shot accompanying a stray bullet as they tore through the ceiling and smashed through the floor. There had to be a way up into the roof, that must be where the third bedroom was.

With his weapon still ready, he stormed back through the house, feverishly looking back and forth for something that would give him a clue where to go.

"Just fucking kids bedrooms and cupboards," hissed Bill, ducking instinctively as another gunshot sounded. As the firing continued, the shots seemed to be less muffled to his side, and Bill looked questioningly at the opened wardrobe. He rapped on the back panel of the wooden armoire with his knuckles, then kicked it, all the time ducking and swearing with each shot. The wooden panel bowed, splintered, then finally caved, and Bill burst through the other side of the wardrobe, finding himself at the foot of a staircase. He dropped his shotgun and barged up the stairs, taking them three steps at a time until he reached the top. The landing had a low, sloped roof, and Bill had to stoop slightly to pass through. He moved quickly, hoping to reach the sniper before he or she had the chance to realise Bill had found their secret room...

And found the blonde woman from the photograph downstairs, cowering on the double bed that took up most of the room, her arms wrapped around a small child: one of the twins he had already seen. Bill paused, his chest heaving as he tried to regain his breath, and lowered his machinegun.

"Please don't hurt us," pleaded the woman, drawing the girl closer.

"Which of you was the sniper?" Bill finally managed, seconds before the solid wooden butt of a hunting rifle came crashing down on the back of his skull. He pitched forwards, dropping his weapon and folding to the floor, slowly swimming into a sea of blackness that rushed up to greet him.

"I was," grunted a rough male voice as he finally gave up his grip on consciousness.

It had been a normal day like any other, or rather, as close to normal as the days could be. Sarah was in her room, playing with her toys, while Cindy had been in the middle of cleaning the kitchen. She'd just offered to make Steve a cup of coffee while he worked out in the garden, tending to the rows of vegetables in the back of the house. Taking a break from the weeding, he looked towards the two concrete slabs, sorrow and despair welling in his heart as he remembered the two children who now lay at rest beneath the ground. Although he'd heard many stories of parents who had buried their children, he never thought that he and Cindy would do the same. They only had Sarah now, though the arrival of their new child in another two months or so would give them something new to keep their minds occupied; though not enough to make them forget.

Just like the death of any other loved one, you could never forget.

Just as he was returning to work, the steady groan of an engine in the distance droned into life. Dropping his gardening tools, he bolted for the back door, grabbing the old hunting rifle that he'd propped up by the step. He burst into the kitchen, where Cindy currently stood over the kitchen sink, her blonde hair tied back behind her shoulders. She turned around to look at him, waddling in an almost comical movement, but her smile faded as she saw his serious expression and the weapon he held.

"Steve? What's wrong?"

"Sounds like someone's coming. Get Sarah, go upstairs. I'll be up in a minute."

"Daddy?"

Steve looked past Cindy, and saw Sarah standing behind them, clutching her favourite doll and rubbing her eyes. She tugged at her favourite purple jumper, pulling her hands up into her sleeves and wiping her nose on the back of one. "What's happening, Daddy?"

"We're going to play a game," Steve said quickly, guiding Sarah and Cindy to the stairs leading up to the attic and the second floor of the cottage. "You like hide and seek, don't you?"

Sarah nodded, smiling slightly.

"You're going to hide with your mum, and then I'm going to try and find you, you think you can do that?"

Again, Sarah nodded, and started to make her way up the stairs, humming happily to herself. Cindy started to follow, but Steve grabbed her hand and held her back. "Make sure she's quiet. I'll have a look, see how things are. I'll tell you when it's all clear."

Cindy stepped forwards, kissed Steve, then began the slow and laborious task of climbing the stairs. Steve rolled the large wardrobe into place over the doorway, then ran through the dining room into the living room, taking up his position by the boarded window and peering through the wooden slats. There seemed to be two people outside, one hanging back while the other crabbed from side to side, slowly advancing on the house.

Swearing under his breath, Steve rushed back to the wardrobe, closing the doors between each room as he went, and clambered into the wardrobe, fumbling with the secret catches he'd installed and releasing the door in the back panel, stepping through the back of the cupboard and fixing the panel back in place before running softly up the stairs. He found Cindy and Sarah hiding in their bedroom, lying on the bed holding one another.

"Is it your turn to hide?" Sarah asked, looking up and smiling as Steve strode in.

"Not yet, honey. We're going to play at being mice, now. Nice and quiet."

Steve moved towards his wife and daughter, wrapping his arms around them and listening to sounds of the house below. Doors clicked open and thudded shut: then a loud clatter, an explosive blast of a weapon. Steve froze, and Sarah jumped, burying her face into Cindy in a bid to stifle any startled screams that may slip out. More thumps and footsteps followed, accompanied by muffled voices as they moved through the house and out the back. Curiosity got the better of him, and Steve carefully made his way over to the skylights in the roof, gently pulling aside the curtains Cindy had decorated to look like roof tiles. The man he'd seen approaching the house now stood near the greenhouse. He crouched near the graves of his children, reached out and touched the concrete slabs, before standing up and turning to face the house again. Steve twitched the curtain closed a little as the man looked up, trying to hide himself, but it was too late. The man pointed up towards the roof, talking to his partner as he moved back towards the house.

"Shit," Steve muttered as he lifted his rifle and slipped it through one of the cracks in the skylight, firing down into the garden. He worked the bolt on the rifle, ejecting the spent brass, and lined up for a second shot when the man opened fire with his own weapon, pelting the roof with bursts of gunfire. Steve dropped to the floor, cursing under his breath as glass and fragments of slate tiles rained down on him. As soon as the onslaught of rapid gunfire ceased, Steve knew they were in the house, working through way through the building as they tried to find the entrance to the second level.

Lowering his weapon, Steve began to fire random shots through the wooden floor, hoping that he may be able to score a lucky hit as he imagined where the interlopers may be. He tracked their movements to the entrance hidden by the wardrobe, heard them knock once on the fake back, then listened as they started to pound on the panel. Knowing exactly where they were, he lifted the rifle and took aim for the doorway, squeezing his finger to deliver the deathblow.

The weapon clicked empty, and Steve panicked, leaving his vigil at the top of the stairs and running for the box of ammunition he kept upstairs in the bathroom. By the time his shaking hands had managed to push the shells into the rifle and primed the device, he had already heard heavy thumping footsteps working their way up the stairs.

"Please don't hurt us," he heard Cindy say, her voice quivering as she spoke.

"Which of you were the sniper?" a loud voice answered. He sounded annoyed and angry, and Steve feared for the lives of his family. He crept up behind the man who stood at the entrance to the bedroom, and smashed the butt of his weapon into the base of the man's skull, swinging the weapon like a club in the confines of the cramped upper level. The weapon made contact with a sickening thud, and the man keeled over, releasing the weapons he held as he crumpled into a heap.

"I was," Steve spat.

Another set of footsteps followed up the stairs, and Steve swung his rifle around, training it squarely on the chest of the woman who appeared on the landing. She blindly took a step forwards before even seeing Steve, but lifted her hands in submission as soon as she saw the rifle looming down on her.

"Keep them up," he snarled, stepping back slowly and indicating for her to follow into the room. She did so, and dropped to her knees beside the unconscious man.

"Christ, Bill! What have you done to him?"

Steve edged around the outside of the room, motioning to Cindy to open one of the cupboards of the nightstand and throw him something from inside. She instinctively knew what he wanted, and threw him the pair of handcuffs they had bought years ago, just on a whim. Though they had both laughed about it at the time, Steve would never have thought they would serve a purpose, or even be used. He passed them to Tara, and urged her to cuff Bill's hands behind his back. She reluctantly did so, then sat next to him on the ground. Steve quickly shuffled forwards and twisted the quick-release catches of the love-cuffs, disabling the emergency release.

"Sarah, you take your mum downstairs for a moment, I'm going to finish up here, make sure these people aren't going anywhere, okay?"

The little girl nodded, then took Cindy by the hand and gently guided her from the room, stepping around the woman and over Bill.

"Why does Daddy have handcuffs?" she asked, but Cindy just hushed her and carried on down the stairs. Once he was sure they were clear, Steve motioned for the woman to sit on the bed, and he moved over to the doorway, making sure he could get a clear shot at either man or woman if he needed to.

"I've got some questions for you," he said, "And I hope I like the answers."

III

The blackness that engulfed Bill slowly subsided and split in two as his eyes flickered open. It felt like he was trapped in a box, unable to move, with wood pressing against his face and one of his sides. Had he been buried alive, left to suffocate beneath the ground? He tried to squirm, trying to find what the limitations of the box was, and found he had his hands to be bound by handcuffs. He was somewhat relieved to realise he wasn't in a box, but lying facedown in the corner of the bedroom. He tried to roll over, to sit up, but his joints were stiff and aching, his movements restricted. He did manage to roll, though, and saw a small pair of feet standing at the door. He angled his head so he could see the figure, and smiled at the young girl watching him. She didn't return the smile, just sniffed and rubbed her nose on the back of her sleeve. She sat down on the floor so he didn't have to strain his neck so much to look at her, and she shuffled closer.

"Hi," she said softly. Bill smiled by way of response.

"Are you a bad man?"

Bill smiled, laughed, then shook his head. "No, I'm not a bad man."

"Have you killed people?"

"You're awfully inquisitive for a little girl," Bill said, trying to skirt around the questions. "How old are you?"

"I'm six and a half," she proudly announced, squaring off her shoulders as she looked at him. "Are you really not a bad man?"

"Really," Bill said reassuringly.

"We had a bad man here once, he'd killed some people. He hurt Mum and Susan. Daddy wasn't here then. What's your name?"

"I'm called Bill," he said, "What about you?"

"I'm Sarah," she said.

"Come out of there," a man shouted from the foot of the stairs. "He's dangerous."

"He's awake, daddy. And he says he's not a bad man."

"I know. Go downstairs, honey, go see if your Mum needs any help," the voice said. Footsteps ascended the staircase outside, and the man from the photograph downstairs strolled into the room. He guided the little girl from the room, then sat on the bed, a pistol resting limply in his hand.

"Bill. That's your name, isn't it? Bill?"

Bill nodded slowly.

"Didn't answer my little girl's questions, did you? *Have* you killed anyone?"

Again, Bill nodded slowly.

"How much of what the woman says is true?"

"Tara? Shit, where's Tara?"

"Downstairs. She's told me her story, which I find quite unbelievable. I was just wondering what lies you were going to spin?"

"I don't know what you find hard to believe. Is it the prison filled with psychopaths and rapists, run by a crazed religious zealot? Or maybe the fact said zealot thought he could control the living dead? Surely it's not the part where the same zealot had one of his men willingly turn people into Rots for his holy army?"

"That's some of the points, yeah. She said you and your friends had devised some plan to out-smart the Marines and get off the island."

"Did she tell you all my friends were wiped out, too?"

"She mentioned it, yes."

"I know it's hard to swallow," Bill sighed, squirming and wriggling discreetly as he tried to slacken his cuffs. "It seems pretty fantastical. But then, isn't the idea of the dead walking just as fantastical?"

"But it sounds like you escaped some very sticky situations, though. More than one man could possibly hope to survive."

"I wasn't always alone, I had my friends sometimes. I guess I'm just good enough at what I need to do to survive."

"Which is killing people?"

Bill didn't reply; there was nothing he could say or do to try and contradict that notion. His captor looked at him once over, then leaned forwards, reaching out to touch the metal cuffs. "I'm going to let you go," Steve finally announced after a few minutes of silence. "If what I've heard is true, you don't seem to be a threat to me or my family. Although you've killed people, it's been those that've threatened your life."

"You know that you tried to kill me," Bill said casually. Steve froze just as he worked one of the locks free. "Hey, I'm just saying."

"You were at the graves of my children. From the stories Tara told me, even dead bodies aren't safe. Food for the creatures, or even... for other uses."

Bill nodded, remembering his first encounters with a gang in the subterranean train tunnels.

"Just as long as you remember if you even *look* the wrong way at my wife or child, I'll kill you."

"Have *you* killed anyone before?" Bill asked as the handcuffs were removed and fell to the floor.

"Yes," Steve answered sharply, without a pause. "One man."

"Sarah's bad man?"

Steve nodded solemnly.

"What happened?" Although the restraints had been removed, Bill remained seated on the floor, crossing his legs. He felt like he was back in school sitting around on the floor while the teacher told his tale. Steve looked down at him, cocking his head curiously. "Why do you want to know?"

"Standard practice, I guess," Bill shrugged his shoulders. "Everyone I've met has a story to tell. I don't want to hurt your family, either physically or mentally, and I need to know what not to mention around them, to avoid any bad feelings I may unwillingly stir up."

"Little Tom caught the plague in the early days. He died out here, in our home. From what we heard in the news on the radio and on television, it was highly contagious. Realistically, if one of us caught it, then we should all have caught it. Rather than hand over the body of our baby boy to the authorities, we decided to bury him out here. He loved playing out there, by the greenhouse, so we buried him there. We spent the next week and a half waiting for the disease to take one of us, we knew from the news that ten days was the maximum incubation of the virus. That time came and passed, without any sign of the plague touching any of us. The riots in the city came, all television and radio signals were killed. Thing is, though, with this place being so remote, no sign of the riots came this far out. We lived our lives untouched by any of the hate and violence happening in the cities."

"Didn't your boy... I mean, he was infected with the plague..."

"Didn't he rise from the dead?" Bill nodded, and Steve leaned in closer, lowering his voice. "As soon as I heard about the dead rising, I didn't believe it, not at first. Like I say, though, we're pretty remote, so we haven't had any walking dead out here, and for Sarah's sake I hope it remains that way. That little girl's been through enough without having to see a corpse shuffling through the fields outside. I've seen one once, though. I headed out to the closest village, it's about thirty miles from here, I wanted to see how people were out there, and if there were any survivors. We knew most the people there, and I figured no one there would turn into an unruly mob. I must've been about three miles away from it, and I saw one of the animals you call Rots out there, helping itself to handfuls of guts from a toppled cow, before switching to another body that lay beside him, this one a farmhand. I didn't hang around, I turned around and came back here straight away.

"The time I was away, though, someone found our secluded house. A man riding a motorcycle rolled up to our house, I don't know if he was watching and waiting for me to leave, or if it was just coincidence he appeared when I wasn't there. He burst in, he was armed with a rifle, rounded up Sarah and Susan into one room, and Cindy in another. He took advantage of my wife first, and then... Susan. He probably would have done the same to Sarah, too, if I didn't get back just then. I caught him by surprise, knocked him senseless, then dragged him around the back before beating him to death. That night I burned his body, then dug up Tom before hammering a metal spike into his head, just to make sure. I did all this without letting my family know. If they knew I desecrated my son's grave... if they knew I'd split a man's head open with these hands..."

He stopped the tale there, looking at his hands as if they were still covered in blood. Bill nodded, stood up and put a reassuring hand on Steve's shoulder. He looked startled at first, then smiled glumly and patted Bill's hand with his own.

"And... What happened to Susan?"

"She took it pretty bad, tried to segregate herself from us. She used to be a bright and bubbly child, so friendly and outgoing. She became very withdrawn, spent a lot of time around Tommy's grave. Looking back, I guess there were signs for us to look for, something we could have done to stop her. We woke up one morning and found her... lying over the grave. She'd... she'd taken a knife from the kitchen... slit her... cut her... her wrists. The bastard had not only taken her innocence, but he was responsible for her taking her life. You never know what goes on in someone's head, can't predict what they'll do..." A tear rolled down his cheek. "Not even your own flesh and blood."

"And Cindy? She was okay?"

"She's heavily pregnant, only has another couple of months to go. We don't know if the baby's okay, obviously we can't go to the hospital or the doctors. There's been some blood loss... it doesn't move as much as it used to, and I can't hear a heartbeat when I try to listen. We just have to wait and see."

"It's been a rough couple of months for everyone," Bill said, unable to think of anything else to say. While he'd lost one person who he classed as his immediate family, Steve had lost half of his, and still faced the possibility of losing more.

"We keep a close eye on Sarah," Steve said, wiping his eyes and standing up. "She's only six, I get the feeling she doesn't fully understand what's happened. We told her Susan caught what Tommy had. I don't know if she even saw what that sick fucker did to her sister. She doesn't talk about it, and I don't like asking about it, in case I stir up old memories. One of my six-year-old babies has already been driven to suicide. I don't want the same thing to happen again."

"I didn't think kids could do things like that," Bill shook his head slowly. "Kids are just... kids, you know?"

"Kids can do anything," Steve looked over at one of the bedside cabinets, at the picture frame there and the three children pictured on it. "They can make you laugh, make you cry..."

"My name's Bill. Bill Reddings," Bill said, trying to move on the conversation and offering his hand in friendship. Steve took it in his own.

"Steven Merrip. My friends call me Steve. Now, can I trust you? Have you got my back?"

"We're all in the same boat here. We'll watch each other's back."

Bill followed Steve down the stairs and into the kitchen, where Tara sat with a mug of black coffee. She smiled at Bill as they entered, and he returned the smile. Sarah sat beside her, a plastic beaker filled with orange juice gripped in her hands, and she timed her drinks to coincide with Tara's, pausing only to wipe her nose on her sleeve.

"Don't do that, honey," Steve said. "Where's you mum?"

"She's asleep in my room. Said she had a headache. Are you staying here with us?"

"If that's okay. I mean, we don't have anywhere else to go, do we?" Bill said, looking to Tara first, then Steve. Both nodded in agreement.

"Good," the little girl said with a smile, then looked towards Tara again. "I like your hair, it's pretty. Do you want to come in my room and play with my toys?"

Not waiting for an answer, Sarah jumped down from her stool and grabbed Tara by the hand, leading her from the kitchen towards her bedroom. Bill perched himself on the vacant stool and finished off Tara's discarded coffee, before looking around the room. Bullets from the rifle were lodged in the floor and several cupboards, and the ceiling was peppered with holes from the same projectiles.

"So, what now?"

"There's some repair work we need to do. And there's plenty of gardening to tend to. Enough to keep us both busy. I'll show you where all the tools are kept."

The next three days saw Bill working steadily, first on repairing the damage to the property from the brief gunfight, then beginning to learn the basics of tending to the vegetable plots in the back garden of the house. Although the jobs were mundane, he welcomed the break from cross-country riding and non-stop gun battles. It almost seemed as if life were returning to some degree of normalcy, and it was something Bill found he was able to adapt to pretty quickly; as if the plague of walking undead had never happened.

To keep as much variety as possible, he alternated between gardening and maintenance, spending a couple of hours on his knees in the dirt, then another two hours tending to odd jobs around the house. He didn't see much of his companions during the day: Tara spent much of her day with Sarah, while Steve was often with Cindy, only appearing every three or fours hours to check on his progress. Bill didn't mind so much, he enjoyed spending time on his own, and it allowed him to work through the jumble of thoughts going through his mind. While working he could 'zone out', just as he did while working in the office, and carry on with whatever task he was doing while running through whatever may be on his mind.

On the afternoon of the third day since sanctuary, Bill had climbed up on to the roof, beginning to replace the roof tiles that had split and shattered when he had first opened fire with his machinegun. As he lay face down on the roof, working at the slate tiles and the nails that fixed them to the wooden frame, the silence of the country retreat was broken by a low hum, like that of an engine in the distance. Peering over the crest of the roof, he could see the bulky shape of a giant vehicle as it lumbered into view. There were a couple of miles of field and hill between the main road and the cottage, but if Tara had been able to spot the house, Bill had to assume that someone else would also be able to.

As if a switch had been flicked, Bill's survival instincts kicked to life, and he leapt down from the roof, landing in a crouch and launching through the open back door into the kitchen.

"Steve," he yelled, grabbing his crossbow from the kitchen counter and slipping a bolt into position. "Steve, I think someone's coming."

Steve appeared at the entrance to the living room, his eyes wild with fear as he fumbled with his rifle. "Someone's coming?" he repeated.

"Main road, looks like a large vehicle, something like a truck. It's not heading this way yet, but it's probably going to pass us by. We have to be ready, in case they see the house and come for a look. Where's Tara?"

"Here," she answered, emerging from Sarah's room, the girl as always not far behind her. "I heard. I'll take her upstairs. Where's Cindy?"

"She's already upstairs, she's asleep in bed. Have you got your pistol?"

Tara patted the leather holster that hung from her belt, and the weight of the pistol that filled it. "Right here."

"And keep away from the skylights," Bill warned, grabbing his submachine gun and storming through into the living room, with Steve hot on his heels.

"Do you think they'll be able to see the house?"

"Why not?" asked Bill, taking position at one of the windows and carefully prying one of the wooden planks from the window. "We saw it. I don't see why someone else couldn't."

The pair watched out the window for five minutes in silence as the large vehicle trundled into view, and ground to a halt on the main road outside the field Bill had ditched his bike. He lifted his crossbow and peered down the scope, using it as a telescope to see what was happening around the vehicle.

The doors opened and three people climbed out the machine, one kneeling down on the edge of the road and examining the ground. The person stood, seemed to confer with his two companions, then pointed out towards the field, and the house across it. Bill swore, rolling to one side away from the window and hopefully out of the line of sight of the men. Steve did the same, gripping his weapon across his chest and softly muttering a prayer.

"They didn't see us," Bill murmured. "We're too far away, they couldn't see us."

"Who are they?" whispered Steve.

"The vehicle looks to be Military, I think I've seen one before. In Manchester, where my friends..."

Steve took another look through the window, his rifle levelled with the men in the distance, and Bill did the same. Sure enough, the men had decided to venture out on foot across the field, the lead man hunched down low over the ground, his two friends providing cover with their heavy weapons. Bill knew instantly they were following the bike tracks, and that they'd reach the ditch and find his bike submerged in the water. Once they found that, they would undoubtedly find any footprints that had been left by Tara or himself.

"Safety off," Bill warned. "Lock and load, they're going to come here. Don't fire until you're sure they're in range."

The men in the field found the crash site of the bike, and two of them knelt down, trying to haul the machine out of the water. They gave up, and one turned back to face the vehicle they'd just left, waving towards the bike, then the house.

"They're on their way," Steve said as the three men started to pick their way towards the cottage, the lead man still tracking the imprints in the muddy ground. One of the men providing cover lifted his hand to his mouth and called out a single-syllable word that echoed wordlessly into the distance. Bill glared through his scope, lowered his weapon and rubbed his eyes, then returned to his scope. They were closer now, close enough to make out some details of the people. Although they all wore clothing covered in urban camouflage patterns, none wore any breathing apparatus or helmets, as Bill thought they would. From what Al had told him before, the government was certain that the plague had been airborne, and everyone in his helicopter had been instructed to wear the correct breathing apparatus. Even during their fake television broadcast, they'd all wore the same equipment. The fact the three men approaching the house wore none didn't sit well with Bill. If they weren't Marines or another branch of the armed forces, that could only mean they were part of a gang that had managed to commandeer the vehicle. It was certainly possible, as Moloch had proven during his occupation of Edgly. Bill targeted the rear-most person first, lining up their head with the crosshair of the scope, and slowly squeezed the trigger.

"Jesus," he said suddenly, lowering his weapon and urging Steve to do the same. He grudgingly did so, placing his rifle down on the ground and grabbing the shotgun Bill had let him use. He stared out the window, then back towards the door leading into the dining room, licking his lips anxiously. "I know them... I think"

Steve lifted the shotgun, pointing it roughly towards Bill. "You know them? Have you been in contact with these men? Told them where we are? You miserable bastard, you tricked us!"

"No," Bill said, standing up and edging slowly towards the door. "It's them... It's... Take another look at them."

Steve did so, still keeping his weapon trained on Bill as he glared out the window.

One of the men providing cover seemed vaguely familiar, spiked blonde hair surrounded by a red headband. The other man wore a red and blue cap, while the third man, the man leading the group by following the tracks, was muscular, seven foot when he stood upright, with a thick black beard covering his chin. The man wearing the cap lifted his hand once more, calling out the same monosyllabic word as before. Only this time, Bill could make out the word clearly.

"Bill!"

Dropping his weapons, Bill stormed out the house, lifting his hands above his head in a gesture of submission and trying to show he was both unarmed, and meant no harm. Three heavy machineguns instantly snapped up, but none opened fire.

"It's me," he shouted, waving his hands frantically as he walked towards them. "Shit, I thought you were dead."

"There's the kid," shouted Al, standing up from the tracking of the footprints and lowering his weapon. "What did I tell you? I knew he'd be all right. Probably shacked up with that dancer for a couple of days of hard lovin'. That's the kid for you," Al's tone was jovial, until he stepped closer to Bill. "You had us worried, you piece of crap. Where the fuck've you been?"

"Hold it," shouted Garth, dropping to his knees and snapping up his weapon. "Bebop, twelve o'clock!"

Al stepped forwards, knocked Bill down to his feet and brought his weapon up to bear on Steve as he stumbled out the house and dropped his weapon, lifting his hands the same way Bill had.

"He's with me," Bill hissed, rolling on to his back then clambering to his feet. "It's all right, he's on our side."

"Christ, kid, don't tell me *that's* the dancer you've been shacked up with for the best part of a week."

"It's not. That's Steve, it's his house we've been living in for past three days. Steve, this is Al, Garth and Clive. The guys I told you about."

"I thought you were dead," Steve said, slowly reaching out and shaking each of the men's hands.

"We get that a lot," Al said with a grin. "Thanks for looking after the kid for me."

Al's usually hard exterior cracked briefly, and he lunged forwards, hugging Bill for a second before he pushed him away. "Where've you been kid?"

"I couldn't remember where we were supposed to meet up, until the sounds of a gun battle drew me to the right place. By the time I got to where I was supposed to, you were all dead, I saw all the Rots eating what was left from the battle. That's when I... well, I guess that's when I thought you'd all been killed by the Rots. There were too many bodies there for me to check them all, and it was too dangerous, too. I just..."

"Assumed we'd bought the farm, right?" Al grinned. "Christ, kid, I'm surprised at you. Jesus, don't you know me at all?"

"So what happened?"

"I'm getting to it," Al said, raising a hand and signalling to Steve to stop asking any questions. "I can only talk at a certain speed. We were at the right place, but I figured we were too early. I let my men have the night off. First thing in the morning, the rescue team turned up, threw us all off. Because a certain kid and his rescued dancer wasn't there, we had to try to stall for a little time. They weren't buying it, and Spanners in there blew the whole deal because he went on about the whole 'briefcase' thing, remember that?"

"Yeah, that's how you got caught out the first time," Bill said, nodding by way of confirmation and remembering the story Al had told him several times. "They pulled that trick again?"

"Yeah, and Spanner's fell for it. Dumb bastard. Anyway, we let our guns do the talking. It was pretty much a stalemate situation, until we were flanked by a group of Rots. I mean, Rots themselves are no problem. A bunch of Marines, that's a problem, but something I can handle. When we're facing both opposing sides, shit, even *I* know when I'm beat. We bolted; I'm not ashamed to admit we ran away. It's not what Marines do, but fuck, kid, we were surrounded by soldiers and shamblers. We ran like shit off a stick, all of us. None of the Marines followed us, they were too busy dealing with the Rots, and although a few of the dead tried to follow us, I guess we were lucky enough to not attract any runners. We went to ground a few miles away, stayed low, and hoped for the best. After a few hours, we came back and cleared up, then claimed that beast over there as our own. There were a few Rots just incapacitated, but not killed: a few Marines that were on the verge of turning, left to die and rise again. We did what we had to do."

"So *Colebrook's Runner's* been left to rust in the middle of Manchester? How'd Garth ever agree to that?"

"Some poor bastard Marine had strapped himself in during the battle, tried to drive away. Rots got him, smeared his guts across the whole of the cab. Buddy kinda sickened of his vehicle after that, didn't want anything to do with it. When I suggested taking the Marine's Bailey over there, he jumped at the chance."

"It's a dream to drive," Garth cut in, waving back at the vehicle. "I've driven some fine vehicles in my time, but they're all like a piece of shit compared to that thing. Wonderful."

"So we took it. The Rots hadn't penetrated it, it was vacant, just a couple of bullet holes and some blood splashes on the side. *The Pride of Colebrook.*"

"Naturally," Bill said, nodding his head.

"So, let's get your shit on board and go. C'mon, we've got places to go, things to do."

"What about Steve?"

"Shit, he can come along," Al said. "It's big and comfortable in there, plenty of room for one more."

"And Tara, don't forget her."

"Dancing chick," Al said, nodding his head. "Wouldn't leave here. Truth be told, kid, she's the only reason we're out looking for you."

"I'm not coming," Steve said, turning back towards his house. "Not with Cindy as far along she is. I've got a family to think of, I'm not just going to drag them out for a dangerous life of..."

"Family?" Clive said, his first contribution to the conversation. "How many people do you have in there?"

"Me," Steve said casually. "Cindy, Sarah. We don't know what the baby's going to be yet."

"You can't expect to raise your children out in the wilderness like this, surely?" Clive said.

"And the life on the road is ideal for a six year old and a newborn baby?"

"Did my daughter no harm," Garth said with a grin. Nobody paid him much attention.

"Much as I like standing around in a field, up to my ass in mud, is there any chance we can come to some arrangement here?" Al finally said. "Work out who's coming with us, who's staying here, who's getting me a cup of coffee, and maybe even a sandwich. You hear that. bitch?" he said, tapping his microphone. "Still waiting on that cup of coffee."

The table in the dining room normally held six people comfortably, meaning that quite a few people had to stand in the cramped room. Cindy had been given one of the chairs, and Steve sat beside her, with Sarah sitting on his knee. She was quite wary of her house suddenly being filled with strangers, and her eyes flitted nervously from face to face. Tara sat beside Steve, holding the hand of the little girl as the conversation went back and forth. Bill stood in the far corner, stepping back from the conversation and taking in all the details as it happened.

Al sat on one of the remaining seats, leaning back on the rear-most legs, his feet kicked up on to the table as he looked around the captive audience. Angel sat on another chair, though she had made sure to pull this as far from Al as the confines of the room allowed her. She watched Bill as he stood silently in the corner, smiling occasionally when he looked her way and caught her eye. Pam sat by close to Al, her hand resting lightly on his knee as she listened to the conversation, not offering any contribution to the discussion.

Both Garth and Steve leant up against the wall, one on either side of the doorway leading into the living room, almost like sentries watching over an inquisition. All his friends had said their greetings to Bill, some warmer than others, while only Pam and Garth had openly welcomed Tara, one because they were friends held captive by the same maniacal despot, the other for more lecherous reasons.

Having removed the military regalia and changed into his normal priest clothing, Clive stood opposite the parents, strolling back and forth in the cramped confines of the room. He hadn't said much since asking for a meeting with the residents of the house, just simply walked back and forth in the dining room.

"How long do you think you can last here?" Clive finally asked. "Vegetables and rainwater will only last for so long."

"We've lasted this long," Steve said, wrapping his arm around his daughter and squeezing his wife's hand. "We can sit this out."

"Until what? Until we get rescued by the Marines? Al, tell them about the Marines, about the documents you found in that vehicle."

Al shrugged his shoulders, reaching into one of his pockets and pulling out a crumpled piece of paper. He unwrapped it and flung it on the table within Steve's reach. He retrieved it, laying it flat out on the table and read through the page of type before him.

"You see," Al said, summarising the contents of the report and pointing towards Bill. "The kid over there guessed this a long time ago, back when we first met up with the bitch. Course, I didn't want to believe it at the time, kept telling him he was crazy. The Marine's have been told to reclaim Britain as soon as possible, through any means necessary. There's more survivors than you'd think, but the only thing is the armed forces are so shit-scared that the plague's going to spread they've got this whole thing about not letting any survivors off the island. Too dangerous, they say. So they decided it was quicker and easier to wipe out everything left on the island."

"Bullshit," Steve barked, snatching the paper away from the eyes of his daughter while he read the orders. Bill stepped forwards, motioned to him to pass the paper, and read it himself while Al continued.

"Bullshit or not, they decided it would be easier to cleanse the island. Civvies, rebels, Rots, the whole fuckin' enchilada. Right there in black and white. Instructions to gather survivors at power stations, airports and seaports under the false pretence of rescue. Then they bomb the poor bastards, culling on a massive scale. Of course it worked, wiping out survivors and the potentially infected, but it was mostly civvies."

Silence fell across the stunned adults in the room, the only sound that of Sarah as she laughed to herself.

"You said a dirty word," she sniggered, her first words since coming into contact with the group of strangers. Al looked at her, grinned a toothy smile.

"Stick around, kid, I know them all, and use them on a regular basis. Fuck. Shit. Bitch. All the words, from the expletive to blasphemous."

"Honey," Steve snapped, pushing the girl from his knee and pushing her towards the door. "Why don't you go play in your room for a little while. We'll be right here, don't worry."

"Okay," she sighed, trudging towards the door leading to her room and grabbing Tara by the hand as she went. She stopped beside Angel, gently tugged her arm. "Do you want to come with me? I've got dolls and ponies in my room."

"I love dolls and ponies," Angel said softly, smiling and following the girl and her friend into her room. She flashed another smile at Bill as she left the room, but he was still scrutinising the document Al had produced.

"You girls play nice," Clive said with a chuckle, watching the child guide the two women from the dining room. He turned back to Steve and Cindy, all traces of his joviality gone. "She's a nice kid. Why do you want her to die?"

"Christ, that's a bit harsh, man," Sylvester said, lowering himself to the seat just vacated by Angel.

"If harsh is the only way he can see the folly of his ways, then that's the road I'm going to have to lead him down," Clive said to his friend, before turning back to Steve and Cindy. "How long do you think it will be until a gang stumbles across you? Or until one of the hollow men seek you out?"

"We've already had one unwanted visitor," growled Steve. Bill lowered the piece of paper he held, passing it back to Al and taking Clive to one side. He quickly explained the situation as best he could, while an awkward silence lingered in the air. Nodding slowly, Clive turned and rested his hands on the back of Al's chair, watching the two parents for several minutes before finally talking again.

"He's told me what happened. I'm sorry, I didn't know. But if it's happened once, it will happen again. Only next time it may not be one man on his own. It may be ten, maybe twenty men, how would you handle that? And if you've had no experience fighting the hollow men, what are you going to do when the first walking corpses approach your home and threaten your family? How would you deal with that?"

"It's my home, I can keep it safe."

"I thought I was safe in my church, until its sanctity was defiled by the hollow men. Normal men can be put down with a bullet, scared off with threat of violence. The hollow men, they're mindless, like animals. Bullet, blade, fire, none can turn back the devils. They keep coming, and won't stop until they get the flesh they crave."

"I can protect my family," Steve muttered.

"And Cindy?" Clive said, waving a hand towards the pregnant woman. "When the time comes for her to give birth, where will you be? At the window with rifle in one hand and torch in the other, smiting the creatures, or by her side? Have you ever delivered a baby?"

"And midwifery is part of the teachings they provide in priest school?"

"We can provide safety in greater numbers."

"And besides, that bitch in there with your daughter, she's had training as a vet, used to help her father with birthing season on the farm. I'm sure she can help. Let the women deliver the baby, me and you can hang around outside smoking cigars. Just like God intended."

"Sexist pig," Pam muttered, taking her hand of his knee and shaking her head.

"Blasphemer," growled Clive.

"He's right," Garth said, finally offering his own thoughts on the matter. "About the safety. I'm a coward, I'll openly admit that. I stuck with Al and his gang because I knew they'd be able to help me out, provide safety. That, and I was threatened with a gun."

With a grin, Al drew his magnum and cocked it before placing it on the table before it. "Do I need to do the same?" he said jovially. Steve licked his lips, looking across the room to the rifle resting against the wall behind Al. Cindy seemed to whiten a little, starting to shake as she looked at the weapon on the table. Al noticed the way Steve looked at the rifle, and chuckled softly. "If you even think about going for that rifle, I feel you should know I could kill you a hundred different ways before you even reach it."

Steve pulled himself to his feet and lifted Cindy by the arm, helping to guide her up from the table and towards the kitchen. "Give us a few minutes," he murmured as he went. With the parents out of earshot, Clive seemed to breathe heavily out, as if he'd been holding it in during his sermon.

"I had no idea you felt that strongly about this family coming along," Bill said, unable to hide his curiosity as he turned to face Al.

"Truth be known, I don't give a shit one way or the other, 'cause at the end of the day, I still get the biggest bed."

"You're all heart, you know that?"

"Hey, everyone here's got their own little talents, something they're good at. If I see potential, I'll take them on board, even if I have to fight to get them to come. They've survived two months, they must have something, even if it's just dumb luck. We could use some luck, especially for what I've got planned."

Bill took up one of the empty seats and watched as the grinning Marine holstered the exposed weapon, then took out a thick cigar and placed it between his lips, clamping it in place with his teeth.

"You're going to love this plan, it's fuckin' magic. Do me a favour buddy, run out to the trailer, grab the orange folder that's on the desk upstairs, and get it back here. Here's as good a place as any to tell you all what I've been thinking."

IV

Garth returned after twenty minutes, red-faced and out of breath, gripping an orange paper folder filled to bursting point with reports and maps, all defaced with the same handwriting. He passed them to Al, who quickly dumped it on the table and let it flop open. He sifted through the papers, pulled out a clump of blue papers held together with a wire spiral, and started to tear pages from it, passing them around the group.

"I found all this when I was poking around the command office aboard *The Pride* out there. A lot of interesting shit there, some of it meaningless to you civvies. However, these reports detail the location of different outposts, bases and forts across the British Isles. Anyone know what these are?"

"That's normally what we use you for," Sylvester said, looking up from the page he held. "You're the military brains."

"Of course *I* know," sighed Al, rolling his eyes as he talked. "I just wanted to know if anyone else knew what they were, save me a little bit of explaining."

"I watched a documentary once," confessed Garth. "I used to like that kind of shit, found it really interesting. They're all modules, aren't they? Like all the fast food joints in the world."

"He's right," Al said, rummaging through the papers and coming up with a set of blueprints and schematics, passing them around the group. "Only thing is, our modules are a little more complex than your local burger joint."

"I would murder someone for a good burger," Garth muttered as he stared at the technical drawings, before passing them on to Bill. Al nodded, missing his fix of prime minced beef as much as Garth. Meat, like many things, were off the menu for a long time.

"Anyway, all Marine command posts come in modules, big chunky concrete buildings, empty shells that can be shipped in by massive Leviathan helicopters, we're talking structures that are fifteen, maybe twenty feet high, walls a foot and a half thick, reinforced by steel girders. The main cornerstone of any Marine construction is this," Al said, tapping a thick finger on one of the photographs spread in front of him amidst the confusion of paper. "A square based pyramid, flat on top, which can act as a gun platform. A squad of twelve men can occupy just one of these units, and they're often set up on their own as an observation outpost. A variety of one-man towers can be set up on top of this, armed with different weapons."

Al froze as he stared at the photo, and was reminded of the observation outpost he had once approached in a helicopter. Hundreds of Rots surrounding the building, pressing in closer, clambering up dead bodies of their fallen kindred in a bid to reach their prey stranded atop the building. Memories of a man launching himself from the top of a tower, missing the lowest rung of the ladder and diving headlong into the clutch of baying flesh eaters at the base of the outpost.

"Al? Baby, you okay?"

Al shook his head, looking at Pam and the worried expression on her face. He shook his head again, muttered it was nothing, returned to the mix of papers on the table.

"Twelve people?" Sylvester asked in disbelief as the photos and schematics reached him. "Can't be very comfortable."

"Marines don't live in comfort, we live to serve. If a typical grunt's given a bed that's too comfy, the poor bastard isn't going to get up when the drill sergeant comes around at five in the morning. And besides, they'd live on a shift rota. Six men on guard duty, another six off and resting. On it's own, it's an outpost, a communication relay, just another link in a chain. Take four outposts, though, and fly in four concrete walls about five foot thick, maybe thirty feet long, you're looking at a base. Enough space for a full complement of about forty-eight troops, maybe a skeleton crew of another ten technicians to run communication equipment, repair shit, maybe look after any vehicles they can get in there. Close to sixty men. Now, before the plague, there may have been one or two of these. Now, these reports indicate there's at least six. They're kitted out with enough supplies and provisions for sixty men to survive for six months without a supply run. And by survive, I mean fresh water and freeze-dried rations. It's survival, but it isn't living."

"What's your point, Al?" Bill asked.

"Until two months ago, there were maybe two of these in Britain. Now, according to these documents, there's six, like I said. Outposts have increased from fifteen to thirty. There's also one fort that's just appeared on the map," he announced, unveiling the final photo from the pile before him.

"A fort? Jesus, Al, why are you telling us all this?"

"Forts are the pinnacle of module-based Marine structures. They're dropped into hot areas in combat zones, and are equipped to withstand major assaults from the most deadly and well-organised attackers. Last time I saw one of these it was in the middle of Brazil, and those Bebop bastards couldn't fucking *touch* us in there. Six of the observation modules, stuck together with another six wall units. A collection of makeshift huts and buildings in the grounds, with a seventh observation module in the middle of the construction acting as a command centre. We're talking about something that can house a hundred and thirty personnel, with enough food and water to keep them content for a year. Fuel reserves, long-range radio, enough munitions to end a war. Like I say, the pinnacle of Marine emplacements. The perfect place to live during a zombie-related holocaust."

"The Marines tried to wipe us out when we tried to hitch a ride with them off the island," Sylvester said, his brow wrinkling into a frown. "What the hell makes you think they're going to let us waltz into a fort and settle down there until the last Rot keels over?"

"Waltz in? Don't be fucking stupid. We're not going to just walk in there; we're going to take over the place."

"I'm not clear on what part of this plan is 'fuckin' magic'," sneered Bill. "You've just said they were equipped to withstand a major assault. A hundred and thirty Marines? What the hell are we going to do against a hundred and thirty armed Marines?"

"You think you're so smart, kid," Al said, glaring at Bill. He'd missed Bill during the days he was absent, and had obviously forgotten that he could be so argumentative at times. "Momma Colebrook didn't raise no fool."

"I didn't know you had a brother," Bill said with a smile, but Al ignored him.

"These reports, if you take time to read them, tell us that the fort, bases and outposts were reduced to operating on a skeleton crew while the hunting parties were organised to water down the number of survivors. That leaves round about thirty men in the fort. I think we can take them."

"There's ten civilians and one Marine here. You really like those odds?"

"There you go again, kid, running your mouth before even thinking things through. Ten civvies? One's a kid, another's seven months pregnant, Preacher-man's still weird about shooting people, then there's the father-to-be and the two dancing chicks who have practically *no* combat experience at all. I make that four civvies and a Marine. Five if you want to include the pacifist preacher-man. He might not be able to fight, but he could at least carry extra ammo for us. He claims he can still smite the hollow men, too, whatever the fuck that means. So, five civvies and a Marine. That's even better, isn't it?"

"We have names," Pam said, sulking at the generic name she'd been given. Al ignored it, concentrating more on the disproving glare of Bill and Garth. "Frigging sadist," the trailer cab driver said, shaking his head.

"That makes the odds even worse. Why the hell would we want to go ahead with this crazy plan?"

"Do you want to spend the rest of your life traipsing around this place in a trailer? Sleeping and living in an unsecured environment, eating scraps of rancid food, drinking stale water, siphoning petrol from abandoned vehicles as we go, until… whenever. Is that any way to live, when instead we could be living like kings? There's supplies in that fort that can keep over a hundred men and women alive for a year. It could keep *us* all going for the rest of our lives. It's a golden opportunity we can't afford to miss. And with them operating on a skeleton crew, it's an opportunity we'd be fools to pass up on."

"Loathe as I am to admit it," Clive said, looking nervously towards Bill, "Al's right. We can't live as nomads forever. How can we expect a family to agree to come live with us if we can't offer them a better home then where they live now? Sly, what do you think?"

"I think it's fucking crazy," he replied, unsheathing the combat knife that dangled from his belt and picking at the dirt beneath his nails with the tip of the blade. "But then, I think driving around the country until we're all wiped out is fucking crazy, too. Jesus, the whole 'walking dead' scenario is fucking crazy. I say we give it a shot. What harm can it do? We're all living on borrowed time, anyway."

"Sounds like the majority rules," Al said with a grin. "If Preacher-man thinks it's a good idea, that's like the word of God or something. This is going to work, trust me. The fort's in Nottingham, about a hundred kilometres away, so we've still got a journey ahead of us. The sooner we get away from here, the better. No time like the present, and all that shit. Soon as the parents decide what they're going to do, we can leave."

As if on cue, Steve entered the room, guiding his wife back to the table. Bill and Clive gave up their seats and the expectant parents graciously accepted the chairs.

"We've talked it through," Cindy said, looking at Steve and licking her lips. Steve nodded, reached forwards and held the hands of his wife. "We've made our decision."

Can't wait, Al thought to himself as his mind started to work through different tactics and plans for the assault, tuning out the world around him.

The entrance to the middle trailer of the Marine vehicle had been an airlock, no doubt installed as the rest of the world still believed, wrongly of course, that the plague was still airborne. As Bill stepped in he expected to be doused with cleansing jets of gas, like he'd experienced when he'd been escorted out of work all those weeks ago, but instead the seven ventilation grilles on the walls and ceiling whirred softly to themselves, their motors straining against whatever alteration Sylvester had done to disable the purifiers.

After leaving the malfunctioning airlock, Bill found himself in a small entrance hall with three separate doors. The one closest to him lead to a small antechamber, the walls lined with metal racks and hooks, each holding a weapon of some description: many of which he hadn't seen even in Al's impressive and extensive collection.

Behind the door next to the small armoury was a kitchen unit, fitted with four cooking plates and a metal washbasin. A refrigeration unit took up half the room, stacked with sealed packets of meat and vegetables. The room had a sterile quality, almost like a medical facility, with a collection of eating implements left out on the bench like discarded tools in an operating room.

Pressing on into the rear of the trailer, Bill found himself in the luxurious living quarters of the trailer. At least, they were luxurious compared to Garth's previous truck. Five bunk beds lined one side of the wall, each compartment fitted with a thick black curtain. Some had been closed, while others had been left wide open, displaying some of the personal affects that had been left on the beds. One held a clump of metallic instruments and wires, linked up to a small pair of speakers: undoubtedly part of the music system Garth had installed in his old trailer. Another exposed bed held a string of prayer beads and a thick bible.

The rest of the room was fitted with a collection of padded seats and metal tables, scattered with magazines and books, while a large and flat monitor screen dominated one third of one of the walls, currently blank. At the rear of the room there was another airlock leading into the rear-most trailer, the cycling and purifying mechanism disabled just as the first one had been. Beside the airlock was a spiral staircase, and after dropping his rucksack on the ground by an apparently unoccupied bed, he made his way up the stairs, his hand resting on the butt of the pistol hanging by his side as he cautiously ascended to the next level.

The upper floor comprised of a medical bay kitted out with five surgical tables, each one padded with a thick mattress and covered by a thin white sheet. Benches lined the outer wall, with a collection of tools and instruments bolted or fastened down to the sterile surfaces with magnets. Drawers and cupboards were locked up tight, while the keys for each lock hung from a large silver hook by the doorway. Bill strolled through the immaculate room towards the far end, where a large wooden door had been set into the wall. Though the rest of the trailer seemed to be metal, the very presence of the wooden door seemed out of place. He reached out, tried to open the door, but the lock simply rattled and the door refused to budge.

"It's locked up," Al announced as he clambered up the stairs and strolled forwards. "It's the officer's quarters. That makes it my room. Me and Pammy need a little privacy every now and then. You gotta go through the med-bay to get there, but no one ever said Marines engineers were practical, just functional."

"What's in there?"

"Bed. Table and chair. A few guns, more of those files I had back in the house."

He reached out and unlocked the door by swiping a plastic card through the electronic lock beside door. It beeped, and the door swung back as the latches were released, revealing a room that wouldn't be amiss in a commanding officer's three-storey mansion. Al strolled in, slid into the thickly padded leather chair and reclined back with a grin on his face, fingers interlocked behind his head. The walls were lined with bookshelves and shallow filing cabinets, and a large bed was pushed up against the wall, the bedclothes clean and smooth, immaculately neat as only a well-trained Marine could manage. Bill looked at the well-presented bed, then towards Al.

"Old habits die hard," he said by way of explanation, then waved around the room. "I know it's modest, just like me, but it's home. Used to be the hideaway of the onboard officer, before the Rots got him. Now it's my pad. Me and Pam sleep in here."

"You two got together," Bill muttered with a smile, looking at the collection of books and running his finger along their exposed spines. None of the titles inspired him to pick one up and flick through it.

"Can I interest you in a drink?" Al asked, pulling open one of the shallow cabinets and pulling out a square bottle of golden brown liquid. He filled two crystal tumblers and sipped one, then pushed it across the table. Bill took it up, but didn't drink from it.

"What's in the back of the vehicle, then? I know you're just dying to tell me."

"Water and fuel reserves. A generator to run all the pretty toys we have here. Storage for a couple of bikes, and a shit load of weapons and ammo. Enough to keep me happy for a good few weeks. There's a bike already in there, military grade, so you can forget about that bike of yours that you trashed out in the field."

"Enough to help us assault a fort?"

"Don't give me any shit, kid. I know you're not hot for the idea, but I'm in charge and the votes were against you. Soon as we get there, it'll be a piece of cake, and we'll have a palace to live in. Trust me, it'll be worth it. Just like in Brazil, when me and the boys took out a Bebop encampment. Good times, good times."

Al stopped speaking, a distant look washing over his face as he remembered his time in combat. He remained silent for a moment, lost in his thoughts, then snapped out of it with a shake of his head.

"Where is this place again? This magic fort that's going to make our life so much easier?"

"Nottingham," Al answered, grabbing a rolled up map and laying it out flat on the table. He tapped the map where a red 'F' had been marked, then traced the roads back up from its location. "About a hundred kilometres south, as the crow flies. Maybe a hundred and twenty after all the twists and turns of the roads. A few days of travel in this beast, it can't go that fast. To be honest, I think the slow pace of this vehicle is getting to Garth, he loved to go as fast as he could."

"Maybe that's why his vehicle kept breaking down on him. You don't think the same will happen to this?"

"*The Pride of Colebrook* is as tough a bastard as its namesake. You could grab one of the XR1 anti-tank rifles out the back there and fire it point-blank into the engine block, this thing would keep on going. Marines and their equipment are built to last. "

"Right, sure," Bill muttered, knocking back the contents of the glass he held before slamming it on the table. His breath caught in his throat as the liquid burned his mouth and stomach, and then coughed violently as he made his way back into the medical room, heading for the stairs. He paused halfway across the room, then turned back and saluted sharply.

"Thanks for looking out for me."

"I don't follow," Al said, pouring himself another glass before abandoning his room and locking up behind him.

"Looking around here, trying to find me. I mean, how long were you looking for me, three days?"

"You're the kid *and* my sergeant; I wouldn't consider making anyone else here a sergeant. That being said, I was ready to write you off as dead two days ago. Someone kept us looking, pretty fucking insistent about it all."

"Garth?"

"Nope, he was too busy poking around in his new toy."

"Clive?"

"Preacher-man was caring, I guess, but all he kept saying was that his prayers would be with you, and that was about it. He didn't try to convince us either way. It was the bitch that kept the search going. I don't know, maybe she missed you or your dick, I couldn't say which one was right. She wouldn't let it go, like a dog with a bone."

"Angel?"

"She likes you, kid. Probably because other than Preacher-man, you're the only other person here who treats *her* like a person. I guess she was just so insistent about finding you so she had someone else to talk to. That, and the fact she missed the sex."

"Give it a rest," he sighed, turning back to the stairs and making his way down to the main living area, where Sarah had arrived. She ran around excitedly, bouncing from chair to chair and rummaging through the magazines that been left on the tables. She looked up at Bill as he entered the room, and stepped back from the table, dragging her sleeve across her nose.

"You all right?" he asked with a smile. The child nodded her head, staring at him as if it was the first time she'd seen him.

"I'll sleep over here," she finally said, skipping across the room and jumping on to one of the beds. It didn't have anything on it or around it to suggest someone had already claimed it as their own. She pulled the curtain shut and giggled to herself as she remained hidden.

Bill left the child to her own devices and made his way to the entrance of the trailer, helping Steve as he began to throw his bags aboard the vehicle.

"You sure you want to do this?" Bill asked as he grabbed the packs and started to move them into the main living area. "It's a pretty crazy plan he's come up with, are you certain this is going to be the best for you?"

"Like he said, he doesn't expect us to go in and fight. You do the hard work, we all reap the benefits. I'd go in and help, but..."

"It's all right. It's going to be a tough fight, maybe even more than we can handle. Much as Al thinks we can handle this, I think he's overconfident and grossly mistaken."

"You've had your chance to make your opinions heard, as have the rest of the team," Al shouted from the upper floor, his voice drifting down the staircase. "Stop your bitching and suck it up, you miserable shit."

"Where's Sarah?"

Bill jerked his thumb in the direction of the bunk beds, and Steven shook his head, dumping his bags and storming off towards the staircase. "I've got to tell him to watch his mouth around my baby. I'm not having her pick up his foul mouth. I'd appreciate it if you'd do the same, too."

"No problem," Bill murmured as he slipped out the trailer, watching as his small group of friends shuffled towards the trailer, their arms heavily laden with provisions taken from the house: cupboards had been raided, and the garden had been dug up, leaving the building as nothing but a vacant shell. Both Tara and Pam guided Cindy across the grassy field, while Angel took up the rear; a bulging rucksack slung over one shoulder and her assault rifle tucked in against the other. Bill waved as she approached, nodding and smiling as people passed him by until only he and Angel remained outside the vehicle.

"Nearly ready to go," Bill said, nodding back towards the massive machine. "Our new family should be settling in pretty soon. Then it's off to Nottingham, and our eventual doom. Are me and Garth the only people who think this is one of the worst plans he could possibly come up with?"

"I know it's a crazy plan, but if it works, we'll be set for life. A new home, somewhere to begin rebuilding our lives."

"Okay then, apparently we *are* the only ones," Bill said sullenly, then put aside all thoughts of the upcoming assault. "Al was talking about the search for me. How you kept it going when he was ready to give up."

"You know what he's like," said Angel, turning away as she spoke. "He'd say anything to hide his emotions, he likes to portray himself as this cold and heartless killing machine. Thing is, he's become smitten with Pam over the past week, and he doesn't try to hide that. All these different emotions are starting to come to the surface: I guess he's not as shallow as we first thought."

"Our little boy's growing up," Bill said with a grin, looking back at the house.

"It reminds me of home," Angel said, lowering her weapon and joining Bill in his lingering observation of the property. "Secluded, a little vegetable garden. An ideal family home. There's no going back, is there?"

"You want to go home?"

"I mean normal life. There's no going back to a normal life, is there? Everything's changed too much."

Bill didn't answer; just put his arm around Angel and softly squeezed her shoulder. "C'mon, we'll have to get out of here, before they go without us."

The pair returned to the vehicle, stopping as the pressurised door on the side of the cabin hissed open and Garth appeared, hanging on to the heavy wheel that locked the door in place.

"Got a minute kid? I want you to see this shit in here."

Sighing, Bill clambered into the cab behind Garth, motioning to Angel to carry on into the trailer, saying he'd follow in a moment.

The cabin of the vehicle was far more spacious than that of Garth's old trailer, fitted out with three large and padded seats. One sat in the centre of the control room and faced forwards, a panel lined with banks of switches, gears and control sticks. The steering wheel had been replaced with a yolk similar to those found in aircraft, a compact control that was more economical in the confined space. Garth sat on this chair, turning it around and facing the doorway, a grin spread across his face.

Behind the main control seat were another two seats, each facing one of the walls covered with monitors and an assortment of controls. Bill took one of the seats, looked over the controls before him, and tapped the blank monitor screens. A couple flickered to life, displaying scenes fed from external cameras dotted around the vehicle.

"Is this shit the bomb or what? I mean, look at this! State of the art satellite navigation, homing devices, advanced targeting systems, motion sensors. Over there we have automated weapon controls, and there we have tracking, radar, surveillance... half of these systems we'll probably never look at, the other half probably don't work. But I'm telling you; it feels damn good to have them all. A little bit of added reassurance. So, what was she like?"

Bill froze, the sudden swing in conversation catching him off guard.

"The dancer, Tara? What was she like? I mean, all those days and nights alone with her, it must get pretty cold at night. You snuggle up to one another to share warmth, one thing leads to another, and then the magic happens. At least, that's the way it happens in all the porn films the Marines have been carrying around."

"Is there something wrong with you, Garth? I mean mentally."

"Not really. Too much time on my own, not enough female companionship, a little overweight, the list goes on. So you're telling me you and her didn't..."

"I'm not even going to answer you. C'mon, lets get this thing moving. We've got a date with a base full of men who're going to kill us."

XVIII
DEATH SQUAD

"It's not often they put up a fight, most are too weak: the rabid ones are the real threats; the fighters that can spread the disease further than a simple cough or a kiss."

I

Pam hovered over the blackened frying pan on the grill, rolling the sizzling and fatty meat that swam in the bubbling grease with a plastic spatula. She could barely face the meat as it cooked, and the smell made her stomach roll as she tried to concentrate on the task at hand. Although Al had instructed everyone to have an early night and a good sleep, he hadn't practiced what he had preached, and the pair had been awake well into the early hours of the morning, indulging in drinking, smoking and sexual gratification.

It was the drink that was keeping making her stomach roll at that moment, the alcohol in her system dulling her senses and the very notion of cooking the greasy food making her sick.

She finally turned the hob off, pouring the sausages and rashers of bacon on to a large metal tray and walking back into the main living area, moving slowly and carefully, making sure she didn't spill any of the searing hot food.

Al looked up from the plans that dominated the table he sat at, grinning and rubbing his hands together as the plate was put down. She had already prepared another three trays of the food, which had been spread around the group of people gathered around the table, and she knew that this would be the last, which meant she could sit down and listen to the plan Al had been working on since commandeering the trailer.

He sat back, reclining as best he could on the restrictive padded seats, casually leaning back and draping his arm over Pam as he shuffled to one side and made room on the chair for her. He lifted a half-smoked cigar from his pocket, placed it between his lips, and rummaged for his lighter, before noticing the scowl on Angel's face.

"It's bad enough you're eating that crap," she said, motioning towards the plate of bacon and sausages. "Don't even think about lighting up those things of yours."

"Can't even give myself cancer without you bitching at me," he said, rolling his eyes and helping himself to a sausage from the plate. "Who do you think you are, my momma? Jesus, bitch, ease up."

"What did I tell you about your language?" Steve said, glowering towards Al.

"You didn't tell me anything," growled Al, eyes flicking from Steve to Cindy, then the child over in the corner as she played with her dolls. "You asked me to watch my language around the girl. She's over in the corner on her own. She can't hear me. Jesus, if you're that strung up on it, send her outside, we're not moving."

"Outside?" laughed Steve, "With the fucking zombies roaming around?"

"Rots," corrected Al as he lit his cigar, and added with a grin, "And watch your language around the girl."

"Arsehole," Cindy grumbled, pushing her tray of food away from her and walking away from the table, heading towards the child and motioning for her to follow her upstairs to play.

"Fucking civvies. Okay then," Al said, drawing everyone's attention back to the meeting as he drummed his knuckles on the table. "We have a fort ripe for the plucking, and we have people with different skill to utilise for this job. Bitch, you're our marksman and spotter. Take out the guards, make sure its all clear before us boys advance on the place. Spanners, you and buddy are our heavy weapons guys; you can lead our charge. Kid, you're the rifleman, I'm the gunner, and together we're the foot soldiers, we provide the muscle."

"What about me?" asked Clive, interlacing his fingers and leaning forwards, pressing his weight down on the table as he did so.

"Do I have any use for a pacifist who refuses to point a weapon at anything other than a Rot?"

"I was included in your initial figures," he said with a grim smile. "One Marine and five civvies, isn't that right?"

"You're right," conceded Al, "We're going to have to have someone to act as a decoy every now and then."

"I know some first aid, too."

"Whoopee," Al said, rolling his eyes at Pam. She sniggered, trying to concentrate on the task at hand. Although she wasn't going in on the assault, she was still interested to know what was going on.

"I don't like it," announced Bill.

"Jesus, I know you don't like it kid. Do you have any better ideas?"

"Plenty. Don't do it for a start."

"Not a viable option. There's too much at stake. Like supplies for the rest of our immediate life."

"Okay then, what weapons does this hunk of crap have? You left the hummer behind, so I'm guessing it's an upgrade, yeah?"

"Mounted heavy weapons," agreed Al, his eyes glossing over. Pam had only seen the same look in his eyes on a couple of occasions; the first had been when they'd first taken control of the vehicle, the second when they'd first made love, and the third now, as he spoke about the capabilities of the vehicle. It gave her an idea about the things he loved more in life. "Mounted machineguns, Vulcan cannons, grenade launchers, missile launchers, everything you could ask for. Thick armour, too, enough to withstand a heavy barrage of gunfire."

"Why not just roll this up to the fort and assault it like that?"

"Too dangerous to the vehicle, the civvies onboard, and the fort itself. It's all about minimising collateral damage. The last thing we want to do is blast the fort with a salvo of grenades, then spend the next five months repairing the damn place. A small-scale foot soldier assault is really our best bet."

"The last thing they'd expect," murmured Angel, nodding slowly to herself. "It makes sense, I suppose."

"I'm out the loop for five days and suddenly the pair of you are reading from the same hymn sheet? What happened while I was away?"

"She finally saw me for who I am. A damn fine leader, role model for children, and by all accounts the worlds' greatest lover. Isn't that right?"

Pam smiled weakly. When the two of them were alone, Al was like another person: kind, caring, sensitive and considerate. But in front of the rest of the group, he always felt like he had to act up. There was nothing she could do to change that, Pam knew that was just the way he was. And even if she tried to explain that to someone, they'd not believe her. She smiled again, wider this time, casting a glance around the group and noting that no one had offered her any looks. They were all either looking at the collection of papers or conversing between themselves. She nodded gently by way of an answer to Al, and moved aside the tray on the table to get a better look at the pictures. She hadn't actually taken any time to look at the documents Al had been studying for days. All the photos depicted their target from a variety of different angles: a Marine fort, each corner unit of the rectangular base manned by a soldier in an elevated guard tower. One photograph showed the door to the fort, a giant blast door made from steel three foot thick that rolled down into the ground to allow entry; another showed a squad of Marines patrolling the grounds around the fort, while a third was that of a wire fence surrounding an open field, with a sign covered in red writing warning of the presence of anti-personnel mines.

"Looks awfully dangerous," she muttered to herself. Hearing her comment, Bill nodded in agreement.

"She's right. Look at this shit, man," Bill growled as he snatched up a handful of photos, frantically shuffling through them. "Guard towers, heavy weapons, squads on guard, minefields! I mean, Christ, what chance do we have?"

Al audibly sighed, turning to one side to address Clive. "How many times do I have to tell you this? Preacher-man, can you tell the kid how many men there are?"

"Skeleton crew," sighed Clive, "Thirty men in total."

"That's right. And Spanners, what about the guard towers?"

"Unmanned when there's insufficient cover, right?"

"Damn straight," Al said, nodding his head and pointing his smouldering cigar at Garth. "And you, buddy, tell the kid about the mines. About how we're just going to roll over them?"

"What?" snapped Garth, his drooping eyelids flickering open in panic as he was fielded a question. Pam understood both his tiredness and his reluctance towards the plan in general. She didn't understand the principle behind attempting to roll over the mines either.

"The mines," Bill said, the wild look in his eyes indicating that his tirade had not yet finished. "He wants you to tell me about the wonderful plan to just drive over the mines."

"Drive over the… Christ, are you fucking nuts? The tyres are thick, they're not indestructible."

"IFF frequencies, don't you remember the hummer back at the bitch's farm? Mines and explosives set up to not blow up when certain vehicles or people go over them? Jesus, why do I bother? All Marine vehicles are equipped with a transponder that sends out an IFF frequency, which mines are set up ignore. Gives us immunity to their munitions."

"Does it work the same for bullets?" Garth asked hopefully. Al ignored him.

"You all know the plan, we're on the move in five, we're about half an hour from the perimeter. Everyone get kitted up, buddy can go warm up the engine. Kid, you and the bitch prep the weapons. Spanners, you make sure we get there; you're the navigator. Preacher-man… Shit, I don't know, say a prayer or some shit like that."

"What can I do?" asked Steve, rising to his feet.

"You look after this place, make sure no Rot or Marine scout tries to get close. We'll go through the basic weapon systems with you, get you up to speed with things. You've fired a rifle, right?"

"Couple of times, yeah."

"We'll get you armed with a shotgun or assault rifle. I'd suggest the shotgun; it's as good a place as any to start. The kid can sort you out with that. Okay, people, let's get moving."

The crowd dispersed from the table, some muttering between themselves, others moving in silence. Pam remained at the table with Al, watching as he worked on the food that had been left by the group.

"What about me?"

"You can help me get ready and look sexy. Think you can manage that?"

She smiled dryly, following him as he pulled himself out of the seat and headed towards the staircase, retreating to his office and his stockade of equipment.

She sat on the bed and watched as he stripped down and changed into a fresh pair of military-style combat trousers, strapping belts and pouches into place before slipping his oversized handgun into its holster. She watched him as he prepared himself, at the tight muscles in his body as he lay down on the floor and proceeded to go through his daily exercise regime. He certainly wasn't her usual type: she would normally stay away from loud-mouthed and arrogant muscle-heads, but in the current situation, his strength and experience was comforting to her, something she needed now more than anything. There was something there between them, though, more than just a physical attraction, and she got the impression he felt it just as much as her.

"What're the tattoos for?" she finally asked as he stood and reached for his flack jacket. Of course it hadn't been the first time she'd seen them, but she'd never really had the opportunity to ask about them: they'd always been involved in other activities.

"My squad's nickname was the Wolvers. I figured the wolf head was a natural choice to have; it proved how dedicated I was to the Marines. I've had it for nearly twenty years."

"And the woman?"

"I like women," he said with a grin. "But then, you already knew that, right? Why the sudden interest?"

"Just curious," she said with a shrug. "Just wanted to get a little insight into who you are."

"A past life, now," he said, returning the gesture. "Just another reminder of what we're never going to have again. What about that one on your ass? I don't ask any questions about that."

"A tribal design," she said, self-consciously touching the ink beneath her clothing. "Just on a whim."

"Beautiful," he said with a grin, grabbing the rest of his weapons and securing them in place. He smiled, then stepped forwards and lifted her up from the bed, setting her on to her feet before him. He gripped the hem of her clothing in his large hands, tugging playfully at it. "You know, it's a shame. I'm all ready to go, but we've got another half an hour to kill. Any ideas what we can do to pass the time away?"

"I might have an idea," she said, smiling seductively as she slipped her top off and wrapped her arms around him.

II

"I've got a bad feeling about this," Bill muttered as he clambered out the disabled airlock, pressing his weapon tight against this chest as he looked towards the fort in the distance. The trailer had pulled up about half a mile away from the building, its bulk hidden behind a large copse of trees and shrubbery. Bill didn't think the vehicle would remain hidden because of its bulk, but Garth was confident in the parking he'd executed.

"I managed to hide my old trailer for almost a month before meeting you. You know what I'm like, I don't go looking for trouble, try to keep as well away from it as I possibly can."

"Al used to say the same thing. He didn't go looking for trouble…"

"It just had a way of finding him, I know. Seems like he's going out his way to find this particular type of trouble, though."

"There's no reasoning with him, not when he's hell-bent on taking control of this fort of his."

"I'm going out to find a suitable nest," Angel announced, stepping down out of the trailer and looking towards a small grassy hill on the other side of the field they stood in. The top of the mound was littered with rocks and scraps of debris, and would prove to be an ideal position for her. She had to get there first, without being seen by the single guard patrolling the ground around the fort that Bill could see from his secluded spot behind the bushes.

"I'm going over to the hill," Angel announced, confirming Bill's suspicion of the ideal sniping position. Al lumbered out the trailer, his arm linked with Pam as she followed him to the door, draped in a silken gown. He kissed her on the cheek, patted her on the buttocks as she retreated into the sanctity of the trailer.

"Keep that bed warm, baby, you hear? We won't be long. What's it looking like, kid?"

"Angel's about to run over to that hill, get a decent position and target the guard."

"Well, why doesn't she just toss a couple of grenades around while she's at it? There's a few magnesium flares in the trailer, she can spark those up, too! Stupid fuckin' bitch, you run over there, I don't care how low you go, the guard will see you and open fire. Those helmets don't just filter out the crap air; they can enhance vision, too. Think about it, use what cover you have."

She looked around for a moment, clearly puzzled, then turned her head skyward. "The trees?"

"As good as anything else we have to offer. You're a tomboy, you could climb a fucking barn, I'm sure you'll have no trouble in getting up that tree. Now get up there, or do I have to light a fire under your ass to get you moving?"

Angel slung her rifle over her shoulder and leapt up, grabbing the lowest branch and hoisting herself into the foliage above them. Both Garth and Bill lifted their gaze and followed her as she moved into the highest of the branches and settled into the crook of a Y-shaped branch.

"Gotta love watching her work that arse," Garth said with a grin, then without removing his gaze addressed Al. "Where'd the silk gown come from? You holding out on us Marine?"

"I found it in my office. Either the officer aboard this crate entertained a lot of women, or he was a transvestite. I've seen the women they let into the Marines – I'm guessing that it's the latter."

"Well, you know what they say about the Marines," Sylvester said with a grin as he emerged from the trailer cradling a grenade launcher. "They're nothing but a bunch of nancy-boys."

"Watch your mouth," Al said, waggling a finger at the mechanic. "That's just the Officers, anyway. Us grunts are nothing but one hundred and ten percent men. Everyone got their radios turned on?"

Everyone nodded in response, tapping the plastic devices hooked over their ears, then looked out through the surrounding foliage towards the fort in the distance. Bill crouched down low and eased himself forwards through the brush, lifting his hands to his eyes to provide some shade from the morning sun as he squinted into the distance.

"Looks like there's just the one guard out there," he announced, turning back to look at the grinning face of Al. "Loathe as I am to admit it, I think you might be right about this mad scheme."

"Course I'm right," he muttered, crouching beside Bill and laying his heavy machinegun on the ground. "That's because I'm large and in charge. Just one guard? I'm sure that's something the bitch can handle no problem. Am I right?"

"I've got him lined up right now, just say the word."

Bill lifted the pair of binoculars he had taken from the armoury and lifted them to his eyes, focusing on the lone Marine stumbling back and forth in front of the large blast door. Unlike most of the Marines he had seen that wore the sealed white coveralls, this particular guard wore camouflage fatigues and heavy body armour, with a cumbersome helmet and filtration mask. He carried a large assault rifle similar to the one Sylvester carried, but seemed to carry it in a sloppy manner, not what Bill would expect from a trainer soldier.

"Heavily armoured," observed Bill, keeping his binoculars trained on the guard. "Will she be able to get him?"

"That's a grade-A military sniper rifle she has, Heckler and Koch's finest long range weapon, loaded with dual-action rounds, a mix of armour piercing and hollow point. First they penetrate, then they flatten and mushroom out to cause massive trauma. A clean shot could smash his head apart. Have faith, and she'll deliver. Everyone ready?" Al didn't wait for a response from anyone. "Take the shot, bitch."

A muffled shot sounded in the trees above, and Bill watched as the figure in binocular dropped to his knees, his partially exposed neck exploding out in a shower of gore and gristle as the high velocity round tore through his flesh. He tensed for a moment, fingers gripping the opened wound, then pitched forwards, crashing face-first to the ground. He seemed to twitch for a few moments, blood gushing from his body and drenching the ground. As the final remnants of his life-fluid ebbed out, the twitching stopped.

"He's down," confirmed Bill, still crouching amongst the bushes. Al stood to his full height and stepped aside from the bushes, raising his own pair of binoculars and pressing them against his eyes. Bill couldn't help but notice that Al's device seemed to be decorated in a lot of flashing lights, switches and buttons.

"What the hell's that thing?"

"Electronic binoculars," Al said matter-of-factly, without removing his gaze from the dead body.

"Where'd you get those from?"

"Rank comes with privilege, my son. Looks clear, let's advance. Spanners, you take point, break out that grenade launcher and do it just like we planned. Buddy, you're up next. The rest of us will come up behind you, give you support."

"That include me?"

Bill turned and saw Clive standing behind them. A pouch hung from his belt with a red cross on it, and he carried the same bulky handgun Al had given him when escaping the domain of the

Messiah.

"You going to use that?" Al asked, attaching the binoculars to his combat webbing and grabbing his weapon without turning to acknowledge the presence of the priest. "I've never carried anyone before in combat, everyone always held their own. I'm not going to start now; even if it *is* our own link to God."

"I'll try my best."

"I suppose that's all you can do. Hang back here with us, don't be a hero. Okay, move out people."

Bill waited for a few seconds as Sylvester and Garth hesitantly advanced out into the field, then he followed behind, his weapon sweeping from side to side as he switched targets between each of the two facing corner units. They both seemed as dead as the countryside around them, but Bill didn't want to take any chances.

As they neared the fort, they passed the body of the lone sentry. Al held up the advancing group as he knelt by the corpse, rolling it over to examine the body and make sure the job had been done correctly. The chest of the soldier didn't rise or fall, indicating he had left this world.

"That's a brutal shot there, bitch. Brutal, and really messy."

"It got the job done, right? Quick and silent, you can't scream or alert your friends if you've had your windpipe blasted out," came a static-riddled reply.

"I might've underestimated you, bitch. I though you were just another piece of eye candy; but there you are, a ruthless killer. I could like this new you."

He returned his attention to the job at hand, motioning for everyone in the field to come over to his position. Garth seemed to pale slightly as he approached the body, hovering a few feet away from it while Al talked and Bill kept monitoring the visible guard towers.

"Okay, no going back now. Remember the plan: both the walls and the blast doors are too much for the grenades, and we don't want to damage the building too much. The walls are just too thick, anyways. There should be a manual override for blast doors just around to the left of the frame out front. It'll be encased in a good, solid layer of armour, but it won't be completely immune to a direct assault. Forts and bases are normally very well protected, and though they have these 'weak spots', they're often very well guarded. This time, we've hit lucky. We'll have one go to get that control box blasted open, then we need to get the controls fried. That's what you've got that flamethrower for, buddy. Oh, and try not to get the fuel tank hit with a stray bullet: you'll go up like a Fourth of July parade."

"I'll what?" Garth blurted, terror in his voice.

"So," Al continued, ignoring him. "We need to get this done first time, no second chances. Think you can manage that, Spanners?"

"I'll give it a shot."

"You've got one chance," Al repeated, waving over to the line of trees they had just left and indicating to Angel that she should come and join them. "As soon as that first grenade goes off, they're going to be out here like flies on shit. If we're not inside, we're going to be caught out in the open and we're going to be cannon fodder. As my momma used to say, easy pickin's."

"She used to say that? It's a shame she never told you not to try and launch an assault on a Marine fort."

"She used to tell me to keep away from girls, not to smoke, drink or curse. Now, lets pull this shit off so I can get back to Pam, my bottle of whiskey and a good cigar. What do you say?"

"Lets do it," Garth muttered grimly, surprising Bill as he stepped forwards and hefted his flamethrower. He shrugged nonchalantly. "Jesus, the big man's hell-bent on getting me killed, why the hell should I fight it?"

"That's the spirit," grinned Al, slapping him heartily on his back. "Everyone get into position, this operation is green."

As Angel arrived beside Bill, flashing a smile as she approached, Sylvester strolled into position five metres in front of the giant blast door. Levelling of his grenade launcher with the large grey metal box affixed to the wall, he cautiously looked from side towards each guard tower before preparing to fire.

"This is the part I like," he muttered to himself, his voice carrying over the radio. With a squeeze of the trigger of his launcher, the weapon burst to life and vomited the explosive shell from within the breech. It hit the target square on and erupted into a flaming blossom of destruction that swallowed the metal box. The blast of the explosion rolled across Bill with a deafening roar, and thick clouds of black smoke twisting away into the sky, gently dispersing to reveal the slagged casing of the box.

"Clear in one shot," Al said with an approving grin as Angel ran up to the gathering. "Don't be distracted by this little bitch, you're up buddy. Torch that bastard."

Garth stumbled closer towards the control box, advancing on the blast doors and lifting his weapon, activating the device and playing a stream of fire back and forth over the already-charred wall and control box.

"It's not doing anything," Garth said, extinguishing his weapon and turning away from the door. Bill could see the box was smouldering and seemed to be glowing white-hot, but nothing else had happened yet. Bill thought for one moment that the plan had backfired, that things hadn't gone as Al had planned, and he glanced over his shoulder towards the line of trees and the trailer beyond it. Could they make it back there before anyone came to look at the disturbance?

"Did I tell you to stop?" Al asked, glaring at the watch he wore. "Keep going, pour on the fire, we're almost through."

Garth did as he was instructed, returning to his task of incinerating the wiring.

"It's not going to work," Bill said, finally voicing his fears and nudging Al the butt of his weapon. "Let's get out of here."

"Too late," muttered Al, still glaring at his watch. "Thirty seconds, they're already on their way to grabbing their shit from the armoury, trying to get in touch with our dead friend back there. By the time we've turned around and are halfway back, they'll be on top of us. We're past the point of no return now. Pour it on, buddy, keep it coming."

After a further ten seconds of intensive incendiary action, Al called off the assault and rushed towards the blackened control box, shielding his face from the heat and donning a thick pair of black gloves as he approached it. He unravelled a length of wire from his utility belt and dived into the box, cursing as the searing metal grazed his skin and sliced his flesh. Bill couldn't see what he was doing, and by the time he had managed to secure a position where he could see the Marine tampering, there was a loud clunk, and then a continuous sound of clicking as gears ground against each other. Al rushed back from the blast door, motioned for everyone to stand by him and raise their weapons in readiness as the giant door slowly lowered into the ground.

"One minute ten seconds," Al announced, not even checking his watch, "They should be leaving the armoury now. By the time the door's lowered, they'll be within range. You took too long buddy. Never mind. Spanners, sling that grenade launcher, assault rifles only. Garth, you might want to sling that flamethrower, break out your shotgun. Preacher-man, for fucks sake make sure you shoot some people this time. Everyone up and ready, here we go. Keep your eyes open; this is going to be an intense firefight. Ready?"

By the time Al had finished his motivational speech, the door had completely lowered, and Al stepped forwards, cautiously leading the band into the compound.

The fort seemed to mimic all the photographs and sketches Al had presented before the mission: a long, rectangular courtyard, the perimeter made of a thick concrete wall and six flat-topped pyramids. By the entrance of the courtyard itself, six large metal tanks had been gathered together, three on either side of the entrance; one group filled with water, the other with fuel. Small metal drums and barrels had been placed around the base of the large containers, some with their tops removed, others still sealed. Al motioned to everyone to follow him as he skittered across the concrete ground and rolled behind the tanks marked with the 'explosive' logo. He motioned for Garth to stand behind the water tanks on the other side of the entrance, eager to keep the naked flame of his weapon away from the flammable liquid.

Bill stood behind Al, following his gaze across the courtyard towards the large and ominous hole in the ground at the far end of the complex. Rising from the depths of the hole, there seemed to be a seventh outpost module, this one topped with a giant satellite dish. Bill could tell by his puzzled expression that Al had not been expecting to find this in the fort.

"This is all wrong," he muttered, scratching his beard. "Those bastards should be crawling all over us by now, and I've never seen anything like that. Looks like this base has a few levels below ground."

"And we know nothing about them."

"Courtyard secure," Angel whispered, whipping her rifle from side to side as she scanned the area. The only place someone could hide was behind the large Humvee parked by the eastern wall, but there was no sign of any people hiding behind it. Even so, Bill kept a close eye on the vehicle, just to make sure.

"Something's fucked up about this place, and I don't like it," Al announced, then looked back towards Clive. "Make yourself useful, run back there and check that soldier the bitch took out. Take his helmet off."

Clive nodded and ran back out the fort, reaching the body and crouching down beside it. Bill watched as he fumbled with the helmet and mask and returned to the fort gripping the breathing apparatus, his face pale and drawn. "He was dead before the bullet hit him. A hollow man."

"I fucking thought as much. Marines would be crawling out the woodwork by now. The base is hot, you hear me? Looks like there's a job for Preacher-man after all. You don't have any problems shooting the Rots."

Clive shook his head grimly. Al looked at Garth and nodded towards the flamethrower he held. "You might want to drop that and grab something with stopping power. The last thing you want is a human torch to come running towards you."

"You know all the right things to say," Bill said with a grin, still eyeing the inert humvee. "I'm going to check that vehicle. Cover me."

Without waiting for a response, Bill ran over to the vehicle in a stooped run, reaching the vehicle and peering inside the interior. Water bottles and discarded rations lay on the seat, and the engine seemed to be ticking. Bill tensed, expecting the ticking to be linked in to an explosive device, but then remembered the boiler in his old house; how it had ticked in a similar way when the water inside started to cool. He waved Al over and motioned towards the engine. Al complied by reaching out with his hand and touching the bonnet of the vehicle, nodding as he did so.

"Another Landmaster, just like the one we used to have, kid. Standard layout, holds six men plus another two gunners on the back. According to the maps I have, the closest Marine base is a hundred miles or so away. I'm guessing they lost contact with the fort and sent a little party out to find out what the deal is. These guys turn up, find the dead have taken over, and start to try to reclaim the base. There must be eight of them, maximum, and from the looks of it they're all downstairs."

"What about the Rot outside?"

"He wouldn't be one of them. Maybe he wasn't present when the hunting party arrived, then wandered back, and part of his dead mind remembered that he had to walk around outside. I'm a trained killer, not a psychologist for the fucking dead. Did everyone get that conversation?"

The rest of the group nodded as they cautiously approached, each understanding the fact that the whole plan had to be completely reworked. Before discussing anything further, Al climbed on to the rear of the vehicle and detached one of the mounted machineguns, grabbing a green canvas bag and unpacking a portable stand and carrying strap for the heavy weapon. He grinned as he brandished the bulky and cumbersome weapon.

"Okay, we get into that building and start going down a level at a time. I've got the mother of all guns here, everyone stick behind me unless I say so. Move it, people, I want to be drunk by sundown."

The group advanced on the gaping hole at the other end of the compound, and Bill peered cautiously over the edge. A metal staircase had been bolted to the side of the hole, leading down one level to a catwalk that spanned the gap between the stairs and the opening of the target building. Bill had never really experienced any problems with heights, but looking down into the dark depths beneath him as he clambered down the stairs brought a sudden dizzying rush to his head. He gripped the handrail with one hand as he shuffled along, his assault rifle raised and aiming towards the doorway just ahead of Al.

"How deep do you think it is?" Garth asked, leaning casually over the edge and peering into the gloom. Al stopped, looked to one side and spat a wad of phlegm into the chasm, making a show of listening for the sound of the sputum coming in contact with the ground while counting silently.

"That how they teach you to count depths of holes in the Marines?" asked Angel, obviously unimpressed at the lo-tech method.

"No, they teach us to toss a useless piece of crap you don't need. Why, you volunteering? Anyway, I get about sixty feet; pretty deep."

Returning to his trek across the catwalk, Al guided the party towards the entrance of the building, a large doorway covered with a pair of thick reinforced doors. They seemed to be sealed shut, though as they neared they could see that the locks on one of the doors had been demolished. Al reached out and touched the ruined latch, parts of it crumbling away beneath his fingers.

"Thermite charge," he mused aloud. "Standard equipment for a breaking and entry or a breaching operation. Looks as if they're trying to reclaim this place. Saddle up, people, we're going in. Stow the heavy weapons, we need assault rifles or shotguns: no grenades. Everyone ready?"

Sylvester and Clive nodded and pulled aside the opened door, and Al motioned to everyone to move in. He stopped as Angel looked hesitantly at the door and smirked to himself.

"What's up, bitch? What's your problem, afraid of the dark?"

"No," she snarled, shouldering her rifle and storming off towards the opening. "The only problem I have is you calling me a bitch."

"Sorry I can't do anything about that," Al shouted as she vanished into the opening. Bill shook his head, and Al shrugged his shoulders.

"Do you have to bicker so much?" Bill asked, watching as Garth cautiously entered the building, his shotgun cautiously leading his way. "Can't you call her Angel, like everyone else?"

"Shit, no," Al said, waving Sylvester and Clive into the building. "I could probably change her nickname to slut, or whore maybe. I mean, it'll take some getting used to, but I'm a Marine, I can adapt."

"That's not really much of an improvement," Bill said, moving towards the door with his rifle raised and ready.

"You're right," conceded Al. "When the two of you are fucking, what do *you* call her?"

"Arsehole," Bill murmured as he stormed into the opened doorway.

"You saying I should just start calling her an asshole? It's not much better than calling her a slut..."

Bill ignored him, finding himself in a small antechamber, the walls of which were covered in ventilation grilles and fans, though none seemed to be operational. Fluorescent lighting tubes hung from the ceiling, each as dead as the headless, bullet-riddled man lying on the floor in a pool of pale and watery blood. The flashlights each person held and played across the contents of the room penetrated the gloom of the disabled airlock, picking up dust motes as they swept from side to side. A handful of spent bullet casings had been scattered across the metallic floor. Though the body had been decapitated, there was no sign of the head in the room. Al crouched low beside the body and inspected the corpse, then looked at the discarded casings.

"Looks like a Rot, just like the lookout out there. Looks like they disabled him with a barrage of gunfire before coming in close and blasting his head off. They probably hauled what was left over the side of the catwalk outside."

"If that's the case, why not the whole body?" asked Bill.

"You ever picked up a dead body? You ever pick up a head?"

"It never came up in my career. Parcels in the office were normally just boxes of paper."

"Trust me when I say a head is much lighter and easier to move. Try picking that corpse up."

Bill politely refused, choosing instead to help open the next set of doors leading into the base itself. Made from the same material as the outer doors, these were not as willing to open as the previous pair, and took a considerable amount of leverage from Bill, Al and Garth. With a squeal the doors finally gave way and slipped open, the pistons in the automatic doors hissing and groaning as they were forced open.

On the other side of the doors was a metal stairway leading down, accompanied by a foul and caustic smell that was all to familiar to everyone there: the smell that permeated the air of every town and city across Britain. Bill wrinkled his nose in disgust and was reminded of the beginning of his journey, when he first entered the underground tunnels that took him towards the Golden Nexus. The smell of decay, thickened with an earthy aroma.

The staircase was poorly lit by a string of bulbs that had been fastened to the wall, and gave a sickly yellow glare to the shaft. Blood spattered the walls and coated some of the stairs, though none had dried yet; each splatter and puddle glistened in the pale light.

"Everyone stay alert," cautioned Al, peering over the handrail and down into the darkness beneath them. "The stairs only go down two levels, but the shaft seems to go the whole way down. If you slip, it's a long way to the ground."

Sylvester led the way, his assault rifle focused on the bottom of the staircase he was descending, while Clive followed a close second, one hand gripping his weapon and the other clutching a small leather-bound bible, rubbing the golden embossed cross on the cover with his index finger.

"How come we're taking the lead?" Sylvester complained to no one in particular. "Shouldn't the big man be in charge here?"

"You're expendable," laughed Al, standing at the top of the stairs and waving people down. "I'm the brains, you're just the hired help."

"He's the brains," Angel repeated as she strolled past him. "Jesus, are we in that much trouble?"

"Keep noise to a minimum, bitch. This area's hot, we have Marines and Rots inhabiting the base and we don't want them to get the jump on us."

"You don't like people getting the jump on you, do you?" she asked with a smile as she started on her descent, obviously referring to their first meeting in the farmhouse. Al snarled, raised his hand as if to strike her, but held off, instead making his own way down the stairs.

Bill followed, and quickly caught up to the group as he found Sylvester and Clive huddled at the foot of the stairs, both following the catwalk as it switched back beneath the stairs and into the main part of the building. Clive held his finger up to his lips to indicate silence, while Sylvester slowly crept forwards along the walkway, his weapon raised.

"Spanners said he heard something," Al whispered as he cocked his head back slightly. "Could be a guard posted to keep the escape route open. He's scouting ahead to see if he can see anything. Get your weapon ready; we could be going into action."

Bill watched as Sylvester reached the opening, then paused as he made a visible effort to listen. He cautiously retreated from the doorway, keeping his weapon trained ahead at all times.

"Sounds like at least one guard, heavy breather, on the other side of that wall."

"Got him," hissed Al, pulling his heavy magnum from his holster and levelling it off with the wall, estimating where the guard may be standing.

"Will that work?" Bill whispered, crouching down on the stairs and watching as the Marine took aim.

"The Eagle's all about penetration," Al said with a smirk. "Just like me."

He squeezed off a round and the weapon snapped back in his hand, spitting the empty casing out into the void. The heavy round tore through the wall and out the other side, impacting with the hidden guard and splashing blood all over the walls. The body of the soldier slumped to one side, toppling into view and crashing against the wall with a sickening crack. Blowing the thick blue wisp of smoke away from the muzzle, he replaced the weapon in his holster.

"I hope it's all that easy," muttered Sylvester as he strolled across the catwalk and through the doorway.

"Marines, Rots, they're all a bunch of mindless shits," Angel said, pushing past Al as she entered the building.

"Mind you don't trip, bitch, I'd hate to see you fall down there."

Pressing on into the base, Al stopped the group as he peered into the gloom of the building, grabbing the flashlight clipped to his belt and playing the light beam across the dull concrete walls. He passed his cumbersome weapon from one hand to another, shifting the weight of the weapon around and looking around the floor. The opening led to a cross junction which had been labelled with a collection of handy arrows, directions and annotations. Al shone his light on them, stroking his beard in contemplation, then nodded to himself.

"Says here there's five more levels to this base. Next level down's the briefing rooms. From there, it's storage and holding cells, then the kitchen and mess hall, command level and finally the barracks and armoury."

Bill followed Al as he read down the list of levels, then looked down the corridor that promised to have the staircase.

"What are you thinking, should we split up?"

"It'll be quicker."

Bill nodded in agreement, lowering his rifle slightly and leaning against the cold concrete wall, relishing the cool material as it touched his skin and seeped through his T-shirt. The underground complex was very hot, and the length of metal pipes that ran the length of the ceiling seemed only to add to the temperature. Al dabbed at his own forehead with the back of his hand and wiped it off on his trousers.

"Naturally I'll take the barracks and armoury level. Buddy, you take the command level, but don't touch anything. In fact, scratch that. Kid, you take the command level, I can trust you with buttons and switches. The bitch can take the kitchen and mess hall: don't forget I'm still waiting for that frigging cup of coffee."

Angel smiled grimly, shaking her head.

"While you're there, how about checking their refrigerator, maybe rustle up a couple of burgers or some bacon. Spanners, you take Preacher-man and check out the storage and holding cells. If there's anyone in them, keep them there until I check them that. You hear that? No Good Samaritan bullshit. Buddy, you look through the briefing rooms. Safeties off, assault rifles at the ready. Now move out, men. Marine's don't get paid by the hour."

III

The level that held the briefing rooms was as dark and deserted as the rest of the base. Although the drab walls had been puckered with heavy calibre weapons fire and splashed with fresh blood, Garth hadn't seen any sign of any other occupant of the base – living or dead – since the guard outside the catwalk had been disposed off.

Garth had taken a few minutes to stroll around the floor after leaving the rest of his friends, his heart racing at the thought of being on his own again. Before meeting Al and Bill, he had avoided any situation that would mean him getting directly into danger. It seemed that ever since meeting the burly Marine, he had done nothing but get into trouble.

"Never been in this much shit on my own, though," he said aloud, adjusting his cap as he finished his sweep of the corridors and started to progress through the actual briefing rooms. He was sure Al would have told him he'd gone about sweeping through the floor in the wrong order, but Al wasn't here, it was just Garth. And he knew how to look after himself, he had done so for a number of years.

Only the last two months have been in a life-or-death situation. With the walking dead.

It certainly wasn't the average cargo haul, not by a long shot.

Stumbling through the rooms, lost in his thoughts, Garth almost missed the legless Rot that was dragging itself across the floor of the first briefing room, the flesh on its face ragged and torn, swinging from side to side as it pulled itself along. It started to drool and moan as it inched towards Garth, teeth clicking together as its jaw went through the motions of chewing before it had managed to even secure a meal. As soon as he spotted the crawling apparition, Garth lifted his double-barrelled shotgun and opened fire, unloading both combat slugs into the skull of the creature. The sphere tore open with a sickening splatter of blood and brains, and fragments of the bone casing spattered against Garth's trousers. He wrenched the weapon open, sent the empty cases clattering to the floor, then slipped two fresh slugs into the breech before slamming it shut.

"Report in," Al's voice crackled over the radio headset. "Who's finger slipped?"

"Me," Garth responded, his voice shaking slightly. "I found a Rot, but it won't bother anyone again."

"You scored the first kill, buddy, that means you get to buy the first round."

"Says who?" Garth asked, moving through the first briefing room and into the next. It was clear of any Rots, though one body had been left slumped over the large table in the centre of the room. This particular body had no chance of resurrecting as one of the flesh-hungry Rots, though: the head was nowhere to be seen. Blood and shell casings covered the floor, each footfall making a wet crunch beneath Garth's trainers.

"Marine rules," Al said. "Jesus, I don't make them up, I just enforce them."

Garth tutted to himself and moved on to the third of the briefing rooms, finding himself looking at a wall covered with surveillance photos of Rots and maps covered with arrows and notes. One collection of colour photos documented a pack of the undead creatures storming a small convoy of civilians. The bloody carnage had been captured in over sixty photographs, depicting people falling to the hands of the carriers; limbs and flesh being torn from the bodies, and discarded bones picked clean of all meat. None of the photos gave any indication that the Marines or whoever had taken the pictures had attempted to intervene in the massacre.

Happy with the job he had done with cleaning out the briefing rooms - the floor was the smallest of those in the building, of that Garth was pretty sure: Al had obviously given him the smallest task - Garth took a seat at the table. He kicked his feet up on to the table, dragged a ceramic ashtray across the sleek surface and frisked himself to find the pocket he'd stored his cigar tube and lighter.

With a triumphant grin, he produced the small aluminium cylinder and unscrewed the top, slipping the cigar out and clenching it between his teeth. He sparked the lighter to life, puffed on the roll of tobacco leaves until it ignited, then lay back, lost in the euphoria that came with the rush of nicotine. He swore under his breath as the flames of his Zippo lighter licked back up his hand and burnt his hairs. He brushed the back of his hand down, dropping the lighter to the table and grimacing at the smell of his burning flesh.

A smell that would accompany several of the photographs pinned to the wall: scenes of Rots stumbling along, their skin and clothing a blazing torrent of flames, and the aftermath of charred heaps of corpses. Garth stood up, stormed over to the walls and ripped the photographs from wall, piling everything up at the far end of the table.

"Bunch of sick bastards," he muttered, finding a laptop plugged in beside the table, lying on its side on the floor. He picked it up, coiling the power cable around his arm and placing it down on the table. The screen flickered to life as the computer sensed movement, displaying an array of windows filled with different pictures, all of a similar subject matter to the photos he'd removed from the walls. All seemed to have a button marked 'play' just below the main picture.

"Snuff films," he hissed, slamming the laptop shut. He'd seen too many things to even consider playing any of the films.

"What've you got, buddy?"

"Sick shit," Garth answered with a grimace, retreating from the pile of pictures and maps. "Looks like your friends have been gathering a lot of information about the Rots."

"Know your enemy," Al responded over the headset. "What have we got?"

"Photos and videos, from the looks of it. Rot attacks, before, during and after. Possible migration or flocking patterns scrawled on different maps. Maybe satellite photos, I'm not so sure."

"Keep hold of everything, I'll run through it later. "

"Even the snuff movies?"

"Yeah. There might be something useful there for us. I'll check them out."

Sighing heavily, Garth returned to his seat and resumed his vigil on the empty room, cigar in hand, where he found himself wondering how his friends were doing in their search, and why he hadn't tried to smuggle a little alcohol into the excursion.

Sylvester and Clive left the stairwell on their designated sub-level, finding themselves looking down a long corridor that ended in a junction. Shining his light around the walls, Sylvester could make out a sign on the far wall. Clive made a visible effort of leaning forwards and squinting, trying to read the writing.

"Storage to the left, holding cells to the right," Sylvester read aloud, knowing that Clive's eyesight wasn't as good as it had once been. Probably due to the countless hours he used to spend at his desk before the rise, reading through the bible or whatever theological article was the current topic of discussion with his fellow priests.

"Which way do we go first?"

"I'm not looking forwards to searching in the cells," Clive admitted, toying sheepishly with his weapon.

"You get used to them," Sylvester said, remembering the days he used to spend patrolling the corridors of Strangeways Prison. And the days that followed years later, when he experienced the cells from the other side after being apprehended by The Messiah and his men.

"It's not the bars I mind," Clive said, cautiously stepping forwards down the corridor. "It's what we're going to find there that I'm not going to enjoy."

"Storage first, then," Sylvester said as he hefted his weapon and turned to the left, following the corridor as it curved around and doubled back on itself into a long corridor lined on either side with heavyset metal doors, each secured with an electronic lock embedded in the wall beside the doorframes. Sylvester led the way down the corridor, rattling each door handle as he went, making sure each room was secure.

"Don't know the codes," Sylvester explained, more to himself than Clive. "We'll have to run through each one with Al once he's finished checking his floor."

The still of the building was shattered by a sound; a deep boom that echoed through the silent corridors, and Sylvester found himself wheeling around on his heel, bringing his weapon up to bear on the vacant corridor behind him. Even Clive flinched, slightly lifting his weapon.

"Report in," the radio in Sylvester's ear crackled to life "Who's finger slipped?"

"Me," a shaking voice responded. It didn't sound like Bill, and it certainly wasn't Angel, meaning it could only be Garth. "I found a Rot, but it won't bother anyone again."

"You scored the first kill, buddy, that means you get to buy the first round."

Sylvester grinned to himself as the banter between the two carried on for a while, then tuned out the conversation as he continued on his search. As he continued checking the doors, he noticed the look on his friend's face. It was an expression he'd seen many times; most recently when the pair had been locked in a cell, and before that, in his garage moments before his friend had pleaded with him to spend a few days out in the country before the raising of the dead.

"What's wrong?"

"Nothing," Clive said with a gentle shake of his head. "Just thinking."

"What about?"

"You ever think about Steele?"

Sylvester stopped mid-stride, freezing at the mention of *his* name. "I try not to think about him. And when I do, I like to think of him burning in the eternal fires of hell for what he did."

"I know. I'm sorry to bring it up with you. It's just… do you think he might have been right?"

"I don't think he's ever been right," Sylvester snapped, turning and leaning against the wall. Clive nodded, pulled out a battered packet of cigarettes and removed one of the crushed sticks before offering them to Sylvester. He refused, but pulled a lighter from his pocket and passed it over. "I think he's one fucked up individual, and the quick death he got was too good for him."

"I'm sorry, Sly, honestly I am. I didn't mean to stir up bad memories. But I keep thinking about everything that's happening here. The dead rising, armies of men turning against one another… you haven't read the bible, have you?"

"You know me, if it doesn't come with a sports section or cartoons then I normally pass it up."

"The final book of the New Testament, the Book of Revelation, it talks about the end days of humanity, when the boundary between the living and the dead vanishes, and the armies of darkness rise up against the followers of God. The battle between Heaven and Hell, that spills over into our world. The dead are judged, and those whose names aren't in the book of life are cast into the lake of fire. Judgement day. Armageddon."

"Sounds crazy, like a fucked up film," Sylvester said, though he could see how the unhinged mind of Frank Steele could interpret the events surrounding the plague into his biblical fantasy. "And you think this is what's actually happening now? That we're all waiting to be judged?"

"Or maybe we *have* been judged. Now I'm not saying I'm Jesus Himself or anything…"

"You believe it?" asked Sylvester, incredulously.

"I'd be a very bad priest if I didn't believe in *something*," Clive countered, finishing his cigarette and flicking it to the floor. "Don't you believe in something?"

After checking the final door to the storage cupboard, Sylvester spun on his heels and marched back towards the holding cells, motioning for his friend to follow him. "My convictions ain't as strong as yours," Sylvester said. "Do I believe in God? Yeah, why not? Do I think that God has judged us? Or that the zombies are the work of Him or even the Devil? Honestly, it sounds like a fairytale."

"Doesn't the walking dead sound like a fairytale, too?"

Sylvester didn't answer, simply followed the corridor, back around and headed towards the holding cells.

"You ready for this?"

Clive nodded grimly, cradling his heavy handgun as he followed Sylvester towards the junction and cells beyond it. As they advanced on the prison, the stale air seemed to thicken and become tainted with a cloying stench of decay. Sylvester paused as the metal bars came into view, and the buzzing of the fluorescent tubes overhead gave way to the droning buzz of a different kind; flies swarming around fresh meat.

The first cell held a male, his head partially cleaved open by the bloodied machete that still lay embedded in the smashed skull. Sylvester turned to one side, trying to avoid the sight of the sliced brains and smashed skull, only to see another prisoner, this one pinned to the wall at her shoulders and stomach by inch-thick metal bolts. Her milky white eyes stared blankly ahead, blood encrusted jaw twitching and drooling as she saw the unobtainable meat on the other side of the cage. Any moans she tried to make came out in a bloody froth at the gash in her throat where her larynx had been cut out.

"What the fuck were they doing here?"

"Mother of God," Clive hissed, stepping forwards and peering into the gloom of the cell holding the woman, pinned like an insect in an entomologist's display case.

"More freak-show stuff?" asked Al, the sudden interruption over the radio startling Sylvester.

"Holding cells," he stammered. "Two Rots, one of them alive, the other dead."

"I've found one down here myself. Still no sign of any other soldiers, though. Are all the other cells empty?"

"We've only looked in the first two," Clive admitted, stepping away from the bars and peering down the corridor at the rest of the cells. Sylvester knew what he was thinking: probably the same thing he was.

What other creatures had been locked up and tortured?

"No living people there then?"

"I'd say no. Anyone would have shouted for help by now once they heard us talking. There could be more of the living dead, though."

"You need to check, and make sure there isn't anything else in there that might bite us in the ass when we move in. What about the storage rooms?"

"Sealed up tight. Electronic locks, no way for us to break in."

"Code's must be somewhere in the compound, maybe on the command level. You catch that kid?"

"I'm listening," Bill announced. "Security codes, any idea what they'll look like?"

"Pieces of paper with numbers written on, how the hell am I supposed to know? Maybe a manual override on one of the control panels."

"There's only a thousand buttons to press," Bill sulked.

"We've all got a job to do here kid. You find a code, Spanners and Preacher, you guys have to clear those cells, kill anything that's been left alive. The bitch still has to make me that coffee, too."

Sylvester shook his head glumly and prepared himself for the chamber of horrors that lay ahead, knowing that what Al had said was true, that that they'd have to clear out each cell.

"I hate this job," he murmured to no one in particular. Clive nodded softly in agreement, lifting his weapon and stroking the cover of his bible with his free hand.

The staircase opened up directly into the mess hall, a large room filled with long metal tables, each one lined on either side by long benches. Angel took a quick count, and could make out fifteen tables. Though it didn't seem enough to seat as many people as Al said the fort could hold, she had to remember that there would always be a squad or two on duty.

The tables themselves were in a state of disarray, with plastic trays scattered across the surfaces like a discarded pack of giant cards. Cutlery and smashed plates littered the floor, covered in pools of blood and surrounded by spent bullet casings of different sizes. The room itself was dark, the only light given off from the five intact tubes humming to themselves.

The moment Angel stepped out of the stairwell, her weapon came up, tucking the toughened plastic stock in the crook of her shoulder and keeping the muzzle raised and pointing forwards as she advanced into the room. As she moved, one of the lights above her flickered and died, taking her one step closer to being left in total darkness. She held her position, hesitant to move, as if each step would eliminate another of the remaining lights. She fumbled with the flashlight mounted on the rifle, switching it on and playing it across the details of the room. The beam of light seemed to give the mess hall an eerie quality, creating obscure shadows that danced and wavered as the beam moved around.

"You going to be all right?"

Startled by the voice, Angel spun on her heels and dropped to a crouching position, facing the figure that stood on the stairs behind her. He lifted a hand to shield his face from the flashlight, laughing softly.

"Didn't mean to scare you," Bill said. "Just checking on you. Are you sure you'll be okay doing this on your own?"

"I'll be okay," Angel said, turning back to the room, adjusting her grip on the rifle.

"Channel six on the headset," Bill said as he vanished back down the stairs. "Like when we left the farmhouse to find the trailer. If you need any help… Just give the word."

Angel smiled to herself as she took another step into the room, then another, slowly creeping through the debris that littered the floor as she proceeded towards the large door at the far end of the room. As she moved, she made sure each isle of the mess hall was clear. No creatures seemed to linger in the darkness, nor were there any signs of a slain soldier keeled over a table in the middle of a meal.

"It's pretty deserted," she said, after taking ten minutes to clear the room and reach the doors. She didn't get any response on the channel Bill had told her to switch to, so returned it to the normal open link as she pushed the door open.

She stood on the threshold of the darkened kitchen, her silhouette stretched out across the tiled floor and crawled up the benches. Other than the beam of light from her gun, there was no other source of light in the kitchen, and Angel was hesitant to enter the darkened room.

She stood in the doorway in silence, listening to the conversation that was taking place on the floor above between Clive and Sylvester while she decided what to do. As the conversation progressed, it became apparent that the Marines had kept Rots in their holding cells, and seemingly tortured them. Or at least, it *sounded* that way. She couldn't say for sure until she saw the cells. Not that she particularly wanted to see them.

But then, where *would* she rather be? Staring at mutilated corpses behind bars, or standing outside a pitch-black kitchen with Christ-knows what lying wait in the darkness? For a moment she envied Clive and Sylvester. At least they knew they were safe from anything if the Rots were locked in the cells. Her thoughts wandered as she tried to study the details of the kitchen, hoping to get a good view from her vantage point without having to commit herself.

"We've all got a job to do here kid," Al's voice carried over the radio, bringing her back to the conversation. "You find a code, Spanners and Preacher, you guys have to clear those cells, kill anything that's been left alive. The bitch still has to make me that coffee, too."

"You want a coffee," Angel muttered, "You can get your arse up here and make it yourself. And bring a flare or something with you."

No one responded to her comment. She thought at least Al would have responded with a jibe or an insult, but nothing. Maybe he'd suddenly grown up, or grown tired of the constant bickering?

No chance of that happening, she thought with a smirk.

She stepped tentatively into the darkness, sweeping her weapon and the beam of light from side to side as she went, picking out the details of the destroyed kitchen. The walls of the room had been smashed and ruined by a heavy gun battle, ceramic tiles cracked and lying in shattered piles on the floor. Blood spattered the walls and coated the countertop, cooking implements scattered across the floor, and metal plates left dented and battered. Large freezer units lay against the walls, their green power lights glowing in the darkness of the room like a gathering of Cyclopes.

"There's been some action down here," she muttered, carefully prodding a pile of plates with the muzzle of her weapon. The top-most plate slowly slid to one side, and Angel quickly reached out with one hand, trying to stop it from moving. She was too slow, and the plate clattered to the ground. Angel hissed to herself, biting her lip and freezing in position, listening for any follow-up sounds that may indicate another person hiding in the kitchen. She remained motionless, holding her breath for a full minute, until…

There…

A slight noise, something wet dragging across the smooth floor of the kitchen, over on the far side of the room. She lifted her rifle, sighted down the muzzle and focused the beam on a glistening creature that feebly crawled across the ground. It wore a white uniform, as a chef would wear, but no self-respecting cook would allow their clothing to become as thickly smeared with blood and dirt as this creature had. The flesh of its forearms had been stripped back, while the skin on its face and lower jaw had peeled off, the creature an apparent victim of a spill involving scalding hot cooking oil. The one eye it had appeared to be that of an Asian, though not enough of the creatures facial details had survived the ravages of teeth and oil to confirm that.

"Just the one, I can manage that," she said, lining up her shot on the pitted forehead of the creature. She was about to squeeze of a single shot, when one of the large freezer units to the side of her burst open and a second Rot tumbled out, its cold limbs flailing wildly and dead fingers locking around her arms. Screaming in repulsion, Angel dropped her rifle and stumbled backwards, her feet sending battered plates and discarded cutlery flying in all directions. The weight of the creature got the better of her, and she felt herself toppling over, crashing to the floor and smashing her head against the wall. She could feel the blood on her head as the sharpened edges of partially destroyed tiles cut into her scalp. Lying on the ground, Angel fought a physical battle with the undead creature atop her and a mental battle to try and remain conscious as the fog of pain seeped into her brain.

The strength of the undead creature rivalled hers, and she could feel her limbs buckle under the relentless strain of the attack. The crawling Rot on the other side of the room seemed to pick up speed, and Angel could barely make out its shape in the darkness as it thrashed its arms from side to side, heaving itself over pots and pans, sending them skittering across the floor in a cacophony of noise that could only lead to her untimely demise.

Concentrating on the Rot pinning her down, her eyes locked with those of the creature, and for a moment, she could see the spark of human intelligence; could feel the warmth of a human as the creature breathed on her.

"Fucking dead bitch," he hissed, his voice rasping as his frozen and cracked lips peeled open. A battered and torn gas mask hung around his neck. "Kill you… fucking kill you!"

"I'm… not… dead," Angel rasped as the crazed Marine locked a thick and powerful hand around her neck, pinning her to the ground.

"Bitch," he repeated, fumbling for the pistol hanging from his belt, managing to retrieve it and place the muzzle against the flesh of Angel's throat. "Kill you all!"

A gunshot sounded in the kitchen, and Angel closed her eyes, thinking that her time had come. She could feel herself slipping from the grip of the Marine, felt the warmth of blood as it oozed across her neck and shoulders, could hear it dripping on the floor. Somehow, she wasn't completely dead: maybe he'd just winged her?

A second and third gunshot made her think she was right; that the soldier was finishing the job, and her eyes fluttered open, expecting to see a bright light at the end of a long tunnel. Instead, she found herself surrounded by darkness.

"You okay?"

A familiar voice from above her made Angel look up, and could see the shape of a man in the doorway, a smoking weapon in his hand. He stepped forwards, lowered his rifle and extended a hand towards Angel. With weak and shaking limbs, she reached out and took the hand she was offered, and Bill pulled her to her feet. Shaking from her experience, she held on to her saviour, fighting to remain upright.

"I've got her," Bill said, addressing the microphone of his headset and rubbing Angel's shoulder with one hand. "Looks like she found another live one."

He pushed the microphone away from his lips, looked down and smiled at Angel. "You okay?" he repeated. Still shaken from her ordeal, it was all Angel could do to nod a response.

IV

"There's only a thousand buttons to press,"

"We've all got a job to do here, kid. You find a code, Spanners and Preacher, you guys have to clear those cells, kill anything that's been left alive. The bitch still has to make me that coffee, too."

Bill sighed inwardly. He'd only made his way halfway down the main corridor of the command level before doubling back on himself when he'd heard the first gunshot: that had been Garth encountering his first Rot. He'd returned to the stairwell the moment that had sounded, until he'd received confirmation that it had been Garth, and he was all right. The excitement over, Bill had returned to his search of the rooms and corridors of the floor.

Of the doors he had checked, all of them had opened up into a small room filled with consoles covered in an array of buttons, switches and dials. He wouldn't know where to begin in searching any of these rooms for a master code, or a manual release for the storage rooms above. He had thought about asking Al for a hand, but it was clear that he didn't have any idea what the codes or release had looked like. It had been slow progress as he moved through corridors and rooms, but as soon as Al had mentioned his cup of coffee, and there had been no response from Angel, he had started to worry. Even in the heat of battle, he knew the two would keep bickering; whether it was friendly banter or malicious name-calling he couldn't say, but it certainly wasn't like Angel to let a jibe from Al slide.

Unless she's on channel six, Bill thought, nudging the switch on his headset to switch to another channel. He scanned through the different channels, but couldn't pick up any other response.

Then came the scream.

It certainly wasn't a masculine scream; only one member in the party currently investigating the Marine fort was capable of producing a scream like it, and despite all the jokes, it wasn't Garth.

"Angel," Bill said, spinning on his heels and looking back towards the stairwell far behind him.

"I heard it," Al announced. "Sounds like our resident whore's ran into trouble. No gunshots, either. Can you get to her?"

"I'm already on my way," Bill answered, yanking back on the mechanism of his rifle and ensuring that there was a round in the chamber. He bounded down the corridor and reached the stairs, charging up the staircase and taking them three at a time. He reached the mess hall, panting heavily, and couldn't see Angel anywhere. She didn't appear to be in the mess hall that he could see, though the door into the kitchen on the far side of the room was open: it hadn't been when he'd checked on Angel before.

He ran through the hall, his rifle raised and ready, flicking the torch on as he ran and skidded to a halt at the doorway. He could hear a scuffling sound, like someone rolling around on rubble and struggling with someone, and he swept his weapon from side to side, shadows growing and shrinking as the source of light swept across the room.

"Bitch," rasped a voice alien to Bill, a hoarse and guttural moan that seemed to drip with venom. "Kill you all!"

Bill instantly targeted the origin of the voice, and brought his weapon about to bear on a Marine sitting astride Angel, her arms pinned down by his legs, one hand wrapped around her throat and the other holding a pistol, which he pressed into her neck. Bill acted instantly, barely aiming, as he loosed a single round. The bullet tore through the face of the Marine, shattering his skull and splashing blood all over Angel and the surrounding area. His hands spasmed, then released their hold over gun and neck as the body keeled over. Bill swung his weapon around once more, spotted the crawling remains of the Rot on the far side of the room, then squeezed off a second shot. This time his aim was off, the lead projectile smashing against the ceramic tiles on the floor and spitting a cloud of debris into the face of the crawling creature. Adjusting his aim, Bill took a third shot, this time obliterating the head of the creature. He swept the weapon back and forth again, then looked down on Angel, her features covered in blood.

"You okay?" he asked weakly, his voice cracking. Had he been too late? She seemed very still, quiet, and there was a lot more blood than he thought there would be. He could see her eyelashes flutter as she blinked, and he sighed in relief, stepping forwards and offering a hand to his prone comrade. She accepted, her limbs trembling, and Bill managed to pull her frame from the floor, supporting her weight as she wrapped her arms around him. For a moment, Bill thought she was going to fall, though she managed to keep herself upright. Bill gently massaged her shoulder with one hand, gently guiding her back from the kitchen.

"I've got her," he announced, hoping that the rest of the team would be as relieved as he was. "What's the situation there?"

"Looks like she found another live one."

"You killed a Marine? I'm impressed. Tell the little bitch I'm proud of her boyfriend."

Bill smiled grimly, making a mental note to do so later on, once she'd recovered from her ordeal and was in the right frame of mind to take any of the shit Al came out with. "You okay?" he asked again. He felt the slight nod of her head as she managed to respond. He didn't need to know the exact details of what had happened, the Marine lying prone on the floor and the opened freezer unit he had caught a brief glimpse of had been told him all he needed to know.

"You finished up there, Garth?"

"Yeah," muttered Garth, "What's up?"

"I need you to get down the mess hall, double check the area and make sure the floor's secure. I'm taking Angel down with me."

"I bet you are," laughed Al, his booming voice drowning out Garth's complaints. Then, in a change of character he would never have expected, the Marine carried on. "Is she okay?"

"A little shaken," Bill said, still holding Angel. "She's lost her com-set, though."

"Wasn't working right," Angel managed to say, turning her face up to look into Bill's eyes. "The microphone broke just before the attack."

Bill held Angel closer, gently massaging her shoulder, then kissed her lightly on the top of her head. It was something he'd often done with Jenny to calm her down when she was upset, and felt it was appropriate now, as one of his friends needed some support. Angel tilted her head back again; a look of surprise in her eyes, and a brief smile flickered across her lips. Letting his assault rifle dangle from the shoulder strap, Bill reached out with his free hand, cupped her chin and tilted her head back a little further, brought his face closer to hers. He could feel the hot warmth of her ragged breathing against his lips, watched as she closed her eyes.

"Jesus frigging Christ," muttered a familiar voice as Garth descended the staircase, his heavy footsteps on the metal staircase deep and thunderous in the silence of the mess hall, announcing his arrival before his legs came into view.

Bill and Angel leapt back from one another, as if they had received an electrical shock from each other, and each looked guiltily towards the stairs as their friend swaggered into view.

"I had it made up there, I was just kicking back and enjoying a good smoke," he grumbled. "I should've kept quiet. You kids're going to be the death of me, you know that? Okay, what've I got to do?"

"Secure the floor. Mess hall seems clear, and there's a couple of dead in the kitchen. Just make sure everything's clean. Remember to check the cupboard and freezers. I'm going to finish my round downstairs."

"What about her?" asked Garth, nodding towards Angel; she was still pale, still trembling slightly from the encounter. "Am I looking after her, too?"

"She can come with me," Bill said, maybe a little too quickly, as he looked towards Angel. "If you want to, that is."

She nodded softly, drawing the handgun from her belt and working the slide before taking a step towards the stairs. Bill followed behind her, then turned back to Garth and waved a gesture of gratitude.

"Don't thank me, just hurry up. I had a real comfy seat up there."

Bill smiled and nodded, then retreated to the stairwell, catching up with Angel and resuming the sweep through the floor. The pair moved in silence; though Bill would have liked to think it was for sake of stealth, he knew that the silence was more than that: it was awkward.

Although there hadn't been a kiss, it had almost happened. If Garth had been a few seconds later, it would have. And how different would things be?

Stop getting sidetracked, scorned Bill. *Nothing* had *happened, there was nothing behind it. I would have done the same to calm down anyone.*

Bill didn't believe that for one minute, though. He could never imagine giving Al a hug to calm him down, nor could he imagine planting a kiss on the forehead of the Marine. But then, he could never imagine Al being shaken to the point of needing comforting like that.

"Are you okay?" whispered Angel, eyes flicking back and forth as the pair entered the largest of the control rooms, a chamber half the size of the mess hall, with rows of computers and banks of desks lining each wall. A giant monitor screen dominated the largest of the walls, and the screen itself seemed to display live feeds from security cameras all over the base. Bill could see all of his friends on the screen: Clive and Sylvester, grimly strolling along in front of the prison cells, turning their weapons on the tortured creatures contained within; Garth rummaging through freezers and storage cupboards, helping himself to packets of snacks that he found. Another depicted Al purposefully striding from doorway to doorway in a long corridor, turning his weapon into the rooms and opening up with them, spraying gunfire from side to side.

"Looks like he's having fun," Angel commented. Bill nodded to himself.

Another camera screen caught his attention; it looked like one of the corridors he and Angel had travelled down to enter the control room. The corridor itself wasn't disturbing to the pair, but rather the four Marines marching down the corridor towards the control room they occupied, their expressionless masked faces giving no clue as to their true intentions, though they were surely murderous.

"We've got company," Bill said, shouldering his rifle and looking around. There were three entrances to the control room, though only two seemed to be currently shut. He ran over to one, checked it to make sure it was sealed tight, and motioned for Angel to do the same for the other one.

"Secure?"

Angel nodded, then the pair rushed towards the final door, the way they had come in, and tried to close that door. It refused to budge, obviously activated by one of the controls in the room.

"Bottleneck," Bill muttered. "Trapped like rats."

"Get Al," Angel whispered. "Get help."

"Al, can you hear me? We're in some deep shit here!"

The barracks of the fort was larger then Al had thought they would be. But then, he couldn't remember the last time he'd been in a Marine establishment large enough to house over a hundred people. The armoury was on the other side of the complex, at the end of a corridor about fifty metres long. The corridor had eight doors spaced evenly along its length, four on each side, and it took all Al's willpower to refrain from running straight ahead to the armoury and whatever wonderful toys it may hold for him. He needed to sweep the floor first, and he knew he had the tools and experience to do it; he just had to hope his troops upstairs could do the same thing. After all, he had given himself the largest floor because he was the most experienced.

The first room he looked into was much like a barracks in any other Marine establishment; a collection of six beds, six footlockers, and six wall-mounted lockers, each locker emblazoned with either a name or a custom motif. Al was thankful that he didn't recognise any of the names on display. He'd lost enough men over the past few months, and didn't want to come across any more former colleagues, whether dead or undead.

He stepped into the room, sweeping the heavy machinegun from side to side, though there didn't seem to be any sign of any creatures in the room. He left the first barracks, entered the second, and found a trio of writhing corpses, each tearing chunks from one another in a feeding frenzy. Blood washed across the floor with each fresh wound, and Al hefted the weapon again, squeezing the controls on the handle and spraying a salvo of high-calibre bullets across the room. The rounds tore through the three blood-drenched animals, smashing their bones and scattering fragments of flesh across the room.

Lowering his smoking weapon, Al grinned and lowered the device, wafting the soft blue-grey smoke away with his hand.

This can be the bitch's room, he thought to himself. She hadn't retaliated to his jibe about the coffee, and he had assumed with a great deal of smugness that he had finally won their bickering. *Guess she realised who's in charge. Big Al, that's who.*

The scream followed not long after he had cleared out the second room and started to head towards the third. He knew who it was, he could tell not only by the tone and pitch but also by the distance. Bill only confirmed his suspicions when he muttered the name of Angel straight after the scream.

"I heard it," he announced, lazily igniting his lighter as he opened a battered cigar case and plucked a cigarette. He didn't rush to her aid, knowing all too well that she could look after herself, and there were other people in the group more willing to risk their neck for her. "Sounds like our resident whore's ran into trouble. No gunshots, either. Can you get to her?"

"I'm already on my way," Bill said, and Al knew he wasn't lying. There was a bond between Bill and Angel that he couldn't interfere with, no matter how hard he tried; but that wouldn't stop him. When he wasn't with Pam, he needed to find another way to keep himself entertained.

Al moved on to the third of the sleeping quarters, this time finding a quartet of undead creatures squabbling over the remains of half a soldier. He had been torn in two with his legs nowhere to be seen, while the head and been pried from the protective helmet and smashed against it, spilling the brains across the deck and ensuring the body didn't rise again in the middle of the meal.

"Disgusting bastards," he muttered to himself, lifting the heavy weapon he carried again, and opened up with another burst of rounds, spraying lead back and forth and putting an end to their existence once and for all. "Spanners can have this room," he mused as he checked each of the beds by prodding them with the muzzle of his weapon. He turned to head back towards the door, and stopped as he heard the voice of Bill. He seemed out of breath as he spoke.

"I've got her."

"What's the situation there?" Al asked, feigning interest.

"Looks like she found another live one," Bill responded. Although he didn't say it, Al knew that meant that another Marine had bought the farm, this time at the hands of Bill; if Angel had been able to kill the soldier, Bill wouldn't have had to run to her rescue. *Unless it was another of her cocktease games...*

"You killed a Marine? I'm impressed. Tell the little bitch I'm proud of her boyfriend."

"You finished up there, Garth?" Bill went on, ignoring Al.

"Yeah," muttered Garth. He didn't sound to happy, and Al guessed what was coming next. "What's up?"

"I need you to get down the mess hall, double check the area and make sure the floor's secure. I'm taking Angel down with me."

"I bet you are," laughed Al, his booming voice drowning out Garth's complaints. His laughter died, and Al spoke in a lower tone of voice. "Is she okay?" It was a question that caught even him by surprise.

"A little shaken," Bill said, still holding Angel. "She's lost her com-set, though."

Jesus, that bitch is going to cost me a fortune in com-sets, he thought, leaving the room and storming out to the next one. This room was devoid of any creatures, Marines or even dead bodies, though it had been given a liberal coating of blood and entrails. The bed closest to the doorway had a book left open on the ruffled sheets, which Al easily identified as a bible, as blood soaked as it was.

"Preacher-man's room," he said with a smile. "It's a sign."

A noise in the distance distracted him for a moment, and Al returned to the doorway, peering out into the corridor and seeing figures shamble from door to door, knocking into one another and moaning incoherently as they brushed past each other. His gunfire had obviously roused the remaining Rots inhabiting the living quarters, though they hadn't managed to home in on the source of the noise.

Yet.

The Rots had an uncanny ability to home in on the nearest source of fresh meat.

Dropping the heavy machinegun to the ground, Al brought his old M249 around into play. The previously mounted weapon he had salvaged from the hummer, though powerful, was wasted on the soft bodies of the Rots. Pulling back on the mechanism before striding back out into the corridor he opened up with his weapon, obliterating the heads of three of the Rots stumbling around the corridor, cutting down a fourth as the rounds tore through its shoulders and spine.

He marched into the next room, swung his weapon around from side to side and blindly opening fire before moving on to the next. If the majority of the Rots were on this level, and they were alerted to his presence, he didn't want to take time to stop and smell the roses.

He kept moving from room to room, peppering each chamber with gunfire before moving on to the next. Clenching his jaw, he continued on past the few creatures he had slain in the corridor, gingerly stepping over the twitching bodies and pausing mid stride to pull out his magnum and hammer a round home into the head of the Rot his machinegun had only clipped. He'd come too far to have his ankles nicked by a paralysed zombie.

The heat of battle died as Al reached the door to the armoury and turned back to look down the smoke-filled corridor he had just stormed through. The thick tang of blood and cordite lingered in the haze that had settled across the corridor, but there wasn't a sound of another creature on the level. It seemed he had effectively wiped out all the creatures on the level.

"I'd like to see one of those damn civvies work their mojo like *that,*" he said, scratching at his beard as he lowered his weapon and worked the mechanism on the weapon, releasing the spent magazine and letting it clatter to the floor. He patted himself down, searching for a fresh drum of ammunition, but couldn't find one.

Maybe I dropped it in the melee, he thought as he looked back down the carnage of the corridor. It may have slipped out of one of his pockets and landed amongst a pile of corpse.

"Hell with that," he hissed, turning back to the door to the armoury behind him. "I'll just grab me a new one."

He was about to open the door, a smile spreading across his lips, when his headset crackled to life again.

"Al, can you hear me? We're in some deep shit here!"

"Fuck me," Al said, slapping the door to the armoury. "Jesus, kid, what's up now?"

"Marines, four of them. They're homing in on us now, they've got his pinned down in the main control room."

"I'm on my way, sit tight," he said, dropping his M249 and running back through the corridor, retrieving the discarded cannon he had left in one of the barracks on his way to the staircase, ensuring a round was still in the breech as he stormed up the stairs. Marines were the hard targets that the heavy machinegun ached for.

"Where am I heading, kid," Al asked as he ventured on to the floor above him, then, "Spanners, Preacher-man, get your asses down here, I need back up."

"On our way," Sylvester said. "Sub-level four?"

"That's right, don't stop to take in the sights. We got four Marines heading for the bitch and the kid. Lock and load, people."

"People?" Clive asked cautiously. "I can't..."

"Suck it up," Al commanded, waiting by the stairwell for his comrades to turn up. "Shoot or be shot, now pull yourself together."

"Even though I walk through the valley of the shadow death, I will fear no evil. For you are with me; your rod and your staff, they comfort me."

"God damn bible-basher," Al hissed. "Now's not the time for preaching."

"Going into battle?" asked Sylvester as he appeared on the stairwell. "It's the perfect time to turn to God for guidance and comfort."

"I've seen too much bad shit happening in battle to believe there's some all-powerful entity watching over us all. In my opinion, he shafts the good people all too often. Look at me!"

Clive appeared behind Sylvester, but didn't rise to the argument. What would it take to get a rise from this man?

"We're on our way, kid. Buddy, is it clear up there?"

"Yeah, just a few more Rots that were lurking in the freezer."

"Come guard the staircase, in case the bastards try to bail. Hang tight, kid, we're on our way."

By the time Al's confirmation came through to Bill that help was coming, the group of Marines had found them, and were laying down a suppressive fire. They were striking equipment and monitors with stray shots, but they didn't seem to care about the collateral damage as much as Al did. With Angel on one side of the doorway and Bill on the other, they had tried to return fire, but couldn't find a pause in the shooting long enough to get a good shot: both had resorted to blindly sticking their guns out over the edge and spraying gunfire from side to side in hope that they hit someone. Obviously this wasn't the case, as the onslaught of gunfire hadn't decreased one iota.

"Not long now," Bill shouted above the din of the gunfire, trying to put Angel's mind at ease as best he could. She gritted her teeth and nodded as hails of bullets cut through the air between them, slapping into a control panel and showering the pair with fizzing blue sparks. The lights in the control room flickered slightly as the bullets struck the controls, and Bill quickly looked up towards the roof. If the lights went out, then he and Angel would at least be granted the cover of darkness, if only for a few minutes. At least, until the well prepared soldiers managed to unpack their night vision goggles they were undoubtedly equipped with.

As Bill waited for the arrival of his friends, the ferocity of the gunfire seemed to half, though the din of the ballistics didn't seem to alter any; it actually seemed to increase.

"We're here," Al announced, his voice followed by the roar of the heavy weapon he carried. Large calibre rounds tore through the room and chewed through the console in front of the open door, covering Bill with shards of the metallic casing and exposed wires. It appeared that Al was no longer interested in preventing collateral damage, either. He reached over for his crossbow and one of the customised bolts he carried, but decided against it, remembering that they were five stories beneath the surface and he didn't relish the idea of being buried alive.

"Glad you could make it," Bill said, ejecting the empty magazine from his rifle and replacing it with a fresh one. "What's it look like out there?"

"Fuckin' pathetic," Al said. Bill could imagine the grin on his face. "You haven't even winged one of the bastards. Haven't you learned anything? Pour the fire on, keep the bastards pinned, don't let them get a shot of in your direction. That's where you went wrong. Now, don't get caught in the cross fire and sit tight."

The Marine lapsed into silence, though his weapon quickly spoke again, this time a thunderous retort that didn't seem to end. An onslaught of bullets tore through the room, this time the murderous assault beginning to chew away at the doorframe and rain plaster and concrete down on Bill. He motioned for Angel to back away from the opening, aware that the high-powered rounds from the cannon could well penetrate the walls and easily take either of them out. Though he knew Al disliked Angel, he didn't think he'd go out the way to kill her.

The automatic fire ceased, then the opposing forces resumed their counterattack, though this time it didn't seem as ferocious as before.

"One down," Al announced. "My cannon's dry, though, I've spent all the rounds. You going to use that thing, Preacher-man?"

"Take it," Clive announced. High-pitched chattering of a light submachine gun quickly followed him relinquishing his weapon, followed by a colourful string of curses from Al.

"Bastards are too well armoured for the nine millimetres. I don't think the assault rifles would take them, either, I've seen that shit they're wearing in combat before. Only high-powered rounds are enough to score the kill.

"Grenades?" Sylvester asked, his tone hopeful.

"Grenades are too much, they'll bring the place down around us. Something a little less powerful should do the job, or maybe even stun them long enough to allow me to get in close and use *Colebrook's Cannon* on the bastards. Anyone got any flash-bangs?"

No one responded, but Bill looked at his crossbow again, rolling the custom explosive bolt between his thumb and forefinger. It packed a punch, but not enough to rival a military-grade explosive projectile.

"My crossbow," he volunteered, cranking the trigger guard to cock the weapon and slipping the bolt into the worn groove of the weapon. "What about my explosive bolts?"

"A decent spread of shrapnel, that should work," Al said, "Get one into the midst of those bastards. They're grouped in a junction, using the walls as cover. Any corner as your target should do the job to disable them all."

Without another word, Bill cautiously made his way back to the door and peered around the corner of the damaged frame, seeing two of the Marines facing away from the control room, obviously watching over the way Al had approached the battle from. Another Marine kept his rifle trained on the doorway, while the forth lay dead on the floor, the helmet of the man smashed wide open and his head smeared across the wall. The sole Marine standing guard on the control room opened up with a burst of gunfire, forcing Bill to return to his hiding position.

"I can't get a clear shot," hissed Bill, leaning against the wall and cradling his weapon in the crook of his elbow. "I need some kind of distraction!"

"What do you suggest, maybe I should bend over and show them my ass? Christ, kid, we've got nothing else to throw at them."

"What about your handgun?"

"I don't like wasting ammo," Al replied.

"It's not wasting it if it's for a good purpose! Just fire the damn weapon, make them duck and cover again."

There was an audible sigh, but no other verbal response, so Bill knew his friend was going to submit and provide covering fire. Five deep, loud shots sounded in the corridor, then another three, and Bill took his chance, rolling out on to the floor, loosing his bolt at his intended target and hoping for the best.

The explosive projectile struck the body of the dead Marine, striking the remains of the helmet and the short bolt flashed to life, tearing apart in a small explosion and showering the three active soldiers with gleaming shrapnel. It certainly wasn't enough to penetrate their armour, though several fragments had lodged themselves in the protective vests of the reeling men: clearly the explosive blast was enough to stun or surprise the trio of armed men, as they stumbled and swayed from side to side, trying to shake off the concussive effect of the blast.

Al took the opportunity to storm forwards, releasing the empty magazine from his smoking weapon and replacing it with a fresh clip. Reaching the Marines, he quickly raised his weapon, pressed the muzzle against one opaque lens of each mans breathing mask and fired, shattering mask, skull and helmet in one smooth action. Within seconds, all four marines lay dead at Al's feet, and he replaced his smoking handgun in his holster, crossing his arms over his chest.

"Four here, one in the kitchen hiding in the freezer, fuck knows why, one dead at the entrance. That's the full six from the Landmaster. All rooms other than the sealed storage rooms and armoury have been cleared. I'm satisfied."

"I thought you said there were also two gunners?" Angel said as she rolled out of hiding. Bill clambered to his own feet first then helped her up.

"I said there was *room* for two gunners, don't you ever listen? Too busy looking out for the next opportunity for you two to fuck, that's your problem."

Angel didn't come back with any retort, simply reddened and looked away. Al didn't follow up with anything, either, instead choosing to lift his hand to his ear and fiddle with his radio.

"You there, buddy?"

"I'm here," Garth responded. "Is it over?"

"It's all clear. Get your ass out there, bring the trailer into the compound. Once you get back, we'll grab a few HAZMAT suits and drag all the dead bodies out. We're going to have us a bonfire tonight. Gentlemen, bitch, we have a new home. Welcome to Colebrook Town. Population, us."

XIX
DEAD CALM

"If you find one infected, there'll invariably be more: the disease doesn't discriminate in the victims it takes."

I

A bitter cold wind swirled around Sarah Merrip as she stoop on the top of one of the corner units of the Marine fort, now known as Colebrook Town by its inhabitants. Pulling at the thick jacket that Al had found for her, she looked out at the countryside surrounding the compound, covering her eyes and protecting them from the harsh glare of the sun as it reflected off the pure white snow that lay like a blanket over the hills and fields.

Sarah was almost nine now, and had spent the last two and a half years of her life within the town walls, where her parents had done their best to keep her wrapped in cotton wool. She already knew about the bad men that lived on the outside, and despite their attempts to keep it from her, she also knew about the zombies: she'd seen the walking dead not long after moving in, from the exact spot she stood at now when she had accompanied Al during some of his guard duties.

She liked Al, and looked on him as an adopted uncle. Of all the adults in the town, he was the only one who didn't really treat her like a child; he talked to her as if she were an equal. Though there were some things he didn't speak to her about, he was a lot more open than the others were. When he'd explained exactly why a group of five men and women were attacking one another, ripping chunks of flesh and gulping it down in one, he hadn't tried to dumb it down, but he'd explained what changes they were going through. Though this had shocked her at first, especially as she knew that the plague that had caused this was also responsible for the death of her brother, she was relieved to know that he had been amongst the first to go, and consequently not return from the dead. At least, that's what her dad had told her when she asked him about it.

After that, she'd been forbidden from attending any of the guard duties, until after the third month of living there, when Al announced that the number of the zombies, which almost everyone referred to as Rots, had dropped to a point where nothing passed the fort by any more. He bragged that he, Sylvester and Garth had been working on the controls and sensors of the fort and had managed to get the motion sensors working, and that he was also going to start planting mines around the perimeter of the enclave. With the town in relative safety now, it was decided that Sarah could go back up on to the roof of the observation outposts, providing it wasn't too late; after all, there wasn't much else for the girl to do in the base.

She liked to climb up on to the roof whenever she could; it gave her a chance to be on her own and think. She'd often find herself remembering the summer days she'd spend with Tom and Susan, playing in the garden, before the plague came. Occasionally she'd remember the day Tom died, or the time Susan was attacked by the bad man, and she'd find herself crying. Sometimes, thoughts of Emma came to her, the sister who had died hours after birth not long after moving into the fort. Though it was sad, she didn't find herself grieving as much as she thought she would. Or should.

Al had taken Sarah under his wing while her mum and dad had dealt with the death of their newborn child. He'd shown her how to help him out as he went through his daily routine of weapons maintenance, and he'd even shown her how to use a small, low powered handgun. This was, of course, something she didn't tell her parents once she was reunited with them; after all, she couldn't imagine her mum would be pleased that she was learning something that could lead to her becoming a potential killer. Both parents were currently trying to keep as calm and relaxed as they could, as they were expecting again, hopefully with better results.

The other adults had been too busy doing their own things for the past thirty months to take that much time out with her. Clive had taken it upon himself to convert the unnecessary holding cells into an area of prayer and worship. He had set up a table as an altar, and left his bible open on it, spending much of his time in prayer or reading the holy book.

Both Sylvester and Garth had turned out to be very similar people, first running necessary repair work and modification to the vehicles they held in the compound, fixing damaged equipment in the base, then turning their attention to the more important task of sectioning off a portion of the mess hall and setting up their own bar. This was the place that everyone went to during their spare time, and despite her age, Sarah was as welcome as anyone else. She liked to go there and listen to the stories people would tell from before the plague, and liked to see people act like fools when they drank too much.

Tara had taken time to get to know the computer systems of the base, and started to look after everything, from food supplies to fuel and energy consumption. Sarah had hoped that she would have spent time with her in the same way she had back in their house, but that had not happened. It had always been the same, though; adults too busy with their daily chores and routines to spend time with the young when they wanted to play. Her dad had been the same, before the plague, but now, he seemed different.

Pam had spent her time working on a multitude of different things, from paintings and sketches to writing poetry and small works of fiction. She shared a room with Al, so Sarah had come into contact with her a lot, and had gotten to know her quite well. Pam had told her that she was going to write down everyone's story about the plague, convinced that once they escaped from the island it would become a bestseller. Sarah had asked several times to read through parts of it, but she had always been told it wasn't suitable for her. She had managed the occasional peek when no one was looking, however, but hadn't been able to follow the stories as they were filled with words she couldn't understand.

Angel spent much of her time above ground. She had spent her time cultivating the soil within the walls of the fort, planting seeds and erecting greenhouses in which she grew marrows and elderberries: ingredients that were essential for the alcoholic drinks that were served in Garth and Sylvester's bar. Of everyone in the compound, Sarah always thought that Angel worked the hardest, harvesting food and tending to crops, while also acting as a doctor to any medical emergencies. She didn't understand why no one offered to help her... especially Bill.

He hadn't committed himself to any of the tasks carried out by anyone else. After moving in, he had helped in clearing the bodies out of the fort with great zeal, insisting that all the bodies should be dragged or driven as far away as possible before being burned. But after returning, he had only helped out a few people with particularly heavy tasks before withdrawing into his shell. If a nine year old could pick up on it, then anyone else in the facility should have too, though it didn't look like anyone had mentioned it to him. After spending months in his room, now he seemed to spend most of his time in one of the raised platforms above the observation outposts, forever scanning from side to side, as if searching for something...

Though Sarah didn't have a clue what.

She turned from the countryside and looked back down into the open complex, at the figure of Angel as she walked back and forth around her crops, periodically checking the greenhouses. Sarah waved down on her, and she returned the gesture, before lifting her gaze one of the raised platforms, and the solitary figure that stood in it, his attention focused out towards the distance.

Bill felt the cold creep in through the many layers of clothing he wore, numbing his fingers and toes, as he remained motionless in the raised platform, eyes trying to focus against the harsh glare of sun on snow, but he didn't move from his self-imposed guard duty. Everyone else seemed to be happy in their roles, or at least able to do something worthy towards the running of the base, by utilising skills they had from their lives before the rise: it seemed everyone had a talent they could put to use apart from him, as there didn't appear to be any post to be delivered to anyone within the town.

Frustrated at his apparent uselessness, Bill had taken it upon himself to take the opportunity to learn and teach himself all the finer points or combat and weapon skills. Where his now-battered folder had stopped, the information database available regarding the Marine's regime and training techniques had been invaluable. Taking a collection of weapons from the armoury before Al had moved in, he would service and strip them, clean them, then reassemble them until he could do it without the help of any training aids. He had aimed to become a better soldier, a more resilient survivor, and by committing himself, he felt he had succeeded; but he wouldn't know for sure until the next time he faced an opponent in battle.

And unlike the rest of his friends, Bill knew that their time within the fort would be limited. Whether it be another day, week, month or even a year, he knew it couldn't last. While everyone else, even Al, had quickly slipped into living life as they had before the plague, Bill lived in a constant state of awareness, deciding to spend as much of his time as possible watching from one of the raised observation platforms. He wasn't sure what had made him this way: maybe it was just a gut feeling he had, but he just couldn't relax the way everyone else had.

Al had always said that he didn't go looking for trouble, it came looking for him, and Bill didn't see any reason why it would stop now. Whether another recon squad from another base was sent out to reclaim the fort, a hunting pack of Rots stumbled across the area, or a rogue gang faction caught wind of them.

"There's an intricate and random pattern of mines laid out there," Al had assured him one night while relaxing in the pleasant confines of *Colebrook's Club*, the unofficial name for Garth and Sylvester's bar. "And that's on top of the motion sensors we've got set up. There's no way anyone can make their way across there without a map, or without an IFF device."

Bill hadn't been convinced, though, and maintained his watch as often as he could.

Another cold wind washed over him, shaking his raised pulpit, and brought with it a sprinkling of snow. Bill wiped his face with the back of his sleeve, but stood fast, watching as the countryside before him slowly became obscured by the thick flakes of snow that washed across his vision. He remained static for a few more minutes, waiting to see if it was a light snow shower, but instead it seemed to increase in intensity.

"Sarah and me are heading back in, Bill. You coming down from there?" Angel's voice crackled in his ear, the signal obviously affected by the bad weather conditions.

"Yeah," he muttered, stepping backwards and making his way down the ladder before making his way down the staircase inside the corner unit and out into the courtyard. Only Sarah stood waiting for him near the entrance to the underground complex, brushing her hair to one side as the wind whipped at her.

"Where's Angel gone?" he shouted in order to be heard over the whine of the wind. Sarah shrugged her shoulders and turned to move back into the lower levels, and Bill went to follow, but stopped as he heard the thick powdered snow crunch beneath boots behind him. He quickly spun on his heels in time to see a mound of compacted snow head for his face. It smacked into his head, stinging his frozen skin and staggering him as the snowball caught him unawares. He blindly staggered forwards, trying to clear his eyes with numb fingers, when a second snowball pelted him, this one crashing against the back of his head. Stumbling forwards, his hands coiled around the jacket of someone, and he heaved with all his might, slipping on the snow and trying to either remain upright or pull whoever it was down with him. Gravity won the fight, and Bill and his mystery assailant tumbled to the floor.

With both people panting and laughing, Bill managed to clear the melting snow from his face and looked at the person he lay atop, saw the warm and welcome grin of Angel lying in the snow.

"Me and Sarah just had a little talk, girl to girl. We decided you needed to lighten up a little, thought that a little snowball fight wouldn't do you any harm."

Bill felt a smile creep across his lips. Although the two had talked in the past two and a half years, they had never been as close as they were at that point: the last time they had, had been just after Bill had rescued her from the wild Marine in the kitchen, when the pair had almost kissed. That was something they'd never talked about. But now, in the position they were in now, like two lovers wrapped in one another's arms, they found themselves in the same compromising position. Bill felt awkward, uncertain of what to do next, until another snowball slapped into the back of his neck, spilling snow down his collar. He turned his head, peering over his shoulder and saw Sarah laughing, kneeling down to grab another handful of snow.

"I'm going to get that kid," Bill snarled, leaping to his feet and charging towards the girl. She nimbly stepped to one side, ducking beneath Bill's arms and smashed another ball against his side before running inside.

"Little bitch," laughed Bill, watching as the girl sprinted across the catwalk and vanished into the darkened opening of the building, then turned to face Angel as she casually strolled towards the walkway herself.

"You put her up to this, didn't you?"

"She's a kid, kids need to play. Plus, it doesn't hurt to let off a little steam once in a while. I haven't seen you crack a smile since we settled down here; you've been so busy on lookout duty to do anything else. If anything, I would have expected Al to be the compulsive soldier, but even *he's* mellowed. You've changed, Bill. More than anyone here."

"I'm keeping realistic about all this," Bill said, following Angel into the building and shaking the flakes of snow from his head. "We're living in a borrowed Marine base, they could try to reclaim it at any time. Gangs, Rots…"

"Rots? We haven't seen any sign of the Rots in months. If the Marines wanted this place, they'd have come for it after we took it over. The gangs probably don't even know this place exists. We're *safe*, stop looking for danger where there is none!"

"Al says trouble always comes looking…"

Angel stopped walking as she reached the top of the stairs leading down into the depths of the complex, turning to look at Bill as she removed her snow-covered jacket and lay it over the railing.

"Al says a lot of things, most of it's crap. Think about that."

She turned and made her way down the stairs, her footsteps echoing into the chasm below as she made her way towards the staircase inside the structure. Bill stood at the top of the stairs for a few minutes, fighting his way out the soaked jacket he wore and hanging it beside Angel's.

"If you're finished rolling around in the snow with that whore, you might want to pay a visit to my little workshop," Al's voice buzzed over the headset Bill wore. He didn't need to ask where the workshop was; just as Bill had his regular haunting ground, so too did Al. If he wasn't in the bar, he would be in the armoury, on the lowest level.

Bill nodded to himself, making his way to the main staircase and casually nodding to Clive as he passed him by. Bill rarely spoke to Clive; the two men didn't share the same outlook on religion, and as Clive spent much of his time in his shrine, the two rarely crossed paths.

He made the rest of the journey without bumping into anyone else, ending his journey outside the thick metal door that opened up into the armoury. He hammered on the door with his fist, hearing a monotone grunt from within that obviously translated into 'come in'. He pushed gently on the metal door, the well-oiled hinges opening soundlessly into the room.

It had been a long time since Bill had been in the armoury, almost a year in fact, sine he'd collected a small cache and claimed it as his own. He distinctly remembered it being filled with weapons, ammunition crates and explosive devices. Now however, half the weapons seemed to have vanished, and were replaced with four large tables, littered with mounds of scrap wood and an assortment of tools. The smell of gun oil and freshly cut wood lingered in the air, the latter reminding Bill of his school days, and the time he spent in the woodwork shop. Al strolled around the room, his T-shirt rolled up and tied over his head in a makeshift bandana, his body and trousers flecked with sawdust and wood shavings. He looked up as Bill took a step into room, grinned and nodded casually, and put down his electric sander, stepping back from the large bench he was working on.

"Hey kid," he said casually, picking up a smoking cigarette from an ashtray and taking a large drag. "Finished with the bitch in the snow?" he casually asked, motioning towards the bank of four monitors balanced on one of the homemade benches. They displayed a number of pictures from different video cameras mounted around the exterior of the base, cycling through a selection of different angles. "Just because I'm not spending my days up a pole waiting for trouble, doesn't mean I'm not on the look out for it."

"What the hell are you doing here?" Bill asked, ignoring what Al was saying. "Woodwork?"

"I've been making a table or three. And chairs, a set of drawers, a couple of cupboards, I've got a nice bed under construction in our room…"

"Woodwork?" repeated Bill, stepping closer to the nearest table. "It looks… well, it looks good. Like a proper table."

"That's because it *is* a table. I've not always been a Marine; I used to help my uncle in his carpentry shop after school. I guess some skills stay with you. Like riding a bike, I guess. Jesus, I needed a skill to fall back on after retiring from the Marines, other than becoming a hired gun."

"Hired gun?"

"I know how to make a good coffee table," Al said with a grin, "But I also know how to make people dead. You stick with what you know."

"And where are all the guns? I can't believe you've got rid of them…"

"Some are in my room, some are in the trailer, others I've hidden around the base. I'm a very organised man, in case you hadn't realised. The woodwork's just a hobby of mine, something to keep me occupied. Fuck knows we all need something to keep some degree of normalcy in our life. Unlike you, you morose mother fucker."

Al stopped for a moment, smiling as he let the last few words echo in his mind. They must have meant something to him, as he chuckled before he carried on. "You spend all your time staring out into nothing, waiting for something to happen. A watched pot never boils, you ever heard of that saying?"

"I know something's coming," Bill said, "I can feel it."

"You've been feeling it every day for two years, kid. Give it a rest. Relax, take up golf or something, there's plenty for you to do. The amount of time we've been here, nothing's happened."

"Is that what you've brought me here for, to have a go at me? Have you been talking to Angel?"

"Some chance," he muttered, pouring himself a glass of bourbon and sipping delicately at it. "I've got better things to waste my breath on. Like cigarettes."

"And you're going to have to stop that, too," Bill said.

Al sighed heavily, pulling an ornately carved chair out from beneath one of the tables and sinking into it, rolling the glass filled with golden liquor around from side to side. "Have you been talking to Pam? She's trying to get me to quit."

"You're going to have to," repeated Bill.

"My father died of lung cancer," Al said, pointing the smoking cigarette in Bill's direction. "By the time they discovered it, it was too late and they couldn't do anything about it. He died at the age of forty-five. My mom begged me to quit; she didn't want me to go the same way. You notice I'm still smoking, right?

"The way I see it," he carried on. "My life's on the line every day of my life. There's no guarantee I'm going to live to the end of my natural life. Hell, I could be tampering with a grenade tomorrow and blow my own head off. Why should I stop one of the few things that I enjoy in life?"

"Because in a while, you're going to run out of them. When you do, what are you going to smoke? With no one to work in factories, or no one to import them from other countries, you'll have nothing."

"Fuck that, kid, I'll smoke weeds and sticks, then I'll convince the bitch to grow tobacco in her greenhouse. She feeds my need for alcohol, she can feed my thirst for smokes, too."

"She spends her days growing food and her evenings looking after any medical emergencies that may crop up. She can't do anything else!"

"You're right," muttered Al. "You don't do anything, you can grow my smokes."

"I've got better things to do," lied Bill, knowing full well that he didn't.

"Like watching for a Rot that isn't coming, or pining over the bitch?"

Bill didn't respond, simply turned away from the conversation and showed his back to Al, focussing his attention to the bank of monitors. "You wanted me to come here for a reason, right?"

"Yeah, that's right. Aside from making fantastic furniture, I've been making adjustments to a few weapons, testing them out in the firing range around back."

"Firing range?" Bill asked. "I wasn't aware we had one?"

"It's an armoury, it'd be pretty piss-poor if it didn't have a shooting range. Look at this," he said, pulling the magnum from the holster he still carried. Bill vaguely recognised it as the large handgun the Marine had always sported, though it appeared to have grown an extra handhold and an extended magazine.

"What have you done to it?" Bill asked, shocked at the fact Al had butchered his beloved handgun. The extra parts were polished to match the colouring of the weapon, so they didn't look out of place. If Bill hadn't seen Al's prized hand cannon before, he probably wouldn't have picked up on it.

"Modified it. Shit, I don't just know my woodwork, I know my weapons too."

"Looks pretty ugly," Bill insisted. Al shook his head in disgust, handled the weapon gently and held it outstretched in one hand, the weight of the weapon perfectly balanced in his palm.

"It's not ugly, it's a thing of beauty. It's got a semi-auto feature now, it can fire bursts of two rounds at a time. The grip at the front adds to the stability of it all. I tried to increase the burst pattern to three, but that tore it apart. Anyway, I found one of these for you. I know how much you like your shotguns, for some reason. The thing was lying in the corner of the armoury, needed little work. It's a beast of a weapon, it'll kick right into you and shatter your ribs if you're not careful. Test it out, go on."

Bill looked at the bulky weapon Al had pointed to, and gently picked it up. It wasn't as heavy as he had thought it would be, and he shouldered it, making his way to the firing range Al had prepared with a wooden target. Toying with the firing selector switch, Bill sighted down the muzzle and squeezed the trigger, grinning as the weapon spat a burst of three shells in rapid succession, the wooden target of a black silhouette shattering and cracking beneath the onslaught of lead pellets. He couldn't help grinning at the power of the weapon he held, and nodded approvingly to Al as he watched the test. The Marine returned the nod, and picked up one of the metal ammunition crates that littered the floor of the room.

"I've also had a chance to pick apart those homemade shells that J-Man had left me, do a little reverse engineering. They're all pretty standard and basic, nothing that's really more powerful than anything that's available in the armoury, except for what's loaded in that magazine. Hard shot. The pellets are replaced with ball bearings, which provide a more powerful punch. While standard shot wouldn't penetrate reinforced glass, these babies can smash through the stuff like it was paper. Just what you need to crush the skull of a Rot."

"What Rots?" Bill said with a grin, pulling the magazine free from the weapon and replacing the expended shells. "I haven't seen any of them for years."

"I know; the remote cameras haven't even picked any up. It's possible they might have just died out. Only one way to find out."

"What are you saying?"

"Road trip," said Al with a grin. "Load up on a few guns, head off into the nearest city or town and grab a few things."

"I thought we were self-sufficient here," Bill said, hefting his new shotgun. "Why the change of heart?"

"That little speech you gave me about cigarettes, you're right. I need to get some more."

"You're going to risk your life to leave our well-protected town and get some *cigarettes*?"

"No, I'm going to risk *our* lives to get some smokes. Plus, we need a few extra things."

"It can't be anything vital. We're well stocked, remember? That was the whole selling point for moving into this place."

"A few of life's luxuries," Al purred, grabbing a machinegun and a duffle bag, then filling the sack with boxes of ammunition. Slinging one of the large sniper rifles over his back, Al replaced his magnum in his holster and moved towards the door of the armoury, motioning for Bill to follow. He did so, carrying his shotgun and following Al as he moved towards the staircase.

"Luxuries?" Bill questioned, "Have you taken leave of your senses?"

"Shit, no," Al growled. "There's just some stuff I really need to get. Ingredients for explosives and weapons, shit like that. I've used up most of the base's supply."

"What on?"

"All those mines I set around the base, the explosive charges in those didn't just grow on trees. Plus, there's all the mortars I've got set up around the perimeter."

"Mortars? You've got this place well protected: more than you let on."

"I don't like coming across as soft. Get on up to the hummer, I'll swing by Preacher-man, tell him what we're up to, get him to keep an eye on my monitors. Go on, I'll be up in five."

Al peeled off from Bill and ran towards Clive's sanctity, leaving Bill to make the journey to the hummer on his own.

He exited the building and found himself surrounded by a whirling blizzard of snow; he could barely see the vehicle in front of him, but knew that it was there. Trudging through the snow, he clambered into the vehicle and turned over the engine, activating the heaters and rubbing his hands over the vents. Five minutes passed before Al appeared at the driver's door, clambering into the vehicle and glaring at Bill.

"What are you doing?" he said with a scowl.

"Warming my hands, it's freezing out there."

"I mean why are you in here? *Colebrook's Second*, what are you doing in here?"

"Going on some crazy journey with you, I thought."

"Grab a bike from the trailer."

"You're crazy, right? I'm not going on a bike in that shit out there."

"You'll take up valuable cargo space," Al argued, looking over his shoulder at the seats behind him. "I guess I could only get half as much whiskey as what I'd planned."

"Whiskey? I thought we were going to get explosives?"

"Molotov cocktails," Al replied without missing a beat. Bill didn't believe him, but didn't press the argument any further. "Preacher-man's okay with us going, he's going to keep in touch as best he can. Range isn't too far with these headsets, even with the boosting equipment on site. Plus, the snow's really going to scramble our signal. He gave us a little something for our journey."

Al opened his palm and unravelled a silver chain with a medallion, wrapping the chain around the mirror and allowing the trinket to dangle. The fob bore an image of an old man, carrying a child on his shoulders as he strode across a river. Bill knew enough about religion to recognise the figure as Saint Christopher, the patron saint of travelling and journeys.

Al knocked the vehicle into gear and trundled forwards, activating the windscreen wipers and tapping a code into the nine-digit keypad on the dashboard. As the vehicle approached the massive blast door of the base, it trundled down into the recess beneath it, allowing them access to the outside world. Al stopped the vehicle just as they left the confines of the base, then entered the code again, turning to one side and watching as the door slowly rose back into position.

"Spanners did a good fix on that," he said, merely as a passing comment before rolling out across the open ground towards the minefield. Bill knew the way they were heading, but also the fact that the hummer had countermeasures installed. That didn't stop him from squirming at the thought of driving over a hundred explosive devices. Al looked at him and laughed, shaking his head.

"IFF transponder, man, I told you before. Garth had the same set-up when we ran the assault on the bitch's farm, the mines won't go off with us on top. We're good to go."

"I hope to god you're right."

"Not God," Al said, flicking the hanging medal. "Saint Chris. He's watching over us today."

"He'd better do a good job," muttered Bill.

II

"This is the fourth shop we've been in," Bill moaned, standing guard by the doorway to the large department store while Al rooted through the dust-laden contents of the lower floor. Bill was extremely nervous, though he couldn't understand why: they'd been out searching through different stores in the town for almost five hours now, the thick snow and wrecked streets not making their job any easier, and the sun was starting to set on them. Under normal circumstances, Al would have been just as nervous as Bill, but in all the time they'd been out, they hadn't seen one single Rot.

"C'mon, Al, it's freezing out here, the snow's still coming down, and we don't know what the hell's lurking out there in the dark."

"Relax, kid. There's no Rots out here. My guess is their food supply couldn't last forever. I'm thinking that maybe after two and a half years they've starved to death."

"Then why haven't we seen any dead bodies?"

"Scavengers," suggested Al, overturning a wooden crate and sifting through the scattered contents. "If the Rots wouldn't eat their dead friends, the local wildlife would. Plus, any bodies would be buried under the snow, and I haven't seen you going out of your way to dig up any snow to have a look."

"Do you really think they could starve to death?" Bill asked, leaving his guard post and stepping into the gloom of the store. He played his flashlight across the room, providing enough illumination to allow Al to make out a packet of unopened cigarettes. He swept the packet up and shovelled it into one of his pockets. Another item in the jumble caught Al's eye, a shining piece of metal that he also scooped up. A golden bracelet decorated with a number of curving lines. He slipped that into his pocket as well, smiling to himself.

"That's for Pam," he muttered to himself.

"C'mon, Al, we've got enough whiskey and other flammable liquids for whatever pyromaniac plans you may have, we found a few useful medical supplies, now you're just fishing for trinkets to give your girlfriend."

""What's the harm? Have a look around, you might find something to give the bitch. Here, what about this?" Al said, grabbing a dog collar and hurling it at Bill. He caught it, looked at it, then dropped it to the floor, shaking his head. "What's the harm, anyway?" asked Al. "We've been living in complete isolation for almost three years. No Christmas, no birthdays, every day rolling into one another. We all need a break from that. Grab that stuffed toy over there, will you?"

Bill marched across the rubble-strewn floor and snatched up the cuddly toy Al had indicated before stuffing it into the bag he carried. "What, so you think you're Father Christmas now?"

"Ho ho ho," Al said, bundling more items from around the store into his sack. "Spirits have been low recently, I guarantee that when we turn up bearing gifts it'll be well received by everyone. The whole point of the fort was to attempt to add some normalcy to our lives."

"So why're you doing this now? I mean according to the calendars in the fort Christmas has passed; it's February now."

"So I'm a little late, sue me. It's the thought that counts. You may want to grab something for your bitch," Al said, adjusting his grip on the bag he carried. Bill shrugged, vanishing off into the gloom of the building. Switching to his head set once he was out of range, Bill's voice came over the earpiece.

"Aren't we just as bad as the looters?"

"Looters? Hell, no. The looters at the beginning of the plague grabbed everything they could because they thought that once the plague passed over, they'd be able to sell everything and live the rest of their lives in the lap of luxury. I'm under no such foolish impression: I know that the plague isn't going to pass over, and we're just stuck here until the end of our lives. So, I'm just trying to break the monotony."

There was no response from Bill, and Al nodded in satisfaction to himself, returning to the vehicle parked outside the building and loading his recent finds into the hummer before standing by the opened driver's door, looking up one end of the street, then the other. It still paid off to be wary, despite the lack of any threats they had seen since leaving Colebrook Town.

Five minutes passed, and Al threw the smouldering cigarette butt down to the snowy ground. It hissed as the hot tip came into contact with the ice-cold snow, quickly extinguishing. There had been no sign of Bill, no words from him, no sign that he was still inside the building. If it had been anyone else but Bill, Al would have been worried, but he knew that he could take care of himself. But still, five minutes to find a little shiny something for a woman seemed a little excessive.

"Still here, kid?"

"I'm here, I'm just looking," hissed Bill. "What's wrong?"

"Nothing," Al muttered, slowly turning from side to side. "Just thought you were taking your time, I didn't know where you'd gone."

"I'm still…. Shit!"

A trio of gunshots snapped Al out of his sentinel stance, and he lifted his machinegun, bolting into the department store and storming through the shop, calling out for Bill.

"Over here," he shouted. "Ran into an old friend."

"A Rot?" asked Al as he stumbled into the darkened secluded area of the shop where Bill stood, a flashlight in one hand and his smoking automatic shotgun in the other. Bill nodded grimly, motioning to the inert figure that lay on the ground at his feet. Al flicked the beam of his torch over the dead body, stopping when the light played over the pummelled shoulders and battered face of the creature.

"New shells can punch through safety glass?" asked Bill with a sneer. "It took three shells to get that bastard down on the ground. Jesus, Al, I thought you said they packed a punch?"

"Bullshit," said Al, kneeling beside the body and unsheathing his knife, poking the dents in the shoulders where some of the blackened ball bearings still resided. "Bullshit, a couple of drums of twenty shells could turn a normal car into Swiss cheese, there ain't no way one of those rotten bastards could take three shells. You must've hit it at the wrong angle."

"Full frontal shot," Bill said, poking the dead creature with the tip of his boot. "I hit the bastard square on. The first shot didn't faze it. The second cracked its skull, and the third finally smashed it open. Something's wrong with this one."

"It's a tough son of a dead bitch, I'll give it that. Look at this," Al said, poking the corpse with the blade of his knife. Thick chunks of desiccated meat peeled away from the creature, flesh dry and deprived of all liquid. Al took a piece of the body, rubbed it between his fingers, and dropped it to the floor. "God-damned dead bastard's as tough as old leather. Touch that corpse."

"I'd rather not," Bill said, declining the invite. Al demonstrated the fact by trying to cut the skin of the creature's chest with his knife. After much resistance, the flesh parted, and Al pried back the skin, revealing a heavily distorted and deformed rib cage.

"I didn't know you can do autopsies," said Bill, crouching down beside Al. "What've we got here?"

"It's a fucking mutant," Al mused, scratching at the thick calcium deposits that ran along the breastbone and ribs of the creature. "What the fuck is all this?"

"Evolution of the plague?" suggested Bill. "Part of the plague is that it dries out the body, so after so long…"

"It turns the flesh to leather and the bones to rock? I don't buy it, kid, that's just too farfetched. What's more likely is that build-up is a congenial genetic bone disorder, and the skin is so tough because it's frozen with the cold. Always a more simple solution, trust me."

"That explanation is certainly more favourable to us," Bill said, clambering back to his feet. "I don't want to run into more of this guy's friends to see which of our theories are correct. Let's get out of here."

Al nodded, clambering to his feet and moving back towards the parked hummer, making sure his friend was behind him as he moved.

They hit the streets in the middle of another snow flurry, the white storm pressing in against them as they started to clamber into the vehicle.

"We got what we needed?" asked Bill, as he climbed into hummer. Al nodded, and was about to slam the door shut and turn the engine over, when he heard a sound in the distant, so quiet it barely made its way to his ears above the howl of the wind. He stopped, holding his head up and trying to pick up on what he thought he heard.

"What is it?" asked Bill, opening his door and stepping out the vehicle, looking over the roof of the vehicle to his companion. "What did you hear?"

Al didn't say anything, just held his hand up for silence. Bill nodded; he knew better than to say anything further.

"Can't you hear that?"

Bill shook his head, and was about to verbally respond, when he paused, as if he was also listening.

"It's a voice," he finally said, confirming Al's suspicions. "It sounds like a mans voice."

Al nodded, jumping down from the hummer and stepping forwards, moving towards the possible location of the sound. The wind bit into him, and he pulled his padded jacket tighter around him, wiping the ice crystals out from his beard and lifting his sniper rifle up, tucking the stock of the weapon in beneath his shoulder and peering through the scope.

The rifle itself was a piece of hi-tech wizardry; something Al had been extremely pleased to find in the armoury. It had a number of different visions and magnifications, and Al decided upon utilising the thermal vision. The screen was a wash of purple and blue, but in the far distance, he could make out a slight discolouration of something.

Al knew that none of the Rots gave off any heat, so the source of the green and yellow blur could only be a person.

"Someone's out there," he whispered, motioning to Bill to come alongside him. He passed over his rifle, offering him to scope. "Do you agree?"

Bill looked through the scope, shrugged his shoulders. "Looks like it. Where are you going?"

"I'm getting in close," Al muttered, slinging his rifle and machinegun, then drawing his magnum. "I want to see who's stupid enough to be caught out in the snow like this."

"You mean besides us? Anyways, does it sound like he's needing help?"

Al didn't respond: he simply started to move towards the possible source of the voice. He didn't need to look back to see if Bill was following, he knew that he'd have his back covered.

The snowstorm seemed to loosen up for a while, and Al thought he could see movement up ahead. He raised his weapon and levelled it off with a dark figure that shifted in the distance: it seemed to stumble from one side of the road to another with an unusual gait in its step. It paused, seemed to turn and face them. Al stopped dead in his tracks, slowly sinking to his knees: his boots crunching as the displacement of his weight compressed the snow around him. The darkened figure wavered from side to side, as if it were in two minds about what to do next.

"Someone who needs our help?"

"I think that's a Rot," Al whispered. "Maybe the Rot had been chasing the man…"

"How'd it show up on your heat vision scope?" asked Bill, crouching down low beside the Marine and pointing his automatic shotgun at the bulk of the target.

"I don't know, ask the bitch when we get back, she's the biologist. Maybe it was the man we saw as he ran from the creature. Give me that shotgun; I'm going to get closer and show you that one of those shells is enough to rip that fucker apart."

Al slipped his magnum back into his holster and exchanged his machinegun for Bill's assault shotgun. Remaining crouched over, he made his way across the snow as silent as he could, the features of the Rot slowly coming into clarity as he passed through the drizzle of snow.

The creature was a blackened mess of charred flesh and ragged clothing; what was left of its smouldering skin hissed as the white flakes of snow fell on to it. A stubby cylinder lay embedded in its chest, the remains of a smouldering flare that had been lodged into its partially exposed rib cage. The eye sockets of its skull were vacant, and it appeared that the creature was stumbling around blindly, though it seemed to sense Al as he approached.

At least that flare explains the heat signature, Al thought as he lifted the shotgun. The creature wheeled towards him as it sensed his presence, and Al smiled grimly as he squeezed the trigger and discharged one of the shells directly into the blackened head of the creature,

Its head snapped back and took a stumbling step backwards, but it didn't fall to the ground. Al froze as the creature rolled its head back in place, part of its flesh now shredded and exposing a skeletal-like grin beneath dried pulpy tissue, Muttering beneath his breath, Al loosed a volley of three shells from the powerful weapon, The creature stumbled back and collapsed against the wall behind him, and although the flesh of the head and shoulders had been shredded by the powerful rounds, the skull itself remained intact, and the creature active.

"Son of a bitch," growled Al, back-pedalling as the creature hauled itself off the wall and hobbled towards him, talon-like fingers groping at thin air in a failed attempt to grab hold of its attacker. Al grabbed his Desert Eagle and swung it up into position, taking aim and squeezing off a burst of two rounds. The heavy shells smashed against the skull of the creature, obliterating the bone and splattering gristle and brain across the snow-covered ground. The charred body dropped to the ground with a sickening crack as limbs buckled and snapped, tearing flesh and shattering bones.

Bill stalked up behind him, handing back the machinegun and retrieving the shotgun from the ground, brushing off the snow as he did so.

"I told you the rounds weren't that good," Bill said, matter-of-factly.

"I don't understand," muttered Al, kicking the body. "They should have done the business on that dead fuck…"

"Where's the guy gone?" Bill asked, quickly reverting his attention back to the main reason why they had deviated from their original plan of leaving the town. "Shouldn't he be somewhere around here?"

"The heat source was that flare," Al said, motioning to the still-smouldering tube lodged between the ribs of the creature. "I don't know where the voice came from. Maybe it was the wind we heard? Or just the creature moaning?"

Though Al was talking, Bill wasn't listening to him, instead he had his head tilted upwards, glaring at one of the opened windows of one of the shops that surrounded them. He nodded upwards, indicating one of the openings.

"I thought I saw something up there."

"Living or dead?"

"I don't know," Bill said, shrugging his shoulders. "Could have been either."

"Then let's go look. I'm not having a sprinting corpse follow us back to Colebrook Town, he'll do nothing but bring more of his friends. It's more than likely going to be a Rot up there, they move in packs. Where there's one, there'll be a couple. Lets go hunting, kid, see if we can bag some more of the bastards. C'mon."

Bill nodded as Al moved into the store, holding his shotgun and bracing the stock of the weapon against his hip, swinging it around from side to side as he went. Al clearly hadn't believed how defective the shotgun shells were, even *after* taking them on his own firing test. It had taken a pair of bullets from his magnum to take the Rot down, and that was something that didn't sit well with Bill. Even *one* round from the magnum should have been enough to put down the undead; hell, before the group had sought refuge in the Marine establishment, a normal shotgun shell had been more than enough to take down the creature.

Bill couldn't shake his doubts as he stalked into the open building behind Al, their weapons lifted and ready to strike at the first sign of trouble.

The building had once been a shop, though any sign of what they may have sold had long since vanished. It may have been a shop that sold vegetables or flowers, as piles of organic-looking mush had been scattered across the floor, each frozen solid by the sub-zero temperatures. The windows were non-existent and the metal frames that made up the front of the shop had been snapped and twisted by something unknown. Whatever it had been, though, it had left behind a lot of blood, and some of its insides: pink and scarlet icicles hung from a bloodied and unrecognisable lump of flesh that had been skewered on one of the metal supports. Crystals of red snow pooled around the base of the bloody shish kebab, and Al couldn't help himself as he prodded at the meat with the tip of his knife.

"Solid as a rock," he observed. "Been there for weeks, maybe longer."

Snow had drifted into the shop through the open windows, and were it not for the window frame and broken walls of the shop, Bill would have found it hard to distinguish where the outside stopped and inside started. It extended about fifteen feet into the back of the room, where the blackened and bloodstained walls opened up to a smashed door hanging loosely from the hinges. Blood spattered one side of the wooden finish of the door, with gouges left in the surface where ragged fingernails had scratched and torn. Fragments of nails still lay embedded in the wood, bloodied and attached to frozen strands of flesh.

"Looks like they were trying to force their way in here," Bill said, following Al as he pushed past the shattered door. "You think that something was trying to tear through the door to get to our mystery yeller?"

"Unlikely, this shit is frozen solid. It could have been here for months."

The doorway opened into a small room with a staircase leading upwards. The wooden stairs had been badly damaged, some of them torn up and smashed, others dented as though a body had fallen on them from a great height: some of the steps looked out of place, as if they were brand new. The plaster on the walls had been all but removed, exposing the burnished wooden slats of the old-style construction, leaving piles of debris scattered across the floor. Both time and the weather had made sure that the dust that would have lingered in the air from the brittle and dry material no longer bothered the breathing of the pair as they stalked through the room. They left footprints in the frozen dirt, and so had the person that had recently passed through. Al crouched down beside the tracks, looking them up and down, then in the direction they headed: the staircase.

"Tall, light build, probably about your height and weight," Al guessed. "He wasn't running; he was talking his time, so he probably didn't even know the Rot was out there. Either that, or he didn't care."

"And he's upstairs?"

Al nodded. By way of response, Bill stood and placed his first foot on the stairs, but before he could venture any further, Al rushed forwards and pulled him back from the staircase. He pointed to each step, indicating that some stairs had footprints on, while some didn't.

"Footprints are on safe steps," Al hissed. "The others are wired to traps."

"How do you know?"

"I'm a Marine, I know my shit. I've tracked Bebops for miles through the rainforests; I know an ambush when I see one. Step where our mystery man's stepped, or you could wind up with your leg blown off. He's replaced a few boards there and there, look."

Sure enough, the newer boards looked as if they had only been laid a few days ago. The way in which the plaster had been taken off the walls also suggested that it had come off with the aid of a small explosive charge.

"Claymores, more than likely, possibly padded out with ball bearings or nails. We hit the top of the stairs, see what the layout's like. You break left, I'll take the right half of the building."

Bill nodded an affirmative, carefully following behind Al as he acted as guide up the explosive staircase, pausing only to work out how to pass a row of four steps, all of which seemed to be rigged. He managed to bypass them by hoisting himself up on to the landing above and hauling his weight up, then turned around to help Bill up.

Once the pair were up, they looked from one side to another, holding their weapons and sweeping them around.

"Remember the plan," hissed Al as he moved off to the right. "And for the love of god, don't go back down by the stairs. I'm not going to drag half a corpse back with me.

Bill nodded, then took the left of the upper floor, finding himself in a large bedroom, which from the looks of things was currently in use.

The room was cleaner than the lower floor, the floorboards covered by a collection of rugs and pieces of carpet. The bed looked as if it had been made in a hurry, ruffled sheets thrown hastily over the mattress and a stack of magazines piled against one wall. Bill carefully looked at the pile, running his fingers down the spines as he read the titles aloud.

"Minx, Dominator, Hi-tech Monthly, Cooking for Beginners… something for all occasions."

"Grab the Minx magazines," Al said, the signal from the radio weakened somewhat, no doubt by the construction of the building. The plasterwork that was coming off the walls exposed a lot of wooden laths, and beneath that, the metal girders that formed the building itself, which could account for the disruption in the system. "There might be some issues there I haven't read."

"I'm not carrying a ton of pornography back to base for you," Bill muttered, stepping away from the magazines and looking at the large wooden desk that occupied one corner of the room. The top was littered with a number of small tools: wire cutters, pliers, screwdrivers, and tweezers, sitting alongside small mounds of plastic explosives and glass containers filled with ball bearings. A wooden crate sat beside the desk, painted a dark green, and bearing a faded paper label proclaiming it to be property of the Army. Bill peered into the crate and saw a number of large metal devices, equipped with a number of spikes and hooks. One flat side of the device had raised letters reading 'this side facing enemy'. He read the words aloud to himself, stepping back from the crate.

"You found the claymores, kid," hissed Al. "I've found jack shit over here."

"Nothing?"

"Empty rooms, half the walls are missing. One room where some dirty bastard's been taking a dump, another room that's been used as a kitchen. Windows shattered, plaster and the structure behind it exposed by small arms fire. Fuck this, kid, I'm coming over to your side."

Bill nodded to himself and moved on into the next room, where he could detect the lingering smell of a meal, the steaming remnants of which were on a plate in the centre of the chamber. Al trotted into the room just behind Bill, sweeping his weapon around as he entered.

"This is the last of the rooms," Bill said, indicating that there was nowhere else for someone to go. Bill leaned over to the window, saw the street below where he and Al had previously stood, and nodded to himself. "This is the window I saw him at. He didn't rush past us on the way up, and these floorboards are creaky as shit, we'd have heard him move around."

"I agree," Al answered, louder than he normally spoke. He pointed over to a wooden crate that Bill had noticed on the way in, though he had assumed it not to be big enough to hide anyone inside. Al, obviously, had other ideas as he carefully stalked over towards the box, the muzzle of his weapon trained on the crate.

"No one home, kid. Let's just bail, we've got what we came for."

With a flash of movement, Al kicked at the crate, deftly lifting it and knocking it aside with his powerful leg. Beneath the hollow box, a man lay on the ground, most of his body lying in a sunken hole in the floor. The moment the crate was removed, the man hiding beneath it leapt to his feet, a shotgun levelled with Al's chest. Much to Bill's surprise, no one fired, and he had to restrain himself not to open fire himself.

"And who the fuck are you?" Al spat, his weapon remaining perfectly a still as he trained it on the man. He wore jeans and a thick woollen jumper, all covered by a black leather trench coat and topped by a close-knit woollen hat. His eyes were wild, frantically skipping from Bill to Al as he tried to take in everything that was happening to him. Bill could see a number of weapons dangling from the combat webbing he wore, though he didn't make a move for any of them, he was more than happy to work with just his shotgun.

"I'm the guy who lives in this building, and I don't remember inviting you in."

"The door was open," grinned Al with a lopsided, cocky smile. "We just let ourselves in."

"Then you know your way out. Don't let me stop you."

"We'll leave," hissed Al. "But we'll take my claymores, if you don't mind."

"I mind, you piece of shit, they're mine."

"They belong to the Army," Al growled. "And right now, I'm the closest thing there is to the Army. So they're mine. I'll take the plastic explosives, too."

"If you do, I'll kill you."

"You're going to shoot me? Not before me or the kid does, trust me. You can't shoot us both at the same time."

"The hole building's wired to explode. Shoot me now, and everything goes up."

Al seemed to hold his breath with this revelation, and Bill waited for a response from either of the two men. If the man could set explosive devices on steps, there was no doubt that he couldn't do the same for a whole building. Bill waited for someone to make the first move.

He didn't have long to wait.

"So, what do you want?" Al finally asked. "We heard you shouting before, why'd you run?"

"The corpses were moving in on me, I had to move. I heard your gunshots before, I thought I'd be able to catch up to you before they appeared, but they were closer than I thought. I lost sight of you in the blizzard, and I knew I had to make it back to safety before more emerged from their hiding places."

"You wanted to be found, but you hid from us when we approached the building. Why?"

"Nerves, I guess," the man said. He seemed to be calming down, the wild look in his eyes dissipating as he became used to the situation. "As soon as I saw you approach the building, and the way you killed the zombie, I just freaked, and hoped you wouldn't have seen me, that you'd just leave me behind. It normally takes five or six shells to even faze one of the creatures, but you killed it so easily... I guess the power of your weapons bugged me out."

Now that the tension in the air was starting to break, the man seemed to be easing back into his normal character. He finally dropped his shotgun to the floor, righting the disturbed crate and taking a seat on it. He looked from Al, to Bill, then back to Al. The man finally managed to crack a smile, shaking his head.

"Shit, I can't believe there's someone alive after all this time... and in my town. Shit, what are the odds?"

"Yeah, what *are* the odds?" Al said, lowering himself to the floor, but keeping the muzzle of his weapon trained in the direction of the man. Bill took this as a cue that they were settling in, and took a seat on the window ledge.

"How long have you been on your own?" asked Al. The man shook his head absentmindedly.

"At least two winters, I think. Jesus, it's good to see someone alive…"

"We can slap each other on the back later," Al said. "How'd you come to be out here on your own?"

"How long've you got?"

"The hummer's not going anywhere, and everyone back home knows we're out, so they won't worry," Bill said, catching an accusing glare from Al as he spoke. Maybe he'd volunteered too much information.

"Where do I start?" asked the man.

"Start at the beginning. If you bore me, I'll tell you to skip on. How's that sound?

III

"All right then," the man said, reaching into his pocket. Both Bill and Al reached for their weapons, but the man held up his hands defensively. "I just want a cigarette. Do you mind?"

"Better give me one," Al said, fishing his lighter out of his pocket and throwing it to the man. He caught it, lit his cigarette, then tossed the crumpled pack of smokes and lighter back to the Marine. He nodded a slight thanks.

"My name's Michael Southern, but my friends call me Mike," he began, looking to Bill and Al, as if waiting for an introduction. Al didn't offer his name in return, and Bill remained just as silent, understanding that he may already have given too much information. "You know all this shit went down almost three years ago, yeah? The whole living dead scenario…"

"I'm vaguely aware of it," Al said, his face stoic. "Go on."

"Well, it happened when me and my friend Steven Hudson were in university, we were both med students. Truth be known, though, we spent more time in our room high on dope or whatever other drugs we could get hold of than we did attending lectures. We just used the whole 'med student' line when we were trying to pick up women."

"I like this guy," Al whispered, just loud enough for the radio mike to pick him up and pass his comments discreetly on to Bill. "He's into the same shit I am."

"Anyway, me and Stevie, we were sitting around one morning, I was on the dope, but he'd decided to go for a morning acid trip. There was a whole load of shit happening outside, but we didn't know what. We had our blinds shut, the light hurt our eyes too much, and we'd sold pretty much everything we had: phones, televisions, computers and radios, just to buy more drugs. Can you believe someone actually *bought* our radio? So anyway, there we were, and the next thing we know, there's a hammering at the door.

"So, me and Stevie leap to our feet, start trying to hide all our shit, we're swallowing half-smoked blunts and flushing tabs of acid when the door bursts in. I'm about ready to piss myself when this happens, and a cop storms the room; he's kitted out with a riot shield, shotguns, pistols, truncheons, an armoured vest, and I'm totally freaking out, thinking its some kind of bust. I throw my hands up in the air, and Stevie retreats into a corner, rocking back and forth, muttering to himself, I mean he goes completely fucking ga-ga."

Michael stood up and started pacing back and forth as he told his tale. Bill could tell by watching him that he was reliving the story within his head as he spoke about it, could see that he was getting carried away with the emotions.

"I'm almost ready to admit to everything, even shit I didn't do, when I recognise the cop, it's Stevies' brother Marcus. And I'm thinking to myself *shit, this ain't no bust!* I mean, Marcus is the main man, he's the dude that gets us almost all of our shit from his contacts; I knew he wouldn't sell us out. He looks at me, then at Stevie, and tells us to pull our shit together. He starts going on about the dead, about how they're attacking people, and I can't do nothing but laugh, I mean it's crazy talk, like Marcus was on a trip of his own. He shook his head, told me he wasn't lying, and that the dead were coming to life. He asked us if we watched the news, but he knew we didn't have a television.

"I'm still thinking the bastard is fucking nuts, but then I realise that he's covered in blood; his uniform is torn up, his riot shield marked with a smudge of blood, and he looks like he's been through the wars. I start thinking that maybe he's telling the truth. He swears blind that it took him almost an hour to travel the mile from the station to the university, and in that space of time he's killed about twenty of the living dead. That's when the craziest thing happens."

Michael stopped telling his tale for a moment, looking from Bill to Al, as if still expecting them to intervene in his tale. Bill motioned with his hand to continue, and Al stared emotionlessly at him.

"Okay, you must've had a fat kid in your class at school? A real fat little shit who always had a permanent sweat stain around their armpits?"

"David Morris," laughed Al, nodding his head enthusiastically. "He was a sweaty little bastard, but no one ever told him about it. That son of a bitch was the star linebacker in the football team, one of the most respected jocks. You didn't speak to him, he spoke to you."

"And you?" asked Bill.

"I was the best damn offensive tackle Jefferson High School had seen in twenty years," Al said, turning to look momentarily at Bill, before returning his attention to Michael once more. "Go on."

"We had this one guy studying medicine, he was in the same lectures as us; Sam Davis, he was immense, and he stunk up the place something not right. You could throw him in a freezer in the middle of December and he'd still sweat like a pig in a slaughterhouse. Anyway, his room stank like a pile of shit at the best of times. The few days leading up to that event, Sam's room was even worse than usual. No one figured they should check on him, and it turned out that he'd been one of the first to go, and left to rot in room while the syndrome worked through his system. He chose that moment to burst on to the scene, storming out his room and attacking Marcus. That cop didn't take no shit from anyone, and just shot Sam, square in the head, dropping him there and then,

"Stevie just went fucking ballistic, he thought he was on some bad acid trip, starting shouting and screaming, rocking back and forth. Marcus tried to calm him down, tried to tell us what was going on, but Stevie was too far gone. Marcus told me to follow him, and leave Stevie on his own. I tried to tell him he couldn't fend for himself, not on the trip he was on, but like I said, Marcus didn't take any shit. He said if I didn't go with him, he wasn't going to come back. I tried to convince him that we should take Stevie, but he just pulled out a pistol and tossed it to him, telling me he could look after himself. Maybe it was the dope in me, or maybe it was the rush of the adrenaline from the whole scenario, but I agreed, and left with Marcus.

"We left Stevie behind in the middle of a shouting fit; then he fired his pistol, and didn't say another word. He'd made his choice, and I'd made mine."

"He didn't take his own brother?" Bill asked. Michael nodded.

"The reason he gave was that Stevie was too much into his drugs, and generally a weak character. I didn't get how he could do that to his own brother. But we went on from the college ground, finding somewhere to hold up for the night, then moving on to a safer location after daylight. The city was going fucking mental, there was shit going on all over; muggings, lootings, rape, the only thing that kept us safe was Marcus' uniform. Even though the whole place had gone to shit, people still held enough respect for the boy in blue.

"After a couple of weeks on the run, as the zombies and gang-bangers seemed to thin each other's numbers out, we eventually found some place to settle down and dig in. Marcus' cop weapons and skills kept us alive most of the time. Then I found out why Marcus had decided to help me out more than his brother.

"Fucking bastard had a hard on for me, tried it on. When I told him no, I didn't fly that way, he practically forced himself on me. I wasn't going to be eaten by no zombie, and I wasn't going to be fucked by a fucking bent cop. So I... I managed to fend him off. Beat the shit out of him, grabbed some weapons and shit, and ran. Next time I seen Marcus, half of his arm was hanging off, both eyes were missing, and his stomach had been torn open. I happily put that bastard out of his misery, then found this place to live in. I've been protecting it from the dead shits for almost two years now."

"That's pretty intense," said Al, nodding and scratching his beard as he mulled the story over. Bill was certainly convinced by the story, the man had told the tale with too much emotion for it to be a fake. "Fuckin' A, that's a hell of a story."

"I found those things, the claymores, in the back of a van near the old police station. There were a couple of dead soldiers around the van, but none of their weapons had any bullets."

"Time's pushing on," Al said, looking at the readout on his watch. "We should probably head back now, if we're not wanting to travel in the dark."

"The snow's clearing up," Bill said, looking over his shoulder out the window behind him. "We might have a clear drive home."

"Good," Al said with a smile, then looked to Michael. "You want to come with us?"

Bill seemed taken aback just as much as Michael.

"Really?" they both asked in unison. Al nodded.

"Shit, I'm not going to leave you here. Grab whatever you want to take and we'll get back."

"Where to?" asked Michael. "How many are there? I've looked on maps for likely places where survivors would gather, but I couldn't see any..."

"Our little base doesn't appear on any maps available to you civvies. It's a military complex, and there's about...." Al paused as he counted up on his fingers, mouthing names as he went. "About eleven people. Twelve including you."

Michael clambered to his feet and started to make his way around the room, gathering weapons and personal artefacts as he went.

"Don't forget those issues of Minx," laughed Al as he watched the young man work his way around the rooms.

"I won't," he replied as he grabbed a satchel and started to load it up. "You can have them all, if you want. Except issue two hundred and seventy three. I want to keep that one."

Al worked his way down the pile, pulling out the issue Michael had mentioned, and smiled to himself while nodding his head, approving of the cover and the contents within. "Redhead special," he said with a grin. "Nice, very nice. Now hurry up, we don't want to spend much more time here."

The hummer ground to a halt within the confines of the army base, Al parking the vehicle in the cone of light cast down on to the ground by one of the overhead spotlights and hauling himself out the vehicle. Bill followed, then motioned for Michael to follow him.

"This is your place?" he asked in awe, turning around on the spot to take in all the details of the base. "It's well defended. Makes my place look very crude."

"This is our home," confirmed Al. "It's well away from the hustle and bustle of city life. We've got machineguns, mines and mortars lining the base. Nothing could get to us without us knowing. We're well dug-in, there ain't no bastard's getting in here."

"That's good to know," Michael said with a grin. "I can finally sleep with both eyes shut."

"I've been there," Al said with a laugh, clapping Michael on his back. "Back in Brazil, we had to sleep with *both* eyes open, the Bebops there were so damn tricky. Man, have I got some stories I could tell you."

Bill shook his head. Although he wasn't entirely sure about Al letting the man return to the fort with them, the Marine seemed to genuinely like Michael, and looked pleased to have another person to tell his stories to. Bill started to unload the contents from the rear of the vehicle, but Al stopped him, shaking his head.

"That shit can wait until tomorrow, kid. What say we make our way over to the bar, get us a little down time before Garth calls for last orders."

"There's a bar here?" asked Michael, awestruck as he continued to stare at the exterior of the base. "This place is fucking awesome!"

Al grinned as he led the way, pausing only to return to the vehicle and grabbing the larger of the sacks from the back of the vehicle, slinging it over his shoulder.

The trio arrived at the entrance to the base, and they crossed the threshold, shaking off the snow and removing their coats, throwing them on any hooks available to allow them to dry off. Moving towards the staircase, Bill smiled to himself as he heard Michael saying 'awesome' over and over again. From the top of the stairs, they could hear music and laughter coming from the bar on the third level down, and it sounded like everyone was in the bar, unwinding after a hard days work. They made their way down the stairs, manhandling the bag of presents between Bill and Al until they emerged in the mess hall.

Placing a number of large tables on their side and reinforcing them with wooden beams and crates, effectively making a room within a room, Garth and Sylvester had sectioned off the corner of the room before bringing in a number of barrels of wine and comfortable seats that had been kept in storage. Al took the lead into the hall, weaving between the tables that remained bolted to the floor and laughing loudly as he approached. Sarah rushed out to greet him, a wide smile spread across her face, and she lunged at him, wrapping her arms around him.

"Missed you," she said. "Where you been?"

"Just out," Al smiled, setting his sack down on the ground. "Isn't it late for you to be up?"

"Dad said I could wait up for you coming back. What you got there?"

"Just stuff," Al said with a grin, lifting the girl up on to his shoulders and motioning to Bill to bring the bag. He did as he was told, following Al into the drinking area with Michael in close pursuit. "Guess who's back in town!" bellowed the loud Marine, putting Sarah down and stepping aside to hold Pam as she approached, kissing her lightly on the forehead. "Is everyone here?"

"Cindy's in bed," Steve announced, summoning Sarah back to her seat and the watered down wine she had been allowed for the night. "She's not feeling too well."

"What about Red?" Al asked, pulling up a seat beside Pam and helping himself to her drink. "Where's she at?"

"Tara had some work to catch up on," Garth said, somewhat disheartened by that. It seemed to Bill that he was carrying a flame for the young woman, but he didn't bring it up with him. Even if he did broach the subject, no one could say what the ex-driver of the group would come up with in his defence, even if it were true. After all, it was Garth's nature to shy away from any and all conflict.

"Aren't you going to introduce us to your new friend?" asked Clive, motioning towards the man still standing in the doorway of the bar area. Bill stepped aside, and Michael took a tentative step forwards, nodding casually to everyone.

"Yeah, why not," Al said, standing up and laying a hand on Michael's shoulder. "This here is Michael, we found him out in the city we were looking at. Michael was a med student and pothead before the rise. I guess he could start looking into taking over the role of the bitch in the medical bay. Which means she can start looking at producing more alcohol, maybe a little tobacco..."

"In your dreams," Angel said. "If I get a little more time to myself, I'll spend it sleeping."

"Screwing the kid, more like it. Anyway, we grabbed a few supplies while we were out, we got some boxes and bags sitting in the hummer we can unload in the morning. I also went to the liberty of getting a few luxuries. Like this."

Al reached into the bag on the floor, rummaged around, and produced a large teddy bear, immaculate in all ways apart from the one button eye that was a little loose. He handed it over to

Sarah; her face lit up as her hands wrapped around the limbs of the toy. She hugged Al, showing her gratitude, then rushed over and presented it to Steve, who smiled and nodded to Al by way of thanks, before ushering her back towards the entrance to the bar. "It's getting late for little girls to be staying up, lets get you back to your mum. You can show her your new toy."

"I love it," she said, grinning and hugging Al again as she walked by.

"What're you going to call it, honey?" asked Pam, stroking the girls hair as she held the Marine tight.

"I think I'll call him Mother Fucker. You call a lot of things that don't you?"

Al laughed aloud, clutching his stomach as he tried to control his chuckles, then shook his head as he caught a glimpse of Steve's expression, both stern and shocked.

"That's one of those words only the adults can use. Call it something else, something nice."

"Cole," she said. "After you."

"That's better," Steve said, pushing her out the drinking area, then he turned to look at the Marine before leaving.

"Thanks, Al. I know what you're trying to do. Bring back Christmas for her. "

"I did it for all of us," Al said, "There's a little something for us all in there. But if you want to get Sarah to bed, I'll keep yours and Cindy's gifts until tomorrow."

"Thanks," he said, shaking Al's hand then pulled him closer, drawing his face closer to his own. "And stop using that filthy language around my daughter. You're the one she gets it from."

"Aye-aye, sir!" Al said, saluting sharply as Steve relinquished his grip. Bill knew enough about Al to know he was being sarcastic, but Steve seemed to think he had gotten his message across, and left the room, heading for their room. "We may as well wait until tomorrow, hand out everyone's together. We'll make a proper day of it. A real Christmas for us all to celebrate."

"I'll whip up a meal for us all," said Garth with a grin. "There's some dehydrated Soya in the kitchen still, I'll whip up a batch and make a dinner. Sly can make some decorations with the spare wiring we have."

"I can fetch down one of the larger plants from the greenhouse," Angel said with a grin. "It's no Christmas tree, but it could work, at a push."

With that, the room started buzzing with suggestions and ideas for the festivities, and Al retired to his favourite corner booth, pulling Bill down with him and helping himself to a tankard of wine.

"See, I told you this was a good idea. We're fucking heroes, kid. Heroes; the guys who brought back Christmas. We're like Santa."

"I knew there was a soft heart under that cold exterior," Pam said, sitting down beside them and laying her head down on Al's shoulder. "You're just a great big teddy bear yourself, aren't you?"

"That's the kind of talk we keep for private," Al murmured, smiling weakly at Bill, trying to dismiss the comment.

"Sarah really likes you," Bill said, watching his friends on the other side of the room as they continued to make their plans, their spirits soaring high as they built up each other's expectation. Michael tried to join in, though he seemed to be flagging, obviously exhausted from his time alone in the infested cities. "When can we expect to see a Colebrook Junior running around the base?"

Al didn't say anything, simply laughed off the remark. "Michael looks like he could do with an early night. We don't really have anywhere ready for him to sleep."

"He can take my room," Bill said. "I'll keep an eye on things here."

"You mean you'll go off and spend the night in the bitch's room, I'm not stupid."

"No, but you're a pain in the arse, Al. I'll tell Michael the news."

Bill rose to his feet then stopped, leaning over closer to Al and speaking in a lower tone of voice. "You sure this is a good idea? I mean we don't know that much about him…"

"You're still looking for trouble where there is none," Al shook his head. "Poor bastard's been out on his own for two years. He's not acting like your typical nutcase, hasn't got a god complex and isn't trying to make cups of tea out of blood and eyeballs. Trust me, the guy seems legit. If it makes you feel any better, I'll turn on the camera in your room and keep an eye on him all night."

"There's cameras in our rooms?" Bill asked, suddenly feeling violated.

"I disabled them years ago," Al shook his head, then leaned in closer, winking knowingly to him. "Well, most of them."

"Pervert," Bill muttered, leaving Al and Pam and making his way across the room to Michael, who was almost dozing even with the celebration and excitement around him. Bill tapped him on the shoulder, jerking him awake, and he glared at him with bleary eyes, taking a few minutes to work out where he was.

"You can spend the night in my room, if you want," Bill offered. "It's on the bottom floor, the door's marked. I can take you down there, if you want…"

"It's okay," Michael said, hauling himself to his feet. "You talk with your friends, plan this all out. I'll make my own way there, don't worry."

"Bottom floor," Bill said again, "Third door on the left, it's got my name written on it."

"Thanks, Bill," Michael said. "I'll find my way, don't worry about me."

With that, Michael made his way out the bar area.

"What do you think of the new guy?" asked Bill as he watched Michael vanish down the stairs.

"Seems decent enough. Just like everyone here, he's been through some shit, suffered some loss."

"Like what?" asked Garth, his interest perked slightly as he looked up from the hastily drawn plan he'd scribbled on the back of a napkin. It depicted a Christmas tree, surrounded by about twenty people. Bill leaned over, looked at the plan and scratched his head.

"He lost family, friends, friends' brothers… what the hell is that you've done there?"

"A Christmas scene," Garth said, proudly. Can't you tell?"

"Yeah. How many people *are* there around the tree?"

"It's just a rough plan. And besides, those three circles are me," he said, patting his stomach and smiling. "I've added a little beef while I've been sitting around here playing barkeep."

"Beef," scoffed Al. "There's a whole fucking cow on you."

"Hey," Garth said defensively. "That's just more of me to love."

"Ain't enough love in the world for you, buddy," Al said, laughing as he grabbed a jug of wine and poured himself a very generous helping. "Now, let's talk Christmas."

Tara sat in her room alone, studying the figures on her computer terminal as she went over them for the third time that night. There were a lot of things that didn't make any sense to her, one of them being the one hundred gallons of petrol that was missing from the central storage tank. She knew from Pam that the loud-mouthed Marine had been spending a lot of time in the armoury, and that he'd used up all the wood that had been stored on site for construction purposes a long time ago; yet he'd been working on his little projects for months. Was it possible that his indulgence in his hobby had led to him siphoning off petrol and leaving the base to find himself fresh supplies of wood? More than likely he was using it for more perimeter defences. Still, there was doubt in Tara's mind.

Al *had* been the one who had imposed a ban on leaving the base. But, his exact words had been that no inexperienced people were to leave the base. He was extraordinarily bigheaded, and the most arrogant person she had ever met. And in her line of work, she had come across a lot of arrogant people. Al obviously thought that he was one of the most experienced men in the base, and so thought that he was exempt from the ban he had imposed.

And after Pam had told her he and Bill had left the base in the hummer that very day to head into one of the towns, her suspicions were confirmed. But one hundred gallons was still a lot to go through,

Unless he's been using the fuel for his power tools.

Her mind made up, she decided to write off the additional consumption as Al's doing, and vowed she would have a word with him in the morning. Or at least, get Pam to pass the message on; catching Al between his room and the armoury was nothing short of a miracle, and he rarely answered the door to anyone while he was working.

Both food and water were holding out okay for the moment, too. Though the frozen supplies of meat and vegetables were steadily diminishing and the giant freezer in the kitchen was gradually getting more and more empty, one of the storage rooms still held a countless supply of dehydrated food rations. Though Al had swore he wouldn't touch them again, Tara would have to make sure he would, when the time came. With the help of Pam's persuasion, she was sure they would be able to convince him to bite the bullet.

"Can't expect to live like royalty forever," Tara sighed as she flicked through the pages of the spreadsheet on the terminal. "Power consumption's normal. Ammunition okay, Garth and Sly have filled in their reports about our vehicles…"

Tara smiled to herself. She liked to keep the base records up to date and as accurate as possible, especially after the state she'd found them when they had first arrived. Though the Marines may have been responsible for the safety of the law-abiding citizens of the world, they couldn't keep records to save their lives.

It was just as well, she thought to herself. Having something to keep her mind occupied meant she could forget about what had happened to the world around her. Or at least, *try* to forget about it.

She sat back from her screen, rubbing her eyes and checking the digital clock on the small table beside her bed. It was late, but despite the sun rising in a few hours, she knew that her friends would be in the bar for a long time yet. She would normally consider heading up to there herself, but she felt like she'd been burning the candle at both ends recently, and retired to her bed, stripping off the thick jumper and combat trousers she wore and slipping into the oversized T-shirt she slept in. She picked up the thick paperback book she had found in one of the footlockers, found the page she was up to, and read through a couple of lines before drifting off to sleep.

She awoke when she heard heavy footsteps outside in the corridor, and assumed that her friends had returned from the bar, though the glowing readout on the digital clock suggested otherwise: she had only been asleep for ten minutes, but it sounded like Bill had returned early. Maybe the expedition had taken it out of him, and he needed an early night. She waited for a few moments, listening to him fumbling with the door to his room, as if he'd forgotten how to open it, though he was more than likely drunk. She heard the door open, but not shut, as if he'd entered to retrieve something before returning to the bar. She tried to turn over and go back to sleep, but his heavy footsteps and thumping on the door had stirred her too much; she was now wide-awake.

"Guess a drink can't do any harm," she muttered, grabbing her trousers and stumbling over to the door, throwing the book down on the bed. She opened the door, and peered into the open room opposite hers. A figure seemed to be shifting around in the shadows within, moving from desk, to drawers, to bed, obviously searching for something.

"You woke me up, Bill," she announced, closing the door behind her with a soft click. He froze, as if deciding what to do next. "You heading back up to the bar? I might join you all after all."

"Bill's still in the bar," the figure announced, standing up straight and turning around to face Tara. His voice didn't belong to any of her friends, but it was strangely familiar. "How've you been, Scarlet?"

Tara felt the blood drain from her face. Al had taken to calling her Red, which she hadn't minded; but only one man had ever called her Scarlet; a man she had thought she'd never see again, and was sure had died. She fumbled blindly for the door behind her, but the doorknob slipped through her sweating fingers, and she felt her legs weaken and buckle beneath her. She slumped to the floor, shaking her head, and watching in terror as the man advanced on her, stepping out the shadows and into the light of the main corridor. Beneath the woollen hat the man wore, she could see curls of dark brown hair, and his eyes glared hungrily at her from beneath the shadows of his low brow. An evil smile spread across his face as he towered over her while she tried to frantically scramble across the floor away from him.

"Well hey there, bitch. Betcha never thought you'd see me again. I never dreamed I'd see you again, yet here you are."

He reached down, grabbed Tara by the hair and heaved her up to her feet before throwing her into Bill's open room. She landed roughly on the bed, almost tumbling over on to the floor on the other side.

Mikey, she thought, uncertain as to how he was even here. He'd been on of the men who had raped her on several occasions in the lair of the Messiah, but she'd thought he had perished in the explosions, or the Rot attacks after. She felt panic well up inside her, the sheer terror of the situation paralysing both her limbs and vocal chords as Mikey advanced on her, slamming the door behind him and wedging a chair up against it.

"I fucked you every night for weeks," he hissed, pulling off his woollen hat and flinging it across the room. "But you never felt it, you and your bitch friends were always off your face on drugs; I'm surprised you can even remember me…"

"How could I ever forget?" Tara finally managed to say, finding enough strength in herself to lash out with her hand, tearing open the skin on Mikey's face with her nails. He stopped his advance and wiped the fresh blood from his cheek, licking it and grinning to himself.

"See, this is the kind of shit I missed out on while you were stoned. This is one of the things I love about you redheads; you're so fuckin' *fiery*," he said, sending Tara sprawling with a vicious backhand that cut her lip open. "No matter how many times I've had you, this'll be the *first* time you've felt it…"

He pinned her down, wrestling with her and tearing her T-shirt from her and smiling as she managed to get a powerful kick to his ribs. Although it was damaging, and she was sure she heard a rib crack, it didn't affect him; in fact, it only seemed to intensify his attack. She opened her mouth to scream, but Mikey punched her once in the gut, then again in the mouth; she felt her jaw crack with the blow, and could taste the bitter taste of blood and the salty tang of tears in her mouth as she tried to catch her breath.

"And I promise, it'll be the last fucking thing you feel."

IV

The ordeal lasted for almost two hours, but despite the fighting, the bruises and the bloodshed, Mikey felt contented. He lay in the bed beside the limp form of Tara, her panting, wilting form surrounded by pools of cooling blood; her cries of agony had subsided a long time ago, and Mikey thought he had killed her during his performance. Only the ragged breathing and sporadic rising and falling of her mutilated chest gave any indication that she was still alive. He reached over, roughly grabbed her broken wrist, and tried to find her pulse. It was there, but it was very weak; she probably had about thirty minutes left before she slipped away, maybe less.

"It's been real special," he said, rolling off the dishevelled bed and replacing the items of clothing that he had taken off during the struggle. Although there had been other women in the past three years or so, none had sported the same shock of red hair the former prisoner of the Messiah had. And Mikey loved a redhead.

He gathered his thoughts, took a last lingering look at the beaten and defeated form of Tara on the bed, and left the room, flicking off the light and cautiously heading for the staircase, moving as quick as he could.

He had quickly been welcomed into the group, and left to wander alone far quicker. Such a sloppy approach to life meant that whatever fate befell them, they deserved it, and they had invited their own destruction; such were the teachings he followed.

On his way down the lower levels, he had passed through a floor marked as the control centre, and had tried to have a look around there, but most of the doors had been locked up: in fact, the only doors not locked had belonged to small storage cupboards filled with reels of insulted wiring and pieces of scrap metal. Mikey had figured out that Bill was pretty high up in the pecking order, and if anyone had keys to the control rooms, either he or the black man would have them. He had hit lucky when Bill suggested that he take his room, and even luckier when Tara, one of the Messiah's dancers, had stumbled across him. Even thinking about her got him aroused, and he was so tempted to head back to the room for one more assault on the woman, but he held back on his urges. Maybe once he'd completed his mission, he would return to the sanctity of the room and the spoiled flower that lay decimated on the bed.

He'd found the key in the room before he'd been disturbed, and had it in his grasp as he climbed the staircase on to the command level, trying it in each door as he went. He finally found the door the key belonged to, and it opened up into a room filled with blinking switches, flashing dials and various different monitor screens showing pictures from security cameras around the base. He wandered into the room, sat down on one of the padded chairs, and ran his hands along the multitude of controls at his dispense, trying to find the controls he needed.

Just as he found what he needed and activated the controls, he heard a commotion from the lower levels of the base.

"Shit," he muttered, twisting dials to the settings he had memorised. "I have to move quick."

Al swaggered down the hallway towards his room, leaning heavily on Pam as they went. He'd had a lot to drink, more than usual, but it was okay because he knew that he could sleep in as late as he needed.

"Soon as everyone's awake, we have our own belated Christmas," he slurred, leaning away from Pam and slamming into the wall for a moment. He laughed to himself and pushed off, latching on to Pam once more. "Make sure you wake me up."

"Aren't you getting up to help get prepared?" she asked, half-pulling the Marine down the hallway.

"Fuck that," he muttered, plucking a cigarette from one of his pockets. Pam took it out of his mouth before he could light it, and he shook his head despondently. "Jesus, I only wanted one. Where was I? Oh yeah, I ain't helping you lot decorate. I was the dumb bastard who risked his ass for the presents. Some other dumb shit can do that."

He stumbled past the open entrance to Bill's room, and stopped, pressing his finger up against his lips. "Don't wake our guest," he whispered loudly.

"Wonder why he didn't shut the door," Pam thought aloud. Al shrugged his shoulders, looking into the darkness.

"Dumb son of a bitch can't use a door, but at least he's capable of using a bed," he observed.

"He looks exhausted," Pam said, pausing to lean into the room. She sniffed at the air and wrinkled her nose at the miasma of smells that lingered in the darkened room. "Smells a little off in there."

Al sniffed the air himself and took a step into the room.

"Something's wrong here," Al said, sobering up and fumbling for the light switch. He flicked the switch, and froze in horror as the saw the grizzly apparition lying on the bed. Al balked, feeling his gorge rise as he found himself unable to tear his eyes away from the prone figure on the bed.

Pam gagged, turning away from the vision of her battered and bloody friend lying naked on the bed, while Al rushed forwards, gently draping a sheet over her form and resting his finger on her neck, finding a weak pulse. She moaned in pain, but didn't try to pull away from the agonising contact.

"What the fuck happened here?" asked Al, but he didn't need an answer. It was obvious that the new person had been responsible for the hideous attack, and it was Al's fault the man was roaming free in the base. He could do the same thing to anyone in the base.

"Pam, get Angel," Al yelled, stepping back from Tara. Pam made no attempt to move, simply stared at the flaccid form on the bed. Al looked over his shoulder and shouted again, this time setting her off into action while he stayed behind with Tara. She tried to speak, but her swollen and bloodied mouth could barely make any coherent words. Crimson saliva trickled down her lips and pooled on the pillow around her and her eyes fluttered wildly as she tried to communicate with Al.

"It's okay, Red," Al said, trying his best to keep his normally loud voice to a low and soothing level. "Pam's gone to get help, don't talk."

After what seemed like hours, people began to pour into the room, Angel in the lead. She knelt by the bed beside Al, appraising Tara, and leaned in closer, whispering to Al.

"She doesn't look good. Broken bones, cuts, bruises... she's had a brutal beating, what happened?"

"What happened?" demanded Garth, echoing the question as he stumbled into the room, pushing people aside and staring slack-jawed at the beaten woman.

"Michael," Al said simply, without looking up from his fallen friend. "It was Michael."

"What?" Garth shouted. "The new guy? You bring in a complete stranger, set him free in our home without knowing anything about him, and he does this?"

Garth made his way over to Al, lifted him up by his collar, and pushed him against the wall. "This is your fault," he said. "This is all your fucking fault."

"It's *our* fault," Bill said, pulling Garth away from Al. "*We* brought him here. Where is he now?"

Everyone present shook their heads, looking to one another for the answer.

"Spread out," Al said, pushing away Garth and moving towards the door. "Pam, you and Angel stay with Tara. Stay in pairs. This fucker is one mental fucking psychopath; don't take any chances, if you get the opportunity, shoot the bastard in the stomach. No one messes with my friends and lives."

Nobody made a move to leave the room, each person had their gaze fixed on Tara and the two women tending to her. Al hissed and barged through the crowd, pulling his Desert Eagle from his holster and stalking off towards the stairwell.

"Check the rooms and the armoury," he called back over his shoulder. "Make sure it's all secured."

If I had infiltrated someone's base, where would I go first? He thought to himself as he reached the foot of the staircase. *Providing I had no weapons, it would be the armoury. But I always have a weapon... so I guess I'd try to get in touch with anyone I had waiting as backup...*

"Son of a bitch," he said, slipping his radio headset on and flicking it to an all-channel broadcast. "I need backup at the command deck. Now."

He stormed up the stairs, peeling off on the command level and working his way through the tight corridor towards the main corridor, his hand sweating as it coiled around the butt of his handgun, different thoughts swirling through his mind as he moved.

Garth had been right about this whole ordeal being his fault. How could he have been so naive? To invite an unknown into *his* own town, then send him off on his own without an escort? There was no way he could have known Michael was a rapist, but he shouldn't have been so trusting. Now, one of his friends had been attacked. And it was his fault. Regardless of what Bill had said, it *was* his fault; Al was in charge, in his eyes. He was the leader. He had become sloppy in his break from action, and in doing so he had endangered his people.

As he approached the main control room, he could hear Michael talking in a low voice, proving Al right: the sneaky bastard had others waiting outside the city wall.

He stormed into the command centre, his gun raised, and he fired two single shots: one punched through the radio console the man was operating, the second through his spine and splashing the controls with his spilled blood. The man slumped to the floor, his spinal column severed and his enlarged wound pumping blood and bile. His radio transmission ended in a blood-curdling scream as he writhed from side to side in agony, clutching his wound and trying to plug it with his fingers.

"Who the fuck are you? What kind of fucking monster are you?"

The man managed a sadistic grin, despite the pain that wracked his body, and spat towards Al, though didn't say a word. Al knelt down on the floor, pushing the smoking muzzle of his handgun into the injury and rolling the weapon around within the cavernous gunshot wound

"What did you do to Red?"

"Have you… you ever fucked a redhead?" the man managed, a lopsided grin spreading across his lips for a second before his look of pain returned. "Fiery little bitches..."

"Who've you spoken to?" he asked, nodding towards the smoking ruins of the radio console. The man laughed softly and coughed up some blood. He tried to wipe his mouth with the back of his sleeve, but couldn't move his arms.

"Answer me," demanded Al, levelling off his weapon and loosing a third round into the man's shoulder. He clenched his teeth in pain, howling and looking towards the ceiling as he tried to fight back the agony.

"Who," Al growled though gritted teeth, "Who were you talking to?"

"Behold…" hissed the man. "Behold he cometh with clouds; and every eye shall see him, and they also which pierced him: and all kindreds of the earth shall wail because of him."

"What the hell are you talking about?" Al said, firing two more shots into the man: one into the other shoulder, another into his already shredded gut.

"He… he who is… is Alpha and O-o-omega…"

"He who is Alpha and Omega," announced Clive as he strolled into the command room, clutching his bible in one hand and a large automatic handgun in the other. "The beginning and the ending, saith the lord, which is, and which was, and which is to come, the Almighty."

"Heathen," hissed Mikey through gritted teeth. Clive lifted his weapon and fired point-blank into his face.

"That's right," he muttered. "Tell that to Saint Peter at the Pearly Gates, see what he thinks about that."

"You killed him," muttered Al, stunned at the fact the priest had killed him. "I didn't find anything out about him; who he was, who he'd called on the radio."

"Tara managed to say a couple of things before she…" Clive looked down at his feet. "Before she passed on: Mikey... and Messiah."

XX
LORD OF THE DEAD

"There's nothing that can fight this scourge: no walls to keep you safe, no magic serum to stop the spread. We learned that too late…"

I

The confines of the ruined chamber he sat in were dark and damp, lit poorly by large metal braziers filled with glowing embers that stood in each corner of the room. The bed in the centre of the room had once been very ornate, the walls once covered with thick velvet drapes; now, the room was nothing but a wreck, with a mattress that reeked of stale smoke and sex, and tattered curtains that covered part of the stone wall. It was humble surroundings, which he could have improved, but he found the modest room comforting.

He lay back on the bed, hands behind his head, while two young women embraced him, one on either side. Both girls were exhausted from their evening performance, but he could not sleep. His mind lazily wandered back through time, to his first encounter with a girl, and he smiled at the warm memories as they washed across him.

She had been older than him, almost three years his senior, but at thirteen years old he had been abnormally strong and unusually well built; many a girl had cast him an admiring glance, but none had interested him until he saw this young vision of Venus, with golden blonde hair and soft, supple curves. The first time they had come together held the sweetest memories for him, though there had been many times in that one night, each as special as the last.

In the darkness of the woods in the dead of night, no one would be able to stumble across them as their bodies became one; no one had been able to see the two adolescents in the throes of passion, nor had they been able to see the beatings. No one had heard the sound of leather slapping against naked flesh, of muffled moans of agony and ecstasy, or flesh tearing and ripping. No one had seen the girl after she had been beaten unconscious, mutilated, and then burned alive. With the teeth of the smoking corpse bashed in with a rock to eliminate identifying the body through dental records, even if the body *was* found, no one would have known who it was, or who she'd been with last.

And she had only been the first. There were so many that no one knew about. So many that no one would *ever* know about.

The pleasant memories lulled him with a soothing and warming sensation, and he gradually felt himself slipping into a well-deserved sleep. Just as he drifted off, and the first moments of a dream began to play through his head, a hammering at the door roused him.

"Enter," he snarled, raising himself from the bed so he was sitting, facing the doorway. The two women stirred and pushed themselves away from the waking man, their chains clattering against one another as they moved. The door slid to one side, and a man dressed in a long flowing leather coat strode into the room. The guard looked towards the man sitting on the bed, but not directly at him. He nodded to himself, knowing why. All under his guiding hand feared the power he wielded, and the touch of God that had left his visage a permanent scar as reminder of this power.

"We have word from one of the scouts, my lord," the guard announced, carefully choosing his words.

"And?" he asked. If this man had disturbed his slumber, he would have to deal with him in the strictest way possible.

"Saint Michael; he said he had found a small band of people living in a military base."

"Military?" he mused as he leaned forwards, his fingers interlocking as he held his hands together. "A military base would certainly help build our army for our eventual assault on those that have imprisoned us." As with most of his chosen saints, Michael had been sent on a pilgrimage across the country to scout for any other survivors, and if necessary, convert their religion to see things his way. So far, there had been several small pockets of survivors that had been encountered, and a few had turned; those that hadn't had been smote at his command.

The guard nodded solemnly, but he seemed as if there was something else he wanted to say. He shuffled uneasily, looking at his feet uncomfortably.

"Is there anything else?"

"His transmission was cut short, but… he said the group contained people he recognised. Heathens."

Pushing the women from the bed, the man in charge rose to his feet, striding across the room and picking up the leather cloak that hung from one of the hooks on the wall. He paused mid-stride, cocking an eyebrow and looking at the guard.

"Saint Michael said that it was those that were responsible for the destruction of our church he had found. Those that killed our Lord."

"Impossible," he spat, turning on the guard. "I was told we had recovered their vehicle from a battleground, that they had been slaughtered…" He stormed over to the guard and slipped his sidearm out from his holster, then pressed the muzzle against the guard's stomach and fired three times. Blood sprayed the wall behind him, and he fell to the floor, coughing and moaning while he lay on the floor. "Evidently, you were wrong."

The women around the bed squealed and backed away from the explosion of violence, but remained reasonably calm.

"Shut up," he screamed, tracing the pits and ridges of his scared face with the tips of his fingers, following the damaged flesh down his left arm and chest, and stopped at his blackened and charred fingers. He had lost one of them, his middle finger, which had been removed at the first knuckle. Though he had been badly damaged in an explosion, almost to the point where he had died, he had risen again: just as he had before.

Frank Steele – The Messiah - retrieved his shroud and laid it over his head, an evil grin spreading across his mouth as he headed towards the opened doorway, just as a trio of armed guards ran down the corridor, alerted by the sounds of the gunfire.

"Prepare the vehicles," he demanded, his fingers lingering on the deepest recesses of his scar tissue. "We're going on a crusade. He that killeth with the sword must be killed by the sword."

"Amen," murmured the guards, bowing their heads before running off. The Messiah grabbed the last man to turn, motioning towards the two women left in his room.

"The journey will be long. Kill the women before we leave."

"Lord?"

"There are more where we are going. Seraphim, my angels that have fallen from grace. They need to be brought back into my fold. Kill those women in there, and load up the meat wagons."

The guard nodded, bowed, then slowly strolled into the bedroom of the Messiah, drawing his sidearm and firing twice, silencing the screaming women.

I could have easily killed them myself, he thought to himself. It had been a long time since he had killed a woman with his hands, and twice as long since he had taken on two at once. Women were like wild animals; if they were cornered, they could put up quite a fight. He enjoyed a challenge every now and then.

Maybe I'll be able to play with the Seraphim for a while…

"Get your gear," Al hissed, pushing Bill aside and running down the staircase, leaving him alone with Clive and the dead body of Michael.

"What's going on?" Bill called after the Marine. He'd been present while Tara had passed on, though not close enough to hear her final words. Only Clive, who had been performing the last rites, had heard her. As soon as she had passed, he had stormed out of the room, and Bill had only managed to catch up as the sound of multiple gunshots had echoed out of existence. Now, Michael was dead, Al seemed to be in a state of near panic, and Clive was the man holding the smoking gun.

"What's going on?" he repeated, this time to Clive. The priest looked at him, then at the dead body, motioning towards it with the weapon he held.

"That was Mikey."

"That's familiar," confessed Bill, peering at the body. It was riddled with bullets, and it was clear that although Al had taken the time to shoot him in the less vital areas, Clive had ended his existence swiftly. "Can't think where from…"

"The self-appointed Messiah," Clive said, his words sending shivers down Bill's spine. "He was one of his men."

"Son of a bitch," hissed Bill.

"It gets better," Clive said, motioning towards the smouldering heap that was the radio. "Al said he was using the radio. That's only something that you do if you've got friends you need to talk to."

"Fuck," whispered Bill. "Do we know how many?"

Clive shook his head glumly.

"Just before I… just before he died, he was quoting lines from the bible. From the Book of Revelation."

"Just like the Messiah," Bill said, scratching his head. "Do you think that… you know?"

"I don't know. We saw him thrown from an explosion, his prison coming down around him, with the hollow men storming his hall, but... I guess it's possible that he's still alive."

"Do you think he's told them where we are?"

"I do," Clive said with a gentle nod. "That's why Al wants us to gather our gear."

"To prepare to fight them?"

"I think he's thinking more along the lines of abandoning the base altogether."

Bill breathed in sharply; if Al was considering abandoning the base, it had to be bad. He slipped his folded headset out from one of his pockets and clipped it over his ear, clicking it on as he did so.

"What's going on Al?"

"Grab whatever shit you want to keep and throw it in *The Pride of Colebrook*, tell everyone else to do the same; then grab your weapons and meet me up top, double-time."

"We're leaving the base?"

"We're preparing for it, if it comes to that."

Bill slapped Clive on his shoulder in a sign of camaraderie, then rushed for the ground level above him, remembering all his weapons had been left in the hummer. He thundered up the stairs and slipped on his jacket before bursting out into the middle of a snowstorm. He waded through the flurry towards the vehicle, heaved open the door and grabbed the shotgun and assault rifle that lay on the back seat, then looked around the courtyard. He pressed the headset close to his ear, hunching over to muffle the wind from his microphone as he tried to reach Al.

"Where are you?"

"Coming up to ground level now," Al said, his breathing laboured as he ran. Bill turned to face the entrance to the underground complex, and watched as Al jogged across the annex, lugging an oversized rifle almost the size of Bill. Al showed no signs of joviality; he was all business. It had been a long time since Bill had seen him like this.

"Angel's coming up here soon as she gets a rifle from the armoury," he said, looking to the corners of the compound, then lifting his gaze to the elevated guard posts before continuing, "So's Sly. Clive and Garth are going to get our vehicle loaded up, and Pam's helping our resident family prepare to move Cindy."

Bill found it slightly discomforting that Al had used everyone's real names, and not the nicknames he had christened everyone with. "Do you think Steele's really alive?"

"I don't know," he said, shrugging his shoulders and quickly regaining his normal demeanour. "Preacher-man managed to wipe out the guy before he could tell us anything."

"Do you think he honestly would have told us if we took him alive?"

"No," confessed Al, slogging through the snow that covered the ground and heading towards one of the corner units of the base. "He wouldn't have said a word, but I'd have enjoyed torturing the sick fucker. Climb that corner unit and keep an eye out. I don't know which direction they'll be coming from."

"You're convinced they're coming?"

"Wouldn't you?" asked Al, his voice trailing off, then picking up on the radio headset as he worked his way up the elevated outpost. "If you had been the victim of an attempted bombing and left to die in the midst of a swarm of Rots, wouldn't *you* want revenge on the people responsible?"

"I guess," muttered Bill, watching as Angel and Sylvester arrived on the scene, each carrying different rifles. Sylvester rushed to one of the three unmanned corner units, while Angel lingered beside Bill, a look of uncertainty on her pale face.

"You okay?"

She shook her head slowly. "Not by a long shot. Tara's gone... I guess I feel a little..."

"Numb? Me too," said Bill, nodding his head in unison with Angel. "It doesn't seem real..."

"Like the last couple of years didn't even happen, I know."

"If it makes you feel any better," Al's voice crackled over the radio, "The son of a bitch suffered before Clive blasted his brains out."

"You think he's still out there? The Messiah?"

"For the sake of all of us, I hope not," Bill said, stepping forwards and wrapping a comforting arm around Angel and squeezing her shoulder. He understood her fears, knowing what had happened to her in the private chambers of the Messiah. "I won't let it happen again; not to you or anyone else here."

But I failed Tara already tonight, he thought glumly.

Angel didn't say anything, just nodded and sniffed, wiping the back of her sleeve across her eyes.

"When you two have a minute," hissed Al, waving from his vantage point, "We need cover up here. Kid, you take the Northern corner, the bitch can take the South."

Bill nodded, motioned for Angel to head towards her designated corner, then rushed to his own, climbing the ladder affixed to the side of the concrete base unit, then moving on to the raised command post. The metal was ice cold beneath his skin, and he felt his flesh stick to the ladder as he clambered up. He swore beneath his breath as he went, feeling layers of skin peel away as he left them attached to the rungs.

"Now what?" asked Angel as Bill looked over his shoulder and saw her waiting in position in her watchtower. He turned his attention back towards the expanse of snow out in the distance, peering though the falling snow flecked his vista.

"We just wait," said Al. "The kid's been doing that ever since coming here, expecting trouble. Looks like it's finally come about."

"I'm not pleased about it," Bill grumbled, the image of Tara fresh in his mind. "How long do you think it'll take for them to come?"

"Do you even think they *will* come?" asked Angel.

"I do," said Clive, gravely. "Jesus returned from the dead; why can't he?"

II

Al's eyes snapped open as a cold hand wrapped around his neck, and each of his muscles tensed. All traces of lethargy leached out his system at the alien touch, and he spun around in the raised podium made for one, his heart pounding and his hand automatically drawing the Eagle from his holster. Was it possible that someone had crept up on him while he had slept through the night? If they had, he deserved it: Marines didn't sleep on duty, but over two years of inactivity had made him sloppy.

His blurry eyes recognised Pam, and he visibly relaxed, his shoulders sagging and his weapon slipping back into its holster. He smiled and nodded to her, and accepted the tin cup filled with steaming black liquid. He sipped it tentatively, feeling the burn of the hot liquid, and then a more familiar burn of alcohol as it slipped down his gullet.

"Irish," Pam said by way of confirmation. "The way you like it."

"My baby knows what I like," he said with a grin. He took another sip, then motioned for Pam to head back down the ladder. "These things aren't built for two people, you'd better get down."

Pam made her way down towards the flat roof of the building, and Al followed, taking a hearty gulp of the liquid she had brought him. He looked from side to side, and saw that Angel and Bill had swapped their positions with Garth and Sylvester.

"Where's the lovebirds gone?"

"Who?" Pam asked, the noticed the vague gesture he made towards the towers previously occupied by Bill and Angel. "Oh, they swapped over about an hour ago. We had to force Bill to give up his position, he was adamant that he wasn't going to go."

"Kid probably feels guilty as hell," said Al. "We brought the bastard in here, didn't even think about whether he could be a killer or a… you know."

"It's no ones fault," Pam said, though she didn't sound entirely convinced. Al knew Tara and Pam had been close, especially after their time spent together in captivity.

"What's been done with Tara?"

"Sylvester wrapped her up in a clean sheet and moved her into one of the storage rooms. He said we'd hold her there until Clive's finished his watch, then he'd deal with the final preparations."

"He still on guard duty?" asked Al, turning to one side and seeing the shape of the priest in the fourth of the manned towers. He seemed to be flicking through his bible, but he kept his eyes fixed on the horizon. "I thought he would have been the first to drop out, either with the cold or the exhaustion. He's a man of God, not a man of war."

"His beliefs run deep," Pam said, wrapping her arms around Al in a bid to share some body heat in the cold environment. The snow had stopped falling some time ago, but a number of icicles and a powdering of snow still encrusted Al's beard. Al kissed the top of her head, and she smiled softly. "He thinks he's the shepherd, and we're his flock. Because one of us died…"

"One of his herd; he thinks that it's his fault?"

"Flock, baby; sheep gather in flocks. And yes, I think that's his line of thought."

"I never saw him act the way he did. He's always been so opposed to killing. I mean, I started it off, but he actually finished it off: I knocked him down, but he wiped him out. Of everyone here who'd ever blast someone in the face… not Clive. Never Clive…"

"Jesus," muttered Pam. It was obvious from her reaction that the details of the execution of Tara's attacker hadn't been disclosed: the only people who knew were Al, Clive and Bill.

Well, the bitch, too. Christ knows Bill will tell her straight away…

"What about little Sarah? How's she doing?"

"The gunshots woke her up," Pam said with a nod. "She doesn't know about Tara yet."

"What can you tell a kid? One of your friends was raped and killed by the stranger we brought in under our own free will? She's been through a lot of shit for a nine year old."

"Maybe Steve and Cindy won't tell her. Try to protect her?"

"It's possible. That bastard must've recognised us the moment he laid eyes on us. We were played like fools, he let us show him where we live, and now… now the remains of a gang of homicidal bastards are going to be knocking on our door. And you know about Steele, he's not fussy when it comes to sexual partners, …"

"They still have to make it across the minefield, right?" asked Pam. "The time they're making their way through the mines, couldn't we just pick them off with a rifle?"

"In an ideal world, if everyone was a fantastic shot, that would be a feasible solution. But the snow's working to our disadvantage. The IFF sensors on the mines generate heat: not much, but enough to slightly melt some of the snow. The vigilant observer could pick their way across that field, given enough time."

"Just have to make sure they don't have the time," Pam said, motioning towards Al's giant rifle. "Is our vehicle loaded up?"

Pam nodded. "Garth moved it around to face the door, ready in case we need to move it. Do you really think it'll go that far?"

"I'm not going to rule it out as an option," Al said. "If it looks like those shits are going to breech the base, I'll blow the gate wide open and get us the fuck out of here. You with me, buddy?"

His question was addressed to Garth, who turned around and waved a confirmation to the question he'd heard over the radio link.

"If it was up to me, I'd bail out as soon as they got to the outskirts of the minefield, but I'm a coward."

"I'm not giving up this place without a fight," Al muttered, shaking his head grimly and finishing off his coffee, swilling around the final mouthful of the liquid and splashing it to one side, getting rid of the dregs of the beverage.

"Looks like we're just playing the waiting game now," muttered Al, his gaze fixed on his feet before raising it up towards the distant horizon. For a moment, he thought he saw a glimmer of something metallic in the far distance, and snapped up the pair of binoculars he had strapped around his neck, pressing the glasses against his eyes and squinting.

The morning sun reflected off the blanket of snow that covered the ground, making it hard for Al to try to make out details of the object that he thought he saw. The glare of the sun on snow proved too much, and he lowered the binoculars, instead lifting his immense rifle and peering through the anti-glare scope of the weapon. It wasn't perfect, but it did cut out a lot of the overwhelming brilliance of the sun.

He played the scope over his target, and could make out the ragged form of an emaciated corpse stumbling along in the snow, limbs stiff and rigid, elbows and exposed knees immovable by the thick encrusted scabs that covered the joints. The tattered rags it wore barely covered the sexless body, and it moved in an erratic manner, almost in a goosestep, kicking up plumes of snow as it jerked across the hilltop like a twisted marionette. The head of the creature was obscured by a helmet, a metal casing covered in dents and spatters of blood that obscured some of the Marine distortion patterns on the object.

Al's first thought was that he was looking at a deceased soldier who had been taken down in the line of duty, his helmet the only remainder of his previous identity. Then a chilling thought raced through his mind, and he lowered the weapon, still staring out into the distance, but knowing that the creature was out of the effective range of the rifle. He turned slowly to Pam and ushered her towards the ladder leading back down into the compound.

"Do me a favour babe, get the kid and the bitch up here, we all need to talk."

Pam slowly descended the ladder, and once she had made it down to the ground, Al followed, bracing his hands and feet on the outside of the ladder and sliding down the frame. He watched as Pam rushed off towards the entrance leading back into the bowels of the base, then turned to the raised watch towers that were occupied, addressing each in turn as he talked over his radio.

"Spanners, Preacher-man, buddy... I need you guys down here now. C'mon, move."

The three men each muttered a response of sorts, then made their way down their respective posts and into the centre of the annex, nodding a greeting to one another as they all met up.

"What's up?" asked Garth, licking his pale blue lips and pulling at the padded jacket he wore. He patted down his pockets, pulled out a crumpled and battered cigar and lit it, puffing on the tattered stogie.

"Shouldn't we be on look out?" Sylvester said, idly toying with his assault rifle, working the bolt and making sure the breech was clear of any obstruction. "They could be here any minute, and we're going to miss them."

"They're already here," Clive calmly announced, adjusting the heavy leather coat he wore. Al frowned at the coat, recognising it as the same one Mikey had been wearing when they'd picked him up. He couldn't understand why he was wearing it, but he didn't ask about it; he had more important things to worry about.

"You saw it, too?" asked Al, looking towards the priest. He nodded solemnly.

"Saw what?" asked Bill as he arrived in the annex, Angel and Pam close behind him.

"Tin pot Rot," announced Al, motioning towards the outer wall with a jerk of his thumb. Bill looked at him blankly, obviously unaware of what he was talking about.

"Armoured hollow men," Clive said, explaining the situation. "The Messiah used the hollow men that wandered Manchester and protected their head, their one Achilles heel."

"And there's some out there?" asked Bill, looking alarmed.

"Just one," said Al, pulling his magazine out the rifle, checking it was filled with the large calibre rounds, then slamming it back home, working the bolt with a loud 'kachunk'. "But you know the old saying: where there's smoke, there's fire."

"The fires of Hell," Clive nodded.

"Right," Al snapped, tossing his rifle in Angel's direction. She caught the heavy weapon and struggled with it while she slung the shoulder strap over her neck. "Here's the plan. The bitch and me are by far the best marksmen in the group, so we'll take them out at a distance. Head armour or not, that rifle uses high velocity, high powered rounds that will punch a hole through reinforced concrete. Even the toughest of ballistic helmets couldn't stop one of these, we'll be able to take out a lot before they even get there, we're the first line of defence.

"Kid, you and Spanners get a couple of XR1's out the rear of the trailer; they're bound to have vehicles, those tank killers should be able to stop them dead in their tracks. Aim for engines, or where you think the engines may be. I'll give you a quick rundown of their use in a minute. Buddy, you stay in the *Pride*, get the engine ticking over in case we need to get out of here."

"I don't have a problem with that," Garth said, his thin lips lifting slightly in the corners.

"Pam, girl, I want you and Preacher-man to concentrate on getting the Merrips in that vehicle, and as many supplies as you can. We're sorted for weapons, but we need some food in there. Personal effects can be left behind. We can replace them: we can't replace people. You got that?"

He turned to look at Clive, who looked emotionless and impassive.

"Got it?

Clive nodded and sighed, but didn't look at him.

"You got a problem with that, Preacher-man?"

"Gods enemies are my enemies," he said, rubbing the butts of the two pistols he wore strapped around his waist, one on either side of him like a cowboy. "I should be striking out at them. He that killeth by the sword must be killed by the sword."

"It took you almost three years to lift a gun and fire it at one person. How are you going to cope when it comes to a field full of them?"

"The Lord will provide me with the strength I need."

"The Lord can help you get those people and supplies into the trailer first, after that we'll see if he can give you the power to snuff out another life. We don't want to use up too many miracles in one day. Now hustle, people, on to the west wall, that's the way they should be coming from."

Bill stood on the flat roof of one of the corner base units, looking at the bulky box-like weapon he held in his hand. The brief tuition that Al had given - point, squeeze and release – had been short, concise and too the point. Al bragged it was a powerful weapon that fired solid slugs of a strong and lightweight alloy designed to penetrate armour and explode after impact. Bill didn't care about the physics or theory behind it, just as long as it did its job. He was doubtful of the power of the weapon, it felt too light and more like a plastic box then a weapon, but if the weapon-obsessed

Marine had boasted on the power of the device, then Bill would at least give it a shot.

He had stood below Angel's raised platform, his gaze focused ahead, though he occasionally glanced over his shoulders to see if there was any sign of attack coming from another angle.

By the time everyone had got into position, the single Rot that Al and Clive had seen was no longer visible. That had been two hours ago, and now it was beginning to snow once more. Tiny ice-cold flakes landed on Bill's forehead and exposed hands, freezing pinpricks spattering his flesh and keeping him alert. At least the cold kept him awake, and almost made him forget he'd only had a couple of hours of sleep.

Almost.

He stifled a yawn and marched from left to right, trying to keep the blood flowing in his legs, while switching the weapon from one hand to another.

"You ever think Al just imagined that Rot?" he asked, looking up towards the podium Angel stood on.

"Maybe. He's just as tired as the rest of us. Clive, too."

"Fuck you, guys," shouted Al from his platform on the other side of the compound. "I saw the Rot through my scope just as clear as I can see the bitch through it now."

Bill looked across, and saw Al leaning over the edge of the platform, the second of the large rifles he had pointed directly at Angel.

"Stop screwing around," hissed Sylvester, looking up to Al from his vantage point beneath him: he was positioned on the roof of the base unit beneath Al just as Bill was Angel. "Is there any sign of them yet?"

"Nothing," sighed Angel. "No sign whatsoever."

"She's right," confirmed Al, swinging his rifle back around towards the surrounding countryside. "Hey, bitch, you want to make yourself useful and go get me that coffee?"

Bill sighed heavily. This was going to be a long vigil.

Clive stood over the body of Tara, her desecrated form hidden by the white sheet that was draped over her. After managing to get Steve, Cindy and Sarah into the trailer, all the time keeping the heavily pregnant woman as calm as possible, Clive had decided that he would attend to the body of Tara before they had to leave the base. He was under no delusion that Al and his small band of warriors would be unable to repel the attackers, and knew that they would have to leave the base at one point. He had to make sure that the body of his friend was disposed of correctly, to make sure she wasn't introduced to the folds of the army of the undead.

Pam had requested that she be present for the ceremony, but Clive had managed to persuade her that he could do it on his own, and didn't need any help. She'd understood, but still wanted to say her goodbyes before the disposal of the body. Clive had let her have five minutes alone, allowing him to gather a couple of things he needed from around the base.

After Pam left the room, her face streaked with tears, Clive stood alone for the moment in his shrine, the church he had built where the prison had once stood, and lit the stick candles he had found in one of the storage cupboards. They gave the altar an eerie and surreal feeling and bathed the room in a pale orange light while casting flickering and dancing shadows.

Clive looked at the thin needle he held, a sliver of metal he had recovered from the kitchen area used to test the juices of cooking meat. This time the device would be used for less wholesome devices. His gaze flickered from the needle to the blood-smeared earlobe of Tara... could he really do this? Could he really do what was necessary to make sure his deceased friend *remained* that way?

He dropped the sharp implement, stepping away from the body and shaking his head. There was no way he could do it. Killing a murderer and rapist was one thing; defiling the body of his former friend was another; something he couldn't bring himself to do.

He grabbed the other object he'd recovered, a large metal crate, and opened it up, looking at the three dark red cylinders within, each topped with a silver pin attached to a ring. He'd used one of the incendiary grenades only once before, on the child that had died hours after birth. One grenade has been more than enough to incinerate the small child, and the ashes scattered across the countryside outside. He was confident that three of the devices would be enough to incinerate the body, and more than likely the entire floor.

He wouldn't be able to do it, though. Not until he knew for sure they were going to have to abandon their base.

"Everyone sit tight," announced Al, his voice sounding over the headset Clive wore hooked around his ear. "Here come the bastards… and it looks like they've brought some of their friends."

Clive nodded to himself, primed the three devices he held, then ran for the staircase, trying his hardest to ignore the muffled thump, then the whoosh of flames as they washed over the room. Though Al was a good Marine and Clive had faith in his ability, he knew the Messiah would not stop until he got what he wanted. He knew that their home was as good as lost.

This chill of the winter air prickled the exposed flesh of the Messiah as he sat on the throne attached the back of the open-top vehicle he rode in. Wind carrying flakes of snow whipped and whirled around him as he glowered at the immense building he could now see in the distance: a uniform military construction made from heavy concrete and metal, the top of them manned by several people. He couldn't make out the details of them, but he knew that they would all be armed, and watching for his arrival. The element of surprise would certainly not be something he'd be able to count upon.

He did, however, have the advantage with the numbers.

Beside him, chained and shackled to the jeep, sat a partially rotten corpse, a hulking creature with dry and leathery skin covered in pale scabbing wounds, its head covered by a rubber gas mask decorated with pieces of bone. He used to be the right hand man of the Messiah, the Baptist who had welcomed hundreds into the fold of the undead army, but he had suffered the fate of the Chosen after one of the prisoners had escaped and engaged him in hand to hand combat. The loss had dealt a harsh blow to the building of his Holy Army, especially with the breach of the dead pit and the subsequent scattering of his forces. Many had to be terminated before order was restored, and the prison had been worthless for his needs. Much of the following year had been spent finding somewhere new to establish his base, a new kingdom for him to rule from...

His search had led him to an old abandoned hospital far north of Manchester, on the borders of Scotland: an ideal building already filled with many of the risen dead in various states. His remaining men had laid siege to the hospital, incapacitated the dead, and secured the building for his own needs. The Everman Memorial Hospital had been a perfect choice, not just for the abundance of Unbaptised Chosen, but because the hospital had an unusually large mausoleum and church attached to the main building: the former of which would be an ideal area to hold some of the Holy Army, while the latter would serve as the main hall of the Messiah.

It had been an ideal place to begin rebuilding his forces, ever close to the watchful eye of God, while the newly appointed Baptist continued the work of the original, reviving the dead and protecting their weak spots with all manner of helmets and protective plating. The original had remained in the ranks of the dead, and acted as the Messiah's own personal bodyguard.

Of course, the creature couldn't think for itself; none of them could, and the Messiah was well aware of this, though he knew that when the time came, the dead would listen to his voice as God projected his will through him. Many of his followers had first laughed at his claims. They had become the first of the Holy Army, and no others had mocked him after the examples had been made.

The most trusted of his followers, the twelve men he trusted his very life with, had each been sent on missions to find more people to aid their cause, either in life or death. Most had chosen life, but none had come across a find like Saint Michael boasted he had: If his claims were true about what was inside the walls of the Marine base he and his forces now stood outside, then not only had they stumbled across a large untapped wealth of military hardware, but also the men and women who were responsible for the destruction of his first sanctuary and the deaths of so many of his followers.

And also my face, he thought, absentmindedly playing with the pitted flesh of his body while he glared at the building. The heretics, who had taken his original seraphim, their beauty a gift from God, would pay a dear price for their ways.

"Grim," the Messiah said, his voice a deep growl as sat back in the throne. The driver of the vehicle, a dark skinned man wearing a black jumpsuit and matching body armour, turned around to face him, a toothy grin partially hidden by the twisted sneer on his face.

"Lord?" he asked, bowing his head slightly in a humbling gesture.

"The heretics know we are coming, I can see them on the ramparts of the fort. This will not be easy."

Grim nodded slowly, pulling a compacted telescope out from one of the pockets in his suit, extending the device, and lifting to his eye, scanning it across the battlements. Grim helped the Messiah from the very beginning of the plague, but his work over the past six months had seen him rise through the ranks in a relatively short time. He had killed colleagues and strangers alike to earn favour with the Messiah, and it had worked: he know looked upon him as a second in command, a leader of his armed forces and his own personal chauffer.

"Three men and a woman on guard," he confirmed, handing back the telescope so his master could look over the opponents facing him. "The woman isn't one of your seraphim."

"No," mused the Messiah, the telescope lingering on the woman standing in the raised pulpit. "She was the harlot who injured me, a fiery woman."

He paused as he remembered the night she had attacked him, had almost bitten through his penis... and the thought brought a burning sensation in the depths of his loin, a longing he'd not experienced in years. He knew she was a strong woman, both physically and mentally, but it was the strong women he enjoyed breaking the most; the humiliation, the physical violence, and then, the eventual submission, the begging and pleading to make it stop.

He'd heard it many times, and it never failed to turn him on.

"It looks like they're well prepared," Grim said, his gaze fixed on the immense structure. "Snipers… do we even stand a chance?"

"Faith," the Messiah said, leaning forwards and placing a comforting hand on Grim's shoulder. "Have faith, and the Lord shall protect and deliver. They may think they're safe, but they are far from it."

The messiah stood up and turned around to address the collection of vehicles that were parked behind him. Vehicles that looked like they had been stuck together with tape and string, sturdy box-like vehicles bristling with spikes and guns, motorcycles and large trailers and vans, almost sixty in total, had followed him across the country: his entire legion of followers. He scratched the wounds on the palms of his hands until they bled, then outstretched his arms, a clear mimicry of the death of Christ.

"My children," he announced, his voice carrying across the snow-covered wasteland they waited in. "My children, our target lies ahead. A den of evil; the synagogue of Satan, protecting the heretics who attempted to destroy us so long ago. They stand ready for us, secure in their city walls, but heed they not the story of the city of Jericho? Where the mighty horn was blown, and the walls came tumbling down?"

He fumbled for a something hanging from his belt, and lifted it, displaying it for all to see. A brass horn, curved around in a circle, the mouthpiece pointing in the opposite direction to the enlarged opening. He pressed it against his lips, inhaled then let the air out with one mighty blow.

The horn uttered a single-toned note, a long and drawn out sound that echoed off into the distance. His men knew what this sound meant, and those that had travelled in the large vans and trailers leapt from their seats, working their way around to the doors and donning heavy safety gear while working at the locks on the gates,

Meat wagons, the Messiah thought as a malevolent grin spread across his face. Already the rest of his troops were backing away from the vans as they opened up and revealed their precious cargo: a horde of the dead in various states of decomposition.

The new Baptist had studied the physiology of the Chosen over the space of two years, comparing different stages, and presented his findings to the Messiah, who had been very interested in the results. The freshly risen dead, the recently Baptised, were often bloated inside and still held a lot of fluid within them; their appetites were no different to a normal person, and most were slow and ponderous, though there were a few exceptions to the rule. As the plague carried on to wear away at the body, draining fluids and tearing flesh, the creatures became different: both appetites and the pace at which they moved increased, as did their ability to soak up damage. Where a normal bullet would have easily decapitated one of the fresher corpses, the older, dried up husks could easily take three or four more times the amount of damage before finally crumbling. They moved like packs of rabid animals, relentless in chasing their prey, and were far more violent than their fresher kin. These elite members of the Chosen made excellent soldiers, though their rabid states made them far harder to herd and control. Despite their weaker bodies and sluggish behaviour compared to the calcified creatures, the Messiah preferred the waterlogged animals to the berserk fury of the more resilient and starving creatures, though that didn't mean he wouldn't use them if he needed to.

"Arise, my children," the Messiah announced, dropping his horn and spreading his arms wide once more. "Break the walls down!"

III

"What's he doing?" Angel asked as she watched the scene unfolding through the scope of her rifle. The Messiah had climbed up on the back of his jeep and seemed to be riling up the crowd of people behind him.

"Looks like he's addressing his doting public," muttered Al.

"Well, shoot the bastard," hissed Bill from the podium below her. Angel could hear his voice in duotone through both the radio piece and the proximity of him on the podium below. Angel felt her finger twitch near the trigger, and gently guided the crosshair over the shape of the man, lining up for a shot on the base of the skull.

"Save your ammo," hissed Al. "The rifle's only effective for one thousand metres, the sneaky bastards've stopped one and a half kilometres away, they're safe for now. You can start picking off the bastards once they're closer."

"What do we do until then?"

"Just wait," Al muttered. "You could always make that coffee I've been waiting for since the assault on your farm two and a half, three fucking years ago."

"You could always piss right off," Angel snapped back, keeping an eye on the Messiah as he fumbled with his belt and lifted a brass horn to his lips. After a few seconds, the echoing tone of a single note rolled across the wall of the base, the delay reminding Angel of the same effect she'd seen with fireworks when she had been younger.

"I've got movement on some of the vehicles," Al said, and Angel panned her scope around, trying to find the targets Al was talking about. Sure enough, doors had been opened up on all the larger of the vehicles, and a number of men wearing protective body armour were running around, grabbing metal snares and plunging them into the darkness of the interiors of the vans and trucks. They started to pull their cargo out on to the snow-covered ground beside the vehicles, and Angel froze, the blood in her veins turning to ice.

"You have *got* to be fucking kidding me," hissed Al, "Un-fucking-believable."

Angel couldn't help but agree with Al's sentiments as she watched groups of the undead being unloaded out of the large vehicles. Their heads were encased with helmets or armour plating affixed directly to the bone by screws and nails, their heads fixed in place and facing forwards by metal pins and frames attached to their skulls and shoulders, effectively immobilising their skulls. Thick pink drool dripped from their obscured mouths and spattered on the snow at their feet, turning it into pale pink slush. They quivered in anticipation as they were lined up along the front of the gathered vehicles. None of them made a move once they'd been positioned, and Angel was quietly impressed, certain that the Messiah had managed to tame and train the creatures.

"They're blind," hissed Al. Angel took a closer look at the protected cranium of one of the zombies, and saw that a metal plate had been fixed in place over the eyes, hinged on the bottom and held in place by a metal pin attached to a thin piece of wire. Angel followed the wire to one of the handlers who stood behind the line, and could see his fist was filled with similar lines: each armoured zombie had their vision obscured by the same drop-down flap, and the release mechanisms in the hands of the various handlers that stood behind the line of the dead.

"How many are there?" asked Sylvester.

"About a hundred, maybe a hundred and fifty so far," guessed Al. Angel quickly panned along the front line, and decided that Al's guess was probably close to the mark. "And the rest of them. They're opening the larger trailers at the back of the group and bringing more forwards. We're looking at… Son of a bitch!"

"What?" demanded Bill, anxious to know what was happening in the field before him.

"The bastards've got *Colebrook's Runner* out there, filled with the dead metal heads. Of all the nerve…"

"They're got my truck out there?" Garth's voice piped up over the network

"It's not yours any more."

"I wouldn't want it if it was filled with Rots."

Angel refocused on the action at hand, and watched as the Messiah seemed to give a final triumphant gesture, a one to symbolise action. The Rot handlers pulled back on the wires, releasing the metal pins on the helmets of the creatures and freeing the drop-down hatches that covered the view ports of the armour. Each creature seemed to jerk awake, as it they'd been asleep in the darkness, though none attempted to turn around, simply staring at the fort in front of them.

"Well, I'm fucking impressed," scoffed Al. "They're not doing anything. He's got a well-trained brick wall there. Crazy bastard."

"Uh… Al?" Angel said, raising her gaze to the three rear-most of the vehicles; something she hadn't seen before, and was quite surprised Al hadn't, either. But then, most Marines hadn't been trained to identify medieval-style mangonels in modern warfare.

The vehicles were transit vans with large wooden arms on the top, and a number of men were working on each vehicle, loading ammunition on to the scooped bucket of the catapult and winching it around until it was pointing in the direction of the fort. As one, each catapult was released…

Angel looked away from her rifle, turning her gaze up to the sky as she saw a three projectiles as they sailed over the field, breaking up as they reached the apex of their journey, then arched down towards the walls of the fort.

"Incoming!" Al screamed, too late as half a ton of rancid offal slapped against the wall of the building, a foul stench instantly assailing Angel's nostrils as the putrid mess slipped and washed down the side of the building. Another trio of rotten and nauseating meat followed soon after, smacking against the walls once more.

The front line of Rots shuddered at the sound of meat slapping against concrete, and as a third wave of meat made contact with the wall, they lurched forwards into a stumbling walk, marching across the snow-covered field as the smell of the fetid meat drifted downwind towards them.

"Smart bastard," Al said, trying not to sound impressed at the plan employed by the sadistic Messiah. "Okay, looks like the dead are advancing. Bitch, hold your fire; our rounds can smash through their armour, but we might as well let the mines do their work first, save our ammo for the vehicles and the people driving them. There's enough mines out there to take care of them all, we'll just need to thin out the ranks and mop up any survivors."

"You're awfully confident about this," Angel muttered.

"Why not? There's a shit-load of explosives out there."

As if on cue, the first of the animals stumbled into the minefield and vanished in an explosive flare, disintegrating flesh and bone and a fiery flash. Smoking lumps of charred flesh and bone fell to the ground around the advancing army of Rots, but they took no notice of their fallen comrade, continuing on their murderous advance on the offal-coated base.

More and more of the creatures set of the mines on their advance, some explosives taking out multiple Rots. The numbers were thinning, but it seemed as if the handlers we pulling more and more of the creatures out the larger vehicles to replace each of the animals that fell. Already the minefield was a charnel waste ground, a flattened expanse puckered with blackened craters and what snow remained splashed with pink gore, littered with twitching remains of the dead soldiers.

Legless zombies hauled their way across the ground, clawing at the ice-cold surface and leaving bloodied trails behind them; armless corpses stumbled around and rolled into ditches and craters, unable to get back up; limbless torsos writhed and squirmed on the floor like worms, their spines arching as they tried to make their way towards the fresh meat on offer.

Within minutes, the minefield had been almost cleared, and Al and Angel opened up with their rifles, decapitating the creatures with their powerful rounds, despite the armour worn by the creatures. While Al's rifle fired at a rapid pace, each deadly bark hurling a piercing lead projectile through the head of an advancing minion of the Messiah, Angel fired at a much slower pace. She hadn't expected the rifle to be as powerful as it was, and each successive gunshot slammed the stock of the weapon against her shoulder, culminating in a tender bruise that constantly received punishment from the firing weapon.

Some of the advancing creatures fell over the bodies of their undead comrades and started to feast on their charred remains, making easy targets, but neither Al nor Angel picked these creatures off; they concentrated their fire on the animals that had reached the wall of the base and were clawing at the walls. Those that still had fingernails lost them as they raked their hands up and down the gore-covered concrete. Even over the sound of gunfire, Angel could still hear the harrowing moans of the animals as they pawed at the walls. Some even started to ascend the sheer walls, their limbs scrabbling and hauling their weight upwards; these were the prime targets of the defensive team: Al was quickly reminded of the outpost he'd seen swamped when he'd first arrived in Britain, and didn't want to see the same thing happen again.

"Fire in the hole," yelled Sylvester, lobbing a handful of incendiary grenades over the side of the building, the devices erupting in a flurry of fire and igniting the creatures. It didn't have an instantaneous affect, and resulted in a number of the undead stumbling around while on fire, knocking into one another and spreading the flames; a burning disease more contagious than the plague the bodies were rife with.

"Lay off on the firebombs," hissed Al. "It doesn't kill them straight away, it just makes them a walking human torch."

"Gotcha," Sylvester confirmed. He stopped throwing the grenades and instead lifted his anti-tank rifle, unleashing a single round with a deafening roar. Angel watched as the powerful round tore through the bodies and skulls of three creatures that were scrabbling over the top of one another, straight down into the ground and erupting in a spray of churned-up snow and dirt.

"A little overkill, dontcha think?" Al asked as he tossed his heavy rifle down on to the roof of the base unit he was positioned on, his ammunition supply obviously depleted. Angel watched as he climbed down the ladder and grabbed his heavy machinegun, marching over to the railings on the platform and firing down into the baying crowd of the dead.

"Keep going with your rifle, bitch," Al yelled over the barrage of gunfire from his weapon. "Tell us what's going on out there."

"They're moving," announced Angel, returning her gaze to the cordon of vehicles on the outskirts of the base. "The vehicles are moving... there're coming towards us."

With the minefield cleared by the relentless and fearless army of dead, Angel watched as the vehicles started their engines and slowly began their own assault, the smaller of the attack craft building up speed and bearing down on the base within seconds. While the drivers of the low buggy-like machines concentrated on weaving around the dead that remained upright and active, the passenger operated whatever weapon was attached to the vehicle; in most cases, it was a heavy machinegun.

"We see them," Bill confirmed, lifting his own heavy artillery and taking aim at one of the buggies. He squeezed off a single shot, and it sailed wide to one side as the target vehicle careened wildly through a series of puckered craters. Bill tried with a second shot, this time catching one of the tyres of the vehicle with a glancing blow. The wheel exploded off in a flurry of burst rubber and shattered axle, and the vehicle lurched out of control, lifting into the air and rolling on to an untouched section of the minefield, blossoming into a flaming wreckage as the explosives that hadn't detonated already erupted into life.

"They're too fast," shouted Sylvester above the repeating din of his own heavy weapon, "I can't get a clear shot!"

With the smaller of the agile buggies swarming around the grounds outside the fort, the larger and heavier vehicles started their ponderous assault. While the smaller vehicles took the time to weave around the undead soldiers still upright, the larger vehicles rolled over them, crushing them under their wheels while the gunners mounted on the vehicles opened up with their own weapons.

Gunfire tore through the air, coming from both sides of the fight, and Angel suddenly felt very exposed on her raised platform as a burst of bullets sprayed against the metal armour of the nest. She stumbled backwards, moving towards the ladder, and lost her balance as another burst of bullets slammed against the tower. Her grip loosened, she started to fall back, teetering on the edge of the platform and feeling the world spin around her. She fell back, and for a sickening moment felt the lurching weightless sensation as she toppled. The tower itself was quite tall, and Angel knew that if she landed awkwardly, she could easily cause some major damage to herself or even kill her. She closed her eyes, hoping for the best and resigned to the fact that she couldn't do anything but wait for the impact on the hard concrete surface.

Her landing was much softer as she had thought, as she felt something warm and soft wrap around her, keeping her upright and preventing her from landing too badly; she felt a sharp pain in her ankle as it buckled to one side, but other than that she was fine. She opened her eyes and saw Bill, holding her up and looking into her eyes. She smiled by way of thanks, and noticed he was almost reluctant to let her go. She felt awkward for a moment, but it was soon broken when Al's bellicose voice sounded over the radio.

"You two want to stop hugging and kill someone, or should me and Spanners do all the hard work?"

"Right," muttered Bill, finally releasing Angel. "Are you all right?"

"A little startled," she said, nodding and pushing Bill away before making her way towards the edge of the platform.

Both Bill and Sylvester continued their barrage of heavy weapons fire, concentrating their assault on the larger of the vehicles, the easier target, as they picked apart the outer layer of armour and smashed through the engines within. The men abandoned their vehicles as they ground to a halt, running to others that were still active, or taking cover behind the inanimate objects. Some were noticed by the slower of the creatures, and had to contend with them, too.

"Heavily outnumbered," grunted Al, blindly spraying suppressive fire from side to side in a bid to cut back the advancing unholy minions.

The sounds of battle were drowned out by the sudden blare of an air horn, and Angel looked up through her scope to see the Messiah in the distance guiding and motioning for one of the articulated trailers to swing around and face the fort. The vehicle backed up slightly, then with a lurch and a second deafening blast of the horn, it lurched forwards, powering towards the fort.

"Destroy that cab," Al shouted, guessing the offensive manoeuvre and directing his attention to the windows of the trailer cab. Angel realised it was their old vehicle that the Messiah had sent hurtling into the fray, but didn't think too much about that. Instead she tried to take out the driver, but she couldn't draw a bead on the grinning madman at the wheel; each of her shots went wild.

Bill and Sylvester tried to cut down the engine of the beast, and both succeeded in finding their mark, their heavy rounds tearing through the grille of the vehicle and smashing the engine to pieces. The damage had been done, but it was too little too late as the vehicle bore down on the length of wall between the base units that were manned by Bill and Angel, and Al and Sylvester respectively. It didn't look like the driver showed any sign of slowing down – or even wanting to.

"Son of a bitch," shouted Al, motioning towards the ladders to get back down into the courtyard behind them. "The bastards're going to breach!"

Sure enough, the momentum of the oncoming juggernaut was enough as the vehicle ploughed into the wall of the fort, shaking the foundation of each of the base units on either side. Angel fell to her knees as the building shook, and she looked to the side as the front cab of the trailer penetrated the wall. The front window was smeared with blood and the smashed remains of the driver's head dripped down the cracked windshield; the impact of the vehicle had taken its toll on him, though he had been more than willing to give up his life for the cause.

"Get the fuck out of here," shouted Al, racing to the ladders and sliding down them into the courtyard. Both Bill and Sylvester complied, but Angel didn't respond straight away, taking time to peer over the edge of the base unit despite the barrage of gunfire that continued to sail overhead. The petrol tanks of the vehicle had been breached, the flammable liquid gushing on to the ground and turning the snow and mud beneath into a quagmire in which the undead waded through to get at the offal that still clung to the wall. She then noticed the collection of barrels and canisters attached to the back of the trailer cab, each emblazoned with a warning of flammable or explosive content.

The plan of the Messiah was suddenly so clear. Breach the walls with a juggernaut, and then blow it up take down the entire wall.

Al's plan to evacuate the roof of the base units suddenly didn't seem so bad.

She ran to the edge and leapt from the roof, landing heavily on her ankle and tipping forwards into a roll in a bid to prevent any further damage to her leg. She scrambled to her feet, hobbling towards their parked vehicle in the quadrangle and saw that Al and Sylvester had already vanished into the opening, while Bill was rushing back to meet up with her, slipping his arm around her and helping her move quicker than she could on her own.

"It's going to blow," she said as they neared the Marine vehicle, though she didn't need to say anything as the breached wall exploded with deafening blast, the reinforced concrete cracking and shattering, hurling chunks of debris into the air and heaving a section of the wall away, revealing an army of flaming undead as they stumbled over the uneven debris, followed by the armed men of the Messiah.

Bill heaved Angel into the trailer and slammed the door shut behind them, then called out to Al.

"We're all in, get us out of here."

Al sat beside Garth in the drivers cabin while punching a series of numbers and characters into the keyboard before him, before taking one last look around the annex on one of the monitor screens.

It had been a wonderful place to live in, offering security and sanctuary. And in a little over a day, he and Bill had brought in a mole and exposed themselves to a deadly assault. Their home had been destroyed, and Al knew they'd never find another one like it.

The loss of a friend and a home in one day, he mused as he finished hammering in the lines of programming into the computer, slapping the enter key and telling Garth to move as soon as the way was clear. The computer screen showed a short countdown as numbers flashed down in sequence, starting at five and working down to zero. At the end of the countdown, the frame of the giant blast door they faced flashed with an explosive blast, and the door slid down into its recessed hole in the ground with a deafening groan. Garth gunned the idling engine of the vehicle, and it stammered forwards, rushing away from the doomed military base and leaving the invading army behind them.

"Simple as that," Garth murmured to himself as the vehicle streaked away from the battleground, rolling harmlessly over the unexploded mines thanks to its IFF decoder. "We had it all, and in a moment we lost it all."

"Nothing lasts forever," Al said by way of confirmation. He looked at one of the monitors that displayed a rear view of trailer, and leant forwards as he saw a number of pursuit vehicles peel away from the base and engage in a chase.

"What's that?" asked Garth as he glanced at the monitor Al was glaring at. "What's happening?"

"Bastards aren't going to leave us alone," he said with a snarl, heading for the door to the cabin and hurling it open. A rush of freezing air filled the cabin, and Al shouted as he placed one foot outside the cabin and on to the thin railing that surrounded the vehicle: it was wide enough to hold one person, as long as they held on tight to the skin of the vehicle as they moved. He didn't have to go outside to get into the trailer they were towing, but he wanted to see how many vehicles were following. When he craned his neck and saw the crowd of pursuing vehicles he wished he hadn't bothered,

"Keep driving, buddy. Don't slow down and keep on the move. Is there any way we can go faster than this?"

"If we dump the rear-most trailer, yeah," Garth said with a nod.

"Hell with that," muttered Al. "Just do the best you can, right buddy?"

Garth gave a nervous smile, than vanished behind the door to the cabin as it slammed shut.

Al inched around the thin ledge, towards the door leading into the middle trailer, and hammered on the door until Bill heaved it open. Al fell in on top of him, then slammed the door shut, briskly rubbing his body to chase away the chill of the winter air that had whipped at his body.

"We've got company, the bastards don't know when they've won."

"It's not just the building they want, it's everything that's in it," said Clive, gripping one of the seats in the trailer as he bounced from side to side. "Including the weapons. And his seraphim."

Now there's a word I haven't heard in a long time, Al thought as he flashed a reassuring smile to Pam. She tried to return the grin, but couldn't quite manage it. Al knew what she was thinking; that the last thing she wanted was to be chained up to the Messiah once more, acting as a sex slave and an object of his depraved entertainment. She didn't need to fear that. There was no way that was going to happen.

"You got a bit of a limp there, bitch?" he asked as he noticed Angel had pulled one of her boots off and was rubbing her ankle.

"I hurt myself when I jumped down," she admitted, furrowing her brow as she rubbed the joint, pulling her foot one way, then the other.

"If you were a racehorse, they'd have to put you down," Al said with a grin. "As it is, you've still got some use. Get yourself up to my room, take your rifle, and pop the window there: once you've done that, you should have a good view of the vehicles as they come up on our side."

"What if they don't come up that side?" asked Bill as he helped Angel to her feet and guided her up the stairs, rifle in hand.

"Me, you and Spanners are going to make sure they do. We're going up top and making use of the weapons up there. Spanners, you want to get those things up there powered up and ready to rock?"

Sylvester nodded and rushed off upstairs, heading for the hatch in the ceiling of the medical level that opened out on to the open gun platform, giving Al a few moments to prepare for the upcoming fight. He lifted his booted foot up on to the table, rolled up his trouser leg and pulled a small holdout pistol from out of the holster strapped around his ankle. It was a small weapon; similar to the one he had provided Bill with when he'd escaped from the Messiah's prison. He looked over the weapon, weighed it up in one hand, and motioned for Sarah to come over to him. He offered the weapon to her, butt first, and she took it from him.

With cold efficiency she pressed down the release catch for the pistol, slipped out the clip and quickly counted the bullets before slamming it back in place and snapping back the slide, thumbing the safety on and tucking it into the waistband of her jeans.

"In case any of them manage to board us."

"You showed my daughter how to become a killer?" asked Steve in disbelief as he stared at his daughter, the innocence of childhood shattered.

"Lower powered handgun, the kid's got to learn somewhere. And I've told her about where to shoot people. Sarah?"

"Dead men have to be shot in the head," she said, rhyming off what she'd learned in her lessons. "Bad men should be shot in the knees or legs."

"Legs?" asked Steve, unable to comprehend the words that his daughter was coming out with. "Why?"

"Because I'd never make a nine year old kill a living human. So instead, she incapacitates them," Al said, pulling a combat shotgun out of a heavy metal locker and tossing it towards Steve. He caught it with a grunt. "Instead, her dad deals with them once they're down. And besides, they might not even manage to board our vehicle. It's just a precautionary, you know? Better safe than sorry."

With those words, he dropped a larger handgun on the table in front of Pam with a grin, then carried on towards the hatch and the exit on to the roof. As he crested the staircase and moved towards the opened hatch on the ceiling that vomited ice cold air, he noticed Bill coming out of his room, casting a final look over his shoulder as he left Angel behind to her own devices from the position she'd been assigned.

"You two better not be using my bed, you dirty little bastards," warned Al as he pulled on a warmer jacket and looked up into the open hatch, and the cloudless sky above him. "You wouldn't be the first to fuck in a firefight…"

"You gave Sarah a weapon in front of her parents?" Bill asked, ignoring Al's jibe.

"It's not my fault mom and pops are so square. Jesus, when I was ten, I owned my own handgun *and* rifle."

"Americans and their guns," muttered Bill as Al boosted him up into the opening, then leapt up behind him, grabbing the lip of the hatch and hauling his weight up on to the gun platform above.

The roof of the vehicle was flat and surrounded by a sturdy metal railing, and each railing had a mounted machinegun attached to it, which could slide the length of the metal bar it was fitted to. A spherical hub in the centre of the platform had four metal wires attached to separate safety harnesses, one of which Sylvester had already strapped on as he worked over the weapons.

"Got three on line already," he announced as Al strapped himself into the safety webbing, then helped Bill on with his own. "Should I power the fourth one up?"

"There's only the three of us up here," said Al, shaking his head. "Conserve the power and the ammo."

Sylvester nodded an affirmative, and the three men stepped forwards, each taking the controls of a weapon and swinging them around to bear on the advancing vehicles.

Though the pursuing buggies were clearly faster than the leviathan they rode, they each seemed reluctant to approach it, no doubt uncertain of the offensive and defensive capabilities of the vehicle. Al decided to give an impromptu demonstration of his weapon, and fired a burst of gunfire, raking the bullets across the ground and causing a couple of the buggies to sway and part, each peeling off to one side.

"Track them, open up soon as they're in range," Al said, nodding towards Bill and Sylvester, They had each decided to take one of the side weapons, while Al took the rear-facing weapon. "Bullets are armour piercing, high velocity. They'll tear through the skins of the vehicles, but they won't be too good on the engines, especially the larger vehicles. Our best bet is to aim for the drivers, rip right through them and make them crash."

"Got it," muttered Bill, swinging his weapon around and tracking the first of the buggies as they ventured nearer. One of the advancing gang members on the back of the nimble vehicle let loose with a staccato of gunfire, bullets bouncing off the armoured hide of the Marine transport. Al watched as Bill let loose with a salvo of his own, and the bullets tore through the man operating the mounted weapon, sending him toppling over the side of the buggy and tumbling across the snow-covered landscape, bouncing off the chassis of the pursuing vehicle.

Al nodded his head gently, impressed with the young warrior. In the past three years they'd spent in the Marine base, only Bill had remained alert, training and honing his skills, watching for trouble. Now, in the face of danger, he was able to prove his worth.

If only I had another five or six of him, Al thought as he opened up with his own weapon, shredding the two men driving one of the pursuing vehicles. It veered wildly off to one side and crashed into one of its sibling vehicles, flipping end over end before vanishing into the cloud of frozen mud and snow kicked up by the wheels of the pursuing fleet.

The exchange of gunfire continued, the three men atop the armed vehicle seemingly in control of the situation as they picked off the advancing buggies one by one. As the number of agile vehicles decreased, Al noticed that the heavier of the vehicles were slowly advancing, large vans armed with larger weapons and carrying more men. Quickly snatching at one of the devices hanging from his belt, he flicked out the compact telescope and lifted it to his eyes, taking in the details of the fleet behind him.

"Son of a bitch," he muttered, dropping the telescope and letting it bounce off the platform he stood on and sending it skittering into the crowd of approaching vehicles. "No one's stayed with the base. They're all coming for us, including their deluded leader, he's riding at the back of the crowd."

"Base is empty," said Sylvester, hammering another burst of rounds home into one of the advancing vans. They shredded one of the doors, but they didn't hit any of the men inside, and the vehicle kept coming after them. Now, the larger of the pursuit vehicles were nearing the escaping military vehicle, and the rest of the convoy was forming a loose circle around the mobile command base. With the larger transports more heavily armoured than the lighter dune buggies, it meant that although the mounted weapons could pack a punch, they weren't able to hit the real, *soft* targets inside. "It's not the base they're after, it's us!"

"The warder speaks the truth," an alien voice hissed over the radios headsets they all wore. They each cast looks of confusion to one another. "And I looked, and behold a pale horse: and his name that sat on him was Death, and Hell followed with him. And power was given unto him over the fourth part of the Earth, to kill with sword, and with hunger, and with death, and with the beasts of the earth.

"Jesus," muttered Sylvester, finally able to place the voice. "Steele. He's hacked into our frequency somehow."

"Lose them," ordered Al, removing his headpiece and casting it over the edge of the railing. Bill and Sylvester did the same, hoping that anyone in the rooms below had done the same. There was a brief lull in the firing of Angel's sniper rifle below, and Al could only assume she had paused to remove her own radio. Better to work in silence then to have the constant voice of evil and deceit buzzing in your ear. Al looked up, and he could see the grinning form of the Messiah in the distance, his mouth still moving as he spoke, unaware that everyone had pulled the plug on his tirade.

"They're not returning fire," yelled Bill over the repeating sound of his weapon discharging, the lack of their communication link meaning the shouting was a necessity. "Why not?"

"Ever seen any films about pirates?" asked Sylvester, motioning with the barrel of his weapon to indicate one of the heavy trailers as it pulled along side them. "They're going to board us. Take us alive."

"Makes sense," hissed Al through gritted teeth. "They want us alive for their pleasure and entertainment. Which is why we haven't been shot – we're easy targets up here for automatic gunfire... We need heavy weapons to blow up those vehicles."

"Ask and the good lord shall provide," bellowed Clive as he clambered up on to the roof, carrying a large metal box secured with a silver padlock. Black stencilled writing indicated that the box should be handled with care as it contained explosives. "I found these in the rear trailer."

"Out-fucking-standing," Al muttered, drawing his magnum and removing the padlock with a single well-aimed shot. The lock fell to the floor, and the casket popped open, revealing two squat cylinders fitted with a variety of grips and a collection of small rockets, each the size of a half-pint glass. He grabbed one of the weapons, loaded one of the projectiles into the launcher, and squeezed off the missile at one of the approaching trailers. It exploded on contact, rocking it from side to side and sending it spinning off to one side, the heavy vehicle sideswiping another of the approaching vehicles and pulling away from the ring of vehicles. Sylvester grabbed the second launcher, loaded it up and took out another of the larger vehicles as it tried to pull up alongside their own.

"That's what I'm talking about," Al screamed in exaltation, lifting a clenched fist into the air and pumping it in celebration. "Load up and blast the bastards. Preacher-man, take the kid back with you, we need as many of these as you can find."

Al watched as the two vanished into the room below, then looked up as one of the articulated trailers pulled away and accelerated ahead, swinging out in a wide arc and blocking the way with its immense side. He quickly scooped up one of the discarded headsets and yelled into the microphone, hoping against hope that Garth would be able to hear him.

"Full speed, buddy, ram that son of a bitch!"

With that, he dropped the headset again and dropped to the floor, motioning for Sylvester to do the same.

The Marine vehicle collided with the side of the gang vehicle, and both lurched and veered off to one side. The blockade tipped, flipped over on to its side, and spun to one side as the heavy cabin of the Marine trailer smashed the downed machine to one side. Confident in the superior weight and handling of his own means of transport, Al leapt up to his feet, grabbed the controls of one of the mounted machineguns and raked bullets across the underside of the transporter, severing brake fluid lines and axles, puncturing the exposed fuel tanks and igniting the stream of clear gasoline as it poured out the holes. The flames licked up into the fuel tank and the vehicle erupted into a fireball, showering smouldering debris and flaming wreckage down on to the weapons platform. Several of the other pursuing motor vehicles smashed into the wide side of the burning husk of a vehicle, adding to the flaming frenzy that consumed the smouldering trailer, but twice as many managed to evade the wreckage.

"That's beautiful," Al said with a grin, wiping an imaginary tear from his eye. The intensity of the battle and the destruction he was causing gave him a satisfying feeling, a warm sensation that aroused his soul and his body, the familiar buzz of adrenaline-fuelled combat that he had missed for so long.

If only Pam were up here, he thought longingly, feeling slightly embarrassed in case his excitement showed through his combat gear. *She may not be able to fire a gun like Spanners, but damn, if she didn't look good.*

Grabbing another missile and slipping it into the opened launcher he had retrieved, he continued his assault on the pursuing fleet.

"Bill and Clive better hurry up," Sylvester shouted, firing his own launcher into the crowd. "We're running out of missiles."

"The kid'll be back," Al said, confident in the abilities of his friend. "We just need to trust in him, and lay down as much covering fire as possible until he comes back."

IV

Bill picked himself up from the floor after the tremendous shockwave that had thundered through the vehicle like a nuclear explosion. Confused, he looked across to Clive as he hauled himself up, and shrugged his shoulders.

"They're ramming us?" he asked, trying to look out one of the tinted windows. He couldn't see much, and tried to inch closer to the porthole to see what was happening when the windows rattled with an immense explosion, and the walls shook as shrapnel smashed against the outer hull. Desperate to know what was going on, Bill fumbled for the intercom on the wall and thumbed the call button for the drivers cab.

"What's going on up there?"

"It's crazy out there, Bill," Garth replied, his voice shaking with panic and fear as he drove the vehicle. "The bastards tried to block us off with a trailer. Al told me to ram it."

"And you did?" asked Bill, surprised that he had actually taken an offensive manoeuvre.

"I had no choice, I couldn't turn to avoid, so I had to do what he said."

"You okay?"

"Surprisingly, yeah. The front of the cab is shot to shit, all dented and battered, but me, I'm good to go, I'm wired…"

Bill clicked off the intercom. Garth certainly wasn't shell-shocked, which he would have expected, and it sounded like he was keeping it together, but he didn't know how long that would last. While Al could probably thrive in a situation like this for hours, and probably had on several occasions, the rest of their team may not have the tenacity to last as long. Already, Bill felt drained from the gunfight, but he knew he had to get back with more launchers and missiles. He motioned for Clive to lead the way, and together the two men stumbled down the staircase into the main living quarters of the truck.

"Everyone all right?"

Both Steve and Sarah clung to Cindy, the three crowded around one of the larger seats and looking fearful. Steve look terrified, his eyes darting nervously from side to side, while Cindy kept her eyes shut, her head tilted backwards and facing the ceiling. Only Sarah responded with a weak smile and gave a thumbs-up signal. Bill smiled back; the young girl had spent a lot of time with Al, and it showed: she was strong, and seemed to be keeping her parents calm; it would normally be the other way around with the parents soothing the child. Pam was looking out one of the windows;

the handgun Al had given her sitting uncomfortably in her hand as she tapped it nervously against her thigh.

"They're trying to board us, aren't they?"

Bill didn't say anything, there was no need to get the parents worked up more than they already were, especially with Cindy being as close as she was to the birth of her child. He thought Pam might have thought about that already, but then, how easy would it be to keep someone calm in the middle of a battle such as this?

Clive pushed on through to the adjoining corridor between the middle and rearmost trailer, and Bill followed. The corridor itself was nothing more than a mesh walkway suspended over a rubber accordion-like structure, designed to keep the two interiors sterile. The walls of the corridor had been punctured by burst of gunfire from the opposing side, the black rubber torn and shredded, allowing the cold of the winter outside to flush the corridor. The door to the rear-most trailer slid open, and the pair stumbled in, Clive instantly moving for the pile of locked crates he knew contained the devices. Bill moved into the depths of the cargo hold, past the bulky two-man motorbike that was locked into position to one side, past the rails of weapons locked down for storage, drawn towards an immense structure that sat at the rear of the hold.

It looked to be nothing more than a chair attached to a number of weapons and pipes, some he recognised, others he had never seen before. He instinctively lowered himself into the operators seat and strapped himself in, knowing he'd found something that would help turn the tide of the battle.

"What's that?" shouted Clive from the front of the cargo hold, looking up from the mound of crates.

"A weapon, I think. Looks like it could cause some damage. It's got no power, though… shame."

A loud clunk sounded from the front of the room, and the lights flickered and dimmed slightly as the machine Bill sat in hummed to life.

"Found the power switch," Clive announced, swaying from side to side as he came and stood beside the powered up machine. The control panel of the weapon flickered to life, scrolling though reams of computer code as the system booted up, and Bill grabbed the control yolk, finding an array of buttons inlaid within each finger indentation; each button obviously controlled different weapons and he mentally counted each button: six different systems.

The machine wasn't quite symmetrical. It was equipped with two of the multi-barrelled machineguns the humvee had been armed with, one on either side of the seat, and had a large box positioned directly over the pilot's chair, a mounted missile launcher with a number of cautions stencilled on warning of exhaust ports and possible blow-backs, and a cluster of grenade launchers mounted on the front. With a soft 'ping', the screen flickered, then displayed a message saying that all weapons were on online, and warning that all operators and technicians should be wearing ear and eye protection. A pair of goggles with built-in ear protectors sat on a shelf beside the device, and Bill reached over and put them on.

"Get those rockets up to Al," Bill said, pressing one of the buttons on the touch sensitive controls and watching as the rear of the cargo bay slowly split open, each half of the doorway pulling to one side and allowing the cold air to rush in with a deafening roar. "I'll see what I can do from here," he continued, now raising his voice to be heard over the din of the ice-cold air that tore through the room. Clive nodded an understanding and grabbed one of the metal lockers on his way out, leaving Bill to fathom the controls of the weapon on his own.

The weapon slowly slid forwards slightly until it was standing proud of the rear of the trailer, each weapon it bristled with almost quivering in anticipation as Bill gently guided the control yolk from side to side; the weapons platform complied by turning smoothly from left to right, providing him with a wide firing arc. The display on the control panel matched his own vision with a computer-generated image, displaying the number of viable targets available to him. Still testing the limitations of his new toy, Bill gently depressed the top-most buttons on his control stick, and the dual machineguns spun quickly to life. He released the button before either of them could build up speed enough to fire any bullets, then swung the device around to target one of the larger vehicles chasing them: a black transit van with a red stripe running horizontally along it. None of the attackers seemed to have noticed the nearby weapons, as the man on top of his target vehicle continued to aim high, no doubt trying to take down Al and Sylvester on the gun platform above. Bill gently fingered the second pair of buttons on the device, waiting to see what the result was. He gritted his teeth.

Nothing.

Then, the control screen flashed to life, and the intended target on screen flash red; a number of calculations scrolled down one side of the screen...

And the box above Bill opened up with a deafening roar, vomiting a high explosive projectile out the launcher and sending it screaming towards the van. The driver saw the projectile coming, and tried his best to execute some form of evasive action, but the missile was locked on, screaming towards it and detonating on impact with a satisfying blossom of fire. The van lifted into the air belching thick black smoke and shedding people from it as it toppled end over end, bouncing off another vehicle and sending that skittering away too. He could imagine Al on the roof of the vehicle, dancing and whooping in joy. He quickly attracted some unwanted attention, and a hail of bullets rained down on the rear of the trailer, singing as they bounced off armour plating and smashed into weapons stored in their racks. In a panic, Bill moved the weapon from side and side and squeezed all six buttons.

The seat vibrated as all the weapons burst to life, simultaneously launching a barrage of missiles and automatic gunfire while scattering a handful of grenades into the ground around the rear of the vehicle. The advancing gang members spread out and dropped back, trying to keep away from the aim of the heavy assault weapons. Many didn't move quickly enough and were disabled by the rapid fire or the explosives that bombarded them. Bill felt alive, on top of the world as he helped repel the advancing minions of the Messiah, until the weapon slowly started to decrease in its offensive capabilities. First the mounted missile launcher stopped firing, silenced as the ammunition was spent, and then followed the grenade launchers as they clicked shut. For a few seconds the mini cannons continued to grind away through their ammo until they spun empty, the ammunition completely depleted. The control panel flashed up a warning advising that the device was empty, and the technician on duty should replace all the ammunition packs. Bill peered over his shoulder into the empty cargo bay, and realised that *he* was the technician on duty. He hammered the button on the display to close the rear door, and leapt out the seat the moment the bay was sealed, hissing and spitting in pain as he momentarily grabbed the cluster of barrels for one of the machineguns and scalded his hand on the white-hot metal. The doors bounced and rattled as they were riddled with gunfire, but then quickly stopped; obviously the gang knew their weapons couldn't penetrate the hide of the monolithic beast they rode in.

Bill frantically searched the rows of ammunition and weapons along the walls of the cargo bay, grabbing anything he thought may fit the machine of destruction. The rear of the device had popped open and spat out a pair of empty boxes, and he had something to compare against the store of ammunition; even if he just found the bullets for the rapid-fire cannons, it would be enough.

"There!"

On one of the upper shelves, tucked behind strong boxes filled with shotgun shells, were a pair of boxes, similar to the empty ones he had found, each with a lid boasting they contained caseless rounds on a disintegrating belt. He carefully manhandled the heavy boxes on to the ground, pulled off the lid as the instructions on the day-glo orange label dictated, then pushed the first of the boxes into the waiting loading slot. He grabbed the first bullets of the chain in the box and fed them into the gears, nipping the tips of his fingers as they pulled in the chain and automatically fed them into the loading mechanism of the first cannon. He grabbed the second box and did the same again, this time making sure he didn't catch his fingers in the cogs and wheels of the mechanism.

Satisfied that the job had been completed to the best of his ability, Bill mounted the weapon again and tapped the button on the control screen that would work the doors. With a hum, they ground open, allowing more of the cold air to rush in. Bill looked up from his control screen, ready to commence with the attack; and froze in panic and fear at the sight he beheld.

During the time he had been loading the machine, Bill had assumed the barrage of gunfire on the rear of the vehicle had ceased because they had come to realise the futility of the attack. He had no idea they had stopped because one of the advancing trucks had managed to pull up beside the vehicle and attach itself to the rear of the vehicle while a group of men readied themselves to breech the vehicle.

The look of surprise on Bill was only equal to the surprise on the face of the front-most gang member, who was squatting near the doors as they opened, a crowbar in one hand and a carjack in the other. In unison, the eight-man boarding party lifted their weapons preparing to open fire on Bill.

Bill's weapons were already up and ready.

They whined to life, and Bill played the controls to the weapons from side to side, shredding and cutting down the eight men in one fell swoop before lowering his aim and cutting through the metal body of the attached van. The driver visible through the windshield vanished in a bloody spray, and the remains of the vehicle fell away to the snow-covered ground, leaving a small piece of the ruined van attached to the trailer with a collection of ropes and cables.

Wiping the spatter of blood from his eyes and face, Bill swung the weapon around, aimed at another of the approaching vehicles – this one a small jeep tearing towards the rear of the trailer, the driver sporting a small handgun that he was firing randomly towards the Marine machine. Bill swung the dual machineguns about, squeezed on the firing controls…

The small speaker situated by the display screen emitted a short sharp buzz, and the screen itself flashed up an error message.

"Runtime Error 27, jam in ammo chamber?" Bill hissed in anger. He leapt out of his seat, avoiding the random pot shots from the driver in the jeep and scalding his hands again on the machineguns, and ran around to the back of the weapon platform, kicking the chair in anger, trying to pry loose the cover on the ammo chamber and remove the jam. The sound of the approaching jeep intensified while Bill feverishly worked, and he knew he wasn't going to clear the blockage in time as he heard heavy booted feet make contact with the metal floor of the cargo hold. He blindly dived for the first weapon he could grab, his fingers curling around one of the assault shotguns Al had given him earlier. He snatched it up, worked the slide to prime the weapon, and leapt out of hiding.

The man that had jumped in through the open door was pale skinned, and wore a number of leather straps wrapped around its body. The head of the man was covered in a gas mask decorated with bones, and Bill instantly recognised him from when he first met him two years ago. The person that had willingly infected himself with the plague moments before he had died; the infected bone saw still protruded from the gapping wound in his stomach.

The Baptist, Bill thought, bringing up his shotgun to bear on the undead as it stumbled towards him. He unloaded three of the slugs into the stomach of the creature, knocking it back with each successive blast in a bid to give him a little more space to work with. He raised his aim and unleashed a fourth slug into the face of the Rot. Its head snapped back with the impact, but the toughened helmet took most of the force of the blast, meaning that although the skull may have cracked, the brain remained intact.

Knowing that the shotgun may not be enough to penetrate the armour, and that he could go through a full drum of ammo before the animal went down, Bill grabbed another weapon, an assault rifle with an underslung grenade launcher, and worked the bolt before riddling the body with bullets. Shattered and bloody, the walking corpse dropped to its knees, its torso spattered with gaping wounds that seeped a thick black liquid. Bill worked the slide of the launcher and fingered the trigger, unleashing the powerful round and striking the creature dead centre. The explosive lodged itself in the exposed organs of the zombie, almost vanishing in the folds of the rotten entrails, and the creature shook as it took another step forwards, as if it was laughing and shrugging off the assault.

Bill threw himself backwards, firing the remains of his clip and rolling away as the grenade finally exploded, washing the room with firelight and showering the contents with a spray of gore and blood.

With his ears ringing from the proximity of the explosion and his skin burning from the blast, Bill clambered to his feet, washing off the clumps of charred flesh that clung to his clothing, and looked down at the mess he had created.

A leg here, a shin there, two smoking arms, a pile of burning flesh that had once been a torso, and the blackened head, still lodged in its protective casing, rolled from side to side with the swaying momentum of the moving vehicle. Remembering his school days, Bill pulled back his leg and kicked the disembodied skull: he'd never been very good at football, but there was no way he was going to pick up the pieces of the corpse to get it out the mobile armoury. He watched as the head flew out the open doors, bounced off the bonnet of the jeep he had completely forgotten about, and sailed past the dark figure that was making its way over the jeep, into the rear of the trailer. Naked, except for the red shorts and dark cape that he wore, and the leather shroud he draped over his head.

"Jesus Christ," Bill hissed, dropping his weapon to the ground as the scarred figure stepped further into the room. He raised his arms out to the side, mimicry of the form of the crucified saviour of mankind. He spoke in a deep, rumbling voice.

"I am!"

XXI
ANGEL OF DEATH

"…The futility of it all is mind-boggling."

I

Frank Steele, the self-proclaimed Messiah advanced on Bill, clenching one fist and reaching behind his back, drawing the blade he had hidden behind him; a flint spearhead on a short wooden handle that could easily be used as a knife. He pressed the flint against his stomach, drawing it across his skin and reopening a healing wound, grimacing slightly as the blood flowed freely down his well-defined stomach.

Okay, thought Bill, backing up and bumping into the door leading through to the next room. *What now?*

He had the option of running from the room, of course, but that would only expose the rest of the vehicle to the onslaught of the maniacal madman. A convicted rapist and paedophile would have a field day with one of his old dancers, a pregnant woman and her nine-year old daughter; backing out was not an option. Bill was the last line of defence between him and them, and he had to make sure they were going to be safe.

He patted himself down, looking for any kind of weapon that would rival the spearhead the Messiah was wielding, and only came up with his extendable baton that was attached to his belt: it certainly wouldn't cut him, but a strong enough blow would certainly break some of his bones.

Not that anything that simple would incapacitate the man. Not only had he been thrown by the explosive device and seriously burned, but also one of his fingers had been removed. The mass of pale scar tissue that covered his upper torso and left arm was a mottled map of ravaged flesh, flecked with lumps of blackened debris that remained imbedded beneath his skin. As he stepped forwards, he pulled the leather shroud from his head and cast it to the ground, displaying the disfiguring burns that pitted his features and the one dead eye that glared blankly at him from behind a permanent scowl. The left side of his mouth seemed to be fixed in a sneer, exposing his yellowed teeth behind his lips; It would take a hell of a lot more than a metal stick to beat him down, especially if he could get up after taking a stick of dynamite in his back.

Maybe he did have a divine gift!

Bill shook his head, dislodging the thought: he couldn't afford to buy into the bullshit that the Messiah weaved like his followers did.

"You bastards," he hissed, taking a step forward and swinging the bloodied blade forwards. "You did this to me, tried to kill me. But I have risen, death is not a barrier, merely the next step."

"Bullshit," Bill spat back, trying to lash out with his baton but missing. "You're just one lucky shit."

"The lord guides my hand," he retaliated, attacking with a simple slash that caught the sleeve of Bill's jacket and tore it open, exposing his arm beneath. If he had been any closer, he would have easily cut through his skin. "For he is my shepherd, and he leads me."

Bill couldn't think of anything else to say other than 'bullshit', and he didn't feel like repeating himself. His eyes flickered across the gun racks on the wall, looking to see if there were any loose and ready for instant use, but they were all locked down tight for storage. By the time he turned to unlock one, the Messiah could quite easily carve his back open and pull out his spine. The assault rifle that lay on the ground was spent, a useless shell, and he couldn't easily put his hands on a magazine: like all the rest of the ammunition, the rounds would be locked up in a box on one of the shelves, and it would take just as long to find the right box. The only weapon that was ready to be fired was the automatic shotgun he had used previously, and it lay on the ground *behind* the Messiah: Bill would have to go through the deranged killer to get it.

"You can't win this, boy," growled the Messiah, grinning sadistically as he shuffled forwards. "I've killed hundreds before you. You won't be the first, and you certainly won't be the last. I've gutted people with blades duller than this. I've killed with my bare hands; wrung peoples necks, beaten people to death, broken bones. I can make this quick and painless, or I can make this long and agonising. It all depends on your actions. Let me make a deal.

"Drop the weapon and I'll kill you quickly, slit your throat. Persist in this useless attack and I'll see that you suffer. Throw your friends to my army of the Chosen; reclaim my Seraphim, make sure I finish my business with the whore who tried to bite my dick off… Is there anyone I missed? Ah, yes, I believe Michael's report mentioned a child…"

"Fucking son of God my arse," Bill swore, lunging again with his baton. The Messiah took half a step back, and Bill pressed on; he was getting closer to the shotgun, and if he could keep up the assault, then there might be an outside chance that he could reach the discarded weapon. Though a Rot could survive three point-blank slugs from the shotgun, he doubted the Messiah would be as resilient. Again, Bill swung his weapon, blade striking baton and forcing the intruder back. He didn't try to hide the surprise from the power of the attack, the shock plainly visible in his disfigured features as he parried and blocked. For one moment, Bill thought he might have gained the upper hand as his weapon smashed down on the Messiah's forearm, and the sound of the bone cracking echoed dimly in the confines of the chamber. He screamed; an agonising shrill yell that told Bill he had at least caused some damage, but he didn't release the blade, nor did he back down. If anything, the pain simply aggravated him more, and leant strength to his attack.

"Your choice is made, child," the Messiah said with a grin. "He that killeth with the sword must be killed by the sword."

He lunged, fainted to one side, then spun around, catching Bill in the side with the blade and opening a small wound just above his hip bone. With a yell he stumbled back, gripping the fresh wound and allowing the Messiah to regain the footing he had lost in the initial attack. Bill was back to square one, only this time he was bleeding, and he knew he would be at a disadvantage. He took a step further back, trying to adjust his position, and twisted his leg awkwardly, a shot of pain racing up and down his leg as he pulled at an old wound, the gunshot he'd received all those years back in Edgly. It rarely gave him any problems, but at that point in time it suddenly decided to flare up again, more than likely a mix between the cold and the physical activity.

"You can't win this," growled the Messiah, taking another step closer. "I have God on my side, what do you have?"

Bill lunged forwards, his baton outstretched, and the Messiah took hold of it with his free hand, spinning around to one side and using Bill's momentum against him, hurling him towards the opening at the rear of the vehicle. Had Bill been thinking clearly, he could have tried to grab the shotgun as he sailed past, but his mind was clouded with a hundred thoughts, most of them about the ways the Messiah was going to kill him.

Seeing his chance, the Messiah dived on to him, roughly grabbing the collar of his jacket and hauling him closer to the edge, rolling his feet out the rear of the trailer and letting his limp legs dangle outside, his boots churning up the snowy wasteland and bouncing off rocks and stones as they ploughed the land. Each knock jarred his bullet wound or affected his fresh lesion, and he gritted his teeth, trying to block the pain out. He knew this was it; that his time would come and any moment the Messiah would let go of his jacket and let his body be crushed beneath the wheels of his jeep that had backed off a few metres.

"I could let you go right now," he hissed, echoing his thoughts. "End it all right now!"

With a grunt, he pulled him back into the trailer and spun around, throwing him down on to his face. He felt the weight of the Messiah as he pinned him down, sitting on his legs and gripping his wrists with both hands, effectively immobilising his limbs: it was clear that he had done this many times before.

"You should never have fucked with me," he whispered, his voice ragged as he breathed erratically, the excitement of the moment getting to him. "The son of God, how could you possibly think you could win? You fucked with me, little man, now I'll fuck with you. I'll make sure you're the last to go, make sure you watch as I take each and every one as my slave, turn the strong, feed the weak to them, and keep the young to satisfy my needs. How's that sound?"

"Like the delusion of a psycho!"

"You're in no position to belittle me," the Messiah said, contempt in his tone of voice. "In fact, you're in my favourite position of all. Submissive."

Bill tried to struggle free, but there was no moving the weight of the large man. If he couldn't fend him off, then what hope would any of the women have?

As if on queue, a rapping sounded on the door between the armoury and living quarters, and both squabbling men froze as the battered door squeaked and groaned open.

"Bill, are you here? We've dealt with all the vehicles and the men who tried to climb on board. Al sent me back here to check on you."

"Angel, run," Bill shouted, trying to get a warning out to the newcomer to the fight. The Messiah didn't waste any time, leaving his position on Bill, planting a foot on the ridge of his spine and using him as a springboard as he sailed across the room, batting Angel to one side and slamming the door shut once more, heaving at the handle and twisting it into a useless coil of metal: the heat and proximity of the grenade explosion had obviously dealt a lot of damage and left some elements of the room in a weakened state; though the Messiah was strong, there was no way he could be *that* strong. *Could there?*

Angel crashed to the floor and moaned softly, but didn't move any more; it sounded as if she had struck her head, and the Messiah slowly circled her downed form, scratching his chin as he mused over the woman. He clearly recognised her as the woman who had tried to injure him in his prison homestead, as he self-consciously cradled his groin.

"Angel?" he said aloud. "Sweet, sweet Angel. How could you *not* be meant for greater things with me with a name like that?"

Bill pulled himself to his feet, shaking off the ache in his limbs as the Messiah stalked around the room, a look of malevolence about him as he seemed torn between the two choices he had.

"Starter or dessert," he muttered to himself, rubbing his hands in glee at the thought of having two people to defile. "Beauty or the beast?"

"I'll make the choice for you," shouted Bill, stooping low to grab the discarded shotgun and levelling it off so it was aimed at the Messiah's stomach. He fired a shot, but his aim was off, and the solid slug the weapon was loaded with slapped into the bulkhead, denting the metal but not punching through the heavy armoured hull. The Messiah rushed forwards, clambering over storage crates and sailing through the air, arms outstretched as he barrelled into Bill and knocked his weapon aside. The pair rolled across the floor, exchanging kicks and punches, and Bill found himself near the edge of the opened trailer once more, and this time he knew it wouldn't be his legs hanging out.

With a rumbling laughter, the Messiah coiled his fingers around the back of Bill's neck and started to press his head closer to the rushing ground beneath him. Though he may have been hell-bent on abusing Bill, he clearly didn't mind what he looked like, and would quite happily defile a man with half his face torn off. It was a forceful show of power and domination, and although Bill had heard of The Messiah raping men, he wasn't flattered that he would be one of them.

"Make you bleed," spat the Messiah, drool trickling down his chin and splashing on the back of Bill's head. "Make you bleed and scream."

Bill struggled frantically, trying to shake the weight of the man of him and regain his footing. As he resisted, he swung his head around from side to side, and could see that Angel hadn't been lying: there was no sign of any other vehicles in the vicinity of the Marine trailer, and it did seem to be slowing down a little.

"Give it up, Steele," he shouted from his obscure vantage point. "You're the last one, everyone else is dead. No more deluded people following you in your twisted little cult. No more dead soldiers. Admit it, you've got nothing."

"Lies," the Messiah screamed, hauling Bill back into the room and slamming him into the inert heavy weapons rig. The sudden jolt of the machine was awarded with a soft mechanical pulsing sound, and the gears within the loading chambers ground together, feeding more bullets into the waiting Gatling guns. A smooth androgynous voice announced that the blockage had been cleared, and the weapon was ready for firing. Not that Bill needed it now.

"My men would not leave me, we can not be stopped. And in those days shall men seek death, and shall not find it; and shall desire to die, and death shall flee and elude them. "

As if to emphasize his point, every other word was accompanied by a punch to the face or a knee to the stomach, and Bill could feel the continual onslaught take its toll on him.

As his bruised skin split and spilled blood, Bill tried to feebly fight back, but the Messiah was beginning to play with him, sensing he was close to winning the fight. Nothing could stop him.

"Hey, Frank!"

The Messiah paused from his assault and turned around, looking over his shoulder to see Angel standing behind him, a fresh cut dripping blood down one side of her face and a rifle armed with a bayonet cradled in her arms and pointing directly at his stomach. Without a second thought, she lunged forwards and plunged the blade into his stomach, angling the weapon to one side and unleashed a burst of gunfire into his abdomen. His smile cracked and he dropped his swollen and bruised hands to his opened wounds as Angel pulled away the rifle, exploring the charred and smoking ruins of the abdominal cavity with the tips of his fingers.

"D… dear God… what have you…"

He dropped to his knees, leaning forwards and displaying the large exit wounds on one side of his back, blood oozing from him as he dropped to the floor wheezing heavily, his body shaking as it was wracked with pain.

Angel dropped her weapon and rushed over to wrap her arms around Bill, keeping him upright and guiding him away from the dying body of the fallen overlord.

"Took your time," murmured Bill, his lips bloody and split, his left eye swollen from the constant punishment. He limped heavily, cursing the wound in his leg and gripping the fresh cut on his side with one shaking hand. "I thought I was going to have to handle him myself."

"I owed the sick bastard one," she said with a smile, dabbing at the corner of Bill's mouth and mopping up a trickle of blood. "Let's get you into the medical bay, we can get you cleaned up. We just need to get the door open."

Bill half-murmured a wordless response and feebly grabbed the twisted handle, trying to work loose the damaged door, but it wouldn't move.

"Where's Al when you need him?" laughed Angel, and Bill nodded with a smile. If they hammered on the door enough, the Marine should hear him, or maybe there was a welding torch stored somewhere in the trailer.

"There is only one man whose strength you can trust in," announced a haunting voice, accompanied by a deep and rumbling chuckle. "Trust in the lord."

Bill spun and froze, feeling the world around him lurch sickeningly as he glared in disbelief at the stooped figure that stood before him, a gory loophole in his stomach letting the light flood into the room from behind him. He rubbed his fingertips into the bloodied cavity, traced a finger over his forehead and nodded solemnly, leaving the mark of the cross on his pale skin.

"I don't fucking believe it," hissed Angel, slapping her thigh for her sidearm.

"Put your fingers in my wound," he offered, gesturing to the hideous wound in his stomach. "For I… I am alpha… alpha and omega… f-first and last… He who is… was… always will…"

"Heard it all before," Angel said, pulling up her pistol and squeezing off five rounds, each lead projectile smashing against his ribcage and sending him stumbling back another step. The final round caught him in the head. It wasn't a well-aimed shot, merely grazing his temple, but it was enough to knock him off balance. He swung out his hands, fingers locking around the multiple barrels of the inert machineguns on the side of the weapon seat. His fingers began to smoulder, the barrels obviously still hot from their recent discharge.

Bill lurched forwards, tumbling into the seat and grabbing the controls of the weapon, fingers resting tentatively over the firing studs. The Messiah wrapped both arms around the muzzle he held, heaving his body up so he could lean over the barrels and look around with bleary eyes, trying to gather his senses and work out what was going on around him. His eyes fell on Bill and the throne of destruction he sat upon, and a look of terror flashed across his pain-riddled face.

"You… you can't do it. I'm injured… I'm unarmed… you're not like me."

"I like to think I have *some* standards."

"Your kind will never be welcomed in my kingdom."

"Thank fuck for that," hissed Bill, squeezing the buttons. The muzzles of the machinegun spun to life, and the Messiah rolled to one side with his limbs flailing. He slipped and caught a stream of rapid-fire bullets as they tore through his shoulder and neck, his body dropping with a thud to the ground below. Using the targeting computer, Bill lowered the aim of the weapon and locked on to the heat signature of the body, unleashing a constant stream of caseless rounds into the corpse until it faded out of distance. Bill looked over the control panel and thumbed the communication button, opening a channel with the rest of the transport.

"Garth, buddy, you there?"

"We're both here, Bill. Me and Al."

"Al, we need you to come back here and get the door open, it's jammed shut. Garth, can you turn around and backtrack about a kilometre?"

"No problems, Al's on his way back there now. What are we turning around for?"

"To do something we should have done three years ago. I want to make sure that bastard's dead."

"That him?" asked Steve, peering over Bill's shoulders as they all glared down on the bloodied and twitching body that lay on the ground, the snow around it stained a deep red as the remnants of the slain person seeped out into the ground. Al nodded solemnly, walking around the carcass.

"Yeah, that's the bastard. Looks like you fucked him up good," he finally announced, glaring at Bill.

"I try my best," Bill grinned, leaning heavily on Angel, who leaned back on him, the pair keeping one another upright. "I just had to see him, to make sure; after the last time…"

"I know," Al said, nodding his head.

"So he's responsible for the gang that flushed us out our home?" Steve glowered, looking back over his shoulder at the inert Marine vehicle, and Cindy who stood by the door, her arm wrapped around Sarah's shoulders.

"He's responsible for a lot more than that," Garth growled, leaning over and paying his respects to the dead by spitting a wad of phlegm on the corpse. "Tara, for one thing. One of his sick fuckers killed her."

No one else said anything, each glaring at the dead body as if they were expecting it to come back to life; everyone expected it to happen.

"I never thought I'd have to see him again," muttered Pam, wrapping her arms around one of Al's thick limbs and pulling him closer. "It reminds me of the time I spent with him. With his gang…"

"And the days spent in their prison," reminded Sylvester, looking towards Clive for a comment. Of everyone gathered around the cadaver, he was the only one who had not said anything. Steve had the most questions about the situation and the person, so he was obviously the most vocal, while others had the occasional sentence to pass comment. He simply nodded his head, glazed eyes focused on the visceral images.

"What do we do with him?" Steve finally asked, feeling like he'd been out in the open long enough, and he was desperate to get back into the trailer.

"Standard body disposal," Al said, shrugging his shoulders. "Incinerate the fucker, make sure he can't end up as food for the Rots."

"Fuck that," Clive finally said, stepping forwards and flicking back one side of the leather coat he wore, pulling one of the Berettas from one of the holsters and levelling off the pistol with the corpse. Without warning, he emptied a full magazine into the body, the slide of the weapon slamming back and forth until it locked itself in the open position. Clive smoothly dropped the spent magazine from the weapon, slapped another one home, then replaced it in his holster. No one said anything, just stared in stunned silence at the desecrated body.

"Had to make sure," he said, turning away from the scene and making his way towards the opened trailer.

"All right," Al said, breaking the silence. "Show's over, folks. Someone grab one of the flamethrowers, make sure that bastard's burned."

"No!"

Clive spun on his heels, raising his hands. "Leave the body. Let the hollow men feed on their master. Call it poetic justice."

Garth turned to look at Al, raising a questioning eyebrow. Al shrugged, watching as the priest pushed past Cindy and Sarah, vanishing into the interior.

"What's up with him?" Steve asked. "I've never seen him so worked up."

"Preacher-man and Frank never seen eye-to-eye," Al said, trying to shepherd the crowd away from the corpse.

"He feels like his whole religion's been perverted by a psychotic sociopath; the man used his own twisted outlook on God as an excuse for rape, molestation and mass murder," Sylvester said, "He holds a grudge against him, and the death of Tara hit him harder than I thought. I guess it all just mounted up on him."

Slowly, one by one, the gathering moved away towards the trailer, until Steve remained with Bill and Angel.

"You did a number on him," Steve said, fumbling for something to say. Though he wanted to get back into the trailer, he felt comfortable enough in the open with Bill and Angel; the pair seemed to be able to look after themselves. Angel nodded, her eyes fixed on the oozing corpse, while Bill kept his own eyes fixed on her.

"Yeah," he agreed, smiling softly. "Bastard had it coming for a while. There were a lot of wrongs to right."

Silence hung in the air once more, but still no one made a move to return. Steve was about to break away, when he heard the sound of snow crushing beneath light feet, and he spun around to see Sarah rushing towards him.

"Dad," she called, rushing towards him. Angel and Bill quickly bunched up behind Steve, forming a barrier between the young girl and the dead body. Steve nodded his appreciation, and dropped to his knees, looking up at Sarah as she skidded to a halt a couple of feet in front of him. He'd forgotten how much his daughter had grown in the past couple of years: both he and Cindy had been so preoccupied with their own problems they had neglected Sarah quite a bit: in fact, Al had looked after her a lot of the time in the base. She'd even stopped calling him Daddy, and now called him Dad. It was obvious that she was growing up fast: she had to with the world the way it was.

"I thought I told you to stay with your mother. Why are you here?"

"Mum sent me."

"She did, did she?" he asked, lifting his eyes towards the open door on the side of the trailer: there was no sign of Cindy. "Well where is she?"

"She went to lie down," Sarah said, matter-of-factly. "She sent me to get you, while Pam and Clive cleaned up the floor."

"Clean up? What happened?"

Sarah leaned forwards, looking at Angel and Bill, before returning her gaze back to Steve. She lowered her voice, so only he could hear her. "She pissed herself."

"Sarah," Steve hissed in anger. "How many times have I got to warn you about your language, young lady?"

"Al says it all the time," Sarah said, pouting and resting her fists on her hips.

"Al's not my nine year old daughter, he's an adult."

"That's a matter of opinion," Angel said with a smile.

"What's wrong with your Mum?" Steve asked, trying to pull focus back to Cindy; he'd have to deal with Sarah and her bad language later on. "Is she all right?"

"After she… messed herself," Sarah said, picking her words carefully, "She went to lie down, muttered something about contraptions."

"Contraptions?" Steve questioned, his mind racing. "Was that the word she used, or was it *contractions*?"

"That one," Sarah said with a grin, nodding her head and smiling. "Contractions."

"Shit," he muttered, striding towards the trailer and grabbing the girl as he stormed past her. She peered sheepishly over her shoulder at the corpse as she was pulled away, and her eyes widened as she saw the bullet-ridden body.

"Is he dead?"

"Hope so," Bill said, striding after the pair and trying to keep himself between the corpse and the child. "When's she due? I didn't think she would be ready to pop yet!"

"She's not. She should have another month; maybe six weeks before she 'pops' as you so eloquently put it. Something must be wrong."

"Like what? Babies are born premature all the time, aren't they?"

"Premature births happen all the time, yes, but they usually have a hospital to hand to deal with the babies. We've got nothing."

"Is it possible you've miscounted?"

Steve placed one foot on the step leading up into the trailer and ushered Sarah into the vehicle, turning around to look at Bill as if he were an idiot.

"This baby'll be our fifth child. We're pretty good at counting shit like this."

"Shit," giggled Sarah as she marched into the trailer, vanishing into the interior. Steve growled in the back of his throat, swearing that once he'd seen to his wife and their newborn, he'd deal with the disrespectful young girl.

He burst into the trailer, eyes darting from side to side as he scanned the faces of each person in the room. Al sat at the large table to one side, a can of lager beside him as he polished one of the stripped-down weapons. Both Clive and Pam were finishing off mopping up the floor, while Sylvester stood at the bottom of the stairs, watching as Sarah powered up them, waving blindly as she went. Garth stood beside Sylvester, wringing his cap with his hands.

"She's upstairs," Sylvester said, pointing out the obvious. Steve nodded a gesture of thanks anyway, and pushed on, looking towards Angel to make sure she was following him; she was the only medic of sorts they had, and he had a bad feeling about what he was going in to.

Something was wrong.

Cindy had been through this several times, and each time had been the same, almost like clockwork, with contractions evenly spaced: one of the attending midwives at the birth of Sarah and Susan had joked they could have set their watches by her contractions. A textbook birth, another had said. Each birth had come with pain, of course, but the agony she was in now was like nothing she'd experienced. It felt like she was slowly being torn apart from the inside out, and she couldn't get comfortable, no matter how she sat or lay. She had managed to waddle up the stairs into the medical bay, and pulled herself up on to one of the secured gurneys, helping herself to a glass of water and gulping it down.

As she tilted her head back and closed her eyes, Sarah bounded up the stairs and rushed to her side, resting her hands on Cindy's shoulder.

"Mum, are you okay? You look sick."

"It's just the baby," Cindy said with a weak smile, trying to conceal her pain as another agonising spasm wracked her body, this one a sharp stabbing pain in her stomach. She gently placed one hand on her abdomen, as if she could suppress the pain, then reached out with her other hand, brushing a few strands of hair away from Sarah's forehead. "I think your brother or sister's ready to come out now. A little earlier than we thought, though."

She smiled, and Sarah returned the gesture.

"Dad's coming up now," she said, her head twitching slightly as the sound of feet pounding on the stairs could be heard. Sure enough, Steve's face lifted into the room, followed by Angel, then Bill, and finally Garth. Steve looked worried, though he clearly tried to hide it from Sarah as she hovered around Cindy.

"What's happening?" Steve demanded, and then looked down to their daughter. "Honey, why don't you go down and keep an eye on Al, huh? Make sure he doesn't get too drunk and cause some damage with his weapons."

Sarah eyed her parents suspiciously, then slowly nodded and stepped back towards the stairs.

"Soon as she's born, I want to know."

"You expecting a new little sister?" asked Angel as she grabbed a white smock and wrapped herself up in the garment. "Do you know something we don't know?"

"It has to be a girl," she said with a smile as she started to descend the staircase. "There's too many boys here."

As soon as she had left the room, and Cindy knew that she was out of earshot, she turned to Steve, her face cracking into a pained expression.

"Something's wrong, Steve. It hurts, it hurts really bad."

"What's happened? What's going on?" he asked, grabbing a metal stool and scraping it across the floor as he took a seat beside her. "What's wrong?"

"Stress," muttered Angel as she grabbed one of the monitors and wired a collection of probes and sensors up to Cindy. "Her pulse is racing, blood pressure's high. This whole situation's done nothing for her or the baby, they're both stressed to shit, and it's induced labour early. How far apart are they?"

"I don't know," confessed Cindy, trying her best to calm herself down and control her breathing. "There isn't any pattern… it just hurts all the time."

"Let's have a look," Angel said, strolling around to Cindy's feet. She looked over her shoulder at Bill and Garth, and furrowed her brow. "You two boys want to give us some privacy?"

Bill nodded, his face a little pale, and he started to back out of the medical bay. Garth didn't move, just watched the scene going on before him.

"Uh… can I help?" he finally said.

"I don't know, can you?"

"I helped with the birth of my daughter," he confessed. "I can remember that pretty well."

"Where were you at the birth of our last child?" Steve demanded, helping himself to a third apron. "We could have used you then."

"I might have been working on this vehicle," he replied in defiance, then shifted his eyes awkwardly towards the floor. "Or I might have been drunk."

"That's wonderful," Steve muttered, grabbing a sponge and wiping it across Cindy's brow. "Can we do anything about the pain? Any meds, painkillers, anything?"

Angel popped the locks on a drawer and slid it open, looking over the contents quickly and efficiently. "I don't think there's anything I can give her here. It's all pre-determined ampoules, set amounts for gunshot wounds, serious injuries... nothing that says it's suitable for labour pains. Nothing that even says it's suitable for a pregnant woman..."

"You must know something you can do," insisted Steve, his tone of voice rising with each word spoken. "You're the doctor!"

"I'm not a doctor," moaned Angel, slamming the draw shut and moving on to another. "I don't know what to give her."

"Blood pressure's raising, pulse is erratic," Garth reported. "Jesus, there must be something we can give her to calm her down."

"Sedative," Angel announced, holding a needle as she spun around and gently held Cindy's arm. "It's not much, but it's all I know I can give you. It probably won't help with the pain, but..."

"Give me it," Cindy demanded, nodding her head. She felt the prick of the needle, barely noticeable against the pain that coursed through her body, and the slow dulling and drowsy sensation that quickly followed. It wasn't enough to make her sleep straight away, but it made her lethargic, and it was enough to make her care a little less about the pain. Time started to drag, or compress, she wasn't sure; she couldn't keep track of anything going on around her.

She was aware of Angel telling her to push, of Steve trying to tell her to breathe, and then a sudden sensation in her gut, as if someone were repeatedly kicking her there. She closed her eyes, trying to concentrate on one thing at a time, pushing herself through the pain barrier, gritting her teeth as the pain became almost intolerable. Words were exchanged, something she couldn't concentrate on until she heard Angel comment on the baby crowning. Or was it Garth that said that? She really couldn't tell, and if she opened her eyes, she couldn't make out which blurring shape spoke.

Unable to fight the call of the sedative any more, she pushed once more, hoping it was enough, and closed her eyes, a sigh escaping her lips as she breathed out.

II

Al sat silently on the large padded seat, one arm wrapped around Pam, the other around Sarah as she sat in silence. The design of the sickbay and the main living area was a marvel of Marine technology, using sound dampening material and acoustics that he couldn't begin to understand, and didn't pretend to. All he knew was that for the past three hours, there hadn't been any news from upstairs.

"I hope it's a girl," muttered Sarah, repeating herself for the hundredth time. Her hands were pale, gripping the stuffed animal that Al had retrieved from the city for her, and she was obviously anxious, awaiting news on the appearance of her new sibling.

"It's taking a long time," muttered Bill, glaring at his watch. "How long's this going to take?"

"It can take hours," Clive announced calmly. "It can take upwards of twenty hours for some women."

"Screw this shit, I'm going out," muttered Bill, grabbing his assault rifle and hobbling over to the door, grabbing his jacket as he went. Al laughed softly and shook his head.

"Sit down, kid, Spanners is on watch; you can barely stand, you need medical attention. Soon as Cindy's squeezed one out, the bitch can take care of you; in more ways than one, am I right?"

"You're an ass," Bill muttered, falling heavily back into his seat.

"Arse," corrected Al with a wide and sheepish grin.

Silence fell over the room once more. Al knew how Bill felt, he was just as on edge as the rest of them; to go from one extreme to another was a shock to the system, and while the adrenaline from the gun battle still rushed around his body, the fact he was forced to sit in a room and just wait for something to happen was killing him. Especially because be had to look after Sarah.

A little more than two years down the line, and I'm still fucking babysitting.

He shook his head morosely, stifling a yawn and managing a tired grin for the sake of Sarah.

"You know, I hope it's a girl," Sarah muttered, lifting her cuddly toy up and hugging it. Al had relieved her of her pistol, and it now sat on the table in front of him. He could clean it out, maybe that would give him something to do for a couple of minutes.

A footfall sounded on one of the steps, and everyone spun their heads to see who it was. Steve trudged mournfully down the stairs, ignoring everyone as he ripped off the white gown he wore, dropped it to the floor and headed straight out the door. Sarah stood to follow him, but Al sensed that something was wrong the minute he saw him, and grabbed her by the arm, keeping her back.

"Al," she said, sounding, as she often did, much older than she actually was; almost an adult. "I need to see my dad."

"Give him a couple of minutes," Al said, then turned to Pam. "Keep her here a moment, I'll go talk to the bitch, see what's going on."

Al stood and moved towards the staircase, slowly climbing them and turning slightly, noticing that Bill was close behind him. He nodded slightly to Al; an indication that he also knew something was going on. The pair climbed into the medical bay in time to see Angel draping a white sheet over the inert form of Cindy and a smaller shape, while Garth tried to keep himself busy by sealing up lockers and cabinets. He didn't look up when the newcomers entered the medical bay.

"Jesus, what the fuck did we miss here?" Al muttered.

Angel spun, jumping slightly at the sound of the new voice, but lowered her face so she stared glumly at her feet. Al could tell from her swollen and bloodshot eyes that she was upset, and knew that it was time to put all jokes aside.

"What happened?" Bill asked, moving forwards and looking blankly at the white sheet.

"We don't know for sure," Garth said, throwing a tray of soiled instruments into a large plastic yellow bin.

"Stress," sniffed Angel, wiping her nose on the back of her sleeve. "Panic. The stress from the gunfight worked her up so much she induced labour herself when she wasn't ready. The baby in turn got stressed out. It choked itself with its umbilical chord, Cindy took it bad and lost a lot of blood... both are... They're both..."

"There was nothing else we could do," murmured Garth, stepping forwards and placing a reassuring hand on Angel's shoulder. She shrugged it off.

"If I was a real doctor..."

"But you're not," Bill whispered, stepping forwards and gently placing his hands on her shoulders, one on each side. "You did the best you could," he said, his tone soothing. Angel accepted his comforting, stepping forwards and nuzzling her face into his shoulder. He winced; she was obviously pressing against one of the wounds he'd received from his fight with the Messiah, but he didn't try to push her away. She sobbed gently, and Bill wrapped his arms around her, reassuring her as best he could.

"Are we forgetting about someone?" Al said, trying to ignore Garth as he dabbed at his face with the back of his sleeve. "Steve, where'd he go?"

"Said he needed to get out of here," Garth said. "Said he wanted to be on his own, give himself some time to sort things out in his head and work out what to do next."

"I think someone should go out and watch him," Al said. "Make sure he doesn't do anything stupid. What about the kid?"

"Me?" Confused, Bill turned his head; now his eyes seemed a little bleary.

"Not you," hissed Al, pointing a thumb to the stairs. "Sarah. What do we do?"

"Steve should tell her, it'll be best that way," Garth muttered. "We're still relative strangers to her. 'Cept for you, Al."

"I'll talk to Steve first," Al announced, making his way towards the staircase. "I'll send Clive up, we can start getting things ready for the... you know."

Al spun, feeling a lump in his throat as his voice tailed off. He needed to keep everything clear in his mind, and he needed to stay strong; not just for his own macho image, he didn't care too much for that right now, but he needed to make sure Sarah had someone strong for support. Steve wouldn't be worth much at the moment, there was no doubt in Al's mind that Steve wouldn't be right for some time. And who could blame him?

Slowly working his way down the stairs, he nodded solemnly to Clive, leaned in close, and whispered a brief account of what had happened to the priest. He tried to keep an impassive face, nodding to himself and murmuring softly.

"I see. I'll see if I can help," he said softly, patting Al on the shoulder as he pushed past him and headed up the stairs.

"Can I go see my mum?" Sarah grinned, leaping to her feet.

"She's tired, sweetie," Al managed, forcing a gentle smile. "Give her some time."

"Preacher-man can go up," she muttered, using one of Al's nicknames and crossing her arms across her chest and pouting.

"To bless the newborn child," Al quickly said. "You know how the god-man is."

"I want to see my mum," Sarah demanded, almost stamping her feet in frustration.

"Well you can't," snapped Al, heading towards the open doorway. He stopped as he reached the threshold of the living quarters, feeling the frosty bite of the gloomy winter evening, and sighed heavily. Wearily turning to one side and looked at Sarah; she was staring at Al in shock, eyes and mouth wide open in astonishment.

"Can… can I see my daddy?"

"I need to talk to him first," Al said, his voice barely a whisper. "Sit with Pam. Please."

Sarah nodded slightly before dropping back to the seat, hugging in close to as she glared at Al. He smiled a thanks, then turned and stepped out into the night, the blanket of snow crunching beneath his large boots.

"Al," Sylvester announced, grabbing the arm of the Marine as he walked by him. Al ground to a halt, half turning to face Sylvester, keeping his eyes on the shape of Steve across the ten metres of distance he had put between himself and the parked vehicle. "Al, what've I missed?"

"Cindy's dead," Al murmured softly. "So's the baby. Something went wrong, the pair died."

"What? *Both* of them?"

Al nodded.

"Fuck," Sylvester swore, hammering a fist against the side of the vehicle. "What's Sarah like?"

"Doesn't know yet. I'm going to have a word with him first, make sure he's okay. I think Sarah should find out from him, not one of us."

Sylvester stared vacantly, absentmindedly nodding to himself more than anyone.

"Should I stay out here? Keep watch?"

"I'm armed," Al said, patting the holster on his right thigh and the heavy magnum that rested there. "Get yourself inside, keep an eye on things in there. I'll talk to Steve." Sylvester nodded, retreating into the confines of the vehicle while Al trudged across the snowy ground towards Steve.

He sat huddled on the ground, hugging his knees as he rocked slowly back and forth, muttering incoherently to himself. He didn't turn around as Al approached, and he wasn't sure Steve had heard him. Lifting his hand to his mouth, he coughed softly before lowering himself to the ground beside Steve. The coldness of the snow seeped through his trousers and numbed his flesh as he tried to adjust and get comfortable on the ground. Steve didn't acknowledge him.

"Do you want to talk about it?"

Steve didn't respond, simply looked out towards the distant horizon, his eyes misted over.

"Steve?"

"No," he answered, his voice dead.

"What about Sarah?"

"In a minute."

"She doesn't know yet. I thought she should…"

"In a minute," Steve repeated, his voice still emotionless, gaze fixed on the distance.

"Right," Al muttered, nodding his head. "In a minute."

The pair sat in silence, and Al glanced at his watch, counting the seconds as they ticked by. He waited for two minutes before broking the silence again.

"Steve, you need to talk to Sarah, the girl doesn't know what's going on…"

"I know," he answered, rubbing his eyes. "I just need… need a little time. Fuck, what happened?" He broke down in tears, tilting his head, sobbing uncontrollably, his tears dripping on to the snow and pitting it as the salty solution melted the ice crystals. "What the fuck did I do?"

"You did nothing," Al said, tentatively laying his hand on Steve's shoulder. He didn't try to shrug it off, which was a start. "There was nothing you *could* do."

"You're right," Steve said, standing up and turning back towards the transporter. "It was that bitch's fault, fucking idiot, she doesn't know what she's doing; she's killed two of my kids, *and* my wife… stupid fucking whore…" He started to storm towards the vehicle, and Al leapt to his feet, quickly intercepting him before he could rush back to the trailer.

"It's not her fault either," Al said, trying to stop himself from shouting; he didn't want Sarah to overhear any of the conversation. "It isn't anyone's fault. It just… it just happened."

"I'll be sure to tell that to Sarah. 'Sorry about your mother, it just happened'. I'm sure she'll understand, and we'll be back to normal in a couple of minutes."

"That's not what I'm saying… It's a fucking terrible thing that's happened, but it wasn't *anybodies* fault."

"My whole family's dead; everyone 'cept Sarah. And I've not been able to prevent *any* of their deaths. What use am I? Husband, father, provider… *protector*? I'm a fucking joke, Al… a fucking joke."

"You're a good father," Al said reassuringly, making sure he was between Steve and the vehicle at all times, if only as a safety barrier in case he decided to bolt for the medical bay again. "And Sarah's a good kid. You've done a good job raising her."

As if on queue, the young girl appeared at the opening, holding hands with Pam who stood beside her. She peered out into the gloom and lifted her hand in a wave.

"Daddy, I want to see my mum. What's going on?"

"In a minute sweetie," Steve shouted, gesturing with his hands that she should return to the warmth of the trailer. "I'll be another couple of minutes."

Sarah nodded slowly, though she didn't look convinced. She backed up into the interior, half-dragged by Pam, leaving Al and Steve alone once again.

"Are you going in there now?"

"In a minute. You got a cigarette on you?"

"Hey, it's me you're talking to," Al managed with a grin. He pulled out a battered silver case from his pocket and popped it open, offering the container to Steve. He took one of the sticks and a match, lit it, then took a deep drag from the cigarette. "Always got a smoke for a friend. Didn't know you did, though."

"I don't. Figured I could do with one to steady my nerves for what I'm going to do."

There were sounds of more shouting and screaming from the trailer, the sounds of a tired child throwing a tantrum, and Al sighed. "She's a real hellcat," he said with a sheepish grin.

"She gets that from her mother," Steve agreed, wiping the corner of his eyes with a finger. "She used to be like that when she was young." He sighed heavily and took another drag from his cigarette. "Do me a favour Al. I'm going to finish this off out here. Will you go in there and take care of Sarah for me? I know I can trust you with her, and she really likes you. Keeps calling you her uncle."

"Really? Yeah, no probs," Al said, gently slapping Steve on the back. "You won't be long, will you? I don't know how long I can keep her under control."

"I'll be a minute. I just need to finish up here."

"Okay," Al nodded in agreement, turning around and trudging slowly towards the opened trailer. "Be careful, there could still be Rots out here."

"I know."

He seems to be taking it very calmly, Al thought as he took another two steps away from Steve. *Maybe we should keep a close eye on him…*

He froze mid-stride as he heard a soft click. It was a sound that was all too familiar to him, a safety catch being released on a weapon. His heart sank, and he spun on his heel as a muffled explosion sounded, and a rain of warm wet liquid splashed across his face. Only metres away from him, the figure of Steve remained upright for a few seconds before keeling over to one side, his shattered head gushing fresh blood on to the pure white snow around the fallen figure.

Al scuttled forwards and dropped to his knees beside the fresh corpse, looking at the smoking handgun that was still clutched in the hands of the dead man. He stared at the body, lost for words at the suicide that had been carried out behind his back. It hadn't been an impulse he'd acted upon, Steve had planned this, more than likely from the minute he had left the trailer. The words he had spoken echoed in Al's mind as he carefully stood up from the body and removed his jacket, draping it over the decimated head.

Will you go in there and take care of Sarah for me…

He would never have guessed what Steve had planned.

"You selfish dumb mother fucker," he said glumly, slowly making his way towards the trailer.

III

It was almost ten hours later by the time silence fell over the vehicle once more. Sarah lay on the larger of the seats, her feet curled up around her and her head resting on Pam's legs as she used her for a pillow. Every so often her body would shudder uncontrollably with a sob, though she remained fast asleep. Al watched the two females from a seat opposite, a frown creasing his brow as he tried to think through the options he had.

Bill wasn't too sure how Al was handling it; in the space of an hour Al had suddenly developed a little family unit, and obviously wasn't too sure about what he could do with the situation. He knew that he wasn't impressed with the cowardly decision Steve had made, and Bill couldn't understand why he had had done what he did. At the beginning of the plague, Bill could imagine a lot of people tried to kill themselves; but almost three years into the plague, with a family still to look after, what could possibly have driven him to do it? The loss of a loved one could certainly alter your state of mind and cloud your judgement; Bill reflected on his last moments of life with Jenny, all those years ago. While everyone around her had been afraid to even *look* at her in case they caught the plague, he had shunned their precautions and put himself at risk while he reassured her as much as he possibly could. In the haze of memories surrounding those days, had *he* considered committing suicide? He couldn't remember.

Hadn't there been a time when he thought he'd lost everyone but Tara, after escaping the Messiah's fortress, and considered it for the briefest of seconds? Despair could do strange things to a sane man's mind.

Was it everyone I was so distraught at losing? He thought to himself as he looked around the room, *or was it just one person?*

Angel sat opposite Bill, a steaming mug of hot chocolate in one hand as she read through one of the medical journals that were stored in the medical bay. She barely noticed anyone else in the room, intent on the small binder and the pages of text and diagrams it contained, brushing her hair back out of her eyes every so often. She looked up as she took a drink and noticed Bill staring at her and smiled weakly before returning to her textbook.

"I'm trying to take in as much as I can," she confessed. She sighed heavily, closing the book and pushing it to one side. "There's too much. How am I expected to know everything?"

"We don't expect you to know everything," Al said, his voice almost a whisper as he watched the two women in his life sleeping. Pam stirred, opened one eye and smiled lazily before slipping back into a deep sleep. "None of us do."

"Even you?" Bill asked quietly, raising an eyebrow. Al nodded slowly.

"Even me."

"Thanks," Angel managed, a hoarse whisper accompanied by a tear forming in the corner of her eye. She wiped at it with her finger, smiling gently. "That means a lot."

"Don't get me wrong," Al said, leaning back slightly and crossing his arms behind his head. "Doesn't mean I *like* you or anything… it just means I don't expect too much from you."

Angel grinned, nodding her head and knocking back the rest of her drink.

"Thanks," she said, standing up and moving towards the food preparation area, throwing the ceramic mug into the sink and filling it with water before returning to the back of the living area and climbing up the stairs.

Bill made his way to his feet and casually walked around the living quarters, past the bunks occupied by Garth, Sylvester and Clive, each in as deep a sleep as the next, and entering the main entryway to the vehicle, taking a look outside. It was early morning, and the sun outside cast an orange glow over the low cloud cover. It didn't look especially nice out there, like it was going to rain, and the rising sun gave off just enough light to pick out the details of the bloodied patch of snow that indicated where Steve had fallen. They had to make sure Sarah didn't see that. It would be bad enough later on in the day when the bodies were burned on the funeral pyre they were going to have to build; but first, they'd have to find somewhere with enough trees to serve their needs.

Sighing to himself, Bill returned to the interior of the vehicle and aimlessly wandered into the armoury, then the kitchen, before returning to the main living area.

"Are you going to pace around all night?" Al asked without looking at him, "Or are you just biding your time before you follow her up?"

"Follow her?" Bill asked incredulously.

"Don't play fucking dumb with me, kid, I'm not just some dumb grunt. I know all about your ulterior motives; strutting around like fuck knows what…"

"Bullshit," hissed Bill. "It's the adrenaline, from the fire fight, you know? The last thing that's on my mind is anything like that."

"Well get some sleep."

"I'm too wired to sleep," Bill said, throwing himself on to one of the vacant bunks and grimacing as pain shot through his body from the various wounds he'd picked up from his battle with the Messiah. His eye didn't seem to be as swollen as it had been, but both the cut and his old bullet wound had slowly started to pulse again; he had been sitting for so long previously that all his aches and pains had quickly worn away, but getting up and walking around had only served to antagonise them.

"We aren't," murmured Garth, pulling one of his pillows over his head. "Shut up."

Bill muttered incoherently to himself and climbed out of his bunk, shuffling towards the staircase, looking over his shoulder at Al who was glaring at him, accusingly.

"Injuries," Bill explained, motioning towards the bloodied patch visible around the rip in his shirt and jacket.

"Of course," he said with an arrogant smile. "*Injuries*. That what you kids are calling it nowadays?"

Ignoring him as best he could, Bill pulled himself slowly up the staircase, limbs aching with each ponderous step, and a soft smile spread across his face as Angel slid into view.

She sat on a metal stool by one of the benches fixed to the side of the room, looking at herself in a precariously balanced mirror and trying to stitch the cut on the side of her head with a curved needle, grimacing in pain and hissing through her teeth each time the needle penetrated her flesh and pulled the lips of the wound closer together. With the drama of the birth and resulting deaths having passed, and Sarah currently sleeping, it was now time to deal with their own injuries as best as they could.

"Need a hand?"

Angel jumped at the sound of his voice, her needle dropping from her hand and dangling from her head by the thin line of brown thread she was using to mend the wound. She nodded, pulling a second stool up beside her and spinning around, ignoring the mirror and offering the dangling needle to him. Bill sat on the stool, grabbed the hooked piece of metal, and gently tilted Angel's head to one side, getting a better look at the wound. It wasn't much more than a flesh wound, but it had been the cause of quite a bit of bleeding, and Bill knew that a head wound should never be something taken lightly. He looked tentatively at the implement he held, moved forwards as if to pierce the skin, then recoiled slightly and shifted in his seat before trying again.

"I won't break, you know," Angel said with a grin.

"I know," Bill smiled back. "I just… I don't know what I'm doing."

"No one here does. Just finish it off, then we'll have a look at you, okay?"

Bill tried his best to finish the job, finally coming to the end of the wound and looping the thread together into a tight knot. Angel then adjusted herself, covering the wound with her auburn hair and straightened herself up. She smiled and tossed the soiled needle into the yellow medical waste bin before unlocking various lockers and drawers to gather what she would need for the examination. Bill followed her with his eyes as she moved, and found himself smiling on more than one occasion, as she had to bend over to retrieve items from the lower of the drawers. His smile faded as she moved behind a pair of tables draped in white sheets, and his gaze suddenly became fixed on them. He motioned softly towards the tables as Angel turned around, a stainless steel tray in hand.

"Is that them?"

Angel didn't say anything; she just walked around the tables and guided Bill's head away from the covered dead bodies.

"I've cooled the room as best I can using the environmental controls, Al showed me where they were," she said. For the first time since entering the medical bay, Bill realised it was indeed cooler than downstairs, and his breath misted in the air as the pair spoke. "She hasn't seen them yet: maybe it'll be best if she doesn't, we should just cremate them as soon as we can, maybe before she wakes up."

"We can't do that," Bill said, casting a wary eye over the array of instruments on the tray: scalpels, needles, clamps, bandages, sutures: "Can we?"

Angel shrugged, more to herself than anyone else.

"I'm only ten years older than her: the last time I saw my parents was when they were dead, and that's how I remember them, most of the time. I can't remember their faces when they were alive, I can only remember their dead eyes…" she wiped a tear from her eye, shaking the memories from her head. "I mean, that's just me, right? She's a tough kid. She'd have to be if she hung around with Al as much as she does. She might be different to me… I'm just saying…"

"I'll speak to Al," Bill said reassuringly. "We'll talk it over."

Angel nodded, her mind put at ease, and then her soft smile reappeared as she began her examination of Bill, gently prodding and poking him as she systematically run through the list of aches and pains he had to complain about.

"Broken or bruised ribs" she murmured to herself, running her hands over his chest. "Knife wound, needs some stitches, though it's not deep enough to hit any organs. Looks like your old scar's been torn open, too, that could do with some stitches. Bruises, minor cuts…"

She shone a penlight in his eyes and moved it from side to side, following his pupils with her own. "Looks like you might have a slight concussion, you complained of a headache and your left eye's a little unfocussed."

She flicked the light off, dropping it to the tray, and for a moment their eyes met, and Bill felt a spark, a moment of chemistry between the two: he wondered who would be first to break the gaze between the pair.

Jenny, he suddenly thought, his memories stirred up by the talk of seeing people in their final moments. It had been a while since he last thought of her properly, and almost three years since she had died. Now his mind decided to open an old wound and conjure images of Jenny lying on her deathbed, gushing watery blood from rapidly opening wounds until a bullet smashed through her skull and the flames consumed her corpse. Images of the days and weeks before flashed through his mind, their love for each other, the time they spent together…

Angel broke off from the gaze first, retrieving a needle and thread before pulling aside his jacket and T-shirt and quickly going to work on his wound.

"It's a lot easier when it's not on the side of your own head," she grinned, working quickly and efficiently. "If you want me to sew up that wound on your thigh…"

"I'll clean that one up myself," Bill said, nodding his head. "I should be able to manage that."

"You'll need a shot of stimulant to avoid any infection, antibiotics or something…"

"I'll sort it out myself, thanks," Bill managed with a shrug of his shoulders. "I'll be good."

Angel shrugged her shoulders, nodded her head, then stood and walked away from him, heading towards the staircase leading back down into the living quarters. "I'll give you a couple of minutes. Don't tape your ribs, though. You might end up giving yourself something like pneumonia or a collapsed lung."

"See? You're learning stuff all the time," Bill chuckled softly.

"Give me a shout if you need a hand," Angel said as she vanished out of sight and Bill sighed heavily, unfastening his trousers and quickly working on his scar, pulling the opened lesion together and closing the bloodied gap. If there had been one to hand, Bill would have gladly considered using a staple gun on the wounds he had, too. He knew doctors often used staples to close wounds, though they had to be different to a normal staple. Still, he would have tried anything to keep himself together, but luckily he didn't have to put his theory to the test, as there was no such device anywhere on the trailer.

Bill slipped his jacket and T-shirt off as slow and careful as he could, not wanting to over-stretch his injured ribs or open the freshly sealed knife wound, then gently prodded his ribs. They ached, hurt even worse when he breathed in and out too deeply, but they didn't feel *loose*, for lack of a better word.

Slipping his jeans back on, Bill stood up and looked once more at the table with the bodies on. Draping his shirt over one arm, he took a hesitant step towards them, reached out and grabbed the corner of the sheet, lifting it up slightly. A small grey foot came into his field of vision, skin dark purple along the bottom of the limb where the blood had come to settle.

He dropped the sheet. He didn't know what morbid curiosity had compelled him to lift the sheet in the first place, but he had seen more than enough.

"Seen enough?"

Bill spun and saw Angel standing at the top of the stairs again, a puzzled expression on her face.

"I had to see, I guess," Bill said. "I had to make sure... that they were still dead."

Angel nodded, stepping forwards and circling the twin tables. She cracked a smile as she spoke. "What kind of fucked up world are we living in where we have to check to make sure the dead stay dead? I know what you mean, though. I keep expecting to see one of them sit up, to see one of them move or start to moan and groan. The sooner they get burned, the better…"

"I know," Bill said, nodding his head, leaning back against the bench. Angel drew to a stop beside him, joining him in his appraisal of the dead bodies.

"I still wonder if there was something else I could have done, something I missed that could have made things different. What if I'd tried to perform a caesarean? Would I have been able to save the baby, or Cindy, or both? Were there any symptoms I could have picked up on earlier?"

"Stop beating yourself up over this," Bill insisted, wrapping an arm around Angel's waist and bringing her in closer to him, holding her for reassurance. She tilted her head to one side, resting it against his shoulder and sighed heavily. Her warmth against his skin and the tickling sensation of her hair against his chest reminded Bill that he was currently still half naked in the cold room, and he almost broke away to put on his shirt. Almost.

"We'll be all right. Trust me."

Bill turned to one side, wrapped his other arm around her, and placed his lip on Angel's forehead, a gentle and reassuring kiss. She gratefully accepted the embrace, seeming to melt into his arms, then placed her lips on his cheek, returning the gesture. Their eyes locked again, faces mere inches from one another, but this time neither one of them turned away. The distance between them closed, Bill leaned over slightly, and their lips touched, bringing an electrifying sensation that he had all but forgotten existed; it washed over him like the shockwave of an explosion, a burst of adrenaline that erased pain he felt and replaced it with a sense of longing, of *lust*, that he couldn't control himself; neither could Angel.

They clawed at one another, tearing at each other's clothing and flesh, their limbs intertwining around each other as they stumbled across the room and slammed to a halt against the door leading into Al's vacant command room. The pair remained there for almost a minute, raining kisses and playful bites down on one another, until the door creaked and gave way, allowing the pair to tumble into the room, falling to the floor with a sharp jolt that brought a sudden burst of pain to Bill: he didn't' care, he had other things on his mind.

Kicking the door shut behind him, Bill watched as Angel walked over to the bed in the room, pulling her top off and letting it drop to the floor behind her, peering over her shoulder with a sultry smile as she unfastened her trousers and let the heavy material slide down her legs, revealing a milky-pale complexion still partially covered by the black lingerie she wore. Bill rushed forwards as she released the catch of her bra, wrapping his arms around her and savouring the sensation of warm flesh against his own. The pair tumbled to the bed, Bill caressing Angel's smooth pale skin while she fumbled with the belt of his jeans, throwing garments of clothing to the floor as the two writhed in ecstasy in each other's embrace.

Concentrating his kisses on the neck and shoulders of Angel, Bill felt himself become surrounded by the warmth of Angel, her nails raking down his back as the pair moved in rhythm together.

For the first time since the plague had first destroyed his life, Bill felt content and at ease.

Angel's eyes flickered open, taking some time to work out where she was: she didn't recognise the room at first, probably because Al had never invited her into his sacred room, If that were the case, why was she in there?

She looked down at herself, at the ruffled sheet that twined around both her and Bill's naked bodies, and the activities of the previous night came flooding back to her. The feeling of lust between the two had been too intense to fight, and the sex had lasted for close to two hours, off and on, before the pair had slipped into a peaceful slumber; for the first time, a sleep unmarred by dreams or memories of the plague or the roaming dead.

Angel propped herself up on one elbow, pulling the blanket around her to provide as much cover as possible while she lay and looked at the sleeping form of Bill.

She'd never expected anything like that to happen to her, and had certainly never expected her first time to be like that. The circumstances around it all confused her, and she furrowed her brow as she tried to work out the reasoning behind it. It had been an eventful day, filled with surprises and loss. Maybe it was all tied in to the feelings that had been stirred up by the deaths of Steve and Cindy; something that had happened to remind them both that life was unpredictable, and something could happen at any given moment. Maybe it had just been the desire for company, human company that wasn't blowing the head off a zombie or firing a gun at you.

Well, there was some shooting involved…

Angel blushed as the obscene thought ran through her mind, and she pulled her loose hair back into a ponytail, tying it off as tight as she could.

"What now?" she whispered quietly to herself. She slipped out from beneath the covers, retrieving her clothes and pulling them on, silently unlatching the door and slipping out the small room into the larger medical bay.

The room was still chilled, the tables still occupied by the silent corpses of their friends. She walked over to one of the sinks and splashed her face with water, wiping it off with a white towel. She turned away from the sink, lost in her thoughts, and jumped at the sight of a tall dark figure at the top of the stairs watching her. He took a couple of steps forwards, looking behind her to the door to the smaller room and the door left slightly ajar.

"You two been fucking around?" he murmured. "In *my* room?"

She didn't respond, trying to keep busy by replacing instruments and clearing up from the previous nights medical examination.

"I notice you're not denying it," Al said.

"I never deny it," Angel said, throwing a metal tray down on to the bench with a clatter. "I normally ignore you, *Bill* normally denies it."

"He wasn't denying it last night," Al said, circling the bodies and looking at the covering sheets, mentally working out which would be the best way to get the bodies outside. "The pair of you managed to make quite a bit of noise last night. I thought you were fighting at first. Should've known better, I guess."

Angel didn't say anything; she had nothing to come back with. She decided that there were more important things to discuss.

"Sarah hasn't been up yet, has she?"

"No, I didn't know what the hell you two were doing, so I kept her downstairs. She's still adamant that she wants to see them."

"We were talking last night, we don't think she should see them. It's easier to remember people for who they were if the last thing you see isn't a pale dead body."

"You talk about this kind of shit while you're screwing around?" muttered Al, half-closing his eyes and peering at her as a snake would.

"No, we talked about it *before*…"

Al nodded knowingly, a slight grin tugging at the corners of his mouth. "Gotcha."

"Asshole."

"Arsehole, you people keep telling me the word's arsehole."

"We tell you anything to keep you quiet," Bill announced, appearing at the doorway to the smaller room and adjusting his shirt. "She's right, though. About Sarah seeing the bodies…"

"The kid becomes a man," Al smiled. Bill ignored him.

"We both don't think it's a good idea for Sarah to see the bodies."

"Well, neither do I," Al said, lifting himself up on to one of the benches. "So that's something we all agree on, for once. Now how do we make Sarah see things our way?"

"We'll need to talk to her," Angel said. Both men nodded, though no one volunteered for the task. Al turned to look at Angel, and then Bill mimicked him.

"Don't suppose you could do it? You know, a woman-to-woman thing?"

"Am I the only woman here?" asked Angel, though she knew there was no point in trying to argue. The only other female aboard the vehicle was Pam, and she didn't have any experiences similar to what Angel had been through, at least as far as she knew. Resigned to the fact, she sighed and nodded. "Okay, I'll talk to her. Is she awake?"

Al nodded. "Pam's trying to get her to eat something first."

"Go get her," Angel said. Al leapt down from the desk and made his way down the stairs, leaving the two alone in an uncomfortable silence. Angel looked at Bill through the corners of her eyes as he shuffled uneasily from side to side, idly playing with the clasps on some of the lockers. One of the locks popped, and a metal tray clattered to the ground, scattering sterile needles across the floor, each still sealed in their plastic wrappings. He dropped to the floor, rushing to pick them up, and Angel did the same, their hands feverishly snatching at the loose implements until their fingers both wrapped around the same needle. Both recoiled from it, as if it carried an electric charge, and looked nervously at one another.

"I think we need to talk," Bill finally managed to say.

Angel nodded slowly as she looked to one side, trying to avoid as much eye contact as she could, and noticed that Sarah had appeared at the top of the stairs, eyes puffed up and her newest stuffed animal dangling from one hand.

"We'll talk later," said Angel, nodding her head and keeping her eyes fixed on Sarah, a faint smile on her lips. Bill nodded a silent response and marched out the medical bay, pushing past Sarah as she stood motionless at the top of the stairs.

Although she was young, Sarah was by no means stupid or naïve: she had woken in the middle of the night and heard the sounds that Bill and Angel had been making. She didn't need to be a genius to know that they had been fighting for almost two hours; probably about letting her see her parents one more time.

"Did you sleep well sweetie?" Angel asked, ignoring the mess that remained on the floor and stepping forwards. Sarah followed with her eyes as she moved, until the white sheets drew her attention away from her. She stepped forwards, her eyes fixed on the cloth that lay between her and her parents' bodies.

"Is that them?"

Angel nodded, moving quickly and placing herself between the tables and Sarah. She dropped to her knees so she was closer to her height, but not in a condescending way, and placed both her hands on her shoulders. She nodded softly.

"Can I see them?"

"You can," Angel said, but her hands clamped down harder on Sarah's shoulder as she went to move towards the tables. "But I don't think you want to."

"I do," Sarah said, nodding her head. "I want to see mum and daddy."

"Listen sweetie," Angel smiled, keeping her voice quiet and subdued. "Did I ever tell you about what happened to my parents?"

Sarah sniffed and shook her head. No one in the group had openly discussed their previous life with her; she knew that the adults had talked about that between themselves, but one of the disadvantages of being the child of the group meant that she wasn't privy to a lot of information.

"A long time ago, I lived on a farm with my Mam and Dad; we had lots of different animals and grew different crops: once the plague came, we had to kill all our animals to get rid of them. When one of the Rots, the dead men… when one of those turned up, it bit my Mam."

She stopped talking, her eyes glossing over as she told her story. Sarah didn't move; she felt strange, actually being told something that she considered 'grown up' talk.

"My Mam was infected…"

"She turned into one of those dead men?" Sarah asked, a wide-eyed look of amazement on her childish face.

"She was infected," Angel continued, wiping her eyes with a piece of paper towelling. "And she passed it on to my dad with a bite. I had to kill both my parents; I saw them both right up until they died, I had to get rid of them. Sometimes, when I think about them, I remember the good times we had: working on the farm, the nights we'd spend around the fire. But sometimes, in the middle of the night, I'd remember them after I'd killed them, seeing them dead...

"If you don't see them, you can't remember them like that. You'll only be able to remember the good times. I guess I'm just trying to give you something I never had the chance to have myself... am I even making any sense?"

Sarah frowned, trying to think through the words Angel had said to her. She thought she knew what she was getting at. Slowly, she nodded a response, her brow remaining furrowed slightly as she tried to piece everything together in her mind.

"So... you're saying if I don't see them, it's kinda like they're not really dead to me, and I can pretend that it never happened? That they just left me here instead?"

Angel wrinkled her own brow in thought for a while, then forced a smile and a nod. "Kinda, yeah, I guess you could look at it that way,"

Sarah was still uncertain, shuffling forwards slightly and reaching out to grab the corner of one of the white sheets. Angel didn't try to stop her, and she gently raised the corner, catching the glimpse of a pale hand far smaller then her own, fingers half-curled into a loose fist. She dropped the material and spoke to Angel, though kept her eyes fixed on the smaller of the bulges beneath the cloth.

"What was it? The baby, I mean..."

"A little boy," Angel answered, looking apprehensively at the flapping corner of the sheet. "Your Mam... I mean your Mum gave birth to a little boy."

"Did they name him?"

Angel shook her head.

"I guess I'll have to do that, I mean I guess that's up to me."

She looked at Angel, her eyes welling up with tears.

"How else will we remember him?"

"As long as it's not Mother Fucker," Angel managed to blurt out with a smile. Sarah found herself laughing gently along with her.

"What about David? My grampa was called David."

"I think that's a nice name," Angel agreed.

Sarah nodded, muttering the name again and wrapping her arms around Angel: she wasn't sure who was consoling who, as they were both upset, but the warmth of another person was comforting, nonetheless. Pulling away from the hold, Sarah hugged the stuffed animal she held once, kissed its forehead, then slipped it beneath the sheet, resting it on top of the infant.

"For you, David," she whispered softly, then stepped back, staring in silence at the sheets for five minutes.

"Okay, I'm finished," Sarah finally said, matter-of-factly. Angel nodded solemnly, and the pair slowly walked away from the medical gurneys, towards the staircase.

IV

"She's a strong little girl," Bill announced, watching as the last embers of the funeral pyre lifted from the glowing mound of ash and danced towards the sky in the wind. Not far from the edge of the pile of smoking debris, Sarah sat between Pam and Angel on a small metal crate, each staring into the shimmering and shifting dust.

"I know," Al finally said, pulling the chewed cigar from his mouth and tapping it against the side of his boot. "A lot stronger than her father was. She'd make her mother proud, too."

"You think she'll be all right? I mean with the history of her sister..."

"I was never really sure about that," Al confessed. "I mean, a six year old killing herself? Does that shit happen? Maybe the truth was she found a knife and played with it, killed herself accidentally. Kids in America used to do it all the time, shoot themselves with their parent's gun when they were stupid enough to leave them lying around. That wasn't a suicidal kid, it was an irresponsible parent. Convincing yourself your kid killed themselves might be easier than admitting that it was your own fucking fault your kid was dead."

"That's a pretty fucking strong conviction you need to have to say that aloud," Bill said.

"He was never quite here with us," Al carried on. "He was always so busy, so preoccupied with rebuilding his family that he ignored the family he had already. I should've seen it, the way he was talking," Al mused, going over it again in his mind. "I should've seen it coming. He asked me to look after her. We'll keep an eye on her, Pam and me, just to make sure. We'll need help, of course."

"No problems, Al, I got your back. We all do."

"I know you do, kid. Thanks."

Bill took a swig from a bottle of water he had found in the kitchen area, swilling it around in his mouth before swallowing it. He grimaced slightly at the stale taste, then nodded out towards the horizon.

"What's the plan now? Back on the road?"

"We can't spend the rest of our lives on the highways of Britain, not with the Rots and the gangs. It ain't no place for a kid, and it ain't no place for a forty-something year old, either."

"Back to the base, then? See what's left of it?"

"The base is wasted," Al said without looking away from three girls sitting on the crate. "I got a good look at it during the fire fight from up top. It looked like one of the fuel reservoirs cooked off, could've been anything from shrapnel to a flaming Rot: ain't gonna be much more there other than rubble and a crater. And even if that weren't the case, there'd still be a hundred tin pot Rots running riot there."

"Nothing we could salvage?"

"Everything was underground, all the entrances would have caved in with the blast. We're lucky we got out with what we did."

"Lucky?" laughed Clive as we walked up to them and sat down beside them, wrapping the folds of his thick leather coat around him. Since the cremation earlier that afternoon and after reciting a few verses from the bible he carried, Clive hadn't said anything to anyone until now. "Not luck at all. God's will."

"Don't," snapped Bill, pointing a finger at Clive. "Don't come here peddling that horseshit. Now's not the time!"

"Everything that happened wasn't the work of god: Tara, Steve, Cindy, David... what kind of god would do that shit to his own? The same god that thought it would be a good idea to raise the dead?"

"Everything is done in accordance with His will," Clive said, reaffirming his beliefs. "The death of a blasphemous heretic and his unholy army..."

"The death of our friend, that girl's mother, brother, and father? That was his will?"

"Her mother and brother, yes. Steve chose his own path, and the kingdom of God doesn't look well on suicide victims; an eternity in purgatory is the best his soul can expect."

Al rolled to one side from his seat and curled his hands around the lapels of Clive's coat, pushing him backwards and on to the ground where he pinned him down, glaring at him with darkened eyes.

"When we want to hear about this bullshit, we'll ask you. Until then, keep your bible-bashing to yourself, and keep the hell away from Sarah; she's not religious, and I don't expect her to come looking for counselling from you, but if she does, you just send her back to me. And if you say *anything* like that to her about Steve, or anyone else, I'll take great pleasure in gutting you with this."

He withdrew his combat knife from one of his holsters and stabbed it into the ground less than and inch from Clive's head, twisting the blade to make sure his point came across.

"Understand?"

"I do," murmured Clive. "It's been a long and hard day. We all need some rest. If you don't mind, I'll retire to my bunk."

Al pulled himself to his feet and turned away from the priest, letting him clamber to his feet himself and retreat into the interior of the vehicle. Both Pam and Angel has heard the commotion and turned around to watch, but Sarah kept her eyes fixed on the dwindling fire.

"There's something wrong with Preacher-man," Al said in a low voice, waving casually to Pam to indicate everything was all right. Bill nodded in agreement, having noticed the change himself. "He's been weird since... well, I guess since Tara died."

"I don't know what to say," Bill offered. "Maybe the reappearance of the Messiah was enough to tip him over the edge?"

"Maybe. Do me a favour, kid. While I keep an eye on the little one, you keep an eye on him, yeah?"

"Yeah," agreed Bill. "Yeah, I'll do that. Maybe have a word with Sly, too?"

"Couldn't do any harm. I'll have a word with Spanners when I get a few minutes, see if he can find out what the priest's bugbear's about."

Silence feel between the two again. A gentle hissing in the distance make them both look up together, and they could see fat drops of rain splash against the steaming ashes.

"Just a shower," muttered Al to no one in particular. "It'll pass."

"So, what *do* we do now?" Bill asked, aware his initial question hadn't really been answered before the irritating priest had turned up and crashed their conversation.

"We rest up here for the night. First thing in the morning, we break out a couple of road atlases; compare them against my charts and maps. Between those we must be able to come up with some safe haven for us."

"Another staff meeting tomorrow, then?"

Al laughed softly. "Seems like our staff's getting less and less all the time."

Bill nodded slowly in agreement as the hisses in the distance increased and the rain slapped against his head, trickling down his forehead and into his eyes. He wiped at them absentmindedly, tipping his head towards the dark skies and catching drops of rain in his mouth.

"It's not going to die down," Al admitted, flicking his cigar into a mound of snow that was already turning into grey slush. "Fact is, it's going to piss it down. Let's get inside, settle down for the night. Sarah!"

The little girl turned around from her seat, tucking back the rattails of hair behind her ears.

"C'mon in, sweetie. It's getting late, and it's beginning to rain."

"I hadn't noticed," she lied, wiping the water from her face with a soaked sleeve. Pam stood up, tapping her shoulder in agreement and motioning her towards the opened trailer.

"C'mon, we'll see if we can get something to eat for you."

"I'm not hungry," the young girl said, pouting and trying her best to remain outside as long as possible.

"I am," Pam said softly, pulling Sarah up from her seat. "And you make the best sandwiches."

"Okay," Sarah sighed, resigned to the fact she would have to go in. She took Pam's hand, and together the two returned to the trailer, collecting Al as they went. Slapping Bill on his back as he rose from his seat, Al joined his surrogate family and returned to the interior of the trailer, leaving Angel and Bill outside.

She stood from her seat, kicked a pile of snow over part of the fire, then strolled casually over to

Bill.

"She's a strong kid," she said, echoing Bill's sentiments. He nodded curtly.

"I was just saying to Al; we'll all have to keep an eye on her, though."

"Of course," Angel replied, before lapsing into an uncomfortable silence. Bill squirmed, taking another drink from his bottle of water before offering it to Angel. She declined, looking towards the open door.

"You coming inside?" she asked. "You'll catch your death of cold out here."

"In a minute," Bill muttered. He was reluctant to go inside with her; unsure as to whether they were going to have their much-anticipated talk from earlier. He wasn't sure exactly what to say to her, and had tried his best to stay away from her for the duration of the day; it wasn't a position he was overly familiar with, and had no idea what he could say to her. He couldn't put two thoughts together about what had happened the previous night, how could he possibly hope to have a conversation with her about it?

"You sure?"

Bill nodded, watching her as she shrugged and strolled into the trailer.

The rain continued to batter against Bill's head as he took one last look around the abandoned fire, then he turned to face the trailer cab. Garth had retired a couple of hours ago to his own bunk, so Bill knew the cab would be empty. Swinging himself up from his seat, Bill skipped over to the trailer cab, heaved the heavy door open and slipped inside, shaking off his jacket and shoes and throwing himself into the large and worn drivers seat. He could see why Garth spent so much of his time sitting in the cabin; he had the best damn seat in the house.

Surrounded by the soothing glow of a hundred different flashing lights and pulsating screens, Bill nestled down into the comforting fabric of the padded seat and peered out into the rainstorm that now lashed against the windscreen. A ghostly pale reflection stared back at him, bloody, battered, and bruised with eyes heavily shadowed by the dark purple bags that clung to the underside of his eyes.

"Ain't you a pretty little thing," he muttered with a lopsided grin.

"You coming in kid?"

"I'm in the cabin," Bill announced into the microphone of the control panel, taking his eyes off the reflection and leaning forwards to activate the radio device before tearing the headset off himself; he was getting a little bit of feedback from the two devices being so close to one another. "Just lock up the trailer, I'll see you guys in the morning."

"Keep an eye on the radar in there," Al said.

"Yeah," Bill murmured, closing his eyes and tilting his head back. "No problems."

XXII
NECROPOLIS

"With the cramped nature of the towns and cities, and people living in each others pockets, is it any wonder the spread was like wildfire?"

I

Daylight stormed into the confines of the cabin, partially filtered by the layers of streaked grime that coated the windows. A light shower of rain still spattered against the glass barriers, and Bill moaned in a low voice as he lazily reached out and flicked one of the numerous switches that covered one of the control panels to one side. The windscreen wipers scraped across the windshield, the sound of worn rubber squealing against the damp and dirty windscreen fully rousing Bill from his slumber. Slapping his hand against his forehead, then grinding the heels of his hands into his eyes, he yawned and pulled himself out of the seat, glaring at the glowing red digits that displayed, among other things, the current time.

"Half six," Bill muttered to himself. He knew it would be another couple of hours before anyone else woke up; he was normally the first to wake up, especially once Al had started to relax more from his military training.

He flung himself back into the seat and spun around, turning to face a bank of monitors and keypads, idly tapping in different combinations according to the sticky labels pressed on to the empty spaces on the framework of the control cabinets.

One screen flashed to life indicating an overhead view of a large expanse of snow-covered countryside, displaying a network of small roads between dilapidated buildings with a pulsing red dot in the centre. The monitor bragged it was a GPS system, and Bill knew enough to realise that the red dot was his current position, and the landscape was actually the surrounding countryside. Taking the controls in one hand and wiping his mouth with the other, he rotated one dial to pull back the camera view, then twisted another to pan the view from side to side, taking in the details of the surrounding countryside.

Just as Al had said, the satellite picture showed a smoking pile of rubble surrounding a dark crater. The impressive Marine technology was obviously linked in to a real-time satellite that hung high above the island, as every so often a wisp of white cloud would float across the screen.

"Just like a video game," he mused as he scrolled the view as far down as it could go. Rivers and road scrolled by until the screen refused to budge, a warning message flashing on the lower half of the screen that the proximity had been reached, and to explore further he would have to link to another satellite. He didn't know how to do that, so he scrolled back a little and shifted to the side, catching sight of the outer edges of a large city. He perked up as soon as he saw the outer limits of the urban sprawl, and a sudden and reckless urge to explore struck Bill, something he hadn't felt for a long time.

"What do we have here?" he muttered, tapping the screen. To his surprise, the display reacted to his touch, bringing up a window on the screen with a list of numbers; the first three were headed with X, Y and Z, which Bill assumed related to coordinates, and the fourth the distance from their current position.

"Not far," he said, tapping his teeth and hissing to himself. "Maybe there's something there for us to use: maybe even somewhere for us to hold out."

Bill grabbed his jacket and slung it over one shoulder as he swung the door open, slipping his arms into both sleeves as the chill of the morning shocked his systems with a refreshing breeze and a light drizzle of rain. He washed his face in the damp spray, wiped it down on his sleeve, and then retreated back into the cab after his brisk shower, softly jiggling the lock of the heavy door between the cab and the trailer behind it and softly opening it.

It was dark inside, and Bill had to pause on the threshold, allowing his eyes to readjust to the dimness of the room before wading across the floor. He could see the shapes of three people lying on the sofa as well as those lying in the bunk beds, and could instantly tell who was who in the gloom, not only by their size and shape, but by the noises they made while asleep. One of the bulky shapes on the sofa with a nasally rattle was his intended target, and he crept forwards, reaching out and placing a hand on his shoulder.

"Al, you awake?"

The man grunted a wordless response and turned away from him, lazily draping an arm over the young girl between him and Pam.

"Al?" Bill insisted.

"Fucks sake," Al hissed, covering his eyes with one hand. "Is this important?"

"There's a city, about sixty or seventy miles away. Looks big."

"It going some place?" he slurred, refusing to open his eyes fully in case it woke him up.

"Well no," Bill answered, scratching his head.

"No?" Al rolled over, facing away from Bill. "Then it can wait until eleven when everyone's awake and we've all had something to eat."

"Five hours away," Bill grumbled. "What can I do for five hours?"

"Go to sleep," moaned Garth, poking his balding head out from beneath his quilt.

"I can't," insisted Bill

"Neither can I," growled Garth, scooping up his hat and hurling it across the room, bouncing it off Bill's head. "Some bastard's making too much noise."

"If you're at a loose end, clean up the weapons trailer," suggested Al. "You made the mess in the first place."

"You're right, how inconsiderate of me," Bill glowered as he shuffled across the darkened room, heading towards the dented door leading to the rear-most trailer. "Next time some homicidal religious nutcase tries to storm our vehicle, I'll just let them waltz aboard and kill us all."

"At least I'd be able to get a decent sleep," Garth hissed.

Bill slid the door open and slipped into the rearmost trailer, cursing under his breath as he heaved the door shut and flicked the lights on.

They flickered to life with a low humming noise, bathing the room in pale blue light from the overhead fluorescent tubes. Bill sighed heavily, as he'd forgotten just how much of a mess the trailer had been left in after the previous battle. Weapons had been dislodged from their rack and left scattered on the floor; crates of ammunition had been broken open, scattering shells and bullets across the floor, and charred lumps of flesh had left to rot in congealed pools of thinned and watery blood. With a look of repulsion, Bill kicked at the lumps of carrion so they bounced and rolled across the floor, slamming into the door at the rear of the trailer. Once he had gathered all the meat, he opened the doors and dumped the remnants of the dead body on to the slush-covered ground behind the trailer and quickly wiped up the tacky spilled fluid with an old rag before discarding that, too.

"Even after society breaks down, I'm still lumbered with the shit jobs," Bill muttered to himself, replacing a collection of assault rifles on their rack, then pawed handfuls of bullets and shells into different boxes. He started off by trying to sort them out into their different calibres, but gave up and instead decided to throw shotgun shells and slugs in one box and all the other bullets into another. He knew it would piss Al off no end, and that fact made the arduous task a little more pleasurable.

With crates finally resealed, magazines stacked and secured and weapons affixed in place, Bill stepped back from his job and nodded in satisfaction before looking to the digital clock that was fastened one of the bulkheads.

According to the readout, he had only been working for an hour: he still had a long time until the rest of the group was awake. He looked around the trailer to see if there was anything else he could do to pass the time away, other than sort out the different types of bullets he had heaped into the same crate. His eyes fell on the dormant motorcycle suspended from the ceiling by a number of chains and ropes, and he smiled softly to himself.

Dare I?

Grabbing a rucksack and filling it with whatever weapons and ammunition he could, Bill stepped over towards the control box for the sling and pulled it open, thumbing the release button. With a soft whine of motors, the two-man vehicle slowly touched down on the decking of the trailer, and Bill started to work at the chains and ropes, releasing it from the rigging. He climbed on to the bike, getting a feel of the weight of the vehicle and sensing the cage of the rear-mounted gunner seat towering over him.

"I don't like that," he said, leaning the vehicle to one side and almost toppling as the weight of the cage and its gyroscopic suspension overpowered him. He wracked his brains to try to remember if Al had ever mentioned anything about it before; he'd seen the remains of one in Manchester when he and Tara had stumbled across the street filled with dead Marines and feasting Rots, but he'd never seen one moving. From the weight of the vehicle, he couldn't imagine tearing up and down a highway like he had on his old bike; nor could he imagine any type of high-speed chase through a town like Edgly.

Knocking down the reinforced kick-stand, Bill swung himself off the bike and looked at the cage, inspecting the underside of the gun mount and running his fingers along the joints, finding a number of metal pins and locking nuts that joined the two together. He dropped to the ground, rolled on to his back and looked at the underside of the carriage, working at the threaded bolts with his fingers: they were welded in place, and there was no way they'd be able to be removed.

Mounting the vehicle once more, Bill rolled the heavy machine down the rear ramp and parked it up a few metres away from the back of the vehicle before slamming the doors shut, sealing up the trailer again. He kicked the bike into life and slowly gunned the engine, sweeping around from the rear of the trailer to the cab at the front in a wide lazy arc. He jumped off the motorcycle and quickly made his way in to the cabin, getting a fix on the direction of the city and jotting it down on a piece of scrap paper that he found on the dashboard before leaping back on to the idling bike. Taping the paper down over the speedometer, Bill cast a final glance over his shoulder at the trailer, silently mulling over what he was about to do.

It's not like I'm going to explore the entire city, he reasoned to himself. *Just a look on the outskirts, see what it's like. I'll be back in a couple of hours, no problem.*

Revving the throttle of the bike, the vehicle sped away from the trailer, kicking up snow and mud and spraying it against the side of the cab as he pulled away from the scene.

Angel's sleep was torn apart as the hideous sound of a chainsaw tore through her mind, and she jolted herself awake, startled by the sound of the revving engine. Bolting over to one of the windows, she pressed her face against the glass in time to see a cumbersome bike swerve and sway away from the trailer. Her initial response was to grab her rifle and wake the others, suddenly aware that one of the Marines still stationed on the island may have stumbled across their encampment. The moment her hand wrapped around her sniper rifle, she felt a large hand wrap itself around her wrist, startling her.

"Al," she hissed, "Someone's found us."

"No, they haven't," he muttered, waving her away from the window. "Your boyfriend's decided to go exploring on his own. Dumb son of a bitch."

"Exploring? Where?"

"He got a hard-on a couple of hours ago about some city he found on the GPS, wanted us all to get up and go looking right now."

"Why didn't we?"

"It's a fucking city, it's not going anywhere."

"Well, we have to go after him."

"Why? He's a big boy, he can look after himself."

"But…"

"He took the only other form of transport we have, bitch. You want to go after him, the only people who can drive this thing is Garth and me. You want to go after him, go wake up sleeping beauty over there."

Angel frowned, knowing fine well that Garth was in no way a morning person, and wouldn't be inclined to help anyone out who woke him before he naturally woke himself up. "Why can't you drive it now?"

"Cause I'm asleep right now," he grinned, returning back to his spot beside Sarah and Pam. "And all this shit right now is just me talking in my sleep."

"You're a bastard, Al, you know that?" snapped Angel, returning to the window. The bike was nothing more than a speck in the distance now, and she felt helpless. Though there was nothing she could do, she didn't move from the window, staring longingly into the distance.

II

The outlaying roads of the city were heavily congested with battered and damaged cars and vans: rusted and decrepit husks of vehicles that were the only reminder to Bill that this place had once been a thriving and bustling city. The ice-cold rain that pelted Bill had washed most of the snow here away, and although the wetness of the downpour didn't penetrate his clothing, the cold certainly did.

He sat in the middle of the road, the engine of his machine ticking over as he surveyed the carnage around him. In almost three years he had all but forgotten what the cities of Britain had become once the dead had started to walk, and although he and Al had paid a visit to one such town only a few days ago, the blanket of snow had helped mask the true desolation.

Further up the road, he could see that the way become completely blocked as buildings around them had crumbled and fallen, mounds of rubble taller than Bill creating walls and barriers before him. Even on a normal bike, he would have had a problem in negotiating the cars and rubble; with the heavy excessive load of the Marine cycle, he wouldn't have stood a chance in hell. Reluctantly, Bill clambered off the machine and unhooked one of the heavy machineguns from the back of the vehicle, strapping it to himself with some excess webbing he found attached to the rear seat before working the firing bolt, making sure it was loaded and ready to fire.

Turning up the collar of his jacket, Bill strolled into the jumble of abandoned vehicles, carefully weaving between the metallic skeletons, ducking behind the larger obstructions, and moving as carefully as he could without drawing too much attention to himself. Since leaving the sanctity of the trailer, he hadn't come across any Rots or other gang members, but that wasn't to say they weren't out there.

He moved briskly through the downpour, his rucksack heavily laden with weapons and bullets knocking against his spine and kidneys with each step, and tried to shift the uncomfortable weight from one side to another, trying to find the happy medium. The cold nipped at his hands and face as he continued to walk, his fingers numb, and he systematically removed one hand from the weapon, flexed his fingers, then replaced it and did the same with the other. He knew that he wasn't carrying any extra ammunition for the M249, but he would have been an idiot to leave it attached to the bike: he'd left the second as there was no way he'd be able to carry both weapons *and* his rucksack.

He reached the first mound of rubble and scrambled to the top, ducking down low and crawling over the ridge. In the valley below him, three Rots crouched over an inert body, tearing at the corpse and squabbling between one another as they fought for the juiciest piece of meat or the largest bloody bone. Bill looked around from left to right, then gently placed the large weapon on the ground and set his bag down, retrieving a pistol from his cache and screwing a silencer on to the opened muzzle. The pistol itself was something special; a hunting pistol Al had taken great pleasure in fitting up with a laser-targeting device. Bill flicked a switch on the side of the laser and rested the barrel of the weapon on a mortar-covered brick in front of him, guiding the red dot on to the base of one skull of one of the creatures. He quickly swung the weapon from side to another, quickly lining up each shot and practicing which he would be able to do the quickest.

Pfft.

The weapon kicked almost inaudibly in his hand, and the round slapped into the back of the creature's head. Bill gawped in amazement as the creature jerked forwards, then clambered to its feet, turning around to look directly at him.

Its skin was tough and dry, like old leather, and as the animal moved it stretched and moved with the thin, bony limbs: it didn't rip or spew watery blood like other carriers of the disease. The falling water splashed against the dry skin, sinking into the dried pores like rain on a desert floor, and it glared at him through shrivelled eyeballs, standing rigid like a soldier to attention. Bill readjusted his aim, lifting the twitching red dot to the forehead of the creature and unleashed a second round. The round smashed against the skull, snapping the head back before jolting back into position; it remained upright, the skin breached by the bullet, the bone beneath dented but not penetrated.

The creature burst to life, lunging forwards and powering up the pile of rubble, rigid limbs flailing wildly as it ran faster than any Rot he had seen before. Bill stood up, lifting the pistol and squeezing the trigger again and again, round after round slamming into the skull and torso, slowing the oncoming creature but not stopping it.

"Christ," Bill muttered, dropping the now-empty pistol and grabbing the machinegun, bringing it about to bear on the creature and unleashing a stream of gunfire into the Rot. The more powerful rounds hammered the animal, finally penetrating the bone and dropping the flesh eater. Although the heavy weapon had a lot more power behind it, it lacked the benefit of a silencer.

As the gunfire roared across the open street, the remaining two zombies clambered to their feet, each in as emaciated a state as the first. Bill lowered the weapon and hosed it from side to side, showering the walking dead with red-hot lead, shredding limbs and cracking bones, toppling the animated corpses and ending their existence. As the retorts of the gunfire echoed off into the distance, Bill lowered the smoking weapon and flexed his fingers, rolling his hands at the wrists and shaking away the vibrations of the weapon that had rumbled through his chilled bones.

The strength of the creatures – and their ability to absorb a number of bullets before toppling – unnerved Bill no end, and he was reminded of the creatures he and Al had seen in the town they had found Mikey in.

"Congenial bone disorder my arse," muttered Bill, recalling his conversation with the Marine at the time. "They're evolving."

Bill swallowed hard, knowing he was right. Ordinarily, a nine millimetre round would have been more than enough to penetrate the skull; now, things were different and the zombies had evolved into something that could take more damage than normal. Bill was more than convinced that it wasn't just the cold that was making the creatures tougher than normal.

"Time to go," he decided, realising that exploration on his own didn't seem like such a good idea, especially if he was facing creatures stronger than he was used to. He spun around on top of the mound, sending chunks of masonry tumbling down around him, and looked towards the bike in the distance... and the horde of Rots that had emerged from their hiding places. A hundred leather-skinned animals with reinforced bones stood between him and his transport, his chances of survival rapidly diminishing as more and more of the animals stumbled into the street. Bill looked over his shoulder, at the four dead bodies that lay at the foot of the mound, and decided the only way he could possibly go was that way, hoping that he could double back on himself and give the crowd of Rots a wide berth. He flung the pistol back into his bag and rummaged through it as he moved down into the valley of debris, pulling out a sawn-off shotgun and sliding solid slugs into the magazine tube. A modified pump-action was a step down from the automatic assault weapons Bill had recently used, but it was the only shotgun he could carry in the rucksack that wasn't too cumbersome.

"Okay, you dead pieces of crap," he hissed, lifting the weapon and firing off one slug at the first of the zombies as they crowned the hill. The slug had more power than the pistol, and it smashed into the skull, punching out the other side of the cranium of the creature and spraying brains on the three rising behind it. One of them lunged on the falling body, ploughing forwards and rolling down the other side, bouncing down the uneven side and landing in an awkward, broken position beside the other fallen Rots. As soon as it stopped moving, the lunging creature buried its maw into the opened skull of the dead creature it had tackled, gorging itself on what brain matter was left. Its feasting was quickly ended as Bill loosed another slug, creating another decapitation.

Backing away from the advancing horde, Bill found himself making his up the other side of the valley, deeper into the city. He felt as if the zombies were herding him deeper into their territory, where they'd have the advantage; If he'd thought about bringing a grenade he could've blasted his way back through to his bike, but he'd only planned on scouting the city, not assaulting it.

God damn it, Bill thought as he blasted another zombie, this time obliterating its neck and sending the severed head toppling to the ground. Even though he'd been on a short recon mission, he should have prepared better. *What was it Al had said? Better to take everything and not need it instead of needing something and not having it?*

"I know better for next time," Bill spat, blindly filling his pockets with shotgun shells from his bag before slinging it back over his shoulder. "If there *is* a next time."

The buildings that towered the streets on either side became more and more complete the further into the city Bill went, providing numerous hiding places that the Rots seemed to revel in: buildings he passed by crawled to life as the dead appeared; they stumbled out of blackened doorways, toppled over decaying windowsills, fell through broken walls and crawled across the ground as the city came to life. A low, constant moan filled the air as the hungry undead advanced on him, a droning sound broken only by the deafening blast of the shotgun as it repeatedly spoke.

Knowing when he was beat, Bill turned from the advancing hordes and sprinted from the evolved Rots, though they didn't give up on their pursuit. While some gave in to temptation and lunged on their fallen comrades, others broke into a sprint after him, their legs and arms flailing wildly as they moved. The runners didn't show any sign of giving up the chase, and Bill knew that he would tire before they did: he had to do something to even the playing field.

But what?

Without any more powerful automatic weapons or any kind of position he could make a stand from, he was only delaying the inevitable by running. Already he could feel his limbs burning as they turned to lead, and he sensed the hungry jaws of the dead nipping at his heels.

Buildings turned into concrete blurs as Bill pushed himself onwards, ignoring the pain that was tearing through his nerves and the warm trickle he could feel dripping down his side: it seemed that he'd popped his stitches. He clutched at his side as he moved, feeling the warmth beneath the cold of his sodden jacket.

The winding street Bill ran through led to an open building, a shop that had been gutted by fire, all the way through to an open back door. It wasn't sanctity, but it would at least create a bottleneck effect that should slow the Rots. Taking a chance Bill lunged into the shop, crashing through blackened timbers and stumbling over uneven debris on the floor until he managed to dive through the doorway. He spun in the middle of his dive, rolling on to his back and bringing his shotgun up to bear on the advancing monsters. He fired and reloaded, again and again, taking out zombies with each shot until there was a large pile of headless bodies blocking the doorway. At that point, the Rots started to struggle to get through, dumbfounded at the fact they couldn't walk through the pile, nor around, and if they tried to climb over they only added to the blockage as another zombie took a slug to the head.

Stepping away from the doorway and quickly looking around behind him, Bill tried to get a fix on where he was. It was a back alley, not very wide, running off to the left and the right. Both sides were blocked off by a wire fence, which wouldn't hold if any Rots happened to see him, and decided to try to climb over or knock down the barrier. The only other way out the alley seemed to be a rusted steel ladder that was fixed to the wall; it didn't look like it could hold his weight, but it was the only viable way out he was really faced with.

Taking the first of the rungs in his hands, Bill slung his weapons over his shoulder and hauled his weight up the wall as the first of the shambling horrors clawed their way over the rotten pile of carcasses. They lunged for him, the razor sharp exposed bones of their fingers wrapping around his leg and ripping at his jeans as he jerked his limb free. He lashed out with his booted feet, though each kick that connected with a skull of a zombie felt like he was kicking a pile of bricks and had no effect. Instead, he turned his attention to the digits wrapping around his other leg, hacking at them with his heel and snapping the smaller bones in the fingers.

Tearing free of the final creature holding him back, Bill finally managed to pull himself up another set of rungs. The ladder creaked and moaned beneath his weight as he carried on climbing, the rusted metal flaking away in his hands and beneath his feet as he clawed his way onwards. He cast a glance over his shoulder as he reached the top and shuddered at the sea of mutilated and deformed faces that stared blankly back at him, each creature moaning and groaning as they anticipated their impending meal.

With only five rungs to go until he reached the top, the ladder shook and lurched violently, and Bill thought the rickety ladder had finally come away from the wall. The rusted rung he held snapped off in his hand, slipping from his sweating palms and sailing into the crowd below, striking a head of one of the Rots. Bill looked up, could see that the ladder remained fixed at the top, and swivelled his head around, assuming that the damage had occurred below him.

At the base of the ladder, the deathly grinning visage of a Rot pulled itself up from the crowd, claw-likes hands locking around rungs as it pulled itself up. Fumbling for his shotgun, Bill angled the weapon downwards and managed to pull the trigger, discharging one slug into the top of its skull. The bullet tore through flesh and bone, exploding out the arched back of the creature and showering the crowd with gristle and gore as it toppled back into the gathering of the dead. The ladder cleared, another Rot took a chance and dived on to the ladder, jerking it once more as it climbed up behind him, snapping jaws dripping with bloodied saliva as it tried to succeed where its brethren had failed. Its movements were more erratic than the previous, with each jerking movement jarring the ladder more and more.

Bill knew that he couldn't hang on the ladder all day, and returned to the task of the climb, finally managing to swing himself over the lip of the roof as the ladder creaked and groaned. His limbs ached and his fingers were numb, as if they'd been submerged in ice water, but he couldn't rest, not with the Rot still on the ladder. Grabbing his shotgun, Bill stepped back and levelled off the weapon, firing the solid slugs point-blank into the fixings of the ladder. The rusted metal on one side of the ladder disintegrated under the impact of the shotgun blast, and Bill worked at the slide before shifting his aim to the other side of the ladder and the one remaining fixture.

The weapon clicked unresponsively.

Cursing to himself, he patted down his pockets, searching for another slug, but nothing came to hand. He dropped his bag and rummaged through the contents, searching for another round he could use that would remove the rest of the ladder, and came up triumphant with his last slug. He slipped the round into the weapon, pumped it into the chamber, then spun and fired, obliterating the ladder. He heard the clatter of the metal ladder as it bounced off the wall and into the crowd below, and he rushed forwards, hoping to see the last of the climbing zombie as it vanished into the sea of clamouring undead.

As he neared the edge of the building, he caught the overpowering scent of decay, and peered over the edge, putting the smell down to the proximity of the crowd. He hadn't expected the Rot to be clinging tenaciously to the wall, damaged fingers dug deep into the wall as it continued to heave itself up, inch by inch. Rusted fragments of the ladder remained embedded in the palms of the creature, oozing blood and mucus.

Muttering under his breath, Bill retreated away from the edge of the roof and rifled through the contents of his rucksack, looking for the knife he knew he had packed: his years in isolation had made him all but forget what the creatures were capable of, and he was instantly reminded of the creature in the early days of the plague that had scaled the walls and ceiling of an underground tunnel. His fingers coiled around the rubber grip of the combat knife, and he pulled it from the bag just as the struggling creature hauled itself over the lip of the roof, a malevolent grimace on its face. Bill lashed out with the knife, a glancing blow that took a slice of leathery skin from its skull and sent it sailing into the baying crowd below. The creature staggered, watery blood seeping from its fresh wound, though it seemed unfazed by the assault. It clattered on to the flat roof Bill stood on, fingers bloody and raw, caked in dust and dirt from the bricks it had been scraping at minutes before, then lunged at him.

Already one step ahead of the zombie, Bill flicked out the blade he held and blocked its arm, feeling the impact from the blow as it knocked the weapon aside. He lunged with the knife once more, this time plunging the dagger into the ocular cavity of the creature and sinking the cold steel up to the hilt in the gaping socket. The moment the weapon pierced its brain the Rot convulsed and spasmed, before stumbling backwards and toppling over the edge and plummeting into the flesh-hungry crowd below.

"Jesus," Bill hissed, letting himself drop to the floor and run a hand through his soaking hair as he took count of the supplies he had left. Only a handful of solid slugs and a box of twenty shells loaded with buckshot remained for his shotgun, the latter having almost no effect on the enhanced creatures; an MP5, fully loaded, along with four magazines filled with a variety of different rounds; normal bullets mixed with armour piercing and hollow-point rounds. Only the armour piercing rounds would have any effect on the thickened skulls, and even then, it would take a couple of rounds to do the job and scramble the brains of the intended target. He had just under half a box of ammo left for the M249, but other than that and the bent and useless defence baton that lay on the floor, he had nothing else to use; his knife was still embedded in the skull of the Rot that was currently being torn apart by the bloodthirsty pack of zombies. He was drastically under equipped, hideously outnumbered, and isolated from the bike and his only way out of the city.

And even then, he thought to himself as he leaned over the edge of the roof and spat on the feasting creatures, *even then, there's no guarantee that this new breed of zombie couldn't catch up with me.*

Bill stood up and glared around the rooftops; it wasn't as if he could leap from roof to roof, either: the gaps between the buildings were too far for him to jump. The only way he could go was through the door that led into the small structure on the roof, leading to the staircase that would take him to the interior of the building. The one good thing that Bill had going for him was that the building was sealed off, at least from the crowded alleyway that was packed wall-to-wall with the undead. If he was lucky, Bill thought that he may be able to dodge from building to building until his friends turned up: all he had to do was set up a signal that let them know where he was.

With his submachine gun drawn, Bill crept into the darkened staircase, each weathered floorboard creaking beneath his weight as he moved lower and lower into the building.

The staircase went down the middle of the building, each doorway boarded from the other side of the door, suggesting to Bill that many people had made their last stand on the other side of the stairwell. If the building was a block of flats, that meant that there could be a hundred more Rots caged in the barricaded rooms and corridors; that didn't sit well with Bill. He moved quicker, down the stairs and into the belly of the structure, his eyes adjusting to the gloom as he progressed deeper and deeper, though not well enough to make out too much detail: although parts of the wall had been smashed out or torn down, the dim light that came in from the dismal outside didn't provide much illumination beyond a couple of feet from the holes.

As he neared the bottom, the silence of the building became broken by the sounds of gentle footsteps and throaty, animal growls: noises that couldn't be produced by a Rot, but could certainly be created by a pack of wild animals. Though the sounds were close to him, he knew that there was no way the creatures could get him: as part of the securing process of the building, the lowest set of stairs had been destroyed by the fire axe left embedded in the smashed timbers of the top stairs. Though he couldn't understand why anyone would leave the axe, a perfectly good weapon in its own right, unattended at the top of the stairs, he thanked them for their gift to him. It was far superior to the knife he had lost, or the twisted baton he had left on the roof, with enough weight and leverage behind it to easily crack open the toughest of skulls with a single blow.

Pulling the only flare he had out of his pack and igniting it, he let it drop from the landing he crouched on into the opened foyer below him, his eyes burned by the sputtering red flames as the device dropped and clattered to the ground.

The eerie glow from the flare doused the foyer area of the building in a crimson glow, giving the pit and the beasts that inhabited it the appearance of the depths of hell. Flickering firelight illuminated the pack of four-legged beasts as they anxiously circled the opening, none of the animals flinching or recoiling from the flare as they circled. While Bill had become used to seeing undead people gather together, he couldn't recall ever seeing a pack of undead animals.

The pack consisted of twelve dogs, each in a varied state of decomposition and mutilation as they circled a prone humanoid figure, every so often one of them lunging forwards and snapping at the corpse, which in turn moaned and tried to lash out after each sporadic attack. It seemed as if the undead dogs were playing with their meal, turning on one another if they ventured too close to each other or tried to steal a piece of their feast.

The hides of the dogs were slick and oozing with pale pink liquid, a stark contrast to the dried husks that lingered outside the building, and Bill gave a sigh of relief: the dry Rots were a lot tougher, these animals could at least be taken out with a normal handgun. He drew the hunting pistol, activated the laser target and lined up a shot on one of the dogs. The weapon kicked in his hand, the muzzle gave a suppressed flash of light, and the skull of the creature exploded, showering the closest animal with ruddy brain and fragments of blood. The pack instantly divided as some kept up their interest in the human corpse, while others savaged the fallen mongrel, tearing strips of flesh from the twitching body.

Bill lined up his second shot and took down a second dog, dividing the pack once again.

"Fish in a barrel," he whispered to himself as the slide of the weapon locked open. He pressed the release catch of the magazine, feeling the smooth metal of the magazine as it slipped over his fingers…

…Tumbled out his grasp…

… And landed on the concrete below with a metallic slap.

Shit!

The pack lifted their heads in unison, cataract-like undead eyes glaring at him and rabid muzzles quivering and dripping with saliva. Bill remained frozen in a crouched position, remembering something he'd heard once: something about hunting animals and their vision being based on movement.

The larger of the dogs broke into a fit of gurgling, half-choked growls and barks, and the rest of the pack followed suit.

"That was *bulls*, you dumb shit," Bill muttered as he clambered to his feet and slapped a fresh magazine into the open weapon. "*Bulls* see movement."

The animals below erupted into a frenzy, galloping around in circles, frothing at the mouth while they sporadically leapt and clawed at the air at the base of the destroyed staircase. Bill holstered his pistol and pulled out his shotgun, removing the slugs from the weapon and loading up a handful of hard shot shells while keeping his eyes trained on the snapping canines. He levelled off the weapon and fired down into the pit, cutting down the dogs, each of the undead animals growling and spitting even as their skulls were crushed beneath the onslaught of the heavy ball bearings.

The roar of the gunshots finally ended, their echoes dying up into the recess of the building as the last of the undead animals keeled over and died. Bill looked down on the bloody soup of slain creatures, shattered bones and spilled brains, and tried to take a head count. It looked like there were enough body parts to account for the pack, and he slung his shotgun over his shoulder as he lowered himself over the edge of the broken staircase.

With its tormentors destroyed, the human corpse on the floor started to haul itself across the floor, grabbing pieces of dead animal and forcing them into its mouth. Bill lumbered up to it, fighting to keep his balance on the slick floor, and raised his axe above his head before bringing it crashing down on the skull of the prone Rot, the blade biting into the thick bone and tearing it apart, adding more brains to the mix on the floor.

"Where the hell's the door?" muttered Bill, heaving the axe from the head of the zombie and looking around the hall. The only door leading out of the room had once been underneath the stairs, but now lay buried beneath the destroyed staircase; it would take him hours to dig his way out. Resigned to that fact, he crouched down on the floor and started to pull away the broken wood and plaster, just as the flare sputtered and died.

He was cast into darkness, and he suddenly felt claustrophobic, like the building was shrinking in around him. The stench of the dead bodies surrounding him started to attack his senses, and he started to feel dizzy. It was all in his head, he knew it, but he didn't like standing around in the dark while he freaked himself out. He spun wildly on the spot, taking in as much details as his eyes adjusted to the darkness, and spotted a glimmer of hope: wooden panels nailed to the wall with slits of daylight between them: not enough to offer much illumination, but enough to make Bill realize that there had to be a window or something behind the panels.

Lifting his axe for a second time, Bill sized up the boards, shifted his grip, and let fly with the heavy weapon.

A lone black crow sat on the ravaged corpse of a human, the soft and rich bounty of its eyes having long since been taken by scavengers, be they living or dead. It shifted its perch on an exposed shard of skull, pecking at the shrivelled brain every so often, while glaring from side to side with its one glassy eye. Rain spattered its bloody face, watering down the tainted blood that trickled from its one vacant eye socket. It squawked, a harsh and rasping cry that echoed down the street, a shrill screech that shattered the steady moaning of the Rots that roamed the paths and roads further in to the boundaries of the city.

Startled by the sudden and violent explosion of panels of wood bursting through a shattered window, the bird launched itself into the air, flapping its wings and shedding greasy feathers as the wood panels splashed in the puddles that littered the road, clattering noisily on the ground. Casting one last look over its flapping wings, the undead crow watched as a bloodied figure stumbled out, and it soared around before swooping down towards the new figure on the street, a promise of fresh eyes and fresh meat.

Bill smiled as he felt the rain splash against his face and watched with interest as the black bird lifted from its feast and circled high in the sky. He pulled himself from the shattered window and lifted his face to the heavens, washing his face with the cold rain that still fell like drops of ice from the dark clouds. A flash of movement caught his eye as he opened his eyes, and a black blur swooped down from the skies, screeching a blood-curdling death cry as it dived towards him.

Bill reacted instantly, swinging his fire axe around like a bat and smashing it into the frail body of the crow. It bounced off the metal head of the axe, its body snapping and twisting as it fell to the floor, wings flapping uselessly as it rolled from side to side in pool of rainwater.

Bill stepped forwards and rolled his boot over the flapping undead bird, grimacing as its bones cracked beneath the weight of his boot. Bill backed away from the grim scene and scraped his boot on the kerb of the pavement, cleaning off as much of the dead bird as possible. Other than the bird and the partially emaciated corpse, the rest of the street was deserted, each side of the road lined with the same abandoned and decrepit buildings as every other town and city on the island. A soft moaning and groaning could be heard, which Bill accounted for as the Rots still trapped on the other side of the building.

He knew it was only a matter of time before the zombies managed to work they way around the building, and he had to move fast: though he didn't know which way would be best if he were trying to get back to his bike. He started to wander blindly down one side of the street, reloading his weapons as he went.

He wandered through the streets for close to ten minutes before realising he was completely lost, and if he couldn't find safe shelter or his bike soon, he would die from pneumonia. His aimless wandering seemed to be taking him *deeper* into the city: the only thing that seemed to be going in his favour was the fact that there didn't appear to be anything in the streets other than dead bodies with their heads either destroyed or removed completely.

Something's not right, Bill mused to himself as he continued to move through the streets. *Something's not right at all.*

III

A further five minutes of walking saw Bill finding an open doorway that he huddled in while the rain passed. Within twenty minutes, the downpour had finally stopped, and Bill emerged from his hiding place, brushing water off his jacket and wringing out his clothing to aid his drying off. In his haste to get to shelter, he had all but forgotten which way he had been travelling in. He looked up one way of the street, then down the other, but nothing struck him as familiar: if he'd seen one derelict building, he'd seen them all.

The bark of gunfire caught his attention, and he snapped up his weapon, suddenly alert and trying to get a fix on the location of the shot as it died in a burst of receding echoes. Could it be that his friends had already arrived? He'd learned his lesson, and he certainly wasn't going to go off investigating on his own for a very long time. He lifted one hand to his ear, trying to adjust the setting on his earpiece.

It wasn't there.

Bill paused for a moment, trying to think. Had he lost his earpiece when he'd dropped down from the broken stairs? Maybe it had fallen off when he'd been trying to escape from the horde of Rots…

Did I even pick it up before I left? He thought to himself. He couldn't remember if he'd picked one up or not. How could he be so stupid as to not pick up his radio?

How could he be so stupid as to go off exploring on his own?

Bill retreated to his shelter once more, only this time it wasn't rain he was hiding from; it was whoever was approaching. Though it could be Al or Angel as they strolled through the city looking for him, there was just as much chance that it could be a member of a gang. He was desperate for his friends to find him, but at the same time he didn't want to shout out or fire off a shot in case he attracted the wrong kind of company. More minutes passed as he hid and waited, slowly turning his head back and forth, looking for any telltale sign of movement in the streets.

In the distance to his right a thick black plume of smoke started to rise towards the sky. There had been no explosion, so Bill could only assume it was a fire that had been set intentionally: maybe as a signal?

He stepped cautiously out from his hiding place, cradling his machinegun as he carefully strolled down the street, his back pressed against the buildings as he went, making sure no one would be able to sneak up behind him. It was a straight road to the fire, and Bill felt his heart quicken as the source of the blaze came into view.

It had been a camp set up in an old shop: canvas tents and stacks of provisions were afire within the building, and a headless corpse twitched at the base of the largest of the opened windows: a recent pillaging of a small village of survivors. Three vehicles stood dormant outside the burning shop, their engines ticking softly to themselves as though they had been active until recently.

Bill stayed where he was, staring in confusion at the sight before him. It looked as if a small gang had been set up here, until a person or persons unknown had wiped them out, but not anyone he travelled with. They would have waited for him while the signal fire burned, where as the perpetrators of this act of violence had clearly and quickly moved on. He was about to take a step towards the burning building to get a closer look, when a flicker of movement caught his eye. He dropped to the floor and shuffled to one side, hiding behind a mound of bricks that had fallen from a damaged building and adjusting his position on the ground to get a better view.

A man dressed in urban combat fatigues and body armour stalked out of an alleyway besides the building, cradling a bulky weapon and swinging it lazily from side to side as he swaggered into the street. He wore the same bulky breathing apparatus as all the Marines that Bill had seen. Had he not been a full foot shorter than Al, Bill would have sworn the two men were one and the same.

"Marines," he muttered to himself, watching as the man's head bobbed up and down, as if in a conversation to someone. If Bill had his radio headset, he was sure that he would have been able to eavesdrop.

The soldier seemed to relax, then turn to one side and signalled to someone out of Bill's line of sight before marching away. His solitary footsteps were joined in unison by a small army, and Bill expected to see a whole squad of Marines following him. While there were Marines in the following crowd, there were others that he hadn't expected to see.

The group that followed the sole Marine stood three men wide and seven men deep; twenty-two people in all, including their leader. The first three of the group were Marines; each carrying similar weapons to the machinegun Bill carried, and behlnd them marched their prisoners. Men and women dressed in rags and scraps of metal were first, each locked in metal stocks with their hands fastened at head-height, each stock linked to the next by a foot of chain. These men and women totalled nine in all and the marched along at a stumbling pace, their legs shaken and weak, blood flowing freely from wounds on their body. The remaining nine figures at the rear of the crowd, these restrained using stocks and lengths of solid metal, were Rots, each thrashing and writhing uncontrollably as they tried repeatedly to lunge on the people in front of them. Lumps of meat dragged along the ground behind the chained zombies, pieces of corpses that had been collected and fastened together with meat hooks and coils of rope. They marched out of sight, and intrigued by the spectacle, Bill slowly pulled himself to his feet and followed the bizarre meat wagon, watching as one of the marines in the group broke rank and unceremoniously stabbed the still-twitching headless corpse with a barbed hook and nodded in satisfaction as the group of prisoners dragged it away with the rest of their grizzly cargo.

What's going on, Bill mused to himself as he scuttled over to one of the ticking vehicles and threw himself behind it, watching as the crowd were led away. Keeping his distance from the rabble, Bill followed them up the street, skipping lightly from side to side, exchanging cover behind a car for cover in the darkness of an alleyway; like a moth to a flame, even though he knew he would get burned, he couldn't help but follow them.

"Where the hell are they going?" muttered Bill as he trailed them through the silent streets: the Marines obviously patrolled these certain streets on a regular basis, as they were devoid of any Rots or corpses; maybe it was one of their patrol routes?

The group of Marines and their prisoners stumbled to a halt at the end of a cul-de-sac where a number of other soldiers had set up the base: numerous small buildings had been erected, metallic huts attached to filtration devices and airlocks, linked to one another by oval tunnels made of thick plastic material. A memory of his life years ago flashed through his mind, a walk through a plastic tunnel just like the ones used in the camp, a dying woman on one side of him and an emotionless soldier on the other. He shook his head, dislodging the dreams of his past as he took in more details of the camp.

A ten-foot metal tower had been constructed, similar to those that had sat atop the base units of the fort they had recently left, and a lone guard stood on watch, a sniper rifle in hand as he lazily panned it from side to side, barely taking any notice of the surroundings. At the base of the tower there lay a small excavator, nowhere near as large as those that had been left in the courtyard of Messiah's prison. It had been used to gouge out a ten-foot drop in the concrete pavement, the rubble of which had been piled up around the streets to serve as protective barriers. The prisoners were unceremoniously unchained from one another and all but two of the people were kicked into the dugout.

A crowd of Marines quickly formed by the rim of the hole, raising their hands in joy as they watched their new prisoners break free of their shackles and turn on one another. Pouches were opened and their contents pulled out, the valuables changing hands as bets were placed over the fight occurring in the pit. Bill could hear the screams of the living and the moans of the dead as they went up against one another, each screaming as flesh was shredded from bone. Bill didn't need to see the sight to picture the fight in its bloody glory. The Marines, not only content with watching the bloody spectacle, moved a video camera mounted on a tripod to the edge of the hole, pointing the camera down into the dugout. The fight went on for five minutes until one of the Marines seemed to laugh and pull a grenade from his belt, and two of his comrades nodded and did the same. They raised the explosive devices and toasted the carnage in the pit as if the grenades were cans of beer, clinking them together before popping the pins and tossing them into the crater.

The captives in the pit stopped fighting and cried out in agony as the grenades erupted into a flash of napalm, engulfing the occupants in a blazing inferno and bathing the gathered Marines in an orange glow. Slapping one another on the back, one Marine collected all the valuables together and forced them into one of his pouches, before all the soldiers went back to their posts, leaving the camera running as the screams from the pit died off into rasping chokes.

Bill sat staring dumbfounded at the tips of the flames as they licked towards the sky, thick clouds of smoke rolling up towards the sky. Finally pulling away from the sight, Bill tried to work out where the two prisoners had been taken, moving closer to the encampment while staying behind cover.

One of the town's buildings that had been built into the structure of the camp was an open-plan building, the front wall of which had been torn down to display the dark and dingy interior, lit by a dim light bulb hanging from the ceiling. Two chairs had been secured to the ground by heavy rivets, the seats facing one another. As Bill crept closer, peering over the bonnet of a blackened car, he could see two Marines, still sealed in their environment suits and mask, as they tore the rags from the two men and tossed them to one side before forcing them down into the seats, securing their ankles and wrists to the arms and legs of the chair with short lengths of barbed wire and pieces of chain. One of the Marines strolled over to the wall and pulled down an oversized switch, activating a pair of halogen lights that flooded the room with brilliant white light. The two Marines set up another camera in the room, then fiddled with the controls to their respirator.

"They secure?" one of the soldiers asked, the newly activated speaker emitting a harsh and metallic voice. Again, Bill found himself reminded of the Marines that had stormed his place of work and rushed him and Jenny away from the building.

"Trussed up like a cheap whore," said the second soldier, his voice distorted by his helmet and breathing apparatus into the same robotic tones as his counterpart. He laughed as he slapped one of the restrained men in the face. "That thing rolling?"

"Live feed's set up to the Old Man's office, and the unit's recording."

"Great," hissed the soldier, giving a thumbs-up to the camera. "Let's get this started."

He turned to the first man he'd slapped and pulled out a lighter and cigarette from his pocket.

"Want one?" he offered, placing the cigarette in the man's lips and lighting it up. The man nodded, taking a drag from the stick before the Marine pulled it from his mouth.

"You shouldn't smoke these things," he said. "They're bad for you. Look."

The Marine turned around and pressed the smoking end of the cigarette against the flesh of the other prisoner. He winced and squirmed as his flesh smouldered, gritting his teeth in pain as the Marine moved the cigarette to another spot on his body, his face this time, burning his fleshy cheeks.

"How many of you are there?" demanded the other Marine, stepping behind the first prisoner and holding his head in place, keeping his eyes open and forcing him to watch as the soldier tortured his companion. "How many?"

"We're all there is," grimaced the prisoner. "No one else."

"What about the son of a bitch who was shooting things up on the other side of the city?"

"I don't know who that was…"

"Why don't I believe you?" asked the Marine, peeling back the eyelid of the prisoner and pressing the cigarette into his eye. The squirming captive screamed in agony, trying to twist his head from side to side, jumping up and down in a bid to move the chair.

"Simon! Jesus, what the fuck're you doing to Simon?" screamed the other prisoner.

"Shut up," hissed the marine holding the cigarette, spinning on his heels and backhanding him. "Maybe if you start telling us what we want to know we won't have to do this."

He dropped the cigarette and strolled over to a table that sat just out of the range of the camera, littered with different implements that could be used in different methods of torture. He picked up a blowtorch and returned to the seats, waving the blowtorch back and forth and running the flame across the shining steel blade of a knife he held.

"Simon, is it?" asked the Marine as he looked at the sobbing man with one eye. "Maybe you want to tell your friend the more he lies, the worse it'll get for you."

"Ray…" muttered Simon, hanging his head and spitting on to the floor. "Tell him… Tell him who it was."

"Fuck's sake, Simon, I don't know who it was!" shouted Ray, their argument drowning out the questions and commands of the two Marines. "Don't give in to them, they want us to argue…"

The Marine holding the knife lunged forwards, slicing the cheek of Simon, the heated blade sinking in deep to the flesh and cutting back to expose the glint of bone. The man screamed in hysterics as the knife ground against the jawbone and he slumped forwards, the pain having knocked him unconscious.

"Wake up, fucker," the Marine said, dropping the knife and slugging the man square in the jaw. His head snapped to one side, splashing blood across his friend and the floor, and his eye fluttered open. The Marine retrieved the dropped blade and with a fit of rage brought the knife crashing down on Simon's forearm, the warmth of the blade aiding it as it sliced through skin and muscle, gliding between the two bones of the forearm and embedding itself in the arm of the chair. The scream of the man was deafening, though it died into a whimper as the Marine worked the blade back and forth, opening the wound more, stepping back slightly as blood arced from the severed arteries in the limb and sprayed across the soldier.

"Your friend *will* die if he doesn't get medical attention. As soon as you answer our questions, we can arrange that. His life is in your hands. Now, who was that person?"

"I've already told you," screamed Ray, tears streaming down his face as he watched the pale visage of his friend as he slowly slipped into unconsciousness once more. The Marine that had previously stood back from the torture stepped forwards with a handful of wires cut to pieces two inches in length. He pushed them under the nails of Simon, ignoring the moans of agony, and played the blowtorch across the wires, chuckling a throaty laugh as the wires began to glow red and sink through the flesh and nails of his fingers. "I told you, I don't know who it was…"

"We believe you," hissed the Marines. "We believe you."

"Jesus, help him! Get a medic!"

"I *am* a medic," said the Marine still holding the knife as he stepped forwards and plunged the blade deep into the stomach of Simon. Holding back the flaps of skin of the mans stomach, he pushed his hands into the opened cavity and withdrew it holding with a handful of quivering pale tubing, pulling out the intestines and laying them in the hands of Ray. "Anyone but a medic would have fucked that up and killed him. As you can see, he's still alive. Just."

Sure enough, Simon was still awake, twitching and rolling his one good eye as the pulsating organ squirmed in the hands of Ray. His hands convulsed in repulsion and the intestinal tract slipped on to the floor like a slimy, blood-covered snake.

"A little clumsy," laughed the Marine, pulling his pistol from his holster and bringing it smashing down on Ray's hands. He screamed, and the gun came down again and again, each blow cracking more than one bone in his hand. He dealt a final blow across Ray's face, the force of the impact cracking his jaw and sending a spray of spittle, blood and teeth splashing across the floor. Laughing, the Marine holding the gun turned and pressed the barrel of the weapon against the head of Simon, unleashing three shots that tore through his skull and painted the wall with blood and grey matter.

Ray was crying as the Marine tilted his head back and pried his mouth open, keeping it open by forcing a transparent plastic tube into his mouth and watching as his companion in torture returned to the table and grabbed a metal cage with a small furry rodent inside; black with a long pink tail, it looked like a rat to Bill. He watched as the Marine opened the cage, picked up the rodent, and dropped it into the opened pipe before waving the blowtorch over the opening, sending the rodent into a violent fury as it tried to escape the heat, burrowing into its surroundings as it tried to escape the flame. Ray spasmed and convulsed as the rodent started to bore down through his gullet; the Marines laughed and cheered, giving one another a 'high-five' as he turned away from the torture scene and left the man to die a horrible death.

"Sick bastards," murmured Bill, sinking to his feet and turning away from the horrific scene. The torture had been needless and barbaric; he felt as if the Marines had known the people didn't know who had been firing weapons. He also sensed the Marines didn't even care, either: as if the torture had been just a form of entertainment.

"Maybe you'd feel different if you had first-hand experience with it," growled a mechanical voice from behind him. Bill grimly turned around and found a Marine standing behind him, the barrel of a combat shotgun pointing directly at his face. He lifted his hand to his mask and seemed to fiddle with the controls, activating his radio link and killing his external microphone. He nodded as he either spoke or listened to his radio; Bill couldn't tell which. Satisfied with the outcome of the conversation, the Marine spoke again.

"Room for one more in the chair," he jeered, motioning for Bill to get up with the barrel of his shotgun while kicking his guns away from him. "Ain't no rats left, but I'm sure we can find something similar."

"I'll bet you can," hissed Bill. The way in which he'd been positioned while watching the torture had kept his body leaning over his axe, and as such, the Marine had no way of knowing that he still had one weapon in his possession. It would be a risky move to try and knock the shotgun aside, but he'd rather die from a gunshot wound than be tortured.

Bringing himself up to his full height, Bill feinted to one side and swung the axe around, the metal head making contact with the barrel of the weapon and batting it to one side at the exact same moment as it discharged. The slug slammed harmlessly into the ground, spitting up concrete as it chewed into the hard surface and the Marine tried to readjust his aim, but Bill was two steps ahead of him; hauling the axe in a reverse motion, the flat side of the axe head smashed into the Marine's arm and cracking bone. The shotgun clattered to the ground and Bill swung again, this time cutting into the Marine's neck. The soldier dropped to the ground, the metallic voice nothing but a gurgle as he tried to scream. Bill continued to swing, again and again, each blow making contact with the neck and hacking away through more flesh and blood.

The axe blade finally severed the head and struck against concrete with a loud clink, and Bill dropped the implement, stumbling to his knees and breathing heavily. The cold air burned his lungs as he tried to catch his breath, and he was suddenly aware of a lot of noise around him.

The Marines in the base had turned their attention to him, opening fire as he ducked low and retrieved his own weapons before scrabbling back, away from the base and rolling behind mounds of debris in order to protect himself. Bullets flew overhead and smashed into the barrier he cowered behind, a non-stop barrage aimed at him. At least he had avoided the inevitable torture, but there was no way he could escape out the street without being cut down by the gunfire. The Marines had cleverly re-engineered the street so there was only one approach, and it was an effective killing field.

Bill angled his M249 over the barrier he hid behind and fired blindly towards the encampment, hoping against hope that he'd be able to take out a couple of the soldiers before they got to him. Groping amongst the debris around him, Bill found fragments of a shattered mirror used to help drivers in blind junction beneath some chunks of sodden plaster. He tossed them to one side and they clattered to the ground, which gave Bill a distorted view of the Marine encampment and soldiers as they advanced on his position, all the time maintaining a constant stream of fire as they took turns to cover one another.

It was clear that Bill was going to die, even more so when the shadows of a second squad of five Marines appeared at the other end of the street, advancing towards him in a pincer attack. Bill let his head sag against the concrete he rested against, knowing that he was beaten. He moved his weapon around, trying to at least cut down some of the soldiers advancing on his rear, but the heavy machinegun clicked unresponsively, its magazine empty. Cursing to himself he tossed the weapon aside and fumbled for his lighter submachine gun. The soldiers stopped, dropped to the floor, and the first of them opened up, launching grenades arcing high into the air.

Bill closed his eyes, fighting back the tears as he waited for the devices to impact and consume him in their fiery wrath.

He felt the kick of the explosions as they bloomed to life behind him, raining soil and debris around him, but nothing else. He opened his eyes, ears ringing as he looked around the battlefield with blurry vision, and saw that one faction of soldiers had opened fire on the other, creating a deadly crossfire that caused both sides to drop and take cover. Bill kept his body pressed against the debris as the battle waged around him, and he blindly fumbled for his shogun as he saw one of the soldiers roll and dive towards him; a large and bulky figure carrying a heavy machinegun and grinning inanely, a smoking cigar clutched in his teeth.

The familiar face mouthed something to him, but Bill couldn't hear: all he *could* hear was the rush of blood in his ears and a distant ringing. The figure leaned in closer, bringing with him the smell of sweat and tobacco.

"You all right, kid?"

The words were muted and metallic, sounding like he was talking into a metal can, and it was all Bill could do to manage a nod, feeling his head swim with the movement.

"Who are you?" Bill felt his mouth move, but couldn't hear anything he was saying, just a dull murmur. The figure grinned, shook his head, then peered over the ridge and opened fire with his weapon. Scalding hot casings toppled down on top of Bill, and he muttered and swore as he brushed them aside.

As the battle raged on, the muted rush of blood in his ears slowly faded away and the roar of gunfire took its place. Bill slowly felt more like himself and he felt like he was able to shake off the concussive effects of the explosion. He looked over at the dark-skinned figure beside him and smiled.

"You feeling better, kid?" he asked with a grin. "You look like shit."

"Feel like shit, too," Bill confessed, fumbling with his weapons as he tried to work the slide or reload them: his fingers seemed unable to follow the most simple of commands.

"Take it easy," Al muttered, unleashing another salvo of rapid fire towards the advancing Marines. "You're suffering from a little shellshock. I guess Spanners isn't as handy with a grenade launcher as he likes to think he is."

"Hey, fuck you, Al,"

Bill looked around, but couldn't see Sylvester anywhere. It was then he realised that Al had slipped a headset on him while he's been dazed from the proximity of the blast. Bill tapped the microphone slowly, blew into it, then rumbled a greeting to the rest of his friends

"I'm thinking about writing a book about stupid, idiotic things that people do," Al shouted as he blindly lobbed three small, egg-shaped grenades over the barrier. "I was going to start off with this little story, but I just couldn't figure out how anything could top this."

"Gimme a couple of days," Bill managed with a grin. "I'll think of something."

The grenades went of with a deafening roar, raising a symphony of cries of agony, followed by the crescendo of a building keeling over. Al clambered to his feet and waved his weapon back and forth, the rapid-fire drumbeat of the gun adding to the orchestra of death he was conducting. He eased his finger off the weapon and lowered the smoking barrel, unleashing a cackle that echoed down the street as all gunfire ceased.

"Clear?" shouted a voice from the back of the street; it sounded like Garth.

"All clear," confirmed Al, stepping out from behind the barrier and slinging his machinegun before drawing his modified Desert Eagle and stalking out into the remains of the battlefield. "Cover me, bitch, just in case."

"Call me bitch again and I'll do more than cover you," Angel's voice promised. Bill smiled slightly and tried to pull himself to his feet as Clive and Sylvester revealed themselves from their hiding positions; Garth had elected to bring up the rear, and there was no sign of Angel at the moment.

"Pam and Sarah stayed in the trailer," Sylvester said as he knelt beside Bill and checked over him for any signs of injury that needed to be treated. "Garth went through the driving of the big rig with Pam, though he said he'd much rather stay back and help guard the trailer."

"I'll bet he did," murmured Bill as he raised his hand in a greeting as the large tanker driver hauled his bulk over mounds of concrete.

"It's not that simple," Garth said, huffing and panting as he leaned over and rested his hands on his knees. "Someone who knows the roads should have stayed with the vehicle in case it needed to pull out, or come further into the city. I was just offering my services…"

IV

"…Where they were most needed," Al growled as he levelled off his magnum and snapped a single round off into the head of the closest body, making sure they remained dead. He wouldn't normally have wasted the magnum rounds, but with the heavy-duty headgear the Marines were wearing, he had no choice but to opt for something that provided maximum penetration. Another couple of steps and Al found another body, which he dispatched with the same execution-style precision.

He turned to look over his shoulder to see Bill, Sylvester and Garth bunched together. It had been foolish positioning like that that had allowed him to take out the remaining Marines with a clutch of high explosive grenades: the layout of the rubble had the marks of an intentional battlefield redesigned to the advantage of the defending soldiers; Al had done it himself when he'd been defending his flat in Edgly. The positioning of the rubble had been intentionally set up with a bottleneck to create a tight kill zone halfway up the street. It had been set up to the advantage of the defending Marines, but in the heat of the battle they'd simply charged ahead, and Al had used their own defence to his advantage as they'd stormed through the bottleneck.

Another body, another magnum shell discharged point-blank to the head. The remainder of the bodies were either buried under mounds of rubble that had dislodged from the narrow opening, or shredded by shrapnel and burning in small fires.

"Everyone's dead," Al confirmed into the radio pickup, turning to wave over to his friends. He heard something shifting behind him, and spun back around to see the blackened form of a burned Rot slowly advancing towards him, smoke rising from its charred limbs as it lunged for him. He raised his handgun, drawing a bead on the forehead of the overcooked creature. He was about to open fire when the eye socket of the smouldering creature erupted into a bloody geyser and the back of its head tore open in a spray of blood and bone fragments. Bewildered, Al looked around, checking to see who it was that could have taken out the zombie.

"You owe me one," Angel's voice carried over the radio link.

"The fuck I do," Al hissed. "The way I see it, it just makes up for one of the many times I *didn't* shoot you when I had the chance."

"I just shot out the eye of a Rot out from a hundred yards. Try not to piss me off, okay?"

"I make no promises, bitch. You get your ass down here; we're going to be moving further into the city, and I'd *hate* to leave you behind."

A second bullet tore through the air and ricocheted off one of the bricks by his feet, inches from his boot. Al spun and stuck his finger up towards the building he knew Angel had taken up residence in during the battle and snorting. Snipers were always the same, bragging about their skills in firing a gun, but shitting themselves the moment a battle flared to life.

"That the next target for me to hit?" Angel asked with a laugh.

"I got a target for you," muttered Al to himself, grabbing his crotch in a lewd gesture.

"I'm not that good a shot yet," responded Angel. "I'm on my way."

Al carried on towards the remains of the Marine encampment, drawn towards the plume of black smoke that rose from the hole in the ground. As he approached, the smell of barbequed flesh assailed his nostrils, and he pulled back, knowing where the blackened zombie had come from, and knowing what had been thrown into the pit. Al pulled another grenade out and primed it, tossing it casually into the crater and making sure everyone in the pit was dead.

As the grenade went off, Al turned away and strolled towards the area that had been set up with a pair of halogen spotlights. Two figures sat strapped to two chairs, the heads tilted to one side and slightly forwards, bloodied chins resting on their chests. Al stepped into the light and examined the first of the corpses. An eye burned out, stomach cut open and intestines draped on to the floor, his left forearm cut open exposing bone, and wires had been inserted under his fingernails. The gunshot wound to his head had been the cause of his demise.

The hands of the second man had been smashed beyond recognition, finger bones sticking out from bruised skin and oozing blood. Pale blue lips wrapped around a plastic pipe told Al that this man had died a while ago, though despite that fact his throat still squirmed and pulsated, as if constantly swallowing. As he watched, the flesh of the throat seemed to rip and tear as the claws of a small rodent broke through the flesh, allowing the rat within his neck to eat its way out.

Al turned away, feeling nauseous as the bloody vermin dropped to the floor and slowly crawled away. He knew what had happened here; he'd even taken part in it himself, though never in such a barbaric manner.

In the Marines it had been in the first weeks of training that all cadets had the notion drummed into them that their enemies were just that: their enemies. They weren't friends, family, fellow countrymen or even humans: the further a Marine could distance him or herself from their enemies, the better. Though torture wasn't condoned in any circumstances in the *public* eye, behind closed doors it was a different story. The public loved to hear about the latest successful raid on a drug cartel's warehouse, but they never questioned where the information came from in order for that military strike to take place. Captured Bebops were tortured for information they knew; specific locations, trade routes or timetables, and the Marines were instructed to go to great lengths to get hold of this information. While most men were toughened enough to take a beating, few could go through the ordeal of having their teeth or fingernails pulled, or worse.

Al had attended several torture sessions, and being able to distance himself from the enemy had helped him get through it and obtain the information he needed. Until now, he had never even given torture a second thought. Until now, though, he had never found himself on the other side of the branding iron, and although he hadn't been tortured himself, the people who *had* been tortured were on his side: survivors of the plague, trying to eke out their existence while the world around them kept getting worse. Al was sickened, not just by the violence the Marines here had committed, but by the fact the he knew *he* was capable of just as horrendous an act, and that three or four years ago it may have been him force-feeding live rats to his prisoners, or wiring them to a car battery, or doing whatever it would take to make them talk.

Al scratched at the shoulder of his uniform absentmindedly, at the chevrons that denoted his ranking as Sergeant as if they burned him. He pulled a small blade from his utility belt and sliced at his clothing, ripping off his chevrons first, then cutting out his name and tossing the material into the flames that licked the bottom of the charnel pit. He sighed softly to himself, feeling his stomach churn as he continued to mull over the thoughts in his mind. He lightly touched the left hand side of his chest, wondering for one moment if it would be possible to peel off the tattoo of the wolf he had, his memorial to the Wolvers, of which he was part of, or at least *had* been, until he had been abandoned. If they were so willing to leave him in the shit, then maybe, after three years, it was finally time to turn his back on them.

"Al? You okay?"

Al turned away from the fire to see Bill standing behind him, his gaze fixed on the flames. He slowly shook his head.

"Fucking Marines, kid. Barbaric assholes, ruthless killers."

"I know. I watched it happen. They threw a bunch of live people and Rots down before watching them fight, betting on them, then torched them alive. Then they started to work on those two poor bastards. There was nothing I could do…"

"I know, kid, I know," Al said, placing a reassuring hand firmly on Bill shoulders. "Marines are a bunch of heartless fucking assholes, the lot of them. Cold hearted mother fuckers."

"I know you are, Al, you're a Marine, you keep telling us," Angel smiled as she advanced on the camp, her rifle slung over her shoulder and blissfully unaware of the atrocities that were waiting for her once she stepped over the threshold of the base. Al snarled and lunged forwards, grabbing her by the wrists and pinning her against the wall.

"Don't label me as one of those psychopathic fuckers *ever* again, you hear me?"

Angel nodded, eyes wide in terror as she tried to pry his fingers off her wrists. He let go and stormed off, allowing Bill to step in and run through what had happened. Al smiled slightly as he realised that he was getting better at talking low enough for the microphone not to pick up his voice. He was learning, albeit at a slower pace than he would have liked. Al strolled back over to the illuminated area, ignoring the bodies as best as he could and peering at something mounted on a tripod. He stepped closer to it, tapped a few buttons on it then looked at the illuminated LCD screen on the side. A flashing red dot indicated that it was recording and a series of cables linked the camera up to a small portable transmitter sitting just behind it. Snarling, Al kicked the tripod over and stamped repeatedly on the electronic box until the casing cracked apart and spewed wires and computer chips across the ground.

"Sick shits were recording it, too. To watch later on… for entertainment?"

Beside the transmitter unit was a number of small shining blue discs in plastic cases each labelled with different titles and dates, going back as far as about a year. He looked at the titles of the video discs, and discovered they weren't so much titles as descriptions of the graphic events contained on them; electrocution, dismembering, hanging, molestation, crucifixion… every form of violence and degradation known to man had been documented on the discs, and Al had no wish to view any of them. Gathering them in his arms, he picked them up and hauled them into the flaming pit, making sure no one was ever going to watch them again. It started to become clear to Al that the Marines were torturing as a form of entertainment more than anything else.

"What now?"

Clive had kept himself busy by giving the last rites to each of the dead Marines he had passed by, and now was standing by the edge of the pit, hands clasped in prayer as he looked down at his feet, his lips working as he uttered sacred prayers to his lord. Sylvester had asked the question and was pacing back and forth along the edge, working the mechanism to his assault rifle and fidgeting nervously.

"First we toss those poor bastards into the fire," Al said, motioning towards the two bodies on the seats. "Then, we go back towards the trailer. There's going to be nothing worth taking from here. Wherever here is, it's too populated, judging by the number of snuff-discs these bastards have made."

"How far back is it?" Bill asked. Al paused for a moment then shrugged his shoulders, turning towards Angel.

"Any idea?"

"Twenty minutes jog, I guess. We could always switch channels and ask Pam to sound the horn, give us something to home in on; maybe even drive further into the city."

"No way," hissed Al. "This squad of Marines aren't alone. They were transmitting the feed from a camera to another location, more than likely their main base camp; this is probably just a scout camp or something, they'll be reporting back to a larger strike force. If Pam sounds the horn, the Marines'll be drawn to her like Rots to a piece of meat. We'll just have to move carefully, and keep an eye out for any other people, alive or dead, and avoid them."

Al started to remove the bodies from the chair, unwinding the wires wrapped around their wrists and ankles and lugging the first of the bodies away. Bill stooped to help him, while Garth and Sylvester manhandled the second corpse; all the time Clive muttering prayers and splashing water from the silver canteen he carried.

"Almost finished with that Voodoo mumbo-jumbo, Preacher-man?"

"All done," Clive growled, frowning as he crossed himself and turned from the pyre.

"Fine. We go back the way we came, okay?"

Al started to move towards the end of the street he and his friend had entered, but froze as he heard something rumbling in the distance: the growl of a powerful diesel engine as it hauled a heavy piece of machinery through the streets. He raised his hands, calling for silence as he feverishly glanced around the cul-de-sac. The doors to the other buildings had been heavily barricaded and it would take hours to shift the wood and rubble, but there were some ladders that had been erected on the side of some of the buildings.

"We need to get out of here," he murmured to himself, waving his friends away from the street and motioning towards the closest of the ladders leading on to the roof of a three-story maisonette. "Something's coming our way, and I don't like the sounds of it."

"Like what?" asked Angel as she rushed for the ladder, scrabbling up the rungs and throwing herself over the lip of the building. Al rushed everyone up the ladder before him, making sure everyone was safe as he watched the far end of the street.

"Sounds like a tank, a real heavy one."

"Tank?" sneered Sylvester. "Jesus, man, I've got a load of grenades, I can crack that bastard open, what's the problem?"

"The problem?" Al scoffed as he lunged on to the ladder and pulled himself up. "The UGMC's primary ground assault vehicle is the Rhino, an armour plated beast armed with twin hundred and twenty millimetre cannons, three Gatling guns and two rocket pods. The problem, my little grease monkey, is that if you're planning on going up against one of those beasts with your little forty mills there, you might as well just paint a target on your forehead and hurl rocks at it."

"C'mon," Bill said, pulling Al up the remainder of the ladder and slapping him on the back. "If Al isn't prepared to go into a fight, it must be a no-win situation. Let's split before this mobile gun platform turns up."

There were no ladders on the other side of the building, and with the proximity of the engine growing closer with each passing moment, the group were forced into taking drastic actions to speed up their escape and drop down from the roof. Though Al had packed a rope, once it had been attached to something secure on the roof it was about seven foot shy of the ground below.

"It's not long enough," Garth said, leaning over the edge of the building.

"It's not short by much," Al said, swinging his legs over the edge and coiling part of the rope around his wrist. "Just a few feet."

"It's easy enough for you to say, you're a giant and I'm a midget in comparison."

"I'm going down first," Al said, leaning back and slowly descending the wall, grimacing slightly as the nylon chord rubbed and burned his skin. "If you're that shit-scared, I'll catch you, how's that sound?"

"My hero," Garth said, clasping his hands and fluttering his eyelashes. "You'd do that for me?"

Al rolled his eyes as he descended the wall, and Angel took up position on the roof, scanning from one side of the street below to the other with the scope of her rifle. Everything was still, and she kept nodding as each of the men asked if it was clear before they slid down the rope. Bill was next after Al, then Clive and Sylvester.

"Still scared?" she asked him as she looked up from her riflescope. Garth nodded, wiping his brow with a rag he pulled from his pocket.

"You go first," he said, motioning towards the rope. "I can't do it. Never been good with heights."

"Get down there," Angel said with a grin, gently patting him on the shoulder. "I'll stay up here, cover you and the rest of our guys down there. Okay?"

"This isn't what I thought I'd be doing when I woke up this morning," Garth complained as he rolled over the roof of the building, the rope wrapped firmly around both wrists as he slowly lowered himself towards the ground. "You guys ready to catch me?"

"God damn, just move your ass, buddy, we don't have all day."

"Don't rush me," Garth insisted, almost grinding to a halt halfway down the rope.

"If it makes you feel any better, the Rhino could easily drive through this building and blow us all to shit."

Angel shook her head as she performed one final check on the street, then moved over to the rope as Garth finally reached the bottom and let go, dropping into the open arms of Al and Sylvester as they waited for him. Angel watched as the two men caught him, and she wasted no time in taking the rope in her own hands and quickly abseiling down the building. She was lighter and quicker than the rest of the men, and knowing that she felt very confident as her boots clicked and scuffed over the surface of the wall. She was halfway down the building when she felt a sickening lurch, and watched, as the world around her seemed to slow down, as the end of the rope at the top of the building lashed into view. She felt a moment of weightlessness as the ground below reached out to grab her, and she felt herself plummet. The drop wasn't enough to kill her, but if she landed badly on the rubble that littered the pavement she could easily be paralysed.

"Gotcha!"

A familiar voice whispered in her ear, and Angel felt a pair of arms wrapping tightly around her, cushioning her impact and catching her before she made contact with the ground. She opened her eyes, not aware that she'd had them shut until that point, then looked blearily around before pushing herself away from Bill and gently lowering herself to her knees, feeling herself shaking slightly.

"When we get back to the trailer, you're all going on a diet," she managed with a grin. "You're all too big to climb ropes."

"All muscle, baby," a still-pale Garth said with a grin, patting his oversized stomach. Al stooped to pick up the length of discarded rope and frowned at the rope, before dropping it and running blindly down the street, calling out behind him as he ran.

"Run, get outta here, find some cover."

"What is it?" Bill yelled as he pulled Angel to her feet and launched into a run. Angel didn't need to hang around; she'd seen the frayed rope that looked as if it had been cut, and heard the banter of gunfire as a Marine on the building above opened fire, strafing the street with high velocity bullets as the group ran from the scene.

"Bastards cut the rope," Al swore as he burst into the confines of an old house, slamming through doors and bursting through shattered windows into the streets on the other side. "They must've had scouts running ahead of the tank, and the fuckers followed us up on to the roof."

"So that means we don't have to go on a diet?" Garth managed, his breathing laboured as he lumbered through yet another house. Angel smiled and shook her head, taking the lead slightly and trying to steer the running crowd back into the right direction: in the blind panic that had followed the Marine opening fire, Al had bolted in the wrong direction. As soon as they burst out the house and entered another street, Angel turned to the right, trying to lead the group away.

"Where you going, bitch?"

"The trailer, it's back this way! You ran off in such a panic that you bolted the wrong way."

"They're back that way. Jesus, don't you ever use your head?"

"But I thought…"

"You didn't think shit," Al sneered, tearing off again to the left and pulling the group away from the direction of the trailer and deeper into the city. "We loop wide around, make sure we don't draw them anywhere near our vehicle."

"How long will that take?" wheezed Bill as he kept pace with Angel.

"City can't be that big, can it?" Sylvester asked.

"It was large on the map," Al bellowed as he stormed into yet another building, this one inhabited by three of the toughened Rots that staggered around the darkened building. Al lifted his magnum as he ran, sending a double-tap into the skull of each of the creatures before they managed to lunge towards them.

"God damn Dry Rots," he hissed, ejecting the spent magazine and letting it clatter to the floor. The house seemed bigger than the others they had passed through: while most houses had been a straightforward run through a couple of smaller rooms, this one had large rooms connected by hallways lined with decorative panelling and expensive piece of art set in heavy wooden frames. It was more of a maze to exit the building, and when they finally did, they found themselves in a street four lanes wide, leading far off to one side where a giant building lay partially obscured behind a jungle of grass and trees that had been allowed to grow out of control.

Al slowly stumbled to a halt, his feet slapping down on the cracked concrete as he stared open-mouthed at the mansion and its overgrown garden. Sylvester stopped beside him, glaring at the building and the rusted iron fence that encircled the grounds, at the guard box that stood vacant by the main gate, and stroked the growth of stubble that covered his chin.

"Place looks familiar," he said slowly, trying to recall the name of the building.

"Can't say it rings a bell with me," Al said, taking the break to reload his weapons and motioning for his companions to do the same. "Anyone else know what it is?"

"Don't you people know anything?" Angel said as she slipped the half-spent magazine in her rifle and replaced it with a new one. "That's Buckingham Palace."

"Where the royal family lives?"

"Between ski trips and pleasure cruises, yeah."

"Doesn't look like there's anyone home," muttered Garth. "Either that, or the gardener's on a sabbatical."

"Another ideal place to lose those psychotic bastards between gunfights," Al muttered, eyeing up the building. "Might even be a good place as any to try and hold out for a while, take some of the fuckers with us."

"Is that wise?"

"A palace is like a castle, right?"

"It's a palace," Angel corrected him. He chose to ignore her.

"So it should be fortified, or at least have something like a small armoury somewhere for the guards that were once stationed here."

"This isn't going to work, is it?" asked Angel as she watched Al move towards the silent palace.

"What other choice do we have?"

Angel looked at Bill and Garth before shrugging her shoulders. She had plenty of other suggestions which she thought were better, but doubtless Al would ignore whatever she said, more out of principal than anything else.

XXIII
CAPITAL PUNISHMENT

"They look upon us as little more than death squads now; the stigma of the men in white sent out to deal with the infected mounting up in the cities."

I

"Major, we're getting a report in from Sector Twelve."

The major looked up from his piles of crumpled paper and glared at the small monitor that sat on his desk. It showed the clean shaven face of one of his lieutenants, bald head bobbing up and down as he viewed a number of different screens before him, looking up occasionally to peer into the camera that fed his image into the major's office.

"What is it?" the major scowled. He knew that lieutenant couldn't see him, he'd disabled his video camera a long time ago to maximise his privacy, but he felt the scowl carried across in his tone of voice.

"We lost contact with Sector Nine about ten minutes ago, and I dispatched part of Sector Twelve as a scouting party over there to check it out. We've received word back that Nine has been wiped out."

"Wiped out?" the major asked, leaning forward in his seat and dropping his pen. "I don't understand... who did it?"

"The scouts reported in a group of six armed rebels fleeing the scene, they were heading deeper into the city."

"I knew there were more of the bastards here. Did Sector Nine have any prisoners? Is it possible these rebels set them free?"

"I don't think so, sir. We received a live feed from there before the soldiers were wiped out; all prisoners were disposed off correctly."

"Does the feed show the six rebels?"

"Sir, yes sir."

"Route it through to my monitor."

The lieutenant nodded, and his image was replaced with the vision of a pit with charred corpses heaped up at the bottom. People were pushed into the pit, then zombies after them: the two different species lunged at one another, tearing chunks of flesh and throwing punches while soldiers stood around the outside of the fight, hurling insults and rocks into the melee. Incendiary grenades followed, and the figures left alive in the pit erupted into flames as the napalm ignited. The major nodded thoughtfully, watching as the picture changed to a view of two men sitting opposite each other as the interrogation process went underway. He smiled; he particularly enjoyed the broadcasts from Sector nine more than any other squadron, purely because they were so inventive in their methods. He'd spend many an hour watching the broadcasts over and over again; it was the only form of entertainment that he and his men got after they'd been stationed on the island to clear it of any remaining infected creatures.

The torture session stopped, and the major watched intently as Marines scrambled down the street, opening fire and ducking for cover behind rubble and cars. The gunfight went on for some time, eventually ending in a salvo of explosions and the group of five men advanced down the street, finally joined by the sixth, this one a woman. They vanished out of shot for a moment, and then one person strolled into view as he examined the corpses, a large and muscular man with dark skin. He looked over the bodies, watched as the rat emerged from the throat of one of the corpses, and looked glumly at his feet. He wore military fatigues, and scratched idly at the chevrons on his shoulder before ripping them off and throwing them aside. The major scratched his neck idly as he watched as the man turned on the camera and hurled it to the ground, killing the picture.

"Gill," he addressed his lieutenant, thumbing one of the buttons on the desk and watching as the same bald man appeared on the screen. "One of those rebels was a Marine. Are there any Marines that have gone AWOL or MIA that we know of?"

"I'm looking through the files now, sir, but there's not a lot to go off. Since the large-scale operation to clean up the island, keeping files up to date has taken a back seat by some squads."

"If he's a Marine, is there any chance that the others are Marines, too?"

"Doubtful," Gill responded, shaking his head. "He seemed to be the only one who moved, fought and dressed like a Marine. You can see him clearly in the combat footage, if you want me to set it away again…"

"No, no need for that. Monitor the different radio channels, and tell our own men to switch to a secured channel."

Gill nodded and worked a number of switches and dials before smiling in satisfaction.

"Channel six," he growled. "I've got them on channel six, I'll pipe it through to you."

The major nodded and listened as the banter as it played through the speaker on his desk.

"I don't like it," murmured one voice, clearly female. She sounded young, and could only be the woman that had appeared on the video. "I don't like this at all."

"We need more weapons if we're going to get out of this alive; fuck knows how many Marines are out there," rumbled a deep, low voice. A voice that was hauntingly familiar to the major.

"Why not just pull out now?" asked a third. "Isn't going into the palace just looking for trouble?"

"How many times have I got to tell you," hissed the deep voice. "I don't go looking for trouble, it comes looking for me. We can't just pull out, that would lead them straight back to our base of operations. Like I've said before, Momma Colebrook didn't raise no fool."

"Colebrook…" the major shouted, slamming his fists on the desk, his mug of coffee jumping and sloshing steaming black liquid over the rim. "Gill, bring up the files on Colebrook; I think he was called Alan, a sergeant…"

"No Alan Colebrook," Gill said as his image was replaced with a scrolling list of names, green text on a plain black background. "There's an Albert Colebrook, a sergeant attached to the Wolvers division, he went MIA about two and a half, three years ago, presumed KIA. Last file note seems to be linked in to a communication made to you."

"That's the fucker, right there," the major spat. "The reason we're stuck on this island wiping out walking corpses and Bebops, the reason we knew people weren't just rolling over and dying when they're infected. The reason I'm sitting in this stinking vehicle."

He stood up and grabbed a battered metal case from the top of a filing cabinet, popping the locks and pulling out a pair of matching hand weapons: gleaming metal knuckle dusters with a wicked blade attached to one side, an old set of matching trench spikes that his great grandfather had used during the second world war. The antiques had been passed down from father to son, generation to generation, and the major intended to pass them on to his own son, providing he managed to get off the island of the walking dead.

"Gill, get us to the palace as soon as possible, and converge all available forces on there too. I want that bastard *alive* so I can deal with him myself. "

The overgrown gardens of Buckingham Palace were almost level with Bill's shoulders as he stalked into the mass of weeds and overgrown bushes, cautiously looking from side to side as he advanced further. The good thing about moving through the undergrowth that had consumed the front of the palace was that anything heading towards them would be unable to hide their advances. However, Bill knew that there could be any number of incapacitated corpses lying on the ground, waiting to snag someone as they strolled by.

"Just like back in Brazil," grinned Al as he stomped through the bushes alongside Bill, his heavy machinegun pulled up and the stock tucked in tight beneath his shoulder. "I ever tell you about the time me and the guys were…"

Al stopped himself before he went any further, remembering the fact he'd vowed to have nothing to do with the Marines after witnessing their barbaric treatment of their prisoners. Bill shook his head grimly, knowing that it would be hard for him to try and adjust to his new lifestyle. Bill slowed down to a snails pace, allowing the rest of his friends to overtake him as he dropped back to the rear of the group, electing to cover them from behind. He'd swapped his heavy machinegun for an assault rifle, which he lifted above the height of the weeds and panned from left to right. The vegetation was damp and the faint stench of moist earth took the edge off the foul odour of decay that lingered around the grounds.

"I don't like it," murmured Angel, her sniper rifle slung over one shoulder and a machine pistol in her hand. She nervously eyed the weeds and the decrepit building in the distance that they headed towards. "I don't like this at all."

"We need more weapons if we're going to get out of this alive; fuck knows how many Marines are out there," Al said, his voice now a low rumbling sound that carried across the field.

"Why not just pull out now?" asked Sylvester as he cracked open his grenade launcher and made sure he had a round loaded. "Isn't going into the palace just looking for trouble?"

"How many times have I got to tell you? I don't go looking for trouble, it comes looking for me. We can't just pull out, that would lead them straight back to our base of operations. Like I've said before, Momma Colebrook didn't raise no fool."

"Didn't Momma Colebrook warn you about chatter on a live radio signal?"

"Fuck," Al muttered, ripping his headset from him and dropping it to the floor. "Everyone lose them. I forgot about those things, the bastards have probably been monitoring our coms once they knew we were here."

"So they know we're heading into the palace," Garth said moodily as he pulled his radio headset from his head. "Probably got a welcome wagon waiting for us inside."

"We'll be okay," Bill said reassuringly, placing his headset in his pocket. "I don't suppose there's any way we can listen in on *their* conversations?"

"They'll be on a secure channel by now," Al said, shaking his head, "We won't be able to listen in."

The mass of grass and weeds started to thin out into random clumps and patches as the group approached the building, the muddy ground partially covered by greenery that had been trampled flat. Pieces of flesh and partially gnawed bones littered the opening, while blood mixed with stagnant water pooled in the centre of the opening, the air above it writhing with clouds of flies and midges; maggots squirmed in the juices of the dismembered limbs, and the earthy scent of the overgrown garden was once again overpowered by the smell of rotting meat. The larger clumps of vegetation closest to the main door quivered and shook. Al hissed a wordless response, and everyone dropped to their knees, weapons trained on the overgrown weeds.

"Looks like they made it here before us," Angel whispered, shifting her grip on her pistol.

"It's not Marines," Al said, his voice low. "There's no pattern to their formation; anyway, they would have cut us down by now. Kid, see if you can get a little closer."

Bill nodded once and started to shuffle forwards, keeping his body low to the ground and using one arm to steady his crouch as he moved. He picked his way through the field of carrion, wrinkling his nose as he neared the foul stench that seemed to linger within the rustling weeds.

"Can you see anything yet?" whispered Al, rocking nervously from side to side.

"Not yet," Bill said, turning around slightly.

The moment his guard was down, the bushes burst to life and a pair of bloodied canine corpses leapt out from their hiding, snarling and gurgling to one another as they launched into a frenzied run, weaving between each of the group. They each tried to track the running dogs with their weapons, though the rapid movements of the living animal corpses proved too quick to open fire without endangering one of the group.

"Bunch up," barked Al, narrowly avoiding the snap of drool-covered jaws as they tried to snag his fingers. "Back to back, track the bastards, try and cut them down."

Dodging from side to side and avoiding the salivating jaws of the undead canines, Bill regrouped with his friends, rolling across the filthy ground and slamming into the legs of Sylvester as he tried to score a hit on one of the dogs. The shot went high, snapping part of its spine instead of smashing its skull. It whimpered and squealed as its hind legs skittered wildly to one side, but it continued to run, dragging its hind legs behind it as it lazily circled the group, growling in the back of its rotten throat.

"Back up," Al spat through gritted teeth, unleashing a salvo of gunfire and riddling the second dog with bullets, downing it as the contents of its skull were splashed across the gore-covered ground. The remaining creature started to weave around bushes in wider circles, dragging its useless limbs behind it. Angel finally managed to bring the animal down with a burst of gunfire, and the animal gurgled a final bloody death cry as it rolled head over heels.

"Job done," Garth said with a grin, blowing off imaginary smoke from his still-unfired weapon. "That wasn't too hard."

In the distance of the overgrown garden a low, guttural howl pierced the air, followed by another, and then a third, each originating from a different point in the garden. Bill looked nervously around from side to side, trying to get a fix on one of the dogs, but the acoustics of the open yard made it seem like they were coming from all over. Weeds swayed all around them as the undead canines seemed to home in on them, the sound of plants and grass grazing against rotting flesh and the footsteps of the animals as they tore through the miniature jungle.

"It ain't over," glowered Al, lifting his machinegun and sweeping from side to side, trying to get a fix on one of the approaching flesh eaters.

"They're everywhere," whispered Sylvester, reloading his assault rifle and glaring into the surrounding plants, as if willing himself the ability to see through the curtain of vegetation. Clive lifted his shotgun and fed fresh shells into the magazine tube, taking time to cross himself as he went.

"Devil dogs," he muttered to himself, panning his weapon as he spun in a tight circle. "Sent by Satan himself."

"I don't think so, Preacher-man," Al said, blindly spraying a short salvo of bullets into the grass. He was rewarded with a high-pitched yelp, and grinned to himself before opening up with a second burst.

"We need something with a wider spread," Bill said above the din of the gunfire, lowering his assault rifle and pulling out the sawn-off shotgun he carried, jacking the modified shells out of the weapon and feeding normal buckshot into the now waiting chamber. "I hope none of those little bastards are tougher versions of zombie dogs."

"Tougher zombies," Al grunted, rolling his cigar around in his mouth as he swivelled and fired again and again, tracking targets in the rustling undergrowth, and most of his shots were awarded with howls and squeals. "Yeah, those tough bastards're harder to put down. Dry Rots, right?"

Bill nodded an affirmative, watching as the muscular man grinned at him, a toothy smile with his cigar clamped firmly between his yellowing teeth. "Tough little shits, need quite a bit of power to break their skulls open. Still, my group of ultimate ass-kickers are more than capable of the job at hand. Heads up, they're closing in."

Bill lowered his shotgun and unleashed load after load of shot blindly into the jungle around them as the howling canines advancing, each person trying to overlap their field of fire to maximise their kill zones while covering one another.

"There's too many of the bastards," Sylvester said with a grimace, the vibrations of his assault rifle carrying through his arm and knocking Bill as he brushed against him. "We need more fire power!"

"I'm on it," Garth announced, and in a moment of bravery uncharacteristic of him, he slung his rifle and pulled up another weapon that Bill noticed he had been carrying: a carbine weapon about a metre long with a heavy red fuel tank in place of a magazine, and a mix of plastic and metal tubes twisted around the junction of the tank and barrel. He clicked a button to one side of the weapon, igniting a small intense blue flame at the end, then stepped forward and unleashed a burst of flaming napalm jelly, spraying it from side to side.

"You stupid bastard!"

Al slapped the weapon away, trying to discourage the foolish act, but it was too late. Already the flames were rushing across the vegetation and drying up the damp roots and shrubs, the intense heat of the fire prickling Bill's skin with sweat and smothering the air around them.

"What's wrong?" Garth demanded, lifting his flamethrower again as he tried to unleash a second spray of napalm. "Animals are afraid of fire, right?"

"Let's ignore the fact that the smoke is going to be a dead giveaway as to where we are, and consider our surroundings," Al said, trying his best to speak in an eloquent voice. He didn't try for very long. "We're in the middle of a fucking overgrown field, you dumb shit. And the animals are mindless, they don't fear anything…"

As if to prove his point, one of the reanimated dogs tore through the flames, its mottled fur a yellow blaze as it ran from side to side, dripping rivulets of burning liquid and flesh from its body as its smouldering jaws snapped and snarled at Bill. He lowered his weapon and discharged a shell into the skull of the animal, the fiery beast keeling over dead at his feet.

The smell of scorched damp vegetation subsided as the overpowering stench of burning rancid flesh and fur filled the air. Black smoke billowed up around the group, the heat of the raging inferno overpowering and suffocating, sucking the air up and away.

"Fucking idiot," Al shouted, spinning around and trying to get a fix on the building they were headed towards. He levelled off his weapon at waist height and fired off a full belt of ammunition, clearing a path before nodding towards the opening he had created. "C'mon, this way," he managed, choking in the heat and smoke of the fire. "Before we get completely cut off and fried alive."

Garth nodded and was the first to move, gripping his weapon tight as he plunged through the overgrown grass, the vegetation whipping at his arms and legs as he moved. Sylvester and Clive were next, moving back-to-back and covering one another as they went, bringing down more and more of the flaming dogs as they leapt through the sheets of fire that covered the field. Bill and Angel joined them, shotgun and machine pistol barking in unison as they took down rogue canines that evaded the weapons fire of the mechanic and the priest. Al was the last to leave, a fresh drum of ammunition in his weapon as he slowly moved backwards, sweeping his heavy machinegun from side to side and cutting down the dogs as they tried to follow their intended prey.

The entrance to the palace that they reached was a heavy oak door, a deep navy blue in colour with heavy, wrought iron handles and doorknockers. One of the doors stood ajar, which Bill assumed had been the way Garth had entered the building, as neither he, Sylvester or Clive had hung around outside to take pictures. Ushering Angel into the palace, Bill turned around and lifted his shotgun, offering cover for his friend. There was no sign of Al, and thick black smoke drifted across the field, the orange glow of the flames muted by the clouds of burnt matter. Baying howls and bloody growls filled the air, and Bill thought that, for just one moment, the undead dogs had taken down Al.

Shapes within the smoke moved, and a large humanoid stepped out of the murk, body streaked with soot and sweat, a black rag tied around his mouth and his clothing smeared in blood. He lowered his weapon as he swaggered into view, cursing under his breath and diving into the open door. Bill fired off the rest of his shells from his shotgun and rolled into the open doorway, gasping for breath and feeling the cold of the interior shock his system as Clive and Sylvester pushed to door shut and locked out the heat of the fire and the fury of the dogs. The animals outside hurled themselves against the barricade as the deadbolts slid into place, claws scratching at the wooden surface, the reek of charred flesh oozing into the darkened room through the cracks in the door.

Everyone sunk to the floor in the room, dropping their weapons to the ground and fumbling in their pockets for spare ammunition, reloading everything they had as fast as the could. The task completed, Al stripped the rag from his face and ran it over his head, polishing his gleaming dome and wiping off the sweat while Angel ran her hands through her hair, brushing away the stray strands that were plastered to her scalp and tightening her hairclips. Clive adjusted his bandana and Sylvester cracked each of his fingers sequentially as Garth pulled his battered and grimy hat from his head and buffed it uselessly against his grimy sleeve. Everyone was quiet, until Al finally broke the silence.

"Way to go, buddy. Un-fucking-believable."

"I thought it would work. It happens all the time in the films, the wild animals kept at bay by the flames. I really thought it would work."

"The reason wild animals are scared is because they're intelligent enough to know that fire will kill them. Mindless zombies are just like you," Al scorned, stepping forwards and poking Garth in the head with his index finger. "Mindless. Stupid."

"How was I to know *that* would happen?"

"You were in the middle of a field," Sylvester announced, sighing as he clambered to his feet and stumbled listlessly towards one of the windows: they were all made from reinforced glass, and although they had all been smashed, the fine web of security wire embedded within had kept them together, giving them a frosted appearance. As he stood close to the window, the flaming animals that raced back and forth outside occasionally lit him up with a putrid yellow glow. "What did you think was going to happen?"

"It was damp... I thought..."

"Forget it," Bill finally said. "What's done is done."

He turned his attention to the room, a dark and cool chamber with dark wooden panelling on the wall and a thick red carpet on the ground. There was a faint smell of rot and decay in the air, though Bill knew that could just be the remnants of the smell from outside, from before the fire started. Pieces of torn grass and chunks of bushes had been uprooted and pulled into the room, piled in the corners and underneath a large mahogany dining table, as if the dogs had made dens in the room. He was sure that the creatures had formed these dens before they turned...

Which meant that there still might be one of the creatures in the palace.

"Look alive, people," Al said, noticing the makeshift dens as Bill did, grabbing his weapon and working a fresh belt of ammunition into the mechanism. "There might be another of the dead dogs lingering around here."

"More?" Garth muttered, lowering his flamethrower slightly. Al grabbed it and took it from him, extinguishing the flame at the barrel and pulling the carry strap over his shoulder.

"More, yes. And I'll keep hold of this, I'm not letting you play with matches any more."

Al led the way, acting as a guide as he took the group deeper into the building. The dark room opened up into a wide hallway, the ceiling arcing high above their heads and the walls covered in the same lavish wooden panelling. Bill dropped back as the group progressed, lost in awe at the scale and majesty of the palace. Though the walls were damp and the wallpaper shredded and torn in several places, exposing bare plaster and wooden laths in some places, Bill could imagine the palace in its prime, with lavish carpets and decorative tapestries; looters had stripped the building bare, though, taking anything they could get their hands on. Chandeliers had been removed, light fittings pulled from the walls, drawers pulled open and emptied on the floor; the wallpaper remaining on the wall was two-toned, ghost images left behind from paintings and pictures that had once hung there and protected the paper, while the exposed covering had slowly paled and faded.

"This place used to be filled with gold and shit like that," murmured Sylvester as they continued to move through hallways and reception rooms filled with debris and dirt. "While the 'peasants' lived their mundane lives outside barely scraping a living, these rich bastards lived in here like..."

"Like kings and queens?" suggested Angel. Sylvester nodded while shrugging his shoulders.

"You know about this place?" Garth asked, incredulously. Again, Sylvester shrugged.

"Terri was big on the royals. We visited this place a few years back..." his voice quivered slightly, a lump forming in his throat. He cleared his throat and carried on. "Well, a few years before the… Before she passed on."

Clive clapped him gently on the back as they carried on, gently massaging his friend's shoulder with the tips of his finger. Sylvester returned the gesture by patting the hand and murmuring thanks.

"So you know this place, but I'm still leading this freak-show?" asked Al.

"We visited *once*, Al, we didn't spend a month in the guest quarters."

"Now's your chance."

"I'll pass, thanks."

The hallway wound around the outside of the building, the windows boarded up and allowing the smallest shafts of light into the room, dust motes whirling and dancing in the faint air currents as the six people cut boldly through the darkened rooms. The passage finally opened up into wide foyer, a tall room with a grand spiral staircase sweeping up one wall of the room and up to a balcony overlooking the entrance hall. The banister was a deep rich mahogany, though the varnish had been scratched and peeled off, fragments of animal claws and fingernails embedded in the hard wood a testament to the source of the damage. The floor was covered with ceramic tiles; each covered in a thick layer of grime and paw prints. A body lay on the ground in the centre of the room, a soldier in a twisted and awkward position, limbs spread akimbo and head pulled to one side. The rubber seal that surrounded the soldier's neck, fixing the emotionless breath mask to the sealed combat suit, had been torn open, as had the soldier's throat. Shredded flesh hung out the wound, raw meat exposed and oozing blood on to the dirty tiles. The doors leading to the outside world remained firmly shut, though the lower half of one of the doors had been smashed away, the ragged edges of the hole covered in a pale tacky blood.

Al lowered his heavy weapon and pulled out his Desert Eagle, moving towards the soldier with a stooped running motion, timidly reaching out and grabbing the mask by its seals before heaving it off. The thick rubber appliance slipped off the head of the Marine with a gentle hiss, and Al gently placed his fingers against the undamaged side of the neck.

"No pulse," he reported, "But he's still warm. Looks like we disturbed a feeding dog with our little gun fight."

Bill stepped forwards, inching closer to the dead body with his shotgun pointing unwavering at the head of the corpse. "That's not what I'm concerned about," he said grimly. "What was he doing here?"

"They're here," hissed Al, dropping into a lower crouch. "They knew we were headed here, and managed to get some of their guys here before we did. They obviously weren't expecting the dogs to be here, though. Leaving one man as a guard, that's just fucking amateurish."

"What about a scout?" asked Angel.

"You say something kid?" Al said, glaring at Bill. He sighed inwardly, having been under the impression that Al had put an end to this behaviour.

"What about a scout?" he repeated. Al nodded with a smile.

"Good thinking, kid, I like your style. Possibly a scout, so we may be in the clear for now."

"I thought if he'd decided he wasn't a Marine any more he'd be a little less of a dick around me," Angel muttered under her breath as she took a step back into the hallway they'd just exited from. Bill followed after her, watching as she knelt on the ground and lifted her pistol, panning it lazily from side to side.

"I think he'll always be like that," Bill said softly, kneeling beside her and speaking in a soft voice so no one else could hear him. "How're you holding up?"

"Fine," she said in a standoffish manner before sighing to herself. "A little disturbed by what those Marines did to their prisoners. A little pissed off with him," she said, nodding towards Al as he circled the corpse, stripping it of ammunition or anything else that may prove useful. "He can be such an arsehole."

"Asshole," corrected Al from across the room, barely looking up from his work. "I'm an asshole, get it right if you're going to badmouth me."

"Whatever," muttered Angel.

Bill nodded slightly, crouching on the ground beside her as the pair of them watched the hallway. "Look, about the other night…"

"Not now, Bill, it's not the time. You had your chance the other night; instead you decided to sleep in the driving seat and ignore me."

"But I… I didn't know what was happening, I didn't know what I wanted…"

"And now you do?" snapped Angel. "Well, why didn't you say so? You know the world revolves around you, lets just put everything on pause while you finally make up your mind."

Bill went to protest, but he jumped at the sound of a weapon being fired. Turning to look over his shoulder, he could see Al standing over the fallen solder, his smoking handgun levelled at the shattered skull that oozed thick grey and crimson.

"He started twitching," he announced, as if he felt he had to explain his actions. "Couldn't let the bastard get up."

Nodding, Bill turned back to look at Angel, but by the time he'd done that she had clambered to her feet and taken position over by the entrance, leaving him alone. Bill stood to try and follow, but she simply shook her head, indicating she didn't want him to follow her.

"Look lively," announced Al. He crouched over the remains of the shoulder, his hand covered in droplets of blood as he held the radio headset he'd retrieved from the corpse by his ear. "This guy may have been a just scout, but his squad's not too far away: they're about to break into the east wing."

"What wing are we in?"

"Do I look like a tour guide?" snapped Al. "Ask Prince Spanners over there, apparently he used to live in here."

Sylvester rolled his eyes, shaking his head.

Al waved frantically with one hand while he pressed the gore-soaked device to his ear, giving a verbal commentary to accompany what was happening over the secured channel.

"They're about to break in through one of the doors," he said, holding his finger up for silence. "It's heavily barricaded and secured, so they've got to break out the heavy equipment, one of the piston-driven battering rams. That's good, those beasts are noisy; we used to use them all the time in Brazil. At least the noise of that thing going off will give us a good idea where they are so we can prepare for them, get a fix on them. Count down, breech in ten, nine eight…"

II

The thick doors of the entrance hall burst open with a deafening roar, the ramming motion of the piston knocking in the doors and spewing fragments of wood into the entrance hall. Slivers of shattered wood hung from the tattered opening, and a trio of soldiers stormed into the building, sweeping their assault rifles from side to side and clearing debris away from the opening with the side of their boots.

"Breech complete," the first soldier said, peering from side to side and motioning for each of the soldiers to take point either side of the hole. "Secure entrance hall."

Diving to each side, the other soldiers took their position, checking the hallways to either side of the foyer before turning their attention to the balcony above them. A figure stood in the darkness, hands resting on the handrail as it glared down on to the tiled surface, swaying slightly from side to side. It made no move to head down the stairs, nor did it try to identify itself. As one the soldiers opened fire, bullets slapping against the body in the head and shoulders, jerking and twisting from side to side before it keeled lifelessly over the balcony, bones and joints cracking and splintering as they crashed against the tiled floor.

"Dead," announced one of the soldiers, running forwards and kicking the shattered skull of the body. "Entrance hall secured."

The soldier turned from the corpse and took two steps away before his head exploded with a deafening clap of thunder. As their comrade crumpled to the floor the remaining soldiers snapped their weapons up and pivoted from side to side, searching for their attacker. A second clap of thunder echoed in the foyer and one of the remaining soldiers dropped to the floor, a bloody and gaping hole appearing in his chest. The remaining soldier anxiously spun in a full circle, unable to fathom where the attack had come from until it was too late.

Al stepped out from the shadows beneath the balcony, his bulky frame previously hidden by a pile of rubble and debris that had once been a marble table. His Desert Eagle already trained on the remaining Marine, he squeezed the trigger and sent a burst of two powerful rounds tearing through the heavy mask that covered his face. He dropped to the floor, convulsing and twitching spasmodically as his life force ebbed away.

"These Marine's ain't so tough," Garth growled as he and Clive pulled themselves from beneath the staircase. Bill and Sylvester rose from their hiding place at the top of the balcony, where they had supported the body of the scout shortly before tossing it over the railing.

"They didn't even check any of the hiding places in this room before announcing that the place was clear," Sylvester said in disbelief.

"God damn greenhorns," muttered Al, relieving the bodies of their weapons and supplies. "The Marines must be scraping the bottom of the barrel for their troops now. I'll bet these bastards have just been drafted straight out the army.

"What's so bad about the army? I thought one armed force was just the same as the next, working to the same common goal," Clive said, helping Angel out from her hiding place next to Al.

"If you weren't a man of the cloth, and if I was still a Marine, that sentence would have been enough to warrant me punching your lights out," Al growled, pointing a finger menacingly at him. "As it stands, you're lucky. There's too much dust and shit in the air, I can't see a shittin' thing. Spanners, you able to see anything through the windows up there?"

Sylvester, still standing on the balcony, leaned forwards, peering through the large windows that stood above the exposed entrance. He nodded softly, casting a wary glance downward, reluctant to take his eyes off the scene unfurling outside.

"There's more soldiers out there, they've got a load of armoured vehicles parked up, and seem to have us locked in their sights," Sylvester blurted, his voice quivering as he spoke. "It's just like in the movies, with the cops surrounding the bad guys… only *we're* the bad guys, aren't we?"

"Hmm," Al said, pulling the bodies of the soldiers to one side and patting them down for any additional useful supplies. Coming away with a clutch of forty millimetre grenades and magazines for the assault rifles, he glared at the opened doorway before pushing the bodies towards the opening with his feet, creating a low barrier of dead bodies. "Let's hope the cops don't decide to send in the SWAT, yeah?"

Sylvester nodded weakly and started to move towards the stairs, but Al held his hand up.

"Stay up there. We're going to make a stand."

Sylvester laughed and continued to make his way down the stairs, but a withering glare from Al stopped him in his tracks. His face crumbled into a look of confusion.

"Jesus, you're serious?"

"It makes perfect sense," Al continued, stacking up the magazines on the ground beside him and mentally counting them up. "We sure as hell can't just walk out the door, and they're on to us anyway: the city's probably teeming with scouts now. The outside walls of this place must be one and a half, maybe two feet thick. What do you say, kid?"

"Easily," Bill said, nodding in agreement. "Solid stone, too."

"It's an ideal place to make a stand, they'll have no weapons that can penetrate that kind of material; if we block off all the hallways leading in to this room, set up a good strong defence, we'll be able to make our stand and take down those bastards."

"Seriously?"

"You want to try to just walk out there, see where that gets you? If they don't shoot you in the gut and leave to die in agony, they'll strap you to a chair and force-feed you live cockroaches or set your clothes on fire and piss on you to put out the flames. We make a stand, we've got no other choice."

"God damn it," muttered Sylvester, hanging his head as he knew the man was right, then looked down towards Clive. "Sorry, man." The priest smiled, nodding his head, and Sylvester drew the grenade launcher from the holster attached to his combat webbing. "So, how do we do this?"

"Glad you asked. The bitch and me are by far the best marksmen we got, so we hang back in the darkness beneath the balcony and act as snipers, keeping the fuckers as far away from the doorway as possible. If they try to rush us, I want buddy there to sit by the door with that nasty little flamethrower of yours, lay down a suppressive field of fire. Kid, you and Preacher-man make sure the hallways are clear and locked down, I don't want any nasty surprises sneaking up on us and trying to shaft us from behind. Spanners, you stay up there and get your grenade launcher ready. There's about twenty grenades down here, not to mention however many you got up there. Get them out the window and into the ranks of the Marines out there."

"Sounds good," Bill admitted, heaving the heavy oak doors shut behind him and locking them before running down the stairs and joining Clive in securing the larger doors on the ground floor. Al retreated to the grim sanctity of the darkness beneath the balcony, loaded with a collection of magazines for him and Angel to share.

"Hi, bitch," he said with a grin, the pair crouching down once again beside the pile of debris they had previously hidden behind. She rolled her eyes, holstering her machine pistol and bringing her rifle up. Al shook his head and lowered the barrel, handing her an assault rifle instead. "We've got hundreds of rounds for these beauties, we may as well use these. Single fire mode, remember we're shooting people and not Rots: while headshots are good, they're not necessary. Try not to hit our buddy as he crouches by the doorway there."

"Have I got to sit here?" Garth whined as he took his position, his flamethrower ready.

"You're our point man," insisted Al. "That's an honorary position, buddy."

"I don't mind if I have a less honourable position."

"I'll bet you don't," muttered Al, then in a louder voice, "Spanners, you want to kick off the party and get this shindig started?"

"What's a shindig?" asked Angel, lifting her rifle and settling in for a long fight as Sylvester unleashed his first grenade, an explosion outside rattling the windows and shaking loose pieces of glass free. Al responded by kicking her in the shin, grinning as he did so.

"Real mature, Al" she snapped, thumbing the selector switch on her rifle to single shot. "Real mature."

"Major," one of the Marines stood to attention, snapping off a sharp salute as the commanding officer clambered out from the airlock of his command vehicle. Under normal circumstances he would have scorned one of his subordinates for identifying a senior officer in a battlefield, but he was easily identifiable regardless: while the soldiers wore dirty, bloodstained HAZMAT suits and identical filtration masks with gold-coloured lenses, he wore a pristine airtight jumpsuit and a helmet with an opaque faceplate, also gold in colour. A thick black belt wrapped around his waist, and from the belt hung two leather holsters, each housing one of his prized trench spikes.

"What's the situation, Sergeant?"

"We've got them pinned down in the entrance foyer in the East wing," he reported, handing over a plastic clipboard with a series of figures and sketches on it. He pointed to different parts of the clipboard as he spoke. "After killing one of our scouts and three of the initial recon squad sent in after breaking the doors in, they opened up with the first shot, a grenade that wiped out one of our hummers. That was about two hours ago, we've been locked in a stalemate since then. They've got a pretty tight defence; someone in there knows what they're doing."

"A Marine, a Sergeant no less," the major said, nodding in agreement. "He knows how to plan and counter operations like this, he served in Brazil for a number of years; he's no stranger to guerrilla warfare or urban combat. How've they got it set up?"

"We think there's one, possibly two snipers keeping the doorway clear, another person with a grenade launcher. We've tried breaking in elsewhere in the castle and working our way through the building, but they've got the hallways hemmed in tight, too, we're sitting ducks if we go in there. We managed to get one man close to the doorway, but they have an incinerator unit set up by the door and he got cooked soon as he reached the open door."

"Very tight. How long do we think they can last?"

"Indefinitely, if they have enough food. We haven't tried blasting through the walls yet, but the architectural plans we have access to on the mainframe network suggests they're twenty two inches thick: we'd have to use C4 to break through, but we can't get close enough without exposing ourselves to a barrage of grenades of sniper fire. So far, eleven men have been killed and a further three men injured."

The major nodded and strolled away from his parked command vehicle, moving towards the burning wreckage of a humvee and the cluster of vehicles parked further back. Shrapnel and smouldering debris littered the ground around the damaged vehicle, as did the charred and blackened remains of the soldiers killed in the blast. The major calmly slid to the ground behind one of the remaining armoured vehicles, its side peppered with sharp metallic slivers that smouldered from their heat.

"Tanks?" the major asked. One of the soldiers, a private that crouched over a heavy radio transmitter that had been wired in to his mask for ease of use, shook his head solemnly.

"They're clogged up in sector thirteen, they're hemmed in by a pack of dead there, they estimate another hour before they can get here, providing the streets remain relatively clear."

"An hour," sneered the major. "Anything could happen. Send in another squad."

"Sir?"

"Another squad, try another assault."

Reluctantly a squad of twelve men formed beside the major, each armed with an assault rifle and a satchel filled with explosives.

"Get to that palace and make a hole in their wall," insisted the major. Twelve vacant and identical respirators started grimly back at him, their rubber faces not betraying any of their emotions. "Your goal is to plant those charges on the wall and break through, or at least expose the structure of the building. Failure to carry this out will result in death, either at their hands or mine."

The soldiers didn't respond, simply kept their gaze fixed on the major.

"You've got your orders, Marines, now carry them out."

The soldiers slowly turned and made their way towards the opening of the palace, staying low and cautiously fanning out to either side of the door. A single rifle shot sounded and one of the soldiers fell, screaming and clutching his stomach as deep crimson blossomed and seeped over his white suit. None of the men advancing on the building stopped to help their fallen comrade, and the major watched coldly as the stomach wound slowly claimed the Marine. The sergeant beside him lifted his weapon to end his suffering, but the major shook his head and lowered the muzzle of the assault rifle with a slight indication of his finger.

"He was careless," the major sneered. "Payback is a bitch, and he's learned the hard way."

Another burst of gunfire, and a second soldier dropped, this time his head obliterated by a rifle round. Shaking his head, the major watched as his group of highly trained men, the best the world's armed forces had to offer, were systematically picked off: another three taken down by sniper fire, five more killed in a grenade that sailed out one of the windows on the higher level, and the final two drowned in a wave of fire that splashed over them.

"Wiped out by amateurs," the major snarled. "The incompetent fuckers deserved it."

He turned and waved his hand towards the guard standing stoic beside the rear of his command vehicle. He nodded by response and clambered up on to the back of the vehicle as he started to unlock the rear hatch.

"Tear it open. I want those bastards dead, except for the Marine… him, I want alive."

Slowly, the major adjusted the controls for his radio, switching to a frequency that broadcast over the public address system that was set up around the encampment.

"Colebrook," he shouted, his voice booming from the speakers. "I know you're in there. If you give yourself up, maybe we'll let your friends go; or at least make sure they die quickly. You're the reason we're here. Come out, give yourself up."

"He knows you?" asked Angel, turning her head slightly to one side as she kept her eyes trained on the doorway. "How does he know you?"

"I was in the Marines for almost twenty years," Al said with a slight grin, balancing an unlit cigarette on his lips as he spoke. "I made some friends, I made some enemies; he could be any one of those."

"He's not offering you a cold one and a pack of cigarettes," muttered Sylvester from his vantage point, "I'm guessing it's someone you pissed off at one point in your illustrious career."

"Hell of a long time to hold a grudge, though," muttered Al, scratching his goatee as he spoke. "Three years off active duty, years in Brazil before that…"

"I can understand someone still holding a grudge," Angel muttered, rolling her eyes. "You're not the easiest man to get along with."

"He sounds familiar, though…" mused Al, listening to the tone of the voice as the speaker continued to talk, trying to pick out any characteristics that he may recognise. There was something there that sounded familiar, but with the voice distorted by the speakers and crackle of the radio link, he couldn't place it.

"You're the reason we're here," the speaker announced again. "The reason I'm here. You and your damn radio transmissions."

"Carter," Al announced with a grin while nodding his head. The name wasn't just familiar to him; Bill turned from the hallway he guarded, a puzzled expression on his face.

"The same Carter we made a fake television broadcast for?"

"And the same bastard I used to get on my home made radio all the time. God damn, they sent the Brass in to the field!"

"Why?"

"Same reason they sent small squads on to the mainland, why they kept bases well stocked: they were trying to conduct a full-scale assault on the island, wipe out the survivors and reclaim the land for their own use. The acting coms officers on duty no doubt logged all the radio broadcasts I made, and they eventually found their way up the ranks. Shit normally rolls downhill, but with fuckups like this, everything documented would probably be scrutinised by the three brain cells the Brass shared. I'll bet they realised how bad it was here, that plague carriers weren't just dropping dead and there were armed militia running riot, they had to step up the attack. And of course, the fact one of their cleanup squads were wiped out by a rogue gang who broadcast a fake television transmission no doubt made them sweat a little more. The Brass must've shit bricks when they realised they'd been outfoxed."

"You're enjoying this, aren't you?"

"It's not very often the grunts pull one over the eyes of the Brass," Al smiled, rummaging through the equipment he'd stripped from one of the Marine corpses. He picked up a battered radio unit, thumbed a few of the grey rubber buttons on the front of the box, then strained to listen to the broadcast: the only audible words seemed to be the speech given by Carter that boomed over the speakers.

"Can't get a word in edgeways," hissed Al. "Spanners, how about you get that bastard's attention and make him shut up?"

The grenade launcher Sylvester held spoke with a hollow thunk, and Al watched as the grenade sailed through the air, bounced once on the ground outside, then erupted into a flaming blossom of shrapnel. The loudspeakers squawked with a screeching hiss of feedback, replaced by the laboured breathing of Carter as he muttered incoherently into his mask.

"Glad that got your attention," Al laughed, standing up from his hiding place and wiring a headset into the coded radio. "Sorry about that, but I *really* couldn't bear listening to any more of your shit. That you, Carter?"

"That's *Major* Carter, soldier," snapped the Marine; he'd killed the transmission to the loudspeakers, and Al worked the controls of the device so everyone in the room could hear it.

"Only to another *Marine*, you dumb-ass fuck-wit. I quit about…" Al made a visible display of looking at his watch, even though he knew Carter couldn't see him. "Maybe six hours ago, something like that. So you can take your military etiquette and shove it up your ass, if there's any room up their with all the dicks of the rest of the Brass that are already in there, *Carter*."

Al spat the major's name as he strolled around the foyer, his weapon slung as he addressed the leader of the soldiers.

"I don't give a shit about your retarded friends in there," the major screamed, his voice seething with anger. "I want you, you miserable bastard, alive. I want to put you through the same hell you've put me through."

"Blow me, you greasy old fuck," Al said with a grin, casually flicking a finger towards the doorway. He knew he was out of his field of vision, but he didn't care. "This is all *your* fault, or at least the higher powers that pull all the strings. If you'd arranged to pick me up after I'd called you the first time, I wouldn't have made all those radio broadcasts, and I certainly wouldn't have went to the trouble of me and my friends organising a certain television broadcast."

"I'll kill you, Colebrook, it's your fault I'm stuck on this fucking island!"

"Right back atcha, asshole." Al spat, furrowing his brow as he talked. "If you'd sent an evac copter when I'd asked for one, I would've stopped making all those broadcasts, and this would've all been your little secret. You want to blame someone for being stuck on this island, blame yourself. Or at the least the coms officer that sent off all the reports up the chain of command."

"There's something going on out there," reported Sylvester from his vantage point, peering out into the rabble of soldiers outside as they swarmed around the rear of the large command vehicle that had parked up outside. Al slipped closer to the doorway, sidling up beside Garth and unsheathing his knife, slipping it around the corner of the doorframe and using the shiny blade to view what was happening.

The rear of the command vehicle had been peeled open, the large doors on the back of the transport pinned back and revealing the shining weapon the technicians swarmed over: a seat attached to a number of pipes, tubes and boxes, each a weapon that Al recognised. Vulcan cannons, flame units, rocket propelled grenades… a very destructive piece of Military hardware that he couldn't help feel was going to be aimed in his direction very soon.

"New toy, Carter?"

The short snap of a rifle answered his question as a bullet smashed into his blade, knocking the knife out of his grasp and sending it skittering across the floor. Al swore, rubbing the jolt of the impact from his hand as he retreated from the doorway.

"Three minutes to give yourself up, Colebrook, then we'll rip your little hideout apart."

The radio went dead, and Al dropped the box to the floor.

"What they got?" asked Bill, still standing by the hallway he'd been assigned to guard.

"Remember that weapon you waxed the Messiah with?"

Bill nodded grimly, fully aware of what they would be facing off against.

"Parked too far away from the reach of the grenade launcher, and me and the bitch couldn't manoeuvre ourselves to get a decent shot without being exposed to their snipers. That stationary gun emplacement will tear through the walls of this castle in less than ten seconds once its running at full power; I guess there's only one option left."

"You're right," Garth said, nodding grimly. "It's been nice knowing you, Al. You really think they'll let us walk if we hand you over?"

"I don't know how you'll be able to walk out of this if I snap your legs," glowered Al. "We're going to have to move out, make a run for it. Kid, Preacher-man, how clear are those hallways?"

"The way is clear here," announced Clive, adjusting his coat and keeping his shotgun levelled off at head height. "I've seen maybe a couple of men approach this way."

"My way seems to be teeming with the bastards. They're well back, but I can see them, I guess they're waiting to rush us on the signal," Bill offered. "I say we take Clive's way."

"Agreed," Al said as he gathered all the weapons and ammunition he had. "You'd better be right about this, Preacher-man, else you'll be going to meet your god sooner than you planned."

Clive didn't respond, simply mouthed a prayer as he prepared himself for the upcoming assault. Al grunted wordlessly as he grabbed the heavy machinegun from the ground, slinging his assault rifle over his shoulder. He motioned for the rest of his team to do so, urging them to move as fast as possible.

"Meter's running," he hissed, stepping beside Bill and crouching down. "The plan is simple; we make noise here and then run like shit in the opposite direction. We cause a distraction; any soldiers over at Preacher-man's hallway will probably relax a little more, then we can charge them and make our way out. Wait for the signal, though.'

"Time's up,' shouted Carter, his voice booming over the loudspeakers once more.

"That's the signal," screamed Al. Both he and Bill opened fire, their weapons spewing smoke and bullets as they aimed at the gloomy corridor. The darkened hallway flickered wildly with the muzzle flashes, creating dancing shadows and picking out he shining metallic bolts and casings of the Marine's weapons. The sounds of their weapons were all but drowned out by the heavy pounding of the weapon outside, the thick stone walls crumbling and breaking apart as the heavy rounds tore through them.

Bill looked over to Al and asked him a question, his words inaudible through the barrage of gunfire. Al couldn't understand anything, but he could take a guess, and nodded, stepping away from the hallway and quickly retreating back to the other hallway, where the rest of his crew lay pressed against the floor, keeping a low profile as the rounds from the mounted Gatling cannons tore through the foyer.

"Move," screamed Al as he lumbered into the hallway with Bill close behind him. With weapons still firing, the group advanced through the hallway as the entrance foyer behind them was ripped to shreds; broken chunks of concrete and fragments of wood rained down from the walls and ceilings, and a thick cloud of grey dust billowed out into the hall behind them.

Marines leapt out of their hiding places behind broken statues and small hidden alcoves, weapons drawn and ready, though each was cut down by rapid fire or point-blank shotgun blasts before they could open fire.

Walk in the park, Al thought to himself as he pulled the discharging muzzle of his M249 from left to right, tearing apart body armour, flesh and bone of the doomed soldiers as they fell to the ground.

The deathly rattle of the heavy weapon outside the palace ceased, and Al could hear muted orders through the thick walls and shattered windows; sounds of the soldiers advancing on the decimated foyer, marching carefully across the grounds towards the demolished front of the palace.

"They're moving through one of the side halls," Carter's voice boomed out. "Don't let them escape."

"Fucking officers, never get their hands dirty" hissed Al, emerging from the hallway in a cramped antechamber littered with charred corpses; blackened limbs still smoking and reeking of scorched flesh, each with their head punctured by a single bullet.

"What the fuck's this?" asked Garth, kicking one of the corpses.

'Must've been a pocket of Rots holding up in the palace. I guess the Marines just killed them outright while they were advancing on us, instead of nailing them to a tree of setting them on fire while they recorded it. Okay Spanners, which way?"

"How the fuck should I know?" snapped Sylvester, levelling off his grenade launcher and sending an explosive round tearing down the hallway they had just ran up, demolishing part of the hall and making it harder for the Marines to follow them. "That'll buy us some time, at least."

"What now?" asked Angel, slamming the stock of her rifle against the ground as she tried to dislodge the round that had jammed in the barrel. Frustrated, she tossed the rifle aside and drew her machine pistol, cocking it with a loud clacking sound. "Sit and wait for them to tunnel through?"

"We need to get back to our vehicle and get the fuck outta here. This is all your fault, kid, you know that?"

"You can chew me out later," Bill muttered beneath his breath.

"I intend to," growled Al, slowly rotating on the spot as he checked out the different exits from the chamber. One would take them towards the front of the building and the soldiers that awaited them there, another was the hallway they had just come from, and the third seemed to snake around the rear of the palace.

"That way," Al said, rushing towards the only logical choice and powering down the hallway, his weapon tucked in tight against his shoulder and ready for any threat or confrontation. He moved as fast as he could, confident that no one, not even Garth, would lag behind: even with his extra weight, fear seemed to give him that extra burst of adrenaline that provided the speed or strength required to get him through. Al hadn't been surprised he'd tried to get out of joining the search party for Bill in the first place, but if push came to shove, he could still hold his own.

The rest of the run through the corridors of the palace was largely uneventful, and it was evident that all the armed forces had converged on the front entrance of the building, certain that the group would not have been able to slip through the net. Al was grateful of that, and the moment he stumbled out a pair of double doors and into the cold dusk that had claimed the city, he felt himself relax slightly. While he knew they were by no means out of danger, he felt more comfortable in an open environment, where it would be harder for him and his followers to be pinned down. At least, that was the theory.

'Now what?" Garth asked, doubling up and leaning over, trying to catch his breath. His face was pale and his lips were blue, with sweat pouring down his brow and soaking his shirt. "Where do we go?"

"It's safe to say Prince Spanners doesn't know much about the back yard of this place, am I right? We need somewhere we can make a stand from. I'll get on the radio, tell Pam where we are and get her to come pick us up."

"I thought you didn't want to put her in danger! I thought you wanted everything kept in a safe zone."

"Desperate times, buddy, they're calling for a desperate measure. I don't want to, but if we can't get our own heavy guns into position, we're not going to stand a chance. We need cover, somewhere we can hold down in safety until it all goes down."

"There's a building over there," Angel announced, pointing to a construct at the other end of the expanse of garden, a structure obscured by trees and covered in a mass of vines and ivy.

"That's no building, bitch," murmured Al, his heart beating faster as he recognised the type of structure and started to jog towards it, beckoning for everyone to follow him.

"Then what the hell is it?" shouted Angel as she burst into a sprint to catch up to the excited ex-Marine.

"Barracks," he explained. "It's the next best thing to an armoury, reinforced walls should be able to take a pounding from those mounted Gatling guns."

"I'd like a little more reassurance than 'should'," Garth wheezed as he moved. Clive looked over and smiled, patting one of the pockets in his coat where he carried his worn bible.

"Have faith in the word of the Lord, and he will protect you."

"Unless his word is written on a sheet of reinforced steel that's ten inches thick, I'm not interested," Garth grinned as they reached the door to the barracks. They had been torn open, the metal barriers lying battered and twisted on the ground, a sure sign that the interior had been breached either by soldiers or Rots: Al wasn't sure which he'd rather face, especially if the undead within were the tougher breed that had reared their rotten heads.

"Bitch, you hang back on the door, keep an eye out for those boy scouts approaching. Take my rifle if it helps. The rest of us split up and clear the inside, make sure it's secure: also, keep your eyes peeled for anything like weapons, if we're lucky there may still be a small cache sitting somewhere."

"*Outside* of an armoury? Do Marines love their weapons enough to sleep with them? What kind of crazy bastard does that?"

"I'm sorry, maybe we haven't met. Albert Colebrook," Al said with smile, extending his hand towards Bill. He slapped it away casually and stepped into the building, getting ready to purge the building as quickly as possible. "I'll call Pam, make sure she gets here as soon as she can."

III

Pam stood on the roof of the main trailer, a thick padded jacket wrapped around her as she watched over the immediate area. They'd parked the vehicle on the outskirts of the city, and if she looked hard enough, she could just make out the shape of Bill's abandoned bike in the distance. It had been the starting point of the search for the impulsive young man, and had been easy enough to find because of the tracking device attached to the machine. Al had gone into great detail as he told the story of how he and Bill had been tracked to an old farmhouse using the same method by a gang once, and the gunfight that had followed.

After three hours, a couple of Rots stumbled across the bike and lazily circled it for a few minutes before a third creature arrived on the scene. Larger than the other two, it launched into an attack and downed one of them, and though the creature fell out of her line if sight, she knew that the fallen zombie was going to end up as lunch for the others.

"Where are they?"

Pam felt her heart race as she spun on her heel, jumping as the soft voice of Sarah carried over the cool and still air that lingered over the city. She smiled softly, motioning with a wave of her hand for the young girl to climb up and stand beside her. She did so, revealing the fact she had a thick green sheet wrapped around her to provide extra warmth.

"I don't know, honey," Pam said, taking hold of the little girls hand.

"Haven't they called in yet?"

"Al said he wouldn't do that. He wants us to stay safe. That's why he called for radio silence."

Sarah nodded her head, a sparkle in her eye as she did so. "Radio silence," she mused. "I thought he just wanted us to turn the volume down on it. He means he's not going to talk to us."

"That's right. You know what Al's like, with his military speak."

"He's funny," Sarah agreed, nodding her head once more. She was silent for a little longer, wiping her nose on the quilt she was wrapped in, then spoke again.

"Sometimes mum and dad didn't talk. Was that radio silence?"

"No," Pam said with a gentle smile. "No, that was something different."

Again, Sarah was silent, squeezing Pam's hand as she looked out into the silent city.

"Do you think they'll be much longer?"

"I don't know, honey. I can't imagine Bill would have gone too far into the city on foot."

"Do you think Al will really do what he said?"

Pam smiled as she remembered the morning, and the tirade of expletives and gestures Al went through as he prepared his weapons and equipment before going into the city, in which he'd promised, amongst other things, to beat Bill senseless and remove his testicles with a blunt and rusted razor. She shook her head. "No, I think he was just joking, I don't think he meant anything by it. He was just angry."

"I get it."

She wiped her nose again, sniffed, then lowered herself to the floor, crossing her legs and drumming her fingers on the metal railing just below one of the mounted machineguns.

"So are you and Al going to look after me now?"

"We all will, honey, all of us."

"But daddy asked Al... I heard him and Bill talking about it the other night."

Pam nodded, aware of the conversation Sarah was talking about. Though everyone had agreed to help look after her, Al said he would take charge of looking after Sarah as much as possible because of what he'd promised Steve moments before he'd killed himself.

"That's right, he did. And I think he will; Al keeps his word."

"Except for when he says he's going to rip someone's balls off and shove them up their ass?"

"Sarah," Pam scowled, trying to stop herself from laughing, "Don't say that."

"Sorry, I forgot I couldn't say that word. Garth told me the word's arse; that's right, isn't it?"

"Get inside," Pam said, motioning towards the hatchway leading back into the vehicle. "I'll make you something to eat."

"I'm not hungry," murmured Sarah as she clambered back down the ladder.

"You have to eat something," Pam insisted as she followed down and moved down towards the kitchen area. Sarah followed, but didn't say anything as she watched Pam piece together a couple of sandwiches made from stale bread and freeze-dried meat. She looked at the sandwich and slowly nibbled at the corner of the bread; then she took a larger bite, then wolfed down half of the sandwich, wiping her mouth with the back of her sleeve.

"More hungry than you thought?"

Sarah nodded meekly, polishing off the snack. She hadn't eaten since the incident with her parents, and Pam was glad to see her finally eat something.

"C'mon, follow me," Pam said, returning back into the main living area and sitting down on one of the seats, curling up on it and unearthing the thick notepad she carried. She opened the book, folded the pages flat, and pulled a plastic biro from her pocket. "I'll tell you a story."

"That's your book about people before the plague," Sarah said; it wasn't a question, but Pam nodded anyway.

"Who do you want to know about?"

"Tell me about Al," she insisted, jumping on to the seat beside her and curling up besides her, hugging into her. Pam smiled and flicked through the pages, finding the page than began with Al's tale. She started to read through her writing, simplifying the larger words she thought Sarah wouldn't understand, and omitting the part of the story where Al's father died of cancer; the death of parents wasn't something she wanted to bring up, and the reason she was telling her the tales was to keep her mind occupied.

She wound up Al's story, and was about to ask Sarah who she wanted to hear next, when the radio headset tucked into her pocket bleeped. She pulled it out and hooked it over her ear, and Sarah dived off the seat and barrelled across the room, grabbing one of the spares and hooking it over her own ear.

"Al?"

"The one and only, baby," Al's voice crackled over the radio, distant and faint.

"How's it going?"

"Fine, it's all good. We found Bill…"

"Does he still have his balls?"

Al laughed over the radio link, his normally deep laughter reduced to a horse chuckle. Pam scowled at the young girl, but she seemed oblivious to it.

"Yeah, he's still got his balls. For now. We've run into a little trouble…"

"Trouble?" Pam cut in, her heart skipping a beat at the thought.

"It's nothing, just a little squad of Marines bugging us. I need you to bring the *Pride of Colebrook* out here as quick as you can. The roads are a little cramped and narrow, but I think there's enough muscle under the hood to plough through most of the blockades you'll come across."

"Where are you?"

"A few miles away from you, easily. There's a control panel in the cabin, it's part of the tracking device I used to find the bike. Go to it and enter 'Bailey mobile command' into the vehicle description. You're looking for a command base assigned to Carter: there can't be that many here that are active. You find that, and we're right there."

"You're in trouble, aren't you?" Pam asked as she moved through the trailer towards the door leading to the driver's cab, pushing her way into the front seat and casting aside the piles of pornographic magazines, gun magazines and empty Styrofoam cups that littered the cramped room.

"I don't go looking for it," protested Al.

"I know; it finds you. I'll get there as quick as I can."

"See if you can work out a few of the automatic weapons on your way," pleaded Al, "And be careful. That beast can suck up a lot of punishment, but it's not indestructible."

"You fill me with confidence," Pam muttered as she tapped the flat plastic keypad set into the dashboard and turned the ignition. The vehicle rumbled to life, the sound of the growling engine shattering the silence as Pam revved up the device.

"Be careful, baby. Take care."

"I will. Love you."

Pam knocked the vehicle into drive and started forwards on her journey, instructing Sarah to sit down beside her and work the tracking computer as Al had instructed.

"Love you too, babe."

Bill looked over his shoulder as Al strolled into the room, pulling the headset from his ear and slipping it into his pocket.

"She's coming?"

"On her way now. I hope she'll be all right."

"She'll be fine, you know she can look after herself."

Al nodded, stepping back towards the main entrance where Angel still stood vigil over the building.

"It's been three minutes," Bill said, stepping up beside his friends. "Any sign of them showing up yet?"

Angel looked at him through the corner of her eye and sighed, then focused back on the palace on the other side of the yard. Bill swore beneath his breath, the looked towards Al.

"Fucking kids," he muttered to no one in particular. "Bitch, it's been a few minutes since we got here. Any sign of them coming out the palace?"

"Nothing yet," she said. "A little movement in some of the windows, but no one's left the building yet."

"Probably moving through it in a standard sweep, making sure we haven't branched off into any other building before leaving to try and flank them."

"Building's clear," Sylvester shouted as he and Clive appeared at the top of the stairs just inside the entrance hall. "Just beds upstairs, two rooms filled with them. Foot lockers have been busted open by looters, nothing's left in them except a few torn photos and some rotten food."

Bill nodded at the report, and heard the unmistakable heavy thumping of Garth as he plodded through the lower floors, appearing with a piece of brown dried meat between his lips.

"What you got there, buddy?"

"Beef jerky. There was a pack of it sealed in a box on top of one of the cupboards in one of the storerooms. I think it's gone off, though; it tastes like shit."

"Beef jerky always tastes like that, that's why it lasts so long. No bastard wants to eat it. Anything else?"

"Something like a cabinet, but it's sealed up, I don't think any looters or scavengers could break into it. Big and metal, looks pretty rusted now. I reckon we all could break into it if we tried."

"What are we waiting for? Bitch, you keep watch here, the rest of you, we'll go crack this puppy open. Lead the way, buddy."

Garth nodded and retreated the way he had come from, everyone following apart from Angel, who stood vigilant by the open doors. Bill paused as he was about to leave the hallway, considering saying something to Angel, but she seemed to be in a bad mood with him. He hurried on to follow the rest of the group as he heard whoops of joy coming from Al.

"What is it?" he asked as he stumbled into the room Garth had lead them to.

A small chamber, the walls lined with empty gun racks and metal cupboards with their doors ripped off, exposing draws that had been pulled out of their runners and raped of their contents, leaving smaller strongboxes strewn across the floor with their lids off and displaying the empty interior of each container. It was evident to Bill that this had once been a small armoury of sorts: nowhere near as large or well stocked as the armoury they had back in their base before abandoning it, and one that had apparently been ransacked a long time ago. Only one thing remained intact in the room: a large metallic sarcophagus that lay on the ground, embedded in concrete. The container looked to have been hammered with a number of blows from a sledgehammer, the hinges attacked with a drill in an attempt to release the pins, and the concrete chipped and chiselled away in parts; all attempts to infiltrate the coffin had been a failure, and the splashes of dried blood on and around the base of the coffin suggested that the would-be looters had either damaged themselves in the process, or had fallen under attack while they had been preoccupied.

"A secured weapons cache," Al smiled. "Something badass is underneath that metal canopy."

"It looks like its sealed up tight," Clive said, kneeling beside the cabinet and rapping his knuckles against the side. It responded with a hollow thump. "Sounds hollow, though."

Sylvester crouched beside him, running his hands and fingers over the painted surface. In some areas the metallic paint flaked away with the slightest brush, indicating that there were underlying signs of metal fatigue.

"Can you get in it?" Al asked, dancing excitedly from side to side, unable to stand still as the tension built.

"I'm not a safe cracker," Sylvester said as he investigated the box. Bill could see Al's shoulders sag as he said that. "But I know enough about cars and bodywork to spot potential weak spots.

Obviously a controlled blast is out the question: I'm guessing whatever is in there may be explosive."

"Could be anything," agreed Al. "It's anyone's guess."

"It seems weaker over here," Sylvester said, indicating one of the corners of the box. "It's been like this for years, easily more than two. The elements have really given it a good going over, I think we could break through it we all give it a try."

"You can unlock it from the inside," Al nodded. "He used to lock rookies up in these crates all the time, see how long it took for them to realise that there was a release catch *inside* the box."

"Well, I hope they didn't decide to lock a Rot in there," Sylvester looked dubiously at the crate. Al shrugged. "Well, they were sadistic fucks, after all…"

Al was first to attack the metal box, tearing a piece of steel from the gun rack on the wall and hammering it against the corner Sylvester had indicated, urging everyone else to do the same. They did so, each man grabbing a different piece of debris and taking their turn to hammer the metal container. Each strike resulted in the sharp snap of metal against metal, and the corner becoming more and more battered. After a full minute of consecutive battering, the weakened metal finally buckled and gave way, and Al help up his hands to call a halt to the battering, this time electing to insert his metal rod into the hole and swing it back and forth, peeling the edges of the ragged hole further and further until Sylvester could tentatively fit his hand inside and, fumbling around blindly, he found the locks themselves and manipulate them from the inside.

The catches clicked, and the heavy door swung open as Sylvester and Al worked the container cover. Al stepped back, biting his lip and inhaling sharply as he looked at the weapons they had unearthed.

"Well? What are they?"

"Portable Gatling cannons, two of them, similar to the guns they used on us before."

He bobbed his head as he silently counted the components in the unsealed casing, smiling as he did so.

"Five drums of ammo, that's about twenty-five hundred rounds. It's a lower calibre than their weapon, so it's not going to be as powerful, but Goddamn, it'll rip through the foot soldiers in no time at all. Only thing is…"

He poked at the contents, pulling open the drums of ammunition and inspecting the weapons.

"Two of the drums have gone bad, the powder looks damp, and I don't think it'll fire. That'll just cause a misfire, we'll have to remove the jam, and that means a complete field strip. The receiver bolt of that cannon looks a little corroded, it should work for a while, but not long; it'll probably snap on us after half a drum, maybe not even that."

"So is that good or bad?" asked Bill, unsure as to whether what Al had said was good or bad news.

"It's brilliant. We'll still have one fully operational cannon, providing the power pack still holds a charge, with enough ammo to hold them off until Pam gets here with our own portable armoury. As long as we can get it set up in time, we should be fine."

"They're coming," Angel called from the front door. Al snapped into action, grabbing the two drums that had been rendered useless by the damp and slinging them to one side, then grabbing two of the good ones and staggering towards the door.

"Kid, grab the other one; Preacher-man, you grab the power pack, Spanners and buddy there can carry the working cannon."

"There's two batteries," stammered Clive as he stepped back, allowing the cannon to be removed from the packaging with an accompaniment of grunts and groans from Sylvester and Garth. "Which one should I grab?"

"Ask your god, he should be able to guide you. Get it out here fast, we don't have much time."

Bill leapt into action and grabbed the one remaining drum, following the activity towards the front of the building. Instead of setting up the cannon by the open front door, Al guided them towards one of the side rooms and set down the drums by one of the windows facing the palace. Bill dropped his load beside them, then peered out into the yard beyond: he could see figures moving back and forth in the shadows, the glimmer of light from the setting sun catching the golden tint of their goggles and giving away their positions. They moved quickly and efficiently, communicating with hand signals and movements that Bill couldn't begin to interpret.

"Form perimeter," Al translated, peering out into the yard through a small set of binoculars as he watched the signals going back and forth. "Establish kill zone, wait for mobile command to arrive; hold fire. Sniper on guard, rest of hostiles hidden, possibly in building."

"That's a lot of flapping over nothing," Garth said as he lowered the cannon on to the ground beside the window. "Why not just radio in?"

"Radio silence, they must think we can still listen in on them. At least that's one thing we have on our side, they can only communicate by line of sight. Position that stand there so we can secure it to the floor."

"Stand?"

"You need a stand, dumb ass, it has to be secured to the ground or else the weapon'll kick all over…"

"I have it. I think," Clive mumbled as he stumbled into the room carrying a bulky black box in one hand and an assortment of tools, cables and accessories in the other. He flung them down on the ground and stepped back, allowing Al to take charge and assemble the device as quick as he could. Metal and plastic clattered against one another as he feverishly worked, constructing the stand and attaching the weapon to the top before bolting the feet to the ground with a heavy rivet gun. Feeding the end of the belt from the first drum into the open mechanism, he stepped back triumphantly and looked towards Sylvester, then motioned towards the wires that were still dangling from the back of the cannon.

"What you want me to do with that?"

"You're a mechanic: hotwire it. I'm a warrior, not a sparky, I don't do wires."

Sylvester stepped forwards and pulled out his knife, shaking his head as he knelt and stripped the protective coating from the wires before working on the plastic guard that covered the terminals of the battery.

The silence that hung in the air as Sylvester worked over the device was shattered by the short sharp snap of Angel's rifle as it barked to life, indicating that the soldiers were moving towards them and were within firing range.

"How long will it take?"

"Give me five minutes," Sylvester muttered, not looking up from his work. Al leaned over to one side and peered out the shattered window, counting the soldiers in his head and mentally working running through their possible plan.

"You've got two," Al said, heading out into the entrance hall and unfolding the bipod on the end of his heavy machinegun and setting it down on the ground. He dropped to his stomach and lay flat on the floor, pressing his body against the ground and the wall and testing his line of sight in comparison to where he could swing the weapon.

"I'll cover from here. Bitch, you go upstairs, you'll have a wider field of fire from there," he said, dismissing Angel with a wave of his hand. He peered over his shoulder and called back; "Spanners, you and Preacher-man take the controls of that cannon: it's simple enough, press the green button to activate the power, swing it left to right, pull the trigger on the handle to fire. A monkey could operate it. Buddy, I want you to use Spanner's grenade launcher, plenty of cover fire, kick up some shit and raise some hell, keep them on their toes. Kid, I need you to provide cover and support with whatever you can; assault rifles, shotguns, handguns, just use whatever comes to hand. Lets rock and roll, people, we've got a mission here: we need to survive."

Bill relieved Sylvester, Clive and Garth of the weapons and ammunition they wouldn't be needing in the battle, carrying it over to a window on the other side of the barracks and setting up camp there, keeping low as he prepared each weapon for the battle.

"That thing ready yet?" Al bellowed as he heaved back on the cocking mechanism of the weapon he cradled.

"Not yet, I've almost got it…"

"Too late!"

Al's weapon shuddered to life, a deafening roar that tore through the empty barracks as he hosed gunfire across the advancing horde of Marines. Bill lifted the first of his weapons and rested it on the windowsill, squeezing the trigger and spraying it blindly from side to side.

"I can't see shit, what's going on out there?"

"They were approaching, we opened fire, they fucked off out of range."

A third weapon opened fire, this one a rifle from up high as Angel took down a soldier with a well-aimed shot.

"I think I got it… I think I got it…"

Sylvester's cries were drowned out as the weapon he had been working on growled to life: though Bill had thought Al's weapon had been loud, comparing it to the new and active cannon was like comparing the mewl of a kitten to the roar of a lion: Bill felt the fillings in his teeth shake and throb as the cannon screamed its bloody death knell. Bill chanced a look over the edge of the window and watched as the soldiers fled from the battle, those that weren't fortunate enough to evade the gunfire being shredded by the heavy weapon. As Bill watched a large army command vehicle rolled into view, the engine inaudible over the banter of the Gatling cannon, and his heart leapt as he thought for one moment that Pam had arrived with their mobile home.

The group of men clad in white coveralls and black facemasks that patrolled the top made him think otherwise as they swung their weapons about to bear on the building he had sought refuge in and peppered the front of the construction with a barrage of heavy gunfire. Bill instinctively ducked as machinegun fire raked across the window frame, spewing concrete and wood over him as the large calibre bullets chewed through the façade.

"They managed to rip through the front of the palace," Bill shouted, gritting his teeth as he slapped another magazine into the assault rifle and fired blindly over his cover; he didn't intend to hit anyone, just make them duck and cover a little. "How long before they break through this building?"

"Ten, maybe fifteen minutes if it's sustained fire," Al shouted back. "Concrete over a solid, reinforced steel shell. There's layers of Kevlar and toughened ceramics in there, too, plenty to stop some rounds, hopefully long enough for Pam to turn up in our vehicle then get us out of here."

"As long as she can handle the vehicle," Garth shouted between explosions from the grenades he launched into the fray outside. "I knew I should've stayed back there, keeping watch over them."

"You would've turned tail and ran at the first gunshot," snapped Al as he pulled back from the main doorway, deeper into the hallway so he was pressed against the base of the staircase. "They're rolling out the big gun again, everyone step back from the walls and get ready."

"I thought they couldn't break through," Bill yelled, crawling away from the window and pushing his weapons across the ground. "What happened to reinforced walls?"

"The bastards're loading up the rocket launchers."

"I thought they wanted you alive," Sylvester hissed as he and Clive shrunk behind an overturned table; the protection it offered from an explosion would be minimal.

"Chemical warheads, gasses, stun grenades, I don't know what's going through those fucker's heads. All I know is they've taken the Marine's code of conduct, set it on fire and pissed on it to put it out."

"They're loaded up, but they're not opening fire," hissed Angel, appearing at the top of the stairs and reporting on the soldier's progress. "What's going on?"

"Rushing the building?" Bill suggested.

"Storming," corrected Al. "What can you see, bitch?"

"I can't see any of the bastards moving in, they're just kinda spreading out around the building, keeping back out of range. Maybe they're going to try and probe our defences?"

"Maybe…" murmured Al, taking the opportunity to reload his weapon while the fighting died down around him. The battlefield around them was silent and deathly still, and Al cautiously lowered his machinegun and stalked back towards the opened doors to the barracks. Bill stalked up behind him, an assault rifle loaded and ready in his hands as he followed the ex-soldier.

"What're you up to, Carter? What're you planning?"

"Talking to yourself?" Bill asked, crouching low as he tried to count the soldiers surrounding the building.

"No, I'm talking to that miserable little shit out there in charge. He's up to something, but I don't know what… the mind of an officer, it's an enigma that the mind of a grunt can never work out."

"Enigma?" queried Bill, raising an eyebrow. "Really?"

"Pam's an educated lady, all this writing she's been doing over the past few years must be rubbing off."

"You're getting smarter?"

"Maybe a little," Al said with a toothy grin. His grin cracked and faded as the penny finally dropped. He dashed back from the doorway, pulling Bill as he went and stooping to grab his discarded weapon.

"Load up and get ready for round two, men. The fucker's are coming around the back; they're trying to flank us. Anyone see a back door to this place when we were looking around?"

"The only windows I could see were the ones at the front, I couldn't see anything else that would let someone in."

"Then get ready, we're about to get a Marine suppository. Keep back from the walls and bunch up. Bitch, get down here; we're going to need all the help we can get. Drop the grenade launcher and pass out the shotguns, this is going to get ugly."

The team quickly grouped together, crouching in as close to the centre of the building as they could, staying clear from any of the walls and looking anxiously from side to side. Five minutes passed without any activity from outside.

"So how do you know they're going to flank us?" Angel whispered, fanning away the plumes of blue-grey smoke that drifted away from the battered and smouldering cigar that Al chewed restlessly on.

"They've surrounded the building, making sure we can't bolt for safety somewhere else; I've seen this tactic before, we used it in Brazil a few times. First the bulk of the squad circles the building, pinning the targets down in their hideout; then the strike team moves in, a highly trained squad that specialises in, normally black ops or something like that, they pin us down."

"How do they break in?"

"They normally drop in from a stealth copter above the target. This place, this whole island, is a no fly zone, so we can rule out that; they're probably going to try breaking in through the walls, explosive shaped charges, things like that."

"And if you're wrong?"

"Well, that's never happened, has it?" murmured Al, tapping ash from the tip of his cigar on to the floor.

Another five minutes passed, and Al cocked his head, trying to listen for the sounds that would give away the approach of the assault squad. Bill joined him, craning his head as he tried to pinpoint the telltale sounds of the attack.

It was deathly silent outside, and Al could hear the occasional muffled cough from the ranks of soldiers outside, the ragged breathing of his team as the tension built up inside them. He knew how they felt, he could feel the flow of adrenaline simmer and boil within him. Somewhere nearby, Al could hear an almost-inaudible hum, low and bass as it seemed to linger around the building.

The back wall of the building suddenly shook and cracked as a muffled explosion sounded, dislodging plaster and tearing apart bricks. Daylight crept in through the cracks and Garth instinctively lifted his weapon.

"It didn't work," called a muffled voice from outside.

"We need to open it up more," shouted another. "We need more explosives."

"They misjudged it?" whispered Angel incredulously.

"Bullshit," hissed Al, shaking his head. "They know how thick the walls are in the building, they know what it would take to break through. It's a decoy."

"Decoy?"

"Get upstairs, quick."

Al lead by example, breaking away from the group and rushing upstairs, weapon raised as he crested the top step and saw a hole in the ceiling, the smoking edges of the fissure blackened where a cutting torch had burned through concrete and melted steel. Five men dressed in black were already in the building, removing thick cords of rope from their combat webbing while another two descended into the room. One of the men looked up, the mechanical goggles he wore glowing a pulsating red and green, and he lifted his weapon, a light assault rifle with a laser target attached to the top.

Screaming a bloody war cry, both Al and the members of the assault squad opened fire.

IV

Major Carter stood behind the perimeter of soldiers that had surrounded the house, grinning to himself behind the opaque screen of the helmet he wore as he watched the last of the assault squad drop into the building from the stealth helicopter that hovered fifty feet above the building.

Having a helicopter on the island had been very risky, especially seeing as if the helicopter fell into the wrong hands it would have been invisible to the command outposts dotted around the coastline; any pilot who managed to secure the vehicle could have flown away from the island without a second glance. Of course, the higher-ranking officials had stipulated that the island was a no-fly zone, and as such a helicopter would be highly inappropriate, and consequently a luxury not permitted on the clean-up details. Something like that would have to be smuggled on to the island.

It had been Carter's final order before he left the *Narcissus* that the helicopter be sealed into a giant cargo crate and shipped on to the island with him. The crate was sealed and locked by an entry code only he knew, and it was kept under constant guard; there wasn't much fuel left, and it had never been used until now. He had sworn to himself he would use it only if the situation became so grave that the mission was lost, and he had to evacuate.

"Desperate times," he chimed to himself as the last man vanished through the hole that had been cut open by the team and the helicopter lifted up and swooped away to one side, retreating to the enlarged cargo pod where it could be sealed up until it was needed again.

"Team is in," reported one of the soldiers beside him.

Gunshots sounded from within the building, a heavy staccato of rapid-fire assault weapons and deep, booming blasts of a shotgun, or maybe a large calibre weapon like a magnum.

"They've engaged the enemy," the same soldier announced, pointing out the obvious. "Squad maintaining radio silence."

The gun battle raged for a couple of minutes before the clatter of discharging weapons turned to the occasional exchange of a burst of shots, and Carter could feel the tension in the air, knowing exactly what was going through the mind of each soldier as they stood guard around the silent barracks. He had been surprised when the rag-tag gang of civilians had managed to piece together the heavy Vulcan cannon and turned it on his men, and the defensive positioning of men in both the palace and barracks indicated that Sergeant Colebrook was a formidable Marine, despite his current AWOL status. Because he was familiar with the tactics of the Marines and the way that they'd conduct the assault, Carter had needed to come up with a new plan to break in, and he prayed that the distraction of the failed explosive breach was enough to give the squad an advantage and complete their mission.

As he watched the building, a figure appeared at the door, a large and bulky one wearing the black armour and jumpsuit of the assault squad. He stumbled backwards out the building, his rifle raised and firing randomly into the darkness of the building as he ran. Returning fire followed him, gunfire snaking across the floor around him as he moved.

"Mother fuckers," screamed the Marine as he stumbled backwards, flinging his rifle down as the receiver clicked empty and drawing his handgun, firing randomly at the building before bursting through the line of soldiers surrounding the building. He scrambled across the floor on his hands and knees, hurling himself so his body was behind one of the battle-scarred vehicles and breathing heavily as he leaned back against the hull of the machine. Carter didn't wait for the soldier to compose himself and make his report, he simply stormed over to him, a pair of sergeants stepping in line behind him as they followed him.

"What happened, Marine?"

"Fuckin' A, man," the Marine muttered, clambering up on to his feet and snapping off a smart, sharp salute. "Sir."

"Are you going to make me ask again, corporal?" Carter said, flicking the insignia on the soldier of the Marine with the back of his gloved hand.

"Sir, no sir. The operation was a failure."

"We can see that," snapped one of the sergeants. "Details."

"They caught us unaware, I think they cottoned on to the fake explosion: they opened fire on us before we even managed to unclip ourselves from the zip lines, that killed three of us outright. The battle that followed was bloody and brutal; by the time they'd managed to whittle it down to Sarge and me, we'd injured the black man and killed some weird bastard who thought he was a priest or something. We tried to retreat, but that bitch they've got with them managed to take him out. I might've clipped her with a round or two, but I made sure I didn't kill her; I want a piece of that ass for Sarge."

"You've seen the way they operate and what they've got? Did you manage to get a good look?"

"Machine guns," the Marine said, waiving his hands vaguely. "Another three or four drums of ammo for that cannon, grenade launchers, shotguns; loaded for bear, sir, and they know how to use them all."

"At ease, Marine," Carter said, clapping him on the shoulder. He visibly relaxed, dropping to the ground once more and nursing a sprained ankle as he did so.

"Orders, sir?" one of the sergeants asked. Carter thought it over for a moment, wiping his hand across his faceplate: he had to get back inside so he could strip down out his suit as soon as possible, and the only way to do that was level the building and wipe out everyone in one swift action. Though he would have loved to torture Colebrook more than anything, he couldn't afford to lose any more men to the resourceful Marine and his group.

"Raze it," he ordered. "Level that building until it's a pile of rubble, and make sure no one's left alive. Bring the chopper back in, make sure it's fully armed and able to take it down. Get the stationary cannon set up in the rear of my vehicle."

"Sir," the black ops soldier yelled, heaving himself to his feet and snapping off another salute. "Sir, I want to operate that cannon."

"You've done your job, Marine, we've got plenty of men able to operate that."

"Sir," the soldier said, reaching out and grabbing Carter by the arm. He froze, his eyes fixed on the golden lenses of the respirator that stared back at him. "Sir, those fuckers wiped out my men. I want payback."

Carter looked back at the building, then to his side as the black stealth copter slid noiselessly into view. He nodded as he peeled the corporal's hand from his arm.

"Sergeant, see that this man is briefed on the cannon and that it's fully loaded; make sure the shells are high explosive, wide shrapnel dispersal. Likewise with the copter, I want total annihilation."

The helicopter hovered into position above the bulk of the squad, the downdraft of the heavy rotors whipping up a storm of mud and dirt around Carter as he stood triumphantly amidst his troops. He raised his arm, his fist clenched, then screamed the command to open fire while dropping his arm.

The missile barrels on the side of the helicopter opened fire first, the smoking projectiles streaking through the air and smashing into the side of the building, erupting into a fiery cloud of napalm and tearing a chunk of masonry from the upper floor, exposing the steel skeleton of the building. The soldiers on the ground opened up with their own weapons, bullets and grenades sailing through the air and impacting against the wall, tearing pieces from their target and slowly exposing more of the metallic bones.

"Where's that cannon?" screamed Carter above the gunfire. "Where is it?"

"I'm on it," screamed the black op soldier sitting at the control. "Calibrating targets, lock on achieved... missiles ready to launch... out-fucking-standing!"

The cannon to the rear of the group opened fire, and Carter snapped his head around as he tracked the missiles with his eyes, watching as the volley of explosive shells tore through the air and smashed into their designated target.

The helicopter erupted into a fiery blossom as it slowly fell to the ground, the troops below dropping their weapons and scattering to one side as the vehicle plummeted to the ground like a stone, any remaining ammo that hadn't been ignited in the initial explosion cooking off as soon as it came into contact with the ground. Pilots and weapons officers stumbled from the flaming wreckage. Soldiers caught under flaming debris and shrapnel cried out and moaned as they tried to pull themselves free from their prison, but all were quickly silenced as the multiple-barrelled machinegun attached to the cannon kicked to life, sweeping from side to side and wiping out the soldiers.

"What the fuck?" demanded Carter, dashing towards the cannon and the crazed operator who sat atop it. As he moved towards the turret he grabbed one of the fleeing soldiers and ordered him to advance on the building before returning his attention to the black ops soldier. "What the fuck are you doing?"

He watched as the soldier drew his weapon and opened fire twice, shattering the heads of the sergeants that lingered beside the major as he approached. The black ops Marine cackled maniacally and reached for the catches on his mask, pulling the heavy rubber breathing apparatus and helmet away from his head.

"You!" Carter stammered, his hands reaching for the brass trench spikes that hung from his belt. The weapons slipped out their oiled scabbards with a smooth movement, and Carter slid his fingers into the holes of the spiked knuckledusters, forming a fist around the melee weapons.

"That's right, fuckhead," shouted Al, leaping down from the mounted weapon, cracking his knuckles and reaching for the combat knife that dangled from his belt. "It's all about you and me, now."

With the staccato of gunfire sounding around him, Al advanced on the crazed major, lazily waving his blade from side to side while the major adjusted his grip on the pair of weapons he sported. Without warning he dived forward, lashing out with his blade. Carter snarled as he parried the blow and retaliated with his own attack. While the steel blade missed Al, the metal knuckles connected with his stomach. Though he wore the heavy armour and protective jumpsuit that he had stripped from the assault squad that he killed inside the building, he could still feel the impact, and knew that enough of the blows would leave a mark. Despite the frail appearance of the old major and Al's misconception of all officers being inept and defenceless, the man was agile enough to avoid another slashing knife attack and retaliate with a barrage of punches, each connecting with the armour he wore. The blades began to dent and rip the protective platings as they came in contact with it, and Al knew that he had to keep on the offensive.

Dropping to the floor and rolling back away from the fight, Al pulled at the release tabs to his armour, shedding the heavy and cumbersome armour and letting it drop to the floor. The moment the flak jacket hit the floor, Al instantly found he had more mobility; though the armour was designed for protection in a gunfight, it certainly wasn't designed with hand-to-hand combat in mind.

The pair circled one another as they measured each other up, Al passing his blade casually from one hand to another while Carter tensed the muscles in his neck, rolling his head and cracking the joints in his upper spine.

"I've been trapped on this island for a year because of your fucking broadcasts," Carter hissed, the sneer on his face visible through the opaque faceplate of his mask, illuminated by the flickering firelight given off by the small fires that burned amongst the scattered debris of the helicopter while the darkening sky became black and overcast. "All your fault, Colebrook."

"I've been stranded here for *three* because of *you*," Al spat back, positioning himself so a piece of flaming scrap metal lay on the ground between him and the major. "You get used to it, the place grows on you."

"A bunch of backward fucking Bebops, worse than the tree crawlers in Brazil," slurred the major, stepping forward with a lunge and tearing through Al's jumpsuit and skin with the tip of the blade before feinting back, away from the blur of Al's knife as he lashed out.

"You wouldn't know half the shit we went through in Brazil, the grunts like me," Al sneered. "We lost men, good men, and all the fucking Brass could care about was the public image: if the corps looked good in the news because we're winning or losing. They never gave a shit about the grunts, but they'd bend over backwards to lick their own asshole if it meant an officer would be saved, and fuck the consequences."

"Is it always so black and white for you? I suppose you think you know better than Military Intelligence?"

Al scooped a smouldering piece of scrap up with his boot and lifted it up, sending it arching through the air. Carter twisted to one side to avoid the flaming projectile and Al lunged forwards, sinking his knife into the gut of Carter and pulling to one side, cutting through the thick material of the protective suit and splashing blood across the ground. Carter dropped to his knees, clutching at the wound with one hand and feverishly fumbling for a strip of sealant material from a roll attached to his belt. Al reached into the tattered top of his jumpsuit and pulled out a metal chain with a number of tags attached to it before flinging it down on the ground.

"Miller," Al said, rhyming off the names on the dog tags. "Mantel, Clarity, Yung, Grem, Rook, Davis… My squad, my soldiers, my friends… dead because of fucks like you calling the shots from your offices and vacation homes."

Taking a step toward the stunned major, Al swung his boot forwards, catching him in the glistening faceplate and cracking the toughened glass with his devastating blow. Carter dropped his roll of sealant tape and screamed, more in panic and terror than anything else, as he clutched the faceplate, trying to protect it. Al stepped forward again, preparing for a second kick, but Carter could see the move coming through his dented faceplate and lunged forward, his trench spikes sinking into the flesh of Al's thigh like the fangs of a snake striking its prey. Al screamed and buckled with the flash of pain that washed over him, and he stumbled back, peeling Carter's hands away from the weapon and leaving the bladed weapons stuck in his leg. Carter regained his composure and finished sealing up his suit, then collected a piece of crumbling masonry that had been ejected from the building after the initial barrage of missiles from the helicopter. He looked down on Al as he raised himself to full height, the faceplate cracked and buckled from the heavy blow Al had delivered, his bloodied suit mended by a criss-cross of tape and resin.

"We all have jobs to do," Carter murmured, feeling the weight of the chunk of masonry in his hand and rolling it around, finding the sharpest point and preparing to bring it crashing down on Al as he rolled around on the ground in agony. "My job was to win the war. Your job was to win it for me. Now... now it's my job to wipe every creature off the face of this island, living or dead. And you're one of them, Colebrook: you and your friends.

"Consider this to be your dishonourable discharge."

"Didn't you get the memo? I quit!" Al shouted as lifted his undamaged leg and kicked out with all his might, catching Carter square on the kneecap and smashing the joint with such force that his knee bent the other way. He screamed again, releasing the piece of rubble and dropping to the floor as his leg gave way, snapped bone tearing through the durable material and blood gushing from the rip. Crying in pain, Carter fumbled once more for his sealant, but Al crawled over to him and knocked it out his hands, sending it skittering across the ground. Grabbing the piece of stone the major had dropped, the roles were now reversed as Al lifted it above his head, bringing it crashing down on the helmet.

The first blow only added to the spider web of cracks that covered the plate, but the second broke through the glass, a small hole no larger than a finger. A third and final blow completely decimated the protective panel and the opaque glass crumpled in, releasing a hiss of purified air and the terrified screams of Carter, as the integrity of the suit was broken.

"It's not even airborne," muttered Al as he gripped his knife and pulled himself upright.

One of Carter's hands slipped from the opening of the helmet to the pistol that hung by his side; what he was planning to do with it, Al had no way of knowing, but he knew that it couldn't be good. He moved quickly and precisely, whipping the blade of his knife around to the side and slicing through the cloth and flesh of the arm moving for the pistol, then brought it racing down into Carter's arm, pinning him to the ground.

Carter's screams of terror and agony quickly slipped into wordless, meaningless babbling as he tried to plead for his life, but seemed unable to string a sentence together. Eyes wild, he frantically tried to reach over and pull the knife from his arm, but with Al's weight on top of him, he was helpless. Grabbing the stone that he'd previously used to crack the helmet, Al hauled the heavy object up, then brought it crashing down on Carter's face, the first blow glancing harmlessly off the side of the helmet. The second fractured the screen further, widening the fissure in the faceplate with the sharpest edge of the rock. A third blow dented the reinforced glass further, and Al felt his fingers briefly make contact with the pallid, sweating flesh of Carter's face.

The blow seemed to enrage Carter even more, and his body bucked and writhed, dislodging the weight of Al and allowing the pinned soldier to fumble for the knife that fastened his limb to the ground. With a cry of desperation, Carter gave up on his attempt to grab the blade and instead started going for the pistol again.

Still clutching his rock and using it like a caveman, Al lashed out and smashed it against Carter's groping fingers, breaking the scrabbling digits and crippling him, before returning his main focus of the bludgeoning to Carter's head. Adjusting his grip on the stone, Al plunged the shaped rock again and again into the opened cavity of the helmet, feeling the skin part first, then the bone crack, finally stopping when the chunk of rubble sunk two inches into the battered skull of Carter and his protests and retaliations had turned to spasms and twitches.

Pulling himself away from the body, Al pushed his back up against the tyres of the vehicle that held the cannon he had previously operated and slowly pried the pair of trench spikes from his thigh with a grimace of pain. The blades weren't barbed or curved, so it wasn't too hard for him to pull them free. It was only then that he realised the extent of the situation around him.

Gunfire rattled around him on all sides, Marines opening fire on the building while his friends inside returned shots of their own, the rattle of different calibre weapons as they sounded off echoing in the cold dusk of winter. Fires raged around him from the stealth aircraft he had taken out, and he looked around for the first weapon he could find: other than the blade and two spikes, there didn't appear to be anything else he could use, he would have to take down a soldier first.

"No problem," he hissed to himself as he retrieved his knife from the bloodied pulp that filled the shattered helmet of the major and swept his gaze around the battlefield: a group of soldiers hiding behind an APC, all armed with assault rifles and machineguns; another group armed with grenade launchers and shoulder-mounted rocket launchers bombarded the building with explosives, while a third slowly advanced on the building, most armed with automatic shotguns or flamethrowers. Even in the midst of chaos, with their commander down, the soldiers kept their formation together, moving methodically and proving themselves to be more formidable than Al had originally thought. He didn't feel like taking on any of the groups of soldiers, but amidst the battle he could make out the clear sound of a heavy duty sniper rifle sounding, and decided that would be his best method of getting a weapon.

It didn't take him long to find the sniper; it seemed that in the midst of the battle, everyone was too busy concentrating on the building, the focal point of the attack, to notice their leader had been killed; the sniper sitting behind a large mound of rubble was so intent on scoring a kill that he didn't even see Al creep up on him, and he certainly wouldn't have heard him over the bark of his rifle going off. The knife, still glistening with the spilled gore of Major Carter, made quick work of the soldier as Al found the weak spot between the rubber mask and the body armour he wore, the blade ripping through fabric and the windpipe of the soldier. As he dropped to the ground drowning in his own blood, Al relieved him of the rifle and made sure it was in working order and fully loaded before taking position, ignoring the choking man at his feet and levelling off the crosshair on the group armed with assault weapons that were approaching the building.

Three successive shots from the rifle smacked into the back of the soldiers' heads, each armoured helmet tearing open as the large calibre round burst through the helmet and tore out the front of their heads. In the heat of the battle, none of the soldiers seemed to notice the direction the gunfire was coming from. He switched his attention to the men wielding the explosive weapons and watched them through the scope as they unleashed a volley of rockets into the building. The front of the barracks, already heavily damaged from the constant assault, finally gave in to the onslaught and the façade of the building sloughed away from metallic skeleton, like rotten flesh slipping from the skull of a Rot, obscuring the front of the building as the debris rained down and mounted up around the openings into the barracks.

"Son of a bitch," Al muttered to himself as he shouldered the rifle, flicked the fire selector switch around to automatic, then stood up and hosed it back and forth across the group of men armed with the explosive projectile launchers, cutting down the men where they stood and lumbering over to them. By that point the final group of soldiers, the ones armed with the machineguns who'd hid behind the APC, had noticed Al. Bullets tore across the ground and raked the bodies of the fallen soldiers, and Al moved quickly and methodically, grabbing one of the discarded heavy rocket launchers and shouldering it. Roughly one metre long, it comprised of three tubes joined together in a triangular formation, each tube holding a high-explosive guided missile. The readout on the electronic panel on the side told him that one of the three tubes had been fired, leaving two shaped charges ready for firing. Dropping to his knees, Al squinted at the small LCD screen that acted as a scope, pointed the weapon at the armoured vehicle the men used for cover, and simultaneously squeezed the firing pins for both tubes.

He'd used the launcher once, a long time ago in Brazil, when his squad had been thrown into combat against a small group of Cartel who had managed to steal an APC and use it against the Marines. There had been a tense moment where Al thought there was no way the squad would have been able defeat the armoured vehicle, until Ping suggested using explosives; it meant destroying the machine, but better turn it into a pile of molten slag then let it fall into the hands of the enemy. It had taken most the grenades that the squad had carried, but they had finally managed to destroy that rampaging vehicle.

Al hoped that the rockets packed a lot more punch than the grenades, as he only had two of them.

He watched through the target screen as the missiles streaked towards the APC and smacked into the surface, and his heart skipped a beat as he thought the rockets hadn't even exploded. The moment passed as the projectiles ripped apart, tearing through the vehicle, lifting it into the air in a blazing inferno and knocking away the soldiers as their airtight suits ignited, smashing their bodies against the ground or other vehicles. Al dropped the useless weapon, punching the air with a fist and whooping in joy. For a moment, his elation was matched with the feeling of victory when he and his squad had obliterated the stolen APC in Brazil, and he couldn't help but dance a small victory jig as he gloated over the remains of the squad he had slain.

"The cream of the armed forces," Al smirked to himself. Then he remembered – he was on his own, with his friends blocked in the barracks. As he turned to look over his shoulder, a large portion of the building fell in on itself with a deafening blow. "Shit," he shouted, running towards the building and pulling frantically at the mounds of rubble, beginning the painful excavation by hand, and hoping that his friends were working on the same area inside.

Pulling away, he paused as he grabbed a large block of masonry, his ears picking up the sound of something in the distance, a constant and low murmuring. For a moment, he thought that the sound was the trailer with Pam at the wheel, approaching the battleground, someone who would be able to aid him in his quest to reveal an entrance or exit into the building. Instead of the loud drone of the engine, he could make out a different constant sound, a low moaning sound that signalled the arrival of a horde of flesh-hungry undead.

Reluctantly, Al spat on the ground, dropped the debris and rushed over to one of the dead soldiers, retrieving one of the assault rifles and checking the mechanism before shouldering the weapon.

If it's not the Marines, it's the god damn living dead, he though to himself with a scowl. He managed to sum it up verbally in one word as he looked around the flaming killing ground for a good tactical place to dig in and prepare for the approaching dead.

"Fuck."

XXIV
DEATH US DO PART

"We can't stop it, can't cure it; that's not what we're here to do now. We're here to control it, try to prevent it spreading any further. Looking at the reports coming in from up and down the country, we haven't succeeded."

I

Bill moaned deliriously to himself as he slowly came around, unaware of where he was. The room was dark, the only source of light coming from the multitude of fires that burned around him. Thick smoke rolled across the ceiling, and all around him, he could see mounds of rubble and broken support beams. He clambered to his feet slowly, his joints aching and his head swimming as his ears roared with the rush of blood. He must have been too close to the last barrage of explosives; not only had they broken down the front of the barracks, but they'd also knocked him flat on to his back and knocked his head against rubble. He tentatively pressed his hand to the back of his head and grimaced, coming away with bloodied hands. He sighed to himself, and felt something crack within him; he certainly couldn't hear it, all he could hear was a hollow ringing from the explosion, and no matter how many times he wiggled his finger in his ear he couldn't dislodge the muting blockage.

Outside the building, he could hear a heavy, deep pulsating sound, what he could only imagine a gun battle to sound like with his damaged ears, and he thought that Al's plan wasn't going as well as planned.

"Everyone okay?" he shouted out, or at least he thought he'd shouted. There was no response, and Bill looked feverishly around finding himself trapped in the room he was in; each doorframe had collapsed on itself, effectively blocking him in. Trying to remember which damaged wall had been the window, Bill immediately got to work in digging at the rubble, tossing aside the debris as he tried to move as fast as he could, despite the wounds he had. The overpowering smoke was starting to fill the room, not only from the fires that raged within his own room, but from the thick black tendrils of choking vapour that snaked into the room through the cracks in the walls and fallen detritus blocking the doors.

Choking and gasping, Bill burrowed feverishly into the fallen wall, hurling aside the broken blocks and feeling the cool air from outside creep through the blockage as he sensed he was getting closer breaking through.

"Come on," he muttered to himself, even though he couldn't hear it himself. "Nearly there!"

Someone had been working on removing rubble from the other side, they had to have been, because he quickly tunnelled through and felt the rush of cool air slapping him in the face and letting the smoke that had built up around him vomit out the hole. He pulled himself out of the opening he had created, hauling his aching body over the uneven surface and gasping for breath, rubbing at his watering eyes as the thick smoke stung them. The stench of burning wood and unsettled dust from the inside of the building was replaced with the unmistakable reeking odour of decay, and Bill looked up, bleary eyed, to see one lone gunman standing in the centre of the clearing that soldiers had gathered around. Gripping an assault rifle in each hand, the familiar figure turned slowly while stepping from side to side, unleashing the occasional burst of fire towards the approaching pack of Rots that were slowly advancing from all directions.

It appeared that Al's plan had worked; there was just an x-factor that he had failed to take into account when explaining his idea, though he seemed to be taking care of the matter as best as he could. He'd seen Bill as he pulled himself free from the building and motioned towards him with a subtle nod of the head before returning to firing the weapons. Bill heaved himself out the small tunnel and flopped on to the floor before rolling shakily to his feet and stumbling over towards Al, moving with as much grace and speed as one of the ghoulish creatures.

"There's a bun?" Al said, without turning to look at Bill as he arrived.

"What?" he replied, shouting even though he didn't need to; the question of the former Marine made no sense to him. Al didn't respond, simply thrust one of the weapons into Bill's hand and signalled to cover the rear.

"Lose this in Ted," Al mumbled. Bill looked at his friend in confusion, watching as he turned back and opened fire on the advancing horde of the undead that was slowly inching their way towards them. Bill shrugged his shoulders and lifted the weapon, trying to focus on the multiple blurred targets as they swayed from side to side. He squeezed off a burst of rounds, missing his mark with each shot, all the time wondering what it was that Al had said. Had the ex-Marine lost his mind?

There's a bun, he wondered, trying to focus on the middle Rot of a blurred trio, assuming it was the real one. The rifle in his hand jumped as he fired, finally managing to down one of the creatures with a muffled burst of gunfire. The proximity of the explosion had knocked his hearing for six, and the gunfire barely sounded like a gunshot at all.

"Where's you gun," he murmured to himself, working over the incoherent words that Al spouted. "Use this instead."

He rubbed his eyes as he tried to focus on the zombies, trying to regain his senses, and thought back to the days he used to go swimming, and the sensation he used to get when he got water trapped in his ear. Taking a momentary break from his firing, Bill closed his eyes, pinched his nose and pressed his lips together while trying to blow out. He could feel the pressure building in his ear canals, felt his skin burn as the blood rushed to his head, and with a sudden stab of pain, his ears popped. The banter of gunshot suddenly changed from muffled to tinny, and the noise of the moaning dead vibrated through his bones as their penetrating murmur assaulted his ears.

"Jesus, kid, what the hell are you doing?"

"I can understand you now," Bill said, shouldering his rifle again. His vision was still blurred, but this time he saw only double instead of triple. He felt a little safer, seeing that the number of assailants had effectively been reduced by a third.

"Oh, *now* you can understand me, because I was talking French a minute ago. Fucking kids… keep focused, we need to thin down the ranks as much as we can until Pam gets here, she shouldn't' be too long, I can hear the engine over these moaning bastards, she must be just… There!"

Sure enough, on the other side of the advancing horde of the undead, the shape of an armed trailer could be seen in the gloom, its air horn sounding like a banshee as it neared them.

"She's not slowing down," Bill said, stepping closer to the building as the vehicle approached. Al followed him, taking a break from gunning down the Rots and watching as the vehicle ploughed through the crowd of walking dead.

While some had continued to advance towards Al and Bill, others towards the rear of the crowd had elected to turn towards the armoured vehicle: these were the first to fall beneath the toughened wheels as the machine swerved wildly from side to side, smashing through flaming debris, rolling over the inert corpses and ploughing through the living dead as it trundled along. One of the weapons on the roof opened up, erratic and random spurts of gunfire that seemed to be aimed in no specific direction, and sliced into the ranks of the creatures on either side of the trailer: though the shots were wild and clearly unaimed, the creatures were packed in so tight it was impossible to miss. The dead fell under the assault, Al and Bill rejoining the fight with the heavy ordinance on their side, cutting a swathe through the seemingly endless ranks and forming a defensive perimeter around the front of the building and entrance to the trailer.

"Get inside," Al hissed, slapping Bill on the shoulder. "You're no use down here, maybe you can do some good on the weapons mounted up top."

"What?" Bill stammered as he jerked a thumb towards the crumbling building. "What about everyone else? They're still trapped in there."

"I'll deal with them," Al promised. "But I need some heavy fire to support me. Get inside, get on the roof and get Sarah inside; she's doing a good job up there, but I know you can do better."

Bill craned his neck to look towards the roof of the trailer, and sure enough, he could see the shadowy figure of the young girl swinging the weapon around from side to side and spraying the undead with automatic fire.

"You teach her to do that?"

"I taught her how to do a lot of things," Al said with a smile, slapping him on the shoulder again. With vision still blurring, Bill stumbled towards the trailer, his assault rifle thundering in his hands as he crabbed to the side, throwing it down on to the ground as he reached the door and heaving it open. He stumbled inside and the door swung shut behind him, instantly cutting off the sound of Al's weapon and the acrid odour of rotting flesh and cordite, though the scent of smoke clung to his clothes as he charged through the trailer, grabbing one of the radio headsets and hooking it over his ear as he moved, flicking the power switch.

"Everyone's trapped inside the building," Bill shouted, climbing the staircase and making a beeline for the hatchway that opened on to the weapons platform. "Al's going to get them out, he needs covering fire. Sarah, I'm coming up there."

Hauling himself up on to the platform, Bill found Sarah struggling with one of the larger weapons as she weaved the weapon back and forth, her face red and drenched with sweat as she wrestled with the controls.

"I'll take that, honey," Bill said, nudging the girl aside and taking over. The stench from the heaving throng of the dead beneath him was overpowering, rancid and sickly sweet, despite the cool temperature; Bill thought that the dead wouldn't smell as strong in the cold of winter; there was a time Bill had also assumed the dead would lie on the ground and rot, which meant his grasp of the basics of biology weren't anything to write home about. "Get below decks, settle down on one of the seats: we'll be going soon, get ready to help anyone who might need it."

He leaned over one side, then the other, and for the first time could see the extent of the dead. The creatures pressed in on the idling vehicle, fifty metres in all directions packed with groaning and wailing animated corpses, their partially chewed fingers and bloodless stumps reaching out for the trailer or the figure of Al below as he whirled around in a circle, armed with two assault rifles again, each stock tucked in between his elbow and his hip as he braced and fired.

"Any time you want to help me," Al screamed, casting a glance up to the roof of the trailer. Bill nodded, though didn't know if Al had seen him. Instead, he gripped the weapon, aimed down and let loose a stream of automatic fire into the heaving mass of animated flesh and bone. Though his vision was still blurred, he had a greater chance of hitting the undead heads when aiming down instead of being at street level.

"Good work, kid," Al said as he flicked his radio link to life. "I'll work on the broken building, you keep those dead pinned back."

Bill nodded to himself, keeping the Rots away from the vehicle and the building while keeping a clear path between the two. No matter how many he cut down, there always seemed to be more to replace them: the fact some of the creatures had elected to consume the fallen soldiers which in turned raised those corpses from the dead didn't help. It seemed to be happening faster than Bill had seen before, but he knew that the virus was changing all the time.

"I'm through," Al hissed, hurling aside rubble and diving into the crumbling building. "I'll be two minutes, keep the area clear."

His weapon fired empty, but Bill knew that he didn't have time to reload it: he moved from the machinegun to the next weapon beside it, a heavy weapon with a thick coated belt feeding into the massive rotating chamber on its base, and squeezed the trigger, not entirely sure what to expect.

The automatic grenade launcher roared to life, spitting forty millimetre rounds into the thriving masses, each round erupting into a spray of darts as the specialised flechette rounds tore through the skulls of the dead and toppled wave after wave of the animals, and Bill felt a grin spread across his face. The tiny, needle-like spikes continued to cut down the dead as the weapon fired over and over again, the brunt of the damage being caused by these and not the small explosive charges given off when the devices erupted.

Bill took a break from the mass carnage he was creating in time to see someone scramble out the hole Al had created, a blond figure wearing a dust-covered trench coat, and Bill held off on using the grenade launcher, stepping along to the next weapon and reverting to a machinegun to make sure his friends weren't hurt by the fragmentation rounds. He carried his own weapon and fired randomly into the crowd as he moved, slamming his body against the side of the trailer as he fumbled for the door and stumbled into the room below, grasping for a comlink as he did so. The previously silent radio in Bill's ear hissed to life, a sharp and rasping noise of an out-of-breath priest panting into a microphone.

"How's it going, Clive?"

"I've certainly had better days, Bill, that's for sure," Clive announced, climbing up on to the platform and grabbing the machinegun Bill had previously operated.

"It's empty," Bill commented, stepping back and motioning to the mounted weapon he had used to cover the priest as he fled from the decaying building. He preferred the grenade launcher, and didn't want to lose his new toy to Clive. "Use this one. You're okay in using it?"

"I've spilled more blood today than I would ever have thought possible," Clive said morosely. "I have sinned enough today, and each death must be remembered; but the hollow men are simply empty vessels, I have no trouble in killing them."

"I'll take that as a yes," Bill said with a grin, thumbing the firing switch once more and releasing a salvo of grenades into the Rots below. "You might want to try clearing some of the corpses from the other side, keep the numbers even."

"I will... Sweet Jesus!"

Bill turned to see what had caused Clive to blaspheme, and saw that some of the creatures had started to climb on to the vehicle: some pounded the roof of the drivers cab, others scraped their rotten fingers across the hull of the vehicle, what nails they had peeling back and flaking off while their bloodied fingertips drew watery trails over the metal. Three of the animals had managed to climb on to the weapons platform and surrounded the two as they lurched forwards. Bill slapped his thigh, where he would normally keep a handgun, but he touched nothing but the denim of his jeans; he was completely unarmed.

With lightning-quick speed, Clive stepped between the three Rots and Bill, flinging back his coat and pulling a double-barrelled shotgun out from a leather scabbard that hung from his belt. He swept the weapon round, levelling it off with the heads of the creatures and discharging a barrel into the face of two of the Rots, leaving only one remaining on the platform. Cracking open the shotgun to reload it, Clive watched in horror as the remaining undead lurched forwards, arms outstretched.

Now it was Bill's turn to return the favour; it had been some time since reading the anarchist's handbook he found in Barkley's DIY warehouse, but he could remember the basics of melee combat, and even though he knew that things like eye gouges and kicks to the groin would do little to no damage, he knew that if he could hit the creature with enough force, he should be able to knock it over the barrier and back into the crowd below.

His shoulder made contact with the rock-hard abdomen of the calcified creature, and it stumbled back, moaning wordlessly as the move caught it by surprise. It swiped for Bill, bloodied and gnarled fingers sailing harmlessly above his head as he ducked to the floor, then he launched upwards and forwards, his left fist curled tightly into a ball as it connected with the bloodied jaw of the creature. He didn't know why he'd used his left hand, he knew he was right handed, but in this instance he was pleased he had launched an attack with the wrong hand: it felt like all the fingers in his hand broke as they smashed against the toughened jaw, and the creature's head snapped back with a sickening crack. It wasn't enough to break the hardened neck bones, but the head of the creature remained tilted back, twisted at an awkward angle as it lurched around on the platform. Bill stepped back, nursing his aching hand and assessing the situation, realising he may have bitten off more than he could chew with the toughened undead creature.

The Rot wore the tattered remains of an army uniform; not the white sealed suit the Marines had worn, but the classic green camouflage fatigues that solders were normally associated with. The webbing that was strapped around its body had started to fray and deteriorate, many of its pouches ripped and empty; of the holsters still left intact, a handgun could still be seen fastened in its holder. Though there was every chance that the pistol had been there for many years, and as such may not have been in such a good condition to fire, but it was the only thing that Bill could get hold of that would act as a weapon. Wrapping his hand around the neck of the creature with one hand to keep its rotten teeth away from him, he fumbled for the weapon, grimacing as his fingers brushed the exposed and dried flesh of the creature. His fingers coiled around the grip of the pistol and then pulled the weapon from its holster. With a single fluid motion he pushed the creature away, cocked the weapon, levelled it with the head of the creature and squeezed the trigger as quick as he could, again and again. The bullets smacked against the head of the creature, smashing against bone and tearing through leathery skin. Each successive round pummelled the skull, finally penetrating the bone with the fifth and final round and sending the creature spinning over the edge. Dropping the blood and flesh-coated weapon, Bill returned to his vigil on the weapons platform to see Clive finishing off the creatures that were climbing over the cabin, swinging the mounted machinegun around from side to side and firing wildly into the crowd.

Grabbing the grenade launcher once more, Bill wheeled it around to face the building, and froze. During the time it had taken for he and Clive to clear the Rots off the vehicle, the passage between the trailer and the building had been engulfed by the sea of the living dead, and some of them were frantically scratching and clawing at the fallen walls: none had worked out that there was already a hole created, an entrance large enough for a man of Al's stature to pass through, but it was only a matter of time before one of them managed to pull themselves through.

"Son of a bitch," snapped Bill, tapping his radio. "Al, they're on to you, the bastards are on to you, there's a crowd tearing at the front of the building… you're going to have to blast your way out!"

The trailer suddenly lurched, and the vehicle slowly began to move forwards, trundling away from the ruined building while the Rots continued to hammer on the sides, their moans demanding the fresh meat that was inside.

"Pam, where're you going? What about Al?"

"I'm down here," Al said as he hauled himself up on to the roof, brushing off the thick layer of dust and soot that covered him from his trek into the building. "Sly and Garth are down below, patching each other up. The Rots were too close to us, we had to bug out of there before it got too hot; there's hundred of them, maybe thousands, fuck knows where they've been hiding up until now. We couldn't spend any more time in the building anyways, it had almost fell in by the time we'd pulled out. We got over here the time you and Preacher-man were dancing with the dead up here."

He peered over Bill's shoulder, at the congregation of undead animals that were forming at the base of the building. "And not a moment too soon, as well. Those bastards move quick."

"How's Angel doing?"

"We… we couldn't find her; we had to leave."

Bill couldn't believe what he was hearing. Was it a joke, the sick kind of joke the ex-Marine was famous for pulling? He didn't look like he was joking, nor did he sound like he was.

"Don't fuck with me, Al, is she down below?"

Al slowly shook his head. Bill looked back towards the destroyed barracks, as the building gradually grew smaller; if Angel had been left inside, that would explain by so many of the creatures were still clawing at the base. Bill's forehead knitted into a frown as he tried to comprehend what Al was telling him, unable to make any sense out of it.

"Garth said she was on the upper level when the walls started to collapse. We couldn't get up there, the stairs were completely blocked by the rubble, we tried but the smoke was too thick and the constant shifting of rubble made it damn near impossible to make a clear path."

"And you left her?"

"There was nothing we could do, if we didn't leave when we did, then none of us would have escaped."

"You've *left* her in there? What happened to that bullshit about not leaving one of your men behind?"

"That's the Marines, kid: I'm not a Marine anymore."

"You're not even a fucking human anymore, Al," Bill spat, throwing a leg over the barrier and assessing the distance between the vehicle and the building.

"No," hissed Al, shaking his head. "Don't even think about it!"

"Father," Bill said, ignoring Al and turning to the priest. He looked surprised, Bill had never addressed him by his formal title; in fact, no one had for nearly three years now. "Say a prayer for us."

He prepared himself for the leap into the unknown, looking for a clear patch of ground amongst the pursuing creatures, and trying to remember the clearest route back to the building. A thick and powerful hand curled around his wrist, holding him back, and he turned to glare at Al.

"We tried our best," assured Al. "We couldn't get to her; it's probably worse in there now; if the falling rubble hasn't blocked her off, then the Rots will get through…"

"I'll try harder," Bill promised, more to himself than anyone else. "Let me go, you've just given me two reasons to move faster."

"You'll need a weapon," Al said, resigned to the fact that he couldn't sway the young man from changing his mind. He slipped his magnum out the holster and handed it over, followed by a bandoleer of magazines for the weapon. Bill looked bewildered at the weapon as he slipped the bandoleer over his shoulder. "You know that's my favourite weapon, kid. Think of it as a reason to come back. And for Christ's sake, be careful you stupid son of a bitch. I'll get Pam to swing the thing around, maybe even get Garth behind the wheel. Take care."

Bill nodded once, then plunged over the edge, dropping to the soft, churned up muddy earth and sinking to his knees the moment he landed, rolling across the mire and coming up with the heavy pistol in his outstretched hands, opening fire on the closest clutch of Rots. The immense weapon kicked in his hands, the shots jolting his shoulder and lifting his aim up and away from his target, catching one zombie in the eye and grazing the temple of another. He launched into a run, keeping his weapon held tight with both hands while weaving between the animated corpses.

The muddy and churned up ground made it tough for Bill to move, though he still had the speed advantage over the lumbering creatures, darting between corpses, rolling across the ground beneath them, and skirting agilely around them, all the time sweeping the powerful handgun around from side to side and decapitating the creatures: no matter how advanced their stages of decomposition or calcification, the large rounds dealt just as much damage, removing their heads clean off with each shot.

The broken building loomed in the distance, a small number of the undead creatures milling round the outside, scratching at the walls and fallen debris. Ejecting the spent magazine and replacing it with a fresh one, he lifted the weapon and fired into the crowd, aiming to score a perfect kill with each bullet in a bid to conserve ammunition. While the Desert Eagle was an extremely powerful weapon, and the boost to his morale and confidence was massive, the ammunition for it wasn't as plentiful as the official military weapons; he figured that Al had given him all the bullets he had before leaving, either as a gesture of good faith or a leaving present.

He slowed down to a jog, then a brisk walk as he neared the building, taking careful aim and assassinating each creature as he neared them, fixing his eyes on the hole Al had created and powering towards it.

Reaching the entrance, he cast a cursory glance into the tunnel through the rubble, making sure it was clear of any Rots before diving back into the dark depths of the building.

II

It was like entering the depths of hell.

Crawling through the tunnel and back into the broken interior of the barracks was a shock to his system, from the extreme cold of the winter evening to the oven-like interior of the building as it slowly cooked. Plaster and paint cracked and flaked from the walls as the fierce heat of the flames washed over them, exposing the bare metal structure beneath. Despite the strengthened metal, the heat was beginning to destroy it, too; the sounds of crackling fire and shifting debris was drowned out by the creaking groan of weakening metal as the skeleton buckled and snapped. As he looked around the room he was in, Bill knew that the building was going to collapse in on itself at any time; he wasn't surprised that Al had evacuated the building when he had, it was too much to risk everyone's lives for.

But not mine.

The room the hole opened up in was the room that had housed the Gatling cannon the team had used against the Marines: part of the weapon was still visible beneath the masonry that had fallen on top of it, the drums of unused ammo scattered across the floor and lying dangerously close to the many fires that littered the ground. He didn't have the time to try and rescue them, to pull them away from the heat: with the building on the verge of collapse, he had to work as fast as he could, find Angel and get out. He stumbled out the crumbling doorway into the wrecked entrance hall, and he could see instantly why Al had given up trying to make it upstairs to search for Angel.

The staircase had crumbled and collapsed in on itself, leaving nothing more than a gaping hole in the ceiling that Bill couldn't reach, no matter how much debris he stood on. If Angel really were up there… how could he possibly hope to get up there? He tried to visualise a path he could use to get up, leaping from mound of rubble to mound of rubble, but nothing seemed to work. His mind working overtime, he levelled his pistol off, aimed at the wall closest to the opening above him, and fired, emptying a full magazine into the wall. He ejected the spent clip, slapped a fresh one into it, then slipped the smoking weapon in his holster and lunged at the wall, his fingers digging into the damaged cement of the surface and his boots kicking into the crumbling material. The material coating the metal skeleton was thick enough to support Bill's weight as he clambered up the surface. He smiled inwardly as he clambered up the wall, his mind wandering to a time where he had enjoyed rock climbing in high school. Ironically enough, he had only done that to get the girl of his pubescent dreams. It hadn't worked then, but he'd found he had a knack for climbing the fake walls presented to him on a weekly basis. He was pleased to see that it was a talent he hadn't lost, although the plastic handholds back then were a lot kinder on his hands.

Deep crimson seeped from his fingertips as he forced them into the gouges made by the high calibre bullets, the edges of the holes rubbing against his skin and mixing with his spilled blood as he painfully edged his way up the wall, his jaw tense and teeth gritted as he ascended.

He reached the last of the hand holes he had made, still a couple of feet short of the damaged landing of the building, but didn't hesitate. He tightened his grip with his left hand, reached for the holstered magnum and drew it, firing blindly over his head and coughing as dust and debris spilled down into his mouth and eyes. Replacing the weapon, he grabbed another of his handholds, hauling himself further up just as he heard the sound of more rubble shifting in the room he had entered through. He cursed under his breath, imagining his only entrance collapsing and sealing him in, but instead he could hear footsteps, the shuffling crunch of boots on debris as something made its way across the room and stumbled into the ruined hallway.

A Rot stood in the doorway, an elderly man with matted hair pressed against the transparent skin of his scalp. Blackened veins spread across the flesh of the man like an obscene tattoo, channels within his skin filled with coagulated blood no longer needed by the creature. With a keening wail, the rotten creature twisted its head upwards and spotted Bill on the wall. It reached out, as if it were trying to pluck Bill from his ascent, then looked at its empty hand, expecting Bill to be there in its grasp. It glared at him with milky eyes, snarled, then lunged at the wall, its fingers brushing against his legs and snatching at the hems of his jeans. The creature was at the right height for Bill to lash out with a foot and catch the animal square in the head. Luck was on his side, for once, and the Rot hadn't mutated into the toughened strain yet: the pulpy head of the animal split like a ripe melon when his steel toe caps made contact, spilling brains and blood as it dropped to the rubble-strewn ground with a breathless sigh.

More sounds came from the room, more movement of rubble and shuffling footsteps, a collection of moans and wails that could only signal the approach of more creatures as the clawed their way into the building.

"Shit," Bill hissed to himself as he finally managed to swing his leg up on to the exposed floorboards of the landing, watching as the shadows of the stumbling creatures appeared at the doorway. They slowly filed out into the hallway, one festering walking corpse after another, each moaning and reaching up towards the landing where Bill stood. One of the corpses leaned over to one side and scraped the wall, its skeletal claws making their own handholds as the animal hauled itself up after him, the bone of its claws screeching as they scraped the metal beneath the surface, its malevolent and skeletal grin dripping bloody drool as it neared its anticipated meal. Bill drew his handgun and fired a single round into the oncoming creature, missing its head but tearing is calcified shoulder apart. It tumbled backwards into the crowd of bloodthirsty creatures and writhed in agony as the crowd tore it apart, the spilled blood and charred flesh only serving to further excite the animals.

"Angel!"

Bill turned back from the landing and looked around. The hole in the ceiling the attack squad had tried to enter the building through opened up to a darkened sky now, the night merely hours away now. It had been an eventful day, and Bill longed for nothing more than to find somewhere quiet he could lie down and rest, but there were a lot of things he had to do before he could even think about resting. Finding Angel was one of them, and getting her out of the building was another. He supposed that meeting back up with his friends would be a third, but he could only meet his goals one at a time.

One at a time.

He skirted the pile of dead bodies, the slain assault team that included the largest man who had been stripped naked to provide Al with his cover, and dashed into the first room he came to. He hoped that she wasn't in there, purely because the floor had collapsed, leaving a crater in the room below that had previously held the metal sarcophagus. From beneath the fallen floor the battered corner of the metal crate could be seen, but there was no sign of Angel.

The next room had been one of the front-facing rooms, one of the rooms that had taken a barrage of grenade and rocket fire and been the first to collapse. Bill thought that Angel wouldn't have been there and turned away from the mound of rubble, sure that she would have been able to run from the window before the rockets hit. He spun back on himself as he saw something that looked familiar, a boot that he recognised, and he rushed to the fallen debris, heaving aside lumps of concrete and pieces of burning wood as he frantically pawed at the mound. His fingers, already bloody from climbing the wall, bled even more as he worked, spraying crimson fluid around as they cast aside the rubble. Slowly, he uncovered the top of the boot, then the leg of a blue pair of trousers, and he knew that he was on to a winner. More rubble shifted as he feverishly worked away, a calf leading to a thigh, then to a hip, then another leg. Taking an ankle in each hand, Bill slowly pulled, gently at first to make sure she wasn't snagged on anything, then more forcefully once he knew it was safe to do so. She slid gracefully out from beneath the rubble, still clutching her battered and broken rifle with one hand. Other than the blood that seeped from a cut on her forehead, she seemed relatively unharmed. Her chest still rose and fell with shallow breaths, though she didn't make a move to get to her feet. Bill knelt by her, muttered her name, gently slapped her cheeks with the back of his hand, but she didn't respond. Bill knew that ordinarily someone in Angel's position shouldn't be moved, or moved as little as possible until it was known for sure that she hadn't received any crippling spinal injury and that moving her wouldn't do any more damage.

Bill didn't have time for back support, neck braces, the recovery position or anything like that. She was breathing, and that was all that mattered at the minute.

He stood, pried the rifle out Angel's hand and slipped one hand beneath her neck, the other beneath her lower back, and stood up, lifting her from the ground and carried her back on to the landing.

The heat from the fire below only served to intensify the rotting stench of the creatures gathered on the ground floor below him, and his appearance there only served to further antagonise the hungry crowd. The only thing that was currently going Bill's way was the fact that the giant hole in the ceiling was effectively acting as a chimney and drawing the smoke away to make sure he didn't choke on the thick black cloud that roiled up around him. He stood on the landing and assessed his options again, jostling Angel to gain a better grip on her.

From below, a thunderous blast of gunfire sounded, and for a brief moment he thought that Al had returned to save him, providing cover and clearing a path through the dead. Bullets tore through the wall and open doorway, cutting into the zombies closest to the door and knocking them down; some with fatal headshots, others with a barrage of gunfire that smashed into their bodies and shattered their limbs and ribcage. Bill soon realised all wasn't as he hoped when the bullets began to tear through the floorboards, and he realised that the drums of ammunition left by the fire had finally cooked off.

Yet another threat to add to the list of things endangering Bill's life. He didn't have time to think about what to do, only react. He gently placed Angel on the landing and patted down the Marine corpses that had been left to rot on the upper floor. His search came up triumphant as he uncovered four grenades and considered his options. One would certainly be enough to clear the crowd of Rots below him, but he wasn't sure he'd have enough to break out the building: He couldn't chance going back out the way he came in, and he didn't have time to try and dig his way out through the fallen rubble at the front of the building. There was no rope he could use to climb out the hole in the roof, and even if there was, how could he get Angel out with him?

Without another thought, Bill rushed to the first room he explored on the upper floor where the floor that had collapsed, and pulled the pins from each grenade before hurling them into the far corner of the room below him and knelt down, hands over his ears and turning away from the grenades.

The simultaneous explosions ripped through the outer wall of the building, peeling off the coating of concrete and plaster, shattering the metal structure and tearing it apart, buckling it outwards. As the smoke cleared, Bill lifted his hands from his head and peered at the wall, at the new opening he had made that would lead him and Angel outside. The gloom of the night on the other side was enticing to Bill, the cool wind that lapped in through fresh hole like the lulling song of a siren. The ceiling above him was a web of cracks and tears, a constant downpour of dust and debris raining down on Bill as he rushed over to retrieve Angel. Though he had punched a way out into the sidewall, it looked like he had significantly shortened the life span of the building: he had to move fast.

Wrapping his arms around Angel and lifting her up from the ground once more, Bill stumbled over to the hole in the floor and peered over the edge: he didn't have time to try and lower Angel down first, he just dropped to the uneven and broken surface with her still in his arms, landing heavily on his ankle and twisting his leg as the debris gave way beneath his feet.

Cursing under his breath and muttering to himself, Bill stalked across the rubble-strewn ground, swaying from side to side as he tried to keep his balance with his precious load in his arms. The debris that tumbled down from the ceiling high above struck him as he moved, each step a struggle as he kept his eyes focussed on the gaping hole the explosives had created. As he reached the threshold of the exit and stepped through, the exposed metal support frame squealed and groaned, the noises giving Bill the extra spurt of strength and speed he needed to lurch out the building and stumble away from the crumbling building. He managed to make it three metres away before finally collapsing to his knees, gently placing Angel on the ground and wheezing heavily, not realising how quickly he had got used to the acrid taste of the smoke-laden air until he was free from the confines of the building, sucking the cold, cleaner air of the outside; it was still laced with the stink of decay, but it was a damn sight cleaner than the thick, sooty air he had previously been breathing.

The building behind him creaked and groaned once more, the sounds uttered by the building louder than those any Rot that Bill had ever come across. He peered over his shoulder, watching as the exposed metal twisted and buckled, collapsing in on itself as the concrete and masonry cracked and peeled away, tumbling to the ground and kicking up clouds of dust that washed over Bill as he leaned forwards over Angel. Chunks of the falling structure bounced off his back and struck his head, but he didn't move, he kept the protective barrier up around Angel as the building continued to collapse.

The sound of shifting rubble finally stopped, and as the dust cleared, Bill sat upright, surveying the surrounding area as his vision swam. He could feel the wounds on his head were bleeding more freely now, he could feel the warm liquid seep down his neck and his vision swam: he shook his head, trying to keep focused. Flames licked up from beneath the mound of rubble that was now the building, casting flickering red light and horrific shadows across the ground around the ruin. Creatures still lingered around the crumbled building, clawing futilely at the rubble and moaning to one another as they came up with a severed limb from the creatures that had been trapped inside when the walls had fallen. Checking on Angel once more to make sure she hadn't been hurt any further, Bill pulled out the heavy handgun, lined up a shot, and squeezed off a single round. The weapon jumped violently in his weakened hand, and the pain that jolted through his arm felt like he'd pulled a muscle in his shoulder. The shot went wild and served to only alert the closest of the creatures that there was fresh meat outside the fallen building that they pawed at. As one the listless creatures spun on their feet and stumbled towards them, some tumbling over masonry, others managing to navigate their way over or around it. Bill lined up another shot, squeezed the trigger, but the weapon didn't fire; the slide was locked back, indicating that it needed a new magazine. Bill fumbled with the release catch, snatched at a fresh clip, then tried to re-aim. His eyes were blurred and unfocussed, and no matter how much he tried to blink, he couldn't clear his vision. Shadows of the Rots fell across him, bringing with them the overpowering stench of rotten flesh and poor personal hygiene, and Bill looked back at Angel while firing blindly into the oncoming fray. He'd tried to rescue her, and had almost succeeded.

It was too bad he had failed.

Taking one of her limp hands in his and returning his attention to the advancing undead, Bill lifted the weapon again and squeezed the trigger. It snapped open, empty again, and he couldn't help but wonder why Al loved such a weapon that such a poor magazine capacity. He fumbled for another magazine, dropped it, and his eyes felt heavy; heavier than the gun itself. Sighing to himself muttering an apology to Angel, Bill accepted his failure as a Rot loomed closer and uttered an ear-splitting roar.

Blood splashed across him as his eyes closed.

After handing his Desert Eagle over to Bill and leaving Clive to man the weapons on the roof, Al had ran back downstairs into the living quarters of the trailer, ruffling Sarah's hair as he walked past with a grin. She smiled back, then turned her attention back to watching Garth and Sylvester tend to each other's wounds.

"How's it going?" he asked, unwrapping a bandage himself and coiling it around his left forearm; it was nothing major, just a flesh wound, but it was enough to warrant attention.

"Not bad," Sylvester admitted, pressing a piece of gauze to his head and dabbing gently at it. "I feel pretty shit about leaving Angel…"

"She was on the top floor," Garth said, pulling out a packet of cigarettes with shaking hands and placing one on his lip. "Right by the window. I'm sure she was… you know, with the first burst of rockets. I… I don't think she could survive that."

It sounded like Garth was trying to convince himself more than anyone.

"Yeah, well, we're turning around," Al announced, moving towards the hatchway that would lead towards the front cabin.

"What?" Garth shouted, no sure whether he should be happy or terrified. "We're going back for Angel?"

"No," grunted Al. "Bill's gone back to get her. We're going to turn around and pick that damn fool up before the building collapses in on itself. Spanners, get your ass up there and help out our resident priest, make sure we keep as many of those bastards away from us as possible. I'm going to get Pam to turn around; hey buddy, you want to take the wheel again?"

"It's what I'm here for," Garth murmured. "Your personal chauffeur."

Al ran on to the drivers cabin, bursting in through the door and seeing Pam wrestling with the controls. She couldn't see where she was going because the windows were obscured by the rotting faces of the undead creatures as the pressed against the glass, leaving bloody and greasy smears on the windscreen. They rattled and hammered on the glass, and the only thing Pam could do to try and dislodge them was to activate the windscreen wipers. One of them scraped back and forth across the window, while the other had snapped off, lodged firmly in the cheek of one of the attacking creatures. The Rots were also on the roof of the cabin, pounding and stamping on the metal plating overhead in a desperate bid to break through.

Pam didn't look back over her shoulder, keeping her eyes fixed on the window, but she smiled softly as she saw Al's reflection in one of the monitors.

"Everyone okay?"

"Angel's still in the building. Bill's gone back to get her. We need to turn around; if we do it when we're going fast enough, we could probably shake enough of those bastards."

Pam nodded in response, but before she could respond, the window before her broke into a thousand shards of safety glass as one of the creatures burst through, spraying blood and spittle all over as it snapped ferociously at Pam and Al.

Instinctively slapping at his thigh, Al cursed as he remembered he had handed over his gun to Bill before he leapt into the undead fray. Instead, he unsheathed a ten-inch combat knife and dived forwards, plunging the steel blade into the eye socket of the Rot up to the hilt. It slid silently off the bonnet, away from the broken window, only to be replaced with another of the animals, snarling viciously as it tried to lash out. Having lost his knife, Al looked around for a weapon in a blind panic while Pam recoiled from the undead intruder, pushing herself back into the padding of the chair and lifting her hands up to protect her face from the spittle and flying pieces of glass.

Garth stumbled into the cabin, ready to take over the driving duty, and blanched as he saw the shape of the Rot leaning in the cabin. Al snatched the machete from Garth's belt and turned back, intent to hack at the skull of the Rot, only this time keeping the blade, when he saw the skeletal hands of the creature curl around the wrist of Pam. Everything seemed to slow down, and Al felt like he was trying to swim through treacle as he dived forwards, blade raised above his head, and helplessly watched as the broken and shattered teeth of the Rot clamped down on Pam's fingers, crunching through the bone of her index and ring finger, pulling away the top two segments of each finger with a bloody spray.

Pam's scream cut through the cabin and she lost control of the vehicle, the machine swinging and swaying wildly from side to side as the squirming and shaking creatures on the front of the vehicle overpowered the unmanned controls. Screaming a blood-curdling war cry, Al lunged forwards, grabbed the soft head of the undead and twisted and pulled at the same time, jarring the spine of the creature and breaking the neck in one swift move. It wasn't enough to kill the undead attacker or snap its spinal column, but it was enough to paralyse it and block the broken window.

"Get out," screamed Al, slicing through the safety harness Pam had fastened herself in with and hauling her out the cabin, back into the main part of the trailer. "Lock the door, seal it up, we're fucked."

Garth did as he was told, while Al leaned over Pam, glaring at the missing fingers that oozed blood and twitched spasmodically. He knew the bite of the dead carried the disease, knew that Pam was as good as dead herself as the plague would spread through her. A thousand different thoughts raced through his mind as he stared helplessly at Pam, a thousand different choices he had to act on before it was too late.

His mind made up, he tore a piece of material from his shirt, wrapped it tightly around her right arm, then Al lifted his hand and brought the knife crashing down on Pam's wrist. The first blow sliced through the flesh and muscle of her wrist, the second cracked the bone, and the third cut through it, completely severing her hand from her arm. She had blacked out after the first strike from the blade, and Garth stared dumbfounded as the ex-Marine worked through the grizzly work. Finally finding a shaky and uncertain voice, Garth managed to speak.

"What the *fuck* are you doing, you sick bastard?"

"Amputating," Al said, matter-of-factly as he grabbed a handful of shotgun shells from one of the pouches on his utility belt. Checking every so often on Pam to make sure she was okay, he went to work on the shells, peeling them open and pouring the gunpowder over the blade of the machete until the metal was all but covered by the black powder, and he pulled out his lighter, igniting the mound and watching as the gunpowder heated the blade.

While the pile of gunpowder cooked, Al broke open more shells, tapped the gunpowder out over the fresh, bloody wound of the stump at the end of Pam's right hand, and ignited that, too. The powder sparked a blazing orange as it sizzled and partially cauterised the wound, giving birth to the slight scent of burning flesh. Al grabbed the knife and pressed the heated metal against the wound, gritting his teeth while the nauseating smell of burning flesh filled the assailed his nostrils.

"Get me bandages, clean bandages, fast."

Garth stood motionless, staring at the macabre sight as Al adjusted the makeshift tourniquet and applied more heat and pressure to the wound.

"Fucking move!"

Snapping out of his trance, Garth nodded and dived for the piles of unused bandages that had been left on the row of seats, grabbing a handful and throwing them at Al.

The bleeding from the makeshift amputation wasn't as bad as Al thought it would have been, and he hoped that he managed to act in time. The infectious bite of the undead was the main method of spreading the plague, and although Al had never heard of someone surviving a bite, he wasn't aware of any attempts to amputate the damaged limb. It may be that if he acted quickly enough he could stop the infection spreading; only time would tell.

As he finished off wrapping the wound, Garth dropped to the floor, shaking his head as he tried to make sense of the events that had unfolded before him.

"What the fuck do we do now?"

"We'll have to wait, see if it stops the spread," Al said, wiping the tears from his eyes and mopping Pam's brow with a piece of unused wadding.

"I know that, but it doesn't do us any good if the controls are occupied by the Rots."

Al looked around, starting to take in the details of the trailer as he started to remove the focus from his fallen lover, and noticed that the sealed door leading to the control cabin seemed to be under a barrage of blows from the *inside*.

"The dead are inside, they've taken over the vehicle. We're sitting ducks in here, it's only a matter of time until they break through: that door's designed for privacy, not restraining a horde of attackers. We're dead in the water."

Al looked around, realising that Garth was right. He had to organise and rally everyone together, get them armed and moving as soon as possible, before the corpses overthrew the vehicle.

"What about Bill? How are we going to get him out of this?"

"I'm thinking," Al said, still kneeling beside Pam.

"We're surrounded by them, there's hundreds of them, they're going to break in here and get us all…"

"Garth!" Al shouted, fixing him with an ice-cold stare. "Keep your shit together. I can't have any fuck-ups here. I need you to get hold of any supplies you can, food, water, anything. Grab it, bundle it up into whatever bags we've got lying around, and get ready to move."

Checking on Pam's heart rate and breathing before standing up, he rushed into the main living area check on Sarah. She was cowering in her bunk, the curtain pulled to one side and her blanket pulled up over her head. She was visibly shaking beneath the material, and Al gently reached into the bunk, pulling away the sheet and slowly exposing her ashen face.

"You okay sweetie?"

She didn't say anything, just shook her head.

"I know; it's all pretty scary. Pam's been hurt really bad, and I need you to prove to me how much of an adult you are. Garth's going to gather as much food as he can, and I need you to help. We're going to have to go for a run out there, but it won't be long."

Sarah shook her head defiantly.

"Honey, we don't have any choice, the Rots… the dead men… they're going to break through any minute now. I need you to help Garth while I get Sylvester and Clive down off the roof and loaded up on weapons. You think you can do that for me? Help Garth?"

Sarah slowly nodded, then reluctantly slipped out of the bunk, keeping the blanket draped around her shoulders. She trudged to the first of the cupboards and slipped out a satchel, placing whatever she could find into the canvas sack. Al smiled to himself as he rushed to the upper floor and climbed up on to the weapons platform. He was greeted by the concerned face of a mechanic and a priest, their weapons swinging wildly from side to side as they took their shots: the continuous thunder of the automatic fire had trickled down to an occasional well-aimed salvo into the crowd below.

"Why've we stopped?"

"Rots smashed through the windscreen, took a chunk out of Pam's hand. We need to bail out, get ourselves to safety someplace else. I've got Garth and Sarah gathering supplies, I need you two to be my point and tail men, carrying as many weapons as possible."

"We're almost out of ammo up here anyway," muttered Sylvester, releasing his grip on his weapon. "What about you, what's your job in all this?"

"I'm carrying Pam," Al said. "I'll help where I can, but I need to be careful with her."

"She's been bitten by the dead," Clive said. "Won't that mean…"

"I amputated," Al said, shaking his head. "Cut her hand off at the wrist, cauterised the wound as best as I could, I don't know if it'll be enough. We'll have to see."

"Fuck," muttered Sylvester. "Okay, where we running to?"

"Back to the building, we'll meet up with Bill, find somewhere from there."

Al looked from side to side and saw that the dead on either side surrounded the main trailer, but the rear-most trailer was relatively clear. He motioned towards the open ground behind the vehicle and returned to the hatchway. "We'll head out the back, run from there. Hopefully, we can cover some pretty good distance before the Rots see us. Last one in lock up the hatch, we don't want them coming in."

Al slid down the ladder and down the stairs to the first floor, finding Garth loading up a final bag while Sarah sat on the ground beside Pam, brushing strands of hair away from her face. She looked up at Al and shook her head; he didn't respond. All the while, the door leading to the control cabin constantly shook and vibrated, slowly buckling inwards.

"Okay, we're getting out of here now. Garth, you got enough food there?"

"All the rations we have," he nodded. "I would have preferred a good bottle of whiskey, maybe some tins of stewed steak. Travel light, that's what I've been told in the past. Rations are packed; we've got enough for maybe a week or two. I'll carry all the bags, the little one can't carry too much anyways."

"She can carry the whiskey," Al said, grabbing two bottles of golden brown liquid from an opened cupboard and rolling two pieces of bandages into the open necks. He handed them to Sarah as she wandered over to him.

"Hold these, don't drop them. I'll tell you when I want them. Okay, everyone into the rear trailer, grab assault rifles and as much ammo as you can. Hold the doors until I'm there."

Garth, Sylvester and Clive nodded and left the trailer, heading into the weapons trailer while Sarah watched as Al picked up Pam, draping one arm over his broad shoulders and wrapping his own around her waist.

"I'm scared," Sarah said, juggling with the two bottles as she watched Al carry the invalid patient. "I can't run that fast, what if they catch me?"

"They won't. Me and Pam can't run that fast either, just keep hold of those and pass them to me when I ask for them, okay?"

Sarah nodded slowly.

"We'll be all right, honey, don't worry. Come on, they're waiting for us."

III

The doors to the back of the trailer swung open and Sylvester leaped down to the muddy, churned up ground, dropping to his knees and sweeping his weapon from left to right. Clive dropped down next to him, and together then shuffled forwards, their assault rifles tucked up into their shoulders and their aim high as they slowly advanced out and to the side, providing cover from the advancing Rots while Garth struggled out the back of the vehicle, heavily laden with bags and carrying a compact submachine gun while helping Al manipulate the form of Pam down on to the ground. She had woken briefly while Sylvester had been preparing his weapons, an M60 strapped over his back and an M16 gripped in his hand. She didn't seem to be fully cognitive, mumbling to herself and nodding her head before dropping back into unconsciousness. Sarah tagged along beside them, a bottle of whiskey in each hand as she stuck by Al's side. Under normal circumstances, Sylvester would have found the image of a nine year old stumbling through the grounds of Buckingham Palace with a pair of whiskey bottles in her hands quite odd and a little out of place. Of course, now, he didn't think that anything was out of place.

In a world where the dead stalked the living, what *could* be out of place?

"I am the first," Clive insisted, stepping ahead and leading the way. He motioned to Sylvester to provide some covering fire. "You are the last. Like Alpha and Omega."

"What did you say?" he asked, cocking his head. Clive shook his head and stepped away from the vehicle, starting to make his way towards the building in the distance.

The gloom of dusk was setting in now, and Sylvester couldn't make out any of the details of the corpses that were advancing until he squeezed off a round from his weapon and the muzzle flash bathed the creatures in blinding white light. He stood to the left of the vehicle and couldn't count how many were there on that side, and knew there could be just as many on the other side of the vehicle. For every creature he dropped with a well-aimed shot, another two seemed to appear, and the group of fleeing people appeared to be facing overwhelming odds. Not two minutes out of the vehicle and he had already had to replace the magazine; he only had another five magazines attached to the combat webbing he wore, and although he carried satchels filled with various ammunition, he knew that it would take too long to stop and fish out a fresh clip. He didn't think that the Rots would be so compliant as to wait while he reloaded.

Several of the creatures clung to the side of the vehicle, trying to haul their undead carcasses over the railing surrounding the weapons platform, their hands grasping tirelessly at the sides of the trailer as they tried to climb up the smooth surfaces. Some had managed to clamber up to the roof, and were banging ceaselessly on the locked trapdoor, oblivious to the fact that their target meals were now outside.

"Change of plan," shouted Al as he motioned for Sylvester to follow him with a nod of his head. "There's too many of them to provide cover for. Lower your weapon and move with us. I'll tell you when to fire."

Sylvester breathed a sigh of relief, and hadn't realised until that point that he'd been holding his breath since Clive left him. He quickly backed away just as the rear-most trailer shook and jostled, while a low and drawn-out moan echoed within the empty confines of the trailer. It sounded as if the creatures that had found their way into the cabin had finally broken through the door, and were now swarming the abandoned trailer.

Al called a halt to the procession and motioned to Sylvester to support Pam while he took one of the bottles from Sarah and ignited his lighter, touching the white rag to the flame and swirling the contents around before hurling the bottle into the opened doors in the rear of the trailer. He reclaimed his injured partner and motioned everyone to hurry up. Sylvester did as he was told and moved. He knew that the flames from the Molotov cocktail might slow the undead animals down, but they wouldn't stop them; they didn't fear the flames, and as such would just walk straight through them.

There was a deafening explosion, and Sylvester felt a rush of air slam into his back, knocking him forwards and making him stumble as he ran. A hint of Al's reasoning behind throwing the incendiary flashed into his mind as he raced through the gloom of dusk, knocking aside any of the faster Rots as they tried to approach them. He hadn't intended on stopping the creatures with fire, but with an exploding vehicle. And with the flaming Rots stumbling through a trailer filled with ammunition and explosives…

Garth trotted to a halt, turning around and watching in grief as a second explosion ripped through the vehicle, tossing aside the zombies that remained erect around it. A glassy look appeared in his eyes as he watched the debris tumble and scatter across the muddy field. Sylvester, his gaze fixed over his shoulder, slammed into the mourning trailer driver without seeing him, and the pair dropped to the ground, limbs wrapping around one another and churning up more mud.

"What the fuck?" screamed Sylvester, hauling himself to his feet before grabbing Garth roughly by the arm and picking him up. "Move, you dumb shit,"

"But… but…"

"We'll get a new one," Sylvester confirmed as he carried on running, dragging Garth. He rubbed at the splashes of mud that covered his face and reluctantly followed.

"New one," muttered Garth, absentmindedly. "I must've missed the armed forces automobile showroom on the way in here. I hear you can pick up a bargain on pre-owned models."

"Stop pouting," hissed Sylvester, continuing on the journey and swinging his assault rifle from side to side as he went. Though Al had told him to move without sighting or opening fire, he felt safer knowing he was ready to act at a moments notice.

The target building in the distance seemed to waver and flicker as Sylvester moved, and he wiped at his eyes, sure that it was an optical illusion, that the heat rising from the burning building was playing tricks with his tired eyes. Part of the building blew outwards with a deafening roar of cascading rubble and slate tiles, spewing debris and twisted infrastructure out the gaping wound that appeared. Everyone stopped running and stared, slack-jawed, at the building as it slowly tumbled and collapsed in on itself. Silence fell across the group, except for the sporadic bursts of gunfire from the rifle Clive held as he tried to keep the advancing horde at bay. Sylvester joined in half-heartedly while keeping an eye on the building and Al, who looked defeated: whether that was because there was a chance that Bill was in there, or because his plan and proposed safe zone had suddenly vanished.

"What now?" demanded Garth. "What do we do now?"

"Calm down," insisted Al. "Keep it together, don't let the kid know you're shitting yourself."

"The kid knows what's going on," whispered Sarah hoarsely, gripping Al's combat webbing and drawing herself closer to him. "The kid knows, and she *is* shitting herself."

Sylvester looked feverishly around, eyeing the field, the crumbling building ahead of them, and the outlying buildings around them. They were further away then the ruined barracks, and possibly just as infested as the grounds of the palace. Far to one side, a copse of ruined trees lurked ominously in the gloom, their branches powdered with a sprinkling of snow; like a haunted forest from a fairy tale, it didn't look inviting, and could be filled with all manner of undead creatures.

"We could've flushed the trailer if we'd tried," Garth whined, leaning over and supporting his weight by locking his hands around his knees. "We could've done it."

"Shut up and stop your fucking whining," Al screamed, checking on Pam's condition while trying to come up with another plan.

"The trailer," Sylvester shouted; "That's it!"

"Shut up about the god damn trailer," shouted Al. "It's gone, if I hadn't blown it up then the fucking Rots would have swarmed the place…"

"Ours is gone… but what about the other one?"

"Other?" murmured Al, silently mouthing a collection of seemingly random words to himself. "You mean Carter's? Goddamn, Spanners, you're a fucking genius. New plan, we're heading towards the other trailer."

"Well, where the hell is it?" demanded Garth.

"Other side of the fallen building," Al muttered, heading towards the building once more, this time aiming for the inert military vehicle that lay beyond.

"Our sanctuary lies beyond the inferno," Clive muttered, ejecting the spent magazine from his rifle and replacing it with another. "Trust in God and he will deliver us."

"You think he'll deliver Bill and Angel, too?" asked Garth as they moved.

"It's hard to say," Clive said as he moved, his assault rifle rattling off rounds as he moved, scoring the occasional hit on an advancing zombie, though most of his shots missed. "The young girl may be saved, I don't know about her beliefs, but Bill is a heathen, he follows no religion or guiding deity other than his own reckless instincts."

"You badmouth all your friends behind their backs, or just your closest?" muttered Al, nearing the smouldering heap of rubble as part of the building that remained. At the distance they were now from the building, they could hear gunshots, which Sylvester put down to the ammunition left inside the burning shell cooking off. He didn't want to be close to the building when the drums of ammunition for the Gatling cannon went off, there was enough force there to bore through the concrete and shred anyone near the rubble; that included the undead creatures that milled around the debris, though those that hadn't been knocked down by the concussive blast and resultant rain of smouldering masonry now seemed to be swarming to the other side of the building.

Had one of the Marines survived Al's wrath and were trying to make their escape?

"Gunshots," he shouted, instinctively ducking and gently lowering Pam on to the muddy ground.

"Isn't it the ammo in the building?" Garth asked, his mind on the same tracks as Sylvester's. Another salvo of shots sounded, and Al shook his head, sure of his diagnosis.

"That's an Eagle sounding off," he said with a grin. "That's my weapon, that's Bill. Preacher-man, you and buddy stay here, look after Pam and Sarah, don't let any of those dead fucks get near them. Spanners, you're with me."

"Pam's already been touched by evil," Clive muttered, looking at the unconscious woman on the ground. "We should just take the child and leave here while we can. Save the bullets."

Al snarled and unleashed a single punch, his fist crashing into Clive's jaw and sending him sprawling backwards, into the mud and the path of an advancing zombie that had it's attention roused by the altercation between the two men. Al stormed forwards, pointing an accusing finger down on the sprawled priest, ignoring the approaching undead creature.

"I don't know what the fuck's gotten into you, you miserable son of a bitch, but if I was going to leave *anyone* to the Rots, it wouldn't be someone like Pam, It'd be a miserable fuck like you who's suddenly turned so bitter and fucking twisted that he's willing to write off people he calls his friends in order to save his own worthless ass. Friends who saved *his* ass, if I remember rightly. Get up and do as I say, or I'll feed you to the Rots, piece by piece. Garth, you're in charge, make sure this self-righteous bastard doesn't do anything he'll regret. Spanners, grab your rifle and come with me."

Sylvester nodded and cautiously followed the ex-soldier, casting a glance over his shoulder and watching as Garth killed the zombie that had approached Clive, and then returned to tending to Pam and allowing the preacher to extricate himself from the mud. Ordinarily, Sylvester would have jumped to his friend's defence, but it turned out that he wasn't the only person in the group that had noticed a change in Clive. Maybe Al's blunt method of confronting a problem would help bring him out of his strange mood and back to normal?

"Stay alert," commanded Al as the pair skirted around the outside of the building, his rifle lifted high and panning from side to side, sighting undead after undead while scanning for any sign of Bill. "You see anything yet?"

"Nothing," Sylvester confirmed, bringing his own rifle up as the silent trailer came into view. The side of the machine was covered with indentations from gunfire and spattered with blood from the battle, though none of the Rots seemed to be homing in on it; their uncanny sense of seeking out living beings seemed to be drawing them towards a small clearing in the middle of the battle ground, where the undead swarmed a figure kneeling on the ground, a gun held in his outstretched hands as he tried to fend off the advancing horde.

"I see him," Sylvester shouted, pointing towards them with a trembling finger.

"Got him," Al said without looking up, lining up a shot as he tucked the stock of the rifle in his armpit and rested his cheek against the top of the weapon. Sylvester swallowed hard, there was no way he'd ever try to make a shot like that; he didn't trust his own aiming skills to even attempt it. He watched helplessly, licking his dry lips and waiting for Al to take his shot. One of the rotting creatures approached Bill as he fumbled with the handgun and another magazine, and he looked down to the ground, as if he had accepted his fate.

"I'll be a son of a bitch, he got her. Chivalrous to the very end," murmured Al as he squeezed the trigger. His weapon barked to life, vomiting a searing hot projectile from the muzzle and sending it crashing through the head of the target Rot. Dark crimson burst from the ruined head of the creature as it keeled over, splashing blood over Bill as he, too, fell to one side.

"You shot him?"

"Relax, the pussy just passed out. Advance, sweep and clear those Rots, make sure none of the bastards lay a finger on the pair. He's fallen *over* the bitch, I don't know whether he did that on purpose or not. You secure them, I'm going to hotwire that vehicle and get us the fuck out of here."

Sylvester nodded and ran forwards, confident in taking the shots he needed now that Bill lay on the ground. His shots were going wild, but the closer he got to the pack of Rots, the more accurate he became, until he was scoring perfect hits with each controlled burst.

He dived to the ground and rolled to a stop beside the unconscious forms of Bill and Angel, quickly checking each for a pulse before resuming his duty and cracking open the heads of the Rots. There didn't seem to be as many as there had before, which was one of the small miracles in life that Sylvester was grateful for, as was the sound of the truck roaring to life behind him. With a triumphant whoop, Al lumbered out the idling vehicle and danced his way across the muddied ground to where the pair lay on the ground. He motioned to Angel, indicating he wanted Sylvester to carry her, then grabbed Bill and dragged him towards the opened trailer.

"Now what?" Sylvester asked, gasping for breath as he hauled the limp girl into the Marine vehicle and placed her on one of the bunks in the living quarters. The vehicle itself seemed larger than the previous trailer, more spacious and comfortable, with heavily padded seats, a thin carpet and a variety of different entertainment mediums installed above one of the heavyset countertops. It looked like it was more than one step up from their previous model, more than likely because this particular vehicle had once been the base of operations for a high-ranking officer. Al laid Bill out on a bunk beside the one Angel occupied, and rushed back towards the front of the vehicle and the open door between the living compartment and the drivers cabin.

"We pick up Pam, Sarah, Garth. Maybe that scumbag priest you call your friend. Then get the hell out of here. I'll drive; you get ready to get everyone aboard. I've done enough sightseeing for the day.

Bill opened his eyes to see white polystyrene tiles above him, a grid of rectangular sheets that were a pale cream in colour and speckled with tiny black indentations. It looked like the ceiling of the break room in the government office he worked in, but he knew that room well enough to know he wasn't there now: in fact, he was a long way from there. He'd had many short naps in that room between his rounds. There had even been the sordid half hour spent in there after one of the office Christmas parties with Jenny…

Jenny, he thought to himself. There was a person he'd lost that he hadn't thought about in the same way he used to. He closed his eyes and sighed heavily. He still felt the loss, even though he didn't think about her all the time. Should he feel guilty about that? About the fact he had moved on with his life, or was at least trying to? All the pining in the world wouldn't bring her back from the dead, and he had done nothing other than grieve her passing during the fortnight he was in quarantine. Did that make the fact he didn't think about her any more all right? He'd gone out of his way to retrieve a photograph of her, yet when was the last time he'd even looked at?

He didn't know.

He didn't even know where it was.

And how did that fit in with his current state of mind, and flurry of mixed emotions that filled his mind as he lay in silence?

Well, not total silence. There was the low, almost inaudible drone of the engine as the trailer trundled along the road it travelled on, and the sound of metal instruments clinking gently against one another as they rolled around surgical trays added to the melody. They were back on the road, probably on another damn-foolish crusade headed by Al.

He tried to move, to pull himself from the bench he lay on, but he felt the bite of black nylon restraints hold him down, and beneath that, the searing pain of his muscles as they groaned in unison. He tried to lift his head, that hadn't been restrained, and tried to look around the medical bay, the muscles in his neck stiff and aching as he moved.

The room had shrunk to a cubical that was eight foot square, and the walls painted a pale grey in colour. Black metallic nozzles hung ominously from the ceiling, and Bill realised that he had seen these before. He was faced with one of two choices. Either he had been dreaming the last three years and was still trapped in quarantine, or he had been captured by soldiers and thrown into a holding cell: that would certainly explain the restraints.

In the corner of the room, huddled in the gloom, a hulking figure sat in silence, the glowing red tip of the cigar he toyed with partially illuminating the grim features of his face. Playing the smoking roll of tobacco across his mouth, he stood up and stepped closer to Bill, dragging the seat he had perched upon across the ground behind him. The metal legs squealed and groaned as they scraped across the floor tiles.

"I didn't know you were into bondage," Bill said as cheerily as he could while Al repositioned the seat. Every muscle in his face ached as he smiled, so he tried to keep that to a minimum. Al returned the gesture with his own grim smile.

"How are you feeling now?"

"Like half a building just fell down on me."

"It didn't 'just' happen, kid. You've been in and out for something like two days now. At least, I think it's been two days… I've had things to do."

"Two days…" Bill mused to himself. Though Al said he had been in and out, he had no recollection of anything during those brief periods of consciousness. "The last thing I remember is… a Rot eating me? Or at least my blood spraying across me. It's all a little fuzzy, to be honest."

"I shot one, must've sprayed you a little. Sorry"

"No worries," Bill said, laughing softly to himself. "It's not like I swallowed any, I'm not infected."

Al nodded his head, his lower lip trembling slightly. "No. You're not."

He cleared his throat with a cough, then wiped his nose with the back of one finger.

"So you jumped off the trailer, ran like shit off a stick to that building, climbed into the building, dragged that bitch out and kept the dead at bay until I came and hauled your ass out of the fire. You know, you're one reckless mother fucker, kid, you know that? A crazy-assed bastard. It's one of the reasons I like you. Crazy and reckless, just like a decent Marine. "

"How is Angel?" Bill said, his mind slowly rebooting and replaying events through his mind. "She wasn't that responsive when I got to her."

"Angel's fine. She's been spending most of her time looking after her patients, reading through medical files. She comes in every so often, changes your dressings, tops up your saline drips."

"Patients?" Bill asked, picking up on the use of the plural. "Who else is injured?"

"No one," Al said quickly, rubbing at his eyes and waving a dismissive hand. "She's… everyone else is okay. It's nothing."

"Al?"

"Nothing. It's nothing."

He stood, seemingly angry with himself, and marched for the door, looking back over his shoulder. Bill thought he could see a hint of light reflect in a tear that rolled down his cheek before he vanished from sight.

"Your boy's awake," Bill heard him almost grunt. "I'll be with Pam."

Bill still had a look of confusion on his face when Angel strolled in, wearing a white lab coat over her normal clothing and clutching a roll of bandages and a small plastic bag filled with a clear liquid. She smiled softly, threw the bandages and saline on to the chair, and stood beside the gurney Bill laid on, towering over him. The smile remained fixed on her face even as she spoke.

"You won't hear me say it often, but Al's right. You were reckless and stupid."

"You're welcome," he murmured by response, then tried to quickly change the subject. "Where the hell are we? This isn't our vehicle, it isn't our sickbay."

"Al blew it up," she muttered as she went about changing the drip Bill was hooked up to. He hadn't even noticed he had been attached to one until she had replaced the bag.

"There's a surprise," Bill muttered, more to himself than anyone else, and then in a louder voice added, "What happened?"

"The Rots broke through the windscreen of the cabin, poured in through the front. Then they broke in through the roof. They were packed in tight around the vehicle, Al decided to call it quits and bail out. The destruction of the vehicle was an accident. He claims. So they took the Marine machine that had been left over from the fight. It's bigger, nicer inside. More like a real place to live in."

"I suppose that's because he was an officer. At least, that's what Al probably said."

"Al hasn't said a lot over the past two days: he's spent most of his time with Pam."

"What happened to her? He mentioned someone, another casualty, but didn't say who."

"When the Rots broke into the trailer, one of them managed to tag Pam; chewed one of her fingers straight off."

"She's infected?" Bill said, sitting bolt upright, or at least trying to. The straps of the bed cut into him and held him pressed against the bench, knocking the wind out of him as he chaffed himself against the restraints.

"We don't know about that."

"Well, she was bitten," Bill reasoned, "We've all seen it before, the bite carries the infection, she has to be infected."

"Al cut her hand off," Angel snapped. Bill didn't say anything, dumbstruck with the revelation. Amputation of an infected limb wasn't anything that had been tried in the past, at least to Bill's knowledge. Whether it would work or not, Bill had no idea; Al had obviously been desperate to try anything that he thought may have increased her chances of survival.

"Is she… is she okay?" he finally managed to ask.

"I don't know," Angel snapped. "When I'm not looking after you or running tests on her, I'm spending all my free time reading through medical journals and files to see if I can work out what the hell is wrong with you and whether she's infected."

Angel's voice continued to raise as she spoke, until she punctuated her tirade by hurling the empty bag from the drip down on to a tray littered with surgical items. They clattered to the ground with a metallic crash, and Angel murmured a wordless sob, slumping to the stool beside the bed. She finally spoke again, a lump in her throat making her voice crack and waver.

"I… I think she's still going to be infected. From what I've read, amputation hasn't worked in past cases. The Marines have tried different methods of… infection and curing. While the prisoners they rounded up were… well, you know what I mean."

Bill nodded softly. He'd seen the way the prisoners had been dealt with in London, and could only imagine the diabolical medical practices that had been carried out behind closed doors. Of course, the plague-infested wastelands would be the ideal place to run all manner of tests, and whichever military scientist or doctor that came up with it would be hailed as a hero, someone who could save thousands, maybe millions of lives. He didn't say anything else; he didn't feel like there was anything he *could* say.

"Does he blame me?" Bill finally managed. "I mean, for Pam being injured."

"He doesn't blame anyone but himself," muttered Angel while checking on the stitches on Bill's wounds. "He says he didn't react quick enough, couldn't protect her. He's convinced himself that it's his fault."

"I see," Bill murmured, watching as Angel looked over his wounds and prodded and poked his ailments. He hissed softly at the pain, though Angel didn't offer any sympathy. She unfastened some of the restraints to allow her to check the full extent of his injuries, and Bill felt like he could breathe easily.

"Broken ribs," she said, appraising the damage. "Deep lacerations, possible concussion. I'm surprised you could walk out of there, yet alone carry me."

Bill was silent, listening to the low hum of the overhead fluorescent tube. Angel continued to work in silence, until she finally gave up.

"Jesus, Bill, what the hell were you thinking?" she finally shouted, scowling at him.

"I guess I wasn't," Bill muttered, feeling like a child being scolded by his mother.

"You're damn right you weren't," she hissed. "Al knows what he's doing, God help us all, and he knew when it was time to pull out of there. What the fuck was going through your head?"

"I guess there were a hundred thoughts rushing through my head," Bill finally announced. "I was thinking about the best way to get in and out without picking up any injuries."

"That worked, didn't it?" she said, sarcastically.

"I was thinking that one of my friends was in trouble, and there was something I could do to save her. While others had given up, I was prepared to keep on fighting. I wasn't going to leave anyone lying in there if there was any chance they were still alive."

Angel shook her head in silence.

"You're an idiot. A reckless moron."

"Is looking our for my friend reckless?"

"Risking your life by running through a field of zombies before diving into a crumbling building to find someone who may or may not be alive is reckless. Blasting apart the wall to an already unstable building is reckless. Sitting in an open field while trying to take out the advancing walking corpses with random shots from a handgun is just plain dumb."

"You needed my help!"

"How did you even know I wasn't dead? What would have happened if you made your way in there and found me dead?"

"I knew you were still alive," muttered Bill.

"What?"

"I knew you were alive," Bill repeated. "I could feel it."

"You're crazy," Angel whispered, finishing her examination of him and stepping over to the doorway.

"A crazy-assed bastard," Bill muttered, nodding his head, "So I've been told. Three years ago, I lost someone who meant the world to me. I sat and watched as she died, and there was nothing I could do to help her or stop the suffering. And when she died, I felt part of me die with her. This time, it was different; someone I cared about was in trouble, and there *was* something I could do. I've already lost someone I loved in this plague: I wasn't about to lose another. I knew you hadn't died, because I didn't feel part of me had died with you…"

His voice tailed off, swallowing hard as he watched Angel while she stood by the door, her hand resting on the handle. She didn't look at him, kept her face covered by part of her hair that hung to one side.

"I love you," Bill said, his voice hushed. "I have done for a while, I've just been afraid to admit it."

"That's interesting to know," Angel said, her voice quivering as she spoke. "Maybe if you told me that when you fucked me instead of two days after; instead of going out your way to ignore, me, maybe things would have been different."

"I tried to tell you," Bill said, pleadingly.

"When was that, exactly? When you went to sleep in the drivers cabin instead of the living area with the rest of us? When you climbed on your motorcycle and rode off on some reckless journey into the middle of some god-unknown town without a second thought for the friends you were leaving behind?"

"No," Bill protested, "No, I…"

"That's right, it was when we were surrounded by armed soldiers in a run down castle. Too little, too late, Bill. I'm going to put this down to concussion. Get some rest, I might be back later."

With that, she left, slamming the door behind her.

It's not like this in the movies, Bill thought to himself in anguish, finding himself relying on films as his guide in life for the first time in years.

Al sat by the bed Pam lay on, anxiously playing with his handgun while listening to the heavy and laboured breathing of the patient on the bed. Time passed while he toyed with the weapon, though he had no way of knowing how long *had* passed.

"Did I do the right thing?" he finally said, loading the handgun and slipping it into his holster. "If I didn't take your hand off, would you still be like this? Would you be better off? Would you be suffering more or less?"

He looked at the stack of papers that he had brought out of Carter's stateroom; every report that had been filed and compiled on the plague had been passed on to all the senior officers in charge of the land based operations, and Carter has been no exception. Those that he had read indicated that there was no cure, no vaccination, and that a very low percentage of the population of the country had a natural immunity to some of the strain. Nowhere suggested that amputation was a viable option to halt infection. But then, they still thought it was airborne, what did they know?

"You're not gone yet, though," he whispered, feeling tears well up in the corners of his eyes and roll down his cheeks. "And you've got to hold on, just a few more days, I've got so many plans and so little time. And when the time comes, I'll be there to end it."

"How's she doing?"

The door to the room swung open and Angel stormed in, hurling down a wad of bandages on to the small steel table beside the bed. She reached out and took hold of Pam's damaged limb, unwinding the soiled cotton wadding and tending to the wound. Al looked at the stump and the folded and seared flesh that had been the product of his own butchery, nurtured carefully by Angel's own caring hands. The flesh was red and inflamed, and blood oozed freely from the injury, red in colour with a few traces of translucent pink liquid seeping from edge of the stitched wounds.

Normally, Al would have tried to hide his tears, especially from Angel, but he was beyond caring; the bickering and banter between the two suddenly seemed far from significant while Pam lay on the bed in a deep slumber.

"No change," he muttered. "Just like every other time you came in."

Angel didn't say anything else, just continued to clean and dress the wound.

"Is Bill all right?"

Angel grunted wordlessly.

"He's okay then," Al said, dabbing his eyes and wiping his face with his shirt.

Another wordless response.

"I thought you'd be happy to see he was okay."

"So did I," murmured Angel.

"What's he done now? He climbed back out the window, went running through the streets looking for another collapsing building to hide in?"

"He told me that he loved me."

"Crazy bastard," hissed Al, unable to fight the grim smile that crept across his lips. "He finally did it."

"You knew about this?"

"I knew he liked you. But then, so did everyone else. I'm guessing you did, too."

Angel remained silent while she finished off working on the bandage. Throwing the soiled dressings into a small plastic bin to the side of the room, she washed her hands and sighed to herself. "Maybe I did, I don't know."

"And I assume you feel the same way about him?"

"I… I'm not sure."

She walked to the doorway and pulled it open.

"Look, Angel."

She paused at the doorway, turning back to look at Al.

"I know I'm the last person you'd ever ask for any advice. Well, maybe the first for weapons advice, and being fucking awesome, but anything like relationships… well, you know what I mean. But if you're ever going to listen to any golden nuggets of advice I may throw your way, it's this."

Al leaned forwards and grabbed Pam's hand, locking his fingers between hers and squeezing softly. "Don't fuck around. You don't know how much time you may have together."

"I'll keep that in mind."

IV

Pam opened her eyes slowly, remembering the action that had taken place over the last couple of days. She had accepted the fact she had lost her hand, and that she may be infected – well, the fact she *was* infected. There was enough evidence to suggest she was infected, what with the watery puss seeping from her wound and the flaking eczema around her joints seeping the same fluid. Al didn't really talk about it, but he didn't have to: she knew it was weighing on his mind even more than it was on her own.

The trailer had stopped moving days ago, or at least what she thought was days ago: with no natural daylight, she only had her own natural body clock to go off, which wasn't very accurate. Al seemed to be visiting her less often, or maybe that was because she was spending more hours awake than asleep. He seemed to keep his distance when he did visit, as if he was preoccupied with something else.

Just his way of coping, she thought to herself. *We all have different ways of coping.*

Her hand ached, sometimes it felt numb, and occasionally the way she lay she could feel her fingernails digging into her thighs. This was, of course, impossible, because the hand in question had been incinerated when the old trailer had been burned. She'd read about it in the past, in the real-life magazines she used to buy to read on the bus on the way to university. Ghost limbs, still being able to feel them after they'd been removed. It had been curious to read about, and even more curious to experience it first hand, for lack of a better term.

It was certainly something to add to her book.

Clive had found a battered old laptop for her, and brought it up for her a day or so ago. She'd spent most of her time trying to finish her work as best she could, compiling everyone's stories while typing as best she could with one hand. She still found her aching stump poising itself above the keyboard while typing, and could feel her muscles and tendons twitch and contract, as if she were still trying to type with both hands. It was unusual, but something she would have to get used to.

At least, she would if she had the time to get used to it, which she didn't.

She reached over to pick up the laptop, then paused and decided not to. Just like everyone aboard, she had a story to tell, but she'd told her own, she'd finished it even before it ended. It was obvious how hers ended, and she'd never know how any others ended.

A gentle rap at the door broke her train of thought, and Sarah skipped into the room, carrying a bundle of white cloth and wearing a sheepish grin. Angel followed her, the same smile on her face. It occurred to Pam that they were both wearing similar dresses. It wasn't the fact they were wearing similar clothing that stood out the most, but the fact that she had never seen Angel in a dress.

"What's going on?" she asked, pushing herself upright and sitting up. She grimaced and hissed through clenched teeth as she forgot about her stump and pushed it into the bedding. Angel rushed forwards to support her, then motioned towards the bundle of clothing that Sarah carried.

"Al sent us up with them, told us to get you changed and ready."

"Ready?" Pam asked, intrigued at the statement. "Ready for what?"

"It's a 'prise," giggled Sarah as she pulled back the covers and started to unravel the bundle of clothing.

The simple task of putting on the white dress would normally have taken five minutes with an injured patient, but the aching limbs weeping puss meant that the trio had to work slowly and in unison in getting the clothing on without smearing it in the leaking body fluids. Angel wrapped as many joints as she could in bandages, in part to reduce the amount of watery blood that stained the dress, but also to add some support to her weakened body. Though she had used her arms do go through the motions of typing, she had remained in bed for days, and her legs were weak and shaking as she swung them over the edge of the bed.

"Don't get up yet," Angel said, producing a metal case and laying it on the bed. She flipped it open and produced a vial filled with a black liquid, then shook it and unscrewed the cap. "Close your eyes."

Pam did as she was told, and something brushed against her eyelashes, a distant feeling from a past life that she couldn't remember.

"Is that what I think it is?" Pam asked, smiling.

"Masala," said Sarah.

"Mascara," corrected Angel with a laugh. "We found some makeup amongst the belongings of one of the soldiers here. Either there had been a couple of female Marines here, or... well, Al said that there were some strange characters in the Marines, I guess he was right."

"Where is he?"

"Outside, waiting for you."

"Outside? What's going on?"

"Something Al's been working on for a while. Your driver's waiting outside."

"Driver?" Pam slowly pulled herself to her feet, grimacing as Angel gently draped her arm over her shoulder and guided her towards the door. The dress she had changed into dragged across the ground as she moved, and what she thought had been white was actually cream in colour, a gown covered in fine lace and mesh. The door opened, and she was startled to see Garth standing at the doorway, wearing an ill-fitting suit and a collapsible metal wheelchair standing in front of him. He smiled, tipping the EuroTruck cap he still wore, and reached out with one hand, guiding her to the wheelchair. She lowered herself into the seat, then sat back as Garth pushed her through the trailer, to a small elevator platform at the rearmost of the vehicle, then through the trailer to the exit. One thing she noticed was the vehicle was vacant; there was no sign of anyone as the four of them moved through the living quarters and made their way outside, down the lowered gangway on to the pavement below.

The vehicle had stopped in the middle of a small village, buildings on either side of them displaying the same scars and disfigurements as every other building she had ever passed. Smashed windows, fragmented doors, riddled with craters and bullet holes, splashed with blood that had dried a long time ago. One side of the street was a row of shops, each as looted as the next, while the other side of the street opened up on to a courtyard that had been the village's market place at one point. Wooden stalls had been overturned and smashed, with scraps of tarpaulin flying from the wooden skeletal frames like flags on a beached shipwreck.

At the end of one of the streets, a large church stood ominously, candlelight flickering behind the stained glass windows of the holy building. Garth wheeled the chair towards it at a leisurely pace, with Angel and Sarah following close behind them, exchanging hushed whispers and giggles between the two of them. Whatever was going on, whatever Al had arranged, Pam was going to find the answer in the church. She could pick up some words amidst the whispers behind her: ceremony was the one that seemed to be repeated the most.

A ceremony in a church, she thought to herself. Al's promise to be there at the end, the progression of the plague and the way it was taking its toll on her body. Did he plan to bring her demise about quickly, before it became too much for her – or Al – to take? A cold sweat prickled her forehead, and Angel quickly checked on her pulse and breathing, making sure she was okay.

The heavy wooden doors to the church swung open as they approached, opened from the inside by Sylvester as he graciously waved them on into the building. His attire had also changed, from the black jeans and grubby shirt he normally wore, to a pair of black trousers and a white dress shirt, with a black tie hanging loosely around his neck, exposing the unfastened top button of the shirt. He grinned and stepped aside, exposing the interior of the church.

The back half of the building was still in a state of disrepair, but the front of the church had been cleaned up: overturned pews had been set upright, the floor of the aisle swept clean, the altar set correctly and every candlestick that had been left in the church – possibly the village – had been set up and lit. Some balanced in brass and gold candlesticks, while others had been clumped together in mounds of melted wax. Flowers had been spread out along the aisle and side of the pews, Snowdrops and Bergenias with an overflowing display of Witch-hazel resting on the altar. Even in the deadlands of Britain, it was pleasing to see that the winter blooms were still obeying the laws of nature, even if the dead weren't.

On the far side of the church, Clive stood in the pulpit, his black coat removed and a freshly pressed black shirt taking place of the tee shirt he had worn, with his dog collar gleaming brightly in the candlelight. A lengthy purple sash had replaced his bandana, and he held his bible in both hands, clutching it to his chest.

Bill and Al stood before him, both wearing black trousers and jackets, standing patiently at the altar. Bill leaned against the pews while Al stood stoically in front of Clive; his feet positioned at shoulder width apart, hands behind his back and clasping one hand with another. Pam smiled to herself as Al didn't flinch when the doors were slammed shut, he stood strait at attention. You could take the man out the Marines, but you couldn't take the Marine out the man.

Garth proceeded to make his way down the aisle, and near the back of the church Sylvester activated a small music centre, the one working speaker playing a version of the wedding march. Pam's grin remained on her face as all the pieces of the puzzle instantly fell into place, and she felt a tear roll down her cheek. She wiped absentmindedly at her face, the brush of her finger against her skin bringing pain and discomfort. The journey up the aisle stopped, and Al finally looked down, a glassy look in his eyes.

"You look beautiful," he whispered. "I hope you don't mind, but I didn't think we had… that we had time to do it properly."

"I don't mind," she whispered, wiping at her eyes again and looking at her hand. The mascara had to be waterproof, her hand wasn't coming away black. In fact, they looked slightly pink.

"Angel and Sarah picked out the dress and arranged the flowers. Everyone else helped clean up the church."

"It's wonderful," she said, looking around and ignoring the pain that coursed through her neck. "I never… never would have guessed."

"Are we ready?" asked Clive, stepping down from the pulpit. Al looked at Clive, then Pam, waiting for her to respond. She nodded slowly, leaning back in her chair and waiting for Clive to begin.

"Dearly beloved," he began after clearing his throat, then stopped. "I'll not lie to you. It's been… well; it's been three years since I've had to do one of these. I'm a little rusty, and can't remember the words exactly, and I understand time is a factor. Just give me a chance.

"We are gathered here today, to join this man and this woman, in holy matrimony. They have come together, under extraordinary circumstances, and have found a unique bond of love and friendship between them, which they invite everyone here today to celebrate. I normally read a passage from the bible, which the couple normally choose. It normally relates to the strength of love, and how our Lord, Jesus Christ, preached to his followers. I think everyone here knows enough about love, what it means, and how it is to lose someone, without me having to go over it."

He calmly looked from side to side, focusing on each person in the church. "We all know what it feels like to lose someone we love. Do we have rings?"

"Here," Al murmured, pulling two rings out his pocket. The were two different sizes, and Pam could see that they were bullet casings, cut and filed down into thin bands of brass. He grinned as he spoke. "I thought I'd try my hand at metalwork instead of woodwork. I don't think it's too bad, all things considered. Nearly lost a thumb, though."

"Better than losing a hand," Pam said weakly with a grimace, trying to show as much good humour as she could while not giving away the fact she was in so much pain with each move she made. Al returned the comment with a grim smile.

"I'm sorry," he muttered, kneeling beside the wheelchair.

"It's not your fault," Pam said. Something she had repeated time and time again to him, though she knew he would never believe it. "Carry on, Clive."

The priest nodded, taking the rings from Al and laying them on the open page of his bible before making the sign of a cross over the top of them with his index finger.

"If you can repeat after me. I, Albert George Colebrook, take thee, Pamela Wingrove."

"I, Al, take thee, Pam," he said, glaring at Clive. "Nobody uses my full name: only Momma Colebrook does." Clive sighed to himself and nodded in resignation.

"To be my lawfully wedded wife."

"To be my lawfully wedded wife," Al said, picking up the smaller of the rings and rolling it between his forefinger and thumb. "To love, honour and obey, for richer, for poorer; in sickness and in health, until…"

He didn't say the rest of the words; they both knew how it ended. He shrugged his shoulders at the look of disbelief on Pam's face. "I've read some books, seen films. I know the general gist of things."

"And I, Pam, take thee, Al, to be my lawfully wedded husband. To have and hold, love and cherish, for richer and poorer, in sickness and in health, until… until…" Pam stammered in her speech, choking back on her words as she pushed onwards, adamant that she would finish the vows, or at least her version. "Until death us do part."

"Place the ring on her finger," Clive whispered. Al nodded and slid the brass ring up her finger. Skin flaked and peeled away as the metal rubbed against her flesh, oozing watery blood and causing a jolt of pain to burn its way up her arm. With teeth gritted and urging him to go on, the ring finally came to a stop near her knuckle, and Pam closed her fist, admiring the handiwork of Al. "It's beautiful," she said with a grin. While he had the pick of every jewellery shop between wherever she was and London, he had instead chosen to make the ring himself, which meant much more to her. Taking the other ring in her shaking hand, she gently placed it on Al's outstretched finger.

"I now pronounce you husband and wife," Clive finally said, closing his bible and smiling. "You may… uh… kiss the bride?"

Al smiled and shuffled forwards, his face inches from Pam's.

"I can't kiss you," Pam whispered, a tear rolling down her cheek. "I'll infect you."

"I can still kiss you," Al cooed, placing a kiss lightly on Pam's cheek. "Like this. C'mon, let's go outside."

Relieving Garth of his duties, Al took control of the wheelchair and spun it on the spot, pushing it back down the aisle, past the faces of the adoring crowd: the tear-streaked face of Angel, the stern face Sylvester tried to wear to hide his quivering lip, the beaming grin on Sarah's face, with Bill, Garth and Clive behind them.

"Where're you taking me?"

"Honeymoon," Al answered, simply. "Round the back of the church. We have to be quick."

Pulling the doors to the church open, Al wheeled the chair out the front door then quickly around the rear of the building, through the graveyard, to a small grassy clearing behind the church that overlooked flowing valleys filled with forests and babbling brooks, each tree and grassy field covered with a sprinkling of white powdered snow. After years of living underground in a concrete bunker or travelling through war-torn cities filled with the living dead, Pam had all but forgotten that places like this had ever existed. In the distance far to the west, the sun was beginning to set, washing the snowy valley before them in pale orange and pink.

"It's beautiful," she whispered, wrapping her hands around Al's has he crouched down beside her. "Where… where are we?"

"Some place in Wales," Al said, slowly and gently lifting Pam to her feet and helping her step closer to the stunning vista. With each step, she could feel the watery mix of blood and puss trickle down her legs as the skin around her knees and thighs cracked and tore. "I can't pronounce it's name, it's got lots of L's and Y's in it. I thought this was the next best thing to sunset on a tropical beach. It took me three attempts to find the perfect church for this. I wanted everything to be right: to be perfect."

"It is," said Pam, feeling herself sway and her legs begin to tremble. Without warning, they gave way and she dropped to her knees, coughing violently and spitting bloody phlegm on to the ground. Al dropped down, slipping a comforting arm around her shoulder and holding her close while her body shuddered, her dry retching tearing drying tissue away from her throat and making her vomit watery blood. "I'm sorry," she said, weeping as she tried to pull herself up from the ground while nursing her bandaged stump. "I didn't want to spoil it."

"You didn't spoil it," he said, tucking an arm under her shoulders, then another under her knees, hoisting her from the ground and cradling her in his arms. "You didn't spoil anything. It's not your fault."

"And this," Pam said, lifting her stump. "This isn't your fault, either. We've been on borrowed time for three years. You know as well as I, It's always been a matter of time."

Hours passed while Al stood at the back of the church, the newlyweds watching the sun sink below the horizon and the moon drift into view. Though the chill of the night was starting to sink in and each breath starting to condense in the cool air, Pam felt on fire, her body burning from the fever that was claiming her body. Maybe if she'd stayed in bed in the medical bay, she would have lasted a little longer, with drips and constant monitoring. But she and Al both knew that would only be delaying the inevitable, and she would rather see the valley and the open sky in her final hours instead of the four walls of a sick bay. And she knew that the final hours had almost ended.

"Still awake?" Al asked. In the time since picking her up, he hadn't wavered or shown any sign of tiring, and had held Pam close, afraid to let her go. She murmured a wordless response; it hurt too much to talk.

"You know that I love you," he said, matter-of-factly. "And that I'd do anything for you."

"Make… make sure you look after Sarah," she rasped, feeling blood gurgle in the back of her throat. She swallowed the noxious mix of phlegm and blood. "That's all I want you to do. Look after her and yourself."

"I will," promised Al. "I'll treat her like she's my own. Like she's *ours*."

"Make sure you tell her that. She's only going to have you, now."

"I will," Al said again, this time a tear rolling down his cheek and dripping on to her face. "No matter how many times I said it in the past, I never felt like I said 'I love you' enough."

"I know how much," Pam whispered with a smile. She could feel the fever dropping from her now, and felt an ethereal calmness wash over her, She knew that her demise was only a matter of minutes away. "And… you know… I love you, too."

She swallowed hard, taking on another load of watery blood, and twisted her face, feeling dried skin cracking and flaking as she did.

"I loved the wedding," she went on, fighting back the tears of pain as she tried to maintain her composure and hide the pain she was in. "And the honeymoon was wonderful."

"I hope the pictures come out good," Al said with a grin. "Paid the photographers a fortune."

"Can't wait to see them," she said. "I didn't get to ask if my ass looks big in this."

"Arse," corrected Al. "You Brits say arse."

"I married an American today," she said, trying to smile. This time, the pain was too much to bear, and she couldn't hide it. "That makes me an American citizen. So I can say ass."

"I love you so much, baby," Al murmured, gently running his fingers through her hair. "I don't want you to go, I don't want you to leave me."

"I have to go," Pam said, closing her eyes. "Tired. Cold. Take... care of... me."

"You know I will," Al said, choking back his tears and sinking to his knees, propping Pam and himself up against the wall of the building. "And you know I'll always love you. Always."

"I know," Pam said, opening her eyes once more to look at her husband. "I... love... you."

She closed her eyes again, smiled softly to herself, and went to sleep.

The night finally succumbed to the day, and Al watched as the sun rose around the front of the church, casting long shadows across the valley that stretched out before him. He still cradled his wife in his hands, rocking back and forth as he watched a flock of birds explode from the forest, rising into the sky with an inaudible flutter of wings and feathers. They streaked overhead, a shower of grey and black feathers falling down on him as he brushed hair from Pam's face.

"Wish you could've seen the sunrise with me," he muttered to the body. "It's beautiful. Just like you."

He sat for another hour, holding the body close to him while the long shadows shrank from the rising sun, sitting patiently, waiting for the inevitable to happen. It was taking longer than he thought it would, but he knew that it *would* happen, regardless of how strong he knew Pam had been.

Had been.

It seemed strange to think of her in the past tense, especially while he still held her in his arms. He held his hand up and stroked the ring he wore, not marvelling at his craftsmanship but the significance behind the ring. He was married.

Was, he chided himself, *I still am*. Just because one of the pair had passed on, that didn't mean they were no longer married. He would always remember her, and she would always be with him. The ring was only a physical memento of the relationship and marriage.

With shaking hands, Al reached out and pulled the ring from Pam's finger as gently as he possibly could, flaying pieces of skin from her as he did so. He threaded the ring through the chain from his old dog tags and slipped it over his neck, rubbing the trimmed down bullet casing with one hand and stroking Pam's hair with another.

As he sat, lost in his thoughts, one of Pam's fingers twitched. He didn't notice at first, but then when she balled one hand into a loose fist, Al paid attention.

He was trained to take notice.

"Fight it," Al whispered. "C'mon, honey, you can do it. Fight it, don't let those fuckers take you!"

The loose fist tightened, and her eyes flickered open, as bright and vigilant as Pam's had ever been. Was it possible she had only been sleeping, and was waking up? Maybe the infection hadn't spread as they had originally thought. Was it possible that the amputation had worked?

"Pam?" Al asked, hopeful she was okay. He knew that she was strong, was it possible that she had managed to pull through the infection? Maybe the amputation, as hasty and slapdash as it had been, had been the right course of action. "Pam, baby, are you all right? It's me, baby, it's Al. Fight it for me, you fight it, I know you're going to be okay."

A moment or recognition flashed through her eyes, and for with a fleeting second, Al felt his spirits soar as he thought she had pulled through. The recognition quickly changed to a vacant and blank gaze, then flashed with a glimmer of animal ferocity. She sat bolt upright, the stale air that lingered in her lungs rushing out with a putrid gurgle, and Al knew straight away what he had to do.

His hand wrapped around the hilt of the blade he carried, and he whipped his arm around behind the skull of the undead woman, pushing the blade into the base of her skull with a crunch, then jerking the blade up and grinding it around from side to side, slicing up the brain inside the skull. He found it more personal to do it this way; he wouldn't have felt right simply shooting her in the head.

The Rot – that's what she was now, just a Rot, an empty shell – slumped silently to one side, rolling on to her back and twitching spasmodically. Al looked at the blade he held, dropped it, then cradled her head in his hands and silently wept, rocking back and forth.

He reached into his jacket, pulling a pair of incendiary grenades clinking the pair together in a mock toast.

"To my wife," he murmured, pulling out the pins and flicking loose the release handles. He felt the springs give with a gentle click, and smiled softly to himself. "To us."

XXV
SHORES OF HELL

"The containment solution is simple: bomb the ports, destroy the tunnels and bridges: allow the plague to live its course unhindered by our futile attempts to curtail it."

I

Bill stood in the doorway to the main living area of the trailer, working his way through a packet of freeze-dried fruit cubes while he watched the church in the distance. It was coming up to midday now, and there still wasn't any sign of Al coming our from behind the church. Though he wanted to go and check on him, he knew that it would be better if he just stayed where he was.

"How long's it been now?"

Angel appeared beside him, carrying her own selection of freeze-dried food in its shiny silver wrapper. Bill shrugged, fishing through his bag of food and flicking out the yellowed chunks; he didn't like them because they tasted like plastic bananas. The red pieces of food tasted like plastic strawberries, but he could live with that. He finally shrugged.

"Maybe twelve hours, give or take. He's been around back since the ceremony ended; he's not tuned in to any frequency or channel, but it doesn't feel right going back there. It's not like we've got anything better to do, right?"

Angel shook her head slowly. "No, you're right."

"Finally talking to me?"

"Looks that way," she said, crumpling up the wrapper to her plastic orange-tasting bar and shoving it into her pocket. "Look, I know you meant well…"

"All reckless idiots do," said Bill. "Just… forget it."

"But I…"

The words died in Angel's mouth as an explosion blossomed to life behind the church, thick black plumes of smoke billowing up from behind the building as a pair of incendiary grenades burst into flames.

"Jesus, Al!"

Bill dropped his packet of food and leaped down from the trailer, taking five running steps towards the church, then shuddering to a halt and casting an unsure glance over his shoulder: what should he do? Even if he ran around to the back of the building, what could he do without any fire-fighting cquipment?

Did they even have anything they could use onboard?

"Sarah!"

Angel was knocked aside as the young girl tore out the trailer, dashing across the opening and heading straight for the church. Bill dropped to his knees and wrapped his arms around her as she rushed by, almost tackling her as his weight and strength instantly overpowered her.

"I've got to see Al," she insisted, pummelling Bill with clenched fists as she struggled in his grip. Although each of the girl's blows were feeble in comparison to the punishment he had taken in the past, each knock seemed to land directly on one of his major wounds: a bruise or a suspected broken bone. "I gotta see, I gotta see."

"He's okay," Bill muttered soothingly, wrapping his arms tighter around the girl to stop her struggling. "It's okay, he'll be all right."

"I need to see," she whimpered, breaking down into muffled sobs as she stopped fighting and relaxed. "I need to see…"

"Relax, sweetie," Angel cooed as she stepped closer, kneeling on the ground and gently stroking Sarah's head, smoothing her hair. "Al's not stupid, he'll be okay."

"But if Pam's dead, he… when my mommy died, my dad…"

"Al's not like that," Angel said, still stroking Sarah's hair.

"Not like what?" asked a familiar voice. Normally a deep, booming and commanding voice, this time it was soft and quiet.

The doors to the church were open now, and the flames were working their way through the building. Bill looked up and could see the fury of the orange and yellow fire as it ripped through the sacred building, the stained glass cracking and falling away from the windowpane, the upturned pews fuelling the conflagration as it spread through the structure. The doors were wide open, and an ominous figure stood in the doorway, arms stretched between each door. Even with his atheistic outlook on life, the sacrilegious appearance was not lost on Bill. Peering around the figure, he could see an inert form laid out on the altar, slowly being consumed by the inferno.

"It's done," he announced, stepping away from burning building and clasping his hands. Sarah broke free from Bill's grasp and stumbled forwards, tears streaming from her face and latching on to Al's leg as he strolled forwards. "C'mon, kid, give me some space."

"I wanna be with you," Sarah complained, clinging tightly to Al and wrapping her hands around his belt. "Don't wanna leave you."

"I want some space," Al growled, pushing Sarah away from him as he stormed towards the trailer. "Leave me alone."

Sarah took two stumbling steps away from Al, her face swollen and puffy from the crying, and fresh tears pooled at her eyes as she watched the ex-soldier remove his suit jacket and toss it on the floor, trudging wearily towards the opened trailer. Bill snagged his arm as he tried to push through him and Angel, forcing him to turn and face him.

"She wants to spend time with you to make sure you're all right," Bill said in a hushed voice.

"I'm all right," Al glowered.

"Be that as it may, she wants to make sure you don't do anything stupid."

"Stupid?"

"All she knows is she thought her father was okay until he went outside and blew the back of his head off."

"Jesus," shouted Al, pushing Bill back away from him. "I'm not her fucking father!"

Al's gaze drifted from Bill to Sarah, her lower lip trembling and quivering, eyes glazing over as she stared accusingly at him and balled her fists. His shoulders sagging, Al dropped to his knees and motioned to her to come towards him. Reluctantly, she slowly stumbled towards his outstretched hands, her eyes overflowing and spilling over her rosy cheeks.

"That's not what I meant," he whispered. "You know that's not what I meant. It's you and me now, honey. You and me."

Wrapping his arms around the young girl and rising to his feet, he turned back towards the trailer, rocking Sarah gently from side to side as he moved. He stopped as he reached the doorway and turned to look over his shoulder, looking directly at Angel while he stroked the back of Sarah's head.

"You sorted that shit out yet, or are you still fuckin' around?"

Angel responded with a slight shrug of her shoulders.

"I told you, Angel; don't fuck around, don't waste any time. I'm going to our... my room."

With that, he stepped into the trailer and vanished into the darkness of the interior.

"What was that about?" Bill asked, surprised not only at the fact Al had offered Angel some actual advice, but the fact he hadn't called her bitch. She looked sheepishly at her feet, kicking at the ground absentmindedly, then strolled across the street and took a seat on the bottom step of the trailer. She motioned for Bill to follow, and he cautiously did as he was told: was he going to get another lecture about how stupid it had been to go back in the building in London?

"Listen," he said, sinking to the step beside her. "I just... I just want to forget the whole thing. Forget it ever happened. I'm sorry."

"Shut up and listen. Have you ever been to a wedding before?" asked Angel. Bill tried to cast his mind back to his life before the plague, where weddings were more of a frequent happening. The last one he had been to had been his old friend, Brian, from where he worked. He slowly nodded, though his memories of the day were a blur. Brian had insisted on an open bar at the reception, and Bill had never been able to turn down a reasonably priced drink.

"There's a lot of traditions that are normally followed, you know that?"

"Some of them. Bride's father pays for the wedding; something old, something new, all that crap, right?"

Angel nodded. "There's also this one."

She leaned in closer to him, close enough for Bill to smell the bottle of perfume her and Sarah had scavenged while looking for clothing. An intoxicating smell: overpowering and alien after years of the earthy smell of the underground or the cloying odour of rotting meat in the cities. She closed in on him, her eyes fluttering shut, and their lips touched. Another electrifying sensation coursed through Bill as the pair kissed, stronger than their last, and he gently reached out to place his hand on the side of her head, holding her there in case she decided to break away.

Their first kiss had been out of lust, an animal instinct to seek solace and comfort in the company of someone else; now there was passion behind the kiss, a love the two felt for one another, but had never been able to fully vocalise.

Angel finally broke away from the kiss, but didn't pull back, instead resting her forehead on Bill's and smiling. Bill tried to focus on one part of her face, but the closeness of her made it too hard for him to make out any details.

"The chief bridesmaid and best man always get together," she grinned. "I guess this means I like you…"

"I like tradition," Bill smiled back, taking her hand in his. "They're there for a reason."

"Promise me one thing, though. Don't be a reckless idiot any more."

"I can't make any promises," laughed Bill. "But I'll try."

"C'mon," Angel said, rising to her feet and heading back into the trailer, leading Bill by his hand. Bill couldn't fight the smirk that crept across his face as he obediently followed.

Bill stepped out the medical room that he had claimed as his own and slowly closed the door, moving as silent as he could so as not to wake Angel while she slept. The room itself wasn't much, barely big enough to be classed as a box room, but it had enough space for three medical gurneys: one which acted as a table and held a collection of weapons, ammunition and equipment, and another two positioned and fixed together to act as a double bed. The gurneys themselves were adjustable in height, which Bill had only found out after throwing his weight down on to one that hadn't been set up correctly. After bruising his tailbone and his ego, he made sure that everything was one hundred percent sturdy before committing any part of his anatomy.

It had been two days since Al had set fire to the church, cremating the body of Pam and making sure no rogue gang or pack of Rots would come along and defile her body or the holy sanctuary that had been prepared for the wedding. Although he had expected him to protest and put up a show of disagreeing with Al's methods, Clive had been strangely quiet when it came to the destruction of the church. Bill peered out one of the reinforced portals that overlooked the smouldering ruins of the building outside and shook his head slowly. Though he spent most of his time in the old stateroom that Carter had used as his base of operations, Al would often take a break from whatever he was doing to stand on the edges of the ruined structure, watching the blackened debris for anything up to an hour as the wind toyed with the ashes and scattered them softly. He was out there at that moment, his nine-year old shadow beside him as always, her hand wrapped around two of Al's oversized fingers.

Though the break in the constant travelling and fighting was nice, Bill couldn't help start to feel trapped and restless. Sylvester had dismantled the quad and motorbike that had been stored in the rear trailer, or at least stripped the engines, and it had been just as well: any working vehicles would only be a temptation to him to go on another solo journey to a nearby infested city.

Or would it? Before he had nothing much going for him in the stake of a future, but now, he had Angel. He finally had her. Much as either of them hated to admit it, Al had been right; there had been a spark between the pair, right from the beginning, though nothing had been openly admitted, purely because it had been a very confusing time for everyone involved. Their first time together had been nothing but sex, but now, they *made love.*

"What're you so happy about?"

Bill found himself at the foot of the staircase, in the main living area. Almost one and a half times the size of the previous trailer, there was a lot more room to move around in, and a lot more spaces to sit and relax. There was also a lot less people. Clive sat at the large plastic dinning table on his own, his bible open while he lazily flicked through the pages. He seemed distracted and wasn't really reading the book, and seemed pleased to see Bill.

"Just thinking," Bill said, shaking his head. "Nothing important."

"Can I have a moment of your time?" the preacher asked, indicating to one of the empty seats. "Please?"

Bill shrugged his shoulders and stepped forwards, pulling out one of the chairs and carefully sliding himself on to the frame. He winced in pain as his aching coccyx ungraciously accepted his weight on the plastic structure.

"Can I ask you a question?"

"You just did," Bill grinned. He seemed to be taking Al's place as the smartarse in the group while he mourned the loss of his loved one; a role-reversal to when the two had first met. "You want to ask me another?"

"You don't have any… religious beliefs, do you?"

"No," Bill agreed, shaking his head and suppressing he laughter.

"In fact, you're very much an atheist, aren't you?"

"I guess," Bill said, squirming uncomfortably in his seat, and it wasn't just the bruised tailbone that made him do that. Bill had never been at home discussing religion with anyone; he'd been in trouble in some of his schools because of his attitude, fallen out with friends, and offended strangers with his outlook. Talking about it with a priest wasn't his idea of a good time, but he gave Clive the benefit of the doubt: he looked troubled, maybe having a heathen to distract him for a few minutes would keep his mind occupied.

"How do you do what you do? How do you live your life without the teachings of any religion to guide you?"

"I guess I've been brought up well," Bill shrugged. "Despite having no parents, no real parents, I mean. Just because I don't follow any religion, doesn't mean I'm a violent sociopath."

"How many people have you killed?"

"Ask Al," Bill snapped, not missing a beat. "He keeps track of everyone's kill count. I'm sure you're not in single digits yourself, now. Times change, people change. Three, four years ago I would never have dreamed of killing another human. Now…"

"Now it's like second nature?" offered Clive. "Do you ever think about the men and women you've killed? Ever remember them?"

"I try not to, it makes sleeping at night easier."

"What about your first? Do you remember the first person you killed?"

"Miller," Bill said, nodding. "Jason Miller. Marine. Infected, but not turned. He only had a rifle, he couldn't use it on himself, and I had to do it for him. I added his tag to Al's collection, but I don't know if he's still got them now. Your first kill was Mikey, wasn't it?"

"No. December nineteenth, twenty thirty-nine, eleven fifteen at night. I killed someone while driving home from the church. It was dark, and I'd had a drink. Not enough to take me over the limit, but enough to inhibit my reactions. He ran out into the road, I didn't react in time. Darren Brewers was only twenty, had his whole life in front of him, and because I over-indulged in the festive spirit, I killed him. His family didn't have a very good Christmas that year. Nor any year afterwards, I'll wager. I was cleared of manslaughter, but given community service. I went to teach the word of

God in the prison, which is where I met Sylvester."

"Who saved you, then you saved him, and now you're here. It may sound fucked up, Clive, but it sounds a lot like destiny, like everything was pre-ordained."

"You're saying God wanted me to kill that young man to get me here today?"

"You said it yourself, I'm an atheist, and I didn't say God made you do anything. If fate hadn't taken my parents from me, who's to say *I'd* even be here now? I would've had a normal life, one school, no moving from foster home to foster home. But I don't think any God killed my parents just to get me here, I mean Jesus, what kind of fucked up deity would do that? Fate, destiny, dumb luck; call it what you will. I don't think God put us in this position, I think we put ourselves in this position."

"Bill," Clive said, closing his book and leaning forwards, pressing his fingers to his temples as he spoke. "Bill, I'm inclined to agree with you. I think… I think I've lost my faith."

"You have?" Bill asked, unable to hide his surprise.

"A long time ago, a child in my parish asked me 'what is God?' It wasn't a question I'd ever been asked before. People always asked *who* God was, and I knew this, and I tried to pass that off as an answer to the youngster; the creator of all life on the planet, the holy father of our Lord Jesus. This didn't satisfy the curiosity of the youngster, he pressed me again with the question, each week for a month. I continued to think this through all my spare time."

"Didn't have much of a social life, did you?"

"Vow of celibacy," Clive reminded him. "Don't really have much interest in grooming myself and attracting the attention of women. In my spare time I read books, think through the great theological quandaries that mankind has come across. I didn't own a television or radio, I found more stimulating ways to entertain myself. I finally worked out the answer to the question.

"God is love."

"And the kid accepted that?"

"It took weeks of bible study and reading texts on the subject, but I finally found it. He loves each and everything he creates, from the smallest insect to the largest tree. Children are very inquisitive. They ask questions no one else would think. They also seem to understand more than an adult; their minds are more open, while an adult's is closed. And it's this thinking that's making me think again about God and his existence."

"I don't follow you," Bill admitted, sitting back in his seat. Again, a shooting pain from his tailbone made him grimace in pain.

"I don't expect a closed-minded person to be able to follow me. The Lord is good, and always triumphs over evil, so by that thinking, love will conquer all."

"But it doesn't, does it? I'm sure your parents loved you. You and… what was her name, Penny?

"Jenny," Bill corrected.

"Yes, I'm sure you both loved one another. Sly loved Terri, Steve loved his family, Cindy loved Steve, Sarah loved her parents, Al loved Pam: an awful lot of love in the world, yet they have all suffered insurmountable loss. Where was God's shining love then? Millions have died, or worse. There's no loving omnipotent being at work here, no one guiding our actions or leading us to safety. If there is a God, why would he forsake his children?"

"Sometimes children have to be left to fend for themselves," Bill offered, feeling he had to justify Clive's beliefs to convince him. "We can't always be lead by our hand by a god."

"There is no god," glowered Clive. "Only man. Man created god, not the other way around. We are in this alone, and have been since the beginning. The more I have thought about this, the easier I find it to kill people. I can feel my grip on my humanity slipping with each time I fire a weapon, each passing second in a gunfight. Each life I extinguish. And I have taken many."

"*You've* been taking count?" Bill asked, incredulously. Clive nodded.

"Before my revelation, I counted to remember how many souls to pray for at night. I didn't know their names, so I kept a tally, a memento, a reminder for each life I took. This headband," he said, indicating the red leather band that was tied around his head. "This was worn by Darren the night I killed him. The coat from Mikey is another reminder. And the rest of them…"

He rolled up the bottom of his shirt and displayed a number of neat incisions around his waist, each made with razor sharp combat blade. None of them seemed to be older than a week.

"Each cut is kill. I made them to remember. Now I can't forget."

"You're fucked in the head," Bill hissed, standing up and backing away towards the door leading out the living area. "What's wrong with you, man?"

"I wish I knew," Clive whispered, looking glumly at the book before him. "I used to find comfort and answers in this. Now, it just seems like lies."

Bill stumbled down the passage and out the open door, half-falling down the steps on to the ground outside. The cracked pavement was slick with frost, and he had to keep his arms outstretched to keep his balance. Garth and Sylvester sat huddled around a metal bin filled with burning wood by the opening of the trailer, a collection of engine parts spread around the upturned crates they sat on.

"You okay?" Sylvester asked, looking up from the handful of washers and sockets he held, his face streaked with grease and oil. He wiped his face with the back of his arm and smeared the dirt further over his cheek. "You look a little freaked out."

"Your friend's the one who's freaked out," Bill said, tipping his head towards the opened trailer. "He's lost it, the crazy fucking psycho."

"What's he doing?" he asked, jostling the handful of washers and sockets he held before scattering them on to the flat surface in front of him.

"Says he's lost his faith, doesn't' believe in god, he's keeping a tally of the people he's killed by cutting himself. He's fucking cracked, you need to get in there and have a word with him."

"Why me?"

"He's your friend, not mine. I don't hang around with crazy members of the God Squad. In fact, I normally kill them."

"I'll have a word with him," Sylvester said, rising from the crate he sat on and heading into the trailer. Bill nodded and slid on to the vacant seat, nodding towards the two figures staring into the pile of debris.

"How long has he been out there?"

"Close to two hours, now," Garth answered, dropping his tools and grabbing a battered hipflask, taking a pull on the alcoholic liquid and smacking his lips. He offered it to Bill, though he refused. "Almost twice as long as normal."

"Have you spoken to him?"

"No," Garth snorted. "No one has. Just let him get on with it."

"This is stupid," snarled Bill, leaping to his feet and storming over to Al. "We can't hang around here for the rest of our lives, we need to have a plan, get moving. Get packed up, we're going to get a move on."

Garth reluctantly did as he was told, gathering the tools and throwing them into the metal chest that sat at his feet before retreating into the trailer. Bill watched as he vanished into the darkness inside, then stepped on to the blackened ground that had once been the doors to the church. He reached out and placed a comforting hand on Sarah's shoulder, then did the same to Al. While the young girl accepted it, Al shrugged it off with a grunt.

"Al."

He didn't respond.

"Al," Bill repeated, grabbing his shoulder again and spinning him around. "Al, we're going."

Al glared at Bill, almost looking through him with a distant look in his eyes, then slowly nodded. "Sarah, honey, go inside and wait for me, I won't be long."

"Okay," she said softly, trudging towards the trailer.

"And keep away from Clive," Bill called back over his shoulder.

"He still acting fucked up?" Al asked, watching as Sarah disappeared into the trailer. Bill nodded slowly. "I still notice these things, kid. He's crazy, but I don't think he's going to do anything to anyone else; he's too busy wrestling with his own inner demons, as it were."

With that, he turned back to stare at the charred rubble, in particular where the altar had once stood.

"Al, did you hear me? We're going."

"Who died and put you in charge?" asked Al, eyes fixed on the ruins.

"You did," Bill said, repeating himself and feeling like he was going around in circles. "Or at least part of you did. We can't sit around here for the rest of our lives waiting for Rots or a gang to stroll into town; we need to move on. There's nothing here for us."

Al grunted.

"Al?"

"I heard you," Al snarled, but continued in a softer tone. "I heard you. I know you're right. We move. Do you know this is all our fault?"

Bill didn't say anything. Was he talking about the infection and demise of Pam or the destruction of the church? He couldn't tell what he was referring to, but he didn't need to ask him to explain himself, he was willing to give up that information himself.

"The plague. It's our fault. I found documents in Carter's room, hundreds of them, paper files, computer files filled with the details. Man made the plague with the intention of using it on another man. It was the next step in biological warfare, some fucking genius had an idea to make something that would spread like wildfire through the jungle, infecting different animals and working its way up the food chain until it wiped out all the Bebops in Brazil. Jungle bases, shantytowns filled with resistance, all of them, infected in minutes and cleared of enemy activity within days. They didn't mean to bring the dead back to life, that just… happened. They fucked up, and it killed an entire nation."

"What?"

"It all makes sense, why else would they send in the Brass? Jesus, the Brass would ordinarily do as little work as possible, bunch of slackers that they are. It was a simple plan: sweep through bases and forts, gather all the incriminating evidence and destroy it, along with every undead corpse and "rebel" scum they come across. Wipe out the threat and the proof; move back in to the cities already built, repopulate the island, the Marines are the heroes, everyone's happy."

"If they were supposed to destroy all this," Bill said, taking the small folded pieces of paper Al produced from one of his pockets and reading through the fading type, "Why'd Carter have a room filled with this shit?"

"Because he's Brass, and they're all the fucking same; he was planning to blackmail the Marines once the place was cleansed. He could get about anything he wanted with all this evidence. Dirty double-crossing bastard."

"You're sure about this?"

"Between organising a wedding and a funeral, I've had some time to read through this. I asked Spanners to have a look; he came to the same conclusion."

"So it was the Marines?"

"Like I said, they made the first part of the plague, the fever, weeping of joints, dehydration, tearing of skin. A nasty mix of whatever they could get their hands on. Fuck knows where the second part came in, the resurrection part and the whole flesh-eating zombie business. Clive would say it was just an act of God."

"Not at the moment he wouldn't," Bill murmured to himself before confirming the plan of action. "So we move. Where to?"

"We need somewhere safe. Secure. Somewhere Sarah can be safe, where you and Angel can screw each other's brains out. Somewhere to settle."

"And where's that? Edgly must be quiet this time of year, we could go back there."

"I'm sick of this god-damn island," he growled, pulling open one of the pouches on his webbing and producing a crumpled packet of cigarettes. He placed one to his lips and snapped his lighter open, igniting the flame with a click of his fingers. He stared into the flickering flame for a few seconds as it wavered near the tip of the cigarette, then shook the lid to the Zippo shut and spat the cigarette on to the ground, crumpling the packet into a ball and shoving it deep into his pockets. "I'm sick of this island, sick of living on the road, pissed off with the Rots and I've had it to my back teeth with the fucking Marines."

"Where'll we go?"

"West. I'm going home."

II

"America?" Angel asked incredulously.

"Fuckin' A," hissed Al, leaning back in his chair and scratching his smooth head, a smile creeping across his lips. "It's been too long, and I miss Momma Colebrook's apple pie and creamed potatoes. Plus we got a lot of years to catch up on."

"I don't want to go," Garth murmured, looking at the map spread out on the before him, and the proposed route that had been laid out in red marker. "I... I need to get to Spain."

"Spain? The hell for?"

"Anna, right?" Angel asked. Garth gave a gentle nod. "Your daughter, you want to go see her."

"I *need* to see her, to make sure she's okay."

"She will be," Al cooed. "You can't go to see her, though. The European coastlines will be too well guarded to even attempt setting foot on continental sands. Damn bastard Marines'll be crawling up and down the beaches like crabs on a cheap hooker. Probably instructed to shoot on sight, too. "

"It's all irrelevant, anyway," Sylvester said with a half-hearted laugh. "Am I the only person who's remembered that we're trapped on this damn island with no boats, planes, trains, tunnels: nothing to get off shore? Ports have been bombed, airplane hangers destroyed, tunnels caved in. We're trapped, so you can think about moving over to the States or Spain all you want, but unless anyone's found a plane lying around, and unless anyone can fly it, then we're pretty much screwed. Am I right?"

"Carter had a gunship," Al went on, throwing a pile of rolled up papers on to the table that the group had gathered around. "A stealth gunship, a specialised military attack helicopter that's the next model up from the Cavalier. The Silent Thunderstorm is undetectable by radar, it could easily slip through the net monitored by the guard towers and patrol boats."

"So you're suggesting we go back *into* London and fix up the helicopter you destroyed?"

"No, if those documents on the table there are right, then there's more than one in the country."

"Explain," Bill said, reaching out and grabbing the pile of papers before starting to leaf through them.

"The Brass," hissed Al through clenched teeth. "They're all the same, all low-life bastards. You know about the blackmail scam he was trying to pull? Turns out the bastard had another major that was in on it. Major Leonard Preston, his partner in crime, also had a stealth helicopter shipped in to him just as he was being stationed on the mainland. They were already plotting and scheming on doing this, months before they even got the orders that they were going to be stationed on the mainland. Carter's journal details some conversations with Preston, they even made a couple of meetings during the past year, conducted in the dead of night where stealth helicopters are invisible to radar *and* the naked eye."

Al retrieved the papers from Bill and shuffled through them before placing a collection of five photographs out on the desk.

"Preston was stationed on the western-most point of Wales hours before Carter received his final communication, which according to his records was just around summer, months ago. Rots overran his position, tore through his platoon and killed them all. And because they were wiped out by mindless animals…"

"The helicopter should be untouched. Brilliant."

"Out-fucking-standing," Sarah muttered, holding a stuffed toy in her hands and kicking her legs back and forth. Al smiled slightly to himself and gently placed a reassuring hand on her shoulder, then leaned over so his mouth was inches from the side of her head. He whispered something in her ear, quiet enough so only she could hear, and she nodded slowly, getting up away from the table and retreating to one of the bunks before pulling the curtain shut.

"Bedtime," he muttered by way of explanation.

"She's picked that up from you," Angel said with a grin.

"Christ knows what Bill's picked up from you," he snapped back, trying to get things back to the way they used to be. A smile flickered across Angel's lips and Al nodded slightly, catching sight of an empty chair that would have normally been where Pam had sat as he dipped his head.

"So, where's the major keep his limo, and who can hotwire it?"

"Theoretically, I can pilot it," Al said, leafing through the paperwork and unfolding a fragment of an ordinance survey map of a heavily wooded area.

"If you can theoretically fly it," Garth asked, rubbing at his jaw as he often did when he was nervous, "Doesn't that mean that you can just as easily and theoretically crash it?"

"Relax, buddy, I've had some lessons, took some training."

"If that's the case, why weren't you a helicopter pilot, how come you're one of the 'grunts' as you call them?"

"I flunked out the tests. Intentionally, of course: you know what happens to Marines once they become pilots? They become lieutenants." Al could feel the words choke in his throat as he spoke. "A fucking officer, man. No way I was going down that road. I'd rather spend the rest of my life as a non-com slogging my guts out than kicking back in the Brass's ready room. I joined to serve and protect."

"Isn't that the police force's motto?"

"Police enforce the law of a town or city. The Marine's jurisdiction is the world."

"Oo-rah," Sylvester said, half-heartedly raising a fist. Al shot him a withering look.

"Okay, fine" Bill said, looking over the map. "You think you can fly the helicopter. Is it able to even *reach* America, and if so, then where is it?"

"The bird won't have anywhere near enough fuel to get us home: it's a seven or eight hour flight in a passenger plane, we'd never manage that. We'd have to commandeer one of the patrolling gunboats in the surrounding waters. Flying in low with our stealth capability, they wouldn't know what hit them until it was too late. We strafe the deck, touch down, trade in our rotor blades for a set of propellers and rudders and take off. Hit somewhere relatively deserted and move on up from there."

"You make it sound so easy," said Angel, sidling up next to Bill and leaning her head against his shoulder while the two of them studied the map. "What's the catch?"

"Catch?"

"We know you too well," Sylvester agreed. "There's always a catch."

"Okay, the major and his men were held out here," Al conceded, tapping a location on the map with his forefinger. "This cliff here overlooks the Irish sea. It's pretty high, surrounded by water on two sides; it's a shear rock face here and here, with a path leading up through a forest here. It's the perfect place to mount a defensive from."

"Not that perfect, eh?"

"Yeah. Neither was ours. We all make mistakes, and we all have to live with the consequences. Now, the real kick in the balls in this case is the fact that there isn't any road leading up to the top of the cliff, the trees are too dense. We'd have to park up in the little village at the foot of the hill here, leave the trailer and walk up through the woods. We need all the manpower and support we have, so we can't leave Sarah behind without leaving someone else behind to look after her. So she's coming with us."

"The place could be crawling with Rots…"

"The place *will be* crawling with Rots. Britain is crawling with Rots. Except for the… I don't know, four and a half, maybe five thousand things that we've killed."

"That seems like a hell of a lot," Bill said as he looked up from the map and nodded towards Clive. "See, I told you he counted." Clive simply nodded, not offering anything to the conversation.

"It's not as high as you think, bearing in mind the millions of people who used to live here. It's just a fraction of the population. So, what does everyone think?"

"Hijack a military helicopter, attack a gunboat then hijack *that* before cruising over to America? I gotta admit," Bill said, leaning back from the table and squeezing Angel's hand while smiling. "It's a crazy and reckless plan, and I promised someone not so long ago that I wouldn't do anything crazy or reckless ever again. But unless anyone else can think of a way for us to pass the time away?"

"I'm in," Angel said. "Anything to get off this island."

"Seems like a sane plan, or at least as sane as I'd expect from you. Who's going to look out for Sarah?" Sylvester asked.

"I'll take her," Al said. "She can ride on my back. We trained with equipment loads in excess of one hundred pounds; I can't see her being any heavier than that. What about you, buddy?"

"I guess I don't have any say in the matter, do I? Majority rules…"

"Once we get to America, we'll get a fake identity and passport set up for you and you can fly out to Spain from there. It's a lot less conspicuous then floating up on the Spanish shoreline, and I'm sure you'd like to see your daughter with a clean haircut and expensive suit, not a tatty old shirt and trousers smeared with blood and shit, stinking of stale smoke and whiskey."

"Why should I appear any different to the last time she saw me?" Garth said with a grin. "Yeah, I'm in. What about you, Clive? God on our side with this one?"

Clive grunted a wordless response.

"I'll take that as a maybe," Al said with a shake of his head. "Okay, it's been a while, but we're back in action. Take a look through the weapons trailer, see what we've got and what you want to use. It's an assault on a nest of Rots, so go crazy. Buddy, you come with me into the cabin, we'll get this thing rolling, we're about half a day away, so we'll probably get there come dusk. We rest up for the night and begin the assault at dawn. Get some rest, people, we've got a big day ahead of us."

Bill lay in the bed beside Angel, one arm draped over her waist and stroking the smooth skin of her stomach while he nuzzled up closer to her, pulling the sheets and blankets tighter around him and smiling as he nibbled softly at the back of her neck. He lay back, looking at the back of her head as he did so and grinned dreamily.

"How long now?"

Angel stirred slightly and raised her head, looking at the glowing electric clock that sat on the table beside their collection of weapons. They had stripped, cleaned and reloaded their weapons before retiring to bed, and were now just waiting for the assault to begin. Al had found a number of clocks and synchronised them all before handing them out, setting alarms to go off at half five in the morning. He claimed that gave everyone enough time to pull themselves together, grab a mug of coffee and have a full English breakfast before going on a killing spree. Bill wasn't sure if he felt like tea and toast before slaughtering a pack of Rots,

"Just after two," she murmured, shuffling back in the bed and pressing herself closer to Bill, listening the rain hammering on the roof above. She sighed, pursing her lips as she frowned to no one in particular. "Do you think this will really work?"

"Course it'll work," Al said, cleaning the barrel of his weapon with an oily rag and peering down the sights. He hadn't had any sleep all night, and although he had insisted Sarah get some sleep, she too had spent the night imitating Al and cleaning her handgun, oiling the moving parts and making sure the barrel was clear of any obstructions. "Have any of my plans ever failed before?"

Sarah scrunched up her face and shrugged her shoulders. Being the child of the group, she often felt she wasn't privy to a lot of the plans and decisions made, though Al tried to keep her in the loop as much as possible, within reason, of course; there were some things that Sarah knew she shouldn't know.

"You still remember what I told you to do to the bad men?"

"Yu-hu," Sarah said, nodding her head and reassembling the small handgun in front of her. "Shoot them in the head. Right here," she said, pointing to her forehead, then crossed her eyes and let her tongue loll from her mouth.

"That's really cute," Al grinned slightly, slapping a magazine into his handgun and heaving back on the slide, placing a round in the chamber before flicking the safety off and sliding the weapon into his holster. "Just remember what I told you and you'll be all right."

"I know," Sarah said, rolling her eyes and looking at the clothing Al had selected for her to wear. A simple black jumpsuit with several pads and plates in different positions; the suit had been designed with the average Marine in mind, and Al had taken a knife to the legs and arms to make it more accommodating for the girl. Though the body of the suit was still bulky, Al had assured her that plenty of straps and webbing would make sure it didn't impede her movements too much. "Stick close by you, if we get any trouble I climb on your back, only fire if I need to, and promise not to shoot anyone on our team."

Al nodded grimly and threaded a belt of ammunition through the open mechanism of a heavy machinegun, then moved that aside and prepared a pair of small submachine guns. Maybe he was planning on taking too much equipment, especially if he was going to be carrying Sarah, too. With his handgun, automatic weapons and ammunition he was looking at carrying twice as much as what he was used to, and Sarah couldn't help but feel he was taking on too much.

"I can look after myself if I need to, you know," she finally said. "I don't want a piggyback."

"I know. I'm not going to carry you all the way; if we get overwhelmed, we drop our weapons and you climb on my back."

"So if I'm on your back, we're in the shit?"

"We're in the shit, yes," laughed Al, leaning over and ruffling her hair. "Just for a change."

Sarah smiled and continued to look at the small silver handgun she had, then her lingering gaze drifted to her hand. She flexed her fingers then made a fist, remembering Pam in her final days.

"Here. For luck. Nothing weird or perverse or anything."

Sarah looked up from her hand to see Al's massive hand outstretched, a small brass ring lying in his palm. She picked it up and looked over it, tried it on each finger but found that it only sat snugly on her thumb.

"Pam's wedding ring," she said. It wasn't a question, but Al nodded a response anyway.

"It's you and me now, sweetie. We stick together, you and me." He looked up towards the ceiling, though seemed to be looking beyond the roof. "We can only hope someone who cares is watching over us from up there. We could really use the luck."

"I think they are," Sarah smiled.

"Bullshit," snarled Clive, crumpling an empty packet of cigarettes and letting it drop to the tabletop before flicking it across the room with a single finger. It smashed against the wall and tumbled to the floor. "I've seen too much to think anything else.'

"What use is a priest who's lost his faith in God?" demanded Garth.

"What use is a tanker driver with no tanker to drive?" Clive snapped back, taking one of the remaining cigarettes from the open carton that Sylvester held in his hand. "It's just a job: is that all I was to you when I believed? A lucky charm, a talisman imbued with magical power?"

Neither Garth, nor Sylvester, answered him. He grunted and shook his head.

"Well, I wasn't much fucking good, was I? How many of my wards died? Five? Six? What good was I? I couldn't protect anyone, despite my prayers, despite my guidance. The years I spent... the years I wasted."

"Wasted?" Sylvester asked, finally lending his voice to the discussion. "The hundreds of people who came to your church looking for answers, the advice you gave out, children baptised, couples married. The lives you turned around... the lives you saved? That's a waste of time?"

"Lives I saved and changed that didn't matter for shit, they're all dead now."

"That's not true, you saved my life when you sent me out to the country."

"And Terri's, too," Clive laughed softly to himself. "Didn't do her any good, either, did it? Despite my prayers, she still died," he continued, spitting the last three words with venom he didn't know he was capable of, nor that Sylvester had ever heard.

"God abandoned us a long time ago. We've been living in hell for the past three years."

"This is why you've been so distant lately?"

"I wouldn't say distant," Garth said, bluntly. "I'd say he's been acting like a dick."

"You're not helping," Sylvester muttered, glaring at him from behind a furrowed brow. "You gotta pull yourself together and *keep* it together. Now, you going to be okay for this mission?"

"I can kill," Clive said with a nod. "Living, dead, there's no difference now. The boundaries between the two have blurred."

"That's not what I asked," Sylvester said.

"Yeah," Garth said. "Can you keep your shit together in your fucked-up head long enough to be useful?"

"Can you?"

"Touché," Garth smiled wryly, getting up and storming away from the table, heading towards the door leading to the weapons trailer.

"Promise me you'll keep your shit together," Sylvester said. "We need everyone in on this, and that includes you. The last thing we need is for you to freak out and lose it half way through the battle."

"I will. Just because I've lost faith in god, doesn't mean that I've lost faith in my friends."

"Good," Sylvester said, standing up from the table and following Garth into the weapons room. It was less than an hour before Al's proposed start time for the mission. "Good. Just hope that your friends haven't lost their faith in you."

III

The door to the trailer rolled open and Al was first out the vehicle, swinging his heavy machinegun from side to side and motioning to the rest of the group to follow. Rain battered his face as he hefted the weapon, shouldered it and squeezed a salvo of shots off, decapitating the closest of the ten Rots that were softly pawing at the sides of the vehicle with their rotting fingers and bloodied stumps. They each turned to face him, instantly lumbering towards him with guttural groans and whimpering moans gurgling in the back of their throats. He cut loose with another volley of gunfire, ripping through the front line of undead defence and stepped away from the vehicle, wading through the ankle-deep mud and motioning to the rest of the group to follow.

"Mind your step," he warned, as Bill was the first to follow. Dropping to his knees he unloaded a slug from his automatic shotgun, obliterating the head and upper torso of an approaching rot with a single well-aimed shot. Al grinned, pleased at the progress of the young warrior: though he had initially began his journey all those years ago with nothing but a scattergun and a submachine gun, both of which required little to no skill to score a hit, he was now adept as a target shooter with quite a large degree of accuracy. Though he still used the same weapons, the shotgun was loaded with solid slugs instead of buckshot, and any automatic weapon he did fire was in controlled bursts and not what the Marines labelled as "panic fire". Though Bill was no Marine marksman, once he got to America he would certainly be able to win a couple of competitions and earn some quick and easy money.

"Slippery as shit," Bill complained as he unleashed another pair of combat slugs and helped Angel down into the mire. While Bill favoured the up-close assault weapons, Angel still preferred her rifles and she dropped to the ground beside Bill, shouldering her long-range sniper rifle and spinning around, covering the team's back from any of the undead horde that may try to shamble up behind them. Her rifle coughed a muffled shot, and another, and Al didn't need to turn around to know that each shot from the silenced weapon meant another of the zombies had been taken down. While Bill may not have been an expert marksman, Angel could give even the most highly trained Marine sniper a run for his money.

With the immediate threat dispatched, Al waved over to the open trailer and watched as Sarah jumped down into the mud, gripping a small shotgun in her pale hands. While a pistol was fine for shots that had time to be carefully aimed, Al needed to make sure she was able to deal more damage and deliver it with a rapid response, if required. Al had dug through the smaller munitions available in the armoury and had decided that the smaller tactical P-3 shotgun would be suitable, armed with the hard shot shell recipe that Al's old squad mate had cooked up. He wasn't comfortable in seeing the innocent young girl carrying a weapon, but it was something he'd seen time and time again in the favelas of Brazil. Children warriors; their innocence taken away by their unstable surroundings; causalities of circumstance.

And look at Sarah's circumstances… he mused quietly to himself.

The clearing the vehicle had been parked in was roughly fifty feet in diameter, surrounded by trees and shrubs, with a small wooden hut and the beginning of a fence merging into a smaller copse of trees. The skeleton of a horse lay by the front of the building, gleaming and bleached bones stripped clean by scavengers and the harsh elements, with a headless Rot, one of the fresh kills, lying over it. To the west rose the hill Al intended to conquer; two rising columns of rock parted by a flowing carpet of naked tree branches, disappearing into a mist-shrouded peak. Anything could be waiting for them in the forest of skeletal tree trunks, and even more in the mist-obscured peaks. The brisk morning air had a salty tang to it, a pleasant smell in comparison to heady odour of rot and decay.

Clive gingerly lowered himself from the trailer on to the muddy ground, looking carefully around and gripping the large-capacity rapid-fire handgun he favoured. His eyes fell on the animal bones, and he nodded grimly.

"And I looked, and behold a pale horse: and his name that sat on him was Death, and Hell followed with him," he announced. Al turned slightly and looked over his shoulder, glaring at him suspiciously with half-closed eyes.

"That Shakespeare?"

"Book of Revelation," Clive said, shaking his head.

"You know, considering you don't believe in that 'bullshit', you're spouting it off an awful lot," Al growled. "What the fuck is it with that?"

"I… I don't know," Clive said, shaking his head.

"If you don't believe, and if you don't know why you're going to say what you say, you should just shut the fuck up and not say *anything*. Now, keep the fuck out of my face and keep your head down. Spanners, keep an eye on the psycho, maybe get a leash for the freak."

Sylvester rolled his eyes as he stepped down, cradling his assault rifle as he would a child, and wheeled casually around on his heels, taking in as many details as he could. While Clive was slowly turning crazier with each passing day, Sylvester was becoming stronger and stronger. Another of his group that would have been a fine Marine, if the Marines hadn't turned out to be nothing but a pack of homicidal crazies and loonies that he didn't give so much as a fuck about.

"Everyone remember where we parked," yelled Garth as he climbed out the trailer and slid the door shut, clicking the latch into place and tapping a few digits into the numeric lock. He pointed at the cabin of the vehicle and made a beeping sound with his mouth, as if setting an imaginary car alarm. "We're just next to the scary cabin with the dead cowboy outside. I want everyone to remember in case we have to come back, because I hate it when we lose our vehicle."

"You're rambling on about nothing," Al said, watching as Garth slung his flamethrower and adjusted the brim of his cap. "You do that when you get nervous. Are you?"

"I'm practically shitting myself here," he confessed. "God damn it, I'm practically shitting myself. What the hell are we doing out here, Al? What the fuck are we doing?"

"We're going home," Al murmured.

"I went to the toilet before we left," Sarah said with an innocent smile. "That way we don't have to stop on the way. Mommy taught me that."

"You can do worse than listen to the little one," Al grinned before turning to the forest he was faced with. It wasn't going to be easy, of that he was sure.

Just like Brazil, only a hell of a lot colder, he thought to himself before waving silently towards the wooded pathway before him. The thick brown trunks of the trees and the shrivelled grass and moss that covered the floor were coated in a sprinkling of morning dew, partially frosted in places. Al breathed out softly through his mouth, watching the mist of his breath spread and evaporate into nothing, and looked longingly at the sealed pouch in his combat webbing that carried the last of his smokes: three cigarettes and two cigars, all of which he had no intention of smoking. The decision to quit hadn't come easy, and wasn't one he had made on a whim. Cancer wasn't his main concern: he'd been smoking one thing or another for almost twenty years, since just after joining the forces, and if he had cancer now, there was nothing he could do. His main priority now, after surviving and escaping the island, was to look after Sarah and set a good example: chain smoking wasn't one of the things he wanted to teach the young girl. Foul language was one thing, but nicotine addiction was something he wanted to keep her well away from. It had been downfall of his father, and it would more than likely be his own demise; he couldn't see anyone shooting him or getting the drop on him, he was too good.

At least, in his eyes he was.

Once they were in the helicopter, he would toss them out into the ocean. Garth would probably bitch about a waste of good smokes.

Shit, maybe I'll keep one cigar for when we touch down home. A last celebration.

They climbed higher up the wooded hill, the gravel-covered path they walked on slowly turning to a worn trail between the grass, the well-treaded loam of the hiking trail seemingly compacted by a hundred pairs of feet. Al stopped mid-stride and knelt down, examining the prints in the mud and carefully appraising the situation. It was more like the Brazilian rainforests now than ever before. Tracking prey through the woods, footprints in the mud, the silent and still forest…

That didn't sit well with Al. If the area was teeming with Rots, as he assumed it would be and as the imprints in the muddy ground attested to, why was it so silent and peaceful? Other than the pack of Rots that had lingered near the trailer, the area was too quiet. In Brazil, the still jungle had often been the prelude to an ambush, but now… Rot's weren't capable of ambushes.

"Everyone stop right now," Al said, lifting his hand up. He felt like he was being watched, but not by the eyes of the dead. "Take cover, everyone, into there," he continued, pointing to a small hollow in the ground surrounded by bushes and small logs. Everyone clambered into the dugout, squatting on the damp mossy ground.

"Something spooked you?" Bill asked, peering over the shrubbery covering the hole.

"Too quiet," murmured Al. "Where's all the undead?"

"Maybe they wondered off?" suggested Garth, his tone hopeful. "Those guys down there, they were probably just the remains of the crew that wiped out the Marines, right? Right?"

"Think about our last three years, buddy. How often have we had a lucky break like that?"

"Well," muttered Garth, adjusting the brim of his cap. "There was… you know, when the… after we…" Garth found himself lost for words, unable to pinpoint any lucky break he had. Finally, he remembered something, and grinned like a schoolboy who'd just heard his math class had been cancelled. "Year and a half ago, we were playing poker, I had a full house and you all had pairs or three of a kind."

"Yeah, I forgot about that one," Al muttered, rolling his eyes. "Something's out there, some kind of… trouble," he continued, looking up the hill and through the thicket of bushes that surrounded the foxhole.

"And trouble has a knack of finding you, right?" asked Angel, peering through the scope of her rifle and slowly scanning the woodland.

"I've got a magnetic personality," Al admitted.

"So what, are we staying in here for the rest of the day? Until someone makes a move? How do you even know you're right?"

"Twigs and branches laid across the ground, too regular to have just fallen from the overhead boughs. They're noise-makers, put there to alert any sentries. We step on them, they snap, *they* know we're coming. And look, over there… shit, I didn't see that before!"

Al pointed up the embankment, fifty yards ahead of their position, where a razor-thin piece of wire had been stretched between two trees. Though he couldn't see the other side of the trees where the wire had been attached, he knew that there would be something like claymores or signal flare launch tubes, anything to either maim or bring attention to them.

"This isn't just a bunch of Rots," hissed Al, grinding his teeth. "Frigging Marines, it has to be."

"It's not just the remains of the previous defences against the Rots, is it?"

"Remember what I just said about lucky breaks? C'mon, kid, no one here's that lucky, not by a long shot. C'mon, we need to regroup back at the trailer, reassess this plan. Slowly, people, and mind where you put your feet. The last thing we need is to set off a landmine."

Al rolled on to his back and swore under his breath before clambering to his feet, already trying to work out in his mind how he could successfully mount an uphill assault on a Marine base. He was about to help Sarah to her feet, when he heard a whistling sound as a projectile tore through the air, then the hollow *thunk* of it something striking one of the trees. He looked to one side and saw an arrow quivering from side to side in the tree closest to him, a small round light blinking on the shaft of the projectile suggesting it was more than just a normal arrow.

The arrow evaporated into a blinding flash, and Al felt his limbs become lead weights. He dropped to the floor, his vision obscured and a high-pitched whine filling his ears. He'd experienced flash-bangs before, though he'd never been on the receiving end of a super-strength version of the device, and it certainly wasn't anything to write home about. He felt dizzy and nauseous, and could tell from the sounds the rest of his friends were making that they weren't fans of the incapacitating charge, either.

"Mother-god-damn-fucker," Al grimaced, his head swimming as he tried to pull himself to his feet but failed miserably.

"Let go of your weapons and stop squirming," ordered a new voice, powerful and commanding. "The more you move, the more it makes you sick. Harbinger, get these people in restraints and get them on their feet. Carry the little one, looks like she's out cold."

"Ja," hissed another voice, a heavy German accent, and Al felt himself being roughly manhandled, felt nylon tags being wrapped around his wrists, then heard the *click-click-click* of the tags adjusting to the wrists of others.

"And bag 'em, make sure they don't learn the way to the Nest. Last thing we want is for someone to escape and tell the rest of them."

"Ja," hissed the second voice, and Al felt a heavy Hessian cloth fall over his head, the rim of the sack lined with a heavy chain to make sure there was no chance of the cloth riding up over his head or coming away with a sudden gust of wind. Though his senses seemed to be returning, the bag on his head dampened them all: the only thing he could sense was the smell of his stale breath in the confines of the sack, a mix of coffee, freeze-dried rations, and the last cigarette he had.

"Move," commanded the voice of the man in charge.

"Where we going?"

"Where Eagles dare," laughed the commanding voice. "I hope you're not afraid of heights."

Captain David "Lance" Lancet sat at the metal desk in his cramped office, scowling at the collection of paper reports that had been gathered for him. He'd read through them several times, and wasn't quite sure what to make. He san back on the leather recliner he had positioned before the metal collapsible table that served as his desk, then ran his fingers through the mess of salt-and-pepper hair that covered his head. Two men sat opposite him, each wearing clothing similar to his own: a jungle camouflage one-piece jumpsuit with a black battle vest and a number of different webbings and straps around their person. Though the clothing was based on the standard Marine issued battle fatigue, the three men had taken to customising it to their own taste. Lance himself had opted to cut the suit at the elbow, forming a T-shirt top. He wore a holster at each side of his belt, a shining Medusa revolver in each holder, and a number of knives tucked into pouches and pockets on his vest.

"What do you make of this?" he finally asked.

The first of the Marines offered his opinion on the matter by simply shrugging his shoulders. Sergeant Günter Hargstrung, the hulking mountain of a man that had taken the nickname of Harbinger. He had completely torn the sleeves from his uniform, and wore a scabbard for a smaller rifle strapped to his back. His hair, a seemingly unnatural platinum blonde, was short and spiky, crowning the top of his square-jawed face. He wore an eye patch over his right eye, and chewed ponderously at a toothpick that he worked from one side of his mouth to another. Behind him, leaning against the wall, was his sniper rifle, a heavy weapon capable of punching though the armour of a tank. Lance couldn't think of another man able to carry and fire the weapon other than the imposing German giant. He could understand English, though he couldn't speak much of the language. Silently, Harbinger turned to face the third Marine in the room.

"Goliath?"

The Marine that had remained silent scratched his jaw. His coverall had been left relatively unscathed by the scissors or knives, though his vest was covered in grenades and explosive devices, many of which could be loaded into the grenade launcher he had slung over his shoulder. He finally spoke, his voice low and rumbling. "My gut instinct is that it stinks of bullshit to me."

"But?" Lance growled, knowing there was more to Sergeant David Johnson's response than that.

"But, I looked into their stories, you know that's what I do. When I'm not researching your shit, I'm blowing it up."

Lance nodded. Since the rest of the squad had been killed, everyone was pulling double duties. Harbinger not only acted as the sniper and lookout for the base, but he was the assistant medic. Goliath was the information officer and the demolitions expert, though at the moment there wasn't much call for the latter skill.

"And a fine job you do," grinned Lance. Harbinger grunted in agreement. "Now, what's the story? How do they check out?"

"The black man claims to be one Sergeant Albert George Colebrook, but also says he wants nothing to do with the Marines anymore. Our records show that there was a Colebrook attached to the Wolvers division, but he and the rest of his squad were killed in action about two, maybe two and a half years ago. Dates a little sketchy."

"So his story's bullshit?"

"Not necessarily," Goliath muttered, tapping the screen of the tablet he held before slamming it on the desk and sliding it across towards Lance. "The KIA status was applied to the squads file by one Major Carter."

"Carter? The asshole that he claims to have killed in London?"

"The very same. I believe this guy, he knows the lingo, knows the details. He can walk the walk and talk the talk. This guy's seen action; his service record shows him in Brazil doing heavy grunt-work, cleaning up the coke fields and flushing cartels out left, right and centre. A lot of black ops and wet-work: assassinations, sabotage, that kind of stuff. An impressive twenty-year career."

"And now he wants to throw it all away?"

"You've read his account, you know what Carter and Preston were up to: sick and twisted shit."

Lance nodded, tapping the screen of the tablet to cycle through the pages of information that Goliath had collected.

"The rest of them are all civilians, and you know that their record keeping skills are somewhat sloppy. The young woman, I found her registered to some agricultural college up north, some college in a backwater hick-town called Ashford, just near this Little Slumberton she talked about. Both the fat one and the scrawny one with long hair could give me the registration numbers of their business; the garage was still active, but the shipping company was dissolved some time ago. The little girl, we've got nothing, but that's not surprising for someone her age. The priest, again, we got nothing, but if you want my opinion, he's a few rounds short of a full clip."

"And the last of the civilians? Bill, was it?"

"Found him on *our* records, strangely enough. He was picked up right at the beginning of the plague, nine days before the dead started… well, you know. He was picked up and thrown in quarantine, his girlfriend at the time was infected."

"But he clearly wasn't," Lance said. Harbinger nodded in agreement, but Goliath shrugged his shoulders before responding.

"We're a little fuzzy on that fact, but I'm guessing he wasn't. The day the whole damn country fell apart, he was scheduled to go under the knife. It's labelled as Autopsy. But we don't know for sure he died. I mean, he's not dead, is he?"

"If he is, he's the most advanced fucking zombie we've seen yet."

"Maybe it's just an assumed identity?" Goliath suggested.

"Taking on the identity of a dead man?" Lance shook his head. "I don't buy that, what's he got to gain? Plus, he's clearly here, alive."

"Could they have forgotten to log it? With everything going to shit…"

"I doubt it. If they had time to schedule an autopsy, they had time to record his death. He was one of the first who showed a potential immunity, the autopsy could have been… well, you know where I'm going with this."

"I know. A lot of sick fucks out there."

Lance rose from the desk and rested his hands on the butt of each pistol at his sides. Each of his men did the same, grabbing their weapons and standing to attention.

"Let's see what our guests have to say."

"Bunch of fucking assholes," Al stormed, pacing back and forth in the small room they had been thrown in. No one had seen anything through the black cloth sacks they had all been forced to wear on their way into the compound.

Bill could hear the sounds of a small settlement as he walked towards the holding building, but the residing Marines – Al had swore blind that their captors were well organised and clearly soldiers in the armed forces – had elected to paint the windows black, both inside and outside. Each had been taken into the adjoining room one at a time and interviewed, the room being kept in darkness while two Marines circled them, asking questions and taking notes. It wasn't as intimidating, as Bill would have thought it would be, and he certainly had expected more from the rough and tumble Marines, especially after the things he had seen happen in London. Maybe Al had been wrong?

"We'll be all right," he muttered, sitting on the ground beside Angel and an arm wrapped around her shoulder. He looked over to Al with a hopeful smile. "Don't you have another holdout pistol strapped to your groin, or a blade up your ass? Something we can use?"

"Arse, kid, you keep correcting me on that. Bastards are professionals too: they patted me down all over and stripped the pistol. Marines; gotta be. Fuckers are soft, though, maybe we can use that to our advantage."

"Advantage?" laughed Garth, hauling himself to his feet and warming his hands by the portable gas heater that occupied one corner of the holding cell. "How can we possibly have an advantage in this dump? We've got a portable heater and a light bulb in here to work with, how can we possibly have an advantage over them?"

"They're soft," hissed Al, keeping his voice low as if he thought their captors were listening at the door. "If Carter or his asshole lackeys caught us like this, the four of us men would be thrown into a pit to be burned live with a bunch of Rots, the priest would be burned as a heretic because, let's face it, he's fucking crazy, and Angel and Sarah would have the shit raped out of them."

He looked down apologetically at Angel and shrugged by way of excusing himself.

"It's true. You've got a nice ass, I've said it before."

"Arse," Angel muttered to herself, leaning in closer to Bill and resting her head against his shoulder and looking at Sarah who lay on the floor beside her, wrapped in a thick grey blanket that had been provided by the Marines.

"These bastards have just thrown us in this room, asking us questions. They're trying to work out what to do with us. That means they're indecisive, and we can make that work for us. We can get the drop on these bastards."

"I'd love to hear your plans," announced a new voice as the door to the room screeched open, vomiting a piercing bright light into the room. Bill lifted his hands up to his face, shielding himself from the light and peering at the trio of figures that stood in the blinding glare of the outside world. "Maybe you'd like to elaborate for us? I'm sure it would make an interesting addition to the story you've all concocted about what's happened in the past three and a half years."

"You say that like you don't believe us," sneered Al, facing off against the three figures and balling his fist. Bill clambered to his feet and stood by his friend, while Sylvester squared off on the other side, evening the odds somewhat. It was three on three, if it came to it.

"You must admit, Colebrook, there's a lot of stuff you've told us that makes it all very hard to swallow. A crazy psycho tracking you across the country with an army of the dead behind him? Taking on a whole Marine platoon? Turning a bunch of civilians into a platoon of your own, taking urban guerrilla warfare to a whole new level?"

"Crazier things have happened," Bill muttered.

"Like the dead walking," Clive announced from the rear of the room, slowly rising to his feet and wrapping his coat around him. "And the rest of the men not killed by these plagues yet repented not of the works of their hands…"

"Shut up, Preacher-man, this ain't the time for your bullshit," Al called over his shoulder, then glowered at the three people who as of yet had not entered the room. "So, you know all about us, who the fuck are you? Preston's men? Some of his sick fucks with no sense of direction, no one to lead you once the Rots wiped him out?"

"Rots didn't kill Preston," announced the man in charge, stepping forwards, out of the glare of the light and into the muted interior of the room. He touched the tip of his fingers to his brow in a half-hearted salute, bowed courteously towards Angel, then smiled and offered a white paper bag to Sarah as she sluggishly pulled herself to her feet and stood behind Al, holding on to his forearm and eyeing the bag suspiciously. The Marine shrugged his shoulders and helped himself to a handful of boiled sweets from the bag before tossing them into his mouth.

"My name," he smiled, "Is Captain David Lancet. And I killed Preston."

IV

The small black boat bobbed up and down on the calm sea, moored three miles away from their designated landing point on the Welsh coastline: a craggy cliff overlooking the calm sea, standing proud and ominous over the placid reflection of a cloudy midnight sky.

Lance sat at the back of the boat, trailing a finger in the icy waters while he slowly chewed the dehydrated ration bar. After a gruelling two-year service in North-West Ireland, where he and the rest of his team had been deep undercover trying to take down a tightly-knit gang that had been heavily involved in trafficking drugs, weapons and people, their mission had been cut short when the plague had reared its undead head, cutting a swathe through the country and decimating their chance at completing their mission or escaping from the island. Shore leave or leave of any other kind was nothing but a pipe dream, and they had found themselves in a very dangerous - and very bizarre - situation.

"Fucking zombies," he murmured, breaking off pieces of the ration and flicking them into the murky waters around him. He had watched two of his squad fall to the plague, both Sparks and Lil' Timmy: each had risen from the dead hours after they died and were tagged and bagged, and had to be put down with a bullet through their head. Another two of his squad had been victims of the zombie aftermath, torn apart by the ravenous hordes as they tried to storm the block of flats they had secured. G-Dog and Raven had been fortunate enough to be killed outright, the undead feasting on their brains so at least they were spared the indignity of rising from the dead. That had left the five of the squad on the run in Ireland, looking for somewhere to hold out. They had tracked across the country over the course of almost a year, losing Carlos in a shoot-out with a gang who resented them passing through their town, and their scout Maverick had taken a nasty tumble into a pit-trap, breaking his leg in several places and contracting an infection that eventually lead to gangrene and the severing of a limb which spelled the end for him. With inadequate medical facilities and personnel, Maverick had taken a turn for the worse, and Lance had put him down like a rabid dog. He knew that it was for the best: not only for Maverick, but also for the rest of the squad. That didn't make it any easier to live with.

"What's that?" asked Goliath, looking up from the book he was reading, flipping up his night vision goggles. "You say something, Lance?"

"Nothing," Lance muttered. "Nothing. Just thinking. What's it looking like out there? Our intel right?"

Harbinger grunted wordlessly and handed over a small stack of papers, each a small photograph three inches square. Lance turned his back to the shoreline and clicked on the small torch that hung from his vest, cupping one hand around the glowing bulb and leafing through the surveillance photos taken through the modified lens of the sniper rifle Harbinger had resting on the bow of the boat. Each picture was a palette of pale green, a digital printout of the night vision scope and showing the details of the encampment that was positioned on the crown of the rocky cliff.

"Seems like a standard Marine set-up," Lance muttered, passing them over to Goliath as he closed his book. "Guards to the rear, one or two, they obviously don't expect anyone approaching from the sea. Most of them should be placed to the front, we can't see them from here. How long until sunrise?"

"Couple of hours," Goliath murmured, glancing at his watch. "This building here seems big, but not too protected from what I can see. If the Old Man's anything like every other officer in the world, he'll be living in luxury in the rear building while his men do the hard work. Rest of his goons are probably in the front of the compound, guarding the miserable fuck's fat ass."

"We hit there first, then. Kill the leader, the rest should follow. Harbinger, move us closer, silent running," Lance ordered, throwing the photographs over his shoulder. They hit the water and fizzed softly, dissolving in the water until there was nothing but a pale mound of foam. The sniper at the front of the boat nodded and stowed his weapon before turning the engine over. It hummed to life, almost silent, and the boat slowly moved forwards, sliding effortless at such a speed that it shifted effortlessly and silently through the water. Dark fret frothed and bubbled behind the boat as it glided across the still sea, and the towering rocks loomed closer.

"We hit the shoreline and climb the cliff, take out the rear guards, then sweep through the compound. Work quickly, silently and methodically, one building at a time. Knives and silenced handguns only, so keep that shotgun and launcher stowed, Goliath. If we can, we'll find Harbinger some high ground to get a little scope action. Sound good?"

"Ja," rumbled Harbinger, gently guiding the boat closer to the shore and navigating around a jagged collection of rocks that pierced the surface of the murky water.

"What intel?"

Lance looked over to the young woman that decided to interrupt his story. He glared at her, trying his best to ignore her.

"What intel?" she repeated.

"You need to keep a reign on your squad, Sergeant," Lance growled, addressing Al but keeping his steely gaze fixed on Angel.

"If I could keep a reign on that bitch my life would've been a lot easier," Al murmured, making no attempt to veil the contempt in his voice while knitting his brows in a deep and ponderous frown. "What intel did you have? Where'd you get it? Were you in touch with someone on the outside?"

"Not that it's any of your damn business, *Sergeant*, but we intercepted a number of coded transmissions while we were holding down a facility on the south-eastern shore of Ireland. Normally bursts of reports about surrounding countryside, the state of play with zombie movement around the area. Goliath managed to triangulate the location of the base, dug up some maps from the database we had, and projected the layout of the place."

"Projected?" scoffed Al, scratching his chin. "That sounds a lot like guessing to me, *mon capitan*. Your boy made up the lay of the land and dumb luck played its part; it just so happened he was right, but any half-assed idiot could look at a hilltop retreat and *guess* how an experienced officer would erect his defences. Jesus, *I* could defend this place. The fucking *kid* could plan out the defence for this place."

"I could?" Bill said, looking up as if he'd only been half-paying attention.

"Not you, Sarah," Al waived his hand dismissively. "Erect a few barriers at the front of the compound, guard towers facing down the mountainside, claymores in the forest, smaller guard posts towards the rear. Any prisoners or barracks, the buildings people may be living in grouped in the centre. Am I right?"

Lance didn't answer. Al beamed and nodded his head. "I'm right."

"If you don't mind, I'd like to carry on with my story?"

"Knock yourself out," Al said, grinning wickedly. "Please."

"How's it looking?" Lance whispered into his coded radio link, crouching down behind a thick, thorn-covered bush. Barely a foot from the heels of his boots, the cliff edge loomed menacingly behind him, yawning like the gaping maw of a ravenous beast. Fifty feet beneath him, frothing water crashed against the base of the cliff and jostled the black stealth craft that had been moored against the slick rock face. He remained frozen in his position, afraid to move in case any sudden shift in his weight made the cliff edge crumble.

"Not that there was any doubt, but I was right," Goliath's hushed whisper came over the radio. "All the manpower seems to be at the front, watching the forest down the other side of the mountain. We can take them out if we move in from the back. How's Harbinger doing?"

Lance carefully moved his head to the side to see the bulky German soldier standing upright, leaning against the back wall of a small warehouse close to where Lance crouched. Two crumpled figures lay at his feet; casualties of war, each with their necks sliced wide open by the machete he was sheathing as Lance watched. Harbinger stepped back slightly so the glistening moonlight fell on his face and hands, and he quickly worked through a series of hand signals and gestures.

"He's going to go high," Lance said, watching the flurry of combat signals. "There's a tree he's going to climb, start planning his killing spree. He says there's two buildings in front of the warehouse, any idea what they are?"

"One looks like an armoury or ammo dump, the other like a holding cell; there's too many guards to suggest it could be anything else," came Goliath's hoarse response.

"Save the two buildings, there's supplies and people in there, and we came to get both. All right, everyone ready?"

"Affirmative," muttered Goliath, the soft click of the slide of his weapon being drawn back carrying gently over the radio link.

"Ja," rumbled Harbinger, his bulk concealed in the height of a thick and heavyset oak tree. The wide limb he perched on rustled and moved beneath his weight, but nothing that looked out of the ordinary: as if it were merely the wind toying with the leaves.

"On my mark…" Lance said, licking his lips and cocking his weapon. "Move."

Lance slowly raised himself out of the bushes and lifted his silenced handgun, moving out from his cover behind the bushes and tapping a single round into the head of the closest guard. He toppled wordlessly to the ground, the crater-like exit wound from the gunshot seeping dark crimson ooze on to the ground and pooling around the corpse.

"One down," hissed Lance, stepping quickly forwards and stooping to drag the corpse into the darker shadows of the surrounding bushes.

"Number two down," reported Goliath from the other side of the compound. "I'm circling back around to meet up with you."

"Drei," announced Harbinger.

"Stay up there, Harbinger, we'll need you for covering fire."

Silent, almost inaudible footsteps approached him, and he spun in time to see Goliath approach, the muzzle of his weapon smoking lazily as he rushed forwards and slapped Lance on the shoulder. Waving his hand, the captain stalked into the confines of the encampment, carefully pressing his body against the walls of the warehouse and peering around the corner.

Two buildings lay in front of him, one a squat and square building, the other a larger rectangular building with boarded windows. One guard stood by the entrance to the square building, leaning against the doorframe and smoking a cigarette while a trio of Marines stood by the door to the other building, each in a relaxed stance: two leaning against the walls while another paraded around in front of them, seemingly in the middle of telling a joke. The silver light of the moon illuminated their grinning and laughing faces, though their noise was kept to a minimum.

"Two each," whispered Lance. "Make your choice."

"I'll take the joker and the loner on the square hut."

"Leaving me the other two," Lance nodded. "Harbinger, keep your eyes open, give us the signal if anything goes down. See if you can spot any of their watchmen out front. We're going in."

Lance and Goliath rolled around the corner of the building, their muffled weapons coughing four times and smashing the skulls of each of the guards. Guns still raised, the pair stalked across the camp to the buildings. Goliath tried to open the door to the square hut, not very hopeful, but was surprised when the lock clicked open and the door swung silently inwards.

"Jackpot," smiled Lance. "What've we got?"

"What do you want?" Goliath grinned, stepping into the room and looking around. "Rifles, shotguns, grenades, couple of mounted machineguns, and enough ammo to boot. A few high-powered handguns, magnums and revolvers: like a dream come true."

"Too much to hope this door isn't locked," Lance murmured, trying the handle. It rattled, but the lock held tight. Appraising the door, he noted that there were two deadbolts on the outside and a couple of padlocks: the external locks were nothing he couldn't deal with, but the key to the door itself was something they'd have to locate if they didn't want to attract too much attention by blowing open the door.

"Need the key," Goliath muttered, echoing Lance's own thoughts. "You think it's on one of those dead guards?"

"I doubt it," Lance muttered, turning back towards the warehouse and feeling bile burn the back of his throat. "I reckon it's in the hands of the Old Man. Stay here, this shit's mine."

"You don't like officers, do you?"

"Just the assholes who keep civvies locked up in a hut and feed them to zombies. Keep it tight, coms open, if you run into any trouble… well, I'm sure I'll hear it."

Goliath nodded and hunkered down beside the two buildings, casting envious glances across the contents of the open armoury, while Lance quickly made his way across to the warehouse, checking the door and finding it to be unlocked. He smiled to himself and slowly teased the door open, slipping into the room and pulling the door closed behind him before snapping the latch into place.

Despite the gloom of the warehouse, Lance could see that it was deceptively larger than it looked from outside. A large mound of machinery and scrap parts took up the main bulk of the room, partially covered by a thick black canvas tarpaulin. Towards the back of the enclosed chamber, the soft glow of a television screen cast a flickering light across the room, the sound muted and lending an eerie quality to the darkened surroundings. Lance shuffled carefully forward and lifted the corner of the tarp, appraising the equipment with an approving nod, then lowered the covering and proceeded deeper into the room, stepping carefully over discarded tools and twisted pieces of metal as he advanced, his weapon lifted and pointed towards the leather recliner positioned before the television set.

As he neared it, he could see the images on the screen, and for one moment he thought the commanding officer was watching an old horror movie. Scenes of a young man and women in the bottom of a pit, clutching to one another in terror as a trio of blood-spattered undead advanced on them. They lunged on the couple, nails and teeth ripping into flesh and bone, spilling blood as the zombies tore them apart with their bare hands, splattering ruddy chunks of dripping flesh on the ground. The truth sunk in as the camera wavered and lifted slightly, exposing a group of Marines on the lip of the pit, cheering, laughing and swapping rolls of notes and cartons of crumpled cigarettes.

Some of the transmissions had hinted at the barbaric sports and games played in the Marine camp, though Lance hadn't dreamed he would ever see anything like that. Something within him snapped, and he grabbed hold of the recliner, spinning it around and levelling off his weapon to the face of the sleeping man in the chair. He grunted, snorted, but didn't wake up: the glass tumbler of whiskey he gripped loosely in his hand slopped dark amber fluids over his hand and thigh. His clothing was grimy and dishevelled, barely recognisable as the field dressing of a major.

"Preston, I presume," Lance sneered, pressing the silencer of his pistol against the forehead of the sleeping soldier. He spluttered, snorted again, then his eyes flickered lethargically open, lazily looking up and down. Drunk and dilated pupils slowly pulled into focus, and a look of half-hearted panic flickered briefly across his face. He was too drunk to fully understand the connotations of what was going on, but tried to pull himself to his feet, spilling his glass and kicking an empty bottle with his foot. He murmured a wordless response, fumbling with thick, unresponsive fingers at the shoulder holster that poked out from beneath the rumpled jacket. He seemed to sober slightly as he realised his weapon wasn't there. His vision focused on the television screen and the morbid scenes that played out on it, and the pair of Medusa revolvers that sat on the bench before it, an assortment of different calibre ammunition scattered around the weapons.

"A Marine is useless without his weapon. First thing you're taught in basic training, you sadistic bastard, right before they mention protecting the people. What the fuck is *that*?" Lance demanded, pointing to the television as the screen was filled with the image of a pair of Rots fighting over the remains of half a human head, pawing at the grisly remains and shovelling what they could into their slack mouths.

"Mu-mu-my ent-enter-tain-munt," grunted Preston, still trying to pull himself to his feet.

The weapon in Lance's hand bucked slightly and the back of Preston's head blew out, spattering his brains across the recliner. He keeled over to one side, flesh and blood slipping out the gaping wound, and Lance unceremoniously pulled him on to the floor. The death of the heartless leader had been too quick, and Lance didn't think the speedy execution had been befitting of the brute. He holstered his pistol and stepped over to the television, lifting the electrical appliance from the bench, staggering over to the corpse and hurling it down on to the ruined head of Preston in a fit of disgust. Pieces of the monitor and shards of skull scattered away from the impact, a brief flurry of sparks showering over the inert body as the tube within the near-antique television burst.

With a greater sense of satisfaction than he had felt after just shooting him, Lance grabbed the revolvers of the major, appraising the old weapons and slipping them into a pouch attached to his webbing before scooping up the collection of bullets and stuffing them into a separate pouch. The Medusa was an interesting weapon, able to use most calibres of ammunition with only a few modifications to them, though weren't widely used throughout the armed forces: Preston had obviously been a collector of weapons. Besides the scattering of shells, he also found a silver key fastened to a loop of wire, and he hooked it with his finger, quickly making his way back to the doorway to the building.

Slipping back out into the darkness outside, Lance slunk through the shadows of the compound, returning to the pair of buildings guarded by Goliath.

"Get the key?" he rumbled, his voice low as he warily eyed the front of the compound. Lance nodded, produced the key and popped the lock on the door, swinging it wide open. The hinges squeaked eerily as the door rolled inwards, and Lance stepped into the room, slapping the wall around the door on a whim: There was some power in the base, that much was obvious through the television being active. His probing fingers found a plastic fuse box, and he threw the switch with a grunt, sending power coursing through the wire veins that lined the room. The three rows of luminescent tubes running the length of the room flickered to life, casting a sickly yellow light over the room, picking out the details of the chamber.

A corridor ran up the centre of the room, surrounded on all sides by thick metal bars spaced six inches apart. On the other side of the bars, slowly rousing from their slumbers and blearily wiping their eyes, a rabble of men, women and children slowly lifted their heads from the concrete surface they slept on. Each wore tattered rags, were covered from head to toe in grime and dirt reeked of faeces and stale sweat. As they gathered their senses and pieced together what was happening, they noticed Goliath and Lance standing in the door and slowly backed away. Lance wasn't surprised, not after the morbid home movies Preston had been in the middle of watching: this group of thirty people may well have once been twice as big, but the snuff movies called for constant re-casting.

Lance stepped forwards, and the group of prisoners took a step back in unison, fear in the eyes of each and every person. Children wormed their way to the back of the crowd, while men stepped forwards, an unspoken vow of protection that seemed to have been formed amongst the prisoners: the stronger men protecting the weaker women and helpless children.

"How do these cages open?" Lance asked, looking around the room: there didn't seem to be any locks on the bars themselves, but an intricate web of ropes and pulleys criss-crossed the ceiling and seemed to feed into a collection of levers in one corner.

"Fuck you," spat one of the prisoners, a man who seemed to stand forward of the crowd: the self-elected leader, maybe? Regardless, it appeared that they weren't going to offer any help, not until they realised they were *being helped* themselves.

"Goliath, work those levers, see if we can get these people out of here. Harbinger?"

"Ja?" the German's voice crackled over the radio, distorted slightly by the rustling of leaves and snapping of twigs.

"Get down here, get those weapons prepped and ready to be handed out."

He didn't wait for the response, instead turned to the group of cowering people and addressed them openly.

"Does anyone here know how to use a weapon? Fire a gun?"

The lead prisoner eyed him warily, keeping his distance and leaning to one side so he could watch Goliath work at the levers and ropes.

"What is this, a new slant on your sick games? Give us a gun, set us free and hunt us down? Fucking the kids and killing their parents isn't enough for you now?"

"You've got some fire in you," Lance muttered, looking up slightly as Harbinger flung the door open and barged in, dragging a heavy metal crate behind him. He set it down, popped the lid and pulled an assault rifle out. He loaded it, cocked it, sighted down the barrel, grunted and placed it to one side before starting on the next. "So, can you fire a gun?"

"You're not here to kill us, are you?" the man slowly asked, his eyes showing a glimmer of hope, the corner of his lips beginning to tug upwards in the birth of a smile. "You're here to help us?"

"Ja," Harbinger hissed without looking up from his work. He'd already prepared six rifles, and was currently working on his seventh.

"Rescue?"

"In a way," Lance admitted. The prisoners seemed to visibly relax, their tightly knit crowd spreading out slightly in the confines of the holding cell. "We have the means, we have the weapons, but we don't have a place to go. We're staying here for now."

"I'm sure the fuck in charge is going to let us do that."

"The fuck in charge is dead," Lance announced, letting that sink in. He lifted the pair of Medusa handguns he had liberated from the grotty dwellings of Preston from his pouch. He hadn't realised in the darkness of the warehouse, but the handle of the weapon was made of pearl and decorated with an ornate pattern. It was more of a collector's piece than he realised. An awed silence fell over the crowd as they recognised the weapons.

"I can fire a weapon," announced one man from the rear of the crowd, raising his hand and stepping forwards. He looked to be in his mid-thirties, his hair wild and unkempt and his gaunt face covered in a thick beard. "Spent a couple of years in the army before an injury took me out."

Lance had to fight back a sneer. The army and the Marines didn't see eye to eye very often, but right now he couldn't afford to let that get between them.

"You seen any combat?"

"A couple of months, yeah," the man admitted. He took another step forwards, and showed signs of a limp as he moved. "Used the old SA102."

"You can use one of those, then," Lance said, waiving to the pile of weapons Harbinger had prepared. "Same principle. Just need to get you out here."

"Middle lever, right lever, then middle again," he volunteered, offering the combination to open the cage. Lance smiled, nodded, and waited for Goliath to complete the sequence. He did just that, and the audible whine of an electric winch could be heard, taking up the slack of some of the ropes overhead, then pulling some of the bars up with a deafening squeal. Lance gritted his teeth, wishing the resident Marines had taken it upon themselves to oil the hinges as the doors peeled upwards, away form the floor.

"They called me Slim," said the first volunteer as he hobbled out the enclosure and grabbed the first rifle. He smiled, showing yellowing and rotten teeth, and Lance returned the gesture, albeit without the yellowed teeth. He could see why he'd been given that name: even before his captivity, it was clear that the man had a slight, gangly frame.

"Now you're called Hopper. Anyone else?"

Slowly, one by one, people started to raise their hands and step forwards, each giving part of their story before accepting their rifle.

"Let's do this," Lance said, returning to the open doorway and lifting his own rifle. The time for stealth had ended, now it was time to mop up the rest of the resistance using whatever force necessary. Goliath brandished his grenade launcher with a malicious grin and stepped out into the night, angling the weapon and firing off a salvo of explosive rounds towards the front of the compound.

Explosions rocked the encampment, bathing the cliff-top settlement in a sickly yellow glare of flames, and the screaming began as Lance and his rag-tag troop began to cut a swathe through the remaining Marines.

XXVI
DEATH FROM ABOVE

"I have requested that the Civil Aviation Authority and Uni Gov continue to keep all air traffic grounded until such a time we are able to combat the disease."

I

"Wait a moment," hissed Al, lifting a hand and pulling himself to his feet. "You're telling me that a bunch of malnourished, untrained civvies under the command of a rogue soldier tore apart a Marine base?"

"You sound surprised; somewhat unbelieving, even," Lance said with a smile. "Look around the room, what do you see? What stands out the most about the squad of people you claim you've guided around this infested island? Our stories are very similar."

Al looked from left to right, nodding at each of his friends as his eyes fell on him: as much as he hated to admit it, Captain Lancet was right. What *were* his friends, if not soldiers? A delivery boy, a student vet, and the driver of a big rig: a mechanic, a priest and a nine-year old girl. But he didn't think of them like that, he hadn't for so long, he couldn't remember when he'd stopped. Bill was his second, able to lead if Al couldn't: Angel was a field medic, and was capable of a lot more than she thought she was, but it would be a cold day in hell before he admitted that to her face. With Sylvester's knowledge of machines and engines, and Garth's partial knowledge and ability to drive more or less anything he sat down to, he had what passed as a technician and driver. Clive, at the moment, was still something of a mystery; his belief of god, or lack thereof, meant he may or may not have a chaplain. And of course, he had Sarah, who had quickly become his adopted daughter. No role as such in the squad, but another responsibility for him.

He stopped mid-thought and frowned. After finding Carter and his band of psychotics, Al had sworn off his ties to the Marines, claiming he no longer wanted anything to do with them, yet he still looked on himself and his friends as a squad with a Marine structure. After twenty years in the UGMC, it really was hard to think any other way.

"Point taken," Al said, shrugging.

"If anything," Lance continued, "I would be more inclined to say your own story was *more* than unbelievable. At least in mine, there was only half an hour or fighting before it ended. It sounds like you've all been fighting for the past three years."

"Feels like thirty," muttered Bill, sitting restlessly against the wall, his hand clutching Angel's. "Like a lifetime."

"So everyone's happy and smiley living here?" Garth asked. Lance nodded slowly.

"It took a while for the people to learn to trust us, but I wouldn't expect any different, not after the shit that had been inflicted on them by Preston. We've been here for months, now, almost a year. We were on the southern coast of Ireland and picked up some chatter, like we told you. The content was… more than disturbing. We came here to put an end to it, which we did."

"How could you be certain Carter wouldn't come over here to explore, pick at the ruins and salvage the equipment?"

"It was a chance, but we were ready for him. Watchtowers, mortars, tripwires…"

"People with custom arrows attached to flash-bangs?"

"Exactly. You could have been Carter's men."

"With a little girl in tow?"

Lance didn't say anything, just raised his eyebrows and gave a grim, knowing smile and nod. Al returned the nod, knowing what Carter's men had been capable of, and that they could well have carried around any number of prisoners with them for 'entertainment' purposes.

"So, you know our story and we know yours," Sylvester said. "What now?"

"We came here for the helicopter," Al reminded him.

"The helicopter?" asked Lance.

"Don't play dumb with me," growled Al, nodding, "The helicopter, it was probably stored in Preston's warehouse. More than likely, the equipment under the tarp you mentioned in your story. You ain't using it."

"The helicopter?" Lance repeated. "Jesus, how do you think we're protecting this place? How do you think it's powered? That thing's been salvaged for parts and weapons since we set up here. It's not flying anywhere."

"Fuck!"

Al kicked the wall, his brute force denting the metal structure, before pacing back and forth.

"Inoperable?"

"Engine's linked up to the generators we have. Weapons are used to protect…" Lance sighed. "Maybe it would be easier if you just came outside and had a look."

It was still raining outside, the clouds overhead looking like thick cotton, heavily laden and spilling their tears over the compound. The dismal grey light of the setting sun cast morose, lengthy shadows across the sodden turf outside the compound, while a large overhead floodlight had been erected above the facility, chasing the gloom away and adding a slight warmth to the air, an artificial sun that heated the ground.

Bill was the first to exit the building that had formerly been their prison, and he stopped, taken aback by the brightness of the light. Shielding his eyes, he looked from left to right, and saw a number of villagers stumble back and forth around them, giving them a wide berth. Disbelieving stares from aged and haggard faces, scowls from troubled children, hushed mutterings and rumours between the villagers. Each person wore layers of ragged clothing, an eclectic mix of civilian and camouflage patterns, and most of the adults carried a weapon of some description, either slung over their shoulder or nestling in holsters dangling from their hips. For a moment, Bill was reminded of an old medieval village with a modern twist, the peasants armed with state of the art firepower.

"We need our weapons back," Al demanded as he stepped outside, Sarah's hand engulfed in his own. He breathed deeply, wiping his brow as the rain trickled down his face and smiling toothily at any villager who caught his eye. Each one seemed to back away.

"You don't need them in here," Lance muttered from behind them.

"If they do, so do we."

"Don't push it, Al," Bill warned him, looking around from his vantage point. It looked as if they had been placed in the same building that the prisoners had originally been kept in, as the building beside it was the armoury, an electronic lock on the side glowing a dim blue and a ragged villager standing on guard, leaning heavily on a wooden crutch.

To one side there was the small warehouse, the ground before it protected from an overhead tarpaulin stretched over four stakes embedded in the ground. Surrounding the warehouse on all sides were small shanty buildings made of canvas and metal, whatever scraps could be pulled and scavenged together to create buildings large enough to house two or three people. Bushes and trees had been cut back, making more space for development.

The other side looked out on the rest of the plateau and an expanse of more shanty buildings. Around all the sides of the compound other than the edge that backed up against the cliff edge, a wall of metal sheets and tree trunks had been erected. They had been attached to trees left rooted in the ground, forming a protective semi-circle of wood and steel.

"How tall's that wall?" Al asked, waving over towards the screen of trees.

"A little over eight foot in most places. We have sentries that patrol it, and there's a catwalk on this side."

"Rots could climb that no problem," Bill said, catching sight of one of the men patrolling the catwalk. His eyes were fixed on the forest below them, a bow gripped in one hand and a quiver of arrows strapped to his back. Beside him stood a smaller figure, a child or a teenager, clutching a rifle and a telescope.

"We know. That's why there's a watch, twenty-four seven. The other side's covered in razor wire, barbs, anti-climb paint, whatever we could find that would deter or slow down any would-be climbers. The military designed and built it, we just extended and modified it."

"So what're you supposed to be showing us?"

"That, for a start," Lance said, pointing to the spotlight, then indicating another three around the camp, positioned at the four points of the compass. "Takes juice to run those babies, we've got a generator set up for each one, and a fifth to generate power for the rest of the base. We salvaged one engine from the helicopter, siphoned off and used all the fuel for that. Weapons were added to the perimeter wall to bolster our defences there. So you see, there isn't anything you can use for your plan, as reckless and crazy as it was."

"You would think so, wouldn't you?" Al said with a grin. "Is there somewhere we can all talk? Somewhere we aren't on public display?"

"There's the warehouse," Goliath suggested, gripping the butt of his shotgun. "We can go there, but don't try anything stupid. You're deep in the heart of enemy territory, don't piss off the natives."

"What kind of stupid asshole would wander into enemy territory, kick up a shit storm and start a revolution?" Al said, an arrogant smile spreading across his face as he wandered towards the warehouse. "This the way?"

Villagers parted as they ventured towards the building, scuttling out of the way and allowing them access to the door, the muttering and murmuring continuing. Al took it upon himself to continue smiling, then started waving and talking to people. Bill shook his head: he knew that Al wasn't being warm or friendly; he was deliberately getting in people's faces and making them uncomfortable. Without his weapons on him, which had only happened once in the three years he had known him, Al was employing the only tactic he knew could intimidate other people.

The door squeaked open and everyone filed into the warehouse, heading towards the back of the room where a large table had been erected. Walking past a hulking piece of machinery under cover that could only be the stored helicopter they had came to seek, Bill was tempted to take a quick look under the protective dust sheet, but feared what form the repercussion of doing so would take. Instead, he took a seat around the table beside Angel, still gripping her hand and stroking the back of her knuckles with one finger.

"You okay?" he asked quietly. She nodded a response.

"Just a little taken aback; all these survivors and no one trying to kill us or eat us. Like a real little town."

Bill smiled, lifted and kissed the back of her hand, then glared at Al as he slapped him on the side of his head.

"Keep focussed, kid, you can do your kissy-face thing later."

He took up a position at the head of the table, allowing Sarah to sit on the table beside him, then instructed Garth, Clive and Sylvester to stand behind him. Lance sat at the other end of the table, with Goliath on one side and Harbinger at the other.

Bill frowned, not knowing where this was going, but imagined this was what it looked like before a war between two countries started: each side had their own demands, their own agenda. God only knew what Al had planned.

"I guess I should start by thanking you," Al started. "And trust me, that doesn't come easy. If there's one thing I can't fucking stand, it's officers. Twenty years in the service, and the only LT that I got on with was Lieutenant Clarity; Johnny C. But thanks for not killing us on sight, giving us a chance. I dare say that if the tables were turned, and if I was on the other side of the bow, that flash-bang would have been a frag."

"Wow," muttered Angel. "I've never known you to apologise."

Al smiled, somewhat sarcastically, then carried on.

"You still have your stealth boat out back?"

"It's in a secure location," Lance confirmed, admitting they had it but letting on as to where it was."

"And in the trailer, we have quite a few documents, satellite surveillance photographs, shit like that. We can see the location of the guard towers out in the sea and pinpoint the closest one. If we can use your boat, we get out there, raid it for whatever fuels and supplies we can get our hands on, return here, and get the helicopter prepped and carry on with our plan. What do you think?"

"Fucking suicide," Goliath muttered. "Even more than your original plan."

"That would leave us a generator down, weapons down…"

"There's a perfectly fine command vehicle at the foot of that hill out there, we get that winched up with the helicopter and you can strip it down for whatever you want. There's a couple of Infinity Dynamos on board, they can be cranked by hand."

"Hey, woah there, that's our vehicle!" hissed Garth.

"We aren't going to need it again, these people here will. What's the problem? The pair of dynamos, the generator, most the ammo, we can't take it with us, and it must add up to the trade-in value of a working helicopter. And how the hell are we going to get it over to America?"

Lance sat and listened to the exchange, a smirk on his face as he followed the discussion with his eyes. Al finally silenced Garth, and turned to look at Lance, waiting to see what his reaction was. "What do you think?" he finally repeated.

"I think you've mistaken this community for a place that barters. We don't *trade*, we *take*. If we wanted your vehicle, we'd take it. And we will. But you put across an interesting proposition. That *thing* isn't doing anything right now; it just sits there on its platform and takes up space. What weapons are on that vehicle down there?"

"You've not had a look yet?" Bill asked, raising an eyebrow. "If the situation was reversed here, Al would have been poking around in there hours ago."

"Mounted machineguns," Al said, leaning forwards as he spoke. "Gatling cannons, rocket launchers, grenades, assault rifles, automatics, handguns, shotguns, bolt-action and automatic sniper rifles, and enough ammo for each to take down a small country… what do you need?"

"We need it all," Lance admitted, sitting back and rubbing at his chin. "And we'll take it all."

"So we have a deal? Fix up the helicopter, we grab more supplies, come back here and finalise the swap, then we'll be on our way."

"We'll need to discuss this," Lance said, motioning towards his two aides and turning around in his seat. Al nodded, and spun on his own seat, motioning for everyone to gather around him.

"I can't believe you're going to give up our ride," hissed Garth.

"When we get to America, we wouldn't be able to ride around in the damn thing anyway. We get there and stay inconspicuous. How inconspicuous is a twenty-four-wheeled trailer convoy armed to the teeth? Accept it and move on. Anyone else?"

"You think they'll buy it?" Sylvester asked, twirling a handful of hair nervously around his forefinger.

"Don't see why not. We've got stuff they want, and we can get even more from a guard tower's supply cache. They'd be idiots not to."

"What if they decide the trailer's enough, and that we don't need to go any further?"

"Simple. We refuse to turn over the trailer. As bold and brash as they are, they wouldn't dare consider losing it if we didn't cooperate and deactivate the anti-tamper self destruct mechanism I turned on just before we left."

"The what? I didn't know you did that!"

"To the best of my knowledge, there isn't one," admitted Al with a grin. "But I bet you anything they don't know that. It's just like playing poker, bluffing and double-bluffing."

"Smart," said Bill, awestruck. "I've never seen you actually use words and intelligence to negotiate deals. It's normally guns blazing and grenades exploding."

"Yeah," agreed Angel, nodding with a smile. "Very eloquent. You know, you would have made a fantastic officer."

"You start to like someone," Al snarled, fixing his steely gaze on Angel and frowning, "Then they go and throw shit in your face. Anyone with anything worth saying?"

"I wish I took one of those sweets," Sarah muttered. Al grinned, ruffled her hair and wrapped an arm around her shoulder.

"Are you finished?" announced Lance. Al coughed, cleared his throat and spun back to face the table, locking eyes with one another. The pair nodded to one another, neither shifting their gaze, as if playing a game of chicken: the first to blink or look away, the loser. Lance was first to break the gaze, and Bill smiled softly to himself: his team had taken the first small victory of the day.

"The boat's out back, locked down against the cliff face. It holds three people, maximum."

"Three," Al muttered, scratching his beard. "Me, the kid and the bitch, I guess…"

"One of the men will be Harbinger," Lance said, matter-of-factly. He seemed dead-set on this, and Bill knew that there was no amount of staring competitions that would change his mind. "He'll keep an eye on the two others on the mission, make sure there's no funny business or double-crossing. Al, Bill, you two will go with him. Between the pair of you, there's the most combat experience. Al's the most obvious choice: you, because you were just thrown into the plague situation without any notification; Mister I-don't-watch-the-news was dropped into a combat situation without any warning and came through the worst."

"What about everyone else?" demanded Bill, glancing around anxiously at the rest of his team.

"The mechanic and the fat bald man need to stay back here and prepare the helicopter. Goliath will help them."

"Fat and bald?" Garth spluttered, looking from side to side for backup from his friends. No one said anything. "Fat and bald?" he repeated under his breath.

"The man of God can give a sermon to the townsfolk. It's been too long since any had guidance from above."

"You listened to our story, right?" Al said, shaking his head. "Preacher-man's losing the plot day by day, doesn't know right now if he's the worlds best God-squad member or a flat-out atheist."

"He can give a sermon. He doesn't have to believe, but the people do. Morale."

"I can do that," Clive nodded. "I can read passages from the bible, answer questions."

"Just keep away from the damn Revelation bullshit," Al snapped. "I don't want to come back and find you pinned to a tree. What about Sarah?"

"We have children here her age," Lance said with a soft smile directed to the little girl. He rolled up the bag of boiled sweets and slid them across the table, into Sarah's waiting hands. She smiled and tore it open, helping herself to them. She offered them around, but everyone refused, much as it pained Bill to do so. He had a sweet tooth, but decided that Sarah wanted them the most. In fact, he hadn't even thought about sweets and sugary treats for years until now. "She can play with them."

"I don't want to," Sarah muttered. "I'm not a kid."

"She's grown up a lot in the past few years," Angel said, smiling at her. "I think she's a lot more mature than some of the people in this room, in particular the fat bald man in the corner."

"Hey," protested Garth, sitting upright and scowling. "I don't like this bitching and name calling, and I don't like the fact you're saying that kid's more mature than me!"

"Tough, she is," Angel said with a smile. Sarah seemed happy enough to eat the sweets, and appeared to have tuned everyone out while she rooted through the paper bag. "She's seen things no one should see, I don't think playing with dolls or bikes are ever going to appeal to her again."

"All the kids here have had a rough time," Lance said defensively. "If they weren't raped by the soldiers, their parents were before being thrown to the zombies and their deaths being recorded for later viewing."

"I'll look after her," Angel said. "That is, if you don't have plans for me to peel potatoes or anything like that."

"Oh no, we keep the women in the breeding pens, make sure they keep popping them kids right out," Goliath said. Bill, or anyone else on his side of the table, didn't pick up the levity of his comment. "Joke," he said, raising his hands in mock surrender. "I was joking!"

"I'll look after Sarah," Angel repeated. "She's kinda like a little sister to me now. Guess that makes you like my adopted father, right Al?"

"That shit isn't even funny," Al growled under his breath. "When do we go?"

"Sun should be set in an hour or so," Lance said, glancing at his watch. "You two, get suited up in the armoury, Goliath can walk down to the trailer with Baldy and grab these documents you need."

"His name is buddy," Al said, aware that the nicknames were his own devising, and he didn't' appreciate the Brass coming along and changing them. In fact, he didn't appreciate the Brass at all; Bill knew this, and was starting to feel the same way. He'd rather Angel came along with them, he knew what she was capable of, but he supposed a military marksman would be just as effective as her. Maybe he just didn't want to be separated from her. It had taken that long for them to get together, he didn't want anything to come between them now.

II

Bill had changed into his new clothes as soon as he had been given them: though he wasn't keen on the one-piece black jumpsuit and it's skin-tight qualities, he had to admit it was warm, comfortable despite it's appearance, and smelled a lot better than his old jeans and T-shirt. He'd struggled into the combat webbing, which he found a lot more uncomfortable than the worn leather belt he'd previously been wearing. Despite the fact it was designed for combat Bill found it very restrictive, but supposed it was going to take a little bit of getting used to. As it was, it seemed to bunch up where it shouldn't, and cut in to him too much. Still, he'd give it a shot, at least the once, before he swapped it for his old fashioned single-strap leather belt.

"Ready," he announced, standing proud in the dim glow of the armoury's overhead lighting.

"No you're not," Al said, shaking his head. Harbinger looked up from cleaning his immense rifle and grinned, exposing perfect teeth and shaking his head. "You've got the damn harness on back to front. Christ sake, take it off and come here."

Feeling like an idiot, Bill unclipped the combat webbing and tossed it over to Al, who quickly adjusted the buckles and fasteners of the harness and told Bill to step into it, quickly and efficiently slipping it into place. Bill nodded, acknowledging it was a lot more comfortable now.

"Might have the most combat experience," grinned Al with much chagrin, "but you can't even put on a frigging harness. Jesus wept, Sarah did it first time."

"Okay," snapped Bill, kneeling beside the two muscular men and looking over the collection of weapons that were in the middle of being prepared. Both were cleaning rifles, each weapon of a similar size but a different design. Bill watched in wonderment as the two Marines worked, and marvelled at how similar they were: same size, same build, working on the same type of weapon. The only difference was that one was pale as a sheet and didn't speak a word of English, while the other was dark skinned and spoke a lot more. In this case, more wasn't necessarily better.

"Sniper, huh?" he asked as he picked up a handgun and slipped it into his holster. It was a simple sidearm that he hoped he didn't have to use; it didn't look anywhere near as powerful or intimidating as the rest of the weapons on parade. "That mean you hang way back behind enemy lines, out the way of danger and take the odd pot shot at your target?"

Harbinger leapt into action, standing up and grabbing the shoulder straps of the webbing, spinning around and hurling Bill against the wall. The rack of weapons beside him shook and wobbled with the force of the impact, and Bill swallowed hard. Harbinger leaned in closer, his face inches from Bill's, and growled in his ear: "Nien."

"At least we know he can say something other than 'ja'," Al said, dropping his weapon and standing up, prising the two apart. "Me and you, Harbinger, we're the same rank, so I can't order you around as such, but I can make suggestions, and I *suggest* you leave my men alone. And Bill, don't antagonise Brutus here. He's our backup for this mission. The last thing we need to do is watch our back in case one of "own guys" draws a bead on us. Okay?"

Both men nodded and slinked off to their respective weapons.

Bill had insisted on taking a shotgun, but Al had nixed that idea, claiming that the stationed Marines were likely armoured, and they needed penetration, not a spread of shot. Instead, he had been handed a Hammersmith TAC1 assault rifle, a robust weapon with a drum of one hundred rounds attached to the underside. Al had shown him how to attach the weapon to his harness, how to reload it, and how to activate the laser target attached to the underside of the barrel. He had protested, stating he'd rather have a grenade launcher, but Al had bluntly said he'd rather he didn't. Obviously the incident in Edgly still lingered in his mind, and if truth were told, Bill was sure he could still hear ringing in his ears in the still of the night from the proximity of the blast.

Al favoured his M82, the powerful rifle he'd lovingly used since finding one on Angel's farm, and the same TAC1 rifle as Bill. He'd also had his modified handgun returned to him, along with a surprising gift of a metal box filled with the heavy rounds.

Harbinger lovingly polished his enhanced rifle, the ThunderKraft Mjolnir. It used the same ammo as Al's own rifle, but managed to put a little extra kick behind the round, offering greater damage. He didn't take the same assault rifle, but instead carried a brace of Hummingbird machine pistols and two hundred rounds for them. They didn't offer as much offensive power as the TAC1, but Harbinger had told Al by using the mute hand signals of Marine combat that he didn't intend to let them get close enough to go on the defensive.

Finally kitted out and tooled up, Al passed a final inspection over Bill and tossed him a thick stick of black waxen face paint.

"Cover your face in this, kid, you and Harbinger stick out like sore thumbs. What do you do about that luminous fuzz on your head, Brutus?"

Harbinger grunted, wiping black smudges across his cheeks and forehead, then grabbed one of the black rags he'd been using to clean his weapons and forced it into one of this pockets before storming out the armoury.

Outside, Angel waited for Bill, smiling as he strolled into view and motioned with one hand to the attire he wore.

"It's nice, really suits you. It really shows off your ass."

"Thought you British said arse," Lance said, looking towards the cliff and the rope ladder he had secured, their route down to the little black boat that waited for them at the base of the cliff.

"Don't get into that," Bill said, grabbing Angel around her waist and holding her close to him. "Take care," he whispered breathily, his lips inches from hers before he kissed her, at the same time pressing a small blade he'd liberated from the armoury into the palm of her hand. He would have rather given her a handgun, but the beauty of the knife, despite the limited range, was that it was small, and could kill an infinite number of people, in theory at least. He didn't need to explain why he'd armed her: protection in case the Marines left in the compound decided to turn on her or Sarah. "You know I love you," he finally managed to say.

"I love you to," she murmured, playfully biting his lip. "Take care."

"Christ sake," muttered Al, barging past them. "It's enough to make you sick. Come here honey."

Sarah rushed forwards and wrapped her arms around Al's neck, getting a solid purchase on him before he raised himself to his full height and hugged the girl back. "You make sure you do as you're told," he chastened, rubbing a streak of black paint on her cheek. "Don't stay up late, we'll be back before sunrise. Do as the bit... do what Angel tells you. And stick close."

"Don't worry Pops," Angel said, peeling herself away from Bill and stepping closer to Al, then raising herself up on her tiptoes and planting a kiss on his forehead. "We'll behave, and I'll have her in bed by ten. We'll just stay up and bitch about men."

Al rubbed furiously at his head, as if the kiss burned him, then strolled off towards the ladder, motioning to Garth to join him and show him the maps he had been working on. Bill waved his farewell and Angel and Sarah then followed towards the ladder, with Harbinger bringing up the rear.

"Garth says there should be a tower about fifteen miles out that way," Al confirmed, consulting an aerial view of part of the coastline. Numerous red dots traced a line around the coast, then veered away towards Ireland, just near to part of the coast surrounded with a blue ring. "They're normally only a couple of miles away from the coast, see, but because we happen to be around the area the towers spread out to ensnare Ireland, we have further to go. Why Preston couldn't just set up his playground of debauchery closer to a tower is beyond me."

"Probably to avoid tracking," Lance muttered. "Get moving, you should aim to get there and back before sunup."

"Sir, yes sir," snapped Al, exaggerating a salute before clambering down the ladder and muttering half-formed sentences to no one in particular. Bill grinned to himself, waved to Angel as he positioned himself at the top of the ladder, and started to make his way down the rope ladder, gripping tenaciously to the swaying rope and wooden construction as he slowly inched his way down the cliff face.

A bitter wind ripped at his clothing and nipped at his exposed flesh, toying with the rickety ladder and the clumps of vegetation that poked out between the soil and rocks that made the cliff wall. A light spatter of rain started to fall with the wind, wetting the wooden rungs of the ladder and making the rails slippery in Bill's fingers. He coiled his fingers, held tight to each slat, and looked upwards grimly. Rain spattered in his face, bouncing off his forehead, and glared at the lip of the cliff, and the rolling dark clouds beyond. What was stopping him from simply climbing back up there and letting the Marines get on with Al's foolish mission; spend some time with Angel before the borrowed time he was living on ran out?

A lumbering form hauled itself over the edge, immense and bristling with weapons: neon white hair glinting in the silvery light of the moon as it peered out behind the precipitating cloud cover. Cumbersome boots slipped over water-covered wood, slowly coming down towards Bill.

That's what was stopping him.

Bill increased the pace at which he descended the rickety ladder, aware that the heavyset German didn't appear overly confident or graceful on the ladder, and he didn't feel like having three hundred pounds of man, weaponry and equipment come crashing down on him. That would knock him from the ladder, and in turn Al would more than likely follow.

"Got it," Al yelled from beneath him, the sound of a metal blade clanging against the cliff face ringing out above the crash of the waves. Bill peered over his shoulder, and noticed that Al had made considerable distance since setting off: maybe the notion of Harbinger bringing everyone down with a clumsy misplacing of an oversized boot appealed to Al as much as it did to Bill. The sound of the stealth boat slapping in the water followed, and Bill quickened his pace: he wasn't looking forward to a boat trip in little more than a dinghy, but at the same time he didn't have much of anything else to look forward to.

He finally reached the bottom of the ladder and graciously took Al's hand as he pulled him into the raft, motioning for him to take position up at the front of boat.

Harbinger finally reached the bottom of the ladder after wrestling with the rope ladder, shrugged off Al's hands as he tried to help him, then stood up in the boat, glaring down on Bill as he adjusted his position and grabbed the black nylon chord that spanned the perimeter of the boat.

"What's wrong?" Bill demanded, looking up at the Marine. The behemoth scowled at him and flashed a quick series of hand signals. Bill looked towards Al for a translation, who complied with a shake of his head.

"He says you're sitting in his seat."

"Didn't see your name on the bench," Bill said with a smirk. Harbinger failed to see the funny side, refusing to give in and take a seat elsewhere in the boat. Instead, he repeated the flash of hand signals.

"Your seat, huh?" Bill muttered, shuffling closer to Al and giving the sniper plenty of space to settle down. "You going to sit up there like a god damn beacon? White hair glowing in the dark like a radioactive helmet?"

Harbinger didn't look around or respond, simply slipped the crumpled square of black material out of his pocket and wrapped it around his head, tying it off in a double knot behind his head and tucking in the loose flaps of material.

"Bandana," muttered Bill, sulking in the middle of the boat between the two bulky soldiers.

"Genius," murmured Al. "That guy right there should be calling the shots up there on the cliff top, and that asshole officer should be down here to pilot the boat."

Harbinger didn't offer a verbal response, but lifted his hand and extended his middle finger, not turning back to look at either of the other passengers to see if they registered his crude gesture or not.

"Guess you ain't got any love for the officers, either. Okay, cast-off," Al muttered, waving to the rope beside Bill. "Let's get this shit on the road."

Angel watched from the top of the cliff as the boat pulled away from the mooring at the base of the ladder and slid across the waves of the blackened sea, the drone of the motor buzzing off into the distance. She held Sarah's hand and stood motionless, watching as the tiny black vehicle faded out of sight. She didn't know how long it was until the sun came up, which was when the first part of the mission was due to be complete, but every hour would feel like a day until she knew Bill was safe, back in the village: the few minutes it had taken for the boat to vanish out of sight felt like it had dragged out into hours.

"Sounds like a pissed hornet," muttered Garth from behind her, digging the toe of his right boot into the dirt and twisting it from side to side, his eyes focused on the excavation at hand before finally lifting his gaze. "They're going to hear them coming before they see them."

Angel twisted her head around and glared at Garth, a deadly look that spoke volumes about how much she would hurt him if he continued to put a negative spin on the task. It was bad enough that Bill had been drafted into the fool's errand, the last thing she needed was for Garth to doubt or jinx the outcome. He held his hands up apologetically by way of surrender.

"I'm just saying, that's all."

"Didn't you listen to that guy's story?" asked Sarah, jerking a thumb over towards Lance, who stood patiently by the armoury and watched as it was locked back up by the limping man who stood on guard. "It can go silent, dummy."

"If you're finished watching them sail off into the night," murmured Lance, diverting his attention from the armoury to the expanse of water beyond the cliff. He let the mood linger for a moment before finally spitting a wad of phlegm over the edge and into the sea below. "The grease monkey's looking at the helicopter, looking at what he needs. Goliath's helping him out, if you want to get down there and help him out."

"I'm good for now," Garth said, waving a hand dismissively.

"It wasn't a request," Lance hissed. "You want to fly the bird, you and your mismatched ragtag band of rebels, you need to get it ready. Get it ready for Harbinger coming back, or as close to ready as possible."

"You can't order me around, I'm not military," snapped Garth, pointing a stubby and dirty finger in the direction of Lance. He growled and took a step forward, and Garth instantly took a step back, cowering slightly from the domineering figure. Angel thought for one moment Garth had finally found his courage, like the lion in that story her mother used to read her. He'd almost stood up to the Marine captain, but quickly backed down once the guttural growl rumbled in the back of his throat.

"I'll go see if Sly needs a hand," Garth announced as he walked away from the cliff top and around to the front of the warehouse, nervously adjusting his cap as he quickly made his escape. "Angel, keep an eye on Sarah."

"He's all shirt and no shorts," Lance muttered with a grin, shaking his head before turning to face the young girl that stood motionless beside Angel. "Are you sure you don't want to play with some of the kids here? I know it's late, but I know a group of them that always get together and play video games until early in the morning. It's not the most constructive of things to waste power on, but you know, they're just kids, they need something to keep them occupied. You want to go see them?"

"I'm not a kid," Sarah protested, sticking close to Angel and squeezing her hand. "I don't play kids games."

"Whatever," muttered Lance, shaking his head and knowing when he was beaten. He could intimidate weaker people all he wanted, but both Angel and Sarah had spent a significant amount of time with Al: it would take a lot to intimidate them. "Just… keep out of trouble: both of you. Hopper, rustle up an escort for these two. Oh, and Miss Green, if you pull that knife on anyone here, I'll make sure it's the last thing you do."

Angel felt her cheeks flush, embarrassed that the captain had spotted the passing of the weapon. Still, knowing she had something she could use to protect her comforted her a little, and she hoped that Lance wasn't going to confiscate it. He didn't make a move for her, didn't ask for it back.

"Just make sure no one does anything to anyone here to warrant me pulling the knife," Angel said, her tone threatening, cool and calm: "And I'll behave."

"Miss Green, if anyone does anything here, I'll pull a knife on them myself. Everyone here's on the same side."

Lance took a step closer, leaned in and grinned. "Trust me, I'm a man of my word."

"That's yet to be seen," Angel muttered, tugging Sarah by the hand and peeling away from the precipice, leaving Lance to contemplate the horizon on his own. Heading towards the flickering light of the campfire that had been started halfway between the warehouse and the towering wooden walls, Angel found herself pulled towards the crowd that had started to gather. Despite the spattering of rain that has started to drizzle from the sky, everyone in the village seemed excited about the upcoming sermon. Villagers eyed Angel warily and the crowd parted as she approached the small bonfire, keeping close the heat and trying to find some shelter from the chilled wind that whistled through the compound.

"C'mon, sweetie, let's see what Clive's doing."

Pacing back and forth in a small wooden hut that one of the villagers had opened up to him, Clive unravelled a length of purple silk, gently pressed it against his lips, then draped the sash around his neck, letting it dangle over the heavy leather coat he still wore. Adjusting his bandana, he produced his weathered bible from the inside pocket of his coat and thumbed through the pages, squinting at the small type in the dim glow given off from the low-wattage bulb that dangled from the ceiling. He didn't have to believe what it was he was saying, just sound like he did; he just had to pick something that was particularly relevant. But what?

Revelation sprang instantly to mind, though the talk of the afterlife, the end of days and the ultimate battle between good and evil may be too much to take onboard, especially the younger members of the clergy that would gather at the hearing. Talk of Revelation may also remind Angel of her time with the Messiah, which was something he didn't want to do. The rabid killer with delusions of grandeur may have believed in what he preached; he may not, but Clive feared becoming what he hated the most. If he continued to travel the same path as Frank Steele, then that was entirely possible.

So what else could he read? By his calculations it was around the end of March, maybe the beginning of April, which meant that under normal circumstances that he would read from the Easter story: Christ's final days on earth and the crucifixion, his burial and rising from the grave. Perhaps not the most *appropriate* of topics to discuss, especially considering the number of undead creatures that lurked beyond the heavily protected walls. That obviously meant that the story of Lazarus was excluded, too.

Maybe something from the Old Testament? Something that would illustrate the plight of the masses, hundreds of people pitted against insurmountable odds that only god could deliver them from... Moses and the Israelites, maybe, and their escape...

"No," he muttered to himself. "No, keep away from the plagues."

Exodus, he finally decided. The tale of Noah's Ark, the story of a pious man being guided by god amidst the maelstrom: surely it would instil belief in the villagers, show that although it may seem that god had abandoned them, he was still watching over his chosen people. He slipped his bible back into his pocket, patted it softly then exited the small hut.

An orange glow enveloped the exterior of the hut and the crowd of people that surrounded it, each person with their gaze fixed on the entrance. A murmur rippled through the crowd as Clive stepped into the glow of the fire and stood by a wooden podium near the entrance to the hut. He removed his bible again, placed it on the makeshift lectern, but didn't open it. Even if he did, the glow from the campfire wouldn't have illuminated a lot of the text. It didn't matter, though, he knew the story off by heart.

"Thank you all for attending," he began, feeling the familiar tingle of the hairs on the back of his neck standing on end: something he used to get when he first started to practice delivering his sermons. "I understand that it's late, but I also understand that visitors to your village are... rare, to say the least. We are just passing through, and I trust you will forgive me. Captain Lancet assures me that service will resume as normal following this impromptu sermon."

Clive smiled reassuringly to the front row of people, those closest to the fire, and hoped that the flickering flames were kind to his features, and didn't add a certain demonic quality. The women and children there returned the smile, and he felt the unease and tension in him dissolve. He wasn't preaching now, he was acting, but it seemed to come naturally.

"Thousands of years ago, before the birth of our Lord, Jesus Christ, there was a man. A follower of the Lord who lived his life as he should. He was kind and good, never raised a hand to another person, helped out whoever he could whenever he could: even while those around him took advantage of one another, squabbled and fought, this man followed the righteous path.

"Now, God had noticed what was happening in his world, and saw that in all the evil that was engulfing his land, but one candle shone in the darkness. He spoke to this man, and told him that he was to build a boat."

"An Ark," whispered one of the children near the front. Clive looked down on her and smiled, nodding his head.

"Yes, he told him to build an Ark. A boat that had enough space for him, his family, and two of each animal from the mainland. God planned to... well, for lack of a better word, to purge the land of the men that had turned evil. Once the Ark had been built, God summoned a rain like the world had never seen before. For forty days and forty nights the rains beat down on the earth; villages on the shores and coasts vanished, then towns and cities further up the mainland were consumed. Soon, entire countries had disappeared, swallowed by the cleansing waters. Hundreds and thousands of people died. Some survived, those aboard the Ark sailed on the rising seas for over a month, until the rain finally stopped.

"Since building the Ark, Noah hadn't heard anything else from God, but his faith was strong, and he knew that he wouldn't abandon him, even in his darkest hour. Each day, he released a bird from the roost aboard the Ark, though each day none returned; until one morning. A dove fluttered down on the deck that fateful day, with an olive branch clutched between its beak.

"Faith had delivered him from the rains; faith and God."

Clive leaned back, unaware that he'd adopted an aggressive stand while he spoke: fingers curled around the edges of the lectern, shoulders drawn and hunched around him. The palm of his hands had rubbed raw against the edges of the makeshift pulpit, and he looked at them for a few seconds, at the blood that trickled down his wrists. It reminded him of someone…

Religious figure, his palms bleeding as he preached to the gathered masses, his words nothing but lies, designed to motivate and compel the men to follow him. I am Alpha and Omega, the beginning and the ending, saith the Lord, which is, and which was, and which is to come, the Almighty…

"Father Ridgedale?" a familiar voice spoke aloud, close the front of the assembly, then followed up with in a hushed tone: "Clive, are you okay?"

Clive looked down and saw Angel in the crowd, with Sarah beside her. He nodded, more to himself than Angel, and wiped his hands on his trousers before continuing.

"This, of course, reminds us all of Psalm twenty six. Twenty six? Maybe twenty four?"

Clive chuckled and openly addressed the congregation, outstretching his arms, palms outward. He caught himself, and quickly readjusted his posture so it wasn't mimicking the crucifixion as much. "You'll forgive me if I can't remember of the top of my head, I'm sure you'll all agree the past couple of years have been somewhat traumatic."

A slight laughter rippled across the crowd, with murmurs and approval and nodding of heads.

"A man died and went up to heaven, and God was waiting for him at the gates. As they entered the gates together, God showed this man's life to him as footprints in the sand. 'But Lord,' asked the man, pointing to the marks in the sand. 'Why are there two sets of footprints?' God smiled and told him that the other set of footprints were his own. The man nodded, and followed the footprints. He noted that, in times of need and when things were looking bad for him, there was only one set of footprints. 'When times were hard, Father, why did you abandon me?' God smiled and shook his head. 'My child,' he said, 'when you faced times of hardship, there's only one set of footprints not because I abandoned you, but because I carried you'."

Clive stepped away from the lectern and closer to the fire, dusting down a tree stump before lowering himself down to it. As he sat there, he felt like he was an elder of an ancient tribe, cast back to the dawn of time, as if the flickering fire before him had just been discovered, and his followers gathered around him were listening, awestruck as he described how he came about the startling discovery.

"You see, times may seem desperate now," Clive said, wrapping up the sermon. It was a lot shorter than he was used to: Sylvester had always said they seemed to go on forever. "And for all God may seem like he's abandoned you," he continued, pointing to a random person in the crowd, then picking another, then another. "Or you, or you; just like it may seem that he abandoned Noah those weeks out at sea, he hasn't gone, he hasn't forgotten about us. God has very wide shoulders, and he bares the burden of us all.

"Now, if you can all join me in the lords prayer."

Clive closed his eyes and proceeded to go through the prayer, listening as the congregation murmured their way through. He could hear Angel and Sarah clearly above everyone else: they had heard him say it a number of times, and had attended a few of his 'sermons' when they lived on the army base, but their voices were drowned out as everyone chimed in with a rumbling 'Amen' at the end. With that, the congregation quickly disbanded, leaving Angel and Sarah, along with Captain Lancet at the rear of the gathering.

"That was nice," Angel whispered, stepping towards him and wrapping her arms around him. "You did good, I think a lot of people got something from it."

"You're right," Captain Lancet announced as he stepped forwards, kicking dirt over the fire as he started to kill the flames. "That's given a lot of people here a boost of faith that they were lacking. You did good, Preacher-man. Real good."

He sat down on the front row of benches, and motioned for the rest of them to join him. Angel complied, joining him on his right, and Clive on his left. Sarah slipped on to the ground between Angel's legs and closed her eyes, resting her head against her right knee. Angel softly stroked her tousled hair, and the young girl quickly slipped into a deep sleep, sighing and muttering softly to herself.

"That story you told," the Marine started, waving vaguely towards the lectern. Clive's vision followed his gesture, and the blood on the edges of the plinth from where his hands rubbed stood out like a beacon to him. He quickly averted his eyes. "Why'd you pick that?"

"Captain? I was told to…"

"Drop the Captain, Preacher-man. Everyone here calls me Lance. Just roll with it."

"Lance," Clive said, feeling awkward as he spoke the name. "I was told to speak to the people and give them something to instil hope in them. Al told me not to go anywhere near the Book of Revelation, which was obvious. The last thing these people needed was for someone to stand beside a blazing fire and preach about the Apocalypse: but Noah's Ark? That shows that God is always looking after his own, and the Psalm? I believe Garth would say that seals the deal."

"And no other reason for that choice?"

"Well, I suppose Bill and Al out there helped me decide, on some deep subconscious level. Those two, and your man as well, out in the middle of the ocean. Remembering them in our prayers, and hoping that God is watching them."

A rumble of thunder sounded in the distance, and a spatter of rain hissed in the dying embers of the fire. Clive looked up towards the sky, closed his eyes and shook his head. *How fitting?*

"That's good," muttered Lance, ignoring the rain as he sat motionless. "See, your story gave me an idea, too. If you've got a couple of moments, Father, I'd like to have a word with you in my office. Well, both of you."

"What about…" Clive asked, trailing off as he motioned towards the sleeping child at Angel's feet.

"Of course, bring her, we can't leave her sleeping out here in the rain. And besides, Angel promised she'd look after her, and the last thing we want to do is piss off Al."

III

"God damn British pissing weather," hissed Al through clenched teeth, pulling the wax-coated black canvas over his head and shoulders as the wind and rain buffeted the small boat. "Are we nearly there?"

Harbinger looked up from the glowing scope on his sniper rifle, and nodded grimly. He held up two fingers on his left hand, and then drummed the fingers of his other hand on the side of his weapon. Bill barely followed the conversation, and guessed that two fingers could have meant anything: two minutes, two miles…

"Twenty minutes." Al translated. "Give or take."

Bill pulled his piece of tarpaulin tighter around him and frowned. Al shook his head, and pushed his left hand out from beneath the sheet.

"Left hand denotes tens, right hand single units."

"Wonderful. What else can you teach me in twenty minutes?"

"Stop," Al commanded, raising a fist and pumping it up and down once. Then he extended one finger and pointed it skyward. "Danger," he continued, then moved his hand around in a slight circular motion. "Circle around. The way you spin your hand denotes the direction: clockwise for right, counter clockwise for left."

Bill copied the motions, slowly mouthing the words as he tried them himself.

"I see," Al continued, pointing to his eyes with two fingers. "Now, try this."

Al performed his own series of hand movements, and Bill slowly tried to follow.

"Stop, I see ten circle around?"

"Close," Al nodded. "Two fingers on right hand, that's single units. Stop, I can see two of them: circle around to the left. Take the basics and fill in the blanks, yeah?"

"I guess," Bill murmured hesitantly. "A lot of gaps to fill in; there's a lot to learn, too."

"Being in the Marines isn't all about shooting guns, killing goons and sleeping with women in different countries. It involves really big guns, am I right? Eh?"

Al playfully slapped Harbinger's chest with the back of his hand, who in return grinned softly and nodded, then motioned to the sniper scope. Al shuffled closer to the weapon and peered through, then nodded in response and started to prepare his own arsenal, pulling his sniper rifle out from beneath the canvas and levelling it off with the target in the distance.

"Get your shit ready, kid," Al hissed, panning slowly from left to right with his weapon. Bill nodded, though his weapons were already set to go off. He grabbed the pair of night vision binoculars that dangled from around his neck and lifted them to his eyes, thumbing the controls on the top of the device and zooming in on the structure on the distance.

A shapeless mound of concrete, floating impossibly in the frothing waters of the turbulent sea, with a flat metallic podium attached to it, raised and supported by a number of metal legs ad supports, with a twisted and broken barrier surrounding the perimeter of the construct: a helipad left in a state of disrepair. From the centre of the mound of concrete rose two structures: one a squat building with a catwalk circling it halfway, the other a tower that loomed over the island like a silent sentinel. Bill couldn't make out any colours other than the pale washed-out greens that the image intensifiers created.

"Looks pretty quiet over there," Bill said in a hushed tone, suddenly afraid to speak in case his voice carried across the storm and into the ears of a listening Marine.

"It's the middle of the fucking night," growled Al, keeping his voice just as low. "Right about now those Marines'll be either fast asleep or jerking off over photos of their girlfriends. It ain't pretty, but it's the truth, am I right Brutus?"

"Ja," Harbinger rumbled. He switched his powered scope for a smaller eyepiece, lifted his eye patch up and pressed the weapon into his eye socket, carefully panning from left to right as the boat encroached on the dark, murky waters surrounding the tower.

"That being said, there should be at least one Marine on duty in the tower. I don't see one. I don't even see a single light over there. Bring us in on a quiet engine, kid, just like I showed you. Nice and slow, easy does it."

Bill nodded and took the controls to the engines, shrugging off the blanket draped around his shoulders and guiding the vehicle onwards as it glided effortlessly through the waves.

The guard tower slowly pulled into view, and Bill felt his body tense as it approached, expecting to come under fire from whatever heavy weapons they had to make sure no infection escaped the island. He swallowed hard, never imagining for one moment he would ever be this close to one of the guard towers that served to contain the plague. He gripped the butt of his weapon with one hand, playing the pinprick of a laser target over the drab grey walls of the building, anxiously awaiting the attack he knew would follow. The boat butted up against the side of the framework that supported the helipad, and Al looped a length of black nylon rope back and forth amongst the support stanchions, securing the boat before nimbly climbing on to the pad and helping Bill make his way up.

"Okay, we move quick and we move fast. Just like every other Marine pre-fab building, it's a generic layout. Bottom floor of the short building is the storage level, upper floor living areas. Beyond that, a staircase into the tower and the observation levels. Ideally, I'd like to burst in through the storage area and grab what we need without letting those bastards know we're here.

Unfortunately, that ain't gonna happen. Instead, we smash the door down, storm the building, and clear it room-by-room using classic break-and-enter techniques. Harbinger, that's you and me. Bill, you cover our sixes, make sure we don't miss anyone. Now, who's got the key?"

Harbinger grinned as he replaced the eye patch over his right eye and produced a squat, triple-barrelled shotgun, unlocking the safety on the weapon and raising it. Al nodded, then bolted across the open helipad, diving in to a roll that ended in a tumbling halt at the sealed doorway to the storage shed and pulled out a can of red aerosol paint. He hastily sprayed a circle around the top and bottom corner of one side of the door, then another in the middle, and motioned for Harbinger to advance next. Bill dropped to his knees and shouldered his own rifle, providing cover as the large man thundered across the landing area, weapon raised. He aimed high, fired, aimed low, fired again, then levelled off the weapon at his hip and unleashed a third shot. With each discharge of the weapon there came a tremendous blast, a cacophonous explosion of gunpowder and a solid ceramic slug pounding against the metal door, tearing through the locking mechanisms of the portal. Al heaved it open, waved over to Bill, then vanished into the darkness of the building with Harbinger close behind.

Bill ran across the rain-spattered landing pad and slipped into the open warehouse, the hiss of rain hitting the ground turning to the hammering drone of the water thumping against the side of the vacuous building. The gloom of the building seemed to consume Bill, until Al sparked a bright white flare to life, tossing it casually on the ground. It rolled around on the grilled floor, casting long and flickering shadows.

"Okay, three shotgun blasts, a door being blown open, and still nothing. Gives a new definition to heavy sleepers. Quickly look around, whatever we can take now we grab. Anything else, you can come back with the Helicopter to stock up after we're finished with it. *Ja?*"

"Ja," grumbled Harbinger.

"JP-9, in that corner," Al announced, waving to one side. "Get the fuel rounded up, then see if you can find something else that we can use to pull the barrels. Unless you fancy swimming back to shore?"

"Well, won't they float on the water? We could tow them behind us…"

"Physics, kid, it's all physics. Weights, densities, temperatures, bullshit like that. They might, they might not. I'm not willing to risk losing any of this stuff if we need it. You willing to forfeit your seat if we loose some juice in the drink?"

"I'll look for a raft or something…"

"No, you'll look out for any sign of the sleeping beauties, me and Harbinger know exactly what we're looking for. Keep them peeled, kid, I'm counting on you."

"Makes me feel a whole lot better," grumbled Bill, squatting down near the spluttering flare and facing the door to the rest of the complex. He perched there for close to forty minutes while his two companions heaved and tossed heavy equipment around the storage facility, gathering what they needed by the door.

"Almost an hour in," Al murmured, stepping back from the collection of barrels that had been collected together and wiping his brow with an oily rag he had managed to find. "Harbinger, can you sort all this stuff out on your own? Get it outside and loaded up. Something stinks like shit here, and I think we should check it out. Bill, get over here."

Bill trudged wordlessly towards the door and crouched down, barely having enough time before Al heaved it open and strolled into the stairwell beyond.

"You're a little nonchalant about this," Bill commented as he followed Al into the stairwell.

"Kid, we blasted a triple-barrelled lock-breaker in the dead of night, but I think we could have used a tonne of plastic explosions. There's no lights on, I don't think there's anyone home."

"Really?"

"If someone let off a bomb outside your house in the middle of night, you'd get up to have a look, wouldn't you? Course you would, that's because you and the bitch are nosey shits and you'd want to know who interrupted your mammoth fucking session. These Marines get maybe five hours of sleep on a shift pattern, between shining shoes, ironing clothes, prepping and stripping weapons down, equipment maintenance… if someone interrupted my sleep when I was in the Marines, I would've been pretty pissed and would have demanded to know who the hell was banging on my door."

"I see," Bill said, nodding, though he wasn't quite sure what that meant. "What's the deal with Harbinger's eye? I never asked about it, I thought he'd lost it in an attack: guess I was wrong. Is it just a fashion statement?"

"Old Pirate mythology," Al grunted. "Real old school. Back in the olden days, Pirates used to wear an eye patch so they had one eye for day vision, and another eye for night vision, like specialised lenses. Improves their vision, makes it razor-sharp, so they can pick out a dust mote in the middle of a sandstorm in the dead of night. Well, maybe I exaggerate that, but they think it does them good."

"So, does it work?" Bill asked, gripping his weapon and rubbing his sweating palms against the reassuring steel of its frame. Al carefully pried open the door leading from the stairwell and into the living quarters, panning the barrel of his own weapon from side to side and playing the beam of the flashlight attached to it across the walls and open doors. This air was still, and tasted stale to Bill. As the pair stepped into the corridor, their feet kicked up clouds of dust and grime, tiny filaments that played and danced in the cone of white light.

"Does it work?" Al repeated, then breathed in sharply through his teeth, hissing and making a show of the fact he was thinking hard about it. "The results are varied. Angel seems to be a good shot…"

"You think we should try her with an eye patch, see if it improves her aim or night vision?"

"I was thinking about throwing a sack over her head, making my life easier."

"Funny man," Bill groaned inwardly as they entered the main barracks. Six beds lined one side of the wall, each with a footlocker sitting at the base of it. Each strongbox remained sealed and secure, a thick and heavy padlock dangling from each hasp. Wall lockers were mounted to the gunmetal grey walls, each locked up just as tight as the boxes at the foot of each bed.

"Shipped out?" Bill queried. Al shook his head.

"You get shipped out, you don't leave all that," Al said, motioning to one of the beds. The sheets had been left unkempt, with a variety of pornographic magazines left littered across the sheets. A bundle of photographs had been scattered across the pillow, a young girl with dark skin and black hair, clutching a young toddler in her arms. "Wife or girlfriend, a young daughter. Even if you were shipped out in a rush, you make sure your carrying pictures of that special girl back home around with you. See?"

Al unfastened a pouch on his combat webbing around his waist and flashed a collection of papers. One was his treasured picture of Caitlin Dillons, another a crumpled photograph of Pam, and a third of Sarah. Though Bill could never remember seeing Al with a camera, it looked as if they'd been taken in the fort they'd lived in for a while. He quickly replaced them in his pouch and grinned sheepishly, as if he was ashamed that he'd revealed something personal about himself.

"So, the place isn't deserted?"

"Maybe," murmured Al, returning to the entrance to the barracks and sticking his head back out into the corridor, peering cautiously from side to side with his weapon following his gaze. "Could be that there's just one guy left, less than a skeleton crew. We'll take a look up the tower, see if there's anyone in there."

"What if there is?"

"Shoot first, ask no questions later. C'mon, kid, the sooner we get this shit sorted out the sooner we can get back and grab that helicopter."

The pair slunk back into the corridor and slowly opened the door to the stairwell; Al peered cautiously up the stairs, while Bill looked down, making sure no one had entered the access while they'd been away.

Cautiously, the pair crept up the metal steps one at a time and found the door leading into the tower locked from the inside. Al grabbed the enlarged metal wheel that acted as the central locking control, braced himself against one of the walls in the narrow passageway, then twisted it. A deafening screech pierced the silence of the station, and Al motioned for cover while he swung the metallic barrier to one side.

Crouching low and panning the muzzle of his assault rifle to and fro, the stale, salty scent that hung in the air was chased away by the fetid stench of rot and decay, and Bill tensed as the outline of a figure was visible in the dim green glow of the monitors. Doing just as Al had commanded, he squeezed off a burst of three rounds with a deafening cry that he felt appropriate. The glaring flash from the discharging weapon made dancing shadows on the distorted and withered features of the corpse, and it shuddered and slumped to one side as the searing lead smashed into the cadaver. His finger still coiled around the trigger, a second burst of gunfire screamed from Bill's chattering weapon and struck the body once more, this time knocking it from the chair and leaving a ruined and shattered husk on the floor.

"Think it's dead?" Al smiled as he pushed Bill aside and strolled casually into the cramped control room. The stench of seared dead flesh and cordite lingered in the air, making Bill gag as he followed into the small room and slid on to the vacant seat. Al quite casually kicked the body aside and lowered himself to the recently vacated chair, slamming his weapon on to the desktop and leaning back in the seat, pulling out a cigar and chomping down on it with clenched teeth. Bill peered at the corpse from where he sat, shaking his head and prodding it with the muzzle of his weapon.

"How long?" Bill asked, his voice quiet as if he was afraid he would wake the dead man,

"Since he's been dead? Fuck knows, couple of months, maybe longer." He snapped out his lighter, flicked it open and lit the cigar, then shrugged. "Guess they needed soldiers elsewhere, probably to clean up the shit on the mainland, so they left the bare minimum behind to monitor the islands."

"One person? That's hardly a skeleton crew, it's just… shit, that's just one guy!"

"The Marines obviously have total confidence in their soldiers on the mainland. This guy," Al said, kicking the corpse with his boot. "This fucker here was just a back-up, a contingency, in case someone suddenly decided to jet the hell off the island at the very last moment. If anything like that did happen, he could blow the whistle and the patrol boats could either scramble fighters or shoot the bastards down. All the sensors are set up on automatic, anyway, this guy was just making sure nothing stopped working."

"Until he died," Bill said.

"Until he killed himself," Al corrected, motioning to the bloodied combat knife that lay on the floor. For the first time, Bill noted that the floor was covered in dried blood, and the same substance covered the blade. Aside from the bullet wounds that covered the corpse, deep gashes in the wrists of the corpse, running the length of his arms, suggested that the soldier had been severely depressed up to the point where he had sliced open his own wrists.

"So, I guess the place is completely deserted?"

"Looks that way. I know when I was stationed on one of these damn towers we were told not to do anything that wasn't in our job description. We weren't described as cleaners, but no fucker would just leave a corpse around to stink up the place. Aside from the obvious hygiene issues, the bastard reeks to high heaven. No, any soldiers stationed here would have dragged this guy out and dumped him in the sea the first chance they had. Harbinger, you hearing this?"

"Ja," the Marine grumbled his response, sounding out of breath as he hauled the cargo around on ground level.

"Take your time, there's no one home. Once we get back, this place can be stripped clean without any worry. Why don't you take five, me and the kid'll come down to give you a hand."

Knowing that the base was abandoned, the trio could take their time in securing their supplies to the rear of the craft, and by the time sun rose on the tower structure, the small black stealth boat had a raft made of emptied barrels hitched to the back, laden with four containers filled with helicopter fuel. Though the surface of the raft bobbed low to the surface of the sea, Al was confident the makeshift platform would hold, and motioned to board and return to the cliff top outpost, their cache secured and their plans one step closer to fruition.

The first thing Bill felt as he hauled his weight over the lip of the cliff was a thin pair of arms wrap themselves around him, accompanied by the sound of Angel talking as she murmured greetings into his shoulder. He returned the embrace, and then turned to help Al complete his ascent. He, in turn, was greeted by a welcoming hug from Sarah.

"Status?" barked Lance, standing by the ladder and watching as his man, Harbinger, clawed at the ground and heaved his considerable bulk over the edge of the precipice.

"Mission complete," Al said with a grin, snapping off a jaunty salute with much gusto.

"Harbinger?" Lance questioned, obviously preferring to hear it from the mouth of his own man. He nodded once, a solid response to the question.

"The tower's dead," Al smiled, lifting Sarah up and shifting her weight over to one side as he stepped away from the edge of the cliff face. As soon as the way was clear, two men who had stood patiently by and watched the reunion slung their rifles over their shoulder and scrabbled down the ladder, pulling lengths of cable behind them that would be used to winch the cargo up once it had been secured. "Turns out there was one guy left there to watch over the tower, and he'd taken about as much as he could. Slit his wrists from wristband to elbow, bled out like a pig in a slaughterhouse. Once we get the shit with the helicopter and boat sorted out, you can get over there and take as much as you need."

Lance shook his head slowly.

"We don't need to do that any more. We need to talk, if you wouldn't mind stepping into our office?"

Lance turned and walked away from the cliff, heading towards the warehouse, and Harbinger obediently followed him, keeping close to his heels like a faithful dog. Al tried to fight the sneer that crawled across his face, but failed miserably.

"This is the part I should've seen coming. We've served our use to the Brass, so now he's going to change the deal and kill us all. Or feed us to the Rots. Or something like that."

"How do you know that?" Bill asked, mid-hug with Angel.

"Because they're all the fucking same, those bastards. They use you for what they can, and then take a shit on you from a great height. Now they've got fuel for their helicopter engine, which powers the base, we've served our purpose."

"You really think that's what's going to happen?" Bill asked as he strolled off towards the warehouse, holding Angel's hand and swinging it back and forth as they walked.

"I'm counting on it," Al warned, pulling a grenade from his bandoleer and looping his thumb through the firing pin before pushing both hand and grenade into his trouser pocket. Bill saw the movement from the corner of his eyes and stopped dead in his tracks.

"You're going to kill us all?"

"Better dead than being dangled from a length of rope and used to fish for Rots. I'm not stupid, kid, I won't prime it until I know for sure we've been screwed over. I may be homicidal, but I'm not suicidal."

Bill allowed Al to overtake him as he stormed onwards, entering the warehouse with a determined expression on his face. The moment he entered, he saw the helicopter that was his ticket off the island, almost fully restored. Garth and Sylvester crawled over the sleek hull like worker ants, while Goliath stood on the ground beside a pile of machinery and tools, supervising the pair as they slowly reconstructed the vehicle. Al stopped in his tracks, looking at the impressive machine, and smiled. The stealth craft was certainly more pleasing on the eyes than the Cavalier gunship. Though not as heavily armed as the gunship, the stealth helicopter was armed with a brace of rocket pods and a forward-facing Gatling cannon, which would be more than enough to take out the surface defences of the gun boat that they'd be attacking. Al relaxed his grip on the grenade and unhooked his finger from the firing pin; Lance appeared to be upholding his end of the deal, at least as far as restoring the helicopter went.

"You're back then," Garth said as he half climbed, half fell off the helicopter, wiping his hands on a greasy rag that hung from his belt.

"Was there ever any doubt?" Al grinned. Garth nodded his head.

"What's happening?" Sylvester asked, following Garth down from the machine and following the growing crowd as they moved towards the desk at the end of the warehouse. Al shrugged his shoulders.

"Brass wants a word with us, probably announcing how they're going to fuck us over this time. Where's the psycho Preacher?"

"Another sermon," Angel responded as she took a seat at the desk. The two groups were still divided, with the three Marines on one end of the table and Al and his friends at the other. "The village really warmed to him, took aboard everything he said and wanted to hear more."

"Did he mention anything about the lord smiting the non-believers or anything like that?" Al asked as he lowered himself to his own seat and leaned back, kicking his feet up on to the table.

"No, he did fine," Lance answered, cutting into the conversation. "In fact, it's because of him that there's been a change of plan."

"Fucking asshole," Al spat, pulling the grenade out his pocket and slamming it down on the table. Both Bill and Angel recoiled, and Harbinger and Goliath snapped their weapons up to target him. Garth and Sylvester stared blankly at the device. "I knew you were going to fuck us over, you always do. I just didn't think the preacher would figure into the equation…"

"Let me talk," Lance demanded, cautiously eyeing Al's fingers as they played with the grenade and picked idly at the priming pin. Still attached to the device, it wouldn't take much to pull it apart and take out the entire warehouse and everyone in it. "Your friend…"

"Ain't no friend of mine, he's a fucking nut case," spat Al.

"Your friend," Lance continued, "Told us an interesting tale during his sermon. You're familiar with the tale of Noah's Ark, correct?"

"The man who parted the Red Sea," Al nodded. "Yeah, I know my shit."

"Apparently, you don't," Angel said, keeping a wary eye on his hands as he tapped playfully on the side of the grenade. "That was Moses."

"But he had an Arc, right?"

"That's different. Noah was the one with the boat full of animals."

"Oh," Al muttered to himself, nodding gently. His face suddenly changed, as if a switch had been thrown in his head. "I'm not taking a bunch of fucking animals with us."

"No, you're going to take the village with you. Every last one of us."

"In the helicopter?" mocked Al. "There's no space in there."

"The plan remains the same up until you get to the boat. Instead of sending back the helicopter, you bring the whole boat back, and we load everyone up.

"We were just planning on a gun boat," Al said, shaking his head. "It'll be too small."

"A gunboat, yes. Instead of that, you'll go for a frigate. We've managed to get the rough coordinates of a frigate, you'll need to fly out to that grid reference and conduct a search from there.

Take control of it and there'll be enough room for the village and all the supplies we can carry."

"We're biting off more than we can chew," warned Al. "There's no way we can do that, even if we left the Preacher-man behind and took the three of you, there's too many soldiers to contend with."

"Too many? You planned an assault on a fort that could have had a hundred soldiers stationed there, a frigate with half as much shouldn't be a problem for you. The helicopter will suffice for the initial attack on the frigate; you can easily eliminate the gun emplacements. This time, I'll go with your group: I can operate the weapons we've installed on the helicopter, and I need Goliath and Harbinger to get the villagers ready to move, pack up what shit they have and get ready."

"What *do* the villagers think of this?"

"They don't know yet. I wanted to clear it with you first before announcing it."

"You mean you wanted to see if we came back alive first," corrected Bill. Lance nodded slowly in his direction. "Touché."

"Who goes in the helicopter?" Garth asked, breathing a sigh of relief as Al finally stopped fiddling the grenade and replaced it in his pocket.

"Everyone," Al said, not giving Lance a chance to reply. "You, me, the kid, even Preacher-man. I'm not leaving anyone behind this time. There's plenty of room in the helicopter, that's not an issue, and I want people who I know and trust watching my back when we get down on that boat. You can sit and keep the engine ticking over if combat isn't your thing..."

"I'm good for any situation," Lance assured him. "I'm proficient in close-quarter combat, and I specialise in demolitions..."

"I specialise in attracting trouble," Al assured him. "But that and demolitions are among the least necessary skills for this thing, I don't want you to sink the fucking boat," Al said, rolling his eyes. "Still, at least you talk English. Not like the monster over there."

Harbinger slowly lifted a meaty paw and extended a middle finger, though he actually seemed to smile slightly when doing it.

"It's agreed then," Lance said, standing.

"It's hardly agreed," countered Al, raising himself to his feet and staring deep into the eyes of Lance. "But there's no point in arguing it out with you, because you've made up your mind. I want it to go on record that I think this is a very fucking bad idea. Kid, you're my witness.

Bill sighed and nodded in agreement.

"So, when's the bird ready to fly?"

"A couple of hours, I think," Goliath volunteered. "We striped it down, but we didn't damage anything in the process, so there isn't anything that takes too long to reinstall. The seats for the rear of the vehicle have been destroyed or lost, we can't track them down..."

"Forget them, this isn't a pleasure cruise," Al said, moving over to the flying vehicle and peering into the empty husk. The pilot and co-pilot seats were in position, but were heavily battered and scuffed, with some of the padding hanging out parts of them. The opened area in the rear of the vehicle was nothing more than a collection of steel plating bolted or welded to the floor and halfway up the walls. Unlike the larger Cavalier gunship, which he had previously travelled in, it was surprisingly spacious in comparison. That being said, the stealth craft held fewer weapons. If the helicopter had been a gunship he wouldn't have had any qualms about taking on a frigate, or at least fewer than he did now. "I'm in the front, Lance's called shotgun. Everyone else can pile in the back, there's plenty of railings you can strap yourself to, just make sure you don't fall out. We leave one of the side doors open and the bitch can take pot shots with her sniper rifle at anyone running around on the deck. We need someone backing her up with an assault rifle; I figure you can do that, kid. The two of you make a reasonable pair."

"Thanks," Bill said, nodding as he clambered into the helicopter. He could just stand upright without having to stoop down, so Al knew that everyone else would be fine. The only person in the group who would have had to walk doubled over was Al himself, and he was one of the lucky ones who was sitting.

"Everyone else should be armed with assault rifles or machineguns, nothing heavy or explosive. A few smoke grenades, maybe, but we don't want the hull breached. The last thing we want is to have to continuously bail water out the lower decks on our way to the States. Sarah, you sit in the back and hold on tight."

"The girl?" Lance said, incredulously. Al grinned and nodded.

"I didn't mind leaving her when we went for the gas, at least not as much. At least the bitch or Spanners could've kept an eye on her. I'm taking my whole crew in with me this time, so there's going to be no one I can trust her with back here."

"You can't expect to baby-sit in the middle of a combat zone," Lance grunted, shaking his head.

"Yet I'm going to baby-sit an asshole officer on this mission?" Al hissed, his voice lowering. "Bad enough I had to watch over the Goon there, now you're lumbering me with your incompetent ass?" he continued, poking a finger at Lance who stood motionless, glowering at the ex-Marine from behind furrowed eyebrows. "No, Sarah can help me keep an eye on you."

"I outrank you," Lance finally interjected, stepping forward and defending his position on the mission. "I'm a god-damn Captain here, and this is a military operation, and as such we're in charge. You're using our resources, and if I say the girl has to stay here…"

Without warning, Al hauled off a punch that connected squarely with Lance's cheek. He stumbled backwards, reeling from the blow and leaning against the helicopter with his left hand, while rubbing his face with his right. The skin was starting to swell already, and a thin rivulet of blood trickled down his face where the dermal layer had been opened. He looked accusingly at Al, who simply flexed his fingers and shook his hand, chasing away the jarring pain from striking the skull.

"This mission isn't military, you haven't been military for years. The minute you turned on a commanding officer and slaughtered his squad is the minute you stopped being a Marine. This place changes people. Look at some of the shit they did to people here, is that any different to the bullshit we put some Cartel members through?"

Lance's mouth opened and closed wordlessly, like a fish gulping air. He finally managed to stammer a response, still cupping his head in his hand. "That was different, we didn't do that kind of…"

"We didn't make them fight Rots, primarily because at the time they didn't fucking exist, but everything else… In the public eyes we followed the Geneva Convention to the letter, following the bullshit rules of engagement and conduct of war. But did we? Really? How many times did you shoot first? How many Bebops did you leave lying around in the dirt, bleeding out from a gunshot wound while you tended to your buddy with a scrape on his knee? How many interrogations did you sit in or get involved in? As long as the public image was squeaky clean, the Brass didn't give a flying fuck how we got the results we did.

"Now we've seen this shit from the other side, it appals us. Do you know why? Because three years ago, that *was* us. *We* were the ones killing, maiming, torturing. We were the good guys: but we weren't good. Far from it, in fact."

Lance wasn't sure where to put himself, fixing Al with a venomous gaze then flicking his eyes across to his cohorts. Neither offered any backup; they were just as flustered as the Captain was, and Al's speech had clearly been unexpected.

"So in conclusion," Al finished with a grin. "This mission wouldn't be going ahead if it weren't for me and the kid taking a boat out to the tower, and it was mainly my idea. You've changed it a little, but it's still my idea. I take my full squad in, plus your Brass-decorated ass, and pull this shit off. Those are my terms, if you don't like it, fuck off and find yourself another pilot."

Al spun on his heel and stormed out the warehouse, followed closely by Sarah, Bill and Angel, and stormed off towards the cliff, looking out over the horizon and nodding slightly to the men that manhandled the fuel drum and ammo boxes up over the side of the drop.

"I love the way you handle people," Bill grinned, standing beside him and joining him in the admiration of the vista. "You've got a special talent."

Al didn't say anything, just nodded a response. The view was tranquil and had a soothing effect on him. He remembered the last time he took the time to admire a view, and thought of Pam, and the area behind the church they had been married in. Though a rolling valley of fields and trees were very different to a calm seascape, it still managed to cool his temper as he reflected on better times.

"Fucking officers," he finally muttered as he took Sarah's hand in his own and squeezed it softly. Bill nodded in acknowledgement, though didn't offer any further comments.

"So what do we do now?" Angel finally asked, lowering herself to the ground and patting the grass beside her. Bill followed her, wrapping his arm around her shoulders, but Al remained on his feet.

"What can we do? I'm sick of officers, but I'm sick of this shit that's going on here, too. We still follow the same plan, it's just a shame that asshole's made it harder for us. If we're heading out tonight, I suggest we get some sleep. I don't know about you all, but I'm tired, and I don't want to be going back into combat without a decent sleep. I'm sure they won't mind if we disappear for a couple of hours. It's the least the bastards can do."

Al stalked away from the cliff top, jerking his head and indicating for Sarah to follow him.

"C'mon, honey, leave Love's New Dream to do… whatever it is they do. We'll see them in a few hours."

IV

The sun lowered on the camp once more, and Bill and Angel were ready to move. Neither of them had been able to sleep; like children on Christmas Eve, they were too busy thinking about what lay ahead to even consider sleep, or how the lack of it would affect them the following day.

They hadn't moved from their perch atop the outcrop all day, sharing each other's body heat as they sat and talked about what would await them in their new life. Angel said she had wanted to try to finish her training as a veterinarian and continue looking after animals, and once they got settled in the states with their new identities Al had promised them, that was what she wanted to do first. Despite everything that had happened, she wanted to pick her life up, more or less, where she had left off.

"What about you?"

"I don't know," Bill confessed. "I don't want to work in an office again, I know that much. In the past three years, I've had pretty much had a free reign over what I can do."

"A new-age traveller?" Angel said with a smirk. "Wandering from town to town, looking for odd jobs to earn a few dollars for a meal and a roof over your head for the night? You can take up playing the guitar, too, maybe do a little busking."

"I can't see us doing that," Bill said with a shake of his head. "I've tried before, I can't play the guitar to save my life." He laughed softly to himself. "Maybe that would work to my favour, they would pay me to stop playing." Angel laughed softly then pressed herself closer, leaning her head on his shoulder.

"You said 'us'," she said with a smile.

"I did?" Bill asked, then shrugged his shoulders. "Yeah, I guess I did."

"So what *does* happen when we get to our new home?"

"With us?" smiled Bill as he tilted his head so his cheek lay on the top and Angel's. "We have a couple of kids, live a normal life where we don't have to fight a walking corpse ever again. I'd be happy if I didn't have to lift another gun ever again, too."

"What about everyone else?"

"Garth makes his way over to Spain, gets together with his daughter. Sylvester opens up a new business. Al adopts Sarah, maybe goes to live with his mother who, as I've been told on numerous occasions, didn't raise any fools. Clive, he'll find himself again, he'll regain his faith. Eventually."

"And that's everyone," muttered Angel.

"Yeah. That's everyone," Bill murmured in melancholy tones. He sighed, remembering the rest of his fallen friends that had accompanied him in his journey. Pam and Tara, captives of the Messiah and friends until the end. Steve, Cindy and the rest of their children; a family torn apart by death and disease. He couldn't help but wonder how things would have played out if they had survived: how different things could have been. Would Garth have plucked up his courage after three years, and finally made his move on Tara? If Steve or Cindy had survived, would Al have grown so close to Sarah? The little girl certainly had a mellowing affect on him, and gave him someone to worry about other than himself. If Pam hadn't become infected, would Al have asked her to marry him? He didn't seem like the type to settle down, but circumstances can change people, as he knew himself more than anyone. He'd killed animals, people, walking corpses… committed acts he wouldn't have thought he was capable of. Now, only a few more soldiers stood between him and his freedom, and a life of pacifism. However, like nations and races before him, he was going to have to buy his freedom with a gun.

"You okay?"

"Just thinking," Bill said, his attention half rising out the mire of thoughts that rushed through his mind before sinking back beneath the surface and lost himself in contemplation once more.

Al had been uncertain of the assault on the frigate, which didn't sit well for Bill. If the cocksure and arrogant Marine part of Al wasn't happy with going up against a life-or-death situation, he wasn't entirely sure he was onboard with the idea, either. It was either all or nothing; there was no runner-up position in the upcoming conflict.

"What if this doesn't work?" Angel asked, as if she could read Bill's thoughts. "What happens then?"

"We're screwed," Bill admitted. "If they shoot us down, then we can't really limp back here, not with a damaged helicopter. If we fail this time, we don't have a second chance. Even if we *do* manage to get back here, they'll probably send out a squad to finish the job."

"Al doesn't sound as if he's brimming over with confidence," Angel agreed. "That's not normal for him, and it's pretty worrying. Where's the comforting arrogance? The cocksure attitude?"

"Don't discount the old man yet," Bill said. "I'm sure he has a couple of tricks up his sleeves."

"How long do we have left?"

Bill looked at the battered and broken watch that still clung to his wrist, and shrugged. Though the watch face hadn't withstood the ardour of war and combat, the strap had held up remarkably well against the test of time. "The sun's coming in pretty low, now, so we don't have long. Maybe we should make our way to the armoury and get ready."

"Maybe," she replied with a smirk. "Or maybe we have a little extra time to ourselves…"

"Al won't mind if we're five minutes late," Bill smiled, wrapping his arms around her shoulders and pulling her close, kissing her lightly at first, then harder as the pair melted into one another.

"He's fucking late," sneered Al as he paced back and forth inside the armoury, his heavy machinegun slung over his shoulder with a thick nylon strap, the muzzle of the weapon pointing uselessly at the ground. "He's always fucking late when he's hanging around with her."

"They're probably having sex," Sarah announced with a sheepish grin as she adjusted the straps of her modified combat suit. Al scowled at the young girl, and she shrugged her shoulders by way of apology. "Well they probably are, I'm only saying. It's not like I said they were fucking…"

"We know," Garth said, ruffling her hair with the palm of his hand and managing a strained smile. "We know. There's just more tactful ways of saying things, that's all."

"I blame the people that are bringing her up, myself," Sylvester countered. Garth laughed heartily and slapped him on the back, while Clive nodded solemnly. Al glowered at them, gritting his teeth. He was about to reply when the doors to the armoury burst open and the missing pair stumbled into the room, adjusting their clothing and laughing, almost in hysterics. The moment they entered, and noticed that everyone was waiting for them, they tried to stifle their laughter and regain their composure. Garth nodded slightly, a welcoming gesture, then rolled his eyes towards Al, who stood in silence: his eyes fixed on the two people, he worked the bolt on his weapon back and forth, waiting for one of them to say something.

"Sorry?" Bill finally offered.

"We got lost," Angel followed up, pulling a flak jacket on over her dishevelled clothing and pulling the fasteners together, cinching the straps tight and looking over the weapons before reaching for a snub machine pistol and a sniper rifle. She began to stow magazines away on her person, and Bill did the same after grabbing a bulky assault rifle. Al finally cleared his throat and the two looked at him.

"You're late."

"We know."

"I preferred it when the two of you *weren't* fucking around, at least we ran according to schedule then. We'll discuss this later; maybe I'll keelhaul you when we get on the frigate. Until then, Bill, you leave that peashooter, grab one of these," he said, slapping the side of the heavy weapon he carried. "Load up, drums of ammo are over there, you might need a couple. Bitch, make sure you get a night vision scope; otherwise you're not going to see what you're shooting at. Buddy, get over to the warehouse, take Spanners with you, make sure everything's running okay and get working on the winch, we need that thing on the roof with the blades deployed ASAP. Preacher-man, you and Sarah grab those two rucksacks and bring them. They're filled with smoke grenades, so try not to jostle them too much. Safeties on, everyone! Kid?"

Bill looked up from the heavy machinegun he was working over as he finally managed to thread the belt of bullets into the received and manually work the first few rounds through.

"Jesus, you're going to have to do that faster in combat. Kid, you and the bitch keep your safeties off and your weapons cocked. You two're going in hot, so be ready to open fire as soon as we see them. The missiles on the chopper have a little more range than that rifle, knocking around a mile, but we're going to wait until we're right on them to open up. And try to keep your hands off one another in the back of the helicopter."

"We'll try," Bill said, trying to keep a straight face, then turned to face Angel and grinned slightly. Al saw the expression on Bill's face and slapped the side of his head with the flat of his palm, not enough to cause any injury, but not soft enough to give the impression he was playing around.

"I'm serious, kid. You two, you're the ones I trust the most. That's why I'm letting you go in as the riflemen: I wouldn't trust anyone else in a moving vehicle with a loaded and primed weapon other than you two. Don't prove me wrong."

"We won't," Bill nodded, and this time his face remained stoic. Angel nodded her own head, confirming the sentiment.

"Now come on, finish getting kitted up and let's go. That frigate isn't going to wait for us."

Al stormed out the armoury with his friends in tow, marched past villagers and nodded casually as they stopped and stared at the people with heavy weapons that were casually walking through their community. The walk to the warehouse the helicopter rested in wasn't particularly long, but over half the village must have been out, watching as the procession of warriors strolled through the encampment and vanished into the storage facility.

Already, the dais the helicopter sat on was being raised as Garth, Sylvester and Harbinger worked in unison on a loop of chains threaded through a series of winches and pulleys. Inch by inch, the thick metal platform slowly ground up the tracks running the height of the building, well-oiled steel sliding against the lubricated tracks, the mechanism clacking as the teeth of internal cogs and gears locked into place, making sure the podium didn't slip back down.

"Put your backs into it," hollered Al as he strode across the open ground, hurling his machinegun up on to the ascending platform as he raced by and grabbed the chains, lending his own muscle to the task. "Where's the Almighty?"

"Lance?" Garth muttered with a grimace as sweat trickled down his brow and dripped into his eyes. He squinted, rubbed his face against his shoulder in a bid to clear his vision before giving up. "He's briefing Goliath on the handover before he goes."

"Typical," Al spat as he continued to work at the chain. The base the helicopter sat on had already raised a third of the way up the shaft, and Bill and Angel were working at securing a number of rope ladders to the edges of the elevator, making sure they had a way to climb up once the raised area had reached its apex. Clive and Sarah stood to one side, working over a second winch, which was slowly peeling the skylight above open. The gloom of night hung above them, as uninviting as it was black. "The Brass never bust their balls to get a job done if they've got a squad of grunts to do the dirty work. Am I right?"

Al playfully punched Harbinger in the arm, and he stared coldly back at him. For a moment, Al thought he was going to haul off a punch, but instead he finally nodded and rumbled his monosyllabic response: "Ja."

"I knew we'd get on," Al announced with a grin, and Harbinger forced a smile in return before diverting his full attention to the chains.

After a further five minutes of wrenching the chains, the landing platform finally clicked into place with a deafening clunk, and the four men stood back from their task, wiping their brow, bending at their knees and waists as they recovered their breath, and silently congratulated each other on a job well done with hearty slaps on the shoulders and back. With the podium locked in place and the skylight rolled back, all that had to be done was unfold the rotor blades of the vehicle and lock them in to place before they were ready to go.

Lance and Goliath finally arrived at the scene, whatever conversation they were having dying off as they saw the assembled troops and the raised platform.

"I didn't think you'd be done so soon," Lance said with a slight smile. Al fought the sneer he was compelled to give him, instead turning to face away from him and moving towards the ladder. "Is everything ready?"

"We need to deploy the rotor blades," confirmed Garth as he watched Al mount the rope ladder and slowly begin the ascent, carefully placing hand over hand, foot over foot, and making his way up one rung at a time. Despite the bulk of the man, Al moved with surprising grace, as if he had spent his entire life climbing ropes and ladders, which was down to the training that had been drummed into him at boot camp. Garth shook his head slightly, knowing that he couldn't do that himself, and looked frantically around for an elevator for himself.

"C'mon," jeered Al as he reached the top of the ladder and hauled himself over the edge of the platform. "This shit isn't going to fly itself, get your lazy asses up here, double-time. Sarah, honey, you take your time."

Leaving his crew to their own devices as they attached their equipment to ropes and clambered up the rickety steps themselves, Al strapped himself into the pilot seat of the helicopter and looked out the convex window, at the roiling sea that loomed in the distance to one side, and the rolling hills and valleys to the other side, crowned with forests and no doubt teeming with Rots.

I won't be sorry to see the back of this shit hole, he mused to himself as he strapped himself into the seat and looked over the controls. It wasn't too different to the models of aircraft he'd taken his lessons in, and he mentally recalled what each control panel or reading was for. The main three he needed to keep an eye on were the fuel levels, the speed and the height. For this moment in time, everything else was unnecessary.

One by one, each of his crew rose over the edge of the precipice and filed in to the helicopter, stowing their equipment in the rear of the vehicle and muttering greetings and confirmations they were ready as they clambered in. Sarah was first, pressing herself against the rear of the bulkhead and standing close to Clive, the pair attaching the battle harnesses they wore to the interior of the vehicle by a thick, heavyset clip. Sylvester and Garth were next, leaning against one side of the helicopter and allowing Bill and Angel to position themselves by the open door, securing themselves to the frame with the same clips, then nodding to Al.

Lance was the last man over the edge, a swagger in his step as he circled the front of the helicopter and headed towards the co-pilot's seat. For a brief moment, as he passed in front of the heavy Gatling cannon mounted on the front of the vehicle, Al considered hitting the fire button, but as his training had been in a different vehicle, he wouldn't have been able to find the button before his opportunity had passed. But then, he wouldn't actually have done it.

Would he?

The door on the other side of the cockpit swung open, and the co-pilot climbed in, quickly strapping himself into the seat and nodding his head towards the bulbous window at the front of the vehicle.

"You're looking rather pleased with yourself," Al observed, running a final check over the different status lights he could remember: everything seemed to be in the green. "What's up with you?"

"Just pleased to get back into the action," Lance murmured with a smile. "Now, take us out there."

Al didn't respond, just flicked the switch for the rotor controls and waited patiently while the folded blades unfurled like the petals of a flower. They slid gracefully into place with a gentle hum, then locked in position with a loud crack as the restraining bolts slid home.

"You sure you can fly this thing?" Bill's voice crackled over the radio headset, trembling with nerves or anticipation. Or maybe it was a little of both.

"Trust me," Al said as he gently warmed up the engine and the blades slowly began to circle, building up their speed from a gradual turning to a whirling blur of metal. The engine and spinning blades roared, and Al found himself grinning slightly, reminded of previous missions in a gunship or troop carrier. The last mission he had been in with a helicopter had seen the destruction of the vehicle and the annihilation of his entire squad: he wanted to make sure that this mission went without a hitch. Casualties were not an option.

He glanced casually over to Lance, who motioned frantically with his hands for him to raise the vehicle.

Well, maybe one would be acceptable…

Teasing back gently on the control yolks, the helicopter shuddered, bobbed slightly, then lifted from the landing platform, hovering in mid-air for a couple of seconds. Grinning wildly, Al cast a glance over his shoulder, looking for approval for his friends. Bill and Angel seemed focused on the open doorway, their weapons lifted and ready for action. Around them, pale faces looked warily from side to side, and though everyone seemed nervous to some extent, Garth seemed to be the worst.

"Don't like flying," explained Garth to anyone who listened. "Don't like crashing, either. Keep us up in the air, Al, that's all I ask of you."

"I'll try," Al said with a grin, knocking the control stick to one side softly, sending a shudder through the vehicle as it jinked to one side. He tried to pass it off as wind buffeting the vehicle, but couldn't help keep back a peel of laughter.

"You're a real asshole, Al," Garth whispered, clutching his rotund gut with one hand, as if he were keeping his stomach and intestines in. "A real fucking asshole."

"I try my hardest," the joyous pilot laughed, tapping the controls forward and taking the helicopter away from the raised platform, his feet working feverishly at the pedals that controlled the rear rotor. "Everyone hold on, we're heading over the sea. If you can't swim, find someone who can. And Preacher-man, if you don't mind, say a prayer for us. You might not believe, but I do."

After close to an hour of flying in a grid pattern over the coordinates provided by Lance, the frigate finally came into view; the dark shape of the vehicle bobbing up and down on the black water. A few portholes glowed dimly in the bleak night, and the bridge of the boat was illuminated a sickly green by the myriad of controls and panels that blinked and flashed in the control room.

"Target acquired," Lance hissed through clenched teeth, sweeping his hands over a bank of controls to bring the weapons systems online. He nodded softly to himself as he eyed the power levels and ammunition indicators, then took the control yolk in his hands and panned it softly from side to side. The motors of the mini cannon mounted on the nose whined and groaned as the barrels of the weapon panned from side to side, mimicking the movements of the joystick.

"Only target the weapon emplacements," Al said, trying to put aside his differences and work as efficiently as possible with the man he disliked. "We need the boat in one piece, remember?"

"Systems detect eight active launchers and flak cannons," the acting weapons officer reported. "Nothing detected on the infrared spectrum, no men on the deck."

"Sleeping?" questioned Angel, shifting slightly from her crouched position on the deck plate, her rifle tucked in tight against her shoulder.

"They wouldn't let them all go to bed at the same time," Al responded. "That would just be inviting trouble. I mean, shit, if someone got hold of a stealth helicopter and flew out to them in the middle of the night, they could blow them out the fucking water. Do we have a lock on the weapons?"

"Two SAM launchers locked on, sidewinders ready for launch."

The missile pods on the side of the helicopter erupted to life, billowing smoke blossoming around the front of the craft as the rockets tore away from their housing with a deafening roar. Angel craned her head around to watch the projectiles smash into the craft and erupt in a fiery explosion, tearing apart the two launchers.

"Retarget," Al shouted, jinking the helicopter around to one side and tilting the vehicle, trying his hardest to keep the helicopter on the move to make a harder target. Bringing up her rifle and pressing the night vision scope against her eye, she panned it from left to right, the pale green outline of the boat becoming obscured by thick black smoke as it rolled across the deck, carried slowly away by the night breeze.

"There's nothing down there," Angel reported, her scope pressed against her eye as she kept watch for any movement on the deck.

"Keep watching, we've knocked on their door and it's only a matter of time until they open up."

Sure enough, one of the hatches on the deck slammed open and a figure stumbled out, the person glowing a sickly, radioactive green in the enhanced scope. Angel didn't miss a beat, squeezing off a round and catching the figure in the shoulder. It spun around and keeled over the railing, knocking its head on the side of the vehicle as it fell into the dark water. It sank beneath the brackish foam, and didn't resurface.

"Got one," she said with a smile.

"Good to know," Al screamed as another salvo of rockets were vomited from the weapons pod. Luminous flares streaked towards the boat, and searing white columns of fire roared to life, the sensors in Angel's scope blanking out and temporarily disabling the image while the intense glare of light chased away the darkness of the night.

"Looks like fireworks," murmured Sarah from behind Angel, the child's voice filled with awe. "Cool."

"I'm glad you approve," Lance muttered as he wrestled with the controls of the weapons and strafed the deck with heavy-calibre automatic gunfire. Sparks danced across the metal skin of the boat, the roar of the multiple-barrelled cannon lost beneath the constant droning of the rotor blades.

"Missile emplacements are down," Al bellowed into his radio, fighting with the controls as he brought the helicopter down closer to the ship, rotating the vehicle and making the broadside of the aircraft face the frigate. "Lance, take out those flak cannons, I want to get closer to land. Bill, you and Angel keep the deck secure while I work my way around to the helipad.

Angel nodded, catching sight of a green blur in her scope as the equipment rebooted and came back on line, a streaking figure that tore across the deck of the craft, bolting from an open hatchway towards an inert machinegun emplacement. Angel tried to snipe the person, but the figure moved too quick for her to follow, and her bullet smashed into the deck, leaving a warm, pale-green blob on the deck in her specialised scope.

"I've got him!"

From behind her, a familiar voice, and then the thunderous *chakka-chakka-chakka* of a heavy machinegun roaring to life, almost close enough to deafen her. She could feel the heat from the muzzle discharge, feel the scalding hot brass cases as they dropped on her shoulder and tinkled to the floor, and feel the vibrations from the discharging weapon as they shuddered down Bill's arm and into his hand that gently rubbed reassuringly at her shoulder.

"Out-fucking-standing," Angel whispered breathily.

The fleeing figure toppled head over heels as a barrage of lead slugs smashed against its torso, limbs and head, obliterating it and sending the bloody carcass toppling over the edge of the frigate into the icy ocean to join its fellow crewmember. He kept the barrage on the upper deck, spraying the weapon from side to side and slicing into anyone that dared leave the sanctity of the craft and try to repel the attackers.

"Coming around to the helipad now," Al announced as the helicopter swung wide around the prow of the ship, arcing far to the left before swooping down on to the vacant pad that sat raised at the back of the craft. "Hold on tight, because landings weren't my forte. Grab your shit and get ready to move: I want Spanners and Preacher-man to secure the pad, the kid and the bitch cover them. Sarah, honey, stick back with buddy for now. Buddy, you make sure that she's all right. If she's hurt, I'll hold you responsible. Okay?"

Murmured responses sounded from all around the helicopter, and each person unclipped their safety harness as the flying machine neared the landing pad. Whether Sylvester and Clive were eager to sweep through the ship or just get out of the helicopter, Angel couldn't say, but they were both quick to leap out the open door and run in a crouch across the deck to take refuge behind a pair of large packing crates that were secured to the deck by oversized and heavy chains.

Providing cover for one another, Angel and Bill hauled themselves from the vehicle and ran beneath the dwindling blades as they joined the two men at the packing crates.

"How many are there?" Al asked. Angel turned back to see the bulky Marine crawling over the helicopter and locking it in position, making sure a sudden wave or jolt in the frigate couldn't dislodge their craft.

"Three dead on the decks," Sylvester announced, a pair of night vision goggles pressed against his face as he carefully peered out from around the crates. "Another two that we watched take a swan dive into the drink."

"Any activity on the deck?" Lance asked, helping in securing the vehicle.

"Negative," Sylvester said, shaking his head slowly. "Whoever came out to watch us arrive must've been mowed down. That's some pretty thorough work, Bill."

"Well, I try…"

"Wait!"

Clive had been conducting his own survey with a pair of goggles, and held up a hand to get the attention of the other three people hiding behind the crates. "Someone's watching us. Check out the bridge."

Angel slammed her rifle down on to the crate and unfolded the bipod mounted on the barrel, steadying her aim as she looked down the length of the craft through her scope.

The boat was about thirty metres wide, and seemed to stretch on forever from where she sat. A wide metal staircase led down from the raised platform to a lower recess in the deck of the ship, a canyon flanked on either side by platforms, with stairs that rose up to a walkway that ran the perimeter of the ship. Every ten metres there sat a gun emplacement, eerily silent and vacant. A few cargo crates littered the chasm on different levels, but high above them all, in the large, four-story structure that sat in the centre of the boat, a room lined almost entirely in glass watched over the length of the ship. Lifting her scope, a solitary figure stood motionless in the bridge, looking down on the landing pad. Although Angel knew it was impossible, it seemed that the figure was looking directly at her through sunken, sallow features. Angel swallowed hard, tensing her muscles as she lined up the red dot of her scope against the smooth forehead of the commander on the deck, took a deep breath, then exhaled as she squeezed the trigger.

Her rifle jerked softly, and she watched through the scope as the glass panel splintered and shattered, and the head of the person in the bridge exploded outwards in a bloody mess, spraying the interior of the command post with blood tinted dark green by both the scope and the muted light of the bridge. Satisfied, Angel lowered her weapon and reported her kill just as Al came bounding up to them, his machinegun resting lazily against his shoulder.

"Stone cold killer, baby," he grinned. "Better them than you."

"They didn't open fire on us," Lance muttered, a bulky shotgun cradled in his arm, obviously referring to the approach on the frigate.

"Man, we didn't give them a fucking *chance* to. We buzzed in low, wiped them out."

"Even the automated defences should have kicked in," Lance argued,

"Bullshit," Al said, dismissing the notion with a vague wave of his hand. "Stealth, man, the copter has stealth capabilities, that would have thrown off all the radars, given off ghost signals and anomalous blips."

"Shame they don't' have stealth suits," Angel said with a grin.

"These suits do have some radar-absorbing facilities," Al pointed out, brushing an imaginary dust mote from his own suit. "Absorbs some body heat signatures, confuses sonar… we're not totally invisible to systems like that, but it helps evade some tracking methods."

"I meant I wish we were totally invisible to the naked eye."

"Yeah, sometimes I wished I couldn't see you, too. Everyone satisfied this deck's secure?"

Angel nodded slowly, and all around her, other heads nodded their own confirmation.

"Cool," Al grinned, waving over to the helicopter and motioning for Garth and Sarah to approach the packing crates. "Phase one is complete. All we need to do is go over every inch of the ship and make sure we secure it. Garth, guard the copter: you and Preacher-man keep an eye on Sarah, too, the rest of us are going to have to go into the lower decks. Spanners, head down into the engineering decks, make sure everything's ship shape."

"That's not even funny," Sylvester said, his face impassive as he registered Al's play on words. "I'm going on my own?"

"Lance can tag along, if you want."

"No, I'm good," Sylvester said, shaking his head and pulling back on the lever of his rifle, making sure the weapon was primed and ready to fire. "He's your baggage, you can look after him."

"Good," Al nodded, patting Sarah on the head and slapping Garth on the back before motioning for the two of them to stand by the helicopter. With a swift nod of his head, he indicated for Clive to follow them. "Move out; Spanners, once we've cleared the rest of the decks we'll tell you, so keep your radio active, crank up the gain so it penetrates all this metal, and be on your guard. There could be a couple of engineers down there."

"Do I shoot them?" Sylvester asked, uncertain of the task ahead.

"If they shoot at you, yes. If they don't, just take out their kneecaps," Al's response was as nonchalant and blasé as ever: as if taking over a military frigate and killing the crew was something he did on a regular basis. "Now move, and don't fuck around."

XXVII
BURIED AT SEA

"Of course we know the truth, we know the origins of this plague, though it goes without saying, those origins must be buried deep and never revealed."

I

The lower decks of the boat thrummed and shuddered as the engines below pulsed and generated power, a deep and rhythmic sound that seemed to vibrate the marrow of Bill's bones as he and Angel carefully passed beneath pipes filled with wiring and through opened bulkheads, systematically checking each cabin and room before moving on to the next.

The first cabin they broke open told a grisly story, a one that instantly set off alarm bells in Bill's head as he looked over the tattered clothing that littered the floor, the spatters of blood and gore that had been sprayed across the wall and floor, and the spent brass casings that littered the ground. A pistol lay in the midst of the scattered shells, the slide locked back and telling the story of a weapon being fired until empty and thrown to one side in blind panic. Al stepped into the room first, barely able to swing his weapon around as he checked out the state of the room.

"Gunfight," he casually announced as he stated the obvious.

"How long ago?" Bill asked, carefully entering behind Al and minding where he placed his feet.

"Two hours," snapped Al. "How the hell am I supposed to know that?"

"You're normally good at shit like this," Angel said, jumping to Bill's defence. Al's chest seemed to puff out slightly at the recognition of his skills, then shrugged it off and knelt beside the weapon and casings.

"Everything's cold. Shells, weapon, and the blood, that's a little on the dry side of tacky. Course, the question isn't when did it happen, but who was shooting at who?"

"Mutiny?" suggested Lance. "The Marines onboard trying to take control of the ship?"

"That's one of the better scenarios," Bill nodded. "The other is that someone else tried to take the ship, like maybe some damn fools on a helicopter thinking they could bite off more than they could chew."

"What about these?" Angel said, motioning to the hull directly opposite to the cabin door and the collection of flattened lead projectiles that lay embedded in the metal. Tiny splatters of blood surrounded them, though nowhere near as much as in the cabin. Al stepped closer to them, pulling out a blade and prying one of the projectiles loose from the wall and turning it over in his palm, using the tip of the blade to move it.

"Bullets," he finally announced. "Probably from the pistol."

"Amazing," Bill muttered sarcastically.

"They've torn straight through a target, but there's not been much blood lost. No arterial spray."

"What does that mean?"

"It means that whatever was shot didn't have much blood in it…" murmured Al, scratching his beard thoughtfully.

"Or not much of a pulse to spray the blood," Bill offered.

"What are you suggesting?" Lance asked, standing in the corridor and looking nervously from side to side, making sure no one approached or tried to get the drop on them.

"He thinks that there's Rots on the boat," Al said.

"That's fucking impossible," Lance growled.

"No it's not," Al said with a grim shake of his head. "I think the same. Can you smell that?"

Lance made a visible act of sniffing the air and shook his head.

"Decay. Death. Something we're so used to, we couldn't smell it when we came down into the lower decks."

"Zombies? Here? What about the Marines who were running around on the deck?"

"They were just running around because… shit, I don't know, I'm not a friggin' zombie psychiatrist, I don't know what they think. Hey, buddy, can you check the dead bodies on the deck?" Al said, addressing Garth on the deck of the ship. "We think they may be Rots, we need someone to check on them." A faint reply came back over the headset, a hissing spray of static punctuated by Garth's voice.

"Fuck off."

"I'll do it," Clive offered.

The comlink fell silent, and Al waited patiently for the response to his request, idly toying with the strap of his weapon while he took a seat on the messy bed. Bill paced nervously back and forth, chewing on one of his fingernails and passing a strained smile at Angel as he waited. He spotted something stuck to the walls of the cabin amidst a spray of gore, and upon closer inspection found the tattered remnants of a fingernail, tiny slivers of flesh hanging from the exposed cuticle. He stopped nibbling at his own nails and lowered his hands, hooking his thumbs over his belt and tapped his toe while he waited. Finally, the silence was broken as Clive's voice, quiet and distant, carried over the radio.

"Mother of God," he whispered harshly, "The bodies… they're… hollow men…"

"Of course they are," Al said with a grin as he glared at Lance. "Just like I said. Okay, I need you to work up and down the deck, make sure all their brains are destroyed, finish them off if you need to. Spanners, you getting this?"

A faint, barely audible response came back, a response that barely seemed like a positive response. It was enough for Al, who nodded with a sharp, jarring motion of his head. "He heard. Let's go."

He stood and stormed out into the corridor, casually pushing past Lance, but making sure he had enough force behind the move to bounce his back off the wall. He continued to move down the corridor, muttering to himself as he went.

"You think we should follow him?" Angel asked. Bill shrugged his shoulders.

"It'd be rude not to."

They lifted their weapons and headed deeper into the bowels of the boat, with Bill's head swimming with thoughts of the Rot presence on the boat. What did that mean? Had an infected creature managed to find its way on to the ship? Or maybe the Marines had voluntarily brought one on to the ship, either for research or entertainment, and it had escaped. He didn't know for sure how it had happened; he probably never would. He just had to accept that it had, and now he and the rest of his friends were faced with another problem to deal with on the ship. Still, he'd rather face off against a ship filled with zombies instead of a boatload of Marines. As loathsome as the undead were, at least they didn't know how to operate weapons, which made their job easier.

He hoped.

The corridor they followed was lined with cabins; the majority of which were spattered with gore; filled with spent bullets and discarded weapons, each telling the same story of a last stand in a confined space. Although it was obvious that the ship was infested with the living dead, they hadn't encountered any in the lower decks. Had all the Rots been wiped out on the upper deck?

Bill got his answer as the corridor opened up into a dining area, the walls heavily coated with spattered blood. Two dining tables ran the width of the room with benches on either side, all bolted to the floor. Tin plates and plastic utensils slid around the tables and on the floor as the ship rocked gently from side to side, slipping through puddles of gore that coved the benches and smearing it even further. On the table furthest from them, a corpse lay stoic on the table, arms and legs hanging limply over the edges of the counter, its face turned away from the group that had entered the room. Bill quickly snapped up his rifle and drew a bead on the creature, though it didn't seem to be moving, despite the number of bite marks that ran the length of the limbs he could see. Fingers had been chewed off, revealing bony stumps that dripped with thick droplets of crimson gore into the pool that surrounded it.

"Zombie," hissed Lance. "Infected, has to be."

"It's not moving," whispered Angel, her voice low and hushed, as if a loud voice would wake the dead from its slumber. "Are you sure?"

"The undead can infect the dead," Al reminded her. "As long as the brain's intact, a Rot can make another corpse rise. Take it easy."

Bill cautiously crept forwards, his weapon tucked in tight against his shoulder as he reached out with his free hand, edging closer to the corpse and stooping to grab one of the metal plates that slipped over the deck. He stopped a couple of feet short, then hurled the plate at the prone figure, watching as the metal disc bounced off the corpse and crashed into the far wall with a deafening echo before dropping to the floor, rolling around its rim with a *clang-a-lang-a-lang* sound until it ground to a halt with a clatter. The corpse refused to move.

"Dead," Bill announced, lowering his rifle slightly and taking a seat on one of the vacant tables, still fixing his gaze on the corpse. Al lumbered up to it, content that the cadaver wasn't going anywhere, and heaved it off the table, using his boot to push the corpse. It fell to the floor with a thump, exposing the face that up until then had been hidden. Flesh had been peeled back from the bone, the skull itself fractured and broken, and chunks of meat hung out the gaping wound.

"That's why he ain't moving," grinned Al. "Rot food."

A low, keening wail sounded in the lower decks of the boat, the harsh moaning sound of Rots as they were roused from their slumber. Footsteps echoed in the metallic corridors, seeming to come from all directions at the same time, and Bill instantly snapped his machinegun up, nodding to Al as he did the same. There were three exits from the wide cabin; one the way they had entered through, and another two leading towards the front of the ship. They'd already checked the way they'd come, so there could only be two places for the Rots to come from.

"Bill, Angel, head left. We'll take the right."

Bill nodded, scuttling over the tables and the blood-slicked benches, helping Angel on her way as they slipped and skidded across the room. They reached the furthest entrance just as the first Rot lumbered into view, a Marine draped in the remains of his old uniform, smeared in blood and dirt, with both of his lower arms severed at the elbow. The grey flesh of his face sagged from the bone, looking as if his face was melting, and one white cataract of an eye swivelled wildly from side to side as it lumbered down the corridor towards them.

Behind it, a second zombie followed, the exposed talons of the bones at the tips of its fingers lodged firmly in the flesh of a severed arm it carried, brandishing it above its head like a club. Its face was just as grey and gaunt as its brethren, eyes shrunken and opaque with disease, spittle dripping from a mouth filled with yellowed teeth in a bloodied trail of saliva and drool, joints raw and exposing flaking muscle tissue beneath.

Bill and Angel opened fire at the same time, the roar of their weapons deafening in the enclosed spaces as their bullets smacked into the dead creatures; the thunderous belch of Bill's heavy machinegun and the high pitched scream of Angel's machine pistol drowned out the moans of the dead as their heads were obliterated. More creatures entered the corridor, joining the throng from offshoot rooms and corridors that couldn't be seen from their vantage point.

The sound of firing increased and Al and Lance opened up with their own weapons, another machinegun and a shotgun joining in with the cacophony of gunfire that rocked the boat.

Gritting her teeth and unfolding the bipod of her rifle, Angel set up the weapon and rested it on the table before her, abandoning her spent machine pistol and taking down each of the shambling creatures as they approached with perfect headshots. Deformed heads, exposed skulls, eyeless faces, twisted and bloodied grins, all vanished in sprays of scarlet and black blood mixed with rotting flesh and chunks of white gristle and meat.

"How many are there?" screamed Bill over the thunder of gunshots, the clatter of brass casings tumbling to the floor, and the groans of the dead as they fell beneath the onslaught.

"Could be twenty, could be a hundred," Al shouted, though his replay could only be heard over the radio headset. "It's a big ship, everyone would be infected."

The response didn't instil Bill with any great confidence, but it seemed that the flow of the dead was finally slowing. What had once been a continuous wave of the dead had reduced to a trickle, and now there was only one or two creatures that ambled aimlessly around, oblivious to any of the people and gorging themselves on the remains of their fallen kindred. Angel finished each one with a satisfying bullet to the head.

"All clear?" Al finally shouted, stepping back from the opening he had been protecting and pulling the mechanism of his machinegun open, unclipping the empty drum, replacing it with a fresh one. Lance surged forwards a couple of steps and punctuated the end of the battle with a selection of well-placed shotgun blasts that decapitated the few bodies that remained intact. Bill imitated Al, heaving open his weapon and threading a fresh belt of brass cases into the loading slot, cranking the thick bolt back and keeping the weapon trained on the pile of carcasses in case one had been missed. Angel retrieved her weapon and ejected the spent magazine before slinging her rifle back over her shoulder and sighed, brushing a few strands of hair away from her face.

"All clear," Bill nodded in agreement.

"Fucking hell," Al murmured, slamming his weapon down on the table and taking a seat on one of the benches. He stared sullenly at the array of dishes and cutlery that lay on the table before him, at the collection of brass cases, then suddenly screamed and swept his hand out across the table, sending dishes, forks and cartridges scattering across the room and crashing into the wall nearest to him.

"Boat's infected," Lance muttered, staring despondently at the pile of dead creatures. "Whole god damn boat's infected. How'd that happen?"

"Well how the hell should I know?" shouted Al, tucking his fingers under the rim of a dish he had missed and flicking it angrily towards the wall.

"What does this mean?" Bill asked; his gaze fixed gloomily on the pile of corpses he had helped create. Angel stood beside him and wrapped her arms around him, burying her face into his chest.

"Means we're fucked," Al said, bluntly. "Boat's filled with Rots. They were probably bored shitless out here on their own and had heard about the fun and games that the other Marines were having on the mainland. They tried to import a little entertainment themselves, and bad shit went down from there. It's going to be harder to secure the boat, and it'll take weeks to shift the stink of rotting flesh, even if we open the doors and windows."

Bill nodded. Already the acrid tang of cordite was drifting from the air, and the underlying bittersweet scent of putrid decay was starting to sink in. He rubbed his face, at the grimy layer of discharged powder residue that coated his face, and wiped the palms of his hands on his trousers.

"Do we press on?"

"Of course," Al insisted, motioning to the mound of corpses in front of them. "Can't let a bunch of dead spoil our plans. There must be a door someplace on the hull on this level that we can throw them out of. Once we do that, we'll be back in business to claim this as our own. Just be careful, and make sure none of them are playing possum. We might need to scramble their brains with a blade before we move them, just to make sure. We've got this deck to deal with, and another two after this. Spanners seems to be dealing with things himself, I can't hear anything down there that indicates he's had any trouble.

"Al?" Garth's voice played wearily over the headset. "Al, we've cleaned out the top deck. They were all dead. Again. Most of them had been taken out with a headshot anyway."

"The bitch is effective in what she does," Al shrugged. "We've got most things in hand here, too."

"We need one of you up here, Al or Lance, whichever one's in charge."

"That'll be me," Al growled, glowering at Lance. Bill looked at him, seeing panic in his eyes as he tried to work out what was happening. "What's wrong, is Sarah okay?"

"I think you'd better come up."

"Where's everyone else?"

Sarah looked up from the drawing she was working on; a piece of yellowing paper and a half-chewed pencil that Clive had managed to retrieve from beneath one of the seats in the front of the helicopter. It was more of a doodle than anything else: silhouettes of humanoid figures standing around a fire, a boat and a helicopter in opposing corners. She'd tried to draw something real to keep her mind occupied while Garth and Clive had thrown the bodies of the bad men over the railings and into the sea. She hadn't been able to focus or pick a specific thing to draw, so instead had picked a couple of things she remembered vividly and drew them. The people around the fire were supposed to be the congregation, and the figure with his arms spread out was Clive, preaching to the crowd as he told the funny story with the man and the boat. The boat and the helicopter were basic pictures, and although she knew she could draw better, she wasn't in the mood. Her fingers were numb from the icy cold winds that whipped the surface of the frigate and rocked it back and forth, and she couldn't sit comfortably without readjusting the compact shotgun that dangled from her belt. She knew how to fire it, but wasn't looking forward to using it if she needed to. She'd fired one like it before, one day she'd spent with Al in the base, and she knew that if she wasn't careful it could hurt her, let alone someone else.

Al stormed across the deck of the frigate, stepping into the dim yellow glow of the portable lanterns that had been set up around the helicopter wearing a worried expression. The sternness of his face seemed to melt slightly as he saw her working over her picture, and his march turned into a gentle canter. He took up a position behind her, peering over her shoulder and watched her pencil strokes.

"Hey, sweetie, what're you doing?" he asked, an obvious question.

"Drawing a picture," Sarah said, rolling her eyes.

"What of?"

"Us," she said, pointing the tip of her pencil at the figure of the preacher. "That's Clive, the preacher man, he's telling the crowd he's going to save them on this," she continued, moving the point around to the boat. "That's Colebrook's ark, we're going to fill it up with all these people." She rolled the pencil back over to the crowd of people around the preacher figure.

"Wonderful," Al forced a smile. "Where am I?"

"Right here," she said, pointing to the lower corner of the piece of paper where a crowd of people were clustered around a large, over-sized male figure. He held an equally oversized weapon on both hands, levelling them off at the gathering people around him as they reached up with thin, stick-like arms. "They're all the dead men reaching out to get you, but they can't get you."

"Like a super hero," Al said, nodding in approval. "I like it. Give me some hair, though. I look bald."

"Silly," Sarah snorted, pushing him away with her elbow. He turned and walked towards the helicopter, and Sarah abandoned her artwork and followed him, playfully kicking at his heels as he went.

"What's going on? I thought something was up when you called."

"We had a radio transmission," Garth said, nodding towards the open cockpit of the helicopter, where Clive sat and looked mournfully at the dials. "It was a weak signal, but it sounds like the village, like maybe Goliath wanting to know how things are going, a progress update, I guess."

"Fucking asshole, he's got one major superiority complex, see if you can call them up," Al muttered, swinging his leg through the open door and resting on the edge of his seat. Clive stared blankly at him, then at the controls and shrugged his shoulders.

"Christ," Al muttered, leaning over and twisting one of the controls, bringing the radio on line and spinning the dial to increase the gain and boost the signal. Sarah shuffled closer to the helicopter, climbing into the interior and standing in the back, hanging on the seat while she watched Al operate the controls and tune in the radio.

The speakers embedded in the floor and ceiling of the helicopter hissed to life, blaring a stream of static before levelling out into steady signal.

"Anyone there?"

There was a pause, then a response came back, faint and distant, almost washed out by the low quality of the transmission.

"Goliath here, who is this? Lance, is that you?"

"No," Al tried adjusting the gain once more, nudged his headset and brought the microphone closer to his mouth. "No, it's Al. What's going on?"

"I told those incompetents you left looking after the helicopter that I needed to speak to the man in charge," Goliath snapped, annoyed with the fact his request had been ignored.

"Yeah, they did, I'm in charge, Lance is just along for the ride. What do you want, Goliath?"

"We've been monitoring a lot of activity amongst the dead in the area, and it looks like there's a lot of them approaching the village now. With weapons and supplies stripped out for the helicopter and your foolhardy plan, I don't think we'll be able to hold them off long enough for you turn around and get the frigate back here. We need an immediate evac."

"We can't do that, there's not enough space or fuel in the chopper to get there and back for everyone over there," Al shook his head.

"Do as many runs as you can," suggested Goliath, a sense of urgency in his voice.

"Draw straws?" Al snorted, shaking his head. "Start doing that and the locals'll start a riot, you'd be dead before the Rots got to you." He paused with a smirk. Maybe that wouldn't be so bad... especially if Lance had remained. *Fucking Brass and the ass kissers... the only good guy out the trio's Harbinger*, Al mused to himself as he slowly scanned the deck of the ship. *Probably because he doesn't speak*. He spotted a number of grey plastic casings fastened to the railings around the side of the ship, then nodded towards them. "Preacher, you and buddy cram as many of those things into the back of the copter here, you could probably fit about three or four of them in. I'll get the bird back in the air and take them back to base."

He returned his gaze to the radio controls and addressed Goliath.

"Get those people prepped and ready, we're going to evac them all together."

"Are you listening to me? You don't have time to turn the frigate around!"

"There's a reason why I'm the brains of this outfit," Al watched as Garth and Clive loaded the first of the grey containers into the back of the helicopter. "I'm bringing about four self-inflating life rafts, they should be large enough to carry everyone out here, or at least most of them: the few that can't get on a raft, they can catch a lift in the chopper."

"That won't work," Goliath started to protest, but Al spoke over the top of him: "You don't know it won't work, asshole, give it a chance."

"What about Lance? Patch me through to Lan..."

Al snapped the radio off and looked over his shoulder, watching as Garth and Clive manhandled another of the bulky cartons into the rear of the vehicle. He grinned to himself as he imagined the irate look that would be on Goliath's face. *Serves him right for being a dick*, he thought, nodding his head.

"We're going to be able to fit one more," Garth announced as he wiped his brow with the back of his forearm. "No more. Will three be enough?"

"Should be, that's great," Al looked across the decking, noticed a coil of nylon rope that was strapped to the railing, and motioned towards it with a slight tilt of his head. "Fetch that, too, use it to strap the rafts down, and make sure the helicopter's clear of any mooring or obstructions. Sarah, honey, you want to get up in here with me?"

"You could get up off your arse and get it yourself," muttered Garth sullenly as he wrestled with the third life raft. "Heavens forbid you should do something yourself."

"You could shut the fuck up, buddy. Or do you want me to take you back to mainland? You loved that trailer so much, you can keep the fucker yourself while we go to America."

"I'll get it," he sighed, looping his arm through the coiled rope as he shuffled past it, balancing his side of the load on one arm while Clive took the brunt of the weight of the object."

"What's happening?" Sarah asked as she jumped into the helicopter and settled down into the thinly padded seat. "Where you going?"

"We're going to get the rest of the people and bring them out here. You and me, you up for that?"

"Like Moses leading his people across the Red Sea," Clive said as he finished loading up the third and final raft, then started to help tie them down to make sure they didn't fall out mid-flight. Al scowled at him, biting his tongue. It was bad enough that he had to put up with asshole officers trying to call the shots, the last thing he wanted to be was likened to a saviour of hundreds and thousands of people or a prophet.

"Packed and strapped," Garth and Clive finished strapping the rafts into the rear of the helicopter. Garth gave a final tug to the ropes, slapped the grey containers then stepped back, watching as Al ran his hands over the controls and brought the engine to life, cycling the rotor blades up to full speed. Satisfied with the performance of the vehicle he motioned to the pair, and they gingerly approached the vehicle, crouching as they walked in fear of being sucked up into the vortex the spinning blades made.

"Go find Bill, tell him and that asshole Lance what's going on: see if they can turn this thing around so we can rendezvous with them closer to shore. Life rafts don't have much of a range; we need to make this happen as quick and as easy as we can. There should be a jetty near the back of the boat, see if we can get that prepped and ready for us coming back. If Lance gives you any shit, throw him in the brig, you got that?"

"Why take Sarah? Why not take one of us?"

"Circling a crowd of Rots in a heavily armed helicopter is a damn sight safer then leaving her aboard a floating tin can that may well be loaded with a horde of the living dead."

"A horde?" Garth murmured, his already pale skin lightening even more. "Aboard this ship? Really?"

"It's nothing personal," Al carried on. "If the job were to just look after my daughter while she drew pictures out here, then you'd be my first choice. But I'd never leave her in a possible close-combat situation, shit, not even with Bill, and especially not with a flaky priest or an overweight driver. Sorry, buddy, but you know it's true."

Daughter? Sarah thought to herself as she watched Al continue to work over the controls of the helicopter. Had his inflection been a casual slip of the tongue, or was he really that close to her? She didn't have time to dwell on it as the whining engine became a fearsome growl, and Al motioned for Garth and Clive to back away as he gently nudged the controls for the helicopter, lifting the vehicle from the landing pad. As he gained more height, he pulled off to the left, peeling away from the ship and spinning back towards the coastal hideout they had originated from.

The drone of the engines filled Sarah's ears once more as the helicopter streaked through the sky, tilting slightly forwards and shaking as Al tried to squeeze as much power out the vehicle as possible. It had taken some time to reach the boat in the first place, but that was mainly because they didn't know exactly where the frigate was. With both positions being known, a regular search pattern had been reduced to a straight line, which meant that the journey would be a lot quicker.

"How long until we get there?" Sarah asked, watching the stick between her knees weaving gently from side to side as it mimicked the movements Al made to keep the vehicle on course. If she hadn't known better, it looked as if a ghost were controlling the vehicle.

"Ten minutes, if I can push it," Al grunted then motioned towards the stick. "Grab that thing, help me keep this thing steady. I guess Lance served more of a purpose than I was willing to acknowledge. Now, when we get there I'm going flank around the outskirts of the village and buy us some time: if the Rots are advancing like Goliath said, I need you to use the guns. Have you ever played any video games?"

"Some," Sarah shrugged her shoulders. "Not a lot. I never got into them. Not like Tommy: he used to love playing on them all the time; sometimes he let me play on them, but he said I was shit. Mum told him off for swearing."

She giggled to herself once, then lapsed into silence, watching out the window as a dark smear on the horizon turned into a spread of cliffs with roaring waves crashing against their base.

"Al?"

"What's up, sweetie?"

"You called me your daughter. On the ship, there, when you were talking to Garth."

"I did," Al nodded his head, his gaze fixed on the unfolding seascape before him. "I'm sorry, I don't mean to replace your parents or nothing. But I promised your father I'd look after you, you know that."

"It's okay," she muttered. "I know you're not my daddy, least not my real daddy. But I know you'll look after me."

"Sometimes, sweetie, I forget just how old you really are," Al shook his head slowly. "You're more mature than Garth, sometimes even more mature than me."

"Wouldn't be hard," Sarah sniggered, smiling. She looked towards Al, seen his grin break into a chuckle, then motioned towards the smudge of land that appeared on the horizon. "What do I need to do?"

"Look at that little screen, whatever the crosshair is over, the gun hits. Stick with the Gatling gun, there's no need to break out missiles on soft targets like the Rots. You want to give it a shot out here?"

"Won't I give away our position?"

"Smart girl," Al nodded, beaming with pride. So young, but she'd picked up the finer points of warfare and assault. Not something any normal child would be well versed in, but this world was different to the world Al had grown up in. "Out here, it won't matter. Plus, the Rots won't be packing anti-air weaponry. I think it'll be safe to give it a shot."

"Okay," Sarah nodded, taking the controls of the weapons in her hands. Even from the rear of the vehicle, she'd seen Lance operate them and seen that they were relatively easy to use. A small joystick that moved the guns mounted beneath the nose of the helicopter, a plastic stud that acted as a firing button, and a small camera attached to the weapons that acted like the sights. She moved the controls, squeezed the firing triggers, and watched as the monitor displayed a blazing stream of tracer fire that spewed from the cannons. She glanced out the window, and watched the same stream of burning bullets stream out the darkening sky and into the sea.

"Fun," she giggled to herself.

"Simple, too," Al said, nodding his head. "Even a child can use them… even a child… so why did I need Lance to come along as co-pilot? Anyone could have done that job…" He shook his head, dismissing the thought. "Here we go, you ready for this? Short bursts, okay?"

Sarah nodded, keeping her eyes fixed on the monitor as the roiling sea that filled her screen became a blur of foliage and felled trees. Grassy hills populated with stumbling figures wandering in erratic patterns, slowly meandering through wooded areas towards the cliff top settlement. Lining up the sights on the first of the faltering corpses, Sarah made sure that it was actually a Rot before firing. The missing limbs and stumbling gait were a giveaway, as was the piece of rotting flesh dangling from its mouth. Sarah squeezed the controls, and watched as the bullets ripped into the zombie and decimated it, coating the creatures beside it with chunks of bloodied flesh and shattered bone. She slowly guided the crosshair to the next target, and then the next, picking off the crowd of advancing undead while Al slowly worked up the incline, concentrating as he kept an eye out for any of the towering trees that may pose a threat to the rotor blades while making slow progress on his ascent.

As Sarah mopped up the remnants of the creatures climbing the woodland path, a few stray shots shredding trees and tearing apart patches of shrubbery as Al slowly turned the nose of the craft from side to side, providing Sarah with a wider range of targets as she slowly manipulated the controls.

The village slowly came in to view, the top of the walls bristling with men and women, each holding rifles and aiming them at the advancing horde. One by one, they raised their arms in jubilation as they saw their saviours loom into view in their flying machine, cutting down the attacking undead. A pair of people in the crowd ignited a set of flares and tossed them into the opening behind the wall, their glowing green flames fuelled by copper salts as they rolled around on the ground.

"Flare is green," muttered Al, bringing the helicopter closer and swinging the vehicle around, giving a final sweep of the hill and making sure all the Rots had been either killed, or incapacitated. "L.Z. is clean. I'm setting it down, hold on sweetie. Might get a little rough."

"Flare is green, L.Z. is clean? Do the Marines make everything a rhyme?"

"It's easier to remember shit like rhymes and limericks under fire. Hold on tight, I'm setting it down."

The helicopter touched down on the makeshift landing pad, the landing gear settling into the damp mud of the surface and the rotor blades winding down. As the motor died, a spatter of rain started the mist the windscreen, a fine spray of precipitation that turned into a spread of thick, finger-sized drops. Al grunted as he cracked open the door to the helicopter and tumbled to the muddy ground, then turned to help Sarah from her perch and setting her down in the mud beside him. She turned slowly around, taking in the details of the village in the dim night, and saw the other two Marines leading the procession of civilians as they approached, weapons slung casually over their shoulders. Al nodded to Harbinger, then cast a sideways glance at Goliath.

"Does Lance know that you're here?"

"Pleasure to see you again too, fuck-face," Al barely looked at him as he turned to begin unfastening the lifeboats loaded into the rear of the vehicle. He paused for a moment, considering the question, then shrugged. "He probably does, by now, anyways. I need as many men as you can spare to get these things unloaded and down to the bottom of the cliff, we're going to head out and meet up with the frigate, and we're going to do it now. The Rots on the hill have been killed, but you and I both know that there's a shit load more out there."

He paused, then motioned to the group of young men standing directly behind Harbinger and Goliath. "You guys, start moving these things, the rest of you gather what you need: any meds, vitals like that. Any suitcase packed with family heirlooms will end up going overboard."

"What about food?" someone shouted from the rear of the crowd.

"There's enough aboard for everyone, at least until we get home. Come on, people, there's a storm coming and you don't want to get caught out in the middle of the drink in a wood and plastic skiff. Move!"

The crowd quickly dispersed, an excited murmur among the group, leaving only the Marines and Sarah around the inert vehicle. Al warily eyed the pair of soldiers, his hand resting on his hip by the butt of his handgun, waiting for one of them to make a move.

"You're really gonna pull this off," Goliath finally said, breaking the silence.

"'Cos he's a hero," Sarah muttered, "And he's gonna save us all."

"Ja," rumbled Harbinger, nodding solemnly. Slowly, Goliath extended his hand and held it out in the open. Al lifted his hand from is weapon, tentatively reached out and took Goliath's hand, shook it once, then lowered it again.

"I guess you really did know what you were doing, huh?"

"Sometimes the grunts know better than the Brass, eh? Now come on, get these people sorted out and into the boats. There should be enough space for everyone."

"Harbinger will be in charge of our little navy. He's familiar with the boats, and he can handle them on the choppy waters better than me. I… get a little sea sick, to be honest. Our original journey here out on the sea was a little rough on my stomach. It took me a while to recover, right Harbinger?"

He raised his eyebrow slightly, nodded his head and rumbled his normal, monosyllabic response before turning and helping everyone with the manhandling of boats down the cliff to the shoreline below. Al looked down on Sarah, then motioned towards the vehicle with a short jerk of his head. "Get back in, honey, we need to be ready to take off. We should probably get up into the air anyway, keep an eye out for any Rots that are still trying to claim that they're king of the hill."

"Mind if I come up with you?"

Sarah eyed Goliath warily, noticing that she wasn't the only one didn't trust him: the distrust was in Al's eyes too, and although the pair had shook hands, it didn't look as if the hatchet had been buried quite deep enough. "What for?"

"If I can't handle the boats, if only make sense for me to ride in the helicopter with you. I can help you with navigation, weapons..."

"We fly in a straight line," Al said bluntly. "Sarah can handle the weapons. Didn't you see her cut down the Rots?"

"I can liaise with Harbinger, then: eyes in the sky that keep the boats together, keep an eye out for anyone that may get in trouble and need our help... Jesus, Al, I can't go out to sea on one of those flimsy little boats."

"We're going to sail to America in a frigate, you telling us now that you suffer from seasickness? You're going to spend the next couple of weeks puking over the edge of the boat, what difference is another hour going to make to you? Seems like you're just delaying the inevitable."

"I can't go in the boats, Al... not if there's an alternative method."

"You can't swim," blurted Sarah, grinning from ear to ear as she prodded Goliath's thigh with her index finger. He scowled at her, shook his head, but Al burst out laughing, slapping his thigh and grinning at Sarah.

"She's got it, hasn't she? You can't swim. Dumb ass bastard..."

"I *can* swim, I'm a Marine, for fuck's sake," Goliath glared at Al and Sarah, almost shaking with rage.

"That don't mean shit," Al shook his head dismissively, "Marine's don't have to swim. I knew a guy in the air force; you think he had to be able to fly with his arms? Saddle up then, you chicken-shit."

"There's more of them!"

Al and Sarah looked up to top of the wall, and the few men that remained on guard were frantically gesturing to the bottom of the hill, preparing whatever weapons they held, and levelling them off on the unseen horde at the foot of the incline.

"Are there any runners?" Al shouted, leaving the side of the helicopter and ascending one of the rusted ladders attached to the balcony surrounding the peak of the barrier. "Any immediate threats?" He reached the platform and snatched a pair of binoculars from a makeshift table, lifting them to his eyes and peering down into the murk below. The downpour of rain didn't make it any easier to see in the dark, but sure enough he could make out stumbling shadows between branches and bushes. "No, no runners. Just a bunch of shufflers."

He turned to the men still at their posts. "Go get your shit sorted out, and help out with the rafts. We'll hold the fort while you all get sorted to go."

The group of men didn't have to be told twice, and as they left, Sarah made her way up on to the podium and stood beside Al, slipping her small hand into his meaty paw. The rain was icy cold, and she wanted to get under some shelter, but Al made no move to seek refuge from the downpour. If he didn't move, then there was no reason for her to move, either. She could see that he was watching the front line of Rots, but he made no effort to lift his weapon and open fire.

"This is the last time you'll see the place, I'd imagine," he finally said. "I wouldn't think anyone would ever come back here. Sad to see it go?"

"No," Sarah shook her head. "My Mum, my Daddy… all my brothers and sisters. This place is all full of sad memories. I'll never forget them, but it's not my home any more."

"There's a home waiting for us across the pond. Momma Colebrook makes the best damn meals I've ever tasted, and I'm sure there's a seat for you at her table. She'll be thrilled to meet you sweetie."

"How's it going down there?" Goliath was pacing back and forth on the ground beside the helicopter, his feet sinking a couple of inches into the mud with each step. He had has hand pressed against the side of his helmet, nodding to himself, then waved to Al to attract his attention.

"Everything's almost set down on the docks. Boats loaded, Harbinger's getting ready to take out the first boat. There's a storm coming, it's going to get rough out there…"

"Sooner they get sorted, the better," Al nodded his agreement.

"We have to take off, too," Goliath shouted above a rumbling roll of thunder. "If it gets any muddier, we're going to have to dig this bird out, and I don't fancy doing that with the dead hammering at the gates."

"Agreed," Al grabbed Sarah and carried her back to the helicopter, almost throwing her into the co-pilot's seat before clambering into the vehicle after her. "Get in the back, there's no seats but I don't give shit about you. Hold on, if you fall out, well, you can swim for it." He chuckled to himself at the thought of losing him overboard into the water, then waited as Goliath retrieved a duffle bag from beneath a tarpaulin and hauled it into the back of the 'copter. Unslinging his rifle and dumping that into the vehicle, too, he climbed into the opening and didn't have to give Al any indication that he was in before the blades whirled up to speed and the vehicle lifted up out of the mud. Al slowly banked the helicopter over to one side, hovering over the cliff and directing an underslung spotlight on to the small fleet of boats as they pushed off from the cliff face and jetted into the oncoming waves. A few faces on the boats turned upwards, gave a weak wave, then returned to holding on to the boats as they slowly moved into the approaching tempest.

"They'll be okay, won't they?" Sarah asked, pulling her headset on and pressing her face against the window of the vehicle and recognising some of the younger children from the camp. The helicopter was scary enough in a storm, but she couldn't begin to imagine what it would be like to be sitting on a life raft in this.

"Of course, Harbinger knows his way around a boat," Al nodded, adjusting his own microphone and headset. "Plus, if it gets really bad, we'll drop a rope and pull the lead boat. You can see that whoever was in charge of getting things set up down there's used their heads; they're all tied together so they can't lose any boats."

"Why don't we just do that now?"

"I'm worried about fuel," Al confided, lowering his voice. "If a car runs out of fuel, you just park it up and walk. Up here, we run out and we'll drop out the sky. I want to avoid putting any more drain on what we've got in tank. Which is why I didn't want that sack of crap to come along with us. As it is… it's going to be tight."

Sarah sat back in silence, her attention now pulled from the armada below to the fuel gauge and it's ever-decreasing figures. She was trying to remember the length of time it had taken to get back to the mainland, and was trying to work out the figures in her head about whether they'd have enough to get back.

"We can manage it," he rumbled in a low voice, reading her mind. "Just. It'll be close."

She continued to watch the readouts in silence, gripping the arms of her seat as the storm buffeted the helicopter and rain battered its hull. Lightning flashed to one side, a sharp crack that briefly illuminated the interior of the helicopter with a burst of yellow-white light.

"Lightning," muttered Sarah as she peered into the distance. She could just see the rolling ship in the distance, and felt herself relax at the sight of it. They were almost home free, just in time for a second burst of lightning flash to the same side again. Sarah turned her head to one side, hoping to catch a glimpse of the forked electricity arcing from the sky, and judge just how far away it was, but she couldn't see anything. Just Goliath, a length of webbing attached to his harness as he stood by the open door, his rifle up in his arms as he slowly panned it from side to side.

Flash!

The weapon he held discharged, the flash of light matching what Sarah had thought to be lightning. The roar of the helicopter engine drowned out the sound of the weapon being discharged, and Sarah couldn't think what he was shooting at. The only thing that they could see from up here would be the flotilla of life rafts below: even if there were anything swimming around in the sea, it would be too dark to see anything to get a clear shot without compromising the safety of the people on the boats.

"What's he shooting at?" she finally asked, nodding towards Goliath. Startled, Al spun his head to one side, then the other, trying to catch a glimpse of the Marine and the weapon he was brandishing.

"He's doing what? Hold that stick, keep this thing steady," he demanded, unfastening the safety straps from the seat and pulling himself into the rear of the helicopter while Sarah timidly gripped the controls for the vehicle, holding it steady as best she could. She hoped that whatever Al was going to do, it was going to be quick: she didn't have a clue what she was doing, and felt like she didn't have enough strength to do anything other than barely keep it in a straight line.

"What the fuck're you doing?" Al screamed, his bellicose voice carrying over the radio, as well as above the constant drone of the engine. "The fuck you shooting at?"

"Fly the helicopter, Colebrook."

"Christ… what the fuck are you doing?"

II

Floating in the sea below the helicopter were four life rafts, their black bodies almost invisible against the dark murk of the ocean. Aboard the rear-most craft, the occupants were screaming at the top of their voices, a pair of men trying to reach over the stern of the boat and reel in a body that lay sprawled on the rolling surface, each crashing wave taking the bloody corpse further and further from the group of boats. A couple of the people at the front of the craft were peering up at the helicopter, some pointing fingers, others brandishing the weapons they still held. The range of the rifles they held weren't enough to cause any damage to the helicopter, but a stray bullet would be enough to take out Al permanently if a lucky shot hit.

He ducked his head away from the window and glared at Goliath; at the smoking weapon he held.

"You shot that poor bastard down there," he snarled, stepping towards him. It wasn't a question, but Goliath nodded a response, anyway. He slowly swung his rifle to one side, pointing it wide of Al and making sure the glow of the red laser target nestled on the back of Sarah's head.

"Make a move on me, soldier, and the little girl gets her brains sprayed across the windscreen."

"Al?" Sarah moaned softly, her small hands gripping the controls shaking softly as she watched the reflections of the two men in the darkened windscreen.

"It's okay, honey, you're doing fine," Al spoke softly over his shoulder, then turned his glowering gaze towards the rebellious soldier, his voice turning into a deep growl: "What *the fuck* are you doing?"

"Think about it, Colebrook: a frigate with what, ninety people? A hundred people? A frigate with that many people just *lands* on the shores of America, and we just disappear into the woodwork? How's that going to work? A smaller group's going to be easier to hide than a fucking village!" Goliath grinned, a lopsided sneer which irritated Al no end.

"And you thought you'd take it upon yourself to what, thin the ranks?" Al sneered, shaking his head. "You going to shoot every fucker down there?"

"Got the rounds right here," Goliath patted the combat webbing that held a trio of magazines. "Unless you want to make it quicker and drop a few explosives on them?"

"You gotta be fuckin' shittin' me," Al shouted. "You risk your collective asses to free those people from the sick fuckers who held them captive, only to cut them loose now, in the middle of the fucking ocean? Jesus, who's fuckin' idea's this? It makes no sense."

"They were in the wrong place at the wrong time, pure fuckin' circumstantial. We'd planned on just getting the fuck out of here, when we found the copter was low on fuel, Lance figured the next best thing to being trapped in hell was being trapped in hell with a bunch of people who'd worship you as their fucking saviours. He had a point; we didn't need to lift a finger all the time we were there."

"And now you're shooting them down? Writing them off?"

"There ain't any space for all of us in the new world," Goliath laughed. "How do we explain a hundred people landing on the shores of America, hungry, thirsty, looking for a means to survive? Ten is manageable, we can work around that: anything more?" Goliath laughed again, shaking his head. "Not a fucking chance."

"Miserable bastard," Al growled, his voice low as he gently edged towards Goliath while simultaneously trying to put himself in the line of fire. "You think we're on board with this? Think we'll let this slide? And Harbinger, is *he* in on this?"

"There's a round here with his name on, too. The two of you are remarkably similar, you know. Only difference is, he's quiet, and you can't stop running your mouth off. Maybe I should plug you instead of him?"

"Try it," Al nodded. "Go ahead. I dare you."

"And leave the kid to fly the helicopter? Fuck, no, you get your ass back in that seat and keep us on course back to the frigate."

"I won't stand for this," Al shook his head, reaching for the heavy handgun that sat in the leather holster at his waist. "Drop the weapon."

"This isn't a fucking western like you watched as a kid, Colebrook: This is me, holding a gun at that kid, and you can't quick-draw yourself to victory here. Don't be a hero."

Al furrowed his brow, weighing up his options as Goliath slowly edged to one side and knocked his duffle bag over, tugging blindly at the straps and opening it.

"I was keeping these for later in case anyone else in your little group gave me any shit, but I guess this'll be the quicker way to deal with the fuckers down there. Prime them and throw them out, sink them."

Al lifted his hand from the butt of his weapon and slowly shuffled forwards, his eyes locked with Goliath's. Slowly sinking to his knees, he fumbled with the bag and finished opening it, pulling a pair of grenades from it and lowering his gaze from the Marine to the handful of explosives he held.

"Prime them and toss them," Goliath repeated, jerking his head towards the opening of the helicopter, and the door he'd previously been sniping from. "Grab some more, get one in each boat. Scuttle them all, let them drown at sea."

"Prime them," Al muttered, pulling the pin out of the first pair and peering towards the opening and the black sky outside. "Then throw them…"

Without looking away, he blindly threw the armed grenades, the explosives spiralling through the air and tumbling to Goliath's feet.

"You dumb fuck," he sneered, quickly lowering his gaze to his feet and making a move to kick them out the door. It was a momentary lapse in concentration, and just enough of an opening for Al to lunge forwards, fists raised, and rammed his shoulder into Goliath's midriff. With the wind knocked out of him, he slumped against the back wall of the helicopter, his rifle clattering from his hands and sliding out the door behind one of the grenades: the second of the explosives still rattled around the confines of the helicopter, knocking against Goliath's boots while he tried to kick out at Al. He backed off, each Marine sizing the other up while both were aware of the ticking time bomb rolling around the floor, though neither made a move to pick it up.

"Standard ten second delay on that thing, Colebrook…" Goliath gasped, still holding his stomach with one hand while he tried to suck air. "How long left now?"

"Five seconds," Al snapped back, as if he had pre-empted the question. "How fast can you move?"

Goliath kept his eyes locked on Al, licking his lips while he weighed up the limited options he had.

"Four seconds," Al continued, listening as the grenade rattled around on the floor. It was closer to Goliath than it was to him, but he knew that if he made a lunge for it, he'd open himself up to attack. He knew that the ball was in his court.

"Three," Goliath responded, a sadistic smile spreading across his lips. "I've got nothing to lose."

"Fucker," Al snarled, diving forwards on to the ground and batting the grenade with one hand clear of the helicopter and out the door. Far below the helicopter, beneath the surface of the raging sea, the first of the grenades erupted harmlessly, spraying a flume of water into the air before washing over one of the life rafts. The second grenade detonated mere seconds after leaving the helicopter, searing the side of the helicopter with a lick of flames and spraying a shot of gleaming shrapnel across its side. The vehicle rocked wildly to its side, knocked by the proximity of the blast, and Sarah screamed as she fought to keep control of the bucking machine. Al snarled, tried to shout out words of encouragement, but the moment he'd made a move to knock out the grenade, Goliath had pounced once he'd made sure the grenade was out of the vehicle and he was safe.

Working his legs, the thick heavy boots of Goliath slammed home into Al's face twice, the hard steel of the toecaps cracking his cheeks and opening the flesh above his eye. The rocking of the craft meant that Al was able to roll away before any more blows cracked his skull, but it wasn't going to protect the rest of his body from an attack. Dropping to his knees to keep a lower centre of gravity and better balance, Goliath pummelled Al's back with tight fists, peppering his spine with bone-cracking punches that left him gasping and fighting for breath.

"Gonna kill you," Goliath spluttered, fumbling for his webbing and his knife that hung from a dangling sheath, a murderous glint in his eyes. "Kill you, and that fucking bitch, then I'm gonna strafe those fuckers down there with rockets, blow them all to fuck. What do you think of that, fucker?"

"I think… think you run… your mouth a lot," gasped Al, rolling to one side and clutching his stomach, trying to shield his softer body parts while writhing in pain.

"Mouthy to the end," Goliath chuckled, moving in for the kill, the silver blade of his knife gleaming in the muted light of the cockpit. "So cocksure and arrogant. You're dead, fucker, what's it going to take to get that through your thick skull?"

"Dunno," Al grunted in response, unfurling himself from his foetal position, and exposing the handgun he'd drawn from his holster while he'd been curled up. He fired a double shot from the weapon, both of the powerful rounds smashing into Goliath's lower leg and pulverising his calf with the powerful magnum rounds. The high-powered rounds splashed meat and blood across the floor and wall of the helicopter, and Goliath bellowed in agony, an ear-shattering scream that cut through the continuous drone of the engine of the craft. Holstering his smoking weapon and leaving the moaning form of the wounded Marine on the ground, Al hobbled into the seat beside Sarah and grabbed the free control yolk, trying to keep the helicopter under control. It wasn't until he took a seat and he looked out the window that he realised that the vehicle was dropping, the craft clearly out of control and sinking lower and lower towards the watery surface. It started to turn, and each full rotation of the craft gave a brief, fleeting glimpse of the frigate in the distance, a beacon of hope that seemed further away now than it ever seemed.

"What's the damage?" he managed to say between laboured breaths. He could feel his eye swelling where he'd been kicked, and could taste the blood in his mouth from the blow to his cheek. It also seemed like he had a couple of loose teeth.

"Engine looks like it's pissing smoke," a pale Sarah said, a lot calmer than Al would have expected she would have been. Maybe she realised she was living on borrowed time, just like Al had some time ago. It was a harrowing thought that a child as young as her was willing to accept that fact, but not something Al could reflect on at that moment. "And we're losing something called hyperbolics."

"Hyperbolics?" Al skimmed his eyes across the array of dials and readouts on the dashboard, looking for what Sarah was talking about. "Where is it, honey?"

Sarah lifted a shaking hand, pointing to one of the readouts on an overhead panel.

"Hydraulics," Al muttered. "Mean this thing's going to be a hell of a lot harder to control, if I can't find the override. Help me find it, sweety, I need to disable it…"

As he looked across the control panel, Al's attention was caught by a glimpse of silver in the windscreen before him, and he weaved to one side, narrowly avoiding the downward, sweeping arc of a combat blade scything through the air and narrowly missing his shoulder. The blade of the knife sank into the padding of the seat, ground against the springs that supports his frame, and Goliath grunted incoherently as he tried without success to pull the blade out for a second lunge.

"Fuckers," he spat, bloody spittle dribbling down his chin and spattering his teeth as he stumbled back from the seat on one good leg, and crashed into the rear of the helicopter before lunging forwards again, this time throwing his weight on to Al and pushing him towards the fluctuating controls, pinning down the flight controls and smashing his head against the windscreen. With the yolk pushed forwards, it only gave the helicopter one sure-fire direction to head in, and it was somewhere the vehicle was already on its way to.

"Get off him," Sarah yelled, throwing herself on to Goliath and raking his face with her fingernails. Blood sprayed and seeped across her fingers as she clawed at him while he continued to pound Al's skull against the canopy of the craft. Cracks and splinters appeared in the glass where his skull was hitting, slowly creeping out with each blow. Summoning up all the strength he had, Al managed to lash out an arm and push her back, sending her tumbling into the co-pilot's seat.

"Brace yourself, honey," he managed to say through gritted teeth while trying to do something, *anything,* to fend off the advances of the injured wild animal that was trying to smash his head through the glass. The spinning vehicle lurched forwards and spiralled down, down towards the sea, and through his one eye pressed up against the glass, Al could see the gurgling black sea rushing up to meet him. He instinctively closed his eyes, and for a moment felt weightless before being violently shaken and hurled from his seat, an icy cold liquid washing over him and swirling around his feet, quickly inching its way up his body.

Darkness consumed him as the freezing water pressed in around him, and he felt the force of Goliath weaken, while the pressure of the sea took his place. Kicking away from the pilot seat and submerged beneath the murky depths, he flailed his arms uselessly, trying to find Sarah in the sinking craft. Even if he could open his eyes under water, the darkness of the sea itself and the brooding clouds overhead meant that he wouldn't be able to see anything anyway. Searching blindly with feverish hands, he groped frantically for Sarah: if he was as panicked as he was, he could only imagine how the young girl would feel in the same situation. He only hoped that she'd been able to get a good breath before the helicopter had hit and went under. His hands wrapped around a thin bar of metal, possibly part of the seat, and then a seatbelt: he was getting closer, he knew it. His numbing fingers snagged a different type of material, and then they brushed against a small, frail wrist. He clamped down and kicked out, pushing himself away from the crashed vehicle and pulling the limp form of Sarah behind him.

It was dark, and for a moment Al panicked, unable to tell which way the surface was, until he felt the natural buoyancy of his body in the salt water and he managed to get his orientation. With burning lungs and stinging eyes, he half kicked, half climbed through the swirling waters, breaching the surface with an almighty scream of elation. Rolling on to his back and keeping Sarah resting on his stomach, he paddled backwards towards the fleet of lifeboats, grunting from the exertion and strain that was being put on his wounds.

"We'll be okay," Al spluttered, trying his best to reassure the girl as he approached the boats, flailing his arms wildly to attract the attention of anyone in the boats, and hoping that they knew it wasn't him who'd been shooting at them.

"Over here," he called, spitting out the salty foam as it washed over his face, but he couldn't hear any response to his pleas for help. What seemed like an eternity passed, and exhausted, Al felt like he was either being ignored or out of earshot. He wrapped both arms around Sarah and contemplated what choices he had left. His handgun was in his holster, he could feel the comforting weight of it against his legs, and knew that he could, if need be, offer a death quicker than drowning,

An overpowering wave crashed over his head, and then a second. With water filling his ears, he could only hear muted sounds, and wasn't sure what was going on around him. With crashing waves and the storm that was surging around him, he was finding it hard to get his bearings anywhere, and he didn't want to thrash around to have a look in case he inadvertently drowned his young ward.

The chances of the two being picked up by any of the life rafts were pretty remote, he was accepting that fact quicker with each passing moment, and he could feel his body becoming heavier and sluggish, more unresponsive as he could ever imagine. Even if he had the forethought to carry a flare gun, he doubted he'd even have the strength or the motor capacity to lift it and fire.

Flare guns, life vests… damn the cheap-ass marines and their cost cutting, he thought to himself, angry at the UGMC, and not for the first time. Though he was willing to accept his own fate, he knew that as long as there was an ounce of strength left in his body, he'd do what he could to protect and save Sarah. He kicked out with legs made of lead and ponderously floated in a direction, any direction, in a vain hope that he was heading the right way. Moaning listlessly as he went, he was startled when a swarm of hands grabbed him and hauled both Sarah and him out the water.

"Sweet fucking Christ," he yelled, feeling the pain of his injuries as he was dumped into the lifeboat, with Sarah beside him. Blankets were thrown on top of the pair, and inquiring hands probed them for injuries and checked them over. Al hauled himself up into a seating position, and looked at Sarah beside him. Pale, lips blue and teeth chattering, she was shaking violently, though she seemed conscious and aware of what was going on. She managed half a smile, nodded her head.

"It wasn't us," Al shook his head, pointing vaguely into the sky at where the helicopter had previously hovered only a few seconds ago. "Goliath…"

"We know," one of the villagers nodded as he wrapped a third blanket around Sarah. "Harbinger told us, he was listening in on the radio."

"You had a conversation with him?" Al laughed, and looked around the surrounding boats for the marksman. Though he was garbed in black, the platinum blonde hair of the oversized man stood out like a beacon, and Al gave a half-hearted wave across the waters. There was a nod in response, and Al smiled. "I knew he could speak," he muttered.

"Ja," coughed Sarah, a grin spreading across her pale face. Al wrapped his arm around her and held her tight, rocking her slightly and looking towards the illuminated frigate in the distance.

"How long until we make it to the frigate? At a guess?"

"Don't know," replied the man who seemed to be in charge of that particular boat. "I'm not a mariner, I just know I have to aim the pointy bit at the front where I want to go, and hope for the best. Maybe another hour? Could be more, could be less."

"Great," muttered Al, prodding his face gently. "I need some painkillers, there should be a medikit somewhere on this boat, I'm looking for a blue phial and an auto-injector, you know what that looks like?"

"Like a gun, yeah," the man nodded, hauling out a grey metal box that was attached to the boat with a length of chain. He popped the locks and opened the lid, rummaging through the contents and producing the grey gun-shaped injector and a packet of small blue containers, each tailored to fit into the injector. Al nodded, smiled, and took them from the man, loading one of the capsules and pressing it against his neck, instantly feeling the numbing rush of the painkiller as it rushed through his system.

"Do you have a concussion?" asked the man, reading the back of the packet of capsules. "Hypothermia, congenital heart defects…"

"You don't read the instructions for shit like this," Al grunted, the shot already revitalising him. "The stuff's a mix of painkillers, adrenaline, testosterone, and some stuff that's got numbers in the middle. It's for use on people who've been shot; in the heat of battle, you don't have time to read instructions. Just use it and hope for the best. Now, let's see about taking some of these blankets and make a shelter for Sarah: she can't take any of these drugs, I know that much."

With the rain continuing to hammer the boats and their inhabitants, Al propped up a pair of blankets over Sarah with an oar on either side of her, making a small shelter for her on the boat, and sat impatiently waiting for the convoy to reach the frigate. With brow furrowed and fists clenched, waiting was all he could do.

III

The frigate was motionless in the dark water, a sleeping leviathan lazing in a pool of murky oil, and the base of the ship's hull was dotted with a number of hooks and ties and different levels, ideal to moor the flotilla of rafts to. The small group of lifeboats bobbed lazily by the oversized craft, each tied to one another as the people aboard carefully clambered over one another to climb the ladder hanging from the lowest point of the craft. A construction made of thick cable and wooden slats, two of the largest and strongest survivors held the ladder on either side while the rest of the group slowly clambered up behind one after another, swaying in the beating wind. Al remained at the bottom, his arms wrapped around Sarah as he waited their turn to climb the ladder. He knew that he would have to carry Sarah up, and as such, it would probably be better if he went last. Al figured he was also the only person there who could be able to climb the ladder without it being secured at the base.

"It should lead you up to a platform by an anti-aircraft gun emplacement. Should have a sealed bulkhead you'll need to unlock to get inside, once you do that, get inside and look for someone who you know's on our side," Al had urged the first of the people who had climbed the ladder. "They need to take down Lance before *he* knows that *we* know what he's been planning."

There was only a handful of people left now, including Harbinger, who was busying himself with working over his sniper rifle, securing it to his combat webbing for his ascent. As he grabbed the ladder and motioned for the two anchoring survivors to make their own way up, Al motioned to him with a gentle nod.

"You really came through for us," he smiled. "Thanks, Harbinger."

He shrugged nonchalantly; watching the last of the survivors ascended the ladder. "Was a dick," he grumbled to no one in particular, a heavy accent that accompanied a grim smile.

"Ja," Al smiled, taken aback slightly by the break in Harbinger's limited conversation and slapping his broad shoulders. "Fucking Brass."

"What'll happen now?" Sarah asked, looking up the ladder and pulling one of her blankets tighter around her frame. Rain bounced off her brow, and she shook it, dislodging the stream of water that cascaded down her cheeks.

"Hopefully, whoever gets in first up there finds the kid, or the bitch; Spanners, at a push. Buddy'll just back away from the fight, and Preacher-man'll try to go preach to the fucker in the bridge, try to get him to confess his sins. In one respect, I hope that they get to him and kill him... but at the same time, I want a piece of that bastard myself. C'mon, the sooner we get up there, the sooner we can get up there and head home."

Harbinger swung his weight up on to the ladder after the last of the villagers had disappeared over the lip of the frigate above, then Al hauled Sarah up on to his shoulders making sure she had a tight grip around his combat webbing before following the other hulking Marine.

"Can the ladder take all our weight?" Sarah timidly asked. Al almost shrugged his shoulders before remembering that if he did, he could well shrug her off his back. "It should do," he finally said, looking below him at the rafts rattling against the side of the ship as they slowly started to slip away from their moorings. He thought that they'd managed to get away just in time, until he saw a dark, shadowy figure latching on to the lower rungs of the ladder and painfully hauling himself up one rung at a time.

"Goliath," Al spat, recognising the figure, then lifted his head. "We've got company, Harbinger."

Despite the injuries that he'd sustained, and the fact that he'd been in the cold waters of the ocean for a couple of hours, he was still coming, intent on their murder. He had a silver blade clenched between his teeth, and for a moment, Al was reminded of the old films he'd watched when he was a boy, with pirates climbing aboard the ships of their prey with cutlasses braced in their mouths. The gleam in the eyes of Goliath, however, was far more murderous than even the most skilled actor had been able to portray.

Spurred on by the advances of the damaged soldier, Al increased his climbing pace, arm over arm with Sarah on his back, trying not to shake the ladder too much above him, while at the same time, trying to shake off the advancing Marine below. Though his joints were frozen and weak from his time in the ocean, Goliath continued his ascent with an unnatural zeal, and for a moment, Al was uncertain if it was actually Goliath, or if he had passed on, and the creature making a mad dash up the ladder was now nothing more than a Rot. The ragged and laboured breathing of the lumbering madman convinced him otherwise, however. Climbing the ladder, Al's body was screaming in agony, and he could only imagine what Goliath was going through: that didn't mean he felt sorry for the bastard.

"Nearly there," Sarah said, peering up the ladder, trying to not sound as scared and panic-stricken as she actually was. "Harbinger's... Al, what's he doing?"

Al pulled his gaze from the ascending, would-be killer to see Harbinger fumbling with this belt, lashing a cable around a pylon sticking out the side of ship and leaning out away from the ladder. He relinquished his grip on the ladder, kicked out, and dropped past Al, attached to the frigate by his improvised zip line as he rushed past Al and Sarah, hurtling past them and pulling out his sidearm as he did so, drawing a bead on Goliath and opening fire.

Bullets sparked off the hull and hammered into the body of Goliath just as his hand curled around Al's foot, his fingers knitting into his bootlaces as the first of the rounds smashed through him: two in his chest, one through his shoulder. Screaming in pain, he turned limp as the agony of the wounds consumed him, and Al almost lost his footing as the sudden dead weight almost tore him from the ladder. He could barely hold Sarah's weight, but the sudden jarring of the extra dead weight almost made him black out himself. Locking his arms around the rung he held, he gritted his teeth and watched through half-closed eyes as Harbinger, still dangling from his improvised abseil, tried to pry off the unconscious soldier.

"Hurry," Sarah shouted over the pelting rain that thrummed against the wall of the ship, voicing her concern for Al and the strain the excessive weight was having on him. Harbinger grunted wordlessly, having obviously used his conversation quota for the day, and tried to untwine fingers from bootstraps, the freezing rain making it hard for him to manipulate the separating of the two. A bitter wind screamed around him, an invisible banshee that made the task his numb fingers had even harder as they tried to work around the taut laces.

"Mother fucker!"

As a jagged bolt of lightning flashed in the sky overhead with an accompanying peel of thunder, Goliath's eyes flickered open and screamed into Harbinger's face, his blade falling away from his mouth and into his free hand, which he brought crashing down in and overhead stabbing motion, sinking his blade into the side of Harbinger's neck and pulling it downwards, releasing his grip on Al and throwing his full weight on to the sinking blade. Harbinger's scream was drowned out by another thunderous clap, his howl overpowered by a screeching gust of air dashing the ladder against the hull of the ship as the blade lodged itself deep in his collarbone. With a flailing of limbs and an ear-splitting roar, Harbinger grabbed hold of Goliath, pinning his arms with his own oversized extremities. The line he was dangling from sang as it strained from the extra weight, drawn taught, spinning, and finally snapping with a crack, the ragged end of the cable lashing against Al's face as both Harbinger and Goliath smashed into the surface of the water. Frantically struggling with the dead weight of the muscular Marine and the snaking cable that wound its way around the thrashing form, the screaming face of Goliath sank beneath the black surface, a spray of froth and bubbles the last thing to escape his lungs.

Swearing beneath his breath, Al laboriously finished his ascent, his mouth turned down in a frown as his thoughts lingered on the sacrifice Harbinger had made for the safety of both Sarah and himself: a frown that turned into a sneer as the thought what he would do to Lance to make him pay for the betrayal.

Turning his gaze to the heavens, he pulled his weight and his precious cargo over the lip of the ship and tumbled on to the deck, the pair lying on the soaking deck as they recuperated from the climb.

The deck itself was eerily quiet, with only the drumming of rain on the metal surface, and a thick, cloying stench that seemed to permeate the cold and damp air. Sarah was first to pull herself around, shrugging off her blanket and rolling on to her front, then lifting herself shakily up on to all fours.

She screamed.

Sitting bolt upright, Al's found his pistol was already in his outstretched hand as he panned it from side to side, the sorrow returning to his face once more as he was faced with a scene of carnage.

That last rumble of thunder obviously hadn't been thunder.

No body had been left whole: each villager had been torn apart by oversized rounds, leaving behind nothing but chunks of unrecognisable meat littered with shards of bone and lumps of gristle, with a carpet of crimson that seeped across the deck and into the sluice channels that carried the excess fluids over the sides of the boat. Directly in front of him, a multiple-barrelled pair of giant machineguns stood silently poised at the decking, a thick cloud of cobalt-blue smoke lingering round their dimly glowing muzzles. Bullet holes scarred the deck, craters pooling with rainwater, blood and offal, and Al slowly pulled himself to his feet, slipping across the carrion-covered platform to the sealed bulkhead that would lead into the ship, wrapping an arm around Sarah and shielding her from as much of the carnage as he could. He placed his hands on the locking mechanism, the bulk of the blood that had sprayed over the handle had already been washed off by the downpour, and cycled it open, quickly rushing Sarah in and slamming the door shut, spinning the lock back into place. He stood motionless for a moment, shaking with cold and anger, and it was only after Sarah fell to her knees sobbing that he realised, he, too, was crying: the rain outside had masked his tears, but now, water still streamed down his face.

"I'm going to fucking kill the bastard," Al swore, holstering his weapon and fumbling for his comset. Miraculously, it was still hanging around his neck, and he brought it up to his mouth.

"Bill, where you and Angel at?"

"We're below decks," came the reply, distorted with an underlying hiss of static. The thick bulkheads were breaking the signal up, but not so much that he couldn't be understood. "Trying to clean out all the bodies. What's wrong?"

The fact Al had called Bill by his given name, and not the nickname he'd come up with a long time ago, raised alarm bells. The fact he'd also said Angel, even more so.

"What about everyone else?"

"Sylvester's in the engine room, think he's keeping an eye on the valves and whatever else is going on down there. Clive's reading the last rites to the bodies of the Rots as we dump them over the edge."

"He needs to come to the portside lock, forty-A. Quick."

"I'm nearby," Garth's voice cut in, a lot clearer than Bills. He appeared at the junction at the far end of the corridor, looking slightly bemused, and gave a half-hearted wave. He dropped his comset, looking at the weeping form of Sarah kneeling on the ground, then at Al, a look of bemusement on his face. "I heard the thunder, sounded like the ship got hit by something, like a lightning strike or something, I thought I'd check it out... where's the helicopter? What's going on here? We didn't hear you land. Is Sarah okay?"

"Keep an eye on her, get her away from here, out on the main deck, find somewhere safe for her."

"It's pissing down out there," Garth started to protest, moving towards the bulkhead behind Al. The marine held back a growl as he slapped Garth back, away from the exit and the grizzly remains that lingered outside.

"Not out there, use your fucking brain for once. And put a fucking raincoat on," Al spat, storming past him. He paused, knelt on the ground beside Sarah, holding her hands in his: his meaty paws dwarfed hers, able to cover both with one hand. "Will you be okay, sweetie? With Garth looking after you?"

She sniffed, nodded, then shakily stood and made her way over to Garth, who took her by the hand and followed Al to the junction he'd just rounded the corner of.

"Where are you going?" Garth asked, moving towards the winding corridor that would lead out to the helipad and the main deck itself. He stopped, moving to hinder Al's retreat by planting his feet shoulder width apart and trying to block the corridor. "Damn it. What the fuck is going on?"

"I had to park the helicopter in the ocean because Goliath thought it'd be a fucking good idea to snipe everyone from the helicopter. He's dead, Harbinger's dead... the entire fucking *village* is dead, just on the other side of that door. The human body can't take a burst of anti-aircraft fire."

"That was the thunder..." Garth mused to himself, making a move to step to one side. "I'll take Sarah, don't worry... Where you going?"

"I need to have a word with Lance," Al growled, cracking his knuckles. Garth watched as Al headed off towards the bridge, then gently took Sarah by the arm and guided her outside, grabbing a thick, heavy waxen poncho that hung by the door. He wrapped it around her, then stepped outside, marching slowly towards the front of the ship and watching the waves ahead of them rolling back and forth.

"You okay?" Garth finally asked, breaking the silence that lingered over the little girl. She nodded softly, refusing to look up from her feet, which she'd been staring at since Garth had taken custody of her.

"You don't need to tell me anything, kiddo, I'll get all the details from Al later on. Rain's dying off, anyway." Small talk wasn't Garth's forte, and he struggled with anything to say to Sarah: although he was desperate to know the details, he didn't want to press her fragile mind for anything further.

"I was so scared," she finally whispered.

"But you're all right now," Garth muttered. "Al promised he'd look after you, right? And he did."

Sarah nodded, looking back over her shoulder at the dark shape of the bridge that loomed over them. She was tired and cold, the adrenaline from the hell she'd been through slowly subsiding, and despite the horror that she'd seen, the mangled carcasses of the villagers that lay halfway down the ship, she knew that she needed sleep. "I know, but…"

Sarah's mutters died off as her head lolled forwards, her chin resting against her chest as she started to snore softly. Garth grinned to himself, wrapped his arm tightly around her and nodded to himself. Maybe there were some things the large bald guy was actually good for. Driving trucks, staying out of trouble, keeping the kids safe…

After barely five minutes, Sarah startled her self awake, an incoherent mutter about something she'd left behind for Michael, and she looked blearily from one side to the other, taking in the details of the saturated deck.

"Al?" she slurred. Garth nodded his head, whispered softly that he was fine, and Sarah smiled to herself, lowering her eyelids and slowly going back over.

She snapped out her dreary state as the darkened bridge exploded into a flurry of rapid explosions, screams and shattering glass. She threw back her poncho and looked at Garth, his gaze following hers towards the control room in the distance that seemed to be quiet once again. The lighter spatter of dying rain splashed against her face, and despite the chill of the water that soaked her clothes, she felt herself break out in a sweat as she caught the blur of a figure garbed in a military outfit tumbling out the shattered remains of one of the windows, twisting and flailing before landing awkwardly with a bone-shattering crack on the deck far below.

"Fuck, Al!"

She leapt up and rushed towards the impact zone, jerking backward and dropping to the ground as Garth snatched at her arms and held her back. From her vantage point she could see the broken body lying on the ground, a mix of jagged bones and bloodied flesh.

"Let me go," she screamed, pushing Garth away as she tried to scramble across the slippery deck plates. She inched closer, but Garth managed to get a secure grip around her, interlinking his fingers and holding her down, despite her protesting. "Get off me!"

IV

"Al!"

One of the doorways leading to the lower decks slammed open, and Bill stumbled out into the main corridor, swinging his head wildly from side to side as he tried to find his friend. He curtly nodded as he stormed past, almost knocking him off his feet.

"Christ, Al, what's going on? I tried raising you, but these headsets aren't worth shit."

"Get out on the main deck, you and Angel, I want you to look after Sarah, make sure she's okay. She's with Garth."

"What's wrong?"

"Ask me in ten. I need to speak to Lance, alone."

"Where's everyone else? We didn't hear the helicopter approach…"

"Dead," Al spat solemnly. "Harbinger's in the ocean, the village is dog food by the portside gun platform."

"Goliath?"

"Roasting in hell, for all I care."

"What's going on?"

Angel appeared behind Bill, a machete in one hand that was stained with blood. "We need to shift these bodies out before they stink the place out."

"You need to do what I tell you," snapped Al, "and go and fucking look after Sarah. Make sure nothing happens to her."

"But…" Angel started to protest, but Al shook his head.

"Just do as you're told," Al ordered, trying not to scowl too much, but failing miserably. Bill looked at him, surprised, then half muttered a "Yes sir," response and half-heartedly snapped off a lazy salute before grabbing his rifle and making his way towards the main deck. Al grabbed his arm before he left, muttering under his breath as he did so. "Look... ah, fuck it,"

Al let go, stalking off deeper into the decks of the ship, heading for the bridge.

"Where you going?" Bill shouted after him, and Al turned around long enough to call over his shoulder. "You know how I said I don't go looking for trouble, it finds me? Well, it's time to break the habit of a lifetime."

The corridors of the ship deeper in the confines of the hull were just like those of the guard tower he had once been stationed on, lined with pipes and wiring that made movement for a man with his stature not impossible, but very hard to negotiate without side-stepping and doubling over at the waist. He finally found a set of stairs that promised to lead up, and he slowly climbed the metal steps one at a time, reaching the heavy metal door that sealed the upper deck from the lower deck and pulling it open. The hinges squeaked softly, and Al stepped into the upper corridors. Any feeling of claustrophobia he may have had in the lower decks was chased away by the open corridors of the bridge and command centre. He could stand tall, take bounding steps; he could even stretch his arms out to either side and *just* touch the walls. He passed open doorways leading into luxurious cabins with thick carpeting, extravagant bedding and ornate furniture. While the cabins in the lower decks were cramped and designed to hold two or three crew members, these rooms were clearly tailored for one person, though they lived in the lap of luxury.

"Fucking Brass," he muttered to himself as he followed the signs for the bridge, coming to another set of ascending stairs, this one a wide spiralling construction, and climbing up them slowly. The murmuring chatter and crunching of machines filtered down to him as he approached the crown of the stairs, leaving the gunmetal grey corridors of the living quarters and stepping into the darkened bridge.

A panoramic vista lay before him, the outer walls around him constructed entirely of glass and looking out over the ship and its aquatic surroundings. Wind and rain spattered the windows, and Al could see the horizon list from side to side as the wind rocked the boat back and forth. While the rest of the ship had been tainted with the permeating scent of death and decay, this room smelled of stale air, but nothing more: as if it had been sealed off by someone as soon as they knew the dead had infected the crew of the ship in a bid to keep them out. If that were the case, why hadn't they sealed themselves in there and called for help?

A figure shifted to one side of Al, a hunched shadow working over a control panel and shifting his weight from one foot to another.

"You never intended to even give those poor bastards a chance, did you?"

Lance stood bolt upright and spun on his heels, looking at Al. He remained secluded in the shadows, only the slightest of his facial features picked out by the glowing green instruments around him.

"I'm waiting for an answer," Al said, shuffling back half a step and leaning back on to a bank of controls. Something clicked on the console, but Al didn't remove himself from the controls or try to switch it off. The boat hadn't blown up, and the bank of weapons that lined the outer shell of the frigate hadn't opened up, so he figured it couldn't have been that important.

"Well..." Lance seemed temporarily lost for words, floundering for something to say. "I didn't know you were back here. The helicopter, I didn't hear it land. There were no proximity alarms that went off. I wasn't expecting to see you."

"Probably weren't expecting to see me ever again," barked Al. "And I'm sure the proximity alarms did go off. Which is why you opened up with the anti-aircraft guns to cut everyone down out there, you fucking bastard."

"I don't know what you're talking about," Lance snapped back, "And I don't appreciate what you're trying to insinuate, Sergeant. I've spent the last two hours trying to work out the navigation console so I can get you and your friends out of here, and now you're spouting some shit about a mass murder? You'd better reign yourself in, Colebrook, if it wasn't for us you'd still be chasing off the zombies trying to eat your black ass."

"What the fuck did you say?"

"I said shut up, and count yourself lucky you're still alive. I don't know what happened out there, and to be honest, I don't give a shit. It's clear something bad happened, and... and I see that Goliath and Harbinger aren't with you. Christ only knows what plan they came up with while I was away from them." Lance laughed nervously, shaking his head. "But those two were always close, I suppose. They could have come up with anything... they could've even come up with this story about the base being attacked by zombies."

"Like they managed to rig the weapons on a frigate they'd never been on?"

"Okay, you got me," Lance raised his hands in mock surrender. "I guess Goliath told you everything. But Jesus, Colebrook, we can't just turn up on American shores with a ship loaded with people and just *disappear* into the woodwork! You know what I'm saying is true..."

"So why even bother?"

"If your protector and saviour was leaving you behind, wouldn't you do anything to keep them where they were? If we left them all alone, it could have been *us* that were smeared across a concrete platform. As it is, we just... pre-empted their moves."

Al said nothing, folding his arms over his chest, waiting for Lance to make his next move.

"So what's the plan now?" Lance finally spoke again, the unnerving silence between the pair finally shattering.

Al didn't reply, simply impatiently tapped his index finger against the swell of his bicep. Lance seemed to hesitate before tapping a string of commands into the console, barely looking at the keypad as he did so. "I'm keying in the coordinates for America, Al. We're going home. What's done is done; we can't change that. We can just move on."

"Just like that?" It was Al's turn to laugh now, incredulous towards the whole situation. "Ninety villagers slaughtered by your hand, two of your friends killed by one another... and you can just move on? Just like that?"

"It's a gift, I guess," Lance nodded, a smug grin on his face. "What do you say, Al? Ball's in your court. A bunch of nobodies in exchange for your friends?"

"I'll admit, I didn't know many of those people very well," Al shook his head. "And I've got my own family to worry about now..."

Lance smiled to himself, nodding his head.

"But then, who's to say you're not going to fuck us over to save your own ass? I know that there were young men, women, fucking *children,* for fucks sake... You're nothing but a fucking animal, a savage no better than any of those other fucking soldiers that baited the dead, made them fight one another for your own amusement..."

"I did this for our fucking *survival,*" screamed Lance. "It's the only way this plan would work! Why can't you understand?"

"I've changed," Al shook his head, watching Lance as his hands slowly moved towards his combat webbing, and the holdout pistol he knew was stored there. "The Marines made everything seem so black and white: but there's too many shades of grey."

"Maybe I did just look out for myself," Lance shrugged. "But I can still run this ship without you. Last chance, Al, pick a side. You're either with me... or against me!"

"No wonder you had such a big fucking grin on your face when you first boarded the helicopter, you'd just cleared all your plans with Goliath. What did you offer him? Promotion? Money? Maybe a chance to fuck your little sister? Hell, I'm sure you're a very generous man, maybe you offered the bastard all three? While we risked our ass to get fuel for the whirlybird, you two shit stains sat and plotted the demise of your friend and the community you'd set up. Heartless mother fuckers, that's all you are."

"Goliath is like any good soldier, he respects the command structure. Something a loose cannon like you couldn't possibly begin to understand. And if you really must know, I said that Goliath could have that little snot-nosed cunt that follows you around like a bad smell."

"Miserable fucker," Al spat, starting to lunge forwards. Lance didn't say anything, simply snatched at the holdout pistol tucked into his webbing and squeezed off a shot. Al reacted just as quickly, snapping up his magnum from its holster and squeezing off a double-burst from his own weapon. A flash of sparks appeared in the air between the two men, then Lance staggered backwards, clutching his shoulder as it blossomed and oozed thick red blood. Al leapt to one side and slammed his body against the bulkhead of the open hatchway he'd entered through as bullets peppered it, the small calibre rounds denting the metal, but not striking with enough force to penetrate the thick steel skin.

"You should've... should've left it, Sergeant," Lance hissed. Al grinned as he could hear the pain in the voice of the other man. "Should've done what you were ordered!"

"I forgot to mention," Al shouted as he blindly fired around his shield, hearing the large rounds smash against instruments and destroy readouts. With any luck, he wouldn't damage anything they needed. "Long time ago, when the rest of you bastards left me for the dead, I decided to give myself a little field promotion. Turns out Colebrook made Commander. So that means I don't take shit from no one. And that includes you and your dead boyfriend."

Lance responded with a wordless scream and another barrage of gunfire that peppered the open hatch. While retreating from the firestorm and pulling a round canister from his belt and tugging the pin from the top, Al counted to three then casually lobbed the canister over the top of the door. The room flashed with a brilliant white light and the sound of a hundred pieces of glass shattering, accompanied by the feeble whimpering of Lance. Al stepped out from behind his cover and levelled off his magnum, aiming directly at the prone figure slumped over a battered control console, its readouts smashed by the impact of the body.

The flash grenade was designed to incapacitate a person by scrambling their senses, and would last just long enough to subdue someone before they regained their motor functions. Al stormed forwards and pulled Lance up by the straps of his webbing, hurled him towards the window, and levelled off his magnum.

"Any last requests?"

"Go... fuck... yourself," wheezed Lance.

"That's not original at all. But then, why would I expect originality from an officer?"

Lance grimaced, then with a deafening roar lurched forwards, urging his useless limbs to work for him. He stumbled into Al just as his weapon fired, and both men stumbled across the bridge with their arms locked around each other, bouncing off consoles and tumbling over chairs. Al felt incredible pain in his side as his recent injuries flared up once more, and felt blood trickle down his fingers and wrists as he wrestled with Lance. They edged closer and closer to the panoramic windows, finally knocking into them and sending a crack through the giant panes.

"Never could stand you grunts," Lance hissed with vehemence as he took hold of the back of Al's skull and smashed it into the window once, twice, three times. He pulled pack, looking at the bloody pulp of skin that covered his forehead and the glistening slivers of glass that had been embedded in his skin by the impacts. "Bunch of idiots and slackers, could never finish anything they started."

"Yeah?"

Al kicked Lance in the kneecaps, grinning uncontrollably as he heard one of the bones snap, regardless of the pain he was in himself. He kicked again and again until he heard more snaps and cracks, and Lance screamed and listed to one side, the bones of his shins smashed in two and tearing through the flesh and material of his clothing. Gibbering uncontrollably, the disgraced Captain clung to one of the consoles, a murderous look in his wild eyes.

"I finished that leg, you miserable piece of shit," Al growled, taking perverse pleasure in the pain the man was clearly in, "And by Christ I'm going to finish the other one."

Al's weapon discharged again, a pair of bullets smashing through the surrounding glass plates and introducing a howling gale into the command deck. Rain lashed against the consoles closest to the window, making Lance's clothing, already slick with blood and sweat, even harder to hold. The pair smashed into the wall again and again, a match of strength that Al found surprising, especially considering the grievous extent of Lance's wounds. It was that survival instinct kicking in, something that all Marines had encountered at one point in their career, the fight or flight that gave the wounded wings: it was something that Al had experienced a few times himself, and it was something he intended to experience again.

A canister slipped from Al's belt and dropped to the floor in the scuffle and exchange of blows, unseen by either of the combatants, and was knocked back and forth by their feet until the pin finally snagged under Al's foot. The grenade detonated, and both men were propelled away from it, the sudden flash and loud blast enough to stun both men as they stumbled deliriously across the bridge, the disorientating effects of the device confusing each of their movements.

Al felt the world spinning and tumbling around him until he finally came to his senses, lying flat on his back with rain spattering his face where he lay. He couldn't move yet, the disorientating effects of the flash bomb still lingering heavily in his system. A dull pain wracked his side, and he was sure he could feel a piece of metal lodged in his flesh between his ribs, the rain washing his wound and thinning the blood he was sure he could feel trickling down his bruised skin. Wind picked at his clothing, finding its way through the close-knit fabric of the numbing his entire body. Somewhere in the maelstrom of wind and hail, he could hear his name being called, distant and ethereal.

"Pam?" he whispered softly, his eyes closed and spattered with rain, diluting his tears.

"Is that you?"

"He's a fucking mess," Bill growled, kneeling on the floor beside the bloodied pulp of the man that lay on the deck of the boat. Despite the tumble he had taken from the bridge, and the number of broken bones that seemed to protrude from the ruptured body, the chest of the fallen man still seemed to rise and fall, albeit in short and shallow breaths.

"But he's still alive," Angel said, standing behind Bill and gently massaging his shoulder. She couldn't look at the bloodied mess, and instead she tried to focus on something else, anything to detract her attention from the near-dead body. "What can we do for him? I'm not much of a medic, I couldn't do anything for him…"

"Put him out his misery," suggested Clive. "If there's nothing you can do for him, it's the only right thing to do."

The crowd surrounding the decimated body bowed their head in silence, the only sound audible over the howling wind and spatter of rain the barest whisper of a struggling breath.

"I say let the fucker suffer."

Bill looked over his shoulder at the crumpled figure that sat atop one of the smaller packing crates, a blanket draped over his bloodied skull and another wrapped around his battered form.

After the gunfight in the bridge had erupted, Bill had rushed from Angel's side, urging her on to meet up with Garth and Sarah as Al had commanded, turning back on himself and rushing in the direction of the shots, or at least the direction he thought the shots were coming from. The harshness of the steel bulkheads served only to distort the sound, sending Bill on a wild goose chase as he followed echoes and ghostly sounds before finally finding the source of the skirmish. By the time he had located the bridge, the only thing he found was the bloody aftermath of the fight. Bullet casings littered the floor, tinkling as they slid into one another as his booted feet skimmed the deck. Pools of blood spattered the deck, crimson puddles that told tales of injuries and grievous trauma; rivulets of the same fluid had been splashed across the walls and consoles, adding to the macabre effect of the battleground. A single figure lay on the floor beside one of the shattered panoramic windows, coated in a slick covering of blood and rain that leaked in through the damaged glass. Though he was muttering nonsensical words and half-formed sentences, he responded as Bill approached him and leaned closer.

"What happened?"

"Crazy old psycho bastard attacked me," moaned the figure, motioning for Bill to help him up. "I attacked him back. Where is the fucker?"

After helping the injured party sit up, Bill leaned out the window and could see the shattered figure that lay on the deck far below.

"He's not going anywhere," Bill said, motioning to the window.

"Good," muttered the man as he crawled along the floor, sending casings scattering as he retrieved the bulky magnum and the smaller handgun from the floor, stuffed them into different pockets, and retrieved a lump of shapeless lead that rolled gently from side to side. He smiled softly to himself, then shook his head.

"Shot right out the air," he mused. Bill wondered if he hadn't fully regained all his senses, but he seemed to speaking more cognitively as he ever had. "Jesus Christ, it's not often that happens. Shot the fucking thing *right out the air!* It was bang on target, if it had hit me it would have killed me. *"Un-fucking-believable."*

Bill looked on in shock as Al pulled back the sheet covering his head and repeated his sentencing for the fallen Marine on the deck.

"You heard me. Let the fucker suffer."

"That's hardly humane, is it?" Clive asked, his voice smooth and calm, a contrast to the seething anger that came with the words Al had spat.

"Humane?" laughed Al. "Humane? Is that what you call turning an anti-air flak cannon on an entire colony of survivors just to serve your own selfish desires? Don't make me laugh, Preacher-man. What Lance did to the villagers, that sick bastard would have done to any one of us if he needed to. Ain't nothing humane about that."

"I have to agree with Al," Sylvester said. Bill was shocked at that, but not as much as Clive, who looked like his best friend had just betrayed him. In a way, he had. "If Goliath and Lance *had* planned all along to wipe out the entire town, who's to say we weren't surplus to requirements, too?"

"It just doesn't make sense," Garth muttered, his eyes flicking nervously from the prone casualty on the ground to the handgun tucked in the waistband of his trousers. Just like everyone else there, he'd had some rough experiences with the dead, and wasn't willing to let his guard down just yet, no matter how relaxed the rest of the crew seemed to be. "Why wait until now?"

"A window of opportunity," Al said, staring at the piece of lead he still clutched. Bill couldn't believe what Al had said about the bullets knocking each other out the air, but sure enough, the chunk of soft lead definitely had the appearance of two bullets that had crashed into one another: the heavy round from the modified magnum having a larger impact on the smaller handgun bullet. He rolled it carefully around in his fingers, deep in thought, then handed it over to Sarah, who stared at the bewildering lump of metal.

"I don't follow," Angel said, stepped back from the dying man on the ground and slipping her arm around Bill's waist. As she did so, he could smell the faint taint of the dead that clung to her clothing, lodged there from shifting the corpses. He probably smelled just as bad. Once everything had been settled, the two of them would have to retire to a room and get cleaned up. He couldn't remember the last time he'd shared a bath with someone, but it was something he was looking forward to. A great deal.

"I don't expect you to," Al said with a mischievous grin. "That's because you're the dumb bitch.

Anyway, from what I can tell, it was something Lance had been scheming for a while, more or less when they first cleared the encampment. Yes, there was a whole towns-worth of people to rescue from the sadist Marines stationed there, but his original plan had been to use the helicopter to escape. That's when they realised they didn't have enough fuel, or a completely competent pilot. So instead of fleeing the island, they made the best of a bad situation and set up the camp. They were living like kings, anyway, the people looked up to them like they were gods. But it always gnawed at the back of Lance's mind: the Marines had abandoned him in the middle of a mission, and he wanted to go home. I mean, who doesn't?"

Garth nodded thoughtfully, his mind obviously filled with thoughts of visiting his daughter, Anna. Sarah sighed and shrugged her shoulders, playing idly with the pair of bullets Al had handed her.

"Some of us can't go back home," she said without looking up from the compacted rounds.

Bill nodded grimly in response to that, the corners of his mouth rising in a slight smile as he appraised the youth. She was a strange one, of that he was sure. Sometimes she would act like the child she was, and other times… other times she could be the most mature of the group. Considering her age and all she'd been through, she'd kept herself together incredibly well. In some respects, she was a role model for the whole group.

"You don't need to go back," Angel said, reaching out and tucking some stray strands of Sarah's hair back behind her ear and smiling softly. "We're all moving forwards, on to a new life."

"Cute," Al whispered with a smirk. "Where was I? Ah, yes.

"Our man Lance was pretty sharp, he knew that he could go out to a guard tower and get more fuel for the helicopter, but who could he send? He didn't want to go himself or send Goliath, it was obviously too dangerous for the people he gave a shit about, and he couldn't send Harbinger on his own. Likewise, he couldn't send civvies on the mission."

"So he waited for a group of suckers to come along and play into his hands?" Sylvester asked, realisation dawning on him, "He let us think that we had come up with this plan ourselves, and he let us go out and risk our arses to do something he was too yellow to do?"

"Bingo," Al said. "Though to my credit, I *did* think of it myself. The fact it was also his plan was just a coincidence.

"So we turn up, he makes it look like he's doing us a favour by letting us go, and sends Harbinger with us 'to keep an eye on things'. Meanwhile, the human pancake and the incredible sinking stone," he said, pointing to the quivering man on the ground first, then jerking a thumb towards the side of the boat to indicate Lance and Goliath's fate respectively, "They were planning out the whole damn operation. Manipulative bastards that they are *made* it look like your God Tale gave him inspiration to deliver the whole town, but in reality he'd been thinking about it for months."

"One thing I don't understand," Clive said, cupping his hand around the end of the cigarette he'd placed in his mouth and flicking his lighter to life. His face was momentarily illuminated by the red glow of the flame. "Why'd he tell us to get a frigate?"

"Authenticity," Al replied. "That way it looks like he's trying to accommodate for the village, and we're none the wiser. The time it takes us to get out here and take the boat, Goliath's all geared up and ready to go. He knew that we wouldn't go without everyone, and he took the chance that we'd be able to be *coerced* into agreeing with this. Goliath was supposed to be executing them on the way, without us noticing maybe, so he can claim they were lost at sea. It's pretty fucking rough out there. The AA emplacement; that was just the backup plan. I don't think he expected us to survive, he must've thought we were in the crowd with everyone else. Hell, maybe he thought that Goliath was in there, too, and he just didn't care about him, either."

"Why'd he have to kill them?" asked Sarah.

"Because he didn't want to bring everyone. His plans didn't accommodate a village. His plans probably didn't cover us. He couldn't let us leave without him, but he couldn't let it appear as if he was abandoning his flock, as it were. After all, imagine what would have happened if this didn't turn out right? The people who had previously adored him'd shun him. He had the boat, but he couldn't guarantee the plan was going to work until we were in the air and on the way."

"So he killed them all off?"

"That's about the top and bottom of it, yeah."

"Fuck," whispered Bill, shaking his head and looking glumly at the twitching mound of broken flesh and bone at his feet. There wasn't much else he could say or do.

"How do you know this?"

"Some I pieced together after it happened. Lance and Goliath told me some of it when I was talking to them. Questions I was asking, answers I was getting. You see, I saw interrogations in Brazil, I know how they work, how you can catch people out. The Brass? Fucking inept, I knew when he was lying; I figured he was scheming something when he insisted he came as the weapons operator. A kid could operate the basics that we needed; a kid *did* operate the weapons. I didn't need a frigging piece of Brass to act as my co-pilot."

"And Goliath was in on it all?" Garth muttered. "He seemed like an okay kinda guy…"

"He was a dick, even Harbinger thought so. Yeah, he told me. And now, the mastermind of it all's going to die. Throw him overboard."

"He'll drown," Clive protested half-heartedly.

"Hey, you wanted to put an end to his suffering: consider it a compromise."

"Allowing a man to slowly drown is hardly ending it quickly," the priest tried to argue his point, but Bill knew there was no point in arguing with Al: his mind was made up.

"My heart bleeds for the fucker," he sneered, spitting a bloody wad of phlegm on the body. "At least this way we give him a chance to fend for himself."

"He's barely alive, he's paralysed, he can't move."

"I've got better things to do then debate this shit. Spanners, you and buddy haul that useless pile of meat over the side."

He hobbled towards the door leading into the lower decks, indicating for Bill to follow him.

"I'm hungry; I've just had a craving for a couple of hamburgers. Let's see what slop we can find in the galley, eh kid? I'm not saying it's a five star restaurant down there, but I guarantee I can make something better than the tin of dog food you ate once."

"You ate dog food?" Sarah asked, scrunching up her face as she followed them, making a 'bleugh' sound as she stuck her tongue out.

"It was a long time ago," Bill said, scowling at Al as he went.

"And I let you kiss me," Angel said with a smile, playfully poking Bill in the small of his back as he followed.

"It was a long time ago," Bill repeated, looking over his shoulder as Garth and Sylvester grabbed the body of the fallen Marine and casually hauled it over the side, listening for the splash of limp flesh against the lapping waves that knocked against the side of the boat. They both quickly jogged back to catch up with the leaving party, while Clive stood at the railings, looking mournfully into the roiling ocean and muttering something to himself, his fingers caressing the leather-bound bible he still carried.

The galley of the frigate was large enough to adequately house enough chefs to feed half the ship while they rested and the other half was on active duty, so it wasn't too crowded for the group of seven people as they worked on their meals.

Clive had finally decided to join them after ten minutes on the deck alone, shrugging off his heavy trench coat and laying it over the back of a chair before busying himself by clearing off a bench and preparing a place for the group to eat. Though it hadn't been vocalised, it would have been easier to eat in the kitchen area instead of trying to wipe down one of the tables in the mess halls: that would come later, after everyone was suitably rested and recovered from the ordeal of cooking.

"Smell that barbecue," grinned Al as he tended to a row of hamburgers on an oversized skillet, working with his head cocked slightly as he listened to the sizzle and spatter of the greasy burgers.

"That's wonderful," Angel said, looking up from the salad she was preparing. "Shame I don't eat meat."

"That's not what I've been told," Al said with a leering grin, winking at Bill. He rolled his eyes and shook his head, retrieving a stack of tin plates from a cupboard. Sometimes it was better to ignore the Marine instead of taking the bait.

"Anyway," he continued. "There's more meat in the soles of my shoes than there is in these burgers. They're all Soya, packed with carbohydrates and proteins. We can't have the best of the best getting fat from eating shit like an actual hamburger. Plus, these things last and last: the use-by date read at something like two thousand and fifty six. But, they do taste absolutely fucking sweet! Like the real thing."

"Looks like cardboard and paper," Bill said as he peered over the shoulder of the cook.

"And that's what it is, but it's good tasting cardboard and paper. Either eat them or don't, I don't give a shit. More for me."

He finished cooking them and carefully placed them on one of the plates Bill offered him, piling them on top of one another and nodding towards the oven.

"How's the bread rolls doing?"

"About ready," Garth grinned as he pulled open the oven and heaved out a tray of easy-bake rolls. He slammed them down on the countertop, gritting his teeth and blowing on the tips of his fingers as he tried to cool the burned digits. "Jesus, they're hot."

"Christ, buddy, be careful, you're going to burn the boat down before we get halfway across the Atlantic."

"Just like you've burned the burgers?"

"Fuck you," Al laughed, waving the spatula he held at Garth. "You don't want them? Don't eat them."

Bill chuckled to himself and shook his head to himself. After years trapped in Britain, spending his waking hours looking over his shoulder and his nights sleeping with one eye open, he never thought he'd return to normalcy. Even when they'd been living in the Marine base, he hadn't allowed his defences to drop: he knew that although they were locked up in their own little bubble, just outside the membrane of safety lay a wasteland patrolled by roaming ghouls and deranged gangs. Now, their fortress of solitude was a boat; surrounded on all sides for miles by water and desolation. With that, on-the-edge lifestyles could be changed. When was the last time he had sat down to a meal like the one he was going to? More to the point, when was the last time anyone had been able to act in the normal mannerisms they were now? Al, unusually jovial and cooking a selection of dubious meat-like products, seemed like a normal person, despite the bandage wrapped around his muscular torso and the gauze that covered the ragged wounds on his forehead. Garth was normally on edge; the only time Bill had seen him relaxed was when he saw him smoke some dope. Now, he didn't need the narcotic to relieve him of the tension, he'd quickly lost himself in the baking task.

Sarah was a child again, at least for now. Al had handed her a deck of cards before cooking, and she sat and played games with Sylvester: a children's game of matching pairs, not the games Bill had played recently which involved flushes, pairs, three of a kind and other things he didn't fully understand. Seeing the two play together reminded Bill of a father and a child playing games, but although Sarah could possibly pass as Sylvester's daughter more than she could Al's, she'd made her decision about who she would look up to as a fatherly figure. Unfortunately.

Angel was in high spirits just as much as the rest of them, preparing food, laughing and joking, humming a few bars of a song to herself every now and then. She even managed to find a way to brush playfully up against Bill every so often, beaming as she did so.

Everything seemed perfectly normal for a dysfunctional family, apart from the gloomy presence of Clive, who's dour countenance served as a reminder that this wasn't actually a pleasure cruise or a holiday; this was the deserved rest after what felt like a lifetime of pain and suffering. Everyone had lost someone close in the holocaust that followed the rise, and while they certainly wouldn't forget them, the needed to move on. Dwelling on the past wouldn't bring anyone back.

"And we're ready," beamed Al, snapping Bill out his trance as he almost threw two serving platters on to the bench Clive had cleared. Everyone dragged a stool over to the bench and sat down except Al, who hadn't quite finished preparing his meal. Carrying seven shot glasses between his fingers, three in one hand and four in the other, he slammed the small drinking vessels down on the table and produced a bottle of golden brown liquid, proudly displaying the black and white label to everyone assembled. Garth seemed to nod in appreciation and Sylvester duplicated the gesture, while everyone else stared blankly at the bottle.

"Bunch of heathens," Al muttered as he went on to unseal the bottle.

"I found this in the store cupboard, hidden behind a sack of flour. Either the cooks were keeping this back for a special occasion, or they'd stolen it from one of the Brass and they wanted to make sure the heat was off before they popped the cork, as it were. Either way, their loss is our gain. This is the finest whiskey ever invented by man. It's a recipe that's hundreds of years old. I drink it, my father drank it, and his father drank it before him."

"So you come from a long line of alcoholics?" Angel asked. Al ignored her.

"There's a tradition my squad had. At the end of a mission, we'd kick back, break open a bottle and salute good old Captain Jack. This, my friends, is the only officer I'd go out of my way to save."

"And you hate the Brass, right?" Garth asked with a smirk, nervously tapping at the shot glass before him, anxiously awaiting the beaker to be filled with the amber nectar.

"Damn right I hate the Brass," Al nodded in agreement. "So you know how good this shit must be. But, aside from that, a tradition is a tradition, none the less. And you, all of you... even the bitch there... you're my squad. And our mission is complete. So if you will?"

He leaned forwards and poured a generous measure in each glass, making sure he didn't spill a drop. The seventh glass he poured less than half a measure and motioned to Sarah.

"You're part of the team too, honey. Go ahead."

"Really?" Sarah said with a coy smile.

"Really?" Angel echoed, her tone disbelieving. "You're giving a child whiskey?"

"We're a team," Al said, reiterating his point. "Now, we all think of something to drink to. I don't make up the traditions; I just uphold them. Any takers to start first?"

No one made a move to raise his or her glasses, though Bill could see that Garth was fighting a losing a battle against his willpower to down the drink in one.

"Fine, I'll start first," Al announced, lifting his drink above his head and pushing it out towards the group, waiting for another person to copy his gesture. "To loves that have been lost; those nearest and dearest to us that have passed on; men and women that we loved and were taken from us."

"To new love found," Bill volunteered, lifting his own glass and knocking it against Al's while looking at Angel. "Finding someone to share your life with without even looking, in the last place you'd expect to find it."

"Acceptable, I guess," Al muttered, nodding his head. "I know what you mean, we've all been there."

"To family lost," Angel said, lifting her own glass and gently clinking it to the two men's raised glasses. "The people that nurtured and supported us, helped us grow strong into the people we are today."

"And to family gained," Sarah beamed, climbing up on to her stool and leaning forward on the table, her glass just reaching the bottom of Al's. She chuckled slightly at something she decided to keep to herself. "The people who will look after us now. Like my big cuddly Al."

"Friends," volunteered, Sylvester, raising from his seat and thrusting out his glass. He winced slightly as he extended his arm, the smallest of bandages showing under his shirtsleeve. Everyone had wounds to heal, both mentally as well as physically. "Those we've gained and lost. The people we'll never forget, the people who'll be with us for the rest of our lives. Those that are with us now in body, and those in spirit."

"The thousands of the dead," offered Clive. Al rolled his eyes, but didn't try to cut him off. Everyone had had his or her say so far, he wasn't about to try and impose censorship now. "Not just friends, families and loved ones we know, but also those we didn't: those whose passing went unnoticed, another soul lost in a sea of millions of dead. We need to remember them every day, and can't afford to forget them. We learn from their experiences and failures. A great nation has fallen, but they should not be forgotten."

"Somewhat random, and a little disjointed," Al said, nodding slowly as another glass entered the collective toast. "But I get what you're saying. I think."

"There's a lot of things going on in my head at the moment," Clive confessed. Al nodded, then turned to face Garth, the only person who hadn't lifted his glass. He looked tentatively at his glass, licking his lips.

"You ain't drinking that until you add to the toast, buddy. It'll take us a few weeks to sail to America: I've got all the time in the world for you to think of this. Sarah thought of one, even the preacher thought of one, no matter how… strange."

"I'm thinking," Garth said, waiving him off with one hand. He finally stood and added his glass to the raised circle. "Got it. To every single one of those bastards that tried to take us down: shooting, stabbing, explosions, car chases. The shits that tried to turn us into Rots. The fuckers who tried to eat us. We beat you, you assholes. We beat you all. You complete pack of bastards."

"Out-fucking-standing," Bill added.

"Un-fucking-believable," Angel finished.

"Oo-rah!" Al whispered, raising his glass a little higher and tilting it slightly.

"Oo-rah," the rest of the group murmured in unison, their glasses clinking together before being brought back towards each mouth

Bill grimaced slightly as the liquid washed down his throat: cool at first, but then a strong, burning sensation that lingered harshly on palette as the thick liquid rolled down into his stomach. Angel gritted her teeth, breathing sharply though her teeth before coughing violently, thumping her chest with a balled fist as she tried to shake something loose. Sarah dropped her glass and sprayed her drink out across the table, coughing violently and twisting her face. Al patted her on the back, trying to help her clear her throat. Garth and Sylvester smiled at one another, then turned as one to face the bottle that sat on the table, hoping Al would call for a second toast. Clive drained his glass, shivered slightly, then slammed the empty container down, shaking his head clear.

"Tastes like burning," Sarah choked, swilling her mouth out with a gulp of water.

"Tuck in, people," Al finally said, sitting back down and pouring himself a generous measure of the whiskey. He offered the bottle to Garth, who almost snatched his hand off. "Plenty more where this came from. After the meal, we get rested up over night, then get this thing ship-shape."

"That was terrible," Angel muttered, acknowledging his play on words with a sad shake of her head. "It was terrible when you said it the first time. It's not getting any better. "

"Yeah," admitted Al, "I'm not too good at clean humour. I got plenty of dirty jokes, though."

"Save them for when the kids are in bed," Garth grinned, gesturing vaguely at Bill, Angel and Sarah.

"What're we calling this thing, then?" Sylvester asked. "Everything's been named after you so far: Colebrook's Runner, The Pride of Colebrook, Colebrook's Cannon… what's this thing called?"

"The boat's name?" Al looked towards Sarah and winked. "Colebrook's Ark. Why break the habit of a lifetime?"

XXVIII
EPITAPH

"The likelihood of anyone surviving this is nil: a one hundred percent mortality rate ensures that no one will live through this ordeal. While we mourn the loss of a nation, we can sleep easy knowing the truth dies with them. "

I

Bill slowly opened his eyes, wiping away the sleep that crusted his eyelids and looked around the cabin he and Angel had called home for the past week. He'd tried his best to keep the place tidy; it wasn't like he had anything else to do on the boat while it ponderously sailed across the Atlantic Ocean, but somehow he always managed to find something else to do. He slowly pulled himself up from the bed and scratched absentmindedly at the back of his head, stifling a yawn and grabbing a clean shirt from the dresser beside him.

The room itself had been a cabin belonging to an officer. Everyone had taken up residence in one of the more luxurious rooms after the initial attempt to clear the wealth of rotting corpses from the lower levels had failed. Some of the bodies were in such a poor condition that the rotten flesh was slipping off the bones as the cadavers were lifted, making the clean up a nightmare. After half an hour battling with one corpse that was quickly turning into a putrid pool of liquid, Al decided to call it a day with the lower decks, and seal off as much of the rooms as they could, instead trying to retrieve as much equipment as they could and bringing it to the upper decks. The only thing he had insisted on had been clearing a safe passage to the engine room, so that area could be accessed easily if they needed to do so. With the sealed decks now acting as a tomb, the frigate had turned into a ghost ship; a cargo hauler of the dead that glided across the still of the ocean towards its ultimate goal. The only reason Bill could sleep easily on top of the rooms piled up with corpses, was that he and Al had systematically worked their way through the crypts and put a bullet through the head of each corpse, just to make sure.

Pulling on the shirt and a pair of crumpled trousers he retrieved from the floor, he stepped over to the sink and splashed some water on his face, trying to wake himself up. The no-spill mug of steaming coffee on the low coffee table told him Angel was awake, but her absence from the main room suggested that she was in the adjoining bathroom. One of the perks of living in the officers' quarters was that they had an all-round better class of living. During the failed cleanup procedure, Bill had seen that the enlisted men who shared their quarters, had the most minimal of furnishings, plastic disposable cups and onc bathroom was shared by around twenty men and women. The officers had a wider range of furnishings, one room per officer with a double bed, and an en-suite bathroom: even their cups were made of a high-quality plastic with a wider base to prevent spillages in a stormy voyage. Bill couldn't understand why Al had wanted to sleep in the lower decks in the first place while these better cabins were available, though he suspected that he was trying to keep a barrier up between himself and the officers, even in death.

Bill grabbed the coffee and took a sip of the hot liquid, twisting his face as the bitter liquid washed his pallet. He wasn't a fan of unsweetened coffee, but supplies were limited on the boat: there was plenty of freeze-dried artificial meat products, but very little actual food: anything that hadn't been sealed in containers or storage crates had inadvertently been tainted by the Rots, or at least had a chance of being tainted. This close to the home stretch, no one wanted to take any unnecessary risks. After sealing the bodies in the lower decks, any provisions not freeze-dried or sealed tight went over the edge.

The bathroom door swung open and clouds of steam billowed out, a figure adorned in a white gown emerging from the midst of the condensation. She smiled softly, towelling her hair dry as she looked at Bill.

"Thought I'd take a shower," she explained.

"I was just thinking about joining you," Bill smiled.

"Not this morning," Angel shook her head. "I've got to check on Al's wounds, make sure everything's healing okay, and you've got to sit with Garth in the bridge."

"Of course," Bill nodded. "How could I forget? So there's no chance of…"

"Not at the minute," Angel shook her head, shrugging off her robe. She already had her underwear on, and quickly snagged a fresh pair of coveralls, stepping into the clothing and zipping it up in one smooth movement.

"Can't we at least get some breakfast first?"

"It's already made. Garth had an early start, whipped up a bunch of powdered eggs and made a couple of fresh loaves. Sarah buzzed us when you were asleep; she and Al are already eating."

Bill nodded as he grabbed his belt and strapped it around his waist, moving to grab one of the pistols that lay on the chest of draws by the door. He paused, looked curiously at the lump of metal, and lowered his hand. He didn't need the weapon, not in the sealed environment they lived in. He wouldn't be able to carry a gun around with him once they docked at America, or at least not openly; he would have to get used to being unarmed. As strangely alien as the notion may seem, he had to start living his life without a weapon by his side.

Linking arms with Angel, the pair left their cabin and took a brisk walk to the galley, a pleasant and comfortable silence between the two while they moved. As they descended a set of curving stairs and headed towards the dining room-cum-kitchen, a pleasant aroma drifted up to meet them, a smell that reminded Bill of breakfast in bed on a lazy Sunday morning.

"Something smells good," Bill announced as he entered the kitchen. He wasn't surprised to see that it was only Al and Sarah that had gathered for breakfast: it had been the same story for the last week. Garth had taken back to his original roots, sitting at the controls of the massive vehicle for hours on end, while Sylvester spent most of his time in the engine room, tinkering with the turbines and keeping everything running. Clive spent most of his days sitting by the prow of the ship and thumbing through his bible. Despite his wavering religious beliefs, he still spent a massive amount of time pouring through the contents of his well-worn book.

"Don't be fooled by it, kid," Al said with a grin, looking up from his plate. "It tastes like paint thinner. The bread, at least, is bread, but the eggs are friggin' horrible."

"I hadn't come to expect anything else from rations," Bill said, sitting down to a tin plate heaped with fresh bread and pale, flaccid mounds of artificial eggs. Bill poked the unidentifiable mound of food with his fork, the metal instrument pushing the greasy substance around.

"It tastes better if you use these," Sarah said, tapping the array of condiments that she had set up in front of her: sauces and spices, some familiar to Bill, others not so. He looked at her plate, and could barely see the mound of powdered eggs beneath the accoutrements she had added.

"How are the wounds today?" Angel asked around a mouthful of bread.

"Painful," Al grinned, gently prodding the bloodied bandage that was wrapped around his head. "Hurts like a bitch."

"It's healing well, though," Angel said. "Or as best as I can expect. It took long enough to get all the glass out. And you're probably going to have quite a scar there."

"It'll just add to my rugged and manly good looks," Al laughed, pushing away his plate. Bill couldn't help but notice that he hadn't touched the artificial eggs, either.

"I can't eat this crap," Bill muttered to himself, grabbing the bread and dropping his fork in the greasy eggs. He sat staring at his plate, thoughtfully chewing the bread as his eyes glazed over.

"What's the matter? Psyching yourself up for another day looking at screens and reading manuals?"

"Garth can read all the manuals he wants," Bill said, waving his hand dismissively. Aside from piloting the boat, this was what Garth did: Al had decided that there weren't enough people to man the ship and have it running the vehicle twenty four hours a day, instead electing to have the vehicle running at full speed for seven hours each day, then weighing anchor for the remaining seventeen hours of the day. Although Garth had protested this, confident he could pull longer shifts, Al had pulled rank and said he didn't want to endanger the boat. Although Garth may have been able to pilot the craft, he wasn't sure that anyone else would be able to monitor things like radar or communications channels over the same length of time. So instead of making the journey from

British waters to the shores of America in a little over a week, the journey would actually take three and a half. Garth was convinced the system would be able to run everything itself, and so he'd spent every waking hour reading the multitude of manuals and documentation stored on the bridge, looking for his own elusive Holy Grail: the instructions for the autopilot and all the related systems.

"Look deep in thought there, kid," Al finally said, tapping his plate with a fork to attract his attention. Bill snapped out of his trance and shook his head.

"Just thinking."

"About?"

"Garth and his crusade to get there a little earlier. He's only trying to get there quicker so he can arrange safe passage to go see his daughter, Christ, even when we *do* get there, how are we going to arrange all that? Won't we need money to get him fake identity papers and a passport?"

"All in hand, kid, it's all in hand."

"What the hell are you up to?"

"Fucking officers. They're all the same," Al said, sitting back in his chair and sipping at the plastic tumbler he cradled in his hands. "A long time ago, there was a tyrannical despot who got his rocks off over watching men and women being tortured. And he was planning on blackmailing the UGMC over some potentially harmful information he had procured through his service. Of course, we killed him."

"And all the paperwork was left behind in the trailer before we left. What's your point?"

"Jesus, kid, just give me a chance. Can you believe this, honey?"

Sarah shook her head and rolled her eyes.

"Anyway, yes, we left all the paperwork and shit in the trailer. It's probably clutched in the hand of some Rot bastard right about now. But remember that Carter wasn't working alone, he also had Preston."

"Who Lance killed, right, I'm with you."

"Lance killed him. Lance came up with this whole fucking scheme of wiping out an entire village just to haul his ass out the fire, you'd better believe that he had the entire thing planned out from the start: he was going to pull the same ploy as the diabolical duo, using the files they'd collated from the two sources. What do I keep telling you? All the Brass are the fucking same."

Al unzipped the larger of the pockets on the legs of his trousers and produced two flat black objects. At first Bill thought they were magazines for a weapon he hadn't yet seen, but then he realised they were portable hard drives.

"Each drive holds fifteen terabytes of information. Each one is filled with video footage, medical reports, project reports, pictures, plague spread estimations and computer simulations: both are proof that the UGMC, and the United Government in general, are responsible for the plague. Lance was going to bribe the government: now, we're going to do the exact same thing. I was often told I could be an officer if only I made the effort, and try to think more like one. So now, I am. At the moment, there are only two of these in existence, and I've got them both. By the time the three weeks are up, there's going to be fourteen of these babies, two each. And the government is going to give us exactly what we want, to make sure none of these hard drives fall into the hands of any prime-time news network."

"Devious," Bill said, nodding approvingly. "Very devious."

"I learn from the best,' Al announced, shrugging his shoulders.

"Where'd they come from?"

"I pulled them out Lance's gear, just after I... you know. I didn't know what they were at first, but if he was hiding them in a pair of shabby briefs then they had to be important. I pulled them, and finally got them hooked up the other night. If we all have two copies..."

A loud sound suddenly exploded in the still of the frigate, a deafening roar that sounded only once before echoing off into silence. The sudden outburst startled everyone sitting at the table, Al dropping his tumbler and kicking back from the table, his hand slightly grazing his thigh and coming up with a handful of magnum, his customised handgun ready to leap into action. Bill slapped at his own thigh, then remembered he'd decided to leave it in their room.

Of all the luck…

"Gunshot," Al reported, confirming Bill's suspicions as he leapt up from his seat, running for the doorway. "Sarah, stay here, keep your head down. Angel, keep an eye on her."

Bill launched himself from the table and followed Al; the two running for all their life was worth as they tried to pinpoint the origin of the sound.

"Sounds like it came from below," Al shouted as he tumbled down the stairs and powered through the lower decks. "Maybe the engine room."

"Are we… in trouble?" Bill managed between deep breaths and stumbling steps. A week of lazing around had quickly taken its toll on him, and he could already feel himself tiring.

"I don't know. Maybe a survivor we'd missed…"

The pair reached the hatchway leading to the engineering section and slammed into the bulkhead that sealed it off from the rest of the frigate, feverishly spinning the locking wheel and hauling the door open. A small antechamber awaited them, with another four sealed hatches leading off in different directions. In the centre of the small room a collection of packing crates had been set up, forming a large makeshift settee that could comfortably accommodate three people. This had been the room Sylvester had set up as his break room: on the other side of the furthest locked hatches was a staircase that descended down into the mechanical innards of the beast they rode in.

Sylvester lounged back on the large homemade seat, his head lolling to one side and displaying the hole that had been drilled neatly through his head by a bullet. The wall behind him was coated with a thick gelatinous material that slowly dripped down on to the floor, a viscous mix of brain matter and blood that lay on the ground at the foot of the wall. Beside the corpse of Sylvester there sat Clive, the still-smoking handgun gripped in both his hands. He looked up at Al and Bill as the two of them burst in, looked at the body, then the weapon, and dropped it, raising his hands and waving them back and forth.

"No, I can explain…"

"You can't explain shit, you deranged mother fucker!"

Clive had awoke from his slumber in his quarters in the early hours of the morning as the sun first lifted itself above the horizon, pulling on his trousers and walking over to the bathroom, standing before the mirror above the white sink and investigating the figure that he was confronted with. A stranger stood before him; a gaunt, sallow face with a pale torso riddled with scars and lacerations, each mark a reminder. He gripped the sides of the sink and leaned forwards, his head resting against the flat, cold mirror.

Who are you?

With all the time he'd had to himself in the last seven days, he'd been asking himself a lot of questions, though as yet hadn't managed to come up with any answers. He wasn't sure when he was going to get his answers.

He splashed water in his face then slowly wandered back into the main living area, grabbing his T-shirt from the back of his chair. He looked curiously at it, wondering why he still insisted on washing and drying the same clothing all the time. He sighed inwardly and slipped the shirt on over his head, then grabbed the red bandanna and tied it off around his skull.

He didn't have much in his room: his coat hung on the back of his door on a rusted metal hook; the chest of drawers by the doorway held his bible and a handgun, loaded with a single round. Other than that, he had nothing else in his cabin.

He slipped one arm into his coat, then swung it on over his head and thrust his other arm into the remaining sleeve. He pushed the handgun into one pocket and the bible into another, then swung his door open and strolled out, looking back and forth as he went.

He normally went outside, watching the horizon while he read through his bible and dwelled upon his thoughts, but today he didn't feel like doing that. With a chill to the air outside and dark skies promising a storm, he was instead drawn to another location, turning towards the corridor cleared to the engineering section, and the smaller room there that Sylvester used as his break area. He knew that Sylvester would spend the next six or seven hours amongst the grease-covered clockwork innards of the leviathan they travelled in. By the time Sylvester emerged from the engineering decks, the storm should have cleared and Clive could continue with his routine outside.

Sure enough, the room had been abandoned by the time Clive arrived in the chamber. Flicking the switch by the doorway, the small bulb that hung from the ceiling flared to life, and he casually dusted off the largest of the crates as he settled down to read through his book. He wasn't sure what to make of the religion he had followed for as long as he could remember: had he devoted his life to a lie? Where his bible had once offered solace and comfort, now it only offered confusion. Parables and passages that once provided answers and guidance now only raised more questions, no matter how much he read it. Could it be that he'd spent his life reading meanings into stories that didn't exist?

The near-silence of the chamber was broken as one of the doors opened, releasing a cacophony of noise as the sealed bulkhead between the room and the engineering decks slammed into the wall and slowly swung back on rusted hinges. Clive looked up from his readings to see Sylvester enter the room, shielding his eyes from the glare of the bulb overhead.

"Jesus," Sylvester muttered, trudging across the room and grabbing a bottle of water that rested on one of the pipes that lined the walls. "The hell're you doing here?"

"Change of scenery," Clive said, smiling thinly. "Didn't think you'd mind."

"Keep your feet off the furniture," Sylvester responded dryly, his lips barely moving as he waived towards the crates. Clive nodded slightly, noticing the way his friend moved as he shuffled across the floor and almost fell into the seat beside him. His skin was pale and clammy, which Clive assumed was because of the time he spent below the decks, but once he was up close, Clive didn't think that was actually the case. Sweat rolled down his brow, trickling down the contours of his face, following the weathered tracks of his skin and dripping off his jawline where it pooled In the crumples of his dirt-stained vest. Each movement he made seemed to bring pain to him, the only comfort he seemed to get came from the bottle of water that he splashed across his face.

"Working hard?"

Sylvester barely managed a nod.

"What are you doing down there?" Clive lay his bible face down on his knees and

"Work," Sylvester muttered, absentmindedly brushing a few strands of hair from his face. Instead of moving them aside, they seemed to come away in his hand. "Just need to make sure everything's up and running; make sure nothing'll go wrong in the next two weeks."

"But you'd be able to fix it," Clive said, sitting up and taking more notice of Sylvester's appearance. He'd seen people like this before, seen the sweating and weakness that Sylvester was showing, the pain of each movement he made. But that was impossible, surely it was just fatigue that had him this way? Sylvester had rarely been seen since the voyage had begun, spending almost all of his time in the machine-filled lower decks. "Why not just sit and relax, wait until something goes wrong? We can't all be proactive like Garth…"

"Because I might not be here," Sylvester said, letting his head loll back as he stared at the ceiling above him. He tried to stifle a cough, placing the back of his hand to his mouth. "I'm tired: so tired."

"All the better reason to have a rest," Clive said.

"Maybe I'll have all the time in the world to rest when I'm dead," Sylvester said flatly.

"How long," Clive finally asked, noticing for the first time the grimy bandage wrapped around Sylvester's upper arm. Each of the rare times Sylvester had made an appearance, in the upper corridors or in the galley; he had always worn a jacket or a T-shirt. The heat of the engine rooms obviously made those garments of clothing unnecessary, so he had stripped down to a vest while surrounded by the engines and the turbines. Beneath the bandage, he could see a thin trickle of pink liquid that seeped out from beneath the cotton wadding and flowed down the curve of his bicep.

"How long?" he pushed again.

"Another day," Sylvester grinned openly, the corners of his lips cracking slightly, spilling salty, pink liquid across his face. Another spray of water from his bottle cleaned his face before he continued. "Maybe two, I'm not sure."

"How?"

"When we first landed. I went into the engineering decks, but I couldn't hear anything that was going on above me: there was too much metal around me, it interfered with the signal from the radio and I couldn't hear shit. Even the gunfire… that was lost to me. Only to be expected, I guess. There's a hell of a lot of noise down there, what with the engines and the generators. Al could have used a handful of grenades and I wouldn't have known."

"So you didn't know any of the soldiers on the upper deck were hollow men?"

"Rots," Sylvester said, trying to correct Clive and simultaneously shaking his head. "No, I had no idea. Not until one of the bastards fell out of a locker on to me. It took me by surprise, and I didn't even realise it had bitten me until an hour or two later; I fell into a pile of old tools, and I was covered in nicks and grazes. Even if I noticed at the time, it would have been too late. I wrapped the bite up, convincing myself that it hadn't been a Rot, just a deranged Marine who had locked himself up in the lower levels and eventually lost his mind, seeing me as a snack instead of his rescuer. I almost convinced myself that I'd heard him talking before I caved his head in with a toolbox, but I knew deep down I was wrong. I tried to delude myself into believing that I was going to be all right, and after four or five days, I figured I'd been lucky. The skin had been broken, but maybe I'd avoided getting any saliva in it."

He hesitantly untied the bandage and peeled it back, revealing the bloodied mass of raw flesh beneath the wrapping. Muscle tissue tensed and flexed as he carefully moved his arm, and a thin mix of blood and pus steadily seeped down his arm as he wiped around the edges of the wound with his finger. For the first time, Clive noticed that the joints of his fingers were covered in sores, his knuckles bloodied and raw; even a couple of his fingernails were missing.

"They say the maximum term before death is ten days, right?"

Clive nodded slowly.

"And you've seen someone die naturally of it, right?"

Again, Clive nodded mournfully, remembering the parishioners of his old church he had delivered the last rites to: back in the day when he believed in his faith. Though he couldn't remember their names, he could remember their faces, and each had a scar on his body as a final resting place.

"How was it? The final hours, I mean."

"It was…" Clive paused. Should he soften the truth of the final hours of an infected soul? Should he sugarcoat the ordeal, or should he tell the bitter truth? He quickly decided that his friend deserved more than lies. "It was agonising; convulsions, vomiting. Some of the dying experienced madness; others suffered hallucinations. Some fell into unconsciousness, while others suffered the torment of the disease tearing their body apart right up until the bitter end."

"I didn't think it would be a cakewalk," muttered Sylvester, his shoulders sagging. As they did so, the neck on his skin wrinkled and cracked, the sheen of sweat that coated his body picking up a pink tinge around the fresh sores.

"Why did you feel you had to keep this a secret? Why suffer in silence when you could look to your friends for support?"

"Because I'm not a fucking cripple," Sylvester said with gritted teeth as he pulled himself to his feet. Muscles tensed and strained as he tried to move his bulk, and more rivulets of blood appeared at his joints. "Do you remember the news reports? The people surrounding hospitals: crowds watching the sick being ferried into incinerator stations by the busload, their faces a mask of pity for the infected. I wanted to spend the last days looked at the same way I had for the last three years, not as a charity case that everyone felt sorry for. I want to be remembered as me, Sylvester, not as that poor bastard who contracted the plague on his way off the island.

"On his fucking way to Salvation," Sylvester repeated, facing away from Clive, his shoulders bouncing up and down as he sobbed silently to himself. "That's the worst thing about it. We were off the island; we were home free. How fucking ironic is that? Three years trapped in the middle of a quarantine zone, not a fucking scratch. Three weeks away from sanctuary, and a fucking Rot catches me on my unawares. What are the chances?

"What are the god damn chances?"

Clive shook his head slowly, not certain what he could say or do.

"So you've been working around the clock to make sure things are going to work for the rest of the journey?" Clive finally said.

"In another two days I won't be much good with a wrench and a spanner," Sylvester murmured with half a smile, which quickly turned into a grimace as a spasm of pain arched through his body. "I'm glad you're here."

"Me?" Clive asked. Sylvester nodded, and he returned to his seat, pulling his arm across his cheeks to wipe his tears. As he did so, skin flaked and peeled away.

"I've done pretty much all I can down there. There's a world of difference between a pickup truck and a military frigate, but as far as I can see everything should run fine for the next month, at least. Now, I feel like my job here's done, and there's nothing more I can do. Its... I guess it's in god's hands now, Clive. I'd like you to give me my last rites before I die."

"I don't know if I can," Clive said, looking at his hands as they tapped nervously against the bible on his knee. "A marriage is one thing..."

"I'm asking you to do this as a friend: as my closest friend. Everything you believed in may not mean shit to you now, but I still believe, and you're the nearest thing we've got to a minister."

"You do? Despite everything that's happened?"

"It's strange," Sylvester said. "You'd think I would be bitter, wouldn't you? Spend my life building up a business, working with my wife, preparing for a future that was never meant to be? But everything that happens has a purpose. I lost everything the day we wandered into the Messiah's prison. I lost Terri, the only person I ever loved. But I also gained a stronger friend then I could ever have asked for. You were confronted with a man who perverted religion, while you stood strong with your beliefs; you helped me through that early loss. However many days or weeks we were locked up in the holding cell for, you were always there to provide solace and comfort. Do you remember?"

"I do," Clive nodded.

"And you remember what you said? Everything that happens is God's will; each action has a purpose. If I hadn't lost Terri, would I have joined with Al and his crusade across half the country?"

Clive shrugged his shoulders. "Who can say?"

"Exactly, who can say? If Terri had survived, I could have gone down a different path. And then who would rebuild the helicopter to get out here? Who would look after the engines and make sure they're fully-functioning?"

"Garth seems to have some idea about what he's doing," Clive offered nonchalantly.

"Garth doesn't know shit about engines and machines; he barely knows which end to kick if it stops working," Sylvester managed with a grin, his skin peeling and weeping as his face wrinkled. "No, I think God made everything happen the way he did because he knew how things would play out. And now, he's decided it's my time."

"Such conviction," Clive muttered.

"I learned it from a close friend," he said, reaching out and patting Clive on the back of his hand. Skin flaked and peeled, sticking to the backs of his hand, but he made no effort to brush them down or pull away from his friend. "Time is short, and I'd like very much if you could do this for me. As a parting gift from an old friend."

Clive nodded softly and opened his bible, solemnly reading the required passages in a hushed voice, all the time watching, as Sylvester seemed to sink into the crates, relaxing as the words seemed to wash over him and cleanse him.

"Do you absolve of all your sins," Clive finally said, closing his book and placing it to one side. "Repent of you misdoings and be welcomed into the Kingdom of God?"

"I do," Sylvester whispered, lips barely moving. He erupted into a fit of coughing that brought a hacking, gurgling sound: blood welled up in his throat, thick with bile and the lining of his innards, and washed over his parched lips. He lurched forwards, the violence of the cough rattling his lungs and bringing up more tainted and bloody mucus. He managed to recover from the coughing fit, then leaned back and nodded his head, whispering to himself once more: "I do."

"Then all we can do is wait," Clive said. "I'll stay with you. I've not been much of a friend to you recently: to anyone, for that matter. I've been distant, I've been… I've not been myself," he said with a certainty that he hadn't felt in a long time. The faith Sylvester displayed was admirable, despite everything that had happened to him: something of an example to follow. Facing deaths door, the last three years of his life plagued by misfortune as his friends and family died around him, and he still believed in the teachings of the lord.

And not the twisted, demented teachings of a sociopath and psychotic killer, he mused silently. If, after everything he had been through, Sylvester could still believe in God, then why couldn't Clive? To accept him into his life once more, to follow his path… maybe everything that happened *did happen* for a reason.

Was it possible that Clive had been tested? The initial encounter with the Messiah in Manchester had only strengthened his beliefs, but after seeing him again outside the fort they had called their home for so long: after apparently raising from the dead, with an army of hollow men behind him to tear their sanctuary apart, his beliefs had *started* to waver. Why would any loving god allow such a sadist to continue existing and hurting other people?

But without the arrival of the Messiah on their doorstep, would they have moved from there, or would they have stagnated in the same place for the rest of their lives? So much had happened since that point, Clive could barely remember it all. Sarah had lost her family, but had gained another in Al: a strong figure who would be more than capable of looking after her in the brave new world they were faced with. Al had also felt a stronger sense of love than he could ever imagine with Pam first, then Sarah, and realised the error of his ways when it came to the Marines: acts he may have participated in, in a different time, repulsed him to the point where he wanted nothing to do with them.

Bill and Angel had come together as one, each coming to terms with losing family and loved ones: had they remained in the fort, would they have eventually paired up? It was unlikely, as the events leading up to their union had been due, in part, to the Messiah's attack. Garth would eventually be reunited with his daughter in Spain, and Sylvester…

Clive looked to his friend, trying not to display the sympathy he had wanted to avoid from the rest of the group.

Sylvester had kept everything together, mechanically speaking, fixing vehicles and machines when they stopped functioning and making sure everything worked as and when it was needed. It appeared that his destiny was also to remind Clive of his faith, and act as an example for him to follow. A beacon he wished he'd paid attention to a long time ago. In alienating himself from his religion, he had also shunned his friends to the point where his very presence seemed to anger Al and make people like Angel and Bill feel uncomfortable. The only person, who he felt acted the same around him, was Sarah.

The innocence of youth, he reflected mournfully.

He opened his bible again and read through the last rites once more, this time with more conviction than the previous reading. As the words poured from his lips, he could feel something inside him, a warm sensation of pride that he hadn't felt in a long time, and smiled to himself. He noticed Sylvester was smiling, too. He obviously realised his friend had found his religion once more.

"Thank you," Sylvester finally murmured as the ceremony finished for the second time. "That meant a lot to me."

"It meant more to me," confessed Clive. "I'll still wait with you. For the next two days, or however long it takes, I'll be here."

"No," Sylvester shook his head; rivulets of blood streaming down his neck and shoulders. "I... I don't want to wait. Here."

He pulled a handgun out that he'd tucked into the waistband of his trousers and offered the butt of the weapon to Clive. "I want you to finish me. I don't want anyone else to do it. Just you."

"I can't kill you," Clive shook his head. "Not like this, please, don't ask me..."

"You have to," Sylvester sighed heavily. "If I kill myself, I spend eternity in Purgatory, you said it yourself. I know Terri's in heaven... I want to go and see Terri."

"I can't kill you..."

"I'm already dead," spat Sylvester.

"Then do this yourself," Clive said, pushing the weapon away. Was this another test? Having just found his faith once more, a test to see whether he would make the right choice between letting his friend suffer for another two days or ending his life right now? Or even a test to evaluate whether he was still a killer...

"Please," Sylvester pleaded: pink, bloodstained tears rolling down his cheeks from bloodshot eyes. "Please. I don't want to turn. Don't want to suffer."

Clive took the weapon from him, looked at it, then placed it to one side before pulling his own pistol from his pocket and evaluating it, mentally comparing the two. They were both the same make, both looked identical to him, though he was sure Al could have told the difference if he had been present. His own weapon felt lighter, and he knew why: his handgun was loaded with a single bullet, while Sylvester's doubtless had a full clip in his. He wasn't sure why he only had one bullet loaded in his weapon: he supposed that maybe, on a subconscious level, he'd expected to turn the weapon on himself. But now, it appeared that the one bullet he'd kept back was for his friend, to put an end to his suffering.

He finally nodded and lifted the weapon, pulling back on the slide and making sure the bullet was still there, still loaded.

"Are you sure you want this?"

"I'm sure," Sylvester nodded, closing his eyes. "I saved your life when I worked in the prison the day you were attacked. Now you can save mine: I'm ready to go."

"I'll never forget you, Sly. We had some wild times, you and me."

"If you loosened up once in a while," Sylvester said, a grin splitting his cheeks and dripping with watery blood. "We would've had a hell of a lot more wild times. We'll be watching over you, you know: Terri and me.

"I know you will," Clive said, levelling the weapon with Sylvester's face and firing point blank into his face. The sudden explosion of the gun made him jump, and as the echo of the shot faded away, the sounds of dripping blood and spatters of gore trickling down the far wall were joined by the gentle sobs of a grieving friend. "I know you will."

He performed a cross over the body of his friend, sat beside him, and bowed his head in prayer, hoping that his spirit would find his way to his wife. And once there, then maybe they would watch over not only him, but also the group as a whole.

He looked up as the one of the doors to the antechamber burst open and Al and Bill stood, their horrified gaze passing from the silent corpse of his friend, to the smoking handgun that still rested in his grip. Startled, he lowered the weapon, shaking his head and waving his hands.

"No," he muttered frantically, floundering as he tried to get his point across. "I can explain…"

"You can't explain shit, you deranged mother fucker!"

A pair of gunshots echoed in the still of the ship: a deep, thunderous pair of explosive rounds that tore the silence apart with their angry screams.

In the lower decks of the ship, the thick heavy muzzle of a powerful handgun lowered towards the ground, a thick tawny vapour of cobalt-blue smoke that filled the air with an acrid tang.

A pair of brass casings toppled to the floor, smoking metal with their opened ends crimped and blackened from the discharged powder.

Al dropped the weapon he held, the heavy modified handgun landing with a solid thud on the deck plating. He dropped to his knees beside the weapon, his hands hanging limply by his side. Bill looked on in shock at the two figures that sat on the pile of crates: Sylvester, with his head punctured by a neat hole in the centre of his face, and Clive with his face and upper-left torso decimated by the powerful magnum rounds. Two empty shells that had once been his friends.

"What the fuck?" muttered Al, staring at the mass carnage he had been part of creating. "Fucking Preacher-man, knew he was going a little crazy, but fuck… They were like brothers!"

"What's going on?"

Bill jumped as the ship-wide intercom burst to life: It hadn't been used very often, and as such was easy to forget about, but Garth's interest had obviously piqued enough for him to ignore his manuals for long enough to activate it.

"Nothing," Al said, turning his head to address the nearest intercom, but keeping his eyes transfixed on the corpses. "Nothing's wrong. Just… keep doing what you're doing."

He motioned to Bill, who leaped forwards and snapped off the intercom, allowing them to have a private discussion that wasn't transmitted across the entire ship.

"What the hell did he do?" Al muttered, retrieving his weapon and angrily pushing it into his pocket before taking a step towards the pair of cadavers. "What the hell did he do?"

"He finally lost it," Bill murmured, though he wasn't sure whether this was a statement to himself, or whether he was trying to answer Al's question.

"I should've seen this coming," hissed Al. "They train you for this shit. Looking out for the guy in your squad that's most likely to lose it: berserker fits of rage, shell shock, psychosis, they teach you to lookout for it all. I should've seen it coming, spending too much time reading that fucking book of his… He didn't even believe… in it."

He stopped talking and took a step closer to the bodies, reaching out to move Sylvester slightly and look at his arm. His face twisted into anger, and he unleashed a long, tortured scream that seemed as loud as his gunshots had been. Bill stepped forwards to see what it was that Al had found, and saw the ragged, gaping wound on his arm that looked unmistakably like a bite.

"He'd been tagged by a Rot. Son of a bitch, he was infected. Jesus, look at his hands, at his fingers… no wonder he's been keeping low, he's almost gone."

"Tell me something I don't fucking know," snapped Al. "Which means Clive hadn't snapped, he was… I guess he'd been asked to do it. Look at Sly, man. Look at Spanners' face. He looks pretty fucking happy for a man who just had a gun pulled on him."

"He asked Clive to…"

Al nodded grimly, and Bill returned the gesture. It made sense that Sylvester wanted the person to put an end to it all be his best friend.

"And I killed Clive," Al muttered, his voice soft, barely a whisper. He grabbed a dark blanket that had been folded and left on top of one of the crates in the corner of the room, tossing it over the bodies. Muttering something Bill couldn't make out he made the sign of the cross over himself, then each body. He stepped back from the body, bowing his head in silent prayer.

"Are you okay?" Bill asked, finally breaking the awkward silence. He had never been very religious, and had always been a little uncomfortable when people practiced their faith around him; that was the main reason he'd never really been that close to Clive.

"No, I'm fucking not okay," Al growled, glaring coldly at the bodies. Already the dark material was taking on a darker colour as the blood seeped into its fibres. "I've just killed one of our friends, because I thought he'd killed another of our friends. I didn't even give him a chance to explain himself. Of course I'm not okay. Don't be so fucking stupid."

He was silent for a little longer, then sighed and let his shoulders sag.

"What the hell are we going to tell everyone? How could I fuck this up so much?"

Bill thought for a moment, sinking to the floor and nodding his head as his mind worked overtime.

"We lie," he finally said.

"The fuck?"

"We lie. Spin a yarn. Sylvester had turned, nobody knew. Clive went to see his friend, didn't realise, and got bitten himself. He asked us to kill him."

"It's good," Al said, clapping a hand on Bill's shoulders. "But that's not what I'm going to do. We tell the truth. Would you tell Angel what really happened?"

"Well… I couldn't lie to her."

"No, I didn't think so. And I'm sure I'd blurt it out to Garth one night when we're drinking. Which would mean only Sarah didn't know, and I don't want to treat her like a little girl when she's more mature than half the adults on this boat. It was an accident, plain and simple. I'll start off by telling her. You tell Angel, then Garth I get the feeling I'm going to have to spend a lot of time with Sarah."

With heavy feet and shoulders drooping, a defeated look in the way he moved, Al slowly trundled out the room with Bill in tow. "We'll sort the bodies out tonight, send them off in style fit for the decent men they were."

Darkness lingered over the outside of the boat, bringing a cutting wind that pinched the cheeks and fingers of Bill as he stood on the stern of the vessel, looking down on the small life raft that bobbed up and down on the surface of the darkened waters. He'd changed his clothing and burned them after helping remove the two bodies from the lower decks and load them up on to the detached life raft, and now wore a padded black leather jacket over a thick, one-piece coverall he'd claimed as his own. Even with the jacket and the heavy jumpsuit, the chill of the freezing winds still managed to find its way through the material and prickle his flesh with goose bumps. Pulling the soft baseball cap down over his eyes, he watched glumly as Al made his way down the rope ladder at the rear of the vehicle, two cans of gasoline strapped clumsily to his back and adding to his already bulky frame.

Angel watched beside him, her arms wrapped around one of Bill's as he gripped the icy-cold barrier that spanned the perimeter of the frigate. Her eyes were red and bleary, and although the tears had stopped some time ago, she still rubbed at her eyes with the back of her hand every so often. Her hair had escaped the tie that normally kept it pulled back in a pony tail, but she didn't try to rectify it: the wind was too ferocious to even try and maintain any semblance of styling while on the outer decks.

Garth stood to the far left, his sizable bulk resting on a dented barrel that lay on its side. He held a cigar limply in one hand, ash dropping from the glowing tip as his knee jiggled back and forth. In his other hand he held Clive's bible, running his fingers along the edges of the worn book. His cheeks were red as if he, too, had been crying, though he insisted it had only been the cold that had caused him to turn that way.

Sarah had taken it worse than anyone, and had bluntly refused to attend the ceremony, instead lying on her bed with her face pressed into her pillow. No amount of cajoling or persuasion had managed to move her, so she had been left alone to her own devices.

Everyone had been affected by the deaths of the two friends, though it was possible that all emotions had been amplified as, for the first time in almost three years, everyone was in a position where they could lower their mental defences and let their true colours show. Though there were still tears spilled on the stern at the time, Bill knew that Clive and Sylvester weren't the only people that were being mourned. While Bill had had the opportunity to grieve his loss in the safety of quarantine, others had not been that lucky. The tears of Angel weren't just for their friends, but for her family: likewise, Sarah was grieving for not only the priest and the mechanic, but also the loss of her entire family.

Al hauled himself back on to the deck, the wind that swirled and eddied around him reeking of the thick, noxious odour of spilled petrol. He nodded grimly to each of the persons assembled, looking mournfully towards the doorway that lead back towards their rooms. It looked like he had expected Sarah to appear while he had been attending to the funeral pyre, and was hurt at the fact that she hadn't. He joined Bill and Angel by the railing and leaned over the side. Garth slowly stood and followed him, joining them at their vantage point and looking down on the small boat as it bobbed up and down, its carbon-fibre hull knocking against the solid steel armoured hull of the frigate.

"Does anyone have anything they want to say?" asked Angel.

"Sorry," murmured Al. Though his face was stoic, impassive as he looked down at the foam and spray that frothed around the base of the two vehicles, tears streaked down his face and dripped from his chin, into the sea far below. "Nothing else I can say or do."

An uncomfortable silence hung over the gathered mourners, with no one able to think of anything. Bill noticed that Angel's eyes were closed, her lips moving slightly in silent prayer, and Garth did the same. Al played absentmindedly with a strip of red cloth, and it took Bill a few seconds to recognise that it was the bandana Clive had insisted on wearing. He tied it off around his upper arm, making sure it was tight, then looked at Bill.

"Keeping the memory alive," he muttered by way of explanation. Bill nodded in agreement, then pulled out a battered and tarnished lighter: the same lighter he had retrieved from the infected Marine he had killed on his first day after being released from quarantine. He had barely used it, he didn't have much call for it, but he flicked it open and sparked the flint in a smooth motion. The oil-soaked wick burst into flames, the fat orange flame flickering wildly as the wind snatched at it.

"Ready?"

Al nodded, and Bill tossed the ignited lighter over the edge, watching as it plummeted towards the small life raft. The vapours from the petrol that had been splashed across the smaller vehicle ignited before the lighter even had a chance to hit the deck, giving birth to a soaring pillar of fire that raced up the edge of the frigate, bringing a greasy smell of oil and the smoking canvas the corpses had been wrapped in. The small length of rope that kept the two boats together disintegrated in the heat of the flames, flaking away into ash that settled on the surface of the water. The flaming boat started to drift away, its slight frame offering no resistance as the powerful waves carried it away from the hull of the frigate. Like a beacon drifting off into the night, the flaming raft sailed into the distance while the four watchers looked on.

Al stepped away from the barrier, muttering something inarticulate to himself, fumbling with the small crate he had brought out for the assembly. He lifted an ornate ceremonial rifle out the box, worked the bolt action with a smooth movement, then raised the weapon and fired blindly.

The sound of the rifle firing was like a crash of thunder, a deafening roar that made Bill jump, and he spun around to see Al, tears streaming down his eyes as he slowly worked the bolt and fired once more, the muzzle of the weapon pointing towards the dark and brooding sky. He worked the mechanism of the rifle over and over, a smooth and regular action like that of a machine. Bill had seen enough films to recognised it as the salute normally associated with the funerals of soldiers that had fallen in the wars, and guessed that as well as the two burning friends that had almost vanished over the horizon, he had finally found an outlet for the grief of his friends that had perished since crashing on the island. He could also mourn the loss of his wife.

The retort of the final gunshot echoed off into the distance as Al finally lowered his weapon, ejecting the empty magazine from the receiver and letting both rifle and clip clatter noisily to the ground amidst the spent casings that littered the deck. Kicking a couple of the brass shells aside, Al took a step forwards and raised his hand, touching the tip of his fingers to his brow in a salute that was aimed towards the burning boat, its occupants, and those that had fallen on the infested island far beyond.

"We have different ways of coping with deaths in the Marines," Al finally announced, breaking the vow of silence that the small crowd had voluntarily undertaken.

"Is it over?"

A weak, shaky voice from the doorway made Bill turn around to see Sarah looking out into the distance, where the smallest of orange specks could be seen.

"It's over," Al confirmed with a nod of his head. "All over."

She gingerly took a few steps out on to the deck, picking her way through the spent shells, and wrapped her arms around Al's waist, sniffing and wiping her eyes with the back of her hand.

"You okay?" Al murmured softly. Sarah's head bobbled up and down. "Okay then," he continued. "We've got another two weeks on this boat. Let's just… I want to go home. Keep it together."

He turned and left the deck with Sarah in tow, returning to the warmth of the inside, and Garth followed, making his way back to the bridge. Bill leaned back on the railing, sighing heavily.

"We'll be all right," he finally announced. "We'll get by."

Angel rested her head on his shoulder and nodded. "I know," she murmured. "We'll have to."

II

The days after the funeral seemed to blur into one for Bill as he sat poised over a number of radar screens and readouts: his task for the journey to monitor everything that went on around the immediate vicinity of the frigate while Garth powered the vehicle onwards. The only reason Bill could tell time was passing and that they were approaching America was that, despite the rain and overcast skies, the temperature was slowly rising all the time. He knew it would be warmer there then it had been in England. Where *wouldn't* be?

"How long've we got now?" Bill asked, looking up from the glowing green screen and towards the view through the oversized windows that surrounded the bridge, ignoring the wooden panels that had been erected to cover over the shattered window that Lance had been hurled through.

"Shouldn't be much longer now," Garth smiled, almost dancing from side to side at the thought of arriving at their destination. For Bill, America was the end of his journey, a new place to rest, but he knew that for Garth it was merely another stepping stone for his ultimate goal: a place for him to clean himself up before he went to visit his daughter. "Maybe another day or two, thank Christ. I tell you, a military frigate is completely different to a yacht."

"Who would've thought that?"

"I know, I know. Their trailers are the same as our trailers, their bikes are like ours, but their boats are completely different."

"I can't wait to get off this frigging boat," Bill muttered. "Three and a half weeks trapped on a floating tin can: it was fun for about a day or two, but then it just became boring as shit. Sitting here watching these screens… I can think of better things to spend a month doing."

"Really?" Garth asked disbelievingly. "I find that hard to swallow. Al's got his guns to maintain and Angel's boning up on all the medical crap that's lying around in the sick bay. Seriously, what have you got to do?"

"I've started drawing," Bill admitted, patting the small pad of paper that he had started to carry around with him. Garth tutted to himself and shook his head.

"Real important shit, then."

"C'mon, you can't tell me you like sitting in here, day in and day out, for weeks on end?"

"I used to be a truck driver, Bill. Long distance haulage, it's what I do."

"I suppose," Bill said slowly, his gaze returning to the screens. "Only thing is, when you're driving a trailer you at least pass some scenery on your way: a funny billboard, a greasy spoon somewhere… out here, what have you got?"

"Well, at least once a day I see either you or Angel leaning over the side of the boat and throwing up. That breaks the monotony a little."

"And that's another thing I won't miss about this frigging ship: motion sickness, sea sickness, whatever the hell it's called. When I'm lying in bed, I feel sick; when I'm walking around, I feel sick. I was fine, *we* were fine at the beginning of this little voyage, but the longer we're out here, the worse it gets. I can't wait to be back on solid ground."

"Al's right about you," Garth said with grin, reaching into his pocket and pulling out a crumpled leather pouch filled with tobacco. He sprinkled it into a small sheet of paper and rolled it up before lighting it. "You would make a great soldier. But you'd make an appalling sailor. Still, soon as we get ashore I can look into investing in some proper smokes. Cuban cigars, I think, are the order of the day. You can't beat them."

"I'll be happy to have a real bed," Bill admitted. "I guess we have different priorities."

"I'll be happy when you get a real bed, too," Garth said with a mischievous grin. "The pair of you keep us awake well into the night on that creaky thing you're sleeping on at the minute. I preferred when the pair of you were moody, sulky and didn't speak to one another. At least I got a good night sleep."

Garth slapped his thigh as he laughed at his own joke, and Bill stifled his own snigger.

"You've got your family here, though." Garth continued, his laughter dying as he continued. "I've still got a hell of a journey left until I see mine again."

Bill nodded his agreement, removing his gaze from the radar screens and opening his pad up, grabbing a well-chewed pencil from his pocket and sketching out the basic outline of a person on the page. He didn't hear the door to the bridge open, nor did he hear the soft, deliberate footsteps that slowly made their way across to behind his seat.

"Whatcha doin?"

He leapt out his seat and dropped his pad and pencil, spinning around to see Sarah leaning over his shoulder, trying to see what he'd been drawing. He smiled softly and sank back into the chair, his heart hammering inside his ribcage as he slowly recuperated from his startle.

"Just a little sketch. I needed to rest my eyes from the radar."

"You need to keep a watch on those screens," Sarah scowled, chastising Bill as she knelt on the floor and recovered pencil and paper. "I'll keep hold of these for now."

She strolled over to the large table that had been set up on the back wall as sat down, pouring herself a drink from the plastic jug of water and setting up the sketch pad before scribbling on a fresh sheet of paper.

"Hey," Bill said, watching as she started to draw over the humanoid form he'd just sketched.

"You've got a job to do," Sarah sang without looking up from her drawing. "I'm just a kid, I need to have things that help my development. Al says I need to be more like a kid so I fit in better when we get to Merica."

"America," Bill said, correcting her as he looked back to the radar.

"America," Sarah repeated, mimicking Bill's tone and mannerism as she spoke.

"Stop that."

"Stop that," she imitated him once more. Bill knew this game; he'd played it himself numerous times when he was younger. And he knew there was only one way to win: he remained silent. Five minutes passed without anything else being said, and Sarah sighed heavily, shaking her head as she realised she'd been bested.

A further ten minutes passed, and Bill stood up, stepping away from his post.

"I've had enough of this shit, Garth, what time is it?"

"Coming up to four. I think. Ship-time, of course: I don't think anyone thought about changing the clocks as we passed through the different time zones."

"Fuck it, I'm going to grab something to eat. You coming?"

"Yeah," Garth said, brushing cold ash from his cigarette off his vest top and grabbing his jacket from beside him. "Yeah, I could do with something to eat. I'll knock the autopilot on first."

"Finally found it?"

"Just now," Garth admitted, almost spitting as he stood up and thumbed a red switch close to his seat. The lights flickered and dimmed slightly, and for a moment Bill had a picture in his mind of the bridge erupting into sparks before blacking out.

It didn't.

"It took you three weeks to find it. Was it worth it?"

"At least I can go take a piss without worrying about the boat straying off course. Other than that, it doesn't do shit."

"Time well spent," Bill muttered, strolling over to Sarah and looking at her drawing. "You coming, too?"

She nodded, pushing her chair away from the table, and Bill went to grab the pad, looking over her work. He could see a boat on the water, with a number of people gathered on it. Above the boat, amongst the clouds, there were a number of people.

"It's good. What's going on here?"

"That's our boat, and that's all of us on the back."

"And the people up here?"

"Angels," Sarah muttered, kicking her toe against the dull grey floor. "It's Mum and Daddy up there watching us, with Pam and Tara. And that's Clive and Sylvester. The stars are my brothers and sisters."

"What about this? Is Al... is he..." Bill looked at the picture, squinting as he tried to make out some of the details and working out how best to word it.

"Is he pissing into the water?" Garth blurted out, looking over Bill's shoulder at the picture and laughing.

"No, he's fishing. Look, he's caught that."

"That's a fish?"

Sarah shook her head, laughing softly to herself. "No, it's a zombie shark."

"That isn't even funny," Garth murmured, his smile fading as he sidestepped over to the window and nervously peering out the window in to the murky water below, looking to see if there were any of Sarah's mythical beasts in the waters around them. "Fuckin' kids, always saying freaky shit like that..."

His voice trailed off as he looked out the window, leaning forwards and squinting into the distance. He rubbed his jaw with the palm of his hand and chewed at his lip, and then: "Grab me that pair of binoculars," he said, waving vaguely towards one of the consoles and the green goggles that lay on top. Sarah acted before Bill could, grabbing them and running across the room to Garth, slapping the binoculars in his outstretched hands.

"What've you got?" Bill asked, storming closer to the window. "Zombie shark? Undead dolphin?"

"Better than that shit: way better than that shit," Garth said, shaking his head as he looked through the vision enhancing equipment. He stumbled away from the window, flicked the ship-wide intercom to life and grabbed the microphone.

"Land ho!" he screamed at the top of his voice, the speaker in the bridge squealing with feedback. His cry echoed off into the distance as each of the speakers simultaneously announced his sighting. Bill felt his heart skip a beat, and he dashed to the window, snapping up the binoculars and focusing his gaze on the distant horizon. Sure enough, a small smudge loomed in the distance: a grey-green blob that held the promise of a new life. He stared at the distant island for what felt like five minutes before passing the binoculars to Sarah. She clambered up on to one of the inactive consoles as she tried to get to a better vantage point.

"What've we got?" demanded Al as he stormed into bridge, pulling a T-shirt on as he moved quickly towards the windows. His hands were covered in grease and oil, some of which seemed to be smudged across his forehead as well. "C'mon, what've we got?"

"Something far away," Sarah said, offering the binoculars. Al refused them; instead pulling out a scope that had previously been attached to a rifle, lifting it to his eye and treating it like a telescope. "I can't tell what it is. Could be just a smudge."

"No, that's land, all right. Why's it not showing on the radar?"

"It must be too far away," Bill suggested. "Beyond the range of the sensors."

"Doesn't matter," Al said, stepping away from the window and moving towards the screens and readouts that Bill had to monitor. He plucked at a few switches and hammered buttons around a black screen, tapping the inert monitor with a grime-encrusted fingernail. "It should be showing on the GPS system: that should be able to tell us exactly where we are… why's it not working?"

Bill looked at the set of screens Al was studying and shrugged his shoulders.

"Well, you should've been looking at it regularly… this thing here, why isn't it working?"

"Because it's got a bullet it in?" Bill suggested, motioning to the side of the monitors where part of the metal casing had peeled away. Al dropped to his knees beside it and fingered the jagged edges of the hole, pulling out an oversized shapeless lump of lead and letting it drop to the floor. It looked remarkably like part of the misshapen lead projectiles that Al had draped from his neck by a piece of leather; the larger of the two bullets, suggesting that it had been one of Al's shots that had put an end to the console.

"Fuck," he muttered to himself.

"What's happening?" Angel rushed into the bridge, her pale features frantically scanning the windows before her for any sign of the Promised Land. She clutched a thick hardback book, which she dropped on the table by the doorway. "Where is it?"

"About seventy miles that way, give or take," Garth grinned, pointing a thumb towards the window. "And it's America?"

"Maybe," Al muttered. "It could be anywhere, we've got no way of knowing. Someone shot out part of the navigation controls."

"But why aren't we heading towards it?" Angel asked, stepping across the bridge and taking Bill's hand in her own. He grinned, squeezed her hand, then wrapped his arm around her waist and stooped slightly, kissing her on the side of her neck. She grinned and squirmed, but didn't pull away.

"I'm on it," Garth nodded, taking the oversized wheel and slowly turning it a few degrees to one side. "Full speed ahead."

"Well, all right," Al said, wiping his hands off on his trousers. "Let's get some shit sorted out. I've been looking through what was in some of the officers' quarters. There's not much in there, but there's enough to piece together a couple of outfits that look reasonably like civilian clothing. At least we won't look *too* much out of place. We'll get a little closer, then drop anchor and row ashore on a life raft: it'll be easier to do that then beach an entire frigate, plus it won't raise as many eyebrows or questions. Grab what you need and we'll be on our way. I've even managed to plunder almost a thousand dollars and some loose change, so we can buy a few basic provisions when we get there. Now, let's hustle and get cleaned up. Three hours, people."

Al left the bridge with an excitable Sarah and Garth in tow, each heading towards their private quarters. Only Bill and Angel remained, staring out the window at the blob of an island that was slowly starting to grow in size, their arms wrapped around one another.

"We've finally made it," Angel said, a soft smile spreading across her face.

"I know. It's hard to believe. Almost three years ago everything was normal in my life. I was in a different place... we all were. But now, we've got a new home, a new life to look towards."

"What are we going to do?"

"Wait until we get our money, I guess. I don't like the idea of living off dirty money, but I prefer that to being rounded up and locked away in a detention camp, or executed. It's something we can talk about on the raft."

"What about *us*?"

"Us?" Bill repeated, dropping his hand into his pocket. He shrugged his shoulders and frowned, deep in thought, until his fingers came into contact with something in his trouser pocket: an object had had long forgotten about, and as his fingers caressed the smooth, metallic surface, a rush of distant memories flashed through his head.

He remembered that cold day in February when he and Al had left the safety of their base and travelled into the closest town to gather gifts for the belated Christmas celebrations. While Al had concentrated on everyone else, Bill had wandered off on his own, intent on finding the perfect present for Angel. It had been then that Bill had made the discovery about the seemingly tougher Rots: but before he had stumbled on the evolved form of undead creatures he had found a small velvet box lying amongst the shattered debris of a display cabinet. Obviously lost under the initial stampede of looters, he had opened the box to find a small gold band, plain at first glance, but closer inspection revealed a number of small, intricate patterns engraved on each face of the ring.

It had been that point that the Rot had attacked him, and he'd pushed the ring into his pocket and forgot all about it in the ensuing battle and chaos that followed in the days and weeks afterwards, until that moment. The very fact it had survived there for this long... although it didn't make him rethink his outlook on religion, it was certainly enough to make him think that this was certainly meant to be.

He pulled out the ring and held it off to one side, rolling it around between thumb and forefinger, then curled his hand into a fist, engulfing the piece of jewellery before presenting it to Angel on his outstretched palm.

"If we're getting new identities with the millions of dollars that Al's going to get for us, why don't we save a little money and get all our documents in the same name?"

Angel looked at Bill, then the ring he held, before returning her gaze to him once more.

"What?"

"I... I want you to..." squirming, Bill stepped in front of Angel and held her hand, then offered the ring once more, gently pushing it on to her finger. "Marry me? I mean I love you, and we're together all ready; we're going to start a new life in a new country, it only makes sense that we..."

"You don't need to explain yourself all the time," Angel whispered, placing a finger on his lips and smiling. A tear rolled down the curve of her cheek, and she dabbed at it with the back of her index finger. "You just need to ask. I will."

Bill grinned and threw his arms around her, lifting her off her feet and spinning around. He dropped her to her feet and stepped back, staring into her eyes and grinning all the time.

"Where'd you get it?" she asked, looking at the ring on her finger. She listened intently as Bill recounted the tale from his journey into the town with Al, then held up her hand as he came to the end.

"You got this for me before we even..."

"I guess I always knew we'd be together," Bill shrugged his shoulders. "Or at least, I hoped we'd be together. It took me almost three years to admit to myself how I really felt, and that's three years I'm not going to get back. That's why I want to spend the rest of my life with you, to make up for the time I've lost."

"I think I've known," Angel admitted. "Maybe not for the full three years, but I think I knew, one way of another. When we first met, I think we were all messed up, trying to come to terms with what was happening. But now... we've all changed."

"Speaking of changing, we need to get into the civvie clothing Al's managed to find," Bill said. "We've only got three hours."

"That leaves us with plenty of time to celebrate," Angel cooed softly, a seductive smile spreading across her face. "C'mon, I'll race you back to our room."

"Late again," Al hissed through clenched teeth as he stood on the deck, watching as Bill and Angel finally burst out the opened doorway, laughing and joking, their arms linked as they almost skipped out into the chill of the night air. "Finally," he said aloud, raising his hands. "I'm pleased you two finally decided to join us."

"Leave it," Bill said, adjusting the collar of the leather jacket he wore. "We just had some things we needed to get sorted out before we left for the mainland."

"That's right," Al nodded, motioning to the second of a pair of winches on the side of the frigate: while he and Garth manned one of them, he intended Bill and Angel to stand watch over the second and slowly lower the raft down into the frothing dark water below. "You two can't screw each other in the raft, you'll have to go for hours without touching each other. Think you can manage?"

"We probably can't wait until the honeymoon," Angel grinned sheepishly, "But we might be able to last a few hours."

Al frowned, glanced at Angel's hand and the band of gold that had appeared there, and shook his head before starting to work the winch. Although he was pleased for the young lovers, the announcement, no matter how casual, only served to remind him of his marriage and the untimely end of it all. Of course the pair hadn't set out to intentionally remind him of what he'd lost, and he couldn't expect them to put their life on hold until he had fully come to terms with his loss, but the memory was still there. Once he managed to get home and speak to Momma Colebrook, maybe he'd be able to begin his own healing process then.

They were about thirty miles from the shore, and despite the darkness, they could still see the dim glow of lights that dotted the shoreline. He didn't know which port of America exactly he was facing, but he knew from all the shore leave he'd taken in his career that if somewhere had a port, there'd be a bar or café right next to it to cater for all the incoming sailors. They could stop there, grab some food, then start making phone calls.

"Okay," he huffed as the four adults worked at the winch, slowly lowering their raft down into the murky water. The small boat landed with a soft splash, and he kicked the rolled-up rope ladder over the side, listening as it unfurled and knocked against the hull of the frigate. "I'll go first, secure the boat and the ladder."

He locked off the winch, motioned for Bill to do the same to his, then descended the rope ladder. It was a short climb, shorter than the descent had been from the cliff top retreat down to the secured stealth boat, and he covered the distance relatively quick, dropping the last couple of feet into the boat. It dipped and bobbed, water lapping over the rim of the boat and knocking against the hull of the frigate as he tried to steady the platform before motioning for the next person to come down.

Sarah was next, carefully clambering over the lip of the frigate and beginning the descent on her own. She moved slowly and carefully, tentatively wrapping her arm around each rung and bracing herself as she took each step one at a time. Once she was within his grasp, Al reached out and plucked her from the ladder, setting her down on the deck of the smaller craft. Garth lumbered down next, almost falling down the ladder as his sweating palms slipped on the smooth metallic ladder. Al grimaced as Garth managed to catch himself, imagining the damage the overweight man could do to the small raft if he fell through from the ladder: he could easily sink the boat if he fell from the higher rungs.

Bill was next down the ladder, moving quickly and efficiently before helping Angel down after him, her normally graceful movements somewhat less elegant than usual. The two settled down at the front of the boat while Garth and Al sat at the back, allowing Sarah to sit in the middle.

"Okay, the anchors are down on the Frigate so it won't float away, just in case we need to get back on board," Al said, grabbing the starter cord and yanking the engine to life. The still of the night air was shattered as the as engine shuddered to life, and Al released the cables that attached the raft to the frigate. The boat lurched and shuddered, then tore away from the mother ship, slowly turning towards the glimmering shoreline as Garth guided the vehicle.

"We're on our way," Al said with a grin, then followed up with a whoop of joy.

"How long until we hit the shore?" Angel asked, her hair flaring out behind her as the wind and the motion of the boat tugged at it. Al shrugged to himself.

"Hours. We're about thirty miles out, I want to take it easy with this thing, it the engine blow's we're fucked, stranded out in here in the ocean. We could row, if that was the case, but we could die before we get there. Plus, if we go any faster, the ride is going to be a hell of a lot rougher, and I know you two might be more than willing to rock the bunk, but you hate to rock the boat."

"Take your time," Bill murmured to Garth, nodding towards the throbbing engine. "No rush."

"Damn right," Al said, leaning back and relaxing, watching as the dim glow of the buildings along the coast slowly crawled towards them. He smiled as Sarah sank back into her seat and rested her head against his leg, then Bill and Angel melt into each other's embrace and wrap a blanket around themselves. Al grabbed a second blanket and draped it over Sarah as she settled down to sleep.

"Soon as we get to mainland," Garth grumbled as the guided the boat, 'I'm going to grab myself some downtime with a real nice whore. Do you know how long it's been since I…"

"I can only imagine," Al snapped, jerking a thumb towards Sarah. "But I'm sure she doesn't need to know. Try to keep your base urges under control, eh?"

"Control this," Garth laughed. Al didn't need to look at what part of his anatomy he was clutching: he simply nodded to himself. "That's what I'm trying to achieve."

A hushed silence fell over the boat as it continued to sail across the dark waters, the drone of the engine fading into the roar of crashing waves, and a few people aboard the life raft started to drift to sleep, Garth included. On more than one occasion Garth's head lolled to one side and the boat followed suit, lazily sliding across to one side. Al quickly knocked the side of his head with the back of his palm, waking him with a start and prompting him to realign his course.

Keeping his eyes closed tight, Al silently prayed that their luck would hold out for the crossing: if a storm broke out during their journey, the small raft would be tossed around and easily capsized. To have reached this far and die on the shores of another country because of the weather would be unfair, especially in light of the odds and obstacles they had encountered.

Darkness slowly started to give way to sunlight after hours of travel, and black clouds started to part, revealing the warm, golden glow of a rising sun as its rays of light probed through the gloomy cloud cover. One by one, the lights that dotted the coastline blinked out, and the smudge of land started to take shape: flat buildings and towering skyscrapers slowly drawing into view, giving Al an early glimpse of the civilisation they were approaching. He leaned forwards and nudged Sarah gently with his boot. The young girl drearily woke up, staring at the distant shore and dreamily rubbed her eyes.

"We there yet?"

"Nearly," he said, grabbing one of the oars that had been stored in the raft and prodding Bill's back with the flat paddle. He snorted and coughed, then gently shook Angel awake, pulling the blanket in tight around her as he looked across the gulf of water and at the distant shoreline.

"Are you okay?" asked Bill. "You look pale."

"Sleeping in a tin bath afloat in the middle of the ocean can do that to you," Angel murmured, fishing out a bottle of water from beneath the blanket and taking a sip. "Feel like shit."

"Look like shit," countered Al, slowly pulling himself to his feet and lifting the detached scope he still carried. He placed it against his eyes, nodded as he panned from left to right, taking in the sights of the shore. He nodded and sat back down beside the motor, slipping his scope back into his pocket.

"We can cover the distance in half an hour if we push this thing flat out. It'll be rough as shit, and it might even stop working, but I think it'll be worth it."

"Rough?" questioned Bill. He was just as pale as Angel now. "How rough?"

"Remember how much you felt like shit after using that grenade at point-blank distance?"

Bill nodded groggily, remembering the incident that had occurred in Edgly almost three years ago.

"Ten times worse, probably. Think you can handle that?"

"No," Bill shook his head, then looked at Angel. "What about you?"

"Sooner we get there, the sooner we can get off this thing. I'll be okay."

"Out-fucking-standing," Al said with a smile, then gently slapped Garth on the shoulder with the back of his hand. "You heard them, the people have spoken. Punch it, buddy, let's pull out all the stops."

"About frigging time," Garth said, working the throttle on the engine and leaning forwards into the wind as the small boat jumped and bounced over the crest of the waves. Al couldn't help but grin at the speed the boat moved, wiping his face as the sea spray splashed up the side of the boat: his smile broadened as Sarah laughed and giggled, a glimpse of the childish joy she should be experiencing in these younger years.

Angel and Bill weren't taking it as well as the young girl, however: they had sank low in their seats, huddling into one another and staring grimly at the floor, each as pale as a corpse. Their ragged breathing was the only thing that reminded Al that they weren't dead, though they certainly felt it.

"I can see land. For real," shouted Sarah, pointing towards the front of the boat. "People! Boats! Look!"

"I see it," grinned Al, clapping his hands excitedly on his thighs. "By Christ, I see it!"

"Don't get too excited," Garth muttered, dipping his hands into the water beside him and splashing it on the motor. Full speed had obviously been too much for the machine, and thick black smoke bellowed out the groaning motor. Orange flames danced and spurted out the engine, scalding Al as the fire washed across his arm and up his face, and he furiously smashed his boot against the casing. With a crack, the housing dislodged and fell back into the water, sinking with a burbling gush of bubbles as it vanished into the murky depths. The bouncing motion of the boat ceased as it slowed down, bobbing up and down on the waves and slowly panning around in a circle as the current toyed with the flotation device.

"You okay?" Garth asked, looking at the singed and blackened flesh that covered Al's arm and face. He nodded with a shrug, brushing at the black soot that covered him, then grabbed both oars and passed one over to Garth. Without saying another word, the two started to row the boat ashore, approaching a number of boats that were moored to different wooden piers and jetties. Pulling the boat through the water with slow, deliberate strokes, the harbour was eerily quiet and deserted. Though Sarah claimed to have seen people from a distance, there wasn't anyone aboard any of the boats or walking along the wooden walkways; hardly surprising, given the fact it was just coming up to four in the morning.

"Where are we?" Bill asked, shakily pulling his weight up from the boat and looking enviously at the catwalks they approached, licking his lips at the thought of stepping ashore.

"Could be anywhere on the eastern seaboard," Al murmured, pulling his oar in and wiping the back of his uninjured arm across his forehead, mopping up the beads of sweat. "Except New York: no sign of Lady Liberty to welcome us home."

"Home," Bill echoed, unfastening his jacket slightly. With the sun coming out, it was starting to warm the air: not too noticeable at first, though certainly promising to bring more heat through the course of the day.

"Home," Angel repeated, sitting up and watching as Al grabbed a length of rope and hurled it across the water towards the closest of the piers, trying to loop the nylon chord across one of the thick, heavy-set iron moorings. He missed the first time, then reeled the rope back in and tried again, this time getting the loop over the metal. He pulled the rope, closed the loop, then slowly pulled the boat in to the catwalk.

Angel clambered quickly out the boat, pulling herself up on to shaky legs and slowly making her way out across the raised pier towards the concrete plinth that held a number of parked vehicles and wooden shacks. Bill clambered up out the boat after her, quickly swapping the rickety and wobbly boat for a less rickety walkway. Garth was next out, helping Sarah up from the boat and following the two young lovers towards the wooden huts. His eyes crinkled in the corner as his mouth turned into a beaming smile, and he dabbed at the thin tears of joy that trickled down his cheeks with the back of his hand. Al looked at the collection of buildings that were decorated with a number of garish and faded placards advertising hotdogs, French fries, popcorn and all manner of candies for sale.

He pulled his own weight out the boat and gathered the small rucksack he'd prepared: a bulky bag filled with a number of different hard drives, all with the same incriminating evidence geared towards exposing the United Government's Marine Corps, the companies and the countries that had funded and supported them. Between the distant buildings and a large green SUV, a number of public telephone boxes sat vacant and silent. Even now, public payphones were still popular amongst criminals and those wanting to remain 'off the grid'. If living amongst the rotting undead wasn't off the grid, Al didn't know what was.

Fishing around in his pocket, he pulled out a handful of loose change and picked out a small number of coins, moving towards the telephones and reaching out to take Sarah's outstretched hand led her onwards.

"Yeah," he muttered to himself.

"Home."